A STRUGGLE FOR ROME

A STRUGGLE FOR ROME

A historical novel by Felix Dahn

Translated from the original German by Herb Parker

ATHENA PRESS
LONDON

A STRUGGLE FOR ROME
Translation copyright © Herb Parker 2005

ISBN 1 84401 444 4

First Published 2005 by
ATHENA PRESS
Queen's House, 2 Holly Road
Twickenham, TW1 4EG
United Kingdom

Printed for Athena Press

CONTENTS

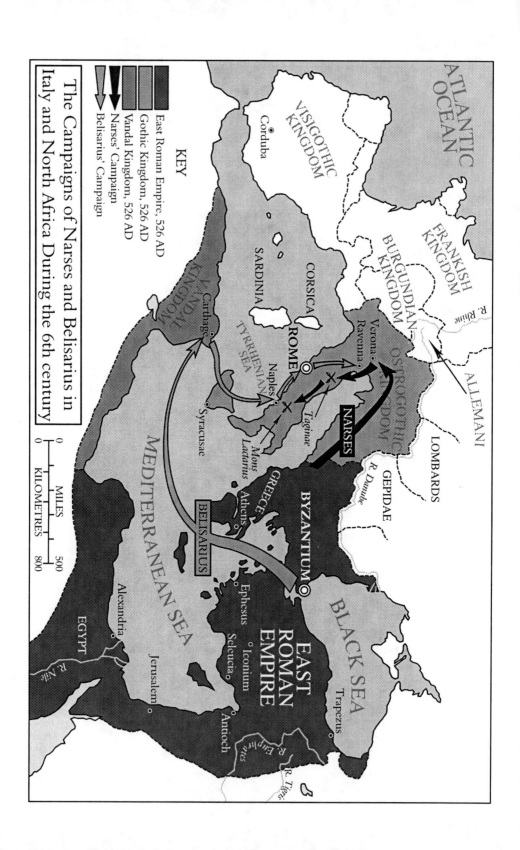

The Campaigns of Narses and Belisarius in Italy and North Africa During the 6th century

KEY

East Roman Empire, 526 AD
Gothic Kingdom, 526 AD
Vandal Kingdom, 526 AD
Narses' Campaign
Belisarius' Campaign

ATLANTIC OCEAN

VISIGOTHIC KINGDOM

Corduba

FRANKISH KINGDOM

BURGUNDIAN KINGDOM

R. Rhine

ALLEMANI

LOMBARDS

GEPIDAE

R. Danube

OSTROGOTHIC KINGDOM

Verona
Ravenna

CORSICA

SARDINIA

TYRRHENIAN SEA

ROME

Naples

Tiginae

VANDAL KINGDOM

Carthage

Syracusae

Mons Lactarius

NARSES

GREECE

Athens

BYZANTIUM

BELISARIUS

MEDITERRANEAN SEA

BLACK SEA

Trapezus

Ephesus

Iconium

Seleucia

Antioch

EAST ROMAN EMPIRE

Alexandria

Jerusalem

EGYPT

R. Nile

R. Euphrates

R. Tigris

0   500   800
MILES

0
KILOMETRES

Italy early 6th Century

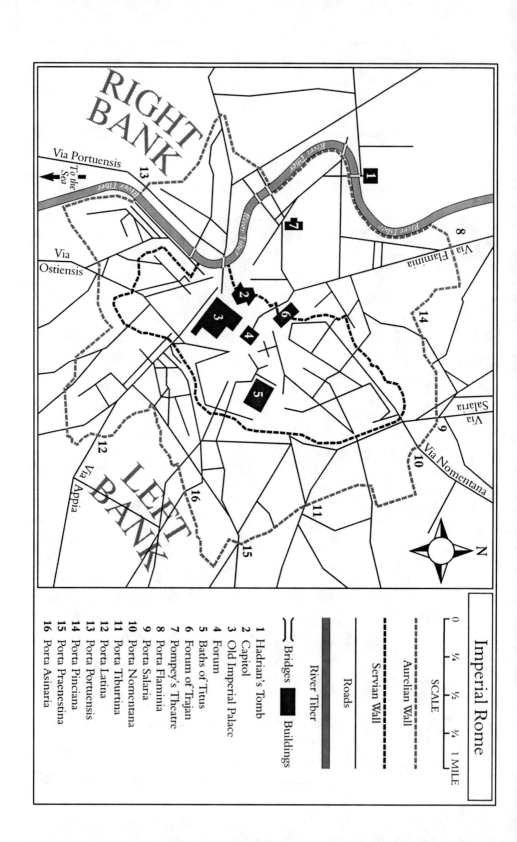

Imperial Rome

SCALE

0 ¼ ½ ¾ 1 MILE

Roads

Aurelian Wall

Servian Wall

River Tiber

Bridges Buildings

1 Hadrian's Tomb
2 Capitol
3 Old Imperial Palace
4 Forum
5 Baths of Titus
6 Forum of Trajan
7 Pompey's Theatre
8 Porta Flaminia
9 Porta Salaria
10 Porta Nomentana
11 Porta Tiburtina
12 Porta Latina
13 Porta Portuensis
14 Porta Pinciana
15 Porta Praenestina
16 Porta Asinaria

RIGHT BANK

LEFT BANK

Via Portuensis

To the Sea

Via Ostiensis

Via Appia

Via Salaria

Via Nomentana

Via Flaminia

River Tiber

N

Translator's Preface

The historical novel *Ein Kampf um Rom* (*A Struggle for Rome*), by the German historian and novelist Felix Dahn, was begun in Munich in 1859, continued in Italy (Ravenna) and completed in Koenigsberg in 1876. It was first published in German later that year.

The work was dedicated to Dahn's friend and colleague Ludwig Friedlaender, and bears as its motto:

"Wenn etwas ist, gewaltiger als das Schicksal, dann ist's der Mut, der's unerschuettert traegt."

(Translation: If there is anything mightier than fate, it is the courage to bear it undaunted.)

The novel is set mainly in sixth century Italy, and partly in Byzantium, and it describes the decline and fall of the Ostrogothic Empire. It has been widely read in German and translated into a number of languages.

The story begins with the death in 526 AD of the great Gothic king Theodoric, who also appears with his *"Waffenmeister"* Hildebrand as "Dietrich von Bern" in Germanic mythology. (The word *"Waffenmeister"* is difficult to translate. It literally means "armourer", but also implies tutor and mentor of a young warrior.) This book describes the fate of the Gothic nation under the various kings who came after Theodoric, until the final annihilation of the entire nation after the battle of Taginae by the Byzantine eunuch and general Narses in 553 AD, thus covering a span of twenty-seven years. Among other source material the author has drawn heavily on the *Gothic Wars* by contemporary historian Procopius, who also appears in the story. The novel closely follows historical fact, and all the major events described in the story actually took place. Judging by the great detail given by the author it is probable that most if not all of that is also historically accurate; to be certain one would need to have access to Dahn's original source material, particularly the writings of Procopius. As far as I have been able to ascertain most of the major characters in the story actually lived, the notable exception being Cornelius Cethegus Caesarius, the Prefect of Rome, who is a figment of the author's imagination, although he may be based in part on one or more real characters. But such a man could have lived, and if he had much of history might have turned out differently.

In my present and entirely original translation I have tried to adhere as closely as I could to the author's words, using limited poetic licence only where a literal translation would have seemed clumsy or stilted to a modern reader. One problem has been with the names of the many characters, nations, places and tribes which appear throughout the book. As far as I reasonably could I have used the names with which an English reader is most likely to be familiar. In the case of well known characters, such as Justinian and Theodora, the choice was easy. Where I could find them I used names as they appear in the *Encyclopaedia Britannica* (i.e. Amalasuntha, Witigis, Totila, Teias, Belisarius), or the names used by Gibbon in his *Decline and Fall of the Roman Empire*, and where all else failed I have simply used the name from Dahn's original. Where it comes to place names I have used modern names for well known cities (i.e. Rome, Naples) and the ancient names otherwise. To the casual reader the words I have used for either a people, a person or a place will not matter, and the historian will soon work out what each name refers to. The word "Arian", where it appears in this book, refers to the so-called Arian religious controversy, and has nothing to do with the "Aryans" which featured so prominently in Hitler's abhorrent racial theories.

Felix Dahn apparently wrote a number of novels, described by his critics as "professorial novels" because of the wealth of historical information woven into them. *A Struggle for Rome* is by far his best-known work, and the only one that has been widely read. I first read *Ein Kampf um Rom* as a twelve-year-old German boy living in China and attending a German school, on the recommendation of my then history teacher, and I have been fascinated with it ever since. Literature, like any other art form, is subjective, but for me there is nothing better than a good historical novel, and as far as I am concerned *Ein Kampf um Rom* has no peer.

It is my hope that the present translation will enable more English-speaking readers to read and enjoy this magnificent, informative and compellingly readable novel, and if so then the four years of my spare time which I have devoted to the present translation will have been time well spent.

Herb Parker
Redcliffe, Queensland, Australia
June 2002

BOOK ONE

Theodoric

Chapter 1

It was a warm and humid night in the summer of the year 526 AD.

Thick clouds lay heavily over the dark plains of the Adriatic coast. It was difficult to make out details of the landscape and its many waterways in the gloom, interrupted only by occasional lightning in the distance, briefly lighting up the sleeping city of Ravenna. Gusts of wind howled through the oaks and pines along the crests of the hills to the west of the city. Once these hills had been crowned by a temple of Neptune, which even in those days had fallen into disrepair, and which today has disappeared entirely, but for a few barely recognisable traces.

It was quiet on this forest plateau, the silence being interrupted only by the occasional boulder torn loose by the storm, which would roll noisily down the rocky slopes, finally splashing into the swampy waters of one of the many canals and ditches which surrounded the fortress city on all sides, except where it bordered directly on the sea.

Now and again a weathered plate would come loose from the inlaid ceiling of the temple and smash itself into a thousand fragments on the marble steps, warning signs that before long the entire structure of the old building would collapse.

But these eerie sounds were as if they did not exist to a man who sat motionless on the second highest step of the temple. He rested, his back against the topmost step, his gaze directed in steady silence toward the sleeping city beyond the plateau.

For a long time he sat thus, apparently waiting for someone. He ignored the heavy raindrops which were beginning to fall, and which the wind blew into his face and into the magnificent white beard which covered almost all of the old man's chest with a blanket of silvery white, reaching down to his heavy metal belt. At last he rose and descended a few of the marble steps. "They are coming!" he said to himself.

The light of a torch became visible, rapidly approaching the temple from the direction of the city. Soon rapid footsteps could be heard, and shortly afterwards three men started to climb the ancient marble steps.

"Hail, Master Hildebrand, Hildung's son!" the torchbearer who led the little group called out as he reached the Pronaos, or antechamber of the old building. He was evidently the youngest of the three men, and he spoke in the Gothic tongue with a peculiarly melodious voice.

He held the flickering light high in the air. It was beautifully worked, the handle of Corinthian bronze topped by a four-sided shade made of ivory. Without hesitation the young man placed the torch into a metal ring that held together the remains of the main central column of the building.

The light of the torch illuminated a face of almost godlike beauty, with laughing pale blue eyes. His long waving blond hair was parted in the middle and reached down to his shoulders. His mouth and nose were delicately formed, almost feminine, and he wore a light golden beard. He was dressed entirely in white. A white cloak of finest wool was held together over his right shoulder by a golden clasp in the shape of an eagle, and under it he wore a Roman toga of the finest silk, embroidered with gold thread. On his feet he wore sandals, fastened in the Roman manner by white leather straps tied in a cross pattern reaching to his knees. His bare arms were covered with broad bands of gold, and as he stood there, resting from the arduous climb and leaning on a tall lance, it seemed as if a youthful Apollo had returned to the ancient temple, just as he might have done in the distant past when it was still resplendent in its former glory.

The second man to arrive bore an unmistakable family resemblance to the first arrival, and yet differed markedly in appearance from the torchbearer. He was a few years older than his brother, and his build was broader and more powerful, of gigantic height and strength. His tightly curled brown hair reached to his bull-like neck, but his face lacked that confident and joyful glow which lit up the features of his younger brother. Indeed, his whole appearance resembled that of a bear, full of strength and raw courage. He wore the hide of a large wolf like a cape, its head crowning his own, and its shaggy fur dripping raindrops. Under the wolf cape he wore a plain woollen garment, and on his right shoulder rested a short, massive club fashioned from the root of a stone oak.

The third man followed with measured step, apparently deep in thought. He was of medium height, with an open face suggesting intelligence, honesty and integrity. He wore the brown cloak, steel helmet and sword of a Gothic foot soldier, and his light brown hair was trimmed straight across his forehead in the ancient Germanic style, as depicted on Roman victory columns. His regular features and his whole appearance suggested calmness, manliness and dependability.

When all three had reached the *cella* of the old temple and greeted the old man the torchbearer called out in a lively tone: "Well now, Master Hildebrand, it must be quite some adventure that caused you to call us together here, into this wilderness and on such a wild night. Speak, what's on your mind?"

Instead of replying the old man turned to the last of the three and asked, "Where is the fourth man I invited?"

"He insisted on coming alone," was the reply. "He turned us all away, but you know his manner well."

"Here he comes now!" said the blond youth, pointing to the other side of the hill, and indeed a man of most unusual appearance was approaching.

The full light of a torch shone on a seemingly bloodless face with an almost ghostly pallor. Long strands of shiny black hair, wet with rain, fell from his bare head to his shoulders in wild disarray, like a cluster of dark serpents. Melancholy eyes with long lashes under arched brows held a hint of inner fire, and a finely shaped aquiline nose contrasted sharply against a clean-shaven mouth and chin. It was the face of a man who had endured much grief and sorrow, and whilst his build and movements were those of a young man in his prime, his soul seemed to have aged prematurely with suffering. His chest and legs were clad in an expertly made suit of armour fashioned entirely of black steel, and his right hand held a battleaxe on a long shaft. He greeted the others by nodding his head and placed himself behind the old man. The latter now gathered all four men together near the column bearing the torch, and began in a subdued voice:

"I have called you together here this night, because there are serious matters which need to be discussed by loyal and dependable men willing to help, and in a place where we cannot be overheard. For months I have looked about me, among our whole nation. You four are the ones I have chosen because you are the right men. After you have heard what I have to say you will understand why you must keep to yourselves those matters which we will discuss this night."

The soldier with the steel helmet looked at the old man seriously and said in a calm voice: "Speak! We will listen and remain silent. What is it of which you wish to speak to us?"

"Of our people, of this our Gothic nation and Empire, which are on the brink of disaster."

"Disaster?" cried the blond youth animatedly. His gigantic brother smiled and raised his head, listening intently.

"Yes, on the brink of disaster," replied the old man, "and you four, you alone can avert it and lead our nation back to glory."

"May heaven forgive you those words!" the torchbearer interjected passionately. "Don't we have our king Theodoric, whom even his enemies call great, the finest warrior and the wisest monarch in the world? And then do we not also have this wonderful, smiling land, Italy, with all its treasures? What in the world can compare with our Gothic Empire?"

The old man continued, undeterred. "Listen to me. King Theodoric, my noble master and more than a son to me, is as you say a very great ruler, and nobody knows his worth better than I, Hildebrand, Hildung's son. More than fifty years ago I brought him to his father in these very arms, a sturdy and lively infant, and said to him: 'He is strong and of noble breed; he will give you much joy.' And as he grew up I made him his first arrow, and washed his first wound. I have accompanied him to the golden city of Byzantium, and there I guarded him with my life. And as he conquered this beautiful country I rode ahead of him, step by step, and in thirty battles I held his shield. I know that he has found more learned advisers since then than his old mentor, but I doubt that he has found anyone more wise, and certainly none more faithful. Oh how strong his arm was, how sharp his eye and how clear his mind! He could be terrible in battle, yet so friendly over a goblet of wine, and when it came to sheer intelligence he could outwit even the wily Greeks. All of these things I had experienced a hundred times long before you, my young falcon, first left the nest.

"But the old eagle's wings have grown tired. His many years of war weigh heavily on him, for he and you and your generation are not able to carry your years as I and my compatriots did. He is ill, mysteriously ill in body and spirit as he lies there in his golden rooms in Ravenna. His physicians remark how strong his arm still is, but every heartbeat could strike him down like lightning, and every sunset could be his last. And who is to become his heir? Amalasuntha his daughter, and Athalaric his grandson. A woman and a child!"

"The princess is wise," said the one with the helmet and sword.

"Yes, she writes letters in Greek to the emperor, and speaks Latin to the pious Cassiodorus, but I doubt that she thinks like one of us, like a Goth. May the gods protect us if she is the one who must hold the helm in a storm!"

"But I cannot see any sign of a storm, not anywhere!" the torchbearer laughed as he shook his blond locks. "From where can it possibly blow? We are at peace with the emperor, the bishop of Rome was appointed by the king himself, the rulers of the Franks are the king's nephews, and the Italians are better off under our shield than they have ever been. I see no danger, not anywhere."

"Emperor Justinus is a weak old man," agreed the one with the sword. "I know him."

"But do you also know his nephew, who is already his right arm and who will soon succeed him? Justinian is as dark as the night and as treacherous as the sea! I know him, and I fear what he has in mind. I accompanied our last group of envoys to Byzantium, and he came to our feast. He thought I was drunk, the fool, not knowing just how much Hildung's child can drink. He questioned me at length about anything and everything one needs to know in order to destroy us. Well, I told him what I wanted him to think, not what he wanted to know, but I know it as surely as I know my own name; this man wants Italy back for the Empire, and he will not rest until he has wiped out every last Gothic footprint from these shores."

"If he can, that is!" growled the giant.

"Right, friend Hildebad, if he can. But make no mistake; he can do a great deal. Byzantium is immensely powerful."

Hildebad shrugged his shoulders in disagreement, causing the old man to ask angrily: "Have you any idea just how strong they are? For twelve long years our great king fought with Byzantium, and even then he could not win decisively. But you weren't even born then," he added, calming himself.

"Very well," the giant's younger brother interjected, "but in those days we Goths fought alone in a foreign country. Since then our nation has gained another half. We now have a home, Italy, and in the Italians we have brothers in arms."

"Italy our home!" cried Hildebrand. "What a delusion! And the southerners our allies against Byzantium? You young fool!"

"Those are our king's own words," the youth replied, defending what he had said.

"Yes, I know them well, those delusions which will eventually destroy us all. We are foreigners here, just as we were forty years ago when we first came down from the Alps, and a thousand years from now we will still be foreign. In this land we will always be Barbarians."

"But why must we remain Barbarians? Whose fault is that but our own? Why don't we learn from them?"

"Be silent!" the old man cried, shaking with anger. "Be silent, Totila. Thinking such as yours has become the curse of my house!" Controlling himself with difficulty he went on: "The southerners are our mortal enemies, never our brothers. Woe betide us if we trust them! If only our king had followed my advice after our victory and wiped all who could carry sword and shield, from babes in arms to old men. They will always hate us, and with reason. Yet we are fools enough to admire them."

There was a pause, and the youth continued in a more serious tone, "Do you really believe that friendship between us and them is out of the question?"

"There will never be peace between the sons of Gaut and these southern people. We are like the man who enters a dragon's golden lair, and forces the dragon's head down with an iron fist. The creature begs for its life and the man has pity, blinded by its glittering scales, and his eyes wander to the treasure in the cave. And what will the poison worm do? As soon as it can it will attack its benefactor from behind and kill him."

"Very well then, let them come, and let this horde of vipers rise against us!" cried the huge Hildebad. "We will smash them, like this!" With those words he raised his club and smashed it into the floor, so that the marble plate smashed into fragments, shaking the old temple to its very foundations.

"Yes, let them try!" Totila added, his eyes aglow with a fire which made him look even more handsome. "If these ungrateful Romans betray us, and if those treacherous

Greeks attack us, then look, old man! We have men like oak trees." He allowed his eyes to rest with loving pride on his brother's huge frame.

The old man nodded agreement. "Yes, Hildebad is strong, very strong, even if he is not quite as strong as Winithar and Walamer and the others I knew in my youth. And strength is a good thing against Germanic peoples like our own. But these southerners fight from walls and towers. They conduct war like an exercise in arithmetic, and in the end they can calculate an army of warriors into a corner where they can barely move. I know of one such master tactician in Byzantium. He is not a man himself, and yet he defeats men. You know him too I think, Witigis."

The last words were addressed to the one with the sword, who had become very serious. "Yes, I know Narses, and I am afraid that what you have said is only too true. I have often had similar thoughts, but they were more like a dark foreboding. You are right! The king is nearing death, the princess is more Greek than Gothic, the Italians false as vipers, and the Byzantine generals veritable magicians in the art of warfare. But happily we Goths do not stand alone. Our wise king has made friends and allies everywhere. The king of the Vandals is his brother-in-law, and the king of the Visigoths his grandson. The kings of Burgundy, Thuringia, the Heruli and the Franks are all related to him by marriage. All nations honour him like a father, and even the Estonians send him gifts of fur and yellow amber from the far away eastern sea. Is all that—"

"All of that is nothing except empty words and pretty trinkets!" Hildebrand interrupted him. "Do you really expect the Estonians with their amber to help us against Belisarius and Narses? Woe betide us if we cannot win alone! These various allies will flatter us as long as they fear us, and once they no longer fear us they will threaten us. I have much experience with such matters as the faithlessness of kings. We are surrounded by enemies everywhere, some open and some secret, and we have not a friend anywhere other than ourselves."

A silence followed, during which they weighed the old man's words. The storm howled through the weathered remains of the old temple and shook the decaying columns.

Witigis was first to speak. He raised his eyes from the ground and said in a firm voice: "The danger is great, but I trust that the situation is not hopeless. Surely you did not call us together just to look helplessly at a threatening future? There must be some way we can help ourselves, and we want to hear from your lips what you think must be done."

The old man took a step toward him and took his hand. "Well said, Witigis, Waltari's son! Yes, I think as you do. We can still avert the worst, and that is why I have asked you all here, to seek your counsel where no enemy can hear us, and to find a way. So let each of you speak and offer your thoughts, and then I will give you mine."

As they all remained silent, Hildebrand turned to the black-haired last arrival. "If you think as we do then you too should give your thoughts, Teias. Why have you remained silent?"

"I am silent because I think differently from the rest of you."

The others were astonished, and Hildebrand asked, "What do you mean by that, my son?"

"Hildebad and Totila do not see the danger. You and Witigis see it with hope. I have seen it long ago, but I do not hope."

"You are too pessimistic," Witigis replied. "How can you surrender before the fight has even begun?"

"Are we to simply perish, our swords in their scabbards, without even a fight and without honour?" cried Totila.

"Not without a fight, my Totila, and certainly not without honour, believe me," Teias replied, his hand on the shaft of his battleaxe. "We will most certainly fight, and fight in such a way that men will never forget it in all eternity. We will fight with courage that will become legend, and with honour and with the greatest glory, but in the end we will not win. The Gothic star is setting."

"Nonsense! I think our star is about to rise higher than ever!" Totila replied impatiently. "Let us go before the king. Hildebrand, you speak to him as you have spoken to us. He is wise, and he will give us guidance."

But the old man shook his head. "Twenty times I have spoken to him, but he no longer hears me. He is tired and wants to die. His soul is clouded by who knows what shadow. Hildebad, what do you think?"

"I think," replied the giant, "that as soon as the old lion has closed his eyes we should mobilise two armies. Witigis and Teias will lead one of them to the gates of Byzantium and burn it to the ground. My brother and I will cross the Alps with the other army and smash Paris, the dragon nest of the Merovingians, into a heap of rubble for all time. Then there will be peace both in the east and in the north."

"We have no ships against Byzantium," said Witigis.

"And the Franks outnumber us seven to one," added Hildebrand. "But you mean well, Hildebad. What do you suggest, Witigis?"

"I advise an alliance of all the northern tribes and nations against Byzantium, properly sworn and secured by an exchange of hostages."

"You trust in others because you yourself are true, my friend. Believe me, only the Goths can help the Goths, but we must remind them that they still are Goths. Listen to me. You are all still young, and each one of you loves and enjoys something. One might love a woman, another his weapons, a third some hope or even a secret sorrow which to him is like a loved one. But believe me, a time will come, a time of need even for the young, when all these joys and even sorrows become worthless, like the dead flowers from yesterday's feast.

"During such times people become soft and pious. They forget what is here on earth, and instead they seek something beyond this life and beyond death. I cannot do that, and I believe that many among us, including you here, cannot do it either. I love the earth, the mountains, the forest, the meadow and the babbling stream. I love the life here on this earth with its fierce hatreds and enduring love, with its violent anger and silent pride. Of the airy life hereafter up in the clouds, about which the Christian priests teach us, I know nothing and I want no part of it. But there is one thing a decent man can cling to, even when everything else is lost. Look at me! I am like a leafless tree in winter. I have lost everything that brought me joy in life. My wife has been dead for many years, my sons are dead and my grandsons are dead, all except one and he is worse than dead for he has become a southerner. All those whom I knew as a boy and in my prime have long been dead and buried, and even my last great love, my king, is tired and not far from the grave. What do you think it is that gives me my will to live?

"What is it that burns under this white beard, that gives me courage and purpose to drive me out on a wild night like this, like a young man? I will tell you what it is. It is that deep urge which is for ever in our blood, the pull toward my and our people. It is a mighty and enduring love to everything that is Gothic, to all those who speak the beautiful tongue of my parents and who live and feel as I do. It alone remains, this love of my people, like a fire which goes on burning in my heart long after no other glow is left. It is the holy of holies, and the most powerful force in a man's breast, to stay with him to the grave, utterly invincible."

The old man's eyes glowed with idealistic zeal. His long white hair fluttered in the wind and he stood there like a heathen priest from a bygone age among the younger men, their fists gripping their weapons.

At last Teias spoke. "You are right. This one flame still blazes where all else has long been extinguished. But it burns in you, in us, perhaps in a hundred or so more of our brothers. But can that save an entire people? No! And can that fire grip the masses in their hundreds and thousands and hundreds of thousands?"

"Yes, it can, my son, and I thank the gods for it. Hear me well. It is now forty-five years since the day when we Goths, several hundred thousand of us, with women and children, were trapped in the inhospitable chasms of the Haemus Mountains.

"We were in a desperate situation. The king's brother had been defeated and killed in a treacherous surprise attack by the Byzantines, and all the provisions he was to bring to us were lost. We sat between bare walls of rock, and suffered so badly with hunger that we were boiling grass and leather. Unscaleable cliffs behind us, the sea in front and to our left, and in a narrow pass on our right the enemy, outnumbering us three to one. Thousands of us had died from hunger that winter, and twenty times we had tried to break through that pass, in vain. We were on the point of despair. And then an envoy came to us from the emperor, offering us our lives, freedom, bread, wine and meat with only one condition. We were to be scattered in groups of four throughout the Roman Empire. We were never again to wed a Gothic woman. We were never again to teach our children our Gothic language or Gothic customs. Even the very name and character of us Goths were to vanish, and we were to become Romans. When he heard that, our king leapt to his feet and called us together. In an unforgettable, passionate speech he put the enemy proposal to us, and then he asked us to choose. Would we rather give up the language, customs and traditions of our people, or would we rather die with him? And his words swept through the hundreds, the thousands and the hundreds of thousands, like a forest fire through dry twigs. A great cry arose from those fine men, like a roaring sea, and with swords flashing they stormed that pass! The enemy were swept away as if they had never been there, and we were victorious and free."

The old man's eyes glowed in proud remembrance, and after a pause he went on: "That alone can save us, now as it did then. Once our Goths know that they are fighting for that ultimate treasure, to preserve their precious customs and the language of their people, then they can laugh at Byzantium's hatred and southern treachery alike. And this, above all else, is what I want to ask of every one of you, with all my heart. Do you feel in your innermost being, as I do, that this love of our people is the ultimate, the finest treasure and the strongest shield there is? Can you truthfully say with me: 'My people are more to me than anything else in the world, and compared to my people all other things are nothing. To my people I will give everything I have, and to my people I will sacrifice myself if need be.' Can you, will you say that with me?"

"Yes, I can. Yes, I will," the four men replied in turn.

"That is good," the old man continued. "But Teias is right. Even now many of us Goths no longer feel like this, and yet if we are to survive they all must. Therefore will each one of you swear to me that from this day you will work tirelessly, night and day, so that you and those of our people with whom you come in daily contact are filled with the spirit of this hour? Many, many of us have been blinded by the glitter of foreign finery. Many wear Greek clothes, and think Roman thoughts. They are ashamed to be called Barbarians, and they want to forget that they are Goths. They have torn their hearts from their breasts, and yet they want to live. They are like leaves from a tree, which the wind can blow into muddy puddles where they will rot. But the trunk of the tree will survive the storm, and with it will live all that adhere to it. That is what you must teach our people, and remind them of it constantly. Tell the young boys the legends of our fathers, of battles against the Huns, of victories over the Romans. Show the men how danger threatens, and how only our Gothic spirit can be our shield. Tell your sisters that they must not embrace a Roman or one who has become one, and tell your wives and your brides that if need be they must be willing to sacrifice everything, themselves and yourselves and your children, for our Gothic people. And then, if the enemy should come, they will find us a strong nation, proud, united and firm, and the enemy will be destroyed like a wave on a rock. Will you help me achieve this?"

"I believe you," he continued, after they had all agreed. "But I still believe in our ancient customs, and the traditions of our fathers. Our aims are more likely to meet with success if we follow those old customs. I therefore ask that you follow me."

Chapter 2

With these words he took the torch from the column and strode through the interior of the temple, past the crumbling main altar and the pedestals of statues long gone, to the posticum at the building's rear. The others followed the old man in silence as he led them down more steps into the open.

After a few more steps they stood under an ancient stone oak, whose majestic crown held off rain and storm like a roof. Under the tree a strange sight met the Gothic men, reminding them at the same time of an ancient custom dating back to their heathen past, which their forebears had brought with them from their distant northern homeland. Under the tree a strip of the dense turf had been cut open, only a foot in width but several feet long. The ends of the strip of turf were still attached to the ground, its centre raised above the ground resting on three spears of different length, which had been rammed into the earth, the longest of them in the centre. The whole arrangement formed a raised triangle, and several men could comfortably stand under it between the spears. A brass kettle filled with water stood in a shallow crevice under it, and beside it lay an ancient slaughtering knife, sharp and pointed, hundreds of years old, with a blade of flint stone and a hilt made from the horn of a mountain steer. The old man approached and rammed the torch into the earth beside the kettle. He then stepped into the crevice, right foot first, and turned to the east, bowing his head. Enjoining them to silence by placing a finger on his lips, he then bade the others to follow his example. Silently the four men stepped into the hole and stood beside the old man, Witigis and Teias on his left and the two brothers on his right, and all five then joined hands to form a symbolic chain. Letting go of Witigis and Hildebad, who were nearest to him, the old man knelt. First he gathered a handful of the black forest earth and threw it over his left shoulder. With the other hand he reached into the kettle and sprinkled a little water behind him on his right. Finally he exhaled deeply into the night air, his long white beard blown about his face by the wind, and waved the torch above his head from right to left.

In a soft murmur he began to speak, as if to himself: "Hear me, old earth, flowing water, light air and flickering flame! Hear me well and mark my words. Here stand five men from the people of Gaut, Teias and Totila, Hildebad and Hildebrand, and Witigis, Waltari's son.

"We stand here in this quiet hour to forge a bond of blood brothers, for evermore and for all eternity. We will be as true brothers in peace and war, for better or for worse. One hope, one hate, one love, one pain as we now combine into the one drop our blood as blood brothers."

With these words he bared his left arm. The others followed suit, holding their bare arms close together above the kettle. The old man picked up the knife, and with one stroke he scratched the skin of his own forearm and those of the four others, so that a few drops of blood from each of them fell in red drops into the kettle. He then resumed his former position and continued to speak:

"And we swear an eternal oath to give up everything we have, house, land and possessions, horse, weapons and cattle, sons, kinsmen and servants, wife and body and our lives to the good and glory of the people of Gaut, the good and noble Goths. And if any one of us should refuse to honour this oath with all its sacrifices—"

At this point he and the others stepped out of the crevice and from under the turf roof. "—then his red blood shall flow un-avenged like the water under this forest grass—"

With that he picked up the kettle, poured the bloody water into the ditch, and then removed it along with the other implements.

"—and on his head the halls of heaven shall fall with thunder, and crush him to death with the might and weight of this turf."

With a single stroke he cut down all three spears, and the strip of turf fell heavily into the crevice with a dull thud. The five men joined hands once more and stood together on the strip of grass which had now been restored to its former state. In a faster tone Hildebrand continued. "And if any one of us should fail to honour this oath and this bond, or fail to defend his blood brothers like a real brother, or to avenge their death, or if he should refuse to sacrifice everything he has to the Gothic people in their need, then he shall for ever be damned. He shall live for all eternity among the dark powers which live under the green grass of this earth. The feet of good men shall trample on the traitor's head, and his name shall be without honour wherever Christians sound their bells or heathens make sacrifices, wherever a mother suckles her child or the wind blows, across the whole wide world. Speak, brothers, is that the fate which must befall a lowly traitor?"

"That is what shall happen to him," the four men repeated.

After a pause Hildebrand broke the chain of hands and said: "Now I want you to know why this place has a special significance for me, as it now does for you, and why I chose this place for what we have done here this night. Follow me!" Picking up the torch he strode ahead to the other side of the ancient tree, exactly opposite where the crevice had been in which they had all stood. To their astonishment they saw yawning before them an open grave, and beside it a slab of rock which had been removed from its former role of resting over it. There, in the depth of the grave, lit by the ghostly glow of the torch, lay three long white skeletons, together with a few rusty weapons, spearheads and the remains of a shield. The four men stared in surprise, first at the old man and then at the remains. Hildebrand looked silently into the grave for a long time. At last he spoke again: "My three sons. They have been lying here for thirty years and more. They fell on this hill during the final battle for the city of Ravenna. They all fell in the same hour, on this day. Jubilantly they threw themselves into the enemy spears – for their people."

He paused. The four men stood, deeply moved, each occupied with his own thoughts. At last the old man raised himself to his full height and looked up at the sky. "It is done," he said, "the stars are growing pale, and midnight has long passed. Go on back to the city all of you, except Teias. Teias, I think you will want to stay here with me. You more than anyone have the gift of sorrow as you do the gift of song. You and I will be guard of honour to these dead."

Teias nodded without uttering a word, and sat down at the foot of the grave where he had been standing. Hildebrand handed the torch to Totila and leaned against the slab of rock on the opposite side to Teias. The other three waved him farewell and descended toward the city, each one of them gravely absorbed in silent thought.

Chapter 3

A few weeks after the nocturnal meeting another meeting took place, also secret and also under the cover of night, but consisting of entirely different people gathered for entirely different reasons.

It took place on the Appian Way near the St Calixtus cemetery, in a buried passage of the catacombs, that complex maze which formed another city under the city of Rome. These secret rooms and passageways were originally burial places and once served as a refuge for the early Christians, and their various entrances, exits and intersections are so difficult to find that their innermost sections should only ever be visited with a competent guide. But the men attending the meeting we shall be witnessing this night were not afraid, for they were well led. None other than Silverius, the Catholic Archdeacon of the old church of St Sebastian, had led his friends from the crypt of the saint's basilica down the steep steps into this section of the labyrinth. Roman priests were said to have passed on their intimate knowledge of the catacombs through the ages, and Silverius knew his way. The men who were gathered here this night did not look as if the surroundings were strange to them, and seemed immune to their gruesomeness. Quite indifferently they leaned against the walls of an eerie semicircle, dimly lit by a bronze lamp, which formed part of a low passageway. The drops of water which regularly fell did not concern them, and if perchance their feet struck a white bone here and there, they merely kicked it aside without looking at it or taking any notice of it.

Apart from Silverius there were a few more priests present, together with a number of Roman patricians, descendants from those old noble families whose members had held almost every important office in Rome for centuries, as their birthright.

Attentively and in silence they watched the archdeacon's movements. The latter carefully scrutinised those present, occasionally casting inquiring glances into the adjoining passages where young men in clerical robes were keeping watch. At last he appeared to be taking steps formally to open the meeting. Once more he approached the tall man leaning motionless against the wall opposite him, with whom he had repeatedly exchanged glances. When the latter nodded silently in response to an inquiring look Silverius turned to the others and said:

"Dearly beloved, gathered here in the sight and name of Almighty God! Once again we are gathered here to do our holy work. The sword of Edom is drawn over our heads, and Pharaoh thirsts after the blood of the children of Israel. But we do not fear those who kill our bodies but cannot harm our souls. What we do fear is He who can destroy our bodies and our souls with everlasting fire. On this night we put our trust in Him who led his people through the desert, and we will never forget that our suffering is for God, and everything we do is to honour His name. Thanks be to Him, for He has blessed our efforts. Small were our beginnings, as were those of the gospel, but already we have grown like a young tree by a flowing stream. In fear and hesitation we first came here, for the danger was great and hope small. The noble blood of fine men had flowed. But today, firm in our faith, we say with courage and with confidence. Pharaoh's throne stands on feet of straw, and the days of the heretics are numbered in this, our country."

"Get to the point!" a young Roman with flashing eyes and short curly hair interrupted. Impatiently he threw back his cloak from his left hip over his right shoulder, revealing the short Roman sword he wore. "Get to the point, priest! What is to happen today?"

Silverius could not quite hide his annoyance, but maintained an outward calm as he went on sharply. "Even those who do not believe in the holiness of our purpose should not deny others the right to believe, especially if it is only to advance their own worldly aims. Tonight, Licinius my impatient friend, another highly welcome member will join our ranks, and his presence here is a sure sign of God's mercy."

"Whom do you propose? Have all the conditions been fulfilled? Will you vouch for him absolutely? Or is there another guarantor?" another conspirator asked, a man of mature years and regular features, who had been sitting quietly on a part of a wall, a staff between his feet.

"I vouch for him, Scaevola," Silverius replied, "in any case his identity is sufficient assurance."

"Not so! The rules of our association demand that someone must vouch for a new member, and I insist on it," Scaevola replied calmly.

"Very well, Scaevola, you incorrigible lawyer, I said I'd vouch for him," the priest replied with a smile as he waved to one of the guards in a passageway to his left.

Two young *ostiarii* led a man into the chamber, and all eyes were on the hooded head of the new arrival. Silverius removed the hood from the man's head and shoulders.

"Albinus!" the others cried in surprise, shock and anger.

Young Licinius grasped the hilt of his sword, Scaevola rose slowly to his feet, and wild shouts came from all directions: "What? Albinus the traitor?"

The accused looked about him anxiously. His flabby features were those of a born coward, and as if seeking support his eyes sought those of the priest.

"Yes, Albinus," the latter replied calmly. "Does anyone here wish to speak against him? Let him do so!"

"Great heavens!" Licinius interjected promptly. "What need is there for words? We all know who Albinus is, a coward and a disgraced traitor!" as anger choked his voice.

"Accusations are not proof," Scaevola took over from the younger man's objections, "but I now ask him myself. Let him confess here and now in front of us all. Albinus, are you or are you not the man who, when the beginnings of our conspiracy became known to the tyrant, saw fit to accuse our noble fellow conspirators Boethius and Symmachus? Although at that time only you were under suspicion did you not also involve them, even though they tried bravely to defend you? Were they not then shamefully executed and all their property confiscated? And didn't you, the real suspect, then swear a despicable oath that you would never again concern yourself in the affairs of this city, after which you saved your hide by just disappearing? Speak! Are you the coward who caused the flower of our fatherland to perish?"

A murmur arose among the conspirators. The accused stood, quietly trembling, and for a moment even Silverius lost his calm. At that moment the man who had been leaning against the wall opposite Silverius rose and took a step closer. That seemed to give the priest new courage, and the latter continued: "Friends, everything you say did happen, but not the way you say it happened. Above all know this: of all those involved Albinus is the least guilty. What he did he did on my advice."

"On your advice? You dare to admit that?"

"Albinus was compromised through the treachery of a slave, who had managed to decipher the secret code his master had used in letters to Byzantium. Once the tyrant's suspicions were aroused any sign of organised resistance could only increase the danger. Boethius and Symmachus rushed to his defence on a noble but foolish impulse, which showed the Barbarians the mood of Rome's nobility and that Albinus was not alone. They acted contrary to my advice, and sadly they paid for it with their lives. What is more their sacrifice was in vain, because the hand of the Lord claimed the faithless slave before he could make any further accusations, and it was possible to destroy the secret letters before Albinus was arrested. Now, do you think Albinus would have remained silent under torture and the threat of death when the mere naming of his fellow conspirators could save him? No, you do not believe that, and Albinus himself did not believe it either. Therefore above all else we needed time. We had to postpone the torture as much as we could, and that was done by way of that oath you call shameful. Admittedly Boethius and Symmachus were executed while all this took place, but at least we could be certain of their silence, even under torture. Albinus himself was freed from prison by a miracle, like St Paul of Philippi. It was said that he had fled to Athens, and that the tyrant was content to forbid his return, but in fact Almighty God had granted him a refuge here in His temple until the hour of freedom comes. In the loneliness of this asylum the Lord has been able to reach the heart of this man in a wondrous way. Undaunted by his near escape from death this man has once more stepped into our midst, and he now offers his entire enormous fortune to the service of God and the fatherland. Please note that he has donated all his property to the church of St Mary, to be used for the purposes of our conspiracy. Do you want to reject him and his millions?"

An astonished pause followed, but at last Licinius cried, "Priest, you are very clever, just like a priest. But I do not like such cleverness."

"Silverius," the lawyer added, "you may take the millions. That is your right. But I was Boethius's friend, and I will have nothing to do with this coward. I cannot forgive him. Get rid of him!"

"Get rid of him!" The cry arose from all sides. Scaevola had put into words what they all felt. Albinus grew pale, and even Silverius was shaken by the contempt he saw all around him. "Cethegus!" he whispered quietly, seeking support.

So far the silent man had observed all with a superior calm, but now he looked up. He was tall and lean but powerfully built, with a broad chest and muscles of steel. A purple edge on his toga suggested wealth, rank and good taste, but the remainder of his attire was concealed under a long soldier's coat, under which well-made sandals were visible. His face was one of those once seen never forgotten.

His thick and still shining black hair was cut short in the Roman manner about his temples and high, almost oversized forehead. Narrow eyes under delicately curved brows seemed to conceal an entire ocean of buried passions, and even more strongly they suggested iron self-control. His sharply defined mouth and clean-shaven chin gave him an air of proud disdain for God and the whole world. As he stepped forward, his calm but noble eyes firmly on the restless group, he commenced to speak in a tone which was neither dominating nor flattering, yet exerted its influence on all those present. Few men were able to bear his presence without feeling inferior.

Calmly he began. "Why do you quarrel about what must be? Surely you know that the end justifies the means. So you do not wish to forgive? No matter, it is not important, but one thing you must do is to forget. That you can do. I too was a friend of the two deceased, perhaps their closest friend, and yet I am determined to forget. I am willing to forget for the very reason that I was their friend. Only he loves them, Scaevola, who is willing to avenge them. For the sake of revenge, Albinus, your hand!"

All were silent, won over more by the personality of Cethegus than his logic. Only the lawyer added a further comment:

"Rusticiana, widow of Boethius and daughter of Symmachus and a most influential woman, is a supporter of our conspiracy. Will she remain so if the traitor joins us? Can she forgive and forget?"

"Yes, she can! Do not believe me, believe your eyes."

With these words Cethegus turned quickly into one of the side passages, which his back had until now concealed. Close to the entrance a veiled figure stood listening. Cethegus grasped the stranger's hand and whispered: "Come now, come!"

"I cannot. I will not!" the reluctant woman replied quietly.

"You must! Come, you can and you will, for I will it so." He threw back her veil, and after another glance she followed him as if she had no will of her own.

They turned into the main chamber. "Rusticiana!" they all cried.

"A woman in our midst," said the lawyer, "that is against our rules."

"Yes, Scaevola, but the rules were made to serve our cause, not the other way round. And you would never have believed from my lips what you now see with your eyes." With that he laid the widow's hand into the trembling right hand of Albinus.

"Look, Rusticiana forgives. Who can now hold out?"

They were all silent, overcome and convinced. Cethegus seemed to have no further interest in whatever was to follow, and with the woman he retreated to the wall behind him. The priest declared solemnly: "Albinus is now a member of our conspiracy."

"But what about the oath he swore to the tyrant?" Scaevola asked hesitatingly.

"It was forced on him, and has been made null and void by the holy church. But now it is time to part, and we have time only for the most urgent business and for the most urgent messages. Here, Licinius, is the plan of the fortifications of Naples. You must have it copied by tomorrow, as it is going to Belisarius. Scaevola, here are some letters from Byzantium, from Theodora, Justinian's pious wife. You must reply to them. Calpurnius, please take charge of this remittance for half a million *solidi* from Albinus and see that it gets to the Major Domo of the Franks. He will use his influence with his king against the Goths. Pomponius, here is a list of patriots from Dalmatia. You are familiar with conditions there, and you know the people. Please check if any important names are missing. Finally I have this to pass on to you. According to letters just arrived from Ravenna today the hand of the Lord rests heavily on the tyrant. It is said that deep sorrow and belated repentance for his many sins are weighing on his soul, and he is far from the solace of the true church. Be patient a little longer. Soon he will be called away by the Almighty's angry voice, and the day of freedom will follow. We meet again on the next *ides*, at the same hour. May the Lord's blessing go with all of you."

The Archdeacon concluded the meeting. The young priests stepped out of the various side passages with their torches and led the conspirators in different directions to the exits of the catacombs, known only to them.

Chapter 4

Silverius, Cethegus and Rusticiana together climbed the steps leading to the crypt of St Sebastian's basilica, and from there they walked through the church to the archdeacon's house immediately next to the church. On arriving there the priest made sure everyone in the house was asleep, except for one old slave waiting up for his master in the atrium by the light of a candle. On a sign from his master he lit the tall silver lamp next to him, and pressed on a spot on the inlaid marble wall. The marble plates revolved on an axis and permitted the priest, who was now holding the lamp, to step with the others into a small room on the other side of the wall. The marble wall closed silently behind them, and there was no sign of any door.

The little room was simply decorated with a tall wooden cross, a prayer stool and a few Christian ornaments against a golden backdrop. Upholstered seats along the walls suggested that at some time in its heathen past this small room might have been used for those intimate and informal little feasts with only two or three guests, described in glowing terms by Horatius. But now the room served as asylum for the archdeacon's innermost religious and worldly secrets. Silently Cethegus sat down, and with the eyes of an art connoisseur he scanned the mosaic opposite him. While the priest was busy pouring wine into goblets from a tall jug and placing a bowl of fruit on a three-legged bronze table, Rusticiana stood opposite Cethegus and looked at him with reluctant admiration. Barely forty years old, she still showed traces of a rare, almost masculine beauty, which had suffered more from too much passion than from her years. Here and there grey hairs specked her rich black tresses. Her eyes were unsteady, and her mouth lined by deep creases. Her left arm resting on the table, she drew her right across her forehead as if in deep thought, staring at Cethegus at the same time. At last she said:

"Tell me this, what power is it that you have over me? I no longer love you. I should hate you, and I do, yet I cannot help myself from doing your bidding, powerless to do otherwise, just as a bird cannot avoid the eyes of a snake. And you lay my hand, this very hand, into the hand of that scoundrel. Just what is the source of your power, evil blasphemer that you are?"

Cethegus listened attentively, but in silence. At last, quite relaxed, he replied: "Habit, Rusticiana, habit."

"Yes habit! A habit that is almost like a form of slavery, and a habit which has been there almost as long as I can remember. It was natural that I, as a young girl, should be attracted to our neighbour's handsome son. I thought that you loved me, for you kissed me. Who could know back then that you are incapable of love? That you can love nothing and nobody, not even yourself? It was a sin that the wife of Boethius gave in to that love which you so playfully re-ignited in me, but God and the church have forgiven me. Yet even today, after I have known you and your heartless ways for decades, and long after the fire of passion has cooled in my veins, still I blindly follow your demonic will. It is madness, enough to make one laugh out loud."

She gave a loud laugh. The priest halted in what he was doing, and cast a sidelong glance at Cethegus. His interest had been aroused. Cethegus leaned back against the marble and picked up his goblet.

"You are unjust, Rusticiana," he said quietly. "What is worse, you are illogical. You are confusing the games of Eros with the work of Eris and the Erynnae. You know that I was Boethius's friend, even though I did kiss his wife, or perhaps because of it. I see nothing special in that, and as for you, Silverius and the church have forgiven you. You also know that I hate these Goths, and I mean really hate them. Furthermore you know that I have the will, and what is more important the ability, to achieve the goal that possesses you, which is to avenge your beloved father and the husband you honoured. That is why you follow me, and you are wise to do so. Admittedly you have a remarkable talent for intrigue, but your impetuousness often clouds your judgment and spoils even your most carefully laid plans. You are wise therefore to follow one who keeps a cooler head than you, that's all. But now you had better leave. Your slave is waiting for you sleepily in the vestibule, thinking you are here in confession with your friend Silverius. Now a confession can last only so long, and she might become suspicious. Please remember me to Camilla, your lovely child, and keep well!"

He rose, took her hand and gently led her to the door. She took her leave with apparent reluctance, nodding a farewell to the priest and casting a last glance at Cethegus, who seemed oblivious to the violent emotions within her. Quietly shaking her head she left.

Cethegus sat down again and emptied his goblet.

"What a strange conflict between you and this woman," said Silverius as he sat down beside Cethegus with his wax tablets, stylus, letters and documents.

"Not strange at all! She is just trying to erase her guilt toward her husband by avenging him. And the fact that she is doing this through none other than her former lover makes her sacred duty that much sweeter. Of course she is not consciously aware of any of this. Anyway, what do we have to discuss?"

The two men now commenced their work handling those matters connected with the conspiracy which they considered were best not discussed with the other members.

The archdeacon began: "The most important thing we have to do today is to determine the exact extent of Albinus's wealth, and how we can put it to best use in the immediate future. There is no question that we need money, a great deal of money."

"Money matters are your speciality," said Cethegus, "I understand them well enough, but they bore me."

"Furthermore we must win over all the influential men in Sicily, Naples and Apulia. Here is a list of them, with detailed information about each one. There are men among them who will not yield to our usual methods of persuasion."

"Give me the list, I will handle it," Cethegus replied confidently as he cut into a Persian apple.

After an hour's intensive work the most urgent business was done, and the master of the house returned the documents to their secret hiding place behind the large cross in the wall. The priest was tired, and looked with envy on his companion, whose steel body and indomitable spirit seemed tireless no matter how late the hour, whatever the exertion. He made a comment to that effect as Cethegus was refilling his silver goblet.

"Practice, my friend, strong nerves and a clear conscience," Cethegus replied with a smile, "that is the whole secret."

"No, seriously Cethegus. You puzzle me in other ways too."

"I certainly hope so!"

"What do you mean by that? Do you consider yourself so superior as to be beyond the understanding of other men?"

"Not at all. I am only just mysterious enough to puzzle others as much as I puzzle myself. You can relax, your knowledge of human nature has not let you down. I do not understand myself any better than you do. Only drops are transparent."

"The key to your being must certainly lie very deep down." The priest went on. "Take the other members of the conspiracy, for example. With each one I know exactly what led him to join us. There is the hot-headed enthusiasm of Licinius, Scaevola's misguided but righteous sense of justice, and in the other priests and myself the urge to serve God."

"Of course," Cethegus replied as he took a draught of wine.

"Others are driven by ambition, or by the hope of cutting their creditors' throats in a civil war, or the sheer boredom of living in this peaceful land under the Goths. Some may be driven by a stranger's insult, and most of us have a natural aversion to these Barbarians, together with a habit of recognising only the emperor as Italy's rightful ruler. But none of these motives apply to you, and—"

"And that is very disturbing, is it not? Does one not rule men by knowing their motives? I am afraid I cannot help you, my pious friend. I really don't know myself what it is that drives me. If only I knew I would gladly tell you and thus be ruled by you. There is only one thing I feel clearly. I simply cannot stand these Goths, these big peasants with their yellow beards. I find their boorish good natures as well as their naivety repulsive. As well as their crudeness and that silly heroism of theirs. The world is ruled by disgusting accidents of chance. Why should this land with its history and with men like, well, like you and me, why should this land be ruled by these northern Barbarians?" He threw back his head in disgust, closed his eyes and took a sip of wine.

Silverius replied: "There is no doubt the Barbarians must go, we agree on that point. And as far as I am concerned once that happens my own goals will have been achieved. All I seek is to free our church from these Barbarian heretics, who deny the godliness of Christ and try to make a pagan idol out of him. I hope that the Roman church will then occupy the pre-eminent place in Christendom, which is its unquestionable due. But as long as Rome is occupied by these heretics, and as long as the bishop in Byzantium is supported by the only rightful emperor—"

"The Bishop of Rome is not the first bishop in Christendom, and not Italy's ruler. And therefore the holy chair of Rome, even if one Silverius should one day occupy it, is not what it should be, the highest office in the church. Isn't that what you want?"

Startled, the priest looked up.

"Do not be alarmed, friend of God. I have known and kept your secret for a long time, even though you never confided it to me. But let us continue." He filled his goblet once more. "Your Falernian wine is well aged, but a little too sweet. Really, from your point of view it would be best if these Goths would merely vacate the throne of the Caesars, not that the Byzantines should take their place. Otherwise the Bishop of Rome would still have a more senior bishop in Byzantium, as well as an emperor. So you don't want an emperor like Justinian in the Goths' place, but rather you want – what?"

Eagerly Silverius suggested. "Either an emperor of our own, an emperor of the western Empire—"

"Who would be a puppet in the hands of St Peter." Cethegus completed the sentence for him.

"Or a Roman republic, a church state—"

"In which the Bishop of Rome would be the ruler, Italy the principal country, and the Barbarian kings in Gaul, Germany and Spain obedient sons of the Church. So far so good, my friend. But first we must destroy the enemies whose spoils you are already distributing. So I will propose an old Roman toast. Beware the Barbarians!"

He rose and raised his goblet to the priest. "But the night is almost over, and my slaves must find me in my sleeping quarters in the morning. Keep well!" He drew the hood of his cloak over his head and departed.

His host followed him with his eyes. "A most important tool!" he said to himself, "but fortunately only a tool. May he always remain just that."

Cethegus walked from the Via Appia, where the church of St Sebastian concealed the entrance to the catacombs, in a northwesterly direction towards the Capitol. His house was situated at the foot of the Capitol, at the northern end of the Via Sacra and northeast of the Forum Romanum.

The cool morning air revived him. He threw back his cloak, took a deep breath and stretched his powerful arms and shoulders. Quietly he said to himself: "Yes, you are a riddle to be sure. Here you are, involved in conspiracies and nocturnal intrigues like a youth of twenty, or like a republican. And why? Why does the youth even draw breath? Because he must, and for the same reason I must do as I am doing. However one thing is certain. This priest may well become Pope, and it may even be necessary. But he must not on any account remain Pope for long, for if he does you can forget about your own dreams, Cethegus, those vague dreams as yet shadowy and unclear. Yet those same ideas may yet become a thunderstorm, with thunder and lightning, and that storm decide my fate. Look there, I can see lightning in the east. Very well, I accept it as an omen."

With those words he entered his house. In his bedchamber, on a cedar table in front of his bed, he found a letter, tied and sealed with the royal seal.

He cut the string with his dagger, opened the double wax tablet and read:

"To Cethegus Caesarius, the Princeps Senatus, from Marcus Aurelius Cassiodorus, Senator. Our king and master lies dying. His daughter and heiress Amalasuntha wishes to speak with you before the end. You are to assume a most important office in the government. Come to Ravenna at once."

Chapter 5

An air of oppressive gloom lay over the royal palace in Ravenna, with its cheerless opulence and its inhospitable spaciousness. The very air seemed heavy.

The old fortress of the Caesars had undergone many a change over the centuries, and many additions and alterations had been made, for the most part quite inconsistent with its original architectural style. Since the Gothic king and his Germanic court had taken the place of the old Imperators its appearance had become totally unappealing. Many rooms which had once served the peculiar customs of Roman life were now unused and neglected, the splendour of the original furnishings unchanged except for the effects of inevitable decay. Cobwebs covered the splendid mosaics in the once magnificent but long disused baths of Honorius, and small lizards ran over the marble framed silver mirrors of what had once been Placidia's dressing rooms. On the other hand, the needs of the more warlike Gothic court had caused many a wall to be torn down, in order to enlarge rooms into drinking halls, military quarters or guardrooms. In addition a number of neighbouring houses had been connected with the palace by way of newly built walls, thus creating a fortress within the city. In the *piscina maxima*, now a dry pond, fair-haired boys were playing their wild games, and the horses of Gothic guards neighed in the marble halls of what had been the *palaestra*. Overall the vast building had a rambling, ghostly appearance, like a barely preserved ruin and an incomplete new construction at the same time. Thus the palace of this king was symbolic of his Roman/Gothic Empire, and of his unfinished yet already decaying political creation.

On the day that Cethegus entered the building again after an absence of many years a cloud of tension, grief and gloom lay over the palace even more heavily than usual, for the soul of its Royal master was about to depart from within its walls.

The giant who had directed the fate of Europe from here for a generation, the hero of his century, who was admired with love or hate in the Orient and Occident alike, the mighty Dietrich von Bern, whose name had become legendary even in his lifetime, Theodoric the great Amalung, was about to die.

His physicians had announced this, not to him but to his advisers, and soon the news leaked out into the city and among the people. Although such an end to the monarch's mysterious illness had not been unexpected, yet the news that his end was imminent filled all hearts with uneasy anticipation.

The faithful Gothic people grieved and feared for their king, but even among the Roman population the predominant mood was one of gloomy expectation. Here in Ravenna, in the immediate presence of the king, the Italians had had ample opportunity to admire the greatness and tolerance of this man, and had experienced many acts of kindness and generosity from him. Many feared that a much harsher Gothic regime might follow the death of the king, who throughout his reign had sought to shield the Italians from the brutality and coarseness of his own people. The one exception had been his latest quarrel with the emperor, which had cost Boethius and Symmachus their lives.

But in the final analysis there was one even greater factor. The personality of this heroic king had been so grand, so majestic, that even those who often wished for the destruction of him and his Empire could not help feeling regret rather than joy now that his sun was about to set.

Such had been the mood in the city since early morning, when the first messengers had been seen hurrying from the palace in a state of great agitation. In the streets, in the squares and in the baths men stood about in pairs or small groups, exchanging what information they had heard, trying to glean more news from a nobleman coming from the palace, and speculating on what might lie ahead. Women and children sat on the doorsteps of their houses, hoping to hear some news. As the day wore on even people from neighbouring towns and villages, particularly mourning Goths, streamed through the city gates into Ravenna. Such agitation and worse had been anticipated by the king's advisers, particularly the *Praefectus Praetorio* Cassiodorus who distinguished himself in those troubled days by maintaining law and order.

Since midnight all means of access to the palace had been closed off and manned by Gothic guards. A detachment of Gothic cavalry was drawn up in front of the building, on the forum of Honorius. Strong elements of Gothic infantry with shields and spears lined the marble steps leading to the main portal.

Only here could access to the palace be gained, on the orders of Cassiodorus, and permission could only be given by one of the commanders of the infantry, the Goth Witigis or the Roman Cyprianus. The latter admitted Cethegus, who now followed the familiar route to the king's rooms. Throughout the palace there were groups of Goths or Italians whose rank entitled them to be there.

The large drinking hall, usually the scene of much gaiety, was almost silent. Young Gothic centurions and officers stood about in small groups or in twos and threes. Here and there an older man, a former companion in arms of the king, stood in a corner trying to hide his obvious grief. A wealthy merchant from Ravenna wept openly. The king, who was about to die, had forgiven him his part in a conspiracy and spared his warehouse from being plundered by angry Goths.

Cethegus walked past all of this with a look of cold contempt. In the next room, which normally served to receive ambassadors from foreign countries, he found a number of wealthy Goths and Gothic noblemen, who were obviously discussing the imminent change of ruler, and what that might mean both to their own particular circumstances and to the nation as a whole.

Among them were three of the leading Gothic nobles of the Balti clan. They were Duke Thulun of Provence, who had defended the city of Arles with great heroism against the Franks, Duke Ibba of Liguria, the conqueror of Spain, and Duke Pitza of Dalmatia, who had defeated the Bulgarians and the Gepidae. All three of them were not only powerful men, but also proud of their ancient nobility which gave them almost equal standing to the Amalungs. They also took pride in their successes in war, which had served to defend and enlarge the Empire. Another prominent member of their clan was Alaric, king of the Visigoths. Hildebad and Teias were also present, and these five men were the leaders of the party which had long sought a tougher policy toward the native Italians, whom they hated and despised. Only with great reluctance had these men accepted the king's much milder policies. Looks filled with hatred from this group met the noble Roman, who evidently sought to witness their king's last hours. But Cethegus calmly walked past them and lifted the heavy woollen curtain which led to the next room, the antechamber to the king's sickbed. On entering he encountered a tall royal lady, dressed in dark mourning clothes and standing silently but without a tear, and greeted her with a nod of his head. In front of her was a marble table covered with documents. She was Amalasuntha, the widowed daughter of Theodoric.

A woman in her mid-thirties, she possessed an exceptional if somewhat cold beauty. Her rich dark hair was parted and arranged in the Greek manner, and her high forehead, large round eyes, straight nose and the pride in her almost masculine features gave her an air of authority, which was further accentuated by her imposing full figure. Dressed as she was in a mourning gown folded in the Greek manner, she looked like a statue of Hera that had climbed down from its pedestal.

A youth of some seventeen years stood beside her, his arm in hers. He was Athalaric, her son and heir to the Gothic crown. He did not look at all like his mother, having taken after his unfortunate father Eutharic, whom a heart disease had claimed while still in his prime. It was therefore with concern that Amalasuntha saw in her son an almost exact replica of her late husband, and it was no secret at court that he was already showing all the signs of that same mysterious illness which had claimed his father. Atahalaric was very good looking, as were all the Amalungs, a clan said to be descended directly from the gods. His dark eyes were shaded by heavy brows and long lashes, and their expression varied from aloofness to dreamy uncertainty. Dark brown locks covered his pale temples, which were lined with fine blue veins. There was a look about him that suggested physical pain or severe self-denial, out of place in such a young face. His almost transparent cheeks were a mixture of marble paleness and unhealthy red, and his tall but stooped frame seemed as if he was always tired. Only occasionally was he capable of surprisingly fast movement. Leaning against his mother, with his mantle about the young head which would soon wear a heavy crown, he did not see Cethegus enter.

A short distance from these two stood a woman, or perhaps still a girl, as if daydreaming near an open window from which she could see the Gothic soldiers guarding the marble steps. She was Matesuentha, Athalaric's sister, and a young woman of startling beauty. Her tall frame and noble bearing were those of her mother, but her more sharply defined features hinted at passionate inner fire, masked only slightly by an assumed air of calm. Her well-formed slender figure was filling out to womanhood, and she was like the statue of Artemis in the arms of Endymion by Agesander. According to legend the aldermen of Rhodes had been forced to ban that statue from their city, because its marble sensuousness was driving the young men of their island to madness and suicide. Her rich, wavy hair was dark red with a metallic sheen, and was of such extraordinary beauty that it had earned her the nickname of "Princess Schoenhaar" (Princess beautiful hair) even among these people whose women had long been famous for their magnificent golden tresses. Her brows and long lashes however were a shining black, and contrasted sharply with her white forehead and alabaster cheeks. Her delicate, slightly curved nose complemented a sensuous mouth. But her most startling features were her grey eyes, not so much because of their indefinite colour as their expression, which could change from dreamy detachment to glowing passion in a split second. Her whole appearance, as she stood there at the window looking out into the night air, was one of seductive beauty, reminiscent of one of those irresistible forest nymphs with which Germanic folklore abounds. Her beauty made such a powerful impact that even Cethegus, who had known the princess for a long time, could not help a feeling of renewed admiration in his cold, burnt out breast.

However his attention was immediately claimed by the only other person in the room, Cassiodorus the king's loyal adviser, and a leading exponent of the well-meaning but hopeless policy of conciliation which had been followed in the Gothic Empire for a generation. The old man's features were disturbed not only by grief over the imminent death of his master, but also by concern for the Empire. Nevertheless they were kind, noble eyes, and he rose to greet the new arrival with uncertain steps. The latter bowed respectfully. The old man's tearful eyes rested on him, and at last he threw himself against the cold breast of Cethegus, who despised him for such weakness.

"What a day!" he complained.

"A fateful day," Cethegus replied thoughtfully, "and it will call for strength and self-control."

"Well said, Patricius, and spoken like a Roman," said Amalasuntha, disengaging herself from Athalaric, "greetings!" She gave him her hand which did not tremble. Her eye too was clear.

"Stoa's disciple is showing the wisdom of Zeno, and her own strength," said Cethegus.

"Let us say that the mercy of God is giving her soul wonderful strength," Cassiodorus corrected him.

Amalasuntha began: "Patricius, the *Praefectus Praetorio* has suggested you to me, as if I had not known you for so long. You are the same Cethegus who translated the first two songs of Aeneis into Greek hexameters?"

Cethegus smiled. "*Infandum renovare jubes, regina, dolorem.* A sin of my youth, my queen. I bought up all copies of it and had them burnt on the day Tullia's translation appeared."

Tullia was Amalasuntha's pseudonym. Cethegus knew this, but the princess did not know that he knew. He had thus found her greatest weakness, and she was immensely flattered. She went on:

"You know the situation here. My father's hours are numbered, and although he is still strong and able the physicians say he could fall down dead at any moment. Athalaric here is heir to his crown. I will be his regent and guardian until he reaches his majority."

"That is the will of the king, and both Goths and Romans have long recognised its wisdom," said Cethegus.

"That is true. But the masses are easily influenced, and these crude men despise the rule of a woman." As she said this, angry lines appeared on her forehead.

"It is contrary to both the Gothic and Roman custom," Cassiodorus remarked, "for a woman—"

"Ungrateful rebels!" Cethegus said, as if to himself.

"Regardless of how we might feel about it," said the princess, "I must accept it as a fact. All the same I know I can count on the loyalty of the Barbarians generally, even though there may be some among them who have designs on the crown, particularly certain members of the nobility. I do not fear the Italians either, here in Ravenna or in most of the cities. What I do fear is Rome, Rome and the Romans."

These words struck a chord with Cethegus, who was now concentrating with every fibre of his being, with a multitude of thoughts racing through his mind. But outwardly he remained icily calm.

With a sigh she added: "Rome will never get used to Gothic rule. They will resist us always, and indeed how could it be otherwise?" It seemed as if at heart Theodoric's daughter was part Roman.

Cassiodorus continued: "What we fear is that, once news of the king's death reaches Rome, there may be a rebellion against the regency of the princess. Such a rebellion could have the aim either of becoming part of the Byzantine Empire, or even of establishing their own separate western Empire with its own western emperor."

Cethegus lowered his eyes as if deep in thought, which indeed he was.

"Therefore," Amalasuntha went on, "we must do everything we can to prevent this happening, long before the news reaches Rome. A determined man, who is absolutely loyal to me, must have the garrison in Rome swear an oath of allegiance to me, or I should say to my son. The most important strategic points and gates of the city must be occupied, the Senate and the nobility intimidated, and my rule firmly established before it is even threatened. For this task Cassiodorus has suggested you. Will you accept?"

As she said this she inadvertently dropped her golden stylus from her hand, and Cethegus bent to pick it up. He had only this one moment to ponder the countless possibilities which her proposal had sent racing through his mind.

Had he and the conspiracy in the catacombs been betrayed? Was this a trap laid by a cunning, power-hungry woman? Or were these fools really so stupid as to offer him, of all people, such an office? And if that was indeed the case what should he do? Should he use this opportunity to seize the initiative immediately and commence the fight and capture Rome? And if so for whom? Byzantium? Or for an emperor of the western Empire, and if the latter, then who would that emperor be? Or was all this premature? Might it be better to be loyal now, for disloyalty later? He had only that moment as he bent down to retrieve the stylus to weigh all these possibilities, but his quick mind needed no more. From a corner of his eye he saw the face of Cassiodorus, trusting and unsuspecting, and as he handed the stylus back to the princess he said, in a forceful tone:

"My queen, I accept the office."

"I am glad, thank you," the queen replied as Cassiodorus shook his hand.

Cethegus continued, "If Cassiodorus suggested me for this office, then he has proved once again his deep knowledge of human nature. He has been able to see through my exterior to the core."

"What do you mean by that?" Amalasuntha asked.

"Your Majesty, appearances could deceive. I have to admit that I do not like to see the Barbarians – I beg your pardon, Goths – ruling Italy."

"Your frankness does you credit, Roman, and I forgive you."

"Furthermore for many years now I have paid no attention at all to affairs of state or to public life. I have abandoned those former interests and passions and lived as a private citizen on my estates, dedicating myself to a life of scholarship and leisurely pursuits."

"*Beatus ille qui procul negotiis,*" the learned women quoted with a sigh.

"But because I do honour scholarship and learning, and because as a disciple of Plato I want to see wisdom rule in my homeland, I want to see a queen rule here who may be Gothic by birth, but who has a Greek soul and the virtues of a Roman. For her sake I am willing to give up my life of leisure, but under one condition. This must be my last official duty. I accept your proposal, and I vouch with my head for the security of Rome."

"Good. Here you will find the various documents you will need, and your authority to act in my name."

Cethegus glanced through the documents. "This is a manifest from the young king to the Romans, with your signature. It will require his signature also."

Amalasuntha dipped her quill into the purple ink, which the Amalungs used just as the Caesars had done. "Come, my son, write your name."

During the whole conversation between Cethegus and his mother Athalaric had stood there, leaning on the table, sharply observing Cethegus, but now he rose. Although a sick man he was accustomed to behaving as a crown prince, and to the authority which went with it. With tremendous feeling he now said: "No! I will not sign. Not only because I don't trust this cold Roman, but because I find it distasteful to find you tampering with my grandfather's crown while he still breathes, like dwarfs aspiring to the crown of a giant. The greatest hero of the century lies dying behind those curtains, and yet all you can think of is how to divide his royal garments!" With that he turned his back and walked to the window, where he placed his arm around his beautiful sister, stroking her hair.

For a long time he stood thus, and she paid no attention to him. Suddenly she came alive as she grabbed his arm and pointed to the marble steps. "Athalaric," she whispered, "who is that man who is just coming round the pillar, the one with the blue helmet?"

"Let me see," the youth replied, leaning forward. "Oh him! He is Count Witigis, a worthy soldier who conquered the Gepidae." He then told her about some of the count's deeds and successes in the last war.

Meanwhile Cethegus looked questioningly at Cassiodorus and Amalasuntha. "Let him be," the latter sighed. "If he does not want to do something then no power on earth can force him."

Any further questions were cut off when the triple curtain separating the king's sickroom from the noise of the antechamber opened. It was the Greek physician Elpidios, who reported that the patient had just woken from a long sleep, and sent him away to be alone with old Hildebrand who never left his side.

Chapter 6

Theodoric's bedchamber had already been used by the Caesars for this purpose, and was decorated in the gloomy splendour of the late Roman style. Detailed reliefs on the walls and golden ornamentation still described Roman victories and triumphs, and heathen deities floated above all this, creating an overall atmosphere of oppressive ostentation.

The couch on which the Gothic king lay presented a marked contrast to this. Barely a foot above the marble floor, it was an oval framework made of rough hewn oak, covered only with a few blankets. Only the precious purple rug covering the sick man's feet and the lion's skin with golden paws, a gift from the king of the Vandals, betrayed the patient's royal rank. All other objects in the room were simple and without ornamentation, almost barbaric in their severity.

The king's heavy shield and broadsword, unused for many years, were hanging from a pillar in the background. At the head of the bed stood old Hildebrand, head bowed, carefully scrutinising the sick man's face. The latter was leaning on his left arm, his majestic and powerful face turned towards his old companion. His hair was thin and showed signs of the many years it had spent under the weight of a heavy helmet, but it was still light brown without any sign of grey or white. His mighty forehead, sparkling eyes, eagle's nose and heavily lined cheeks spoke of a lifetime of great challenges and achievements, and of the ability to cope with them. It was a regal and exalted face, yet despite the fierce grey beard it also showed the benevolence and peace-loving wisdom for which Theodoric was famous. For a generation these qualities had brought about a golden era in Italy, and raised the Empire to heights of glory which had become legendary even in his lifetime.

For a long time the king allowed his golden brown eagle eyes to rest on his gigantic nurse with loving grace. Finally he stretched out his thin but still strong hand and said: "Old friend, the time has come to say goodbye."

The old man sank to his knees and clutched the king's hand to his broad chest.

"Come, old friend. Do I now have to console you?"

But Hildebrand remained on his knees, raising only his head so that he could look his king straight in the eye. The latter said: "I know, Hildung's son, that you have inherited from your father and from your ancestors a deep knowledge of man and his illnesses, and that you know far more of such things than all the Greek physicians and the other quacks who attend me. Above all you are more truthful than they are. So I will ask you what I myself feel. Must I die today, before nightfall?"

As he said these words the king looked into his old friend's eyes in a way which would tolerate no deception. But Hildebrand had no intention to deceive; he had regained his composure and strength.

"Yes, King of the Goths, heir of the Amalungs, you must die. Death's hand has already passed over your face. You will not see the sun set again."

"Thank you!" Theodoric replied without batting an eyelid. "The Greek whom I just sent away has been lying to me of whole days, and I need what little time I have left."

"Do you want me to call the priests again?" Hildebrand asked, but without enthusiasm.

"No, they cannot help me, and now I no longer need them."

"Your sleep has strengthened you immensely, and lifted the veil from your soul which has clouded it for so long. Hail Theodoric, Theodomer's son, you will die a king and a hero!"

"I know," the latter smiled, "you did not like to see the priests near this bed and you are right. They did not help me."

"And who did help you then?"

"God, and myself. Listen carefully, for these words will have to be our farewell. I am going to thank you for your loyalty for fifty years by confiding in you, and only you, what has been torturing me. I have not told Cassiodorus or even my daughter. What are the people saying? For that matter what do you yourself think has caused my great sadness, which struck so suddenly and plunged me into this illness?"

"The local people say that it was remorse over the deaths of Boethius and Symmachus."

"And did you believe that?"

"No. I could not believe that you would regret spilling the blood of traitors."

"You were right. Perhaps their deeds did not merit the death sentence according to their laws, and I did love Boethius dearly. But they were traitors a thousand times over. Even though they were Romans I regarded them more highly than the best among my own people. And their thanks were to wish my crown upon the emperor and to write flattering letters to Byzantium. They preferred Justinus and Justinian to Theodoric's friendship. No, I have no regrets on their account. But guess again, what did you believe?"

"My king, your heir is a mere boy, and you have enemies all around you."

The sick man knitted his bold brows: "You are nearer the mark. I have always known what my Empire's weakness was. Many nights I have lain awake with concern over just that, after putting on a brave and confident face the previous evening during the feast. Old friend, I know that you thought me too confident. But I could not afford to let anyone see a sign of weakness or see me sway, not friend nor foe, otherwise my throne swayed too. But I sighed when I was alone, and bore my worries alone too."

"You were wisdom itself, my king, and I a fool."

"Look," the king went on, stroking the old man's hand with his own, "I know everything about me of which you approved, and also of which you disapproved. I also know of your blind hatred for the southerners. Believe me, it is blind, as perhaps my love for them was also blind." He sighed and paused.

"Why do you torture yourself?"

"No, let me finish. I know that this Empire, this my life's work, can fall and fall only too easily. And perhaps my own generosity towards these Romans is to blame. So be it! No work of man lasts for ever, and if posterity lays the blame at my feet for being too benevolent then I will bear that."

"My great king!"

"But Hildebrand, one night as I lay awake, worrying about the dangers threatening my Empire, another guilt oppressed my soul; not of goodness but lust for fame and bloody violence. May the gods have mercy on me if the Gothic people are to perish as punishment for Theodoric's crime! He, his picture appeared before me!" The sick man was now speaking with effort, and hesitated for a moment.

"Whose picture? Whom do you mean?" Hildebrand whispered, moving closer.

"Odoacer!" Theodoric whispered almost inaudibly. The old man lowered his head. At last the king broke the silence: "Yes, old friend. This hand – you know it well – slew the mighty hero while he was dining, as my guest. His blood spurted hot into my face, and his breaking eyes looked at me with undying hatred. A few months ago in a nightmare his bloody, angry image appeared before me like a god of revenge. It was as if my heart convulsed, and a terrible voice inside me said: For this one bloody deed your Empire will fall and your people will perish."

After a further pause Hildebrand took up the conversation once more, looking stubbornly at his king.

"My king, why do you torture yourself like a woman? Have you not slain hundreds with your own hand, and your people thousands on your command? Did we not come down into this land from the mountains, through thirty battles, wading up to our ankles in blood? What is the blood of one man in comparison to all this? And think back to how things stood at the time. For four long years he had resisted you, as the mountain lion resists the bear. Twice he drove you and your people to the brink of disaster. Your Goths were being decimated by the sword as well as by hunger and pestilence. At long last, after a fiercely stubborn resistance, Ravenna fell, forced into surrender by starvation. Your conquered enemy lay at your feet at last. And then you were warned that he was planning treason. He planned to resume the fight one more time, and he planned to do it by ambushing you and your people in your sleep that same night. What were you to do? Face him openly? If he was guilty that would have achieved nothing. So you courageously took the initiative and beat him to the punch, by doing to him in the evening what he would have done to you later that night. And how did you then exploit your victory? This one deed saved your people, and avoided another round of desperate bloodshed. You pardoned all his people, and for thirty years you have allowed Goths and Romans to live together in this land as if it were heaven. And now you want to torture yourself over this one deed? Listen to me! Two peoples will thank you for it in all eternity. And I, I would have slain him seven times over!"

The old man halted, his eyes flashing fire. He looked like a furious giant. But the king shook his head.

"Old warrior, you mean well, but all that solves nothing. I have told myself the same things a hundred times, and much more persuasively than you put it, but it does not help. He was a hero, the only one who bore comparison with me. And I slew him out of suspicion, jealousy, even – I must admit it – out of fear, fear of having to wrestle with him one more time. That was and always will be a crime and an outrage. Excuses would not buy me peace, and a gloomy sadness came over me. Ever since that night his image has haunted me, whether I was asleep or awake. Then Cassiodorus started sending me bishops and priests. They heard my confession, saw my remorse and forgave all my sins, but they could not help me either. Peace would not come to me, for even though they forgave me I could not forgive myself. Perhaps it is something I inherited from my heathen ancestors, but I cannot escape the ghost of my murdered foe by hiding behind a cross. I cannot believe that I am absolved from my bloody deed by the blood of an innocent god who died on the cross."

Hildebrand's face lit up happily at this, and in a subdued voice he said: "You know, I have never been able to believe in these priests and their crosses either. Oh please tell me, do you still believe in Thor and Odin as I do? Did they help you?"

The king smiled and shook his head. "No, you incorrigible old heathen! Your Valhalla is not for me either. But I will tell you what did help me. Yesterday I sent the bishops away and I thought, and I prayed and I called to God. I became calmer. At last I fell into a deep sleep, such as I had not known for months. And when I awoke I was no longer plagued by self-reproach. I was calm and able to think clearly, I decided that what is done is done, and no miracle of God can undo it. Very well then, let them punish me. If He is indeed the God of Moses then let Him punish me and my whole house unto the seventh generation. I submit myself and my people to the revenge of the Lord, and He can destroy us for He is just. But because He is just He cannot punish this noble Gothic people for another's crime. He cannot destroy a nation to avenge a crime committed by their king, and I know that He will not. And if these people are to perish then I know it has nothing to do with my misdeed. I and my house alone will pay for that, and I am ready to submit to His justice. And so a feeling of peace came over me, and I am able to die with courage."

He was silent. Hildebrand bowed his head and kissed the hand that had slain Odoacer.

"That was my farewell to you, and my legacy and my thanks for a lifetime of loyalty. Now let us devote what time is left to our Gothic countrymen. Come, help me get up. I cannot die in these cushions. My weapons are hanging over there, please give them to me. Don't argue! I can, and I will!"

Hildebrand had to obey. With his help the patient rose from his sickbed with vigour. He threw a purple robe around his shoulders, put on his belt and sword, and placed the crowned helmet on his head. He stood leaning on his spear, his back resting against the room's thick central column.

"Now please call my daughter, and Cassiodorus, and anyone else waiting outside."

Chapter 7

Thus the king stood quietly, while Hildebrand drew back the curtains on both sides so that bedroom and antechamber were again one room. Those waiting outside – several more Goths and Romans had joined the original number – approached the king with astonishment and in respectful silence.

The latter spoke: "My daughter, have the letters been prepared to Byzantium, announcing my death and my grandson's succession?"

"Here they are," Amalasuntha replied.

The king glanced through the papyrus scrolls. "To the emperor Justinus, and a second letter to his nephew Justinian. He will of course be wearing the diadem before long, and is already his master's master. I can see from the beautiful parables that Cassiodorus composed them. But what's this?" His face became grave. "This is too much of a good thing, where it says: 'and so I commend my youthfulness to your illustrious protection.' Protection? Woe betide us if you have to rely on protection from Byzantium. It is sufficient for Theodoric's grandson to end the letter with: 'In friendship I remain.' And here is another letter to Byzantium, but to whom? To Theodora, the illustrious wife of Justinian? What? To the circus dancer, the lion tamer's shameless daughter?" His eyes flashed with anger.

"She has much influence with her husband," Cassiodorus interjected.

"No, my daughter will not write to a harlot who has sullied the honour of all women." He tore up the papyrus scroll, and handed back the other letters to Cassiodorus.

"Witigis, my brave warrior, what will be your task after my death?"

"I will go to inspect our garrison at Tridentum."

"There is no man better suited to that task. But you have still not expressed the wish I granted you after the battle with the Gepidae. Is there still nothing you desire?"

"There is, my king!"

"At last! I am glad. Speak!"

"Today a poor prison warden is to be tortured because he refused to torture an accused criminal, and he struck a superior officer who tried to force him. My king, please set the man free. The practice of torture is disgraceful, and—"

"The warden is free, and from this moment torture will no longer be used in the Gothic Empire. See to it, Cassiodorus. Noble Witigis, give me your hand. So that all will know just how high you have always been in my esteem I now give you Wallada, my thoroughbred warhorse, as a reminder of this hour of parting. And if ever you find yourself in danger on his back, or—" he whispered very quietly "—or if he is about to fail you, whisper my name in his ear. Now, who is to guard Naples? Duke Thulun was too severe. The people of Naples are a happy people, who can only be won over by a cheerful man."

"Young Totila is to assume command of the port there," Cassiodorus replied.

"Totila! A fine young man with a sunny outlook, a real Siegfried and a favourite of the gods! A good choice, for no heart can resist him, but of course these southerners—" he sighed before continuing "—who will secure Rome and the Senate for us?"

"Cethegus Caesarius!" Cassiodorus replied, and indicated the latter with his hand. "This noble Roman."

"Cethegus? I know him well. Look at me, Cethegus!"

Reluctantly the latter raised his eyes, which he had lowered to evade the king's searching look. But by using all his vast willpower he bore the piercing eagle eyes, which seemed to penetrate to his very soul.

"It was most strange, Cethegus, that a man like you should have kept himself away from affairs of state for so long, and from our royal presence. Either that, or it was dangerous. Perhaps it is even more dangerous that you return – now – to serve the state."

"It was not my wish, my king!"

"I vouch for him," Cassiodorus added.

"Quiet, friend. No man can vouch for another, indeed barely for himself. But—" he maintained his searching look "—this proud man, with the look of a Caesar, will not betray Italy to Byzantium!"

Cethegus had to endure one more look from the golden eagle eyes. Suddenly the king grasped his arm, so tightly that the Roman almost winced with pain, and whispered to him: "Listen to what I now tell you, as a prophesy of warning. No Roman will ever again grace the throne of the Occident. Don't argue. You have been warned. What is all that noise outside?" He turned quickly to his daughter, who was issuing quiet instructions to a Roman messenger.

"Nothing, father. Nothing important, my king."

"What? Secrets from me? By my crown, are you trying to rule while I still breathe? I heard the sound of foreign tongues outside. Open the doors!"

The door connecting the antechamber to the hall outside was opened. Among the numerous Goths and Romans there several strange figures could be seen, small strange-looking men in jackets of wolf hides, wearing pointed caps and long shaggy sheepskins hanging from their backs. Surprised and overcome by the king's sudden appearance, they sank to their knees as if struck by lightning.

"Ah, envoys from the Avars, that bunch of thieves near our eastern borders! Have you brought the tribute which you owe?"

"Your majesty, we still bring it this time, furs, woollen rugs, swords and shields, here they are. But we hope that next year – we thought we would ask if—"

"You thought you would see if old Dietrich von Bern had grown weak with age? You hoped I might be dead? And that you might refuse tribute to my successor? You are mistaken, spies!"

He picked up one of the swords the envoys had brought as if to examine it, together with its sheath. He took it in both hands, grasping it firmly by the hilt and by its point. Quickly he exerted pressure with his powerful hands, and threw the sword in two pieces at their feet. Calmly he said:

"You Avars use shoddy swords. Now come, Athalaric my heir. They don't believe you can wear my crown. Show them how you can handle my spear."

At this the youth flew to the king's side, the fire of ambition giving colour to his usually pale features. He picked up his grandfather's heavy spear, and hurled it with tremendous force against one of the shields which the envoys had leaned against a pillar. The spear pierced the shield completely and penetrated some depth into the pillar itself. Proudly the king placed his hand on his grandson's head and called out to the envoys: "Now go home and report what you have seen!"

He turned away, and the doors closed, leaving the astonished Avars outside. "Now give me a goblet of wine, perhaps my last. No, I want it undiluted, the Germanic way!" He pushed the Greek physician aside.

"Thank you, old friend Hildebrand, for this drink which you handed me so faithfully. I drink to the glory of the Gothic people!"

Slowly he emptied the goblet, and placed it firmly on the marble table.

And then, suddenly like lightning, it struck him just as the physicians had long predicted. He staggered, clutched his chest and fell backwards into Hildebrand's arms. The latter knelt down slowly, lowering his king onto the marble table while cradling his head with the crowned helmet in his arms.

For a moment all held their breath, but the king did not move. With a loud cry Athalaric threw himself over his grandfather's lifeless body.

BOOK TWO
Athalaric

Chapter 1

It was not without good reason that both friend and foe either feared or hoped for grave dangers threatening the young Gothic Empire. It had been less than forty years since Theodoric, at the emperor's behest, had crossed the Isonzo River with his people to take both crown and life of the adventurer Odoacer, to whom a rebellion by the Germanic mercenaries had given the throne of the western part of the old Roman Empire. All the wisdom and greatness of King Theodoric had not been able to remove that sense of insecurity, which in a way was part of the very nature of his bold creation. In spite of the benevolence of his regime the Italians, not that one can blame them, felt the reign of foreigners to be a disgrace to their national pride. Furthermore the foreigners were hated with a double intensity, for they were seen not only as Barbarians but also as heretics. According to the prevailing contemporary view the western and eastern parts of the Roman Empire were seen as two parts of the one indivisible entity, and once the Caesars of the Occident were no more, the emperor of the eastern Empire was seen as the only rightful ruler of Italy. Thus the eyes of all Roman patriots and of all orthodox Catholics in Italy were directed toward Byzantium. It was from Byzantium that they hoped the long-awaited liberation from the Goths would come, from the Barbarians, heretics and tyrants. And Byzantium had both the will and the means to fulfil these hopes. Even though the subjects of the emperor were no longer the Romans of Caesar's or Trajan's day, nonetheless the eastern Empire possessed tremendous power, based on a long-established system of government together with an abundance of learning and science. Byzantium's power was superior to that of the Goths in every way.

As has already been said, there was no shortage of desire to use these superior powers in order to destroy the Barbarian kingdom, particularly as the relationship between the two governments had from the beginning been based on mistrust, barely concealed hate and deceit. Before their conquest of Italy the Goths had been settled in the region of the River Danube, and had formed an alliance with Byzantium. That alliance had been unsatisfactory to both sides, due partly to the ambition of the Gothic kings, and even more so because of the duplicity and deceitful conduct of the emperors, so that the uneasy truce erupted into warfare every few years. On several occasions Theodoric, who had been honoured by the emperor in times of peace as Consul, *Patricius* and adopted son of the emperor, had led his armies before the very gates of the Imperial city.

In order to avoid this constant friction the emperor Zeno, who was a very capable diplomat, found a typically Byzantine solution to put an end to the troublesome Gothic wars. That solution was to make the Goths a present of Italy, which they first had to wrest from Odoacer's iron grip. This solution not only removed the Goths from the immediate proximity of his own capital, but it also ensured that two potentially dangerous enemies were now fighting each other instead of Byzantium.

Whichever side ultimately won the struggle in Italy Byzantium stood to gain. If Odoacer won, then the Goths and their terrible king, to whom heavy tribute had to be paid every year, were eliminated for ever. On the other hand, if Theodoric won then the usurper Odoacer, whom Byzantium had never recognised, was defeated and punished. Furthermore, as Theodoric was acting in the name and at the behest of the emperor, it meant that the two halves of the Empire would again be reunited, at least in theory, as a result of a glorious victory.

However this grand strategy did not end the way it was intended. As soon as Theodoric had won and established his own rule in Italy, his great mind and vast abilities rapidly secured for him supreme power in his own right. Even though formalities were still observed, in reality there could be no question of any subservience to Byzantium.

Theodoric deferred to the emperor's instructions in a formal sense only when it suited him, for example as one way to soften the animosity toward Gothic rule on the part of the Italians. In fact he reigned over both Goths and Italians, not as governor in the name of Byzantium, but in his own right as "King of the Goths and Italians". Not surprisingly this led to the emperor's displeasure, and open warfare broke out repeatedly between the two Empires. Therefore there could be no doubt that Byzantium would be only too willing to end the suffering of the Italians by ridding them of the yoke of Barbarian rule, just as soon as Byzantium felt strong enough. The Goths on the other hand had no real allies against these enemies, both internal and external. Theodoric's fame and his policy of building ties by marriage with the other Germanic rulers had won for him only a kind of moral support, but not any tangible reinforcement of his own military strength.

The Gothic Empire, which had been planted with just a little too much daring and trust in the midst of an entirely alien world of Roman culture, lacked direct contact with other Germanic tribes which had not as yet been Romanised. They lacked the infusion of fresh Germanic elements, such as those which constantly rejuvenated the Empire of the Franks, which in turn was also being established around this era. At least the northeastern part of the latter Empire had been spared the decay which was an inevitable part of Roman influence. On the other hand the small island of Gothic culture, surrounded on all sides by a hostile sea of Roman life and customs, grew smaller and weaker every year.

While Theodoric lived, the mighty creator of this daring work, his reputation and the very glamour of his name were enough to cover up the weaknesses of and dangers to his kingdom. But the Goths had every reason to await with trepidation the moment when their endangered ship of state was to be steered by a woman or by a sickly youth. They feared insurrection by the Italians, interference from the emperor, defections from conquered neighbouring countries and attacks from hostile Barbarian tribes. If the moment of danger passed quietly and without major incident then this was due to the tireless efforts of Cassiodorus, the king's well proven minister and friend. For weeks he had been active, and now that Theodoric was dead he redoubled his efforts. In order to maintain peace among the Italians he had released a manifest to Italy and all the provinces, announcing as an established fact Athalaric's succession to the throne under his mother's guardianship. This was accepted without causing so much as a ripple. At the same time representatives of the new king were despatched to all parts of the Empire, firstly to seek and accept assurances of allegiance, and secondly to reassure the people that the new government would respect the rights of Italians and provincials alike, and that it would maintain and even exceed the benevolence and generosity of the dead king, particularly toward his Roman subjects.

At the same time strong elements of the Gothic armies were despatched to the borders and to key cities. Their aim was to discourage, by a show of Gothic military might, enemies of the kingdom from starting hostilities. The relationship with the Imperial court in Byzantium was renewed and secured by the sending of envoys, and also by the sending of letters. These letters were composed with great diplomacy and in a suitably subordinate tone, so as to preserve the illusion of subservience to and dependence on Byzantium.

Chapter 2

Apart from Cassiodorus there was one other man who played a most important role during these days of change, and in the eyes of the court he did so most satisfactorily.

The man in question was none other than Cethegus, who had assumed the important office of Prefect of Rome. As soon as the king had closed his eyes he had rushed immediately from the palace and out of Ravenna to the city on the Tiber, which had been entrusted to his care, arriving there before the news of the King's death.

Even before daybreak, he had assembled the senators in the *Senatus*, in the hall of Domitian near the Janus Geminus to the right of the arch of Severus. He had surrounded the building with Gothic troops and informed the surprised senators of the impending change of government. Many of the same senators he had seen only recently in the catacombs, where he had helped to incite them to rebellion against the Barbarians. Finally he hastily forced them to swear oaths of allegiance to Athalaric, not without making reference to the spears of a thousand Gothic soldiers, which could easily be seen outside.

He then left the *Senatus*, keeping the city fathers locked up until he reached the Slavic amphitheatre, where he had convened a public meeting of Roman citizens, again within sight of strong Gothic forces. By means of a masterly speech he was able to inspire the easily influenced *Quirites* in favour of the young king. He listed the generous deeds of Theodoric, and promised similarly benevolent rule from his grandson, who he said had already been recognised throughout Italy, and in particular by the city fathers of Rome. Finally he announced that, as the first part of Amalasuntha's reign, there was to be general feasting of the Roman people together with seven days of games in the circus. The games were to consist of chariot races with twenty-one Spanish teams, as well as other feature events.

A thousand or more voices broke into loud cheering, praising the regent and her son, but the name Cethegus was heard most of all. The people, wild with joy, dispersed, the detained senators were released, and the city of Rome had passively accepted the change of ruler without incident. The Prefect himself rushed home to his house at the foot of the Capitol, where he locked himself in and promptly started on his report to Amalasuntha.

It was not long before there was a furious knocking on Cethegus's heavy front door. It was Lucius Licinius, the young Roman whom we met in the catacombs, who was striking at the door with the hilt of his sword so that the whole house reverberated. With him were Scaevola the lawyer, who had been among the detained senators, and Silverius the priest. Both had grave expressions on their faces.

Carefully the *ostiarius* looked at the three men through a secret hole in the wall, admitting them only after he had recognised Licinius. The furious youth stormed along the familiar passage through the vestibule and the Atrium into Cethegus's study. When the latter heard the rapidly approaching footsteps he rose from the *lectus* on which he had been reclining as he worked, and sealed the letters he had written into a capsule, the domed end of which was made of silver. "Oh, the liberators of the fatherland!" he said with a smile as he rose to greet them.

"Despicable traitor!" Licinius shouted at him, his hand on his sword. He could speak no more, as he was livid with anger. Threateningly, he partly withdrew his sword from its scabbard.

"Halt!" Scaevola, who had caught up with the youth, gasped as he restrained the latter's sword arm. "First let him defend himself, if he can."

Silverius, following, added: "It is impossible that he should have betrayed the cause of our holy church."

"Impossible?" Licinius laughed, "What? Are you mad or am I? Did he not cause us, noble Romans, to be detained in our homes? Did he not bar the gates and incite the mob to swear allegiance to the Barbarians?"

Cethegus continued for him: "Did he not trap the honourable city fathers, three hundred of them, in the *curia* like mice in a trap? Ha! Three hundred of the noblest mice in Rome!"

"And now he mocks us, are we to tolerate that?" Licinius cried as Scaevola went pale with anger.

"Well, what would you have done, if you had been free to act?" Cethegus asked calmly, crossing his arms across his broad chest.

"What would we have done? Exactly what we, and you, had talked about a hundred times. As soon as news of the tyrant's death reached here we would have killed every Goth in the city, proclaimed a republic and elected two consul—"

"Named Licinius and Scaevola, that's the main thing!" Cethegus remarked calmly, "And then?"

"And then? Freedom would have triumphed!"

"Foolishness would have triumphed!" Cethegus roared at the surprised patriots. "What a good thing your hands were tied! You would have killed all hope, and for all time. Look at me, and then thank me on your knees!"

As he said this he took some papyrus documents from another capsule and handed them to Licinius and Scaevola. "Read it. The enemy was forewarned and had his noose expertly placed around Rome's neck. Had I not acted as I did Count Witigis with ten thousand Goths would at this moment be at the northern gate, young Totila with the fleet from Naples would be blocking the mouth of the Tiber from the south tomorrow, and Duke Thulun would be marching on Hadrian's tomb and the gate of Aurelian with another twenty thousand from the west. If you had harmed the hair of a single Goth this morning, what would have happened?"

Silverius breathed a sigh of relief, and the other two were embarrassed and silent. At last Licinius regained his composure. Courageously, eyes afire, he said: "We would have resisted the Barbarians behind our walls."

"Yes, my Licinius, the way I am going to restore our walls we would have held them off for ever, but the way they are now not a single day!"

"We would have died as free citizens," Scaevola said.

"You could have done that in the *curia* three hours ago," Cethegus smiled with a shrug. Silverius stepped toward him with outstretched arms as if to embrace him, but Cethegus drew back.

"You have saved church and fatherland, you have saved us all! I never once doubted you," the priest said. Licinius grasped the Prefect's hand, which the latter willingly offered.

"I did doubt you!" Licinius cried with admirable candour. "Forgive me, great Roman. From this day my sword, which a moment ago was to have pierced your heart, will be for ever at your service. And when the day of freedom does come let us have no consuls, but let us join in saying *Salve* Cethegus, Dictator!" His eyes gleaming, he ran from the house. The Prefect's eyes followed him with a look of satisfaction.

The lawyer followed Licinius, and said in parting: "Dictator yes, but only until the republic is secure!"

"Indeed," Cethegus smiled, "then we will awaken Camillus and Brutus, and take up the republic where it left off a thousand years ago, won't we, Silverius?"

"Prefect of Rome," the latter replied, "you know that I had aspirations to lead our fatherland as well as our church, but from this hour that is no longer so. You lead, and I will follow. Promise me only one thing, freedom of the Roman church and free elections of the Pope."

"Agreed!" said Cethegus, "as soon as Silverius has become Pope. It is a bargain." The priest left with a smile on his face, but also deep in thought.

For some time Cethegus silently followed the three of them with his eyes. At last he said to himself: "Go! You will not overthrow any tyrant. You need a tyrant!"

This day and this hour were of decisive importance to Cethegus. Almost without any conscious effort on his part he was carried by the torrent of events. His mind was embracing new horizons, and goals that he had never before dared set himself, or of which he had at best only dreamed.

In this historic moment he saw himself as the only master of the situation; both the major political parties of the day, the Goths and their enemies the conspirators, were completely in his hands. And suddenly the mainspring in the breast of this man, which he had thought dormant for decades, drove him once more into intense activity. His almost boundless desire to rule, which to him was a basic need almost like air, took possession of him and drove him to concentrate all his inherent abilities, honed by the experiences of an eventful life, into feverish action once more.

Cornelius Cethegus Caesarius was the descendant of a very ancient and immensely wealthy Roman family, whose founder had established the fame of his house as a general and a statesman serving Caesar during the Civil Wars; it was said that he was an illegitimate son of the great Dictator. Cethegus had inherited from his forebears many-sided talents and desires, and his wealth had given him ample opportunity to develop the former and indulge the latter to the fullest extent possible in his time. He had received the most thorough education then available to a young Roman aristocrat.

To begin with he had studied the arts under his early tutors. Later he attended the best schools in Berytus, Alexandria and Athens, where he studied law, history and philosophy with outstanding results.

But all this failed to satisfy him. He sensed the breath of decay in the learning of his day. In particular, his study of philosophy served to destroy in him the last vestiges of religious belief, without putting anything positive in its place. When he returned from his studies his father introduced him to government service, as was the custom of those times, and the gifted young man rapidly rose to positions of ever-increasing importance.

Then, quite suddenly, he dropped out. Having become thoroughly familiar with the workings of government he no longer wished to remain a cog in the great machinery of an Empire, an Empire which not only restricted his freedom but which also served a Barbarian king. At about this time his father died, and suddenly Cethegus became not only master of himself but also the controller of incredible wealth. With the same dedication which had characterised all his pursuits he threw himself into the wildest turmoil of life, lust and pleasure. He quickly tired of Rome, and undertook long journeys to Byzantium, to Egypt and even to India. There was no luxury and no pleasure, innocent or otherwise, which he did not sample. Only a body of steel could have endured the exertions, privations, excesses and adventures of these travels.

After twelve years he returned to Rome. It was rumoured that he would erect grandiose buildings, and people looked forward to the full life of a rich patrician developing in his villas and estates, but they were to be disappointed. Cethegus contented himself with building a house at the foot of the Capitol, small but comfortable and in the most exquisite taste, and lived in the large city like a hermit.

Quite unexpectedly he published an account of his travels, together with descriptions of the little known people and countries he had visited. The book was a huge success. Cassiodorus and Boethius sought his friendship, and the great king wanted him at his court. And then, suddenly, he disappeared from Rome. Whatever caused him to do so remained a mystery in spite of all the enquiries and inquisitiveness of friends and enemies alike.

Gossip at the time had it that poor fishermen found him one morning, on the banks of the Tiber, unconscious and close to death.

A few weeks later he turned up again near the northeastern borders of the Empire, in the inhospitable countries along the Danube, where a bloody war was raging with the Gepidae, the Avars and the Slavs. There, on the Gothic side, he fought these wild Barbarians with death-defying bravery, and pursued them into their hiding places among rocky mountains with select mercenaries, whom he paid out of his own pocket. And when the Gothic general entrusted him with a small force to undertake a raid he went and attacked Sirmium instead, the fortified capital of the enemy, and he captured it with a display of generalship which was in no way inferior to his bravery. During all this time he shared the privations of his troops, sleeping every night on the frozen earth. After peace had been concluded he travelled once more to Gaul, Spain and Byzantium. Finally he returned to Rome and for some years he lived in a state of embittered leisure, withdrawn from public life. He refused all the honours which Cassiodorus tried to force upon him, be they to do with war, civil administration or academic pursuits. He appeared to have no further interest in anything at all except his studies.

A few years before our story begins he brought back with him from Gaul a handsome youth, to whom he showed Rome and Italy, and toward whom he exhibited all the love and concern of a father. It was said that he planned to adopt him, and as long as his young guest was with him he appeared to be coming out of his self-imposed solitude. He invited the young noblemen of Rome to glittering parties in his villas, and whenever he accepted a return invitation he was the most charming of guests. But as soon as he had sent young Julius Montanus off to Alexandria to study, with an impressive retinue of pedagogues, slaves and servants, he suddenly retreated back into his impenetrable shell, apparently angered by God and the world. It was only with the greatest difficulty that Silverius and Rusticiana had persuaded him to abandon his hermit-like existence and take part in the conspiracy in the catacombs. He told them that he was willing to become a patriot out of sheer boredom. And indeed, until the king's death he appeared to be taking part in the conspiracy only with obvious reluctance, even though he and the archdeacon were its leaders.

All this had now suddenly changed. He had an irresistible urge to try himself at every possible intellectual pursuit, to overcome all difficulties, to leave all rivals in his wake, and to be the undisputed master in everything he did. As soon as he had mastered any one challenge he immediately threw to one side the laurels of victory and looked for another, but until now nothing had given him complete satisfaction. He had tried art, science, self indulgence, bureaucracy and warfare. He excelled at them all like none other, yet they all left him unfulfilled. He had to rule, to be undisputed master, to conquer all adversity with superior strength and intellect, and then to lead an iron regime over those he had subordinated. This is what he had always, unconsciously, aspired to. Only in this one role would he ever feel satisfied and content.

And so it was that at this hour his broad chest filled with deep breaths. He, who had always been so icy cold, was aglow at the thought that he was now in control of the two great powers of his time, Goths and Romans. And out of this feeling of power a deep conviction came over him, that for him and his ambition there was only one goal that would make life worthwhile, a goal beyond the reach of any other mortal. He liked to think of himself as being descended from Julius Caesar, and he felt the blood of Caesar rise in his veins at the thought: Caesar, Imperator of the Occident, emperor of the Roman world!

Months ago this flash of lightning had first crossed his mind, not a wish and not a thought, rather more like a dream. At first he was shocked at his own boldness, and amused at the same time. He, Cethegus, restorer and emperor of the Roman Empire? While Italy shook under the tread of three hundred thousand Gothic soldiers? The greatest of all the Barbarian kings, whose fame filled the then known world, sat firmly on his throne in Ravenna. And even if Gothic might could be broken there were the Franks beyond the Alps and Byzantium beyond the sea; both would be reaching for the rich prize of Italy with greedy hands, two mighty Empires against him, one man.

It was only too true: he stood alone among his people. He knew his countrymen only too well, and he despised them as unworthy descendants of great ancestors. He had to laugh at the daydreams of Licinius and Scaevola, who wanted to restore the republic with these so-called Romans. Yes, it was true; he did stand very much alone.

But it was precisely this that stirred his ambition. In this moment, after the other conspirators had left him and after his own superiority had become clearer than ever both to them and to himself, in this moment that which had been merely a dream and almost a game became a firm resolve in his mind.

With his arms crossed over his powerful chest he started pacing the room with purposeful steps, like a caged lion, and started talking to himself.

"Drive out the Goths with a capable people behind me, and not let in the Franks or the Greeks, that would not be difficult. Another man could do that also. But to do it alone, entirely alone, more hindered than helped by these men without spine or will, that would be to achieve the impossible. To make these sops into heroes, these slaves once more into Romans, and then make these clerics and servants of the Barbarians masters of the world once more, that and that alone is worth striving for. To create a new nation, a new era, alone, one man alone with nothing but the strength of his will and the power of his intellect – no mortal has ever done that! That would be more than even Caesar achieved – he led legions made up of warriors and heroes. And yet, if it can be thought it can be done. I who thought it will do it! Yes, Cethegus, that is a goal! That is worth living for and if need be dying for. To work, Cethegus, and from this moment nothing else matters but this one great goal."

He stood still before a giant statue of Caesar sculpted from white marble, a masterpiece by Arkesilaos and a perfect work of art. According to family tradition Caesar himself had given it to his son, and it formed the shrine of this house, standing opposite the writing divan.

"Hear me, immortal Julius, great forebear! Your descendant is tempted to wrestle with you. There is something greater even than that which you achieved; even to aim at a higher goal than you is an immortal ambition, and to fall from such dizzy heights would be the most magnificent death imaginable. Hail me, for that I know once more why I am alive."

He strode past the statue and cast a glance at the military map of the Roman Empire, which lay rolled up on the table.

"First crush these Barbarians – Rome – then re-conquer the north – Paris! Then regain the rebellious eastern Empire and make it obedient once more to mighty Caesar – Byzantium! And then further, ever onward, to the Tigris, the Indus, further than Alexander, and then back through Scythia and Germany to the Tiber – your course, mighty Caesar, which the dagger of Brutus cut short. And so, greater than you, greater than Alexander – oh, stop, intoxicating thoughts, stop!"

And the icy Cethegus was ablaze with a mighty passion, more powerful than any even he had known. His blood pulsed through his temples. At last he placed his burning forehead against the cold marble chest of Caesar, whose marble face looked down upon him with serene majesty.

Chapter 3

This day was to become a decisive one, not only for Cethegus but also for the catacomb conspiracy, for Italy and for the Gothic Empire.

Up until this time the patriots, under a number of different leaders, had made little progress, largely because they could not agree on the means to be used to attain their goals, or even the goals themselves. All this changed dramatically from the moment Cethegus, who was by far the most gifted man among the conspirators, took the reins of the party firmly into his strong hands.

All the previous leaders of the conspiracy, apparently including even Silverius, willingly accepted the Prefect as their leader, who had so convincingly demonstrated his vast capabilities and saved their cause. It was only now that the conspiracy became a real danger to the Goths.

Cethegus himself went to work immediately, working tirelessly day and night to undermine the power and security of the Gothic regime. Using his great capacity to see through people, to win them over and then to rule over them, he was able day by day to build the party's numbers, strength and means.

But he was also able, through clever foresight, to allay any suspicions on the part of the Goths on the one hand, and to prevent a premature uprising by the conspirators on the other. It would have been easy to suddenly, on the one day, attack the Barbarians all over the peninsula, to begin the uprising and then to call in a Byzantine army to complete their victory, particularly as Byzantium had been waiting for just such an opportunity for a long time. But that would not have achieved the Prefect's secret aims, and would merely have exchanged Gothic rule for Byzantine tyranny.

As we are well aware Cethegus envisaged an entirely different eventual outcome, and in order to achieve his aims he had to establish himself in a position of strength and influence in Italy, such as no other man possessed. He had to become the most powerful man in the country, even if secretly, long before the first Byzantine set foot on Italian soil and before the first Goth had fallen in battle. He had to be so far advanced in his preparations that the Barbarians were in effect driven from Italy by the Romans, led by Cethegus, with only minimal assistance from Byzantium. Thus, once victory was complete, the emperor would have no alternative but to leave the government of the liberated country to its liberator, even if nominally he would rule initially as governor in the name of Byzantium. Cethegus would then have gained the time and the initiative to stir up national pride against the "Greeks", as the Byzantine rulers were contemptuously called in Italy.

It was true that for two hundred years, since the days of the great Constantine, the glamour of ruling the world had passed from Rome to the golden city on the Bosporus, and the sceptre of the sons of Romulus had passed to the "Greeks". Even though the eastern and western Empires were supposedly one in theory, and a seat of culture and civilisation as opposed to the world of the Barbarians, nonetheless the "Greeks" were hated and despised by the Romans, just as they had been in the days when Flaminius had declared the conquered Hellas to be a freed slave of Rome. That old hatred was now compounded by envy, and therefore a man who could drive the Byzantines from the country after ridding it of the Goths could be certain of enthusiastic support in the whole of Italy. The crown of Rome and rule over the western Empire would be his certain reward. And should it then be possible to drive the Italians and their newly re-awakened nationalism as Romans into a war of aggression across the Alps, and if Cethegus should succeed in re-establishing Roman imperialism on the ruins of the Franks' Empire in Paris and at Aurelianum, then it might no longer be too daring to try and win back the rebellious eastern Empire as well. And so the city on the Tiber might once more become the capital of the world, just as it had been in the days of Trajan and Hadrian.

But if these distant glittering goals were to be attained, then every step along the steep and treacherous path had to be taken with the utmost caution, and one false step could ruin everything. If he was to rule Italy as its emperor, then above all else Cethegus had to have Rome, for it was only in Rome that his ambitions could be realised. Therefore the new Prefect devoted the utmost care to the city which had been entrusted to him. Rome had to become, physically as well as symbolically, a fortress and a seat of government, obedient to and possessed by him alone. His office gave him the perfect opportunity to do just this, for it was the responsibility of the *Prefectus Urbi* to look after the welfare of the people as well as the security and general upkeep of the city. Cethegus knew to perfection just how to exploit the rights and privileges which these duties involved in order to further his own goals. He had won over all classes of the Roman population with ease. The nobility honoured him as the head of the conspiracy, he ruled the clergy through Silverius, and the latter was the right hand and widely tipped successor of the aging Pope. Furthermore Silverius was showing a devotion to Cethegus which even he found strange.

Finally he managed to tie the lower classes of the population to himself, not only by providing grandiose circus games and regular food distributions out of his own pocket, but also by undertaking a series of major works. These provided work and sustenance for the people for years at the expense of the Gothic treasury.

He persuaded Amalasuntha to give an order to effectively restore the fortifications of Rome, which had suffered from the ravages of time, repeated sieges and neglect since the days of Honorius. The order was to restore the fortifications of Rome rapidly and completely, "to honour the eternal city" and "as protection against a Byzantine attack" as Amalasuntha fooled herself.

Cethegus himself had drawn up the plans for this huge undertaking and, as future sieges by Gothic and Byzantine armies were to show, in doing so he displayed a degree of generalship verging on genius. With tremendous drive and sustained zeal he went about converting the huge city, with its circumference of many miles, into a first class fortress. The thousands of workmen knew very well whom they had to thank for their well paid work. Every time Cethegus showed himself on the walls, instructing, checking or even lending a hand, he was loudly cheered. And the trusting queen in Ravenna went on pouring million after million of *solidi* into a structure which was to become an impregnable fortress, against which the flower of her nation's fighting men was soon to perish.

The most important point in the fortifications was Hadrian's tomb. This magnificent building, which Hadrian had built from large blocks of marble without mortar, was located only a stone's throw from Aurelian's gate in those days, towering over both it and the wall at that point. Cethegus had recognised how this solid structure, which in its present position served as a fortified bastion which might well assist a force attacking Rome, could easily be converted into the city's main defence. He had twin walls built from Aurelian's gate to and around the tomb, and so the towering marble fortress now formed an impenetrable defence of Aurelian's gate, which could no longer be taken by storm, all the more so because the Tiber formed a natural moat immediately below. High up on the walls of the mausoleum stood three hundred beautiful statues of marble and bronze. Some of them had been placed there by Hadrian himself and his successors; they included the Divus Hadrianus himself, his handsome favourite Antonius, the Pallas "guardian of the city", a sleeping faun and many others.

Cethegus was pleased with his conception and loved this place. Every evening he would walk here, surveying "his" Rome with his eyes and checking on the progress being made with the fortifications. For this reason he had added a number of beautiful statues from his own private collection to those already there.

Chapter 4

But if Cethegus was to succeed in furthering his aims there was a second task he had to accomplish, and it called for much more caution. If he was to be in a position in Rome – "his" Rome as he liked to call it – where he could independently offer resistance to the Goths, and a Byzantine army as well if need be, then he needed not only walls but soldiers to defend those walls. At first he thought he might meet this need by way of forming a personal bodyguard of mercenaries, as was the custom with many high officials, statesmen and generals. In Byzantium, for example, both Belisarius and his rival Narses had long had such personal bodyguards. By using old connections made during his travels in Asia, and by using his immense wealth, he was able to attract into his service a number of the courageous mountain tribes of Isauria, who in those days played much the same role as the Swiss mercenaries of the sixteenth century. However this method had two major limitations.

In the first place he could hope to employ only limited numbers of mercenaries without exhausting his financial resources, which he needed badly for other purposes as well. He could afford enough Isaurians to form the backbone of an army, but not an army as such. Secondly it was impossible to import these mercenaries into Italy in large numbers without arousing Gothic suspicion. Thus bringing them in involved much cunning and considerable risk to himself. He could import them only singly or in pairs, under the pretext that they were his slaves, freedmen, clients or guests. He spread them around his various villas scattered through the peninsula, and even employed some as sailors on his ships in Ostia, or as labourers in Rome.

In the final analysis, therefore, it had to be the Romans themselves who had to re-establish and then defend Rome, and hence he had to get his countrymen used to bearing arms again.

Unfortunately for Cethegus, Theodoric had wisely excluded the Italian populace from military service, except for a small number who were regarded as being particularly reliable. During the unsettled last days of his reign, while the prosecution of Boethius was under way, a law had been passed making it illegal for any Italian to bear arms. Admittedly this law had never been strictly enforced, but even so Cethegus could not hope that the queen would permit him to establish a fighting force of any significant number of Italians, as this would be contrary to her great father's law as well as the Gothic interest.

Cethegus therefore persuaded Amalasuntha that she could win the hearts of the Romans by an entirely harmless small concession, namely by relaxing Theodoric's much hated law just a little. He suggested to her that he be permitted to set up a small garrison of Italians for the defence of Rome, consisting of only two thousand men, whom he would equip and train personally. He managed to convince her that the people of Rome would thank her for even this token gesture that the eternal city was no longer defended only by Barbarians. Amalasuntha was a lover of Rome, and her greatest wish was that the Roman people should love her in return. She therefore willingly gave her consent, and Cethegus immediately set about forming his "home guard", as he was to call it. In a proclamation to the people he recalled "the sons of the Scipios to the arms of old", he made the young noblemen from the catacombs into "Roman knights" and "tribunes", and he promised every Roman volunteer to double the official Gothic pay out of his own pocket. Out of the many thousands who now answered his call he selected the most suitable, equipped the poorer ones and made gifts of swords and helmets to those who distinguished themselves. But most importantly he made a practice of discharging his soldiers as soon as they had been adequately trained, making them a gift of their arms, and promptly replacing them with fresh recruits. Hence at any given time only the two thousand men permitted by Amalasuntha were in service, yet within a short time many thousands of well trained and well armed Roman soldiers were at the disposal of their leader, whom they worshipped like a god.

While Cethegus was busy thus building his future capital and training his future Praetorian Guard, he had to constantly mollify the enthusiasm of his fellow conspirators, who were clamouring for an immediate start to hostilities. He urged them to wait until his preparations were complete, which of course only he could determine. At the same time he kept up steady correspondence with Byzantium. His aim was to ensure that he could count on their help when he wanted it, and that they would be ready to invade Italy the moment he called them. On the other hand he wanted to make sure that they would not appear before he was ready, or in such strength that they would be difficult to get rid of again.

What he wanted from Byzantium was a good general who was not a good statesman, with an army strong enough to support his Romans, but too weak to win without them or to remain in the country against their will. As we will see in the events that follow, many things developed just as the Prefect wished them to, and others did not. The Goths still thought themselves secure in their possession of the prize over which Cethegus was already haggling in his mind with Byzantium. The Prefect's efforts were directed at dulling them into a false sense of security, splitting them into factions where he could, and ensuring that a weak administration remained in control.

The former task was not difficult. With typically Germanic arrogance the Goths had great confidence in their own strength and despised all their enemies, overt or covert. We have already seen how even a highly intelligent and clear thinking young man like Totila was difficult to convince that danger lay ahead. The smug stubbornness of a man like Hildebad was more typical of the general attitude among the Goths, and furthermore there was no shortage of competing factions.

Apart from the ruling Amalungs there were two other prominent noble houses within Gothic society. There was the Balti clan, with the three dukes Thulun, Ibba and Pitza at the heads of its three main branches. Secondly there was the wealthy Woelsung clan, led by the brothers Duke Guntharis of Tuscany and Count Arahad of Asta. As well as these there were many others who conceded little to the Amalungs in terms of rank or glory, and each of them was zealously guarding his own position close to the throne.

Among the Goths there were many who endured only with reluctance the reign of a boy under the guardianship of a woman, and who would have liked nothing better than to bypass the royal house in accordance with the ancient traditions of their people, electing a proven warrior as their king. On the other hand the Amalungs also had their faithful following, who would have condemned any such idea as treason.

Finally the whole nation was split in two camps anyway, those who supported the benevolent rule of the Amalungs, and those who favoured a harder line. The latter group had long been dissatisfied with the mild rule of Theodoric and his daughter, particularly as far as the Italians were concerned. They now wanted to punish the Italians for their secret hatred with brutality, which was what they believed should have been the policy when the country was first conquered. Much smaller in number were their counterparts who, like Theodoric himself, were sympathetic to the more advanced civilisation of their conquered foe, and who sought to raise the cultural level of their own people accordingly. At the head of this party was the queen, Amalasuntha.

Cethegus saw it as being in his interest to maintain this woman as head of state, because she and her weak regime promised that the dissatisfaction and fragmentation already in evidence among her people would become lasting, and consequently the Gothic national strength would in time weaken. Her ideals precluded any development of Gothic nationalism, and the Prefect shuddered at the thought that a strong man might manage to gather together the scattered strength of these Germanic people into a unified and powerful fighting force once more.

There were times when he was seriously concerned at the domineering traits which were starting to show in this woman, even more so than the occasional sparks of concealed fire which Athalaric showed from time to time. Should mother and son show these traits more frequently, then he would have to use the same zeal to overthrow them as he had used so far to prop up their regime. For the time being he could still revel in the mastery he had gained over Amalasuntha. He had achieved this very rapidly, not only by exploiting her passion for learned discussion, but by making it appear as if her vast learning was superior in all respects to his own. Cassiodorus, who was often a witness to these discussions, could not help feeling regret at the way this once razor-sharp mind seemed to have become rusty through lack of use.

Cethegus's deep understanding of human nature had enabled him to reach an even more vulnerable spot in this proud woman's make-up. Her great father had not been blessed with a son, but only with this one daughter, and from early childhood she had heard the constant wish for a male heir, not only from her father but from the mouths of the people. The highly talented woman felt it an affront that she should be considered inferior to a possible brother merely because of her sex, and that a brother was generally accepted as being more able and better suited to wear her father's crown. As a child she had often cried bitter tears because she had not been born a boy.

As she grew up, of course, she was to hear the wish for a son less often, and only from her father's lips. Everyone else at court praised the princess's great intellect, considerable talent and masculine courage. This was not merely flattery either. Amalasuntha was indeed an extraordinary creature in every respect, and her capable mind and resolute will, as well as her cool toughness and lust for power, far exceeded the accepted limits of gentle femininity. The knowledge that her future husband would gain with her hand the most influential position in the country, if not the crown itself, did little to limit her self-assurance. In time her driving ambition was no longer to be a man, but to show that she, a woman, was as equal to the demands of government as any man, and that fate had chosen her to disprove once and for all the assumed inferiority of her sex.

The marriage of the cold princess to Eutharic lasted only a short time, and was not a happy union. Eutharic was from another branch of the Amalung family tree, and was a gifted man with high ideals, but he died from a severe illness after a few years. It was only with the greatest reluctance that Amalasuntha had submitted to her husband, and as soon as she was widowed she raised her proud head once more. She became obsessed by the ambition to realise her favourite dream as guardian and regent to her son, and she wanted to reign with such obvious ability that even the proudest men would humbly acknowledge her as being their worthy ruler. We have already seen how the expectation of becoming ruler enabled this cold soul to endure even her father's death with comparative calm.

She assumed the duties of government with the greatest zeal, and worked with tireless dedication. She wanted to do everything herself, and pushed the aging Cassiodorus to one side because in her opinion he was unable to keep up with her own quick and able mind. She would not tolerate advice or help from any man.

Jealously she guarded her position at the top as sole ruler of the Gothic Empire. Among her advisers there was only one to whom she would listen gladly and often, the one who praised the manly independence of her mind frequently and publicly, and who still more often seemed to be secretly admiring those same qualities in her, without ever trying to dominate her. In short she trusted only Cethegus. She was convinced that he wanted nothing but to serve her ambition, and to help her realise all her thoughts and plans with conscientious attention to detail. Unlike Cassiodorus or the Gothic leaders he never opposed her favourite plans, but encouraged her to pursue them instead. He was instrumental in helping her surround herself with Romans and Greeks, and excluding the young king from the business of government as much as possible. Gradually he influenced her to remove from court one by one her father's old Gothic friends, because they felt entitled to voice many a word of criticism in view of their rank and past service to her father. More and more she saw the Goths as ignorant Barbarians. Money which had been designated to buy warships, horses and weaponry for the Gothic forces was used instead, on the advice of Cethegus, to further learning or the arts, or on the beautification and fortification of Rome. In short he helped her in everything which would estrange her from her people, make her nation defenceless and her regime hated. And if he did have a plan of his own he knew how to conduct negotiations with the queen in such a way that she became convinced the plan had come from her alone. Cethegus, she thought, was merely doing his best to help her carry out her wishes on her explicit instructions, as well as obeying her orders faithfully and promptly.

Chapter 5

In order to gain and then maintain the necessary influence with the queen, Cethegus found it necessary to spend a great deal of time at court, far more time than he could afford without neglecting his other interests in Rome. For this reason he strove to surround Amalasuntha with persons who would save him the need to be constantly in Ravenna, and who would at the same time serve his interests and keep him well informed. It so happened that a number of Gothic noblemen had angrily left Ravenna, and their wives needed to be replaced at court. Cethegus therefore toyed with the idea of using this opportunity to introduce Rusticiana to the court, the daughter of Symmachus and widow of Boethius, but this was no easy task. The families of these two executed men had been banned from Ravenna in disgrace, and it was therefore necessary to first influence the queen in Rusticiana's favour.

Cethegus soon achieved this aim by playing on the noble woman's compassion for the deeply disgraced family of the executed traitors. Amalasuntha had never wanted to believe in the guilt of the two noble Romans, whose guilt had never been proven, and in addition she had always honoured Rusticiana's husband Boethius as a great scholar and teacher. Finally Cethegus managed to convince her that pardoning this family would do more than anything else to win her the hearts of the Roman population, who would applaud her action, be it one of mercy or one of justice. And so the queen was easily persuaded to extend compassion, but it was much more difficult to persuade the proud and temperamental widow to accept it. Rusticiana's entire being was filled with anger against the royal house and with thoughts of revenge. Cethegus even had good reason to fear that, once Rusticiana was in the constant company of the "tyrant", she would be unable to control her almost boundless hatred and thereby betray herself. Repeatedly Rusticiana had rejected his proposals, in spite of the tremendous influence he had over her.

Then, one day, they made a surprise discovery which was to lead to the Prefect's wishes being realised.

Rusticiana had a daughter Camilla, barely sixteen years old. She was a beautiful girl with dark eyes illuminating a very pretty and typically Roman face. Her slender body had only just grown to maturity, and her movements were quick and light like those of a gazelle. Within this lovely body there dwelled a sensitive young mind and a lively imagination. She had loved her unfortunate father with all the devotion of childhood, and the blow which cost his head left her with deep emotional scars. Her dreams were filled with mourning and sadness, together with passionate admiration of his martyrdom for Italy.

Before her family's fall from grace she had been a popular guest at court, but after the fateful blow she and her mother had fled across the Alps to Gaul, where an old family friend had offered them a refuge for some time. Camilla's brothers Anicius and Severinus were at first also condemned to death, but later their sentences were commuted to banishment from the Empire. As soon as they were released from prison they rushed directly to the imperial court in Byzantium, where they immediately started agitating against the Goths. Once the storm had passed the two women returned to Italy, where they led a life of quiet grief in the small house of a former slave named Corbulo in Perusia. From there, as we have seen, Rusticiana had managed to find her way to the conspirators in Rome.

Summer had arrived, the time of year when wealthy Romans were in the habit of fleeing the humid heat of the cities in favour of their cool villas in the mountains of Sabinia or on the coast. The two noblewomen found it difficult to endure the smoke and dust in the narrow streets of Perusia. With many a sigh of regret they thought of their beautiful country estates near Naples and Florence, which along with all their other possessions had been confiscated by the Gothic treasury.

One day the faithful Corbulo appeared before Rusticiana with a strangely embarrassed look on his face. He had long noticed how the *patrona* was suffering under his unworthy roof, and how his work as a stonemason had caused her and her daughter much discomfort. For this reason he had recently bought a little country estate, a very small one, with a house that was smaller still, up in the mountains near Tifernum. Of course there could be no comparison with their former villa near Florence, but there was a little permanent spring, oaks and cherry trees to give ample shade, and the ruins of an old temple overgrown with ivy. He had planted roses, violets and lilies in the garden, just as he thought Domna Camilla liked them. And so he begged the two women to mount mule and litter, and to move into their villa like other noblewomen.

The two women were deeply touched by the old man's loyalty, and gratefully accepted his kind offer. Camilla, who was looking forward to this change of scene with almost childish joy, was happier and more cheerful than she had been at any time since her father's death. Impatiently she insisted on making an immediate start, and left that same day with Corbulo and his daughter Daphnidion. Rusticiana was to follow with the slaves and the luggage as soon as she was able.

The sun was already setting behind the hills of Tifernum when Corbulo, who was leading Camilla's mule, reached the small clearing from which the little estate could first be seen. He had long looked forward to seeing the child's delight when he would show her the nicely situated little house from here.

But instead he stopped in astonishment, shielding his eyes with his hand to make sure the sun was not blinding him. He looked about him to make sure he was in the right place, but there could be no doubt. There, where the forest bordered on green meadow, was the grey statue of the border god Terminus with its pointed head, which served Corbulo as a landmark. It was certainly the right place, but the little house could not be seen. Where it should be there was a dense thicket of pines and plane trees, and the other surroundings too were completely changed. Where there had been cabbages and carrots there were now hedges and beds of flowers, and where there was formerly nothing but a ditch and a road bordering the small property there was now a delightful pavilion.

"May the mother of God and all the higher gods help me!" Corbulo cried, "am I bewitched or is it this area? Something magical has happened, whatever it might be." His daughter handed him a charm she wore on her belt, but she could offer no explanation either, as this was the first time she had seen the new house. And so there was nothing else for it but to drive the mule to utmost haste, and father and daughter ran down the hill with the animal, jumping with joy.

As they came closer Corbulo did find the little house he had bought behind the trees, but it had been rejuvenated and beautified almost beyond recognition.

His surprise at the change which had come over the whole area soon turned to superstitious fear. At last he stopped, his mouth open, and dropped the reins to burst forth in a mixture of Christian and heathen oaths. Suddenly Camilla, who was just as surprised, called out: "Look, there is the garden where we used to live, the *viridarium* of Honorius in Ravenna, the same trees, the same flower beds, and even the little temple of Venus near that small pond, just like the one on the coast in Ravenna. Oh how beautiful, and what lovely memories it brings back! Corbulo, how on earth did you do it?" Her eyes were brimming with tears of happiness.

"May the devil and all the evil spirits torture me if I did that! But here comes Cappadox with his clubfoot. At least he is not bewitched! Speak, you old Cyclops, what has happened here?"

The gigantic Cappadox, a broad-shouldered slave, limped towards them with an uneasy smile, and amid many interruptions and astonished questions he told a strange tale indeed. Three weeks ago, a few days after Cappadox had been sent to the estate to manage it for his absent master, a distinguished Roman had arrived with a large train of slaves, workmen and heavily laden carts. He asked if this was the estate which the stonemason Corbulo had bought on behalf of the widow of Boethius, and when this was confirmed he introduced himself as the *Hortulanus Princeps*, i.e. the chief superintendent of gardens in Ravenna. An old friend of Boethius, who did not dare mention his name for fear of the tyrant, had instructed him to take care of his widow and daughter, and he was to restore, re-decorate and beautify their residence with all the means at his disposal. Cappadox was not to spoil the surprise by saying anything to his master, and he had been detained at the villa kindly but firmly. The superintendent immediately devised a plan, and his workmen and slaves started work without delay.

A number of neighbouring properties had been bought at high prices to enlarge the original estate, and then a flurry of demolition and building, digging and planting, hammering and sawing, plastering and painting had commenced, so that poor Cappadox was driven nearly out of his wits. If he tried to interfere or ask a question the workmen would laugh in his face. If he tried to escape the superintendent would wave his hand, and half a dozen strong arms would hold him. And this, the narrator concluded, had been going on continuously until the day before yesterday. Then suddenly they were finished and had left.

Cappadox continued: "At first I was afraid, when I saw all these costly wonders appear out of the ground. I thought I would be in deep trouble if Master Corbulo had to pay for it all in the end. I tried to inform you, but they would not let me leave, and in any case I knew that you would not be at home. And when I saw the unbelievable amount of money the superintendent seemed to have, and how he threw gold pieces around the way children throw pebbles, I calmed down and just let things happen. Master, I know you can put me in blocks and have me beaten, but why? Because you are the master and I Cappadox the slave. But it would not be just, Master, because you bade me look after a few cabbages, and under my care they have become a garden fit for an emperor."

Camilla had long since dismounted, even before the slave had finished his tale. Her heart beating with joy, she ran through the garden, the summerhouses and the house itself. She flew along as if she had grown wings, and Daphnidion could barely keep up with her. One cry of delight or surprise followed another. Every time she rounded a corner, or another clump of trees, again and again a picture from that other garden in Ravenna appeared before her delighted eyes. But the biggest surprise was yet to come. When she entered the house itself she found a little room, furnished and decorated just like the room she had once occupied in the former villa, perfect down to the motifs in the woven curtains and her favourite harp on the little tortoiseshell table. This was the room where she had played her last childish games, and dreamed her first girlish dreams. At last the weight of memories and gratitude for such a generous display of friendship overcame her, and sobbing with joy she sank down on the soft cushions of the *lectus*. Daphnidion could barely calm her as she cried, again and again: "There are still some noble hearts, and a few friends of the house of Boethius." And she offered a prayer of thanks to God.

When her mother arrived next day she was no less surprised, and immediately wrote to Cethegus to ask him which of her late husband's friends might be her mysterious benefactor. Secretly she hoped that it might be Cethegus himself, but the latter was just as surprised as she was and could offer no explanation. He suggested that she should watch carefully for any clues which might help solve the puzzle, and indeed the secret was to be revealed very soon.

Camilla never tired of walking through the garden, and drawing comparisons with that other garden she had loved so much. Often these walks led her beyond the garden and into the adjoining forest, and the cheerful Daphnidion accompanied her on these walks, the two girls having become firm friends. Several times Daphnidion had warned the *Patrona* that a forest faun must be following them, as they often heard rustling in the grass or bushes near them. But Camilla laughed at her superstition.

One day the girls, driven deeper into the forest than usual by the heat, found a lively little spring, gushing forth from the rock in a clear and plentiful stream. But it did not flow along any defined course, and the girls were able to catch a few drops of the cool water only with difficulty. Camilla cried: "What a pity so much of this lovely water is wasted. You should have seen the Triton spring in the *Pinetum* in Ravenna. A stream of clear water used to pour from the bronze sea god's mouth into a seashell made of brown marble. What a pity!" And they continued on their way.

A few days later they came back to the same place. Daphnidion, who was leading the way, suddenly stopped with a sharp cry, silently pointing to the spring. It had been tamed, and a stream of water now poured from a Triton's head into a delicate brown basin shaped like a seashell. Daphnidion now firmly believed that this must be the work of ghosts and turned immediately to flee, shielding her eyes with her hands so that she would not see the spirits, which she considered very dangerous. She ran straight back to the house, calling to her mistress to follow. But Camilla did not frighten so easily, and a thought flashed through her mind that the secret listener who had overheard them last time was probably not far away now, enjoying their surprise. Searchingly she looked about her, and her eyes caught sight of a wild rose bush, whose branches were moving. Quickly she walked toward that spot, and presently a young hunter stepped toward her from the bushes, armed with bag and spear.

"I have been discovered!" he said quietly, evidently embarrassed.

But Camilla drew back with a cry of terror. "Athalaric, the king!"

A torrent of thoughts and feelings raced through her head, and semi-conscious she sank down on a patch of grass near the stream. The young king stood before her slender figure for a few seconds, with a mixture of shock and delight. Thirstily his burning eyes feasted on her lovely face and noble features as she lay before him. Like lightning a flash of crimson crossed his face, and at last he sighed, his hand on his rapidly beating heart. "Oh love of my life! If only she were mine I could want for nothing else ever! Even if I could just die now, with her, I could not wish for more!"

She moved her arm, and this brought him back to his senses. He knelt down beside her and splashed some of the cool water from the well on her forehead. She opened her eyes. "Barbarian! Murderer!" she cried shrilly. Pushing his arm aside she sprang to her feet and fled like a startled doe.

Athalaric did not try to follow her. "Barbarian, murderer!" he sighed to himself with deep pain, and buried his feverish face in his hands.

Chapter 6

Camilla returned home in such a state that Daphnidion could not help thinking that the Domna must have seen nymphs or even the forest god Picus himself.

But the girl threw herself into her startled mother's arms with violent emotion. The raging torrent of her emotions gave way to a stream of hot tears, and it was some time before she was able to offer coherent answers and explanations to Rusticiana's worried questions.

A heavy struggle of conflicting emotions filled Camilla's young soul.

When she was growing up into a young woman at the court in Ravenna it had not escaped her how the pale youth often looked at her with a strange, dreamy look in his eyes, and how he listened to her voice with rapt attention. But she had never become consciously aware that he was attracted by her. Whenever she caught the young prince looking at her thus she would return his stare frankly and openly, which immediately caused him to lower his eyes. They were both children then, and it had never occurred to her what might be going on inside Athalaric – indeed he barely knew himself. Nor had it ever occurred to her to wonder why it was that she too liked to be near him, and how she liked to share his bold ideas and fantasies, so different from those of her other playmates. Often she would walk with him silently, through the gardens in the twilight, where he would often speak to her quite suddenly as if in a dream. And yet his words always made sense to her, and she felt that she fully understood the poetry of youthful idealism which they contained.

And then the catastrophe of her father's sudden death sharply and abruptly tore the delicate fabric of this blossoming affection. Not only was the heart of this passionate Roman girl filled with mourning for her murdered father, but she was also filled with burning hatred for his murderers. Boethius had always displayed an attitude of arrogant condescension toward the Goths, even during his days in favour at the court. Since his death everyone in Camilla's circle, her mother, brothers and family friends, had seethed with hatred and contempt, and that hatred was not only directed at the bloody murderer and tyrant Theodoric. They hated with equal fervour all Goths, and above all the king's daughter and grandson, because in their eyes they shared his guilt by failing to prevent him. And so the girl had barely given Athalaric another thought. If she heard his name mentioned or if, as happened occasionally, he appeared in her dreams, all her hatred of the Barbarians concentrated on him. Perhaps this was because, subconsciously, she had developed an affection for the handsome prince, although her conscious mind rejected any such possibility with all her might.

And now this evildoer had dared to strike at her unsuspecting heart with such a cruel trick!

As soon as she had seen him step from the thicket and recognised him she had known immediately who had been responsible for the transformation of the spring, and indeed the whole villa. It was him, the hated enemy and member of the accursed house, her father's murderer, the Barbarian king! All the joy she had experienced these last few days, as she had walked through the house and garden, had evaporated. This mortal enemy of her people and her family had dared to give her joy and pleasure! For him she had offered prayers of thanks to heaven! Not only that, but he had had the temerity to follow her steps, to listen to her words, and to fulfil her most secret wishes. And at the back of her mind, even more terrifying, was the question of why he had done it. He loved her! The tyrant of Italy, surely he could not hope that the daughter of Boethius – no! It was too much! With painful sobbing she would bury her face in her pillow until, at last, an exhausted sleep would come over her.

Before long Cethegus, who had been hastily summoned, arrived at the villa. At first Rusticiana had wanted to follow her own and Camilla's initial impulse and flee from the villa and the king's hated nearness, so that she could hide her child as far away as possible on the other side of the Alps. But so far Camilla's condition had prevented any departure, and as soon as the Prefect entered the house all the excitement seemed to settle down before his cold eyes. He went into the garden alone with Rusticiana and there, leaning against a laurel tree, he listened to her emotional tale with calm attention.

"And now tell me," she concluded, "what must I do? How can I save my poor child? Where can I take her?"

Cethegus opened his eyes, which had been half closed as was his habit when he was thinking or concentrating hard.

"Where to take Camilla? To the court, to Ravenna."

Rusticiana responded angrily: "This is no time for your cruel jokes!"

But Cethegus quickly rose to his full height.

"I am not joking. Quite the contrary, I am in deadly earnest. Be quiet and listen to me. The fate which will ultimately destroy the Barbarians could not have placed a more wonderful gift at our disposal. You know how completely I control Amalasuntha, but what you do not know is how powerless I am against that stubborn young idealist. That sick boy is the only one among the Goths who, although he may not have seen through me, suspects me. And I don't know whether he hates me or fears me more. It would not concern me so much if the youth was not so determined and so consistently successful in his efforts to oppose me. You will understand that his word weighs heavily with his mother, often more heavily than mine. And all the time he is becoming older, more mature and more dangerous. His mind is mature well beyond his years, and he is starting to play an increasingly effective role as adviser to the regent. He always opposes me, and he often wins. Only the other day he succeeded, against my wishes, in having command of the Gothic troops in Rome given to that black galled Teias, in my Rome! In short, the young king is becoming very dangerous, and until now I have not had the slightest control over him. Now, to his peril, he loves Camilla, and through her we can control him."

"Never!" Rusticiana cried, "not while there is breath in my body! Me, at the tyrant's court? And my child the beloved of Athalaric? Boethius's daughter? His bloody shadow would…"

"Do you want to avenge that shadow? Do you want the Goths destroyed? Yes? If that is the end you want, then you must also want the means to achieve it."

"Never! I swear it!"

"Woman, do not anger me! Don't resist me! You know me well. Did you not promise me obedience, blind and unconditional obedience, when I promised you revenge? Was that not your oath? I seem to remember that you swore that oath on all the saints, and that you and your children should be cursed in all eternity if ever you were to break it. It is wise to be careful with you women, so now obey or fear for your soul!"

"You terrible man! Am I to sacrifice all my hatred to you and your schemes?"

"To me? Who is talking about me? All I am doing is to look after your affairs, and your revenge. The Goths have done me no wrong. It was you who tore me away from my books, and who appealed to me to help you destroy these Amalungs. Don't you want to any more? Very well then, I will return to Horatius and Stoa. Farewell!"

"Stay, stay! But must Camilla become the sacrifice?"

"Nonsense! Athalaric will be the sacrifice. She is not to love him, only control him. Or do you fear that she might really fall in love with him?" Cethegus added, looking sharply at her.

"How dare you even think that? My daughter love him? I would sooner strangle her with these hands."

But Cethegus had become thoughtful. "It is not the girl I am concerned about," he said to himself, "I care little about her. But if she loves him, and after all the Goth is a handsome youth, intelligent and idealistic... Where is your daughter?" he added aloud.

"In her room. But even if I wanted her to she would never agree. Never!"

"We will try. I will go to her."

They went into the house. Rusticiana was about to go into the room with him, but Cethegus pushed her aside.

"I must have her alone," he said, and stepped through the curtain. When she saw him the lovely girl rose from the cushions on which she had been resting and brooding. From childhood she had become used to seeing in this clever, older man her father's friend and a trusted adviser. She therefore greeted him trustingly, much as a patient greets a physician.

"You know, Cethegus?"

"Everything."

"And you bring me help?"

"I bring you revenge, Camilla."

That was a new and powerful idea to her. Until now she had thought only of flight and escape, or at most angry rejection of the royal gifts. But now – revenge! Revenge for the pain of these last few days, and for the shame she had suffered. Revenge against her father's murderers! Her mental wounds were still fresh, and her hot Roman blood pulsed through her veins. Her heart rejoiced at Cethegus's words.

"Revenge? Who is going to avenge me? You?"

"You will avenge yourself, Camilla. It will be sweeter that way."

Her eyes flashed. "Against whom?"

"Against him. Against his house, against all our enemies."

"How can I do that? I am just a weak girl."

"Listen to me, Camilla. I will tell you, Boethius's noble daughter, something which I would tell no other woman on earth. There exists a strong conspiracy of patriots, which will wipe out these Barbarians without leaving a trace of them in our land. The sword of revenge hangs over the tyrant's head, and your fatherland and your father's memory are calling on you to bring it down on them."

"Me? I am to avenge my father? Go on!" Camilla cried, her face aglow as she brushed her black hair from her temples.

"A sacrifice is called for. Rome demands it."

"My blood, my life, anything! I will die like Virginia!"

"You will live to see victory. The king loves you. You must go to Ravenna, to the court, and through that love you must destroy him. Only you have control over him, and you shall avenge yourself by destroying him."

"Destroy him?" Camilla sounded deeply moved as she asked this question, almost inaudibly. Her voice was trembling, and her bosom heaving, reflecting her inner struggle. With tears in her eyes she buried her head in her hands.

Cethegus rose. "Forgive me. I did not know you were in love with the king."

A cry of anger, as of physical pain, was the anguished girl's response. She jumped up and grasped his shoulder.

"Who said that? I hate him! I hate him more than I ever thought I could hate anyone."

"Then prove it. I do not believe you."

"I will prove it," she cried, "he shall die! He must not live!"

As she said it she threw back her head. Her eyes flashed, and her black hair flew about her shoulders.

She loves him, thought Cethegus, but it does not matter because she does not know it. She also hates him, and that alone she knows. It will work.

"He shall not live," she repeated. "You will see how I love him!" she said laughing, "what do you want me to do?"

"Follow me in all things."

"And what can you promise me in return? What will he suffer?"

"An all-consuming love to his death."

"Love for me? Yes, that he shall!"

"He, his house and his Empire shall fall."

"And will he know that, through me…?"

"He will know it. When do we leave for Ravenna?"

"Tomorrow! No, today, there is still time." She stopped and clutched his hand. "Cethegus, am I beautiful?"

"One of Italy's most beautiful women."

"Ha!" she cried, shaking her head and its flowing tresses, "he shall love me and perish! Let us go to Ravenna! I want to see him, I must see him, now!"

And with those words she stormed from the room. Her entire being was now possessed by the desire to be with Athalaric.

Chapter 7

They left the villa that same day for the capital. Cethegus had sent a messenger ahead with a letter from Rusticiana to the queen, in which Boethius's widow declared that she was now willing to accept the invitation to return to court, which had been extended to her repeatedly via the Prefect. The letter also implied that Amalasuntha's gesture was being seen not so much as an act of mercy, but rather as a sign that Theodoric's heirs were trying to right the wrong they had committed. The wording sounded as if it had come directly from Rusticiana's heart, and Cethegus knew that taking this stand would not only do no harm, but would remove any suspicion which the sudden change of heart may have aroused. The queen's reply reached them while they were still en route, bidding them welcome at court. Upon arrival in Ravenna they were received with every possible courtesy and honour by Amalasuntha, surrounded by slaves of both sexes and accommodated in the same rooms which they had previously occupied, much to the delight of the Roman ladies.

These gestures however also served to severely anger the Goths, who despised Boethius and Symmachus as traitors, and who interpreted the latest happenings as a silent condemnation of their great king Theodoric. The late king's last remaining friends angrily left the court, which by this time had become almost entirely Romanised.

Meanwhile the diversion caused by the journey and arrival in Ravenna, as well as the time which had elapsed, had done much to calm Camilla. And her anger had all the more time to settle as it was to be several weeks before she saw the young king again. Athalaric had fallen seriously ill.

The story doing the rounds at court had it that the king had gone to Arentium with only a few companions, to enjoy hunting, the mountain air and the baths. While there he was said to have become overheated while hunting, causing him to take a cool drink from a spring, and this in turn had brought on a renewed attack of his old illness. In fact his followers had found him unconscious beside the spring where he had encountered Camilla.

The story had a strange effect on Camilla, and her hatred of Athalaric now changed at least in part to silent pity, and even a degree of self-reproach. Yet on the other hand she thanked heaven that any further meeting with Athalaric had been delayed because of it. Since arriving in Ravenna she had dreaded this meeting, just as much as she had longed for it when she was still far from him in Tifernum. And when she went for walks through the beautifully kept palace gardens she could not but admire the care with which Corbulo's little property had been modelled on their example.

The days and weeks passed. Nothing was heard of the patient except that he was slowly recovering from his illness, but still confined to his rooms. The physicians and courtiers around him often praised his patience and courage, even while he was in great pain, as well as his gratitude for the smallest act of kindness and his dignified and gentle manner. But when Camilla caught herself thirstily taking in these words of praise she would say sternly to herself: "But he did nothing to prevent my father's murder." At this her face would flush with anger, and she would hold her clenched fist to her heart.

One hot night in July Camilla, who had been tossing and turning restlessly for hours, at last fell into an uneasy sleep in the early morning hours. She was plagued by nightmares, and it seemed as if the ceiling of her room with its heavy ornamentation was pressing down on her. Directly over her head was a beautiful and youthful likeness of the god Hypnos, the god of sleep, created by some distant Hellenic sculptor.

She dreamt that the god of sleep was assuming the paler, more serious features of his brother Thanatos. Slowly the god of death lowered his face toward hers. Steadily he came closer, and his features became more and more distinct. Already she could feel his breath on her forehead, and his lips were almost touching her mouth. Then suddenly, to her horror, she recognised the pale face and dark eyes. This god of death was Athalaric, and with a cry of terror she sprang up.

The pretty little silver lamp had long gone out, and dawn was breaking, its light illuminating her room. A red glow shone dully through the stained glass windows. She pushed open the window and rose from her bed. Somewhere a cock crowed, and the first rays of the sun were rising out of the sea, of which she had an unobstructed view from her window across the palace gardens. She could bear it in the stuffy room no longer, and so she drew a loosely flowing robe about her shoulders before silently making her way through the sleeping palace and down a flight of marble steps into the garden.

Here a refreshing morning breeze was blowing off the sea and into her face, and she rushed out toward the sun and the blue Adriatic Sea, which bordered directly on the high walls of the eastern part of the royal gardens. A gilded trellised gate with ten broad steps of hymettic marble beyond it led down to the little harbour which was a part of the palace gardens. In the harbour pretty little gondolas with beautifully made oars and sails of purple linen were gently rocking to and fro, fastened to the bronze ram's heads in the quay with silver chains. On the palace side of the gate there was a spacious semicircular section of the garden, surrounded by shady pines. Its surface was made up of carefully tended lawns, crossed with little paths, and here and there could be seen small beds of flowers, their perfume filling the morning air. A little spring flowed down the banks into the sea, and in the centre of the semicircle stood an ancient temple of Venus. A single tall palm rose above it, and fiery red saxifrage was growing in the empty niches of its outer walls. To the right of the closed gate stood a bronze Aeneas, but the Julius Caesar on the left had collapsed centuries ago. In its place Theodoric had erected a statue of Amala, the mythical ancestor of his dynasty. Here, between the statues and sitting on the steps one could enjoy a lovely view of the sea through the trellised gate, with its bushy islands and their lagoons, and a poetic group of sharp cliffs known as the Needles of Amphitrite.

It was an old favourite spot of Camilla's, and she now headed for this place, sweeping the morning dew from the grass as she ran along narrow paths, her gown slightly raised. She wanted to see the sun rising over the sea. She was just rounding the back of the temple and about to place her foot on the first of the steps leading down to the trellised gate, when her eyes caught sight of another figure, dressed in white, sitting on the second step to her right, looking out to sea.

She recognised the brown silken hair. It was the young king.

Their meeting had been so sudden that there had been no time to think of evasion, and the girl stood on the first step as if rooted to it. Athalaric sprang to his feet and turned quickly, a light red colour flushing across his marble face, but he was first to regain his composure and the first to speak.

"Forgive me Camilla, but I did not expect to see you here at this hour. I will go and leave you alone with the sun." With these words he gathered his white cloak about him.

"Stay, king of the Goths. I have no right to chase you away – nor do I wish to," she added.

Athalaric took a step closer. "Thank you. But I must ask a favour of you. Please don't betray me to my physicians or to my mother. They lock me in so carefully all day that I have to escape them before the day has even begun. This fresh sea air is doing me good, I feel it. It cools me. You will not betray me, will you?" He spoke calmly, and looked at her with natural ease.

This calm and ease confused Camilla. She would have been much more courageous if he had shown more emotion, and she saw his calmness with pain in her heart, but not because of the Prefect's schemes. She shook her head in silence and lowered her eyes.

At this moment the sun's rays reached the spot where they were standing. The old temple and the bronze of the statues shone in the morning light, and a broad band of shimmering gold stretched from the east across the mirror smooth sea.

"How beautiful!" Athalaric exclaimed, carried away by the scene before him, "look at that bridge of light and brilliance."

She too looked out to sea, and her thoughts were with his. Slowly, as if lost in memories, he went on. "Do you remember, Camilla? Do you remember when we used to play here as children, when we dreamed together? We said that this golden road, painted on the sea by the sun, leads to the islands of the blessed."

"To the islands of the blessed," Camilla repeated. Silently she could not help admiring the tenderness and ease with which he, avoiding any reference to their last meeting, spoke to her in a way which completely disarmed her. "Look how those statues are glowing, that wonderful pair, Aeneas and – Amala! Camilla, I owe you an apology."

Her heart started beating faster. Now he would talk about the transformation of the villa, and their meeting at the spring. Blood rising to her cheeks, she waited in silent anticipation.

But the youth continued calmly: "You know how often we used to stand here, you the Roman and I the Goth, competing with one another in praising the relative merits of our people. You would stand under Aeneas and speak of Brutus and Camillus, of Marcellus and the Scipios. And I, leaning against the shield of my ancestor Amala, would praise Ermanaric, Alaric and Theodoric. But you spoke better than I did. And often, when the glory of your heroes threatened to outshine mine, I would laugh at your dead and say that the present and the future belonged to my people."

"Well, and now?"

"Now I no longer speak as I did then. You have won, Camilla."

And as he said this he seemed prouder than ever before. The look of superiority on his face angered the Roman girl, already irritated as she was by the implacable calm with which the young king stood opposite her. She and Cethegus had made such great plans, counting on his passion. She just could not understand this calm. She had hated him because he had dared to show his love for her, and now her hatred burned anew because he was able to conceal that love. With the intention of hurting him she said slowly: 'So you concede, do you, king of the Goths, that your Barbarians are no match for the nations of humanity?'

"Yes Camilla," he replied calmly, "but only in one respect, and that is luck. Luck of fate as well as luck of nature. Look at that group of fishermen over there, hanging out their nets on the olive trees by the beach. How beautiful they are! Whether moving or standing still, despite their rags each one of them looks like a statue. Look at that girl with the amphora on her head! Or the old man there, lying on the beach with his head resting on his arm, and looking out to sea. Every beggar among them looks like a dethroned king. How beautiful they are! They are sure of themselves, and they are happy. A glow of luck hangs over them, as it does over children or noble animals. That is what we Barbarians lack."

"Is that the only thing you lack?"

"No, we lack the luck of fate too. My poor, glorious people! We have been swept off course into a strange world, a world in which we cannot prosper. We are like an alpine flower, which a storm has carried down here into the hot plains. We cannot take root here. We wither and die."

As he said this he looked out to sea with a melancholy look in his eyes. But Camilla was in no mood to ponder a king's prophetic words about his people, and asked coldly: "What did you have to come here for? Why did you have to cross the mountains, which God has erected as an eternal barrier. Why?"

Without looking at her Athalaric said softly, as if to himself: "Who knows why a moth flies toward a bright flame, again and again? Without heeding pain until at last it has been devoured by the beautiful, seductive enemy. Why? Because of a sweet madness. And it is that same kind of madness which has lured my Goths away from their oaks and pines to these laurels and olives. They too will get their wings burned, and nothing will deter them. And who can blame them? Look about you. Look how blue the sky is, and the sea. Look how the tips of the pines and the temples glow there, reflected in the mirror of the sea. And over there, beautiful hills rise. Floating on the sea are lovely islands, bountiful with grapes and elms aplenty. And caressing it all is this soft, warm air, which gives everything such a special charm. Look at the miracles of form and colour which the eyes drink in and the senses breathe! That is the magic spell which will always tempt us, and which in the end will destroy us."

The young king's intense emotion did not fail to make an impression on Camilla. The tragic power of his thoughts gripped her, but she did not want to be overcome. Inwardly she was wrestling with her emotions, which were becoming softer towards him, but coldly she said: "What? A whole people attracted by a magic spell, against all reason?" Coldly and dubiously she looked straight at him.

But she was shocked to see an immediate transformation in the young king. It was as if a flash of lightning had sprung from the youth's dark eyes, and passion long suppressed suddenly erupted from the very depths of his being. With intense emotion he cried:

"Yes, believe me! A whole nation can follow a foolish infatuation, a sweet and fatal madness, a deadly longing, just as – just as one person can. Yes Camilla, there is a force in our hearts, stronger than will or reason, which can sweep us away into disaster, our eyes wide open. But that is something you have not yet learned, and I hope you never will, never. God be with you!"

With that he turned quickly into a path to the right of the temple, overgrown with vines, which hid him immediately not only from Camilla but also from the palace windows.

The girl remained standing, deep in thought.

His last words rang strangely in her ears. For a long time she stood there, looking out at the sea, with strangely mixed feelings. At last she turned back toward the palace, in a totally changed mood, and returned to her room.

Chapter 8

On the same day Cethegus arrived in the capital and called on the two women. He had rushed from Rome on urgent business, and had just come from a meeting of the council of advisers to the regent, which had been held in the sick king's rooms. His hard features showed suppressed anger.

"To work, Camilla," he said angrily, "you are taking too long! This cheeky boy is becoming more difficult every day. He is resisting me, and Cassiodorus, and even his mother. He confers with dangerous people like Witiges, Hildebrand and their friends. He writes and receives letters behind our backs, and he has even managed to persuade the queen to only call meetings of her advisers in his presence. And during these meetings he crosses all our plans. That must stop, one way or another!"

"I no longer hold out any hope of influencing the king," Camilla said seriously.

"Why, have you already seen him?"

The girl remembered her promise to Athalaric not to betray him, and in any case it was contrary to her own feelings to betray him or reveal the meeting that morning. She therefore evaded his question and said: "If the king even resists his mother, the regent, surely he will not be ruled by a young girl?"

"Golden innocence!" Cethegus smiled, and let the conversation rest as long as the child was present, but secretly he implored Rusticiana to see to it that her daughter should have contact with the king. This was now possible, as his health was improving. At the same time, as his health recovered, his mind and his will were also maturing rapidly. He was becoming stronger and more self-confident. It seemed as if opposing Cethegus strengthened him in body and soul.

Thus it came about that he was able to spend many hours in the spacious gardens, and it was here that his mother and the family of Boethius often found him in the evenings.

And while Rusticiana was conversing with the queen, appearing to return her favour with genuine friendship and listening attentively to everything she said so she could report it word for word to the Prefect, the two young people walked together through the shady gardens.

Often the small group would embark in one of the gondolas in the little harbour, with Athalaric himself working the oars to steer toward one of the small green islands, which lay out in the clear blue sea not far from the bay. On their way home they would hoist the purple sail and allow the fresh westerly wind, which usually accompanied the sunset, to carry them back slowly and effortlessly. At other times the king and Camilla enjoyed their walks and gondola trips alone, with only Daphnidion for company.

Amalasuntha recognised that there was a risk this might increase her son's affection for Camilla, which had not escaped her. But she placed the beneficial influence this association seemed to be having on her son ahead of all other considerations. In Camilla's presence Athalaric tended to become calmer, more cheerful and kinder towards his mother, whom he otherwise often treated quite harshly. He also seemed able to control his feelings with a confidence which seemed doubly strange in the sickly, excitable youth. Last but not least, the queen was not disinclined to the idea of such a union, which promised to completely win over the Roman nobility and wipe out all memory of the executions of Boethius and Symmachus.

Within the young girl a strange transformation was taking place. Day by day she came to know the young king, his sensitive manner, imaginative mind, sincerity and his poetic side. Gradually she felt her anger and hatred declining, and it was only with difficulty that she could remind herself of her father's fate as a talisman against the spell the king held over her. More and more she was able to separate fairly in her mind the Goths and the Amalungs, who had brought about her father's death, and more and more she came to ask herself if it was fair to hate Athalaric for a tragedy which he had not caused, but merely failed to prevent. Moreover she did not know if he could have prevented it even if he had tried, for he had been young. In her heart she wanted to forgive him completely, but she mistrusted her own feelings, fearing them as if they were a black sin against her father and her country.

She noticed with trepidation how indispensable the noble youth was becoming to her, and how strongly she longed to hear his voice and look into his dark eyes. She was afraid of this sinful love, which she could deny to herself only with difficulty. The only weapon she had to fight it was his assumed guilt in connection with her father, and she clung to this defence with all her might. Thus she swayed between conflicting emotions, her inner struggle made all the more difficult by Athalaric's calm self-confidence. After all that had happened she could not doubt that he loved her – and yet! Not one syllable, not one look gave any hint of that love. The remark he had made when he left her so suddenly at the Venus temple was the most meaningful one he had made, in fact the only significant word to escape his lips until now.

She could not even guess at the inner struggle the youth had been through himself, until in the end his love for her was still there, but he resigned himself to her hatred. Still less could she suspect where he had found the strength for such resignation. Her mother was even more surprised at his apparent coldness. "Patience!" she said to Cethegus, with whom she often conferred behind Camilla's back. "Patience! Soon, within three days, you will see a changed man in him."

"It would be high time," Cethegus replied, "but how can you be so confident?"

"I am relying on a method which has never yet failed."

"Surely you don't propose to give him a love potion?"

"Indeed I do, in fact I have already done it."

Cethegus smiled sarcastically. "So even you, the widow of the great philosopher Boethius, subscribe to such superstition! In the madness of love all women are the same."

"It is neither superstition nor madness," Rusticiana said calmly. "The secret has been in my family for over a hundred years. An old Egyptian woman gave it to my great great grandmother by the Nile, and ever since no woman of my house has loved in vain."

"That requires no magic, yours is a beautiful family," was the Prefect's laconic reply.

"Save your jokes. The potion works without fail, and if it hasn't worked until now—"

"So you have already tried, you reckless woman! How could you, without it being noticed?"

"Every evening, when he returns from a walk or a trip in the gondola, he drinks a cup of spiced Falernian wine. His physician prescribed it, and it contains a few drops of Arabian balsam. The goblet always stands ready on a marble table in front of the Venus temple. Three times now I have managed to pour some of the potion into it."

"Well," said Cethegus, "it has not had much effect so far."

"Only your impatience is to blame for that. The herbs must be picked during a new moon, which I knew, but because of your haste I picked them during the full moon and as you see it did not work. But last night was a new moon, and I went to work with my golden scissors. If he drinks now—"

"You are a second Locusta! I think I will place my faith in Camilla's lovely eyes. Does she know of this?"

"Not a word to her, she would never tolerate it. Quiet, here she comes." The girl entered, quite excited and with her face aglow, a strand of her black hair loosely about her slender neck.

"Tell me, you two wise and worldly adults, what do you make of this? I have just come from the ship. He has never loved me, the conceited Barbarian. He pities me! No, that's not the right word. I can't work it out." With this she burst into tears and threw herself into her mother's arms.

"What happened, Camilla?" Cethegus asked.

After taking a deep breath she began: "He often has a peculiar look about his mouth and eyes, as if he was the one who had been hurt by me, as if he had made some great sacrifice for us, and as if it was up to him to forgive us."

"Immature boys often see it as a sacrifice when they fall in love."

Camilla's eyes flashed with anger at these words as she turned to confront Cethegus. "Athalaric is no longer a boy! You should not belittle him like that!"

Cethegus remained silent, but a surprised Rusticiana asked; "Don't you hate the king any more?"

"To the death, but he should be destroyed, not belittled."

"What happened today?" Cethegus asked again.

"Today that puzzling cold, proud look was on his face again, but more clearly than ever before. A coincidence caused him to put it into words. We had just landed. A beetle had fallen into the water and he bent to pick it up. But the little creature struggled against its rescuer, and with the claws in its head it bit deeply into his finger. I commented on how ungrateful it was, but Athalaric smiled bitterly as he placed the beetle on a leaf and said that we always hurt those the most who have done the most for us. And as he said it he cast a proud, melancholy look over me. And then he quickly took his farewell and turned away, as if he had said too much." She was breathing heavily and clenching her small fists. "I will not bear this any longer. That proud man will either love me or he will die!"

"That he shall," Cethegus said almost inaudibly, "one or the other."

Chapter 9

A few days later yet another independent action on the part of the young king caught the court by surprise. He himself called a meeting of the regency council, a right which until that time only Amalasuntha had exercised. The regent was more than a little surprised when a messenger from her son summoned her to his chambers, where the king had already assembled many of the highest officials in the land about him, among them Cassiodorus and Cethegus.

The latter had at first decided to stay away, so that he would not appear to be recognising the right which the boy had assumed. He sensed that nothing good would come of it, but then he changed his mind for that very reason. "I must not turn my back on danger, but face it head on," he said to himself as he reluctantly started his walk to the king's chambers. When he arrived there he found all the invitees already assembled, with only the regent herself missing. Athalaric rose as she entered. He was wearing a long *abolla* of purple, Theodoric's crown glistening on his head and his sword rattling under his cloak. He rose from his throne, which was situated in front of a niche closed off by a curtain, and walked towards her to lead her to a second, higher throne, which was however situated on his left. When all had taken their seats he commenced: "My royal mother, brave Goths and noble Romans! We have summoned you here in order to make our wishes known to you. This Empire is threatened by dangers which only we, the king of this nation, can avert."

Such words had never before been heard from his mouth. All were silent, including Cethegus who thought it best to hold his tongue until the right moment. At last Cassiodorus began: "Your wise mother and your faithful servant Cassiodorus—"

"Our faithful servant Cassiodorus will be silent until we, his lord and king, ask for his advice. We are not pleased, not at all pleased, with the things which our royal mother's advisers have done, or failed to do. It is high time that we ourselves saw to the affairs of government.

"Until now we have been too young and too ill. We no longer feel too young or too ill. We hereby make it known that the regency will shortly be abolished, and we ourselves will assume power."

He halted. Everyone remained silent, as nobody wished to follow the example of Cassiodorus, only to be humbled into silence.

Amalasuntha, who was dumbfounded by this sudden display of energy and resolve on the part of her son, spoke at last: "My son, the age of majority, according to the laws of the emperor, is—"

"Let Romans follow the emperor's laws, mother. We are Goths and we live by Germanic law. Gothic youths reach their majority when the assembled Gothic army declares them fit to carry arms.

"We have therefore decided to call a general mustering of our armed forces in Ravenna, to which all military leaders, dukes, counts and free Goths are invited, as many as will answer the call. They will arrive at the next midsummer festival."

The entire assembly was silent with shocked surprise.

"That is only fourteen days away," Cassiodorus said at last, "will it be possible to deliver all the invitations at such short notice?"

"They have already been delivered. Hildebrand, my old mentor, and Count Witigis have seen to it."

"Who signed the decrees?" Amalasuntha asked firmly.

"I did, dear mother. I had to show those who are invited that I am mature enough to act on my own initiative."

"And without my knowledge!" said the regent.

"Without your knowledge, because otherwise I would have been forced to do it against your will."

He paused. All the Romans present were stunned by the sudden resolve of their young king. Cethegus alone immediately resolved that this general mustering had to be prevented from happening at any cost. He saw the very foundation of his plans tottering. Gladly he would have risen to his feet in support of the regency, which was disappearing before his eyes, using the full power of his oratory. Several times he would have loved to cut the bold youth down to size with his own superior intellect, but something held him back, and he held his tongue in check, his thoughts spellbound as if by some magic.

He thought he heard a noise in the niche behind the curtain, and concentrated his eyes on that spot. Behind the curtain, which did not quite reach to the floor, he could see the feet of a man.

True, he could only see as far as the ankles. But those ankles wore armour made of steel, fashioned in a most unusual manner. That leg armour looked somehow familiar, and had to be part of a complete suit of armour made in the same way. He also somehow felt that the man wearing that armour was someone he hated, very dangerous to him, but he could not work out who his enemy could be. If only he could see that armour up to the knees! Quite against his will his eyes were drawn to that curtain again and again, and he guessed and guessed. This kept his mind tied in knots, at the very moment when everything was at stake. He was angry with himself, but could tear neither his eyes nor his thoughts away from that niche. The king however, who had encountered no resistance so far, continued.

"Further, we have recalled the dukes Thulun, Ibba and Pitza, who had angrily left this court, from Gaul and from Spain. We find that we are surrounded by far too many Romans, and not nearly enough Goths. Those three worthy warriors, together with Count Witigis, will examine the defences of our Empire, and our armies. They will also check our ships and our fortresses and repair any damage. They will be here soon."

"They must leave again immediately," Cethegus said to himself quickly, but his thoughts ran on. "That man is hidden there for a reason."

The royal youth went on: "Further we have recalled Matesuentha, our beautiful sister, to court. She had been banished to Tarentum because she had refused to marry a much older Roman man. She, the loveliest flower in our nation, shall return and adorn our court."

"Impossible!" Amalasuntha cried. "You are now interfering in the rights of your mother as well as those of your queen."

"I will be head of the family as soon as I reach my majority."

"My son, you know how weak you were just a few weeks ago. Do you really think that the Gothic army will declare you fit to carry arms?"

At this the king blushed almost purple, partly from embarrassment and partly from anger. But before he was able to reply a rough voice by his side spoke: "Don't let that worry you, my queen. I have been his mentor and his tutor, as I was of the great Theodoric, and I tell you that he is a match for any foe. When old Hildebrand declares a man fit to carry arms then all Goths will accept it as a fact." Loud acclaim by all the Goths present confirmed what the old man had said.

Again Cethegus thought to intervene, but a movement behind the curtain distracted him. There stood one of his greatest enemies, but who?

"There is one further matter we wish to announce," the king began again, casting a glance toward the niche which did not escape the Prefect's notice.

Could it be an accusation against him, Cethegus? Is the king trying to catch me off guard? That he will never do. And yet he was surprised when the king suddenly called out in a loud voice.

"Prefect of Rome, Cethegus Caesarius!"

He winced, but quickly regained his old self-control. He bowed his head and said: "My lord and king."

"Have you nothing to report to us from Rome? What is the mood of the *Quirites*? What do they think of the Goths there?"

"They are respected as the people of Theodoric!"

"Do the Romans fear us?"

"They have no reason to fear you."

"Do they love us?"

Cethegus would have liked to say they had no reason to love the Goths either, but the king continued.

"So there is no sign of discontent? No cause for concern? Nothing special is happening?"

"I have nothing to report to you."

"Then you are poorly informed, Prefect, or else your intentions are suspect. Do I, barely risen from my sickbed in Ravenna, have to tell you what is happening in Rome right under your nose? The workmen on your walls are singing derisive songs about the Goths, about the regent and about me. Your legionaries are making threatening speeches during their exercises. Most probably there is already a widespread conspiracy with senators and priests heading it, which assembles at night in unknown places. A fellow conspirator of Boethius, the banished Albinus, has been seen in Rome, and do you know where? In your garden!" The king rose, and all eyes were focussed on Cethegus with surprise, anger or anticipation. Amalasuntha trembled for the man she trusted. But the latter was once more fully in control of himself. Calmly, coolly and silently he looked the king straight in the eye.

"Defend yourself!" the latter called out to him.

"Defend myself against a shadow? A rumour? An accusation without an accuser? Never!"

"There are ways to force you."

A mocking sneer appeared on the lean face of Cethegus. "No doubt I can be murdered on mere suspicion. We Italians have much experience of this! But you will never convict me. Against brutality there is no defence, only against justice."

"You will receive justice, we assure you. We will charge the Romans present here with the task of investigating your case, and the senate in Rome will pass sentence. You may choose a defender."

"I will defend myself," Cethegus said calmly, "but what is the charge? Who stands to accuse me? Where is he?"

"Here" cried the king, and drew back the curtain. A Gothic warrior in a full suit of armour made from black steel stepped forth. We know him. It was Teias.

The Prefect's hatred caused him to lower his eyes, but the other man spoke: "I Teias, Tagila's son, accuse you Cethegus Caesarius of high treason against this Gothic kingdom. I accuse you of having harboured the banished traitor Albinus in your house, and of protecting him from the law. That offence carries the death penalty. Furthermore you plan to subjugate this land to the emperor."

"That is not true," Cethegus replied calmly. "Prove your charges."

"Fourteen nights ago, with these very eyes, I saw Albinus enter your garden," Teias continued, turning to the judges appointed by the king. "He was coming from the Via Sacra, wearing a cloak and a broad brimmed hat. For two nights already this shadowy figure had slipped past me, but this time I recognised him. When I approached him he vanished through a door, which was slammed shut from inside, before I could apprehend him."

"Since when does my worthy colleague, the brave commander, play at being a spy?"

"Since he has had a Cethegus by his side to help him. Even though the fugitive escaped me, this scroll fell from his cloak. It contains the names of Roman aristocrats, and alongside each name there are symbols of an undecipherable secret code. Here is the scroll." He handed the scroll to the king, who read aloud. "The names are Silverius, Cethegus, Licinius, Scaevola, Calpurnius and Pomponius. Count Teias, can you testify under oath that the man you saw was Albinus?"

"I can."

"Very well then, Prefect of Rome. Count Teias is a free, honourable Goth of impeccable standing. Can you refute that?"

"Yes, I refute that. He is not impeccable. His parents lived in an invalid and incestuous marriage. They were cousins, and the church has condemned their cohabitation as well as their offspring. He is a bastard and cannot testify against me, a noble Roman of senatorial rank."

An angry murmur ran through the assembly, and many of the Goths uttered cries of disgust. Teias's pale face grew paler still, and he trembled. His right hand reached for the hilt of his sword, and in a toneless voice he said: "Very well, I will defend my honour with my sword. I challenge you to a duel, so that God may be the judge, in life or in death."

"I am a Roman and I do not live by your bloody barbaric customs. But even if I were a Goth I would not duel with a bastard."

"Patience," said Teias as he slowly returned the half drawn sword to its scabbard. "Patience, my sword, your day will come."

The Romans in the room breathed a sigh of relief.

The king spoke again: "Be that as it may, the charge is sufficiently proven to have the said Roman arrested. Cassiodorus, you will try to decipher the secret code. Count Witigis, you will hurry to Rome and arrest the five suspects, and you will search their houses as well as that of the Prefect. Hildebrand, you will arrest the accused, and relieve him of his sword."

"One moment," said Cethegus, "I guarantee with everything I own that I will not leave Ravenna until this matter is resolved. I demand trial as a free man, as is a senator's right."

"Take no notice of him, my son," old Hildebrand cried, "let me seize him!"

"Don't," said the king. "He will receive justice, strict justice, but not brutality. Let him go. The accusation must have caught him by surprise, and he shall have time to prepare his defence. Tomorrow at the same hour we meet here again. This meeting is now closed."

The king motioned with his sceptre, and Amalasuntha rushed from the room in a state of great agitation. The Goths went happily to join Teias, and the Romans quickly ducked past Cethegus, avoiding him. Only Cassiodorus walked firmly toward him, placed a hand on his shoulder and said:

"Can I help you?"

"I will help myself," Cethegus replied, and strode proudly from the room.

Chapter 10

The sudden and severe blow, which the young king had so unexpectedly administered to the very foundation of the regency, soon filled the palace and the city with surprise, fear and joy. The family of Boethius received their first news of what had taken place from Cassiodorus, who came to ask Rusticiana if she would go and help calm the stricken regent. They asked many eager questions of course, and at last he told them the whole story in detail. Although he was obviously displeased, his tale showed clearly how courageous and decisive the young king must have been. Camilla listened eagerly to every word, her soul filled with pride, pride in her beloved, love's happiest emotion.

"There is no doubt," Cassiodorus concluded with a sigh, "Athalaric is against us. He has sided completely with the Gothic party, with Hildebrand and his friends. He will destroy the Prefect. Who would have believed it from him? Rusticiana, again and again I have to remind myself how very differently he behaved during your husband's trial."

Camilla was now listening with rapt attention, hanging on his every word.

"We were convinced then that he would always be the most devoted friend and zealous protector of the Romans."

"I know nothing of that," Rusticiana said.

"It was hushed up. The death sentence had been pronounced over Boethius and his sons. All of us, particularly Amalasuntha, pleaded with the king for mercy, but his anger was implacable. When I begged him, again and again, he finally lost his temper and swore by his crown that anyone who dared to plead for the traitors one more time would pay for his boldness in the deepest dungeon. That silenced all of us except one, the boy Athalaric. He alone would not be intimidated, and he cried and he begged and he hugged his grandfather's knees."

Camilla trembled and caught her breath.

"And he would not desist until at last Theodoric, in a violent rage, struck him a fierce blow and flung him from his presence to the guards. The angry king kept his word, and Athalaric was led away to the castle dungeon. Boethius was executed immediately."

Camilla had to hold on to one of the columns in order to stay on her feet.

"But Athalaric did not suffer in vain. The next day the king greatly missed his favourite at the table. He thought of the courage with which he, a mere boy, had pleaded for his friends when grown men had been intimidated into silence. At last he rose from the table, where he had been sitting deep in thought for some time, and personally went down into the dungeon. There he unlocked the door, embraced his grandson, and on his pleading he allowed your sons to live, Rusticiana."

"I must go to him, I must go at once!" Camilla said to herself in a choking voice, and with that she rushed from the room.

Cassiodorus continued. "In those days Romans and their friends could see in the future king their best ally, and now – my poor mistress, his poor mother!" He departed lamenting.

For a long time Rusticiana sat there, stunned. She could see the very foundation on which she had built her plans for revenge crumbling before her eyes, and fell into a morbid brooding. As she sat there the shadows from the tall towers of the castle around her grew longer and longer. She was aroused from her introspection by the firm footsteps of a man, and shot up in fright. Cethegus stood before her, his face cold and dark but icily calm.

"Cethegus!" cried the troubled woman, and tried to grasp his hand. But she drew back when she felt the coldness inside him. "All is lost!" she sighed, remaining standing.

"Nothing is lost. All we need to do is remain calm, and we need to be quick," he retorted, looking quickly around the room. When he saw that they were alone he reached into the folds of his toga. "Your love potion did not work, Rusticiana. Here is another one, much stronger. Take it." Quickly he pressed a small phial of dark lava stone into her hand. Rusticiana looked at him with fear and foreboding.

"Do you suddenly believe in magic and potions? Who brewed it?"

"I did, and my potions never fail."

"You!" A cold shudder ran through her.

"Don't ask questions, don't wonder and above all don't delay! It must happen today, do you hear? Today without fail."

But Rusticiana still hesitated and looked at the little phial in her hand. Cethegus approached her closely and gently placed a hand on her shoulder. Slowly and deliberately he said: "Do you understand what is at stake here? Not only all our plans. No, blind mother, much more. Camilla is in love. She loves the young king with all her heart and soul. Is the daughter of Boethius to become the tyrant's harlot?"

With a loud cry Rusticiana drew back. What had been an evil premonition these last few days had now become a certainty. With one more look at the man who had spoken the gruesome words she hurried away, clutching the little phial in her fist.

Calmly Cethegus followed her with his gaze, and slowly said to himself while smoothing the folds of his toga: "It is strange. I had long thought myself no longer capable of such strong emotion, but now life is once more a challenge. Once again I can strive, hope and fear, and even hate. Yes, I hate that boy, who has the temerity to interfere in my schemes with his childish hand. He wants to resist me, to stand in my way. Him! In my way! Very well then, let him bear the consequences."

Slowly he walked from the room and turned toward the regent's audience chamber, where he deliberately showed himself to the masses, helping to restore the calm of shaken Roman courtiers by his own self-confidence. He saw to it that he had plenty of witnesses to every step he took that fateful day. When the sun went down he went into the gardens with Cassiodorus and a few other Romans, in order to discuss his defence for the following day. In vain he looked for Camilla.

As soon as she had heard the end of Cassiodorus's tale Camilla had rushed into the palace courtyard, where the king was in the habit of indulging in weapons practice at this time of day, with other young Goths. She just wanted to se him, nothing more, but later she would speak with him and beg him to forgive her the terrible wrong she had done him. She had abhorred him, and rejected him. She had hated him in the belief that he was tainted with her father's blood. She had done this to him, to him who had sacrificed himself for her father and saved her brothers!

But she did not find him in the courtyard. The important events of the day kept him in his study. His companions were not exercising today, but stood in groups praising the courage of their young king.

Camilla soaked up this praise joyously. Blushing with pride and happily daydreaming she walked into the garden, where she sought her beloved in all his favourite places. Yes, she loved him. She could now admit this to herself boldly and joyfully, for he had earned her love a thousand times. What matter that he was a Goth, a Barbarian? He was a noble, magnificent young man, a king, and the king of her soul. Repeatedly she drew away from Daphnidion, who was accompanying her, so that she would not hear how she kept repeating his beloved name to herself over and over. At last she reached the Venus temple, where she daydreamed sweetly about her future, now clearly before her like the golden glow of dawn. Above all she resolved that she would explain to the Prefect and to her mother tomorrow that they must no longer count on her help against the king. And after that she herself would beg his forgiveness with tender words of love, and then – and then? She did not know what would happen then, but blushed with joyful anticipation as she dreamed on.

Red, sweet-smelling blossoms fell from the bushes, swaying in the evening breeze. A nightingale sang in the dense oleander bush next to her, and a clear spring ran past her to the blue sea as the waves broke almost silently at her feet. It was as if all of nature was paying a tender tribute to the love blossoming within her.

Chapter 11

She was finally aroused from her daydreaming by the sound of footsteps rapidly approaching along the sand path. The walk was so quick and the step so firm that at first she did not suspect it was Athalaric. But it was the king, totally changed in his bearing and appearance, more masculine, stronger and more resolute. He was holding his head high, which he otherwise often allowed to drop down to his chest, and Theodoric's sword was swinging by his side.

"Greetings, greetings, Camilla," he called out to her in a loud, excited voice, "seeing you is the nicest reward I could wish for after such a day." He had never spoken to her like this before.

"My king," she whispered with a blush, her brown eyes looking at him once more before she lowered them. My king! She had never addressed him thus, nor had she ever looked at him like this.

"Your king?" he said as he sat down beside her, "I am afraid you will not be calling me that when you hear about all that has happened today."

"I know everything."

"You know? Well then, Camilla, be just. I am no tyrant." She thought to herself how noble these words were, seeking to excuse his finest deeds.

"You see, I do not hate the Romans – heaven knows, they are your people! I honour them and their former greatness, and I respect their rights. But I must also defend my kingdom, Theodoric's great creation, firmly and if need be without pity or mercy. Woe be to anyone who dares raise a hand against us in anger. Perhaps," he went on more slowly, "perhaps this kingdom has already been judged and its fate decided by the stars. Be that as it may. I, as the king, must stand or fall with my kingdom and its people."

"What you say is true, Athalaric, and spoken like a king!"

"Thank you, Camilla! How fair and just you are today, and how kind! Since you are so kind I will entrust to you the secret of how I was healed. You see, I was a sick, misguided dreamer, without aim or purpose, and without joy, just contentedly drifting toward death. And then suddenly my soul became aware of the dangers threatening this kingdom, and that stirred me to concern myself actively with the fate of my people. And that concern grew in my breast, and with it grew a mighty love for my Gothic countrymen. That love has given me strength, and compensated for much other pain to which I had become resigned. As long as this nation prospers, what does my happiness matter? And that thought has made me strong and healthy, so that now there is no task to which I do not feel equal."

He sprang to his feet, stretching out his arms. "Oh Camilla, this inactivity is gnawing at my vitals. If only I could mount my horse and charge into battle! Look, the sun is setting. How inviting the sea looks, with the sunlight reflected in its mirror. Come in the boat with me." Camilla hesitated. "Your servant? Oh let her be. She is resting happily by the spring, under the palm trees, sound asleep. Come, come quickly before the sun goes down. Can you see the golden road on the water? It's beckoning us!"

"To the islands of the blessed?" the lovely girl asked, with a blush and a far away look in her eyes.

"Yes, come to the islands!" he replied happily. Quickly he lifted her into the gondola, unfastened the silver chain from the quay and cast off. Standing at the stern of the boat he took the oar, rowing and steering at the same time like a true Germanic boatman. He cut a picturesque figure.

Camilla sat in front, near the bow, on a *diphros* or collapsible Greek stool. She looked into his aristocratic face, lit by the setting sun, as his dark hair fluttered in the breeze. The rower's regular, powerful movements were a delight to watch, and they were both silent as the gondola cut through the water.

Fluffy red evening clouds were moving slowly across the sky, the light wind from the shore bringing with it the perfume of almond blossoms. All about them was peace and harmony. At last the king broke the silence. Pushing the boat forward with a powerful stroke of the oar he said: "Do you know what I am thinking? How beautiful it must be to steer a kingdom, a nation, many thousands of people, safely through wind and waves to happiness and glory with a firm hand. What were you thinking, Camilla? You looked so lovely, so they must have been good thoughts." She blushed once more, and looked away into the water. "Please Camilla, do speak openly and frankly in this beautiful moment."

"I thought," she whispered softly, her small head still turned away, "I thought how lovely it must be to be guided through the sea of life, through all turbulence and danger, by a trusted beloved hand."

"Camilla, believe me, even a Barbarian can be trusted."

"You are no Barbarian. Anyone who thinks sensitively, acts nobly, masters his own weakness and rewards ungratefulness with graciousness is no Barbarian. He is as noble a human being as any Scipio ever was."

Delighted, the king stopped rowing so that the boat stopped. "Camilla, am I dreaming? Are you really saying those words? To me?"

"Yes Athalaric, and more, much more! I beg you to forgive me for having rejected you so cruelly. Believe me, it was only fear and unjust hatred."

"Camilla, my pearl!"

The latter, who was facing the shore, suddenly cried: "What's this? They are following us. The court, the women, my mother."

It was true. Driven by the Prefect's terrible demand Rusticiana had gone to look for her daughter in the garden, but did not find her. She ran to the Venus temple, but in vain. Looking about her she suddenly saw them, her child alone with him, in the boat far out to sea. Furiously she rushed to the small marble table, where the king's slaves were just mixing his evening drink. She sent them down to the quay to get a gondola ready, thus gaining an unobserved moment at the table, and then went down the steps toward the boat with Daphnidion, whom her angry shouting had awakened. At this moment the Prefect and his friends appeared out of the dense thicket, as their stroll had also brought them to this spot. Cethegus followed her down the steps to help her into the boat.

"It is done," she whispered to him, and the gondola pushed off. It was at this moment that the young couple noticed movement on the shore. Camilla rose, expecting the king to turn the boat around, but the latter cried: "No, they shall not take this hour from me, the most wonderful moment of my life. I must revel in more of your sweet words, Camilla, you must tell me more, tell me everything. We will land on the island over there. Let them find us!"

With that he started rowing with all his strength, so that the little boat darted through the water as if it had wings.

"Go on talking, please."

"Oh my friend, my king, don't make me." He saw only her lovely eyes, her glowing face, no longer paying any attention to the direction in which the little boat was speeding. "Wait, when we get to the island, then you will tell me—"

One more powerful stroke of the oar, and suddenly there was a dull splintering crash. The boat had struck a rock and bounced back from the rock shuddering.

"Great heavens!" Camilla shouted, jumping to her feet and looking toward the bow of the boat, where she saw a veritable torrent of water rushing toward her.

"The boat has foundered – we are sinking," she cried, growing pale.

"Come over here to me and let me see," Athalaric cried as he sprang to her aid. "Oh, those are the needles of Amphitrite – we're doomed."

The Needles of Amphitrite, which as we know were visible from the terrace of the Venus temple, were two narrow and sharply pointed cliffs between the shore and the nearest island. They barely broke the surface, and the slightest wind caused the waves to break over them, making them hard to see. Athalaric knew how dangerous this spot was, and had always easily avoided it, but this time he had been looking only into the eyes of his beloved.

With a single glance he summed up the situation. They could not escape. A plank in the bottom of the boat had been smashed in the collision with the rock, and water was pouring through the hole in huge quantities. The boat was sinking by the second.

He could not hope to reach the nearest island by trying to swim there with Camilla, and Rusticiana's boat had only just pushed off. In an instant he weighed up the situation and realised their plight. With shock in his eyes he looked at the girl. "Beloved, you are going to die," he cried in despair, "and I, I alone am to blame." He embraced her passionately.

"Die?" she cried, "oh no! Not so young, we cannot die now. I want to live, live with you." She clung firmly to his arm, her tone and her words cutting through his heart.

He tore himself free and looked about for a way to save them. He looked all around, but in vain. The water was rising with alarming speed, and the boat sinking rapidly. He threw the oar away. "It is over, beloved. Let us say farewell."

"No, never! I will not be parted from you again. If we are to die – oh, away with the restraints which bind the living," and she pressed her head lovingly against his chest. "Oh let me tell you, let me confess how much I love you, and for how long, since – since for ever. Oh God, I loved you even when I thought I had to hate you, despise you. Yes, you shall know how much I love you." And she covered his face with kisses. "Now I want to die too, better to die with you than live without you. But no—" she tore herself away from him "—you must not die! Leave me here, jump, swim, try to reach the island. Alone you might make it. Try, and leave me here."

"No," he cried in ecstasy, "I too would rather die with you than live without you. At last, after longing for so long, I have found fulfilment! We belong together from this moment. Come Camilla, beloved, let us jump."

They were both filled with the thrill of love, mixed with anticipation of imminent death. He drew her to him, placed his arm about her, and together they mounted the stern of the boat which by this time was only just out of the water. They were about to jump when suddenly they both gave a cry of hope. A ship in full sail was rounding the narrow headland, which reached into the sea a little distance from them, with lightning speed.

Their cry was heard on board the ship, where their plight was quickly recognised. Perhaps they even recognised the king. At once forty oars, dipping into the water in two rows, made the little ship fly before the wind even faster. The men on deck called out to them to hang on, and soon – it was high time – the bireme lay beside the gondola, which sank the moment the young couple had been pulled aboard through a hatch in the lower deck. It was a small Gothic warship, and the Amalung banner of a rising golden lion was flying from the masthead. Aligern, a cousin of Teias, was in command.

"Thank you, worthy friends," Athalaric said when he had found his voice again, "thank you! You have saved not only your king, but also your queen."

Soldiers and sailors alike gathered around the happy youth, who was holding the weeping Camilla in his arms. "Hail, our beautiful young queen!" the red-haired Aligern rejoiced, and the crew joined him in a thundering chorus: "Hail, hail our queen!" At this moment the sailing ship passed Rusticiana's rowing boat, and the latter was aroused from her state of dumbfounded terror by the shouts of joy from the ship. Her terror had begun the moment two rowing slaves had seen the danger the young couple were in, at the same time realising they could not possibly get there in time to save them.

Now she came to and looked wildly about her. She was astonished – was that a dream she was seeing? Was that really her daughter snuggled against the chest of the young king aboard a Gothic ship, gliding proudly past her? Was she really hearing voices shouting "Hail Camilla, our young queen?"

She stared at the passing apparition, speechless. But by now the fast sailing ship had already passed her boat and was heading for the shore. It dropped anchor just off the small harbour, a boat was lowered, the young couple together with Aligern and three sailors jumped into it, and in no time they were ascending the small steps into the garden, where Cethegus, his companions and a crowd of other people had gathered. Many had observed the danger threatening the little boat from the palace or the garden, and they now came to greet the rescued pair. Among wishes of goodwill and cries of blessing Athalaric climbed up the steps.

"Look," he said as he reached the terrace in front of the temple, "look, Goths and Romans, your queen, my bride. The god of death has brought us together, right Camilla?" She looked up to him but received a mighty shock. The excitement and the sudden change from terror to joy had had an all too powerful effect on the barely recovered youth. His face was as pale as marble. He stumbled, and gripped his chest as if gasping for air.

"Oh my God!" Camilla cried, fearing a recurrence of his old complaint. "The king is not well. Quickly, his wine, his medicine!" She ran to the table, grasped the silver goblet which stood ready, and pressed it into his hand.

Cethegus was standing close to them, and he watched every move.

Already Athalaric was raising the goblet to his lips, but suddenly he lowered it again and smiled. "You must drink to me, as befits a Gothic queen at her own court," and he handed her the goblet. She took it from his hand.

For an instant a burning urge flashed through the Prefect's mind to rush over, grasp the drink from her hand and spill it. But he held himself back. If he followed his impulse he was certainly lost. Tomorrow he would be convicted not only as a traitor but as a poisoner as well, and he would certainly be executed.

All his plans, his ideas, his world, the future of Rome, all would be lost. And for what? For a young girl who was in love with his mortal enemy, and who had shamelessly deserted him. No, he said silently to himself, clenching his fist, it is she or Rome, so it must be she. And calmly he watched as the girl took a sip from the goblet, which the king then emptied at a single draught. He shuddered as he replaced the goblet on the marble table. "Come up into the Palatium," he said, wrapping his cloak around him, "I am cold." And he turned to go.

At that moment his eye met that of Cethegus. He stood still for a moment and looked the Prefect straight in the eye.

"You here?" he said sombrely and took a step toward him. Suddenly he shuddered again, and with a loud cry he fell on his face beside the spring.

"Athalaric!" Camilla cried, and threw herself over him. Old Corbulo was the first of the servants to come to her aid. "Help," he called, "he is dying – the king!"

"Water, water quickly!" Cethegus said aloud. With quick resolve he grasped the goblet, bent down, rinsed it quickly but thoroughly in the water, and bent over the king. Cassiodorus was holding him while Corbulo looked after Camilla.

The various spectators stood about the two lifeless figures, shocked and speechless.

"What has happened? My child!" Rusticiana, whose boat had just landed, rushed to her daughter's side. "Camilla," she despaired, "what is wrong?"

"Nothing!" Cethegus replied calmly. "She has only fainted. But the young king has had a heart seizure. He is dead."

Book Three
Amalasuntha

Chapter 1

Athalaric's sudden death hit the Gothic party like a thunderbolt from a clear blue sky, particularly as their hopes had been raised so high earlier that very day. All the new initiatives which the king had ordered, in accordance with their wishes, were suddenly paralysed. Once more the Goths were without an effective representative in a state which the queen now ruled entirely unopposed.

Early on the following day Cassiodorus called on the Prefect, whom he found calmly and soundly asleep.

"How can you sleep like a child after such a devastating blow?"

"I slept," Cethegus replied as he raised himself on his left arm, "with a new feeling of security."

"Security? For you perhaps, but what about the Empire?"

"The Empire was in much greater danger from this boy than I was. Where is the queen?"

"She is sitting by her son's casket, speechless. She has been there all night."

Cethegus sprang to his feet and cried: "That must not be! It is not good! She belongs to the state, not to a corpse, the more so because I have heard rumours about poison. The young tyrant had many enemies. Is there any further news on that?"

"Nothing conclusive. The Greek physician Elpidios, who has examined the body, did find some unusual symptoms. But he says that, if indeed poison had been used, then it must be a new and very secret one which is quite unknown to him. The cup from which the poor youth took his last drink did not show the slightest trace of any suspicious substance. The general opinion is that all the excitement caused his old heart complaint to flare up again, and this is what killed him. But I am glad that you were seen by witnesses the whole time after you left the regency council. Grief makes people suspicious."

"How is Camilla?" the Prefect inquired further.

"I believe that she still has not regained consciousness, and her physicians fear the worst. But I came here to ask you something. What happens now? The queen has spoken of dropping the inquiries against you."

"That must not happen!" Cethegus cried. "I demand that the inquiry be conducted. Let us go to her."

"Are you going to disturb her at her son's casket?"

"Yes I am. Do your delicate feelings prevent you from doing likewise? Very well, follow me after I have broken the ice."

He bade his visitor farewell and summoned his slaves to dress him. Shortly afterwards, dressed in a dark grey robe as a sign of mourning, he strode into the basement where the young king's body was lying in state. Guards and some of Amalasuntha's women were guarding the entrance, whom he ordered with an authoritative tone to make way. Silently he entered.

It was the same hall, with the same old curved ceiling, which had once served as the place where the bodies of dead Caesars were embalmed with salves and combustible material prior to cremation. The quiet basement, with walls panelled in dark green serpentine amid short Doric pillars of black marble, never saw the light of day. The only light which fell on the sombre Byzantine mosaics on golden backgrounds came from four pitch torches, which illuminated the young king's stone sarcophagus with unsteady light.

There he lay, on a mantle of deep red purple, his helmet, sword and shield near his head.

Old Hildebrand had wound a wreath of oak leaves around his head, and his noble features were at rest, his facial expression stern, pale and handsome.

At his feet, dressed in a long veil of mourning, sat the tall figure of Amalasuntha, her head supported by her left arm, which in turn rested on the sarcophagus. Her right arm hung limply by her side, and she could weep no more tears. The only sound to disturb the deathly silence was the gentle hissing of the torches.

Cethegus entered noiselessly, not unmoved by the solemn beauty of the scene before him. But a moment later he had cast aside these feelings of sympathy, and calmly he said to himself: "What is needed now is clear thinking, and to remain calm." Softly he stepped closer and took Amalasuntha's limp right hand.

"Rise, noble lady, you belong to the living, not the dead."

Startled, she looked up at him. "You, Cethegus! What are you doing here? What are you looking for?"

"I am looking for a queen."

"Oh, I am afraid you will find only a grieving mother!" Amalasuntha sobbed.

"I cannot believe that. The Empire is in danger, and Amalasuntha will show her people and the world that even a woman can rise above her personal grief for her country."

"Yes," she replied, rising to her feet, "that she can. But look at him. How young, how handsome he was! How could heaven be so cruel?"

"Now or never," thought Cethegus and said aloud: "Heaven is just, sometimes severe, but never cruel."

"What are you talking about? What had my son done wrong? Do you dare accuse him?"

"No, I do not. But a portion of holy scripture has been realised through him, where it says to honour thy father and thy mother, that thy days be long upon the land which the Lord thy God giveth thee. That commandment is also a threat. Yesterday he sinned against his mother, dishonouring her with spiteful rebellion, and today he lies here. I see the finger of God in that."

Amalasuntha hid her face. She had forgiven her son his rebellion many times over as she sat by his sarcophagus, yet nonetheless she was deeply affected by this line of thinking and by these words. Also her grief was starting to give way to that other feeling she loved, the habit of power.

"My queen, I believe that you plan to drop the charges against me, and that you have recalled Count Witigis. The latter may be, but I demand a full trial and formal acquittal as my right."

"I have never doubted your loyalty, and woe betide me if ever I have cause to. I know of no conspiracy. All charges are dropped, and the matter is over and done with."

She seemed to be waiting for him to reaffirm his loyalty. Cethegus was silent for a while. At last he said quietly: "My queen, I do know of a conspiracy."

"What did you say?" Amalasuntha cried, giving him a threatening look.

"I have chosen this time and this place," Cethegus continued as he glanced at the sarcophagus, "to prove my loyalty to you once and for all. Hear me, and then judge me!"

"What will I hear?" Amalasuntha cried, her full attention now aroused, determined that she would be neither deceived nor inveigled into clemency.

"I would be a bad Roman, my queen, and you would have to despise me, if I did not love my own people above all else, and my proud nation which even you love, even though you are a foreigner. I knew, as you know, that hatred against your people as Barbarians and heretics still smoulders in Roman hearts. That hatred was exacerbated by your late father's severe last acts. I suspected that there might be a conspiracy, so I looked for it and found it."

"And remained silent about it!" the queen replied, rising angrily.

"Remained silent until today. The fools wanted to call on Byzantium to invade Italy, and subject themselves to the emperor after the Goths had been destroyed."

"Despicable traitors!" Amalasuntha cried passionately.

"Fools! They had already gone so far that there was only one way to hold them back. I became their leader."

"Cethegus!"

"By doing this I gained valuable time, and was able to keep noble but misguided men from disaster. Slowly I was able to open their eyes to the fact that their plan, if it did succeed, would only exchange a mild rule with a despotic tyranny. Finally they saw this, and followed me. Hence no Byzantine will set foot on this soil until I call him – I or you."

"I? Are you mad?"

"Nothing is impossible for mankind, as your favourite Sophocles said. Let me warn you, my queen, of imminent and extreme danger, which you apparently do not see. There is another conspiracy which threatens you, your freedom and your right to rule, and which is much more dangerous than the Roman foolishness of which I have already spoken. There is a Gothic conspiracy right here at court, under your very eyes, and yet you do not see it."

Amalasuntha paled.

"Yesterday you saw, to your shock and surprise, that your hand no longer held the reins of this Empire, and nor did your noble son, who was only a tool in the hands of your enemies. As you know, my queen, many of your people are bloodthirsty Barbarians, rough and eager for plunder. They want to burn and devastate this land, where Virgil and Tullius lived. You know that your rebellious nobility hates the tremendous power of the royal house, and seeks to be its equal. You also know that many of the crude Goths think a woman unfit to rule over them."

"I know it," she said, proudly and angrily.

"But what you do not know is that all these parties have united against you. They are firmly united against you and your pro-Roman policies. They want to either overthrow you, or force you to comply with their wishes. Cassiodorus and I are to be removed from your side. Our senate and our rights are to be abolished, and the kingdom is to become a mere shadow. There is to be war against the emperor, and brute force, extortion and plunder is to be the lot of the Romans, my people."

"You are only conjuring up visions of terror!"

"Was what happened yesterday just a vision of terror? If the arm of heaven had not intervened, would you, like me, not have been robbed of power? Do you really believe that you were still the mistress of your Empire, or for that matter even of your own house? Are they not already so powerful, people like that old heathen Hildebrand, that peasant Witigis or that sombre Teias, that they often openly opposed your will? They did so in the name of your son, of course, whom they already had completely in their power. Did they not recall those three rebellious dukes? And your recalcitrant daughter?"

"True! What you say is all too true!" the queen sighed.

"Once those men gain power, then farewell science, art and culture! Farewell Italy, mother of mankind. Farewell scrolls of white parchment as they burn, and farewell, shattered remains of once beautiful statues. Blood and force and brutality will fill this land, and the children of future generations will say that this happened under Amalasuntha, Theodoric's daughter."

"Never! That must never happen! But—"

"You want proof? I am afraid that you will have proof soon enough. Even now you can see that you cannot depend on the Goths if you want to prevent these terrible happenings. Only we Romans can protect you against these awful possibilities, we Romans to whom you belong in any case because of your cultured mind. When that terrible time comes, when those noisy Barbarians surround your throne baying for blood, then let me gather about you those men who once conspired against you, the patriots of Rome. They will defend you and themselves at the same time."

"Cethegus," the troubled woman said, "you rule men so easily. But who, tell me, who will vouch to me for the patriots, and for your loyalty?"

"This document, my queen, and this one here! The first one contains the names of all the Roman conspirators, and as you can see there are several hundred names. The other one contains the names of the Gothic conspirators, although naturally I could only guess many of them. But I guess very well. With these documents I give both parties, as well as myself, into your hands. There is nothing to stop you exposing me as a traitor at any time, I who have sought your favour more than anyone. Or, if you will, you can sacrifice me to the anger of your Goths, as I no longer have any followers. You can do with me as you wish, and as soon as you wish. I stand entirely alone, with only your favour to sustain me."

The queen had quickly perused both documents, eyes aglow. "Cethegus," she cried, "I will remember your loyalty in this fateful hour!" Deeply moved, she extended her hand to him.

Cethegus inclined his head slightly. "One more thing, my queen. The patriots, who are now your friends as well as mine, know that the sword of fate hangs over their heads, as well as the hatred of the Barbarians. Shocked and frightened men need something they can cling to. Please let me assure them of your royal support and backing, by placing your own name at the top of this list, so that I will have a tangible sign of your favour to show them."

She took the golden stylus and the wax tablet, which he held out to her, and after hesitating for only a moment she quickly wrote her name and handed tablet and stylus back to him. "Here, may they always remain as loyal to me as you are."

At that moment Cassiodorus entered. "My queen, the Gothic nobles await you. They seek an audience."

"I am coming! They shall hear my wishes," she said firmly, "but you, Cassiodorus, shall be the first to hear the decision I have made here in this grave hour, and which the whole Empire will hear shortly. From this moment the Prefect of Rome shall be the first among my advisers as he is the most faithful. His shall be the place of honour, both in my trust and by my throne."

A surprised Cassiodorus led the queen up the dark steps. Slowly Cethegus followed them, and holding the wax tablet high in the air he said to himself: "Now you are mine, Theodoric's daughter. Your name on this list will serve to divide you from your people for ever."

Chapter 2

When Cethegus had emerged into daylight from the crypt and was about to follow the queen, he became aware of the sound of flutes, such as were then customarily played upon the death of a Roman patrician. At once he guessed the significance of these sounds.

His first impulse was to avoid the procession, but then he decided to remain. "It has to be faced some time, so it may as well be now," he thought. "I must also know how much she knows."

The sound of the flutes came closer and closer, accompanied by the monotonous singing of mourning women. Cethegus stepped into a darkened niche on the narrow path which the small procession was about to enter. The group was led by six young noble Roman maidens, dressed in grey mourning robes and carrying lowered torches. Next came a priest carrying a tall cross, and after him a number of former slaves whom the family had freed, Corbulo at their head. The flute players were next, and after them, carried by four Roman maidens, came an open coffin covered with flowers. Here, on a white linen sheet, lay the body of Camilla, dressed as a bride with red roses in her dark hair. There was a look of peace about her, and a contented smile played on her slightly open mouth. Behind the coffin staggered her unfortunate mother, her hair in disarray and staring unseeingly in front of her. She was supported by several matrons, and a number of slave women concluded the procession, which gradually disappeared into the crypt.

Cethegus recognised the weeping Daphnidion and stopped her. "When did she die?" he asked calmly.

"Oh master, a few hours ago! Oh my poor, kind, beautiful Domna!"

"Did she regain consciousness?"

"No master, she did not. Right at the end she opened her big, lovely eyes one last time, and she seemed to be looking around for something. 'Where is he?' she asked her mother. 'Oh I see him,' she cried then, and raised herself from her pillows. 'Child, my child, where are you going?' my mistress cried. 'Over there,' she said with a radiant smile, 'to the islands of the blessed!' and then she closed her eyes and sank back into her pillows. That lovely smile remained on her face and she was gone, gone for ever!"

"Who had her brought down here?"

"The queen. She found out what had happened and ordered that her son's bride was to be laid in state and buried next to him."

"But what did the physicians have to say? How could she die so suddenly?"

"Oh, the physician only saw her briefly. His mind was still occupied with the king's death, and the mistress would not have a strange man touching her daughter. I suppose her heart must have broken – surely one can die from that. Quiet, they are coming!" The procession returned in the same order as before, but without the coffin, and Daphnidion joined it. Only Rusticiana was missing. Calmly Cethegus paced the lonely passage, looking for her.

At last the broken woman appeared at the top of the steps. She staggered and seemed about to stumble, when he firmly took her arm. "Rusticiana, take a hold on yourself!"

"You here? Oh God, you loved her too! And we, you and I, have killed her, murdered her!" She collapsed against his shoulder.

"Quiet, woman!" he whispered, looking around him.

"Oh God, I, her own mother, have killed her. I mixed the drink which killed him."

Cethegus thought. "Good, at least she does not know that Camilla also drank from that cup, let alone that I saw her do so." And then he said aloud: "It was a cruel stroke of fate. But think what would have happened if she had lived! She loved him."

"What would have happened?" Rusticiana cried, stepping back from him. "Oh, if only she was alive! What would it have mattered if she had become his betrothed, his wife even, if only she had lived!"

"But you forget – he had to die."

"Had to die? Why did he have to die? So that you can carry out your proud, arrogant schemes! Oh you are an unbelievably selfish man of ice!"

"They are your plans, which I am carrying out, not mine. How often must I repeat that? You called the god of revenge, not I. So why accuse me if he demanded a sacrifice from you? Think again. Farewell!"

But Rusticiana grasped his arm violently. "And is that all you have to say to me? Not a word, not even a tear for my poor child? And you expect me to believe that you acted for me, and for her? To avenge us? You have never had a heart, and have never loved her. You have never loved anyone! In cold blood you let her die – a curse on you! Damn you to all eternity!"

"Be silent, you madwoman!"

"Silent? Never! I will talk, talk and curse you. If only I knew of something which is as dear to you as Camilla was to me! Oh if only I could see the only remaining joy in your life perish, so that I could watch you fall, to perish in despair. If there is a God in heaven then that day must surely come!"

Cethegus smiled.

"So you don't believe in any heavenly power that can avenge a wrong? Very well, then believe in the revenge of a heartbroken mother! You shall tremble! Right now I am going to the queen to tell her everything. You shall die!"

"And you will die with me!"

"I will die with laughter on my lips, if only I live to see you perish!"

She was about to hurry away, but Cethegus gripped her arm. "Stop, woman! Don't you think I had the foresight to protect myself against the likes of you? Your sons, Anicius and Severinus, who were banished from Italy, are secretly in Rome, in my house. You know that there is a death sentence over their heads if they are caught here in Italy. One word from you and they will die with us. You may then bring to your dead husband not only his daughter, but his sons as well, all dead through your actions, and their blood on your hands." Quickly he disappeared around a bend in the passage.

"My sons!" Rusticiana cried, and collapsed on the marble floor.

A few days later the widow of Boethius, with Corbulo and Daphnidion, left the Ravenna court for ever, despite the queen's efforts to hold her.

The faithful Corbulo took her back to the little villa near Tifernum, which she now bitterly regretted ever having left. There, on the spot where the Venus temple had stood, she built a small basilica, and in it she buried an urn containing the hearts of the two lovers.

She prayed often, her impassioned appeals to God being partly for Camilla's salvation, and partly for revenge against Cethegus, whose real role in Camilla's death she did not even suspect. She merely sensed that he had used both mother and daughter as pawns in his demonic game of chess, and that he had coldly risked the girl's life and happiness without compunction. Constantly she prayed for revenge.

There was to be a time when the Prefect's guilt would be fully revealed to her. The revenge for which she prayed would also have its day.

Chapter 3

At the court in Ravenna a mighty struggle was taking place. The Gothic patriots had been not only saddened but stunned by the sudden death of their king, but they were soon stirred into action once more by their leaders. The high regard which old Hildebrand enjoyed, the calm strength of the recently recalled Witigis and the restless energy of Teias were constantly at work. We have already seen how these men were able to influence Athalaric to act independently of the regent. Now they were able to enlist more and more support among the Goths against Amalasuntha's regency, in which the hated Cethegus was taking on an ever more dominant role. The general mood among the Gothic army, as well as that of Ravenna's Gothic population, was ready for a decisive coup. It was only with great difficulty that old Hildebrand could restrain his impatient friends, so that they would conserve their strength until the day when, supported by powerful allies, they could be certain of victory.

Those allies were the three dukes Thulun, Ibba and Pitza, whom Amalasuntha had driven from the court, and whom her son had recalled. Thulun and Ibba were brothers, and Pitza their cousin. A third brother of the first pair, Duke Alaric, had been sentenced to death for alleged conspiracy years before and then fled, not having been heard from since. All were members of the famous Balti dynasty, which had worn the crown of the Visigoths, and which ranked almost equal to the Amalungs in terms of prestige and tradition. Their ancestry, like that of the royal house, could be traced right back to the gods. Their wealth, their huge estates, their dependent colonies and their famous deeds in war served to further enhance their dynasty's power and glory. There was a rumour among the populace that Theodoric had at one time considered bypassing his daughter and her then infant son, and for the sake of the Empire making the powerful Duke Thulun his heir.

The patriots were now ready to revive this concept following Athalaric's death, in the event that Amalasuntha could not be dissuaded from taking the path she had chosen.

Cethegus could see the storm coming. He could see how Gothic national pride, awakened by Hildebrand and his friends, was turning more and more against the Romanised regency. Reluctantly he had to admit to himself that he lacked any real power to contain the general feeling of dissatisfaction. Ravenna was not Rome, his Rome, where he controlled public works, and where he had been able to get the citizens used to arms again and accept him as their undisputed leader. Here in Ravenna all the troops were Gothic, and any attempt to arrest Hildebrand or Witigis was likely to provoke open rebellion. He therefore made a bold decision to untangle himself from the web which tied him down in Ravenna. The single masterstroke needed to do this was to move the queen to Rome, using force if necessary. In Rome he had arms, followers, and above all he had power. Once in Rome Amalasuntha would be entirely under his control, and the Goths could do what they liked. It would change nothing.

Much to his delight the queen received his plan enthusiastically. She longed to be away from these walls, where she seemed more like a prisoner than a head of state. She longed for Rome, for freedom and for power. Quickly, as always, Cethegus made the necessary arrangements. He could not avail himself of the shortest route, which was overland, because the Via Flaminia and all other main roads leading into Rome were patrolled by Gothic troops under the command of Witigis, and he therefore feared that their flight might be discovered too soon and prevented. He therefore had no alternative but to travel at least part of the way by sea, but he could not count on any of the Gothic warships in the port of Ravenna for this purpose.

Fortunately the Prefect remembered that the ship owner Pomponius, who was also one of the conspirators, was at that time hunting down pirates along the eastern Adriatic coast with three triremes, manned by reliable Roman crews. He therefore sent a message to Pomponius to appear in the bay of Ravenna on the night of the festival of Epiphanias. While the city was occupied with these festivities, and under cover of darkness, he hoped to reach the ships safely and easily with Amalasuntha. The ships were to take them past the main Gothic positions to Teate, and from there the road to Rome would be short and quite safe.

With this plan in mind, and as his messenger had safely reached Pomponius and returned with the latter's promise to arrive punctually, the Prefect could allow himself to smile with contempt at the growing hatred of the Goths, who regarded his favouritism with Amalasuntha with undisguised anger. Repeatedly he urged Amalasuntha to be patient, and not to provoke an open confrontation with the "rebels" by a premature display of her royal anger, which could so easily ruin all his plans.

The festival of St Epiphanias had arrived, and the people were gathered in huge crowds in the basilicas, and in public places within the city. The various jewels from the Gothic treasury were secretly packed, as were the most important documents from the royal archives. It was midday. Amalasuntha and Cethegus had just advised their friend Cassiodorus of their plan, and although the latter was at first shocked by the boldness of the plan he soon saw the wisdom in it. They were about to leave the royal chambers when the noise of the crowd outside, which had been audible for some time, suddenly increased in intensity. The sounds became louder and louder, and loud threats accompanied by the rattling of arms and loud cheering could be clearly distinguished.

Cethegus drew back the curtains from the large window facing the outside, but already only the last of the people gathered outside could still be seen, the remainder having already poured through the palace gates. What the cause of all this tumult might be Cethegus could not even guess.

Already the turmoil could be heard ascending the palace steps, and sounds of quarrelling with servants, isolated fighting and the sound of heavy footsteps were coming closer and closer. Amalasuntha did not flinch, but firmly grasped the dragon shaped armrests of her throne, to which Cassiodorus had led her.

Meanwhile Cethegus confronted the approaching masses. "Halt!" he cried from the door of the chamber, "the queen will see nobody!"

For a moment there was silence, and then a powerful voice called out: "If she will see you, Roman, then she will see her Gothic brothers. Forward!"

Again the sound of a thousand voices filled the palace, and a moment later Cethegus had been pushed to the back of the room by the irresistible force of the crowd, although he personally was not threatened or harmed in any way.

The leaders of the crowd stood immediately before the throne. They were Hildebrand, Witigis, Teias, a huge Gothic soldier whom Cethegus did not know, and next to him – there could be no doubt – the three dukes, Thulun, Ibba and Pitza, all fully armed, three magnificent warrior figures. The intruders bowed before the throne, and then Duke Thulun faced the crowd once more with the demeanour of a born ruler and called out: "Gothic men, please wait outside a little longer. We will try to settle matters with the regent in your name, and to reconcile our differences. Should we not succeed then it will be time for action, and you know what kind of action I am talking about."

The crowd willingly obeyed his command with cries of joy and dispersed into other parts of the palace.

"Daughter of Theodoric," Duke Thulun began, his head proudly held high, "we have come here because your son, the king, recalled us. Unfortunately we do not find him alive. We know that you are not pleased to see us here."

"If you know that," Amalasuntha replied with regal dignity, "then how dare you appear before us? Who authorised you to force your way to our throne, against our will?"

"Necessity, noble lady, urgent need, which has been known to break through stronger barriers than a woman's whim. We have been asked to present to you the demands of your people, which you will grant."

"Watch your language, Duke Thulun! Do you know whom you are addressing?"

"The daughter of the Amalungs, whose child I honour even where she errs, and even when she commits grave wrongs."

"Rebel!" Amalasuntha cried as she rose majestically from her throne, "you are speaking to your king!"

But Thulun smiled. "You would be wiser to remain silent on that point, Amalasuntha. King Theodoric charged you with the guardianship over your son, even though you are a woman. That was against our laws, but we did not interfere as it was a family matter. He wanted your son, a mere boy, to succeed him, and that too was unwise. But the Gothic nobles and the Gothic people honour the blood of the Amalungs and the wish of a great king, who until then had always acted wisely. But your great father never wished, and we would never have agreed if he had, that a woman should wear the crown and rule over us. A spindle must never rule over swords and spears."

"So now you no longer recognise me as your queen?" she cried indignantly. "What about you, Hildebrand, Theodoric's old friend, do you also deny me?"

"My queen," the old man replied, "may you yourself prevent my ever having need to deny you."

Thulun continued: "We do not deny you, at least not yet. I said what I said only because you made such an issue of your right, and because you must understand that you have no right. But we do honour noble blood, and by doing so we honour ourselves. Because of this, and because at this moment the Empire is in grave danger of serious disunity and even civil war, we do not propose to lay claim to your crown at this time, even though we have every right to do so. I will now list for you the conditions under which you may continue to wear it."

Amalasuntha was suffering almost unbearably. Gladly she would have let her executioners take care of this proud head, which dared to speak to her in such terms. But she knew she was powerless and had to endure it. Tears were about to form in her eyes. With one last great effort she managed to suppress those tears, but the last of her strength drained away as she did so. Supported by Cassiodorus she sank back into her throne.

Meanwhile Cethegus had approached her from the other side. "Agree to everything!" he whispered, "it is all being forced on you and therefore null and void. Remember, Pomponius comes this very night."

"Speak," said Cassiodorus, "but please pay her the respect of sparing her feelings as a woman."

"Ha-ha," Duke Pitza laughed, "but she does not want to be treated as a woman. She thinks she is our king."

"Quiet, cousin," Thulun reprimanded him, "she is of noble blood, as we are. To begin with," he went on, turning to Amalasuntha, "you will dismiss the Prefect of Rome from your side. He is known to be an enemy of the Goths, and he must not advise our queen. Count Witigis will take his place."

"Granted!" Cethegus replied himself.

"Secondly you will issue a manifest that no order coming from you is valid from now on, unless it has been countersigned by Hildebrand or Witigis, and that all new laws must be verified and approved by a general assembly of your people before they become law."

Amalasuntha made to rise angrily, but Cethegus held her arm. "Pomponius is coming tonight!" he whispered, before adding aloud: "Also granted!"

"The third demand," Thulun began again, "is one which you will grant with as much pleasure as it gives us to make it. We three Balti nobles never learned to bow our heads in this palace. The roof here is too low. It is best if Amalungs and Balti live far apart, like eagle and falcon. The Empire needs our strong arms near its borders. Our neighbours are of the mistaken belief that this Empire was orphaned the day your great father went to his grave. Avars, Gepidae and Slavs are hopping across our borders with impunity. In order to discipline them you will mobilise three armies, each of thirty thousand men, and we three will lead them, as your generals, to the north and to the east."

"Now they want control of the armed forces too," Cethegus thought to himself, "not bad." He then added aloud, with a smile: "granted!"

"And what do I have left?" Amalasuntha asked, "if I grant you all this?"

"The golden crown on your white forehead," Ibba said in reply.

Thulun spoke once more: "I believe you know how to read and write, like a Greek. Very well, such talents should not be wasted. This parchment here should contain all that has been agreed to. I had my slave draw it up."

He handed the document to Witigis for verification. "It is so? Good. Now you will sign it, Princess. Fine, we are now finished. Now it is your turn, Hildebad, to speak with that Roman there."

But Teias stepped in front of him, his right hand on his sword, trembling with uncontrollable hatred. "Prefect of Rome," he said, "blood has flowed, precious Gothic blood. That blood will serve to consecrate the bitter war which will break out shortly. Blood for which you will pay!" Anger choked his voice.

"Ah, don't make such a fuss about it!" Hildebad, for he was the huge Gothic soldier mentioned earlier, said as he pushed Teias aside. "My golden brother can spare a little superfluous blood, and the other fellow lost a lot more than he could afford. Here, you black devil," he called out to Cethegus as he held a broad sword under his nose, "do you recognise this?"

"Pomponius's sword!" the latter said, growing pale and taking a step backwards. Amalasuntha and Cassiodorus asked, shocked: "Pomponius?"

"Yes," Hildebad laughed, "Terrible, isn't it? I am afraid your little boat trip is off."

"Where is Pomponius, my skipper?" Amalasuntha asked furiously.

"At the bottom of the sea, with the sharks, my queen."

"Damn you to hell!" Cethegus cried, no longer able to control his anger, "how did that happen?"

"Oh, it's quite a little tale. You see, my brother Totila – I believe you know him – was lying in the port of Ancona with two small warships. Your friend Pomponius had been making a lot of noise for some days, and he boasted so much that in the end even my unsuspecting brother became suspicious. Suddenly one morning your friend disappeared from the port with his three triremes. Totila became suspicious, set full sail, and gave chase. He caught up with Pomponius near Pisaunum, intercepted him and boarded his ship with myself and a few others to ask him what he was up to."

"He had no right to do that, and Pomponius will have refused to give him an answer."

"Oh yes, my precious Cethegus, he gave an answer all right. When he saw that there were only seven of us, alone on his ship, he laughed and said: 'Where am I going? To Ravenna you milksop, where I will rescue the queen from your claws and take her to Rome'. As he said this he gave his men a signal. When we saw this we too raised our shields, and our swords flew from their scabbards. By Thor, that was a hard fight, seven of us against thirty of them. Fortunately it did not last long before our boys on the nearest ship heard the sound of iron on iron, and in no time at all they had lowered their boats and clambered over the side like cats. Now we had superior numbers, but the skipper – I must give the devil his due – would not surrender. He fought like a madman and thrust his sword through my brother's shield and into his left arm, so that blood spurted everywhere. But that made my brother mad too, and he ran his spear through his opponent and felled him like a slaughtered ox. As he lay dying he said: 'remember me to the Prefect, and give him back my sword which was his gift. Tell him that nobody can conquer death, otherwise I would have kept my word.' I promised him that I would deliver his message. He was a brave man. Here is his sword."

Cethegus accepted it silently.

"The ships surrendered, and my brother escorted them back to Ancona. I hurried here on the fastest of our own ships and met the three dukes in the port, just in the nick of time."

A pause followed, during which Amalasuntha and her supporters considered their situation. Cethegus had agreed to all demands without any attempt at opposing them, firmly counting on escape that evening, and that was now no longer possible.

His plan, his beautiful plan, had been foiled by Totila, and at that moment the name Totila became deeply engraved in the Prefect's mind by hatred. He was finally disturbed in his bitter brooding over revenge by Thulun, who cried: "Well, Amalasuntha, are you going to sign now, or would you rather we called the Gothic people together to elect a new king?"

Cethegus quickly regained his composure as he heard these words. He took the tablet from the duke's hand and handed it to her, saying in a low voice: "I am afraid you must, my queen, you have no other choice." Cassiodorus handed her a stylus, she wrote her name, and Thulun took back the tablet.

"Good," he said, "we will now go and tell the Goths that their Empire is safe. Cassiodorus, you will come with us in order to show the people that no force was used to achieve this."

Upon a sign from Amalasuntha the senator did as he was told, and followed the Gothic men to the forum in front of the palace. When the queen saw herself alone with Cethegus at last she jumped to her feet violently. She could no longer control her tears, and passionately struck her forehead with her hand. Her pride had been deeply wounded, and this hour had affected her more profoundly than the death of her husband, or even the loss of Athalaric. Weeping openly she cried at last: "So that is why men are always superior. Because they can always use brute force when all else fails, nothing but raw, clumsy brutality. Oh Cethegus, everything is lost!"

"Not everything, your majesty, only a plan." Coldly he added: "I wish you luck. I am going to Rome."

"What? You are leaving me alone now? You, who advised me to make all those concessions, who caused me to lose my throne, you are leaving me? Oh how I wish I had stood up to them, then I might have remained queen, even if they put the crown on that rebel Thulun's head!"

"Yes," Cethegus thought, "it might have been better for you, but certainly worse for me. No, no able ruler, and no warrior, must ever wear this crown again." Quickly he recognised that Amalasuntha was no longer of any use to him, and just as quickly he abandoned her to her fate. Already he was looking around in his mind for another tool with which to implement his plans. But then he thought better of it, and decided to reveal some of his thoughts to her. He hoped that this would stop her acting independently, and thereby handing the crown to Thulun on a platter.

"I am leaving Ravenna, mistress," he said, "but that does not mean I am deserting you. Here I can no longer be of any use to you. They have banished me from your side, and they will be watching you."

"But what am I going to do about these concessions, and about these three dukes?"

"Wait, and for the time being go along with them. After all, the three dukes are going to war, and perhaps they will not come back."

"Perhaps!" Amalasuntha sighed, "what's the use of perhaps?"

Cethegus took a firm step closer. "They will not return – as soon as you wish it to be so."

The shocked woman trembled. "Murder? My God, what are you plotting?"

"That which is necessary. Murder is the wrong word. It is really more self-defence, or perhaps just punishment. If you had the power right now you would certainly have every right to kill them. They are rebels. They have forced your royal will to their bidding. They have killed your skipper. They richly deserve to die."

"And die they shall," Amalasuntha whispered to herself, clenching her fist. "They shall not live, those brutish men who dared to compel a queen. You are right. They shall die."

"They must die, they and – and the young sailor hero!"

"Why Totila too? He is the most handsome youth in the country."

"He will die," Cethegus snarled through clenched teeth, "I wish he could die ten times over."

Suddenly a flood of hate was burning within him, and the violence with which it erupted from his icy nature caught the queen by surprise. Quickly and softly he continued: "I will send you three trusty men from Rome, three Isaurian mercenaries.

You will send them after the three dukes as soon as they reach their camps. Listen carefully. You are sending them, you as the queen, because they are executioners and not murderers. The three of them must die on the same day. I will take care of Totila myself. The blow and the shock of it will catch everyone by surprise, and while the Goths are still reeling I will hurry to your side from Rome. I will come with men and arms, to save and protect you. Farewell!"

Quickly he left the hapless woman, whose ears were filled at that moment with the sound of wild cheering from the Gothic crowd assembled in the forum outside the palace, acclaiming the success of their leaders and the defeat of Amalasuntha.

She was feeling very much alone, deserted by everyone.

Her troubled mind half suspected that the Prefect's last promise was little more than an empty consolation, to soften the blow of his sudden departure. Sorrowfully she sat there, resting her head on her hands, and for a time she was totally absorbed in her own dark thoughts, groping desperately for a way out of her plight. Suddenly there was a rustling of the curtains, and a palace official stood before her. "Envoys from Byzantium are outside, seeking an audience. Justinus has died, and his nephew Justinian is now emperor. He sends you his brotherly greetings, and offers you his friendship."

"Justinianus!" the troubled woman cried from the depth of her soul. She saw herself standing entirely alone, robbed of her son, threatened by her own people, deserted by Cethegus. In vain had she searched about for help from any and every quarter, unable to muster support. Now she took a deep breath and again she said, almost with a sigh of relief: "Byzantium – Justinian!"

Chapter 4

A traveller coming from Florence will find, as he approaches Faesulae, the ruins of what was once the villa on the right side of the road. It seems as if ivy, saxifrage and wild roses have been competing in a race to cover the ruins. For centuries peasants from the nearby village have been carrying away the stones for retaining walls for their vineyards on the hillsides all around. Yet the remains clearly show what was once a portico with columns, the main building and the walls. Weeds grow prolifically on the lawn of a once beautifully tended garden, of which nothing remains today except for the marble basin of a spring which dried up centuries ago. Only an occasional lizard uses it now to sun himself.

But in the days of Amalasuntha it looked very different here, and the "Villa of the patron of Faesulae," as the area was known at that time, was inhabited by happy people. The house was lovingly cared for by capable women's hands, and the well tended garden filled with the cheerful laughter of children. The slim Corinthian pillars in front of the house were covered with climbing roses, grapevines adorned the flat roof, and the whole house looked warm and friendly. The winding paths in the garden were surfaced with white sand, and the ancillary buildings, which served as servants' quarters or as store rooms, displayed a cleanliness and a feeling of order such as one did not normally associate with local slaves.

It was almost sunset. The field hands and country maids were just returning from the fields, wagons piled high with hay approached, pulled by horses of obviously non-Italian origin. Shepherds were coming down from the hills with their herds, accompanied by large, shaggy, happily barking dogs.

The most lively part of this colourful spectacle was taking place just in front of the main gate. A few Roman slaves were driving panting horses pulling a cruelly overloaded wagon, accompanied by much shouting, cursing and threatening gestures. Instead of whips they were using sticks tipped with metal spikes, and they kept driving these spikes into the tortured animals, always into the same spot, which rapidly became an ugly wound. Despite this progress was slow, and the wagon jerked forward only a little bit at a time. Now a stone blocked the left front wheel, making any further progress impossible. But the angry slave did not notice it.

"Move, you beast and child of a beast," he screamed at the trembling horse, "Get going, you Gothic good for nothing!" A fresh blow with the spike was followed by another desperate jerk, but the wheel just would not go over the stone, and the tortured animal fell to its knees, threatening to overturn the entire wagon. "Just you wait, you lazy nag!" he shouted and struck at the terrified animal's eye. But he only struck once before he himself collapsed under a mighty blow, as if struck by lightning.

"Davus, you evil dog!" roared a bear-like voice, and a huge Goth was standing over the fallen slave. He seemed to be almost twice as tall, and at least twice as broad as the frightened tormentor of the unfortunate horse. A stream of blows from the Goth's rough stick descended on the back of the screaming slave.

"You miserable swine," the big man concluded with a kick, "I'll teach you how to treat a creature at least six times better than you. I think you torment the stallion, you wretch, because he is from the other side of the mountains. Let me see you do that once more and I'll break every bone in your body. Now get up and unload the wagon. You will carry every bale the horse couldn't manage into the barn on your back. Now get going!" The chastised slave got up, gave his master one more hate-filled look and limped away to do as he was told.

Meanwhile the huge Goth had managed to get the horse back on its feet, and busied himself washing its wounds with wine and water from his own drinking flask. He was obviously devoted to the animal.

He had barely finished when a boy's voice called urgently from the nearby stable: "Wachis, Wachis, quickly, come here!"

"I am coming, Athalwin my boy, what's the trouble?" He was already in the doorway of the stable, next to a handsome boy of seven or eight years, who was angrily pushing back his blond locks from his reddened face as he barely suppressed tears of anger in his bright blue eyes. He was holding a beautifully carved wooden sword in his right hand, waving it threateningly at the brown slave standing opposite him, with clenched fists and a stubborn look on his face.

"What's the trouble?" Wachis repeated as he crossed the threshold.

"The big red stallion has nothing to drink again, and look here! Two horse flies have attached themselves here, high up on his chest, where he can't reach with his mane and it's too high for me. When I told that horrid Cacus over there he would not obey me. I am sure he swore at me in Roman, which I don't understand." Wachis stepped closer, threateningly.

"I only told him," Cacus said as he slowly withdrew, "that first I will eat my millet gruel. The animal can wait. In our country people come before animals."

"Is that so, you sop?" Wachis replied as he killed the flies, "Well, with us a horse gets fed before its rider. Get moving!"

But Cacus was strong and stubborn. Throwing his head back he said: "We are in our country here, and so we follow our customs, not yours!"

"Now look here, you accursed black devil, are you going to obey or not?" Wachis said angrily, about to strike the slave.

"Obey? No! You are only a slave like me; my parents were living in the house here when you and your kind were still busy stealing cows and sheep beyond the mountains."

Wachis dropped his stick and rolled up his sleeves. "Now, my dear Cacus. I still have a bone to pick with you anyway, you know what about. So let's get it over and done with once and for all."

"Ha!" Cacus laughed sarcastically, "You mean about that flaxen-haired wench Liuta? I don't like her any more in any case, the Barbarian. She dances like a young cow."

"That does it!" Wachis said calmly, and walked steadily toward his opponent. But the latter wriggled out of the Goth's grip like a cat, drew a knife from his gown and threw it at Wachis, who ducked so that the knife missed his head by a whisker and buried itself in the doorpost.

"Right, you murderous little worm!" cried the giant as he threw himself at Cacus, when suddenly he felt himself being held from behind. It was Davus, who thought he would use this opportunity to gain revenge.

But now Wachis became very, very angry.

He shook off Davus and grabbed him by the neck with his left hand. With his other hand he caught Cacus by the chest, and now with bear-like strength he was banging their heads together, accompanying every blow with an exclamation. "Now – my boys – that's for the knife – and that for attacking me from behind – and that's for the young cow…" Who knows for how long this strange litany might have gone on had not a loud voice interrupted him.

"Wachis, Cacus, break it up I say!" a strong female voice was calling to them, and a magnificent-looking woman in a blue Gothic dress appeared before them. She was not particularly tall, but she was imposing, her build strong rather than slender. Her golden brown hair was wound about her head in thick braids, and her regular features gave her a firm look. Her blue eyes, which were almost too large, suggested honesty, dependability and self-reliance, and her bare arms suggested that she was no stranger to hard work. A large bunch of keys was hanging from the broad belt around her homespun gown. Standing there, with her left hand resting firmly on her hip, she made a commanding gesture with her right hand.

"Oh Rauthgundis, my strict mistress," Wachis said as he let go, "do you have to have eyes everywhere?"

"Everywhere my servants are up to no good. When will you learn to get along with one another? I can see that you southerners are lacking the master's firm hand. But you, Wachis, should not be giving me cause for worry as well. Come Athalwin, come with me."

She took the boy by the hand and they walked to the corner of the yard, where she filled her apron with grain to feed the chickens and pigeons, which gathered about her immediately.

For a while Athalwin watched her silently. At last he said: "Mother, is it true what they say? Is Father really a thief?"

Rauthgundis stopped what she was doing for a moment and looked her son straight in the eye. "Who has been saying that to you?"

"Who? Oh, that nephew of our neighbour Calpurnius. We were playing on the big haystack on his meadow over near the fence, and I showed him how all the land on the right side of the fence was ours, as far as you could see, where the creek was glistening in the sunlight and where our field hands were mowing our wheat. And then he became angry and said: 'Yes, and all that land used to belong to us, and your father and grandfather stole it from us, the thieves.'"

"I see. And what did you say to that?"

"Nothing, Mother. I just threw him down the haystack so that he landed at the bottom, with his legs up in the air. But now I would like to know if what he said was true."

"No child, it is not true. Your father did not steal it. But he did take it openly from our Roman neighbours, because he was better and stronger than they were. Strong men and brave warriors have done this in the same way for thousands of years. And the Romans, back in the days when they were strong and their neighbours weak, they did it most of all. But now come, we must see to the linen which is bleaching in the sun over on the hillside."

As they turned their backs on the stables and walked toward the grassy hill nearby they heard the sound of a horse, approaching rapidly down the old Roman road. Quickly Athalwin reached the top of the hill and looked out along the road.

A horseman on a huge brown stallion was galloping down along the road from the nearby heights toward the villa. He was a fully armed Gothic soldier, his helmet and the lance across his back glistening in the setting sun.

"It's Father, Mother, it's Father!" the boy cried and ran down the hill as fast as his young legs could carry him, to meet the approaching horseman.

By now Rauthgundis had also reached the top of the hill. Her heart was beating. She shielded her eyes against the setting sun as she watched her child run down the hill, and quietly and happily she said to herself: "Yes, it is he. It's my husband!"

Chapter 5

Meanwhile Athalwin had reached his father, and was busy climbing up his leg into the saddle. Lovingly the soldier helped his boy up, and sat him in the saddle in front of him. He then spurred the horse into a full gallop so that Wallada, once Theodoric's warhorse, flew along the road toward home. As he recognised his home and his mistress the fine animal neighed happily, and joyfully he and his riders approached the house.

At last the rider had reached his goal, and he dismounted with the boy. "My darling wife!" he said, as he gave her a hearty hug.

"My Witigis!" she sighed happily in reply, aglow with the joy of reunion, "welcome to your home and family."

"I promised to get here before the new moon, but it was very difficult—"

"But you kept your word."

"My heart drew me here," he said as he put his arm around her and slowly walked with her toward the house: "Athalwin, it seems that Wallada is more important to you than your father." He smiled at his son.

The boy was carefully leading Wallada by the reins. "No father, but please let me carry your spear as well – we peasants here have not had it this good for a long time." And then, as he dragged the heavy spear along with great effort, he called out loudly: "Hey Wachis, Ansbrand, father is thirsty after his long ride!"

Smiling, Witigis stroked the boy's blond head as he rushed ahead of them to lead the way. "Well, how are things here?" he asked, looking at Rauthgundis.

"Fine, Witigis. We have brought the harvest in. The grapes have been pressed and the hay is mostly stacked away."

"That is not what I wanted to know," he said, pressing her to him, "how are you yourself?"

"As well as can be expected of a woman who misses her beloved husband," she said, looking up at him, "and there is only one cure for that, and that is plenty of good hard work. I often think how hard it is for you out there, among strange people, in camp and at court, where nobody looks after you lovingly. So I keep saying to myself that at least he will find everything in order as it should be when he does have a chance to come home, with a welcome waiting for him. You see, that's what makes all the hard work dear to my heart, and gives it meaning."

"You are my ever-capable wife. But aren't you working too hard?"

"Not at all, work is good for me and keeps me healthy. But the constant frustration and strife with the slaves and hired hands is one thing I do find painful!"

Witigis stood still. "Who is it that dares to hurt you?"

"Oh. The Italian field hands and the slaves, and the Roman neighbours. They all hate us, and may heaven help us if ever they no longer fear us. You have no idea how cheeky our neighbour Calpurnius is when he knows you are away, and the Italian slaves are stubborn and cannot be trusted. Only our Gothic hands are dependable."

Witigis sighed. They had now reached the front of the house, and they sat down at a marble table among the columns of the portico. "You must always remember," Witigis said, "that our neighbour had to give us one third of his land and his slaves."

"And kept two thirds and his life – he should be thankful!" Rauthgundis replied, contempt in her voice.

As she finished speaking Athalwin came skipping around the corner with a basket of apples, which he had picked. After him came Wachis and the other Gothic field hands with wine, meat and cheese. They greeted their master with hearty handshakes, and the latter in turn greeted them with: "Thanks; you have done well. The mistress has been praising you. But where are the others, Davus, Cacus and the rest?"

"Begging you pardon master," Wachis said with a smirk, "they have a bad conscience."

"Why? What has happened?"

"Oh, I think it's because I spanked them a little – they are slightly embarrassed." The others laughed.

"Well, that won't hurt them," Witigis remarked, "go and have your meal now. I will have a look at what you have been doing tomorrow." The men left. "What's the problem with Calpurnius?" Witigis asked as he poured himself a goblet of wine.

Rauthgundis blushed and thought before replying. Then she said: "It's about the hay from the meadow up on the hillside. Our hands had mown it, and during the night he shifted it into his barn. Now he won't give it back."

"He'll give it back," he said calmly as he drank.

"Yes!" Athalwin interjected excitedly. "I think so too. And if he won't give it back, why, that's better still. Then we'd call a feud, and I would go over there with Wachis and the other armed hands, like a real army with real arms. He always looks at me so nastily, the black devil."

Rauthgundis bade him be silent and sent him to bed. "Very well, I'm going," he said, "but Father, next time you come home you will bring me a real weapon, won't you, instead of this stick here?" With those words he skipped into the house.

"The strife with these Italians will never end," Witigis sighed, "even the children are carrying it on. The whole business is far too much trouble for you, and I am sure that will help to persuade you even more readily to accept what I am going to suggest to you. Come back to the court with me, to Ravenna."

Rauthgundis looked at him, almost stunned with surprise. "You are joking!" she said in disbelief. "You never wanted that. In the nine years which have passed since I became yours it has never entered your head to take me to court. I doubt if anyone in the nation even knows that there is a Rauthgundis. You have always kept our marriage a secret," she smiled, "like some guilt."

"More like some treasure," Witigis replied, placing his arm around her.

"I never asked you why, Witigis. I was and am happy with things the way they are, and I have always thought that you must have your reasons."

"I did have a very good reason, but not any more. Now I can tell you everything. A few months after I found you up there in your lonely mountain home, and learned to love you, King Theodoric had the strange notion that he wanted me to marry his sister Amalaberga, the widow of the king of Thuringia, because she needed a man's protection against her terrible neighbours, the Franks."

"You were to wear their crown?" Rauthgundis asked, eyes aglow.

"Yes," Witigis replied, "but I decided that I would rather have Rauthgundis than queen and crown, and I said no. He was very annoyed, and he only forgave me in the end when I said that I would probably never marry. At that time I could not hope that you would ever be mine. You know how your father mistrusted me, and resisted our marriage. And when you finally did become my wife, I thought it prudent not to show him the woman for whom I had spurned his sister."

"But why have you kept it a secret from me all these nine years?"

"Because I know my Rauthgundis," he said, looking straight into her eyes with utmost sincerity. "You would always have thought about what I might have lost with that crown. But now the king is dead, and I am permanently tied to the court. Who knows when I will again be able to rest under this roof, in the peace of these columns?"

In a few words he then told her of the Prefect's fall, and of the position he now held at Amalasuntha's side. Rauthgundis listened attentively, and when he had finished she affectionately squeezed his hand. "I am so glad, Witigis, that the Goths have finally realised what a treasure they have in you. And you seem happier than usual, I think."

"Yes, I have been happier since I have been able to help carry the load of responsibility in these troubled times. It was much more difficult just standing there, watching the burden pressing down on my people, and unable to do anything about it. But I do feel sorry for the queen; she is almost like a prisoner."

"Well, it serves her right! Why did she have to meddle in the affairs of men? That would never have occurred to me."

"You are not a queen, Rauthgundis, and Amalasuntha is very proud."

"I am ten times as proud as she is, but I am not so vain. She can't ever have loved a man, and understood his manner and his worth. Otherwise how could she want to take the place of men?"

"These things look different when you are at court. Come back with me, and you will see for yourself."

She rose and replied calmly: "No, Witigis, the court is not for me and I am not made for the court. I am the child of a mountain peasant, and I have no courtly graces. Look at this brown neck," she laughed, "and at these rough hands. I can't pluck the strings of a *lyra*, or read pretty verses. I would not fit in at all well with fine Roman ladies, and I would give you little to be proud of."

"Are you trying to tell me you are not good enough for the court?"

"No, Witigis, not at all. I am too good for the court!"

"Well, both you and they would have to learn to get along, and to respect one another."

"No, I could never do that. They may feign respect toward me because they are afraid of you. But I could never respect them, or even pretend to. Every day I would tell them to their faces that they are shallow, false and evil."

"So you would rather do without your husband, for months at a time?"

"Yes, I would rather do without him than be around him having to play a part that is foreign to me, so that I could not be myself. Oh, my Witigis," she said intensely as she put her arm around his neck, "think who I am and how you found me.

"Up in the Alps, where the last Gothic settlements nestle against the mountain peaks at our northern border, where the young Isara River gushes forth out of stony chasms into the open plains of the Bajuvars, that is where my father's mountain farm lies, my former home. I knew of nothing except hard work on the lonely mountain slopes in summer, and spinning with the maids in the smoke-blackened hall in winter. Mother died when I was very young, and my brother was killed by the Italians. And so I grew up very much alone, alone with my old father, who is as faithful but also as hard and unyielding as his beloved mountains. Of the world either side of our mountains I saw and knew nothing. Sometimes I would look inquisitively down into the valley, where a horse laden with salt or wine was making its way. On many a summer evening I would sit on the mountain peak and watch the glorious setting of the sun, far away to the west. I often thought about all the things the sun must have seen in the course of a long summer's day, since it rose far away to the east on the other side of the Oenus. And I wanted to know what it looked like, on the other side of the Brenner Mountain, where my brother went and never came back. And yet I also thought about how beautiful it was, in our lonely green mountain retreat, where I could hear the stone eagle call, and where I could pick lovely flowers which would not grow down in the plain. Perhaps I might hear a wolf howling outside the stable door at night, so that I would have to chase him away with a flaming torch.

"During the autumn and during the long winters I had plenty of time to think. When the fog hid the tops of the tall pines, when the mountain wind blew the rocks from our straw roof, and when the sounds of distant avalanches filled the air, then I would think to myself about the world outside. And so I grew up, knowing nothing about the world beyond the next forest, alone, at home with my thoughts and my quiet life on a lonely mountain farm.

"And then you came along – I remember it to this day…" and she paused, recalling happy memories.

"I too remember it exactly," said Witigis. "I was leading a detachment of a hundred soldiers from Juvavum to relieve a garrison in Augusta on the Licus River, and I had become separated from my men and lost my way. It was a hot day, and I had been wandering in the trackless wilderness for hours when I saw smoke rising above some pines. I soon found the hidden house and walked through the gate. And there, at the well, stood a magnificent-looking girl about to hoist the bucket."

"I got a terrible fright, for the first time in my life, when the tall man in a brown cloak walked into our yard, with his curly beard and shiny helmet."

"You blushed right up to your temples, and I asked you for a drink of water. Never had I seen a lovelier picture than when you bent down to lift the heavy bucket onto the edge of the well with your strong arms. And then you poured me a drink into a wooden mug. Your golden brown tresses fell across your black bodice, and your cheeks were like peaches. Oh how fresh and blooming you were, and how capable you looked. And you have remained just as fresh, just as blooming and just as capable ever since."

"And so that I might go on blooming for you, my Witigis, please don't take me to court. Even here in the valley, just south of the Alps, I often find it too hot and humid for my liking, and sometimes I just long for a breath of fresh mountain air among my pines. But at court, in those small golden rooms, I would wither and die. Please leave me here. I'll manage our neighbour Calpurnius. And I know that you think often of your home, your wife and your son, even when you are in the palace."

"God knows I do, often and with longing. Very well then, you remain here, and may God be with you, my dear and precious wife."

The second morning after this Witigis rode back along the plateau. The leave-taking had affected him deeply, and it had taken most of his willpower not to show the feelings which had almost overcome him. How very much this worthy man's heart clung to that wonderful woman and his boy!

Wachis rode along behind him, and was not to be denied the pleasure of accompanying his master at least part of the way. Suddenly his horse was alongside that of Witigis. "Master," he said, "there is something I know and you don't."

"Oh? Then why don't you tell me about it?"

"Because you have not asked me to."

"I am asking you now."

"Well, once one is asked, of course, one has to talk. The mistress has told you that Calpurnius is a bad neighbour?"

"Yes she has. What of it?"

"But she did not tell you since when?"

"No, but do you know since when?"

"Yes, since about half a year ago. One day Calpurnius met your wife in the forest, alone as they both thought. But they were not alone. There was a third person present, taking a nap in a ditch."

"And that lazybones was you?"

"You have guessed correctly. And then Calpurnius said something to the mistress."

"What did he say?"

"That I could not understand. But the mistress made no bones. She raised her hand and slapped his face so hard you could hear it for several hundred paces. That I did understand. Ever since that day Calpurnius has been a bad neighbour, and that is what I wanted to tell you, because I did not think that the mistress would want to worry you with the worthless devil. But I think it is better that you do know about it. Look, just by coincidence there is Calpurnius now, standing at his front door. Do you see him? And now farewell, dear master." With those words Wachis turned his horse around and galloped home.

Witigis felt the blood rising to his temples, and rode to his neighbour's door. The latter tried to disappear into the house, but Witigis called out to him in such a commanding tone that he had to stay where he was.

"What do you want of me, neighbour Witigis?" he asked, blinking.

Witigis pulled up his horse right next to Calpurnius, and then he held his clenched, heavily armoured fist right under his nose. "Neighbour Calpurnius," he said calmly, "if ever I should have reason to strike you in the face, you will never get up again."

Calpurnius drew back, rather surprised and somewhat afraid.

Witigis spurred his horse, and calmly and with dignity he rode on his way toward Ravenna.

Chapter 6

Cethegus, the Prefect of Rome, was lying stretched out on the comfortable cushions of the *lectus* in his study. He was relaxed and in good spirits.

The inquiry had ended with his full acquittal; only a sudden and unexpected search of his house, such as the young king had ordered but his death had prevented, could have brought about his undoing. He had been able to convince the Gothic government that work on Rome's fortifications should be continued, with the attendant costs supplemented from his private means, which served to further enhance his standing in the city. The previous night he had called a meeting in the catacombs, where all reports had been favourable. The numbers as well as the resources of the patriots were steadily increasing.

The tougher measures adopted by the Gothic government since the recent events in Ravenna could only serve to further increase dissatisfaction among the Italian population. More important still, Cethegus was now in complete control of all aspects of the conspiracy. Even the most jealous and ambitious among his fellow conspirators saw the need to leave the leadership to the most gifted man among them, at least until the day of liberation dawned.

The mood among the Italian population was now such, and anti-Gothic sentiment so strong, that Cethegus could seriously entertain the idea of starting the fight without help from Byzantium, as soon as Rome's fortifications were complete. He told himself over and over that it was one thing to call in the liberators, but getting rid of them again was another matter. More and more he came to love the idea of ruling Italy on his own, after liberating it on his own.

Luxuriantly Cethegus stretched and laid aside Caesar's *Civil War*. Resting his head on his left arm he said to himself: "The gods must still have great things in store for you, Cethegus. Every time you fall you land on your feet like a cat. Yet when things are going well the gods are also willing to talk to you. But trust is much too dangerous and the only true god is silence. Yet one remains human, and it is human to want..."

At that moment a slave entered; it was Fidus, his old *ostiarius*. Silently he handed his master a shallow golden bowl with a letter in it, and turned to go. "The messenger is waiting," he said.

Cethegus picked up the letter with indifference, but as soon as he recognised the wax seal he cried out animatedly: "From Julius! Just what I need at a time like this!" Quickly he broke the seal, untied the strings holding the bundle of tablets together, sorted the tablets in order, and started to read. His usually cold face suddenly glowed with a joyous warmth.

"To Cethegus the Prefect, his Julius Montanus.

"How long is it, my fatherly teacher" (by Jupiter, thought Cethegus, that sounds frosty), "since I have sent you a letter? For much too long I have owed you the greeting which is your due. Last time I wrote it was from the banks of the Ilissos, where I tried to find traces of Plato in the desolate grove of Academos, but did not find them. I know that my letter was not a happy one. The sad old philosophers wander about in deserted schools, under pressure from the emperor and hindered further by suspicious priests and the indifference of the masses. They aroused nothing in me but pity. My soul was in darkness, and I did not know why.

"I berated myself for my ingratitude toward you, the most magnanimous of all benefactors." (He has never given me such unbearable names before, thought Cethegus.)

"For two years now I have been travelling through the whole of Asia and Hellas, feeling like a Syrian king with your wealth at my disposal, and accompanied by your slaves and freedmen. I saw and enjoyed all the beauty and all the wisdom of the ancients, and yet my heart remained discontent, and my life without meaning. Nothing gave me what I needed, not Plato's idealism, not the gold and ivory of Phidias, not Homer and not Socrates.

"At long, long last, here in Naples, the blooming city blessed by the gods, I have found that which I have always lacked and searched for in vain, although I did not then know it.

"In place of dead wisdom I have found warm, living happiness." (He is in love, at last! You dry old *hyppolite*! Thanks be to you, Eros and Anteros!) "Oh my teacher, my father! Do you know what joy it is to call another heart, another human being who understands you completely, your own for the first time?" (Oh Julius, the Prefect sighed with rare feeling, did I ever know it!) "To whom you can bare your soul, completely and openly? Oh if ever you have known such joy then rejoice with me, and give sacrifice to Zeus the fulfiller! At last, for the first time, I have a friend."

"What's this?" Cethegus cried as he angrily jumped to his feet, with a look of jealous pain in his face, "how ungrateful!"

"As I am sure you must realise I have never, until now, had a real friend, someone I could trust and in whom I can confide. You, my teacher…"

Cethegus threw the tablets down on the little table and got up to pace the room. "The first foolishness of youth!" he then said calmly, and he picked up the tablets and resumed reading.

"You, so much older, wiser, better and greater than I, you have burdened my soul with such a weight of gratitude and admiration that I could never quite bring myself to bare it with you. Also I have witnessed all too often how you ridicule any such softness or warmth with your piercing wit. Whenever I was with you a stern look on your proud face always killed any such feelings in me, just as frost kills the first violets of spring (well, at least he is honest). But now I have found a friend, open, warm, young and idealistic as I am, and this has brought me a joy such as I have never known before. It is as if we have the one soul in two bodies. Together we spend sunny days and moonlit nights walking through these divine fields, and there is no end to our happiness. We never run out of things to talk about. But I must bring this letter to a conclusion. He is a Goth (What next? Cethegus thought with feeling) and his name is Totila."

Cethegus allowed the hand holding the tablet to drop for a moment. He said nothing. He merely closed his eyes briefly, and then calmly went on reading.

"And his name is Totila. I was walking through the Forum of Neptunus the day after my arrival in Naples, and I stopped to admire some statues which a sculptor had exhibited there for sale. Suddenly a grey-haired man wearing an apron rushed at me from a doorway, covered head to toe in plaster, with a chisel in his hand. He grabbed me by the shoulder and shouted: 'Pollux, my Pollux, I have found you at last!'

"I thought the old man was mad, and said: 'I am afraid you are mistaken. My name is Julius and I have just come from Athens.'

"'Nonsense,' the old man cried, 'your name is Pollux and you come from Olympus.' And before I knew what was happening he had ushered me through his door. Once inside the house I realised who the old man was. He was the sculptor whose work I had been admiring.

"There were a number of other half finished statues in his workshop, and he told me that he had been planning to do a group sculpture of the Dioscurian Gods for some time. He had recently found a perfect model for Castor in a young Goth. 'But in vain,' he told me, 'I have been imploring heaven to give me an idea for my Pollux. He must resemble Castor, because like him he is a brother of Helena and a son of Zeus, so there has to be a strong resemblance in facial features and in build. And yet they must also be different, the difference just as pronounced as the similarity. They must belong together and yet each one must be an individual. For weeks I have been doing the rounds of all the baths and gymnasiums in Naples, in vain. I could not find a suitable model. And then a god, Zeus himself, brought you to my door, and it struck me like lightning! There is my Pollux, standing there just as he must be, and you are not leaving this house alive until you have promised me your head and your body.'

"Gladly I agreed to the old man's demand that I come back the next day, and I became even more agreeable when I learned that he was Xenarchos, the finest sculptor in marble and bronze that Italy has seen for a long time. Next day I came back and found my Castor – it was Totila. I cannot deny that the tremendous resemblance surprised me, even though Totila is older, taller, stronger and much better looking than I am. Xenarchos says that we are like lemon and orange. Totila has lighter skin and hair than I have, and Xenarchos swears that this is just how the two gods resembled each other, and also differed from each other. And so we met, and among Xenarchos's statues we became friends. We did indeed become Castor and Pollux, close and inseparable as they were. People already call us by those names as we walk through the streets arm in arm.

"But our new friendship was to be sealed even more firmly very soon by a threat which could easily have cut it short.

"One evening, as was our custom, we had walked through the Porta Nolana toward the baths of Tiberius, where we planned to seek relief from the heat of the day. After we had bathed we were in a jovial mood – you will scold me for it – and just for a laugh I put on my friend's white Gothic mantle and placed his helmet with the wings of a swan on my head. Smiling, he agreed to the exchange and put on my *Chamys*. Peacefully engaged in conversation we were walking back to the city through a pine forest. It had just become dark.

"Suddenly a man leapt out of the *taxus* bushes behind me, and I could feel cold steel against my throat. But in the next instant the would-be murderer lay at my feet, Totila's sword through his chest. Only slightly wounded, I bent down to the dying man and asked him what reason he had to hate me so much that he tried to murder me. He looked me in the face and whispered, just before he died: 'Not you, Totila, the Goth.' And then he twitched and was dead. You could tell plainly from his clothing and from his weapons that he was an Isaurian mercenary."

Cethegus put the letter down for a moment and pressed his hands to his temples. "Madness of chance," he said, "what could you have led to?" And then he finished reading.

"Totila said that he had a lot of enemies at court in Ravenna. We reported the incident to Uliaris, the Gothic commander in Naples, who had the body searched and enquiries made, but without result. But this serious event did serve to seal our young friendship in blood, and it has bound us together more firmly than ever. And so the seal of the Dioscuri, which you gave me as a farewell gift, has turned out to be a good omen. And I ask myself at times to whom I owe this happiness. I owe it to you, and you alone, because it was you who sent me here to Naples, the city where at last I found everything I have ever wanted. May all the gods and goddesses reward you for it! But I see how this letter speaks only of me and of my new friend. Do write soon and tell me how things are with you. *Vale.*"

A bitter smile played about the Prefect's mouth, and again he paced the room, controlling his emotions with difficulty. At last he stopped and said to himself: "How could I be so – so immature as to be annoyed! The whole thing is quite natural, even though it is naïve. You are ill, Julius! Wait, I will write you a prescription for a cure." With an expression of cruel joy on his face he seated himself on the writing *lectus*, took a papyrus scroll from its bronze vase, dipped a quill into the red ink contained in an agate inkwell shaped like a lion's head and started to write.

"To Julius Montanus Cethegus, Prefect of Rome.

"Your touching epistle from Naples has amused me greatly. It shows that you are now going through the last sickness of childhood. When you are over it you will be a man.

"In order to expedite this cure I hereby give you the best possible prescription. You will immediately visit the merchant Valerius Procillus, my oldest friend in Naples. He is the wealthiest merchant in the Occident, and made his fortune from dealing in purple. He is a bitter enemy of the emperor in Byzantium, whose predecessors had his father and brothers killed. He is also a republican like Cato, and for that reason alone he is my friend. But his daughter Valeria Procilla is the most beautiful Roman woman of our time, and a true daughter of the old heathen world. Antigone or Virginia would have been pleased to have her as a friend. She is only three years younger than you, and therefore ten times more mature. Nonetheless her father will not refuse you her hand, once you tell him that Cethegus is wooing her for you. You will fall hopelessly in love with her at first sight.

"You will fall in love with her even though I tell you so in advance, and even though it is my wish. In her arms you will forget all the friends in the world, for when the sun rises the moon pales. By the way, did you know that your Castor is one of Rome's most dangerous enemies? And I once knew a certain Julius who said, in fact swore: 'Rome above all else!' *Vale.*"

Cethegus rolled up the papyrus, and then tied it and sealed it with his amethyst ring which was fashioned in the shape of a beautiful head of Jupiter. He touched the silver eagle on the marble wall, and outside the vestibule a heavy striker struck the silver shield of a toppled Titan, with a sound like a bell. The slave entered.

"Let the messenger bathe, then give him food, wine, one gold piece and this letter. At sunrise tomorrow he will take it back with him to Naples."

Chapter 7

Several weeks later we find the Prefect in an entirely different circle, seemingly quite inconsistent with either his ambition or his age.

During the first few centuries after the conversion of Constantine the Roman world was influenced and characterised by a strange coexistence of Christianity and paganism. Among the glaring but peaceful contradictions which this created was a mixture of festivals of both the old and new religions. Apart from the great festivals of the Christian calendar the happy festivals of the old gods were also celebrated, even though they had long lost their original religious meaning and significance.

The people were willing to give up their belief in Jupiter and Juno together with heathen ritual and sacrifice, but not the games, the festivals, the dancing and feasting which had been a part of their former religion. The church had always shown the wisdom to passively tolerate what it could not change in any event. Even the heathen *Lupercalia*, which combined primitive superstition with wild celebrations of every kind, were only abolished in the year 496 AD, and then only with great difficulty.

Some of the more harmless festivals, such as the festival of Flora, continued on for very much longer, and some of them are still celebrated in Italian villages today, retaining much of their original meaning. In our story the festival of Flora had arrived. Once it had been celebrated on the whole of the Italian peninsula with games and dancing, especially by the younger generation. Even in the days of our story Flora was still celebrated with feasting and drinking at the very least.

The two Licinius brothers and their circle of friends had arranged a feast for the main day of the Flora festival, those friends consisting of young Romans mainly from the nobility or of patrician rank. Each guest, as is still often the custom in our society, brought with him a contribution of food or wine. The feast took place in the house of Kallistratos, a rich and likeable Greek from Corinth, who had settled in Rome to enjoy a life of artistic leisure. His house was located near the gardens of Sallustus, and had come to be regarded as the centre of good living and fine culture. Apart from Rome's wealthy nobility many artists and scholars frequented the house, together with those young Romans who had been so occupied with their horses and chariots and dogs that they had little time to devote to the affairs of state, and who had therefore been untouched so far by the Prefect's influence.

Cethegus was therefore delighted when young Lucius Licinius, who had become one of his most enthusiastic followers, brought him the Corinthian's invitation. "I know," the young man said timidly, "that we cannot offer conversation or intellectual stimulation worthy of your mind. I suppose that, if Kallistratos's Falernian and Cyprian wines don't tempt you, you will decline his invitation."

"No, my son, I am coming," Cethegus replied, "and I am tempted not by old Cyprian wines but by young Roman men."

Kallistratos was proud of his Greek heritage, and had built his house in the Greek manner right in the heart of Rome. It was built in the style of the golden age of Pericles, resulting in a simplicity which contrasted sharply with the ostentation common in those days. Access to the house was through a narrow passageway leading to an open courtyard, surrounded by pillars, with a fountain of brown marble in the centre. Among other rooms the northern wing of the building contained a dining hall, and it was here that our small gathering took place. Cethegus had chosen not to come for the *coena*, or main feast, but rather to the nocturnal drinking bout which followed, known as the *commisatio*. Hence on his arrival he found his young friends already in the luxurious drinking chamber, with its walls inlaid with tortoiseshell, where delicate bronze lamps had already been lit. The guests were reclining on the horseshoe-shaped *triclineum*, wearing wreaths of roses and ivy. As Cethegus set foot in the room he was met by an intoxicating aroma of wine and flowers amid flickering torches and glowing colours.

"*Salve* Cethegus!" the host called out, meeting him. "You will find only small company here."

Cethegus ordered his slave to untie his sandals. The slave was a beautifully built young Moor, whose scarlet tunic served to accentuate rather than conceal his magnificent body.

"Quickly, choose a wreath," Kallistratos urged him, "and take your place of honour up there in our midst. We have elected you in advance to be our festival king."

Cethegus had made up his mind to win these young men over. He knew how well he could do this when he wanted to, and he wanted to tonight. Thus he chose a wreath of roses and took hold of the ivory sceptre handed to him by a kneeling Syrian slave. As he adjusted his diadem of roses he waved his sceptre with mock authority: "In that case I hereby put an end to your freedom!"

"A born ruler!" Kallistratos cried, half serious and half in jest.

"But I will be a benevolent tyrant! Here is my first law: one third of water, two thirds of wine."

"Well, well!" Lucius Licinius called out and drank to him. "*Bene te!* You lead a reckless regime. Equal parts is normally our limit."

"Yes, friend," Cethegus smiled as he lowered himself on his place of honour. "I studied drinking among the Egyptians, who drink only straight wine without any water. Hey waiter – what's his name?"

"Ganymedes; he comes from Phrygia. Well built, isn't he?"

"Very well, Ganymedes, obey your Jupiter and place one *patera* of Mamertinian wine in front of each guest. You had better give Balbus two – he is from the country." The younger men laughed.

Balbus was a wealthy Sicilian, and owned a great deal of property there. He was still quite young, but already very fat.

"Ha," the drinker laughed, "with ivy about my head and amethyst on my fingers I will resist the power of Bacchus."

"Very well, what stage are you up to with your wine?" Cethegus asked, waving to the Moor standing behind him, and who now placed a second wreath of roses around his master's neck.

"The last one was Settinian cider with Hymettian honey. Here, try some!" Those words were spoken by Piso, the roguish poet whose witty epigrams were snapped up by the book dealers as fast as he could write them, but whose finances were in a constant state of poetic disorder. He handed the Prefect what we would call a trick cup. It was a snake's head of bronze, and if one attempted to drink from it in the normal manner it would shoot a jet of wine into the drinker's throat. But Cethegus knew the game, drank carefully and gave the cup back. "I prefer your dry jokes, Piso," he laughed, and grabbed a tablet with writing on it from the folds of the poet's tunic.

"Oh, give it back," said Piso, "they are not verses, quite the contrary! It is a summary of my debts for wine and horses."

"Well now," Cethegus replied, "I took them, and so they are now my debts. You can come and collect your receipt from me tomorrow, but not without paying me something in return. I want one of your nasty little epigrams about our pious friend Silverius!"

"Oh Cethegus," the poet cried, both delighted and flattered, "just how sarcastic can a man be for forty thousand *solidi*? May heaven have mercy on the holy man of God!"

Chapter 8

"And what about the feast itself? How far have we got with that?" Cethegus asked, "the apples already? Are these the ones?" He was looking at two fruit baskets made of palm leaves, standing on a bronze table with ivory legs, piled high with apples.

"Ha! I triumph!" Marcus Licinius laughed, the younger brother of Lucius, who indulged in the then fashionable pastime of modelling in wax. "Now what do you think of my art, Kallistratos? The Prefect thinks that the wax apples, which I gave you yesterday, are real."

"Really?" Cethegus exclaimed with feigned astonishment, as the unpleasant smell of wax had not escaped him. "They are really good, and even the best of us can be deceived with art like that. Where did you learn? I would very much like to have some fruit like that to display in my hallway."

"I taught myself," Marcus replied proudly, "and tomorrow I will send you my new Persian apples, seeing that you are one who appreciates true art."

"But the feast is over now, isn't it?" the Prefect asked, resting with his left arm on the cushions.

"No," the host replied, "I will now confess. Seeing that I could not count on our festival king arriving until the drinking hour, I have arranged a little late supper to go with our wines."

"Oh you fiend!" Balbus cried, wiping his lips, "now you tell us, after I have eaten so many of your snipes with figs!"

"That's against the rules!" Marcus Licinius cried.

"It will ruin my manners!" Piso added with mock consternation.

"Say, is that what you call Hellenistic simplicity?" Lucius Licinius asked.

"Quiet, friends," Cethegus consoled them, and added a quotation: "A Roman resolutely endures even unexpected adversity."

"A Hellenic host must adapt to his guests," Kallistratos said in half apology, "I was afraid you would not come back if I had only offered you the customs of Marathon."

"Very well then, but at least tell us what we still have to face," Cethegus exclaimed. "You, announcer, read the list of dishes. I will then decide which wines are to accompany them."

The slave was a fine-looking youth from Lydia, wearing a gown of blue Pelusian linen slit to the knees. He was standing behind the Prefect by a cypress wood table, and read from a little tablet which he wore on a gold chain around his neck: "Fresh oysters from Britain in tuna sauce with lettuce."

"With that we'll have the Falernian wine from Fundi," said Cethegus without thinking. "But where are the goblets? A good wine can only be really enjoyed from the right cup."

"They are on the table over there!" A wave of the hand from the host and the curtain, which until then had obscured a corner of the room from view, fell away. A cry of astonishment rose from the tables.

The splendour of the precious goblets, and the exquisite taste with which they were displayed, took even these pampered eyes by surprise. A large silver carriage with golden wheels and bronze horses stood in the centre of the marble table top, similar to the carriages which were used to display the booty from a campaign in Roman triumphs. The precious booty in this case was a collection of goblets, glasses and bowls of every conceivable shape, made from a wide range of materials, and arranged with impeccable taste in apparent disarray.

"By Mars the victor," the Prefect laughed, "the first Roman triumph in two hundred years. A rare sight. May I destroy it?"

"You are just the man to bring them back," said Lucius Licinius passionately.

"Do you think so? Well, let's try! For the Falernian wine we will use those chalices there, made from the wood of the turpentine tree."

"Thrushes in wine from Tagus, with asparagus from Tarentum!" the slave continued.

"With that we will have the red Massica from Sinuessa, out of the amethyst goblets.

"Young turtles from Sicily with flaming tongues."

"In the name of holy Bacchus, stop it!" Balbus cried. "You are subjecting me to the tortures of Tantalus. I don't care what I drink from, amethyst or turpentine wood, but I cannot endure this recital of delicacies fit for the gods with a dry palate any longer. Death to Cethegus the tyrant if he lets us starve another moment!"

"I feel as if I was the Imperator, and I hear the faithful people of Rome. To save my life I give in to your wishes. Slaves, serve!"

The sound of flutes could now be heard coming from the antechamber, and six slaves emerged walking in time to the music. They were dressed in white tunics and red mantles, with ivy wound around their richly oiled locks. Each guest was handed a fresh hand towel of the finest Sidonian linen, bordered with soft purple.

"Oh," cried Massurius, a young merchant who dealt mainly in slaves of both sexes, and who enjoyed the dubious reputation of being Italy's leading authority on such merchandise, "the safest towel is a soft head of hair" and with those words he stroked the hair of Ganymedes, who was kneeling beside him. "But I hope those flutes are female, Kallistratos! Remove the curtain and let the girls in."

"Not yet," Cethegus ordered, "drinking comes before kissing. Without Bacchus and Ceres, you know—"

"Venus is the one who freezes, not Massurius."

The sound of lyres and zithers could now be heard coming from the side chamber, and a procession of eight youths dressed in shiny golden green silk entered, among them a food preparer and a carver. The other six carried dishes on their heads; they walked past the guests in time to the music and stopped in front of the citrus wood table used to prepare the food. While they busied themselves there castanets and cymbals sounded from yet another direction. The large double doors revolved about the bronze-clad columns, and a swarm of slaves entered, dressed in the beautiful costumes of Corinthian Ephibi. Some served bread in finely worked bronze baskets and some kept the insects at bay with fans of ostrich feathers and palm leaves, while others filled the wall lamps with oil from double-handled jars or swept the floor with brooms of Egyptian reeds. The remainder helped Ganymedes to fill the goblets, which were already circulating freely.

The conversation now became more lively as the wine started to do its work, and Cethegus, who gave the appearance of being totally absorbed by the atmosphere even though he was completely sober, set about captivating the young men with his own youthfulness.

"What do you think?" asked the host, "Shall we play dice between courses? The dice are over there next to Piso."

"Well, Massurius," Cethegus asked with a mocking glance at the slave dealer, "do you want to try your luck against me again? Will you have a wager against me? Syphax, give him his dice!" he commanded the Moor.

"May Mercury preserve me!" Massurius replied with mock horror. "Don't gamble with the Prefect! He has inherited the luck of his ancestor Caesar."

"*Omen accipio!*" Cethegus laughed, "I accept that, together with Brutus's dagger."

"I tell you, he is a magician! Just recently he won a wager from me with this brown demon." And he tried to throw a fig into the slave's face, but the latter cleverly caught it with his shining teeth and ate it with obvious enjoyment.

"Well done, Syphax," Cethegus praised him, "roses out of your enemy's thorns! You can become a juggler when I set you free."

"Syphax does not want to be free. He only wants to be your Syphax and save your life, as you saved his."

"What's this? Your life?" Lucius Licinius asked with shocked surprise.

"Did you pardon him?" Marcus asked.

"More than that, I bought his life."

"Yes, with my money!" Massurius growled.

"Now you know that I immediately gave him your lost wager as a *peculium*."

"What's this about a wager? Tell us about it, it might give me an idea for an epigram," Piso asked.

"Let the Moor tell you himself. Speak, Syphax, you may."

Chapter 9

Without hesitation the young slave stepped into the middle of the horseshoe formed by the tables, his back to the door. Quickly his keen eyes scanned those present, and then he fixed them glowingly on his master. Everyone admired the youthful strength of his body and the beauty of his well muscled limbs. His only clothing was a precious scarlet loincloth, his brown body otherwise being quite naked.

"It is easy to tell a story after the pain of it has subsided. My home is in the sun's favourite land, where a hundred palms shade the evergreen oasis, known only to us, the lion and the spotted panther. But one godless night the enemy found our old hiding place. They were Vandal horsemen, and there was no escape. Smoke from our burning tents rose red and black through the tops of the cedars, and screaming women and children were fleeing everywhere. Suddenly I was struck by a flying spear.

"I woke up in the slave hold of a Greek ship, bound hand and foot. They had bought us, myself and many men and women of my tribe; I had not been able to save anything except my god, the white snake god, whom I carried hidden in my belt. They took us to Rome, where I was bought by one whose name shall be cursed in all eternity."

"It's our friend Calpurnius," Cethegus interrupted.

"And no star shall guide him through the dark night – let him perish of thirst in the hot sand!" The Moor gnashed his teeth with fierce hatred. "He often beat me for no reason at all and let me starve. I remained silent and prayed to my god for revenge. He was angry that I was able to bear his fury so calmly.

"He did not know that Syphax carries his god with him always, in the form of a white snake. One morning he approached my bed while I was asleep, and saw it curled around my neck. He was frightened, even though I told him that his teeth were not deadly, only his revenge. That made him angry. He tried to strike me and said: 'Kill the worm!' In vain I implored him on my knees. He struck me, and then he tried to strike my god. When I shielded my god with my body he became even angrier and cried: 'Kill the viper!' How could I obey? Then he called his slaves and commanded them: 'Take the creature from him and boil it alive. He shall eat his god.' I was horrified to hear such unspeakable blasphemy. And then they grabbed me and tried to take the snake from me. But my god gave me the strength of desperation, which is like that of a wounded tiger, and with a cry of rage I leapt amongst them.

"I struck the accursed blasphemer down with this fist, reached the door of the house and escaped into the open, with thirty slaves after me. It was a matter of life and death."

The guests were listening intently, and even Balbus put down his goblet, which he had been raising to his lips.

"I can run quite well. My three cousins and I often chased the swift antelope until it dropped from exhaustion. And the slaves were slow and heavy.

"But they knew the city and its streets, while I did not, and that made it an uneven contest. My pursuers divided into groups of three or four men, and cut off my escape through the side alleys and lanes.

"Fortunately I had picked up a heavy iron poker at a blacksmith's shop I had passed, and two or three times I used it to ward off my attackers, or to strike those who suddenly appeared in front of me. But in my heart I knew that this chase could not go on for long. As quick as I was, and however slow they were, in the end I had to lose.

"And at that moment my god, whom I had been holding firmly against my chest, sent me my great master," and his eyes sparkled as he said it, "my master, the mighty one, powerful as the lion of Abaritana and clever as the elephant, as good as rain after a long drought and as glorious as—"

"Now you are not narrating at all well, Syphax, so I had better complete the story. I was just coming from the entrenchments near Hadrian's tomb."

"Your lovely favourite spot, where you have placed all the statues of the gods," Kallistratos interrupted.

"And I was turning into Trajan's Forum from the base of the Capitol. There I found a crowd of people, shouting and yelling as they watched a manhunt with great curiosity. The Moor shot towards us like an arrow from the Forum of Nerva, his pursuers far behind him. But at that same instant six or seven of Calpurnius's slaves entered the Forum right beside me, ready to catch him as soon as he got there. 'He is done for!' said a familiar voice beside me. It was Massurius, who was just coming from the baths of Augustus.

"'To whom does he belong?' I asked. 'Our master is Calpurnius,' answered the slave who was standing beside me. 'Then I pity the poor wretch,' Massurius said to me, 'he punishes slaves by tying them up right to their necks, and then he puts them into his fishpond to be eaten alive by his perches and pikes.'

"'Yes,' said the slave, 'Syphax struck him down, and as he rose the master told us to feed the dog to the pikes, and that whoever brought him in was free.'

I looked at the Moor, who had almost reached me running along the Forum. 'He is too good for the fishes,' I said, 'what a magnificent build! Just look at him. I will wager that he makes it.'

Just at that moment the fugitive reached the first row of slaves, who tried to prevent him from entering the Via Julia, but in a flash he broke through them and was racing towards us.

'And I will wager a thousand *solidi* he does not make it – look at the lances over there,' said Massurius. Five slaves with lances and throwing spears were standing immediately in front of us. 'It's a wager!' I cried, 'a thousand *solidi*!'

He reached us. Three spears flew at once, but the nimble Moor ducked under them like a panther and then, leaping high into the air, he jumped right over the lances of the other two. Out of breath he fell to the ground at my feet. He was bleeding from a number of stone and arrow wounds, and already the whole mob from the Forum Julium was bearing down on him. In desperation he looked around him and tried to turn right into the street of the peace temple, which would have taken him straight back to the house of his master. I saw the portal of the small basilica of St Laurentius, open in front of us. 'Over there!' I called out to him."

"In my language! He can speak my language!" Syphax cried.

"I think he can speak any language," said Marcus Licinius.

"'Over there,' I repeated, 'you will find asylum over there.' Like lightning he flew up the steps, and was already on the top step when a stone struck him, causing him to fall. In an instant the first of his pursuers reached him and tried to grab him. But like an eel Syphax twisted out of his grip and pushed him down the steps, and then he leapt through the door into the church."

"And you had won your wager," Kallistratos said.

"Yes, I had, but not he. The priests of St Laurentius may guard their right of asylum ever so zealously, but at the same time they have very little pity for a heathen. They gave him asylum for a day, but when they found out that he had struck his master to protect his snake they gave him a choice. Either he had to become a Christian and surrender the snake, or else it was Calpurnius and the pikes.

"Syphax chose death. I heard about it and went to see the angry Calpurnius, from whom I bought not only his revenge but also the life of this slender lad, the handsomest slave in Rome."

"Not a bad bargain," Marcus remarked, "the Moor is loyal to you."

"I think he is," Cethegus replied. "Stand back, Syphax, it looks as if the cook is about to bring us his masterpiece."

Chapter 10

It was a six-pound turbot, which had been fattened with goose livers for many years in Kallistratos's seawater pond. The much-prized *rhombus* was served on a silver platter, with a little golden crown on its head.

"By all the gods and the prophet of Jonas!" Balbus stammered as he allowed himself to fall back onto his cushions, "that fish is worth more than I am."

"Quiet, friend," Piso warned, "so that Cato does not hear you. Remember that he said: 'doomed is the city where a fish is worth more than an ox.'" Loud laughter and cries of "*Euge belle!*" drowned out the protests of the half-intoxicated Balbus.

The fish was dissected and found to be utterly delectable.

"Now, slaves, take away this dull red wine. The noble fish shall swim in equally noble liquid. Syphax, now is the time for my contribution to this banquet. Have them bring the amphora which the slaves outside have been cooling in snow. Serve it in the yellow amber chalices."

"What are you offering us, some rare treat from a strange country, no doubt?" Kallistratos asked of Cethegus.

"You had better ask 'from which quarter of the world', if I know this much-travelled Odysseus," Piso added.

"That is something which you will have to guess. And if you can correctly guess it, if any one among you has tasted this wine before, then I will give him an amphora of it, as tall as this one."

Two slaves, wearing garlands of ivy, dragged the heavy brown vessel to the table. It was made from porphyry and was of a most unusual shape, covered in hieroglyphics and its opening well sealed with gypsum.

"Holy Styx! That must come straight from the Tartarus. What a gloomy-looking object," Marcus laughed.

"But it has a white soul. Show us, Syphax." The Nubian took the ebony hammer which Ganymedes handed him, carefully broke away the gypsum, removed the palm bark stopper with silver tongs and poured out the layer of oil which floated on top. He then poured out the sticky white liquid, which gave off a heady aroma as he poured. They all drank, sipping slowly, tasting and wondering.

"A treat for the gods!" Balbus said as he set down his goblet.

"But it is as strong as liquid fire," Kallistratos added.

"No, I don't know this one!" said Lucius Licinius.

"Nor I," Marcus agreed.

"But I am delighted to make its acquaintance," Piso declared as he held out his empty goblet to Syphax.

"Well," the host asked of the last of his guests, who had been sitting on his right but who so far had not uttered a word, "Furius, great mariner, adventurer, visitor to India and world navigator, is even your great knowledge to be put to shame?"

The man whom Kallistratos had thus addressed raised himself a little from his cushions. He was a handsome, athletic man of some thirty years, with a weather-beaten face, deep black eyes, gleaming white teeth and a beard trimmed in the Oriental manner.

But before he could speak, Kallistratos quickly interrupted: "By Zeus Xenius, I don't think that you two know one another."

Cethegus studied the stranger with his usual penetrating look. "I know the Prefect of Rome," said the silent one.

"Well, Cethegus, and this is my volcanic friend Furius Ahalla from Corsica, the wealthiest ship owner of the Orient, as deep as the night and as hot blooded as fire. He owns fifty houses, villas and palaces on every coast of Europe, Asia and Africa, twenty galleys, a few thousand slaves and sailors and—"

"And a very talkative friend," the Corsican concluded. "Prefect, I feel sorry for you, but the amphora is mine. I know the wine." He took a pewit egg and broke the shell with a golden spoon.

"I doubt it," Cethegus replied mockingly.

"I do. It is Isis wine from Memphis." Calmly he sipped the golden red egg.

Cethegus looked at him in astonishment. "You have guessed it," he said, "where did you come to taste it?"

"In the same place as you, of course. As you know it flows from only the one source," the Corsican smiled.

"That's enough of your secrets. Let's have no riddles here!" cried Piso.

"Where did you two martens find the same nest?" Kallistratos asked.

"Well," said Cethegus, "you may as well know. In old Egypt, particularly in Memphis, there are still a few men, and particularly women, who cling tenaciously to their old religion despite the monks and priests who share their desert land. They still worship Apis and Osiris, but it is the sweet goddess Isis whom they serve with special fervour. They have fled from the surface, where the cross of the Christian church now reigns supreme, down into the secret womb of mother earth, where they practise their holy madness. In a labyrinth under the Cheops pyramid they still have hidden a few hundred jars of this great wine, which was once used to intoxicate the chosen during their orgies of joy and of love. The secret is passed on from generation to generation, and there is only one priestess at any one time who knows the whereabouts of the cellar, and who has the key.

"I kissed the priestess, and she led me into the cellar. She was a real wildcat, but her wine was good. As a farewell present she gave me five amphorae of it to take with me on the ship."

"I did not get that far with Smerda," said the Corsican. "She let me drink in the cellar, but as a souvenir I only got this," and he bared his brown neck.

"A stab with the dagger of jealousy," Cethegus laughed, "I am glad the daughter took after her mother. In my time, when the mother let me drink, little Smerda was still a child. But be that as it may, long live the holy Nile and sweet Isis." With this the two men drank to one another.

But each of them secretly resented having had to share a secret, which each of them had thought to be his alone.

But the others were captivated by the mood of the otherwise icy Prefect, who was chatting with them in the lively manner of a young man. Now that the favourite topic of young men in their cups had been raised, namely amorous adventures and tales of conquests in love, he related an almost inexhaustible string of stories and anecdotes, most of which he himself had experienced. All listened to him with rapt attention and asked questions. Only the Corsican remained silent and cold.

"Say," said the host as the laughter following another anecdote had subsided, "tell us this, man of the world, lover of Egyptian Isis priestesses, Gallic druidesses, raven-haired daughters of Syria and my own beautiful sisters in Hellas, you know and appreciate them all but tell us, have you ever loved a Germanic woman?"

"No," Cethegus replied as he sipped his Isis wine, "I have always found them too dull."

"I don't know about that," Kallistratos answered, "I think that is going too far. I tell you, not that long ago I felt a burning passion for a Germanic woman, who was not dull at all."

"What's this? You, Kallistratos of Corinth, countryman of Hellena and Aspasia, were aroused by a Barbarian? Oh treacherous Eros, bewilderer of the senses who puts men to shame!" the Prefect scolded.

"Yes, it was a bewilderment of my senses, if you like. Certainly I have never experienced anything like it."

"Tell us about it! Tell us!" the others urged.

Chapter 11

"Very well," said the host as he smoothed the wrinkles on his cushions, "I will tell you, even though my part in it is not one of which I am especially proud.

"A few weeks ago I was returning home from the baths of Abaskantos at about the eighth hour.

"Outside my house on the street there stood a woman's litter with four slaves, and outside my front door stood two veiled women, with their *calanticae* pulled over their heads. One of them was dressed like a slave, but the other one was dressed in a very tasteful and expensive manner, and by what little I could see of it her figure was divine. What graceful step, what delicate ankles and slender feet! When I approached both of them fled back into the litter, and in a flash they were gone. But as for me, you know that a sculptor's blood runs in the veins of every Greek, and that night I dreamed of those ankles and that graceful step.

"Next day, as I opened my door to go to the bibliographers in the Forum, I saw the same litter hurrying away. I must confess, without being vain, that I was hoping that I might have made a conquest for once, and I certainly wanted to. My doubts disappeared altogether when I returned home at the eighth hour; there was my stranger, alone this time, but before I could speak she had slipped past me and into her litter. I could not follow the fast clip of the slaves, and so I went into my house, full of happy thoughts. As I entered my *ostiarius* said: 'Master, a veiled slave woman is waiting for you in the library.'

"My heart beating wildly, I hurried into the room. Sure enough, it was the same slave I had seen the day before. She drew back her mantle, and a very pretty, intelligent-looking and dark skinned woman was looking at me slyly. I'd say she was a Moor or a Carthaginian. 'I ask a messenger's reward,' she said, 'Kallistratos, I bring you glad tidings.'

"I took her hand and tried to stroke her dark cheek – for he who desires the mistress kisses the slave – but she laughed and said, 'No, not Eros sent me here, but Hermes. My mistress—' I was listening attentively '—is a great, a great patron of the arts. She offers you three thousand *solidi* for the Ares bust in the niche next to the door of your house."

The young men laughed out loud, Cethegus with them.

"Yes, you can laugh," the host continued, nodding agreement. "But I did not laugh at the time. My dreams so abruptly shattered I said crossly: 'It is not for sale.' The slave offered me five thousand, and then ten thousand *solidi*, but I turned my back on her and reached for the door.

"And then the little snake said: 'I know that Kallistratos of Corinth is angry, because he was hoping for amorous adventure but is offered only money. He is a Greek, loves all things of beauty, and is burning with curiosity to see my mistress.' She was so right that all I could do was smile.

"'Very well,' she said, 'you shall see her. And then I will renew my last offer. If you still refuse it, then at least you will have satisfied your curiosity. Tomorrow at the eighth hour the litter will return. Be ready with your Ares.'

"And she slipped away. Restless, I remained behind.

"I could not deceive her, for my curiosity was indeed very much aroused. I firmly made up my mind not to part with the Ares, but to see the art lover just the same, and waited impatiently for the appointed hour. At last it came, and with it came the litter. I stood waiting at my open door. The slave stepped out.

"'Come,' she said to me, 'you shall see her.'

"Trembling with anticipation I approached. The purple curtains of the litter half opened and I saw—"

"Well?" called Marcus, leaning forward, goblet in hand.

"Something I will never forget! A face, friends, of a beauty I had never even dreamed could exist. Cypris and Artemis in one! I was as if blinded. I just cannot describe her. The curtains closed and I sprang back. Then I took the Ares from its niche and handed it to the Punian. I refused her gold and stumbled back into my house stunned, as if I had seen a nymph."

"Well now, that's really something," Massurius laughed. "After all, you are not usually a novice in the works of Eros."

"But how do you know she was Gothic?" Cethegus asked.

"She had rich red hair, milky white skin and black eyebrows."

"All ye gods in heaven!" Cethegus thought to himself, but he said nothing and waited. None of those present spoke her name.

"When did all this happen, did you say?" he asked of the host.

"A month ago."

"That fits," Cethegus calculated in his mind. "That was when she was coming from Tarentum through Rome to Ravenna, and rested here for three days. It must have been Matesuentha." But he said nothing, as it was obvious that none of the other guests knew her.

"And so," Piso laughed, "you sacrificed your Ares for a look. A very poor bargain! This time Venus and Mercury ganged up on you together. Poor Kallistratos."

"Oh," said the latter, "the bust was not worth all that much. It was a modern work. Jon in Naples made it about three years ago. But I tell you this. I would gladly have given a Phidias for that sight."

"A traditional head?" Cethegus asked, feigning indifference, and seemingly looking at the bronze jar standing in front of him.

"No, the model was a Barbarian, some Gothic count, Watigis or Witigas, how can anyone remember those boring barbaric names!" Kallistratos answered as he concluded his story and started peeling a peach.

Cethegus was deep in thought as he sipped from his amber goblet.

Chapter 12

"Yes, the Barbarian women are not hard to take," cried Marcus Licinius, "but may Orcus swallow their brothers!" and as he said it he ripped the wreath of white roses from his head, replacing it with a fresh one. Flowers wilted quickly in the heat. "They have not only robbed us of our freedom, but by the daughters of Hesperia, they even best us in love. Only the other day the lovely Lavina slammed her door in my brother's face and admitted that redheaded Aligern."

"Who can fathom the taste of a Barbarian?" the scorned Lucius commented, shrugging his shoulders as he reached for his Isis wine for consolation. "You know her too, Furius. Don't you think that she has become confused in her tastes?"

"I don't know your rival," the Corsican replied, "but there are lads among these Goths who could well be dangerous with women.

"And that reminds me of an adventure, which I only found out about recently, although admittedly it is as yet unfinished."

"Go on and tell us about it," Kallistratos encouraged him as he dipped his hands into a bronze basin of warm water, being handed to him by a slave, "perhaps we will find an ending."

"The hero of my story," Furius began, "is the handsomest young man among the Goths."

"Ah, young Totila," Piso interrupted while his goblet was being refilled with iced wine.

"The very same. I have known him for many years and I like him, as must anyone who has ever set eyes on his sunny face, quite apart from the fact—" and here a dark shadow crossed the Corsican's face, like a sad memory, and he hesitated for a moment "—that I am obligated to him for other reasons."

"It sounds as if you are in love with the blond boy," Massurius teased as he threw a packet of Pizentian biscuits to his slave to take home.

"No, but he has done me many favours, as he tends to do for everyone he deals with, and he was often in charge of the harbour garrison in the Italian seaports where my ships landed."

"Yes, he has done a great deal to strengthen the Gothic navy," said Lucius Licinius.

"And their cavalry too," Marcus added, "he is the best horseman among his people."

"Well, I last met him in Naples. We were both pleased to see one another, but no matter how hard I tried I could not persuade him to come and join one of the late and merry banquets on my ship."

"Oh, your ship's banquets are both famous and notorious," Balbus remarked, "you always serve only the finest of wines."

"And the fieriest of wenches!" Massurius added.

"Be that as it may, Totila always offered an excuse of having business to attend to, and could not be persuaded otherwise. Now I ask you! Business in Naples, after the eighth hour? Where even the most industrious people are lazy? They were excuses of course, and I decided to catch him out. One night I silently sneaked around his house in the Via Lata. Sure enough, on that very first night he came out, looked about him very carefully, and much to my astonishment he was dressed as a gardener. He wore a wide brimmed hat pulled down low over his face, and had an *abolla* wrapped around him. I followed him silently. He walked right through the city toward the Porta Capuana. Right next to the gate there is a thick tower, and in it lives an old patriarchal Jew, whom King Theodoric entrusted with the responsibility for the gate as a reward for his great loyalty.

My Gothic friend stopped outside the gate and quietly clapped his hands. And then a little side door of iron, which I had never noticed before, opened silently and Totila slipped inside as quietly as an eel."

"Oho," Piso interjected with enthusiasm, "I know the Jew and Miriam, his beautiful bright-eyed child. The loveliest daughter of Israel and pearl of the Occident. Her lips are like pomegranates, her eyes are deep blue as the sea, and her cheeks have the rich aroma of a peach."

"Well said, Piso," Cethegus smiled, "your poem is delightful."

"No," Piso replied, "Miriam herself is living poetry."

"The Jewish wench is certainly proud," Massurius grumbled, "she scorned me and my gold with a look as if no woman had ever been bought for money."

"Imagine that," said Lucius Licinius, "so that arrogant Goth, who walks about as if he was carrying the stars of heaven on his blond head, has stooped to bedding a Jewess."

"That's what I thought, and I made up my mind to tease the lad about his poor taste at the first opportunity. But that was not to be. A few days later I had to go to Capua, and left before sunrise to escape the worst of the heat. Just as dawn broke I was driving through the Porta Capuana, and as my coach rattled past the Jew's tower I thought enviously of Totila, who I imagined was enjoying the bliss of tender arms. But as I passed the second milestone beyond the gate I saw the figure of a man coming toward me in the opposite direction, carrying empty flower baskets and dressed as a gardener as before – it was Totila. So he was not lying in Miriam's arms! The Jewess was not his lover, but perhaps his confidante, and who knows where the flower blooms that this gardener tends so devotedly. Lucky devil! Just think, the Via Capuana is lined with the villas and pleasure palaces of the noblest families in Naples, and the most gorgeous of women glitter and bloom in those gardens."

"By my soul," Lucius Licinius cried as he raised his goblet to his lips, "the most beautiful women in Italy live there – a curse on the Goths!"

"No!" Massurius shouted back, glowing from the effects of the wine. "A curse on Kallistratos and the Corsican, for telling us strange love stories and whetting our appetites, just as the stork serves the fox nectar in tall glasses, from which he cannot drink. Come, worthy host, bring on the girls if indeed you have organised some. There is no need to raise our expectations any higher."

"Yes, the girls, the dancers, the singers!" the young men noisily concurred.

"Halt," the host replied, "where Aphrodite approaches she must walk on a bed of flowers. This glass, Flora, is for you!" He jumped to his feet and hurled a precious crystal wineglass against the panelled ceiling, where it shattered into many pieces.

As soon as the glass struck the beams of the ceiling the entire panelling rose upwards like a trapdoor, and a thick shower of flowers of many types rained down on the heads of the astonished guests. There were roses from Paestum, violets from Thurii, myrtles from Tarentum, almond blossoms and many others, which soon covered the mosaic floor like a thick layer of snow. The tables, the cushions and even the heads of the guests were equally covered in a blanket of flowers.

"Never," said Cethegus, "has Venus arrived at Paphos more beautifully."

Kallistratos clapped his hands. At this sign the wall directly opposite the *triclineum* divided, accompanied by the sound of lyres and flutes. Four exceptionally beautiful girls in scanty Persian gowns of transparent pink gauze danced out of a thicket of flowering oleander bushes, playing cymbals.

Behind them came a wagon in the shape of a seashell, with golden wheels, pushed by eight young girls. Four pretty flautists in Lydian gowns of purple and white, with mantles embroidered in gold, walked ahead of the wagon. On the wagon lay, covered in roses, Aphrodite herself. She was an extraordinarily beautiful girl, a luxuriously seductive temptress, half reclining on a bed of cushions and wearing nothing but the thin belt of the three graces copied from Aphrodite.

"Holy Eros and Anteros!" Massurius exclaimed and leapt from his couch into the group with uncertain step.

"Let's draw lots for the girls!" Piso suggested, "I have a new set of gazelle bone dice. Let's consecrate them!"

"Let the festival king distribute them," Marcus suggested.

"No, freedom, at least let us have freedom in love," Massurius cried as he grabbed the arm of the goddess, "and let's have some music. Hey there, music!"

"Music!" Kallistratos ordered.

But before the cymbal players were able to start playing again the entrance door was violently thrown open. Pushing aside the slaves who tried to stop him, Scaevola stormed in, deathly pale.

"Here I find you at last, Cethegus! In a moment like this?"

"What's the trouble?" the Prefect asked calmly, removing his wreath of roses.

"What's the trouble, you ask! The fatherland sways between Scylla and Charybdis. The Gothic dukes Thulun, Ibba and Pitza—"

"What about them?" Lucius Licinius asked.

"They have been murdered!"

"Triumph!" the Roman exclaimed, letting go of the dancer he was holding in his arms.

"A fine triumph!" the lawyer retorted angrily. "When the news reached Ravenna everyone blamed the queen. They stormed the palace, but Amalasuntha had fled."

"Where to?" Cethegus asked, jumping to his feet.

"Where to? She is on a Greek ship, on her way to Byzantium!"

Cethegus silently set down his goblet on the table, and furrowed his brow.

"But the worst of it is that the Goths want to depose her and elect a king."

"A king?" Cethegus asked. "Very well, I will assemble the Senate. The Romans too shall choose."

"Whom or what are we going to choose?" Scaevola asked.

But Cethegus did not have to answer. In his place Lucius Licinius called out: "A dictator! On your feet and to the Senate!"

"To the Senate!" Cethegus repeated majestically. "Syphax, my cloak."

"Here, master, and your sword," the Moor whispered. "I always take it with me, just in case."

Host and guests alike stumbled after the Prefect who, the only one among them who was completely sober, led them from the house and into the street.

Chapter 13

A few weeks after the feast of the *Floralia*, a rather short man stood in one of the long and narrow rooms of the Imperial Palace in Byzantium. He was unimpressive in appearance, and seemed to be deep in thought.

All around him it was quiet, and he was quite alone.

Although it was still broad daylight outside, the round window which opened onto the courtyard of the huge building was draped with heavy gold embroidered rugs. Equally precious carpets covered the mosaic floor of the room, so that our thinker made no sound as he paced up and down.

The room was filled by a dull half light, and its golden walls were adorned with a long row of small white busts, representing all the Christian Imperators since Constantine. A huge cross of solid gold, as tall as a man, hung on the wall above the writing divan.

Each time the man passed the cross as he paced up and down the room he bowed his head in front of it, for a splinter of what was claimed to be the original cross was set in glass in its centre.

At last he stopped before the world map, which covered an entire wall. It was drawn up on parchment bordered with purple, and represented the *Orbis Romanus*. After a long, searching look at the map the man sighed, and covered his face and eyes with his hands.

They were not attractive eyes, nor were they set in a noble face, and yet much was written on that face, both good and bad. The restless gaze of the deep-set eyes suggested alertness, and a cunning and suspicious mind. Deep lines, more from worry than age, had etched themselves into the high forehead and thin cheeks.

"If only I knew the answer!" he sighed once more, rubbing his bony hands together. "It drives me constantly. It is as if a ghost has entered my breast and it drives me, on and on. But is it an angel of the Lord, or is it a demon? If only someone could interpret my dream! Forgive me, almighty God, forgive your most devoted servant. You have cursed those who interpret dreams.

"And yet King Pharaoh dreamed, and you permitted Joseph to interpret his own dream. Jacob saw the gates of heaven open up in a dream, and all their dreams came from you. Should I – dare I risk it?"

Once more he paced up and down uncertainly, and who knows how much longer he might have gone on doing so if the curtain at the end of the room had not been silently raised.

A *valerius*, glittering with gold, prostrated himself before the little man and crossed his arms on his chest.

"Imperator, the patricians you summoned are here."

"Patience," the little man thus addressed replied, seating himself on a couch which was encrusted with gold and ivory. "Quickly, the silver shoes and the *Chamys*."

The palace servant removed the thick soled sandals from his master's feet, and replaced them with silver shoes with equally thick soles and high heels, which served to make their wearer seem an inch or two taller. A folded mantle, covered with gold stars, was draped around the monarch's shoulders, and the servant kissed every item of apparel as he touched it. After a further bow – this humiliating Oriental gesture had only recently been reinforced at court – he left.

Emperor Justinian placed himself in his "audience position", resting his left arm on a broken column from the temple in Jerusalem, which had been cut down to match his height, and faced the entrance.

The curtain was drawn back, and three men entered after first prostrating themselves just as the slave had done. Yet these were the three leading men in the Empire, which was evident not only from the richness of their dress, but also from their proud heads and aristocratic faces.

"We have summoned you here," the emperor began without returning their submissive greeting, "to hear your advice – about Italy. We have given you all the necessary information regarding the situation there, including the letters from the queen and the documents from the patriotic party. You have had three days in which to study and consider them. You speak first, *Magister Militum*."

He pointed to the tallest of the three, a splendid and heroic figure of a man, who wore a suit of armour richly decorated with gold. His large brown eyes spoke of loyalty and confidence, and a strong straight nose and well rounded cheeks gave his face a forceful and youthful look. His broad chest and his powerful arms and thighs had a Herculean look about them, but his mouth indicated gentleness and kindness in spite of the fierce round beard.

"Imperator," he said in a deep, resonant voice, "Belisarius always gives the same advice. Let us attack the Barbarians! I have just smashed the Vandal Empire at your command, with fifteen thousand men. Give me thirty thousand, and I will lay Theodoric's crown at your feet."

"Well said," the emperor responded, obviously pleased, "your words have done me good. What do you say, Tribonianus, prince among my law scholars?"

The man thus addressed was a little shorter than Belisarius, but not as broad shouldered, or powerfully built. His high forehead, calm and serious eyes and firm mouth suggested a formidable intellect coupled with forthrightness and honesty. "Imperator," he said, choosing his words carefully, "I warn against this war. It is unjust."

Justinian retorted angrily: "Unjust? To take back part of the Roman Empire is unjust?"

"Was a part. Your forebear Zeno agreed under a contract to leave the Occident to Theodoric and his Goths, once they had overthrown the usurper Odoacer."

"Theodoric was to be a governor representing the emperor, not the king of Italy."

"Agreed. But once he became king, as he had to because Theodoric could never serve a lesser man than himself in emperor Anastasius, your uncle Justinus and yourself recognised both him and his kingdom."

"Only out of pressing need. Now that the danger is over, and I am in a position of strength, I take it back."

"That precisely is what I call unjust."

"You are being clumsy and awkward, Tribonianus, and as ever a stubborn stickler for the law. You do well compiling my laws, but I will never again seek your advice in political matters. What has justice to do with politics?"

"Justice, oh Justinianus, is the only enduring policy."

"Nonsense, Alexander and Caesar thought otherwise."

"True, but firstly they did not complete their tasks, and secondly…" he hesitated.

"Well, and secondly?"

"Secondly you are not Caesar or Alexander."

All were silent. After a pause the emperor said calmly: "You are very frank, Tribonianus."

"Always, Justinianus."

Quickly the emperor turned to the third man. "And what is your opinion, *Patricius?*"

Chapter 14

The man to whom these words were directed quickly banished from his lips the smile of detached amusement, which the lawyer's discourse on morality in politics had produced.

He was a crippled, little man, considerably shorter even than Justinian, inducing the latter to lower his head even more than was necessary when speaking to him. He was bald, with his cheeks the sickly yellow colour of wax. His right shoulder was higher than his left, and he dragged his left foot, which caused him to lean on a black crutch with a golden handle. But his eyes had the piercing look of an eagle, and the power in those eyes ensured that even this miserable figure of a man could not be described as ugly or repulsive. It was those very eyes which gave his otherwise plain face a look of intellectual greatness, but his features also spoke of much past suffering. Altogether his face could only be described as fascinating.

"Imperator," he now said confidently in a firm voice, "I advise against this war, for the present."

The emperor's eyes twitched with displeasure: "Are you also troubled by questions of justice and morality?" he asked, almost scornfully.

"I said for the present."

"And why is that?"

"Because necessity comes before whim. One who needs to defend his own house should not break into the houses of others."

"And what is that supposed to mean?"

"It means this. From the west, from the Goths, no danger presently threatens this Empire. The enemy who could destroy it, and quite possibly will do so one day, comes from the east."

"The Persians!" Justinian said, disgust in his voice.

"Since when," Belisarius interrupted, "since when does Narses, my great rival, fear the Persians?"

"Narses fears nobody," the latter replied, "not the Persians, whom he has defeated, nor you who was defeated by them. But he knows the Orient well. If it is not the Persians then it will be others coming after them. The storm which threatens Byzantium is brewing near the Tigris, not the Tiber."

"What do you mean by that?"

"I mean that it is shameful for you, my emperor, to have to buy the title 'Romans' by which we still call ourselves, from Chosroes the Persian Khan every year with many hundredweight of gold."

The emperor's face reddened noticeably: "How can you interpret gifts and aid money as tribute?"

"Gifts! If they are not forthcoming one week after the due date Chosroes, son of Cabades, burns your villages. Aid money! He uses it to pay Huns and Saracens, your most dangerous enemies."

Justinian was pacing rapidly through the room. "What, then, do you advise?" he asked finally, halting in front of Narses.

"Do not attack the Goths without need and without reason, while you can barely hold the Persians at bay. I advise you to concentrate all the might of your Empire and stop these shameful tributes, to put an end to the devastation of your borders, to rebuild the ruined cities of Antiochia, Dara and Edessa, and to win back the provinces in the east, which you lost in spite of Belisarius's brave sword. Next, you should fortify your borders from the Euphrates to the Araxes. And when you have completed all these necessary works, which I fear you will not be able to do, then and only then you may try to gain those laurels which now tempt you so."

"You do not please me, Narses," Justinian said bitterly.

"I have known that for a long time," the latter replied.

"You are not indispensable!" Belisarius said proudly. "Don't listen to these faint-hearted doubters, my great emperor. Give me the thirty thousand, and I will wager my right hand that I can capture Italy for you."

"And I will wager my head, which is worth a lot more," Narses retorted, "that Belisarius will not conquer Italy, not with thirty, not with sixty and not with a hundred thousand men."

"Oh?" Justinian asked, "who can do it then, and with what force?"

"I can," Narses replied calmly, "with eighty thousand."

Belisarius was livid with rage, but remained silent because he could not think of a reply.

"Even you, with all your conceit, have never rated yourself that highly above your rival," the lawyer remarked.

"Nor am I doing so now, Tribonianus. You see, the difference is this: Belisarius is a great hero, which I am not. But I am a great general, which Belisarius is not. And only a great general will defeat the Goths."

Belisarius stood up to his full height, clutching the hilt of his sword with his clenched fist. It seemed as if he was about to crush the cripple's head. But the emperor spoke in his place: "Belisarius not a great general? Narses, your envy is blinding you."

"I do not envy Belisarius anything, not even his health," Narses sighed softly. "He could be a great general if he was not such a great hero. Every battle he has ever lost he lost because of too much heroics."

"Nobody can say that of you, Narses," Belisarius interjected bitterly.

"Certainly not, Belisarius, for I have never lost a battle."

An angry reply by Belisarius was cut off by the entry of the *valerius* through the curtain.

"Alexandros, whom you sent to Ravenna, my lord, has landed an hour ago and asks—"

"Bring him in, bring him in!" Justinian cried impatiently as he jumped up from his couch. He motioned to the ambassador, who was prostrate on the floor, to rise: "Alexandros, you return alone?"

The ambassador, a handsome and still quite young man, repeated: "Alone."

"But your last report said – how did you leave the Gothic Empire?"

"In the midst of great confusion. I wrote to you in my last report that the queen had decided to rid herself of three of her most arrogant enemies. If the attempt failed she would no longer be safe in Italy, and in that event she asked my permission to board my ship, to take her to Epidamnus. From there she would then flee here, to Byzantium."

"To which I agreed. What happened with the assassination attempt?"

"It succeeded, and the three dukes are no more. But a rumour reached Ravenna that the most dangerous of the three, Duke Thulun, was only wounded. That influenced the queen, who was already concerned over large hordes of Goths gathering in front of her palace, to seek refuge aboard my ship. We promptly weighed anchor, but after we had left the harbour and had reached the vicinity of Ariminum Count Witigis overhauled us with a superior force. He came on board and demanded Amalasuntha's return, vouching for her safety until the matter was formally investigated by a full congress of her people. When she learned from him that Duke Thulun had also died from his wounds, and also that Witigis and his friends did not yet believe her guilty, she agreed, particularly as she had reason to fear that force would be used against her if she did otherwise. But before returning to Ravenna with Witigis she wrote you this letter on board the *Sophia*, and sends you these gifts from her treasury."

"We will look at those later. Continue, what is the situation in Italy now?"

"Favourable to you, oh Imperator. The exaggerated reports of the Gothic rebellion in Ravenna, and of the queen's flight to Byzantium, quickly raced right through the country. There have already been a number of clashes between the Romans and the Barbarians. In Rome itself the patriots wanted to start fighting on their own, to elect a dictator in the senate, and to implore your help. But all that would have been premature once the queen was in the hands of Witigis. Only the genial leader of the catacombs conspiracy was able to prevent it."

"The Prefect of Rome?" Justinian asked.

"Cethegus. He did not trust the rumours. The conspirators wanted to ambush every Goth in the city and proclaim you emperor, meanwhile electing him dictator. But in the *curia*, even though they literally held daggers to his breast, he said no."

"A brave man!" Belisarius remarked.

"A dangerous man!" Narses added.

"An hour later news of Amalasuntha's return reached Rome, and everything remained the same. But that black Teias had sworn to turn Rome into pasture if a single drop of Gothic blood was shed. I heard all this during my journey along the coast to Brundusium. But I have even better news! I have found eager friends and allies of Byzantium, not only among the Romans but among the Goths themselves, in fact among members of the royal house itself."

"And who might that be?" Justinian asked.

"In Tuscany there lives Amalasuntha's cousin Count Theodahad. He is extremely wealthy and owns large estates there."

"Is he not also the last male member of the Amalung dynasty?"

"Indeed he is the last. He hates the queen, and his wife Gothelindis, who is a clever but evil daughter of the Balti clan, hates her even more. He hates her because she stands in the way of his boundless greed, in particular his attempts to acquire the properties of all his neighbours. She hates the queen passionately, for reasons which I have not been able to determine, but I believe they go right back to when both princesses were only girls. In any event her hatred is deadly. Now these two have promised me that they will help you regain Italy in any way they can. She seems to be content merely to see her hated enemy fall from the throne, but he of course demands a rich reward."

"He shall have it."

"His help is important because he already owns half of Tuscany, and can easily ensure that it falls into our hands. The noble Woelsung family owns the other half. His ambition, once Amalasuntha is toppled, is to succeed her on the throne, and that would also serve us well. Here are letters from him, and from Gothelindis. But read the letter from Amalasuntha first. I think it is very important."

Chapter 15

The emperor cut the purple ribbons which held together the bundle of wax tablets and read: "To Justinianus, Imperator of the Romans, Amalasuntha, Queen of the Goths and the Italians!"

"Queen of the Italians," Justinian laughed, "what a crazy title."

"From your envoy Alexandros you will learn how Eris and Ate are running wild in this country. I am like a lonely palm, which is being torn to pieces by strong winds blowing in opposite directions. The Barbarians are becoming more hostile towards me every day, and the Romans will never forget that I am of Germanic origin, no matter how much I try to get closer to them. Until now I have been able to deal resolutely with all these dangers, but I cannot go on doing so unless at least my palace and my royal person are safe from sudden violence. Regrettably I cannot rely absolutely on any of the factions in my country here.

"I therefore now appeal to you, as my brother in royal dignity, for help. The majesty of all sovereigns as well as peace in Italy must be protected.

"I beg of you to send me a reliable force of men, a bodyguard—" the emperor looked significantly at Belisarius "—a force of a few thousand men with a leader who is totally dedicated to me. They shall occupy the palace in Ravenna, which is a fortress in itself. As far as Rome is concerned, this force must above all keep the Prefect Cethegus away from me, and even destroy him if that becomes necessary. He is as powerful as he is duplicitous, and has suddenly deserted me in the very danger into which he himself has led me. Once I have overthrown my enemies and secured my Empire, as I trust in heaven and my own strength I will do, I will return your troops and their leader to you with rich presents. *Vale!*"

Justinian was clutching the tablets in his fist. Eyes aglow, he looked straight in front of him, and a look of mental and intellectual might gave his face an air of majesty. It was obvious at this moment that, along with many weaknesses and much pettiness, there lived in this man a spark of greatness too, the greatness of a diplomatic genius.

"With this letter," he said at last, "I hold Italy and the Gothic Empire in my hand." Majestically he now strode through the room, taking giant strides, even forgetting now to bow before the cross.

"A bodyguard – she shall have it! But not a few thousand men, many thousands, too many for her comfort, and you, Belisarius, will lead them."

"Don't forget to look at the gifts," Alexandros reminded the monarch, pointing to a chest of rosewood inlaid with gold, which the *valerius* had put down beside him. "Here is the key." He handed over a small tortoiseshell box, sealed with Amalasuntha's seal. "Her picture is in there too," he added in a slightly raised voice.

As soon as the envoy raised his voice, unnoticed by all but him, the head of a woman appeared silently through the curtains, and two gleaming black eyes were looking sharply at the emperor. The latter opened the treasure chest, quickly pushed all the precious gifts aside, and reached for a modest little boxwood tablet with a narrow golden frame. A quite unintentional cry of astonishment escaped his lips, and his eyes sparkled as he showed the picture to Belisarius: "What a magnificent woman, look at that majestic forehead! You can see she is a born ruler, a king's daughter." With that he looked admiringly at Amalasuntha's noble features.

At this moment the curtain rustled, and our eavesdropper entered.

She was Theodora, the empress, a seductively beautiful woman. All the cosmetic arts of that era of immense luxury, together with all the means an Empire could muster, were employed for hours each day in order to preserve this beauty, in itself outstanding but already affected at an early age by a life of unrestrained licentiousness.

Gold dust gave her blue-black hair a metallic sparkle. It had been combed upwards from the nape of her neck, in order to better show off her beautiful head and slender neck.

Eyebrows and lashes were dyed black with Arabian mascara, and the red colour of her lips had been applied so expertly that even Justinian, who kissed these lips, never suspected that nature might have been given a helping hand with Phoenician purple. Every hair on her alabaster white arms had been carefully removed, and the delicate pink of her fingernails occupied a slave girl for a long time every day.

And yet Theodora, who at that time was not yet forty, would have been an extraordinary beauty even without all these tricks.

Certainly this face could not be called noble. Her strained, shining eyes did not look capable of a great or even proud thought. A habitual smile played about her lips, suggesting where the first wrinkle would appear in time, and her cheeks showed signs of tiredness and even exhaustion, especially around the eyes.

But as she now floated toward Justinian with her sweetest smile, delicately raising her heavy gown of deep yellow silk with her left hand, her whole appearance was one of stunning and almost magical beauty, not unlike the aroma of Indian balsam which accompanied her.

"What is it that pleases my royal master so? May I share his pleasure?" she asked with a sweet, flattering voice. Those present prostrated themselves before the empress, almost as humbly as they had previously done before Justinian.

The latter was alarmed at the sight of her, as if he had been caught red-handed, and tried to hide the picture in the folds of his *Chamys*. But it was too late. The sharp eyes of the empress had already spotted it.

"We were admiring," he said, somewhat embarrassed, "the – the beautiful workmanship of the golden frame." Reddening, he handed her the picture.

Theodora smiled: "Really there is little to admire in the frame. But the picture is not bad. The Gothic queen I suppose?" The envoy nodded. "Not bad, as I said, but barbaric, severe and unfeminine. How old is she, Alexandros?"

"About forty-five."

Justinian looked questioningly at the picture, and then at the envoy. "The picture was made about fifteen years ago," the latter said, as if by way of an explanation.

"No, you are wrong," said the emperor, "here is the year according to consul and her reign. It was made this year."

There was an embarrassed pause, and the envoy stammered: "Painters flatter, like—"

"Like lackeys," the emperor concluded. But now Theodora came to his aid.

"Why are we discussing pictures and the age of strange women when the Empire is at stake? What news does Alexandros bring? Have you made up your mind, Justinianus?"

"Almost. I only wanted to hear your advice, and I know that you favour war."

As soon as he had said this Narses calmly said: "Why, master, did you not tell us at the beginning that the empress wants war? We could have saved our words."

"What? Are you saying that I am my wife's slave?"

"You had better guard your tongue," Theodora said angrily, "many men who thought themselves invulnerable have been stabbed by their own sharp tongues."

"You are not being at all cautious, Narses," Justinian warned.

"Imperator," the latter replied calmly, "I have long abandoned caution. We are living in a time, in an Empire and at a court where every word which one does or does not speak can bring about disgrace or downfall. And since every word can bring about my death, I may as well die for words which please me."

The emperor smiled: "You must admit, *Patricius*, that I put up with a great deal from you."

Narses approached him: "You are a great man, Justinianus, and a born ruler, otherwise Narses would not serve you. But Omphala made even Hercules small."

The eyes of the empress glowed with deadly hate. Justinian was becoming alarmed.

"Go," he said, "I wish to confer with the empress alone. You will hear my decision tomorrow."

Chapter 16

As soon as the others had left the room, Justinian went over to his wife and kissed her on her white temple. "Forgive him," he said, "he means well."

"I know," she replied, returning his kiss. "For that reason, and because he is indispensable against Belisarius, he is still alive."

"You are right, as always." And he placed his arm about her.

"I wonder what's on his mind?" Theodora thought to herself, "whenever he is affectionate like that it is usually a sign of a bad conscience."

"You are right," he repeated, walking up and down the room with her. "God has denied me the kind of mind which wins battles, but He has given me instead these two men of victory – fortunately there are two of them. The rivalry between these two secures my throne much better than their friendship ever could. By himself either one of these two great generals would be a constant threat to the Empire, and my Empire would totter the day they ever became friends. You are still fanning their hatred, I trust?"

"That is only too easy to do. There is a natural enmity between them as there is between fire and water. I report in delicious detail every sarcastic remark Narses makes to my friend Antonina, to whom Belisarius is not only husband but also obedient servant."

"And I report every coarse remark Belisarius makes to the excitable little cripple. But now to our business. After receiving the report from Alexandros I have virtually made up my mind to march into Italy."

"Whom do you propose to send?"

"Belisarius of course. He promises to do with thirty thousand what Narses would undertake only reluctantly with eighty thousand."

"Do you think that such a small army will be sufficient?"

"No, but Belisarius has pledged his honour that he will succeed. He will use up all his might, and yet he will not quite succeed."

"And that will do him a lot of good. Since his victory over the Vandals his pride has become unbearable."

"But he will do three quarters of the work. Then I will recall him, set out myself with sixty thousand, take Narses with me and finish off the last quarter with ease. Then I will also be a general and a victor."

"Well thought out!" Theodora said, with honest admiration of his cunning, "your plan is sound."

"Of course," Justinian said as he stopped with a sigh, "Narses is right, and in my heart I have to admit it. It would be better for the Empire to repel the Persians rather than attack the Goths. It would be a safer, wiser policy. Because as he says, our ruin will one day come from the east."

"Let it come! That might take centuries yet, and by that time all that will remain of Justinian in this world is his fame, for having recaptured not only Africa but Italy too.

Must it be your task to build for eternity? Let those who come after you look after their present, and you look after yours."

"But what if future generations were to say: 'if only Justinian had defended instead of attacking the end result would have been better.' What if they say that Justinian's victories destroyed his Empire?"

"Nobody will say that. Men are blinded by the glitter of fame. And there is one more thing…" As she said this, a look of deep and sincere conviction displaced the flattering smile from her face.

"I think I know what you are thinking, but say it anyway."

"You are not only an emperor, you are also human. Therefore you must concern yourself with the future of your own soul even more than you do with the affairs of your Empire. On your way to the throne, indeed on our way to the throne, with all its glory, many a difficult step had to be taken, and many a bloody deed had to be done. The lives and the treasure of many dangerous enemies – enough!

"It is true that we are using a portion of this treasure to build a temple of holy Christian wisdom, a temple of victory, which alone will ensure that our names become immortal on this earth. But as far as heaven is concerned – who knows? Who knows if we have done enough?

"Let us—" and her eyes were aglow with a sinister fire "—let us eradicate the infidels, and seek to find our way to Christ's forgiveness over the dead bodies of His enemies."

Justinian squeezed her hand. "The Persians are also enemies of Christ, in fact they are heathens."

"Have you forgotten what the patriarch taught? Heretics are seven times worse than heathens! They were shown the true faith, but they have spurned it. That is a sin against the Holy Ghost and will never be forgiven, on earth or in heaven. But yours is the sword which is destined to defeat these Arians whom God has cursed. They are Christ's worst enemies, for they know Him and yet they deny that He is God. You have already overthrown the heretic Vandals in Africa, and choked their heresies in blood and fire. And now Italy calls you, Rome, the city where the blood of the apostles flowed, the holy city. Rome must not serve these heretics any longer! Justinianus, give Rome back to the true faith!"

She paused. The emperor sighed deeply, and looked up at the huge gold cross. "You have uncovered the deepest recesses of my heart. That is what drives me to these wars, these victories, more strongly even than fame and honour. But am I able, am I worthy to achieve so much that is great and noble, to the honour of God? Does He really want to perform such a great work by means of my sinful hand? I have doubts, and often I wonder. And the dream I dreamt last night, did God send it? What does it mean? Is He telling me to attack, or to leave well enough alone. Your mother, the soothsayer of Cyprus, had great wisdom and the ability to interpret dreams. She would have known."

"The gift is hereditary, as you know. Didn't I predict the outcome of the war against the Vandals for you, from a dream?"

"You did, and you shall interpret this dream for me also. You know that I hesitate in carrying out even the most perfect plan, if an omen speaks against it. So hear me. But—" he looked at his wife, almost as if he was a little afraid "—remember that nobody can help what he dreams."

"Of course not. God sends them!" And to herself she added: "I wonder what I will hear?"

"I fell asleep last night while I was still weighing up in my mind the last report about Amala – about Italy. I dreamed that I was walking through a landscape with seven hills. There, asleep under a laurel tree, lay the most beautiful woman I had ever seen. I stood in front of her and admired her. Suddenly a roaring bear leapt from a bush on my left, and a hissing snake came out from among some rocks on my right, both about to attack the sleeper. She awoke and called my name, so I quickly picked her up, pressed her to my breast and fled with her. Looking back I saw how the bear tore the snake to pieces, and the snake bit the bear to death."

"And the woman?"

"The woman kissed me lightly on my forehead and then suddenly disappeared. I woke up reaching out for her in vain. The woman," he added quickly before Theodora had had time to think, "is of course Italy."

"Of course," the empress replied calmly, but her bosom was heaving. "Your dream is an excellent omen. The bear and the snake are the Barbarians and the Italians, fighting over the city of the seven hills. You tear it away from them both, and let them destroy each other."

"But I don't keep her – she gets away again."

"No, she kisses you and disappears into your arms, just as Italy will be absorbed into your Empire."

"You are right!" Justinian cried as he jumped to his feet. "Thank you, my clever wife. You are the light of my soul. Yes, I will dare it! Belisarius shall go!"

He was about to call the *valerius*. But then, suddenly, he stopped, took her hand and said with lowered eyes: "There is one more thing."

"Aha," thought Theodora, "here it comes."

"Once we have destroyed the Gothic Empire and moved into the palace in Ravenna with help from the queen herself, what – what is to become of her, the queen?"

"Well," Theodora replied innocently, "what is to become of her? Why, the same as what happened to the dethroned Vandal king. She will have to come here, to Byzantium."

Justinian heaved a deep sigh of relief: "I am pleased that you have found the right solution," and with genuine pleasure he squeezed her delicate little white hand.

"More than that," Theodora went on. "The more certain she is of being received with honour here, the more likely she is to agree to our plans. So I will write to her myself, a sisterly letter of invitation. If the worst comes to the worst, she will always find an asylum next to my heart."

"You have no idea," Justinian responded eagerly, "just how much you will aid our victory by doing that. Theodoric's daughter must become totally estranged from her own people and drawn over to us. She herself shall lead us into Ravenna."

"But it also means that you cannot send Belisarius with an army straight away. That would only make her suspicious and difficult. She must be completely in our hands, and the Barbarian Empire destroyed from within, before the sword of Belisarius ever leaves its scabbard."

"But he will need to be somewhere close to Italy, from now on."

"Yes, somewhere around Sicily. The unrest in Africa is a good pretext for sending a fleet into those waters. And as soon as the net is set, the arm of Belisarius will have to close it."

"But who is going to set the net in the first place?"

Theodora thought for a while, then she said: "The greatest mind in Europe. Cethegus Caesarius, the Prefect of Rome, my old friend."

"A good solution. But not he alone. He is a Roman and not my subject, and thus I cannot depend upon him absolutely. Whom shall I send? Alexandros again?"

"No," Theodora said quickly, "he is too young for such a task. No." She thought in silence for a while, and at last she said: "Justinian, to show you how I can put personal hatred aside where the Empire is concerned, and where the right man must be chosen, I myself will suggest my enemy. Send Petros, Narses's cousin, the Prefect's fellow student and a clever rhetorician – send him."

"Theodora," the emperor embraced her happily, "you really are a gift from heaven. Cethegus – Petros – Belisarius. Barbarians, your fate is sealed!"

Chapter 17

On the following morning the empress rose cheerfully from her thickly upholstered couch. Its soft pillows were covered with yellow silk, and filled with the soft neck feathers of the crane.

In front of the bed stood a tripod with a silver basin, made to represent the ocean, and in the basin lay a solid golden ball. The empress's soft hand casually lifted the ball and let it drop back into the basin, which resulted in a clear ringing sound. That sound brought a Syrian slave girl, who slept in the antechamber, into the room. She approached the bed with her arms crossed over her chest, and drew the heavy curtains of violet Chinese silk. Next she picked up a soft Iberian sponge, which lay in a crystal bowl soaking in ass's milk, and with it she started to carefully sponge away the mass of oily dough which had covered the face and neck of the empress during the night.

Once the dough had been removed she knelt on the floor beside the bed, her face almost touching the floor, and raised her right hand toward the empress. Theodora took the hand, carefully placed her foot on the girl's neck, and then lowered herself elastically to the floor. The slave girl rose and placed a richly embroidered pink dressing gown about the shoulders of her mistress, who had been sitting on the edge of the palm wood bed clad only in her under-tunic of the finest silk.

The girl then bowed, turned toward the door, called "Agave!" and disappeared. Agave, a beautiful young girl from Thessalia, entered, wheeling before her a little washing table of citrus wood, which she placed before her mistress. The table was covered with countless small bottles and jars. Next she began to gently rub Theodora's face, neck and hands with soft cloths, first dipped into a variety of salves and wines. "We will leave the main bath until midday," said Theodora as she rose from her bed and sat down on a colourful armchair, covered with otter fur.

Agave brought over an oval basin of turpentine wood, with a veneer of tortoiseshell on the outside, and filled with delightfully perfumed water, into which she placed the slender white feet of her mistress. Next she loosened the golden net which held the empress's black hair during the night, so that her blue-black tresses could fall freely over her shoulders. Finally she wound the purple bosom band around the empress, bowed and left with the call: "Galatea!"

An aged slave woman took her place. Galatea had been the young Theodora's wet nurse, lifelong companion and, it must be said, procuress in the days when she was merely the daughter of Acacius the lion tamer and, even though barely out of her childhood, already the depraved darling of the great circus. All the twists and turns, all the humiliations and reverses which this adventuress had endured on her changing path toward the throne of an Empire had been shared by Galatea.

"How did you sleep, my little dove?" she asked, handing her an amber bowl containing an amber essence, sent in huge quantities as tribute each year by the city of Adana in Sicily for the empress's toilet.

"Well, I dreamed of him."

"Of Alexandros?"

"No, you fool, of handsome Anicius."

"But Alexandros has been waiting outside in the secret niche for hours."

"He is impatient," her small mouth smiled, "let him in." She lay back on the long divan, pulling a covering of purple silk over herself, but ensuring that her pretty ankles were still visible.

Galatea bolted the main entrance, through which she herself had come in, and then crossed the chamber to a bronze statue of Justinian in the opposite corner. As soon as Galatea touched a secret spring the seemingly immovable colossal statue immediately moved aside, revealing a narrow opening in the wall which was normally completely hidden by the statue. A dark curtain had been drawn across the opening. Galatea raised it, and the handsome envoy Alexandros rushed into the room.

He threw himself on the floor at the feet of the empress, grasped her hand and covered it with passionate kisses.

Gently Theodora withdrew her hand. "It is very careless, Alexandros, to admit one's lover whilst dressing. What was it the poet said? 'Everything serves beauty. But seeing that being created, which pleases only when complete, is not a joyous sight.'

"But I promised you before you left for Ravenna that I would grant you admission during the morning hour some day, and you have richly deserved your reward. You have dared much for me – Galatea, grip the tresses more tightly!" Galatea had commenced the task of arranging her mistress's magnificent hair, which she alone was entrusted to do.

"You risked your life for me." And again she offered him two fingers of her right hand.

"Oh Theodora!" the young man exclaimed, "for this moment I would gladly die ten times over."

"But," she went on, "why didn't you let me have a copy of the Barbarian woman's last letter to Justinian?"

"It was no longer possible, as everything was happening too quickly. I just did not have time to send a messenger from my ship. In fact it was only with the greatest difficulty that I was able to get a message to you yesterday, about her picture being among the gifts. You came in at the right moment."

"Yes. I wonder what would become of me if I did not pay Justinian's guards and retainers double what he pays them? But you really are the most careless of all envoys! That business about the date on the picture was very clumsy."

"Oh, most beautiful daughter of Cyprus, I had not seen you for months. I could think of nothing but your overwhelming beauty!"

"In that case I suppose I will have to forgive you – the black headband, Galatea – you are a much better lover than you are a statesman. That is why I decided to keep you here. Yes, you were to have returned to Ravenna. But I thought I might send an older envoy, and keep you here for myself. Don't you agree?" She smiled, her eyes half closed.

This made Alexandros more passionate and more courageous. He sprang to his feet and pressed a burning kiss on her lips.

"Stop, you naughty boy, you are violating a monarch," she scolded him, and gently slapped his cheek with a fan of flamingo feathers. "That's enough for today. Tomorrow you may come back and tell me all about the Barbarian beauty. No, you must go now. I need the rest of this morning to see someone else."

"Someone else?" Alexandros cried, taking a step backwards. "So it's true what they whisper in the gymnasiums and baths of Byzantium! You, ever-faithless woman, have—"

"A friend of Theodora's must never be jealous!" The empress laughed, but it was not a pleasant laugh. "But this time you need not worry – you will see him yourself. Now go!"

Galatea gripped him by the shoulder and, although he resisted, pushed him behind the statue and out of the room without further ado.

Theodora now sat upright, and closed her flowing undergarment with her belt.

Chapter 18

Galatea promptly reappeared with a small, bent man, who looked much older than his forty years. His features were intelligent but too accentuated, and together with piercing eyes and a thin mouth they gave him a rather unpleasant sly look. Theodora returned his obsequious bow with a slight nod of her head, while Galatea commenced painting her eyebrows.

"Empress," the old man began fearfully, "I am amazed at your daring. What if someone was to see me? All the cunning and scheming of the last few years would come undone in an instant."

"But nobody will see you, Petros," Theodora replied calmly. "This is the only hour when I am safe from Justinian's oppressive affections. It is his prayer hour, and I have to make the best of it. May God preserve his piousness! – Galatea, the morning wine. What? Surely you are not afraid to leave me alone with this dangerous seducer!" The old woman left with a contemptuous grin, and soon returned with a jug of warmed and sweetened wine in one hand, and a cup of honey and water in the other.

"I could not arrange our meeting in church today, as we usually do, and where you give a fine impersonation of a priest in the dark confessional. The emperor will summon you before the church hour, and by then you must be fully informed."

"What is to be done?"

"Petros," Theodora said as she leaned back luxuriously, sipping the sweet mixture which Galatea had prepared, "today is the day we have long waited for, where all our cleverness and hard work of the last few years will be rewarded, and you will become a great man."

"It is about time," Petros remarked.

"Now don't be impatient, friend – Galatea, a little more honey. In order to put you in the right frame of mind for the business before us, let me remind you of the past, and the start of our – our friendship."

"What for? Why is that necessary?" the old man asked uncomfortably.

"For a number of reasons. Firstly you were a cousin and adherent of my mortal enemy Narses, and hence my enemy too. For years you worked against me in the service of your cousin. You did me little harm, but you did not do much for yourself either, because the virtuous Narses never does anything for his relatives, so that he cannot be accused of nepotism like so many other courtiers. Hence he never promoted you, and you suffered want and remained a simple scribe. But an intelligent head like yours is resourceful. You falsified and you doubled the emperor's tax edicts. The provinces were not only paying Justinian's taxes, but a second tax as well, which Petros and the tax gatherers shared between them. For a while it went perfectly, and then one day—"

"Empress, I beg of you—"

"I am almost finished, friend. But one day, unfortunately for you, there was a newly appointed tax gatherer, who cared more for the favour of his empress than he did for the promised share of the booty. He agreed to your proposition, let you forge a document for him, and – brought it to me."

"The miserable traitor," Petros grumbled.

"Yes, it was bad," Theodora smiled, setting her cup aside. "I now had all the evidence I needed to have you, the confidant of that wretched cripple I hate so much, beheaded. It was tempting, but I chose to exchange quick revenge for enduring advantage. I called you to me and gave you a choice. Either you died, or you henceforth served me. Wisely you chose the latter, and so we have been working together all these years, even though the world thinks we are still mortal enemies. You told me of every plan Narses made, even before it was complete, and I rewarded you well. You are now a rich man."

"Oh, it is hardly worth mentioning."

"Come, ungrateful one, my treasurer knows better. You are very wealthy indeed."

"Very well, it is true, but I do not have rank or honour. All my former fellow students are patricians, prefects and men of rank. Cethegus in Rome or Procopius in Byzantium, to name but two."

"Be patient. As from today you will rise very quickly. I always had to hold back something you really wanted to tempt you. Now listen. Tomorrow you will leave for Ravenna as an envoy."

"An Imperial envoy?" Petros cried delightedly.

"By my influence. But that is not everything. You will receive explicit instructions from Justinian to destroy the Gothic Empire, and to pave the way through Italy for Belisarius."

"Those instructions, do I follow them or foil them?"

"You follow them. But you will receive one further instruction, which Justinian will charge you to carry out before all else. You are to rescue Theodoric's daughter from her enemies at all cost, and bring her here to Byzantium. Here is a letter from me, inviting her warmly to my bosom."

"Very well," said Petros as he pocketed the letter, "I will bring her directly here to you."

Theodora shot up like a coiled snake, so that even Galatea drew back with fright. "Not if you value your life, Petros, never! That is why I am sending you. She must not come to Byzantium! She must not live!"

Petros let the letter fall, taken aback. "Oh empress," he whispered, "a murder?"

"Be silent!" Theodora hissed, demonic fire in her eyes. "She must die!"

"Die? But why, empress?"

"That is no concern of yours. No, stop, I will tell you. It will give your cowardice an incentive. Listen—" she gripped his arm and whispered in his ear "—Justinian, the traitor, is falling in love with her."

"Theodora!" Petros exclaimed, shocked. "But he has never even seen her!" he stammered.

"He has seen her picture. He already dreams of her, he is infatuated with that picture."

"You are so beautiful, and you have never had a rival."

"She is younger, and I will see to it that I never do have a rival."

"You are so clever, you are his adviser, privy to his most secret thoughts."

"That is exactly what he is starting to find troublesome. And note this! Amalasuntha is a king's daughter! She is a born ruler, while I am the lion tamer's child.

Ridiculous as it may sound, now that he wears the purple Justinian tends to forget that he himself is the son of a goatherd. Himself an adventurer, he has started to inherit the madness of kings. He is starting to rave about the majesty of royal birth, and about the mystique of royal blood. I have no defence against such whims. There is nothing I fear from any woman in the world, but this king's daughter." She jumped to her feet and clenched her fist.

"Beware, Justinian!" she said as she paced through the room. "Theodora has tamed and bewitched lions and tigers with these hands and with these eyes. Let's see if I cannot also keep this fox in purple faithful." She sat down again. "Enough, Amalasuntha dies!" she added, suddenly calm once more.

"Very well then, but not by my hand," Petros replied. "You have enough servants who are used to blood – send one of them. I am a man of words, not of blood."

"You will be a man of death if you do not obey. You, my enemy, are just the one to do it. None of my friends can kill her without arousing suspicion."

"Theodora," Petros warned, forgetting himself, "to murder Theodoric's daughter, a born queen—"

"Ha!" Theodora laughed fiercely. "So the born queen blinds even you, you miserable worm. All men are fools, even more than they are villains. Listen to me Petros, on the day news of her death reaches me here from Ravenna, that very day you will be a senator and a *patricius*."

These words made the old man's eyes sparkle, but cowardice and pangs of conscience were stronger even than ambition. Firmly he said: "No! I would rather leave the court and abandon all my plans."

"You will abandon your life, you miserable coward!" Theodora shouted angrily. "So you thought yourself free and out of danger because I burnt that forged document before your eyes all those years ago? You fool, it was not the real document! Look here, I hold your life in my hand."

From a capsule full of documents she withdrew a yellowed parchment, and showed it to the frightened Petros, who now fell to his knees without offering further resistance.

"Command," he stammered, "and I will obey."

At that moment a knock was heard on the main door.

"Away with you!" cried the empress. "Pick up my letter to the Gothic queen from the floor and think well. *Patricius*, if she dies, torture and death if she lives. Now be gone!"

At those words Galatea pushed the stunned man out of the secret exit, returned the bronze statue to its correct position, and went to open the main door.

Chapter 19

A woman of imposing appearance entered, taller and of a more solid build than the delicate empress. She was not as seductively beautiful as Theodora, but younger and fresher, a healthy, natural beauty.

"Greetings Antonina, my beloved sister! Come to my bosom!" the empress called out to the new arrival, who was bowing deeply.

The wife of Belisarius obeyed silently. "How hollow her eyes are becoming!" she thought to herself as she rose to her feet again.

"What coarse ankles the soldier's woman has!" the empress said to herself as she mustered her friend.

"You are blooming like a rose," she said out loud, "how the white silk brings out the freshness in your cheeks! Have you any news of – of him?" she asked, toying indifferently with a fearsome weapon which was lying on the table. It was a small lancet on an ivory shaft, with which clumsy or simply unfortunate slave girls were often stabbed an inch deep into their arms and shoulders by their angry mistress.

"Not today," Antonina whispered with a blush, "and I did not see him yesterday."

"That I'll believe," Theodora thought to herself and then, whilst stroking Antonina's arm, she said aloud: "Oh how I will miss you! Soon, perhaps next week, Belisarius will put to sea and you, the most loyal of all wives, will accompany him. Which of your friends will go with you?"

"Procopius," Antonina replied, "and – the two sons of Boethius."

"Aha," the empress smiled, "I understand. In the freedom of camp life you hope to enjoy the handsome young man more, without being disturbed. While the hero Belisarius fights battles and captures cities—"

"You have guessed it. But I have a request to ask of you. You have of course done well. Alexandros, your handsome friend, is back, and even near you he remains his own master, a mature man. But young Anicius, as you know, is constantly watched over by his elder brother Severinus. Severinus thinks only of freedom and revenge against the Barbarians, and he would never tolerate this tender – friendship. He would get in the way of our relationship a thousand times. So please do me a favour. Severinus must not follow us. Once we are aboard with Anicius please find a way to keep his older brother in Byzantium, either by some pretext or by force if need be. You can do it easily – you are the empress."

"Not bad," Theodora smiled. "What a cunning campaign. I see you are learning from Belisarius."

Antonina turned red from head to foot. "Oh, do not say his name. You know best where I learned to do those things which make one blush."

Theodora cast a flashing glance at her friend, who went on: "Heaven knows, Belisarius was no more faithful than I, until I came to this court. It was you, empress, who taught me that those selfish men, full of war and politics and ambition, neglect us women once they are our husbands. Once they own us, they no longer respect us. You taught me that it is no sin to accept those innocent attentions and flattery, which our tyrannical husbands refuse us, from a friend who is still hopeful and therefore attentive. As God is my witness, my vain and weak heart desires nothing more from Anicius than the sweet incense of adulation, which Belisarius refuses me."

"Luckily for me he will soon find that boring." Theodora said to herself.

"And yet even that, I fear, is a wrong against Belisarius. Oh how great he is, how noble, how magnificent! If only he was not altogether too great for this small heart!" and she covered her small face with her hands.

"Miserable coward," the empress thought, "she is too weak for pleasure, just as she is too weak for virtue."

Agave, the pretty slave girl from Thessalia, entered with a large bunch of beautiful flowers.

"From him," she whispered to her mistress.

"From whom?" the latter asked. But now Antonina was looking up, and Agave gave a warning signal with her eyes.

The empress gave the flowers to Antonina in order to occupy her. "Please put them in the marble vase over there."

As Belisarius's wife obeyed, with her back turned, Agave whispered: "Well, from him, whom you kept hidden here all day yesterday, from handsome young Anicius…" the child added, blushing.

But scarcely had she uttered the careless word when she screamed and held her left arm. The empress struck her in the face with the still bloody lancet. "I will teach you to have eyes as to whether men are handsome or ugly," she whispered fiercely. "You will have yourself locked into the spinning room for four weeks – immediately – and you will never show yourself in these rooms again. Now be gone!"

The weeping girl left, holding her head.

"What did she do?" Antonina asked, turning around.

"She dropped the perfume bottle," Galatea said quickly, as she picked up the small phial from the carpet. "Mistress, your hair is ready."

"Let the slaves in to dress me, and anyone else who is waiting outside. Would you like to have a look through these verses while you are waiting, Antonina? They are the latest poems by Aratorius about the deeds of the apostles, very good reading. This one here, about the stoning of St Stephanos, is particularly good. But you read and be the judge."

Galatea opened the main doors wide, and a whole swarm of slave girls and attendants came in. Some cleared away the used toilet articles, some burnt incense in small pans or sprayed balsam through the room, but the majority were busy about the person of the empress, who was now completing her attire. Galatea removed her pink dressing gown. "Berinice," she called, "the Melesian tunic with the purple stripe and the golden flounce. Today is Sunday."

While the experienced old woman, who alone was permitted to touch the empress's hair, skilfully inserted the jewelled golden needle into the knot at the back of her head, Theodora asked: "What news is there from the city, Delphina?"

"You have won, mistress!" the latter replied as she knelt down with the golden sandals. "Your colours, the blues, won over the greens in the circus yesterday, both on horseback and in the chariot race."

"Triumph!" Theodora rejoiced, "a wager of two hundredweight of gold – it's mine!"

At this moment a servant girl entered, carrying a bundle of letters. "News? From where? From Italy?" Theodora called out to the girl.

"Yes mistress, there is news from Florence, from the Gothic duchess Gothelindis – I recognise the seal with the gorgons on it. There is also news from the deacon Silverius."

"Give them to me!" Theodora commanded, "I will take them to church with me. Elpis, my mirror!" A young slave girl approached, carrying an oval, highly polished solid silver mirror some three feet high, set in a gold frame encrusted with pearls and supported by a strong ivory base. The poor girl had a most demanding job. Her task, while her mistress was completing her wardrobe, was to follow her every move with the heavy mirror, so that the restless empress could view herself continually as she dressed. She knew that she would be punished if she was slow to follow even a single movement.

"What is there to buy, Zephiris?" Theodora inquired of a dark-skinned Libyan freedwoman, who was just handing her a pet snake for its morning caress. The snake lay in a small basket.

"Nothing much," the Libyan replied, "come Glauca," she went on, as she took a richly embroidered white and gold *Chamys* from a clothes press. She held it carefully in her outstretched arms until Glauca took it from her and then, with just a single throw, placed it about the shoulders of her mistress in elegant folds. She then placed a white belt around Theodora's waist to hold the garment in place, and fastened the ends with a golden clasp around Theodora's ankles. The clasp had once represented the dove of Venus, but now stood for the Holy Ghost. Glauca was the daughter of an Athenian sculptor, who had studied the art of drapery for many years, and for that reason had been bought by the empress for several thousand *solidi*. She had but this one task to perform each day.

"Some perfumed soap balls have just arrived from Spain," Zephyris reported. "A new Milesian fable has appeared, and the old Egyptian is back again—" she spoke very quietly "—with his Nile water. He says it is infallible. The queen of Persia was barren for eight years, and...?"

Theodora turned away with a sigh, and a shadow crossed her smooth face. "Send him away," she said, "there is no longer any hope of that." For a moment it seemed as if she would sadly withdraw into herself.

But then she roused herself, motioned to Galatea, and went over to her bed. She took a withered ivy garland from her pillow, and handed it to the old woman with the whispered words: "For Anicius, send it to him." Then aloud: "My jewellery, Erigone!" The latter, assisted by two other slaves, laboriously carried the heavy bronze chest towards her mistress. Its lid was decorated with a relief showing the workshop of Vulcanus, and secured to the trunk by the empress's personal seal. Erigone showed that the seal was intact, then broke it and opened the lid. Several of the girls in the room stood on their toes, hoping to catch a glimpse of the shining treasures. "Do you still want the summer rings, mistress?" Erigone asked.

"No, the time for them has passed. Give me the heavier ones, the ones with the emeralds." Erigone handed her earrings, ring and bracelet.

Antonina looked up from the verses she was reading.: "How beautifully the green of the emeralds contrasts with the white of the pearls!"

"It is one of Cleopatra's treasures," the empress replied indifferently, "the Jew who sold them swore under oath that was the origin of the pearls."

"But you must hurry," Antonina reminded her friend, "Justinian's golden litter was already waiting when I came up."

"Yes mistress," a young slave girl said anxiously, "the slave at the sundial has already announced the fourth hour. You must hurry, mistress!"

A stab from the lancet was the reply. "Do you dare to admonish your mistress?" Turning to Antonina she added in a whisper: "Men must never be spoilt. They must always wait for us, never we for them. My ostrich feather fan, Thais. You can go, Ione, the Cappadocian slaves shall carry my litter today."

And with that she turned to go. "Oh Theodora," Antonina said quickly, "please do not forget my request."

"No," the latter replied, halting suddenly, "of course not. And just to make quite sure," she smiled, "I will place the matter in your own hands. My wax tablet and stylus!" Galatea brought them quickly. Theodora started writing on the tablet and whispered to her friend: "The Harbour Prefect is an old friend of mine. He will obey me without question. You can read what I am writing:

"To Aristarchos the Prefect, Theodora the Empress.

"When Severinus, the son of Boethius, tries to board the ship of Belisarius please prevent him from doing so, using force if necessary, and send him over to my chambers. He has been appointed as my chamberlain.' Is that satisfactory, dear sister?"

"Perfect, thank you!" the latter replied, delighted.

Suddenly the empress called out loudly: "Merciful heaven, we almost forgot the most important thing! My charm, my Mercury! Please, Antonina, there it is." The latter turned quickly in order to fetch the little golden Mercury, the empress's inseparable good luck charm, which was hanging by a silk ribbon near the bed. While Antonina's attention was thus diverted, Theodora quickly crossed out the word 'Severinus' with the golden stylus, and replaced it with 'Anicius'. She folded the tablet shut, tied it and sealed it with her Venus ring.

"Here is your charm," Antonina said, as she returned.

"And here is your order!" the empress responded with a smile. "You may give it to Aristarchos yourself at the moment of departure. And now let us go. To church!"

Chapter 20

In Naples, the Italian city which would be the first to feel the storm clouds now gathering in Byzantium, nobody knew of any approaching danger. In those days two magnificent young men walked together almost daily, either along the heights or through the city itself, absorbed in lively discussion and enjoying their young friendship. One had brown, the other golden hair. They were Julius and Totila.

What a beautiful time it is when an as yet pure young soul in the first fresh morning breeze of life, not yet stale or disillusioned but intoxicated instead with proud dreams of the future, meets up in close friendship with another human being of similar youthful, optimistic temperament. It is a time when deep, unselfish friendships can come about, enabling a unique relationship to develop between the two souls, where each can be quite certain that the other will fully understand him.

When the garland in our hair has wilted as we enter the autumn of our lives, we may smile about those dreams we entertained when we were young, and about youthful friendships. But it is not a smile of ridicule, but rather something akin to longing, as we think back to the first sweet smell of spring.

The young Goth and the young Roman had found one another at the right age for such a bond of friendship to develop, and their respective personalities complemented each other almost perfectly. Totila's sunny being had retained the full bloom of youth. Laughingly he looked out upon a laughing world; he loved his fellow man, and his happy and helpful nature quickly won for him the hearts of all those with whom he came into contact. He believed only in that which was good, and that in the end goodness must always win out. When he did encounter something bad or evil on his path through life, he would grind it into the dust with all the fury of an archangel. At such times the enormous strength and power in him, which formed another aspect of his being, would break loose, and he would not let up until the hated element had been totally destroyed and erased from his life. But once the disturbance had been removed it was forgotten just as quickly, and once more his soul knew only love and harmony for the world around him and all the people in it. Proudly and happily he enjoyed being young, and he lived for the golden present with joy in his heart and every fibre of his being. He would stride through the streets of Naples singing, the heart-throb of all the young girls and the pride of his fellow Gothic warriors, almost as if he were a God of joy. And yet the heroic part of him, which was to develop so fully later, already lay dormant beneath his cheerful exterior.

The bright magic of his personality was such that it even infected his much more quiet and introspective friend, Julius Montanus. The latter possessed a softer and more sensitive personality, almost feminine. Orphaned early in life, and then overpowered by the vastly superior intellect of Cethegus, he had grown up lonely and surrounded by books. He was more hindered than helped by the joyless learning and culture of his time, and had developed a serious, almost doleful outlook on life. He had a strongly developed tendency to self-denial, and looked upon the world around him in the light of strong religious conviction, so that he tended to be almost melancholy. Totila's sunny friendship came at just the right time, and it helped to light up even the furthest recesses of his soul so strongly that it made him not only more cheerful, but also stronger and more resilient, to the point where he would duly recover from the heavy blow which his very friendship with Totila was to bring down upon his head.

We will let him tell us about it himself, in a letter to the Prefect.

"To Cethegus, the Prefect, Julius Montanus.

"I was at first deeply hurt at your cold reply to my heartfelt last letter to you, in which I described my new friendship, although I am sure that was not your intention. In due course, however, your letter was to increase the depth and the joy of that very friendship in a way you could never have imagined or wished.

"The pain which you caused me initially soon turned to pity. I was hurt at first that you should so coldly and sarcastically dismiss my deepest feelings as the daydreaming of a sick boy, but soon this hurt turned into pity for you. How sad that a man like you, so richly endowed with all the powers of an exceptional mind, should be so sadly lacking in matters of the heart. I pity you, that have never known devotion and selfless love, the *caritas*, or love of your fellow man. To you these things are more an object of ridicule than of belief, but for me every day of pain brought them closer to me. Oh, what you have missed by never having experienced the greatest joy of all! Please forgive me for being so frank. I know that I have never before spoken to you in this manner, but I have only recently become the person I now am. Your last letter was critical of what you termed elements of childishness in me, and perhaps not altogether without cause.

"But I believe that those last traces of childhood have now disappeared, and I now speak to you as a changed man. Your letter, your advice, your 'medicine' did indeed make me into a man, but not the way you had intended. Pain, pure and holy pain, is what it brought me, and it subjected to a hard trial the friendship it was meant to destroy. I thank merciful God that my friendship with Totila was not destroyed, but rather strengthened and sealed for all time. Hear me now, and know what heaven did with your plans.

"As much as your letter did hurt me, I immediately obeyed out of habit and went to call on your friend Valerius Procillus. He had already left the city and moved into his delightful villa. I found in him a much travelled and experienced man, and a keen friend of freedom and of our fatherland. His daughter Valeria, however, is a treasure!

"Your prophesy was right! My intention to close my heart to her melted at the sight of her as fog melts before the sun. It was as if Electra, Cassandra or Virginia stood before me. But, even more than her beauty, it was the splendour of her wonderful soul that mesmerised me, as it opened up to me very soon. Her father immediately invited me to stay as a guest under his roof, and I was about to enjoy the most wonderful days of my life with her. Her soul is the poetry of antiquity.

"Her lovely voice lent new magic to the songs of Ashylos and Antigones. For hours we would read aloud together from their plays, and she was a magnificent sight when the spirit of a play took hold of her. Her dark hair would flow freely about her face, and her eyes would flash with a fire almost not of this world.

"There is another side to her, which may yet cause her a lot of pain and suffering, but which also lends her the greatest appeal. I think you will know what I mean, as you have known her family and its history for many years. You know better than I do how Valeria was dedicated by her pious mother from birth to lead a lonely life of religion, and never to marry. But then her father, whose outlook is more worldly than religious, bought her freedom for the price of a church and a monastery, which he had built. But Valeria believes that heaven will not accept dead money in place of a living soul, and she does not feel that she is free of her obligation. That obligation, which her mother placed upon her, is always on her mind, although she thinks of it with fear rather than love.

"You were right when you wrote that she was a child of the old heathen world, through and through. That she is, very much her father's daughter, and yet she cannot free herself from her mother's Christianity, renouncing all else. For her that religion is not a blessing, but rather the inescapable consequences of that promise weigh her down like a curse. This fine woman bears the burden of these two conflicting forces within her always. Her inner struggle tortures her, and yet at the same time it has made her an even more noble creature.

"Who can know how this conflict will ultimately be resolved? Heaven alone knows, which guides her destiny. For me personally her inner struggle has an almost morbid fascination, for as you know I too have been struggling with both Christianity and Philosophy, trying to reconcile the two. To my surprise these days of introspection have strengthened my beliefs, and it almost seems as if earthly joys lead to heathen wisdom, but only pain and suffering lead to Christ.

"When I became aware of this love growing inside me, I was full of joyous anticipation. Valerius, who had probably been won over by you beforehand, apparently looked upon our mutual affection with favour. Perhaps his only objection to me is that I do not share with sufficient enthusiasm his dream of a renewed Roman republic, nor his hatred of the Byzantines, whom he regards as the mortal enemies not only of Italy but of his house as well. Valeria, too, soon developed affection for me, and in time this may well have brought her into my arms. But I am grateful to either God or fate, I do not know which, that it was not to be. To sacrifice Valeria to an almost indifferent marriage would have been a sacrilege. I do not know what it was that prevented me from saying the words which would have made her mine. I loved her deeply and yet, every time I plucked up almost enough courage to ask her father for her hand, I had the strange feeling that I was about to take something which belonged to another, that I was not worthy of her, or at least that I was not the other half of her soul which fate had intended. And so I remained silent and said and did nothing.

"One day at about the sixth hour – it was very hot and humid – I sought out the coolness of a marble grotto in the garden. I entered through the oleander thicket, and there she lay, asleep on the soft lawn. She had one hand on her gently moving bosom, and the other under her head, still wearing the garland from the morning meal. I stood trembling before her. Never had she been so beautiful! I leaned over her and admired her noble features, which were as if made of marble. My heart was beating wildly, and I bent down to kiss her tender red lips.

"And suddenly my conscience screamed inside me. What you are about to do is wrong! It is theft! Totila! My whole being seemed to be calling his name, and quietly I crept away as I had come.

"Totila! Why had I not thought of him before?

"Bitterly I reproached myself that I had forgotten the brother of my heart over my newfound happiness.

"I was determined, Cethegus, that your prophesy would not come true, and that this love would not estrange me from my friend. He too must see Valeria, and admire her as I did, and once he approved of my choice I would ask for her hand, so that Totila could share our joy.

"The following day I returned to Naples to fetch him. I described Valeria's beauty to him, but I could not bring myself to speak of my love for her. He was to see her for himself, and guess everything. When we arrived at the villa she was not in her rooms, and so I led Totila into the garden. Valeria is a keen lover of flowers and tends them expertly. We entered a section of the garden which is lined by *taxus* bushes, and suddenly she appeared before us. She was standing in front of a statue of her father, which she was decorating with freshly picked flowers from the bosom fold of her tunic.

"The picture she thus presented was incredibly beautiful. This gorgeous young woman, framed by the green of the *taxus*, standing in front of the white marble, her right hand raised in the most appealing way. The sight of her had an utterly overpowering effect on Totila. With an unintentional cry of astonishment he stopped immediately in front of her, speechless.

"She looked up and trembled, as if struck by lightning. The roses fell from her garment, but she did not even notice them. Their eyes had met, their cheeks glowed – I saw both their destiny and mine decided before my eyes in but a single instant. They were in love at first sight!

"Painfully, like a burning arrow, the certainty of it pierced my soul. But that undiluted pain only lasted for a moment. As soon as I looked at them, these two wonderful human beings, I found a tremendous joy entirely free from envy that they had found each other. It was as if they had been made for one another, and they seemed to instantly become one, like the morning glow and the morning sun. And now I also recognised what that strange feeling had been, which had kept me from wooing Valeria, and which had brought his name to my lips. God and the stars had willed it so, and it was not up to me to interfere.

"Please forgive me if I stop at this point. I am still selfish enough that even now – I am ashamed to admit it – my heart still winces at times instead of beating joyfully at the happiness of my friends.

"Quickly and inseparably, like two flames, their souls became one. They love each other, and are as happy as the eternal gods. I have been granted the joy of seeing their happiness, and of helping them keep the fact from her father, as he is unlikely to give his child to a 'Barbarian' as long as that is all he sees in Totila.

"I have kept my love and my knowledge of that fateful promise from my friend. He does not even suspect anything, and he shall never know something which could only serve to dull his happiness. You can see now, Cethegus, how God has diverted your plan from its intended goal. You wanted me to have this treasure of Italy, and instead you gave it to Totila. You tried to destroy our friendship, and instead of that the fire of holy renunciation has sealed it for ever. You tried to make a man of me through the joy of love, and instead I became a man through love's pain. *Vale!*"

Chapter 21

We will omit describing the Prefect's reaction to the letter, and instead we will accompany the two friends on one of their evening walks along the delightful coast near Naples.

After an early *coena* they had walked through the city and out through the Porta Nolana which, already partly decayed, bore reliefs showing the victories of a Roman Imperator over Germanic tribes.

Totila stopped to admire the beautiful workmanship. "I wonder who the emperor is?" he asked his friend, "on the victory chariot there, holding the winged lightning in his hand like a Jupiter by Tonanius?"

"It is Marcus Aurelius," Julius replied, and went to move on.

"No, wait!" Totila said, "who are the four long-haired prisoners pulling the chariot?"

"They are Germanic kings."

"I can see that, but from which tribe? Look, here is the inscription: '*Gothi extincti*', the Goths are extinct!" With a loud laugh the young Goth struck the marble column with the palm of his hand, and quickly walked through the gate. "A lie in marble!" he called out, looking back. "I'll wager the Imperator never thought that one day a Gothic naval commander in Naples would call his boasts a lie."

Julius was thoughtful: "Yes, humanity is like the changing leaves on a tree. I wonder who will rule this land after you Goths?"

Totila stopped in surprise: "After us?"

"Well, surely you don't think that you Goths will last for ever?"

"How should I know?" Totila replied, walking on slowly.

"My friend, Babylonians and Persians, Greeks and Macedonians and apparently even we Romans all had our allotted time. They all blossomed, ripened and faded away. Why should you Goths be any different?"

"I don't know," was Totila's uneasy reply, "I have never thought about it. It has never occurred to me that a time might come when my people—" He stopped, as if it was a sin even to speak the thought out aloud. "How can anyone imagine a thing like that? I would no more think about that than I would about – death!"

"That is just like you, my Totila!"

"And it is like you to torture yourself and others with such nonsense."

"Nonsense? You forget that it has already become a reality for me, and for my people. You are forgetting that I am a Roman. And I cannot deceive myself as many of my countrymen do. It is over with us! The sceptre has passed from us to you. Do you think I could just forget that you, my closest friend, were a Barbarian and an enemy of my people?"

"By the sun's glow, that is not so!" Totila interrupted eagerly. "Am I to find this madness even in you, my gentle friend? Look about you. When, I ask you, when has Italy blossomed more gloriously than now, under our shield? Hardly even in the days of Augustus! You are teaching us wisdom and art, and in return we give you peace and protection from outside invaders. How could anyone wish for a more perfect combination? Harmony between Goths and Romans can bring about an entirely new era, more beautiful than ever before."

"Harmony? But it does not exist. To us you are a strange people, different in speech and religion, in customs and traditions, and added to that there is half a millennium of hatred. Once we took away your freedom, now you are taking ours. An eternal chasm yawns between us."

"You are trying to destroy my greatest ideal!"

"It is but a dream."

"No, it is the truth, I feel it. Perhaps one day I will prove it to you. I plan to make it my life's work!"

"You are building your castle on a dream. There will never be a bridge between Romans and Barbarians!"

"If that is so," Totila replied vehemently, "I don't see how you can live, how can you look on me—"

"Don't say it," Julius said seriously. "It was not easy at first. Trying to stop living for my people alone was perhaps the most difficult thing I have ever had to do, but at last after much thought and inner struggle I did it. My faith in the Almighty, who has already done much to bring Romans and Goths closer together as He alone can, helped me through this crisis. At last I overcame my prejudices, and found peace in being able to reconcile these conflicting emotions in my heart. You see, I am already a Christian in that I live for all mankind, not just my people. I am no longer only a Roman. I am a man, a human being, and that is why I can love you, a Barbarian, like a brother. We are both citizens of the Empire of humanity, and that's why I can go on living, even though I have seen my people die. I live for humanity, and all men are my people!"

"No," Totila cried animatedly, "I could never do that. I can and want to live only among my own people. Gothic customs are the only air which my soul can breathe. Why shouldn't we be able to go on for ever, or at least as long as there is a world? What do Persians and Greeks have to do with it? We are made of better stuff! Just because they wilted and perished, does that mean we too must perish? Right now we are in the full strength of our youth! No, if ever a day should come when the Gothic star falls, then I hope my eyes will not be there to see it. Oh merciful God in heaven, don't let us be sick and ailing for centuries like those Byzantines, who can neither live nor die! No, if it must be, then send us one last terrible war and allow us all to fall nobly and quickly, every last man among us, with myself in the forefront!" Totila had aroused himself into a state of warmest enthusiasm. He leapt from the marble bench, on which they had been sitting, raising his spear high into the sky.

"My friend," Julius said, looking at him fondly, "how beautifully your enthusiasm suits you! But think, if ever there should be such a war between your people and mine, and should I—?"

"You would fight with your own people, of course, if ever there should be such a fight. Do you think that would harm our friendship? Never! Two warrior heroes can inflict wounds on each other to the bone, and still be the best of friends. Ha, I would be delighted to see you running at me as part of a phalanx, spear in hand!"

Julius smiled. "My friendship is not of so fierce a nature, you wild Goth. These questions and doubts have troubled me bitterly and for a long time, and all the philosophers I studied put together did not bring me peace. It was only when I realised that I was here on earth to serve only God in heaven, and all mankind instead of only one nation, only then—"

"Calm yourself, friend," Totila cried, "where is this humanity you dream of? I don't see it. I see only Goths, Romans and Byzantines! But I know nothing of some supernatural humanity up there in the clouds, above the real people in the world. For me there is no other way. I cannot just shed the skin in which I was born. I am a Goth. I think in Gothic words, not some general language which serves all mankind, because there is no such thing. And because I can only think like a Goth, I can only feel like a Goth. I can recognise and respect other nations, of course. I admire your art, your learning, and in some ways even your state, in which everything is so well ordered and arranged. We can learn a great deal from you, but I neither could nor would swap with any nation of angels. Ha, I love my Goths, and at the bottom of my heart I prefer Gothic faults to Roman virtues."

"I feel very differently, and yet I am a Roman!"

"You are not a Roman! Forgive me, friend, but there is no longer any such thing, or I would not be the naval commander of Naples. Only a man who no longer has a nation can feel as you do. Anyone who is part of a still living nation must feel like me!"

For a while Julius was silent, then he said: "And if that were true, then I am a fortunate man, for I have lost the earth and gained heaven. What is a nation, a state, the earth? The home of my immortal soul is not anywhere down here! It yearns for that other kingdom where everything is so very different."

"Stop there, my Julius," said Totila as he stopped, leaning on his spear. "Let me stand and live here, to enjoy all that is beautiful, and to do what is good to the best of my ability. Of your heaven I want no part! I respect your beliefs, and your dreams, but I do not share them. You know," he added with a smile, "I am a heathen, incorrigible like my Valeria – our Valeria. Now is a good time to think of her. Your lofty dreams have almost made me forget the most precious thing in this world. Look, we are back at the city wall, and the sun is going down in the west, quickly as it always does in this southern land. I am to deliver the seeds which were ordered for the garden of Valerius before sunset. Only a very poor gardener," he smiled, "forgets his flowers. Farewell, I am turning off to the left."

"Give Valeria greetings from me. I am going home to read."

"What are you reading now, still Plato?"

"No, Augustinus. Farewell!"

Chapter 22

Totila strode rapidly through the streets of the outer city, avoiding the densely populated centre, heading in the direction of the Porta Capuana and the watchtower of Isak, the Jewish gatekeeper. The tower, located immediately to the right of the gate, was a massive multi-storeyed stone structure with a domed roof. On the top level, immediately below the battlements, there were two large rooms which served as the gatekeeper's living quarters. Here is where old Isak lived with Miriam, his beautiful child.

The larger of the two rooms held the heavy keys to the main gate, and to the various other doors of the important tower structure, arranged in strict order and hanging on one wall. On the opposite wall hung the old gatekeeper's curved horn and broad spear, not unlike a halberd, and in front of them on a woven mat sat old Isak, his legs crossed under him. He was a tall, raw-boned man, with the eagle's nose and the high curved brows typical of his race. Holding a long staff between his knees, he was listening attentively to the words of a plain-looking young man, evidently also Jewish, whose hard and sober face showed all the mathematical and reasoning ability for which Jewish people are noted.

"So you see, father Isak," he was concluding in an unpleasant and monotonous voice, "mine have not been idle words, and they come not only from my heart, which is blind, but also from my head, which can see. I have shown you the letters and documents which prove every word I have said. This is my appointment as chief architect of all the aqueducts in Italy, for fifty gold *solidi* a year plus ten *solidi* extra for every new construction. I have just finished rebuilding the ruined aqueduct of this very city, Naples, and this purse contains ten pieces of gold, which I have duly received. So you see that I am able to support a wife, and in addition I am the son of your cousin Rachel. So there is no reason why you would not give me Miriam, your daughter, to be my wife and to take care of my house."

But the old man stroked his beard thoughtfully and slowly shook his grey head. "Jochem, Rachel's son, my son, I tell you – don't!"

"But why? What can you have against me? Who in Israel can say a word against Jochem?"

"Nobody. You are just and honest and industrious. Your work is good and you are prospering before the Lord. But have you ever seen a nightingale mate with a sparrow, or a slender gazelle with a beast of burden? No, because they don't belong together. Now you take a look for yourself, and then tell me if you and Miriam belong together." With his long staff he carefully and silently opened the heavy green woollen curtain a little, which closed off the adjoining room.

Already the two men had been hearing soft, silver sounds, and now they were able to see into the simple but attractive room. A young girl was standing in front of the broad Roman window, which offered a spectacular view of Naples, the blue ocean and the distant mountains. In her arms she was holding a strange, stringed instrument, and her whole appearance was one of surprising beauty. The setting sun's red glow illuminated the room, giving the girl's white gown and face an enchanting glow, at the same time accentuating her black hair. Her dark blue eyes had the look of a dreamer as they scanned the city and the sea, their owner deep in thought. Piso the poet had called those eyes dark ocean blue. As if in a dream she was plucking the strings of her instrument very gently, while her half open lips whispered rather than sang an old, melancholy song:

"By the rivers of Babylon sat, crying, the people of Juda.
Will there ever be a day when the people of Juda need cry no more?"

"Cry no more," she repeated dreamily and rested her head on the arm holding the harp.

"Look at her," the old man said, "is she not lovely as a rose in the gardens of Sharon, and as the noble hind in the mountains of Hiram? Is she not perfect in every way?"

Before Jochem could reply a soft knocking could be heard, three times, against the iron door below. Miriam rose quickly, startled from her daydream, brushed her hand over her eyes and rushed down the narrow steps leading to the door below.

Jochem went to look out of the window, his face distorted with anger. "Ha, the accursed Christian," he snarled, clenching his fist. "That proud blond Goth again! Father Isak, is he the stag for your little hind?"

"Son, do not speak words of derision to Isak. You know that the youth has his heart set on a Roman girl, and he is not thinking about the pearl of Juda."

"But perhaps the pearl of Juda is thinking of him?"

"With gratitude and joy, as a lamb thinks of the strong shepherd who saved it from the wolf. Have you forgotten the last time the wretched Romans were after Israel's treasure, when they burned down the holy synagogue with evil fire? Have you forgotten how a horde of these evildoers hunted down my child in the street, as a pack of wolves hunts a white lamb, and how they tore the veil from her head and her gown from her shoulders? Where was her companion when that happened? Where was Jochem, my cousin's son? He had run away in great haste at the first sign of danger, leaving the dove to the claws of the vultures!"

"I am a man of peace," Jochem replied uncomfortably, "unaccustomed to the sword of violence."

"But Totila is used to the sword, as the lion of Juda once was, and the Lord is with him. He was passing by, alone, and when he saw what was happening he dived among the cheeky thieves, struck down their ringleader with his sword, and chased the rest away as a falcon scatters the crows. Then he carefully wrapped her veil around my still living child, supported her shaky steps, and led her home unharmed, into the arms of her old father. May Jehovah reward him for it with a long life, blessing every step he takes."

"Very well then," said Jochem, gathering his documents together, "I will go, and this time it will be for many moons. I will travel across the great ocean to do some very big business."

"Big business? With whom?"

"With Justinianus, the emperor of the Orient. He is building a great church in the golden city of Constantine, to honour the wisdom of the Lord. A part of it has collapsed, and I have drawn up a plan and design to reconstruct the building."

At this the old man jumped vehemently to his feet, and stamped on the floor with his staff. "What? Jochem, Rachel's son, you want to serve the Roman? The emperor whose ancestors burnt the holy city of Zion and turned the temple of our god to ashes? And you want to build a house of heresy, you, the son of the pious Manas? Woe be to you!"

"Why do you cry woe, not even knowing what for? Can you tell, from smelling a piece of gold, whether it came from Jew or Christian? Does it not weigh the same, and look just as beautiful?"

"Son of Manas, you cannot serve both God and Mammon."

"But are you not serving the heretics yourself? Is that not a Gothic watchman's horn on the wall? Are you not the keeper of keys for these Goths, opening and closing their gates, and guarding their fortress?"

"Yes, I am," the old man replied with pride, "and I will go on guarding for them, night and day, as a dog guards his master. As long as there is breath in Isak no enemy shall walk through that gate. The children of Israel owe them and their great king a debt of gratitude. He was as wise as Solomon, and his sword was that of Gideon! We owe them as much as our fathers owed to the great king Cyrus, who freed them from Babylon. These Romans have destroyed the temple of Jehovah, and scattered our people across the earth. They have beaten and ridiculed us, burnt our cities, plundered our treasure chests and violated our women everywhere in our lands, and they have written many cruel laws against us. And then this great king came from the north, whose seed Jehovah shall bless, and he rebuilt our synagogues. Everything the Romans had destroyed they had to restore with their own hands and their own money. He protected the peace of our houses, and anyone who harmed us had to pay for it as if he had harmed a Christian. He let us keep our God and our beliefs, and he guarded our trade. We could again celebrate the Passover in joyful peace, for the first time since the temple still stood on the heights of Zion. When a Roman nobleman stole Sarah, my wife, by force, Theodoric had him beheaded the same day, and my wife was returned to me unharmed. These things I will remember as long as I live, and I will serve his people until the day I die. And then people in all the lands on earth will be able to say once more: 'he is as loyal and as grateful as a Jew'."

"I hope that the Goths will not repay your loyalty with ingratitude," Jochem replied as he prepared to leave, "I have a feeling that I will ask for Miriam's hand once more, and for the last time. Perhaps, father Isak, you won't be quite so proud by then." He then strode out through Miriam's room towards the stairs, where he met Totila. With an ugly bow and a piercing glance he squeezed past Totila, who had to stoop in order to pass under the door, closely followed by Miriam.

"There are your gardener's clothes," she said, without looking up, "and here near the window I have your flowers ready. You said the other day that she loves white narcissus, so I got some for you. They smell beautiful." And her lovely voice was silent.

"You are a good girl, Miriam," Totila said as he took off his helmet with the white swan wings and placed it on the table. "Where is your father?"

"May the peace of the Lord rest on your golden locks," the old man said as he entered the room.

"Greetings, faithful Isak!" Totila cried as he removed his long white cloak, replacing it with a plain brown one which Miriam handed him from a hook on the wall. "You good people! Without you and your loyal silence the whole of Naples would know about my secret. How can I thank you?"

"Thank us?" Miriam replied, looking at him with her deep blue eyes, "you have already thanked us in advance for all time."

"No, Miriam," the Goth replied as he pulled the broad-brimmed hat down low over his eyes, "I have become very fond of you both. Tell me, father Isak, who is that little man I have often seen here, and whom I just met again on the stairs? I have a feeling he has his eyes on Miriam. Please speak freely, if she is only short of money for a dowry, I would be glad to help."

"It is not money that is lacking, but love," Isak replied calmly.

"Well, I can't help you there. But should she choose someone else – I would like to do something for my Miriam." And he laid his hand on the girl's shining black hair with a friendly gesture. It was only a very light touch, but Miriam suddenly fell to her knees as if struck by lightning, her arms crossed over her bosom and her head bowed very low. She slid to the floor at Totila's feet like a flower heavy with dew.

The latter, shaken, took a step backwards. But in an instant the girl was on her feet once more: "Forgive me, it was only a rose. It fell down near your foot."

She placed the flower on the table, and she was so composed that neither of the two men gave any further thought to the incident. "It is already getting dark – hurry, master," she said calmly and handed him the basket with the flowers.

"I am going. Valeria too is indebted to you. I have told her a great deal about you, and she always asks after you. She has been wanting to meet you for some time. Well, that might soon be possible – today should be the last time I will need this disguise."

"Are you going to elope with her?" Isak cried. "Bring her here if you do. She will be safe here!"

"No," Miriam interjected, "not here, no, please no!"

"Why not, you strange child?" the old man asked angrily.

"This is no place for his bride – this room – it would not bring her luck."

"Calm yourselves," Totila said, already at the door, "an open courtship is going to take the place of all this secrecy. Farewell!" And as he said this he stepped outside. Isak took his spear, the horn and a few keys from the wall, and followed Totila outside in order to make his evening rounds.

Miriam remained alone upstairs. For a long time she remained standing in the same place, motionless, her eyes closed. At last she brushed her hands over her cheeks and temples and opened her eyes. It was quiet in the room. The first rays of moonlight were just coming in through the open window, casting a silver shadow on Totila's white cloak, which was hanging over a chair. Quickly Miriam rushed over to the chair and covered the garment with burning kisses, and then she picked up the shining helmet with the swan wings, which was lying on the table beside her. She embraced it with both arms, and held it tenderly to her breast, and then she held it in front of her for a while, admiring it. At last she could no longer resist the temptation, and quickly she lifted it up and placed it on her own head. She trembled for an instant as it touched her forehead, then she brushed back her hair and for a moment she pressed the cold steel firmly with both hands to her burning temples. She then removed the helmet and, looking shyly about her, carefully put it back in its former place. Now she went over to the open window, and looked out into the pleasant evening and the moonlight. Her lips moved gently as if in prayer, but the sounds which came from them were the same as before:

"Beside the rivers of Babylon sat, crying, the people of Juda.
When will the day come, Zion's daughter, which brings an end to your sorrows?"

Chapter 23

While Miriam was silently looking up at the first stars, Totila had soon reached the villa of the wealthy merchant Valerius, situated about an hour's walk from the Porta Capuana.

The turnkey referred him to old Hortularius, Valeria's freedman who was responsible for the care of the gardens. He was the young lovers' confidant, and so he accepted the flowers from the young gardener, which he was ostensibly delivering from the leading flower seller in Naples. He then accompanied Totila to his simple bedroom on the ground floor, which had low windows opening onto the garden. The new flowers were to be planted very early next morning, before sunrise, so that in accordance with the ancient secrets of Roman gardeners the first ray of the sun to touch the flowers in their new bed would be the beneficial morning sun.

Impatiently the young Goth sat waiting in the small room with a jug of wine, longing for the hour to arrive when Valeria could bid her father good night after the evening meal they shared. Again and again he looked up at the sky, trying to estimate the time from the appearance of the stars and the moon's movement. He drew back the curtain covering the window. It was very quiet in the big garden, and only a spring could be heard in the distance, splashing gently to the accompaniment of a few cicadas in the myrtle bushes. The warm breeze carried with it the delightful scents of roses and other flowers, and a nightingale started to sing its lovely song, far away in the pine forest beyond.

At last Totila could contain himself no longer. Without a sound he swung his legs over the marble windowsill. The white sand on the narrow path could barely be heard under his feet as he hurried along in the shadows of the bushes, avoiding the moonlight. He slid past the dark *taxus* bushes and the dense olive grove, past a tall white marble statue of Flora glowing ghostlike in the moonlight, and the fountain with its six dolphins blowing water from their nostrils. Quickly he now entered a narrow alley formed by laurel and tamarind trees, and a moment later he had reached the stalactite grotto, where the nymph of the spring leaned over a large urn made of dark stone.

As he entered a white figure appeared from behind the statue. "Valeria, my beautiful rose!" Totila cried, passionately embracing his beloved, who tried gently to soften his impetuosity.

"Don't, my dearest," she whispered, gently withdrawing from his arms.

"No, sweetest one, I don't want to let you go. Oh how I have missed you – it seems like an eternity! Can you hear the nightingale? Can you feel how the soft breath of the summer night and the smell of honeysuckle tell us of love? They are all telling us to be happy! Oh let us hang on to these golden hours. My soul is too small to grasp all this happiness, your beauty, our youth and this glorious summer night. The full joy of life is surging through my heart in mighty waves, as if it is trying to burst with joy."

"Oh my friend! How I would love to abandon myself to the joy of these hours, but I cannot. I don't trust this intoxicating perfume or the opulent warmth of this night. It will not last. It holds something evil. I cannot believe that our love will be a happy one."

"My dearest little fool, why ever not?"

"I don't know. That same inner conflict which has ruled all my life curses me here too. I would dearly love to abandon myself to this happiness, like you. But a voice inside me warns me constantly: it will not last – you will not find happiness."

"So you are not happy in my arms?"

"Yes, and no! The fact that I am deceiving my dear father troubles me. You see, Totila, what I admire most about you is not your youthful strength, or your looks, or even your great love for me. The thing about you which fills me with pride and joy is your soul, bright, open and honest. I have become used to your walking through this dark world like a god of light, clear and brilliant like a star. Your courage, your belief in yourself, your faith in all that is good and your cheerful integrity are my pride and joy. It is as if anything small or mean or dull must vanish when you approach, and that is what makes me happy. I love you with all my heart and soul, and that is why I cannot bear anything secret or hidden, not even in the joy of these hours. We are stealing these hours, and it can no longer remain so."

"No, Valeria, and it will not remain so. I feel just as you do, and I too hate the lie of this masquerade. I will bear it no longer, and I have come to put an end to it. Tomorrow I will put this disguise aside and speak to your father, openly and honestly."

"That is the best decision, because—"

"Because it has just saved your life, young man!" A deep voice suddenly interrupted them, and a man emerged from the grotto's dark interior, returning a sword to its scabbard.

"Father!" Valeria cried, surprised but courageously composed. Totila put his arm about her protectively.

"Get away from the Barbarian, Valeria!" Valerius commanded.

"No, Valerius," Totila replied, holding his beloved even more tightly, "from now on her place is here with me."

"You insolent Goth!"

"Listen to me, Valerius, and do not be angry with us because we have deceived you. You heard it yourself, the deceit was to have ended tomorrow."

"You are lucky that I did hear it. I was warned by my oldest friend, and yet I could not believe that my daughter would – would go behind my back. And when, in the end, I had to believe it I resolved that you would pay for your treachery with your blood. Your decision saved your life. But now flee! You will never see her again!"

Totila was about to reply angrily when Valeria was first to speak, as she stepped between the two men: "Father," she said calmly, "listen to me, your child. I will not try to excuse my love, because it is holy and as necessary as the stars. It needs no excuse, and my love for this man is my whole life. You know me. Truthfulness is the essence of the daughter you raised, and I tell you now, I will never part with this man!"

"Nor I with her," Totila added vehemently as he took her hand in his.

The young couple stood before the old man, erect in the moonlight. Their noble faces bore a look almost of rapture, and they were so beautiful as they stood there together that the angry father could not help but be touched. Softly he said: "Valeria, my child!"

"Oh my father! You have always guided my every step with such love and devotion that until now I have barely missed my dead mother, although I have mourned her often. Now, in this hour, I miss her for the first time. Now, I feel it, I need her to speak for me. At least let the memory of her do so! Please father, try to see her before you, and remember the moment when she lay dying and called you to her side for the last time, as you have told me so often, to charge you with my happiness as a holy promise."

Valerius pressed one hand to his temple, and his daughter dared to take the other. He did not withdraw it. A fierce inner struggle was taking place in him, and at last he spoke: "Valeria, without knowing it you have spoken a powerful word. It would be wrong of me if I now kept from you something on which you touched quite unsuspectingly. So I will tell you of the promise I made to your mother on her deathbed. Her mind was still troubled by that other promise, even though we had long obtained absolution from it. She said to me: ' If our child is not to become the bride of heaven, at least promise me that you will honour her own free choice. I know how Roman girls are often given away in marriage, against their will, and without love. Such a union is wretchedness on earth, and an abomination before the Lord. My Valeria will choose well. Promise me that you will entrust her to the man of her choice, and to none other.' And I promised that I would do so as I held her trembling hand. But give my child to a Barbarian? No, no, never!" And with an effort he freed himself from her embrace.

"Perhaps I am not such a Barbarian, Valerius," Totila began. "At least I am the best friend the Romans have among my own people. Believe me, it is not your countrymen I hate. The people I hate and detest are my enemies as they are yours – the Byzantines!"

That was a lucky word, for in the old republican's heart hatred of Byzantium was the other side of his love for freedom and for Italy. He was silent, and his eyes rested on the young man, thinking.

"My father," said Valeria, "your child could not love a Barbarian. Please get to know him. If you still call him a Barbarian after you have done so I will never be his. I ask nothing of you but this: get to know him, and then decide whether my choice is a worthy one. All the gods love him, and all men cannot help but like him. You alone cannot be the only one who rejects him." And she took her father's hand.

"Oh get to know me, Valerius," Totila begged as he grasped the old man's other hand with feeling and sincerity.

Valerius sighed, and at last he said: "Come with me to your mother's grave. It is over there among the cypress trees that the urn with her heart rests. Let us think of her there, the noblest among women, and let her shadow speak to us. If it is indeed true love, Valeria, and your choice a worthy one, then I will keep the promise I made to her."

Chapter 24

A few weeks later we find ourselves in Rome, in the familiar study with the statue of Julius Caesar, where the Prefect Cethegus was in conversation with Petros, the emperor's emissary, or rather the emissary of the empress, whom we met in an earlier chapter.

The two men had already spent several hours talking and reminiscing about old times. They had once been fellow students, as we have already learned, and while they were talking they had emptied several jugs of fine old wine. They had just left the dining chamber for the privacy of the study, so that they would be able to discuss more confidential matters without being disturbed by slaves or servants.

"As soon as I had satisfied myself," Cethegus concluded his report on the most recent events, "that the bad news from Ravenna was only rumour, possibly unfounded but certainly exaggerated, I reacted to the excitement of my overly eager friends with the greatest possible calm. That hothead Lucius Licinius almost ruined everything with his idolisation of my person. He was constantly demanding that I should assume the dictatorship, so much so that he literally held a sword to my breast and said that I would have to be forced to save the fatherland. He told so many tales out of school that he endangered all our plans. It was lucky that the black Corsican, who for reasons of his own seems to have thrown in his lot with the Barbarians, thought him to be more intoxicated than he really was. At last news came that Amalasuntha had returned, and so finally a measure of calm returned to the people and to the Senate."

"And you," Petros replied, "have saved Rome from Barbarian revenge a second time, an invaluable service for which the whole world, and particularly the queen, is deeply indebted to you."

"The queen, poor woman!" Cethegus shrugged his shoulders, "who knows how long she will be allowed to remain on the throne by the Goths, or by your masters in Byzantium?"

"Oh, you are very much mistaken there!" Petros interjected eagerly. "My mission, above all else, is to support her throne, and my main reason for being here is to seek your advice as to how this might best be done," he added slyly.

But the Prefect leaned back against the marble wall and looked at the emissary with a smile: "Oh Petros, oh Petre, why must you be so devious? I thought we knew one another better."

"What do you mean by that?" Petros asked, embarrassed.

"I thought that it was not for nothing that we studied law and history together in Berytus and in Athens. I thought that even in those days, when we as young men spent many an hour exchanging pearls of wisdom, we had always agreed that the emperor must one day drive these Barbarians from Italy, so that he might rule once more in Rome as he does in Byzantium. And as I still think as I did then I very much doubt that you will have changed either."

"I seek only to serve my master, and Justinian—"

"is of course full of enthusiasm for Barbarian rule in Italy!" Cethegus interrupted.

"Of course," Petros replied uneasily, "there could be circumstances—"

"Petre," Cethegus now exclaimed angrily, "no more empty phrases and no more lies! They are wasted on me. You see, Petros, you still suffer from the same old fault. You are too sly to be clever. You think that you must always lie, and you never have the courage to be truthful. But one must only lie when one is certain one can do so with complete conviction. How can you be so stupid as to try and deceive me that the emperor does not want Italy back? Whether he chooses to support the queen or to topple her is, I think, only a matter of whether he thinks he can reach his goal better with her or without her. Apparently I am not to know his true intentions. But despite all your cunning, next time we meet I will tell you to your face exactly what your emperor has in mind."

A bitter, malicious smile appeared on the emissary's lips: "So you are still just as arrogant as you were when we debated in Athens!" he said venomously.

"Yes I am, and you will no doubt recall that in Athens I was always first, Procopius second, and you only ever third."

At that moment Syphax entered. "Master, a veiled lady awaits you in the Zeus room," he reported.

Petros grinned. He was glad that the discussion had thus been interrupted, as he felt distinctly inferior to the Prefect: "I wish you luck on such an interruption."

"You are the lucky one!" Cethegus smiled, and left the room.

"Proud Roman, you will live to regret your arrogance," Petros thought to himself.

When Cethegus reached the room, named after a statue of Zeus by Glykonos of Athens, he found a woman richly dressed in the Gothic manner. As he entered she removed the hood of her brown cloak.

"Countess Gothelindis," the Prefect asked in surprise, "what brings you here?"

"Revenge!" she replied in a hoarse, ugly voice, and moved very close to him. Her features were well defined, but she was by no means ugly; in fact she could have been called beautiful but for the fact that her left eye was missing and a huge scar disfigured the whole of her left cheek. As the blood rose to the passionately angry woman's face it seemed as if the wound bled anew, and she clenched her fist fiercely with every word. Her one grey eye exuded such deadly hatred that Cethegus took a step back.

"Revenge?" he asked, "against whom?"

"Against – I will come to that. Forgive me for disturbing you," she said, regaining her composure, "your friend Petros, the emissary from Byzantium, is with you, is he not?"

"Yes, how did you know?"

"I saw him enter your *porticus* before the *coena*," she said indifferently.

"That's not true," Cethegus thought to himself. "I let him in by the garden entrance. So they must have prearranged to meet here, and I am not supposed to suspect that. What do they want with me?"

"I don't want to keep you long," Gothelindis continued, "I have only one question to ask of you. Please answer briefly yes or no. I can destroy that woman, Theodoric's daughter, and I want to do so. Are you with me or against me in that?"

"Oh friend Petros," thought the Prefect, "now I know what you have in mind with Amalasuntha. But I had better find out how far you two have already progressed."

"Gothelindis," he began slowly, "so you want to topple the queen. I gladly take your word for it, but I doubt very much that you can."

"Listen, then decide for yourself. The woman had the three dukes murdered."

Cethegus shrugged. "Some people believe that."

"But I can prove it."

"And how can you do that?" Cethegus asked doubtfully.

"Duke Thulun, as you know, did not die immediately. He was assassinated on the Via Aemilia near my villa in Tarentum. My men found him and brought him to my house. He was of the Balti clan and my cousin, as you probably know, and he died in my arms. I too am of the Balti clan."

"Well, and what did he say in his fever?"

"Fever nothing! Even as he fell Duke Thulun struck his murderer with his sword and he did not get far. My men searched for him and found him dying in a nearby forest. He confessed everything to me."

Almost imperceptibly Cethegus clenched his teeth. "Well, who was he, and what did he say?"

"He was," Gothelindis replied sharply, "an Isaurian mercenary, a supervisor of the reconstruction work on the battlements of Rome, and he said: 'The Prefect sent me to the queen, and the queen sent me to Thulun.'"

"Who, apart from yourself, heard this?" Cethegus asked.

"Nobody. And nobody shall hear of it as long as you support me. But if you don't, then—"

"Gothelindis," the Prefect interrupted, "do not threaten me! It will not help you. You should know that threatening me will only make me bitter, but it will not force my hand. If need be I will let you accuse me openly. You are known as Amalasuntha's bitter enemy, and your unsupported testimony – you were careless enough to admit that nobody else heard the confession – will destroy neither her nor me. You cannot force me to fight the queen, but perhaps you can persuade me if you can show me that doing so is to my advantage. And to that end I will give you an ally. You know my friend Petros, don't you?"

"Yes, I have known him for many years."

"With your permission I will ask him to be present during our discussion."

He returned to the study: "Petros, my visitor is the Countess Gothelindis, Theodahad's wife. She wishes to speak to both of us. Do you know her?"

"Me? Oh no, I have never seen her!" the emissary said quickly.

"Very well, follow me." As soon as they entered the Zeus room Gothelindis greeted him with the words: "Greetings, old friend, what a surprise to meet again!"

Petros was silent. Cethegus, his hands folded behind his back, was enjoying himself thoroughly at the expense of Petros. After a painful pause he began: "You see, Petros, always too sly, always needless intrigue. But come, do not allow one failed trick get you down. So the two of you have conspired to topple the queen, and you are trying to win me over to help you. If I am even to consider it I must first know exactly what your intentions are, once you have achieved your goal. Whom do you plan to put in Amalasuntha's place? The way is not yet clear for Justinian."

They were both silent for a while. His clear understanding of the situation, and the ease with which he had seen through them, had caught them by surprise. At last Gothelindis spoke: "Theodahad, my husband, the last of the Amalungs."

"Theodahad, the last of the Amalungs," Cethegus repeated slowly as he swiftly weighed in his mind all the advantages and disadvantages of such a move. He considered that Theodahad, unpopular with the Goths and placed on the throne by Petros, would soon be entirely dominated by Byzantium, and might thus bring about the catastrophe sooner than Cethegus desired by calling on the emperor for military aid.

He considered also that it was desirable to keep the emperor's armies away from Italy for as long as possible, and so he decided to support Amalasuntha and retain the existing status quo. This would gain additional time for him in which to make his preparations. All this he had weighed and decided in a mere moment. Calmly he asked: "How do you propose to attain your goal?"

"We will demand of the woman that she abdicates in favour of my husband, under threat of accusing her of murder otherwise."

"And what if she refuses?"

"Then we will carry out our threat," said Petros, "and cause a storm among the Goths, a storm which—"

"Which will cost her life," Gothelindis cried.

"It may cost her crown," Cethegus agreed, "but if it does the heir to it will not be Theodahad. No, if the Goths elect a king, his name will not be Theodahad."

"How very true!" Gothelindis hissed.

"The Goths might very easily elect a king who would be much more troublesome to us all than Amalasuntha. And so I will be frank with you. I will not support your plan. I will support the queen."

"Very well then," Gothelindis cried angrily as she reached for the door, "so there will be war between us. Come, Petros."

"Calm yourselves, my friends," the emissary replied, "perhaps Cethegus will change his mind when he has read this document." And he handed the Prefect the letter which Alexandros had delivered to Justinian from Amalasuntha. Cethegus read it, and his face darkened.

"Now," Petros commented derisively, "do you still want to support a queen who has already condemned you to destruction? Where would you have been if she had carried out her plan, and if your friends had not been there to protect your interests?"

Cethegus barely heard him. "You fool," he thought, "as if that was what troubles me! As if the queen did not have every right to condemn me. I cannot blame her! But the careless woman has already done what I only feared from Theodahad. She has destroyed herself and endangered all my plans. She has already called a Byzantine army into Italy, and now they will come whether she still wants them or not. As long as Amalasuntha is queen Justinian will play the part of her protector." Now he turned to Petros in feigned shock, handing the letter back to him: "If she was to carry out her resolve and remain on the throne, how soon can your armies land?"

"Belisarius is already on his way to Sicily," Petros replied, quite proud of himself for having managed to intimidate the arrogant Cethegus, "his fleet could lie off the coast near Rome in a week."

"This is terrible!" Cethegus exclaimed, this time genuinely.

"You can see," said Gothelindis, "that she is out to destroy you, even though you had planned to support her. Beat her to the punch!"

"And in the name of my master, the emperor, I now beseech you to assist me in destroying this Gothic Empire, and in giving Italy back her freedom. You and your great mind are much appreciated at the Imperial Court, and after our victory Justinian has promised you – the honour of a senator in Byzantium."

"Could it be possible?" Cethegus cried. "But not even this, the highest of honours, drives me more strongly than my disgust for this ungrateful woman, who now threatens my life as a reward for all my services to her. You are sure, are you not, that Belisarius will not land so soon?"

"Calm yourself," Petros smiled, "this hand of mine will call him when the time is right. But first Amalasuntha must be replaced by Theodahad."

Cethegus thought to himself: "That's good. I have gained time, so I have gained all. Belisarius shall not land until I am able to greet him at the head of a well armed Italy." Aloud, he said: "I am yours, and I think I can persuade the queen to place the crown on your husband's head with her own hand. Amalasuntha shall surrender the sceptre of her own free will."

"She will never do that!" Gothelindis exclaimed.

"I believe she may. Her nobility of spirit is even greater than her thirst for power. There are many ways to destroy one's enemies, even through their virtues," Cethegus said, as he was thinking: "I am sure of what I am about.

"And so I greet you, Queen of the Goths," he concluded, with a slight bow.

Chapter 25

Amalasuntha, the queen, was biding her time once the three dukes had been disposed of. Their removal as leaders of the Gothic nobility, which was opposed to her, had given her a slightly freer hand. Yet, on the other hand, the coming national assembly of her people at Regata near Rome was not far away. There she would have to clear herself completely of any suspicion of murder, or lose her crown or even her life. Witigis and his supporters had promised her their protection only until that time. She therefore now concentrated all her powers to consolidate her position as well as she could.

She could no longer hope for any help from Cethegus, having seen through his cold self-interest. Yet she hoped that the Italians and the catacombs conspiracy, with her own name at the head of the list, would prefer her rule to that of an alternative king elected by the rough and ready Gothic party, given that she had always displayed strong pro-Roman tendencies. She longed for the arrival of the bodyguard she had requested from the emperor, so that she would have a crutch to lean on as soon as danger threatened. She was also busy trying to make more friends among the Goths themselves.

She recalled many of her father's old followers to Ravenna, eager supporters of the Amalung dynasty, and old warrior heroes who were highly regarded by her people. Among them were a number of former companions in arms of old Hildebrand, almost as old as he. One of them was the white-bearded Grippa, Theodoric's cup bearer, who was held in almost as much esteem as Hildebrand himself. She heaped honours upon Grippa and some of the others, and entrusted Grippa with the command of the fortress of Ravenna, making him and his followers swear that they would always guard it for the Amalung dynasty.

By surrounding herself with some of these highly regarded men she had been able to create a counterbalance against Witigis, Hildebrand and their faction, and there was little Witigis could do to stop her from honouring Theodoric's followers, as it was in no way endangering the state. But Amalasuntha also needed support against the noble and influential Balti clan, and the would-be avengers of the three dukes. Her sharp eye saw likely allies in the noble Woelsung family, the third-ranking clan among the Goths after the Amalungs and the Balti. They owned vast lands in central Italy, and had enormous influence. At that time the heads of their clan were two brothers, Duke Guntharis and Count Arahad. She had in fact thought of a most effective way to win them over. In return for the friendship of the Woelsung clan she was willing to offer no less a prize than the hand of her beautiful daughter.

In an ornately decorated room in Ravenna mother and daughter stood opposite one another in a serious, but far from friendly, discussion. The Junoesque figure of the queen was pacing through the narrow room, in strong contrast to her usual calm. From time to time she would cast an angry glance at the gorgeous creature standing before her, eyes lowered, one arm resting on her hip and the other on a marble table top.

"Think well," Amalasuntha exclaimed passionately as she stopped pacing, "and change your mind. I will give you another three days to think it over."

"That is not necessary. I will always speak as I am doing now," Matesuentha replied without raising her eyes.

"Just tell me what you have against Count Arahad!"

"Nothing, except that I don't love him."

The queen did not appear to hear this at all. "Surely this is quite a different matter from the time when you were to be married to Cyprianus. He was old and, perhaps to his detriment in your eyes, a Roman."

"Nevertheless I was banished to Tarentum because I refused."

"I was hoping that strictness might bring you to your senses. For months I kept you distant from the court, away from your mother's heart—" Matesuentha's lovely lips distorted to a bitter smile "—but it was in vain! I recalled you."

"You are mistaken. It was my brother Atahalaric who recalled me."

"Another suitor has now been suggested to you. He is young, very good-looking, and a noble Goth of the highest rank, whose family now ranks second in the Empire. You know, or you must at least suspect, how my throne is threatened by enemies all around, and how I need the support of powerful friends. He and his warrior brother have promised to support me with all their power and influence. Count Arahad loves you, and you – you reject him. Why? Just tell me why!"

"Because I do not love him."

"That is idle girls' talk. You are a royal princess! You must place your own wishes second to those of your dynasty and of your nation."

"I am a woman," said Matesuentha as she raised her flashing eyes, "and I will not surrender my heart to any power on earth or in heaven."

"Is that my daughter speaking? Look at me, foolish child. I have aspired to and achieved much that is great. As long as men admire all that is noble they will mention my name. I have gained every glory there is to be gained in this world, and yet…"

"You have never loved. I know that," her daughter sighed.

"How can you know that?"

"It was the curse of my childhood. True, I was only a child when my beloved father died. I did not know then how to say it, but even so I could feel that his heart lacked something when he lovingly embraced Athalaric and myself, and kissed us with a sigh. Because of this I loved him even more. I sensed that he was searching for love, that he needed love but it was denied him. Now of course I know the answer to what puzzled me then. You became my father's wife because, after Theodoric, he was next in line for the throne. You became his not for love but out of a thirst for power and a desire to rule. His was a warm heart, and yet you offered him nothing but cold pride."

Surprised, Amalasuntha stopped in her tracks: "You are very daring today!"

"I am your daughter."

"You speak about love so knowingly, as if you know more about it at twenty than I do at forty. You are in love!" she exclaimed suddenly, "and that's why you are being so stubborn."

Matesuentha blushed, but said nothing. "Speak!" her angry mother shouted, "admit it or lie to me!"

Matesuentha lowered her eyes, and remained silent. Never had she been so beautiful.

"Are you going to deny the truth? Are you a coward, princess?"

Proudly the girl raised her eyes: "I am not a coward, and I deny nothing. Yes, I am in love."

"And with whom, you wretched girl?"

"That is something no god will wrest from my lips." As she said this she looked so utterly determined that Amalasuntha made no further attempt to find out.

"Very well," she said at last, "my daughter is no ordinary woman. And so I will ask of you the extraordinary, and that is to sacrifice everything for the ultimate dream."

"Yes mother, I carry a very great dream in my heart. It is my highest aim, and to that I am willing to sacrifice everything."

"Matesuentha," said the queen, "that is unworthy of your royal heritage! Look at you. God has blessed you with a beauty in body and soul which makes you one in thousands. You were born to be a queen."

"I want to be a queen of love. They all praised me for my beauty as a woman. Very well then, I have set myself as my life's goal to be a woman, to love and be loved, to be a whole woman."

"A woman! And that is your whole ambition?"

"Yes it is, and oh how I wish it had also been yours!"

"And Theodoric's granddaughter cares nothing for crown and Empire? Do you care nothing for the Goths, your people?"

"No, mother," Matesuentha replied earnestly: "I am almost ashamed to admit it, but I cannot force myself against my feelings. The word 'Goths' means nothing to me. Perhaps it is not my fault, as you have always thought little of the Goths and despised them as Barbarians. Those were my first impressions, and they remained with me. And I hate this crown, this Gothic Empire. In your breast it has taken the place of my father, my brother and me. To me the Gothic crown was never anything but a hated, alien symbol."

"Oh, my child! Woe be to me if I was the cause of this. But even if you won't do it for the Empire, then do it for me. Without the Woelsungs I am as good as lost. Do it for the sake of my love."

With that she took her daughter's hand, but Matesuentha withdrew it with a bitter smile: "Mother, don't profane the noblest word of all. Your love? You have never loved me, nor my father or my brother."

"My child! Whom then did I love, if not you?"

"The crown, mother, and this accursed Empire. You loved only to reign. How often did you push me away from you before Athalaric was born because I was a girl, and you wanted an heir to the throne. Think of my father's grave and—"

"Please, enough," Amalasuntha begged.

"And Athalaric? Did you love him, or was it only his right to the throne you loved? Oh how we children cried, time and again, when we sought a mother and found only a queen."

"You have never complained before, only now that I am asking something of you."

"Mother, even now you are not asking it for yourself, but only for your crown, your reign. Put down that crown, and you will be rid of all your problems. That crown has brought no happiness to any of us, only pain. It is not you who is threatened. To you I would gladly sacrifice everything. It is only the throne, the crown, your idol and my curse. Never will I sacrifice my love for that, never, never!" And she crossed her white arms over her bosom as if trying to shield the love within it.

The queen was now thoroughly angry: "You selfish, heartless child! You admit that you have no feeling for your people, or for the crown of your great ancestors. You will not answer the call of honour or that of your family's reputation. Very well then, you will listen to the voice of force. You refused my love, so now you shall have my anger. Within the hour you will leave Ravenna with your servants. You will go to Florence as a guest in the house of Duke Guntharis. His wife has invited you, and Count Arahad will accompany you on the journey. Now go! Time will bend your stubbornness."

"No eternity will bend me!" Matesuentha replied, then rose and left the room without another glance.

In silence the queen followed her with her eyes. Her daughter's accusations had made a deeper impression on her than she would admit. "Love for power?" she asked herself. "No, that is not what drives me. I feel that I can protect this Empire and make it a happy one. That's why I love this crown. But I could sacrifice this crown as I could my life, I am sure of it, should the well-being of my people demand it. Could you do that, Amalasuntha?" Doubtfully she placed her hand on her heart.

She was awakened from her thoughts by Cassiodorus, who entered slowly, his head bowed.

"Cassiodorus," Amalasuntha exclaimed, shocked by the look on his face, "do you bring bad news?"

"No, only a question."

"What question?"

"My queen," the old man began, "I have served your father and you faithfully for thirty years, a Roman serving the Barbarians, because I honoured your virtues, and because I believed that an Italy which was no longer capable of freedom was safest under your rule, which has been just and mild. I continued to serve even after the blood of my friends Boethius and Symmachus flowed, who I still believe were innocent. They died after public trial, not by murder. I had to honour your great father even where I did not agree with him. But now I come to ask of my friend of many years, of my pupil if I may say so, of Theodoric's daughter a single word, a 'yes'. If you can say it, and I pray to God that you can, then I will go on serving you for as long as this grey head is able."

"And if I cannot?"

"If you cannot, oh queen, then I must bid farewell to you and my last friends in this world."

The old man was deeply moved. "What is your question?" the queen asked firmly.

"Amalasuntha, as you know I was far away at the northern borders of the Empire when revolt erupted here, when that terrible news came and the dreadful accusation was made. I believed nothing, but hurried back here as fast as I could. I have now been here two days, and not an hour passes, and there is not a Goth I meet, but that I hear that awful accusation over and over. It weighs heavily on my heart, and you too seem changed. I don't want to believe it. One true word from you will dispel any trace of doubt."

"Why so much talk?" she cried, "get to the point. What is your question?"

"Just reply with a simple 'yes'. Are you innocent of the deaths of the three dukes?"

"Even if I was not, they thoroughly deserved to die."

"Amalasuntha, I beg of you, say 'yes'!"

"You suddenly seem very concerned about the Gothic rebels."

"I beg of you," the old man pleaded, falling to his knees, "Theodoric's daughter, say 'yes' if you can."

"Stand up," she said, turning away from him, "you have no right to ask such a question."

"No," said the old man, calmly regaining his feet, "not any more. From this moment on I no longer belong to this world."

"Cassiodorus!" cried the queen, shocked.

"Here is the key to my rooms in the palace. In them you will find all the gifts I have ever received from Theodoric or yourself, all my documents and my badges of rank. I go now."

"Where to, old friend, where to?"

"Into the monastery I founded near Squillacium in Apulia. From now I will devote myself only to the works of God, away from the affairs of kings. My soul has long sought peace, and now there is nothing left in this world that is dear to me. Before I go I will give you just one piece of advice. Put down the sceptre out of your bloodstained hand. You can no longer be a blessing to the Empire, only a curse. Think of your soul's salvation, Theodoric's daughter. May God have mercy on you."

And he was gone before she could recover from her shock. She wanted to hurry after him, to call him back, but as she reached the curtain she was met by Petros, the emissary from Byzantium.

"Queen," he said quickly and quietly, "stay and hear me, it is most urgent. Others are following close on my heels."

"Others? Who?"

"People who are not as friendly to you as I am. Do not deceive yourself. The fate of your Empire hangs in the balance. You can no longer save it, so save what you can. I repeat my earlier suggestion."

"What suggestion?"

"The one I made yesterday."

"You mean your disgraceful proposal of treason? Never! I will report this insult to your master, the emperor, and ask him to recall you. I will no longer negotiate with you."

"Queen, there is no longer time to spare your feelings. The next emissary is called Belisarius, and he comes with an army."

"Impossible!" the queen exclaimed, feeling deserted by all. "I take back my request."

"Too late. Belisarius's fleet has already reached Sicily. Yesterday you dismissed the proposal I made to you, thinking it was my own idea. Hear me, it was the emperor himself who made it, a last sign of favour."

"Justinian, my friend and protector, wants to destroy me and my Empire!" Amalasuntha cried, now at last sensing the terrible truth.

"Not destroy you, but save you! He wants to win back this Italy, the cradle of the Roman Empire. The unnatural and impossible Gothic state has been judged and found wanting. Leave the sinking ship! Justinian offers you the hand of friendship, and the empress an asylum near her heart. All you have to do is to hand over Naples, Rome, Ravenna and all fortresses in Italy to Belisarius, and then allow all Goths to be disarmed and led away over the Alps."

"Worm! Am I to betray my people as you have betrayed me? Alas, I saw your treachery too late! I appealed to you for help, and now you want to destroy me."

"Not you, only the Barbarians."

"These Barbarians are my people, and they are the only friends I have. I see that now, and I will side with them always, come what may."

"But they will no longer side with you."

"How dare you? Get out of my sight and out of my court!"

"So you don't want to listen? Mark my words well, oh queen. I can only vouch for your life on my conditions."

"My people and my army will vouch for my life."

"I doubt that. For the last time I ask—"

"Be silent! I will not surrender the crown to Justinian without a fight."

"Very well," Petros said to himself, "others will have to do it. Come in, friends!" he called out aloud.

Cethegus emerged from behind the curtain, his arms crossed over his chest. "Where are Gothelindis and Theodahad?" Petros whispered. His dismay did not escape the queen.

Cethegus replied: "I left them outside the palace. The two women hate one another too fiercely, and that would spoil everything."

"You cannot be called my kind angel, Prefect of Rome," Amalasuntha said sternly, taking a step back.

"I might be this time," Cethegus whispered, moving closer. "You have refused the offer from Byzantium? It is what I would have expected from you. Dismiss the treacherous Greek." Petros left the room.

"What do you want, Cethegus? I no longer trust you!"

"No, instead of trusting me you have trusted the emperor, and now you have seen the result."

"I certainly have," she said dolefully.

"My queen, I have never lied to you, and in this one respect I have never tried to deceive you. I love Italy and Rome more than I do your Goths, and you will remember that I have never tried to hide that from you."

"I do remember, and I cannot blame you for it."

"My dearest wish would be to see Italy free. If it must serve a master, then I would rather have you and your Goths than the tyranny of Byzantium. That has always been my ideal, and still is. In order to keep Byzantium at bay I want to support your regime, but now I must tell you frankly: you and your government can no longer be supported. If you were to go to war against Byzantium the Goths would no longer follow you, and the Italians would not trust you."

"And why not? What is it that divides me from the Italians and from my own people?"

"Your own deeds. Two unfortunate documents, which are now in the hands of Justinianus. You yourself were the one who called his armies into your country, a bodyguard from Byzantium!"

Amalasuntha grew pale. "You know—"

"I do, and unfortunately I am not alone in that. My friends, the conspirators from the catacombs, know it also. Petros has told them about the letter. They are cursing you."

"So I have only my Goths."

"Not any more. The Balti clan and their vast band of followers are not the only ones after your life. The conspirators in Rome are so angry with you that they have resolved to tell the world, as soon as the fighting starts, that your name is at the top of that list of conspirators, against your own people. That document is no longer in my possession, but in the archives of the conspiracy."

"Traitor!"

"How was I to know that you would correspond with Byzantium behind my back, thereby turning my friends against you? You can see that Byzantium, Goths and Italians are all against you now. If war was to break out now, under your leadership, disunity would divide Italians and Barbarians, nobody would obey you, and your Empire would fall a helpless victim to Belisarius. Amalasuntha, there is a sacrifice to be made, and in the name of Italy, your people and mine, I now demand it of you."

"What sacrifice? I am willing to do anything."

"The highest, your crown. Give it to a man who can unite Italy, Goths and Italians against Byzantium, and that way you can save both your people and mine."

Amalasuntha looked at him searchingly, her breast heaving with emotion. At last she said: "My crown; it has always been very dear to me."

"I have always thought Amalasuntha capable of any sacrifice."

"Can I trust your advice this time?"

"If my advice was agreeable to you, you would have cause to doubt. If I was flattering you, and pandering to your pride, you might have cause to distrust me. But I am advising you to swallow the bitter pill of abdication. I appeal to your selflessness and your noble mind. Do not disappoint me."

"Your last piece of advice was a crime," Amalasuntha said with a shudder.

"I held your throne by any available means, as long as it could be held, and as long as that served Italy. Now it is harmful to Italy, and I demand of you that you love your people more than your sceptre."

"There you are not wrong, by God! I have not hesitated to sacrifice the lives of others for my people—" she liked to dwell on this idea, which soothed her conscience "—I will not refuse to make that sacrifice now, but who will be my successor?"

"You rightful heir, to whom the crown belongs, the last Amalung."

"What? Theodahad, the weakling?"

"True, he is no hero, but he is Theodoric's nephew, and heroes will obey him if you place him on the throne. And consider this: his Roman schooling has endeared him to the Romans, and they will stand by him. A king of the type Hildebrand or Teias might want would cause them to hate and fear him."

"And rightly so," said the queen. "But Gothelindis as queen?"

Cethegus took a step closer to her and looked her straight in the eye: "Amalasuntha is not so small-minded as to allow the petty squabbles of women to influence her when great decisions are called for. I have always thought of you as being greater than your sex. Prove it now, and decide!"

"Not now," Amalasuntha replied, "my face is burning, my heart is beating wildly and my mind is confused. Let me compose myself overnight. You have expressed your faith in me, and your belief in me that I can make such a sacrifice, and for that I thank you. You will hear my decision tomorrow."

BOOK FOUR

Theodahad

"To Theodahad it seemed a kind of misfortune to have neighbours."

Procopius, *Gothic Wars I, 3*

Chapter 1

The following morning a manifest announced to the astonished population of Ravenna that Theodoric's daughter had relinquished the crown in favour of her cousin Theodahad, and that he, the last male member of the Amalung dynasty, had ascended the throne. Both Goths and Italians were asked to swear allegiance to the new ruler.

So Cethegus had calculated correctly after all.

The unfortunate woman's conscience had been weighed down with many a foolish deed, now compounded by bloody guilt. Those who have a noble nature tend to seek penance, and to ease their conscience by sacrifice and self-denial. She had been greatly moved by the accusations of her daughter and of Cassiodorus, and so the Prefect had found her in the right frame of mind. She had followed his advice for the very reason that it was so bitter, and indeed so determined was she to do what she could for the benefit of her people, and redemption for her crime, that she had set herself even further self-humiliation as her goal.

The change of ruler had taken place without incident.

The Italians in Ravenna were by no means ready to stage a rebellion, and Cethegus had no difficulty persuading them to wait for a more opportune moment. In addition the new king was well known for his partiality to Roman culture, and popular because of it.

The Goths, on the other hand, did not at first take too kindly to their new king. Admittedly Theodahad was a man, and that alone gave him a pronounced edge over Amalasuntha, and he was also an Amalung. These considerations weighed heavily in his favour against any other possible contender for the crown. Other than this, however, he was by no means well regarded among the Gothic nation. He was unsoldierly and a coward, his soul was effeminate, and his body soft and flabby. He had none of the qualities which Germanic people normally demanded of their kings. He was filled with but a single passion, an insatiable lust for gold, land and other wealth. The owner of vast estates in Tuscany, he was constantly involved in legal disputes against every one of his neighbours. By way of cunning, force and the weight of his royal birth he had been able to expand his land holdings in all directions by acquiring neighbouring estates. As his contemporary Procopius said of him: "To Theodahad it seemed a kind of misfortune to have neighbours." Furthermore his character was that of a weakling, and he was completely under the influence of his strong-willed but malicious wife.

The ablest among the Goths were far from pleased to see such a king on the throne of Theodoric. Amalasuntha's manifest had barely become known when Count Teias, who had only just arrived in Ravenna with Hildebad, summoned the latter together with Witigis and old Hildebrand. He bade them join him in adding further to the disaffection among the people, to take over the leadership and to place a worthier man in Theodahad's place.

"You know," he concluded, "how favourable the mood of the people is right now. Since that night in the Mercurius temple we have agitated incessantly among the

Goths, adding to their dissatisfaction. Clearly we have achieved much, such as the rise of young Athalaric, the victory of the epiphany feast, the recall of Matesuentha and getting rid of Amalasuntha. Yes, we did all those things. But now the time has come to act once more. Are we to accept that a woman's place should be taken by a man who is even weaker than a woman? Do we have nobody in the Gothic nation more worthy than Theodahad?"

"By thunder and lightning, he is right!" Hildebad cried, "away with these withered Amalungs! Let us elect our own hero king, raise him on the shield in the true Gothic way, and then start attacking in all directions. Down with Theodahad!"

"No," said Witigis calmly, "not yet! Perhaps the day will come when that has to be done, but it must not happen until it is absolutely necessary. The Amalungs have a great following among the people. We would have to use force to wrest his wealth from Theodahad, or the crown from Gothelindis. Even though we may win through in the end, they would be strong enough to give us a long and bloody fight, a civil war.

"War between the sons of one nation is something terrible, and only absolutely unavoidable necessity can justify it. That has not yet arisen. Let Theodahad prove himself. As he is weak he should be easily led. And if he should fail then there is still time."

"Who can say if there will still be time?" Teias warned.

"And what do you say, wise old Hildebrand?" Hildebad asked, somewhat influenced by the reasoning which Witigis had just expounded.

"Brothers," the old man replied as he stroked his long beard, "you have a choice while I do not. My hands are tied. Along with the other old followers of our great king I swore an oath that, as long as his dynasty survived, nobody not of his house should wear the Gothic crown."

"What a foolish oath!" Hildebad cried.

"I am old, and I do not call it foolish. I know the value of having a rigid order of succession, such as it has always been practised among the Goths. And the Amalungs are sons of the gods," he concluded.

"Theodahad is a fine god's son, I must say!" Hildebad laughed.

"Be silent!" the old man cried angrily. "That is something you no longer understand, you modern people. You and your pitiful brains want to grasp and understand everything. You have lost all feeling for mystery, for miracles and for the magic which flows in our blood. That is why I do not speak to you of such things. You no longer understand them. But I am almost a hundred years old, and you will not change me. You may do what you want. I will do as I must."

"Very well," Teias relented, "be it on your heads. But once this last Amalung is gone, then what?"

"Then his followers will be free of that oath."

"Perhaps," Witigis concluded, "it is as well that your oath saves us from having to choose. We certainly do not want any ruler whom you cannot acknowledge. Let us go then and calm the people. We will tolerate this king – for as long as we can."

"But not one hour longer!" said Teias as he stormed out angrily.

Chapter 2

Theodahad and Gothelindis were crowned with the ancient crown of the Gothic kings that same day.

A great feast was taking place in Theodoric's royal palace and in the normally quiet gardens, which had been the setting for Camilla's love of Athalaric. All the notables were there, both Gothic and Roman, and the noisy feasting lasted all night. The new king, who was not fond of wine or the customs which accompanied Barbarian feasting, had retired early.

Gothelindis, however, was thoroughly enjoying herself, basking in the glory of her new-found rank. Proudly she sat on the purple throne, the golden crown in her dark hair. Her ear seemed intent only on the many shouts of rejoicing, celebrating the names of her husband and herself. And yet deep in her heart there was but the one joy, the thought that all this noise must reach down to the royal tombs, where her hated enemy Amalasuntha was mourning by the sarcophagus of her son.

Among the crowd of guests, most of whom were always happy as long as they held a full goblet in their hands, many a more serious face could also be seen. There were many Romans who would have liked to see the emperor sitting on the vacant throne, and many Goths could not accept a king like Theodahad without concern, at a time when the Empire faced many dangers in the months ahead.

Among the latter was Witigis, whose thoughts seemed far away rather than dwelling under the roof of the richly festooned drinking hall. His golden goblet stood before him untouched, and he barely took any notice of Hildebad's last call to drink with him. At last, long after the lamps had been lit in the hall and stars appeared in the sky, he stood up and went outside into the green darkness of the garden.

Slowly he wandered among the *taxus* bushes. His eyes were on the sparkling stars, and his heart was at home with his wife and son, whom he had not seen for months. At last his wandering took him to the little Venus temple by the bay, with which we are already familiar. He was looking out at the moonlight reflected on the smooth sea when something glistening caught his eye. It was a suit of armour, with a small Gothic harp beside it. A man was lying in the soft grass before him, and his pale face rose toward Witigis in greeting.

"Teias! I find you here? Did you not attend the feast?"

"No, I was with the dead."

"My heart was not on the feast either. My mind was at home with my wife and child," Witigis said, sitting down beside his friend.

"With wife and child," Teias repeated, with a sigh.

"Many asked after you, Teias."

"After me? Was I to sit next to Cethegus who took my honour, or Theodahad who took my inheritance?"

"Your inheritance?"

"Well, in any case it is now his. His slaves now plough the place where my cradle once stood." Silently he stared ahead for a long time.

"You don't seem to play the harp any more. And yet you are renowned as the best harpist and singer among our people!"

"Just as Gelimer, the last king of the Vandals, was the best harpist among his people. But there is no way they would lead me through Byzantium in triumph!"

"You don't sing very often now?"

"Almost never. But I can feel it, a day will soon come when I will sing again."

"A day of joy?"

"No, a day of ultimate, final mourning."

For a long time both men were silent.

"My Teias," Witigis said at last, "during all the trials of war and peace I have found you to be as true as my sword. And even though you are so much younger than I am, and it is not easy for an older man to befriend one so much younger, yet I think of you as my closest friend. And I know that you care more for me than you do for the companions of your youth."

Teias took his hand and pressed it. "You understand me, and you respect the way I am, even where you do not understand it. The others! And yet, there is one whom I love a great deal."

"Whom?"

"Him whom everyone loves."

"Totila!"

"I love him as the night loves the morning star. But he is so full of life, so optimistic; he can't understand that others must be and remain dark and gloomy."

"Why must they remain so? You know that I am not a curious man. And so, if I ask you in this serious hour to lift that veil a little, which hangs over you and your sadness, I am doing it only because I would like to help you. And because the eye of a friend often sees more clearly than one's own."

"Help? Help me? Can you awaken the dead? My sorrow is as final as the past. Only someone who has once, like me, felt the pitiless wheel of fate, blind to everything tender or noble, grinding everything before it with irresistible force, can understand how I feel. I have known a fate which crushed everything good before it, leaving only evil. Fools might call it the wise providence of God, that inevitability which rules the world and the men in it. He who has experienced that remorseless and never-changing rhythm of the unfeeling wheel at the centre of the world, which creates and destroys life with every turn, can never be like other men. He renounces everything once and for all, and nothing can ever cause him to fear again. But of course, he has also forgotten for ever how to smile or laugh."

"I am horrified. May God preserve me from such an outlook on life. How did you come to acquire such a dreadful wisdom so young?"

"My friend, you will never fathom truth by thought alone, you must experience it. And you can only understand how and what a man thinks if you know the life he has led. I may seem like a dreamer to you, a weakling who likes to hide in his sorrow. But I respect and value your trust and your friendship, so let me share with you just a part of my sorrow. As for the larger part of it, the immensely larger part, I will keep that to myself for now," he said painfully, his hand on his heart, "perhaps a time will come for that too. Let me tell you this night how the star of misfortune shone over my head from the moment I was conceived. You will remember, because you were there, when the false Prefect called me a bastard aloud in front of everyone, and then refused to duel with me. I had to tolerate it. I am worse than a bastard…

"My father, Tagila, was an able warrior but not a nobleman, free but poor. Ever since he first wore a beard he had loved Gisa, his brother's daughter. They lived far away at the Empire's furthest eastern border, on the cold Ister River, where we are constantly at war with the wild Gepidae and the thieving Sarmatians. The people there have very little time to worry about the church and the ever-changing edicts issued by its councils. For a long time my father could not wed his Gisa. He owned nothing but his helmet and spear, and he was in no position to prepare home and hearth for a wife.

"At long last fortune smiled on him. During a war against the Sarmatian king he captured the latter's fortified treasure tower on the Alutha River. All the vast treasures which the Sarmatians had accumulated from their thieving and plundering over the centuries were stored here, and they became his booty. As his reward Theodoric made him a count and called him to Italy, where he bought extensive and beautiful estates in Tuscany, between Florence and Luca. But his luck was not to last long.

"I had just been born when some villain, some cowardly wretch, accused my parents of incest to the bishop in Florence. They were Catholics, not Aryans, and they were cousins. According to church law their marriage was null and void, and the church commanded them to separate. My father just took his wife in his arms and laughed at the ruling of the church. But the anonymous accuser would not rest..."

"Who was the swine?"

"Oh, if only I knew! I would find him and get to him, even if he was enthroned among all the horrors of Vesuvius! He would not rest. Without let-up the priests pressured my poor mother, and tried to frighten her by working on her conscience. It was in vain. Steadfastly she clung to both her god and her husband, and she defied the bishop and his envoys. And if my father found a priest on his property he would give him such a greeting that the priest never came back.

"But who can fight those who purport to act in the name of God? The defiant couple were given a last ultimatum. If they had not separated by the time set by the bishop they would be excommunicated, and everything they possessed would be confiscated by the church.

"My father, by now quite horrified, rushed to the court in Ravenna in order to seek a lifting of the cruel edict. But the wording of the council's ruling was very clear, and Theodoric could not risk offending the Catholic church by challenging its rights. When my father returned from Ravenna, in order to flee with his Gisa, he looked with horror upon the place where his house had stood. The ultimatum had expired, and the threat carried out. His house had been destroyed, and his wife and child had disappeared.

"Furious, he stormed through the length and breadth of Italy looking for us. At last, disguised as a priest, he found Gisa in a cloister at Ticinum. Her son had been taken from her and dragged off to Rome. My father made all the necessary preparations to flee with her, and at midnight they escaped over the wall. But when my mother missed the morning prayer they searched her cell and found it empty. Serfs from the cloister followed the horse's tracks. They were overtaken, my father fell after fighting grimly and my mother was forcibly taken back to her cell. Finally her grief and the inhuman discipline in the cloister combined to send her insane, and in the end she also died. Those were my parents!"

"And you?"

"Old Hildebrand discovered me in Rome. He had been a friend of my father and my grandfather, and had fought alongside them both. With help from the king he took me away from the priests, and had me brought up with his own grandsons in Regium."

"And what about your estates, your inheritance?"

"It fell to the church, which in turn sold it to Theodahad, almost as a gift. He was my father's neighbour, and now he is my king!"

"My poor friend! But what happened to you later on? There is only vague talk. They say you were once a prisoner in Greece…"

Teias rose: "Let me remain silent about that for now; perhaps another time. Once I too was fool enough to believe in happiness, and in the kindness of a loving God. I paid dearly for it, and will never make that mistake again. Farewell, Witigis, and do not be angry with Teias because he is different from others."

They shook hands, and soon Teias had vanished into the darkness.

For a long time Witigis looked up at the stars, as if seeking answers to the sad revelations his friend had made. He longed for a glow of peace and clarity, like the stars, but a heavy mist had risen and obscured the sky. There was darkness all around him. Witigis rose with a sigh and, deep in thought, went in search of his lonely soldier's bed.

Chapter 3

While Goths and Italians feasted in the halls of the Palatium they had no way of knowing that, in the king's chambers far above them, a discussion was taking place which would have far-reaching consequences both for them and for their Empire.

The envoy from Byzantium had followed the king unobserved. And the two of them had been negotiating in secrecy for some time. At last it seemed as if they had reached agreement, and Petros was about to read out once more what they had agreed and drawn up together. But the king interrupted him: "Halt!" the little man whispered, looking as if he was about to disappear into his purple robes, "there is one more thing!"

He rose from his beautifully curved chair, crept silently through the room on his toes, and raised the curtain to make sure nobody was listening. Satisfied, he returned and grabbed the Byzantine by the gown. The light of the bronze lamp, flickering in the breeze, was playing on the ugly man's sallow cheeks, while his eyes were half closed as if squinting: "one more thing. If these beneficial changes are to occur it will be desirable, even necessary, to render a few of the most obstinate among my Barbarians harmless."

"I had already thought of that," Petros nodded in agreement. "There is the old half heathen Hildebrand, that ruffian Hildebad, Witigis…"

"You know your people well," Theodahad grinned, "evidently you have already had a good look around. But," he whispered in his ear, "there is one you have not named, and he above all must go."

"And he is?"

"Count Teias, Tagila's son."

"Is that melancholy dreamer so dangerous?"

"He is the most dangerous of them all, and my personal enemy to boot! It goes back to his father."

"How did that happen?"

"He was my neighbour near Florence. I had to have his fields, and pressed him to sell, but in vain. Ha!" he smiled slyly, "in the end they became mine anyway. The holy church broke up his incestuous marriage, confiscated his property in the process and sold it to me – ah – at a very reasonable price. I did render the church certain services in the process – your friend, the bishop of Florence, can tell you the whole story."

"I understand," said Petros, "why did the stupid Barbarian refuse to sell you his land willingly? Does Teias know?"

"He knows nothing. But he hates me, if for no other reason than that I – ah – bought his inheritance. He looks at me so fiercely, and that black dreamer is a man who would strangle his enemy at the very feet of God himself."

"Is that so?" Petros said, suddenly very thoughtful. "Well, enough of him, he shall not harm us. Now let me read the entire agreement to you once more, point by point, and then we will sign it.

"Firstly: King Theodahad will renounce the throne of Italy and the various Italian provinces and islands, which together form the Gothic Empire, in favour of the emperor Justinian and his heirs and successors. Just so there is no misunderstanding, the Gothic provinces in question are Dalmatia, Liburnia, Istria, Pannonia, Savia, Noricum, Raetium and the Gothic part of Gaul. Theodahad promises to open to the emperor, without offering any resistance, Ravenna, Roma, Naples and all other fortresses in the Empire."

Theodahad nodded.

"Secondly: King Theodahad will do everything he can to ensure that the entire Gothic army is disarmed and led across the Alps in small groups. Selected women and children will follow the armies of the Imperial general, and the rest taken to Byzantium as slaves. The king will see to it that any resistance on the part of the Goths will be in vain.

"Thirdly: In return for the foregoing the emperor Justinian will allow King Theodahad and his wife to retain their royal titles, honours and privileges for life, and fourthly—"

"I want to read this paragraph myself," Theodahad interrupted, reaching for the document. "Fourthly: The emperor shall allow the king of the Goths to retain not only all the estates and treasures which he will nominate as his private property, but also the entire Gothic royal treasure, containing an estimated forty thousand pounds of minted gold. Further, he will retain the whole of Tuscany as his private property, from Pistoria to Caera, from Populonia to Clusium, and finally he will transmit to Theodahad for life one half of all the official income from the Empire, which by this deed will be restored to its rightful ruler. Say, Petros, don't you think I could ask for three quarters?"

"You can ask it, but I very much doubt that Justinian will give it to you. I have already exceeded the extreme limits of my authority."

"We will ask it anyway," the king said, altering the figure. "Then Justinian will have to bargain with me and grant me other benefits instead."

A false smile was visible on the envoy's tight lips: "You are a clever businessman, oh king." And silently to himself he added: "But this time you have miscalculated after all."

At this moment the sound of heavy garments dragging on the floor of the marble passage outside could be heard approaching, and soon afterwards Amalasuntha entered, dressed in a long black cloak and a black veil covered with silver stars. Her face was pale, but her bearing was that of a queen, despite the loss of her crown. Her face spoke of overwhelming grief, regally endured.

"King of the Goths," she began, "forgive me if a dark shadow from the world of the dead appears once more on your festive day. It will be for the last time."

Both men were shocked by her appearance.

"Queen!" Theodahad stammered.

"Queen! Oh how I wish I had never been one! I come to you, cousin, from the coffin of my noble son, where I have been doing penance for my blindness, and seeking God's forgiveness for my guilt. I came up here to you, King of the Goths, to warn you against the same blindness, and the same guilt."

Theodahad's unsteady eye avoided her serious, searching look.

"It is an evil guest," she went on, "who I find with you here as your confidant at this late hour. The only place for a king is among his own people. I saw that too late, at least too late for me, but not too late, I hope, for your people and mine. Do not trust Byzantium. Byzantium is a shield which crushes those whom it purports to protect."

"You are being unfair," Petros retorted, "and ungrateful."

"Don't, my royal cousin," she continued, "do what he asks. Don't agree to proposals which I refused. We were asked to hand over Sicily and to provide three thousand soldiers to the emperor to be used in any of his wars. I refused to be party to any such disgrace. But I see," she said, pointing to the parchment, "that you have already struck a deal with him. Withdraw now, while you can. They will always deceive you."

Theodahad, afraid, picked up the document. He looked suspiciously at Petros.

The latter now stepped forward to face Amalasuntha: "What do you want here, queen of yesterday? Do you dare to stand in the way of this Empire's rightful ruler? Your time and power are past."

"Leave us!" Theodahad added, a little more courageous. "I will do as I see fit. You will not succeed if you are trying to come between me and my friends in Byzantium. Look, we will conclude our bargain before your very eyes." And he signed his name to the document.

Petros smiled: "You are just in time to sign as a witness."

"No," Amalasuntha replied, as she looked threateningly at the two men. "I arrived just in time to thwart your plan. From here I will go directly to the army, and to the national gathering which is to take place shortly at Regata. There I will personally uncover, before all my people, your requests, the plans from Byzantium, and the treachery of this weakling of a ruler."

"You will not be able to do that," Petros retorted calmly, "without incriminating yourself as well."

"I will incriminate myself. I will reveal all my foolishness and admit all my bloody guilt, and I will gladly suffer the death which I deserve. But this self-incrimination will at least serve to warn my people, to arouse them from Aetna to the Alps. A whole world of arms will be ready to greet you, and by my death I will save my Goths from the danger into which I led them so foolishly while I lived."

With these words she rushed from the room, afire with a noble zeal and determination. Theodahad looked at Petros, at a loss as to what to do next. For a long time he could find no words, but at last he stammered: "Help me, advise me – what am I to do?"

"Advise? There is only one advice. The madwoman will destroy both herself and us if we let her. She must not be allowed to carry out her threat. You must see to it."

"Me?" Theodahad cried, terrified. "I cannot do such things! Where is Gothelindis? She alone can help."

"And the Prefect," Petros added, "send for them!"

The two persons thus named were soon summoned from the festive halls to the royal chambers. Petros informed them about what Amalasuntha had said, but without disclosing that the agreement between himself and Theodahad had been the cause.

He had barely started speaking when Gothelindis interrupted: "Enough! She must not be permitted to do what she is planning. Her every step must be watched; she is not to speak to any Goth in Ravenna, and above all she must not leave the palace!" She hurried outside in order to place trusted slaves outside the doors leading to her chambers. A moment later she returned. "She is praying aloud in her room," she said disdainfully. "Come, Cethegus, let us disturb her prayers."

Cethegus had been following these events in silence, leaning against a marble pillar with his arms crossed over his chest. He saw the need to gather the reins in his own hands once more, and to tighten his grip on the situation. He could see that Byzantium was moving more and more into the foreground. It had to stop.

"Speak, Cethegus," Gothelindis urged again, "what needs to be done?"

"Our first need is for clarity," the latter replied, standing up straight. "Every conspiracy must have a purpose, and that purpose must be clear to all the conspirators – otherwise they will always hinder each other with mutual mistrust. You have your aims, and I have mine. Your aims are obvious, as I pointed out to you the other day. Petros, you want Justinian to rule over Italy in place of the Goths, and you, Gothelindis and Theodahad, want the same thing, in return for rich reward in terms of revenge, wealth and honours. I also have my aims – what would be the point of denying it? My clever Petros, surely you would never believe that my only aim is to be your tool, and my only ambition to be a senator in Byzantium? So I too have my purpose, but the combined wisdom of the three of you will never figure it out because it is too obvious. And so I will tell you myself what it is.

"The stone-hearted Cethegus has one great remaining love, and that love is for my Italy. That is why I, like you, want the Goths out of Italy. But unlike you I don't necessarily want Justinian in their place, thus jumping from the frying pan into the fire.

"Petros, as you know I am an incorrigible republican, as we both were when we were students in Athens. I am a republican still, and what I would like best is to throw the Barbarians out without letting you in. There is no need to report this to your master, Petros, I told him myself in a letter long ago.

"Unfortunately that is impossible. We cannot do without your help, but I want to keep that help to the absolute minimum. No foreign army, not even one from Byzantium, must step on this soil except to receive it from Italian hands, and then only at the last moment of desperate need. Italy shall be more of a gift by the Italians to Justinianus than a conquest by his armies. We want to be spared the blessings of generals and tax collectors, which Byzantium freely bestows on the countries it liberates. We want your protection, but not your tyranny."

A hint of a smile appeared on the envoy's face, but Cethegus pretended not to notice it and went on: "So hear my conditions. I know that Belisarius is near Sicily with a fleet and an army. He is not to land, but to turn back for home. I have no use for a Belisarius in Italy, at least not until I call him. If you, Petros, don't send him that order immediately, then from this moment we will go our separate ways. I know Belisarius and Narses and their military rule, and I also know what benevolent masters these Goths are. And I feel sorry for Amalasuntha; she was a mother to my people. Therefore choose now between Belisarius and Cethegus. If Belisarius lands now, then Cethegus and the whole of Italy will side with the Goths. We will see if you can manage to capture a single sod of this land if that happens. If you choose Cethegus, then he will break the might of the Barbarians, and Italy will surrender to Justinian as his bride, not as a slave. Now, Petros, choose!"

"You arrogant man!" Gothelindis said, "do you dare to set conditions to us, your queen?" Threateningly she raised her hand.

But Cethegus gripped that hand with an iron fist, and calmly pulled it down again: "You can forget the play-acting, queen of one day. Only Italy and Byzantium are negotiating here. If you forget how small and powerless you are, then you will need to be reminded. You will sit on that throne only as long as we keep you there." As he said this he stood in front of the furious woman so calmly and with such majesty that she was silent. But her look was one of eternal hatred.

Meanwhile Petros had made up his mind: "Cethegus, for the moment Byzantium can only achieve its aims with your help, and nothing without it. If Belisarius turns back, will you side with us, absolutely and irrevocably?"

"Absolutely."

"And Amalasuntha?"

"I am willing to sacrifice her."

"Very well," said the envoy, "it is agreed."

On a wax tablet he wrote a brief order to Belisarius to return home, and handed it to the Prefect: "You may deliver the order yourself."

Cethegus read carefully, and placed the tablet into his tunic. "It is in order. We have a deal."

"When will Italy attack the Barbarians?" Petros asked.

"Early next month. I am going to Rome. Farewell!"

"You are going? Are you not going to help us destroy that woman, Theodoric's daughter? Do you still feel sorry for her?" Gothelindis asked, bitter accusation in her voice.

Cethegus turned at the door: "She has been judged, and her judge is leaving. Her executioners may now take over." Proudly he left.

Theodahad, who had been speechless with surprise as he watched what had been going on, now grasped the Byzantine's hand in terror and cried: "Petros, in the name of God and all the saints, what have you done? Our agreement and everything depends on Belisarius, and now you are sending him home?"

"And letting this upstart triumph!" Gothelindis hissed.

But Petros smiled, and the smug look on his face suggested that his slyness had won out. "Calm yourselves," he said, "the all-conquering Cethegus has been beaten this time, outwitted by the despised Petros." He took Theodahad and Gothelindis by their hands, looked about him carefully and whispered: "In front of that letter there is a small dot. When Belisarius sees it he will know that he is not to take the content of the letter or the order seriously, but to ignore it. Oh yes, one soon learns the art of writing letters at court in Byzantium."

Chapter 4

During the two days following the nocturnal meeting with Theodahad and Petros Amalasuntha felt like a prisoner, although whether this was real or imagined was not entirely clear to her.

The moment she left her own chambers, or whenever she turned into one of the many passages and corridors within the palace, she had the feeling that she was not alone. Strange figures silently appeared and disappeared, seemingly as intent on watching her as they were on not themselves being seen. She could barely visit her son's grave without the feeling that she was being watched. Several times she asked for Witigis or Teias, but in vain. By order of the king they had left the city the very next morning after the coronation festivities. She started to feel alone, and surrounded by enemies all around her.

On the morning of the third day heavy autumn rain clouds lay heavily over Ravenna as Amalasuntha rose from her bed after yet another sleepless night. She walked over to the window sill, only to find a raven eerily sitting there. With a hoarse cry it slowly flew off through the gardens. The deposed queen was in low spirits, and could not help feeling even more depressed by the heavy morning fog rising from the lagoon, the dark clouds and the loneliness and gloom around her. With a heavy sigh she looked out at the landscape before her, her heart heavy with worry and remorse.

Her only consolation was the thought that she could still save the Empire by humbling and incriminating herself before her people, even at the cost of her own life. She did not doubt in the least that the relatives of the three slain dukes would execute their duty of revenge to the fullest extent, in what was sure to become a blood feud. With such thoughts in mind she walked through the empty halls and corridors of the palace towards her son's grave, seemingly unobserved this time, where she intended to re-affirm her determination to save her people by her own self-sacrifice.

As she was ascending again from the vault, after having spent a considerable time there, and as she was about to turn into a dark passage, a man dressed as a slave rushed out towards her from a dark niche. As he pressed a small wax tablet into her hand before disappearing into a side passage she had a feeling that she had seen his face before.

She immediately recognised the handwriting of Cassiodorus.

And now she also remembered who the mysterious messenger was. He was Dolios, her old minister's faithful scribe. Quickly she hurried to her rooms, hiding the tablet in her clothing. There she read: "I was sad when we parted, but not angry, and I don't want you to leave without having had the chance to confess, so that your immortal soul may yet be saved. Flee from this palace and from this city, as your life is not safe here even for another hour. You know Gothelindis and her hatred. Trust nobody except my scribe, and be at the Venus temple at the bottom of the garden at sunset. My litter will await you there and take you to safety at my villa on the Bolsen lake. Follow my advice and trust me."

Deeply touched, Amalasuntha put the letter down – oh faithful old Cassiodorus! So he had not entirely abandoned her after all. He still cared for his long-time friend and feared for her life. And that delightful villa on the lake! It was the place where, many years ago in the bloom of her youth, she had been the guest of Cassiodorus. Here too was where she had married Eutharic, the noble Amalung, and here she had spent the proudest days of her youth, surrounded by all the trappings of power and glamour of her rank.

She was normally a tough woman, but her soul had taken a battering by misfortune, and with all her heart she longed to see the site of her greatest joys once more. That emotion alone drove her to accept the advice of Cassiodorus, but even more than that she was driven by fear. It was not fear for her life, for she was willing to die, but rather fear that her enemies might yet prevent her from warning her people and saving the Empire. Finally she recalled that the road to Regata near Rome, where the great national gathering would soon take place as it did every autumn, would take her past the Bolsen lake. That meant she would actually be helping to achieve her plans by starting now in that direction. But she wanted to be quite certain, in the event that she failed to reach her journey's ultimate destination, that her voice of warning would reach her people. She therefore composed a letter to Cassiodorus, as she could not be sure of finding him at the villa. The letter would contain her full confession and a full revelation of all the Byzantine plans and Theodahad's treachery.

Behind closed doors she wrote the painful words. Tears of gratitude and regret fell onto the parchment while she wrote, and she then sealed it and gave it to the most loyal among her slaves, who was to deliver it safely to the Squillacium monastery in Apulia, which was where Cassiodorus now lived.

The remaining hours of the day passed slowly for the former queen. She had grasped the hand of friendship which had been extended to her, with all her heart. Her mind was filled with reminiscing and hope, and with a mental picture of the villa on the lake; a precious asylum, where she hoped to find peace and rest. So as not to arouse suspicion among her unseen guards she was careful to remain in her rooms, and at last the sun was down.

Amalasuntha hid only a few documents and valuables under her cloak and then, waving her slaves aside, she hurried quietly from her bedchamber into the wide passage leading into the garden. The thought of being seen by one of the usual spies, and of being stopped by him, made her tremble. Frequently she looked about her, even looking into the niches where statues stood. But everything was quiet, and this time she was not being followed. Still unobserved she reached the palace steps leading down to the garden, of which she now had a clear view. Carefully she scrutinised the path leading to the Venus temple, but it too was clear.

Only a few dry leaves rustled down the sandy path as she passed, blown by the evening breeze, which was driving mist and cloud before it in ghostly shapes. It was eerie in the grey darkness of the garden, and Amalasuntha felt chilly as the cold evening wind tugged at her cloak and veil. She took one last look at the dark mass of the palace behind her, where she had ruled so proudly, and from which she was now fleeing, lonely and pursued like a criminal. She thought about her son, whose remains rested deep within the palace, and of her daughter, whom she herself had banished from these walls and from her side.

For a moment it seemed as if the poor, deserted woman would be overcome by sorrow. She swayed, and with an effort she clung to the broad banister of the terrace.

She remained upright, but a kind of fever shook her body as the full horror of being utterly deserted took hold of her.

"But my people!" she said to herself, "and my repentance – I must finish it, and I will." Strengthened by this resolve she hurried down the steps and turned into the bushy path leading across the garden to the Venus temple. She walked quickly, trembling every time she heard the wind rustling through the leaves.

She was breathless when at last she had reached the little temple, and she looked carefully about her. But there was no sign of any litter or slaves. Everything around her was quiet, only the branches of the trees were sighing in the wind.

Suddenly she heard a horse neighing nearby. She turned to see the figure of a man coming rapidly toward her from the other side of the wall. It was Dolios. He signalled to her, looking about him carefully. Amalasuntha hurried toward him and followed him around the corner. There before her was the familiar sight of Cassiodorus's travelling carriage, a comfortable *carucca* from Gaul with adjustable shutters of the finest carved wood, pulled by three speedy Belgian Manni horses.

"You must hurry, mistress," Dolios whispered as he lifted her up into the soft cushions. "A litter is too slow for the hatred of your enemies. We must hurry and be very quiet, so that we will not be noticed."

Amalasuntha looked about her once more. Dolios opened a side gate of the garden and led the carriage through it. Two men stepped out of the bushes. One took the driver's seat and the other swung himself onto one of the two waiting horses. She recognised them as trusted slaves of Cassiodorus. Like Dolios both were armed. Dolios carefully closed the garden gate and drew the shutters of the carriage. He mounted the second horse and drew his sword: "Let us start!" he said.

And the little procession raced off into the night as if death was following on its very heels.

Chapter 5

Amalasuntha was filled with feelings of gratitude, of freedom and of being secure at last. Her mind was busily planning how she would make good all she had done wrong in the past.

In her mind's eye she could already see her people, saved by her warning voice from Byzantium and from the treachery of their own king. She could hear the brave army's cries of enthusiasm, baying for the blood of her enemies, yet at the same time ready to forgive her. Such dreams filled the hours, the days and the nights of her journey. Without let-up the little procession raced ahead, changing horses three or four times a day, and so they covered mile after mile as if they had grown wings.

Dolios watched carefully after the royal personage entrusted to his care, guarding the carriage with his drawn sword while his companions fetched food and wine from stopping places along the way. But this ceaseless hurry and dedicated watchfulness was beginning to cause Amalasuntha new concern, and more and more she had the feeling that they were being followed.

Twice, in Perusia and in Clusium, as the carriage stopped she thought she could see a second *carucca* entering the city behind them, also escorted by mounted guards. But when she mentioned it to Dolios he spurred his horse at full speed back toward the gate, and promptly returned to report that he could see nothing. From then on she saw nothing more to cause her concern, and the breakneck speed with which they neared their destination gave her cause to hope that, even if her escape had been detected, her enemies would by now have been left far behind, exhausted.

And then an accident, insignificant in itself but ominous because of the circumstances in which it happened, suddenly spoiled the former queen's optimistic mood.

They were just past the little town of Martula. It was a region in which a desolate and treeless heath stretched in every direction, with only a few reeds in the muddy ditches at the side of the old Roman road providing some variety. The reeds, disturbed by the night wind, whispered eerily. Here and there the road wound its way between low walls, covered with vines, or between old Roman tombs, mostly in a sad state of decay. Pieces of stone which had once been part of them were scattered about, and made the going difficult for the horses.

Suddenly the carriage stopped with a jolt, and Dolios ripped the door open. "What has happened?" Amalasuntha cried, frightened, "are we in the hands of our enemies?"

"No," replied Dolios, who had always seemed a taciturn and gloomy man to her, but who on this journey had been almost alarmingly silent, "a wheel has broken. You will have to get out and wait while it is repaired."

At that moment a heavy gust of wind extinguished his torch, and she could feel cold raindrops on her face. "Get out? Here? Where do I go then? There is not a house or even a tree to give a little shelter from the wind and the rain. No, I would rather stay here in the carriage."

"The carriage will have to be lifted to repair the wheel, so you will have to get out. There is an old tomb over there, which will give you some shelter."

Although very frightened, Amalasuntha obeyed, and walked through the stone fragments around her to the right side of the road, where a tall monument was visible on the far side of the ditch. Dolios helped her over the ditch in the darkness. Suddenly she heard a horse neighing nearby, behind her carriage, and she stopped in surprise.

"It is only our rearguard," Dolios said quickly, "come!" He led her through the damp grass to the small hill where the monument stood. When she reached the top she sat down on the stone lid of a sarcophagus.

Dolios had suddenly vanished in the darkness, and in vain she called out to him to come back. Soon afterwards she could see his torch once more, back on the road, giving a flickering red glow in the night mist. The storm made the hammering of the slaves, who were busy repairing the wheel, barely audible.

And so the daughter of the great Theodoric sat there, lonely and fleeing for her life, by the side of an ancient road in the middle of a foul night. The storm tore at her cloak, and the rain had soon soaked her through to the skin. She could hear the wind among the cypress trees behind her, sighing eerily, and ragged storm clouds were racing across the sky, allowing only an occasional ray of moonlight to briefly penetrate the pitch dark night. Fear was taking hold of her.

Gradually her eyes became accustomed to the darkness, and she was able to make out the shapes of objects in her immediate vicinity. Suddenly her hair stood on end with horror – she thought she could see another person sitting on the other side of the sarcophagus, directly behind her. It could not be her own shadow, it was too dark for that. It seemed to be a smaller figure wearing a voluminous cloak, its arms resting on its knees and its head on its arms, staring down at her.

She held her breath. She thought she could hear whispering, and feverishly she strained every nerve to hear. There, there it was again. "No, no, not yet!" she seemed to hear. Silently she stood up, but the other figure did not appear to move. She could clearly hear the sound of steel on stone.

Now utterly terrified, the poor woman cried out in desperation: "Dolios! Help me! Bring a light!" She tried to rush down the hill, but her knees failed her and she fell, gashing her cheek on a sharp rock.

Dolios was there with his torch in a flash. Silently he raised the bleeding woman to her feet, but did not ask any questions. "Dolios!" she cried, composing herself, "give me the torch. I must see what that was, or what it is."

She took the torch, and resolutely walked around the corner of the sarcophagus. There was nothing to be seen, but now in the torchlight she could see that the monument was not an old one like the others, but had evidently only been erected recently. The white marble showed no signs of decay, and the black letters of the inscription looked new.

Spurred on by that strange inquisitiveness which fear often instils in people, she held the torch close to the base of the monument, and read the inscription in the flickering light: "Eternal glory to the three dukes of the Balti, Thulun, Ibba and Pitza. Eternal damnation to their murderers."

With a cry Amalasuntha fell back, and Dolios carried the semi-conscious woman back to the carriage. She covered the rest of the journey barely conscious, sick in body and spirit. The closer they came to the island, the more feverish became her joy of anticipation, and the more she longed for that asylum. But at the same time her joy was mingled with a kind of foreboding. With growing apprehension she watched the trees and bushes on the roadside rush past at ever increasing speed. At last the steaming horses stopped.

She lowered the shutters and looked outside. It was the cold and eerie hour where the first faint light of dawn starts to struggle with the still, all-powerful night. It seemed that they had arrived on the banks of the lake, but she could not see its waters because of a deep grey fog which concealed everything around her. There was no sign of the villa, or even of the island. To the right of the carriage, nestling among the reeds, there stood a little fisherman's hut. The reeds were swaying in the wind, and it seemed to her that they were warning her, beckoning her away from the lake.

Dolios had gone into the hut, and a moment later he came back and lifted his charge from the carriage. He then led her silently across the meadow and toward the reeds. There, on the bank, lay a small ferryboat, seeming to float more in the fog than the water.

An old man in a grey tattered cloak was sitting at the helm, his long white hair blowing wildly about his face. He seemed to be dreaming, his eyes closed, not even opening them when the former queen stepped aboard the small craft and sat down on a small folding chair in it.

Dolios went to the bow and took up two oars. The slaves stayed with the carriage.

"Dolios," Amalasuntha cried, concerned, "it is very dark. Will the old man be able to steer in this fog, without a light on either shore?"

"A light would not help him, queen, he is blind."

"Blind?" the frightened woman cried, "then let us land. Go back!"

"I have been navigating this lake for twenty years," said the old man, "no man with sight knows the way as well as I do."

"Were you born blind then?"

"No. Theodoric the Amalung had my eyes put out because he thought I had been hired to murder him by Duke Alaric of the Balti, Thulun's brother. I was a servant of the Balti and a follower of Alaric, but I was as innocent as was my master Alaric himself, who was banished just the same. A curse on the Amalungs!" he cried, tugging angrily at the helm.

"Be silent, old man!" Dolios commanded.

"Why shouldn't I say what I have been saying with every stroke of the oar for twenty years. A curse on the Amalungs! It gives me rhythm as I row. A curse on the Amalungs!"

The fugitive queen looked at the old man with a shudder. He was indeed steering with absolute confidence in a straight line, his cloak and his white hair flying in the wind. There was fog and silence all around her, and only the sound of the oars could be heard in the silence. It seemed to her as if Charon was rowing her across the River Styx into the grey land of the shadows. Feeling feverish she wrapped her cloak more tightly about her. A few more strokes of the oars, and they had landed.

Dolios lifted the trembling woman out of the boat, and the old man turned the boat around and rowed back just as confidently as he had come. Amalasuntha followed him with her eyes until he vanished into the fog.

And then she thought she could hear the sound of oars once more, those of another boat, quickly drawing closer. She asked Dolios the reason for this sound.

"I hear nothing," the latter replied, "you are too overwrought. Come into the house." Supported by him she staggered up the steps which had been hewn into the rock, and which led up to the castle-like villa. Because of the fog she could see very little of the garden, which she remembered so vividly, and which stretched along both sides of the path. She could barely even make out the rows of trees.

At last they reached the high portal, a bronze door in a black marble frame. Dolios knocked with the hilt of his sword, sending an echoing sound through the vast hall, and the door opened.

Amalasuntha remembered how she had once entered this very same door as a young bride by her husband's side, how the door had been made almost impassable with flowers, and how the gatekeepers, who had been a newly married couple like themselves, had greeted them so cheerfully.

The gloomy-looking slave with the untidy grey hair, who now stood before her with a torch and keys, was a stranger to her.

"Where is Fuscina, the wife of the former *ostiarius*? Isn't she in the house any more?" she asked.

"She drowned in the lake long ago," the old slave replied indifferently and walked ahead of them with the torch. Amalasuntha followed, shuddering inwardly as she visualised the cold, dark waves over which she had just travelled, and which had taken the happy woman's life. They walked through courtyards and halls, all deserted, their footsteps resounding in the emptiness. The entire villa seemed like a mausoleum.

"Is the house uninhabited? I will need a slave woman."

"My wife will serve you."

"Is there anyone else in the villa?"

"Only one other slave. A Greek physician."

"A physician? I will—"

At that moment dull blows could be heard against the main door, through which they had entered just a few moments before. Terrified, Amalasuntha took the arm of Dolios. "What was that?" she asked, as she heard the door closing again with a heavy thud.

"It was only someone seeking admission," said the *ostiarius* and unlocked the door of the room which had been prepared for the fugitive. She was greeted by the musty air of a room which had not been opened for a long time, but she was deeply touched as she recognised the familiar walls decorated with tortoiseshell. It was the same room which she had occupied twenty years before. Overcome by her memories she sank down on the small *lectus*, which was covered with dark coloured cushions.

She dismissed the two men, drew the curtains of the bed about her, and was soon overcome by an uneasy sleep.

Chapter 6

For a long time she lay thus, she did not know how long, half asleep and half awake, and picture after picture raced past her restless eyes. There was Eutharic with his painful smile, and Athalaric in his sarcophagus, seemingly beckoning her to join him. Then there was Matesuentha's accusing face, fog and clouds and leafless trees. Suddenly there were three angry warriors with pale faces and blood on their clothes, and with them the blind boatman from the land of shadows. Once more she thought she was back on that lonely heath, at the base of the monument to the three Balti warriors. Again there was a rustling behind her. A hooded figure seemed to be bending over her, coming closer and closer until she thought she would suffocate. Fear gripped her. Suddenly she awoke from her dream, sat up and looked about her – no, it was not a dream – there, behind the bed curtains was a rustling sound, and a hooded shadow vanished through the wall. With a loud cry Amalasuntha tore open the curtain, but there was nothing to be seen.

Had she only been dreaming after all? In any case she could not bear to be alone any longer with her fears, and she pressed an agate knob on the wall, which rang a gong outside. In a moment a slave appeared, by the look of his face and clothes an educated man. He introduced himself as the Greek physician. She told him her tale of terror, and of her feverish dreams these last few hours. He told her that it was a result of all the excitement, and that she might have caught a chill during her journey. He prescribed a warm bath and left in order to arrange it.

Amalasuntha remembered the magnificent baths which, located in two levels, one above the other, occupied the entire right wing of the villa. The lower level of the octagonal building, intended for cold baths, was connected directly to the lake, its water filtered through sieves which kept out impurities. The metal ceiling of the lower level also served as the bottom of the warm baths located on the upper level. It was divided into two semicircular halves, which could be retracted into the walls of the building so that the two levels became one towering whole. It could then be filled entirely with lake water, and be used for swimming and diving as well as ablution purposes.

Normally however the metal plates formed the bottom of the warm baths, which occupied the upper level, and which were a labyrinth of some one hundred pipes with countless dolphins, tritons and medusas, which served to introduce scented waters mixed with various oils and essences. Graceful steps led from the gallery, where one disrobed, down into the shell-shaped basin of the actual baths.

While Amalasuntha was still reminiscing about these rooms, the wife of the *ostiarius* appeared in order to conduct her to the baths. They walked through vast halls and libraries, from which Cassiodorus's familiar scrolls and books were noticeably absent, toward the garden. The slave woman was carrying towels, oil flasks and a jar of ointment. At last they reached the actual baths building of grey marble, and they walked past the room which served for ball games and gymnastics before or after the bath. They left behind them the dressing rooms and heating chambers and hurried directly to the *caldarium*, or warm baths. Silently the woman opened a door in the marble wall.

Amalasuntha entered and was standing on the small gallery surrounding the basin. A flight of steps in front of her led down to the basin, from which warm and delightful smells were rising. Light entered from above through an octagonal dome of ground glass, and near the entrance there were some cedar steps leading to the diving board. All around the gallery and the actual baths various reliefs concealed the pipes and heating arrangements. Without a word the woman put down the towels and other utensils on the soft carpet covering the gallery floor, and turned to go.

"From where do I know you?" Amalasuntha asked, looking at her thoughtfully, "how long have you been here?"

"For eight days." And she opened the door.

"And for how long have you been serving Cassiodorus?"

"I have always served only the Duchess Gothelindis."

At the mention of that name Amalasuntha sprang to her feet with a cry of terror and grabbed for the woman's gown, but too late. She was already outside, and the key could be heard turning in the lock. In vain she looked for another exit, but there was no escape. Suddenly an overpowering terror came over the queen. She began to feel that she had been cruelly deceived, and that there was a dreadful secret hidden here. Her heart was filled with mortal fear, and flight was the only thing she could think of.

But there seemed to be no avenue of escape. The inner sides of the doors were plates of impenetrable marble, and they were so tightly shut that not even a needle could enter a crack. Desperately she searched, but only the dolphins and tritons returned her stare. At last her eyes came to rest on the head of a Medusa directly opposite her, its hair a nest of snakes, and a cry of despair issued from her lips. The Medusa's face had been pushed to one side, and the oval opening under the snake hair was filled by a living face. Could it be a human face?

The trembling woman clung to the marble wall of the gallery and leaned forward to see better. Yes, there could be no mistake, she was looking at the distorted face of Gothelindis, hate glowering from her one eye.

Amalasuntha fell to her knees and hid her face: "You? Here?"

A hoarse laughter was her reply. "Yes, Amalung woman, I am here and so are your last moments! This island and this house are mine! They will be your tomb! Dolios and all Cassiodorus's other slaves are mine too, sold to me eight days ago. I lured you here, and I followed you here like a shadow. For endless days and nights I have curbed the burning hatred in my heart so that here, at last, I can fully savour the sweet taste of revenge. I am going to watch for hours as you writhe before me in mortal terror, and I want to see how fear reduces your arrogance to a miserable wreck, until you beg for mercy at my feet. Oh yes, I am going to drink a whole ocean of revenge!"

Amalasuntha rose to her feet, wringing her hands: "Revenge? For what? Why this deadly hate?"

"Ha! So you even have the effrontery to ask? Certainly decades have passed, and happy people forget quickly, but hatred has a long memory. Have you forgotten how one day two young girls played under the *plantana* trees on the meadow outside Ravenna? They were the first among their playmates, both young and both pretty, one a king's daughter and the other a daughter of the Balti. The girls were to elect a play queen, and they chose Gothelindis because she was even lovelier than you and not so lordly. They chose her once, twice in succession. But the king's daughter stood by, consumed by boundless pride mingled with jealousy. And when they chose me for the third time, she picked up the sharp, pointed garden shears—"

"Oh stop, Gothelindis, enough!"

"And threw them at me. The shears found their mark. I fell to the ground, crying and bleeding. My whole cheek was a gaping wound, and my eye was pierced. Oh how that hurts, even now!"

"Forgive me, Gothelindis!" the captive queen wailed. "You must have forgiven me long ago."

"Forgive? Me forgive you? Am I to forgive you for taking my eye and my beauty? You had won, and won for good. Gothelindis was no longer a threat to you. Disfigured, she mourned in silence, avoiding people.

"Years passed. And then one day there came to the court in Ravenna the noble Eutharic, from Spain, the Amalung with the dark eyes and the gentle soul. He, although himself ill, took pity on the half blind girl, and he talked to her, full of goodness and kindness. He did not care that she was ugly, so ugly that almost everyone shunned her. Oh how that did my thirsting soul good! And it was decided, in order to bridge the ancient hatred between the two families, that the poor daughter of the Balti should become the wife of the noblest among the Amalungs. That hatred between the two families went back many years. Even Duke Alaric of the Balti had been executed on the strength of an anonymous and unproven charge.

"Then you heard about it, you who had disfigured me, and you resolved to take my beloved from me, not because you loved him but out of pride. You just had to have the leading Goth and next male heir to the throne and crown for yourself. That was what you resolved, and you achieved it, because your father could not refuse you anything. And so Eutharic soon forgot his pity for the one-eyed ugly duckling once the hand of a beautiful royal princess beckoned. As a consolation – or was it to ridicule me – I was also given an Amalung, that miserable coward Theodahad!"

"Gothelindis, I swear to you, I never had any idea you loved Eutharic. How could I—"

"Of course, how could you suspect that your ugly former rival would aim so high? Oh you accursed wretch! If you had at least loved him and made him happy I would have forgiven you everything. But you never did love him, because you could only ever love the sceptre. You made him miserable! For years I watched him by your side, unloved, depressed, chilled to his very heart by your icy pride. You caused him such sorrow by your coldness that you effectively murdered him at an early age. You had stolen my beloved and driven him to an early grave. Revenge! Revenge for him!"

The loud cry of "Revenge!" reverberated around the building.

"Help me! Help me!" Amalasuntha cried, and ran along the gallery wall, desperately seeking an escape.

"Go on and shout. Nobody will hear you here except for the god of revenge. Do you really think I curbed my hatred all this time for nothing? I could have so often reached you in Ravenna, if I had wanted to, with a dagger or with poison, but no! I led you here. That night at the monument to my cousins and an hour ago beside your bed I held back my arm from striking you only with the greatest effort. You shall die slowly, inch by inch, and I want to watch as your terror mounts hour by hour."

"Oh you dreadful woman!"

"What are a few hours against the decades for which you have been torturing me, with my disfigurement, with your beauty, and by having my beloved. But make no mistake, you will pay for it now!"

"What are you going to do?" the terrified victim cried, still frantically seeking a way out.

"I plan to drown you very slowly in these baths, these fountains which your friend Cassiodorus had built. You have no idea of the tortures of jealousy and helpless fury I endured in this house while you shared Eutharic's bed! Not only that; I was one of your attendants and I had to serve you. In these very baths, arrogant woman that you are, I loosened your sandals and dried your proud limbs. And in these baths you shall die!"

With that she pressed a spring. The bottom of the large basin in the upper level, the circular steel plate, divided into two halves and disappeared into the walls on either side. With terror the prisoner saw the enormous depth gape at her feet.

"Think of my eye!" Gothelindis cried. At the same time the floodgates opened in the lower level, and suddenly the waters of the lake were pouring in, thundering and hissing, rising higher and higher with terrifying speed.

Amalasuntha could see certain death before her eyes. There was no escape, and no pleading would placate her demonic foe. But now the old Amalung pride and courage came back to her, and so she composed herself and resigned herself to her fate. Among the many reliefs depicting Greek myths she saw close to her a statue of Christ's death. This gave her renewed courage, and she threw herself down before the marble cross, gripping it with both hands. She prayed silently as the waters rose higher and higher, and already they were licking against the gallery steps.

"You want to pray, murderess? Get away from that cross!" Gothelindis cried fiercely. "Think of the three dukes!" Suddenly the dolphins and tritons on her right started to spew out streams of hot water, and white steam squelched from the pipes.

Amalasuntha jumped up and hurried over to the left side of the gallery. "Gothelindis, I forgive you. Kill me, but please, I want you to forgive me too for what I have done to you."

The water rose and rose. Already it had covered the top step, and the floor of the gallery itself was under water. "Me forgive you? Never! Think of Eutharic!"

And now steaming jets of water hissed at Amalasuntha from the left as well. She fled to the centre, directly opposite the Medusa's head, which was the only place the water jets could not reach. If she could manage to climb onto the diving platform here she might hold out a little longer. Gothelindis seemed to be expecting this, and obviously planned to enjoy her prolonged agony. Already water was splashing her feet; she fled up the brown steps and leaned against the balustrade: "Hear me, Gothelindis! My last request! Not for me – for my people, for our people. Petros wants to destroy us all, and Theodahad—"

"Yes, I knew that this accursed Empire would be your last concern in life. But despair! It is already lost! Those stupid Goths, who for centuries have preferred Amalungs to Balti, are doomed, sold out and betrayed by an Amalung. Belisarius is coming, and there is nobody to warn them."

"There you are wrong, you fiend, they have been warned. I, their queen, have warned them. Long live my people! Death and destruction to their enemies, and mercy for my soul!"

And with one quick leap she threw herself from the balustrade into the raging waters, which swallowed her instantly.

Gothelindis stared fixedly at the place where she had stood. "She has vanished," she said, and then looked into the water. Amalasuntha's bosom band was still floating on top of the waves, and slowly Gothelindis said to herself: "Even in death this woman has bested me. Oh how short was my revenge after so long a hatred!"

Chapter 7

A few days after these events a number of high-ranking Roman officials were assembled in the chambers of the Byzantine envoy in Ravenna. They included notables from both the church and the nobility, among them two former bishops from the eastern Empire, Hypatius and Demetrius.

The faces of all those present showed great excitement as the skilful Petros closed his address with the following words: "This is why I have asked you all here, noble Romans and worthy bishops from both Empires. In the name of my emperor I now put before you, openly and formally, our imperial protest against all of the treacherous and violent deeds which have been secretly perpetrated against the noble woman. She vanished from Ravenna nine days ago, probably abducted from your midst by force, she who had always been a friend and protector of Italy. On the very same day the queen, who is known to be her bitter enemy, also vanished. I have sent out messengers in all directions, but as yet there is no news. If…"

He could not complete his sentence. There was a dull noise coming from the Forum of Hercules, steadily growing louder, and soon footsteps could be heard in the vestibule. The curtain was thrown open, and one of the envoy's Byzantine slaves rushed into the room, covered in dust.

"Master," he cried, "she has been murdered!"

"Murdered!" the words were repeated around the room.

"By whom?" Petros asked.

"By Gothelindis, in the villa on the Bolsen lake."

"Where is her body? Where is the murderess?"

"Gothelindis claims that the former queen drowned in the baths, because she had been tampering with the controls without understanding how they worked. But it is known that she followed her victim on her heels from the moment she left here. Goths and Romans hurried to the villa in their hundreds so that they can conduct her body here in a solemn procession. The queen fled from the revenge of her people, and is now in the fortress of Ferretri."

"Enough!" Petros cried indignantly, "I am now going to hurry to the king, and I will call on you worthy men to follow me. I will need you as witnesses when I report what has happened, to Justinian." Immediately, at the head of the group, he hurried to the palace.

On their way they came across masses of people in a state of shock and indignation. The news had swept through the city like wildfire, and by now everybody knew.

When the crowd recognised the envoy from Byzantium and the nobles of the city they opened a path for them, which closed again the moment they had passed. The crowd then followed them to the palace, where they threatened to tear down the gates. The number of people in front of the palace, and the noise, grew by the minute. In the Forum of Honorius the people of Ravenna were gathering. Already they were combining their grief over their former benefactress with the hope that this might now finally spell the end of Barbarian rule. The Imperial envoy's appearance increased this hope, and the mood of the people in front of the palace was growing ugly. No longer were Theodahad and Gothelindis the only ones under threat.

Meanwhile Petros and his companions had reached the chambers of the helpless king. The latter's resolve had disappeared along with his wife; he feared the angry crowd, and had sent for Petros to seek his advice and support. Not only had it been he who, with Gothelindis, had decided that Amalasuntha was to die, but he had also been involved in the manner of doing it. It therefore seemed to Theodahad only reasonable that Petros should now help him face the consequences of that deed, and he was thus very much dismayed when, on greeting Petros with open arms, he found the latter in a threatening mood.

"I call you to account, king of the Goths," Petros cried even before he had passed through the door. "In the name of Byzantium I demand that you account for Theodoric's daughter. You know that Justinian had promised her his special protection. Every hair on her head is therefore holy, as is every drop of her blood. Where is Amalasuntha?"

The king stared at him in utter surprise. He admired the convincing act Petros was putting on, but could not fathom the reason for it. He did not reply.

"Where is Amalasuntha?" Petros repeated threateningly, taking a step forward, his followers close on his heels.

"She is dead," Theodahad replied, taking a backward step and becoming frightened.

"She has been murdered," cried Petros, "and the whole of Italy knows it. She has been murdered by you and your wife. Justinian, my great master, was this woman's protector. Now he will be her avenger. In his name I now declare war on you, you and your bloodthirsty Barbarians, war against your whole nation."

"War against you and your whole nation!" the Italians repeated, carried away by the might of the moment and now unleashing the hatred they had harboured for so long. Like a tidal wave they descended upon the trembling king.

"But Petros," the king stammered, terrified and alarmed, "surely you remember our contract, and surely you will—"

But the envoy took a papyrus scroll from his cloak and tore it in half. "Any bond between my emperor and your bloodstained house is now severed. You yourselves, by your gruesome deed, have forfeited any protection you might have had. No contracts. War!"

"My God!" Theodahad wailed, "anything but war and fighting! What is it you demand, Petros?"

"Surrender! Withdrawal from Italy! You and Gothelindis will be taken to Byzantium, and there you will be judged before Justinian's throne. There—"

But his speech was interrupted by the sound of a Gothic horn, and a strong detachment of Gothic soldiers rushed into the room with drawn swords, led by Count Witigis.

As soon as they had heard the news of Amalasuntha's death, the Gothic leaders had assembled the most important men in the nation for a meeting by the Porta Romana, in order to discuss how they would maintain order. They had appeared in the Forum of Honorius at just the right time, as the crowd was becoming more and more threatening. An occasional dagger could already be seen blinking in the sunlight, and here and there was heard the cry of: "Down with the Barbarians!"

These gestures ceased and the voices became silent the instant the hated Goths could be seen approaching in closed formation from the Via Palatine. The Goths marched diagonally through the crowd, without meeting any resistance, and while Count Teias and Hildebad were busy securing the gates and terraces of the palace, Witigis and Hildebrand had reached the king's chambers just in time to hear the envoy's last words. The troops drew up to the right of the throne, where the king had retreated. Witigis, leaning on his long sword, stood directly in front of the Greek and looked sharply into his eyes. There was a pause.

"Who dares to play Lord and Master here, in the royal house of the Goths?" Witigis asked calmly.

Petros, as soon as he had recovered from his surprise, replied: "You are not acting wisely, Count Witigis, when you protect murderers. I have called him to justice in Byzantium."

"Have you no answer to that, Amalung?" Hildebrand cried angrily.

But the king's bad conscience gagged his voice.

"So we will have to speak in his place," said Witigis. "Listen carefully, Greek, and you too, you treacherous and ungrateful citizens of Ravenna. The Goths are a free people, and they recognise no master and no judge on this earth."

"Not even for murder?"

"If evil deeds are committed among us, then we judge and punish them ourselves. It is no concern of foreigners, least of all that of our enemy, the emperor in Byzantium."

"My emperor will avenge this woman, whom he could not save. Deliver her murderers to Byzantium!"

"We would not even deliver a Gothic field hand to Byzantium, much less our king!" Witigis replied.

"In that case you will have to share his guilt and his punishment, and in the name of my emperor I declare war on you. Tremble before Justinian and Belisarius!"

A wave of joyous applause among the Gothic soldiers was the response. Old Hildebrand went over to the window and called out to the assembled Goths below: "Hear this, Goths, good news. War, war against Byzantium."

His words unleashed a deafening pandemonium down below, as if an ocean had broken its banks, and a thousand voices joined in the refrain: "War. War, war against Byzantium!"

This reaction could not fail to impress Petros and the Italians, who were surprised at the power of the Goths' enthusiasm. In silence they looked on as the Goths were shaking hands and congratulating each other. Then Witigis, his head lowered, stepped forward once more and solemnly placed himself beside Petros. Slowly and deliberately he spoke: "Very well then, war! As you have just heard, we do not fear it. It is better by far that we have an open war, than the hidden, cancerous enmity of the last few years. War can be a good thing, but woe be to the aggressor who starts this war without reason or just cause. I can see the years ahead of us, many, many years of bloodshed and killing and ruined cities. I can see burning ruins, devastated crops and corpses floating down the rivers. Hear us well! Let the responsibility for all of this be on your heads. For years you have been agitating, and we have stood by quietly and endured it. Now you have thrown us into this war, needlessly, judging where you have no right to judge, and interfering without cause in the internal affairs of a nation as free as your own. Be it on your conscience! That is our reply to Byzantium."

Petros listened to these words in silence, then he turned without another word and left with his Italian supporters. Some accompanied him to his residence, among them the bishop of Florence.

"Worthy friend," Petros said to the latter as they parted, "those letters from Theodahad regarding that certain matter, which you kindly allowed me to see, could you let me have them? I need them, and they can be of no further use to your church."

"The case was decided long ago," the bishop replied, "and the estates have been irrevocably acquired. The documents are yours."

The envoy now bid farewell to his friends, who hoped to see him back in Ravenna soon with the Imperial army, and then hurried back to his chambers. Once there he immediately despatched a messenger to Belisarius, commanding him to begin an immediate attack.

He then wrote a detailed report to the emperor, closing with the following words: "And so, my emperor, it would seem that you have reason to be pleased with the services of your most loyal subject, and with the situation here. The Barbarian nation has been split into factions. On the throne there sits a king who is despised by his people, who is incompetent and treacherous. The enemy has been caught by surprise with no time to mobilise, and the Italian population everywhere has been won over for you. We cannot fail! Unless a miracle happens these Barbarians will have to fall to us, almost without a fight.

"And here again, as has happened so many times, my illustrious emperor appears as the protector and avenger of justice. It is a remarkable coincidence that the trireme on which I have been travelling is called *Nemesis*.

"There is only one thing which saddens me enormously. Despite my loyalty and my earnest efforts I was not able to save the life of Theodoric's unfortunate daughter. I beg of you to at least assure the empress, who has never been favourably disposed towards me, that I did make every effort to do everything I could for the late Queen of the Goths. The empress had expressly charged me with her care during our last discussion.

"As regards your enquiry about Theodahad and Gothelindis, by whose help the Gothic Empire will be delivered into our hands, I will respond, with your permission, by quoting the first rule of diplomacy: it is too dangerous to have people at court who share our deepest secrets."

Petros sent this letter ahead as quickly as he could via the bishops Hypatius and Demetrius, who were to return to Byzantium via Brundusium and from there overland through Epidamnus directly to Byzantium. He himself intended to follow a few days later, travelling slowly along the coast in order to gauge the mood of the local people everywhere, inciting them further where he could. From there he was to sail via the Peloponnesus and Euboea to Byzantium, for the empress had instructed him to travel by sea and given him messages to deliver in Athens and Lampsakos along the way.

Even before leaving Ravenna, Petros was going over in his mind how successful his mission in Italy had been, and he looked forward to the reward which would now await him in Byzantium. He would return twice as rich again as he was when he had left. He had never admitted to Gothelindis that he had come with instructions to destroy Amalasuntha. Instead, he had impressed on her the danger of falling into disfavour with the emperor and empress, and how it was only reluctantly and on payment of large sums that he allowed himself to be won over to her plan to kill the former queen. In effect, he had been using her as a pawn in his own deadly game of chess. He was looking forward to the certain honour of being made a patrician on his arrival in Byzantium, and more particularly he longed for the day when he would be able to face his arrogant cousin Narses, who had never promoted him, as an equal.

"Everything has gone exactly as I wished," he said to himself with satisfaction as he was sorting through his papers. "And this time, my proud friend Cethegus, my cunning proved to be very successful after all. And the little master of rhetoric from Thessalonica managed to go further with his short steps than you did, with your proud aggressive gait. Now I only have to see to it that Theodahad and Gothelindis don't escape to the court in Byzantium, because that would be altogether too dangerous. Perhaps the empress's question was intended as a warning. No, this royal pair must vanish from our paths."

He had his host called, and said his farewells to him. He also gave him a small dark coloured vase of the type used for the keeping of documents. He sealed it with his own ring, which bore a delicately carved scorpion, and wrote a name on the wax tablet attached to the vase. He then said to his host: "Find this man during the coming Gothic national assembly at Regata and give him this vase. Its contents belong to him. Farewell, and I hope to see you again soon, here in Ravenna." He left the house with his slaves and went on board his ship. While the *Nemesis* carried him away his mind dwelt on the honours which awaited him.

As his ship was finally approaching the harbour of Byzantium, the envoy looked with pleasure on the lovely white marble villas in their lush evergreen gardens, and reflected that he would soon be living there too, as a patrician and a Senator. At the request of the empress he had sent news ahead of his imminent arrival by way of one of the fast Imperial sailing ships as it was leaving Lampsakos.

Just before the *Nemesis* entered the harbour of Byzantium she was greeted by the magnificent pleasure ship belonging to the empress. As soon as the latter vessel recognised the *Nemesis* she struck her purple flag, and bade the *Nemesis* to stop. A short time later a messenger from the empress stepped aboard the galley. It was Alexandros, the former Imperial envoy to Ravenna.

Alexandros handed a letter from the emperor to the captain of the *Nemesis*, which the latter read with shocked surprise before turning to Petros: "In the name of the emperor Justinian! You have been found guilty of forgery and misappropriation of tax money over a period of many years. You have therefore been sentenced for life to the metal mines at Cherson, in the lands now occupied by the Ultziagirian Huns. Furthermore you abandoned Theodoric's daughter to her fate at the hands of her enemies. The emperor would have been willing to accept from your letter that you were not to blame for this, but the empress has been inconsolable over the death of her royal sister, and she revealed your old crimes to the emperor. Also, a letter from the Prefect Cethegus to the emperor informed the latter that you and Gothelindis had planned the death of the former queen together in secret. The empress has convinced the emperor of your guilt in this matter also. Your property is confiscated. Finally the empress asked me to tell you—" he whispered into the ear of the now completely shattered man "—that you yourself, in your clever letter, had advised her to destroy those who share dangerous knowledge. Captain, you will conduct the convicted and sentenced criminal to his destination immediately."

Alexandros returned to the royal ship *Thetis*, and the *Nemesis* turned, left the harbour of Byzantium behind and carried away her prisoner, never again to be a part of the world or of humanity.

Chapter 8

Since his sudden departure for Rome we have lost sight of our friend Cethegus, the Prefect, who had been extremely busy during the last weeks of our story. He could see that events were now gathering momentum and that the final outcome was drawing near, and so he looked into the future with confidence. The whole of Italy was united in hatred against the Barbarians, and who else but he could give direction and unity of purpose to this hatred? Only he could utilise that hatred to full advantage, he, the head of the catacombs conspiracy, who was now also the undisputed master of Rome.

And master of Rome by this time he most definitely was. His legionaries were now fully trained and equipped, and the fortifications almost complete. His workmen had worked feverishly, day and night, for months. And now he thought that he had also succeeded in preventing the imminent appearance of a Byzantine army in Italy, which he regarded as the main danger to his ambitious plans. Reliable messengers had informed him that Belisarius's fleet, which until now had been at anchor near Sicily, had indeed sailed toward the coast of Africa, apparently to suppress piracy.

In his own mind Cethegus knew, of course, that eventually a landing of a Byzantine army in Italy was inevitable. In fact he could not do without it, needing their additional strength to topple the Barbarians.

But it was vitally important to him that this appearance of the emperor's army would be no more than the additional strength he needed to finish off the war. For this reason it was necessary, before Belisarius had even set foot in Italy, that he should initiate an uprising of the Italians. This uprising had to be so successful that the later cooperation from the Greeks would appear as only a relatively minor contribution to the eventual outcome of the war. That way he would have to recognise the emperor as the ruler of Italy in a formal and superficial sense, only the real power in the country would be himself.

With this aim in mind he had laid his plans carefully and extremely well.

As soon as the last tower on the walls of Rome was complete, the Goths were to be attacked simultaneously throughout the whole of Italy. All the fortified cities were to be taken at the one stroke, particularly Rome, Ravenna and Naples. Once the Barbarians were forced out of their fortified cities into the open countryside there was little reason to fear that they would re-conquer the Italian fortresses, especially as the Goths were known to be ignorant in siege warfare.

At that stage it would be acceptable for an allied Byzantine army to appear, and help to finally drive the Goths back over the Alps. Cethegus meant to see to it that the liberators would also be prevented from setting foot in any of the more important fortresses, because that would make it more difficult to get rid of them later.

A basic condition of the whole plan was that the Goths should be caught completely by surprise on the day the Italians launched their attack. Once war was likely with Byzantium, much less an actual declared state of war, it was unlikely that the Barbarians would be caught napping, allowing their fortresses to be taken from them in this manner. Now that Cethegus had seen through the real purpose of

Petros's mission, he had to reckon on the appearance of Justinian's armies at any moment, and it had been only by luck that he had been able to keep Belisarius away a little longer. He therefore decided that he could not afford to lose another moment.

On the day the Roman fortifications were finally complete he had called a general meeting of the catacomb conspiracy, which was to finalise plans for the attack, determine the moment to strike, and confirm Cethegus as the leader of the whole uprising. He felt confident he would be able to overcome any opposition from those who were afraid, or who only wanted to fight in the name of Byzantium, by having them carried away with the enthusiasm the younger conspirators were sure to display, once he promised them an immediate fight.

Even before the appointed day news of Amalasuntha's murder had reached Rome, as had the news of the confusion and factionalism among the Goths, and Cethegus longed impatiently for the hour of decision. At last the final unfinished tower on the Aurelian gate was complete. Cethegus himself drove in the last nails, and as he listened to the blows of the hammer he felt that the fate of Rome and of Italy were being forged at the same time.

Subsequently he gave a feast for the thousands of workmen in Pompey's Theatre. Most of the conspirators had also showed up for the feast, and Cethegus had used this opportunity to demonstrate his almost boundless popularity among the people. This had the desired effect on the younger conspirators, but there was a small group, Silverius among them, who withdrew from the tables with dark looks on their faces.

The priest had long recognised that Cethegus wanted far more than being a mere tool in the hands of the emperor, that he had his own plans, and that these plans could prove to be very dangerous to both the church and to his personal influence. He therefore resolved to topple his daring ally as soon as the opportunity presented itself, and as soon as he could do without Cethegus. He had not found it difficult secretly to incite the jealousy of many a Roman against the man whose grip on Italy grew stronger daily.

Finally Silverius had managed to use the presence of the two bishops from Byzantium, Hypatius and Demetrius, who were openly negotiating with the bishop of Rome on religious matters, but who were at the same time carrying out secret negotiations with Theodahad. Silverius used this circumstance to advantage, and via the two bishops he established close contacts with both Theodahad and Byzantium.

"You are right, Silverius," Scaevola grumbled as he was leaving the theatre, "the Prefect of Rome is Caesar and Marius rolled into one."

"He is not spending those enormous sums for nothing, and we cannot afford to trust him too much," the mean Albinus warned.

"Dear brothers," the priest warned, "be careful not to condemn one of our number unjustly. He who does so deserves the fires of purgatory. It is true of course that our friend controls the fists of his workmen just as surely as he does the hearts of his young 'knights'. That is good, for it means that he will be able to use both in order to break the tyranny—"

"And help establish another tyranny!" Calpurnius remarked.

"That he will not, not as long as daggers still kill as they did in the day of Brutus," Scaevola scowled.

"There is no need of bloodshed. Always remember," said Silverius, "the closer the tyrant, the more oppressive the tyranny, and the more distant a ruler the more bearable his rule. The heavy weight of the Prefect can be counterbalanced by the heavier weight of the emperor."

"Indeed," Albinus agreed, who had received large sums from Byzantium, "the emperor must become master of Italy."

"That means," Silverius said to Scaevola, who was becoming angry, "that we must use the emperor to hold down the Prefect, and the Prefect to hold down the emperor. Look, we have reached my house. Let us go inside. I want to tell you in confidence what is to happen at tonight's meeting. It will surprise you, and it will surprise others even more."

Meanwhile the Prefect had also hurried home from the feast, in order to gather his thoughts and to prepare for the important work which lay ahead. It was not his speech that he was thinking about. He had long decided what must be said, and he was an outstanding orator to whom words came as easily as did thoughts. He therefore preferred to let the inspiration of the moment take the place of carefully prepared phrases, as this was a more effective way of conveying what was on his mind when the time came.

But he had to struggle with himself in order to achieve inner calm. His passions were inflamed to a degree which was strange to him.

He recalled the steps he had so far taken toward his goal, ever since that goal had first gripped him. In his mind he went over the short distance still to be covered, and the difficulties and obstacles still to be overcome. He also weighed his ability to surmount those hurdles, and in the end this gave him a confidence in victory which filled him with youthful enthusiasm and zeal.

He was pacing the room with giant strides, and the muscles in his arms were as tense as they would be when battle began. He strapped on the broad and victorious sword of his earlier campaigns, and grasped its eagle-shaped hilt as if determined to fight two worlds at once, Byzantium and the Barbarians, in order to win his Rome. He then stood opposite the giant statue of Caesar, and for a long time he looked silently into his ancestor's marble face. At last he grasped the Imperator's hips and shook them violently: "Farewell," he said, "and give me some of your luck on my way. That's all I need!" Quickly he turned and hurried from the room, through the atrium and into the street, where the first stars already greeted him.

More of the conspirators than ever before had gathered in the catacombs this night, as invitations had gone out throughout Italy for a decisive meeting. There were men present from all strategic points, and from the border posts of Tridentum, Tarvisium and Verona near the Alps, to Otorantum and Consentia on the Ausonian sea. All had sent representatives, as had the other famous cities of Italy. They included Syracusae and Catana, Panormus and Messana, Regium, Naples, Cumae, Capua and Beneventum, Antium and Ostia, Reata and Narnia, Volsinii, Urbsvetus and Spoletum, Clusium and Perusia, Auximum and Ancona, Florence and Faesulae, Pisa, Luca, Luna and Genoa, Ariminum, Caesena, Faventia and Ravenna, Parma, Dertona and Placentia, Mantua, Cremona and Ticinum (Pavia), Mediolanum, Comum and Bergamum, Asta and Pollentia, and from the northern and eastern coast of the Ionian Sea there were Concordia, Aquileja, Jardera, Scardona and Salona.

There were serious-faced senators and grey-headed mayors of ancient cities, which their ancestors had ruled for centuries. There were clever merchants, broad-shouldered farmers, lawyers and bureaucrats, and finally a considerable number of clerics of every rank and every age. They were the only properly organised group, and they obeyed Silverius absolutely.

As Cethegus, still hidden in one of the small side passages, surveyed the crowd in the grotto he sighed, and his face broke into a derisive smile. Apart from a general hatred of the Barbarians, which was not nearly strong enough to steel these men for the heavy sacrifices and hardships which would be needed to pursue their political goals, he wondered what various and often small motives might have been involved in bringing this group together.

Cethegus knew exactly what it was that motivated some individuals among them, and he had learned to control them by exploiting those weaknesses. In the end he had reason to be thankful; he would never have been able to control real Romans as thoroughly as he controlled these conspirators.

As Cethegus looked over the conspirators gathered here, each of them a patriot driven by his own motives, he went over in his mind just what it was that held this group together. Some were there because they hoped to win some title in Byzantium, some simply because they had been bribed, some because they sought revenge for some past insult, and some because they owed money to the Barbarians or simply because they were bored. And as Cethegus pictured in his mind how he would be facing a Gothic army with these men as his allies and his fighting force, he was almost frightened by his own recklessness.

It was therefore refreshing to him when the bright voice of Lucius Licinius drew his attention to a small group of the young "knights", who really did look like warriors, and whose faces and eyes spoke of courage and patriotic pride. They were indeed like the Romans of former times, and so he did have some reliable supporters after all.

"Greetings, Lucius Licinius," he said as he emerged from the darkness of the passage. "You look ready and armed to the teeth, as if you were heading directly from here to face the Barbarians."

"I can barely contain myself for hatred and for joy," the handsome youth replied. "Look, I have recruited all these young men, for you and for the fatherland."

Cethegus looked about him, greeting those present: "Are you also with us, Kallistratos, you cheerful son of peace?"

"Hellas will not desert her sister Italy in her hour of need," the noble young Greek replied, placing his hand on the beautifully carved ivory hilt of his sword. Cethegus nodded to him and then turned to the others, Marcus Licinius, Piso, Massurius, Balbus, all of whom had been ardent followers of the Prefect since the *Floralia* feast, and who had now brought their brothers and their friends. Cethegus looked around the group searchingly, as if he missed one particular face among them. Young Lucius Licinius guessed what was on his mind: "Are you looking for the black Corsican, Furius Ahalla? You cannot count on him. I did find him and speak to him, but he told me he was a Corsican and not an Italian, that his trade was blossoming under the Gothic regime, and that he therefore wanted to stay out of the fight. And when I pressed him further – I would very much have liked to have him with us, for he is brave and rich and commands thousands – he cut me off with the words: 'I will not fight against Totila.'"

"Heaven knows what it could be that binds the wild Corsican to that young milksop," Piso remarked.

Cethegus smiled, but knitted his brows as he said aloud: "I think we Romans are enough," and the hearts of the young men beat faster.

"Open the meeting," Scaevola urged the archdeacon angrily, "you can see how he is buttering up the young men – he will win them all over in the end. Interrupt him! Speak!"

"In a moment. Are you sure Albinus is coming?"

"He is coming. He is waiting for our messenger at the Appian gate."

"Very well then," said the priest, "God be with us!" He stepped into the centre of the rotunda, raised a black cross and began: "In the name of Almighty God and the Holy Trinity! Once again we have gathered here in the darkness of night to discuss deeds which will bring us light. It may be for the last time, because the son of God, whom these heretics refuse to honour, has blessed our efforts to further His glory and defeat His enemies. But after God we owe thanks first and foremost to the noble emperor Justinian and to his pious wife, who hear our sighs of suffering daily, and help where they can. Finally we owe thanks to the Prefect, who has worked ceaselessly to further the aims of our master, the emperor—"

"Stop, priest!" Lucius Licinius interrupted. "Are you calling the emperor in Byzantium our master here in Italy? We have no wish to serve the Greeks in place of the Goths. We want to be free!"

"We want to be free!" his friends echoed in a chorus.

"We want to be free, certainly!" Silverius continued. "But we cannot do that by our own efforts alone, only with the emperor's help. And don't believe for one moment, friends, that your idol here, your leader Cethegus, thinks any differently. Justinian has sent him a valuable ring – his likeness in precious stone – as a sign that he approves of what the Prefect is doing for him. And the Prefect accepted the ring. Look, he is wearing it now."

The young men looked at Cethegus, surprised and disappointed. The latter stepped into their midst. There was an uncomfortable pause.

"Speak, Imperator!" Lucius Licinius cried, "disprove what they are saying! Tell them that Silverius is wrong about the ring."

But Cethegus nodded his head as he removed the ring: "It is as he says. The ring is from the emperor, and I did accept it."

Lucius Licinius took a step backwards.

"As a sign of what?" Silverius asked.

"As a sign," Cethegus replied, the suggestion of threat in his voice, "that I am not the ambitious egotist for which some people take me. As a sign that I love Italy more than my own ambition. Yes, I also counted on Byzantium, and was willing to concede the leadership to the emperor. That is why I accepted this ring. But I no longer count on Byzantium, which hesitates and hesitates, and that is why I brought the ring with me tonight, to give it back to the emperor. You, Silverius, seem to be his representative. Here, give your master back his token, and tell him that he hesitates too long. Tell him that Italy will help herself."

"Italy will help herself!" the young knights rejoiced.

"Consider well what you are doing!" the priest warned, barely restrained anger in his voice. "I can understand the hotheadedness of these young men, but I find it strange that the hand of a mature man, my friend, should reach out for the unattainable. Think of the numbers and the wild strength of these Barbarians! Think how long it has been since Italian men have wielded swords, and how every fortress in the country—"

"Be silent, priest!" Cethegus thundered, "you know nothing of these things! You understand how to interpret psalms, and how to guide souls to salvation. That is your profession and you have every right to speak on those matters. But when it comes to war and fighting and the affairs of men, then let those speak who understand war. We will let you have the whole of heaven, but we insist that you leave the earth to us. Roman men, the choice is yours. Do you want to wait, in the hope that one day Byzantium might wake up and remember Italy? You might all be tired old men by then. Or do you want to fight for your freedom with your own swords, like the Romans of old? Of course you do, I can see it in your eyes. How? They say that we are too weak to liberate Italy. Are you not the descendants of those same Romans who conquered the world? As I address you now, man for man, there is not a man among you whose name does not speak of heroism and past glory. Decius, Corvinus, Cornelius, Valerius, Licinius – do you want to liberate your fatherland with me?"

"We do! Lead us, Cethegus!" the youths cried, ecstatic.

After a short pause the lawyer spoke again: "My name is Scaevola. Where names of Roman heroes are mentioned, it would do well to remember the family in which cold-blooded heroism is hereditary. I ask you, you hothead Cethegus, do you have anything more than a daydream like these young fools? Do you have a plan?"

"More than that, Scaevola, I have victory in my grasp! Here is a list of every fortress in Italy. On the next *ides*, in exactly thirty days, they will all fall into my hands at a single stroke."

"What? Are we to wait another thirty days?" Lucius asked.

"Only until those assembled here have had time to return to their cities, and until my messengers have covered Italy. You have waited more than forty years already!"

But the impatient zeal of the young men, which he himself had inflamed, would wait no longer. They began to grumble openly.

Silverius was quick to recognise this change in mood of the meeting. "No, Cethegus," he cried, "we cannot wait that long! We cannot bear the Barbarian tyranny a moment longer – shame on him who tolerates it another day! I have better news, young men! The army of Belisarius should be marching through Italy within the next few days."

"Perhaps," said Scaevola, "we should not follow anyone who is not called Cethegus?"

The latter smiled: "You speak of daydreams, not of reality. If Belisarius was to land, I would be the first to join him. But he will not land. That is what turned me against Byzantium – the emperor has not kept his word."

Cethegus was playing a very dangerous game, but he had no choice.

"You could be wrong, and Belisarius might live up to the promises of his emperor much sooner than you think. His fleet is near Sicily."

"Not any more. He has turned for Africa and home. You can forget him."

The sound of hurried steps could now be heard, and Albinus entered: "Triumph!" he cried, "Freedom! Freedom!"

"What news do you bring?" the priest asked joyfully.

"War! Salvation! Byzantium has declared war on the Goths."

"Impossible!" Cethegus said, almost inaudibly.

"Freedom! War!" the young men rejoiced.

"There is no doubt about it!" Another voice spoke from the passage – it was Calpurnius. "And more than that! The war has started. Belisarius has landed on Sicily, near Catana. Syracusae and Messana have already fallen, and he has taken Panormus with his fleet. He has crossed into Italy, from Messana to Regium. At this very moment he stands on our soil!"

"Freedom!" Marcus Licinius cried.

"The population is joining him everywhere. The Goths have been caught by surprise, and are fleeing from Apulia and Calabria. He is forging through Bruttia and Lucania irresistibly toward Naples."

"Lies, all lies!" Cethegus said, more to himself than the others.

"You don't seem happy about the victory of our cause? But the messenger has ridden three horses to death! Belisarius has landed with thirty thousand men."

"Anyone who still doubts it is a traitor!" Scaevola exclaimed.

"Now let us see," Silverius taunted, "whether you will keep your word. Will you now be the first to join Belisarius?"

Cethegus saw his whole world sinking before his eyes. All he had achieved had been in vain – worse, he had done it all for a hated enemy.

Belisarius was in Italy with a strong army, and he, Cethegus, was powerless and deceived, beaten. Any other man might have given up at this point, but in the Prefect's make-up there was no room for despair. His giant structure had crumbled, and his ear was still deaf from the blow, and yet he had already made up his mind to start afresh. His world had vanished, but he did not have time to grieve over it. He would create another! All eyes were on him.

"Well? What are you going to do now?" Silverius repeated.

Cethegus did not look at him. He turned instead to the meeting and said calmly: "Belisarius has landed. He is now our leader. I am going directly to his camp." With these words he went toward the exit, fully composed, past Silverius and his supporters.

Silverius was about to add another taunt when he caught the eye of the Prefect, which seemed to be saying to him: "Don't rejoice too much just yet, priest! I will get even with you for this!"

Silverius, the victor, remained silent and did not move as his defeated enemy left the rotunda.

Chapter 9

The landing by Belisarius and his army had caught Goths and Italians equally by surprise.

The last manoeuvre Belisarius had made toward the southeast had served to completely mislead all who were trying to predict the movements of the Imperial fleet. Of our Gothic friends, the only one in southern Italy at the time was Totila. In vain he, as the naval commander in Naples, had sent warning after warning to the government in Ravenna, as well as begging for the means to defend Sicily. We will see later in this story how all those means, which might have enabled him to avert the events threatening his nation, had been taken from him, and how this was to cast a serious shadow into his personal life as well, taking from him the luck which until now had always been on his side.

It had not taken him long to win over the noble, if severe, Valerius, who could no more resist the likeable youth than most other people. We have already seen how his daughter's pleading, the memory of his wife's dying wish and Totila's openness and frankness had influenced the old man the night they first met.

Totila remained at his villa as a guest. Julius was called in by the young lovers to further their cause, and their combined efforts finally caused the old man to soften his initial hard stand. This was largely because Totila, among all the Goths, was more like a Roman than any other by way of his education, way of thinking and benevolence. After all, he knew the Italian language and both Italian and Greek literature better than most Italians, and he loved and respected the culture of the old world, however much he loved his own Goths at the same time.

Finally the old Roman and the young Goth were united by their shared hatred of Byzantium. Whereas the hero's soul of a Totila hated the treachery and the tyranny of his nation's arch enemies as daylight hates the night, in the case of Valerius his whole family tradition was in absolute conflict with the emperors and with Byzantium. His aristocratic family had always been identified with the republican opposition to the Caesars, and many of his ancestors had paid for their political views with their lives, as far back as the reign of Tiberius. Neither he nor those who thought like him had ever recognised Byzantium, which he regarded as the ultimate in tyranny. What he sought was to keep away the greed, the religious intolerance and the Oriental despotism of Justinian from his Latium at any price. Furthermore, his father and his brother, on a trading trip to Byzantium, had been arrested by one of Justinian's predecessors out of greed, and then executed with the confiscation of all they owned in the eastern part of the Empire. Thus the old patriot's political hatred was reinforced by personal pain. When Cethegus invited him to join the catacombs conspiracy he had gladly accepted, the thought of liberating Italy foremost in his mind. Any approach from Imperial party supporters, however, had been rejected with the words: "Better death than Byzantium."

And so it was that the two men resolved together that they would tolerate not a single Byzantine in their country, which the Goth loved almost as much as the Roman.

The lovers took care not to try and extract any kind of commitment from the old man this early. For the time being they were content with the freedom to meet and be together whenever they wished, and they waited patiently until he would be so used to seeing them together that the idea of a permanent union between them would become acceptable to him. And thus our young friends lived through golden days. Apart from their own happiness, the young lovers rejoiced in the father's growing acceptance of Totila, and Julius in his own way was also happy to see the young lovers' bliss, which was the result of his own noble selflessness. His searching mind, which had not been satisfied with the teachings of old world philosophy, turned more and more to the search for inner peace through self-denial.

Valeria, on the other hand, was an entirely different character. She was the personification of her father's very Roman ideals. He had directed her upbringing after the early death of her mother, and from him she had learned much about the old ways of her pagan ancestors. She looked upon Christianity, to which she had been dedicated at birth and from which she had been taken again later by equally forced means, as a power to be feared. She neither understood nor loved Christian teachings, even though she could not isolate her thoughts or feelings from them. As a true Roman maiden she saw with pride how Totila's eyes glowed with warlike fire as he discussed Byzantium and her generals with her father, giving early signs of the hero figure he was later to become.

And so, when her loved one was suddenly called away from her arms by the call of duty as a soldier, she was able to accept it with composure. As soon as the Byzantine fleet had appeared off Syracusae, the young Goth had been irresistibly gripped by the instinct and desire to fight. As commander of the southern fleet it was his duty to observe the enemy and defend the coast, and thus he quickly mobilised his ships and sailed towards the Greek fleet, requesting an explanation for their sudden appearance in these waters.

Belisarius, under instructions not to appear hostile until told to do so by Petros, gave a peaceful and plausible explanation, pretending that he was there to counter unrest in Africa and piracy. Totila had to be satisfied with this reply, but in his heart he was certain there would be war, perhaps only because he wished it so. He therefore took all necessary measures, sent messengers with warnings to Ravenna, and above all tried to at least defend the old fortress of Naples against attack from the sea. The fortifications of the old city on the landward side had fallen into disrepair during the long years of peace, and the old garrison commander Count Uliaris could not be shaken from his proud but mistaken sense of security, any more than his hatred and contempt of the Byzantine "Greeks."

Generally speaking, the Goths suffered under the dangerous misapprehension that Byzantium would never dare to attack them, and their treacherous king gladly encouraged them in this belief. Totila's warnings therefore went unheeded, and indeed a whole squadron of ships was taken from him and moved to Ravenna, ostensibly to be relieved, but the ships which were to take their place never arrived.

Totila had nothing except a few small coastal vessels with which, as he told his friends, he could barely track the movements of the large Byzantine fleet, let alone prevent them. These developments influenced Valerius to leave his villa near Naples, and to visit some of his properties near Regium in the south of the peninsula, where Totila thought the enemy would attack first. His idea was to try and save at least some of his most valuable possessions from this area, and transfer those valuables to Naples, as well as making the necessary preparations for a protracted war. Julius was to accompany him on the journey, and Valeria could not be persuaded to remain alone in the empty villa. Totila had assured them that there was no danger at least for the next few days.

Thus the three of them, accompanied by a few slaves, left for the main villa near the Jugum pass north of Regium. Built right on the edge of the sea, the villa in fact extended in part out into the sea itself, a legacy of the kind of luxury which Horatius had condemned many years before.

On arrival Valerius found that his affairs here were in a bad state. His managers, who had become slack during their master's long absence, had handled his affairs badly, and it was with displeasure that he realised he would have to remain here for weeks rather than days before his inspecting, organising and punishing could put things right.

Meanwhile signs of approaching danger increased day by day. Totila sent one warning after another, but Valeria declared that she could not leave her father alone in the present danger, while the latter refused to flee from the "little Greeks", whom he despised even more than he hated them.

And then one day they were surprised by two boats arriving in the little villa's harbour almost simultaneously, one containing Totila and the other Furius Ahalla. The two men greeted each other, surprised but also pleased, as old acquaintances, and together they walked through the garden to the villa. On arrival there they parted. Totila gave the pretext that he wanted to visit his friend Julius, whilst the Corsican wished to conduct some business with Valerius, with whom he had enjoyed a mutually beneficial business association over a number of years.

Valerius was therefore pleased when he saw the intelligent, courageous and good-looking seafarer enter. After a cordial exchange of greetings, the two merchants turned to their books and their accounts as there was a considerable amount of business they had to transact.

After some initial discussions the Corsican rose from his figures and said to his host: "So you see, Valerius, that Mercury has blessed our alliance anew. My ships have brought you purple and precious cloth from Phoenicia and Spain, and they have taken your valuable merchandise from last year to Byzantium and Alexandria, to Massilia and Antioch. The result has been one hundredweight of gold more profit than last year, and it will go on increasing from year to year, as long as the worthy Goths guard the peace and the laws of this country." He was silent, as if waiting.

"As long as they can go on guarding!" Valerius sighed, "as long as these Greeks keep the peace. Who can be sure that the wind will not bring Belisarius and his fleet to our shores this very night?"

"So you too are expecting war? Confidentially, it is more than likely, it is a certainty."

"Furius!" the Roman cried, "how can you know that?"

"I have just come from Africa, and from Sicily. I have seen the emperor's fleet; one does not send a fleet of that size against pirates. I have spoken to some of Belisarius's commanders too, and they dream of Italy's treasures day and night. Sicily is ready to join with the enemy as soon as the Greeks land."

At this Valerius grew pale with emotion. Furius noticed it and went on: "And that is the main reason why I hurried here, in order to warn you. The enemy will land somewhere close to here, and I knew that your daughter had accompanied you here."

"Valeria is a Roman."

"Yes, but these enemies are the wildest of Barbarians. The army which the emperor has unleashed against Italy consists of Huns, Massageti, Scythians, Avars, Slavs and Saracens. Woe be to your beautiful child were she to fall into their hands."

"That she will not!" Valerius replied, his hand on his dagger. "But what you say is right, she must be taken to safety."

"But where in Italy can you find safety? Soon the waves of this war will close over Naples and Rome, and even the walls of Ravenna will only just stop them."

"Do you think these Greeks are that strong? Byzantium has never yet sent anything to these shores but pretenders, pirates and thieves!"

"Perhaps not, but Belisarius is a son of victory. Whatever happens, there will be a long war, and many of you will not live through it."

"Of you, did you say? Are you not fighting with us?"

"No, Valerius! As you know, only Corsican blood flows in my veins, despite my adopted Roman name. I am neither Roman, nor Greek nor Goth. I hope that the Goths will win this war, because they keep order on land and sea, and because my trade has blossomed under their rule. But if I was to fight openly on their side, then the tax collectors and accountants in Byzantium would confiscate everything belonging to me anywhere in eastern ports, in both ships and goods, and that is three quarters of everything I own. No, what I plan to do is to fortify my island – as you know, Corsica belongs to me – in such a way that neither of the combatants will worry me very much. My island will remain a bastion of peace while the seas and countries around it are resounding to the sound of war. I will protect my asylum as a king guards his crown, or a bridegroom his bride. And that—" his eyes were flashing and his voice trembled with emotion "—that is why, here, today, I want to say something which has been on my mind for years." He paused, overcome with emotion.

Valerius could sense what was coming next, and he was far from happy about it. For years he had enjoyed the idea that one day he might entrust his daughter to the wealthy and powerful merchant, the adopted son of an old friend, whose affection for Valeria he had long suspected. As much as he had grown to like the young Goth, he would have preferred his old business partner as a son-in-law. He also knew the Corsican's boundless pride and furious anger, and if he refused he had cause to fear that their old friendship would immediately turn to burning hatred. There were many terrifying stories of the man's violent nature and sudden outbursts, and Valerius would gladly have spared himself and his friend the pain of refusal.

But the latter went on: "I think that we are both men who talk of business matters in a businesslike way, and so in accordance with old custom, I am speaking directly with the father first and not the daughter. Give me your child to be my wife, Valerius. You know a part of my wealth, but only a part. It is much greater than you think. As proof I will give you double her dowry, however large it might be—"

"Furius!" Valerius interrupted.

"I think that I am a man who can make a woman happy. In any event I am able to protect her like no other man in these troubled times. Should Corsica be threatened I can take her on one of my ships to Africa or Asia. On every coast there would be waiting for her not a house, but a palace. She will have no reason to envy even a queen. I will treasure her more than I do my soul." He halted, very emotional, as if waiting for a speedy reply.

Valerius remained silent; he was trying to think of a way out. It was only for an instant, but even the suggestion that the father could have doubts infuriated the Corsican. Instantly his blood boiled, and his handsome brown face, almost tender a moment ago, was contorted with rage and turned a terrifying red colour. "Furius Ahalla," he said hastily, "is not used to making an offer twice. It is usual for men to grasp my wares with both hands the moment they are first offered. I am now offering myself. By God, I am certainly not inferior to my purple—"

"My friend," the older man began, "we are no longer living in the strict times of old Roman customs, and the new faith has almost robbed fathers of the right to marry off their daughters. If it was up to me, I would give her to you and no other, but her heart—"

"She loves another!" the Corsican hissed, "whom?" And his hand flew to his dagger, as if he was determined that his rival would not live an instant longer. There was something of a tiger in this movement, and in the flashing of his rolling eyes. Valerius sensed how deadly this hatred could be, and did not want to reveal who the other man was.

"Who can it be?" Furius whispered, half to himself. "A Roman? Montanus? No! Oh, oh no, not him – say no, old friend, say it is not he!" and he grabbed at the older man's robes.

"Who? Whom do you mean?"

"The one who landed with me, the Goth whom everyone loves. Yes, it must be him, it must be Totila!"

"It is he," Valerius said, and tried to take the other man's hand as a gesture of consolation, but he had to let go of it again immediately. A convulsive spasm had taken hold of the Corsican's body, powerful and strong as he was; he was holding both hands out in front of him as if trying to strangle the agony which pained him. Then he threw back his head and violently struck his own temples with clenched fists, laughing out loud.

Valerius watched this display of rage in terror. At last the fists came down and revealed a face as grey as ashes. "It is over," he said in a trembling voice. "It is a curse which follows me! I am not to find happiness with a woman. Once before – just before fulfilment! And now – I know it – Valeria's inner strength and her calm nature would have brought peace even into my wildly tempestuous life. I would have become different – better. And if that was not to be—" here his eyes flashed again "—then it would have been almost as satisfying to murder him who stole this happiness from me. Yes, I would have wallowed in his blood and torn his bride away from his corpse – and now it has to be him! He is the only man to whom Ahalla is indebted – and how indebted!"

He was silent, nodding his head as if lost in memories. "Valerius," he cried, suddenly pulling himself together, "I will yield to no man on earth! I would not have tolerated having to stand back for anyone else. But Totila! I will forgive her for refusing me, because she has chosen Totila in my place. Farewell, Valerius, I am putting to sea, to Persia, India, I don't know where – but everywhere I go I will be taking this hour with me!" He turned quickly, and an instant later he had gone. Soon afterwards his fast little boat was taking him away from the villa's little harbour. With a sigh Valerius left the room to look for his daughter. In the atrium he met Totila, who was already taking his leave again. He had only come to urge a speedy return to Naples.

Belisarius had again turned away from Africa, and was now off Panormus. A landing in Sicily or in Italy itself could occur any day now, and despite Totila's urging the king would not send any ships. During the next few days he planned to leave for Sicily himself, in order to obtain some certainty as to what was happening there. That would leave his friends entirely without protection, and he impressed on Valeria's father the pressing need for an immediate return to Naples overland. But the old soldier would not hear of flight from the despised Greeks. He could not and would not leave his business affairs for another three days, and it was only with the greatest difficulty that Totila managed to persuade him to accept a small force of twenty Goths as protection if the worst should happen. With a heavy heart Totila went aboard his boat, and his men rowed him back to his ship.

Meanwhile it had become dark, and when he reached his ship a dense mist hid everything in his immediate vicinity. Then he heard the sound of oars from the west, and a ship rounded the small headland, visible by the red light high on its mast.

Totila listened and asked his watch: "There is a sail on our left. What ship is it? Who is its master?"

"They have already signalled from the lookout," came the reply, "Merchantman, Furius Ahalla, had been at anchor here."

"Where is he headed?"

"To the east – to India!"

Chapter 10

On the evening of the third day after Totila had sent the Gothic soldiers, Valerius finally concluded his business and started preparations for their departure the following morning. As he was having his evening meal with Valeria and Julius he spoke about the prospects for continued peace, which he thought the young hero's desire for war might have underestimated. To him, as a Roman, the thought that "Greeks" should invade his precious Italy under arms was utterly intolerable.

"I too want peace," Valeria said, thinking, "and yet…"

"Well?" Valerius asked.

"I am certain," the girl concluded, "that it is only in war that you will learn to love Totila as he deserves. I know that he would fight for me and for Italy."

"Yes," Julius added, "there is a hero within him, and more than that, he has the mark of greatness."

"I know about greatness," Valerius replied.

At that moment the heavy footsteps of armed men could be heard on the marble floor of the atrium, and soon afterwards young Thorismuth entered, Totila's shield bearer.

"Valerius," he said quickly, "have your wagons and your carriages prepared. You must leave immediately."

The three of them sprang to their feet. "What has happened? Have they landed?"

"Speak," said Julius, "what is on your mind?"

"Nothing that concerns me," the young Goth laughed, "and I did not want to frighten you any sooner than I had to. But now I cannot remain silent any longer. Yesterday morning the tide washed up a corpse—"

"A corpse?"

"A Gothic crewman from our ship. He was Alb, the helmsman on Totila's ship."

Valeria turned pale, but remained composed: "It could be coincidence. He may have drowned."

"No," the Goth replied firmly, "he did not drown. There was an arrow in his chest."

"That proves there has been a naval fight, nothing more!" Valerius interjected.

The young Goth went on unperturbed: "But today all the villagers who pass through here daily on their way to Colum did not come. And a rider I sent to Regium as a scout has not returned."

"That still proves nothing," Valerius stubbornly maintained. His mind would not accept the thought that the hated "Greeks" had landed while there was a glimmer of hope. "The road has often been blocked by the sea before."

"But when I myself advanced along the road to Regium a short time ago and held my ear to the ground, I could hear the earth trembling from the sound of thousands of hooves. They are coming this way with lightning speed. You must flee!"

Now Valerius and Julius reached for their weapons, which were hanging on pillars in the room. Valeria, breathing deeply, placed her hand on her heart. "What is to be done?" she asked.

"Occupy the pass at Jugum," Valerius ordered, "where the road runs through it. It is very narrow, and can be held for a long time."

"I already have eight of my Goths guarding it, and will hurry to them as soon as you are mounted. Half of my men will guard you, but now you must hurry!"

But even before they could leave the room a Gothic soldier, covered in mud and blood, stumbled into the room: "Flee!" he cried, "they are here!"

"Who is here, Gelaris?" Thorismuth asked.

"The Greeks! Belisarius! The devil!"

"Speak!" Thorismuth commanded.

"I got as far as the pine forest at Regium without seeing anything suspicious, admittedly without meeting another soul on the road. Then, as I was passing a thick tree trunk and looking eagerly ahead, I suddenly felt something jerk at my neck as if my head was being torn from my shoulders, and an instant later I was lying under my horse on the ground—"

"You are a bad horseman, Gelaris!" Thorismuth scolded him.

"Indeed, when one has a noose of horsehair thrown around one's neck, and a lead ball against one's head, then it takes a better horseman than I am to stay in the saddle. Two demons, like mandrakes, jumped out of the bushes and over the ditch, tied me to my horse, took me between their own shaggy ponies and – phew!"

"Those are Belisarius's Huns!" Valerius cried.

"They raced off with me, and when I came to again I was in Regium, right among the enemy. Here I found out what is going on. The queen has been murdered, war has been declared, the enemy has taken Sicily by surprise, and the whole island has gone over to the emperor."

"And the fortified city of Panormus?"

"Fell to the fleet, which forced its way into the harbour. The ships' masts were higher than the walls of the city; they shot at the defenders from the mast tops and then they leaped down on top of them."

"And Syracusae?" Valerius asked.

"Fell through the treachery of the Sicilians. The defending Goths have been murdered, and Belisarius rode into Syracusae under a hail of flowers, throwing gold pieces about to the applause of the people."

And where is the naval commander? Where is Totila?"

"Two of his three ships have been sunk, rammed by triremes, his own ship and one other. They say he jumped into the sea fully armed – and – so far – he has not been found."

Valeria collapsed silently onto a couch.

"The Greek general," the soldier went on, "landed at Regium yesterday, in the middle of a stormy night. The city received him with rejoicing. He is now ordering his forces, and he intends to hurry to Naples. His advance guard, the yellow-skinned horsemen who brought me in, had to turn back immediately and take the pass. I was to guide them there. I led them a long way astray – to the west – into the swamps – and escaped in the dark – but they shot at me – with arrows – and one hit – I can't go on." The man collapsed on the ground in front of them.

"He is done for," Valerius said, "they use poisoned arrows! Come, Julius and Thorismuth, take my daughter to Naples along the road as quickly as you can. I will go to the pass and guard your rear." Valeria's pleas had no effect, and the old man's face looked as if he was determined to do as he had said. "Obey! I am the master of this house, a son of this land, and I will ask Belisarius's Huns what they want in my fatherland. No, Julius! You must look after Valeria. God be with you!"

While Valeria, her Gothic escort and most of the slaves hurried away along the road to Naples, Valerius with his shield and spear stormed out of the villa at the head of half a dozen armed slaves, out through the garden and toward the pass, which was situated not far away where his estates began near Regium.

The rocks on the left, or northern, side could not be scaled, and on the right side to the south the cliff fell away sharply into the sea, which often flooded it at high tide. The opening to the pass was so narrow that two men with shields, standing next to each other, could close it off like a gate. Thus Valerius had reason to hope that he could hold the pass long enough, even against a vastly superior force, to allow the fugitives a good headstart. As the old man rushed along the narrow path between the sea and his vineyards through the moonless night, he saw a light out to sea on his right, some distance away. It was obviously a ship, and that frightened him for a moment. Could it be that the Byzantines were going to attack Naples from the sea? Were they going to send armed men against him from the rear? But if that were so, would there not be more lights? He turned to ask the slaves, who had followed him from the villa very much against their will, but in vain! They had vanished into the darkness of the night, running away the moment their master took his eyes off them.

And so Valerius was alone when he reached the pass. Two Gothic guards were holding each of the two entrances to it, while the remainder were in the middle, eight men in all. No sooner had Valerius passed the first two soldiers than the sound of hooves could be heard close by. A moment later two horsemen could be seen approaching at full trot, rounding the last turn in the road before the pass. Both were holding torches in their right hands, and these torches gave the only light to be seen, the Goths having taken great care to do nothing which would reveal their small numbers.

"By the beard of Belisarius!" the first rider said, slowing his horse to a walk, "this road is so narrow here that there is barely room for an honest horse – and there is a pass ahead, or – halt! Who goes there?"

He reined in his horse and carefully stretched forward, holding the torch out in front of him, so that he presented an easy target in front of the pass, in the light of his own torch.

"Who goes there?" he called out again. And then a Gothic spear flew through the air, piercing his armour and his heart. "Enemies!" the dying man cried out as he fell backwards from his saddle.

"Enemies! Enemies!" the man behind him cried, threw his torch away into the sea and raced back, while the fallen rider's horse faithfully remained with its master's body.

Nothing could be heard now in the still of the night except the hooves of the fleeing horse and the sound of the sea against the cliff below. The hearts of the men remaining in the pass were beating faster in anticipation. "Remain cool now, men," Valerius told them, "don't be tempted to leave the pass, any of you. You in the first row, hold your shields close together, and hold your spears out in front of you. We here in the middle will throw. You three at the back will hand us spears and keep your eyes open."

"Master," the Goth behind the pass said, "the light! The ship is coming closer and closer."

"Keep your eyes on it, and call out when—"

But the enemy was already coming. The two riders who had acted as scouts were part of a force of fifty mounted Huns, with a few torches. As they rounded the bend leading to the pass, the scene became one of flickering light interspersed with pitch darkness.

"It was here, Sir!" the rider who had previously escaped said, "be careful!"

"Move the dead man back, and the horse!" said a rough voice, and the leader of the group took a step toward the entrance, torch in hand.

"Halt!" Valerius called out to him in Latin, "who are you, and what do you want?"

"It is my place to ask you the very same question!" the leader replied in the same language.

"I am a Roman citizen, defending my fatherland against thieves."

Meanwhile the leader had taken a quick look around, sizing up the situation in the light of his torch. His trained eye saw immediately how narrow the pass was, and that there was no way around it.

"My friend," he said, taking a pace or two backwards, "so we are allies. We too are Romans and want to liberate Italy from her thieves. So make way and let us through."

Valerius, whose aim was to gain time by any means he could, replied: "Who are you, and who sent you?"

"My name is John. Justinian's enemies call me 'the bloody', and I am the leader of Belisarius's light cavalry. The whole country from Regium to here has welcomed us with open arms, and this here is the first obstacle we have encountered. We would have been a lot further advanced by now if some dog of a Goth had not led us into the thickest swamp that ever swallowed a decent horse. We have lost precious time, so don't hold us up any more! Your life and property are safe, and I can promise you rich reward if you will show us the way. Speed is victory! The enemy is dumbfounded, and they must not regain their senses until we stand before Naples or, better still, Rome. 'John,' my master Belisarius said to me, 'since I cannot order the storm wind to sweep through the country ahead of me, I am ordering you to do so'. So get out of the way and let us through." He spurred his horse.

"Tell Belisarius that, as long as Genius Valerius is alive, he will not advance another step in Italy. Go back, you bunch of thieves!"

"You madman, are you siding with the Goths against us?"

"I would side with the devil, as long as it was against you."

The leader looked about him once more, to the right and to the left, and then said: "Listen, you really could delay us here for a while, but not for long. If you let us pass you shall live. If you don't, then I will have you tortured first, and then impaled!" He raised his torch, looking for a weak spot in the defences of the pass.

"Go back," Valerius cried. "Shoot, friend!" A bowstring hummed, and an arrow struck the rider's helmet.

"Now just you wait!" said the latter, and spurred his horse backwards. "Dismount!" he ordered, "all of you!"

Bu the Huns did not like being parted from their horses. "What Sir, dismount?" the nearest one asked.

John struck him in the face with his fist. "Dismount!" he thundered once more, "do you think you can slip through this mousehole on horseback?" And he flung himself out of the saddle. "Six will climb the trees and shoot from above. Six will lie flat on the ground and shoot lying down, and crawl forward along the sides of the road. Ten will shoot standing, at chest height. Ten will guard the horses. The other twenty will follow me with spears as soon as the arrows have been fired. Forward!" He handed his torch to one of his men and picked up a spear.

While the Huns were following his orders, John mustered the situation once more. "Surrender!" he cried.

"Come on, we're ready," was the Gothic reply.

John waved, and twenty arrows flew at once. A cry of pain, and the foremost Goth at the head of the pass fell. An arrow from a Hun in the trees had struck him in the forehead. Quickly Valerius took his place, his shield in front of him. He was just in time to stop the furious onslaught of John, who had immediately charged into the breach with his spear. Valerius parried the spear thrust with his shield, and struck at the Byzantine with his sword. The latter stumbled and fell. The Huns behind him withdrew.

And now the young Goth next to Valerius could not resist the temptation to finish off John, and leapt out of the pass with his spear. But that was what John had been waiting for. With the speed of lightning he picked himself up off the ground, pushed the surprised Goth over the cliff on his right, and almost the same instant he was on the right side of Valerius, which was not protected by his shield, and thrust his long Persian knife deep into Valerius's side with all his might.

Valerius collapsed, but the three Goths behind him were able to push back John, who had already entered the pass, with their shields. John went back to order another rain of arrows.

In silence two of the Goths were guarding the pass once more, while the third held the bleeding Valerius in his arms.

Suddenly the guard from the rear of the pass ran toward them through the pass itself: "The ship! Sir, the ship! They have landed, and they are going to attack us from the rear. Flee! We will carry you – somehow we will find a place to hide among the rocks."

"No," Valerius replied, trying to get to his feet, "I want to die here. Lean my sword against the wall—"

But suddenly the blaring sound of a Gothic horn could be heard from the rear. Torches flashed, and a force of thirty Goths stormed into the pass, Totila in the lead. "Too late, too late!" he cried out painfully, "but follow me, men! Revenge! Attack!"

Furiously he broke out of the pass with his foot soldiers armed with spears, and the clash on the narrow road between cliff and ocean was terrible indeed. The torches went out in the turmoil, and only the breaking dawn gave a faint grey light. The Huns, although they outnumbered their audacious attackers, were taken by complete surprise at the sudden retaliation. They thought a whole Gothic army was following, and tried desperately to get to their horses and flee. But the Goths had reached the place where the animals were waiting at the same time as their riders, and in wild confusion men and horses tumbled down the cliff.

John himself tried to get his fleeing troops to make a stand, by beating at them with a whip, but in vain. Their rush threw him to the ground, but he picked himself up again and threw himself at the first Goth he saw. But he received a poor reception, for it was Totila, and John recognised him: "Accursed flaxen head!" he cried, "so you didn't drown after all?"

"No, as you can see!" cried the latter, and struck him on the helmet with his sword, using such force that the blade cut right through the helmet and into his skull. He stumbled, and that was the end of any resistance. The nearest riders were only barely able to lift their injured leader onto a horse, and they raced off with him as fast as they could. The battlefield was cleared.

Totila hurried back to the pass, where he found Valerius with his head lying on his shield, his eyes closed. He knelt down at the dying man's side and pressed Valerius's hand to his chest. "Valerius!" he cried, "Father! Don't die! Don't leave us like this. Say at least a word of farewell." The dying man opened his eyes.

"Where are they?" he asked.

"Beaten and in full flight!"

"Ah, victory," Valerius sighed with relief, "so I can die victorious. And Valeria, my child, she is safe?"

"She is. As soon as I had been saved from the sea after a naval encounter I hurried here, to Naples, to warn you and to save you. I landed near the road, between your house and Naples. That is where I met her, and found out about the danger you were in. One of the boats from my ship took her on board and then to Naples. I hurried here in the other boat to save you, but alas, I was able only to avenge you!" And he lowered his head to the dying man's chest.

"Do not mourn over me, I die in victory! And you, my son, are the one who made it possible." Valerius stroked the youth's long blond locks affectionately. "And I am also indebted to you for Valeria's safety. Oh how I hope that one day I will also be indebted to you for saving Italy as well. You are the man who can save our country too, despite Belisarius and Narses. You can – you will – and let my beloved child be your reward."

"Valerius! My father!"

"She shall be yours! But swear to me—" and he raised himself with the last of his strength on one elbow to look directly into Totila's eyes "—swear to me, on Valeria's honour, that she will not be yours until Italy is free, and until not a single Byzantine remains on our sacred soil. Then, and only then, she is yours."

"I swear it," Totila cried, gripping his hand with emotion, "I swear it, on Valeria's honour."

"Thank you, thank you my son, now I can die happily. Say farewell to her for me, and tell her that I have entrusted her to your care – her and Italy." With those words he lay back on his shield, crossed his arms over his chest, and was dead.

For a long time Totila held the dead man's hand to his chest.

Suddenly a blinding light woke him from his daydreams. It was the morning sun, rising in golden splendour over the mountains. He stood up and looked towards the rising sun, and at that moment the sea glowed in the early morning sunlight, and the glow seemed to extend over the whole land.

"By Valeria's honour!" he repeated softly, with deepest feeling, and then he raised his hand to the morning light as if swearing an oath. Just as the dead man beside him had done he found strength and consolation in the promise he had just made, and the sacred duty he had undertaken inspired him. Thus strengthened, he gave orders that the body was to be taken on his ship and back to Naples, to the family vault.

Chapter 11

While these portentous events were taking place the Goths, of course, had not remained idle. But any really effective steps towards their defence had been paralysed, indeed deliberately thwarted, by the treachery of their own king.

Theodahad soon recovered from the shock of war being declared by the envoy from Byzantium, because in his own mind he still firmly believed that it had only been done to preserve external appearances, and to protect the honour of the Imperial court. After all there had been no further opportunity to speak to Petros alone, and the latter had to have some pretext to justify the appearance in Italy of Belisarius and his army, which had of course long been agreed to as the means for attaining their mutual goals. To Theodahad the thought of having to fight a war was quite unbearable, but he had been able to keep it from his mind by wisely remembering that it took two antagonists to fight a war. "If I don't defend myself," he thought, "the attack will soon be over. Let Belisarius come. I will do my best to make sure he does not encounter any resistance, which can only worsen the emperor's attitude towards me. If the general reports to Byzantium that I aided him in every way I could, then surely Justinian cannot do other than honour his contract with me, or at least the major part of it."

And this was the principle on which he had been acting. He recalled all Gothic forces, both on land and on the sea, from southern Italy, where he expected Belisarius to attack, sending them instead in huge numbers to the eastern borders, to Liburnia, Dalmatia and Istria. He had also sent strong Gothic forces to the west, to Gaul. As a pretext he claimed that Byzantium had attacked Salona in Dalmatia with a small force, and that Byzantium had exchanged ambassadors with the kings of the Franks. Therefore, he claimed, the main attack should be expected on land in Istria, where the Byzantines would attack with their allies, the Franks, on the Rhodanus and the Padus.

The apparent movements being made by Belisarius seemed to support these beliefs, and so the impossible situation occurred where the Gothic armies, ships and war supplies were being taken at great speed from the very areas where attack was imminent. Thus the whole of lower Italy, as far north as Rome and indeed almost to Ravenna, had been virtually stripped of troops, and all defensive measures had been neglected in the very regions where the enemy would shortly strike the first blows.

The Dravus, Rhodanus and Padus regions were alive with Gothic arms and soldiers, whereas in Sicily, as we have just seen, even the most essential boats for observation purposes were lacking.

Even the impatient urging of the Gothic patriots did little to change the situation. The king had been able to get Witigis and Hildebad out of the way by sending them, with armies and instructions, to Istria and Gaul. The ever-suspicious Teias was fiercely opposed by old Hildebrand, who clung stubbornly to his faith in the last of the Amalungs.

But the one thing which did more than anything else for Theodahad's courage was when his queen was returned to him. Soon after the declaration of war Witigis had led a strong Gothic force to the fortress of Ferretri, where Gothelindis had sought refuge with her mercenaries. There he had persuaded her to return to Ravenna of her own free will, giving her his personal guarantee that she would be safe until her formal trial during the coming national gathering near Rome. These conditions were acceptable to both sides. The Gothic patriots, now that war had been declared, felt the need to avoid further weakening within their own ranks by any further conflict among their own leadership.

Witigis was acting out of his own great sense of justice, wanting to see that Gothelindis received the right to defend herself. But even Teias could see that, now that the enemy had publicly made the serious accusation against the whole Gothic nation that one of them had murdered their own queen, only a formal and public trial could salvage the Gothic national honour.

Gothelindis herself looked to the future and to her own trial with confidence. Even though many people thought her guilty, she thought she could count on there being insufficient evidence of her deed. After all, hers had been the only eye to witness the death of her rival, and she knew she would not be convicted or punished without very strong evidence.

She therefore willingly allowed herself to be taken to Ravenna, where she was able to instil renewed courage into her husband. She hoped that, once the trial was over, she would soon find protection against further attacks in Belisarius's camp or, later, at the Imperial court in Byzantium. The royal couple's confidence about the eventual outcome of the trial received a further boost due to the fact that the Franks were arming. That gave them a pretext to send the dangerous Teias away also, who now had to join Witigis and Hildebad in the north-west with a further army. With Teias went many of the Gothic party's most eager supporters, thousands of them. So Gothelindis now had cause to hope that, by the time the national gathering took place, the gathering would only be a small one, with few if any of her enemies present. At the same time both she and Theodahad worked ceaselessly to ensure that there would be as many of their own supporters as possible at the gathering, on the day of decision. They also directed their efforts to seek the support of Amalasuntha's old enemies and the powerful Balti dynasty, with branches throughout the Empire. Thus the royal couple had gained confidence, and Gothelindis had persuaded Theodahad to personally defend her at the trial. She hoped that such a display of courage, combined with respect for the royal house, might be sufficient to silence her attackers from the very beginning.

Surrounded by their supporters and a small bodyguard, Theodahad and Gothelindis left Ravenna for Rome, where they arrived a few days before the national gathering was due to begin, taking up residence at the old Imperial Palace.

The assembly was to be held not immediately outside the walls of Rome itself, but in an open field called Regata some distance from Rome, between Anagni and Terracina. Early in the morning on the day he was planning to leave for Regata alone, Theodahad was just taking his leave from Gothelindis when a name both unexpected and unwelcome was announced, that of Cethegus. The latter had not made an appearance during the several days they had been in Rome, having been fully occupied completing the fortifications.

As he entered Gothelindis was shocked by the expression on his face: "My God, Cethegus! What evil tidings do you bring?"

But the Prefect frowned for only an instant when he caught sight of her, then he said calmly: "Evil tidings? Only for those whom they affect. I come to you from a gathering of my friends, where I have just learned what the whole of Italy will soon know. Belisarius has landed."

"At last!" Theodahad exclaimed. The queen could not conceal her obvious pleasure at this news either.

"Don't rejoice too soon! You may regret it. I have not come to demand that you explain yourselves, or your friend Petros. He who deals with traitors must expect to be told lies. I have come only to tell you that you are now most certainly doomed."

"Doomed? Nonsense, we are safe now!"

"No, queen. When Belisarius landed he issued a manifest, in which he says that he has come to punish Amalasuntha's murderers. A reward and his mercy are on offer to those who turn you in, dead or alive."

Theodahad paled. "Impossible!" Gothelindis cried.

"And the Goths will soon know whose treachery it was that allowed the enemy to land with virtually no resistance. But there is more. I have been instructed by the citizens of Rome, as their Prefect, to guard their interests in these stormy times. In the name of Rome I now arrest you, and I will deliver you to Belisarius."

"You would not dare!" Gothelindis cried, reaching for her dagger.

"Be quiet, Gothelindis, there is more to be done here than to murder a helpless woman in her bath. I am willing to let you escape – after all what do I care if you live or die – for a cheap price."

"I will pay any price!" Theodahad stammered.

"You will deliver to me the documents concerning your agreements with Silverius – be silent! Don't lie to me! I know that you have been secretly negotiating for a long time. Once again you have done a pretty deal, with land and with people. I want the bill of sale."

"The deal is off now, and the documents worthless. Take them! They are hidden in the basilica of St Martinus, in the sarcophagus next to the crypt!" His fear indicated he was telling the truth.

"Very well," Cethegus replied. "All exits from the palace have been sealed by my legionaries. I will now go to look for the documents. If I find them in the right place, I will issue orders for your release. Then, if you want to escape, go to the gate of Marcus Aurelius and mention my name to the tribune of the watch. His name is Piso. He will let you go." With those words he left, leaving the royal couple alone with their helpless fear.

"What do we do now?" Gothelindis asked, more of herself than her husband. "Do we flee or fight?"

"What do we do now?" Theodahad repeated. "To fight means to stay here. Nonsense! Let us get away from here just as quickly as we can. To flee is our only chance!"

"And where do you intend to flee to?"

"First of all to Ravenna – at least for the time being that is safe. There I will raise the royal treasure and then, if I have to, I will go to the Franks. What a pity I have to surrender all the money I have hidden here in Rome. All those millions of *solidi*!"

"Here?" Gothelindis asked attentively, "have you hidden treasures in Rome as well? Where? Are they safe?"

"Yes, too safe, in the catacombs! It would take even me hours to find them in those dark labyrinths, and minutes are now life and death. And after all life is worth more than *solidi*! Follow me, Gothelindis, so that we don't lose a moment. I am going directly to the gate of Marcus Aurelius."

He left the room, but Gothelindis remained behind, thinking. His words had given her an idea, a plan, and she weighed the possibility of resisting, of putting up a fight.

Her pride would not permit her to give up the throne. "Gold is power," she said to herself, "and only power makes life worth living." Her resolve was firm. She thought of the mercenaries from Cappadocia, whom the king's meanness had caused to leave her employ. They were still in Rome, waiting, leaderless, awaiting shipment to their own country. She could hear Theodahad hurrying down the steps and calling for a litter. "Yes, go on and flee, you miserable coward!" she said to herself, "I am staying here."

Chapter 12

On the following morning the sun rose majestically out of the sea, and its rays shone on the polished weapons of many thousands of Gothic warriors assembled on the vast field of Regata.

There were Goths from every province of the vast Empire, in groups or in families, many with wives and children. They were assembled for the annual review of the Gothic army, which occurred every autumn.

Such a national gathering was two things at the same time, the Gothic nation's most joyous festivity as well as a solemn occasion. Originally, in heathen times, the focal point of such a gathering had been the great sacrificial feast, which took place twice a year in spring and in autumn, and for which all the various tribes and families of a nation would gather in order to pay homage to their common gods. There were also other aspects to such an assembly, including bartering, a market, games and a review of the army. Finally the assembly had the ultimate say in matters of law and order, and it made all major decisions about war or peace, and about relationships with other states.

Even in the Gothic nation, in which the king had assumed many rights which were formerly exercised by the people, and which had become entirely Christian, the annual national gathering had an almost sacred significance, even though its old heathen origins were largely forgotten. The remnants of their old Germanic freedoms, with which even the great Theodoric had not dared tamper, lived on and in fact underwent a powerful revival under his much weaker successors.

It was still the prerogative of the entire nation of free Goths to determine punishment, even though one of their counts might be conducting the trial in the name of their king, and would ultimately have the responsibility of executing the verdict. On many previous occasions Germanic peoples themselves had accused their kings of murder, treason or other serious crimes before such a national gathering, judged him and sentenced him to death. A Germanic warrior was proud of the fact that he was his own master and subservient to nobody, not even the king where that would interfere with his freedom. He would therefore go to the *Ting* fully armed. There, in the company of his fellow countrymen, he would feel secure and strong as he saw the freedom, power and honour of his nation in living images and deeds before his eyes.

But this particular gathering had special significance for the Goths. When the invitations went out to assemble at Regata, war with Byzantium was to be expected or had already broken out. The people were looking forward to the fight against the hated enemy, and to a mustering of their military might. This time, even more than usual, the gathering was to be combined with a general mustering of the armed forces. In addition at least those Goths who lived in the regions nearer to Rome knew that here, at Regata, there was to be a trial and judgment of those accused of murdering Theodoric's daughter. The great excitement which this news had produced exerted a strong pull on the people to draw them to Regata.

Whereas many of the arrivals had sought shelter with friends and relations in nearby villages, huge crowds had gathered several days before the actual assembly on the field of Regata itself, situated some two hundred and eighty stadia (or about thirty-six Roman miles of a thousand paces) from Rome. Here they were camped either in huts or light tents, or even under the open sky. These crowds were already up and about in the very early hours of the great day, and while they were sole masters of the huge field they used their time for a variety of games and entertainment.

Some swam or bathed in the clear waters of the River Ufens (or "-Decemnovius because it flows into the sea at Terracina after nineteen Roman miles), which traversed the vast plains. Others demonstrated their skill in leaping over rows of spears, or they danced almost entirely naked to the rhythm of swirling swords. The most fleet of foot among them would race against their horses, keeping pace with them at top speed. On reaching the end of the race, still clinging to the horse's mane, they would swing themselves onto their unsaddled backs with a confident leap.

"What a pity," young Gudila cried, who had won this contest and was now pushing back his long blond hair from his forehead, "what a pity Totila is not here! He is the best rider in the nation, and in the past he has always beaten us. But now, with my new black stallion, I would like to challenge him once more."

"And I am glad he is not here," Gunthamund laughed, who had just come second in the same contest, "otherwise I don't think I would have come first in the spear-throwing contest yesterday."

"Yes," said Hilderich, a magnificent young warrior in shining armour, "Totila is good with a spear. But black Teias is better still. He will tell you the rib he is going to hit in advance."

"Pah," grumbled Hunibad, an older man who had been watching the youngsters, "all that is only play. When the going gets really tough, when the enemy is pressing you from all sides and there is no room for throwing, that's when a man's only friend is his sword. And that's why I like Count Witigis of Faesulae.

"Now there is a man to my liking! Oh, how he fought and split skulls in the war against the Gepidae! That man cuts through steel and leather as if it was straw. He is even better than my own Count Guntharis, the Woelsung, in Florence. But what would you boys know about such things? Look, there are the first arrivals coming down the hills. Let's go and meet them!"

People were now arriving in droves from all directions, on foot, on horseback and in wagons or carriages. The field became a hive of buzzing activity, and as more and more people arrived the noise soon became a muffled roar. The horses were tethered at the riverbank, where most of the tents were, and the wagons arranged into a rectangular barricade. Hour by hour the crowd was growing and streaming through the camp.

Friends and former fellow soldiers would find and greet each other, many of them not having met for years. It was a very colourful picture, the old Germanic equality having long ago disappeared from the Empire. There were distinguished-looking nobles, who had settled in the wealthy cities in Italy and lived in the palaces of former senators, and who had long acquired the way of life of the luxury-loving Italians. By the side of such a duke or count, from Mediolanum or Ticinum, with his purple robes over his golden suit of armour, there stood a huge, rough-hewn man, a Gothic peasant from the deep oak forests in Moesia on the Margus River. Around his shoulders he wore a shaggy wolf skin, which he had probably taken from its original owner in some wild forest, and his rough tongue now sounded strange to some of his half Romanised fellow Goths. There were also peaceful shepherds from Dacia, who did not have houses or even a fixed place to live, but who wandered with their herds from meadow to meadow as their ancestors had done a thousand years before, when they had first brought their herds over from Asia. There was a rich Goth, who had married a Roman moneylender's daughter in Rome or Ravenna, and who had learned from his father-in-law how to do business in the Roman manner, counting his profits by the thousands. Next to him stood a poor alpine herdsman, whose simple wooden hut stood near a bear's cave by the thundering Isarcus River, and whose lot it was each day to graze his thin goats on the sparse mountain meadow.

So different were the thousands gathered here that it seemed as if they were from many nations, not one, and yet the ancestors of each one of them had answered the great Theodoric's call and followed him westwards, away from his homelands, many years before.

And yet they all felt like brothers, and like the sons of the one nation. They spoke the same proud language, they had the same golden hair, the same pale skin, the same sparkling eyes, and above all the same proud feeling in their breasts of standing here, on this soil, as victors. Their fathers had wrested this soil from the Roman Empire for them in a fair fight, and they in turn would defend it to the last!

The huge crowd was like a gigantic swarm of bees as it grew and grew, and the confusion looked as if it would never end.

But suddenly the unique sound of a Gothic horn sounded from the top of the hill, in solemnly drawn out notes. Instantly the hum of voices died down, and all eyes turned attentively to the hill, from which a procession of venerable old men was approaching. There were some fifty of them in flowing white robes, their heads adorned with oak leaves, and each carried a white staff and an ancient stone axe. These were the *sajones* and *frondiener*, or ceremonial servants, of the court. Their solemn duty was to arrange the opening, conduct and closing of the *Ting*.

On arriving in the plain they greeted the assembled warriors by sounding the horns three times, and the warriors returned the greeting in accordance with ancient custom by rattling their weapons.

Immediately the boundary markers began their work. They divided into two groups, to the right and left, carrying strings of red wool. The wool was then tied around sticks of hazel wood, driven into the ground twenty paces apart around the entire plain, and the *Sajones* accompanied their activities with the chanting of ancient verses. Exactly in the east and in the west the woollen strings were raised by being tied to lance shafts of a man's height, making two gates to the site of the *Ting*, which was now completely enclosed. In front of each entrance stood two guards with drawn axes, in order to keep away any who were not free, as well as foreigners and women.

When this task was completed the two oldest men stood, one under each entrance gate, and called out in loud voices:

"The enclosure is defended, according to ancient Gothic custom.

Now, with God's help, let justice be done."

The silence which followed these words was replaced, gradually at first but then with increasing force, by a pandemonium of questioning, arguing and anxious voices.

The crowd had noticed, even as the *sajones* were approaching, that they were not led by a count who normally conducted proceedings in the name of the king. But they did expect that the king's representative would at least appear while the ceremony of enclosing the *Ting* took place. But when this task had been completed, and the old men had issued the call for proceedings to begin, still no count or other representative of the king had appeared, and he alone could open the *Ting*. Thus the attention of those present was now on this very noticeable gap. As some searched for the count or royal representative, others remembered that the king had promised to appear before the people in person, in order to defend his queen against the accusations being levelled against her.

But now that enquiries were to be made, and questions asked, of the king's friends and followers, the suspicious fact emerged that there was not a single friend, relative, follower or servant of the royal house present. These persons had been expected to appear in support of the accused, and many of them had been seen in the streets and surroundings of Rome in the last few days.

This was strange indeed and aroused suspicion. For a while it seemed that the entire proceedings were endangered by the noise, and by the non-appearance of a representative from the king. In vain several speakers had already tried to make themselves heard.

And then, suddenly, a sound which drowned out all else was heard from the centre of the assembly, like a war cry of terrifying force. In the centre of the enclosure they could now see the tall figure of a man, whose back leaned against a stone oak. He was holding a hollow bronze shield to his mouth, and into the shield he was shouting the Gothic war cry with all the power his voice could muster. When he lowered the shield they recognised the face of old Hildebrand, whose eyes seemed to be flashing fire.

Rousing cheers greeted the great king's old armourer and mentor. Like his master, Hildebrand had already become a living legend among the Goths, an almost mythical figure. When the turmoil died down, the old man began: "Good Goths, worthy men! You may find it strange that you do not see a count nor any other representative from the man who is wearing your crown.

"Don't let it concern you. If the king thinks that he will hinder our court in this manner, then we will prove him wrong. I can still remember the old times, and I tell you this: the people can hold court without a count, and determine justice without a king. You have all grown up with new customs and in new times, but Haduswinth here is only a few winters younger than I am, and he will bear out what I have to say. The people alone have power, and the Gothic people are free!"

"Yes, we are free!" a chorus of a thousand voices replied.

"We will elect our own count to preside over the *Ting*, if the king will not send us his," Haduswinth cried, "there was law and justice before there ever was a king. And who knows ancient customs better than old Hildebrand here, Hildung's son? He shall be our count."

"Yes," was the universal response, "Hildebrand shall be Count and preside over the *Ting*."

"By your own free choice I am your count, and I regard myself just as properly appointed as if King Theodahad had issued a document to say so. For centuries my ancestors have presided over Gothic justice, so come *sajones*, help me to open the proceedings."

At his signal twelve of the *sajones* hurried to his side. On the ground in front of the oak tree there were the remnants of an ancient altar of the forest god Picus. The *sajones* cleaned up the site, arranged the largest of the stones, and leaned two large rectangular stone slabs against the tree on either side, so that they formed an imposing judge's chair. And so, from the altar of the ancient Roman god of forests and of shepherds, the newly appointed Gothic Count conducted his court.

Other *sajones* placed a flowing blue robe around Hildebrand's shoulders, made of wool with a white collar. Then they placed an oak staff in his hand, and to the left of his head they hung a steel shield in the branches of the tree.

Then they lined up in two rows, to his right and to his left. The old man struck the shield with his staff, so that it rang out loudly, and then he turned to the east and said: "I order peace, silence and goodwill! I order justice and forbid injustice, impatience and anger and the show of weapons, and anything else which could offend against the peace of the *Ting*. And I ask you here and now: Is this the year and the day, the time and the hour, the place and the occasion, to hold a free court of free Gothic men?"

The Goths standing closest to him now stepped forward and repeated in a chorus: "Now is the right place, under the tall sky and under a rustling oak. This is the time, while the sun is rising, to hold a free court of free Gothic men on Gothic soil, captured by the swords of our forefathers."

"Very well then," old Hildebrand continued, "we are assembled here to hear two charges: A charge of murder against Gothelindis, the queen, and serious charges of cowardice and idleness in times of great danger against Theodahad, our king. I ask—"

At that moment his speech was interrupted by the loud sound of Gothic horns, rapidly approaching from the west, coming closer and closer.

Chapter 13

The astonished Goths now turned in the direction from where the new noise was coming, and saw a group of horsemen rushing downhill toward the site of the *Ting*. The reflection of the sun on the shining weapons of the new arrivals made it difficult to make out who they were, even though they were closing quickly.

And then old Hildebrand stood on his raised throne, held his hand in front of his eyes which, despite his age, were as sharp as those of a falcon, and promptly announced: "Those are Gothic arms! The flag has a set of scales on it, that is the family coat of arms of Count Witigis. And there he is himself, at the head of the group. The tall one to his left is our strong friend Hildebad. Why are the generals returning? Their armies are by now supposed to be well on their way to Gaul and Dalmatia." A torrent of astonished voices arose, asking, shouting greetings.

Meanwhile the leading riders had arrived and leapt from their steaming mounts. Their leaders, Witigis and Hildebad, walked through the cheering crowd to the hill on which Hildebrand's throne stood.

"What?" Hildebad cried, still out of breath, "you sit here and hold court, as if there was peace everywhere, whilst the enemy Belisarius has landed?"

"We know," Hildebrand replied calmly. "We are here to discuss with the king how best to deal with him."

"With the king?" Hildebad laughed out loud, bitterly.

"He is not here," said Witigis, looking about him, "that only makes us more suspicious. We turned back because we had reason to harbour grave doubts about our mission, but more of that later! Go on as you were; everything should go according to law and order. Quiet, friend!" He pushed the impatient Hildebad aside, and modestly joined the others to the left of the judge's chair.

When silence had been restored the old man continued: "Gothelindis, our queen, has been charged with the murder of Amalasuntha, Theodoric's daughter. I now ask of you, are we just in holding court here, and in judging her who is thus accused?"

Old Haduswinth, leaning on his long club, stepped forward and said: "The strings which form the border of this site are red. It is the place of the people to judge red blood crimes, over warm life and cold death. It may have been done differently in recent times, but we have the right to sit here and to hear this charge."

"Among the whole nation," Hildebrand went on, "serious charges are being made against Gothelindis, and in our hearts we all think her a murderess. But who will accuse her of murder here, before this court?"

"I do!" said a clear voice, and a young Goth in shining armour stepped forward, his hand on his heart.

A murmur of approval went through the crowd: "He loves the beautiful Matesuentha." ... "He is the brother of Duke Guntharis of Tuscany." ... "He is courting her" ... "He is here as her mother's avenger!"

"I am Count Arahad of Asta, son of Aramuth, of the noble Woelsung family," the young man went on, an appealing touch of colour in his face. "I am not related to the murdered woman, but the men in her family, particularly her cousin and king Theodahad, will not exercise their duty of avenging her murder. In fact Theodahad himself is guilty of aiding and abetting the crime. Therefore I, a free Goth of noble family and unsullied reputation, as well as a friend of the unfortunate former queen, now act as her avenger in place of her daughter Matesuentha. I accuse Gothelindis of murder. I demand her blood!"

Amid the loud cheering of the crowd the handsome young man drew his sword, and pointed it directly at the judge's chair.

"And your proof? Tell us—"

"Halt, Count of the *Ting*," a serious voice now spoke. Witigis stepped forward, toward the accuser. "You are so old, Master Hildebrand, and you know the law so well. Are you going to let the mood of the crowd dictate your judgement? Must I, a much younger man, remind you of the first law of all justice? I hear the accuser, but not the accused."

"No woman may attend the *Ting*," Hildebrand said calmly.

"I know that, but where is her husband Theodahad, to act in her stead?"

"He has failed to appear, even though you have my word that he was invited, as well as the word of these messengers," said Arahad, "Step forward, *sajones*." At this two of the old men stepped forward and touched the judge's chair with their staffs.

"In that case," Witigis went on, "let no man say that among the Goths a woman was judged and sentenced without being heard or defended, no matter how much she was hated. She has a right to justice and to the protection of the law. I will therefore act as her defender." And he calmly stepped toward the young accuser, drawing his own sword just as the latter had done. There was a pause of honest admiration.

"Are you denying the charge?" the judge asked.

"I say it is not proven!"

"Prove it!" the judge said, turning to Arahad.

The latter was not prepared for a formal hearing, and certainly not prepared to be opposed by a man of Witigis's stature and calm strength. He was thus at somewhat of a loss. "Proven?" he replied impatiently. "What more proof is needed? You, I, all of us know that Gothelindis bore Amalasuntha a deadly hatred for many years. Amalasuntha disappears from Ravenna, and her murderess disappears at the same time. The victim is next seen in a house belonging to the murderess, dead, and the murderess flees to a fortified castle. What further proof do you need?" Impatiently he looked at those around him.

"And on that hearsay you dare to accuse your queen of murder in open *Ting*?" Witigis said calmly. "May a day never come among the Gothic nation where people are judged on evidence like that. Justice, men, is light and air! Woe be to the nation which makes hatred law. I too hate this woman and her husband, but where I hate I am doubly severe with myself." And he said these words so simply and with such noble calm that the hearts of all the Goths present went out to this simple, good and decent man.

"Where is the proof?" Hildebrand asked again. "Did you see it happen? Do you have a witness? Is there any other proof? Has the accused admitted her crime?"

"Proof?" Arahad repeated angrily, "I have none beyond my own firm conviction."

"In that case—" said Hildebrand, but he was not able to finish his sentence, for at that moment one of the *sajones* had managed to get to him through the crowd and said to him: "There are Roman men at the entrance, seeking an audience with you. They say they know everything about the former queen's death."

"I demand they be heard," Arahad cried eagerly, "not as plaintiffs but as witnesses for the plaintiff."

On Hildebrand's signal the *sajo* hurried away and came back through the crowd leading the Roman men. The leader of the small group was a man, bent by old age, and dressed in a coarse cassock with a rope around his waist, the hood of the gown hiding his face from view. All eyes were on the old man, questioningly, for he had a strange look of poverty and humility about him, yet rare dignity also.

When he reached Hildebrand's chair, Arahad looked briefly into his face and drew back in surprise.

"Who is the man you have called upon to bear witness to what you have said? An unknown stranger?" asked Hildebrand.

"No," Arahad replied as he drew the old man's hood aside. "He is a man whom you all know and honour. He is Marcus Aurelius Cassiodorus." A general cry of astonishment arose among the crowd.

"That was my name," said the witness, "in the days of my worldly life. Now I am just Brother Marcus."

"Well, Brother Marcus," Hildebrand asked, "what have you to tell us about the death of Amalasuntha? Tell us the whole truth and only the truth."

"That I will do. But you must know, above all, that it is not a desire for human justice which brings me here. I have no wish to avenge her death, for God has said: 'I will punish'. No, I am here to carry out the last command which the poor victim, the daughter of my great king, gave me." He withdrew a papyrus scroll from his gown. "Shortly before she fled from Ravenna she directed these lines to me, to be communicated to the Gothic people as her testament. Here is what she wrote: 'Hear the gratitude of a shattered soul for your friendship! The knowledge of your unswerving loyalty, even more than the hope of safety, draws me to you. Yes, I will hurry to your villa on the Bolsen lake! After all it is on the way to Rome and to Regata, where I want to admit and pay for my guilt before my Gothic people. I will die if I must, but not by the treachery of my enemies. I would much rather die by the sentence of my own people, whom I blindly led to disaster. I deserve to die, not only because I had the three dukes murdered – everyone shall know it – but even more so because of the stupidity which caused me to place my people second to Byzantium. If I get to Regata alive I want to warn my people with the last of my strength. Beware of Byzantium! It is as false as hell itself, and peace between them and us unthinkable.

"But I also want to warn you of the enemy in your midst.

"King Theodahad is planning treason, and he has sold Italy and the Gothic crown to Petros, the envoy from Byzantium. He has done what I would not do, and sold my people out to the Greeks. Be careful, be united, and be strong! If only I can make good in death all the sins I have committed in life!"

The crowd had heard the words in deep silence as Cassiodorus delivered them with a trembling voice, seemingly coming from the next world. Even after he finished the silence continued, a mute testimony to the sorrow and compassion of the Gothic nation.

At last old Hildebrand spoke again: "She has failed us, and she has done penance for it. Daughter of Theodoric, the Gothic people forgive you your misdeeds, and thank you for your loyalty."

"May God forgive her also, Amen!" Cassiodorus added. "I never invited Amalasuntha to the villa, because I could not. A fortnight earlier I had sold all my estates to Queen Gothelindis."

"So she, misusing your name, tricked her enemy into coming to the villa," Arahad added, "can you deny that, Count Witigis?"

"No," the latter replied calmly, turning to Cassiodorus. "Can you also prove that Amalasuntha did not die accidentally, and that it was Gothelindis who brought about her death?"

"Step forward, Syrius, and speak!" Cassiodorus said, "I will vouch for this man's truthfulness."

A slave stepped forward, bowed and said: "For twenty years I have been in charge of the lake floodgates and the fountains and baths of the villa on Lake Bolsen. Nobody other than me knew their secrets. After Queen Gothelindis bought the villa all Cassiodorus's slaves were removed, and replaced by a few slaves belonging to the queen. I alone remained.

"Then early one morning the Princess Amalasuntha landed on the island, and shortly behind her the queen. The latter called for me immediately and told me that she wanted to take a bath. She ordered me to give her all the keys to the baths, and to explain to her all the workings of the fountains, floodgates and pipe work. I obeyed and gave her the keys and the plan, but I took great care to warn her not to open all the floodgates or all the pipes at once, because doing so could endanger her life. But she angrily ordered me to go away, and then I heard her order her bath slave to fill the kettles with hot water, not warm as usual.

"Concerned for her safety, I went and stayed in the close vicinity of the baths. After a while I heard a mighty gushing and hissing, from which I could tell that she had opened all the floodgates after all, against my advice, letting in the full force of the lake. At the same time I could hear the hot water hissing as it rose up the walls on all sides. I also thought I could hear a muffled cry for help, and so I hurried to the entrance of the baths in order to save the queen. You can imagine my surprise when I saw the queen, standing fully clothed, at the familiar controls at the centre of the baths, near the Medusa's head. She was pressing the springs and exchanging angry words with someone inside the baths. I was becoming suspicious of what was happening, and that made me terrified, and so I hurried away, luckily without being seen."

"You coward!" said Witigis, "you suspected what was happening, and you just crept away?"

"I am only a slave, master, and not a hero. If the angry queen had noticed me I certainly would not be standing here now to accuse her. Almost immediately after that I heard the cry that the Princess had drowned in the baths." A tumult of murmuring and shouting ran through the crowd.

Arahad cried, rejoicing: "Now, Count Witigis, do you still want to defend her?"

"No," the latter replied calmly, returning his sword to its scabbard, "I will not protect a murderess. My duty is done." With those words he went to join the other accusers on the left.

"You, free Gothic men, must now judge her and pass sentence," Hildebrand said, "my duty is only to execute the sentence which you impose. So I ask you now, men of this court, what do you think of the charge which Count Arahad has made against Gothelindis, the queen? Is she guilty of murder?"

"Guilty! Guilty!" a thousand voices echoed, with not one dissenting.

"She is guilty!" the old man said, rising to his feet. "Speak, plaintiff, what punishment do you demand?"

Arahad raised his sword straight up against the sky: "She is guilty of murder. I demand that she dies!"

Before Hildebrand could direct the question to the people, the crowd had erupted in anger. Every sword flew from its scabbard and flashed against the sky, and every voice cried: "She shall die!"

And these words rolled across the plain like a fearsome roll of thunder, carrying the majesty of the people's court before them, reverberating for many miles into the distance.

"She shall die by the axe," said Hildebrand. "*Sajones*, go and search for her until you have found her."

"One moment," the strong Hildebad said, stepping forward, "our sentence will be difficult to carry out as long as she is the wife of our king. Therefore I demand that the court should now also hear the charges which have been laid against Theodahad, who has ruled this nation of heroes in so cowardly a fashion. I lay these charges. Hear me well! I charge him not only with incompetence, but with treason.

"I will say nothing of the fact that Gothelindis could hardly have cooled her hatred against Amalasuntha without the king's knowledge. I will also say nothing of the fact that Amalasuntha told us of Theodahad's treachery with her last words. But is it not true that the entire southern part of the Empire has been stripped of men, arms, horses and ships, so that the wretched Greeks were able to capture Sicily and land in Italy without a fight? My poor brother Totila, with merely a handful of men, is facing the enemy entirely alone.

"Instead of protecting his rear the king also sent Witigis, Teias and me to the north. We obeyed reluctantly, because we had a good idea where Belisarius was likely to land. We advanced slowly, expecting to be recalled at any hour, but in vain. The dark rumour that Sicily was lost was already circulating through the land, and the local population were making gestures of contempt at us as we marched north. In this way we marched along the coast for a few days. Then this letter from my brother reached me:

"'Has my brother forgotten me too, like the king and the whole Gothic nation? Belisarius has taken Sicily by surprise. He has landed in Italy, all the population is joining him, and he is advancing irresistibly against Naples. Four times I have written to King Theodahad for help, but in vain. Not a sail came. Naples is in the greatest danger. Save us, save Naples and the Empire!'"

A cry of anguish ran through the thousands of Gothic men.

"I wanted to turn around immediately with our whole army, but Count Witigis, my commander-in-chief, would not hear of it. But I did persuade him to let the troops halt, and hurry here with a few horsemen to warn and avenge. Revenge, revenge is what I seek against King Theodahad, not only because he is weak and stupid, but because he has deliberately sacrificed the south of Italy to the enemy. This letter here proves it. Four times my brother warned him, begged him, but in vain. Theodahad gave my brother and the Empire to the enemy on a plate. Woe be to us if Naples should fall, or of it has already fallen! Ha, he must not rule any longer, nor shall he live, the man who did all that. Tear the Gothic crown he has disgraced from his head, and down with Theodahad! He too shall die!"

"Down with him! He shall die!" the people thundered in a mighty echo.

The strength of the crowd's fury and indignation seemed to be carrying everything before it, and it threatened to crush anyone who tried to resist it. Only one man remained calm among the angry crowd, and that man was Count Witigis. He leapt onto one of the old stones under the oak tree, and waited until the turmoil had subsided somewhat. Then he raised his voice and spoke, once more with the simple clarity which suited him so well: "Countrymen and fellow Goths! Listen to me! You are unjust in your sentence, and you do wrong. Woe be to us if the Gothic nation, which from the time of our forefathers has always prided itself on its sense of justice, allows hatred and violence to ascend its throne in place of justice. Theodahad is a weak, bad king. He shall no longer reign over us! Give him a guardian if you like, as you would with a minor. Depose him if you want to. But you have no right to call for his blood or to demand his death! Where is the proof that he has betrayed us? How can you be sure Totila's letters reached him? You see, now you are silent. Be on your guard against injustice, because it is injustice that destroys the Empires of man!"

Witigis looked great and noble as he stood there, on the rock and in the full light of the sun, full of strength and dignity.

The eyes of the crowd rested on him admiringly, on him who seemed to be so much in control of the situation, and who towered above all of them with his calmness and his sense of right and wrong. But before Hildebad and the people could find an answer to this man, who seemed like justice come to life, the attention of everyone present was again diverted to the thick forest to the south, which crowned the horizon, and which seemed to be suddenly coming to life.

Chapter 14

The sound of speeding horses and the clatter of arms could be heard coming from that direction, and soon afterwards a small group of horsemen emerged from the forest. There was a single rider way out ahead of them, a man on a pitch-black horse, who was riding as if he was racing the storm wind itself. His long black hair and the black horse's tail which adorned his helmet were fluttering in the wind. Bent over his foaming mount he was driving the animal at a furious pace until he reached the southern entrance to the *Ting*, where he swung himself out of the saddle.

A world of the fiercest hatred burned in the black eyes of his deathly pale face, and all on whom his look fell got out of his way as best they could. He ran up the hill as if he had wings, leapt onto the stone beside Witigis, and held a scroll high into the air as he cried out, as if with the last of his remaining strength: "Treason, treason!" and then he collapsed as if struck by lightning.

Hildebad and Witigis sprang to his aid. They had barely been able to recognise their friend. "Teias, Teias!" they called out to him at the same time, "what has happened? Speak!" and Witigis repeated: "Speak! The Gothic Empire is at stake! Speak!"

As he heard those words the man of steel rose again, with what appeared to be superhuman strength. Looking about him he spoke, in a hollow voice:

"We have been betrayed, fellow Goths, betrayed by our own king. Six days ago I received orders to march to Istria, and not to Naples as I had requested. I was becoming suspicious, but I obeyed and put to sea with my troops. Then a violent storm blew up in the west, and it carried a number of smaller ships in our direction, which it had blown off course. One of them was the *Mercurius*, the fast mail ship belonging to Theodahad. I knew the vessel well, as it once belonged to my father. As it sighted our ships it tried to escape and I, becoming suspicious, went after it and caught it. On board I found this letter, from the king to Belisarius: 'You will be pleased with me, great general. All the Gothic armies are at this moment northeast of Rome, and you can therefore land without facing any danger at all. I have destroyed four letters from my naval commander in Naples, and thrown his couriers into the dungeon. As my reward I now expect that you will carry out your part of our contract, and let me have the purchase price in full very soon.'"

Teias let the letter drop, and an impotent fury of gasping and groaning went through the crowd.

"I turned back and landed immediately, and I have been racing to get here ever since. For three days and nights I have been riding non-stop, and I have ridden eight horses to death. I cannot go on." He stumbled, and collapsed into the arms of Witigis.

Now old Hildebrand jumped up onto the highest stone of his chair, standing well above the crowd. He then tore the lance bearing a small bust of the king from the Goth who was holding it, and held its shaft with his left hand. With his right he now raised his stone axe: "He has sold and betrayed his people for yellow gold? Down with him, down, down!" One blow from his axe smashed the bust into fragments. His action was like the first clap of thunder which unleashes a threatening thunderstorm, and the tumult which followed was as if the fury of the elements had now roused this nation, which had just been so cruelly wounded, into a veritable tempest of anger. "Down, down with him!" the words resounded a thousand times, accompanied by a loud rattling of arms.

When the tumult had died down somewhat Theodoric's old mentor raised his deep voice once more and declared solemnly: "Hear this, God in heaven and men on earth, all seeing sun and blowing wind, and know that this Gothic people, free and of ancient fame and born to arms, has rid itself of its former king Theodahad, son of Theodis, because he has betrayed his people and his nation to the enemy.

"We take from you, Theodahad, the golden crown of the Goths and the Gothic Empire, the right to Gothic protection and the right to live. And this we do not unjustly, but in full accordance with the law. We have always been free, and would rather do without king than freedom. And no king stands so high that he does not have to face the justice of his people when he commits murder and treason.

"And so I now take from you crown, Empire and life. You shall be a fugitive from your own people, without honour, without truth and without lawful protection. Wherever Christian people go to church or heathens offer sacrifice, wherever fire burns or the grass is green, wherever ships sail and shields shine, as far as heaven reigns over the expanse of earth, wherever a falcon flies with the wind under its wings you shall be denied shelter and the company of good people. You shall be welcome nowhere except in hell. Your property shall be divided among the Gothic people, and your flesh and blood among the ravens of the air. And whoever finds you shall kill you and go unpunished, whether he finds you in a house or in a hall or on the road, and by doing so he shall earn the gratitude of all Goths. I ask you now, is that what shall happen?"

"It shall be thus!" was the refrain of thousands as they struck their shields with their swords.

Barely had Hildebrand stepped down from the stone when old Haduswinth took his place. Throwing back the shaggy bear skin he said: "We are rid of our disgraceful former king! He will find his avengers. But now, worthy men, it is time for us to elect a new king. Never have the Goths been without a king. As far back as our traditions and our songs go, our ancestors have always raised one of their number onto his shield, a living image of Gothic might, Gothic fame and Gothic fortune. As long as there are Goths they will have a king, and as long as we can find a king our nation will survive. Now, above all, we must have a leader. The Amalung dynasty rose gloriously as the sun, and its brightest ray Theodoric shone for many years, but now it has been shamefully extinguished in Theodahad. Come, Gothic people, you are free! So freely elect a king, the right king, who will lead you to honour and to victory. Your throne is empty, my people, and I now invite you to elect a new king!"

"Elect a king!" the chorus of thousands repeated, this time solemnly.

Now Witigis stepped onto the *Ting* stone, removed his helmet and raised his right hand: "You know it, God up there in the stars. It is not disobedience or wantonness that drives us, but the sacred right of extreme need. We honour the tradition and the rights of our kings, and the glory of our crown. But that glory has been disgraced, and therefore in this time of great need we exercise the people's greatest right. Heralds shall go to every nation on earth and say it out loud: we have done what we are about to do, not because we despise the crown, but because we honour it.

"But whom shall we choose? There are many worthy men in this nation, of old nobility, with a strong arm and a clever mind. There are probably several who are worthy of the crown. How easily could it happen now that some prefer this one, and others another? But for heaven's sake let us not have discord among us now, with the enemy in our land. Therefore let us first swear solemnly: whoever gains the majority of votes, be it only by a single voice, he and no other shall be accepted by us all as our king. I swear it, now swear it with me."

"We swear it!" the Goths repeated.

But young Arahad did not join them. Love as well as ambition was burning in his heart. He considered that his house, now that the Amalungs and the Balti had fallen, was the noblest in the nation, and he also hoped that he might win the hand of Matesuentha if he could offer her the crown. The oath had barely been spoken when he stepped forward and cried out aloud: "Gothic men, whom shall we choose? Think well! One thing is clear, we need the arm of a young man against the enemy, but that alone is not enough. Why did our ancestors elevate the Amalungs? Because they were the oldest and noblest family among us, descended from the gods. Very well, the brightest star is no more, so think of the second brightest, think of the Balti!"

There was only one remaining male heir of the Balti, a grandson of Duke Pitza and still only a boy. Alaric, the brother of dukes Thulun and Ibba, had been banished and disappeared years ago. Arahad now supposed that the Goths would not choose this boy, but would turn to the third star instead. But he was mistaken. Old Haduswinth stepped forward and shouted:

"Nonsense nobility and dynasty! Are we serfs to nobility, or are we free men? By the god of thunder, we are not going to stand here and count ancestors while Belisarius is in our country. I will tell you, boy, what it takes to make a king.

"He needs a strong and a brave arm, that's true, but he needs more than that. The king must be a guardian of the law and our shield in times of peace too, not just our leader in war. The king must have a mind which is always calm and always clear, as the clear blue sky, and the thoughts and ideas of justice shall rule his mind as the stars rule the heavens. The king must have steady strength, but even more so he must be fair to all. He must never lose himself in love or hate as we, the common people, might do. He must be just and kind not only to his friends, but just even to his most hated enemies. I tell you, Arahad, a man in whose breast courage, justice, loyalty, strength and moderation live side by side is the stuff of which a king is made, even if his father was the lowliest peasant."

The old man's words were greeted with loud acclaim, and Arahad stepped back somewhat shamefaced. But the old man went on: "My good Goths, I think we have such a man! I will not tell you who he is, but leave it to you to tell me!

"I came here from our Carantanian border, high up in the mountains where the wild Turbidus foams and turns the very rocks into dust. For more than a generation I lived there, proud, free and lonely. I heard little of the doings of men, or even the deeds of my own people, unless a salt trader happened along because he had lost his way. And yet, even in those lonely mountains, the fame of one of our heroes reached my ears above all the others. He was a man who never drew his sword unjustly, and who never sheathed it again without having gained victory. Again and again I heard his name when I asked: who will protect us after Theodoric dies? I heard his name at the recounting of every one of our victories, but also in connection with every wise work of peace. I had never seen him, but I longed to see and meet him. Here, today, I have seen him and heard him. I have seen his eyes, which are clear and kind as the sun. I have heard him speak. I have heard how he helped even his most hated enemy to law and justice. I have heard how he alone remained cool and calm, when blind hatred threatened to carry the rest of us away. And in my heart I thought: that man has the makings of a king. He is strong in war and just in peace, as hard as steel and as clear as gold. Goths, that man shall be our king. Tell me his name!"

"Count Witigis, yes Witigis, hail King Witigis!"

As the roar of the crowd resounded across the field a dreadful shock came over the modest and unassuming man. He had been standing by the side of Haduswinth following every word he said, and only beginning to suspect toward the end of the old man's speech that it was he himself being praised. But now, as he heard his name called out by thousands, one overpowering emotion came over him: "No, this cannot be. It must not be!" He tore himself loose from Teias and Hildebad, who were shaking his hand, and shook his head as if defending himself. "No!" he cried, "No, friends, don't do this to me! I am an ordinary soldier, not a king. I may be a good tool, but not a master craftsman. Choose another, worthier man!"

He held both hands outstretched, as if begging the people. But the thundering echo: "Hail King Witigis!" was their only reply. And now old Hildebrand stepped forward, took his hand and said aloud: "Don't, Witigis. Who was it that first swore he would recognise the king who had a majority of even one voice? You can see that you have every voice, and yet you want to fight it?"

But Witigis shook his head and pressed his hands to his temples. Now the old man stood very close to him and whispered in his ear: "What? Do I have to admonish you even more strongly? Must I remind you of that night when you took the oath: 'everything for the sake of my people'. I know how you are, and that this crown will be more burden to you than joy. I feel that it will bring you great and bitter sorrow rather than joy. And yet that is why I now demand that you accept it."

Witigis remained silent and placed his hands over his eyes. The delay had already been too long for the people, who were busy preparing the broad shield on which to raise him. Already they were streaming up the hill to touch him and shake his hand. The cry arose anew, impatiently now: "Hail King Witigis!"

"I demand it, on your oath! Are you going to keep your oath or break it?" Hildebrand whispered.

"I will keep it!" Witigis replied, now firmly resolved, and with neither false modesty nor vanity, he turned to address the crowd: "You have chosen, my people. Very well, I am yours. I will be your king."

And every sword, all over the field, flew from its scabbard with the deafening cry: "Hail King Witigis!"

Now old Hildebrand stepped down from the *Ting* chair and said: "I now vacate this chair, for it is fitting that our king should occupy it. But let me act as Count of your *Ting* just once more.

"I cannot place around your shoulders the purple which the Amalungs have graced for generations, nor hand you their golden sceptre, so take my cloak and staff as a sign that you are our king because you are just. I cannot place Theodoric's golden crown on your head, so let me crown you with the fresh leaves of the oak, which you are so very much like in strength and steadfastness." With those words he broke off a young branch from the old oak, and wound it around the head of Witigis. "Come, Gothic soldiers, now it is your turn to perform your shield duty."

As soon as he had spoken Haduswinth, Teias and Hildebad took one of the ancient broad shields of the *sajones*, raised their king on it, now resplendent in his cloak and oak crown, and showed him to the people by raising the shield to their shoulders: "Look at him, fellow Goths, look at the king you yourselves have chosen, and swear your allegiance to him." And they did so, standing proudly erect rather than kneeling, and their heads held high. Thus they swore loyalty to the death to their new king.

Now Witigis jumped from the shield, ascended his throne under the oak and cried: "As you have sworn me loyalty I will promise you clemency. I will be a mild and just king. I will defend right and fight wrong. I will remember that you are all free as I am, my equals and not my serfs, and I will devote my life, my happiness and my everything to you, my Gothic people. That I now swear to you in the name of God and on my oath." And lastly, taking the *Ting* shield down from the tree, he said: "The *Ting* is closed, and I now dissolve this gathering."

Immediately the *sajones* struck down the sticks holding the red woollen string around the *Ting*, and the crowd mingled in colourful confusion. Even the Romans, who had only been allowed to watch the spectacle from a distance, and who had not known freedom like this for five hundred years, were now permitted to mingle with the Gothic men, to whom they sold food and wine.

Witigis was making his way to one of the tents on the riverbank to be with his friends and the leaders of his army, when a man in Roman clothes, apparently a wealthy merchant, made his way to the king's vicinity and eagerly inquired about Count Teias, Tagila's son.

"I am he. What do you want, Roman?" the latter said, turning around.

"Nothing, Sir, except to give you this vase. As you see, the seal on it, in the form of a scorpion, is intact."

"What is the vase to me? I am not buying anything of the kind."

"The vase is yours, Sir. It is full of scrolls and documents which belong to you, and a friend entrusted me to give them to you. I beg of you, take it."

With those words he had pressed the vase into the hands of Teias and vanished into the crowd. With indifference Teias opened the seal and took out the documents, scanning them casually. But then, suddenly, a burning red colour inflamed his pale cheeks, his eyes were aglow and he bit into his own lip. The vase fell from his hands, and with feverish haste he forced his way through to his king, to whom he said in a toneless voice: "My King, King Witigis, I must ask a favour!"

"What is the matter with you, Teias? My God! What do you want?"

"Leave! Leave for six, even three days! I must go away!"

"Away? To where?"

"To revenge! Here, read it. The devil who accused my parents of incest and drove them to despair, death and insanity – it's him – I have suspected it long ago! Here is his letter of accusation to the bishop of Florence, in his own hand. It is Theodahad!"

"It is indeed he, Theodahad," said Witigis, looking up from the letter. "Go then, but make no mistake. You will no longer find him in Rome. He will have fled long ago, and he has a big headstart. You will never catch him."

"I will catch him, even if he is travelling on the wings of the storm eagle."

"You will not find him!"

"I will find him, even if I have to look for him in the deepest recesses of hell, or in the very lap of the Christian god in heaven."

"He will have fled with a strong bodyguard," the king warned.

"I will pluck him from the midst of a thousand demons. Hildebad, your horse! Farewell, King of the Goths. I will execute the sentence of the people."

BOOK FIVE

Witigis – Part One

*"And the Goths chose as their king Witigis,
a man not of noble birth,
but of great fame for his bravery."*

Procopius, *Gothic Wars I*

Chapter 1

The sun was slowly setting over the green hills of Faesulae, bathing in its golden glow the columns of the simple villa in which Rauthgundis reigned as mistress.

The Gothic field hands and the Roman slaves were busy finishing their work for the day. One field hand was bringing the young horses in from the meadow, where they had been grazing. Two others were leading a herd of fine cattle down the slopes from the hills and into their stables, whilst a young goatherd drove his charges on with Roman oaths, because they persisted in nibbling the salty saxifrage among the crumbling walls by the wayside. Some of the Germanic hands were putting ploughs and other implements in their places within the enclosed yard. A Roman freedman, a very learned and distinguished individual, the chief gardener himself, was just leaving the site where the results of his aromatic science bloomed.

From the horse stables there emerged our little friend Athalwin, his face crowned with his own golden locks: "Cacus, now don't forget to put a rusty nail into the drinking bucket. Wachis told me especially! Otherwise he will have to beat you again when he comes home." And with that he threw the door shut. "Endless trouble with these southern slaves!" the little master of the house said to himself, proudly and full of his own importance. "Since father has been away and Wachis followed him into camp everything rests on me. Mother, dear God, can handle the maids, but the male hands and the slaves need the firm hand of a man."

And thus the little boy strode across the yard, very serious. "And they don't seem to have proper respect for me either," he said, pursing his cherry red lips and frowning. "And where is that respect to come from? I am almost nine years old, and they still let me walk around with a thing like a cooking spoon," and he tore at the wooden sword in his belt with disgust. "They could at least give me a hunting knife, a proper weapon. Like this I can do nothing and I look like nothing."

And yet he looked so delightful in his short, sleeveless white linen robe, which his mother's loving hands had spun and sewn, and embroidered with a red thread. He looked like an angry little Eros.

"I would like to run up into the hills and bring Mother back a bunch of the wild flowers which she loves so much, far more than our most precious garden flowers. But I have to take another look around before they shut the gate, because before he left the last time Father said to me: 'Athalwin, you make sure you take care of things while I am away, and look after your mother! I am depending on you!' And I shook hands with him on it, so now I must keep my word."

And so he strode along the yard, past the front of the house, mustering the buildings to his right and left, and was just about to turn to the back of the yard when the barking of the young dogs drew his attention to a noise by the wooden fence which surrounded the whole yard.

He went over to the corner in question and stopped in complete surprise. There, sitting on the fence, or rather climbing over it, was the strangest figure of a man. He was a tall and thin man of mature years, dressed in a coat of very coarse woollen cloth such as the mountain shepherds wore. A mighty wolf skin, crude and unembellished, hung from his shoulders like a cloak. In his right hand he carried a huge stick with a steel tip, which he was using to fend off the dogs who were angrily jumping up at him. The boy hurried to him: "Stop, stranger! What are you doing on my fence? Get down and out, at once!"

The old man stopped for a moment and looked at the handsome boy enquiringly.

"Get down, I said!" the latter repeated.

"Is that the way you greet a tired traveller in this house?"

"Yes, if the tired traveller climbs in over the back fence. If you are an honest man, and you really have some business with us, the big gate is wide open. Come in that way."

"I know that myself, if I wanted to come that way." And he started to climb down into the yard.

"Stop!" the angry boy cried, "you are not coming in that way! Get him, Griffo and Wolfo! And if you are not afraid of these two young dogs I will call the old one. Then you had better watch out! Hey, Thursa, don't let him in!"

At his call a huge grey wolfhound came racing around the stables, barking furiously, and looked as if she was about to make directly for the intruder's throat.

But the moment the animal had spotted the old man her fury suddenly turned to joy. She stopped barking and jumped up to greet the old man, tail wagging, as the latter climbed down calmly from the fence into the yard. "Yes, Thursa old girl, we'll stick together, won't we?" he said, and then: "Now tell me, young man, what is your name?"

"My name is Athalwin," the boy replied, shyly taking a step backwards, "but you, I think you have bewitched Thursa – what is your name?"

"My name is the same as yours," the old man replied in a friendlier tone. "And it is nice that you have the same name as I do. Now don't be upset, I'm not a robber. Take me to your mother, so I can tell her how bravely you defended your home."

And so the two adversaries strode peacefully into the hall, Thursa bounding ahead and barking happily.

The Corinthian atrium of the old Roman villa, with its rows of columns, had been converted by its Gothic housewife into the great hall of a Germanic household with only a few minor changes. In the absence of the master of the house the hall and the tables in it were not arranged as they would be for a festive occasion, and for the time being Rauthgundis had moved her maids from the women's quarters. On one side was a long row of Gothic maids, busily spinning, and on the opposite side a row of Roman slave girls, occupied with the more delicate work. In the middle of the hall Rauthgundis walked up and down, winding yarn herself as she did so, keeping a watchful eye to the right and to the left. Her blue dress of homespun linen was held by a belt of steel rings, which also bore a bunch of keys as her only adornment. Her dark blond hair was combed back and gathered in a simple knot. There was much simple dignity in her appearance as she strode up and down, inspecting and checking as she went.

She went over to the youngest of the Gothic maids, who was sitting right at the bottom of the row, and bent down to speak with her: "Good work, Liuta," she said, "your thread is smooth, and today I have not seen you looking at the door as often as usual. Of course," she added with a smile, "there would be little point, as Wachis won't be coming through that door for some time." The young girl blushed, and

Rauthgundis placed her hand on her smooth hair: "I know," she said, "you were quietly angry with me because I made you spin for an extra hour night and morning all this year, even though you are engaged. It was cruel, wasn't it? But you see, it was for your own good. Everything you have spun this year with my best yarn is yours; I am giving it to you for your dowry. Now next year, your first year of marriage, you won't have to spin at all."

The girl took her hand and looked her in the eye, a tear of gratitude running down her cheek. "And they call you severe and hard!" was all she managed to say.

"Kind to those who are good and strict with the lazy. Everything I manage here belongs to my husband and is my son's inheritance. That is why I have to be strict."

Now Athalwin and the old man appeared in the door. The boy wanted to call out to his mother, but his companion put a hand over his mouth and watched unobserved for a while as Rauthgundis went about her work, praising here, correcting there. "Yes," the old man said to himself at last, "she looks magnificent, and she certainly seems to be mistress of the house – and yet, who can know everything that goes on?"

But then Athalwin could no longer contain himself. "Mother," he cried, "there is a strange man here. He has bewitched Thursa and he wants to talk to you. He climbed over the back fence. I don't understand it."

At that the stately woman turned with dignity toward the entrance, shielding her eyes against the rays of the setting sun, which were coming through the door. "Why are you bringing our guest here? Take him to the great hall. His place is not here with me."

"No, Rauthgundis, you are wrong. Right here, with you, is where I belong," the old man replied, stepping forward.

"Father!" she cried, and threw herself at his breast. Athalwin watched them, bewildered and not a little displeased. "So you are my grandfather who lives up there in the northern mountains! Well, welcome Grandfather! But why didn't you say so in the beginning? And why didn't you come through the gate like other honest people?"

The old man held his daughter in his arms and looked searchingly into her eyes. "She looks happy and blooming," he murmured to himself. And then Rauthgundis pulled herself together; quickly she looked around the hall. Every spindle had stopped, except Liuta's, and all eyes were staring at the old man.

"Will you stop staring and start spinning, you nosey magpies?" she called out sternly. "You, Marcia, were so busy staring you dropped the flax – you know the custom, you do an extra spool. The rest of you can call it a day. Come, Father, Liuta will fix a warm bath for you, and meat and wine."

"No!" her father replied. "When the old peasant is up in the hills he has only the waterfall for his drink or his bath. As for food, my rucksack is out there near the back fence. Have someone bring it. I have my speltbread and my cheese from sheep's milk, bring me those. How many cows have you got out there on the pasture, and how many horses in your stables?" It was his first question.

An hour later – it was already dark and little Athalwin had gone off to bed, still shaking his head about his grandfather – father and daughter were walking outside in the moonlight. "There is not enough air in there for me!" the old man had said. They talked seriously and at length as they walked through the yard and through the garden. Now and then the old man would ask a question about the household or about the buildings and equipment he saw, but there was no tenderness in his tone. Only an occasional look at his child betrayed him.

"Now forget about rye and horses," Rauthgundis said with a smile, "and tell me how you have been getting along yourself all these long years. And tell me what it was that finally brought you down from your mountain to visit your child after all this time."

"How have I been? Lonely, and the winters have been cold. No, up in our mountains it is not nice and warm like here," he said, almost accusingly. "Why did I come down? Well, last year my stud bull fell to his death on the mountain, so I came down here to buy another one."

At that Rauthgundis could contain herself no longer. Lovingly she threw her arms around the old man's neck and said: "And you could not find another bull any closer than here? Don't lie, mountain farmer, not to your child and not to yourself. You came because you had to, and because at last you could no longer bear the homesickness for your own child."

The old man halted and stroked her hair. "How did you know that? Well, it's true. I had to come down here myself and see how you are, and whether your Gothic count is looking after you."

"He treats me like the apple of his eye," she replied happily.

"Oh? Then why isn't he home with his wife and child?"

"He is with the army, in the service of the king."

"Yes, and that's the whole trouble! Who needs a king, and why does he have to be in his service? But tell me, why don't you wear a golden bracelet? A Gothic woman from the southern valleys came past my hut once, five years ago, and she wore a gold band as wide as my hand. And I thought to myself: that's how your daughter wears it, and I was happy about it, and now…"

Rauthgundis smiled: "Am I to wear gold for the eyes of my maids? I only wear jewellery when my Witigis is here to see it."

"I hope he deserves it. But you do have golden bangles and rings like the other Gothic women down here, don't you?"

"More than others, chests full of them. Witigis brought home a lot of booty from the war against the Gepidae."

"So you are quite happy?"

"Very happy, father, but not on account of the gold bangles."

"Is there anything you can complain of? Just tell me if there is! Whatever it might be, your old father will see to it that it is put right."

At that Rauthgundis stopped. "Father, don't talk like that! It's wrong of you to say it, and wrong of me to hear it. Why don't you shake off that silly idea that I had to become miserable just because I went down into the valley to live? I almost think it is only that fear which brought you down here."

"Yes, that's what it was!" the old man replied hastily, beating the ground with his stick. "And you call your father's innermost conviction a silly idea? Is it silly that I find it difficult to breathe down here? Is it silly that our fine, tall Goths have become little brown men down here? Is it silly that all evil has always come from these southern valleys, for longer than anyone can remember? This land is soft and treacherous. Where do the avalanches always come from, which wreck out huts? From the south. Where does the poison wind come from, which ruins men and beasts? From the south. Why do my cows and sheep fall only when they are grazing on a southern slope? Why did your mother die the first time she came down here, to Bolzanum, that hot and humid city? One of your brothers came down too, and joined Theodoric's army in Ravenna, where the Italians stabbed him to death over a goblet of wine. Why is any field hand useless once he has been in the south, even for one winter? Where did our great hero Theodoric learn the accursed art of government, with taxes and torture and jails and writing? What did our fathers know of all these things?

"And where does all deceit come from, all luxury, all weakness and all cunning? From here, from this accursed southern valley, where people live crammed together in their thousands like worms, and where each breathes the poisoned air of another. And then one day a man comes up to my mountains and takes away my healthy and unspoiled child, to take her down to this land of ill fortune! Your husband has much in him that is good and worthy, I am not denying that! If only he had built himself a hut up there in the mountains with me, I would have gladly given him my best brace of oxen. But no, he had to bring her down here to this swampy valley. And he himself bows his head in the golden halls of Rome and in the raven city, Ravenna. Certainly I resisted for a long time, but then—"

"But in the end you gave in."

"What was I to do? After all my cheerful and healthy girl was actually ill with longing for this man of ill fortune."

"And for ten years this man of ill fortune has made your daughter happy."

"If only it were true!"

"Father!"

"And remains true. It would be the first time anything good came from the south. Look, I detest this plain so much that I have not come down here all these years, so that I had never even seen my grandchild. And there was a very good reason why I finally did come down this time."

"So it was not love? Not your heart?"

"Indeed it was, but it was the fear in my heart. There has been an evil sign. Do you remember the beautiful beech tree next to the mountain spring, to the right of the house? I planted it the day you were born, according to ancient custom. The tree, like yourself, grew strong and healthy, although in the year after you left it was a little sad and sickly looking. But the others could not see it, and laughed at me.

"Well, the tree recovered and looked fresh and green once more. But one night last week there was a thunderstorm up there in the mountains, more violent than most I have seen. And next morning, when I went out of the door, the trunk had been split in half by lightning and the crown had been washed away by the stream – to the south."

"It is a shame about the dear old tree! But can that frighten you?"

"It was not all. That evening, after my day's work, I sadly dug out the poor stump and put it on the fire in the hearth, so that the tree which had been my child's sign and symbol would not rot by the wayside, wretched and ignored. I took it very much to heart, and for a long time I sat there thinking and worrying about your husband, and more and more I had my doubts. And as I pondered I looked into the fire, in which the remains of the old tree were burning to ashes.

"Then I fell asleep, and in my dream I saw you and Witigis. He was dining in a golden hall among proud men and beautiful women, magnificently dressed, but you were standing outside the door, dressed in beggar's rags, crying bitterly and calling out his name. But he only said: 'Who is that woman? I don't know her.' And that's why I could stay up on my mountain no longer. Something drew me down here; I had to see for myself how my child was down here in the valley, and I wanted to catch him by surprise – that's why I didn't come through the front gate."

"Father," Rauthgundis retorted angrily, "one should not think such things, not even in a dream. Your mistrust—"

"Mistrust? I trust nobody except myself. And that bolt of lightning and that dream were a sign to me, and I know it clearly: Some misfortune threatens you! Avoid it! Take your boy and come up into the mountains with me, only for a short while. Believe me, you will learn to like it again up there in the fresh air, where one can look out over all the countries of the world."

"Are you asking me to leave my husband? Never!"

"Did he not leave you? To him the court and the king are more important than wife and child. Let him have his way."

"Father," Rauthgundis now said very firmly, gripping his hand, "not another word! Didn't you love my mother? If you did, then how could you speak like that about my husband? My Witigis is everything to me; he is light and air and life itself. And he loves me with the whole of his loyal heart. We are one! And if he deems it right that he should work away from me, to do what he sees as his duty, then that is right by me. He is conducting the affairs of his nation. Nothing shall come between him and me, nothing! Not a word, not a whisper and not a shadow! Not even a father!"

The old man was silent, but his mistrust would not leave him alone. After a short pause he began once more: "Why, if he has such important work to do at court, why won't he take you with him? Is he ashamed of a peasant's daughter?" Angrily he struck the ground with his stick.

"Your anger is confusing you! A moment ago you were angry because he took me away from your mountain into the valley of the southerners, and now you are angry because he won't take me to Rome, where I would be right in their midst!"

"I am not suggesting that you do it! But he should want you there. He should not be able to do without you. But I suppose the king's general would be ashamed of a peasant's child."

But even before Rauthgundis could reply a horseman galloped toward the gate, which was now closed, and struck it several times with his battleaxe from outside. "Open up! Open up!"

"Who is that?" the old man asked cautiously.

"Open up! This is no way to treat a messenger from the king!"

"It's Wachis," Rauthgundis said, opening the heavy bolt which held the gate shut, "what brings you back so suddenly?"

"So it is you yourself to open the gate for me!" the faithful man cried, "Oh, hail and greetings, Queen of the Goths! The master has been elected king of the nation! These my own eyes saw him raised high on the shield. He sends you greetings, and bids you and Athalwin to join him in Rome. You are to leave in ten days!"

Amid all the shock and surprise, all the joy and all the questioning, Rauthgundis could not help looking at her father with joyful pride in her eyes. Finally she threw herself against his chest and wept with joy: "Well, father?" she said, freeing herself at last. "What do you say now, Father?"

"What do I say? Now the misfortune I have seen coming is here! I am going back to my mountain this very night!"

Chapter 2

While the Goths were meeting at Regata, the great army led by Belisarius held the city of Naples surrounded, posing an immediate and serious threat.

As rapidly and as irresistibly as fire in dry grass the Byzantine army had rolled from the southernmost tip of Italy right up to the walls of the city, without encountering any resistance. Thanks to Theodahad's orders not even a single company of a hundred Goths was to be found in these parts.

The brief encounter at the Jugum pass was the only hold-up the Greeks met. The Roman populations of Bruttia with the cities of Regium, Vibo and Squillacium, Tempsa and Croton, Ruscia and Thurii, of Calabria with the cities of Gallipolis, Tarentum and Brundusium, of Lucania with the cities of Velia and Buxentum, of Apulia with the cities of Acheruntia and Canusium, Salernum, Nuceria and Campsae, together with many other towns and cities received Belisarius with rejoicing, and he in turn announced to them liberation from the Barbarian yoke and heresy in the name of the emperor Justinian and the true faith. As far as the Aufidus in the east and the Sarnus in the south-west Italy had been wrested from the Goths, and it was not until the hostile waves met the walls of Naples that their fury was somewhat checked.

The camps of Belisarius and his army could indeed be called magnificent displays of war and military might. In the north, before the Porta Nolana, lay the camp of Bloody John. The Porta Nolana and Via Nolana had been entrusted to this able commander, together with the task of capturing and securing the road to Rome. Here in the sweeping plain, on the fields which had been tilled by the industrious Goths, Massageti and yellow Huns exercised their ugly little mounts. Alongside them were Persian light mercenaries, in linen armour, armed with bows and arrows. Then there were heavy Armenian shield bearers, Macedonians with ten foot long *sarissa* lances and great masses of cavalry from Thrace and Thessalonica as well as Saracens, all forced to spend their time in hated idleness while the siege was under way, and doing their best to fill in their time with forays into the interior of the country.

The central camp, to the east of the city, was that of the main army, and in its centre stood the great general's tent of Belisarius, made of blue Sidonian silk with a purple flag on top. Here too is where the personal bodyguard of Belisarius stood, whom Belisarius personally paid and equipped, and to which only handpicked men were admitted. They were men who had distinguished themselves three times in battle by extraordinary bravery. From this bodyguard came Belisarius's disciples and his best leaders; they wore gold-encrusted helmets with red plumes of horse hair, the best available chest and leg armour, bronze shields and broad swords and lances. The main body of infantry was positioned here also, consisting of eight thousand Illyrians, the only really good troops the Empire could still provide itself. But here also were hordes of Avars and Bulgarians, together with Sarmatian and Germanic tribesmen such as Heruli and Gepidae. Byzantium had to hire these mercenaries for great sums of money in order to make up for the shortage of able-bodied men among its own population. Each of these groups was led by its own tribal chiefs. The remainder of the main army was made up of many thousands of Italians, who had either emigrated or gone over to the enemy.

Lastly there was the southern camp, stretching along the beach, and commanded by Martinus, who was in charge of siege machinery and equipment. Here is where the catapults stood, together with ballistas, battering rams and throwing machines. Among them were Isaurian allies and troops supplied by Africa, which had only just been recaptured from the Vandals. There were Moorish and Numidian cavalry, Libyans and others in abundance.

There were also single mercenaries and adventurers from almost every Barbarian people of the three continents, from the Danube, the Rhine, from Asia and Africa. There were Bajuvari, Franks, Burgundians, black Negroes and yellow-haired Britons. This colourful army, made up of various Barbarian tribesmen, formed the core of the army with which Justinian wanted to drive the "Barbarian" Goths out of Italy and liberate the Italians. All outposts were commanded by members of Belisarius's bodyguard, and their chain stretched right around the city from the Porta Capuana to the sea itself.

Naples, however, was poorly fortified and had only a very small garrison. There were less than a thousand Goths in the city, and their task was to defend their city's extensive fortifications and indeed Italy herself against an army of forty thousand.

Count Uliaris, the commander of the city, was a brave man and had sworn on his beard that he would not surrender the fortress. But even so it is unlikely that he would have withstood the superior force and tactical ability of Belisarius for long, had it not been for the fortuitous coincidence of the Greek fleet being recalled to Byzantium. As soon as Belisarius had mustered his forces after landing and ordered a general advance against Naples by land and sea, his fleet commander Konon sent him an order from the emperor, kept secret until now, for the fleet's immediate return to the Greek coast. The pretext given was that the fleet was to bring reinforcements, but the real reason was to transport the emperor's nephew Prince Germanus and his lancers to Italy. There he was to watch Belisarius's progress, hindering it where necessary, and as commander-in-chief to look after the interests of Justinian, who mistrusted Belisarius. The latter, clenching his teeth in anger, had to stand by and watch his fleet sail away at the very moment he needed it most. It was only with great difficulty that he managed to persuade Konon to send him four triremes, which were still cruising near Sicily.

Hence Belisarius had been able to besiege the city from the northeast, east and southeast with his land army. The west, which was the road to Rome and defended by the Castellum Tiberii, had been kept open with great effort by Uliaris, and Belisarius had been unable to blockade the harbour or access to the sea.

At first he consoled himself with the thought that the Goths had no fleet, and would therefore be unable to gain much advantage from this circumstance. But he was about to be crossed for the first time by an opponent whose ability and courage were quite extraordinary, and whom he would learn to fear even more in the future. That opponent was Totila. No sooner had Totila reached Naples, buried Valerius and dried Valeria's first tears, than he threw himself with relentless energy into the task of creating a fleet out of nothing.

He had been commander of the fleet at Naples, but weeks before King Theodahad had ordered his fleet out of Belisarius's way to Pisa, despite Totila's protests, on the pretext that it was to guard the mouth of the Arnus River. Hence at the beginning Totila had only three small guardships, of which he had lost two near Sicily, and he had arrived in Naples believing any form of naval resistance to be impossible. But when he heard the unbelievable news that the Byzantine fleet had returned home, he immediately regained hope. And so he would not rest until he had created for himself a small fleet of some twelve ships, made up of large fishing boats, merchant vessels, harbour barges and hastily repaired wrecks from the wharves. Admittedly his little fleet would withstand neither a storm at sea nor a single warship, but it performed excellent service in keeping the beleaguered city supplied with food and other vital supplies from Bajae, Cumae and other cities to the northeast. In addition he was able to observe the enemy's movements near the coast, and to annoy him with incessant attacks. Time and again Totila would land with a small force in the enemy rear to the south, then march inland for some distance and attack here, there and everywhere. Again and again he was able to surprise and defeat a sizeable enemy force, scattering it, and after some time he had created such alarm and uncertainty that the Byzantines would only venture forth in large numbers, and then never far from their camps. At the same time these successes gave much encouragement to the hard-pressed troops of Count Uliaris in Naples itself.

But despite all this Totila could not help but realise that the situation was already extremely serious and that, as soon as a few Greek ships appeared off Naples, it would become hopeless. He therefore used a part of his fleet every day to take away those inhabitants of Naples who could not fight, taking them northward to Bajae and Cumae. He firmly rejected proposals by the rich that these refugee ships should be available only to those who could pay, and he accepted rich and poor alike on board his ships to take them to safety. Repeatedly and ever more urgently Totila had begged Valeria to flee on one of these ships, in the care of Julius, but she did not want to be parted from her father's coffin nor from her beloved, whose praises she enjoyed hearing from almost everybody in the city. And so she calmly went on following her grief and her love, living in her father's house as before.

Chapter 3

During these first days of the siege Miriam was to experience the greatest joy of her own love, and at the same time its ultimate pain and torment. She saw her beloved more often than usual, because the Porta Capuana was an important point in the fortifications, and the naval commander had to visit it often. In the tower of old Isak, Totila and Count Uliaris met daily to conduct their council of war. It was Miriam's habit, as soon as she had greeted the men and placed a simple meal of fruit and wine on the table, to slip down into the little garden just behind the tower. That small space had once been the courtyard of a temple of Minerva, the goddess of city walls. In heathen times it had been a popular custom to erect a small altar to Minerva near the main gates of a city.

The altar had disappeared centuries ago, but the mighty olive tree, which had once shaded the sacred statue of the goddess, still stood. Around it were the flowers which Miriam's loving hand grew there, and which she often picked for the bride of her beloved. Directly opposite the olive tree, whose gnarled roots rose above the ground to reveal a dark opening in the foundations of the ancient temple, Christians had placed a large wooden cross over a small prayer stool, made from one of the marble steps which were once part of the old temple. In those days people liked to use former sites of worship to the old gods, although they were now regarded as demons, to practise the new Christian faith.

The lovely Jewish girl would often sit under this cross for hours with old Arria, the widow of the former assistant gatekeeper. After the early death of Isak's wife she had watched over little Miriam like a mother as she grew up among her flowers. For years Miriam had listened as the pious old woman prayed to her Christian God, and in this way much of the Nazarene's teaching about love and light had found its way into the growing girl's heart.

Now that the old woman had reached a stage, through old age and blindness, where she herself needed help, Miriam repaid her earlier kindness by acting as her nursemaid with a deeply felt loyalty. Arria accepted the devotion, and was deeply touched by it. Her old heart was full of gratitude, as well as love and pity for this beautiful creature. She had long recognised Miriam's great love for the young Goth, but had never mentioned it to the shy young girl.

On the evening of the third day of the siege Miriam was walking, deep in thought, down the broad steps leading into her garden. Her eyes scanned the flowers, and she stopped on the lowest step, leaning on the balustrade. Arria was kneeling on the prayer stool, her back turned, praying aloud. She would not have noticed Miriam approaching, had it not been for the fact that winged life suddenly appeared in the quiet courtyard. In the branches of the olive tree a number of white doves nested, beautiful white birds who had been Miriam's only playmates. When they saw the familiar white figure on the steps they all flew up to greet her, flying about her head. One sat on her head, and another on her outstretched right wrist.

"It is you, Miriam! Your doves told me!" Arria said, turning around. The lovely girl descended the last step, slowly so as not to frighten the birds, as the evening sun shone through the leaves of the olive tree into her peach-coloured cheeks. It was a beautiful scene.

"It is I, mother!" Miriam replied, sitting down with her. "And I have a request to make of you. How," she added softly, "does your saying go about life after death, in your religion? 'I believe in the communion...'"

"I believe in the communion of the spirit, resurrection of the flesh and an eternal life. What made you think of that?"

"Well," Miriam replied, "the singer of Zion says that we are facing death right in the midst of life. And that applies especially to us right now. Don't arrows and stones fall into our streets almost every day? But – I still want to pick some flowers!" she added, getting to her feet.

Arria was silent for a moment. "But the young Goth has already been here today. I heard his voice."

Miriam blushed slightly: "They are not for him," she said softly, "they are for her."

"For her?"

"Yes, for his bride. I saw her today, for the first time. She is very beautiful. I want to give her some roses."

"Did you speak to her? What is she like?"

"I only saw her, but she did not notice me. I have been watching the palace of the Valerians for some time, since she has been here. Today she was being lifted into a litter, on her way to the basilica. I was standing behind one of the columns of the house."

"Well, and is she worthy of him?"

"She is very beautiful, and she has an aristocratic bearing too. She looks as if she is clever, and good as well; but," Miriam sighed, "not happy. I want to give her some roses... Mother," she said a little while later, as she rejoined the old woman with a bunch of beautifully perfumed flowers, "what does that mean: the communion of the spirit? Are only Christians to live together like that? No, no!" she went on, without waiting for a reply, "that cannot be. Either everybody, all good people or..." and she sighed. "Mother, in the book of Moses it says nothing about people rising from the dead. Oh, it would not be so bad," she said as she gathered the roses into a bunch, "to finally rest completely! To sleep and sleep in an endless and dreamless night, to rest from living! I wonder if there is such a thing as life without pain? Without longing? Without a silent wish that can never be fulfilled? I just cannot imagine it."

And she stopped what she was doing and rested her head in her hands. The doves flew away, as their mistress was taking no notice of them.

"The Lord," Arria said solemnly, "has prepared a holy place for His flock, where they will neither hunger nor thirst. No sun shall burn them, nor shall they suffer any discomfort. For the Lord our God shall lead them to eternal springs, and wipe all the tears from their eyes."

"All the tears from their eyes," Miriam repeated after her, "go on, it sounds wonderful."

"There they shall live, and never wish for anything, like the angels, and they shall see God. He will spread the peace of shady palms over them, and they shall forget love and hate and pain and everything which touched their hearts on earth. I have prayed for you a great deal, Miriam, and the Lord will have mercy on you too, and take you into His flock."

But Miriam silently shook her head. "No, Arria, I think that eternal sleep would be better than that. How can a soul let go of something which has been its whole life? How can you put aside your deepest, innermost being and still be the same person? How can I be happy and forget what I love? No, only what we love makes life worthwhile. And if I had to choose between all the joys of heaven and having to give up what is in my heart, or keeping my love with all its longing – no, I don't envy the blessed their heaven. I would choose my love and all the pain that goes with it."

"Child, don't speak like that! Don't blaspheme! Look, what is there that is greater than a mother's love? Nothing on this earth! And yet, in heaven, that too will no longer exist. The love which attracts a woman to a man is a golden dream, but a mother's love is an iron band, which is everlasting and which ties one with never ending pain. Oh my Jucundus, my Jucundus! Oh how I hope that you will come back again soon, so that I can see you down here once more before eternal night covers my eyes. Up there in heaven even the love of a mother for her son will disappear in the eternal love of God and the saints. But I would so like to see him once more, and to embrace him and touch his beloved head with my hands. Do you know, Miriam, I hope and I trust in God. Soon, very soon, I will see him again."

"Oh no, you must not die, Arria!"

"No, I did not mean it like that. I will see him again here on earth. I must see him come back the same way he went."

"Mother," Miriam said softly, as if trying to convince a child, "how can you still believe it? Your Jucundus disappeared thirty years ago!"

"And yet he could come back! It is not possible that the Lord ignored all my tears and all my prayers these last thirty years. What a wonderful son he was! He cared for me and earned my livelihood with his hands, until he became ill and could no longer handle axe and shovel, so that we suffered need. And then he said to me: 'Mother, I cannot bear to see you suffer any longer. You know that there are treasures of the old heathen priests buried in the ruins of the old temple, under the olive tree over there. Father went in there once, and came back with a golden bangle. I am going in there, as far as I can, to see if I can't find some of that gold. God will protect me.' And so I said Amen, because our need was great, and I knew that the Lord would protect a pious widow's only son.

"And we prayed together for an hour, here in front of the cross. And then my Jucundus got up and went into the hole there, under the roots of the olive tree. I listened to the sound of his footsteps until they faded away in the distance.

"He still has not come back. But he is not dead, oh no! Not a day passes that I don't think: today God will bring him back. Wasn't Joseph away for many years in the land of the Egyptians? And yet Jacob's eyes were to see him again. And I have a feeling that I will see him again, today or tomorrow. Last night I dreamt that I saw him coming out of that hole there in a white robe, his arms outstretched. I called his name, and we were re-united for ever. And that's how it will be, for the Lord hears the prayers of those who are sad, and they who trust in Him will not be disappointed."

The old woman rose, pressed Miriam's hand, and went into her little house.

Meanwhile the full moon had risen and now it illuminated the little garden with an almost magical glow, interrupted only by the heavy shadows of the tower. The roses smelt beautiful. Miriam stood up and looked at the cross. "What a powerful faith! What a solace for those who believe! Such gentle teaching! Is it really like that? Is that man on the cross up there, with his head bowed in mortal agony, really the Messiah? Has he gone up to heaven to look after his flock like a good shepherd? But I am not one of his flock! Miriam can have no part of that kind of solace. My solace is my love with all its suffering; it has become my very soul. Am I to drift along among the stars one day, without my love? No, for then I would no longer be Miriam! Or will I take it up there with me, and then stand back to watch the Roman girl at his side through all eternity? Are they to live up there in eternal splendour, with me following in a lonely haze, just so I can see the white hem of his gown glow from afar? No, oh no! It would be so much better to bloom like my flowers here, to bloom in the sunshine of love, to glow and to smell sweet for a short time until the sun dries them up, the same sun which awakens them and then destroys them. And then I would wither, like my flowers, to eternal rest and peace, having paid for the foolishness of longing for the light…"

"Good night, Miriam, keep well!" a melodious voice called out.

Almost taken by fright she looked up, only to see the Goth's white mantle disappear around the corner, with Uliaris leaving in the opposite direction. Quickly she flew up the steps and watched the white mantle, glowing in the moonlight, for a long time until at last it had disappeared in the distant shadows.

Chapter 4

Twice each day Totila and Uliaris met in this way, reporting their successes and their losses, and discussing their prospects of saving the city.

But on the tenth day of the siege Uliaris hurried on board Totila's "flagship", a rotten old fishing vessel, where the naval commander of Naples lay sleeping on the deck, covered only by a torn sail. "What has happened?" Totila cried, jumping to his feet still half asleep, "The enemy? Where?"

"No, no my boy, this time it's still Uliaris and not Belisarius who wakes you. But by thunder, it can't go on much longer."

"Uliaris, you are bleeding – your head is bandaged!"

"Pah, that was only a stray arrow, luckily not a poisoned one. I got it last night. I must tell you, things are bad, worse than yesterday. Bloody John, may God strike him down, is digging away at our Castellum Tiberii like a badger; once he has that then goodbye Naples! Yesterday evening he completed an entrenchment on the hill above us, and now he is shooting burning arrows at our heads. I tried to throw him out last night, but I could not. There were seven of them to one of ours, and I got nothing out of it except this arrow wound to my old grey head."

"That entrenchment must go," Totila said, thinking.

"The devil, I agree with you, but it won't move! But there is more. The population is becoming difficult. Every day Belisarius has a hundred blunt arrows shot over the wall with his 'call for freedom'. They do more damage than a thousand sharp ones. Already my poor lads are having stones thrown at them from rooftops here and there. If that should get worse! With a thousand men we can't fight forty thousand Greeks outside and thirty thousand Neapolitans inside. And so I think—" His face looked foreboding.

"What are you trying to say?"

"We will have to burn down part of the city, at least the outer city…"

"So that the people will love us more? No, Uliaris, they shall not have just cause to call us Barbarians. I know a better way – they are hungry. Yesterday I brought in four shiploads of oil and grain and wine; I will distribute them among the people."

"Give them oil and grain if you like, but not the wine! I want that for my Goths. They have been drinking cistern water for days already – ugh!"

"Very well, you thirsty heroes, you can have the wine."

"Thank you. Now, is there still no word from Ravenna? From Rome?"

"None. My fifth messenger left yesterday."

"May God strike down our wretched king! You know, Totila, I don't think we are going to get out of these rotten walls alive!"

"Nor do I!" Totila said calmly, and offered his guest a goblet of wine.

Uliaris looked at him. Then he drank and said: "My golden boy, you are as true as the day is long, just like this wine of yours. If I am to die here, like an old bear among a pack of forty dogs, at least I am glad I got to know you so well over it, you and your wine." With that rough gesture of friendship the grizzled old Goth left the ship.

Totila sent grain and wine to the defenders in the Castellum, which they enjoyed thoroughly. But when Uliaris looked out of the tower of the Castellum next morning he rubbed his eyes in disbelief. There, on top of the entrenchment on the hill, a blue Gothic flag was fluttering! Totila had landed in the enemy's rear during the night and taken the position by storm.

But this new piece of daredevil achievement aroused Belisarius's anger, and he swore to put an end to the young Goth's activities. He was therefore delighted when the four warships arrived from Sicily just at this time. He ordered them to enter the harbour of Naples immediately, and to put an end to the activities of the Gothic "pirates". The four mighty triremes arrived that same evening, and anchored outside the entrance to the harbour. Belisarius himself with his following went to the coast, where he feasted his eyes on the sight of the sails bathed in the glow of the setting sun. "The rising sun shall see them sail into the harbour despite that accursed youth," he said to Antonina, who was with him, and turned his horse back to the camp.

On the following morning, even before he had risen from his camp bed, Belisarius was conferring with his legal adviser Procopius, who was reading out a draft report to Justinian. Suddenly Chanaranges, the Persian leader of his bodyguard, rushed into the tent and called out: "The ships, general, the ships have been taken!"

Belisarius jumped up from his camp bed, furious, and cried: "He who says that shall die!"

"It would be better," Procopius remarked, "if the one who did it was to die instead."

"Who was it?"

"Oh general, it was the young Goth with the flashing eyes and the shining hair."

"Totila!" Belisarius bellowed, "That Totila again!"

"Some of the crews were on the beach, with my outpost, and the remainder were below decks asleep. Suddenly, around midnight, there was a flurry of activity all around, as if a hundred ships had suddenly emerged out of the sea."

"A hundred ships! He has ten cockleshells!"

"In a few moments, long before we were able to get there from the beach to help, the ships had been boarded and their crews captured. One trireme, whose anchor rope could not be severed quickly enough, was set on fire, and the other three ships were taken to Naples."

"They arrived in the harbour even earlier than you thought, oh Belisarius!" Procopius remarked. But Belisarius had already regained his full composure. "Now the audacious boy has warships, and he will become quite unbearable. There must be an end to it, and it must be now!" He placed his magnificent helmet on his majestic head. "I wanted to try and spare the city and the Roman population, but I cannot do so any longer. Procopius, summon my generals here, Magnus, Demetrius, Constantinus, Bessas and Ennes, and Martinus, the master of my siege machinery. I will give them plenty to do. Those Barbarians shall not savour their victory for long; they shall get to know Belisarius instead!"

Soon afterwards a man appeared in the tent of his commander-in-chief who, despite his breastplate, looked more like a scholar than a warrior. Martinus, the great mathematician, was a gentle and peace-loving man, who for a long time had found fulfilment in the quiet study of Euclid. He could not bear the sight of blood, and would not harm a flower. But one day his mathematical genius led him to invent a new missile thrower of immense power. He had stumbled on this discovery as if in passing, and showed his design to Belisarius. The latter was delighted, and would not even allow Martinus to go back to his study. Instead he dragged him directly to the emperor, and forced him to become "Master of Artillery to the *Magister Militum per Orientem*," namely Belisarius himself. He received an excellent salary, and was contractually obligated to design and build one new war machine every year. Now the gentle mathematician looked on with dismay as the terrible weapons of destruction, which he had invented, smashed down the walls of fortresses and the giant portals of castles, spread inextinguishable fire in the streets of Justinian's enemies and killed people in their thousands. He did enjoy the mathematical challenge each year, and devoted himself to it with tireless energy. But once he had solved the problem he thought with horror of the effects which his newest invention would have. He therefore appeared before Belisarius with a sorrowful look on his face.

"Martinus, master of the compasses," the general called out to him, "now is your chance to show me what you can do! How many catapults, throwing machines and ballistas do we have together?"

"Three hundred and fifty, Sir!"

"Good! Distribute them around the entire siege line! Up in the north, at the Porta Capuana and the Castellum I want the battering rams in position! Those walls must come down, even if they are made of diamond! From the middle of your camp I want the missiles aimed upwards, so that they will land in the streets of the city. Make an all-out effort and don't stop for a minute for twenty-four hours! Use relief troops if you have to, and let every machine do its part."

"All the machines Sir? Even the new ones?" Martinus asked. "The new incendiary Pyroballistas too?"

"Yes, those most of all!"

"Sir, they are dreadful! You don't know the effect they have yet!"

"Very well, I want to get to know them and try them out."

"On this beautiful city? On this city which belongs to the emperor? Do you want to capture a heap of rubble for Justinian?"

Belisarius did have a compassionate soul: "What else am I to do?" he asked angrily. "These pigheaded Barbarians and their daredevil Totila are forcing my hand! Five times I have offered them a chance to surrender. It is madness! There are less than three thousand men behind those walls. By the head of Justinian! Why won't those thirty thousand Neapolitans rise and disarm the Barbarians?"

"They probably fear your Huns more than the Goths!" Procopius commented.

"Then they are poor patriots! Go Martinus! Naples must burn within the hour!"

"It will take less than that," the mathematician sighed, "if it has to be. I have brought a knowledgeable man who will be able to help us and make the task easier. He is a living plan of the city. May I bring him?"

Belisarius signalled agreement, and the guard brought in a Jewish-looking man. "Ah, Jochem the builder!" Belisarius said. "I remember you well from Byzantium. You wanted to build the St Sophia church, did you not? What came of it?"

"Begging your pardon, Sir, nothing!"

"Nothing? Why?"

"My plan was to cost only a million *solidi* of gold, and that was not enough for His Imperial Holiness. The more a Christian church costs, the holier it will be, and the more it will please the Almighty. A Christian demanded double and was awarded the contract."

"But I did see you building in Byzantium?"

"Yes, Sir, the emperor liked my plan. I changed it a little, took out the altar, and built a riding school."

"You know Naples exactly? From inside and outside?"

"Yes Sir, like I know my own purse."

"Good, then you will help direct and aim the machines against the walls and the city. The houses of those friendly to the Goths must come down first! Go to it, and do your job well, otherwise you will be impaled. Away with you!"

"The poor city!" Martinus sighed, "but you will see, Jochem, the new Pyroballistas are very accurate, and so easy to use that a child could operate them. And they work beautifully!"

And now an enormous activity began all along the camp, pregnant with disaster. The Gothic guards on the walls watched with concern as the heavy machines were drawn up to the walls, each pulled by twenty or thirty horses, camels, donkeys or oxen, and placed into position along the siege line. Totila and Uliaris, very worried over this new development, hurried onto the walls and tried to take countermeasures. Sacks of earth were lowered in those places which were threatened by the battering rams, lighted torches were made ready to set the machines on fire as they approached, and boiling water, arrows and stones were made ready to be used against the crews and the traction animals. Already the Goths were laughing at their cowardly enemies as they saw the machines halt a long way from the walls, much further than the range of normal machines allowed, and certainly out of range of the defenders on the walls.

But Totila did not laugh. He was dismayed when he saw the Byzantines calmly unharness the traction animals and set the machines.

"Ha-ha!" young Agila laughed, standing next to Totila, "are they going to shoot at us from there? Why not from Byzantium, across the ocean? That would be even safer!" He had barely said this when a forty-pound rock smashed both him and the battlement on which he had been standing into eternity. Martinus had trebled the range of the ballistic machines. Totila recognised that the Goths would have to stand by entirely defenceless as the enemy hurled missiles at them at will.

Now terrified, the Goths sprang from the walls and sought refuge from the hail of missiles raining down on the streets, the houses and the churches, but in vain! Thousands upon thousands of arrows, spears, rocks, stones and heavy pieces of timber flew over their heads; huge boulders came flying through the air and smashed through the timber and tiles of the roofs, no matter how strong they were, while the battering rams smashed ceaselessly against the Castellum in the north. While the thick hail of missiles literally darkened the sky above, the sound of falling rocks, smashing timber and the screams of the wounded filled the air. The population, terrified, fled trembling into their cellars and basements, cursing Belisarius and the Goths in turn. But the wounded city had not yet experienced the worst.

In the marketplace, near the Forum of Trajan, there stood a large open structure which served as a ship's chandler's store, full of dry timber, flax, ropes, tar and the like. Suddenly a strange missile came hissing through the air, struck the timber, and in the next instant the timber was well and truly alight. The flame, feeding on the ship's supplies, spread with lightning speed. The beleaguering troops outside greeted the sight of smoke with loud cheers, and busily directed their missiles in the direction of the blaze, so as to make fire-fighting more difficult.

Belisarius rode over to Martinus. "Well done," he said, "wizard of the compasses. Who aimed the shot?"

"I did!" Jochem replied. "Oh, you will be pleased with me. Do you see the big house over there, to the right of the fire, with the flat roof and the statues on it? That is the house of the Valerians, the greatest friends of the people of Edom. Watch, in a moment it will be alight!"

The firebrand flew hissing through the air, and a moment later a second flame rose from the stricken city.

Procopius now galloped along and called out: "Belisarius, your general Bloody John sends you greetings. The Castellum Tiberii is on fire, and the first wall is down." And so it was! Very soon there were four, six and even ten houses alight in every part of the city.

"Water!" Totila cried, riding furiously through the burning streets to the harbour, "come on out, citizens of Naples, and put out the fires in your houses. I cannot spare a single Goth from the walls. Get empty barrels from the harbour to every street! Form bucket brigades! Get the women into the houses… What do you want, girl? Leave me – oh, it is you, Miriam? You here? Among the flames and the arrows? Go away, what are you looking for?"

"You," the girl replied. "Don't worry. Her house is on fire, but she is safe."

"Valeria! My God, where is she?"

"With me. In our solid tower she is safe. I saw the flames coming from her house and I hurried there. Your friend with the gentle voice carried her from the ruins; he was going to the church with her. I called out to him and led them under our roof. She is bleeding from a stone which hit her on the shoulder, but she is not in danger. She wants to see you, and so I came to look for you!"

"Thank you, child. But come, you must get away from here!"

He grabbed her quickly around the waist and swung her up into the saddle in front of him. Trembling, she put both arms around his neck. He held his shield protectively over her head, and galloped at top speed through the smoking street to the Porta Capuana.

"Oh, if only I could die now, at his breast, if I can't die with him!" Miriam prayed.

In the tower he saw Valeria, lying on Miriam's bed, under the care of Julius and her slaves. She was pale and weak from loss of blood, but calm and composed. Totila flew to her side, as Miriam stood by the window, her heart beating furiously, looking out at the burning city.

As soon as Totila had satisfied himself that the wound was indeed only slight, he jumped to his feet and said: "You must get away from here, immediately! This very hour! In another hour Belisarius may have stormed these walls. I have filled all my ships with fugitives once more. They will take you to Cajeta, and from there you will be able to get to Rome. Once you are there, hurry to Taginae, where you have estates. You must go! Julius will go with you."

"Yes," the latter added, "for we have a place to go to."

"A place to go to? Where?"

"Gaul, my homeland. I can no longer bear to watch this terrible war! You know yourself, the whole of Italy is rising up against you, on the side of your enemies. My fellow citizens are fighting under Belisarius – am I to fight with them against you, or with you against them? I cannot do either, so I am leaving."

Totila turned silently to Valeria.

"My friend," she said, "it seems to me that our lucky star has gone out for ever, and that our love is ill-fated. No sooner had my father taken that oath from you before the throne of God than Naples falls, the third largest city in the Empire."

"Don't you trust our sword?"

"I trust your sword, but not your luck! When I saw my father's house collapsing, for me that meant the pillars of my hopes collapsed too. God be with you and keep you, because we will be parted for a long time. I will do as you say and go to Taginae."

Totila and Julius hurried outside to make sure there would be a place for her on one of the triremes. Valeria rose from her bed, and in a moment Miriam rushed over to help her fasten her sandals.

"Don't! You are not here to serve me," Valeria said.

"I do it gladly," Miriam whispered in reply. "But please permit me one question." Her eyes met Valeria's, with unusual intensity in them. "You are beautiful and clever and proud – but tell me, do you love him? You can leave him now? Do you love him with a hot flame, which consumes everything else, do you love him like…"

Valeria pressed the girl's lovely head to her breast, as if trying to conceal her. "Like you love him? No, my sweet sister! Don't be frightened! I have suspected it for a long time, from his reports about you. And I saw it clearly the first time I saw you looking at him. Don't worry, your secret is safe with me, and nobody will find out about it. Don't cry, and don't tremble, my sweet child. I love you very much on account of your own love, and I do understand it completely. I envy you for being able to give yourself entirely to the emotions of the moment the way you do. A hostile god has given me a sixth sense, which always looks to the future, and I can only see a long dark path before us, with much pain along the way, and it will not end in the light. But I have to admit to you that your love is more noble than mine, because it is hopeless. My hope lies in ruins also. It might have been better if he had discovered the fragrant rose of your love, because I fear that Valeria will never be his. But God be with you, Miriam! They are coming. Remember this hour, and think of me as your sister. And thank you, thank you for your beautiful love."

Miriam had been trembling like a child caught unawares, and her whole being wanted to flee from the all-seeing Valeria. But the way the other woman spoke overcame her shyness, and tears of emotion flowed down her glowing cheeks. With intense emotion, trembling with shyness and embarrassment and tears, she pressed her pretty head against the bosom of her friend.

Now Julius could be heard coming to fetch Valeria. They had to part, and Miriam dared to take just one quick look at the Roman woman's face. Then she sank to the ground before her, embraced her knees, pressed a burning kiss on Valeria's hand, and vanished into the next room.

Valeria rose, almost as if she was in a dream, and looked about her.

Near the window, in a vase, was a fragrant red rose. She kissed the flower, hid it near her bosom, and then with a movement of her hand she quickly blessed the friendly place which had offered her asylum. Then she turned with determination, and followed Julius to the harbour in an enclosed litter, and there she took a quick farewell from Totila before boarding the ship with Julius. In a moment the ship had left the quay and sailed from the harbour and out of sight.

Totila looked on as if in a dream, until the ship had gone from view. He could see Valeria's white hand wave farewell, and watched the fleeing white sails disappear, oblivious to the missiles falling around him. He was leaning against a pillar, and for a moment he forgot the burning city, himself and everything else.

It was young Thorismuth who woke him from his daydream.

"Come, general," he called out to Totila, "I have been looking for you everywhere. Uliaris wants to talk to you. Come – what are you standing there for, staring into the sea in a rain of arrows?"

Slowly Totila pulled himself together. "Do you see that ship over there? There they go!"

"Who?" Thorismuth asked.

"My happiness and my youth," Totila replied, and went to look for Uliaris.

The latter informed him that he had just accepted an armistice for three hours, for which Belisarius had asked in order to begin negotiations. "I will never surrender! But we must have time to repair our walls. Are there no reinforcements coming from anywhere? Have you still no news from the king?"

"None."

"Damn! More than six hundred of my Goths have already fallen from these hellish missiles. I can no longer man even the most important positions! If only I had at least another four hundred men!"

"Well," said Totila, thinking, "I think I can get them for you. In the Castellum Aurelianum, on the road to Rome, there are some four hundred and fifty Goths. Until now they have firmly insisted that they have ridiculous orders from King Theodahad not to reinforce Naples. But now, in this extreme emergency? I will go there myself during the armistice, and do everything I can to bring them here."

"Don't go! You will not get back until after the armistice has expired, and by then the road will no longer be free. You will not be able to get through!"

"I will get through, if not by force then by cunning. Just make sure you hold out until I get back! Come, Thorismuth, on your horse and let's go!"

While Totila and Thorismuth were racing through the Porta Capuana with a few mounted Goths, old Isak was using the armistice to rest and to take a little food and wine. He had been on the walls without a break since the bombardment began, and was enjoying the brief respite. While Miriam was bringing him his meal, listening at the same time to his report about the advances the enemy had made, they heard the sound of hurried and uncertain footsteps on the stairs, and a moment later Jochem stood before them.

"Son of Rachel, where do you come from in this evil hour, like a raven before a disaster? How did you get in? Through which gate?"

"Let that be my worry. I have come, father Isak, to ask one more time for your daughter's hand – for the last time in this life."

"Is this a time to court and to wed?" Isak asked impatiently, "the city is burning, and the streets are full of corpses."

"Why is the city burning? Why are the streets full of corpses? Because the people of Naples are on the side of the people of Edom. Yes, now is a good time for courting. Give me your child, father Isak, and I will save her and you. I alone can do it." And he reached for Miriam's arm.

"You, save me?" she cried with disgust, taking a step backwards. "I would rather die!"

"Ha, so you are still proud!" her angry suitor hissed. "Perhaps you would rather be saved by the blond Christian? We will see if the accursed Goth can save you, from

Belisarius or from me. Ha, I will drag him through the streets by his yellow hair, and I will spit into his pale face."

"Get out of my house, Rachel's son," Isak cried, rising and taking up his spear. "I can see that you are on the side of those outside the walls. I have to go, there is the call of the horn. But let me tell you this: Many more of you will fall before you finally climb over these rotten walls."

"Perhaps," Jochem grinned, "we will fly over them like the birds of the air. For the last time, Miriam, I ask of you: leave this old fool and the accursed Christian. Believe me, the rubble of these walls will soon cover them. I know that you have carried him in your heart, and I forgive you for that, only now become my wife." And once more he reached for her arm.

"You will forgive me for my love? Forgive something which is as far above you as the sun is over a worm? Would I be worthy of ever having even seen him, if I became your wife? Go, get away from me!"

"Ha!" Jochem cried, "my wife – you will never be my wife! But you will squirm in these arms, and I will tear the Christian out of your bleeding heart, so that it will convulse in despair. We will meet again."

With that he vanished from the house, and in a moment he was out of the city.

Miriam, troubled by a nagging fear, hurried out into the open. She wanted to pray, but not in the drab synagogue. She wanted to pray for him, and so she wanted to pray to his god. Hesitantly she dared to go into the basilica of St Mary, from which Jews had often been driven with curses in times of peace. But now the Christians did not have time for cursing. She knelt in a dark corner among the pillars and soon, deep in prayer, she had forgotten herself and the city and the world. She was with him and with God.

Meanwhile the last hour of the armistice had expired, and the sun was already approaching the sea on the horizon. The Goths were repairing and patching the walls as best they could, clearing the dead and the rubble out of the way, and putting out the fires. As the hourglass ran out for the third time, Belisarius was standing outside his tent with his generals, waiting for the signal of surrender to appear on the Castellum Tiberii. "I don't believe it!" John whispered to Procopius. "Anyone who fights the way that old man has done until now will not lay down his arms. It's better this way too, because then there will be a ruthless storming of the walls, with a good plunder and plenty of booty."

Count Uliaris appeared on one of the battlements of the Castellum, and stubbornly flung a spear among the waiting soldiers outside the walls.

Belisarius jumped to his feet. "They want their own destruction, the stubborn fools! Very well, they shall have it! Come, generals, prepare to take the city by storm. Whoever is first to plant our banner on the wall shall have one tenth of all the booty."

The generals went in all directions, driven by ambition and by greed. Bloody John was just going around the aqueduct, which Belisarius had destroyed in order to deprive the city of water, when a soft voice called out to him.

It was already so dark that John could make out only with difficulty who the caller was. "What do you want, Jew?" John said, as he was in a hurry. "I don't have time. I have work to do. I must be first into the city."

"You will be, Sir, without any effort, if you will follow me."

"Follow you? Do you know a way over the wall, through the air?"

"No, but under the wall, through the earth. I will show you the way if you promise me a thousand *solidi* and a girl I want as booty."

John halted: "I agree to your demand. Where is this way?"

"Here!" Jochem replied, and struck the stones with his hand.

"What? The aqueduct? How do you know?"

"I built it. A man can crawl through it if he bends down low. There is no water in it now. I have just come out of the city the same way. The aqueduct ends in an old temple near the Porta Capuana. Take thirty men and follow me."

John looked at him sharply. "And if you betray me?"

"I will walk between your swords. If I lie you can strike me down."

"Wait!" said John, and hurried away.

Chapter 5

Shortly afterwards John reappeared with his brother Perseus and about thirty determined Armenian mercenaries, who carried small hatchets in addition to their swords. "Once we are inside," said John, "you, Perseus, will open the small gate on the right of the Porta Capuana at the same moment as we unfurl our flag up on the wall. That will be the signal for my Huns to rush in through the small gate. But who defends the tower at the Porta? We have to have him first."

"Isak, a great friend of the Edomites; he must fall!"

"He will fall," John declared, and drew his sword: "Forward!" He was the first to enter the actual pipe of the aqueduct. "You two, Paucaris and Gubazes, take the Jew between you. At the first sign of anything suspicious – down with him!"

And so they progressed along the pipe, either walking stooped or crawling on their hands and knees, John in the lead and the Armenians after him, in total darkness and careful to avoid making any noise.

Suddenly John said softly: "Take the Jew, down with him! Enemies – arms! No," he added quickly, "it was only a snake slithering past. Forward!"

"Now to the right!" said Jochem, "the aqueduct leads into a passage from an old temple."

"What's this? Bones – a skeleton! I can't stand this any more, the rotten air is choking me! Help!" one of the men sighed.

"Leave him there! Forward!" John ordered. "I can see a star."

"That is the daylight of Naples," said Jochem, "only a little further to go."

John's helmet struck the roots of an old olive tree, which spread in the atrium of the old temple and across the entrance to it. We know the tree.

Trying to avoid the roots John's helmet struck the side wall of the passage with a loud metallic sound; he stopped in alarm, but could hear only the fluttering of numerous doves, which flew away out of the branches of the tree at the disturbance.

"What was that?" a hoarse voice above him said. "How the wind whistles among the old stones!" It was the widow Arria. "Oh God," she said, prostrating herself on the ground before the cross once more: "deliver us from evil and don't let the city perish until my Jucundus has come back! What if he can find no trace of his city, or his mother? Oh, please let him come back the way he went. Let me see him just once more as I saw him that last night, rising again from the roots of this tree."

She turned to the opening. "Oh dark passage, into which my happiness disappeared, give him back to me! God, bring him back to me out of the same hole." She was standing directly before the opening, her hands folded, and her eyes directed piously to heaven.

John hesitated. "She is praying!" he said softly, "am I to kill her while she prays?" He stopped, hoping that she might finish her prayer and turn to go. "It is taking too long, I can't help God!" Quickly he rose from the roots. The old woman saw him rising out of the ground with her half blind eyes, a shining figure of a man.

A look of ecstasy appeared on her face. She spread her arms with delight and called out: "Jucundus!" It was her last breath, for in the same instant John's sword pierced her heart. Without so much as a cry of pain, a smile on her lips, she sank down dead on the flowers – Miriam's flowers.

John turned, helped his brother Perseus out of the hole, and then the Jew and the first three of his men. "Where is the small gate?"

"Here, to the left, I will go and open it!" Perseus led his men to the gate.

"Where are the steps to the tower?"

"Here, to the right," said Jochem. It was the staircase leading to Miriam's room. How often had Totila slipped in through here! "Quiet, the old man is stirring."

And indeed it was Isak. He had heard a noise from above, and looked down from the steps with his torch, his spear in his hand: "Who is that down there? Is it you, Miriam? Who comes there?" he asked.

"It is I, father Isak," Jochem replied, "I came to ask you again—" and he took another step upwards, silently as a cat. But Isak could hear the sound of weapons.

"Who is with you?" he called out, and came around the corner holding his torch in front of him. As he did so he could see the armed men hiding behind Jochem. "We are betrayed!" he shouted. "Die, you stain on Hebrew honour!" and with that he thrust his broad spear with great anger into Jochem's breast. The latter, unable to retreat, fell backwards down the steps. "Betrayed!" Isak cried once more.

But in the next instant Bloody John had cut him down, jumped over his body and rushed to the battlement on top of the tower, where he unfurled the Byzantine flag. Immediately the blows of axes could be heard below, the small gate fell down, and the Huns raced into the stricken city in their hundreds, with loud cries of rejoicing.

That was the end, and by now it had become quite dark. Some of the Huns ran through the streets, murdering as they went, while others broke down adjoining gates to let their comrades in.

Uliaris and the few remaining Gothic defenders hurried over from the Castellum, hoping to drive out the insurgents, but in vain; a javelin struck him down. The last two hundred surviving Goths, who were still with him, fell fighting around his body.

And now that the Imperial flag was flying on the walls the citizens of Naples rose also, led by Roman patriots such as Stephanos and Antiochos the Syrian. Castor the lawyer, who had been an eager supporter of the Goths, was killed trying to stop them. Thus the local population disarmed single Goths in the streets, and then sent a deputation to Belisarius, congratulating and thanking him as he rode into the city through the Porta Capuana, surrounded by his glittering staff.

But Belisarius was far from pleased, and furrowed his brow in anger. Without checking his horse he said sternly: "Naples has cost me fifteen days, otherwise I would be outside Rome or even Ravenna by now. How much do you think that has cost the emperor in justice, or me in glory? For fifteen days your cowardice and your hostile attitude allowed a handful of Barbarians to rule over you. The penalty for those fifteen days will be only fifteen hours, fifteen hours of plunder and looting. There will be no murdering as the people of this city are now the emperor's prisoners of war, and there will be no arson as this city is now a fortress belonging to Byzantium. Where is the Gothic commander? Dead?"

"Yes," John replied, "Count Uliaris fell. Here is his sword."

"I did not mean him!" Belisarius replied. "I mean the young one, that Totila. What happened to him? I must have him!"

"Sir," said one of the wealthy Neapolitans, the merchant Ascepliodotus, stepping forward, "if you will spare my house and my warehouse from the plundering, I will tell you."

But Belisarius gave a signal, and two mounted Moorish lancers took the trembling civilian between them. "Rebel, do you dare to make me conditions? Talk, or I will have you tortured!"

"Have mercy, Sir!" the frightened man cried, "the naval commander hurried out of the city with a few mounted men during the armistice, in order to fetch reinforcements from the Castellum Aurelianum; he could be back at any moment."

"John," Belisarius ordered, "that man is as valuable as the whole of Naples. We must catch him! Have you occupied the road to Rome as I ordered? Have you occupied the gate?"

"Nobody could have left the city in that direction," John replied.

"Good, now quickly! We must find a way to lure him inside. Take down our flag, and hoist the Gothic banner again on the Castellum Tiberii, and on the Porta Capuana too. Arm the Neapolitan prisoners and place them on the walls. Anybody who warns him, even with a blink of the eye, is a dead man! Put Gothic clothing and weapons on my bodyguards. I want to be there myself! Have three hundred men in the vicinity of the gate, and let him in as if nothing has happened. As soon as he is inside close the gate behind him. I want him taken alive! I must have him for my triumphal march in Byzantium."

"Please give me the task, my general," John requested. "I still owe him retribution for a cut he dealt me in the past." And he flew back to the Porta Capuana, where he had all the bodies and other signs of struggle removed, and made his other arrangements.

And then a veiled figure forced her way closer. "In the name of God's mercy," a lovely voice pleaded, "let me near, men! I only want his body, oh please take care! His white beard – oh my father!" It was Miriam, who had been driven back to her home by the sound of plundering Huns at the Porta Capuana. With the strength of despair she pushed back the spears and took Isak's pale head in her arms.

"Get away, girl!" the nearest soldier called out, a very tall Bajuvar by the name of Garizo, who was a Byzantine mercenary. "Don't hold us up! We have to clear the way! Into the ditch with the Jew!"

"No, no!" Miriam cried, and pushed the man back.

"Wench!" the latter cried out angrily and raised his axe.

But Miriam held her ground fearlessly, holding her arms protectively over her father's body, and looking up at the soldier with glowing eyes. The soldier stopped, as if paralysed: "You have a lot of courage, girl!" he said, lowering his axe, "and you are beautiful too, like the wood nymph of Luisacha. What can I do to help you? You are quite enchanting to look at."

"If the god of my fathers has touched your heart," Miriam's appealing voice begged, "then help me bury him in the garden there. He dug his own grave long ago, next to Sarah, my mother. His head must point to the east."

"So be it!" the Bajuvar replied, and followed her. She carried the head, and he the knees of the body. A few steps took them into the little garden, where they found a large stone under weeping willows. The man rolled it aside, and they placed the body in the grave, its head pointing east.

Without words, and without tears, Miriam stared down into the grave. She felt so weak now, and so alone. Softly and compassionately the Bajuvar rolled the heavy stone back over the opening. "Come," he said.

"Where to?" Miriam asked, in a hollow voice.

"Well, where do you want to go?"

"I don't know! Thank you," she replied, and took an amulet from around her neck and handed it to him. It was made of gold, and was a coin from Jordan. It had come from the temple.

"No!" said the man, and shook his head. He took her hand, and placed it over his eyes.

"There," he said, "that will do me good for the rest of my life. But now I must go. We have to catch that Count, Totila. God be with you."

The mention of his name struck deep chords in Miriam's heart. Once more she looked at the silent grave, and then she slipped out of the little garden. She tried to get out of the city, but found the gate already lowered. Beside it there were men in Gothic armour, and she looked about her, perplexed.

"Is everything ready, Chanaranges?"

"Everything, Sir. He is as good as caught."

"Listen – outside the wall! Horses! It's them! Back, woman!"

A handful of horsemen were galloping toward the gate along the road leading north.

"Open the gate!" Totila cried from afar.

Thorismuth spurred his horse alongside his leader. "I don't know, I don't like it," he said, "the road was deserted, and the enemy camp there looks deserted too. There are no more than a few watch fires burning."

At that moment a Gothic horn sounded from the battlement. "He certainly has no idea how to blow a horn!" Thorismuth commented angrily.

"It will be an Italian," Totila suggested.

"Give the password," a voice called from above, in Latin.

"Neapolis!" Totila replied. "Did you hear that? Uliaris has had to arm the civilian population. Open the gate! I bring good news!" he went on, addressing himself to the men on top of the wall, "there are four hundred Goths right behind me. Italy has a new king!"

"Which one is it?" a voice asked quietly on the inside.

"The one on the white horse. The first one!"

"Open the gate!" Totila called out once more, and the gate opened slowly. Gothic helmets filled the entrance, torches flared, and there was a sea of whispering voices. Thorismuth looked ahead searchingly, his hand shading his eyes. "There was a national gathering at Regata yesterday," Totila went on. "Theodahad has been deposed, and Count Witigis…"

Now the gate was open, and Totila was about to spur his horse, when a woman rushed from the rows of soldiers and threw herself before the hooves of his horse: "Flee!" she cried, "The enemy is upon you! The city has fallen!" But she could not finish what she was saying; a lance pierced her breast.

"Miriam!" Totila cried, horrified, and pulled his horse back.

But Thorismuth, who had been suspicious all along, was quick to act. With one blow from his sword he cut through the rope holding the gate open, and the latter came crashing down in front of Totila.

A hail of spears and arrows flew though the grating of the gate. "Open the gate! After them!" John called out from inside, but Totila would not budge.

"Miriam! Miriam!" he called out, in the depths of pain and despair. And then she opened her eyes once more, with a last look at him, full of love and agony. That one look told everything, and it penetrated deeply into Totila's heart. "For you!" she breathed, and fell backwards, lifeless. He forgot Naples and the mortal danger he was in. "Miriam!" he called out again, holding his hands out to her.

An arrow grazed the chest of his horse, and the noble animal reared up backwards. The gate was starting to rise. Thorismuth, acting once more with quick determination, grabbed the reins of his commander's horse, pulled it around and gave it a sharp hit on the rump with the flat blade of his sword, so that it shot away from the gate. "Let's run," he called out to Totila, "they will have to be fast if they want to catch us." And the two riders flew back along the road they had come, along the Via Capuana. John pursued them for a while, but gave up because of the darkness, and because he did not know the road. Totila and Thorismuth soon met up with the relief force from the Castellum Aurelianum. They halted on the crest of a hill, from which they could see the city with its walls and battlements, lit up by the fires of the Byzantine guards on the walls.

Only now did Totila shake off his pain and come out of his stunned state. "Uliaris!" he sighed, "Miriam! Naples – we will meet again." And he signalled their departure for Rome.

But from this hour onwards a shadow had fallen over the soul of the young Goth. Miriam had made a permanent place for herself in his heart.

When John brought his horsemen back from their fruitless chase he cried, as he leapt from his mount with anger in his voice: "Where is the wench who warned him? Feed her to the dogs!" And he hurried to report the failure of his mission to Belisarius.

But nobody knew where the body of the beautiful girl was. The crowd thought that the horses had trampled her to pieces. But there was one man who knew better, Garizo the Bajuvar. He had carried her out of the tumult in his arms, gently like a sleeping child, into the little garden nearby. There he rolled the stone from the grave which he had closed only a short time before, and carefully he placed his charge by her father's side. And then he stood there for a long time, looking at her.

From a distance he could hear the noise of the city being plundered. In spite of Belisarius's orders the Massageti were burning and murdering everywhere, not even sparing the churches. In the end the general himself had to restore order by charging among them with drawn sword, at the head of his bodyguard.

There was an almost holy glow on her face, so that he did not dare to kiss her, much as he wanted to. So he turned her face to the east, and laid a rose from the garden next to her heart. Then he wanted to leave, and take part in the plunder, but something would not let him, and each time he turned back again. In the end he spent the night as the death watch by the grave of this lovely girl, leaning on his spear.

He looked up at the stars, and spoke an ancient heathen blessing, which his mother had taught him long ago back at home on the Liusacha. But it did not seem enough, and so he added a Christian prayer for good measure, with deep feeling. As the sun rose he carefully closed the grave with the stone and left.

And thus Miriam vanished without a trace.

But the people of Naples, who secretly loved Totila still, told of how a beautiful protecting angel had come from heaven to save him, and had then risen again and returned to whence she had come.

Chapter 6

The fall of Naples occurred a few days after the national gathering at Regata. Totila had only got as far as Formiae when he met his brother Hildebad, whom King Witigis had sent ahead with a few thousand men to reinforce Naples until he could get there himself with a much larger army to relieve the city. As the situation now stood the best thing the two brothers could do was to retreat to Regata and join the main army, where Totila made his report about the last days of Naples. The loss of the third largest city and the third most important fortress in the land forced a complete change to the entire Gothic strategy.

Witigis had mustered his troops at Regata, of which there were some twenty thousand men in all. Together with the small force which Count Teias had brought back on his own initiative, these were the only immediately available troops. Until such time as the strong armies which Theodahad had sent to far away Gaul, Noricum, Istria and Dalmatia could return, the whole of Italy was in danger of being lost, even though those armies had now been ordered to return as speedily as possible.

Nevertheless the king had decided to deploy his twenty thousand men into the fortress of Naples. There he had intended to resist the enemy, who now outnumbered him three to one in that region, until reinforcements arrived. Now that Naples had fallen to Belisarius, Witigis had to give up the idea of meeting him in battle, at least for the time being. Rashness was as far removed from his calm, courageous mind as was timidity.

In fact the king had to make an even more difficult decision. After Totila's arrival the Goths in the camp outside the walls of Rome had been giving vent to their feelings by cursing Belisarius, the traitor Theodahad and the Italians, and some of the younger men were becoming restless and expressing displeasure with their king, who would not lead them against the enemy, even though there were four of them to every Goth. While the army grumbled thus about their inactivity, the king had to face the need to withdraw even further. With a heavy heart he decided that, for the time being, even Rome would have to be abandoned and left to the enemy.

News arrived every day about the rate at which the army of Belisarius was growing. He led an additional ten thousand men out of Naples alone, both as hostages and as fellow fighters, and the Italians were streaming to his flag from all directions. No fortress or city was strong enough to offer Belisarius any resistance between Naples and Rome, and the smaller cities along the coast opened their gates to the enemy with rejoicing. The Gothic families from these areas fled into the king's camp, and told of how Cumae and Atella had surrendered the day after Naples fell. Soon afterwards Capua, Cajeta and even the strongly fortified Beneventum followed. The vanguard of the Byzantine army, Huns, Saracens and Moorish cavalry, was already at Formiae. The Gothic army expected and wanted a battle before the walls of Rome.

But Witigis had long recognised the impossibility of facing Belisarius, whose army by then might number a hundred thousand men, in open battle with a mere twenty thousand. For a while he hoped that he might defend the mighty battlements of Rome, the great work of Cethegus, against the Byzantine juggernaut. But soon he had to abandon that idea as well.

Thanks to the Prefect's efforts the population of Rome numbered more fit men, fully trained and equipped with arms, than it had done for centuries. Hourly the king received more evidence about the political sympathies of these men. Even now the Romans only barely concealed their hatred of the Barbarians, and that hatred was no longer restricted to angry looks and heckling. Already a stage had been reached where the Goths could only show themselves well armed and in sizeable groups. Lone Gothic guards who had been knifed from behind were being found almost daily.

Witigis was well aware that these Romans were led by able and powerful men, namely the leaders of the Roman nobility and clergy. He realised that, as soon as Belisarius appeared outside the walls, the population would rise up against the Goths, and in league with the enemy outside the walls they would soon crush the relatively small Gothic garrison on the inside.

And so Witigis made the difficult decision to give up Rome, together with the whole of central Italy, and to retreat to the well fortified and reliable stronghold of Ravenna. Here he would complete his very inadequate mobilisation, and unite all Gothic fighting men around him. Then, once he had an army of comparable strength to that of the enemy, he would seek out Belisarius and offer him battle.

This decision was, for Witigis, a personal sacrifice. He too had inherited his share of the traditional Germanic lust for a fight, and for him it was not easy to retreat instead of lashing out at the enemy as best he could. But there was even more to it than that. The Goths would not think well of a king, who had been chosen for his courage in place of the coward Theodahad, and who then commenced his regime by fleeing.

He had lost Naples in the first days of his reign. Was he now to voluntarily abandon Rome and half of Italy also? And even if, for the sake of his people, he could thus contain his own pride, how would his people think of him? These Goths were a proud, impatient people, with scant respect for their enemy. Could he hope to retain their loyalty, could he indeed force it? The role of a Germanic king was more to advise and suggest than to give orders and command. Many a Germanic king in the past had been forced into battle by his people, against his own better judgement, and faced defeat. Witigis feared a similar fate, and one night he was walking up and down in his tent at Regata, with much on his mind and a heavy heart.

Suddenly hurried steps approached, and the curtain was torn aside: "Come, King of the Goths," a passionate voice cried out, "this is no time for sleeping!"

"I am not asleep, Teias," Witigis replied calmly, "how long have you been back?"

"I have only just ridden into the camp. The night dew is still on me. Firstly: they are both dead."

"Who?"

"The traitor and the murderess!"

"What? Did you slay them both?"

"I do not slay women. I followed the sham king Theodahad for two days and nights. He was on his way to Ravenna, and had a big headstart. But my hatred was even stronger than his fear, and I caught up with him at Narnia. Twelve slaves accompanied his litter, but they were not of a mind to die for the miserable wretch. They threw away their torches and fled.

"I pulled him out of the litter and pressed his own sword into his fist, but he fell to his knees and begged for his life, and then he tried to deal me a treacherous blow. So I slew him like a sacrificial animal with three blows, one for the Empire and two for my parents. Then I hanged him with his golden belt from an oak tree by the roadside. Let him hang there, to feed the birds of the air and as a warning to all the kings on earth."

"And what happened to her?"

"She found a dreadful end!" he replied with a shudder. "When I got to Rome from here the only thing I could find out was that she had decided not to follow the coward. He fled alone, but Gothelindis called his Cappadocian guard together and promised them mountains of gold, if they would stay with her and retreat to the fortified city of Salona in Dalmatia. The mercenaries hesitated, and asked to see the gold first, so Gothelindis promised to bring it and vanished. The next time I came through Rome, of course, she had been found."

"What happened?"

"She had dared to enter the catacombs, alone without a guide, to find a treasure buried there. She must have lost her mind in the labyrinth, and could not find her way out. Mercenaries who went to look for her found her still alive. Her torch had gone out, but was almost wholly preserved, so it must have gone out soon after she entered the catacombs. There was madness in her eyes, and the fear of death, darkness and despair had taken their toll on this evil woman. She died as soon as they brought her out into daylight."

"How dreadful!" Witigis exclaimed.

"How just!" Teias replied, "but there is more."

Before he could begin Totila, Hildebad, Hildebrand and other Gothic leaders hurried into the tent. "Does he know yet?" Totila asked.

"Not yet," was Teias's reply.

"Revolt!" cried Hildebad, "revolt! On your feet, King Witigis, defend your crown. Lay the boy's head at his feet!"

"What has happened?" Witigis asked calmly.

"Count Arahad of Asta, that conceited dandy, has rebelled. Immediately after your election he rode off to Florence, where his elder brother, the proud Duke Guntharis of Tuscany, lives and rules. The Woelsung clan have a large following there, and they have called on Goths everywhere to defend the 'royal lily', as they call her. They say that Matesuentha is the rightful heir to the crown, and they have proclaimed her as queen. She was staying in Florence, and so she immediately came under their control. It is not known whether she is the prisoner of Guntharis, or the wife of Arahad. But we do know that they have hired mercenaries, Avars and Gepidae, and they have armed the entire following of the Amalungs, as well as their own numerous Woelsung clansmen and friends. They are calling you the peasant king, and they aim to capture Ravenna!"

"Oh send me to Florence with only three thousand men!" Hildebad cried angrily. "I will bring you back this queen of the Goths as well as her lover in a birdcage."

But the others looked worried. "It looks bad!" Hildebrand said gravely. "Belisarius with his one hundred thousand in front of us, behind us the snake pit called Rome, all our might still fifty miles or more away, and now civil war and rebellion in the very heart of the Empire! May thunder strike this land!"

Witigis remained calm and composed as always. He brushed his hand over his forehead, thinking, and after a short pause he said: "Perhaps it is as well this way, now we have no choice. Now we must go back."

"Back?" Hildebad asked angrily.

"Yes. We cannot afford to leave an enemy in our rear. Tomorrow we will break camp and go—"

"Forward against Naples?" Hildebad asked.

"No! Back to Rome, then to Florence and Ravenna! This fire of rebellion must be put out before it gets a proper hold."

"Are you saying that you intend to flee from Belisarius?"

"Yes, Hildebad, but only so that we can come back stronger than ever! Even a bowstring holds back its lethal force before it fires the deadly arrow."

"Never!" Hildebad exclaimed. "You can't do that! You must not!"

Witigis calmly went over to him and placed his hand on his shoulder: "I am your king. You yourself chose me. Louder than any of the others you called out: 'Hail King Witigis!' You know it, and God knows it, I did not reach out for this crown! You placed it on my head; take it back if you no longer have faith in me. But as long as I am wearing it you must trust me and obey me; otherwise all of you will be lost along with me."

"You are right," the tall Hildebad said, his head bowed. "Forgive me! I will make up for it in the next battle."

"Come, my generals," Witigis concluded, placing his helmet on his head. "You, Totila, will go as quickly as you can to the Frankish kings with an important mission; the rest of you go to your men and prepare to break camp. Tomorrow at sunrise we leave for Rome."

Chapter 7

A few days later, on the evening of the day the Goths entered Rome, we find the "young knights", Marcus and Lucius Licinius, Piso the poet, fat Balbus and the young lawyer Julianus engaged in a confidential discussion with the Prefect Cethegus.

"I take it that this is the list of blind followers of the future Pope Silverius, who are more suspicious of me than anybody. Is the list complete?"

"It is. It is a great sacrifice I bring you, general," Lucius Licinius replied. "If I had followed my heart and gone looking for Belisarius straight away, I would already have played a part in the siege of Naples, instead of listening to the cat and mouse game of the clergy and teaching the plebeians how to march."

"They will never learn again anyway," Marcus added.

"Be patient," Cethegus said calmly, without raising his eyes from a papyrus scroll he was holding. "You will have your chance to brawl with these Gothic bears soon enough, and for long enough. Don't forget that brawling is only a means to an end, not an end in itself."

"I am not so sure," Lucius said doubtfully.

"Our aim is freedom, and freedom requires strength," Cethegus replied. "We must get these Romans accustomed to shield and sword once more, otherwise—" but he did not complete his sentence, as the *ostiarius* announced a Gothic warrior. The young Romans exchanged looks of displeasure.

"Let him in!" Cethegus replied, concealing his documents in a capsule. A young man in the brown cloak of a Gothic soldier rushed into the room, a Gothic helmet on his head, and eagerly embraced the Prefect.

"Julius!" the latter replied, coldly taking a step backwards, "so we meet again! Have you become entirely a Barbarian? How did you get here?"

"My father, I am accompanying Valeria under Gothic protection. I come from the smoking ruins of Naples."

"I see," Cethegus said angrily, "did you fight with your blond friend against Italy? That is not right for a Roman, is it Lucius?"

"I have not fought at all, and I do not intend to fight in this wretched war. Woe be to them who started it."

Cethegus mustered him with a cold stare: "It is beneath my dignity to explain to you that such an attitude is disgraceful for a Roman. I am disappointed in you for being such a defector, Julius. You should feel ashamed of yourself in front of your fellow Romans here. Look here, Roman knights, and you will see a knight without thirst for freedom, without any hatred against the Barbarians!"

But Julius calmly shook his head. "You have not yet seen Belisarius's Huns and Massageti, who are supposed to be bringing you freedom. Where are these Romans of which you speak? Has Italy risen to shake off her shackles? Is she still able to do so? Justinian is at war with the Goths, not us. May heaven help the nation which is liberated by a tyrant."

Cethegus secretly agreed with him, but he did not want to sanction such words in front of strangers. "I want to debate this philosophy with Julius alone. You will let me know if anything happens with the pious friends of Silverius, won't you?"

The young tribunes left, looking disdainfully at Julius.

"I don't want to hear what they say about you!" Cethegus said.

"It matters little to me. I follow my own ideas, not those of others."

"He has become a man," Cethegus said to himself.

"And my innermost and most noble thoughts, which condemn this war, are what brings me here. I have come to save you, and to take you away from this clammy air, from this world of falsehood and lies. I beg of you, my friend, my father, come with me to Gaul."

"Not bad!" Cethegus smiled. "I am to give up Italy the very moment her liberators are coming? You may as well know it, I am the one who called them here. I started this war which you now curse."

"I thought as much," Julius said sadly, "but who will liberate us from the liberators? Who will end this war?"

"I will," said Cethegus, calmly and with the ring of greatness in his voice. "And you, my son, will help me. Yes Julius, even your fatherly friend, whom you call so cold and sober, has his secret passion, although it is not for the eyes of girls or for Gothic friendships. Leave those childish games to children, for you are now a man. Give me one last pleasure in my lonely life. Be my companion in the coming fight, and then inherit my victories. Rome, freedom, power are at stake! Young man, is it possible that these words don't rouse you? Just think," he went on, more warmly now, "imagine these Goths and Byzantines – I hate them as much as you do – wearing each other out, and on the remnants of what was once their might a new Italy will rise, Rome in all her former glory! Once more the ruler over Orient and Occident will reside on the Capitol! Think of it, a new Roman world rule, even prouder than your namesake Julius Caesar dared dream. Once again there will be order, blessing and the fear of Rome throughout the world—"

"And the ruler of this world Empire will be – Cornelius Cethegus Caesarius!"

"Yes, and after him Julius Montanus. Come, Julius, you are not a man if this goal does not tempt you!"

Julius spoke in honest admiration: "I feel dizzy! Your goal is as high as the stars, but your paths, they are not straight. If only they were straight, then, by God, I would walk them with you. Go and call up the youth of Rome, call them to arms, and then call out to the Barbarian armies: 'Get out of holy Latium!' Fight an open war against the Barbarians and against tyranny, and I will gladly fight and fall by your side!"

"You know very well that is impossible."

"And for that very reason it is your goal!"

"You fool, can't you see that it is ordinary to make a thing from good material, but that it is divine to create out of nothing, using only one's own creative energy, a whole new world?"

"Divine? By cunning and lies? No!"

"Julius!"

"Please let me speak frankly, that is why I came. If I could only call you back from your demonic path, which will certainly lead you to darkness and destruction! You know how I admire you, and even love you. But the things I hear Greeks, Goths and Romans whispering do not fit in with such admiration."

"What are they whispering?" Cethegus asked proudly.

"I don't want to believe it, but everything terrible that has happened in recent times: the deaths of Athalaric and Camilla, the fall of Amalasuntha, the Byzantine landing – your name comes up again and again, like a demon who creates everything that is evil. Tell me plainly that you are not guilty of dark—"

"Boy!" Cethegus blew up angrily, "do you dare sit in judgment and confession over me? First learn to understand the end before you criticise the means. Do you think that world history is made up of roses and lilies? He who wants greatness must do great things, whether lesser men call them good or bad."

"No, no, no! With my whole heart, no! Cursed is any goal which can only be achieved by committing crimes. Here is where our ways must part."

"Julius, don't go! You are turning down what has never before been offered to a mortal. Let me have a son, for whom I can fight, and to whom I can leave my life's work."

"It is full of evil and lies and blood. Even if I were to step into your shoes right now – I don't want your inheritance, never! I will go now, so that my image of you will not become any more tarnished. But I beg of you: when the day comes – and it will come – that you are finally revolted by all the blood and evil and the goal itself which demands such deeds – then – then call me. I will hurry to your side, wherever I might be, and I will free you from the demonic forces that rule you, whatever the cost, even if it costs my life."

There was a touch of sarcasm around the Prefect's lips, but he thought to himself: "He loves me still. Very well, I will call him when the work is complete; then we will see if he can resist it, if he will refuse the throne of the world." Then he said aloud: "Very well, I will call you when I need you. Farewell." And he dismissed the deeply moved youth with a cold gesture of his hand.

But as the door closed behind him the Prefect, that man of ice, took a little relief of finely worked bronze from a capsule, and he looked at it for a long time. He was about to kiss it, but suddenly there was that mocking smile on his lips once more. "You should be ashamed of yourself before Caesar, Cethegus," he said, and put the medallion back in the capsule. It was the head of a woman, and she looked very much like Julius.

Chapter 8

Meanwhile it had become quite dark, and a slave brought in a lamp, made in Corinth in the shape of an eagle. It held the sun in its beak, filled with aromatic Persian oil. "A Gothic warrior stands outside, Sir, and he wishes to speak with you alone. He looks like an ordinary man. Shall I tell him to leave his weapons outside?"

"No," Cethegus replied, "we do not fear the Barbarians. Let him enter." The slave left, and Cethegus grasped the hidden dagger in his tunic with his right hand.

A tall, magnificently built Goth entered, his face concealed by the hood of his cloak, which he threw back as he entered.

Astonished, Cethegus took a step closer: "What brings the king of the Goths to me?"

"Please keep your voice down!" Witigis replied, "nobody needs to know that you and I are negotiating. You know that my army moved into Rome yesterday and today. What you don't know is that we will leave Rome again tomorrow."

Cethegus was listening attentively.

"You find that strange?"

"The city is well fortified," Cethegus replied calmly.

"True, but the loyalty of the Roman population is less dependable. Beneventum has already gone over to Belisarius. I have no wish to be crushed between Belisarius and you Romans."

Cethegus took care to remain silent; he did not know what this conversation was leading to. "Why did you come to me, King of the Goths?"

"Not to ask you how far the Romans can be trusted. Not even to complain how little they can be trusted, no matter how much benevolence Theodoric and his daughter heaped on them. I have come to discuss a few matters with you, simply and honestly, for our mutual benefit."

Cethegus was taken aback by the man's straightforward, open and honest approach, which he had to secretly admire, even though he would have much rather despised it. "We will leave Rome, and soon after that the Romans will welcome Belisarius. That will happen, and I cannot prevent it. I have been advised to take the leaders of the Roman nobility with me as hostages."

This shocked Cethegus, and he had difficulty concealing it.

"You above all, *Princeps Senatus*."

"Me?" Cethegus smiled.

"I will leave you here. I know very well that you are the soul of Rome."

Cethegus looked down. "I accept the oracle," he said to himself.

Witigis went on: "That is why I will leave you here. Hundreds who call themselves Romans want the Byzantines as their masters. You, you do not want that." Cethegus looked at him questioningly. "Do not deceive me, and do not even try to deceive me. I am not a man of trickery and deception, but I do understand the nature of men and what drives them. You are too proud to serve Justinian. I know that you hate us. But you do not love the Greeks either, and you will not tolerate them here any longer than you have to. That is why I am leaving you here. Represent Rome against the tyrants, for I know that you love this city."

There was something about this man which Cethegus could not help but admire. "King of the Goths," he said, "you speak with the clarity and the greatness of a king, and I thank you for that. Nobody shall say of Cethegus that he does not understand the language of greatness. It is as you say; I will keep my Rome Roman as best I can."

"Good," said Witigis, "I have been warned against your treachery, and I know a great deal about your clever plans. I suspect that there is a lot more, and I have no weapon against falsehood. But you are not a liar. I know that you cannot resist a manly word, and trust disarms even an enemy if he is a man."

"You do me honour, King of the Goths. Allow me to give you a word of warning. Do you know who are the warmest friends of Belisarius and Byzantium?"

"I know it, Silverius and the priests."

"Correct. And do you also know that, as soon as the old Pope Agapetus has died, Silverius will become bishop of Rome?"

"So I have heard. I was advised to take him as a hostage also, but I will not do it. The Italians hate us enough as it is. Also I don't want to disturb the hornets' nest of the clergy. I fear martyrs…"

Cethegus would have liked to be rid of the priest. "He will become dangerous once he sits on the chair of St Peter."

But Witigis would not be swayed: "Let him! The fate of this country will not be decided by priests."

"Very well," Cethegus replied, holding out the papyrus scroll. "I have here the names of his most enthusiastic friends, quite by coincidence. They are important men." He tried to get Witigis to take the list, and so get rid of his most dangerous enemies by having the Goths take them as hostages.

But Witigis would not take the scroll. "Keep it. I don't want any hostages at all. What would be the point of beheading them? As far as Rome is concerned you and your word will be my security."

"What do you mean? I cannot keep Belisarius out."

"I am not asking you to. Belisarius will come, but you can depend on it, he will also leave again. We Goths will defeat this enemy, perhaps only after a hard fight, but we will win it. But then there will be a second struggle, a struggle for Rome."

"A second struggle?" Cethegus asked calmly, "with whom?"

But Witigis laid his hand on the other man's shoulder and looked him straight in the eye, with a look as clear as the sun itself. "With you, Prefect of Rome!"

"With me?" Cethegus tried to smile, but could not.

"Don't try to deny that which is most dear to you, man! It is unworthy of you. I know for whom you built the walls and the battlements and the towers around this city, not for us and not for the Greeks! You built them for yourself! Don't deny it! I know what you are planning, or at least I sense it. So be it! Are Goths and Greeks to fight over Rome, and not Romans? But listen to me: don't let another long war decimate and exhaust your people and mine.

"Once we have defeated Belisarius and thrown him out of Italy, our Italy, then Cethegus, I will wait for you outside the walls of Rome, not for a battle between our people, but for a duel. You and I, man against man, will decide who shall have Rome."

There was such greatness in the eyes and voice of the king, such authority and dignity, that the Prefect was quite confused. He wanted to secretly despise the almost naïve simplicity of this Barbarian. But it seemed to him that he would never again be able to respect himself if he did not respect and honour this simple greatness, and reciprocate it. And so he replied, without even a hint of sarcasm in his voice: "You are dreaming, Witigis, like a Gothic boy."

"No, I think and act like a Gothic man. Cethegus, you are the only man in Rome for whom I have sufficient regard to speak like this. I have seen you fight against the Gepidae; you are worthy of my sword. But you are older than I am, so I will give you a shield start!"

"You Goths are a strange people," Cethegus said impulsively, "what strange Germanic fantasies!"

But now Witigis furrowed his brow in anger: "Fantasies? Woe be to you if you are not able to feel in your heart what I am saying. Woe be to you if Teias was right! He laughed at my plan and said: 'The Roman will never be able to grasp that!' And he advised me to take you with me as a prisoner. I thought more of you and of Rome. But let me tell you this: Teias has your house surrounded. If you are so small-minded, or so cowardly, that you do not understand what I am proposing, then we will take you from your Rome in chains. Shame on you for having to be forced to act with honour and greatness!"

Now it was Cethegus's turn to become angry. He did feel shamed. This chivalrous streak was something foreign to him, and he was annoyed that he could not make fun of it. It annoyed him too, that he was being forced to do something which he was not being trusted to do voluntarily. A furious hatred against the distrust of Teias, as well the brutal frankness of the king, welled within him, and he would have dearly liked to plunge his dagger deep into the big Goth's broad chest. A moment ago he had almost given his word out of a feeling of soldierly honour. But now a very different feeling took hold of him, a rather ugly feeling of glee. They had not trusted him, the Barbarians, and instead they had belittled him; now they would most certainly be betrayed! He stepped forward, a piercing look in his eye, and shook the king's hand: "It is a bargain!" he cried.

"It is a bargain!" Witigis replied, firmly returning the handshake. "I am glad I was right, and not Teias. Farewell, and look after my Rome for me. I will ask for it back in a fair fight." With that he left.

"Well?" Teias asked outside, quickly advancing with the other Goths, "shall I storm the house?"

"No," Witigis replied, "he gave me his word."

"I only hope he keeps it!"

But that caused Witigis to take a step backwards angrily. "Teias! Your own gloomy attitude is making you unjust! You have no right to doubt the word of a hero, and Cethegus is a hero."

"He is also a Roman. Good night!" Teias replied, sheathing his sword, and departed with his men.

Cethegus went to bed that night, not at all happy with the situation. He was angry with Julius. He was very angry with Witigis, and even more so with Teias. But most of all he was angry with himself.

The following day Witigis assembled the people, senate and clergy of Rome once more near the baths of Titus. Speaking from the highest step of the staircase leading up to the proud building, which was occupied by leaders of the Gothic army, Witigis gave a short address to the Romans.

He told them that he would shortly be abandoning the city, but that he would return soon. He reminded them of the mild Gothic regime, and the benevolence of Theodoric and Amalasuntha. Then he asked them to resist Belisarius courageously, if he should approach, until the Goths came back to relieve the city. The Roman legionaries, now once more used to arms, together with Rome's strong walls made a long resistance possible. Finally he asked for an oath of loyalty and allegiance, and called upon the crowd to swear solemnly once more that they would defend their city against Belisarius to the last. The Romans hesitated. Their thoughts were already in the Byzantine camp, and they shunned the idea of a false oath.

But at that moment the sound of muffled singing could be heard coming from the Via Sacra. A great procession of priests could be seen approaching past the Slavic amphitheatre, singing psalms and waving incense. Pope Agapetus had died during the night, and Silverius, the archdeacon, had been hurriedly chosen as his successor.

The army of priests approached very slowly and solemnly, the insignia of the bishop of Rome being carried ahead, with silver-voiced boys singing sweet and yet solemn hymns.

At last the Pope's litter approached, open, spacious, richly decorated with gold and made in the shape of a ship. The bearers walked slowly, step by step, in time to the music. They were surrounded on all sides by the eager people, who were seeking the blessing of the new Pope. Silverius was dispensing same ceaselessly, nodding his clever head to the right and to the left.

A large number of priests and a detachment of mercenaries armed with spears closed the procession, which stopped once it reached the centre of the square.

The Gothic warriors, who were of the Arian faith, watched defiantly from their positions at all the exits from the square as the proud and ostentatious procession passed, representing a church which was hostile to them. The Romans, on the other hand, greeted the arrival of their spiritual leader all the more eagerly, expecting him in due course to relieve their consciences in respect of the oath they were about to take.

Silverius was just about to start his speech to the assembled people when the arm of a very tall Goth reached over the edge of the litter, plucking at the bishop's cloak of gold brocade.

Annoyed at the undignified interruption, Silverius turned to face the Goth with a stern look, but the latter was undeterred. Plucking at the cloak again he said: "Come, priest, the king wants you. Go up to him!"

Silverius would have found it far more fitting if the king had come down to him, and Hildebad seemed to read something to that effect in his face. Then he called out: "That's how it's going to be, so duck your head, my little priest!"

With that he forced one of the bearers to kneel, by using the firm pressure of his hand on the bearer's shoulder. All the bearers now knelt, and with a sigh Silverius got out of the litter and followed Hildebad up the steps.

When he reached Witigis the latter took his hand, stepped forward with him to the edge of the steps, and called out: "Men of Rome, your priests have chosen this man here as your bishop. I approve of their choice. He shall be Pope as soon as he has sworn allegiance to me and taken the oath of loyalty from you. Swear, priest!"

Silverius hesitated, but only for an instant. A moment later he had regained his composure, turned to the people with an unctuous smile, and then to the king: "You are commanding?" he asked.

"Swear," cried Witigis, "that during our absence you will do everything in your power to keep this city loyal to the Goths, to whom it owes so much, to assist us in every way, but to harm our enemies. Swear loyalty to the Goths!"

"I swear it!" Silverius said, turning to the people. "Now I, who have the power to commit and absolve the souls of the pious, ask of you Romans, surrounded on all sides by Gothic arms, to swear as I have done."

The priests and a few of the nobles seemed to have understood, and raised their hands to swear the oath without hesitation. And then the rest of the crowd no longer hesitated either, and the entire square resounded to the cry: "We swear loyalty to the Goths."

"Thank you, bishop of Rome," said the king, "we will depend on your oath. Farewell Romans! We will meet again soon." And he descended the broad steps, followed by Hildebad and Teias.

"Now I am only curious to know…" said Teias.

"Whether they keep it?" Hildebad interjected.

"No, not at all. But how will they break it? I am sure the priest will find a way."

And the Goths departed through the Porta Flaminia with flags flying, leaving the city to its Pope and its Prefect, while Belisarius was approaching in forced marches along the Via Latina.

Chapter 9

The city of Florence was a hive of warlike activity. The gates were closed, numerous guards were marching along the walls and battlements, the streets were full of Gothic warriors and armed mercenaries, and the clatter of arms could be heard everywhere. The Woelsung brothers, Guntharis and Arahad, had chosen the city as their base and stronghold, and had made it the temporary headquarters for their armed revolt against King Witigis.

The two brothers themselves were living in a beautiful villa, which Theodoric had built in a suburb on the banks of the Arnus, but still within the city walls.

Duke Guntharis, the elder of the two, was a respected warrior, and for many years he had been Count of the city of Florence. Properties belonging to the wealthy Woelsung family were situated all over the city, built by serfs and former settlers, and their power in the city and surrounds was virtually without bounds. Duke Guntharis was determined to use that power to the fullest extent.

His imposing figure, fully armed and with his helmet on his head, was now pacing up and down the marble-lined room. His younger brother, unarmed and dressed in normal clothes, was leaning deep in thought against a table covered with documents and parchment scrolls.

"Make up your mind and get on with it, my boy!" Guntharis was saying: "That is my last word on the matter. This very day you will bring me a 'yes' from that stubborn child, or I – do you hear me? – or I will go myself and get it. But then she had better beware! I know better than you how one must deal with moody women and girls."

"Brother, you would not do that!"

"By thunder, I would! Do you think I am going to risk my head, or compromise the fortunes of our family, to protect your tender feelings? Now or never is the time for the Woelsungs to take over as the first ranking family in this nation at last, as is our due, and from which we have been excluded for centuries by Amalungs and Balti. If the last daughter of the Amalungs becomes your wife, then nobody can dispute your right to the crown, and you can count on my sword to defend it and hold it secure on your head against this peasant king Witigis. But it must not drag on much longer! As yet I have no news from Ravenna, but I am afraid the city would open its gates only to Matesuentha, not to us, or at least not to us alone. Whoever has her also has Italy. Once Naples and Rome are lost, that leaves Ravenna as our only powerful fortress, and it is the one we must have. That is why she must become your wife before we go to the raven city; otherwise it will become known that she is more our prisoner than our queen."

"Who could wish for that more fervently than I? But I can't force her, can I?"

"No? And why not? Go and find her, and then win her, one way or another. I am going to the walls to reinforce the guards there. By the time I return I want an answer!"

Duke Guntharis left, and with a sigh his brother made his way to the garden, to seek out Matesuentha.

The garden had been designed by a knowledgeable freedman from Asia Minor. In the background it had a wooded slope, and in front of it the lovely green meadow from the original forest had been retained, without any beds or terraces. A sparkling little stream flowed through the meadow with its flowers and oleander bushes, making a particularly appealing whole.

A young woman was lying in the green meadow, by the bank of the stream. She seemed to be playing with the rippling waves one moment, and with the flowers the next. Apparently daydreaming she was looking into the water, and now and again she would toss a violet or a crocus into the stream, watching with slightly parted lips as the water carried it away.

Close by her shoulder there knelt a young girl in Moorish dress, evidently a slave, busily making a garland of flowers. It was almost finished, and anxiously the attractive young girl looked at her mistress every few moments, to ensure that her garland making had not been noticed by her mistress. But the latter seemed to be absorbed in her daydreaming.

At last the pretty garland was finished, and with a sparkle in her eyes the slave girl placed it on her mistress's red hair. Then she bent forward to catch the eye of her mistress, but the latter had not even noticed the flowers touching her hair. That made the little one cross, and with a pout she cried: "But mistress, by the palms of Auras, what are you thinking about? Where were you with your mind just now?"

"With him!" Matesuentha whispered, opening her lovely eyes.

"White goddess, I cannot bear this any longer!" the little one cried, leaping to her feet. "It is just too much, and the jealousy is killing me! You are not only forgetting me, your gazelle, but you are even neglecting your own beauty over this invisible man. Just take a look into the water, and see how beautiful your red hair looks in contrast to the dark violets and the white anemones."

"The garland is lovely!" Matesuentha said, taking it off and casually tossing it into the stream, "what sweet flowers! Go and greet him from me."

"Oh my poor flowers!" the slave cried, looking after them, but she did not dare to complain further. Sitting down again, she said: "Just tell me how all this is to end. We have been here for many days now, and we still don't know whether we are here as a queen or as a prisoner. We are certainly in the power of other people, and we have not been able to set foot outside your rooms or this garden. We know nothing of what is going on in the big, wide world, and yet you are still happy and contented, as if all this was meant to be so."

"It was meant to be so."

"Oh? And how will it end?"

"He will come and set me free."

"Well, my white lily, I admire your confidence. If we were at home in Mauretania, and if I saw you looking up to the stars at night, then I might think you read it all in the stars. But like this? I just don't understand it at all..." And she shook her black locks. "I will never understand you."

"Yes Aspa, you will and you shall," Matesuentha replied, getting to her feet and placing one arm affectionately around the black girl's neck, "your loving loyalty deserves a reward, and the reward I am about to give you is the greatest thing I have to give."

A tear welled up in the girl's dark eye. "Reward?" she asked. "Aspa was stolen by wild men with flowing red locks. Aspa is a slave. Everybody had scolded her, and many have beaten her. You bought me as one buys a flower, and you stroke my cheek and my hair. And you are as beautiful as the sun goddess, yet you speak of reward?" And she leaned her little head against the bosom of her mistress.

"You are my little gazelle!" the latter said, "and you have a heart of gold. I am going to tell you everything, which nobody knows except me. You see, I had a joyless childhood too, without love, and yet my heart longed for tenderness and love. My poor mother had wanted an heir to the throne with all her heart, and she was sure she would bear one. But she had a girl, and treated her with harshness, coldness and reluctance. Once Athalaric was born the harshness grew less, but she became colder still, and all love and care was devoted to the heir to the crown. I might never have noticed it, if I had not seen the exact opposite in my much softer father. I could feel how he also suffered from the hard coolness of his wife, and often the sick man would press me to his chest with a sigh, and sometimes a tear.

"Once he was dead and buried, it seemed to me as if all love in the world had died with him. I saw little of Athalaric, as he was being educated by different teachers in a different part of the palace. Of my mother I saw even less, and then usually only if I was to be punished. And yet I loved her so much. I could see how my ladies in waiting and my teachers loved and hugged their own children, and how they cuddled and kissed them. My whole heart longed for love like that, but it never came.

"And so I grew up, like a pale flower without sunshine. My favourite place was the grave of my father Eutharic, in the palace garden in Ravenna. There I used to seek from a dead man the love I could not find among the living; as soon as I could escape I would hurry there, to long and to cry. This longing grew stronger the older I became. I had to conceal my feelings in the presence of my mother, because she despised me for showing them.

"When I grew from a child into a young woman I often noticed people looking at me, as if admiringly, but I thought it was pity and I was hurt by their looks. And so I would flee to my father's grave more often than ever, until somebody reported me to my mother. I was accused of being seen crying there, and of coming back quite distraught. Angrily my mother forbade me to ever visit the grave again, except in her company, and accused me of despicable weakness.

"But then my heart rebelled, and I went on visiting the grave despite her orders. Then one day she caught me there herself. She beat me, even though I was no longer a child. She took me back to the palace, where she scolded me severely. She threatened to banish me from her side for ever, and in the end she angrily asked God why He had punished her with such a child. That was too much.

"Miserable beyond words I decided to run away from this mother, whom I seemed to have only so she could punish me, and to go away where nobody knew me. I had no idea where to go, and would have liked to join my father in his grave.

"When evening came I sneaked from the palace, and hurried to the beloved grave once more for a tearful farewell. The stars had already appeared in the sky when I slipped from the garden and the palace, and hurried through the dark streets to the Porta Faventia. Luckily I managed to slip past the guard and out into the open, and for some time I continued to walk along the road, straight ahead into night and misery.

"But a man was coming toward me along the road, in a soldier's clothes. As he was about to pass me he suddenly came closer, looked into my face and gently put his hands on my shoulder: 'And where are you going, maid Matesuentha, alone so late?'

"I trembled at his touch. Tears welled from my eyes and I sobbed: 'Into despair!'

"And then the man took both my hands and looked at me, so friendly, so kind and so concerned. Then he dried my tears with his cloak and said, in the kindest voice: 'Why? What is it that tortures you so?'

"The tone in his voice was so gentle and so compassionate that I was touched and deeply moved. But once I looked into those kind eyes I could no longer control myself. 'Because my own mother hates me, and because there is no love for me here on this earth.'

"'My child, my child! You are ill, and talking nonsense. Come, come back with me. You? Just you wait! One day you will be a queen of love.'

"I did not then understand what he meant, but I loved him immensely for those words, and for his kindness. I looked into his eyes, helpless, questioning, admiringly. I was trembling and shaking. He must have been touched by that, or perhaps he thought it was the cold. He took off his warm cloak and placed it around my shoulders, and then he slowly led me back to the gate, following deserted streets, through the city and to the palace.

"I followed him like a helpless, unsteady child, without a will of my own, leaning my head against his chest. He carefully kept my head and face covered with his cloak, and he was silent, stopping now and again to dry my tears. We reached the palace steps, unobserved I thought. He opened a door, gently pushed me inside, and squeezed my hand: 'Be good,' he said, 'and don't be upset any more. Your turn for happiness will come, and love enough.' He gently laid his hand on my head, closed the door behind me, and went back down the steps.

"But I was leaning against the half closed door on the inside, and could not move. My feet would not move, and my heart was beating wildly. And then I heard a rough voice address him: 'Whom might you be smuggling into the palace in the middle of the night, my friend?'

"He replied: 'Is that you, Hildebrand? Don't betray her, will you? It was the child Matesuentha. She became lost in the city, in the night, and she feared her mother's anger.'

"'Matesuentha!' the other man said, 'she is becoming more beautiful every day'. And then my protector said—" She hesitated, blushing fiercely.

"Well?" Aspa asked, looking at her mistress with big eyes, "what did he say?"

But Matesuentha pressed Aspa's hand closer to her bosom. "He said," she whispered, "he said: 'that one is going to be the most beautiful woman on earth!' "

"He spoke the truth there," the little one replied, "why do you have to blush over that? It's true, isn't it? But go on! What did you do then?"

"I sneaked into my bed and I cried, tears of grief, of joy and of love, all at once. That night a whole new world opened up to me, a heaven almost. He liked me, I felt it, and he had called me beautiful. Yes, now I knew it: I was indeed beautiful, and I was delighted about it. I wanted to be beautiful, for him! Oh how happy I was! My chance encounter with him had brought sunlight into my darkness, and blessing into my life. Now I knew that it was possible for people to like me, and even to love me! Carefully I looked after the body which he had praised. From the sweet emotions in my heart a gentle warmth came over my whole being, and I became softer and more feeling. Even my mother's severity towards me became less and, once I started returning her coldness only with love, she became more loving. Every day hearts became more kindly disposed toward me because I became softer toward them, to everyone.

"I had him to thank for all this; he had spared me from flight into disgrace and misery, and had won for me a whole new world of love. From that moment I have lived only for him." She stopped for a moment, and placed her left hand on her heaving bosom.

"But mistress, when did you see him again? Have you spoken to him, or is your love only a memory?"

"I never spoke to him again, but I saw him once. On the day Theodoric died he was commanding the palace guard, and that was when Athalaric told me his name. I would never have dared inquire after him for fear of betraying my flight and my secret. He was not at court, and if he ever did appear there I was away at one of the villas."

"So you know nothing further about him, about his life or his past?"

"How could I inquire? My feelings would have given me away. Love is a daughter of silence and of longing. But I do know something of him, and of our future."

"Of your future?" Aspa smiled.

"Every solstice old Rudrun used to come to the court, where she would receive strange herbs and roots from Theodoric, which he had brought for her from Asia and from the Nile. It was the only reward she ever asked for having predicted his whole future for him when he was a boy, and everything she had foretold came true, down to the last detail. She used to mix liniments and brew potions: they called her 'the forest woman' aloud, but when she was out of earshot they would call her 'Wala the witch'. Except for the priests, who would have opposed it, everyone at court knew that the king had her foretell the whole year ahead for him every solstice. And when she came out of his chambers my mother and Gothelindis would call her and ask questions, and what she predicted never failed to come true.

"And then, at the next solstice, I too plucked up courage. I waited for the old woman and, when I found her alone, lured her into my room. I offered her gold and jewels if she would foretell my future for me.

"But she laughed and pulled out a little amber phial, and then she said: 'Not for gold! But for powerful blood from a pure child of royal blood.'

She cut a vein in my left arm and caught the stream of blood in her phial. Then she looked searchingly into the palms of both my hands, and finally she chanted: 'He whom you hold high in your heart will give you the utmost glory and the greatest happiness, but also the most acute pain. He will be your consort, but never your husband.' And with that she was gone."

"That's not much consolation, as I understand it."

"You don't know the old woman's predictions; they are always dark and mysterious like that. She adds a threat to every prediction, just in case. But I believe in light, not darkness. A prediction comes true the way one takes it: I know he will be mine, and that he will bring me glory and happiness. I am willing to bear any pain which might go with that; pain on his account is pure joy."

"I admire you, mistress, and your faith. So it's on the prediction of this witch that you have refused the hands of all the kings and nobles, Vandals, Visigoths, Franks and Burgundians, who have courted you? You even refused Germanus, the noble prince from Byzantium. And are you still waiting for him?"

"Yes, I am waiting for him! But not only because of the prediction. There is a little bird living in my heart, which sings to me every day: 'He will be yours, he must be yours!' I know it with absolute certainty," she concluded, raising her eyes to the sky and returning to her earlier daydream.

Rapid footsteps could now be heard coming from the villa. "Ah," cried Aspa, "your handsome suitor! Poor Arahad, you are wasting your efforts!"

"I am going to put an end to this today!" Matesuentha said, rising. There was angry determination in her eyes and face, which told of the Amalung blood in her veins. There was a strange mixture of burning passion and melting softness in the young woman. Aspa was often astonished at the restrained fire in her mistress. "You are like the mountains of the gods back in my country," she said once, "snow on top and roses around your waist, but inside there is a searing fire, which often pours out over snow and roses alike."

Meanwhile Count Arahad emerged from a bushy path and bowed before the beautiful woman, with a colouring in his cheeks which suited him well. "I come," he said, "my queen—"

But she rudely interrupted him. "I hope, Count Arahad, to finally put an end to this game of lies and force. I will bear it no longer! Your impudent brother suddenly attacks me in my rooms, a defenceless orphan in mourning over my mother. He calls me a queen and a prisoner in the same breath, and for weeks he has been holding me in captivity here. He has brought me purple, and he has taken my freedom. And then you keep pursuing me with your futile courtship, which will never succeed. I refused you when I was free! Do you think, you fool, that a child of the Amalungs will listen to you while she is in your power? You swear that you love me? Very well then, respect me. Honour my wishes, and let me go free. Or tremble when my liberator nears!" Threateningly she advanced toward the dumbfounded youth, who was quite at a loss for words.

Now Duke Guntharis was approaching with hasty steps and with fire in his eyes.

"Come, Arahad," he cried, "get it over with. We must leave immediately. He is approaching with a large force."

"Who?" Arahad asked hastily.

"He says he is coming to set her free. He has won, the peasant king, and defeated our outpost at the Castrum Sivium."

"Who?" Matesuentha now asked eagerly.

"Well," Guntharis replied angrily, "you may as well know it now; I can no longer keep it a secret from you anyway. Count Witigis of Faesulae."

"Witigis!" Matesuentha sighed with a deep breath, her eyes shining.

"Yes, the rebels at Regata proclaimed him king, forgetting the rights of the nobility."

"He, my king!" Matesuentha said as if in a dream.

"I would have told you when I first greeted you as queen, but there was a bust of him in your room, adorned with garlands, which seemed suspicious to me. Later I saw it was a coincidence, it was a head of Ares."

Matesuentha remained silent, and sought to cover up the blush covering her face.

"Well?" Arahad cried, "what is to be done?"

"We must leave now. We have to get to Ravenna before him. Florence, the fortress, will hold him up for a while, and in the meantime we will gain Ravenna. Once you have slept in Theodoric's palace with his granddaughter the whole Gothic nation will be ours. Come, queen! I will have your carriage made ready; you will leave for Ravenna surrounded by our troops within the hour." And the two brothers hurried away.

Matesuentha looked after them, fire in her eyes: "Yes, take me away, captive and in chains. My king will strike at you like an eagle from the sky, and free me from your power. Come Aspa, our liberator is coming!"

Chapter 10

The Goths had barely turned their backs on Rome when Pope Silverius, the day after his ordination, called a meeting of leaders of the clergy, the nobility, officials and citizens of Rome at the baths of Caracalla, in order to discuss with them the fate of St Peter's holy city. Cethegus had also been invited.

Silverius opened the meeting by suggesting the hour had come at last to shake off the yoke of the heretics, and to despatch envoys to Belisarius, the representative of Justinian, who was Italy's only rightful ruler. They were to hand over to him the keys of the city and to seek the protection of him and his army against Barbarian revenge. A very young priest and an old and honest blacksmith expressed doubts on account of the oath they had taken, but these were brushed aside by Silverius, who reminded them of his apostolic power to either make an oath binding or to dissolve it. He also made reference to the presence of Gothic arms at the time the oath was taken. After that the vote was unanimous, and the Pope himself, Scaevola, Albinus and Cethegus were chosen as the envoys.

But Cethegus spoke against the decision; he had been listening silently to the discussion and refrained from voting, but now he stood up and spoke: "I oppose the decision, but not because of the oath. I have no need of apostolic powers to absolve me, as I did not swear it. My concern is the fate of this city. Let us not needlessly incur the wrath of the Goths, who may after all return one day. They would not excuse such a blatant breach of an oath because of apostolic power. Let us be either wooed or forced by Belisarius; if we just throw ourselves at his feet we will surely be kicked like dogs."

Silverius and Scaevola exchanged meaningful glances. "Such thinking," the lawyer said, "will surely please the emperor's general no end, but it does not alter our decision. So you are not coming with us?"

Cethegus rose: "I will go to see Belisarius, but not with you," he said, and left the gathering.

After the others had left the meeting, the Pope said to Scaevola: "That will finish him. He declared himself opposed to handing over the city in front of witnesses!"

"And he himself is going into the lion's den."

"He shall not leave it again. You did draw up the deeds of formal charges against him, did you not?"

"Oh yes, long ago. I was afraid that he would try to assume control of the city by force, and now he is going to Belisarius of his own free will! Now the proud man is doomed!"

"Amen!" Silverius added. "May the same fate befall anyone who seeks to oppose St Peter with worldly ambition. We will leave at the fourth hour, the day after tomorrow."

But the holy father was mistaken. The proud man was not doomed just yet.

Cethegus had hurried directly to his house, where the Gallic travelling coach was already harnessed and ready for him. "We leave immediately," he called out to his waiting slaves, "I will just get my sword."

In the vestibule he met the Licinius brothers, who were waiting for him impatiently. "This is the day," Lucius called out to him, "which you have promised us for so long!"

"What has happened to your trust in our courage, our skill and our loyalty?" Marcus asked.

"Patience!" Cethegus replied, with raised index finger, and went into his room. In a moment he returned, his sword and a number of documents under one arm, and a sealed scroll under the other. His eyes were gleaming: "Has the outermost iron gate at Hadrian's tomb been finished?" he asked.

"It is finished," Lucius Licinius replied.

"Has the grain from Sicily been stored in the Capitol?"

"It has."

"Have the weapons been distributed, and the battlements on the Capitol completed, as I ordered?"

"All done, Sir," Marcus replied.

"Good. Take this scroll, and open it tomorrow, as soon as Silverius has left the city. Follow it to the letter. Not only your lives and mine are at stake, but Rome herself as well! The city of the Caesars will be witness to your deeds. Now go, until we meet again!"

His eyes sprayed fire into the hearts of the young Romans. "You will be satisfied with us!"—"You and Caesar!" they cried, and hurried on their way.

Cethegus jumped into his carriage with a rare smile on his face. He was very happy. "Holy father," he said to himself, "I still owe you a debt for the last meeting we had in the catacombs, and now I will pay it. Down the Via Latina!" he called out to the slaves aloud, "and drive the horses as fast as they will go!"

The Prefect had a headstart of more than a day over the much slower papal delegation, and he used it well. His tireless mind had conceived a plan whereby, in spite of Belisarius having landed in Italy, he would still remain master of Rome. And now he went about putting that plan into practice by all available means.

As soon as he reached the vanguard of Belisarius's army near Capua he had its leaders, Bloody John and his brother Perseus, conduct him to the main camp. When he arrived there he did not ask for the general, but requested that he be led directly to the tent of the lawyer Procopius of Caesarea.

Procopius had been his fellow student at law school in Berytus, and the two great minds had forged a strong friendship. But it was not so much friendship which led Cethegus to this man. Procopius knew more than anyone about Belisarius's political past, and was probably also privy to his future plans.

Procopius received his friend joyfully. He was a man with a fresh outlook, healthy common sense and a sound knowledge of human nature. He was one of the few scholars of his time who had not lost the ability to think simply and clearly amid the artificiality of law schools of the day. His open face and high forehead spoke of an eager intellect, and his still youthful eyes suggested that he loved all that was good.

Once Cethegus had washed away the dust of his journey by taking a luxurious bath, his host did the rounds of the camp with him before returning to his tent for dinner. He showed him the various sections of the camp, the most important troop units and the tents of the main leaders. In each case he explained in a few words the main qualities and peculiarities of each of them, and his often colourful past.

There were Bessas and Constantinus, both sons of rough Thrace, who had worked their way up from being mercenaries. They were brave soldiers, but without education, and with all the conceit of self-made men. They regarded themselves as indispensable supports to Belisarius, and as his worthy successors.

Then there was the aristocratic Iberian Peranius, of the Iberian royal family. The Iberians were the hostile neighbours of the Persians, and Peranius had given up his fatherland and his right to the throne out of his hatred for the Persian oppressors, and now he served in the Imperial army.

Valentinus, Magnus and Innocentius were daring leaders of the cavalry, while Paulus, Demetrius and Ursicinus commanded the infantry. Ennes, the Isaurian chieftain, led Belisarius's Isaurian mercenaries. Aigan and Askan led the Massageti, Alamundarus and King Abocharabus the Saracens, Ambazuch and Bleda the Huns, and Arsakes, Amazaspes and Artabazes the Armenians, Phaza having been left behind in Naples with the remainder of the Armenians. Azarethas and Barasmanes led the Persians, and Antallas and Cabaon the Moors. Procopius knew them all and pointed them out. He was sparse with his praise, but when he was critical he spoke with a sarcastic wit and sound knowledge of his subject.

They were about to turn into the quarters of Martinus, the peaceful destroyer of cities, when Cethegus stopped and asked: "And to whom does that silk tent on the hill belong, the one with the purple flags? The troops guarding it seem to be carrying golden shields."

"There," Procopius replied, "lives his indomitable lordship, the chief superintendent of Purpura snails in the greater Roman Empire, on whom the Empire relies for the vital service of supplying purple dye for the Imperial wardrobe, none other than Prince Areobindos himself, on whom God may smile."

"He is the emperor's nephew, isn't he?"

"Indeed he is. He married the emperor's niece Projecta, which is his greatest and only achievement. He has been sent here with his Imperial guard to annoy us, and to see to it that we don't win too easily. He has been given the same rank as Belisarius, although he knows as little about war as Belisarius does about Purpura snails. Furthermore he is to become Governor of Italy."

"Interesting," said Cethegus.

"When we pitched camp he absolutely insisted on having his tent on the right-hand side of Belisarius. We would not agree. Luckily God in His infinite wisdom provided that hill there, thousands of years ago, to resolve our contest of rank. Now, as you see, the prince is on Belisarius's left, but on a higher hill."

"And to whom do the colourful tents belong, over there behind Belisarius's quarters? Who lives there?"

"There," Procopius replied, "lives a very unhappy woman, Antonina, wife of Belisarius."

"Is she unhappy? The celebrated second empress? Why?"

"That is a subject not suitable for discussion in a public place within the camp. Come into my tent – the wine should be cool enough by now."

Chapter 11

Inside the tent soft cushions were arranged around a beautifully worked bronze table, which Cethegus admired. "That is a piece of booty from the war against the Vandals. I brought it with me from Carthage. And these cushions once adorned the King of Persia's bed. I captured them after the battle of Dara."

"You are a very practical scholar!" Cethegus smiled. "How did you manage to change so much since our days in Athens?"

"I certainly hope I have changed!" Procopius replied, and started to carve the leg of venison in front of him, the slaves having been sent away. "You know, I wanted to make philosophy my profession, and to become a wise man of the world. I listened to the teachings of Plato, the stoics and the academics in Athens, and I studied and studied until I was both ill and stupid. Alas, I did not study philosophy alone. In accordance with the praiseworthy custom of our century I had to study theology as well, and so I spent a further year pondering whether Christ, who is one with God the father of all mankind, was also the father of his virgin mother, thus making him his own grandfather. Finally, with all this study, I was in danger of going out of my mind, which a kind nature has endowed with a not inconsiderable intellect.

"Fortunately I became mortally ill, and the physicians forbade me from living in Athens any longer, or from reading any books at all. They sent me to Asia Minor. I managed to save only one volume of Thucydides in my satchel, and that one book was my salvation. During the boring journey I read and re-read his beautiful story of Hellenic deeds in war and peace, and now I noticed with amazement that the doings of men, their passions and their virtues and their sins, were really much more interesting than all the formulae of pagan logic. Of Christian logic I would prefer to say nothing at all.

"When I got to Ephesus and walked through the streets, quite suddenly a wonderful revelation came over me. I was walking across a great square. There, in front of me, stood a church of the Holy Spirit, built on the ruins of a temple of Diana. On one side of it was a ruined altar of Isis, and on the other a Jewish synagogue. And suddenly it struck me! They all believed, and still believe, that they alone know the truth about the supreme being. But that is impossible! It seemed to me that the supreme being has no need to be recognised by us, and nor would I if it was me. Yet the supreme being created men so that they can live, work and move about the earth. And this living, working and enjoying oneself is really the only thing that matters. If one wants to think and reason, then one should think about living and the like.

"As I stood there thinking thus I heard the sound of trumpets. A splendid-looking group of mounted soldiers was approaching, at their head a magnificent man on a bay horse, handsome and as strong as the god of war himself. Their weapons gleamed, their flags fluttered in the breeze, and their horses were frisky. And I thought to myself: 'They know why they are alive, and they don't need to ask any philosopher.' And as I looked at the horsemen admiringly, a citizen of Ephesus struck me on the shoulder and said: 'You don't seem to know who that was, or where they are going. That was the hero Belisarius, and he is leading his troops to war against the Persians.'

'Thank you, friend!' I replied, 'that's where I am going too.' And so it was within the hour.

Belisarius soon appointed me as his legal adviser and confidential secretary, and ever since then I have had two professions. By day I create history, or help create it, and by night I write history."

"Which do you prefer?"

"My friend, unfortunately I prefer writing. But the writing would be even more enjoyable if the history itself was better. Mostly I don't agree at all with what we do, and I only help in doing it because it is better than doing nothing or preaching philosophy. Slave, bring the Tacitus!" he called through the tent door.

"The Tacitus?"

"Yes, friend, we have had enough Livius for the moment. You see, I always name my wines after their historical character. This noisy piece of history we are making here for example, this war against the Goths, is not at all to my liking. Narses is right; we should be able to defend ourselves against the Persians first before we attack the Goths."

"Narses? What is my clever friend doing?"

"He envies Belisarius, but does not show it. Narses is a man who plans wars and battles. I would not be at all surprised to learn that he had already conquered Italy, on paper, before we even landed."

"You do not seem to be a friend of his, and yet he is a very great mind. Why do you prefer Belisarius?"

"I will tell you," Procopius replied as he poured the Tacitus. "My misfortune is that I was not Alexander's or Scipio's historian. Ever since I recovered from philosophy, and theology, I long to be with people, with real living people of flesh and blood. I am revolted by these emaciated emperors and generals and bishops who try to solve everything with their minds alone; we have become a crippled generation, and our days of heroic deeds are behind us. Only honest Belisarius is still a hero like the heroes of old. He could be besieging Troy with Agamemnon! He is not stupid; in fact he has a great deal of intelligence, but it is the intelligence of a noble wild animal out to catch its prey, to do its job. And his work is heroism!

"I derive much pleasure from his broad chest and flashing eyes and mighty thighs, with which he can tame the wildest of stallions. And it is a joy to me whenever his blind lust for a good scrap triumphs over all his strategic plans. I love seeing him race right among the enemy in battle, fighting like a wild boar.

"Of course I can't tell him that I enjoy seeing this, because if I did there would be no holding him, and he would be cut to pieces in three days. On the contrary, I hold him back. He calls me his brains, and he tolerates it because he knows it is not cowardice. Many times I, with my layman's intelligence, have had to get him out of a tight spot which his stubborn heroism got him into. The funniest of all these stories is the one about the horn and the tuba."

"Which of them do you play, oh my Procopius?"

"Neither, only the trumpet of fame and the whistle of mockery!"

"What was that about the horn and the tuba?"

"Oh yes, we were entrenched around a mountain stronghold in Persia, which we had to have because it controlled the road. Already we had bloodied our heroic heads several times trying to take it by storm, and my angry master swore 'by Justinian's slumber', which to him is the holy of holies, that he would never have the retreat sounded before this fortress Angalon. Now it so happened that our vanguard was often attacked from the fortress. We, from our high camp, could see the attackers breaking out of the fortress, but our forward positions at the base of the mountain could not. I therefore suggested that we should sound the retreat every time we saw danger approaching, as a warning signal to our vanguard.

"But that suggestion met with a most unfriendly reception. Justinian's slumber was so holy that an oath sworn on it was irrevocably binding! And so our poor lads had to let themselves be taken unawares by the Persians almost every day. And then I had the bright idea of suggesting to our hero that, if he wanted our men to retreat, he should have the signal to attack sounded, but with a horn instead of a tuba.

"That made sense to our honest friend Belisarius. And so whenever we sounded the horn to attack, our men ran away like startled rabbits. I almost died laughing! But it did the trick; neither the oath of Belisarius nor Justinian's slumber were compromised, our men were no longer slaughtered, and in the end the stronghold fell. You know, I often scold him jokingly and even mockingly about his heroic deeds. But secretly I like to watch him in action, and it warms my heart. He is the last of the heroes!"

"I don't know about that," Cethegus replied, "you will find many a fire eater like that among the Goths as well!"

Procopius nodded thoughtfully: "I can't deny that I find much that I like in these Goths. But they are stupid."

"Stupid? Why?"

"They are stupid because they don't advance against us nice and slowly, arm in arm with their yellow-haired brothers. If they did that they would be irresistible! Instead of that they forced their way into this Italy all by themselves, like a piece of wood into a glowing furnace. They will perish on account of it! They will burn, as you will see."

"I hope to see it. And what then?" Cethegus asked calmly.

Procopius appeared vexed by this question, and replied: "Yes, what happens then? That's the annoying part! Belisarius will become governor of Italy, because the prince of snails won't last a year, and he will waste his best years here while there is more than enough work for him with the Persians. And then I, as his historian, will have nothing to record save how many wine skins we consume each year."

"So, once the Goths are defeated, you want to see Belisarius out of Italy again?"

"Of course! His laurels and mine grow in Persia! For some time I have been trying to think of a way to get him out of here again."

Cethegus was silent. He was pleased to have found so powerful an ally for his own plans. "And so the lion Belisarius is ruled by his brains, Procopius?" he said aloud.

"No!" Procopius sighed, "the opposite is what rules him, not brains but his wife, Antonina."

"Antonina? Tell me, why did you call her unhappy?"

"Because she is only half a woman, and a paradox. Nature made her a loyal, worthy woman, and Belisarius loves her with all the might of his great soul. Then she came to the court of the empress. Theodora, that beautiful devil, is made as much for adultery and intrigue as Antonina is made for virtue. I doubt if the circus wench ever felt even a twinge of conscience. But I don't think she could bear to have an honest woman near her, whom she would have to despise. She would not rest until, by her own devilish example, she had awakened her friend Antonina's coquetry. Now Antonina experiences the torture of her own conscience over her dalliances with her admirers. She loves her husband, in fact she worships him."

"But still? How can a hero, a Belisarius, fail to satisfy her?"

"Just because he is a hero! He does not flatter her, no matter how much he loves her. She could not bear to watch as the empress's lovers exhaust themselves with verses, flowers and gifts, and not enjoy such attentions herself. Her downfall was vanity. But she is not at all happy with these dalliances."

"Does Belisarius suspect anything?"

"Not in the least! He is the only man in the Empire who does not know what concerns him more than anyone. I think it would kill him, and for that reason alone Belisarius must not become Governor of Italy in peacetime. Here in the camp, during the turmoil of war, there are no flatterers to tempt the vain woman, and she has no time to hear them anyway. Because, as if in penitence over the verses and flowers – I am sure she is not capable of anything more than that – Antonina excels all other women in her sense of duty. She is friend and co-general to Belisarius; she shares with him the dangers of the sea and the desert, and of war. She works with him night and day, unless she happens to be reading a flatterer's verses! Often she has rescued him from the claws of his enemies at court. In short, she is only good for him in war, here in the camp, which is also the only place where his own greatness flowers!"

"Now," said Cethegus, "I know enough about things as they are here. Let me speak openly: you want Belisarius out of Italy after his victory, and so do I. You want it for his sake, I for the sake of Italy. You know that I have always been a republican…"

That caused Procopius to push his goblet aside and look at his friend thoughtfully: "That is true of all young people between fourteen and twenty-one years. But the fact that you are still one I find very – very unhistoric. You are trying to create a republic out of this Italian rabble, our most praiseworthy allies against the Goths? They are no longer any good for anything, except perhaps tyranny!"

"I won't argue that!" Cethegus smiled, "but I would like to save my fatherland from your tyranny."

"I can't blame you!" Procopius smiled. "The blessings of our rule are, shall we say, rather heavy!"

"A native governor under the protection of Byzantium would suffice for the time being."

"Of course, and his name would be Cethegus!"

"If necessary, even that!"

"Listen," Procopius said seriously, "let me warn you against just one thing. The air of Rome breeds proud and ambitious plans. There, as the master of Rome, one does not want to be second to anybody on earth. But believe the historian: the Roman era of world rule is over, and nothing will bring it back."

Cethegus became indignant. He thought of the warning he had received from Theodoric. "Historian of Byzantium, I know my Roman affairs better than you. Let me take you into my confidence about our Roman secrets; then tomorrow morning, before the deputation from Rome gets here, arrange an audience for me with Belisarius – and be assured of a great success." And now Cethegus began to outline to the astonished Procopius a broad picture of the secret historic events in the recent past, and his own plans for the future, but wisely keeping his ultimate goal to himself.

"By the ghost of Romulus!" Procopius cried when he had finished. "So you are still creating history on the Tiber! Here is my hand, and you can count on my help!

Belisarius will win, but he shall not govern Italy. Here, let us empty a jug of dry Sallustus on that!"

Early the following morning Procopius arranged an audience with Belisarius for his friend, from which the latter returned very pleased.

"Did you tell him everything?" the historian asked.

"Well, not quite everything!" Cethegus replied with a smile: "one must always have something left to say."

Chapter 12

Shortly afterwards the camp became the scene of unusual activity. The rumour of the holy father's imminent arrival, which flew ahead of his golden litter, had brought the soldiers forth from their tents with the force of religious fervour, reverence, superstition and ordinary inquisitiveness. They left their dinner tables, their games and whatever else they were doing to hurry towards him. It was only with great difficulty that the leaders were able to restrain those who were on duty or on guard, and the faithful hurried for miles to meet their spiritual leader. Now they conducted his procession into the camp, together with hordes of people from the local rural population. Peasants and soldiers insisted on carrying the Pope's litter instead of the original donkeys, even though the Pope modestly protested in vain, and the procession came ever closer, now numbering in the thousands. Constant cheers of: "Hail the bishop of Rome, hail St Peter!" were heard everywhere, while Pope Silverius was dispensing his blessing without let-up, but nobody gave any thought to his companions Scaevola and Albinus.

Belisarius was watching the mighty spectacle from his tent on top of a hill with a serious look on his face. "The Prefect is right!" he said after a while: "This priest is more dangerous than the Goths. That over there is a triumphal procession if ever I saw one! Procopius, have the Byzantine bodyguard outside my tent relieved as soon as the negotiations start; they are Christians and might just be a little too faithful. Have Huns and heathen Gepidae replace them."

He then returned to his tent, where soon afterwards he received the Roman deputation, surrounded by his leaders. Procopius had managed to convince Prince Areobindos of the importance of the mission, which had to take place that day, and which only he could capably handle.

Surrounded by a glittering clerical following, the Pope approached Belisarius's tent. A huge crowd tried to follow him, but as soon as the Pope with Scaevola and Albinus had passed through the narrow lane leading into the camp, guards barred their way with felled lances and would allow neither priests nor soldiers through.

Silverius turned to the leader of the guards with a smile, and gave him a short lecture based on the biblical text: "Let the little ones come to me, and do not bar them." But the Gepidae chieftain shook his shaggy head and turned his back; he did not understand Latin except for basic military commands.

So Silverius smiled once more, blessed his followers again and calmly continued on his way to the tent. Belisarius was sitting on a chair covered by the skin of a lion; the beautiful Antonina was on his left sitting on a panther's hide. Her ailing soul had hoped to find solace and help from the successor to St Peter, but when she saw the face of Silverius, with its look of worldly wisdom, her heart sank.

Belisarius rose as the Pope entered. The latter, without so much as inclining his head, walked straight toward him and placed both hands on his shoulders as if in blessing. He had to reach upwards with some difficulty to do this, as Belisarius was a good foot taller than the Pope. He tried to press Belisarius to his knees, but the general remained firmly standing, like an oak, and Silverius had to bless him standing up.

"Are you coming as an envoy of the Romans?" Belisarius began.

"I have come," Silverius replied, "in the name of St Peter as the bishop of Rome, to hand over the city to you and to the emperor Justinian. These good people," he went on, pointing to Scaevola and Albinus, "followed me like limbs follow the head." Scaevola, annoyed, was about to interject, as that was not the way he understood the situation, but Belisarius motioned him to remain silent.

"And so I bid you welcome in Italy and in Rome in the name of the Lord. Enter the walls of the holy city to protect the church and the faithful against the heretics! Once there praise the Lord and the cross of Jesus Christ, and never forget it was the holy church that smoothed your path and built the road into Rome for you. Almighty God has chosen me as His tool, to lead the Goths to a foolish sense of false security and to have them leave the city blindly. It was I who won the city and its inhabitants over to your side, and defeated the efforts of your enemies. By my hand St Peter now hands you the keys to the city, so that you may protect and defend it. Never forget these words!" And with that he handed the keys of the Porta Asinaria to Belisarius.

"I will never forget them!" Belisarius replied, and motioned to Procopius to accept the keys from the Pope's hand. "You spoke of the efforts of my enemies. Does the emperor have enemies in Rome?"

With an exaggerated sigh Silverius replied: "General, do not ask! Their nets of intrigue have been torn, and they are harmless. It is not the place of the holy church to accuse them, but rather to forgive them and turn everything for the best."

"It is your duty, Holy Father, to reveal to the emperor any traitors who may be hiding among his Roman subjects. I now call on you to tell me who the emperor's enemies are."

Silverius sighed again: "The church does not thirst for blood."

"But it must not hinder the arm of worldly justice!" Scaevola interjected. The lawyer now stepped forward and handed Belisarius a papyrus scroll. "I accuse Cornelius Cethegus Caesarius, the Prefect of Rome, of insulting behaviour, insubordination and revolt against the emperor Justinian. This document here contains details of the charges with full proof. He has called the emperor's regime tyranny. He resisted the landing of Imperial troops to the best of his ability. Finally, only a few days ago, he alone voted against opening the gates of Rome to you."

"And what penalty do you seek?" Belisarius asked, scanning the document.

"According to the law the penalty is death," Scaevola replied.

"And according to the law," Albinus added, "his property should be divided equally between the Imperial treasury and his accusers."

"And may God have mercy on his soul!" the bishop of Rome concluded.

"Where is the accused?" Belisarius asked.

"He said he would go and look for you, but I doubt that his bad conscience will permit him to come."

"You are mistaken, Bishop of Rome," Belisarius replied, "he is already here."

As he said this a curtain at the back of the tent fell, and the Prefect Cethegus stood before his astonished accusers, who leapt to their feet in alarm. Silently, but with a devastating look in his eyes, Cethegus took a few steps forward until he was standing on the right side of Belisarius.

"Cethegus came to me earlier than you," the general continued after a pause, "and he also got in ahead of you when it comes to making accusations. You stand before me as a heavily accused man, Silverius. Defend yourself before you accuse others!"

"I? Accused?" the Pope smiled. "Where can one find a man who will accuse, much less judge, the successor to St Peter?"

"In the absence of your master, the emperor, I am the judge."

"And the accuser?" Silverius asked.

Cethegus half turned towards Belisarius and said: "I am the accuser! I accuse Silverius, the bishop of Rome, of criminal acts against the injured majesty of the emperor, and of high treason against the Roman Empire. I will prove my charges immediately. Silverius intends to take control of Rome and a large part of Italy away from the emperor and, ridiculous as this might sound, to establish a clerical Empire here in the land of the Caesars. He has already taken the first step to implement this – shall I call it a crime or madness? Here is a contract which he concluded with Theodahad, the previous king of the Barbarians – you will note his signature here. In it the king sells, for the sum of one thousand pounds of gold, the city of Rome and its surroundings for thirty miles to the successors of St Peter for all time, in the event that Silverius becomes Pope. All rights are listed, and they include jurisdiction, the making of laws, government, taxes, duties and even the power to wage war. According to its date this contract is three months old. Therefore, at the same time as the pious archdeacon was calling in the emperor's army behind Theodahad's back, he also entered a contract behind the emperor's back, to rob him of the fruits of his efforts and to secure them for the Pope in perpetuity. I will leave it to the emperor's representative to judge how such cleverness should be rewarded. The morality of serpents is regarded in a very particular way among the chosen of the Lord. Among us laymen such actions—"

"Disgraceful treason!" Belisarius thundered, jumping to his feet and taking the document from the Prefect. "Look here, priest, your name! Can you deny it?"

The effect of this accusation and proof on those present was tremendous. The face of everyone showed a mixture of surprise and annoyance, together with anticipation as to how the Pope would defend himself. Scaevola, the short-sighted republican, was more surprised than anyone at these designs of his dangerous ally to rule Italy. He hoped that Silverius would be able to counter this accusation convincingly.

The Pope was indeed in a precarious situation. It looked as if the accusation could not be disproved, and Belisarius's angry face would have been enough to frighten many a more timid soul. But at this moment Silverius showed that he was in no way inferior to either of his opponents, the Prefect or the hero of Byzantium. Not even for an instant did he lose his composure. He did avert his eyes for an instant, as if in pain, when Cethegus produced the document from his garment, but he was able to maintain at least the outward appearance of unshakable calm in spite of the thundering voice and furious eyes of Belisarius. He knew that at this moment he would have to defend his life's ambition, and that gave him great strength. He did not bat an eyelash.

"How much longer do you intend to remain silent?" Belisarius roared.

"Until you are capable and worthy of listening to me. You are possessed by Urchitophel, the demon of anger."

"Speak! Defend yourself!" Belisarius replied, calmer, and sitting down.

"The accusation of this godless man," Silverius began, "only serves to bring out into the light an ancient right of the holy church, much earlier than might otherwise have been the case in these uncertain times. It is true, I did make that contract with the king of the Barbarians."

A murmur of disgust went the rounds of the Byzantines.

"But I did not negotiate with the then ruler of the city, the Gothic king, out of worldly ambition or to acquire new rights. No! As the saints are my witnesses, I did it only so that an ancient right of St Peter would not be allowed to lapse."

"An ancient right?" Belisarius asked, annoyed.

"An ancient right!" Silverius repeated, "a right to render effective something which, until now, the holy church has allowed to rest. Her enemies now make it necessary for her to put the matter before you. Therefore hear, representative and general of the emperor, that the right which Theodahad ceded to the holy church under the contract in question was her right two centuries ago; the Goth merely confirmed it.

"In the same place where the Prefect's sacrilegious hand found this document, he could also have laid his hand on another document, on which our original right is based. The pious emperor Constantine, who was the first of Justinian's predecessors to turn to Christ's teachings, answered the urgings of his saintly mother Helena and crushed all his enemies with the help of the saints, particularly St Peter. In grateful recognition of this aid, and to prove to the whole world that crown and sword alike must bow before the cross of the holy church, he made a gift of the city of Rome, her surroundings and neighbouring cities to St Peter and his successors for all time. The deed confirming this gift also bestowed upon St Peter and the church all the rights and privileges of worldly government, such as jurisdiction and taxation and administration, so that the holy church would have a sound basis for carrying out her worldly as well as her spiritual obligations to her flock. This gift was recorded in a properly prepared legal document, and the curse of Gehenna awaits any who question it. I now ask of the emperor Justinian whether he is willing to honour the undertaking given by his predecessor Constantine, whom God loved, or whether he wishes to overthrow it from motives of worldly greed and ambition, thereby incurring eternal damnation upon his head."

The bishop's speech, delivered with all the conviction of holy dignity and the skill of an accomplished orator, had an immediate and powerful effect. Belisarius, Procopius and the generals, who had been about to sit in angry judgement over the priest a moment earlier, now felt as if it was they themselves who had been judged and found guilty by the legality which now faced them.

It seemed as if the heart of Italy was irretrievably lost to the emperor, and given instead to the rule of the church. There was an ominous silence among the Byzantines, who had been so dominating just a few moments before, and the priest stood triumphant in their midst, a clear victor. At last Belisarius, who was anxious to try and shift the burden of having to fight with the bishop, or the shame of being bested by him, turned to Cethegus: "Prefect of Rome, what do you have to say in reply?"

Cethegus stepped forward, a barely perceptible touch of mockery about his lips. He bowed and began: "The accused makes reference to a document. I believe that it would cause him great embarrassment if I were to demand that he produce it here and now. However I do not wish to oppose the man who calls himself the head of Christianity like an angry lawyer. I concede that the document exists."

Belisarius made a gesture of impotent frustration.

"I am willing to do even more than that! I have saved the Holy Father the trouble of having to produce the document, which he would find difficult, and with my own sacrilegious hand I have brought it with me instead."

He withdrew a yellowed parchment from a capsule under his arm and looked alternately at its contents and at the faces of Belisarius and the Pope, obviously enjoying the tension.

"More still! I have been examining the document for days with the searching eyes of an implacable enemy, and with the aid of lawyers even more able than I am – such as my friend Salvius Julianus – to the last syllable to find some flaw in its validity. It was in vain. Even the sharp brain of my honourable and learned friend Scaevola would not be able to find a fault with it. Every legal detail and every clause are impeccable and unassailable. Indeed I would have liked to be acquainted with the Protonarius of the emperor Constantine; he must have been a legal mind of the highest calibre." He paused, and his eyes rested mockingly on Silverius, who was wiping the perspiration from his brow.

"Well then," Belisarius asked, very agitated, "the deed is in perfect order. Does that not make it legal?"

"True!" Cethegus sighed, "the deed is legally perfect. It is a pity therefore that..."

"What?" Belisarius interrupted.

"It is a pity that it is a fake."

A cry rose from the lips of everyone present. Belisarius and Antonina sprang to their feet, and everyone in the room took a step closer to the Prefect. Only Silverius staggered a step backwards.

"False?" Belisarius cried as if rejoicing, "Prefect, friend, can you prove that?"

"I would certainly not have said it otherwise. The parchment on which this document is written shows every sign of great age: there are cracks, worm holes and stains of every kind, all that one could ask for, so that sometimes it is even difficult to read the writing. However the document only seems to be so old as the result of great cosmetic skill. As many women go to great lengths to look young, someone has gone to even greater lengths to make this document look old. It is a genuine parchment from the Imperial parchment factory in Byzantium, which Constantine founded, and which still exists today."

"Get to the point!" Belisarius cried.

"But it is probably not known to everyone – apparently it also escaped the Holy Father – that the year of manufacture of this parchment is marked, right at the bottom, on the left, by a stamp showing the names of the consuls of the year, in barely recognisable letters. Now watch carefully, my general!

"According to its text the document claims to have been written in the sixteenth year of Constantine's reign, the same year in which he closed the heathen temples and, as the document rightly states, a year after the elevation of Constantinople to the capital of the Empire. The consuls of the year are shown quite correctly as Dalmatius and Xenophilos.

"Therefore it can only be said to be a miracle, in this case one which God worked against His own church, that one already knew in the year 335 AD exactly who would be consul in the year following the deaths of the emperor Justinus and King Theodoric. Because the stamp down here on the edge of the parchment, which the scribe evidently failed to notice – it really is difficult to see unless the document is held to the light like this, can you see, Belisarius? – had three crosses on it, which the scribe blindly put there. But I with my 'sacrilegious' but skilful hand removed these crosses and you see, there it is: 'Justianus Augustus, sole consul in the first year of his reign.'"

Silverius swayed, and supported himself on a chair.

"Therefore the parchment of the document which the emperor's Protonarius wrote two hundred years ago was pulled from a donkey's ribs in Byzantium only a few months ago. Admit, oh Belisarius, that this is where the realm of reason ends and the supernatural begins. Here a miracle of heaven must have taken place, therefore honour the will of heaven." He handed the document to Belisarius.

"By Justinian's slumber, it is so!" Belisarius rejoiced. "Bishop of Rome, what have you to say in reply?"

Silverius had regained his composure with great difficulty: he could see his life's work disappearing into the ground before his very eyes. In a barely audible voice he replied: "I found the document in the archives of the church a few months ago. If it is as you say, then I was deceived as you are."

"But we are not deceived," Cethegus smiled.

"I knew nothing of that stamp, I swear it by the wounds of Christ!"

"I believe that, even without your oath, Holy Father," Cethegus interrupted.

"You will realise, priest," Belisarius said rising, "that there will have to be the most thorough inquiry into this matter."

"I demand it," Silverius replied, "as is my right."

"You will get it, have no doubt! But I would not dare to sit in judgment here; only the wisdom of the emperor himself can determine what constitutes justice in a case like this. Vulcaris, my faithful Heruli chieftain, I hand the bishop over to you. You will immediately put him on board a ship and take him to Byzantium."

"I raise objection!" Silverius said. "Nobody can judge over me except the full council of the holy church. I demand that I return to Rome immediately."

"Rome you will never see again! As for your legal rights, the emperor Justinian and Tribonianus will decide those. Your companions Scaevola and Albinus were your co-accusers against the Prefect, who has now been proven to be the emperor's most faithful and able ally. They too are under grave suspicion, and Justinian will decide to what extent they are innocent. They will also be taken to Byzantium in chains. Get aboard ship! Go out through the back door of the tent over there, not through the camp. Vulcaris, this priest here is the emperor's most dangerous enemy. You are responsible for him, or I will have your head."

"I will vouch for him," the giant Heruli warrior replied, as he stepped forward and placed his heavily armoured hand on the bishop's shoulder. "Come priest, to the ship! He will die before anyone gets him out of my clutches."

Silverius could see that any further resistance could only provoke violence, which would injure his dignity. He therefore yielded and walked alongside Vulcaris, who did not take his hand off his shoulder, to the back door of the tent. One of the guards opened it.

He had to walk right past Cethegus. Silverius bowed his head so that he would not have to look at his adversary, but he could hear the Prefect softly whispering to him: "Silverius, this hour was my revenge for your victory in the catacombs. Now we are even!"

Chapter 13

As soon as the bishop had left the tent, Belisarius rose excitedly from his seat, hurried toward the Prefect and embraced him. "Please accept my gratitude, Cethegus Caesarius! I will report to the emperor how today you have saved Rome. You will receive your just reward."

But Cethegus smiled: "My deeds reward themselves."

This hour of mental combat, with its anger, fear, tension and triumph had exhausted Belisarius more than half a day of fighting with sword, shield and helmet. He needed rest and refreshment, which he asked for, and dismissed his generals, not one of whom left the tent without a word of tribute to the Prefect. The latter saw how his ability and great hidden intellect were now recognised by everyone, even Belisarius himself; to him it felt good to think that in this one hour he had destroyed the clever bishop and also humbled the proud Byzantine. But he did not stop for long to savour the fruits of victory. His mind knew the dangers of resting on his laurels; laurels intoxicate.

He resolved to follow up his victory immediately, and to fully use the advantage which he had at this moment over the hero from Byzantium, while the impression he had made was still fresh. Now was the time to get ready for the main offensive, which he had long been planning. While his own eyes were following the departing leaders with such thoughts in his mind, he did not notice another pair of eyes resting on him with unusual intensity. They were the eyes of Antonina. The events she had just witnessed had had a strangely mixed effect on her. For the first time she had seen the god she admired, her husband, ensnared by the wiles of another, in this case the clever priest, without being able to do anything to help himself. Only the superior intellect of the diabolical Roman had saved him.

Initially the humiliation which her pride had suffered through her husband filled her with hatred against the all-powerful Roman. But this hatred did not last, and the more clearly the Roman's mental superiority came to the fore, the more her initial hatred made way for admiration and respect. The one thing she now felt was that the church had outshone her Belisarius, and Cethegus had outshone them both. And out of this she developed a fervent wish that she never wanted this man to be her husband's enemy, but only his friend and ally. In short, Cethegus had made a very important conquest in the form of Belisarius's wife, and what is more, he was to learn that very soon.

The beautiful woman, normally so full of self-confidence, went over to Cethegus with her eyes lowered; he looked up at her, and she blushed from head to foot. "Prefect of Rome," she said, "Antonina thanks you. You have done a great service for Belisarius and for the emperor. We want to be your friends."

Procopius, who had remained behind in the tent, followed these events with astonishment. "My Ulysses has bewitched the witch Circe," he thought to himself.

But Cethegus recognised how this woman was bowing at his feet, and what power that gave him over Belisarius. "Beautiful *Magistra Militum*," he said, raising himself to his full height, "your friendship is the greenest laurel to adorn my victory. I will put it to the test immediately. I beg of you to be my witness, with Procopius here, to a discussion I am about to have with Belisarius."

"Now?" Belisarius asked impatiently. "Come, let us first celebrate the fall of the priest at the table and with a jug of wine." He went toward the door. But Cethegus remained calmly in the middle of the tent, and both Antonina and Procopius were so much under his spell that they did not dare follow their master. Finally Belisarius himself turned and said: "Does it have to be right now?"

"It does," Cethegus replied, and led Antonina back to her chair.

At that Belisarius also turned back: "Speak then, but make it brief."

"As brief as possible. I have always found with great friends and great enemies alike that candour is either the strongest bond or the best weapon. I will now act accordingly. When I said: 'My deeds reward themselves,' what I meant was that I did not take control over Rome away from the treacherous priest for the benefit of the emperor."

Belisarius pricked up his ears at once. Procopius, frightened by his friend's excessive daring, motioned him to desist. Antonina's sharp eyes had noticed this, and hesitated, suspicious of the apparent understanding between the two friends. This in turn did not escape Cethegus. "No, Procopius," he said, to Belisarius's surprise: "our friends here would have realised immediately that Cethegus is not a man whose ambition is satisfied by a smile from Justinian. I did not save Rome for the emperor."

"For whom then?" Belisarius asked, very serious.

"In the first place, for Rome herself. I am a Roman. I love my eternal Rome. It must not become subservient to that priest, but at the same time it must not become a slave to the emperor. I am a republican!" he said, proudly holding up his head.

A smile crossed the face of Belisarius, for suddenly the Prefect no longer seemed so overpowering. Procopius shrugged his shoulders, and said to himself: "I just don't understand it." But one person to whom this audacious direct approach did appeal was Antonina.

"Of course I could see that we could only overthrow the Barbarians with the help of Belisarius and his sword. Unfortunately I also know that the time is not yet ripe for me to realise my ultimate dream of republican freedom. First the Italians must once more become the Romans of old. This generation has to die out, and so I recognise that for the time being Rome can only find protection against the Barbarians under Justinian's shield. That is why we are willing to bow to that shield, for the present."

"Not bad!" Procopius thought, "the emperor is to protect them until they are strong enough to chase him away by way of thanks."

"Those are dreams, friend Prefect," Belisarius said compassionately, "what practical results have they?"

"The result that Rome is not to be handed over to the emperor and his whim unconditionally, with tied hands. Justinian has not only Belisarius to serve him. Think what might happen if the heartless Narses was to succeed you—" the hero furrowed his brow "—that is why I will now list for you the conditions under which the city of the Caesars will receive you and your army."

But that was too much for Belisarius. Furiously he jumped to his feet, his eyes aglow and his eyes flashing: "Prefect of Rome!" he roared with his lion's voice, "you are forgetting yourself and your position. Tomorrow morning I will leave for Rome with my army of seventy thousand men. Who is to stop me from entering the city, without any conditions?"

"I am," Cethegus replied calmly. "No Belisarius, I am not mad. Look at this plan here, of the city and its fortifications. I am sure that your trained eye will recognise even better than mine how strong they are." He produced a piece of parchment and spread it out on the table.

Belisarius looked at it indifferently, and cried immediately: "That plan is wrong! Procopius, give me our plan out of that capsule. Look here, these ditches are filled in now, and that wall has been torn down. The gates are defenceless, even though your plan shows them to be of immense strength. Your plan is out of date, Prefect of Rome."

"No, Belisarius, your own plan is the one that is out of date. These ditches and walls have been rebuilt."

"Since when?"

"Since last year."

"By whom?"

"By me!" Belisarius looked at the plan, taken aback.

Antonina looked at her husband anxiously. "Prefect," the latter said at last, "if that is so then you certainly understand siege warfare. But to defend these walls you need an army. Empty walls will not hold me up."

"You will not find them empty. You will admit that an army of twenty thousand men could defend Rome – this Rome here, my Rome – for a year and a day even against Belisarius. Let me tell you then that at this moment those fortifications are defended by thirty-five thousand armed men."

"Are the Goths back?" Belisarius cried. Procopius stepped closer.

"No, those thirty five thousand are under my command. For years now I have been recalling the effeminate Romans to arms, and training them ceaselessly in their use. Thus right now I have thirty cohorts, each numbering almost one thousand men, ready to fight."

Belisarius was struggling with his own frustration.

"I will admit," Cethegus went on, "that these forces would be no match against an army of Belisarius in a pitched battle. But I assure you that they can fight most ably from those walls. In addition I have also hired seven thousand hand-picked Isaurian and Abasgan mercenaries out of my own private means. I have gradually brought them to Rome, to Ostia and surrounding villages without arousing suspicion. You doubt me? Here are the lists of the thirty cohorts, and this is the agreement with the Isaurians. You can now see clearly just where you stand. Either you accept my conditions, in which case Rome and those thirty-five thousand men are yours. Rome, my Rome, which you say yourself is terribly strong, is yours, and so is Cethegus. Or you reject my conditions, in which case your entire offensive, which is based on speed, will be foiled. You will be forced to besiege Rome for many months, and the Goths will have all the time they need to reorganise themselves. They will return to relieve the city with a numerical superiority of three to one, and only a miracle will then save you from utter annihilation."

"Or your death this instant, you devil!" Belisarius thundered, and no longer able to control himself he drew his sword. "Come, Procopius, seize the traitor in the name of the emperor! He dies this instant!"

Procopius stepped between them, terrified and uncertain, while Antonina grasped her husband's arm and tried to restrain him.

"Are you two in league with one another?" the furious hero cried, "Guards! Guards!"

Two lancers rushed in from each of the two entrances, but even before they entered Belisarius had torn himself loose from Antonina and flung Procopius aside as if he were a child. Belisarius was immensely strong. Now, his sword raised for one terrible blow, he rushed at the Prefect.

But suddenly he stopped and lowered the weapon, which had already touched its intended victim's chest.

Cethegus had remained standing like a statue, not moving a muscle, coldly looking at his furious adversary. There he stood, a smile of infinite contempt on his face.

"What is that look for, and why are you laughing?" Belisarius asked, hesitating. Procopius motioned unobtrusively to the guards to withdraw.

"It is pity for your fame as a general, which a moment of blind anger almost destroyed for ever. If your sword had found its mark you would have been doomed."

"Me?" Belisarius laughed. "I would have thought you were doomed."

"And you with me. Do you think me so stupid that I would blindly place my head into the lion's mouth? It was not difficult to foresee that the first instinct of a great hero like yourself might well be to strike me down with your sword. I have therefore taken appropriate precautions. As from this morning Rome is in the hands of my blindly loyal friends, as a result of written instructions from me. They are in complete control of Rome. Hadrian's tomb, the Capitol, all the gates and towers of the walls and fortifications are at this moment occupied by my Isaurians and my legionaries. I left orders to that effect with my tribunes, all able young men, in the event that you arrive in Rome before me." He handed a papyrus scroll to Procopius, who proceeded to read from it.

"To Lucius and Marcus Licinius, Cethegus the Prefect. I have fallen, a sacrifice to the tyranny of Byzantium. Avenge me! Call the Goths back immediately. I demand it from you on your oath. The Barbarians are better than Justinian's bloodhounds and tax collectors. Hold out to the last man, and give the city to the flames before you let a tyrant's army have it."

"So you see," Cethegus went on, "that my death would not open the gates of Rome for you. On the contrary, they would be closed to you for ever. You would have to lay siege to the city; or come to terms – with me."

Belisarius looked at Cethegus with anger, but there was also a touch of admiration in his eyes for the courageous man who dared to make him conditions right among the thousands of his own army. He sheathed his sword, flung himself in a chair and asked: "What are your conditions for handing over Rome?"

"There are only two. Firstly you will give me command over a small part of your army. I must not be a stranger to your men."

"Agreed. As Archonius you shall have two thousand of my Illyrian infantry, and one thousand Moorish and Saracen cavalry. Will that be enough?"

"Absolutely. Secondly, my independence from you and from the emperor relies entirely on the fact that I control Rome, and that must not end once you arrive there. Therefore the entire right bank of the Tiber with Hadrian's tomb, and on the left bank the Capitol and the southern wall up to and including the gate of St Paul, will remain in the hands of my Isaurians and legionaries and under my command until the end of the war. You will occupy the remainder of the city on the left bank, from the Porta Flaminia in the north to the Porta Appia in the south."

Belisarius tool a look at the plan of the city. "You have thought that out well! From those points you can force me out of the city or block the river any time you choose. It is out of the question!"

"Then you had better prepare to fight the Goths and Cethegus together, before the walls of Rome."

Belisarius leapt to his feet. "Go! Leave me alone with Procopius. Cethegus, you will await my decision."

"Until tomorrow," the latter replied. "At sunrise I will return to Rome, with your army or – alone."

A few days later Belisarius entered the eternal city with his army via the Porta Asinaria.

Tremendous rejoicing greeted the liberator, and a rain of flowers poured over him and his wife, who was riding to his left on a small white palfrey. Every house had been festively decked out with garlands and gaily coloured bunting.

But the liberator who was being thus fêted did not look happy. He looked fiercely up at the Capitol and at the walls, from which the banners of the city's legionaries, fashioned after the Roman eagles of old, looked down on him in place of the dragon banners of Byzantium.

Outside the Porta Asinaria young Lucius Licinius had turned back the vanguard of the Imperial army, and the mighty gate did not rise until the Prefect Cethegus had appeared on his magnificent black stallion Pluto with Belisarius. Lucius was astonished at the transformation which had come over his much revered friend. The cold, strict reserve had gone; he seemed to be taller and more youthful, and there was a look of the joy of victory on his face and in his whole appearance. He was wearing a tall helmet, richly decorated with gold, and capped by a mighty purple horse's plume which came right down to his breast armour. The latter was a masterpiece from Athens, and every one of its many small plates showed a relief in silver, depicting some Roman victory.

Cethegus, thus magnificently adorned and with the look of victory on his face, outshone not only Belisarius the *Magister Militum* himself, but also the magnificent procession of generals and leaders which followed him, led by Procopius and Bloody John. In fact it was so obvious that the crowd noticed it also, as soon as the procession had passed a few streets, and before long the cry "Cethegus!" became as loud as or louder than the cry "Belisarius!"

Antonina's sensitive ears noticed this, and each time the procession paused she listened uneasily to what the people were saying. Once they had passed the baths of Titus and reached the Via Sacra near the Flavian Amphitheatre, they were forced to slow down by the huge crowd, and even to halt for a while. A small triumphal arch had been erected for them, through which they could pass only slowly.

"Victory to the emperor Justinian and Belisarius, his general" was written on it. As Antonina was reading the inscription, she heard an old man ask questions of his son, obviously knowing little of what was going on. "Tell me, Gaius, the fierce looking one on the red stallion—"

"Yes, he is Belisarius, as I told you," the son replied.

"Is he? But that magnificent-looking warrior on his left, the one with the triumphant look on the black horse, he must be Justinian himself, his master, the Imperator?"

"Heavens no, Father. The emperor is sitting peacefully in his golden rooms in Byzantium writing laws. No, that man is Cethegus, our Cethegus the Prefect, the one who gave me the sword. Yes, he is a man after my own heart. My tribune Licinius told me the other day that Belisarius would never see a Roman gate from the inside unless Cethegus wants it so."

Antonina urged her mount on with a sharp blow from her silver whip and sped through the triumphal arch.

Cethegus conducted Belisarius and his wife as far as the Pincius Palace, which had been made ready for them. Here he took his leave, so that he could assist the Byzantine leaders with quartering their troops, partly in houses and public buildings within the city, and partly in tents outside the walls.

"When you have recovered from the efforts – and honours – of the day, Belisarius, I will expect yourself, Antonina and your leading generals in my house for the evening meal."

A few hours later Marcus Licinius, Piso and Balbus appeared in order to fetch the invited guests. They accompanied the litters bearing Belisarius and Antonina. The others went on foot.

"Where does the Prefect live?" Belisarius asked on entering the litter.

"As long as you are here, near Hadrian's tomb by day, and in the Capitol by night." Belisarius was taken aback, and gradually the little procession approached the Capitol.

Belisarius was amazed to see the walls and battlements, which had lain in ruins for hundreds of years, restored to tremendous strength. When they reached the narrow entrance to the Capitol, which was in effect a fortress within the fortress of Rome, they found a mighty iron gate, which was firmly closed as if in time of war. Marcus Licinius called out to the guards.

"Give the password!" a voice called from within.

"Caesar and Cethegus!" the tribune replied. At that the gate swung open, and a long cordon of Roman legionaries and Isaurian mercenaries came into view, the latter clad in iron up to their eyes and armed with double-edged battleaxes. Lucius Licinius stood at the head of the Romans, his drawn sword in his hand. Sandil, the Isaurian chieftain, stood at the head of his countrymen. For a moment the Byzantine general hesitated, overwhelmed by this display of might in granite and iron.

And then it became light in the dimly illuminated room in the background; music could be heard, and in a moment Cethegus approached, accompanied by flautists and torchbearers, without armour. He was wearing an ornate gown of purple silk with a wreath on his head, such as was customary for the host of a festive occasion. With a smile he stepped forward and said: "Welcome! May flutes and tubas tell it to all the world. The most beautiful hour in my life has come! Belisarius, my guest in the Capitol."

And then he led his silent guest into the fortress to the sound of trumpets and fanfares.

Chapter 14

While these events were taking place among the Romans and the Byzantines, decisive happenings were also occurring on the Gothic side.

Duke Guntharis and Count Arahad had left Florence with their captive queen for Ravenna, leaving only a small garrison behind, and were hurrying to Ravenna in forced marches. If they could reach this fortress, which was regarded as impregnable, before Witigis, who was close on their heels, and if they could capture it before Witigis got there, they would then be in a position to dictate almost any terms to the king. It was true that they had a good headstart, and they hoped that their pursuers would be delayed for a good while by having to besiege Florence. But they lost this headstart almost entirely because the cities and fortresses on the most direct route to Ravenna all declared themselves for Witigis. This compelled the rebels to make a large detour, firstly to Bologna in the north, which had joined their side, and then to the east at right angles to Ravenna.

Nevertheless, when they had reached the swampy surroundings of the coastal fortress, and when they were only half a day's march from its gates, there was still no sign of the king or his army. Guntharis allowed his troops to rest for the remainder of the day, as it was almost evening in any case, and sent only a small group of cavalry ahead under the command of his brother. They were to announce to the Goths in Ravenna the imminent arrival of the main army.

But it was only the first hour of daylight on the following day when Count Arahad returned to the camp in flight, with his greatly reduced force. "By the sword of God," Guntharis cried, "where are you coming from?"

"We come from Ravenna. We reached the outermost gate on the city wall and requested admittance, but we were firmly refused. I then showed myself personally to old Count Grippa, who commands the city. He told me stubbornly that we will hear his decision, and that of the Goths in Ravenna, tomorrow. That decision would be told both to us and to the army of the king, of which segments were already approaching the city from the southeast."

"Impossible!" Guntharis cried angrily.

"I had no alternative but to leave again, even though I could not understand our friend's attitude for a moment. I thought that the talk of the king's imminent arrival was only an idle threat from the old man. But then we were attacked, while my troops were looking for a dry place to bivouac south of the city, by mounted enemy troops led by that black Count Teias of Tarentum. They charged with the cry: "Hail King Witigis!" and after a fierce fight we were thrown back."

"You are crazy," Guntharis cried, "do they have wings? Was Florence blown away from their path by the wind?"

"No! But I found out from peasants that Witigis marched towards Ravenna by the coastal route via Auximum and Ariminum."

"And left Florence in his rear, unconquered? He will regret that!"

"Florence has fallen! He sent Hildebad against the city, and he took it by storm. Like an angry bull he smashed the Mars Gate down with his own hand, and ran through it!"

Guntharis heard these evil tidings gloomily, but then he quickly made his decision. He left immediately for the city to try and take it by storm in a single blow.

The attempt failed, but at least the rebels had the satisfaction of seeing that the fortress, possession of which would decide the civil war, did not open its gates to the enemy either. The king had made camp to the southeast, before the port city of Classis. The well trained eye of Duke Guntharis soon saw that the swamps to the northwest also offered a secure position, and he quickly pitched his well fortified camp in that area.

And so the two opposing armies, like two impatient suitors after the one reluctant bride, had forced their way close to the capital on both sides, yet the city did not seem to want either of them.

The next day two Gothic deputations from Ravenna left by the northwestern and southeastern gates respectively, the Porta Honorius and the Porta Theodoric, and they took the important decision made by the Goths in the city to both warring factions, one deputation to the Woelsungs and one to the king.

The decision they announced must have been a very strange one indeed, because the leaders of both armies kept it very secret. In apparent agreement among themselves they saw to it that not a word of it reached their troops. The envoys were immediately conducted from the commander's tent back to the city gates, under the strict supervision of armed men, who saw to it that they spoke to nobody.

But the effect the envoys had on both camps was remarkable in other ways also. On the rebel side there was a violent argument between the two commanders, followed by a heated confrontation between Duke Guntharis and his beautiful captive, who according to rumour was saved from the Duke's anger only by the intervention of his brother Arahad. After that the rebel camp assumed the calm of perplexity.

The reaction in the king's camp was rather more eventful. The first reply offered by the king was to storm Ravenna with the whole of his loyalist army. Hildebrand, Teias and the army heard this order with amazement. They had been hoping that the gates of the powerful fortress would open to them freely very soon. Contrary to Gothic tradition the king told nobody, not even his closest confidants, what the envoys had told him, or why he had issued the order to storm the city.

Silently but with heads shaking the army prepared for the sudden attempt to storm the walls, but with little hope of success. Their attack was bloodily repulsed. In vain the king drove his Goths again and again at the steep stone walls. In vain he was the first to climb the storm ladders three times. From early dawn until dusk the attackers stormed without let-up, but they made no progress whatever, and the fortress preserved her ancient fame of impregnability. When at last the king was carried out of the fight, having been rendered unconscious by a stone thrown from the wall, Teias and Hildebrand led the tired troops back to their camp.

The mood of the army during the night that followed was sombre and depressed. There were considerable losses to mourn, and nothing had been gained except the conviction that the city could not be taken by storm. The Gothic garrison of Ravenna had fought alongside the inhabitants on the walls, and the king of the Goths was camped outside his capital, the finest fortress in the Empire, laying siege to it! This was the same fortress they had hoped would offer them refuge and time to arm for the coming confrontation with Belisarius. But the worst part of it was that the army blamed the king for the whole unfortunate civil war, and the need for it. Why had negotiations with the city suddenly been broken off? Why hadn't the reasons for it been told to the army, if they were honest reasons? Why was the king shunning the light?

Miserable and depressed, the troops sat around their fires or lay in their tents, attending to their wounds or repairing their weapons. There was none of the usual sound of singing around the tables, and when the leaders walked among their men many an angry word was heard, and many an accusation against the king.

The following morning Hildebad and his troops arrived in the camp from Florence. He had heard about the bloody fiasco with a heavy heart, and wanted to go to the king immediately. But as the latter was still unconscious under the care of Hildebrand, Teias took him into his tent and answered his questions.

After a while old Hildebrand entered, with a look on his face which caused Hildebad to jump from his bear skin in alarm. Even Teias inquired immediately: "What is the matter with the king? His wound? Is he dying?"

The old man sadly shook his head: "No, but if I am guessing correctly, and if I know him and his honest and decent soul, it would be better for him if he did die."

"What do you mean? What are you implying?"

"Just calm yourselves," Hildebrand said sadly, sitting down. "Poor Witigis! I fear that the time to speak will come soon enough!" And then he said no more.

"How was he when you left him?" Teias asked.

"The wound fever has gone, thanks to my herbs. Tomorrow he will be able to ride again. But he said strange things while he was hallucinating – I hope they were only feverish dreams, otherwise I feel great pity for the poor, good man."

There was nothing more to be gleaned from the old man. A few hours later Witigis called the three leaders to him. To their astonishment they found him fully armed, and standing up even though he had to lean on his sword for support. His helmet in the form of a crown and the royal sceptre of the white wood of an ash with a sphere of gold were lying on the table beside him. The three friends were shocked at the deterioration which had come over the face of their king and friend, normally so calm and good-looking. He must have gone through a bitter struggle with himself, and such an inner struggle of conflicting loyalties, duties and responsibilities was something which his honest and straightforward character could not endure.

"I called for you," the king said with an effort, "to receive and support my decision in this difficult situation. How great have our losses been today from the storming of the city?"

"Three thousand killed," Teias replied, very serious.

"And more than six thousand wounded," Hildebrand added.

Witigis closed his eyes painfully, and then he said: "There is nothing else for it. Teias, order a second storm attempt immediately."

"What? What was that?" the three of them cried at once.

"There is no alternative," the king repeated. "How many men did you bring with you, Hildebad?"

"Three thousand, but they are dead tired from the march. They cannot fight today."

"So we will have to storm on our own again," Witigis replied, reaching for his spear.

"King," Teias said, "yesterday we did not gain even a single stone of the fortress, and today you have nine thousand less!"

"And even the men who are not wounded are tired, with their weapons and their courage and their spirit broken," Hildebrand added.

"We must have Ravenna!"

"We will not take it by storm!" was Teias's retort.

"We will see about that!" Witigis replied.

"I besieged the city with my great king," Hildebrand warned. "He stormed it seventy times, in vain. In the end we starved it into surrender – after three years."

"We must storm," Witigis replied, "give the command."

Teias was about to leave the tent, but Hildebrand held him back. "Stay," he said, "we must not withhold anything from him. King! The Goths are grumbling. They will not follow you today. Another storm is impossible!"

"So that's how it is!" Witigis said bitterly. "A storm is impossible? Then there is only one thing to do, what I should have done yesterday, and then those three thousand Goths would still be alive.

"Hildebad, take that crown and sceptre there. Go into the rebel camp, and lay them at young Arahad's feet; tell him he is to marry Matesuentha. My army and I are ready to hail him as our king." And with that he fell onto his bed exhausted.

"You are talking in a fever again," old Hildebrand said.

"That is impossible!" Teias concluded.

"Impossible! Is everything impossible? Fighting is impossible? And abdication is impossible? I tell you, Hildebrand, after the message from Ravenna there is no other way!" He was silent.

The three friends exchanged meaningful glances. At last the old man asked: "What was the message? There may yet be a way out. Eight eyes can see more than two."

"No," Witigis sighed, "not in this case. There is nothing to see here, otherwise I would have told you of it long ago, but still it would lead to nothing. I have been turning it over in my own mind, again and again. There is the parchment from Ravenna – read it, but say nothing to the men."

Hildebrand picked up the scroll and read: "The Gothic warriors and the people of Ravenna to Count Witigis of Faesulae!"

"What cheek!" Hildebad interjected.

"To Duke Guntharis of Tuscany and Count Arahad of Asta. The Goths and the citizens of Ravenna hereby declare to the two leaders outside their gates that they, loyal to the holy Amalung dynasty, and in grateful remembrance of the many unforgettable and benevolent deeds of our great King Theodoric, will remain loyal to that dynasty as long as even one member of it is still alive. We therefore recognise only Matesuentha as the legitimate mistress of both Goths and Italians. We will open our gates only to Queen Matesuentha, and we will defend our city to the last against any other party."

"They are madmen!" Teias said.

"I cannot understand it," Hildebad added.

But old Hildebrand folded the parchment and said: "I understand it very well. As far as the Goths are concerned, you should know that the garrison and the commanders of the city are all Theodoric's old followers. Those men swore to our great king that they would never prefer any other king to members of his family. I too took that oath, but I thought only of the male members of the dynasty, never the women.

"That is why I had to support Theodahad, and why I was able to pay homage to Witigis only after that coward's treachery. But old Count Grippa and his men in Ravenna think that they are also tied to the women of the Amalung dynasty by that oath. You can depend on it, these old warriors are the oldest in the Empire and Theodoric's former companions in arms. They would rather be hacked to pieces man by man than betray their oath, however they interpret it. And by Theodoric's memory, they are right! As far as the native population is concerned, they are not only grateful but smart too. They are hoping that Goths and Byzantines will fight it out in front of their city walls. If Belisarius wins, who claims he is here to avenge Amalasuntha, then he cannot punish the city for being loyal to her daughter, and if we win they will claim that the Goths in the city forced them to close their gates to us."

"Be that is it may," the king interjected, "now you will understand why I acted as I did. If the army had come to know about that message, then many more might have lost heart and gone over to the Woelsung camp, who have the princess in their power. I only had two options, take the city by force or abdicate. We tried the former yesterday in vain, and you tell me it can't be tried again. So there is only one thing left to do. Let Arahad marry the girl and wear the crown! I will be the first to acknowledge him and to defend his Empire by the side of his brave and able brother."

"Never!" Hildebad cried, "you are our king and will remain so. I will never bow my head to that young fop! Let us move against the rebels tomorrow; I will drive them from their camp and bring back the princess, whose hand will supposedly open those gates for us as if by magic, into our tents."

"And once we have her?" Teias asked, "what then? She is of no use to us unless we can greet her as our queen. Do you want that? Haven't you had enough with Amalasuntha and Gothelindis? Do you want petticoat rule a third time?"

"May God preserve us from that!" Hildebad laughed.

"That is what I think too," Witigis added, "otherwise I would have adopted that course long ago."

"Very well then, let's stay here and starve the city out!"

"We can't," Witigis replied, "we can't wait. In a few days Belisarius could come climbing down from those hills there and annihilate me, Duke Guntharis and the city, one after the other. Then farewell Empire and Gothic nation. There are only two choices: storm—"

"Impossible!" Hildebrand said.

"Or give in and abdicate. Go Teias, take the crown. I can see no other way!"

The two younger men hesitated. And then old Hildebrand spoke, with a serious and sad look in his face, but also looking with great affection at the king: "I see a way out, a painful one, but the only one. You will have to take it, my Witigis, and if your heart breaks seven times because of it."

Witigis looked at him inquiringly, and even Teias and Hildebad were astonished at the gentleness in the voice of the flint-hard old man.

"You go outside," the latter indicated, "I must speak to the king alone."

Chapter 15

The two Goths left the tent in silence and paced up and down outside, awaiting the outcome. Now and then Hildebrand's voice could be heard coming from the tent. In a long speech he seemed to be trying to persuade the king to do something he did not want to do, and now and again there would be an exclamation of protest from the king.

"What could the old man have in mind?" Hildebad wondered, halting for a moment, "do you know?"

"I sense it," Teias sighed, "poor Witigis!"

"The devil! What do you mean?"

"Don't press me," Teias replied, "we will all find out soon enough." And so a considerable time passed.

The king's voice was becoming louder and more pained. It seemed as if he was struggling mightily against whatever it was that Hildebrand was trying to get him to do.

"Why is the greybeard torturing our valiant hero king?" Hildebad exclaimed angrily. "It sounds to me as if he is trying to murder him. I am going in there to help him."

But Teias held him back by the shoulder: "Stay," he said, "I think it has to be like this."

While Hildebad was trying to pry himself loose, a clamour of voices could be heard coming from the far end of the camp. Two guards were trying in vain to restrain a huge Goth who, showing all the signs of a long and hard ride, was trying to force his way into the king's tent.

"Let me go, friend," he cried, "or I will cut you down!" And he raised a huge battleaxe threateningly.

"Impossible! You will have to wait. The army's top leaders are with him in the tent."

"I don't care if all the gods in Valhalla are with him in that tent, and Jesus Christ too. I have to see him now! First the man is a husband and a father, and then he can be a king. Let me go!"

"I know that voice," said Count Teias, coming closer, "and the man too. Wachis, what are you looking for here in the camp?"

"Oh Sir!" the faithful man exclaimed, "am I ever glad to see you! Tell these good men to let me go, so I won't have to cut them down. I must get to my poor master immediately."

"Let him go, or he will keep his word. I know him. Now, what do you want of the king?"

"Please, just take me directly to him. I bring him bad, evil news from his wife and child."

"Wife and child?" Hildebad asked, astonished. "Does Witigis have a wife?"

"Very few know about it," Teias replied. "She almost never left her estate, and never came to court. Almost nobody knows her, but the few who do hold her in the highest regard. I know of no other woman like her."

"You are right there, if you have ever been right, Sir," Wachis said with a choking voice. "The poor, poor woman and oh, the poor father! But let me inside. The mistress Rauthgundis is following directly behind me. I must prepare him."

Teias, without asking any further questions, pushed Wachis into the tent and followed with Hildebad.

They found old Hildebrand calmly sitting on the king's bed, his bearded chin resting on his hand, which was gripping his stone axe. Thus he sat there motionless, looking fixedly at the king, who was pacing up and down very agitated, and so carried away by his own emotions that he did not even notice Wachis and the others entering. "No! No! Never!" he cried, "That is cruel! Criminal! Out of the question!"

"It has to be!" Hildebrand replied, without moving.

"No I say!" the king cried and turned around so that he was facing Wachis and almost touching him. For a moment he looked at him absently, and then the faithful servant threw himself at his feet, crying aloud.

"Wachis," the king exclaimed with a start, "what do you bring? Are you coming before her? Stand up – what happened?"

"Oh master," Wachis sobbed, still on his knees, "seeing you tears my heart in two! I can't help it! I have avenged it as best I could."

Witigis gripped him by the shoulders and pulled him to his feet: "Speak, man! What is there to be avenged? My wife?"

"She is alive, she is coming here, but your child…"

"My child?" he said, growing pale. "Athalwin, what happened to him?"

"Dead Sir, murdered!"

A cry like that of a mortally wounded animal broke forth from the father's tortured breast. He covered his face with both hands, and Teias and Hildebad moved closer to him sympathetically. Only Hildebrand remained motionless and stared fixedly at the group.

Wachis could not endure the long, silent pause. He tried to touch his master's hands, but then held back as he saw two great tears on the tough warrior's brown cheeks. He was not ashamed of them.

"Murdered!" he said at last, "my innocent boy! By Romans?"

"Cowardly devils!" Hildebad cried, as Teias clenched his fists, his lips moving silently.

"Calpurnius!" Witigis said, looking at Wachis.

"Yes, Calpurnius! News of your election had reached our estate, and your wife and son had been summoned to your camp. Oh how Athalwin rejoiced that he was now the son of a king, just like Siegfried who slew the dragon! Now he too wanted to go off in search of adventure and slay dragons and giants. Then your neighbour returned from Rome. I noticed that he looked even more hostile and more envious than ever, and I carefully watched your house and your stables. But as for watching over your boy – who would have thought that children are no longer safe?" Wachis shook his head in despair.

"The boy could hardly wait to see his father in the military camp, with all the thousands of Gothic warriors, and to see battles being fought at close quarters. From that hour he threw away his wooden sword and said: 'A king's son must have an iron sword in time of war'. So I had to find a hunting knife for him, and sharpen it too. And from that day he would run away from the mistress Rauthgundis every morning, with his sword in his hand. If she asked: 'Where are you off to?' he would only laugh and reply: 'To adventure, dear Mother!' and skip away into the forest. Around midday he would come back, tired and with torn clothes, and terribly proud of himself. But he would not say a word, except that he had been playing Siegfried.

"But I had my own ideas about that, and one day I noticed bloodstains on his sword, so I followed him into the forest unobserved. Sure enough, it was as I thought. I had once shown him a cave in the rocks, and warned him to be careful of it because poisonous vipers live there by the dozen, just above the creek. He asked a lot of questions at the time, and I explained how every bite was deadly, and how a poor woman picking berries had died instantly when the poison worm bit her naked foot. He drew his wooden sword and wanted to charge right amongst them, and I only restrained him with great effort.

"Now I remembered the vipers, and I trembled at the thought that I had given him an iron weapon. Soon I found him in the forest, right among the rocks in the midst of thorny shrubbery; he was pulling out a big wooden shield, which he had made himself and hidden there. A crown had been freshly painted on it.

"Then he drew his sword and leapt into the cave, with a triumphant cry.

"I looked around me, and there lay half a dozen or so of the big snakes from earlier battles, strewn about with their heads cleft in two; I followed him in and, worried as I was, I could not bring myself to disturb him as he fought so heroically! He drove a huge fat viper from its hole by throwing rocks at it until it reared up against him, hissing. Then, just as it was about to strike, he flung his shield in front of him like lightning and cut the worm in two with a single stroke. I called him and scolded him thoroughly, but he looked at me defiantly and said: 'Just don't you go and tell mother, because I will do it anyway! Until the last dragon is dead!' I threatened to take his sword away. 'Then I'll fight with the wooden one, if you'd rather have that!' he replied, 'and what a disgrace that would be for a king's son!'

"For the next few days I took him with me rounding up horses, which he enjoyed thoroughly, and I thought that we would soon be leaving anyway.

"But one morning he got away from me again, and I went to work by myself. Coming back I took the path along the river, sure of finding him near the cave, but I could not find him. All I saw was his sword belt, torn and hanging in the thorns, and his shield, trampled to pieces on the ground. With a fright I looked about me and searched, but..."

"Quickly, quickly, go on," the king cried.

"But?" Hildebad asked.

"But I could see nothing among the rocks. Then I noticed a man's footprints in the sand, and I followed them. They led me to the edge of a rock, where it falls steeply away. I looked down, and there I saw..."

Witigis was tottering, barely able to stand.

"Oh my poor master! There was the little body, stretched out on the ground by the river. How I got down that cliff face I'll never know, but I was down there in no time. There he lay, still clutching his little sword, lacerated from the sharp rocks, and his blond hair covered in blood..."

"Hold it," said Teias, as Hildebad grasped the poor father's hand as he sank back on the bed, groaning.

"My child, my sweet child, my poor wife!" he cried.

"I could feel the little heart still beating, and brought him around with water from the river. He opened his eyes and recognised me. 'You have fallen, child,' I said.

"'No,' he replied, 'I did not fall, I was pushed.' I grew rigid with horror. 'Calpurnius,' he whispered, 'suddenly came around the corner of the rock as I was fighting the vipers. 'Come with me,' he said, and tried to grab me. He looked angry and treacherous. I drew back. 'Come,' he said, 'or I will tie you up'. 'Tie me up?' I cried, 'my father is king of the Goths, and yours too. Don't you dare touch me!' Then he became very angry and struck at me with a stick, and came closer, but I knew that some of our hands were cutting wood nearby, and so I called out for help and withdrew to the edge of the cliff. Frightened, he looked about him, because the men must have heard me; the sound of their axes suddenly stopped. Then, suddenly leaping forward, he said: 'Then die, you little worm!' and he pushed me over the cliff.'"

Teias bit his lips. "The wretch!" cried Hildebad, and Witigis uttered a cry of pain.

"Make it short!" said Teias.

"He lost consciousness again. I carried him in my arms to the house, to his mother. In her lap he opened his eyes once more. His last breath was to give you his love."

"And my wife? Hasn't she despaired?"

"No master, that she has not! She is a woman of gold, but of steel too. When the boy had closed his eyes for the last time she pointed silently out of the window, to the right. I understood what she meant, that was where the murderer's house stood.

"Then I armed all your field hands and led them over there to exact revenge. We laid the murdered boy on your shield and carried him in our midst to avenge his murder. Rauthgundis came with us, a sword in her hand. We laid the boy down in front of the gate to the villa.

"Calpurnius himself had fled on his swiftest horse to join Belisarius. But his brother and his son and about twenty slaves were in the courtyard; they were about to mount their horses and follow him. We raised the cry of 'Murder!' three times, and broke in.

"We slew every one of them, and then we burned the house down over its inhabitants. Mistress Rauthgundis stood and watched the whole thing, by the side of her child. She stood there, leaning on her sword, keeping watch and never uttering a word. Next day she sent me on ahead to look for you. She followed me soon afterwards, as soon as the little body had been cremated. And since I lost a day because of rebels who tried to bar my way, she could be here at any moment."

"My child, my child, my poor wife! That is the first reward this crown has brought me. And now," he cried out to Hildebrand with all the force of his enormous grief, "you are trying to force me to do that cruel, that unbearable thing!"

Hildebrand rose slowly to his feet. "Nothing is unbearable if it must be borne. Even winter is bearable, and old age, and death. They all come without asking if they are bearable. They come, and we bear them, because we must! But I hear the voices of women, and the rustling of women's clothing. Let's go."

Witigis turned away from him, toward the door.

There, under the door of the tent, dressed in a grey gown and black veil, stood Rauthgundis, his wife, a small urn of black marble pressed close to her breast.

There was a cry of painful love, and of loving pain, and husband and wife were in each other's arms.

Silently the men left the tent.

Chapter 16

Once outside the tent, Teias held the old man back for a moment by his coat sleeve: "You are tormenting the king for nothing," he said. "He will never agree to it. In any case he cannot, certainly not now."

"How do you know…?" the old man interrupted.

"Quiet; I sense it, just like I sense all misfortune."

"Then you will realise that he must do it, there is no alternative."

"He himself will never agree to it."

"But – you mean she may do it herself?"

"Perhaps!"

"She will," said Hildebrand.

"Yes, she is a miracle of a woman," Teias concluded.

During the next few days, while the royal couple lived quietly absorbed in their own grief, barely leaving their tent, it so happened that there began to be a lot of contact between the outposts of the king's army and the Gothic garrison in Ravenna. Forced into inactivity by the virtual armistice, both sides spent their time quarrelling and blaming each other for the civil war.

The king's men argued that the garrison had, in time of greatest need, closed the most powerful fortress in the Empire to their elected king. On the other hand the Goths in the city condemned Witigis for not allowing the Amalung princess what they thought was her due.

One day old Count Grippa happened to overhear such a debate as he was doing his rounds on the walls of Ravenna. Suddenly he stepped forward and called out to the men beyond the wall, who were praising their king: "Is that so? Is it also noble and decent that, instead of giving an answer to our message, he storms our walls like a madman? And yet he could so easily have spared all that Gothic blood! All we want is for Matesuentha to be queen. But does that mean he cannot still be king? Is it such a great sacrifice to share his crown and his bed with the most beautiful woman in the world, with the Princess Schoenhaar whose beauty the singers praise in the streets? Was it better for thousands of brave Goths to die instead? Well, let him go on storming if he wants to! We'll soon see what breaks first, these walls or his stubbornness."

These words made a deep impression on the Gothic troops outside the walls. They could think of nothing to say in defence of their king. They knew as little about their king's marriage as the rest of the nation, and even the presence of Rauthgundis in the camp had done little to change that. Indeed the manner of her arrival had hardly been that of a queen. Thus they hurried back to the camp greatly agitated, and told their comrades what they had heard, and how the stubbornness of the king had been the reason so many of their brothers had been sacrificed. "That's why he has kept the message from the city secret!" they shouted.

Soon groups started forming in all corners of the camp, small and quietly at first, but growing larger and noisier, discussing the situation among themselves. It was not long before they openly criticised their king with the frankness which set Germanic peoples of their time apart from the Byzantines, who would never dare to criticise their emperor, even secretly.

There were other factors at work too, such as the retreat from Rome, the disgrace of their defeat outside Ravenna, grief over their sacrificed brothers and anger at the secretive way in which the king had been behaving. Before long a veritable storm of discontent against the king was raging in the camp, which was no less effective for not yet having broken out openly.

Of course this mood within the army did not escape its leaders either, and the threatening words were barely hushed even when they passed a group of men on their rounds through the camp. But there was little they could do about it, because any attempt to punish signs of insurrection would only serve as a catalyst for open rebellion.

Often, when Teias or Hildebad wanted to intervene with a few calming words, old Hildebrand held them back: "Let the flood rise a little more," he said, "and when it is high enough I will stem it. The only danger is…" he mumbled to himself.

"That those in the rebel camp beat us to the punch," Teias interjected.

"Correct, you know all. But that is not very likely just yet. Defectors from the rebel camp tell us that the princess is still steadfastly refusing. She threatens to kill herself rather than become Arahad's wife."

"Pah," Hildebad offered, "I'd be willing to take a chance on that."

"Because you don't know the passionate creature! She is a child of the Amalungs, and she has inherited her grandfather Theodoric's blood and fiery soul. In the end she will give us a bad time of it too."

"Witigis is a rather different suitor to the boy from Asta," Teias whispered.

"I think I'd count on that too," Hildebad added.

"Let him have a few more days of peace," the old man advised. "he has to come to terms with his own grief first, and there is nothing we can do with him until then. Don't disturb him now, and leave him alone in his tent, with his wife. I will be forced to disturb them soon enough as it is."

But the old man was to be compelled to call his king from his grief much sooner than he had thought, and for a very different reason.

The national assembly at Regata had issued a law against any Goth who went over to the Byzantine side, which meant a shameful death for any such defector. Admittedly such cases were rare, but they did occur, particularly in areas where only a few Goths lived among a predominantly Italian population, and where mixed marriages were common. Old Hildebrand bore a particularly violent grudge against these traitors, whom he saw as a disgrace not only to themselves, but to the nation as a whole. He had been the main instigator of the law against defection and desertion, but so far there had been no need to put that law into effect, and many had almost forgotten it. But suddenly the Goths were to be forcibly reminded of it.

Belisarius had not left Rome with his main army, and it was his intention to use that city as the main base for his movements in Italy for a while longer. But Belisarius had sent a number of smaller troop detachments in pursuit of the retreating Goths, to forage and harass them, to create confusion, and in particular to take over the numerous small castles, fortresses and towns where the Italian population had driven out the Barbarians or slain them. Once there was no garrison to keep them in check, the native population was simply encouraged to proclaim allegiance to the "Emperor of the Romans", as he called himself in Greek.

Such happenings occurred almost daily, particularly after the Gothic cause appeared all but lost following the king's retreat from Rome and the revolt in Florence. Many cities and fortresses surrendered to Belisarius, sometimes threatened by the appearance of enemy troops outside their gates, and sometimes not.

As most of these cities preferred to preserve at least the appearance of having been forced to surrender, in the event that the Goths should prove victorious after all and come back, this was another reason why the Byzantine commander-in-chief sent out these small troop detachments. They usually consisted of a mixture of Byzantine troops and Italians, led by defectors who knew the area and local conditions. These small patrols, encouraged by the continuing Gothic retreat, ventured far into the land, and every castle they occupied served as a base for still further forays.

One of these foraging patrols had recently taken the Castellum Marcianum, situated on the top of a rocky plateau near Caesena, not far from the king's camp. Old Hildebrand, to whom Witigis had given the supreme command after he himself was wounded, saw these dangerous enemy gains with anger, and that anger was further aggravated by the treachery of Italian defectors. And as he did not want to use his troops against Ravenna or Duke Guntharis, with whom he still hoped to come to terms peacefully, he resolved to strike a lusty blow against these cheeky foragers.

Scouts had reported that, the day after Rauthgundis arrived in the camp, the new Byzantine garrison in the Castellum Marcianum now even had the temerity to threaten Caesena, an important city in the rear of the main Gothic camp. Fiercely Theodoric's old armourer swore that these cheeky daredevils would be annihilated. He placed himself at the head of a detachment of one thousand cavalry, which left in the direction of Caesena in the still of the night, with straw wrapped around the horses' hooves to muffle them.

The surprise attack was a complete success. The Goths managed to get as far as the forest at the base of the plateau unobserved. Here Hildebrand divided his force in two. One half he dispersed all around the forest. The other half were ordered to dismount, and he led them silently up the rocky slope to the Castellum. The guards were taken by surprise, and the Byzantines, who now faced a vastly superior force, fled down the hill into the forest, where most of them were taken prisoner by the Goths in ambush. Flames from the burning castle illuminated the countryside for miles around.

But there was one small group which retreated fighting across the small river at the base of the rock, across which there was only a very narrow bridge. Here, Hildebrand's mounted Goths in pursuit were held up by just one man; judging by his richly decorated armour he was a leader.

The tall, slim and apparently young warrior – his visor was tightly closed – fought like a desperate man, covering the flight of his own men, and he had already struck down four Goths.

When old Hildebrand reached the spot he watched the uneven contest for a while, and then he called out to the lone warrior: "Give yourself up, brave man! I guarantee your life!"

The Byzantine seemed to be taken aback by the old man's voice, and for an instant he lowered his sword and looked straight at him. But a moment later he leapt forward furiously and then back again, having severed an arm of the leading Goth with his sword. The Goths withdrew a pace or two from this terrible foe. But now Hildebrand became even more angry: "Attack!" he cried, "no more mercy now! Aim with your spears!"

"He is invulnerable against iron!" one of the Goths called out, a cousin of Teias. "I have hit him three times – I can't wound him!"

"You think so, Aligern?" the old man laughed angrily, "let's see if he is invulnerable against stone too."

And with that he hurled his stone throwing-hammer – he was almost the only Goth who still persevered with this ancient heathen weapon – straight at the Byzantine. The mighty stone axe crashed down directly on the proud helmet of the brave warrior, who fell as if he had been struck by lightning. Two men were quickly on the spot and opened the visor of his helmet.

"Master Hildebrand," Aligern called out in surprise, "this is no Byzantine."

"And no Italian either," Gunthamund added.

"Look at his blond hair – he was a Goth!" Hunibad offered. Hildebrand drew closer – and stopped with a start.

"Torches," the old man cried, "bring some light… Yes," he said fiercely, picking up his stone hammer, "he was a Goth. And I – I killed him," he added with icy calm in his voice. But his fist trembled somewhat as it gripped the shaft of the hammer.

"No Sir," Aligern cried, "he is alive. He was only knocked out. He is opening his eyes."

"He is alive?" the old man asked with a shudder, "the gods can't want that!"

"Yes, he is alive!" the Goths repeated, sitting the man upright.

"Then woe betide him and me! But no! The Gothic gods have placed him in my power! Tie him to your horse, Gunthamund, firmly! And if he gets away it will be your head instead of his. Let's go!"

Back at the camp Gunthamund asked the old armourer what was to be done with the prisoner.

"Give him a bundle of straw for tonight," the latter replied, "and prepare the gallows for him in the morning." With these words he went to the king's tent and reported the success of his mission.

"We have among the prisoners," he concluded gloomily, "a Gothic deserter. He must hang before sunset tomorrow."

"That is very sad," Witigis replied with a sigh.

"Yes, but it is necessary. I will call the council of war to judge him in the morning. Do you want to take the chair?"

"No," said Witigis, "I'd rather not. I will have Hildebad act in my stead."

"No," the old man replied, "that is not right. As long as you lie here in the tent I am commander-in-chief, and it is my duty as well as my right to lead the council."

Witigis looked at him: "You look angry, and cold! Is he an old enemy of your family?"

"No!" Hildebrand replied.

"What is the prisoner's name?"

"Hildebrand, like mine."

"Listen, you seem to hate this Hildebrand! You may judge him, but beware of excessive severity. Remember that I like to exercise mercy wherever possible."

"The welfare of the Goths demands that he dies," Hildebrand replied calmly, "and he will die."

Chapter 17

Early next morning the prisoner was led to a meadow in the north, with his head concealed. This was the "cold corner" of the camp, where the leaders and many of the soldiers had gathered.

"Listen," the prisoner said to one of the guards, "is old Hildebrand present on the site of the *Ting*?"

"He is the head of the *Ting*."

"They are Barbarians, and will always remain Barbarians! Do me a favour friend – I'll give you this purple scarf in return – and go to the old man. Tell him I know I must die. But I would like to save myself and my family – did you get that? My family! – the disgrace of the gallows. Ask him to send me a weapon secretly." The Goth, it was Gunthamund, went looking for the old armourer, who had already opened the *Ting*. The procedure was very simple. The old man had the law passed at Regata read out loud first, then had witnesses describe how they caught the prisoner, and then he had the prisoner himself brought forward, his head and shoulders still concealed by a woollen sack. The Goths were just about to remove it when Gunthamund made his way to Hildebrand's side and whispered something in his ear.

"No," the old man said aloud, frowning. "Tell him that the disgrace to his family is what he did, not the punishment for it." Then, turning to the crowd, he added in a loud voice: "Show them the traitor's face! It is Hildebrand, son of Hildegis!"

A cry of astonishment and horror went through the crowd.

"His own grandson!"

"Old man, you must not go on judging here! You are being cruel against your own flesh and blood!" Hildebad cried, jumping to his feet.

"All I am doing is to exercise justice, which is the same for everyone," Hildebrand replied icily, stamping his staff on the ground.

"Poor Witigis!" Teias whispered to himself.

But Hildebad sprang to his feet and hurried to the camp.

"What do you have to say in your defence, Hildebrand, son of Hildegis?" the old man asked the prisoner.

The prisoner hastily stepped forward, his face red with anger rather than shame, but without even a trace of fear. His long yellow hair was fluttering in the wind. The crowd was carried away by sympathy; news of his courageous fight had already become common knowledge, and now his youth, his good looks and not least his identity said much in his favour. He allowed his eyes to roam over the crowd, and then proudly looked the old man straight in the eye: "I condemn this court! Your laws do not affect me! I am a Roman, not a Goth! My father died before I was born, and my mother was a Roman, the noble Cloelia. I have never regarded this barbaric old man as being a relation of mine, and I despise his severity as much as I reject his love. He forced his name on me, a defenceless child, and took me away from my mother by force. As soon as I could I ran away from him. I have never called myself Hildebrand, for my name has always been Flavius Cloelius. My friends are Roman, my thoughts have always been Roman, and my life is Roman. All my friends joined Belisarius and Cethegus; was I to be the only one not to do so? Kill me if you like! You can and I have no doubt you will. But at least admit that it is murder, not justice. You are not sitting in judgment over a Goth, you are murdering a Roman, because my soul is and always will be Roman."

The crowd heard this defence in silence, and with mixed feelings.

But then the old man rose to his feet wrathfully once more. His eyes spewed fire, and his hand shook with anger. "Miserable wretch!" he shouted, "you are the son of a Gothic man, that much you admit. Therefore you are a Goth, and if you regard yourself as a Roman then that alone is reason enough why you should die! Take him, *sajones*, to the gallows!"

At that the prisoner stepped forward once more: "Be cursed then, you nation of crude animals! I curse all of you, Barbarians that you are, and you most of all, you old man with the heart of a wolf! Never think that your savagery and cruelty are any credit to you, Goths, nor will they do you any good! You will be swept away out of this beautiful country, and not a trace will remain to say you were ever here."

Upon a signal from the old man the *sajones* threw the sack over his head once more and led him away to a hill, where a large oak tree had been bared of its leaves and branches. And then the eyes of the crowd were distracted in the direction of the camp, from which the sound of hooves was rapidly approaching.

It was a group of horsemen with the royal banner, Witigis and Hildebad in the lead. "Stop!" the king's voice called from afar. "Spare Hildebrand's grandson! Mercy! Mercy!"

But the old man pointed to the hill. "Too late, king!" he cried out aloud. "The traitor is dead, and that is a fate which must befall any of us who forget our nation. The nation comes first, King Witigis, and after that come wife and child and grandchild."

This action on the part of old Hildebrand had a great effect on the army, and an even greater one on the king. Witigis could feel the added weight which any demand the old man made would now have, as a result of his own personal sacrifice. And so he returned to his tent with the knowledge that putting up any resistance would now be much more difficult. Hildebrand did not waste the opportunity to exploit his advantage, and the mood of the moment. That evening he went, with Teias, to the king's tent.

Husband and wife were sitting silently on the camp bed, hand in hand. The little black urn stood on the table before them, and beside it lay a small golden capsule made like an amulet, with a blue ribbon. A small Roman lamp gave a dim light. As Hildebrand shook the king's hand the latter looked him in the face; one look was enough to tell him that the old man had come with the firm resolve to enforce his will now, whatever the price.

Those in the tent seemed to be silently shuddering at the mental struggle and anguish about to take place.

"Mistress Rauthgundis," the old man began, "I have difficult matters to discuss with the king, and it will offend you to hear them."

The woman rose, but not in order to leave. A look of deep sorrow and great love for her husband lent her features a kind of solemn nobility. Without removing her hand from that of her husband she laid her other hand on his shoulder.

"Go ahead, Hildebrand, I am his wife, and I demand to bear half of whatever it is you have to say."

"Mistress…" the old man warned again.

"Let her stay," said the king, "are you afraid to tell her to her face what you have in mind?"

"Afraid? No! I would say it to a god, face to face, that the Gothic nation means more to me than you. So hear me then…"

"What? You are going to say it? Spare her, spare her," said Witigis, placing a protective arm around his wife.

But Rauthgundis looked him straight in the eye and said: "I know everything, my Witigis. As I was walking through the camp last night, unrecognised in the darkness, I heard your soldiers speaking critically of you, and praising this old man here. I listened, and I heard everything he is demanding of you, which you have refused."

"And you said nothing?"

"What for? There is no danger, because I know that you will not send your wife away, not for a crown and not for a bewitchingly beautiful girl. Who can part us? Let this old man threaten! I know full well that no star in heaven is more secure than I am in your heart."

This confidence had its effect on the old man, and he knitted his brow: "It is not you I have to reason with, Witigis. I ask you here, in front of Teias. You know how things are. Without Ravenna we are lost, and only Matesuentha's hand will open Ravenna to you. Are you going to take that hand or not?"

At that Witigis rose to his feet: "Our enemies are right when they call us Barbarians! Look at this magnificent woman here, in her grief and unsurpassed in loyalty, standing opposite this heartless old man. And in front of him is the urn with the ashes of our murdered child. And now he tries, with all his might, to drag the husband away from this poor woman, and from these ashes, into a new marriage. No! Never!"

"An hour ago representatives from every unit of the army were on their way to your tent," the old man replied. "They meant to enforce what I am asking of you. I held them off only with great difficulty."

"Let them come!" Witigis cried, "they can only take my crown, not my wife."

"He who wears a crown no longer belongs to himself, but to his people."

Witigis grasped the crown helmet and laid it on the table in front of Hildebrand: "Here, once more and for the last time, I give this crown back to you all. God knows I never wanted it. It has brought me nothing but these ashes here. Take it back, and let whoever wants to do so marry Matesuentha and be king."

But Hildebrand shook his head. "You know that will lead to certain disaster. We are already split into three parties. Many thousands would never recognise Arahad. You alone are what is holding everything together. If you go, then we will fall apart like a bundle of twigs, which Belisarius will snap in two one by one, with playful ease. Is that what you want?"

"Rauthgundis, are you not able to make a sacrifice for your nation?" Teias now said, stepping closer.

"Noble Teias, are you also against me now? Is that what you call friendship?"

"Rauthgundis," the latter replied calmly, "I hold you in the highest esteem, above all other women. That is why I am now asking of you what I would ask of no lesser mortal."

Hildebrand began once more: "You are the queen of this nation. I know of a Gothic queen from the heathen times of our ancestors. Her people were suffering with hunger and pestilence, and their swords were not victorious. The gods were angry with the Goths. Then Swanhild asked the oaks of the forest and the waves of the sea for advice, and they whispered to her: 'If Swanhild dies the Goths will live, and if Swanhild lives her people die.' Swanhild did not even turn for home one last time. She thanked the gods and leapt into the waves. But of course that was in heathen times."

Rauthgundis was not unmoved. "I love my people," she said, "and since nothing remains of Athalwin but a lock of his hair here in this capsule, I too would be willing to give my life for my people. I am willing to die, yes," she cried, "but to live and to know that this man of my heart loves another – no!"

"Loves another?" Witigis cried passionately, "how can you even speak like that? Don't you know that this tortured heart of mine now beats only to hear the beautiful sound of your name? Have you not felt, even as we stand here beside this urn, that our hearts will always be one? What am I without your love? Tear my heart out of my chest and give me another one in its place; then, perhaps, I will let go of Rauthgundis. Indeed," he called out to the two men, "you are both fools, and you don't know what you are doing. You are so foolish that you do not even know that my love for this woman, and her love for me, are by far the best part of poor Witigis. She is my good star! If there is anything worthy about me, then it is her you must thank for it. She is the one I think of in the thick of battle, and her image before my eyes gives strength to my arm. And when I need to find the best and noblest solution to a problem of government I think of her, of her calm and clear soul and mind, and of her utter loyalty and goodness. Oh – this woman is my life and my soul; take her away and your king will be but a shadow whom both luck and strength have deserted!"

With that the king wrapped his arms around Rauthgundis, deeply moved. She was quite astonished, almost shocked. Never before had this steady, solid man, who liked to keep his feelings and his love to himself, spoken like this of her and his love for her. Not even when he was courting had he shown such passion, and yet now that he was about to lose her it came to the surface with a vengeance.

Shaken and very deeply moved she returned her husband's embrace. "Thank you, thank you for this painful hour," she whispered. "Yes, now I know it, your heart and soul are for ever mine."

"And will remain yours," said Teias softly, "even if another woman is called his queen. She will share only his crown, never his heart."

These words had a profound effect on Rauthgundis, and she looked up at Teias, her eyes wide open.

Hildebrand noticed this, and thought the time ripe to strike his main blow: "Who could ever touch your hearts?" he said, "you would indeed be a shadow bereft of luck or strength if you refuse what I am asking and thereby break your sacred oath, for he who breaks his oath is less than a shadow."

"His oath?" Rauthgundis asked, trembling, "What have you sworn?"

But Witigis sank back on the seat, hiding his face in his hands.

"What did he swear?" she repeated.

And then Hildebrand spoke slowly and deliberately, aiming every word at the hearts of the hapless couple: "It was a few years ago when a man, with four friends, entered a powerful covenant at midnight. Under a holy oak tree the turf was cut open and he swore by the ancient earth, the flowing water, the flickering flame and the light air. And they let their red blood mingle, so that they became brothers for ever and a day.

"They swore a solemn oath to sacrifice their all: son and family, life and limb, wife and weapons for the well-being and the glory of the Gothic nation. And if one of the brothers ever refused to honour his oath, whatever sacrifice it might bring, then his blood was to flow un-avenged as the water flowed under the turf in the forest. The halls of heaven were to thunder down upon his head and crush him. And he who should forget his oath, or who would not sacrifice everything for the good of the Goths when the need was there and a brother urged him, he shall be for ever in the power of the dark forces who live beneath the earth. Good people shall walk over the head of the worthless one, and his memory shall vanish without trace. If anyone should think of him he should do so with a curse, and his soul shall be condemned to eternal torture. And his name shall be without honour as far as the wind blows over the wide world, wherever Christians go to church or heathens make sacrifices.

"Thus five men swore that night, and they were Hildebrand and Hildebad, Totila and Teias. And who was the fifth? He was Witigis, Waltari's son."

Quickly the old man brushed back the king's gown over his left wrist. "Look, Rauthgundis, the scar from that cut is still there. But the oath has vanished from his soul, the oath he swore before he became king.

"And when the Gothic men in their thousands raised him on the shield at Regata, he swore a second oath: 'I dedicate to you, my Gothic people, my life, my happiness, my everything; I swear it by the highest god in heaven and on my honour'. Now, Witigis, Waltari's son, King of the Goths, I remind you of that double oath in this grave hour of need. I now ask of you, are you willing to sacrifice everything, like you swore, your happiness and your wife, for the welfare of the Gothic nation?

"I too have lost three sons for this nation. And I have sacrificed my grandson, the last male member of my family. Without so much as batting an eyelid I sentenced him to die, for the sake of the Gothic nation. Will you now keep your oath and do the same? Or will you break it and be without honour among the living and cursed among the dead? Speak, which do you choose?"

Witigis writhed in agony at the terrible old man's words.

And then Rauthgundis rose to her feet. With her left hand on the heart of her husband she raised her right against Hildebrand as if fending him off, and she said: "Stop, leave him alone! It is enough, and has been for a long time now. He will do what you demand. He will not break his oath and be without honour among his people because of his wife."

But Witigis jumped to his feet and embraced his wife as if she was about to be torn from him that very instant.

"Go now," she said to the men, "leave me alone with him."

Teias turned to go, but Hildebrand hesitated.

"Go," she said again. "I promise you on my child's ashes, when the sun rises in the morning he will be free," and she laid her hand on the urn.

"No!" Witigis cried, "I will not drive my wife away! Never!"

"You won't have to. It is not you who is driving me away; I am leaving you. Rauthgundis will go, to save the honour of her people and her husband. Your heart will always be mine, I know that, and after today it will be mine more than ever. Now go! That which needs to take place between us now is for nobody to witness."

The two men left the tent in silence, and they walked quietly together along the camp lane. At the corner the old man stopped.

"Good night, Teias," he said, "now it is done."

"Yes, but who knows if it was for the best? That was a noble, a very noble sacrifice, and it will be followed by many more. And yet, it seems to me to be written in the stars up there that it is all in vain! But we still have our honour to preserve, even if victory is to be denied us. Farewell!"

With that he wrapped his dark cloak about his shoulders and vanished like a shadow into the night.

BOOK SIX

Witigis – Part Two

Chapter 1

On his arrival back at the camp King Witigis found everything in a state of utmost confusion, and the urgent necessities of the moment forced him to forget his grief and gave him plenty to do.

He found the army in complete disarray, and divided into several factions. He could see clearly that total collapse of the Gothic cause would have been the result if he had laid down the crown or abandoned the army.

Several groups were ready to be on their way immediately. Some wanted to join old Count Grippa in Ravenna, some wanted to join the rebel camp, and others were about to leave Italy by fleeing northwards across the Alps. Finally, there was no shortage of those who urged for the election of a new king, and even in this there was no agreement, and various factions stood facing each other threateningly.

Hildebrand and Hildebad were still able to hold together those elements who would not believe that their king had fled. The old armourer had declared that, if the king had indeed fled, then he would not rest until he too had ended like his predecessor Theodahad. Hildebad severely reprimanded anyone who dared suggest that Witigis would do such a thing. Between them Hildebad and Hildebrand had occupied the roads into both the city and the rebel camp, and they threatened to use force of arms if necessary to stop any movement in either direction. Meanwhile Duke Guntharis had also heard of the confusion and was slowly moving against the royalist camp.

Everywhere he went Witigis met restless masses, departing fragments of the army, threats, insults and arms raised threateningly. A bloodbath could break out in any corner of the camp at any moment. Quickly he made up his mind as to what had to be done; he hurried back to his tent, put on the crown helmet and took the golden sceptre in one hand. Then he mounted the mighty warhorse Boreas and rode off through the camp lanes, followed by Teias who was carrying the blue royal banner of Theodoric above his head.

In the middle of the camp he met a mob of men, women and children (these were quite usual in a Gothic people's army) slowly moving towards the western entrance to the camp.

"Let us out!" the crowd yelled. "The king has fled, the war is over and everything is lost. We just want to save our lives!"

"The king is not a fool like you," Hildebad replied, pushing the leader back.

"He is a traitor," the man cried, "who has abandoned and betrayed us over a few women's tears."

"Yes," cried another one, "he slaughtered three thousand of our brothers and then he ran away!"

"What you are saying is a lie," a calm voice replied, and Witigis came around a corner of the lane.

"Hail King Witigis!" the giant Hildebad rejoiced, "Can you see him there? Haven't I been telling you? But it is time you came, or things might have become grim."

Then Hildebrand came galloping from the right with a few horsemen. "Hail to you, King, and glory to the crown on your helmet! Ride through the camp, heralds, and tell everyone what you have seen. Then let the people cry out aloud: 'Hail King Witigis, the loyal one!' "

But Witigis turned away from him sadly.

The heralds shot away like arrows, and in a few moments the cry rose like thunder from every point in the camp: "Hail King Witigis!" and even those who had been quarrelling only moments before were now united in the cry: "Hail King Witigis!"

His eyes scanned the thousands before him with the pride only great suffering can bring. And behind him Teias said softly: "You see, you have saved the Empire."

"Come, lead us to victory!" Hildebad cried. "Guntharis and Arahad are approaching. They think that they will find us leaderless, and they hope to take us by surprise while we are quarrelling among ourselves. They will soon realise they have made a terrible mistake. Let us go and attack them now! Down with the rebels!"

"Down with the rebels!" the soldiers repeated, glad to have found an outlet for their pent-up feelings.

But the king calmly bade them to desist. "Silent! No more shall Gothic blood flow as a result of Gothic arms. Wait here, men. Hildebad, open the gate for me. Nobody is to follow me, I will go to the rebel camp alone. You, Count Teias, will command the camp until I return. And you, Hildebrand," he raised his voice, "ride over to the gates of Ravenna and tell all men there to open their gates to us. Their request is granted, and we will move into Ravenna before nightfall, we, King Witigis and Queen Matesuentha."

He spoke these words so forcefully and so solemnly that the men received them with silent respect.

Hildebad opened the gate; rows of rebels could be seen approaching rapidly in closed formation, and as the gate opened their war cry could be heard far and wide.

King Witigis handed his sword to Teias and slowly rode out to meet the rebels. The gate closed behind him.

"He is seeking death," Hildebrand whispered.

"No," Teias replied, "he is seeking the welfare of the Goths, and he will bring it back with him."

The enemy troops hesitated uncertainly when they recognised the lone rider. Next to the Woelsung brothers, who were riding in the lead, rode a leader of the Avar mercenaries whom the rebels had hired, armed with bows and arrows. The latter now shaded his sharp little eyes with his hand and cried: "By the stallion horse god, that's the king himself! Now boys, aim like you have never aimed before, and the war will be over!" And he tore his small bow from his shoulder.

"Stop, Khan Warchun!" Duke Guntharis said, placing his heavily armed hand on his shoulder. "You have just made two serious mistakes in the one breath. First you called Count Witigis a king, but I'll forgive you for that. And then you want to murder someone who approaches us unarmed, as an envoy. That may be customary among the Avars, but it is not so with us Goths. Leave my camp with your men at once!"

The Khan was taken aback and looked at Guntharis in astonishment: "What? Now? Straight away?"

"Yes, now!" Duke Guntharis repeated.

The Avar laughed and motioned to his men: "It's all the same to me. Come, children, we'll go and join Belisarius. Strange people, these Goths! Bodies like giants and hearts like children!"

Meanwhile Witigis had reached them. Guntharis and Arahad mustered him with searching eyes. Apart from the old simple dignity which Witigis had always possessed, there was now also a new majesty, that of extreme pain manfully endured.

"I have come to speak to you for the sake of the Goths. Let brothers kill each other no more! Let us move into Ravenna together, and then jointly fight Belisarius. I will marry Matesuentha, and the two of you shall be the two men nearest to my throne."

"Never!" Arahad cried passionately.

"You are forgetting," Duke Guntharis said proudly, "that your bride is in our camp."

"Duke Guntharis of Tuscany, I could respond by saying that we too will soon be in your camp. We are more numerous than you, and no less brave. Furthermore, Duke Guntharis, right is on our side. I do not wish to speak to you in this manner. But I do want to remind you that it is the welfare of the Gothic nation which is at stake here. Even if you should win you would be too weak to defeat Belisarius alone. We are only barely strong enough for that together. Give in!"

"No, you give in!" the Woelsung replied. "If you are so concerned about the welfare of the Gothic nation then lay down that crown. Can you not make a sacrifice for your nation?"

"I can, and I have. Do you have a wife, oh Guntharis?"

"I have a wife, who is very precious to me."

"Very well. I too had a very precious wife. I have sacrificed her for my people. I have let her go so I can marry Matesuentha."

Duke Guntharis was silent. But Arahad cried: "Then you did not love her!"

At that Witigis rose up in the saddle, his grief and his love growing to giant proportions. His face glowed in anger, and he cast a devastating look at the shocked youth: "Do not prattle about love, and don't blaspheme, you foolish boy! Because you see red lips and white limbs in your dreams you dare speak of love? What do you know of the loss which that woman means to me, the mother of my dear slain child! She was a whole world of love and faithfulness. Don't anger me, boy, for my soul is still wounded. I have only been able to contain my grief and my despair with great difficulty. Don't anger me so that they break out anew!"

Duke Guntharis had become very thoughtful. "I know you, Witigis, from the war against the Gepidae. Never have I seen a commoner strike such aristocratic blows! I know that there is nothing false in you, and I know how love binds a man to a lawful wife. And you have sacrificed your wife for your people? Then you have sacrificed a great deal!"

"Brother!" cried Arahad, "what are you saying? What have you in mind?"

"I have in mind that I will not see the house of the Woelsungs shamed in matters of honour and decency. Noble birth, Arahad, demands noble deeds! Tell me one more thing: why did you not sacrifice your crown, or indeed your life, rather than give up the wife you love?"

"Because it would have meant the certain demise of the Empire. Twice I wanted to surrender the crown to Count Arahad, and twice the leaders of my army swore that they would never recognise him. Three or four alternative kings might have been chosen, but I give you my word: Count Arahad would never have been recognised.

And so I tore my precious wife from my bleeding heart. Now, Duke Guntharis, it is your turn to think of the Gothic nation. The noblest bloom on the tree will die with the tree, once Belisarius lays an axe to its roots. I have given up my wife, the crown of my life. Can you not give up the hope of wearing a crown?"

"They shall not sing in Gothic halls that the commoner Witigis was more noble than the first among the nobility! The war is over! I honour you, my king!" And the proud Duke went down on his knee before Witigis, who raised him to his feet and embraced him.

"Brother, brother! What are you doing to me? What a disgrace!" Arahad cried.

"I consider it an honour!" Guntharis replied calmly. "And as a token that my king sees what I have done not as cowardice but as a noble gesture of homage, I ask a favour from him now. Our family has for generations been displaced from its rightful place in the nation by the Amalungs and the Balti."

"You have regained that place in this hour," Witigis replied. "The Goths shall never forget that it was the noble-minded Woelsungs who saved them from civil war."

"And to signify that fact I now ask of you that you grant us the right to carry the Gothic banner before the army in every battle from this day onward."

"So be it!" the king replied, shaking his hand. "Nobody could carry out that task more nobly or more worthily."

"Very well, now let us go to Matesuentha," Guntharis said.

"Matesuentha!" Arahad cried, who had until now been watching the reconciliation as if in a trance, as it put an end to all his hopes and aspirations. "Matesuentha!" he repeated, "You have reminded me just in time! You can take the crown from me, I don't care about that, but not my love, nor my duty to protect my beloved. She turned me down, but I love her to the death. I have protected her from my brother, who tried to force her to become mine. No less will I now defend her if you both try to force her to become the wife of our hated enemy. Her hand, more precious than any crown, shall remain for ever free!" Quickly he swung himself on his horse and galloped away at full speed toward the camp.

Witigis watched him depart with concern. "Let him go," said Duke Guntharis, "united we have nothing to fear. Let us go to reconcile our armies, as their leaders have become reconciled."

So Guntharis first led the king around among his own men and urged them to pay him homage, as he himself had done, and which they did gladly. Then Witigis took the Duke and his leaders over to his own camp with him, where the king's verbal victory over the proud Duke was considered by the royalist Goths to be a miracle of diplomacy.

Meanwhile Arahad had assembled a small force of about a hundred loyal followers from among the vanguard of the rebel army, and he now rode back to his own camp with these men as quickly as he could.

A short time later he stood before Matesuentha's tent, and she rose with displeasure as he entered. "Do not be angry, Queen! This time you have no right to be. Arahad comes to perform the last duty of his love. Flee, you must follow me." And in the heat of the moment he reached out for her small white hand.

Matesuentha took a step backwards and placed a hand on the broad golden belt which held her garments together. "Flee?" she said, "flee to where?"

"Across the sea! Over the Alps! It does not matter, to freedom! Because the greatest danger now threatens that very freedom."

"My freedom is threatened only by you and your brother."

"Not by me any more! And I can no longer protect you. As long as you were to become mine, I could protect you, and I could honour your wishes even where that meant being cruel to myself. But now…"

"But now?" Matesuentha asked, growing pale.

"They have destined you for another. My brother, my army and my enemies both in the royalist camp and in Ravenna, they are all agreed! Soon a thousand voices will call you to the bridal altar as a sacrifice. I cannot bear to think about it! Your soul, and your beauty, defiled as a sacrifice to a loveless marriage!"

"Let them come," Matesuentha replied, "we will see if they can force me!" And she grasped the dagger which she wore in her belt firmly in her hand. "Who is the new despot who threatens me?"

"Do not ask!" Arahad cried, "your enemy, who is not worthy of you, and who does not love you; he – follow me! Flee, I can already hear them coming!" Indeed the sound of hooves could be heard approaching.

"I will stay here. Who would dare to try and take Theodoric's grandchild by force?"

"No! You must not fall into their unfeeling hands, where you will not be loved. They don't love you, but only your beauty and your right to the crown! Follow me…"

At that moment the curtain of the tent was drawn aside, and Count Teias entered. He was accompanied by two Gothic boys, dressed festively in white silk.

They were carrying a purple cushion, covered by a small silken veil. He advanced to the centre of the tent and bent his knee before Matesuentha. Like the boys he was wearing a garland of evergreen rue leaves about his helmet. But his eyes and his voice were solemn as he spoke: "I greet you, Queen of the Goths and the Italians!"

She mustered him with astonished eyes. Teias rose, stepped back to the boys, and took a golden tiara and another evergreen garland from the cushion. Handing them to her he said: "I hand you the bridal garland and the crown, Matesuentha, and I now invite you to your wedding and your coronation. Your litter stands ready for you."

Arahad went for his sword.

"Who sends you?" Matesuentha asked. Her heart was beating furiously while her hand clutched the dagger.

"Who else but Witigis, the King of the Goths."

At those words Matesuentha's glorious eyes flashed with ecstasy; she raised both arms to heaven and said: "Thank you, heaven, your stars do not lie, and nor did my heart. I knew it well." And then she grasped the glittering diadem with both hands and pressed it firmly into her fiery red hair. "I am ready, lead me," she said, "to your master, and mine." And she took the arm of Teias with her left hand in a royal gesture. Teias respectfully led her outside.

But Arahad stared after the disappearing woman speechless, his hand still on the hilt of his sword. Finally Euric, one of his followers, went to him and laid a hand on his shoulder: "What now?" he asked, "the horses are ready and waiting. Where to?"

"Where to?" Arahad replied, rousing himself. "Where to? There is only one way left open to us, and we will take it. Where can I find the Byzantines and death?"

Chapter 2

On the seventh day following these events a magnificent feast was about to get under way in the forum and the royal palace of Ravenna.

The citizens of Ravenna, as well as Goths from all three parties, were surging through the streets and the canals – in those days Ravenna was a city of canals not unlike Venice today – in order to admire the huge garlands, arches of flowers, and flags which were flying from every rooftop. This was going to be the occasion for celebrating the marriage of the Gothic royal couple.

Early in the morning the entire Gothic army had held a solemn gathering outside the city walls. The king and queen appeared on milk white horses, and dismounted before all the people. They then stepped under a huge stone oak, and there Witigis had placed his right hand on his bride's head, while she placed her left foot into his golden shoe. With that their marriage was concluded according to ancient Gothic custom, and the soldiers cheered in their thousands. The couple then entered a carriage decorated with green branches, and drawn by four white steers. The king swung the whip, and thus they drove into the city followed by the army. There a second ceremony, a Christian marriage, followed the earlier partly heathen Germanic one. The Arian bishop blessed the couple in the Basilica Sancti Vitalis and they exchanged rings.

Nobody thought about Rauthgundis.

The church was not yet powerful enough to enforce its requirement that a marriage could not be dissolved; wealthy Romans and certainly Germanic peoples still often divorced their wives at will. Thus if a king chose to do the same in the national interest, and without objection from his wife, then that was unlikely to cause any opposition.

From the church the procession moved on to the palace, where a magnificent feast had been prepared in the halls and in the gardens.

Here the whole Gothic army and the entire population of Ravenna were feasted magnificently, in the Forum of Hercules and the Forum of Honorius, in the streets surrounding the palace and on a number of ships at anchor in the port. Meanwhile the Gothic leaders and the nobles of the city dined with the royal couple in the garden rotunda or in the great drinking hall which Theodoric had added to the old Roman palace.

However little the situation in the country and the king's mood were suited to feasting, it was necessary to reconcile the citizens of Ravenna with the Goths, and the various Gothic factions with one another; it was hoped that the wine of the feast might wash away the last traces of animosity.

The best view of the royal table and the other festivities in the garden and the park could be had from a small room which had been chosen as Matesuentha's bridal chamber. Its only window looked out over the garden, and beyond the garden to the sea.

Aspa, the faithful Numidian slave girl, had requested the right to decorate this room as her reward for long and faithful service, and for three days already she had been busying herself there. She said: "Neither these gloomy Romans nor those ruffian Goths know how to prepare a bridal bed for the most beautiful woman in the world, but in Africa, the land of miracles, we know about these things."

And how well she had succeeded, even if it was in the fantastic manner of her own country. She had converted the small chamber into a world of fantasy. The walls and ceiling were lined with white marble, but Aspa had covered the whole of the walls and ceiling with several layers of red silk. Together with the thick carpets on the floor these muffled every sound, so that one could walk through the room in total silence. Only the window sill showed some white marble to contrast with the red silk.

Across the window she had hung a curtain of yellow silk, and all the light in the little room came from a small lamp hanging from the ceiling in the centre of the room; it consisted of a silver dove with wings of gold, flying from a vase filled with flowers. In its claws the dove carried a shallow bowl made from a single piece of chalcedony, a gift from the Vandal kings regarded as a rare piece.

In this bowl a little red flame was burning, fed by strongly aromatic cedar oil. The lamp cast a dreamy half light over a fairytale double bed standing under it, which was half covered in flowers. Aspa had created the bridal bed as the two halves of an open seashell, joined in the middle. The two oval halves of the bed, which was made of citrus wood, rose only a few inches above the carpeted floor, and a lined linen bedspread had been arranged over the pillows and rugs, giving the whole an orange golden glow.

But the real ornamentation in the room was the abundance of flowers, which Aspa's imaginative hand had arranged and strewn throughout the entire room in accordance with her own peculiarly exotic taste. Even the walls, blankets, doors and of course the bed itself were covered in flowers. There were the laurels and oleander of Italy, Sicilian myrtle, beautiful alpine rhododendrons and magnificent irises from Africa; every single bloom had been carefully arranged in just the right spot, and yet it seemed that they had all blown there by accident. On either side of the bed stood a large rose tree, and the red and white blooms on the trees added to the multitude of flowers on the bed and on the carpets. Last but not least an arch of fragrant honeysuckle decorated the door, which was the only entrance to the room. Everywhere the eye might rest, a flower had been skilfully placed.

The stars were already in the sky, and outside it was getting dark. In the room Aspa had lit the little lamp, and was now busy putting the last touches to the room, smoothing a fold here, adjusting a flower there. Meanwhile a Roman slave girl was cooling the wine with snow on a bronze table, while another sprayed balsam through the room.

"A bit more on the myrtle there, like this!" Aspa said, spraying a generous libation across the bed.

"Stop!" the Roman girl protested, "it is enough. Just the fragrance of the flowers alone is enough to stun the senses, and the roses and the honeysuckle are almost overpowering. I would get dizzy in here."

"Ah," Aspa laughed, "what did the poet say? Happiness never comes to those who are sober, but approaches only in the intoxication of ecstasy. Let's close the window now."

"Let me just watch a little longer," a third slave girl begged, "it is just too beautiful! Come, Frithilo," she said to a Gothic maid standing next to her, "you know all those proud men and women down there. Tell me, who is that on the king's left, in the golden armour? He is drinking to the king's health."

"That is Duke Guntharis of Tuscany, the Woelsung. But I wonder where his brother is in this hour, Count Arahad of Asta."

"And the old one next to the king, with the grey beard?"

"That's Count Grippa, who commands the Gothic garrison in Ravenna. He is talking to the queen. How she is laughing and blushing! She has never looked so beautiful."

"But the bridegroom is a fine looking man too – what a magnificent man! The head of Mars, but the neck of Neptune. But he does not look happy. A little while ago he was staring into his goblet for a long time, and knitting his brow – the queen saw it – until old Hildebrand called out to him from the other side of the table. That caused him to look up with a sigh. What could a man possibly have to sigh about, next to that goddess of a woman?"

"Well," the Gothic girl replied, "perhaps his heart is not made of stone after all. Perhaps he is thinking of the other one, his rightful wife before God and man, whom he sent away."

"What? What did you say?" the other three girls asked at once.

But suddenly Aspa flew right between the girls: "Will you stop that foolish talk at once, Barbarian! Be on your way! One such word, even one syllable where the queen can hear it, and you will have reason to remember me!"

Frithilo wanted to reply. "Quiet," one of the Roman girls cried, "the queen is leaving."

"She will be coming up here."

"The king is staying behind, only the women are following her."

Soon the procession approached, led by torchbearers and flautists. After them followed a number of Gothic noblewomen, among them Treudigotho, the wife of Duke Guntharis, who walked beside the bride, and Hildiko, Count Grippa's daughter. Ravenna's noblewomen concluded the procession.

When they reached the threshold of the bridal chamber Matesuentha took her leave from her following, handing her veil to the young girls and her belt to the older women.

Most of them went back to the feast in the garden, and some went home. But six Gothic ladies, three women and three maidens, settled down as guard of honour outside the bridal chamber, where rugs had been made ready for them. Gothic custom demanded that they spend the night there, together with an equal number of Gothic men who would accompany the groom.

When Matesuentha entered the room she could not contain a gasp of astonishment. "Aspa," she cried, "you have done this just beautifully. It is a miracle!"

The African crossed her arms over her chest and, delighted at her mistress's pleasure, bowed before her.

The bride drew her to her bosom and whispered: "You knew what was in my heart and my dreams! But," she continued with a deep breath, "how oppressive it is in here! You gorgeous flowers are enough to intoxicate me."

"The gods come in the fiery intoxication of ecstasy!" Aspa replied.

"How lovely those violets are, and that purple lily there; it's as if the goddess Flora flew through this room thinking a lovely dream of love, and lost her most beautiful flowers as she passed through. I feel as if I am experiencing a miracle of revelation here, and it is running over me hot and strong. But it is humid in here. Help me remove the heavy crown and the jewellery." And with this she removed the heavy crown from her hair.

Aspa combed her rich red tresses behind her ears, and removed the golden needle which had held them together behind her head. The other slaves removed the golden clasp, shaped like a coiled snake, which held her heavy gold embroidered purple gown over her left shoulder. The gown fell away and revealed the maiden's tall and perfectly proportioned body, now clad only in the sleeveless undergarment of white Persian silk. Her arms were adorned with two heavy golden bracelets, inlaid with emeralds, which were part of the ancient Amalung treasure.

Aspa watched with delight as her mistress stood before the wall mirror, combing her loose hair with a golden comb. "How beautiful you are! How enchantingly beautiful! You are like Astaroth, the goddess of love – never have you been as beautiful as you are at this moment." Matesuentha took a quick look in the mirror. She knew, or rather felt, that Aspa was right, and she blushed.

"Go," she said, "and leave me alone with my happiness." The slave girl obeyed. Matesuentha hurried to the window, which she opened quickly as if trying to escape from her own thoughts. The first man she saw was Witigis, standing in the light of the hanging lamps in the garden below.

"There he is again! Always he! How can I escape from him, from my sweet fate?"

Quickly she turned; there, against the wall immediately opposite the window, stood a white marble bust, glowing in the light from the lamp. She knew the bust well; Aspa had not forgotten the Ares head, which had been her faithful companion during her years of longing. "You again!" the bride whispered, and placed her white hand before her eyes. "And if I close my eyes and look inside me, again I see his picture, nothing but his picture, in the deepest recesses of my heart. That picture will completely possess me yet! Oh, and I so want to be possessed!" she cried softly, standing immediately in front of the bust. "I want to be! How often when night came, my Ares, have I looked up to you like a star, until peace and calm came to me from looking at your strong, great face. And how beautifully this longing and hoping has been fulfilled! He who once dried the tears of a crying child and guided her home, he will now also calm all my fears and build a true home for me in his heart. During all these dull years, through the last few months of fear and danger, I always had that one sure feeling in my heart: It is to be! That which you believe in will happen to you! Your saviour will come, and hold you against his strong chest, so that no danger can threaten you. Oh, unspeakable heavenly mercy, it is true! I am his! Thank you, thank you a thousand times, whatever you are, the power above the stars which guides the fates of people so wonderfully and so kindly. Oh yes, I want to earn this happiness. I want that he should walk in heaven! They say that I am beautiful, and I know that I am, through him. I want to be beautiful, for him! Oh heaven, let me keep my beauty. They say that I have a strong, noble spirit; oh God, give it wings so that I can keep pace with him. But God, let me rid myself of my faults, my fiery temper, my stubbornness and my thirst for freedom. I want only to bow to him, to surrender for ever to my strong and glorious master. Oh Witigis!" she cried and sank to her knees, almost overcome with emotion. Then she looked up at the bust again, tears in her eyes. "I am yours! Do what you will with me and with my soul! Destroy me if that is your wish! But admit that you are happy, happy through me."

And she bent her beautiful head to her folded white hands.

Then, suddenly, she rose with a start. A strong light was flooding into the room. The king was standing at the open door, and numerous Goths and others were outside with lighted torches.

"Thank you, friends," the king said in a serious voice. "Thank you for accompanying me. Go now and enjoy yourselves for the rest of the night," and he was about to close the door.

"Halt!" said Hildebrand, opening the door again so that Matesuentha could be clearly seen. "Look here, everyone; the man and woman who were married today are here together happily in their bridal chamber. You will now see Witigis and Matesuentha exchange their first kiss as husband and wife."

Matesuentha trembled. She swayed, and lowered her eyes as colour flooded her cheeks.

The king stood at the door, undecided. "You know the Gothic custom," Hildebad said aloud, "act accordingly!"

Quickly Witigis made up his mind. Taking the trembling left hand of Matesuentha he pulled her toward him, and lightly touched her forehead with his lips. Matesuentha quivered.

"Hail to you both!" cried Hildebrand. "We have witnessed the bridal kiss, and henceforth we confirm your union as complete! Hail King Witigis, and hail his beautiful wife, Queen Matesuentha!"

The others repeated the cry and then Hildebrand, Count Grippa, Duke Guntharis, Hildebad, Aligern and the brave *bandalarius* (flag bearer) of the king, Count Wisand of Volsinii, settled down with the six women and girls outside the bridal chamber. Witigis now closed the door, and they were alone.

Witigis took a long look about the room. The first thing Matesuentha did – his kiss was still burning on her forehead – was to move instinctively as far away from him as she could. Thus somehow – she herself did not know why – she had moved into the furthest corner of the room, by the window. Witigis seemed to notice it. He was standing near the threshold, his hands leaning on his huge sword. The sword, in its scabbard, was almost chest high, and he was holding it like a staff in his right hand.

With a sigh he took a step forward, his eyes directed calmly at Matesuentha. "Queen," he said, his voice sounding formal and solemn, "do not fear me! I think I know what you are thinking, and what in your girlish innocence you fear. It had to be. I could not spare you. The nation's welfare demanded it; I reached out for your hand because it has to be and remain mine. But I have already tried to show you during these last few days that your privacy and your modesty are sacred to me. I have avoided you, but now we are alone for the first time. I would have liked to spare you this ordeal too, but it could not be done. You know, I think, the Gothic custom of the bridal guard of honour, and in our case it is important that we do not offend against it. When I entered this room tonight and saw the colour rising in your cheeks, I would rather have laid my tired head to rest on a hard rock in the loneliest mountain wilderness. But it was impossible. Hildebrand and Count Grippa and Duke Guntharis are guarding our door, and there is no other way out of this room. If I tried to leave you, there would be uproar and ridicule and conflict, and perhaps even renewed fighting. You will have to endure me near you for this one night."

He took another step forward and removed his heavy crown. Then he also removed his purple robe which, like Matesuentha, he wore gathered over his left shoulder.

Matesuentha was leaning against the far wall, speechless and trembling. Her silence depressed Witigis, and in spite of his own suffering he felt pity for the girl. "Come, Matesuentha," he said, "don't remain angry with me. I tell you it had to be. Let us bear nobly what has to be borne, and let us not be embittered by small things. I had to take your hand – your heart remains free. I know that you don't love me; you cannot, you must not love me. But believe me, my heart is upright and sincere, and you will be able at least to respect the man who shares your crown. Let us be friends, Queen of the Goths!"

He went over to her and offered her his right hand. Matesuentha could contain herself no longer; she grasped his proffered hand and sank to her knees before him, so that he was taken aback.

"No, don't turn away, you glorious man!" she cried. "There is no escaping you! Take me, take all and hear all. You speak of force and fear and injustice which you did to me. Oh Witigis, I have been taught that a woman must always hide her feelings wisely, and must only yield to love when asked to do so, no matter how much her heart might long for fulfilment. She should never – but away with this foolishness and false modesty! Let me be foolish! No, not foolish, but frank and great, like your soul! Only greatness deserves you. Witigis, you speak of force and fear – you are wrong! There is no need – gladly..."

Witigis had been listening to her for a while in amazement. At last he thought he understood. "It is great and beautiful of you, Matesuentha, that you feel like this for your people, giving up your own freedom for their sake of your own free will. Believe me, I honour you for that, and I did the same as you. I took your hand only for the sake of the Gothic nation, but I cannot love you, now or ever."

At those words Matesuentha grew rigid, and turned as pale as a marble statue. Her arms fell slack by her sides, and she stared at him with wide open eyes: "You do not love me? You cannot love me? So the stars lied after all? Tell me, am I not Matesuentha, whom you have called the most beautiful woman on earth?"

But the king resolved to put an end quickly to this emotional outburst, which he did not understand. "Yes, you are Matesuentha, and you are beautiful, and you share my crown but not my heart. You are consort to the king, but not wife to poor Witigis, because my heart and my life will always belong to another. There lives a woman whom they tore away from me, but to whom my heart will always belong, Rauthgundis, my wife in life and in death!"

"Ha!" Matesuentha cried, trembling as if racked by fever and raising both arms, "and yet you dared..."

Her voice failed her, but her eyes spewed fire at the king. "And yet you dare!" she cried once more. "Away! Get away from me!"

"Quiet," said Witigis, "do you want to alert the listeners outside? Control yourself! I do not understand you."

Quickly he drew the mighty sword from its scabbard and laid it along the edge of the double bed, where the two halves joined.

"Do you see the sword here? Let it be for ever the cold, sharp barrier that divides us, your soul and mine. Calm yourself. It will always divide us. Lie down and rest on the right side of its edge, and I will stay on the left. Thus let this night divide our lives for ever, like the sword here!"

But within Matesuentha's breast the most powerful emotions were raging, in a terrible and threatening conflict of anger, love and now also burning hatred. Her voice failed her, and all she could think of was to get away from him at all costs. She rushed for the door.

But Witigis firmly grasped her arm. "You must stay!" She trembled once more and collapsed on the bed, unconscious.

Witigis looked down at her calmly. "Poor child," he said, "the overpowering perfume in this room has confused her, so that she no longer knew what she was saying. But what is your girlish confusion compared to the agony which Rauthgundis and I have had to endure?"

Gently he laid the unconscious girl down on the right side of the sword and covered her with a rug.

He himself sat down on the carpet on the left side of the bed, his back leaning against the cushions. His armour rattled as he moved. For a long time he sat thus, his head lowered and his lips resting on a lock of blond hair, which he wore in a capsule around his neck. But no sleep would come to his sad eyes.

As soon as the first cock crowed the guard of honour left their post, led away by flautists who came to fetch them. Immediately afterwards the king left the room in full armour.

The flutes had also wakened Matesuentha.

Aspa, who was silently approaching, suddenly heard a dull thud, and she hurried into the room. There she saw the queen standing, leaning on the king's long sword, staring at the ground before her.

The Ares bust lay at her feet, smashed to pieces.

Chapter 3

The church and monastery at the foot of the Appeninus north of Perusia were glowing in the light of the late afternoon sun. It was that same monastery, high on a rocky outcrop above the township of Taginae, which Valerius had built to absolve his daughter from that promise to become a nun.

The monastery was built of the dark red natural stone of this region, and there was a quiet little garden within the rectangle of its walls. Cool arcades lined the four sides of the garden, with statues of the apostles, and decorated with mosaics and frescoes on a golden background. All of this artwork was done in the serious, joyless character of the Byzantine period, and most of it represented scenes from the scriptures, particularly the Revelation of St John, the favourite book of that era.

There was a solemn peacefulness everywhere, and all outside life seemed to be completely excluded by the strong, high walls. The garden consisted mainly of cypress and thuja trees, which had never known the song of a bird. The strict discipline of the monastery would not tolerate the presence of birds, for the sweet song of the nightingale might disturb the pious inmates in their prayers.

Both the interior and exterior layout of the monastery had been designed by Cassiodorus for Valerius, its donor, along similar lines to the men's monastery at Squillacium in Southern Italy, which Cassiodorus himself had founded. Cassiodorus had possessed thorough theological learning, and even in his days as a minister to Theodoric he had been a strong advocate of strict church discipline. It is therefore not surprising that his pious but severe and unworldly outlook manifested itself in every aspect of his creation, both great and small. The twenty maidens and widows who lived their religious lives here passed their days in prayer and the singing of psalms, in penitence and self castigation. But they also performed many good Christian works by seeking out the poor and ailing of the area in their huts, nursing their bodies and nurturing their souls.

It made a solemn and poetic, but also very serious impression to see one of these pious women walking along the dark cypress paths, in their grey habits and tight fitting white *calanticas* on their heads. It was a form of dress which Cassiodorus had adopted from the Egyptian Iris priestesses. Now and again they would stand before one of the shrubs, many of which were trimmed in the shape of a cross, and cross their arms over their chests. They were always alone and always silent, gliding past one another like silent shadows. All conversation was strictly forbidden save for what was absolutely necessary.

In the middle of the garden there was a small spring of dark stone, surrounded by cypresses, with a few seats carved into the marble. It was a beautiful, quiet spot. Wild roses formed an arbour, which almost hid a gloomy, rough stone relief showing the stoning of St Stephanos.

Sitting by the spring, reading from a bundle of papyrus scrolls, was a lovely virginal figure clad in a snow white gown, held by a golden clasp over her left shoulder. Her dark brown hair, which was arranged in soft waves, was crowned by a garland of ivy. She was Valeria, the Roman.

Here, in these remote but secure walls, she had found refuge after her father's house in Naples had ceased to exist. These lonely surroundings had made her more pale and more serious, but her eyes still glowed with all her former proud beauty.

She was reading very attentively. The contents of the book she was holding seemed to be lively and absorbing, because her lips were moving unconsciously as she read, until at last she could be heard softly whispering the words:

"And he married his daughter to the worthy warrior Hector. She was coming toward him now, her servants following behind her, and carrying at her breast the tender and still very young boy, Hector's only son, like a star high up in the heavens. Silently Hector looked upon his son, a smile on his face, but Andromache approached him with tears in her eyes. Gently she squeezed his hand and began to speak urgently to him: 'Your mad courage will destroy you yet! Do you not care for your little boy, nor me who will soon be Hector's widow? Soon your furious enemies will kill you, rushing at you mightily all at once. If you were to die, then it would be best for me if the ground could swallow me up. My future would never know consolation if fate was to take you from me; no, only grief! My mother and my father have long gone, and you alone are now mother, father and all to me...'"

She read no further; her large round eyes became moist and her voice failed her. She bowed her head.

"Valeria," said a kindly voice as Cassiodorus bent over her shoulder. "Tears over the book of solace? But what is this I see – the Iliad? Child, I gave you the Holy Gospel."

"Forgive me, Cassiodorus, but my heart remains loyal to gods other than yours. You may find this hard to believe, but the more I am exposed here to the shadowy business of earnest renunciation of the world outside, the more desperately my soul clings to the last threads that still tie me to that outside world. My mind is for ever torn between love and foreboding."

"Valeria, you have not found peace here in this house of peace. Very well then, you should leave us. You are, after all, free and the mistress of your own mind. Go back to that colourful world outside, if you think you can find happiness there."

But she shook her beautiful head. "That is no longer possible. Two conflicting forces are fighting within me, and whichever of them finally wins I will always be the loser."

"Child, don't speak like that! You cannot compare those two forces, the blessings of heaven and the lust for life on earth."

"Woe is to those," she went on as if talking to herself, "into whose souls fate has planted that double-edged dagger, which pulls one upwards to the stars one minute, and down to the flowers below the next. They will never know happiness either way."

"It is true, my child," Cassiodorus said as he sat down beside her, "that you carry within you the heritages of both your worldly father and your pious mother, not yet reconciled with one another. Your father was a Roman of the old world, rough, brave, self-assured, striving for power and gain. But I fear that he was insufficiently affected by the power of the spirit, which seeks it's home only in the world beyond this life. Indeed, my friend Valerius was more heathen than Christian. And beside him there was your mother, pious and gentle, and coming from a family of martyrs. She was seeking heaven and ignoring earth, and I suppose that you have also inherited a part of her as well."

"No," Valeria replied, standing up and throwing back her head in a gesture of determination. "I feel only my father's nature in me, and not a single drop of my blood leans that other way. My mother was ill a great deal, and died when I was very young. I grew up under the care of my father. Iphigenia, Antigone, Nausicaa, Cloelia, Lucretia and Virginia were the friends of my youth. Few priests were seen in the house of my father, the merchant, and when he sat down to read to me in the evenings it was from Livius, Tacitus and Virgil, not the holy book of the Christians. And so I grew up to my seventeenth year, my mind directed only to this world, because even the virtues which my father praised and practised were only to do with the state, the house and his friends. In those days I was happy, and my soul was not tormented by conflict."

"You were a heathen despite the water of baptism."

"I was happy. Then, on a journey, we came here to these walls for the first time, with their tomb-like seriousness, and heavy dark shadows entered my soul. Here is where I found you, and you revealed to me what until then had been carefully kept from me, namely that my mother had dedicated me to a life of chastity and religion here in the monastery, if only God would keep her and her child alive. And you told me how my father, to whom this whole idea was quite unbearable, had later bought my freedom back from heaven, admittedly with the full concurrence of the bishop of Rome, by building this church and monastery here instead of surrendering his daughter."

"That's how it was, child, with one fourth of his entire fortune! You need not worry yourself about that. The successor to St Peter, who has the power to bind or absolve, approved the exchange and the dissolution of that oath. You are free!"

"But I do not feel free! Not since that hour! Whatever you and my father say, deep inside me a voice says: 'Heaven will not accept dead money in place of a living soul. Fate will not sell for money that which it has once possessed'. The dark, threatening power of that faith, which has remained foreign to me and which resides here in these walls, has some powerful right to rule over my soul, and it will not let go. I am in its power. I belong to that force, unwillingly, resisting as much as I can, but I cannot escape. The world of self-renunciation, of pain and thorns is my lot, not the world of my Homer, and the golden world of flowers and sunshine, towards which my whole being still leans. As much as I try to forget, those shadows cross my soul again and again. They are there, threatening, at the back of every joy, just like that sinister picture of the martyr there behind the roses."

"Valeria, it seems that you hate that which you should honour."

"I do not hate it, but I fear it. There was a time," and for a fleeting moment a look of happiness appeared on her face, "when I believed that the dark shadows had been defeated for ever by a brilliant God of Light. When I first saw the laughing eyes of the young Goth, and when his sunny soul embraced me, when so much youth, beauty, love and happiness suddenly surrounded me, then I did think for a little while that I might be free of that oath for ever. But it did not last.

"That dark god of pain knocked unmistakably against the thin golden wall, which I had built between him and myself, and his blows came ever closer. War breaks out, my dear father falls and takes with him to the grave a fateful oath from my beloved. The house of my ancestors disappears into ashes and rubble, and I am forced to flee from my city, which then falls to the enemy. Only the sacrifice of a precious life saves my beloved for me, and then the tide of war carries him far away.

"And as I wake from the effects of these blows I find myself here, in this great tomb, in the place of my destiny. Oh you will see that heaven will never be satisfied with just an empty tomb; it will also demand the living body which belongs in it."

"Valeria! You should have been called Cassandra."

"Yes, because Cassandra saw the future, and her visions came true!"

"As you know, we promise rich reward for any soul that forgets about earthly pleasures for the sake of heaven. But God does not force sacrifices. And that is why I tell you that you are tormenting yourself with these futile self-accusations for nothing. The Pope has absolved you, and therefore you are free."

"No Pope can absolve a soul. The Pope may accept money, but fate will not. You will see that everything I foresee with dread will be fulfilled. I will never be happy, I will never be Totila's wife, and this place will…"

"And suppose it was so? Are you so intent on seeking hope and happiness? Certainly you are still young. But child, let me tell you this: the sooner you make a break from these things, the greater the sorrows you will be spared. I have tasted the world with all its false joys and honours, and I have found them all to be hollow and treacherous. Nothing on this earth can give fulfilment to a soul which is not of this earth. Only those who recognise that fact can hope to escape from a world of restlessness and sin. Your home, your real home, is in the world beyond the grave. Your entire soul longs…"

"No, no, Cassiodorus!" the Roman girl cried out passionately, "my entire soul longs for happiness here on this beautiful earth! I belong to the earth, and on it I feel at home. Blue skies, white marble, red roses, glorious scented summer nights – oh you are so beautiful!

"Those are the things which I want to breathe and enjoy with all my senses! Anyone who can enjoy those things is happy, and woe be to those who cannot! Of the next world my fearful soul knows nothing. Mist, shadows, grey uncertainty and nothing else lie beyond the grave. What was it Achilles said?

"'Do not try to console me about death! You cannot, Ulysses. I would rather work in the fields as a paid hand for a humble man, whose estate is small and poor, than rule the shadows of the dead for ever.'"

"That is how I feel too. I could not bear the thought that I would never feel the warmth of the golden sun again, and oh, how I long to be happy in this beautiful world, in the beautiful land of my fathers. You cannot have any idea how I dread the disaster which I can feel coming ever closer, irresistibly, just as the shadows on that wall over there are growing slowly, but with a certainty nobody can change. Oh if only there was a way to slow down the dreadful shadow of my life as it approaches to claim me!"

Then, suddenly, there came from the direction of the entrance a bright, vigorous sound, very strange indeed within these walls which normally heard nothing louder than the soft chorus of the women and virgins. The trumpet blew the cheerful, warlike call of the Gothic cavalry, and that sound penetrated Valeria's soul with a strong, reviving effect.

The old gatekeeper came running from the main building. "Master," he shouted, "there are some impudent horsemen outside the wall. They are making a lot of noise, and demanding meat and wine. I cannot get rid of them, and their leader – there he is already."

"Totila!" Valeria cried joyfully, and flew toward her beloved, who was coming toward her in full shining armour, rattling as he walked, and with his white cloak around him.

"Oh, you bring air and life!"

"And new hope and old love," cried Totila, and they were in each other's arms.

"Where did you come from? You have been away from me for so long!"

"I have come directly from Paris and Aurelianum, from the courts of the Frankish kings. Oh Cassiodorus, how well off they are beyond the mountains! They have it so easy! They have no need to fight heaven and earth and history to preserve their Germanic culture. The Rhine and Danube are close by, and countless Germanic tribes live there in their old, undiluted strength. Compared to them we are like a lonely outpost, a single rock, lost because foreign elements are gnawing away at it on all sides. Therefore," he said, rising to his full height, "it is all the more memorable and glorious to establish and preserve an Empire of Germanic peoples right here, in the land of the Romans! Your fatherland holds such miracles, Valeria. It has become ours also. How my heart rejoiced when I saw olives and laurels once more, and the deep blue sky. And I could feel it clearly inside me: if my great people can remain victorious here, in this wonderful country, then humanity will see its greatest epoch right here."

Valeria grasped her enthused beloved's hand.

"And what did you achieve?" Cassiodorus asked.

"A great deal! Everything! At the court of the Merowing king Childebert I found envoys from Byzantium, who had almost won him over to invade Italy as their ally. The gods – forgive me, father – Heaven was on my side and gave weight to my words. I was able to change his mind. At worst he will remain neutral. I hope he will send an army to help us."

"Where did you leave Julius?"

"I accompanied him to his beautiful home city of Avenio, where I left him among blooming almond and oleander trees. He is walking there now, almost never with Plato in his hand, but usually with an Augustinus, dreaming of eternal peace on earth, of goodness and God's kingdom! It is certainly beautiful in those green valleys, but I don't envy him his leisure there. The greatest thing on this earth is one's people, and the fatherland! My own greatest wish is to fight for my Gothic nation here in Italy. Everywhere I went on my return journey I urged men to arms. Already I have encountered three strong contingents on their way to Ravenna, and I am leading a fourth to our worthy king. Then, at last, we will be able to start advancing against these Greeks, and then: Revenge for Naples!"

And his eyes flashed as he raised his spear – he made a very handsome sight.

Valeria threw herself at his breast delighted. "Look, Cassiodorus, this here is my world! My joy, and my heaven! A man's courage and the gleam of arms and the love of nation and fatherland, a soul moved by love and hatred – is that not enough to fill a human breast?"

"Indeed it does, while we are young and happy! Only pain leads us to heaven."

"My pious father," said Totila, with his arm around Valeria. "It is not fitting for me to argue with you, an older and better man. But I am made differently. If ever I am tempted to doubt that there is a benevolent God who rules this world, then it is only when I see pain and undeserved suffering. When I saw the good Miriam's eyes break my despairing heart cried out: 'Is there no God?' In happy times, and when the sun shines, I feel the presence of God, and his mercy reveals itself to me. I am sure that He wants men and women to be happy and enjoy themselves. Pain is His holy secret, and I am certain that even that riddle will be solved for us one day. But meanwhile let us joyfully do our part on earth, and let no shadow darken it for too long. Let us part with that thought in mind, Valeria, because I have to leave and hurry to King Witigis with my men straight away."

"You are leaving me? Already? When, where will I see you again?"

"I will see you again, take my word for it. I know that a day will come when I can lead you out of these grave walls into life's sunshine, with every right! Meanwhile don't let anything depress you too much. A day of victory and of happiness will come, and it makes me feel good to think that I am fighting for my people and for my love at the same time."

Meanwhile the gatekeeper had come back with a letter for Cassiodorus. "I too must leave you, Valeria," he said, "Rusticiana, the widow of Boethius, calls me urgently to her deathbed. She wants to lighten her heart of some old sin. I am going to Tifernum."

"We are going that way, and you will come with us, Cassiodorus. Farewell, Valeria!"

After a brief farewell the young woman saw her beloved on his way. From a small tower on the garden wall she watched him disappear in the distance, after he had swung himself in the saddle in full armour. His men followed, their helmets glistening in the evening light. The blue flag fluttered cheerfully in the wind, and it gladdened her heart to see this scene of life, strength and hope. For a long time her eyes followed the small procession, but once it faded from sight the fresh courage she had gained from its unexpected appearance departed with it. Fearful foreboding arose in her again, somehow reminding her of Homer's words: 'Do you not see how handsome, how strong is Achilles? Yet fate and death await him too, and his life will fly from him in the tumult of battle, whether an arrow strikes him down or a spear.'"

And with a sad sigh the young woman left the garden for the gloomy walls of the monastery as the night set in.

Chapter 4

Meanwhile King Witigis in his capital Ravenna had busied himself, using every art and skill of the experienced general.

Every week, and indeed every day, saw large and small detachments arrive in the city from those armies which King Theodahad had sent away to the far borders, and the king worked tirelessly to arm, equip, organise and train the huge army, which would eventually number one hundred and fifty thousand men.

Theodoric's rule had been peaceful, and only small forces in the border regions had recent experience of fighting, against Gepidae, Bulgarians and Avars. During the thirty years of peace much of the Gothic military machinery had become rusty. Hence the capable king, ably supported by his friends and generals, had his hands very full indeed. The arsenals and dockyards were emptied out, huge store houses were built in Ravenna, and between the triple walls of the city countless blacksmiths and weapons makers were set up, who now had to work ceaselessly day and night to meet the needs of the warrior king and his rapidly growing army. The whole of Ravenna had become a huge armed camp, and the sound of blacksmith's hammers, neighing horses and the war cry and sound of Gothic arms were everywhere.

In the midst of all this activity Witigis had been able to put his own personal agony aside as best he could, and he eagerly looked forward to the day when he would be able to lead his great army against the enemy. But in spite of his eagerness to get on with the fight he had not forgotten his duties as a king, and thus he had sent Guntharis and Hildebad to Belisarius as envoys to negotiate for peace on the most reasonable of terms.

Thus fully occupied by the affairs of war and the state, he had not given much time or thought to his queen. In any event he thought that giving her maximum freedom, and leaving her alone, was the best course of action he could take. But Matesuentha, since that disastrous wedding night, had become possessed by a demon, a demon of insatiable revenge. Love turned to hate is the worst hate there is.

Her deep and passionate nature had caused this man to become an idol in her mind. Her pride, her hope and her love had all been directed only at this one man, and she had expected that her dreams would be satisfied and fulfilled as surely as the sun rises. And now she had to admit to herself that he had brought her love out into the open without reciprocating it, and that she, although his queen, had to compete for his love with that other woman still in his heart, almost like a criminal. And he, to whom she had looked as her liberator and saviour, had subjected her to the greatest insult and shame of all, a marriage without love. He had taken her freedom and not given his heart in return. And why? What was the underlying reason for this crime against her? It was the Gothic Empire, and the Gothic crown!

In order to preserve those he had not hesitated to ruin Matesuentha's life. "If he had not returned my love, I would be too proud to hate him for it. But he draws me to him, and calls me his wife as if to mock me. He leads me along until my love has almost reached fulfilment, and then he casts me aside, unfeelingly, to unspeakable degradation and shame. And why? Why all this? For the sake of an empty sound: 'Gothic Empire', and for a dead golden crown. Woe be to him, and to the accursed idol for which he sacrificed my heart! He shall pay for it, and he shall do so by seeing his idol perish. He walked unfeelingly with his boots over my own idol, his revered image, and defiled my beautiful love for him. Very well, it will be idol against idol! He shall live to see this Empire destroyed, and his crown hacked to pieces. I will shatter his dream, for which he sacrificed my soul, and I will smash his Empire as I smashed his bust. And when, at last, he stands before the ruins, wringing his hands in despair, I will call out to him: 'That is how shattered idols look!'"

And so, with the irresistible sophistication of passion, she started to accuse and persecute the unfortunate man who had suffered more than she, and who had sacrificed not only her but his own and his wife's happiness for the fatherland. Fatherland, Gothic Empire, these sounds found no sympathy in the ears of a woman for whom they had meant only suffering since her childhood, and against which she had constantly had to defend her freedom. She had been living solely for one selfish passion, and now all she could think of was revenge, to destroy this Gothic Empire to get even for the destruction of her own dreams. Oh, if only she could shatter the Empire with a single blow, like the bust!

But with the madness of this hatred came a demonic cleverness too. She was able to conceal her deadly hatred and lust for revenge from the king, just as she concealed the love she still bore for him in her innermost heart. She even managed to display an outward interest in the Gothic cause, which seemed to be the only bond between her and the king, and which indeed it was, albeit in a very different sense. She knew that she could only harm the hated king and hurt his cause by knowing all the secrets of that cause intimately, and by knowing it's weaknesses as well as its strengths.

Her high position made it easy for her to find out everything she wanted to know. Respect for her huge following alone meant that the precise state of the army and Empire could not be kept from the Amalung princess. Count Grippa supplied her with all the information he himself heard, and she in turn personally took part in the more important discussions as they took place in the king's chambers. Thus Matesuentha knew as much as the king himself about the strength and dispositions of the army, about the most likely strategic plans, and about the hopes and fears of the Goths. Now she longed for an opportunity to use this knowledge against king and Empire, as soon as possible and as damagingly as possible.

She could not hope to get in touch with Belisarius herself. Hence her thoughts turned quite naturally to the apparently neutral Italians around her, who were really very much on the Byzantine side, and with whom she could maintain regular contact easily and without arousing suspicion. But every time she went over their names in her mind, there was not one among them who seemed able and strong enough for her to confide to him her deadly secret, namely that the Gothic queen herself was anxious to help destroy her Empire. These insignificant and cowardly men – the more able had long gone over to Belisarius or Cethegus – were neither worthy of her trust, nor did they appear to be a match for Witigis and his friends.

Certainly she used a number of subterfuges to find out from the king and the Goths themselves which of the Romans they considered their most dangerous and significant enemy. In all these enquiries the one name alone arose over and over again, the Prefect Cethegus. But how was she to make contact with him? She would not dare entrust any of her Roman slaves with so dangerous a mission as a letter to Rome.

Aspa, the brave and intelligent Numidian, shared the hatred of her mistress for the Barbarian who had scorned her, but not the love which her mistress still secretly bore him, and she had eagerly offered to find a way to get to Cethegus. But Matesuentha did not want to expose the girl to the dangers of a journey right through Italy in time of war. Already she was reconciling herself to having to postpone her revenge until the offensive against Rome, continuing meanwhile to find out all she could about the Gothic plans.

Thus one day she was walking back toward the city from the council of war, which had taken place in the king's tent beyond the walls. Now that mobilisation was nearing completion, and the day of a counter-offensive against Belisarius was drawing closer, the king had left his palace and pitched his simple tent among his troops. Perhaps another reason was to get away from her.

Going over what she had just witnessed in her mind, and seeking ways in which she might use that knowledge, the queen was slowly walking through the outermost row of tents, a swampy arm of the Padus on one side and the tents on the other. She was avoiding the noise and congestion of the main part of the camp, and was alone except for Aspa, who was accompanying her. While she was thus strolling along absentmindedly, taking little notice of her surroundings, Aspa's sharp eyes noted a group of Goths and Italians who had gathered around the table of a juggler, who was evidently showing tricks which, judging from the laughter and applause, few of his audience had seen before.

Aspa hesitated for a moment to witness these wonders also. He was a young, slender lad, and judging by his white skin and long yellow hair he was of Celtic origin, although his black eyes looked rather out of place. He really was performing near miracles on his primitive stage. One moment he leapt high in the air, somersaulted and landed on his feet, and next time on his hands. Then he consumed burning coals with evident enjoyment, spitting out coins in their place. Next he swallowed a dagger a foot long, and a moment later withdrew it from his hair, only to throw it high in the air with three or four other razor-sharp knives, which he then caught with unfailing skill by their handles. Every new feat brought fresh applause.

But the slave girl had already delayed too long. She looked to see where her mistress was, and noticed that her path had been barred by a group of Italian bearers. They appeared not to know the Gothic queen, and were forcing their way right past her to the water, with a lot of noisy horseplay. They seemed to be showing one another some object which Aspa could not see, and throwing stones at it.

She was just about to hurry after her mistress when the juggler on the table let out a piercing cry. Aspa turned with a fright, and saw the man take an enormous leap over the heads of the spectators, like an arrow, and charge at the Italians. In an instant he was right among them and for a moment, bending down, he vanished in their midst. Then, suddenly, he appeared again; first one, then another of the Italians fell down from blows of his fists.

In a moment Aspa was at the queen's side, who had quickly moved away from the brawl, but to Aspa's astonishment she stopped there, pointing at the group with a finger.

And indeed they were witnessing a very strange spectacle.

With unbelievable strength and even greater agility the juggler managed to keep a dozen or so of his attackers at bay. He was defending himself furiously, leaping at one opponent, twisting, ducking and weaving, then suddenly leaping forward again and pulling another attacker down, or striking him with a strong blow of his fist. And all this he managed to do without a weapon, and with only his right hand; his left seemed to be holding something to his chest, as if guarding or protecting it. So the uneven contest went on for several minutes. The juggler was pushed closer and closer to the water by the angry, noisy crowd, and then suddenly a knife flashed. One of the bearers, angered by a severe blow, drew a knife and leapt at the juggler from behind. The latter collapsed with a cry, his enemies on top of him.

"Get up! Pull them apart! Help the poor man," Matesuentha called out to the Gothic soldiers, who were now approaching from the deserted table. "I command it, the Queen!"

The Goths rushed to the scene of the struggle, but even before they could get there the juggler, freeing himself from his attackers for a moment, leapt high in the air and out of the turmoil. Now the man, with the last of his strength, ran straight toward the two women, pursued by the Italians whom a handful of Goths could not restrain. What a sight! His Celtic tunic hung in shreds from his body, some of his yellow hair was dragging behind, hanging from his back, and alas, black hair could be seen under the wig, and the white neck was evidently joined to a brown body. With a last, desperate effort he reached the two women, and he recognised Matesuentha: "Save me, protect me, white goddess!" he cried, and collapsed unconscious at Matesuentha's feet. Already the Italians were upon him, the leading one flashing a knife.

But Matesuentha spread her blue cloak over the fallen man: "Go back!" she said with dignity, "let him go! He is now under the protection of the Gothic queen!"

The startled bearers withdrew. After a brief pause the one with the knife said: "Oh? Is he to go unpunished, the dog and son of a dog? And five of us lying here half dead? And me with three teeth less than I had yesterday? And still no punishment for the dog?"

"He has been punished enough," Matesuentha replied, pointing to the deep knife wound in his neck.

"And all that over a worm," cried a second one, "a snake which slipped from his satchel, and at which we threw stones."

"Look there, he is still holding the serpent to his chest. Take it from him!"

"Kill him!" the others cried.

But by this time a number of Gothic soldiers had arrived on the scene, and they made sure their queen was obeyed. They roughly pushed the Italians back, and formed a protective cordon around the fallen man. Aspa had been watching closely, and suddenly she sank down beside the juggler with her arms crossed.

"Aspa, what is the matter? Get up!" Matesuentha said, surprised.

"Oh mistress," the latter stammered, "this man is not a Celt! He is one of my people. He prays to the snake god! Look at his brown skin here below his neck, as brown as Aspa's... And here – there is something written. There are characters tattooed on his chest, the secret writing of my homeland," she rejoiced. And she started to read, pointing her finger at the tattoo.

"This juggler seems suspicious. Why the disguise?" Matesuentha said. "He'd better be arrested."

"No, no mistress," Aspa whispered. "Do you know what the tattoo says? Only I can decipher it for you."

"Well?" Matesuentha asked.

"It says," Aspa whispered softly, "'Syphax owes his life to his master, the Prefect Cethegus'. Yes, I recognise him now, he is Syphax, Hiempsal's son, a friend and frequent guest of my tribe. The gods have sent him to us."

"Aspa," Matesuentha said quickly, "you are right, the gods have indeed sent him, the gods of revenge. Come you Goths, place this wounded man on a stretcher and follow my slave here to the palace with it! From now on he is in my service."

Chapter 5

A few days later Matesuentha went to the camp once more, this time without Aspa. The latter would not leave her wounded countryman's sickbed by day or night, and Syphax was recovering quickly under her care, her herbs and her incantations.

This time King Witigis himself had fetched his queen, with his full retinue. The most important council of war yet was to be held in his tent. The last of the reinforcements were expected to arrive today, and Guntharis and Hildebad were also expected back with Belisarius's reply to their offer of peace.

"A fateful day!" Witigis said to his queen, "Pray for peace."

"I am praying for war," Matesuentha replied, staring rigidly ahead.

"Does your woman's heart thirst for revenge that much?"

"Revenge alone is all that I now want, and revenge will be mine!"

With that they entered the tent, which by now was filled with Gothic leaders. Matesuentha acknowledged their respectful gestures of greeting with a proud nod of her head.

"Have the envoys returned?" the king asked old Hildebrand, taking his seat, "If so have them brought in."

Upon a signal from the old man the curtains on one side rose, and Duke Guntharis and Hildebad entered, taking deep bows.

"What do you bring, peace or war?" Witigis asked eagerly.

"War! War, King Witigis!" the two men exclaimed at once.

"What? Does Belisarius refuse the concessions I offered him? Did you convey my proposals to him in a friendly, persuasive manner?"

Duke Guntharis stepped forward and said: "I met the general in the Capitol, where he is the Prefect's guest, and I said to him: 'Witigis, the king of the Goths, sends you greetings.

"In thirty days he could be standing before these gates with one hundred and fifty thousand armed and able Gothic soldiers. A slaughter and a struggle for this holy city would then commence, such as her blood-soaked fields have not seen for centuries. But the Gothic king loves peace even more than he loves victory. He is therefore willing to hand over the island of Sicily to the emperor Justinian, and he is also willing to provide the emperor with thirty thousand Gothic troops as his allies in all of his wars, provided you vacate Italy and Rome immediately, as they belong to us by right of conquest as well as by treaty with the emperor Zeno, who agreed to let Theodoric have Italy if he could overthrow Odoacer'. That is what I said, according to your instructions.

"But Belisarius laughed and called out: 'Witigis is most generous to let me have Sicily, which is already mine, and in return I will give him the island of Thule. No. The agreement between the emperor Zeno and Theodoric was made under duress and is therefore invalid. As far as the right of conquest is concerned that is now in our favour. There will be no peace except under the condition that the entire Gothic nation lays down its arms and retreats over the Alps, with the king and queen going to Byzantium as hostages.'"

A murmur of indignation swept through the tent.

"Without replying to his demand we turned our backs in anger and walked out. 'We will meet again in Ravenna,' he called out after us. Then I turned around," Hildebad said, "and cried: 'We will meet again outside Rome!' Come now, King Witigis, to arms! You have tried everything you could to secure peace, and in return you have received the ultimate insult. Now let us fight! You have hesitated and mobilised long enough! Now lead us into the fray."

Now the sound of trumpets could be heard coming from the camp, followed by that of speeding horses approaching. A moment later the curtain over the entrance to the tent rose and Totila entered, in full shining armour and with his white cloak. "Hail to you, my king, and hail my queen," he said with a gesture of respect. "My mission is completed. I bring you friendly greetings from the Frankish king. He was ready to attack you with an army, which was in Byzantium's pay, but I was able to change his mind. His army will not invade Italy against the Goths. Count Markja of Mediolanum, who was guarding the Cottian Alps, is now free, and he and his thousands are following on my heels. On my way back I gathered whatever troops I could, and I have also added the garrisons from various castles along the way to my force. One more thing: Until now we have been short of cavalry, but I have brought you six thousand warriors on magnificent horses, who want nothing else but to give their horses work to do in the plains before Rome. All of us have but the one wish: Lead us now to fight, to fight for Rome!"

"Thank you friend, both for yourself and your cavalry. Tell me, Hildebrand, what is the strength of our army now? Tell me, generals, how many men does each of you lead? Notaries, take it down!"

"I lead three thousand men on foot!" Hildebad cried.

"And I forty thousand on foot and on horseback with shield and spear," said Duke Guntharis.

"I have forty thousand on foot, with bows, spears and lances," said Count Grippa of Ravenna.

"I have seven thousand with knives and clubs," Hildebrand added.

"And also we have Totila's six thousand cavalry, and fourteen thousand select battleaxe bearers with Teias – where is he? I miss his presence here! Finally I have fifty thousand men on foot and on horseback of my own," the king concluded.

"That makes one hundred and sixty thousand in all," the *protonarius* wrote, and handed the parchment to the king.

A glow of warlike pride came over the king's serious face. "One hundred and sixty thousand Gothic men: Belisarius, are they to lay down their arms before you without a fight? How much more rest do you need before we can march?"

At that moment the black figure of Teias burst into the tent. He had heard the last question. His eyes spewed fire, and he was trembling with rage: "Rest? Not for another hour! The time has come for revenge, King Witigis! A terrible atrocity has been committed, and that now cries out to heaven for revenge. Lead us into battle immediately!"

"What has happened?"

"One of Belisarius's commanders, Ambazuch the Hun, has had the fortress Petra surrounded with his Huns and Armenians for some time, as you know. There was no sign of relief far and wide. Only young Count Arahad – he was probably seeking death – attacked the large besieging force with a handful of men, and fell in a brave fight. The few Gothic soldiers in Petra defended themselves desperately, because all the women and children from the surrounding areas had fled here, many thousands of them. Finally hunger forced them to open their gates in return for an undertaking that they would be permitted to withdraw from the area unhindered. The Hun swore that he would not shed a single drop of Gothic blood. He entered the city and ordered all the Goths to assemble in the great basilica of St Zeno, which they did, more than five thousand of them, old men, women, children and a few hundred soldiers. And when they were all in there together…" Teias halted with a shudder.

"Well?" Matesuentha asked, turning pale.

"The Hun closed and locked the doors, surrounded the building with his troops and – burned the five thousand to death, including the church and all."

"And the agreement?" Witigis cried.

"Yes, that is what the desperate people in the church cried too, through smoke and flames. 'The agreement,' the Hun laughed, 'has been fulfilled. Not a drop of Gothic blood has been spilt. The only way to get rid of the Goths out of Italy is to burn them out, like field mice and vermin'. And so the Byzantines stood there and watched while five thousand Goths, old men, women and children – do you hear me, King Witigis? Things like that are happening and you, you send peace envoys! Come, King Witigis," the furious man cried, ripping his sword from its scabbard, "if you are a man then lead us now to revenge. The spirits of the slaughtered five thousand will march ahead of us! Lead us to fight! Revenge for Petra!"

"Lead us to war! We want revenge!" was the resounding cry in the tent.

Witigis rose with calmness and strength: "It shall be so! The worst has happened, and the ultimate atrocity has been committed against us. Our best armour now is our right! Let us march now to fight!"

He handed the parchment scroll to his queen, and grasped the royal banner, the blue *bandum*, which was hanging above his chair.

"You see here Theodoric's ancient banner, which he carried from victory to victory. Certainly it is now in less able hands than his were, but do not despair! You know that over-confidence is not my way, but this time I will tell you in advance: in this banner there is an early victory, a great, proud, vengeful victory. Follow me outside. The army will march immediately. Generals, order your forces: to Rome!"

"To Rome!" the tent resounded, "to Rome!"

Chapter 6

Meanwhile Belisarius was making preparations to leave the city with the main part of his army. He had entrusted John with the care of Rome.

He had decided to seek out the Goths in Ravenna. He had gained great confidence for two reasons. The first was his run of victories, thus far uninterrupted by any mishap. The second reason was the successes of his raiding parties which, with the help of Italian defectors, had been able to occupy the entire country as far as Ravenna, including all cities and fortresses. Thus he felt certain that the war would soon be over, and all he had to do to complete the rout was to crush the last remnants of the helpless Barbarians in their last remaining refuge.

Once Belisarius himself had conquered the entire south of the peninsula, including Bruttia, Lucania, Calabria, Apulia and Campania, and then Rome and Samnium, he had sent his subordinate generals Bessas and Constantinus on ahead to conquer and occupy Tuscany. With them he sent the lancers of his personal bodyguard under the leadership of the Persian Chanaranges, the Armenian Zanter and Aeshman of the Massageti.

Bessas encircled the fortress Narnia. Being located on top of a high mountain, and surrounded on three sides by the River Nar, Narnia was regarded as being virtually invincible by the means of siege warfare available at that time. There were only two access roads, from the east and from the west, by way of a narrow mountain pass and an old bridge dating back to the days of Augustus. But the Roman civilians managed to overpower the Gothic garrison of fifty men, and opened the gates to Bessas and his Thracens. Constantinus was able to capture Spoletum and Perusia in a similar manner, without having to strike a blow. Meanwhile, on the eastern side of the Ionian Sea, another of Belisarius's generals, Comes Sacri Stabuli Constantinus, had avenged the deaths of two other Byzantine leaders, the *Magister Militum* for Illyria, Mundus, and his son Mauricius, who had fallen earlier in the war near Salona in Dalmatia. He had occupied Salona, and forced the remaining Goths to retreat to Ravenna. From Tuscany, as we have already seen, Justinian's Huns were already forging through Picenum and as far as Aemilia.

In these circumstances Belisarius thought that the Gothic peace proposals were merely a sign of weakness, and it never occurred to him that the Barbarians could launch a counter-offensive. In addition to all this he was driven by a strong urge to leave Rome, where he detested having to play the part of the Prefect's guest. Once in the open field again he would surely regain the upper hand.

Cethegus left the Capitol in the capable care of Lucius Licinius and followed Belisarius and his army, warning him in vain against over-confidence.

"Why don't you stay behind the stones of the Capitol, if you fear the Barbarians?" Belisarius had replied proudly.

"No," the Prefect had replied, "watching Belisarius being defeated is an opportunity too rare to be missed." Indeed Cethegus would have dearly liked to see the proud general humiliated, as his fame was just too great, which in turn attracted the Italian population to him in large numbers.

Belisarius had led his army out of the northern gates, and assembled them in a camp a few stadia from the city in order to muster and regroup. The strong influx of Italian defectors alone made that necessary. He had also recalled Ambazuch, Bessas and Constantinus into the camp with their troops, leaving only small garrisons behind in the cities they had captured.

Dark rumours of an approaching Gothic army had been spreading through the camp, but Belisarius would pay no heed to them. "They would not dare," he had replied to warnings by Procopius, "they are hiding in Ravenna and trembling at the approach of Belisarius."

Late that night Cethegus was lying on his camp bed, wide awake, with a lamp burning. "I cannot sleep," he said to himself, "the air seems to be full of the sound of arms, and it smells of blood. The Goths are coming. They are probably coming through Sabina, on the Via Casperia and the Via Salaria."

Suddenly the curtains of the tent rustled, and Syphax rushed into the tent, quite out of breath.

"I already know what you are going to tell me," Cethegus said, jumping to his feet, "the Goths are coming."

"Yes master, they will be here tomorrow; they are aiming for the Porta Salaria. I had the queen's best horse, but that Totila, who leads the vanguard, rides like the wind through the desert. And here in the camp nobody suspects anything."

"The great general," Cethegus smiled, "has not posted guards or placed outposts."

"He was relying on the fortified tower on the Anius Bridge, but…"

"Well, the tower is sound and strong."

"Yes, but the garrison in it, Roman citizens from Naples, went over to the Goths as soon as they saw that young Totila was leading their vanguard. Belisarius's bodyguard, who tried to resist, were bound and delivered to Totila, including Junocentius. The bridge and the tower are in Gothic hands."

"That will make it interesting! Have you any idea how strong they are?"

"Not an idea, master, I know exactly. I know as much about their dispositions as their king does. Here is a list. Matesuentha, their queen, sends it to you."

Cethegus looked at him searchingly: "Are miracles now happening to destroy the Barbarians?"

"Yes master, they are! That beautiful woman wants to destroy her people all because of one man, and that man is her husband."

"You are mistaken," Cethegus replied, "she already loved him as a girl, and she bought his bust."

"Yes, she loved him. But he did not love her. And the marble bust was smashed on their wedding night."

"Surely she did not tell you all this herself?"

"No, but Aspa, my countrywoman and her slave, told me. She loves me and told me everything. And she loves her mistress, almost as much as I love you. Matesuentha wants to destroy the Gothic Empire with you as her ally. She will write to you by means of the secret writing of our tribe. And if I were Cethegus, I would take that queen of sunshine for my wife."

"I would, if I was Syphax. But the news you bring is worth a crown. A cunning woman out for revenge is worth legions! Now look out, Belisarius, Witigis and

Justinian! Syphax, you have earned a reward. You may ask for anything except your freedom. I still need you."

"My freedom is to serve you. A favour: Let me fight by your side tomorrow."

"No my panther, I don't need your claws as yet, only your stealth. You will say nothing to anyone about the nearness or the strength of the Goths. Put my armour on for me, and give me the map of the Via Salaria from the capsule there. Now go and fetch Marcus Licinius and Sandil, the leader of my Isaurians." Syphax disappeared, while Cethegus took a look at the map. "So that is where they will come from, from the northwest down the hills. Woe be to anyone who tries to stop them there. Then comes the deep valley in which we are camped, and here the battle will be fought and lost. Behind us in the southeast our position follows a deep stream, and we will be thrown back into it without fail. Then a stretch of flat country – what a lovely field for the Gothic cavalry to pursue us! Still further back a dense forest at last, and a narrow canyon with the ruins of the old Castellum Hadrianum. Marcus," he called out to the latter, who was just entering, "my troops are leaving. We will follow the stream back to the forest, and if anybody asks tell them we are going back to Rome."

"Back to Rome? Without a fight?" Marcus asked incredulously, "surely you know that there is a battle ahead?"

"That is exactly why!" With that he went outside, in order to wake Belisarius in his tent. But he found him already awake, and Procopius was with him. "Have you heard, Prefect? Fleeing peasants report a small force of Gothic cavalry coming. The daredevils are riding to their doom; they think the road to Rome is free," And he proceeded to dress and put on his armour.

"But the peasants warn that the horsemen are only the vanguard. A terrible Barbarian army is following," Pocopius warned.

"An idle scare! They are afraid, these Goths. Witigis would not dare to come looking for me. In any case I have built a tower to defend the Anius Bridge, fourteen stadia from Rome. Martinus built it to my plans; it alone will hold up the Barbarian infantry for at least a week, even if a few nags did swim the river."

"You are wrong, Belisarius! I know that the whole Gothic army is approaching," Cethegus replied.

"Then go home, if you are afraid."

"I will make use of your permission to do just that. I have contracted a fever these last few days, and my Isaurians are suffering from it too. With your permission I will retreat to Rome."

"I know that fever," said Belisarius, "it will go away as soon as they have a wall between themselves and the enemy. Be on your way! I need neither you nor your Isaurians."

Cethegus bowed and left. "Until we meet again, oh Belisarius. Give the signal for my Isaurians to depart," he said aloud to Marcus back in his tent. "And my Byzantines too!" he added softly.

"But Belisarius has…"

"I am their Belisarius. Syphax, my horse." As he was mounting, a group of mounted Roman soldiers approached, with torchbearers in the lead.

"Who goes there?" their leader called out, "Ah, it is you, Cethegus! Are you leaving? Surely you do not plan to leave us now, in this time of greatest danger?"

Cethegus leaned forward. "Calpurnius! I did not recognise you, you look so pale. What news do you bring of the Gothic vanguard?"

"Fleeing peasants say," Calpurnius replied fearfully, "that it is sure to be more than a raiding party. They say it is the Barbarian king, Witigis himself, rapidly approaching through the Sabina. They say he is already on the left bank of the Tiber. If that is true then resistance would be madness – disaster! I will follow you."

"No," Cethegus replied sharply, "you know that I am not superstitious, but I dislike riding with the Furias of doomed men. Your punishment for that cowardly child murder will catch up with you soon enough, and I have no wish to share it."

"There are voices whispering in Rome who say that Cethegus does not spurn a comfortable murder at times either," Calpurnius replied fiercely.

"Calpurnius is not Cethegus," said the Prefect as he galloped away proudly. "Meanwhile greet Hades for me!" he called out.

Chapter 7

"Accursed omen!" Calpurnius snarled, and hurried to Belisarius: "Order the retreat, quickly, *Magister Militum*."

"And why, my fine fellow?"

"It is the Gothic king himself that approaches."

"And I am Belisarius himself," the latter replied, donning his magnificent golden helmet with the white plume of a horse. "How could you leave your post with the vanguard?"

"To report this to you, master."

"And I suppose no messenger could have done that for you? Listen, Roman, you are not worthy of being liberated. I believe you are trembling, you coward. Get back to your post! You will lead our cavalry in the first attack; you two, my bodyguards Antallas and Kutugur, will take him between you. He has to be brave, do you hear? If he tries to run away strike him down! That is how one teaches Romans courage.

"The camp criers have just announced the last hour of night. In another hour the sun will rise, and it must find our entire army up on those hills. Go! Ambazuch, Bessas, Constantinus and Demetrius, we go to meet the enemy."

"Master, it is as they say," Maxentius, the most devoted of the bodyguards, reported: "countless Goths are coming!"

"They are two armies against one of ours," another leader, Salomo, reported.

"I count Belisarius as one entire army."

"And the plan of battle?" Bessas asked.

"I will make it in the face of the enemy, whilst Calpurnius and his cavalry delay him. Forward, give your orders, and bring me my horse." And with that he left the tent while the generals flew in all directions, giving orders and making arrangements.

Within a quarter of an hour everything was moving toward the hills. The Byzantines did not take the time to strike camp, but their sudden departure caused a great deal of confusion. Infantry and cavalry became mixed up in the dark, moonless night, and in addition news of the Barbarian approach en masse had caused a fall in morale.

There were only two rather narrow roads leading into the hills, resulting in much congestion and many a hold-up. Thus the army reached the hills much later than Belisarius had estimated, and as the scene was lit by the first rays of the rising sun Calpurnius, who was leading the vanguard, saw the sunlight reflected from Gothic arms on every hilltop and vantage point. The Barbarians had beaten Belisarius to the punch and Calpurnius, shocked at this discovery, sent a message to his commander-in-chief.

Belisarius in turn could see that it would be impossible for Calpurnius and his cavalry to storm the hills, and he therefore sent Bessas and Ambazuch with the core of the Armenian infantry to storm the hills by way of the wide road. Constantinus and Demetrius led the left and right wings respectively, and he himself drew up his bodyguard as a backstop in the centre. Calpurnius, glad of the change in plans, placed his cavalry beneath the steepest part of the hills, on the left side of the road where an attack looked unlikely. His intention was to await the result of the storm attempt by Bessas and Ambazuch, and then to pursue the fleeing Goths or receive the retreating Armenians.

Up on the heights the Goths were spread out over a great distance in battle order. Totila and his cavalry had been first to arrive. Teias, whose battleaxe bearers were still a long way behind, had joined him. He was filled with a lust for battle, and had asked to be relieved of any command, so that he could involve himself in the fighting wherever he chose. Hildebrand had arrived soon afterwards, and the king with the main force was just behind him. Duke Guntharis, with his own and Teias's men, was still on his way.

Teias had sped back to the king with the speed of an arrow. "King," he said, "Belisarius stands below those hills there. By the god of revenge he is lost! He has been foolish enough to advance against us. Don't be shamed by letting him attack first."

"Forward!" King Witigis cried, "Gothic soldiers, attack!" A few moments later he had reached the ridge of the hills and could see the valley before him. "Hildebad – the left wing! You, Totila, will charge with your cavalry here in the centre, down the road. I will lie in readiness to the right of the road, to follow you or to cover you if necessary."

"There will be no need," Totila replied, drawing his sword, "I give you my word – they will not halt my charge down those hills."

"We will throw the enemy back into his own camp," the king continued, "then we will take the camp and throw them into the stream just behind the camp there. What is left you, Totila and Teias, you and your cavalry can chase across the plain to the gates of Rome."

"Yes, once we have gained that pass there, in the wooded hills behind the river," said Teias, pointing with his sword.

"It seems to be still unoccupied. You must get there at the same time as the fugitives."

At that moment the banner bearer, Count Wisand of Vulsinii, the army's *bandalarius*, approached the king: "My king, you have promised to grant me a wish."

"Yes, because at Salona you unhorsed the *Magister Militum* for Illyria, Mundus, and his son."

"You see, somehow I have a grudge against *Magistri Militi*. Please, for today, relieve me of the banner, and let me go looking for *Magister* Belisarius. His horse, the red Phalion, is so famous, and my own stallion is getting old and lame. And you know the ancient Gothic right: 'Throw the rider and take his horse'."

"That is perfectly legal under Gothic law!" Hildebrand added.

"I must grant your wish," said Witigis, taking the banner from the hands of Wisand, who quickly galloped away. "Guntharis is not here, so you carry it today, Totila."

"I cannot, my king," the latter replied, "I cannot carry a banner if I am to lead my men against the enemy."

Witigis next motioned to Teias. "Forgive me, King," Teias replied, "I think I will need both arms today."

"What about you, Hildebad?"

"Thank you for the honour, but my intentions are the same as the others."

"What?" Witigis cried, almost angry, "must I carry my own banner because none of my friends will accept the honour I am offering?"

"Give me Theodoric's flag then," old Hildebrand said, taking hold of the mighty shaft. "I am not so anxious to be involved in more fighting, but I am glad to see the younger ones so eagerly after fame and honour. I will guard it today as I did forty summers ago." And at once he moved to the king's right side.

"The enemy infantry is advancing up the hills," said Witigis, rising in the saddle.

"They are Huns and Armenians," said Teias, who had exceptionally sharp eyes, "I recognise them by their tall shields!" Then, spurring his black horse, he cried: "Ambazuch leads them, the murderer of Petra!"

"Forward, Totila," the king commanded, "and out of those troops I want no prisoners!"

Quickly Totila galloped to the head of his men, who were drawn up on top of the hill just beside the road. His expert eye took a quick look at the Armenian armour, as they advanced slowly up the hill in deep columns. They were carrying heavy shields, as tall as a man, and short spears for throwing or thrusting.

"They must not be allowed to throw their spears!" Totila called out to his mounted men. He ordered them to strap their light shields on their backs and told them that, at the moment they clashed with the enemy, they were to carry their lances in their left hand and not their right as usual. They were to simply wind the reins around their wrists and switch their lances from right to left over the manes of their mounts. Thus, when they clashed, they would strike at the right side of their opponents, which would not be protected by their shields. "As soon as you have charged – they will not be able to withstand our thrust – withdraw your lance by the arm strap, draw your swords and cut down anything still left standing."

He now drew up his men in two columns on both sides of the road. He himself led the main force along the road itself. He had decided to let the enemy advance halfway up the hill, and both groups of fighters were awaiting the coming clash with breathless anticipation.

Ambazuch, an experienced soldier, was advancing slowly and calmly. "Let them come really close, men," he ordered, "until you can feel the breath of their horses in your faces. Then, and not before, throw your spears, aiming low at the chests of the horses, and then draw your swords. That's how I have beaten every cavalry charge I have ever encountered yet!"

But this time it was to turn out differently. When Totila gave the signal to attack it seemed as if a thundering avalanche was rolling down the hill and over the shocked enemy. Like the storm wind the glistening, rattling, snorting mass raced down the hill, and before the front row of the Armenians had found time to raise their spears they had been mown down as if they had never stood, pierced by the long Gothic lances on their unprotected side.

All this had happened with lightning speed, and as Ambazuch was about to give orders to his second line, in which he himself stood, he found his second column mown down too, the third scattered and the fourth, under Bessas, struggling to offer some form of resistance to the terrible Gothic riders, who were only now drawing their swords. He wanted to halt the charge, so he hurried back and yelled encouragement to his men. Just then Totila's sword reached him, and one blow split his helmet. He sank to his knee and held out the hilt of his sword to the Goth. "I surrender," he cried, "I am yours!"

Totila's hand was already reaching out to accept the weapon when the voice of Teias shouted: "Think of the fortress Petra!" A sword flashed, and Ambazuch fell with his head cleft in two. At that the last of the terrified Armenians took flight, carrying Bessas away with them. The entire force was annihilated.

King Witigis and his men had been following Totila's victory with cries of joy. "Look, now the Hunnish cavalry directly below us are turning against Totila," the king said to Hildebrand. "Totila is attacking them, but they are much more numerous. On your way, Hildebad, hurry down the road and go to their aid."

"Ah," the old armourer cried, leaning forward in the saddle and looking over the precipice, "who is that tribune there, on the horse between two of Belisarius's bodyguards?"

Witigis bent forward. "Calpurnius!" he yelled with a piercing cry. And with that the king himself rode straight down the hill, not bothering to look for a path, directly at the hated Calpurnius. The fear that he might escape made him forget everything else, and he raced down the hill as if the god of revenge had given him wings, over rocks and bushes and ditches – there was no holding him!

For an instant terror gripped old Hildebrand; never had he seen a ride like it. But the next moment he raised the blue banner and shouted: "Follow him! Follow your king!" And thus suddenly the main part of the Gothic army descended upon the Hunnish cavalry, first the mounted Goths and those on foot behind them, leaping from rock to rock and sliding down the hill on their shields.

Calpurnius looked up. He thought he heard his name called, by a voice shrill with anger, and it sounded to him like the trumpet of judgment day. As if struck by lightning he turned and tried to flee. But the Moorish bodyguard on his right held his reins: "Stop, tribune!" he said, "the enemy is over there!" It was Antallas, pointing at Totila's cavalry. And then a cry of pain pierced the air, and made both him and Calpurnius look to their left. There his other bodyguard, Kutugur the Hun, was just falling from his horse, struck by the sword of a Goth who had suddenly appeared from nowhere. And behind this one Goth the steep hillside, which looked as if it could not be climbed, was alive with descending Goths. Suddenly the Hunnish cavalry was trapped, Totila's men on one side and this new enemy on the other.

Calpurnius recognised the Goth. "Witigis!" he cried in terror and let his arm drop. But his horse saved him. Frightened by the fall of the Hun, and wounded as well, the animal bounded away in a wild gallop.

Antallas threw himself furiously at the Gothic king, who seemed to have charged entirely on his own, leaving his army far behind. "Down with you, you daredevil!" he cried. But in the next instant he had been cut down by the sword of Witigis, which seemed to be sweeping from its path anything which still stood between it and Calpurnius. At breakneck speed Witigis pursued him, straight through the lines of Hunnish cavalry who scattered at his approach, terrified at the fury of this solitary charge.

Calpurnius had managed to regain control of his horse, and he now sought protection behind his strongest cavalry. In vain! Witigis did not let him out of his sight, and gave him no chance to escape. No matter how hard he tried to hide among his men, or how rapidly he tried to flee, he could not escape the eagle eyes of the king. Witigis was slaying anything and everything which tried to get between him and his son's murderer.

Group after group, platoon after platoon of men dissolved under the avenging father's terrible sword. The swathe cut by the fleeing Calpurnius and his pursuer had split the main Hunnish force in two, and they were unable to close ranks again. Before

Totila could arrive on the scene the old banner bearer Hildebrand had broken through their right flank with cavalry and infantry, and divided the enemy in two.

By the time Totila arrived there was nothing left for him to do but pursue fugitives. One wing was quickly surrounded by Totila and Hildebrand and annihilated, while the larger force on the other wing tried to fall back on Belisarius.

Meanwhile Calpurnius raced across the battlefield as if he was being chased by the furies of hell. He had a huge headstart on Witigis, who had been forced to cut a path for himself through the enemy lines no less than seven times. But a demon seemed to be driving Boreas, the Goth's horse, and he was coming ever closer to his intended victim. Already he could hear Witigis calling out to him to stand and fight when his horse finally collapsed under him. Even before he had regained his feet Witigis was standing before him. He had leapt from the saddle and now, without a word, he kicked Calpurnius's sword toward him, which the latter had dropped. Driven by the courage of desperation Calpurnius rallied. He grasped the sword and threw himself at the Goth like a tiger. But right in the middle of his leap he fell backwards.

Witigis had struck him one mighty blow, right through his helmet and almost splitting his head in two. The king set one foot on the corpse and looked at the twisted face, then he sighed deeply: "Now I have my revenge! Oh if only I could have my child instead!"

Belisarius had been watching this unfavourable opening to hostilities with anger and concern. But his confidence and his composure did not desert him as he watched the Armenians of Bessas and Ambazuch swept away, and Calpurnius and the cavalry scattered and overrun.

He could now see the great numerical superiority of the enemy, but he still persisted with an advance along the entire front, leaving a gap in the centre to receive remnants of the fleeing cavalry.

But the Goths noticed this straight away and, led by Witigis and then Totila and Hildebrand behind him, they pursued the enemy with such fury that it looked as if they would reach Belisarius's line at the same time as the fugitives, and might even break through the Byzantine centre there and then. That was something which Belisarius could not allow to happen, so he filled the gap with his own bodyguard on foot and called out to the fleeing cavalry to turn and fight.

But it was as if the terror of their fallen leader had infected them all. They feared the sword of the Gothic king behind them more than the threats of their own general in front, and so they approached at top speed as if they were trying to cut down their own infantry.

A moment later there was a terrible collision! A thousand voices cried out in fear and anger, and for several minutes a wild confusion of cavalry and infantry were fighting one another, with the Goths hacking away at both. Suddenly there was a scattering in all directions, together with Gothic cries of victory.

The bodyguard of Belisarius had been mown down, and the centre of his main force broken. He now ordered retreat into the camp. But it was no longer a retreat, it was a rout in full flight. The troops of Hildebad and Guntharis had arrived with Teias on the battlefield, and the Byzantines saw their entire position overthrown. They despaired of resistance, and were falling back on their camp in great disarray. They might yet have reached the camp but for a new, unexpected obstacle in their way.

Belisarius had set out so confident of victory that he had ordered all the wagons, the supply train and the herds, which in accordance with the custom of the time followed the army, to follow the troops along every road. And now everywhere the fleeing troops came up against this slow, cumbersome procession of animals and wagons, which were difficult to move out of the way. The result was boundless delay and confusion. In no time soldiers and baggage attendants were fighting hand to hand, and the columns were splitting up among the carts, boxes and carriages. In some the desire to loot surfaced, and they started to plunder their own baggage train before it fell to the Barbarians. There was fighting, cursing, threatening and complaining everywhere, interrupted by the sound of splintering carts and the bleating and roaring of frightened animals.

"Abandon the baggage train! Set the wagons on fire! Send the cavalry through the herds!" Belisarius ordered, cutting a swathe for himself with his bodyguard in good formation. But it was in vain. The confusion became worse and worse, and it looked as if nothing could untangle the mess.

And then he almost despaired. The cry: "The Barbarians are upon us!" sounded from the furthest rows of his own men. And it was no idle alarm. Hildebad with his infantry had reached the plain, and his leading troops now clashed with the defenceless rabble. There was a massive movement forward, and a thousand voices cried out in fear – in anger – in pain. The bodyguards tried to stand and fight, but could not. The cries of the wounded, crushed and mangled arose everywhere, and then suddenly the greater part of the wagons went crashing down on both sides of the road, taking with them their loads, their animals and the thousands who were intermingled with them.

And so the road was free, and in complete confusion the stream of fugitives fell back on the camp. With loud victory cries the Gothic infantry followed, effortlessly finding targets for their spears and arrows among the fleeing mass. Meanwhile Belisarius was having great difficulty trying to fight off repeated attacks by Totila and the king with the Gothic cavalry. "Help, Belisarius!" cried Aigan, the leader of the Massageti mercenaries, riding out of the maelstrom and wiping blood from his face: "My countrymen have seen the black devil himself among our enemies today. They will not stand and fight for me. Help! Usually they fear you more than the devil!"

Belisarius gritted his teeth as he looked over to his right wing, which was fleeing scattered over the plain, pursued by the Goths. "Oh Justinianus, my Imperial master, how badly have I kept my word to you!"

By now the hilly terrain was weakening the effectiveness of the pursuing cavalry and Belisarius, leaving the task of covering the retreat to the camp to the experienced Demetrius, rode right among the fugitives with Aigan and his mounted guards.

"Stop!" he thundered, "stop, you cowardly dogs. Who flees while Belisarius stands and fights? I am right among you, so turn and fight, so that victory will yet be ours!" And he opened the visor of his helmet to let them see his majestic, leonine face.

So powerful was the effect of the great hero's charisma, and so great their faith in his luck and ability to snatch victory from defeat, that indeed all those who saw the figure of their general high up on his horse did stop, and then turned to face the Gothic onslaught with cries of encouragement. Here at last the flight had come to a halt.

And then a huge Goth approached, easily making way for himself. "Hey, I am so glad you tired of running at last, you speedy little Greeks. I am quite out of breath from chasing after you. You are certainly better than us in the legs. Let's see if your arms are as good. Ha, what are you retreating from? From him on the brown horse there? What is so special about him?"

"Sir, he must be a king among the Byzantines. We can barely endure his furious eyes."

"Who might he be? Ah – it must be Belisarius! I am delighted," he called out to him, "that we meet at last, you brave hero! Now get down from your horse and try the strength of your arms against mine. I am Hildebad, Tota's son, and as you see I am also on foot. What? You won't?" he cried angrily, "do I have to drag you down from your nag?" And he weighed his huge spear in his right hand.

"Back off, Sir," Aigan cried, "that giant can hurl whole trees."

"Yes, Sir, run for it, or at least duck," one of the men repeated.

But Belisarius, his short sword drawn, calmly approached the young Goth more closely. The log-like spear flew through the air, aimed straight for Belisarius's chest. But an instant before the spear found its mark there was a sharp blow from Belisarius's sword, and the spear fell harmlessly three paces to one side.

"Hail Belisarius, Hail!" the Byzantines cried, encouraged, and charged at their opponents anew.

"Now that was a good parry," Hildebad laughed grimly. "Let's see if your fencing skills will help you against this one too." Bending down, he picked up a huge, jagged boulder from the field at his feet. First he swung it slowly back and forth, then he lifted it with both hands above his head and hurled it with all his might at the charging Belisarius. A cry from his followers, and the hero of Byzantium fell backwards from his horse. That was the end.

"Belisarius dead! Woe! All is lost!" they cried as the tall figure vanished from sight, and as fast as they could they ran for the camp, without thinking. A few individual men kept running, without stopping, until they reached the gates of Rome.

The lancers and the shield bearers resisted the Goths with death-defying bravery as best they could, but it was in vain. It was only with great difficulty that they saved their commander, but the battle was lost.

The first deadly blow from Hildebad's sword was caught by the faithful Maxentius, who stopped it with his own breast. But here a mounted Goth finally fell from his horse, a man who had reached Belisarius immediately after Hildebad, and who had slain seven bodyguards to get through to the *Magister Militum*. His own men found him later with thirteen wounds. But he remained alive, and was to be one of the few to fight though the whole war and survive – Wisand the *bandalarius*.

Belisarius by now had been lifted back on his horse by Aigan and Valentius and his strapper, and had quickly regained consciousness. Vainly he raised his general's baton and shouted commands; they no longer heard him and did not want to hear. Vainly he swung his sword at fleeing troops all around him, and in the end their momentum carried him right back into the camp.

Here he succeeded once more in delaying the Goths, who were following up their advantage with great effect, by making good use of a fortified gate and tower. "We have lost our honour," he said dispiritedly, "let us now save our lives." With these words he had the gates of the camp closed, without regard to the masses of his own men who were still outside.

An attempt by the impetuous Hildebad to force his way into the camp without further ado was foiled by the strong oaken walls and gates, which resisted spears and stones. Leaning on his spear, momentarily at his wits' end, Hildebad caught a moment's respite from the searing heat. Then Teias came around the corner. Like the king and Totila he had dismounted and was studying the defences.

"That accursed wooden fortress," Hildebad called out to him, "neither stone nor iron are of any use!"

"No," Teias replied, "but fire is!" With his foot he kicked a heap of ashes nearby. "These are the guards' fires from last night, with plenty of twigs left for fuel. There is still a glow here! Come here, men, quickly! Stoke the fires with your swords and throw on more fuel! Throw fire into the camp!"

"You wizard!" Hildebad rejoiced, "quickly boys, burn them out like a fox in a hole! The fresh northerly wind will help." In no time at all the fires were burning again, and hundreds of firebrands were being hurled into the dry timber of the palisades. And it was not long before flames were roaring skywards. The thick smoke, carried into the camp by the wind, blew into the Byzantines' faces and made defending the walls impossible. They retreated to the interior of the camp.

"If only I could die now!" Belisarius sighed. "Clear the camp! Out by way of the Porta Decumania, and then back to the bridges behind us in good order and formation!"

But the order to abandon the camp also meant the end to whatever order and discipline remained. As the gate resounded from the blows of Teias's axe, and the charred timbers crashed and splintered, the fleeing soldiers tore open all the gates leading to Rome. A moment later the black warrior came racing through fire and smoke, like a demon of fire. He was the first Goth into the camp. Now the fugitives streamed out through every gate, including the main gates on both sides of the camp, and they surged in the direction of the river in utter disorder. The first of them managed to reach the bridges safely and without being pursued; they had a good headstart until Hildebad and Teias were able to force Belisarius out of the burning camp.

But suddenly there was a new terror! Gothic horns were sounding in the very near vicinity. Witigis and Totila, as soon as they knew the camp was theirs, had remounted their horses with their men, and now they were charging at the flanks of the fleeing Byzantine army from both sides.

Belisarius had just galloped out of the Porta Decumania and was hurrying toward one of the bridges, when he saw the masses of Gothic cavalry charging down on both sides. But still the mighty warrior did not lose his composure. "Forward as fast as you can, to the bridges!" he commanded the Saracens. "Cover them!"

But it was too late. There was a dull crashing sound, soon followed by another. The narrow bridges had collapsed under the weight of the fleeing army, and now the Hunnish cavalry and the Illyrian lancers, Justinian's pride, tumbled into the swampy waters in their hundreds.

Without hesitating Belisarius drove his mount straight into the foaming waters, which were already coloured with blood, and reached the other side swimming. "Salomo, Dagisthaeos," he called out to the speediest of his Praetorians as soon as he had reached the other side, "take a hundred of my mounted guards and hurry to the narrow pass as fast as you can. Ride down any fugitives in your way. You must get there before the Goths, do you hear? You must! It is our last slim chance."

Both obeyed and galloped away like lightning.

Belisarius gathered what he could of his scattered forces. The Goths, like the Byzantines, were delayed for a time by the river. Suddenly Aigan exclaimed: "There is Salomo galloping back, Sir!"

"Belisarius!" the latter cried from afar, "everything is lost! There are already arms in the pass. The Goths have already occupied it!"

And then, for the first time on this day of disaster, Belisarius knew fear in his heart. "The pass is lost? If that is so then not one man of the emperor's army will escape. Then farewell Antonina, life and fame! Come Aigan, draw your sword! Let us not fall into Barbarian hands alive."

"Master," said Aigan, "I have never heard you speak like this."

"It has never been like this. Let us dismount and die." He already had one foot out of the stirrup, ready to dismount, when Dagisthaeos came speeding to the scene: "Have courage, general!"

"Well?"

"The pass is ours! They were Roman weapons we saw. It is the Prefect Cethegus. He held it in secret."

"Cethegus?" Belisarius cried, "is it possible? Are you sure?"

"Yes Sir, quite sure. Look, it was high time." And indeed it was. A group of Gothic cavalry, sent by King Witigis to reach the pass before the fleeing Byzantines, had just forded the river. They had now cut off Belisarius's own cavalry and reached the vital pass before them. But just as they were about to charge into the pass, Cethegus broke out of the gorge at the head of his Isaurians, and after a brief encounter he was able to drive the surprised Goths to flight.

"The first glimmer of victory on this black day!" Belisarius cried. "Follow me to the pass!" And so the general led his remaining men to the pass in better order and with relative calm.

"Welcome to safety, Belisarius!" Cethegus greeted him, wiping the blade of his sword. "I have been waiting for you here since daybreak. I knew very well that you would come to me."

"Prefect of Rome," Belisarius replied, dismounting and offering Cethegus his hand. "You have saved the emperor's army, which I had lost. I thank you."

The Prefect's fresh troops held the pass as if it was an impenetrable wall, letting through the fleeing Byzantines one by one, and easily repulsing attacks from the first tired pursuers who, despite having a full day of hard fighting behind them, had followed them across the river.

Before darkness fell King Witigis drew his troops back to spend the night on the field of battle. Meanwhile behind the pass Belisarius and his generals ordered and regrouped the remnants of their army as best they could, as they arrived singly or in small groups.

When Belisarius had thus managed to collect together a few thousand troops once more, he rode over to Cethegus and said: "What do you think, Prefect of Rome? Your troops are still fresh, and ours must have a chance to even the score. Let us break out one more time – the sun will not set for a while yet – and turn the result of the day's fighting in our favour."

Cethegus looked at him amazed, and quoted Homer's words: "Truly, mighty one, you have uttered a dreadful word. You are insatiable! Do you find it so difficult to come out of a battle without victory? No, Belisarius! Over there Rome's battlements are waiting for us; lead your tired men there instead. I will hold this pass until you have safely reached the city, and I will be content if I can manage to do that."

And so it was to be. Under the circumstances Belisarius had less chance than ever of persuading the Prefect to act against his will. So he gave in and led his army back to Rome, where he arrived as night fell.

For a long time the Romans on the walls did not want to let him in because, covered as he was in dust and blood, nobody recognised him. Furthermore scattered fugitives had reported that Belisarius had fallen in the battle, and that all was lost. Finally Antonina, who had been anxiously waiting on the wall, recognised him. He was admitted through the Porta Pinciana, which has from that day been known as the Porta Belisaria.

Fire signals on the walls, between the Porta Pinciana and the Porta Flaminia, informed the Prefect that Belisarius had safely reached Rome. Cethegus could now execute his retreat in good order, under cover of night and almost without harassment from the tired victors.

Only Teias with a handful of men followed through as far as the hills, where the Villa Borghese is today, through to the Aqua Acetosa.

Chapter 8

On the following day the whole of the huge Gothic army appeared before the eternal city, surrounding it in seven camps. And so the memorable siege began, which was to demonstrate the military genius and ingenuity of Belisarius, and to no lesser degree the bravery of the beleaguerers.

The citizens of Rome had observed with dread from their walls how there seemed to be no end to the Goths. "Look, Prefect, they will flood right over your walls."

"Yes, in breadth! But we will see if they can get over them. Without wings they will not enter Rome."

Ravenna was guarded by two thousand men, left behind there by the king, and he had also sent Count Uligis of Urbssalvia and Count Ansa of Asculum to Dalmatia, in order to wrest this province, together with Liburnia, from the Byzantines. They were to find reinforcements by hiring mercenaries in Savia, and recapture the important stronghold of Salona. The entire remainder of the Gothic army lay before Rome. The Gothic fleet, against the advice of Teias, had also been sent to Dalmatia rather than being used against Portus, the harbour of Rome.

But the entire circumference of Rome and her extensive walls had been encircled by the king and one hundred and fifty thousand men.

In those days Rome had fifteen main gates as well as a number of minor ones. The Goths were holding the greater and weaker part of the city completely surrounded by six camps, stretching from the Porta Flaminia in the north (east of the present day Porta del Populo) to the Porta Praenestina. This included all the walls east of the Porta Flaminia to the Porta Pinciana and the Porta Salaria, and from there to the Porta Nomentana (southeast of the Porta Pia) and the so called "closed gate," the Porta Clausa. Finally the encirclement included the Porta Tiburtina (today the Porta San Lorenzo) and the other gates along the bank of the Tiber. All of these gates were on the left bank of the river.

In order to prevent the besieged from destroying the Milvesian Bridge, and thereby cutting off the Goths not only from crossing the river but also from the whole area between the right bank and the sea, the Goths had established a seventh camp on the right bank of the Tiber, on the Field of Nero between the Milvesian Bridge and the Vatican Hill. Thus the bridge was covered by a Gothic camp, which also threatened the bridge of Hadrian and the road into the city through the Porta St Petri, as the inner Porta Aureliana was called in those days, according to Procopius. It was closest to Hadrian's tomb. But the Porta St Pancratia on the right bank was also being closely watched by the Goths.

The camp on the right bank was commanded by Count Markja of Mediolanum, who had been recalled from the Alps and from observing the Franks. But the king himself also spent a lot of time here, examining Hadrian's tomb carefully and often.

The king had not assumed command of any particular camp, leaving himself free to concentrate on the overall command. The other six camps were commanded by Hildebrand, Totila, Hildebad, Teias, Guntharis and Grippa. The king had ordered each of the seven camps to be fortified by means of a deep ditch. The earth which had thus been dug out was used to build a high earth wall, which was in turn reinforced with timber as a defence against possible sorties on the part of the defending Byzantines.

But Belisarius and Cethegus had also distributed their commanders and their troops among the various gates and sections of Rome's defences. Bessas had been put in command of the Porta Praenestina in the east (now known as the Porta Maggiore), and Constantinus was in charge of the severely threatened Porta Flaminia, to which the Gothic camp commanded by Totila was dangerously close. Constantinus had closed it off almost completely by means of marble blocks taken from temples and palaces.

Belisarius himself made his main camp in the north of the city, which was the weakest part of the area he had been given by Cethegus to defend.

The western and southern sections were held, jealously and immovably, by the Prefect.

But here in the north Belisarius was master. He settled between the Porta Flaminia and the Porta Pinciana (now Porta Belisaria), at the same time planning sorties against the Barbarians. The other gates he entrusted to the leaders of his infantry, Paranius, Magnus, Ennes, Artabazes, Azarethas and Chilbudius.

The Prefect had occupied all the gates on the right bank of the Tiber, the new Porta Aurelia on the Aelisian Bridge near Hadrian's Tomb, the Porta Septimiana, the old Aurelian gate (now known as the Porta Pancratia) and the Porta Portuensis. In addition he also held the Porta St Paul on the left bank. It was only from there onwards that the gates were occupied by Byzantines, the nearest one being the Porta Ardeatina under the command of Chilbudius.

The beleaguerers and the beleaguered proved to be equally tireless and inventive in planning attack and defence. For a long time the main Gothic effort was aimed at demoralising the Romans, with no attempt at storming in the early stages, and consequently the main concern of the defenders was to foil these aims.

The Goths, now masters of the surrounding countryside, tried to deprive the defenders of water by cutting each of the fourteen magnificent aqueducts which supplied the city. As soon as Belisarius heard this he immediately ordered all the openings of these aqueducts into the city to be walled off. Procopius had told him: "After you yourself, Belisarius, crept into Naples by way of such a water pipe, the Barbarians might also stumble on the idea, and after all it would not look in the least inglorious to them if they were to crawl into Rome along the same heroic path you yourself used."

Thus the beleaguered Romans had to do without their beloved baths. There was barely enough water in the wells for drinking, at least in those parts of the city remote from the river.

But by cutting off the water it seemed that the Goths had also deprived the defenders of bread. All the water driven mills of Rome were now inoperative, and so the grain which Cethegus and Belisarius had stockpiled in the city could no longer be milled. With great forethought Cethegus had bought grain from Sicily, and Belisarius had obtained supplies by confiscating grain from the surrounding countryside.

"Let the mills be driven by donkeys and cows!" Belisarius ordered.

"Most of the donkeys and cows, oh Belisarius," Procopius replied, "were smart enough not to be locked in here with us. We have only just enough to slaughter for our immediate food needs. They can hardly be expected to mill the grain first, and then still have enough meat left on them to cover the bread they have milled for us."

"Then call Martinus. Yesterday on the riverbank, as I was counting the Gothic tents, I had an idea."

"An idea which Martinus will now have to translate from an inspiration of Belisarius into something practically feasible. Poor man! But I will go and fetch him."

By the following evening Martinus and Belisarius had constructed the world's first ships' mill by joining boats together in the fast flowing Tiber. When he saw it Procopius said admiringly: "The bread from this mill will give mankind more joy than your greatest deeds. The flour thus ground tastes of – immortality!" And indeed these mills, invented by Belisarius and built by Martinus, replaced the useless water mills for the entire duration of the siege.

What Belisarius had done was to anchor two ships in the river, behind the bridge which is now called the Ponte San Sisto. Mills were laid across their flat decks, so that the wheels were driven by the flowing river, which flowed through the narrow arch of the bridge with considerable force.

The beleaguerers, to whom these activities had been reported by defectors, now strove to destroy the new inventions. One night they threw logs, trees and rafts into the river upstream of the bridge, and indeed they managed to smash all the mills. But Belisarius had them repaired, and he also had strong chains fitted across the river just above the bridge. These chains were designed to catch anything floating downstream which threatened the mills.

But the chains were not only intended to protect the mills. They also served to prevent the Goths from coming down the river in boats or on rafts, and invading the city from the water without needing a bridge.

Witigis was now making full preparations to try and take the city by storm.

He had wooden towers built, higher than the tallest battlements, mounted on wheels and pulled by oxen. He also had storm ladders brought in large numbers, together with four dreadful battering rams, each operated by fifty men. The deep ditches were to be filled with countless bundles of reeds and twigs.

Belisarius and Cethegus, on the other hand, had the walls equipped with ballistas and powerful bows, which could hurl huge spears over long distances with tremendous force. The gates were protected by "wolves," large logs with spikes, which were dropped on the attackers when they came close enough. Finally they had the space between the moat and the Barbarian camp strewn with barbed hooks and the like.

Chapter 9

Despite all this the Roman population was saying that the Goths would have scaled their walls long ago, had it not been for the Prefect's uncanny foresight.

It was very strange indeed. Every time the Barbarians prepared for another attempt to storm the walls, Cethegus would go to Belisarius and warn him, telling him in advance exactly where and on what day the attempt would be made. Every time Hildebad or Teias tried to overrun a gate or take a battlement by a sudden strike, Cethegus foretold it, and the attackers would meet with twice the usual number of defenders. Every time the chains across the Tiber were to be broken in a night attack, Cethegus seemed to sense it and he would send ships and fire boats against the enemy.

Thus it went on for many months. The Goths could not conceal even from themselves that they had made no progress at all since the siege started, despite numerous attacks having been made.

For a long time they endured these mishaps, and this constant anticipation and foiling of their plans, with unbowed courage. But eventually frustration not only overcame the masses, especially as food was becoming scarce, but even the king's mind was becoming clouded with a deep depression, as he saw all his strength, his endurance and his strategic skills foiled as if by some evil demon. And whenever he returned to the royal tent from yet another unsuccessful attack, tired and bowed, his queen's proud eyes would rest on him with a mysterious but unbearably ominous expression, so that he had to turn away with a shudder.

"It has happened exactly as I foresaw," he said gloomily to Teias, "my luck left me with Rauthgundis, as did all the joy in my heart. And that Amalung daughter walks about me, silently and gloomily, as if she was my living evil star."

"You may be right," Teias replied. "Perhaps I can lift the evil spell for you. Give me leave for tonight."

On the same day, at almost the same hour, Bloody John asked Belisarius for leave on the same night. Belisarius refused him. "Now is not the time for nocturnal adventures," he said.

"There won't be much pleasure in walking about among damp walls and Gothic lances, looking for a fox which is smarter than the two of us together, many times smarter in fact."

"What do you have in mind?" Belisarius asked, now interested.

"What do I have in mind? To put an end to the accursed position in which we are all placed, not least yourself, my general. For months the Barbarians have been lying outside these walls, and they have gained absolutely nothing from it. We shoot them down from behind our walls like boys shooting pigeons, and we can laugh at them. But who is it really that achieves all this? Not you, the emperor's general, as it should be; in fact it is that icy Roman, who can only laugh when he is ridiculing someone. He is sitting up there in the Capitol and laughing at the emperor, the Goths and, if I may say it, most of all he laughs at you. How is it that this man, who is an Ajax and an Odysseus in one, knows all the Gothic plans just as if he himself had a seat on Witigis's council of war? Some say it is through his *demonium*, others say it's his *eregia*. Still others say that he has a raven, who can listen and talk like a person, and whom he sends into the Gothic camp every night. Maybe old women and Romans believe that, but not my mother's son. I think I know who the raven and the *demonium* are. I am certain that the information can only be coming from the Gothic camp itself; let me see if I can't drink from the same fountain in his place."

"I have thought about that for some time myself, but I could see no way to find out."

"I have had his every step watched by my Huns. It is damnably difficult, because that brown Moorish devil follows him like a shadow. But Syphax has been missing for days, and that makes it easier. Now: I have been able to find out that Cethegus has left the city on many a night, sometimes by the Porta Portuensis on the right bank, and sometimes by the Porta St Paul on the left bank, both of which he holds occupied. My spies did not dare to follow him any further. But tonight – I think he will go again tonight – I do not intend to let him out of my sight. But I would have to wait for him outside the gate, because his Isaurians would not let me through. I will stay behind in a ditch during a patrol outside the walls."

"Good. But as you say, there are two gates to be watched."

"That is why I have chosen my brother Perseus to come with me. He will guard the St Paul gate, and I the Porta Portuensis. You can depend on it, by sunrise tomorrow one of us will know the Prefect's *demonium*." And indeed, one of them was to learn its identity.

Immediately opposite the Porta St Paul, about three arrow shots beyond the outermost defences of the city, there was a huge ancient building. It was the Basilica Sancti Paulus extra muros (St Paul's chapel beyond the walls), the last remains of which did not disappear until Rome was besieged by the Bourbons many centuries later. Originally it had been a temple of Jupiter Stator, the building having been dedicated to the Saint only for the previous two centuries. A huge bronze statue of the god still stood, but the flaming bolt of thunder in his right hand had been replaced by a cross. In all other respects the statue of the tall, bearded man fitted its new name very well.

It was around the sixth hour of night. The moon stood high over the eternal city and cast its silver light over the battlements and over the plain beyond, between the Roman defences and the basilica, which in turn cast its shadows over the nearby Gothic camp.

The watch had just changed on the gate of St Paul. But seven men had gone outside, and only six had come back. The seventh turned his back on the gate and walked out into the field.

He picked his way carefully, taking pains to avoid the numerous hooks, poisoned arrowheads and traps which had been strewn about everywhere, and which had brought about the demise of many a Goth. The man seemed to know them all and avoided them easily, but he was just as careful to avoid the moonlight, seeking the shelter of overhanging parts of the wall and the shadows of trees.

When he had reached the outermost ditch he looked around him and stopped in the shade of a cypress tree, which had lost its branches to missiles from the ballistas. He could see nothing living, and now he hurried to the church with rapid steps. Had he looked back once more he might not have done so.

Because as soon as he left the tree a second figure appeared out of the ditch, which bordered within three paces on the shadows on the other side of the tree. "Done, proud brother John, this time luck has smiled on the younger brother. Now Cethegus and his secret are mine." Carefully he followed the first man.

But suddenly the first man disappeared from sight as if the earth had swallowed him. It was right by the outside wall of the church, and yet when Perseus got there he could see neither door nor opening.

"There is no doubt," the would-be listener said to himself, "the little tryst is to take place inside the church. I must find a way to get in."

But the wall could not be climbed at the spot where he was. Testing and searching as he went, the spy walked softly around the corner. But it was in vain; the wall was of the same height all around. He lost almost a quarter of an hour searching. At last he found a gap in the stones, and squeezed himself through it with difficulty. Now he was in the outer courtyard of the old temple, into which massive Doric columns were casting broad shadows. By exploiting their cover along the wall he reached the main building.

He looked through a crack in the wall, which had betrayed its existence by a slight draught. Inside everything was dark, but suddenly he was almost blinded by a bright ray of light. When he opened his eyes again he saw a strip of light in the grey darkness – it was coming from a lantern, which had suddenly appeared. He could see clearly what the lantern illuminated, but not who was carrying it. He could clearly distinguish the Prefect Cethegus, who was standing right in front of the statue of the apostle, and seemed to be leaning against it. In front of him stood a tall, slender woman, whose dark red hair shone in the light of the lantern.

"By Eros and Anteros, that's the beautiful Gothic queen!" the eavesdropper thought, "not a bad little rendezvous, be it for love or politics. Hark, she is speaking. A pity I missed the earlier part of the conversation."

"So listen well. Tomorrow something dangerous is being planned for the day after tomorrow, outside the Porta Tiburtina."

"Good, but what?" the Prefect's voice asked.

"I could not find out any more details, and even if I do find out I will not be able to tell you later. I cannot risk meeting you here again, because…" and she spoke more softly.

Perseus pressed his ear close to the crack to catch what was being said. As he did so his sword struck the stone, and now a ray of light fell upon him.

"Listen!" a third voice called out softly. It was the voice of a woman, and it belonged to the lantern bearer. Perseus recognised a slave girl in Moorish costume as she now turned to the source of the noise, and in so doing appeared in the light of her own lantern. For a moment everything was quiet in the temple. Perseus held his breath. He knew his life was at stake as Cethegus went for his sword.

"Everything is quiet," said the slave, "a stone must have fallen on one of the metal fixtures outside."

"I will not go to the tomb outside the Porta Portuensis any more either. I am afraid I am being followed."

"Who?"

"The one who never sleeps, it seems. Count Teias." The Prefect's lips set a little harder.

"And he is also involved in some mysterious plot on the life of Belisarius himself. The attack on St Paul's Gate is only a diversion."

"Belisarius will not escape unless he is warned. I somehow fear that they are lying in ambush somewhere in greatly superior numbers. Count Totila is leading them."

"I will warn him!" Cethegus said slowly.

"If the attempt should succeed…"

"Don't worry yourself on that account, queen! I am just as concerned for the safety of Rome as you are. And if the next attempt to take the city by storm fails, then according to my reckoning they will have to abandon the siege, no matter how persistent they have been. And that, my queen, is entirely due to you. This night, perhaps the last time we will meet, let me reveal to you just how much I admire you. It is not often that Cethegus is astonished, and he seldom admits it when he admires someone. But you I do admire, my queen. How you have foiled the Barbarian plans with death-defying courage, and with diabolical cunning! Truly, Belisarius did much, and Cethegus more, but Matesuentha did most of all."

"Oh if only that were true!" Matesuentha replied with flashing eyes. "And if that crown falls from the head of that wretch…"

"It will have been by your hand, of which Rome made use. But queen, you cannot let it end like that! As I have come to know you these last months – you must not go to Byzantium as a captive Gothic queen. Your beauty, your mind, your strength and your courage are made to rule, not serve, in Byzantium. So think about it, once the tyrant has been overthrown. Won't you go the way I showed you?"

"I have never thought beyond his fall," she replied darkly.

"But I have, for you! Truly, Matesuentha," and his eyes rested on her with admiration, "you are – beautiful beyond description. It is a source of great pride to me that even you could not awaken love in me and distract me from my goals. But you are too beautiful, too precious to live only for revenge and hatred. Once we have attained our goal – then to Byzantium! But as more than an empress – as the conqueror of an empress!"

"Once I have attained my goal my life is finished. Do you think I could endure the thought of having destroyed my people for sheer lust of power? No, I was able to do it only because I had to. Revenge is now my life and my love, and…"

Suddenly, from the front of the building, there came the call of an owl, loud and shrill, once – twice – in rapid succession. Perseus was amazed as he saw the Prefect press quickly at the statue's throat, and how it opened silently into two halves. Cethegus slipped into the opening, and the statue closed again silently. Matesuentha and Aspa, however, sank to their knees as if in prayer.

"So it was a sign! There must be danger!" Perseus thought; "but where is it coming from? And who warned them?" He turned, stepped forward, and looked to the left, in the direction of the Gothic camp.

But that caused him to step out into the moonlight, and into the sight of Syphax, who was standing guard in an empty niche in front of the main building, and who until now had been looking only to the left, or Gothic side.

From there, from the left, a man was slowly approaching. His battleaxe glistened in the moonlight.

But Perseus could see another weapon flash; it was the Moor, who was silently drawing his sword from its scabbard. "Ha," Perseus laughed, "by the time those two are finished with one another, I will be safely back in Rome with my secret." A few quick bounds, and he was back at the gap in the wall, through which he had entered.

For a moment Syphax looked doubtfully to the left and right. On his right he saw an escaping spy, whom he had only just noticed. On his left a Gothic warrior was entering the courtyard of the temple. There was no way he could get to and kill them both. So, suddenly, he called out at the top of his voice: "Teias! Count Teias! Help! A Roman! Save the queen! There, to the right along the wall, a Roman!"

In an instant Teias was by the side of Syphax. "There," the latter cried, "I will protect the women in the church!" And he hurried into the temple.

"Stop, Roman!" Teias called out, and went after the fleeing Perseus. But Perseus did not stop. He had run to the wall and got as far as the gap through which he had entered, but in his hurry he could not force his way through again. So, with the strength of desperation, he swung himself up on the wall. He was already starting to lower himself down the other side when Teias's axe flew through the air and struck him on the head. He tumbled backwards over the wall, taking his newly found secret with him.

Teias bent over him, and recognised the face of his dead adversary. "Perseus," he said, "Bloody John's brother." And immediately he climbed the steps leading into the church. On the threshold he was met by Matesuentha, and behind her Syphax and Aspa with the lantern. For a moment the two of them mustered one another suspiciously.

"I am in your debt, Count Teias," the queen said at last, "I was threatened during my lonely prayer."

"You choose a strange time and place to pray. Let's see if the Roman was the only enemy."

He took the lantern from Aspa and went into the interior of the chapel. A little while later he returned with a leather shoe in his hand, inlaid with gold. "I found nothing except – this sandal near the altar, in front of the apostle. It is a man's sandal."

"It was a votive gift from me," Syphax said quickly. "The apostle healed my foot. I had a thorn in it."

"I thought you believe only in the snake god?"

"I believe in anything that helps."

"In which foot was the thorn?"

Syphax hesitated for an instant. "The right," he said quickly.

"A pity," Teias replied, "the sandal was cut for the left foot." He stuck it in his belt. "I must warn you, queen, against such midnight prayers."

"I will do what I regard as my duty!" Matesuentha replied haughtily.

"And I will do mine." With these words Teias led the way back to the camp, with the queen and her slaves following in silence.

Before sunrise Teias stood before Witigis and reported the whole matter to him.

"What you say is not proof," the king said.

"But grounds for grave suspicion. You have said yourself that you find the queen sinister."

"For that very reason I will not do anything based on mere suspicion. Sometimes I wonder if we did not do her an injustice, almost as grave as that against Rauthgundis."

"Perhaps, but these nocturnal wanderings?"

"I will put an end to those, for her own safety if nothing else."

"And the Moor? I don't trust him. I know that he goes missing for days at a time, and then suddenly he appears back in the camp. He is a spy."

"That he is," Witigis replied. "He is my spy. He comes and goes with my knowledge, into and out of Rome. He is the one who has told me about all the important happenings so far."

"And not one bit of information has been of use. What about the false sandal?"

"It really was a votive sacrifice, for theft. He confessed it all to me even before you came. While waiting for the queen he became bored and started to rummage about in a basement of the church. There he found a number of old priest's clothes and buried ornaments, which he kept. Later, fearing the apostle's wrath, he wanted to avert that wrath and in his heathen way he offered this sandal from the loot as a sacrifice. He described it to me exactly; golden strips along the sides and an agate knob on top, with the letter "C" on it. So you can see that it all fits. He must have known the sandal, so it can't have been lost by a fugitive. And he promised to bring me the other sandal as well, as proof. But above all else he has betrayed a new plan to me, which will put an end to all our problems, and which should lead Belisarius himself into our hands."

Chapter 10

Whilst the Gothic king was telling his friend about his plan, Cethegus was standing before Belisarius and John, having been summoned to the Porta Belisaria at a very early hour.

"Prefect of Rome!" the general shouted at him as he entered, "where were you last night?"

"At my post, where I belong, at the St Paul's gate."

"Did you know that last night one of my best commanders, John's brother Perseus, left the city and has not been seen since?"

"I am sorry to hear that. But as you know it is forbidden to go outside the walls without permission."

"But I have reason to believe," John cried passionately, "that you know quite well what became of my brother, and that your hands are stained with his blood."

"And by Justinian's slumber!" Belisarius shouted furiously, "you will regret it. No longer will you rule over the emperor's army and his generals! The hour of reckoning has come. The Barbarians are as good as destroyed. Now we will see whether the Capitol falls when your head rolls."

"Is that the way it is, Belisarius?" Cethegus thought to himself. "In that case watch out!" But he remained silent.

"Speak!" John shouted. "Where did you murder my brother?"

Before Cethegus could reply Artasines, one of Belisarius's Persian bodyguards, entered. "Master," he said, "there are six Gothic warriors outside. They bring the body of Perseus. King Witigis said to inform you that he fell last night by the axe of Count Teias, and he sends you the body for honourable burial."

Cethegus walked out proudly: "Heaven itself calls your malicious accusations lies." But the Prefect made his way back slowly and thoughtfully to his house via the Quirinal and the Forum of Trajan. "You threaten me, Belisarius? Thank you for the hint. Let us see if we cannot get along without you."

Back at his house he found Syphax, who had been impatiently waiting for him, and who now made his report. "Above all, master," the slave concluded, "have your sandal binder whipped. You can see now how badly you are served when Syphax is away. Also kindly give me your right shoe."

"I should not give it to you and let you struggle for telling such cheeky lies," the Prefect laughed. "That piece of leather is worth your life now, my panther. What can you give me in return for it?"

"Important information. I know all the details of the proposed attempt on Belisarius, time, place and the names of the conspirators. They are Totila, Teias and Hildebad."

"Each one on his own is enough for the *Magister Militum*." Cethegus said happily, more to himself than to Syphax.

"I imagine, master, that you have once again set a nice little trap for the Barbarians! On your orders I have informed them that Belisarius himself plans to leave the city by the Porta Tiburtina tomorrow, in order to forage for supplies."

"Yes, he is going with them himself because the Huns, who have been caught so many times, no longer dare to go alone. He will lead a mere four hundred men."

"And now the three conspirators are going to prepare an ambush of a thousand men against Belisarius near the tomb of the Fulvians."

"You have indeed earned the shoe with that information!" Cethegus said, and threw it over to Syphax.

"King Witigis on the other hand will make what is only a token attack against the gate of St Paul as a diversion. I will now go to Belisarius as you have told me, with a message that he should take three thousand men with him and destroy the three Goths and their force."

"Not so fast!" Cethegus replied calmly. "You will tell him nothing!"

"What did you say?" Syphax asked in astonishment. "Unless he is warned he is doomed!"

"One must not interfere with the general's guardian angel again, at least not so soon. Let Belisarius put his lucky star to the test."

"Hey," said Syphax with a sly smile, "is that what you want? Then I would rather be Syphax the slave then Belisarius the *Magister Militum*. Poor widow Antonina!"

Cethegus was about to stretch out on his bed when Fidus, the *ostiarius*, announced: "Kallistratos of Corinth."

"Always welcome."

The young Greek with the gentle face entered. His face had more colour than usual, and it was obvious that some special reason brought him here.

"What is it you bring that is beautiful, other than yourself?" Cethegus asked in Greek.

The young man opened his glowing eyes: "A heart full of admiration for you, and the wish to prove it to you. I beg of you to let me fight for you and for Rome, like the Licinius brothers."

"My Kallistratos! What concern of yours are our bloody dealings with the Barbarians, you our peace-loving guest and the most likeable of all the Hellenic peoples? Keep away from this grave and serious business. Attend to your heritage instead, that of beauty."

"I know very well that the days of Salamis are long gone, like a myth, and that you iron Romans never did think of us as strong. That is hard to accept, but made easier by the fact that you are the defenders of our world, our art and our culture against these Barbarians. You in this case means Rome, and to me Rome means Cethegus. That is how I see this war, and so you see that it does concern even a Greek."

Obviously pleased the Prefect smiled: "Well, if Rome to you means Cethegus, then Rome gladly accepts your offer. Henceforth you are a tribune of the *Milites Romani* like the Licinius brothers."

"I will thank you for that with my deeds! But there is one more thing I must confess to you, for I know that you do not like to be caught by surprise. I have often noticed how dear Hadrian's tomb is to you, and particularly the statues of the gods which decorate it. The other day I counted these marble sentries and found that there are two hundred and ninety eight. So I have decided to complete the three hundred, and I have added two Letoids, which you praised so highly, the ones of Apollo and

Artemis. I have had them placed there as a gift to you, dedicated to the future of Rome."

"You dear, young wastrel. What have you done there?"

"Something which is good and beautiful," Kallistratos replied without artifice.

"But remember that the tomb is now part of our defences. If the Goths should storm…"

"The Letoids are standing on the second wall, the inner one. But I don't think that the Barbarians will reach Cethegus's favourite place ever again. Where could the beautiful statues be safer than in your stronghold? The wall on which they now stand seems to me to be the best temple for them, because it is the safest. Let my gift be a lucky omen at the same time."

"That it shall be," Cethegus cried animatedly, "and like you I believe your gift is in a safe place. But permit me in return…"

"You have already allowed me to fight for you!" the Greek laughed and was gone.

"That boy is very fond of me," Cethegus said as he watched him go, "and I am no different to other fools, I like that! And not only because his liking for me gives me control over him."

A moment later steps sounded in the vestibule, and a tribune of the *Milites* was announced.

He was a young warrior with noble, but very serious features. He had a very strong and typically Roman face, prominent cheekbones, a straight and stern forehead and deep set eyes. His face suggested strength, determination and willpower.

"Well, Severinus, son of Boethius, welcome! Welcome, my young hero and philosopher. It is many months since I have seen you. Where do you come from now?"

"From the grave of my mother," Severinus replied, looking searchingly at Cethegus.

The latter sprang to his feet. "Rusticiana? My old friend? Dead?"

"She is dead," Severinus said abruptly. Cethegus tried to take his hand, but Severinus withdrew it.

"My son, my poor Severinus! And did she die – without a word for me?"

"I am here to bring you her last words. They were meant for you!"

"What did she die from?"

"Sorrow and remorse."

"Sorrow," Cethegus sighed, "I can understand that. But what did she have to be remorseful about? And if her last words were meant for me, what were they?"

At that Severinus stepped right up to Cethegus, so close that their knees touched, and looked him straight in the eye as if he was trying to see straight through him: "A curse on Cethegus, who poisoned my soul and my child!"

Cethegus looked straight back at him: "Did she die insane?" he asked coldly.

"No, murderer! She lived an insane life only as long as she trusted you. On her deathbed she confessed to Cassiodorus and to me that it was her hand which gave the poison you brewed to the young tyrant. She told us the whole story. Old Corbulo and his daughter Daphnidion were supporting her. 'I only found out later,' she concluded her story, 'that my child also drank from the deadly cup. And there was nobody there to arrest Camilla's arm as she drank, because I was still out in the boat and Cethegus was in the *plantana* arcade'. And then old Corbulo grew pale and cried: 'What? The Prefect knew that the cup was poisoned?' – 'Certainly,' my mother replied, 'when I met him in the garden I told him: It is done!' Corbulo was silent with horror, but Daphnidion cried out painfully: 'Oh my poor Domna! So he murdered her! He was standing there, right by my side, and he watched as she drank.' – 'He watched her drink?' my mother asked in a tone which will haunt me for the rest of my life.

'He watched as she drank!' the girl repeated, as did her father. 'Oh, then let his accursed head become possessed by the lowest of demons! Revenge, God in heaven and devil in hell, and revenge, my son, on earth for Camilla! A curse on Cethegus!' And then she fell back and was dead."

The Prefect remained where he stood, not moving, but he quietly gripped the dagger in his tunic. "And you?" he asked after a pause, "what did you do?"

"I knelt down beside her body and kissed her cold hand, and I swore to her that I will fulfil her dying wish. Woe be to you, Prefect of Rome, poisoner and murderer of my sister! You will not live!"

"Son of Boethius, do you plan to become a murderer on the say so of a feeble former slave and his daughter? Is that worthy of a hero and a philosopher?"

"Not murder! If I was a Goth I would challenge you to a duel according to their barbaric custom, which now seems to me very appropriate. But I am a Roman, and I will seek my revenge the Roman way, legally! Beware, Prefect, there are still judges in Italy. The war and the enemy have kept me away from these walls for many months, and in fact I have only just reached Rome today, by sea. But tomorrow I will lay charges in the senate, with your fellow senators who will also be your judges. We will meet again there!"

Suddenly Cethegus barred his exit. But Severinus cried: "One takes precautions when one deals with murderers. Three friends have accompanied me here, and if I do not return within the hour they will come looking for me with the Lictors!"

Cethegus was quite calm again. "I only wanted to warn you against disgracing yourself. If you want to accuse your family's oldest friend of murder on the evidence of a slave and the ravings of a dying woman, without proof, then do so. I cannot prevent you. But first another matter. You have become my accuser, but you are still a soldier and a tribune. You will obey when your general commands."

"I will obey."

"Tomorrow Belisarius plans a sortie, and we also expect the Barbarians to storm. I have to defend the city, but I fear that danger threatens the lion of a man! I must know that he is well guarded. Tomorrow you will – this is an order – accompany Belisarius and guard him."

"I will guard his life with my own."

"Very well, tribune, I depend on your word."

"And you can depend on mine: we will meet again after the battle, before the senate. I look forward to both fights equally. Until we meet again – before the senate."

"We will never meet again," said Cethegus as the footsteps of his departing visitor grew faint in the distance. "Syphax," he called out aloud, "bring wine and the main meal. We must strengthen ourselves – for tomorrow."

Chapter 11

Early the next morning there was a great deal of activity both in Rome and in the Gothic camp.

Matesuentha had been able to get some information, but not all. She had heard about the plot by the three men to ambush Belisarius, and also of an earlier plan to conduct a token attack on the St Paul's gate as a diversionary tactic. What she did not know was that the king had changed his plans. In great secrecy he had made a decision to exploit the great general's absence from the city on this day, by making one last all-out attack rather than the diversionary tactic planned earlier. One final attempt was to be made to see if Gothic heroism was not, after all, a match for the Prefect and his walls, and for the military genius of Belisarius. The Gothic council of war fully understood the gravity of this decision. If, like all the previous attacks, this one also failed – Procopius had counted sixty-eight battles, sorties, attempted storms and other engagements up until this day – then no further effort could be expected from the exhausted and greatly weakened army. Consequently, on Teias's demand, all those present swore to observe absolute secrecy regarding the plan to everyone, with no exceptions.

That is why Matesuentha had learned nothing of the plan from the king, and even Syphax with his bloodhound nose could only find out that something major was being planned for this day. Even the Gothic soldiers themselves did not know what that was.

Totila, Teias and Hildebad had left with their cavalry around midnight, and had set up an ambush south of the Via Valeria near the Fulvian tomb, which Belisarius would have to pass. They hoped to complete their mission in time to play a major role in subsequent events around Rome later in the day.

While the king with Hildebrand, Guntharis and Markja was organising troops within his camp, Belisarius and some of his bodyguards had left Rome before sunrise by the Porta Tiburtina. Procopius and Severinus rode on either side of him, and Aigan carried his banner, which had to accompany the *Magister Militum* on all occasions. Constantinus, to whom command of the "Belisarian" half of Rome had been entrusted, had doubled all guards on the walls, and had had his troops quartered immediately behind the walls, fully armed. He conveyed orders to the Prefect to take similar precautions with the Byzantine troops under his command. The messenger met him on the wall, between the St Paul's and the Appian gates.

"So Belisarius thinks that Rome is not safe unless he is here to defend it," he said mockingly, "but I think that it is he who is safe only while my Rome protects him. Come, Lucius Licinius," he whispered softly to the tribune by his side, "we must always be prepared for the eventuality that one day Belisarius will not return from one of his heroic exploits. Were that to happen then some other strong arm would have to pick up the reins of his army."

"I know to whom that arm would belong."

"It may mean a brief fight with those of his bodyguards who are still in Rome, in the baths of Diocletian or at the Porta Tiburtina. They must be crushed right there in their camps before they realise fully what is happening. Take three thousand of my Isaurians and deploy them, without attracting attention, around the gate, and above all cover the baths for me."

"But where do you want me to take them from?"

"From Hadrian's tomb," Cethegus replied after a little thought.

"And the Goths, general?"

"Pah, the tomb is secure. It will defend itself. If they do storm there they first have to cross the river from the south, and then they have to scale those icily smooth walls of marble, my joy and that of the Corinthian. And in any case," he smiled, "just take a look up there; you will see an army of marble gods and heroes. They can defend their temple against the Barbarians by themselves. You see, as I have already told you, they are aiming at the St Paul's' gate here," he concluded, pointing to the Gothic camp where a strong detachment of troops could be seen leaving in that direction.

Licinius obeyed, and a little while later he was leading three thousand Isaurians, about half the force which normally defended the tomb, across the river and down the Viminalis to the baths of Diocletian. He then relieved Belisarius's Armenians at the Porta Tiburtina with three hundred Isaurians and legionaries.

Cethegus himself now turned toward the Porta Salaria, where Constantinus was acting as Belisarius's deputy. "I must have him out of the way," he thought, "when the news gets here." When he got there he said to Constantinus: "As soon as you have repulsed the Barbarians, no doubt you will want to break out and go after them, won't you? What an opportunity to earn laurels while your commander is away!"

"Certainly," Constantinus cried, "they will learn that we can beat them even without Belisarius."

"But you will have to aim more carefully," Cethegus said, taking a bow from a Persian archer. "Do you see the Goth over there, the leader on horseback? He shall fall." Cethegus despatched the arrow, and the Goth fell from his horse, shot through the throat. "And my bows mounted on the walls? You use them badly. Can you see that oak tree over there? There is a Gothic commander standing in front of it, in full armour. Watch!" He aimed the wall bow and fired; a moment later the Goth was nailed to the tree, the arrow having pierced him and his heavy armour.

At that moment a mounted Saracen came galloping along: "Archon!" he addressed Constantinus, "Bessas asks you to send him reinforcements to the Vivarium, by the Porta Praenestina. The Goths are attacking in strength."

Doubtfully Constantinus looked at Cethegus. "It is a prank!" the latter replied, "the only real attack is against St Paul's gate, and that is well defended, I know that for certain. Tell Bessas that he has taken fright too soon. By the way, in the Vivarium I still have six lions, ten tigers and twelve bears for the next circus carnival. Let them loose among the Barbarians for the time being! That will provide entertainment for the Romans as well!"

But already a bodyguard was hurrying down the Mons Pincius: "Help, Sir, help! Constantinus, your own Porta Flaminia! There are countless Barbarians! Ursinicus asks for your help!"

"There too?" Cethegus asked in disbelief.

"We need help for the broken section of wall between the Porta Flaminia and the Porta Pinciana!" a second messenger from Ursinicus cried.

"There is no need to defend that stretch of wall! You know that it is under the special protection of St Peter, that's enough!" Constantinus replied calmly.

Cethegus smiled: "That's certainly true today. It will not even be attacked."

And then Lucius Licinius came running along breathlessly: "Sir, to the Capitol quickly, where I have just come from. All seven enemy camps are spewing Barbarians at once from every camp gate. They are about to launch a storm on all fronts against every gate of Rome at once."

"Hardly," Cethegus smiled. "But I will come up. But you, Marcus Licinius, are responsible to me for the gate here. It must be mine, not Belisarius's. Go! Take your two hundred legionaries there!"

He mounted his horse and rode along the foot of the Viminal to the Capitol. Here he met Lucius Licinius and his Isaurians. "General," the tribune addressed him, "it is getting serious out there, very serious! What about the Isaurians? Does your order still stand?"

"Have I taken it back?" Cethegus asked severely. "Lucius, you and the other tribunes will follow me. You Isaurians will place yourselves between the baths of Diocletian and the Porta Tiburtina under your chief Asgares." He did not believe that any danger threatened Rome, and he thought he knew what the Goths really had in mind. "This apparent all-out attack," he thought, "is only so that the Byzantines will forget about the danger to their commander outside the gates."

Soon he reached one of the towers of the Capitol, from which he could see over the whole plain. It was filled with Gothic arms, and was a magnificent spectacle. The entire might of the Gothic army was pouring from every camp, surrounding the whole city. Evidently the attack, against all gates at once, had been carefully planned.

The first rows of the circle which stretched three quarters of the way around the city consisted of archers and throwers with slingshots in mobile swarms, to clear the parapets of defenders. Behind them came battering rams, wall breakers and other siege equipment, either taken from Roman arsenals or fashioned after Roman models, however crudely. They were propelled by horses and cattle, and manned by troops who had virtually no offensive weapons, but were armed with broad shields to protect themselves and the traction animals against missiles from the defenders. Close behind them came the troops who would conduct the main attack, in deep ranks and fully armed, with knives and axes for hand-to-hand fighting. They were also carrying long, heavy storm ladders. The three lines of attackers approached very calmly and in very good order from all sides, marching with an even pace everywhere. The rays of the sun reflected from their helmets, and the call of Gothic horns could be heard at regular intervals.

"They have learned something from us," Cethegus cried with the joy of a seasoned warrior. "The man who deployed these men understands the art of war!"

"Who would that be?" asked Kallistratos, who stood next to Lucius Licinius, clad in magnificent armour.

"No doubt the planner is Witigis, the king," Cethegus replied.

"I would never have thought that simple man was capable of it."

"There is much about the Barbarians which is difficult to follow."

Cethegus now rode down from the Capitol across the river, to the wall near the Porta Pancratia, where the next attack seemed to threaten. There, with his following, he climbed into the corner tower.

"Who is the old man there, with the long white beard, leading his men with a stone axe in his hand? He looks as if Zeus missed him with his thunderbolt in the battle of the giants," the Greek asked.

"That's Theodoric's old armourer. He is moving against the Porta Pancratia," the Prefect replied.

"And the one in the rich armour, on the brown horse with a wolf's head on his helmet? He seems to be moving against the Porta Portuensis."

"He is the Woelsung Duke Guntharis," Lucius Licinius replied.

"Look!" said Piso, "on the eastern side, across the river as far as the eye can see, Barbarians everywhere."

"But where is the king himself?" Kallistratos asked.

"That's the main Gothic flag in the middle. He is stopping there above the Porta Pancratia," the Prefect replied.

"He alone stands motionless with his strong force, three hundred paces back." Salvius Julianus said.

"Is he not going to fight himself?" Massurius asked.

"That would be unlike him. But let us get down from the tower and onto the wall. The fight is about to start," Cethegus concluded.

"Hildebrand has reached the ditch."

"My Byzantines are standing over there, under Gregory. The Goths are aiming well. Quickly Massurius, send my Abasgan archers and my best sharpshooters there; tell them to aim at the traction animals!"

Soon fighting had started on all sides, and Cethegus noted with displeasure that the Goths seemed to be making progress everywhere. The Byzantines seemed to be missing Belisarius; their shooting was erratic and they seemed only too willing to retreat, while today the Goths were attacking with death-defying spirit. Already the moat had been crossed in several places, and Guntharis had ladders in place by the Porta Portuensis. Meanwhile old Hildebrand had placed a battering ram in position, and secured it against missiles with a solid roof. Already the first blows against the timbers of the gate could be heard over the noise of battle. This familiar sound shocked the Prefect, who had just arrived here. "Apparently," he said to himself, "they are going to attack in earnest now their diversionary tactic has worked."

Another resounding blow followed. Gregory the Byzantine looked at him questioningly. "That has to stop, and very soon!" Cethegus cried angrily, tore the bow from the nearest archer and hurried to the top of the wall beside the gate: "Here, archers and throwers! Follow me!" he cried, "bring the heavy stones. Where is the nearest ballista? Where are the scorpions? That protective roof has to go."

But under the roof Gothic sharpshooters were standing at the ready, eagerly peering through the ports in the roof at the battlements above. "It's no use, Haduswinth," young Gunthamund said angrily, "I have just taken aim in vain for the third time! Not one of them dares to poke his nose over the parapet."

"Patience," the old man instructed, "just keep your bow at the ready! Sooner or later one of them will show himself. Get a bow ready for me too. Just be patient."

"That's easier for you with your seventy than me with my twenty years."

Meanwhile Cethegus had reached the pinnacle. His eyes searched the plain, and he saw the king in the distance, motionless in the Gothic main centre position, on the right bank of the Tiber. This disturbed him. "What could he have in mind? Could he have learned that a general should not fight himself? Come Gaius," he called out to the young archer who had followed him, "you have good eyes. Have a look over the battlement with me here – what is the king up to?" And he leaned over the parapet. Gaius followed his example, looking out eagerly.

"Now, Gunthamund!" Haduswinth cried down below. Two bowstrings sounded, and the two lookouts fell.

Gaius fell shot in the forehead, and an arrow splintered under the rim of the Prefect's helmet. Cethegus wiped his forehead with the back of his hand.

"You are alive, my commander?" cried Piso.

"Yes, my friend. It was very well aimed. But the gods must have need for me yet; it's only a scratch," said Cethegus, and adjusted his helmet.

Chapter 12

A moment later Syphax was flying up the marble steps. His master had strictly forbidden him from taking any part in the fighting: "The Barbarians must not kill you, nor recognise you. You are indispensable as Matesuentha's slave and spy for King Witigis," Cethegus had told him.

"Woe, woe!" he cried, with such exaggerated agitation that his master noticed it, knowing the Moor's usual calm manner. "What a disaster!"

"What happened?"

"Constantinus is seriously wounded. He was leading a sortie out of the Porta Salaria, and was immediately met by Gothic storm troops. A stone hit him in the face, and they only managed with great difficulty to save him and get him on top of the wall, where I caught him as he collapsed. He named the Prefect to take his place. Here is his commander's baton."

"That's impossible!" cried Bessas, who was following on Syphax's heels. He had come to request reinforcements in person, and had arrived just in time to hear the news. "Or had he already lost control of his senses when he said that?"

"If he had named you he would certainly have lost control of his senses," Cethegus said calmly, accepting the baton and thanking the clever slave with a wink of his eye. Bessas uttered a furious oath and hurried away from the parapet. "Follow him, Syphax; don't let him out of your sight," the Prefect whispered.

Then an Isaurian mercenary came hurrying along. "Reinforcements, Prefect! To the Porta Portuensis! Count Guntharis has placed many ladders against the wall there."

Then Cabao, the leader of the Moorish archers, galloped along: "Constantinus is dead, will you take his place?"

"I will replace Belisarius," Cethegus replied proudly: "Move five hundred Armenians from the Appian gate to the Portuensis."

"Help, help to the Appian gate! All the defenders on the battlements have been shot down!" a Persian mercenary on horseback reported, "the first line of defence is half lost. Perhaps it can still be held, but not easily. But if we lose it we will never be able to recapture it!"

Cethegus waved to his legal adviser, now his tribune, Salvius Julianus: "Go, my lawyer friend: *Beati possidentis!* – take one hundred legionaries and hold that battlement at any cost until further help arrives."

He looked down from the top of the wall once more. Beneath his feet the battle was raging, and the thundering blows of Hildebrand's battering ram sounded again and again. But what concerned him most of all was the mysterious calm of the king in the background, still standing there motionless. "Just what does he have in mind?"

And then a terrible crashing sound came from below, followed by loud cries of victory by the Barbarians. Cethegus did not need to ask what caused the noise. In three bounds he was down below.

"The gate has been smashed!" his men cried out to him in terror.

"I know! We ourselves must now be the gates of Rome!" Clutching his shield more firmly he stepped right up to the right wing of the gate, which was indeed showing a broad gap in it. Already the battering ram was delivering another blow at the splintered planks next to the hole. "One more blow like that and the gate will fall down completely," cried Gregory the Byzantine.

"Right, and therefore there must not be another such blow. Come over here with me, Gregory and Lucius. Milites, get ready with lowered spears! Get torches and firebrands! We are going to break out! As soon as I give the signal open the gate, and throw the battering ram, roof and all, into the ditch."

"You are very brave, my general!" cried Lucius Licinius, as he joined his commander with delight.

"Yes my friend, because now bravery makes sense!"

The column was ready and set to attack, and the Prefect was about to draw his sword as a signal to start the attack. Suddenly there was a lot of noise behind him, even louder than the noise made by the storming Goths. There were cries of woe and the sound of horses, and then Bessas made his way to the Prefect, grabbing the latter's arm as his voice failed him.

"Why are you holding me back in a moment like this?" the Prefect cried angrily, and pushed him away.

"Belisarius's troops," the Thracen stammered in shock, "are badly beaten and now stand outside the Porta Tiburtina, begging to be admitted. Furious Goths are hot on their heels. Belisarius was caught in an ambush! He is dead!"

"Belisarius has been taken prisoner!" a defender from the Porta Tiburtina cried, running along quite out of breath. "The Goths, the Goths are here! They are outside the Porta Nomentana and the Tiburtina too!" came the cry from the street.

"Belisarius's banner has been captured! Procopius is defending his body!"

"Have them open the Porta Tiburtina, Prefect!" Bessas urged, "all of a sudden your Isaurians are there. Who sent them there?"

"I did!" Cethegus replied, thinking.

"They will not open the gate without orders from you! Save his – Belisarius's – body!"

Cethegus hesitated – he was holding his sword half raised. "His body, he thought, "I will gladly save."

Then Syphax came running along. "No, he is still alive!" he whispered in his master's ear, "I saw him from the battlement. He is still moving, but he will be taken prisoner any moment. The Gothic cavalry is bearing down on him fast; Totila, Teias – they will be upon him in no time!"

"Give the order to open the Porta Tiburtina!" Bessas urged.

But the Prefect's eyes flashed; that look of proud, daring determination came over him, giving him what was almost a demonic beauty. He struck at the smashed remnants of the gate before him with his sword: "Forward, to the attack! First Rome, then Belisarius! Rome and triumph!" The gate flew open.

Such a daring act on the part of the defenders was the last thing the attacking Goths expected. Already confident of victory, they thought that the defenders would by now be almost completely demoralised. They were scattered around the gate, not in battle order, and were completely taken by surprise. In no time at all the charge by the closed column out of the gate had thrown them into the deep ditch behind them.

But old Hildebrand did not want to abandon his battering ram. Standing up to his full height he smashed helmet and head of the Byzantine Gregory with his stone hammer. But in the same instant Lucius Licinius pushed him into the ditch with the point of his shield. Cethegus hacked through the machine's ropes with his sword, and now it too crashed into the ditch on top of the old man.

"Now throw fire into the wooden machines which still stand," Cethegus ordered. A moment later they stood in flames, and the victorious Romans were back inside their walls. But there Syphax called out to his master: "Revolt, master, there is mutiny and violence! The Byzantines will not obey you any more! Bessas called on them to open the Porta Tiburtina by force. His bodyguards are threatening to attack Marcus Licinius and to slaughter your Isaurians and your legionaries with their Huns."

"That they will regret!" Cethegus cried fiercely. "Bessas, I will remember this! Go, Lucius Licinius, take half the remaining Isaurians! No, take them all! You know where they are. Attack the Thracen bodyguards from the rear, from the Porta Clausa. And if they won't yield then mow them down, without mercy! Help your brother! I will follow in a moment!"

Lucius hesitated for a moment. "And the Porta Tiburtina?"

"Remains closed!"

"And Belisarius?"

"Stays outside."

"Totila and Teias are already upon him."

"All the more reason to keep the gate shut. First Rome, then everything else. Obey, tribune!"

Cethegus remained behind in order to arrange for the necessary repairs to the Porta Pancratia. This took considerable time. "How did it go, Syphax?" he asked the slave in a low voice, "Is he really alive?"

"He is still alive."

"They are clumsy, these Goths!"

Then a messenger arrived from Lucius. "Your tribune reports that Bessas will not give in! The blood of your legionaries has already flowed at the Porta Tiburtina. And Asgares and your Isaurians are hesitating to attack. They don't believe that you are serious."

"I will show them that I am serious!" Cethegus cried, leaping on his horse and riding off at the gallop.

He had a long way to go, across the Tiber via the Janiculum Bridge, past the Capitol, through the Forum Romanum, through the Via Sacra and the arch of Titus, leaving the baths of Titus on his right, over the Esquilin and finally through the Porta Esquilina to the outer Porta Tiburtina, a path which took him right across the entire city from west to east.

Here, behind the gate, stood the bodyguards of Belisarius and Bessas in a double formation. One group was about to overpower the Prefect's legionaries and Isaurians under Marcus Licinius, and open the gate by force, while the other group stood with lowered spears facing the other detachment of Isaurians, whom Lucius Licinius was vainly ordering to attack.

"Mercenaries," Cethegus cried, halting his steaming horse right before their lines, "to whom did you swear allegiance, to me or to Belisarius?"

"To you, Sir," the leader Asgares replied, stepping forward, "but I thought…"

The Prefect's sword flashed and the man fell, mortally wounded. "You are paid to obey, you treacherous rabble, not to think!"

The mercenaries stood there, terrified. But Cethegus calmly commanded: "To the attack! Follow me!" And the Isaurians obeyed him. One moment more and fighting would break out in Rome itself as well.

But at that moment a terrible cry arose, drowning out all other sounds, coming from the direction of the Porta Aurelia in the west. "Woe, all is lost! The Goths are upon us! The city has fallen!"

Cethegus paled and looked back to see Kallistratos come galloping along, blood streaming from his face and neck. "Cethegus," he cried, "it is over! The Barbarians are in Rome! They have scaled the wall!"

"Where?" the Prefect asked, in a toneless voice.

"At Hadrian's tomb!"

"Oh my general!" cried Lucius Licinius, "I did warn you."

"That was Witigis!" said Cethegus.

"How did you know that?" Kallistratos asked, surprised.

"Enough, I know." It was a terrible moment for the Prefect. He had to admit to himself that, in relentlessly pursuing his design to destroy Belisarius, he had for a moment forgotten Rome. He clenched his teeth.

"Cethegus has left Hadrian's tomb bare! Cethegus has brought disaster upon Rome!" Bessas cried at the head of the bodyguards.

"And Cethegus will save it!" cried he. "Follow me!"

"And Belisarius?" Syphax whispered.

"Let him in. First Rome, then everything else. Follow me, legionaries and Isaurians!" And he flew back the way he had come, like the storm wind. Only a few mounted men were able to keep up with him, whilst his infantry, legionaries and Isaurians, followed him at a running pace as fast as they could.

Chapter 13

Outside the Porta Tiburtina things had begun to calm down, the Gothic cavalry having been called away from what was now not a vital engagement. Together with all available men they were to proceed around the city and across the river to the Porta Aurelia, through which the city had just been entered. Every available Gothic soldier was needed there. The cavalry, swinging right, raced off in the direction of that gate, where all the Gothic forces were now converging. But their own infantry, which was storming the five gates between them and their goal, the Porta Clausa, Nomentana, Salaria, Pinciana and Flaminia, delayed their progress so long that they arrived too late to take part in the decisive engagement at Hadrian's tomb.

The reader will recall the location of the Prefect's favourite place, opposite Vatican Hill and about a stone's throw from the Porta Aurelia, to which it was connected by walls. Everywhere except in the south, where the river served as its defence, the tomb was protected by massive new walls. The *Moles Hadriani* itself was a mighty round tower of the strongest construction, surrounded by a courtyard. The Tiber flowed beyond the first or outer wall in the south. Normally the courtyard and the battlements on the outer wall were manned by the Isaurians, whom the Prefect had withdrawn this time as part of his plan to destroy Belisarius. But what did stand on the battlements of the inner wall was the numerous marble and bronze statues, which thanks to the gift by Kallistratos now numbered three hundred.

The Gothic king had deliberately adopted a waiting position on this day, behind the main fighting, on the field of Nero between the Porta Pancratia and the new Porta Aureliana, where Count Markja was normally in command. His plan was that a simultaneous all-out attack on all the city's gates must scatter the defending forces. As soon as a weakness appeared at any point, through defenders being moved, he intended to exploit that weakness immediately.

With this plan in mind he waited patiently, and had given orders to all his commanders to inform him the moment a gap appeared anywhere in the defences. He had to endure many an impatient word from his own men, who had to stand by idly while their comrades were advancing everywhere. For a long time they waited thus for a messenger to call them so that they could at last join in the fray.

In the end it was the king's own sharp eyes which noticed that the familiar battle standards and thick spears of the Isaurians had disappeared from the outer wall around Hadrian's tomb. He watched the spot carefully; they were not replaced, and the gap not filled. Once sure he leapt from the saddle, gave his horse a blow on the chest with the flat of his hand and said: "Go home, Boreas!" which sent the intelligent animal straight back to the camp. "Now forward, my Goths! Forward, Count Markja!" the king cried, "across the river over there. Leave the battering rams here, but take your shields and storm ladders. And take your axes. Forward!" Soon he was rushing down the steep southern riverbank at a running pace.

"No bridge, king, and no ford?" a Goth behind him asked.

"No, friend Iffamer, swim!" and the king jumped into the filthy water, which briefly closed above the plume of his helmet. Moments later he had reached the far bank, the first of his men with him. Soon they stood at the high outer wall of the tomb, and the men looked up, questioningly, with concern.

"Ladders!" cried Witigis, "don't you see? There are no defenders! Are you afraid of high stone walls?" In a few minutes the ladders had been placed, the wall scaled, the few defenders slaughtered, and the ladders drawn up and placed against the inside of the wall down into the courtyard.

The first man into the courtyard was the king himself. But here the Gothic advance was slowed for a while, because Quintus Piso and Kallistratos were now manning the battlements on the inner wall, having hurried here from the Porta Pancratia with a hundred legionaries and a handful of Isaurians. They were hurling a thick hail of spears and arrows at the Goths, who were descending into the courtyard in twos and threes; their ballistas and catapults were also having a devastating effect. "Send for help, go to Cethegus!" Piso cried up on the wall, and Kallistratos flew on his way.

"What shall we do?" Markja asked, by the side of Witigis, as Goths were falling around him.

"Wait until they have used up their ammunition." Witigis replied calmly. "It can't last much longer. In their fright they are shooting and throwing much too quickly. Do you see? Already there are more stones than arrows. And the javelins have stopped."

"But the ballistas, and the catapults?"

"They will not harm us in a moment. Get ready to storm. See? The hail is getting very thin. Now get your ladders ready, and your axes. Now, quickly, follow me!" In a fast charge the Goths ran across the courtyard.

Only very few Goths had fallen thus far, and already they were standing in front of the second, inner wall, with a hundred ladders in place. Now Piso's ballistas and catapults were useless because, having been set to shoot at long range, they could not be re-set to shoot straight down quickly enough. Piso saw it and paled: "Javelins! Get javelins and spears! Otherwise all is lost!"

"All spent!" Fat Balbus gasped cheerlessly at his side.

"Then it's over!" Piso sighed, lowering his arm with the gesture of a desperately tired man.

"Come, Massurius, let us flee!" Balbus urged.

"No, let us die here!" cried Piso. Already the first Gothic helmet was appearing over the top of the wall.

But then the sound: "Cethegus, Cethegus the Prefect!" arose from the city side. And indeed it was he. Quickly he leapt up on the battlement and with one blow of his sword he severed hand and arm of the Goth who was just about to swing himself onto the parapet. The man screamed and fell.

"Oh Cethegus!" Piso cried. "You have come just at the right time!"

"I hope so," the latter replied, and overthrew the ladder in front of him. Witigis had been standing on it, but was able to jump clear. "Now we must have missiles, spears, lances. Nothing else will help," he cried.

"There is not a missile left far and wide," Balbus replied. "I hope you have brought your Isaurians?"

"They are still a long way behind me!" Kallistratos cried, who had just appeared behind the Prefect.

The number of ladders and helmets appearing over the parapet was increasing, bringing extreme danger with them. The situation was desperate as never before.

Wildly Cethegus looked about him. "Missiles!" he cried, stamping his feet, "we must have missiles, spears, anything!" Suddenly his gaze fell on the huge marble statue of Zeus, standing on the pinnacle to his left. An idea went through his mind in a flash, he leapt over to the statue and, with an axe, he severed the statue's right arm complete with the thunderbolt in its fist. "Zeus," he cried, "lend me your thunder! What are you holding it for, and not using it? Come men, smash the statues and hurl the pieces on the heads of the enemy!" His example was being followed even before he had finished speaking. The panic-stricken defenders attacked the gods and heroes with axes and hatchets, and in a few moments most of the magnificent figures had been smashed to pieces. It was a terrible sight! Here an imposing emperor Hadrian on horseback burst in two, there a beautiful Aphrodite on her knees, and elsewhere the lovely marble head of an Antonius crashed down on a Gothic shield of buffalo hide. Fragments and splinters of marble and bronze flew in all directions, covering the pinnacles in dust. Masses of stone and metal were crashing down, smashing helmets and shields, armour and limbs of the storming Goths and the ladders on which they stood.

Cethegus looked on in awe as the gruesome work of destruction went on. But the situation had been saved. Twelve, fifteen, twenty ladders now stood without the men who had been crowding them like ants only moments before, and a similar number lay smashed at the foot of the wall. Surprised by this sudden hail of marble and bronze, the Goths withdrew for a moment, but then Markja's horn called on them to storm once more, and again the massive missiles rained down on them.

"Oh Cethegus, what have you done?" Kallistratos wailed as he stared at the ruins of the statues.

"That which had to be done!" Cethegus replied and hurled the last remaining remnant of the Zeus statue over the wall. "Did you see that? Two Barbarians at once!" Satisfied, he looked down.

And then he heard the Corinthian cry: "No, no, not this one! Not my Apollo!"

Cethegus turned to see a giant Isaurian raise his axe, about to bring it down on the statue's head. "Fool, do you want the Goths up here?" the savage asked, and took another swing.

"Not my Apollo!" the Greek repeated, and embraced the god protectively with both arms.

Count Markja on the nearest ladder saw this, and thought that Kallistratos was about to throw the statue down on him. So he struck first, and his javelin pierced the Greek through the middle of his chest. "Oh Cethegus!" he sighed, and was dead. The Prefect saw him fall and knitted his brows: "Save his body, and spare his two gods!" he said briefly, and overthrew the ladder on which Markja was standing. He had no time to say or do more, because already another and even more critical danger threatened.

Witigis, who had half fallen and half jumped from his ladder, had been standing close to the wall, under the hail of stone and metal fragments, looking for another opening. Ever since the initial attempt to scale the wall with ladders had been foiled by the unexpected new hail of gods and heroes, he held little hope that the wall could still be won. As he stood thus, thinking and looking for an opening, the heavy pedestal of a Mars Gradivus smashed to the ground beside him, bounced up again and struck a marble plate on the wall. And to his surprise the plate, which had seemed to be a block of the hardest stone, smashed and crumbled into small bits of mortar. In its place a small wooden gate became visible, only thinly camouflaged, which had served as an entrance for the stone masons and workmen as they restored the huge building.

As soon as Witigis saw the wooden gate he cried out triumphantly: "Here, you Goths, here! Bring your axes!" And already his own battleaxe was smashing at the thin planks, which looked anything but strong.

The Prefect's ear heard this new, fateful sound with foreboding. He paused in his bloody work above and listened. "That's iron against wood, by Caesar!" he said to himself and ran down the narrow marble steps, which led from the top of the second wall down its inner surface to the tomb's dimly lit interior.

Another blow sounded, louder than any before it, followed by a dull crashing and splintering, and then joyful Gothic cries of victory. As Cethegus reached the lowest step the gate went crashing inwards into the courtyard, and King Witigis appeared on the threshold.

"Rome is mine!" he cried joyfully, dropping his axe and drawing his sword.

"You lie, Witigis, for the first time in your life!" Cethegus retorted fiercely and leapt at the Goth with such force, striking at the king's chest with the point of his shield, that the latter took a step back in surprise.

The Prefect made good use of this one step, and now he himself stood on the threshold, filling the narrow gate completely. "Where are the Isaurians?" he cried.

But Witigis had allowed only a moment to elapse before he recognised his adversary. "So we meet in a duel over Rome after all!" And now it was his turn to attack. Cethegus, anxious to completely fill the gap left by the gate, used his shield to cover his left side. His right arm with his short Roman sword was not able to defend his right side sufficiently, and the thrust of the Goth's long sword, not adequately parried by Cethegus, pierced the rings of his armour and penetrated deep into the right side of his chest.

The Prefect staggered and was about to fall, but he did not fall. "Rome, Rome!" he said with a last effort, but remained on his feet.

Witigis had taken a step backwards in order to finish off his enemy with a new charge. But at that moment Piso on the wall above recognised him, and hurled a magnificent sleeping faun at him, which was lying there with its feet already hacked off. It struck the king on the shoulder, and he fell. Count Markja, Iffamer and Aligern carried him out of the fight.

Cethegus saw him fall, and then he himself collapsed on the threshold of the gate. The protective arm of a friend caught him, but he no longer knew who it was. He lost consciousness.

But then another familiar sound, delightful to the Prefect's ear, brought him back to his senses. It was the tuba of his legionaries and the battle cry of his Isaurians who had now, at long last, arrived on the scene at a running pace. Led by the Licinius brothers they hurled themselves at the Goths, who were disheartened by the fall of their king. Attacking in considerable strength, the defenders forced their way out through a breach in the first wall, which had meanwhile been made by the Goths who had forced their way inside, with considerable bloodshed.

The Prefect saw the last of the Barbarians fleeing, and then his eyes closed once more. "Cethegus!" cried his friend, who was holding him in his arms, "Belisarius lies dying, and now you too are doomed?"

Now Cethegus recognised the voice of Procopius. "I don't know," he said with the last of his strength, "but Rome – Rome is safe!" And then he lost consciousness.

Chapter 14

After the all-out effort put into the storming and its repulsion, which had started at sunrise and ended at dusk, a long pause of exhaustion followed in both the Gothic and Roman camps. The three commanders, Belisarius, Cethegus and Witigis, were to spend weeks convalescing from their wounds.

But the virtual armistice was even more the result of a deep depression which had taken hold of the Gothic army, after the victory for which they had given their all was snatched from them at the last moment, when it had seemed already theirs. They had done their utmost all day long, their warrior heroes had outdone one another in bravery again and again, and yet both their plans, the one against Belisarius and the one to storm the city, had failed. And while King Witigis, with his steady temperament, did not share the low morale of his men, nevertheless he could see all too clearly that from that bloody day onwards the siege would have to be conducted differently.

The Gothic losses had been enormous. Procopius estimated them at thirty thousand dead and about the same number wounded. They had hurled themselves at the walls all around the city, and exposed themselves to the missiles of the defenders, with death-defying courage, and they had fallen in their thousands, especially at the Porta Pancratia and at Hadrian's tomb.

Since the attackers had also suffered far more than the protected defenders in the preceding sixty-eight engagements, the great army which King Witigis had led against the eternal city months before had shrunk terribly. Furthermore, hunger and pestilence had been raging for some time in the Gothic tents. Bearing in mind his huge losses, together with the low morale of his men, Witigis had to give up the idea of trying to take the city by storm. His last hope, and he did not deceive himself as to how slim that hope was, lay in trying to starve out the fortress. The area around Rome had been completely stripped of anything edible, and it now seemed a matter of which side could endure hunger and deprivation the longest, or which side could manage to obtain supplies from afar. The Gothic fleet, still busy off Dalmatia, was sorely missed.

The Prefect was first to recover from his wounds. After being carried away from the gate he had guarded with his body, he spent two days hovering between sleep and unconsciousness. When he finally opened his eyes on the eve of the second day, the first thing he saw was the face of the faithful Moor, who was sitting on the floor at the foot of his bed, never taking his eyes off his master, the snake coiled about his arm.

"The wooden gate!" was the first word from the Prefect's lips, barely audible. "The wooden gate must go. It must be replaced by blocks of marble…"

"Oh thank you, thank you snake god!" the slave rejoiced. "Now my master is saved. And you too. And I, master, have saved you." With that he prostrated himself with his arms crossed, and kissed his master's bedstead. He did not dare to touch his feet.

"You saved me? How?"

"When I laid you down on these cushions, so deadly pale, I fetched the snake god and brought him here. I showed you to him and I said: 'You see, the master's eyes are closed. Help him open them again. Until you help him you will not receive another crumb of bread or another drop of milk. And if they do not open again, then on the day they cremate him Syphax will burn too, and you, great snake, will burn with me. You can help, so help or roast.' That's what I said to him, and he did help."

"The city is safe. I feel it, otherwise I could not have remained unconscious so long. Is Belisarius alive? Yes! Where is Procopius?"

"In the library with your tribunes. The physician said today you would awake or…"

"Die? This time your snake god still managed to help, Syphax. Bring in the tribunes."

Soon the Licinius brothers, Piso, Salvius Julianus and a few others were standing before him. Deeply moved, they wanted to rush to his bedside, but he motioned them to calm themselves. "Rome thanks you, through me. You have fought like – like Romans! That is the highest praise I know!" As if in thought he looked along the line they had formed by his bed, and then he said: "there is one I miss, my Corinthian! I know that his body is safe, because I entrusted it to Piso with the two Letoid statues. Have a plate of Corinthian marble placed on the spot where he fell in his memory, then place the Apollo statue and the urn with his ashes above it, and write on it: 'Kallistratos of Corinth died here for Rome; he saved his god but his god did not save him.' Now go, we will meet again soon, on the battlements. Syphax, now bring me Procopius, and bring me a large goblet of Falernian wine too."

"Friend," he called out to Procopius as he entered, "it seems to me that before this feverish sleep overcame me I heard someone whisper: 'Procopius has saved the great Belisarius'. An immortal deed!

"History will thank you for it, so there is no need for me to do so. Now sit down here and tell me the whole story – but wait, first adjust my cushions so that I can see my Caesar once more. Looking at him does far more for me than any medicine can. Now talk!"

Procopius looked at the reclining man searchingly. "Cethegus," he then said in a serious tone, "Belisarius knows everything."

"Everything?" the Prefect smiled, "that is a great deal."

"Leave the jokes aside, and don't belittle nobility of mind, especially as your own mind is noble."

"Me? Not that I know of."

"As soon as Belisarius regained consciousness, Bessas immediately told him the whole story in minutest detail. He told how you ordered the gate to remain shut while Belisarius lay outside it in his own blood, the furious Teias hot on his heels. He told how you ordered his bodyguards to be cut down because they tried to open the gate by force. He reported every word you said, even your cry: 'First Rome, then Belisarius'. Bessas demanded your head in the council of commanders, and I trembled for you. But Belisarius said: 'He did right! Here, Procopius, take him my own sword and the entire armour I wore on that day, as my thanks'. And in his report to the emperor he dictated the words: 'Cethegus saved Rome, and only Cethegus! Send him the Patriciate of Byzantium!' Those were his words."

"Thank you, but I did not save Rome for Byzantium."

"There is no need for you to tell me that, you incurable Roman."

"And what thanks did you get, you who saved his life?"

"Quiet! He knows nothing of that, and he is never to hear about it."

"Syphax, wine. That much nobility of mind is more than I can bear. It makes me weak! Now, how did the little jaunt on horseback go?"

"Friend, that was no jaunt, but the most dreadful earnest I have yet encountered. Belisarius went within a hair's breadth of being killed."

"Yes, those Goths always miss by just one hair. They are clumsy oafs, all of them."

"You sound as if you are sorry Belisarius did not perish."

"It would have served him right! I warned him three times. He should have learned by now that what is fitting for a young ruffian is not necessarily seemly for an old commanding general."

"Listen," said Procopius, "you earned the right to speak like that at Hadrian's tomb. Before that, if you had but dared degrade the great man's heroism…"

"You thought I was speaking out of envy for the brave Belisarius! Did you hear that, immortal gods?"

"Yes, admittedly your laurels from the campaign against the Gepidae…"

"Don't remind me of those boyish pranks! Friend, one must defy death when it counts, but otherwise it is best to love life with all due care. Only the living rule and laugh, not the silent dead. That is my homespun wisdom – call it cowardice if you like. So, your ambush? Make it short. What happened?"

"I will be brief. After we had reconnoitred the area, which seemed clear of the enemy and just right for food gathering, we turned our mounts back to the city, the few sheep and goats we had found in the middle, Belisarius at the head, and young Severinus, John and I by his side. Suddenly, as we came out in the open after going though a village, Gothic cavalry charged at us from the wooded sides of the road. I could see only that they greatly outnumbered us, and urged that we should attempt to flee right through the middle of them along the Via Valeria to Rome. But Belisarius replied: 'There may be many of them, but not too many,' and he charged at his attackers to the left, trying to break through their lines. But we received a hostile reception. The Goths rode and fought better than our Mauretanian mounted troops, and their leaders Totila and Hildebad – I recognised the former by his yellow hair and the latter by his huge size – were obviously aiming for the commander Belisarius himself. 'Where are Belisarius and his famous courage?' the tall Hildebad cried so that it could be heard over the noise of the fighting.

"'Here!' my general answered immediately, and before we could restrain him he was facing the giant. Hildebad did not hold back and struck him a mighty blow on his helmet, so that horsehair plume and crest fell smashed to the ground, and Belisarius's head was down on the neck of his horse. Already the giant was about to deliver a second, deadly swing; but young Severinus, the son of Boethius, was there in an instant and caught the blow with his round shield. But the Barbarian's axe went through the shield and cut deeply into the fine young man's neck. He fell!" Procopius halted for a moment in painful remembrance.

"Dead?" Cethegus asked calmly.

"An old freedman of his father's carried him out of the fight, but he died before reaching the village."

"A beautiful death!" said Cethegus. "Syphax, a fresh goblet of wine!"

"Meanwhile Belisarius had rallied, and now he thrust his spear at the Goth's breastplate with such force that he fell right off his horse. We cheered loudly, but young Totila saw his brother fall, and in an instant he had forced his way through the lances of the bodyguard to Belisarius. Aigan, his flag bearer, tried to shield him, but the Goth's sword struck his left arm. He tore the flag from the now disabled hand and threw it to the nearest Goth. Belisarius let out a roar of rage and turned to meet him, but that Totila is as quick as lightning. Before he knew what was happening our general was struck on both shoulders. Belisarius swayed in the saddle and started to slowly fall from his horse, which was hit by a javelin at the same time, throwing it to the ground. 'Give yourself prisoner, Belisarius!' cried Totila.

The general had just enough strength left to shake his head, and then he sank to the ground completely. I dismounted quickly, threw him over my own horse and entrusted him to the care of John, who gathered fifty bodyguards about him and fled with him out of the fight and into the city."

"And you?"

"I went on fighting on foot. Now that our rearguard had arrived – we had to abandon the supplies we had foraged – I was able to turn the engagement against Totila, but not for long. By now the second contingent of Gothic cavalry was upon us too. That black Teias bore down on us like a hurricane, and his charge broke straight through our right wing, which was first to face him. Then he smashed through my own front, which was fighting Totila, from the flank, and he scattered our entire force. I gave up the engagement as lost, jumped on a riderless horse and went after Belisarius. But Teias had also recognised the direction in which Belisarius was fleeing, and chased after us furiously. On the Fulvian Bridge Teias caught up with the bodyguards. John and I had placed more than half of our remaining bodyguards on the bridge to defend the river crossing, under the brave Pisidian Principus and the giant Isaurian Tarmuth. There they fell, all thirty of them, the two leaders last. From what I heard Teias and his sword personally accounted for them all. The flower of Belisarius's bodyguard fell there, together with some of my closest friends, Alamundarus the Saracen, Artasines the Persian, Zanter the Armenian, Longinus the Isaurian, Bucha and Chorsamantes the Massageti, Kutila the Thracen, Hildeger the Vandal, Juphrut the Moor and Theodoritos and Georgios the Cappadocians. But their deaths bought our escape. We caught up with our infantry behind the bridge, whom we had left there, and they managed to occupy the enemy cavalry long enough until the Porta Tiburtina opened at long last to admit our wounded commander. Then, as soon as I had left him safely in Antonina's care, I hurried to Hadrian's tomb, where I heard that the city had been taken, and where I found you near death."

"And what has Belisarius decided to do now?"

"His wounds are not as serious as yours, and yet he is recovering more slowly. He has granted the Goths the ceasefire they asked for in order to bury their many dead."

Cethegus rose from his pillows: "He should have refused it! Why defer the decisive final struggle now? I know these Gothic steers; their horns are blunted from storming, and they will be tired and vulnerable.

"Now is the right time to strike the final blow, which I have thought of long ago. Their huge bodies will not take kindly to the heat out there. They will take even less well to hunger, and worst of all to thirst! A Germanic savage must drink when he is not snoring or brawling. Now all we have to do is to intimidate their cautious king a little bit more. Convey my regards to Belisarius, and my thanks for his sword is this advice: He is to send the much feared John with eight thousand men this very day through the Picenum against Ravenna. The Via Flaminia is open and there will be little opposition on it, because Witigis has withdrawn the garrisons from all the fortresses and brought them here. Right now we can win Ravenna much more easily than the Barbarians could ever win Rome. But as soon as the king sees Ravenna threatened, his very last stronghold, he will hurry to save it at any price. He will withdraw his army from these unconquerable walls and become the hunted instead of the hunter."

"Cethegus!" Procopius cried, jumping to his feet, "You are a great general!"

"It is only one of my interests, Procopius! Go now and convey my best wishes to the great victor Belisarius!"

Chapter 15

On the last day of the ceasefire Cethegus was already sufficiently recovered to appear once more on the walls of Hadrian's tomb, where his legionaries and Isaurians greeted him with loud cheering. His first mission was to go the tombstone of Kallistratos, where he laid a wreath of laurels and roses on the black marble slab. While he was organising repairs and reinforcements to the fortifications from here, Syphax brought him a letter from Matesuentha.

It sounded laconic enough: "Put an end to it soon! I cannot bear to witness this misery much longer. The burial of forty thousand men from my people has torn my breast asunder, and all the songs of mourning seem to be directed against me. If that goes on much longer it will destroy me. Hunger is raging terribly in the camp. Their last hope is a large shipment of grain and cattle, coming from northern Gaul. The ships will be near Portus in about two weeks. Act accordingly, but put an end to it quickly!"

"Triumph!" said the Prefect, "the siege is over. Our little fleet has been lying idle at Populonium thus far. Now it shall find work to do. That queen is like Erynnis to those Barbarians." And he himself went to see Belisarius, who received him with noble magnanimity.

During that same night, the last night of the ceasefire, John marched out of the Porta Pinciana, then swinging left along the Via Flaminia. His goal was Ravenna. And messengers hurried on fast boats to Populonium, where a small fleet of Roman ships had assembled. The fighting for the city, even though the ceasefire was over, had stopped almost completely. About a week later the king left his sickbed for the first time, and in the company of his friends he took a walk through the tents. Three of the seven camps, formerly swarming with life, were now completely deserted and had been abandoned. Even the four remaining camps now seemed sparsely populated. Deadly tired, without complaint but also without hope, the emaciated Goths lay in front of their tents, consumed by hunger and fever.

There was not a friendly word of greeting to cheer the worthy king on this painful walk, and they barely opened their tired eyes at the sound of his footsteps.

From the interior of the camp came the groans of the sick and dying, who were succumbing to their wounds, hunger or disease. Only with difficulty could enough fit men be found for even the most urgent guard duty. Those on watch dragged their spears behind them, too tired to carry them upright or on their shoulders.

The king and the other leaders came to the defences in front of the Porta Aurelia, where a young archer lay in the ditch, chewing at the bitter grass. Hildebad called out to him: "Gunthamund, what's that? Your bowstring has broken. Why don't you fit a new one?"

"I can't, Sir. The string broke yesterday when I fired my last arrow. And the three lads with me and I between us don't have the strength to put on a new one."

Hildebad gave him a drink from his flask. "Did you shoot at a Roman?"

"Oh no, Sir. A rat was gnawing at the corpse over there. Luckily I hit it and the four of us shared it."

"Iffaswinth, where is your uncle Iffamer?" the king asked.

"Dead, Sir. He fell behind you as he was helping to carry you away, in front of that accursed marble tomb."

"And your father Iffamut?"

"He is dead too, Sir. He could not tolerate the poisonous water from these puddles any more. The thirst, King, burns even more than the hunger. And this leaden sky just will not rain."

"Are you all from the Athesis Valley?"

"Yes, Sir King, from the Iffinger Mountain. Oh, what lovely spring water we have at home!"

Teias spotted another soldier drinking from his helmet some distance away. His face grew even blacker. "Hey you, Arnulf!" he called out to him, "you don't seem to be suffering from thirst?"

"No Sir, I drink often," the man replied.

"What do you drink?"

"Blood from the wounds of the newly fallen. It's repulsive at first, but in desperation one gets used to it."

Witigis walked on with a shudder. "Send all my wine into the camp, Hildebad. Let the guards share it."

"All your wine? Oh King, that's easy. You only have one and a half jugs left. And your physician Hildebrand has ordered that you should drink it to get your strength back."

"And who will give these men their strength back, Hildebad? Their need is turning them into wild animals!"

"Come home with us," Totila suggested, "this is not a good place for you to be."

Back in the king's tent the friends sat silently around the lovely marble table, on which some stone-hard mouldy bread had been served up on golden dishes, together with a little meat. "It was the last horse from your royal stables," said Hildebad, "except Boreas."

"Boreas will not be slaughtered! My wife and child have sat on his back." And Witigis rested his tired head on both hands; there was a renewed, long pause. "Friends," he began at last, "we cannot go on like this any longer. Our nation is perishing in front of these walls. I have come to a difficult and painful decision."

"Don't say it yet, oh King!" Hildebad cried. "In a few days Count Odiswinth of Cremona will arrive with the fleet, and then there will be plenty of everything."

"He has not arrived yet!" Teias cautioned.

"And as far as our losses are concerned, as serious as they are," Totila said encouragingly, "won't they be replaced by fresh troops when Count Ulithis arrives from Urbinum with the garrisons the king has withdrawn from fortresses between Rome and Ravenna, to fill our empty tents?"

"Ulithis has not arrived yet either," said Teias. "I hear that he is still in Picenum. And even if he does arrive eventually, that will only make the lack of food and water in the camp more serious."

"But remember the Romans in the city are starving too!" said Hildebad as he smashed the hard bread against the table top. "Let's see who can stand it the longest!"

"I have thought about it often during these grave days and sleepless nights," the king continued slowly. "Why? Why did it all have to work out like this? Again and again I weighed justice and injustice in my mind as well as I could, between the enemy and us. But in all good conscience the only conclusion I can come to is that right is on our side. And surely we did not fail to do our part when it came to strength and courage."

"You least of all," Totila added.

"Nor did we flinch from making the heaviest sacrifices!" the king sighed. "And now, if there is a God in heaven, just and good and powerful, then why does He allow this great, undeserved misery to happen? Why must we be conquered by Byzantium?"

"But we must not let ourselves be conquered," cried Hildebad. "I have never thought much about our God. But if He were to let this happen, then one would have to take heaven by storm and smash His throne with clubs!"

"Don't blaspheme, my brother!" said Totila. "And you, my worthy king, have courage and have faith. Yes, there is a just God, who rules above the stars. And that is why, in the end, our just cause must triumph. Courage, my Witigis, and hope to the end."

But the deeply depressed man sadly shook his head: "I have been able to find only one way out of this madness, this doubting God's justice. We cannot be suffering unless we deserve it in some way. And since our nation's cause is just beyond doubt, there must be some secret guilt attached to me, your king. The ancient songs from our past tell us how, again and again, a king sacrificed himself to the gods when defeat, pestilence and poor crops plagued his tribe for years. He would take upon himself the hidden guilt which seemed to be hanging over his countrymen, and pay for it with his life, or by sacrificing his crown and going off into exile by himself, a fugitive without nation and without peace. Let me lay down this crown, and take it from this head, which has brought it neither luck nor hope. Choose another with whom God is not angry! Choose Totila, or…"

"You are talking nonsense in your fever!" Hildebrand the old armourer interrupted him. "You, loaded with guilt? You, the truest of us all? No, let me tell you children something, you whose fathers lost their old strength with their old religion, so that you now know of nothing to console your troubled hearts. The way you are talking, without hope, is making me feel sorry for you!" And his grey eyes looked at his friends with a rare glow: "Everything that brings us joy or pain here on earth is insignificant. Down here there is only one thing that matters, and that is to be a true and just man, a worthy and honest one, and to die in battle is better than to die in bed. Then the Valkyries come to carry the worthy hero on red clouds from the bloody battlefields to Odin's great hall, where all the other heroes will greet him with full goblets.

"And then he will go riding out to the hunt each day, or to games of arms in the morning, and every evening he will return to wine and song in a golden hall in the twilight. There will be beautiful maidens to caress the young heroes, and the older men will exchange the wisdom of their years with the heroes of the past. And I will meet them all again, the strong companions of my youth, the brave Winithar and Waltharis of Aquitania and the Burgundian Guntharis. And I will see him whom I have longed to meet for so long, the great Beowulf from the ancient past of the Cherusci, the first man to defeat the Romans, of whom Saxon singers still sing and tell. And once more I will carry shield and spear for my great master, the king with the eyes of an eagle. And so we will live on in all eternity in light and in pure joy, forgetting the earth down here and its little woes."

"That is a lovely poem, you old heathen!" Totila smiled. "But what if that no longer brings consolation to us here and now? What does it do for real, heart-rending sorrow? You say your piece too, Teias, you gloomy guest. What are your thoughts on all this suffering? Your sword is always there when we need it; why will you not give us your thoughts too? Why do we no longer hear the sound of your harp, you, the finest harpist and singer among us?"

"What I think," Teias replied, "might be even more difficult for you to bear than all this sorrow. Let me remain silent for a little longer, my sunny friend Totila. Perhaps a day will come when I will answer you. I might even play the harp again, if by then there is so much as one string left on it." And he left the tent.

Outside, in the camp, a strange and mysterious noise had started, mostly of shouting, questioning voices.

The friends had watched Teias go in silence. "I know what he is thinking," old Hildebrand said at last. "I have known him since he was a boy. He is not like other men. There are some in the northern land who think as he does. They do not believe in Thor and Odin, but only in necessity and their own strength. It is almost too much for a human heart, and it certainly does not make one happy to think like that. I am surprised that he can sing and play the harp at all."

At that moment Teias tore the curtains open and re-entered the tent. His face was even more pale than before, and his dark eyes flashed, but his voice was calm as usual as he spoke: "Break camp, King Witigis. Our ships have fallen into enemy hands in Ostia. They sent Count Odiswinth's head into the camp. And they are having the captured cattle slaughtered on the walls of Rome by Gothic prisoners, before the eyes of our sentries. Large reinforcements are on their way from Byzantium under Valerian and Euthalius. A victorious fleet has brought Huns, Slavs and other troops from Byzantium into the Tiber. And Bloody John has marched through Picenum..."

"And Count Ulithis?"

"John has defeated and killed Count Ulithis, taken Ancona and Ariminum, and..."

"Is that still not all?" the king cried.

"No, Witigis! You must hurry! He threatens Ravenna; he is only a few miles from the city."

Chapter 16

The day after this news arrived, so disastrous for the Goths, Witigis abandoned the siege of Rome and led his greatly reduced and demoralised army out of the four remaining camps. The siege had lasted a whole year and nine days. Much of the Gothic strength had been expended on the siege, so much courage, so much effort and so many sacrifices, and yet it had all been in vain.

In silence the Goths marched past the proud walls, against which their strength and their luck had foundered. Silently they endured the scorn and derision which the Romans and the "Romaeans" (or Byzantines) called out to them from the safety of their battlements. The Gothic anger and grief were so great that they took no notice.

But when Belisarius's cavalry, breaking out of the Porta Pinciana, tried to harass the retreating Goths they were fiercely repulsed. Count Teias was leading the Gothic rearguard.

Thus the army moved in rapid marches from Rome along the Via Flaminia to Ravenna through Picenum, avoiding fortresses and the cities of Narnia, Spoletum and Perusium, which were occupied by the enemy. Witigis arrived in Ravenna just in time to suppress the dangerous mood of the population, which had already entered into secret negotiations with John when they heard of the Barbarian misfortune.

As the Goths approached John took refuge in his most recent conquest, Ariminum. In Ancona Konon, Belisarius's fleet commander, lay with warships and Thracen lancers.

But the king did not by any means lead the whole of his army into Ravenna, and along the way he had distributed many of his men among the various fortresses there. He left one thousand men under Gibimer in Clusium in Tuscany, another thousand in Urbs Vetus under Albila, and five hundred under Wulfgis in Tudertum. In Auximum he left four thousand under Count Wisand, the brave *bandalarius*, in Urbinum two thousand under Morra, and five hundred each in Caesena and Monsferetrus. He despatched Hildebrand to Verona, Totila to Tarvisium and Teias to Ticinum, because the northeast of the peninsula was also under threat by Byzantine troops coming from Istria.

He took these actions for other reasons as well. For one thing he wanted to delay Belisarius on his way to Ravenna. Secondly, in the event of a siege, he did not want to be exposed to hunger again due to the sheer size of his army. And finally, in the event of a siege, he wanted to be able to harass the enemy from the rear, from several directions. His immediate aim was to avert the danger which threatened his main base of Ravenna, and to use his badly eroded forces to concentrate on defence until relief arrived. For this relief he was counting on the expected arrival of foreign auxiliary troops, Lombards and Franks, and once they were on the scene he would be able to take the offensive once more.

But his hopes of delaying Belisarius on his way to Ravenna by way of these Gothic fortresses did not eventuate. Belisarius contented himself by surrounding them with just enough troops to act as observers, and went on his way to the capital and the last remaining real stronghold of the Goths, without taking the time or trouble to capture every city and fortress along the way. "Once I have struck the heart a mortal blow," he said, "the fists will open by themselves."

★

And so it was not long before Byzantine tents surrounded Theodoric's capital, on three sides, from the port of Classis to the canals and tributaries of the Padus, which formed the main western defences of the fortress city. Ravenna was in effect completely surrounded.

Admittedly the proud old city had already lost much of the gloss with which it had glowed for two centuries as the residence of the Imperators. Even the renewed glory which the golden reign of Theodoric had brought to the city had disappeared since the start of the war.

Nevertheless the city, which was similar to Venice today, and which in those days was still well populated, must have made quite an impression! How different must it have been from what it is today, where the casual explorer wandering the lonely streets is met by empty plazas and basilicas, creating an impression no less melancholy than the vast swamps beyond the city walls.

Where there was once a great deal of activity on land and water in the port of Classis, where the proud triremes of the Imperial Adriatic Fleet once floated, today there are only swampy meadows in which wild buffaloes graze. The streets are a muddy swamp, the harbour is filled with sand and silt, and the people who once lived here have vanished. Only a single huge round tower now remains from the Gothic era, next to the sole remaining, lonely basilica of Saint Apollinare in Classe Fuori. Commenced by Witigis and completed by Justinian, it is now an hour's travel from human habitation, standing sadly in a swampy plain.

The powerful fortress by the sea was regarded as impregnable, which is why the emperors had chosen it as their residence as their might declined and the Barbarian threat to Italy grew to a dangerous level. The south-eastern side was protected by the sea, which in those days bordered right on the city, even extending into Ravenna itself.

On the other three landward sides nature and man had woven a labyrinth of canals, ditches and swamps of the Padus delta, in which any army laying siege would become hopelessly bogged and entangled. And those walls! Even today their mighty remains fill us with awe. Before the invention of firearms, their enormous thickness, and the height even more than the number of towers on them, were enough to repel any attempt to take the fortress by force. Theodoric had been able to take this, the last refuge of Odoacer, only by starving the city into submission after a siege of almost four years.

Belisarius tried in vain to take the city by storm immediately after his arrival. His attack was resolutely repulsed, and he had to content himself with surrounding the city on all sides and then, like the Gothic king before him, to starve it into eventual surrender. However Witigis could afford to look forward to a long siege with confidence. With the caution and foresight which were characteristic of him he had, even before the departure for Rome, accumulated huge stocks of all kinds of foodstuffs, particularly grain. To store them he had had large warehouses built, in the enormous marble circus of Theodosius. These extensive wooden structures, built immediately opposite the palace and the basilica Sancti Apollinaris, were his pride, his joy and his solace. It had not been possible to transport much of these supplies to Rome through a hostile countryside where enemy troops were constantly active, and with careful management these supplies would suffice to feed the population and the reduced army for at least two or three months. By that time, as a result of newly initiated negotiations, an auxiliary Frankish army was expected to arrive and relieve the city. The arrival of that army would, of course, also mean the end of the siege.

But all of this was known to, or at least suspected by, Belisarius and Cethegus as well as Witigis. And so they searched constantly for ways in which the fall of the city could be expedited. Naturally the Prefect tried to use his secret connections with the Gothic queen for this purpose. But for one thing communication with her was now much more difficult, because the Goths kept very careful guard on all exits from the city. Also Matesuentha seemed to have changed markedly, and no longer as willing to serve as a tool as she had been before.

She had expected a quick defeat and humiliation of the king. The long, drawn out war had tired her, and at the same time the protracted suffering of her people, from war, hunger and disease, had started to affect her deeply.

Finally a sad change had come over the king. Normally a healthy, strong and confident man, he now suffered from a silent but bitter grief, and that touched her deeply. Even though she still accused him of having spurned her love and yet forced her to marry him for the sake of his crown, and although she still thought she hated him for it with all her heart and soul (which to a degree she did), yet this hatred was in fact only unrequited love. And when she saw him now, bent and almost broken by the failure of his campaign and the suffering of his people, to which by her treachery she had contributed to a very large degree, the sight of him had a strange effect on her passionate, yet hard nature.

In the first moments of pain and anger she would have been delighted to see his blood flow. But to watch him tearing himself apart with this self inflicted grief, that was something she could not bear. Another factor which contributed to her own more tolerant mood was the fact that the attitude of the king toward her had also changed since their arrival in Ravenna. She took this to mean that he was beginning to have regrets at the way he had forced himself into her life.

Believing this, her behaviour toward the king during their infrequent meetings, which always took place in the presence of a third party, had also softened. Witigis on his part saw this as a pleasing attempt on her part to ease the tension between them, and he rewarded her with praise and kindness. All of this was enough to influence the impulsive woman to refuse the Prefect's propositions, even on the rare occasions when they still reached her via the clever Moor.

But the Prefect had learned from this source, even during the march on Ravenna, that the Goths were expecting help from the Franks, even though that became common knowledge later. Consequently he had wasted no time in resuming his relations with the various rulers and nobles whom he already knew, particularly the Merovingian puppet kings at the courts of Mettis, Aurelianum and Suessianum (today Metz, Orleans and Soissons). By this means he hoped to persuade the Frankish kings, whose treachery at that time was almost proverbial, to break off their alliance with the Goths.

After having friends carefully prepare the groundwork, he had written to King Theudebald in Mettis, to the effect that he should dissociate himself from a lost cause, as the cause of the Goths had been since the failed siege of Rome. The letter had been accompanied by rich gifts to the king's weak and corrupt *major domus*, who was an old friend of the Prefect. Now the Prefect awaited a reply as each day passed; all the more so as the changed behaviour of Matesuentha had greatly reduced his hopes of a quick end to the war.

The reply arrived at the same time as a letter from the Imperial Court in Byzantium, on a day which was to prove equally fateful for the heroes both inside and outside Ravenna.

Chapter 17

At daybreak one day early in the siege Hildebad, impatient at such a long period of inactivity, had led a furious sortie against the Byzantine camp from the Porta Faventia, which had been entrusted to his care. Initially he made rapid gains, burning some of the siege machinery and spreading terror everywhere.

Without doubt he would have caused even greater havoc, had it not been for the fact that Belisarius, on that day, displayed his great generalship and his personal heroism. Without helmet or armour, he hurled himself first at his own fleeing vanguard, and then at the Goths, and by a great personal effort and considerable bravery he was able to halt the Gothic advance. After that he manoeuvred his two flanks so skilfully that Hildebad's retreat was in serious jeopardy. In the end the Goths had to surrender all their gains and hurry back to the city to avoid being cut off.

Cethegus, who had been camped with his Isaurians outside the Porta Honoria, hurried to his aid, but found the struggle already over by the time he arrived. Afterwards he could not contain himself from going to Belisarius's tent and expressing his admiration both as a general and as a warrior. Antonina eagerly soaked up this praise. "Really, Belisarius," the Prefect concluded, "the emperor Justinian will never be able to repay you for this."

"You are right there," Belisarius replied with pride. "My real reward is his friendship. I could never do what I have done, and what I am still doing, just for this commander's baton alone. I do it because I really love him. With all his weaknesses, he is a very great man. If he would only learn just one thing, and that is to trust me. But be patient; he will learn it yet."

Now Procopius entered and handed his general a letter, which had just been delivered by an Imperial envoy. Forgetting all his tiredness, with his face beaming joyfully, Belisarius jumped up from his chair and kissed the purple strings which held the bundle of wax tablets together and sealed it. He then cut them with his dagger and opened the letter with the words: "From my master and emperor himself! Ah, now he will send me the bodyguards and the long overdue pay for the men, for which I have been waiting, and repayment of the gold which I have advanced out of my own pocket."

And he started to read.

Antonina, Procopius and Cethegus watched him carefully as he read. His face darkened more and more, his broad chest started to heave as if in a struggle, and his hands started to tremble. Antonina, becoming concerned, went over to him, but even before she could speak Belisarius let out a cry of suppressed anger, hurled the Imperial letter on the ground and stormed out of the tent. His wife went after him as quickly as she could.

"Now Antonina is the only one who may dare face him," said Procopius, picking up the letter. "Let's see, probably another piece of Imperial ingratitude," and he started reading: "The beginning is the usual formalities – aha, now it becomes more interesting:

"'At the same time we cannot hide our disappointment that, after your earlier boasts, the war has not been brought to a conclusion more rapidly. We also believe that such a more speedy conclusion would have been possible, if a more concerted effort had been made against the Barbarians. Accordingly we are unable to accede to your wishes to send you the remaining five thousand men from your bodyguard, who are still in Persia, nor the four hundredweight of gold you have requested from your palace in Byzantium.'

"It is true, as you say quite superfluously in your letter, that they are both your property. Furthermore your resolve, expressed in the same letter, that you wish to conclude this war out of your own means deserves to be called loyal and worthy, especially considering the state of the Imperial finances. However, as you also quite correctly point out in your letter, everything you own is at the beck and call of your emperor. Your emperor now considers that further expenditure of your men and money in Italy would serve no purpose. With your concurrence, of which we are confident, we have decided that these means are best deployed elsewhere. Accordingly your troops and treasure have been made available to your colleague Narses, so that a more rapid conclusion to the war in Persia can be brought about.' Ha! Incredible!" Procopius interrupted himself.

Cethegus smiled: "That is the thanks of a master for the services of a slave."

"The end looks interesting too." Procopius went on. "It goes on to say: 'Any increase to your power in Italy seems all the less desirable to us as we receive warnings every day about your boundless ambition.

"'Only the other day you are reported to have said, over a goblet of wine, that the sceptre developed from a commander's baton, and the baton from a stick! These are dangerous thoughts and unseemly words.

"'As you see we are well informed about your ambitious dreams.

"'This time we will content ourselves with giving you a warning, without punishment. However we are disinclined to give you any more wood for your baton, and we remind you that the tallest and proudest treetops are closest to the bolt of Imperial lightning.'

"That's disgraceful!" cried Procopius.

"No, it's worse, it's stupid!" Cethegus replied. "That is tantamount to driving loyalty itself to rebellion."

"How right you are!" Belisarius cried, racing back into the tent and having just heard the last few words. "Oh, he deserves revolt and mutiny, the ungrateful, malicious, disgraceful tyrant!"

"Be quiet! In the name of all the saints, you will destroy yourself!" Antonina implored him, trying to take his hand.

"No, I will not be quiet!" the angered man shouted, pacing up and down past the open door of the tent, outside of which Bessas, Acacius, Demetrius and many of his other commanders stood listening in amazement. "The whole world shall hear it. He is an ungrateful, treacherous tyrant! Yes, you deserve to be toppled by me! If only I was capable of doing what your timid heart fears, Justinianus!"

Cethegus took a look at those standing outside, who had obviously heard everything. Eagerly motioning to Antonina to try and silence her husband, he went over to the entrance and drew the curtains. Antonina thanked him with a glance and went over to her husband once more. But the latter had now thrown himself to the ground by his camp bed, struck his chest with his clenched fists and stammered: "Oh

Justinianus, is this what I deserve in return for what I have done for you? Oh too much, it is just too much!" And suddenly the great man broke into racking, sobbing tears.

At that Cethegus turned away in disgust: "Farewell, Procopius," he said softly, "it revolts me to see men cry."

Chapter 18

Deep in thought the Prefect walked out of the tent and made his way, skirting around the camp, to the entrenchment in front of the gate of St Honorius, some distance away, where his Isaurians were dug in. It was southeast of the city, near the seawall of Classis, and his walk led him some distance along the beach.

Much as the lonely walker was occupied by his great ambition, which had become the focal point of his life, and much as his mind was preoccupied with the unpredictability of Belisarius and waiting for a reply from the Franks, yet his attention was diverted, if only in passing, by the extraordinary appearance of the countryside, the sea, the sky and the whole of nature.

It was October, but it seemed as if the season had changed weeks ago. There had been no rain for almost two months, and not a cloud, not even a wisp of mist had been seen over the swampy landscape for days. It was just before sunset and now, suddenly, Cethegus noticed a single round black cloud above the sea in the east. It was ominously pitch black, and had evidently just appeared. The sun, although not hidden by fog, seemed to be giving no light. There was not a breath of air, not even the slightest wave rippled the water, and far and wide not a leaf stirred. Not even the reeds in the swamp moved.

There was not the sound of an animal, nor the flight of a bird. A strange, thick smog, like sulphur, seemed to be lying over land and sea, making it difficult to breathe. Mules and horses clawed impatiently at the planks to which they had been tied in the camp, and a few camels and dromedaries, which Belisarius had brought from Africa, hid their heads in the sand.

Our lonely wanderer looked about him several times. "It's sultry this evening," he said to himself, "if I was in Egypt now I would say that the 'wind of death' is coming. Sultry everywhere, inside and outside. I wonder on whom the pent-up elements of nature will vent their anger tonight?"

With that he went into his tent, where Syphax said to him: "Master, if I was at home, today I would believe that the poisonous wind of the desert is coming," and he gave his master a letter.

It was the reply from the Franconian king! Cethegus tore open the large, ornate seal. "Who brought it?"

"A messenger who, when he could not find the Prefect, asked for Belisarius. He demanded to be told the quickest route through the camp. That's why Cethegus missed him."

Eagerly Cethegus read: "Theudebald, King of the Franks, to Cethegus the Prefect of Rome. They were clever words you wrote to us. Even wiser words were not committed to writing, but were communicated to us by our *major domus*. We are not disinclined to act accordingly. We accept your advice and your gifts. Our alliance with the Goths has been dissolved by their misfortune; let them blame that, and not a change of heart on our part, for our decision.

"All men who are pious and wise should have nothing to do with those whom heaven has deserted. It is true that they have paid the wages of the auxiliary army in advance, several hundredweight of gold, but in our eyes that is not an obstacle. We will retain these treasures as surety until they cede to us those cities in southern Gaul which fall within the Empire of the Franks, as decreed by God and by nature.

"But as our offensive has already been prepared our brave soldiers, who have been looking forward to the fighting, are enduring the boredom of camp life only with displeasure. We are therefore willing to send them across the Alps just the same, but against the Goths, not for them. But of course it will not be for the emperor Justinian either, who continues to refuse us the title of King, who calls himself 'King of Gaul' on his coins, who will not allow us to mint coins in our own image, and who has offended our honour in other, quite unbearable ways. We rather think that we might expand our own Empire into Italy.

"Now we know that the emperor's entire strength in Italy lies in his general Belisarius, and also that the latter has many reasons to be unhappy with his ungrateful master, both old and new. Therefore we now propose to call on that hero to proclaim himself emperor of the Occident, and to rebel against his former master in Byzantium. To this end we will assist him with an army of one hundred thousand of our warriors, in return for which we ask only for a small part of Italy, from the Alps to Genoa.

"We think it unlikely that a mortal would refuse this offer. If you choose to cooperate with us in our plan we can promise you the sum of twelve hundredweight of gold and also, in return for two of those hundredweight of gold, we will include your name in the list of companions at our table. The envoy who delivered this letter, Duke Liuthari, is instructed to communicate our proposal to Belisarius."

Cethegus had finished reading with growing agitation, and now he blew up: "An offer like this, at this hour? In his present mood? He will accept! Emperor of the Occident with one hundred thousand Franconian warriors! He must not live!"

And with that he hurried to the exit of his tent, but when he got there he suddenly stopped: "Fool that I was!" he smiled coldly. "Still hot blooded? Of course, he is Belisarius and not Cethegus! He will not accept. That would be like the moon suddenly rebelling against the earth, or a tame housedog suddenly becoming a fierce wolf. He will not accept! But now let us see how we can use this greed and treachery on the part of the Merovingian. No, King of the Franks," and he smiled bitterly as he crushed the letter in his hand, "as long as Cethegus lives, not a footstep of Italy's soil!"

And now he took a rapid walk through the tent, then a second, slower one, and then a third. At last he stopped, and there was a flicker of movement on his mighty forehead: "I have it!" he rejoiced. "Come, Syphax!" he cried, "Go and call Procopius."

And as he strode through the tent once more his glance fell on the letter from the Merovingian, which had fallen to the ground. "No," he smiled as he picked it up, "No, King of the Franks, you shall not even have so much Italian soil as this letter covers."

Procopius soon appeared, and the two men spent most of the night in deep, serious discussion. Procopius was almost overwhelmed by the Prefect's enormously ambitious plans, and for a long time he would have no part of them. But the great man had used his vast intellectual capacity to ensnare his friend, and he held him in a vicelike grip with compelling arguments. He dismissed every objection with convincing logic before it even arose, and he did not relent from weaving his tight and unbreakable net around the struggling Procopius until finally the latter had no more strength to resist.

The stars paled, and as Procopius and his friend parted the first light of day already illuminated the east. "Cethegus," he said on rising, "I admire you. If I was not already historian to Belisarius, I would like to be your historian."

"It would be more difficult," the Prefect replied, "but also more interesting."

"The clarity and sharpness of your mind almost frighten me! It must be a sign of the times, like a poisonous coloured flower in a swamp. When I think how you destroyed the Gothic king through his own wife..."

"I had to tell you that just now. Unfortunately I have not heard from my beautiful ally for some time."

"Your ally! Your means are..."

"Always suitable for the task in hand and the aim in mind."

"Not always! But just the same, I will go along with you just a little way further, because I want my hero out of Italy as soon as possible. Let him gather laurels in Persia, not thorns here! But I will go no further than..."

"Than your goal, that's understood."

"Enough. I will speak with Antonina straight away, and I don't doubt I will succeed. She is bored to death here, and she can't wait to get back to Byzantium, not only to renew old friendships but also to destroy some of her husband's enemies."

"A good, and bad, woman."

"But Witigis? Do you think he might consider a revolt by Belisarius a possibility?"

"King Witigis is a very good soldier and a very bad psychologist. I know of a much more able mind who thought it possible for a moment. And you are going to show him everything in writing. And now more than ever, now that the Franks have deserted him, he will clutch at anything. So don't worry about that! Just make sure of Antonina."

"Let that be my worry. By midday I hope to be in Ravenna as an envoy."

"Good! And don't forget to speak to the lovely queen for me."

Chapter 19

At midday Procopius did ride into Ravenna. He was carrying four letters: the letter from Justinian to Belisarius, the letters from the Franks to Belisarius and Cethegus, and a letter from Belisarius to Witigis. Procopius had written the last letter, and Cethegus had dictated it.

The envoy had no idea how he would find the Gothic king and his queen. For some time now the direct mind of the king had not exactly faltered under the pressure of sustained disaster, but it had made him gloomy and introspective. The murder of his only child and the heartrending separation from his wife had shaken him severely, but he had borne them so that the Goths might be victorious. But now that very victory had stubbornly eluded him. In spite of every effort on his part the cause of his people had worsened more and more with every month of his reign, and with the single exception of the battle on the way to Rome fortune had not smiled on him even once.

The siege of Rome, begun with such proud hopes, had ended with the loss of three quarters of his army and a painful retreat. Fresh setbacks and more dismal news followed like the blows of a club on his helmet, and they had increased his depression to a point where his mood was now one of morose hopelessness.

It seemed as if, day by day, almost the whole of Italy was being lost except for Ravenna. Even while he was still in Rome Belisarius had sent a fleet against Genoa, under Ennes the Isaurian and Mundila of the Heruli. Almost without striking a blow their troops captured the important port, and from there almost the whole of Liguria. They won Mediolanum because its bishop, Datius, invited them, and from there they went on to gain Bergamum, Comum and Novaria. In Clusium and half ruined Dertona the disheartened Goths surrendered to their enemies, and were led out of Italy as prisoners. Urbinum was captured by the Byzantines after a courageous struggle, and similarly Forum Cornelii and the whole of Aemilia were captured by Bloody John. Gothic attempts to recapture Ancona, Ariminum and Mediolanum failed.

But there was still more bad news for the embattled king.

Hunger had once more started to rage in Aemilia, Picenum and Tuscany. There were neither men nor oxen nor horses to pull the ploughs. The people were seeking refuge in the mountains and forests, baking bread from acorns and eating grass and weeds. Terrible diseases were rampant as a result of the inadequate and unhealthy food they were forced to eat. In Picenum alone five thousand people died from hunger and disease, and still more succumbed in Dalmatia on the other side of the Ionian Sea. The living were like walking skeletons on their way to the grave. Their skins were like leather, quite black, and their eyes protruded from their faces; their intestines felt as if they were on fire. Vultures scorned these victims of pestilence, but people greedily ate the flesh of their dead fellow men. Mothers killed and devoured their newborn children. On one particular farm near Ariminum only two Roman women were left. Between them they murdered and ate seventeen people, one after the other, who had sought refuge with them. The eighteenth intended victim managed to wake up before they could strangle him in his sleep; he killed the two werewolf women and brought the fate of their seventeen earlier victims to light.

And finally the hope of help from the Franks or the Lombards was to prove futile also. The former, who had been paid huge sums for the promised relief army, simply stayed away without a word. Messengers from the king, sent to urge speed and performance of the obligations which had been paid for in advance, were being held at Mettis, Aurelianum and Paris. No reply of any kind was received from these courts. The Lombard king Audoin, on the other hand, announced that he would make no decision without consulting his warrior son Alboin. Unfortunately the latter had gone off with a large following to seek adventure. Perhaps he might come to Italy one day – he was very friendly with Narses. He would then have a look at Italy and advise his father and his people as to what decisions they should make regarding this land, Italia.

It was true that Auximum had been holding out for months against all the efforts of a strong besieging army, which Belisarius himself led before their walls, accompanied by Procopius. Belisarius was personally in command of the siege. But it tore at the heart of the king when a messenger, who just managed to crawl into Ravenna wounded and with great difficulty, after making his way through both encircling armies in a journey of three days, conveyed the following message from the heroic Count Wisand, the *bandalarius*: "When you entrusted Auximum to me, you told me that I would thereby be guarding the key to Ravenna, and indeed the Gothic Empire. I was to resist until you would come, soon and with a relieving army. We have resisted both Belisarius and hunger, but where is your relief army? Woe be to the Empire if what you said is true, and if those keys fall into enemy hands with our fortress. Therefore come and help us, not so much for our sakes as for the sake of the Empire."

This messenger was soon followed by another, an enemy soldier by the name of Burcentius, who had been bribed with much gold. His message was to deliver a short letter, written in blood: "We have nothing left to eat except the weeds growing between the stones. We cannot possibly hold out for more than another five days." On his return with a reply from the king the messenger fell into the hands of the besiegers, who burned him alive before the walls of Auximum in sight of the Goths.

Oh, and the king could do nothing to help, no matter how much he wanted to.

The handful of Goths in Auximum still held out, even though Belisarius had deprived them of water by cutting off the aqueduct, and by poisoning the last remaining well with the corpses of men and animals and with lime. Any attempt to storm the fortress was still being bloodily repulsed by Wisand, and on one occasion Belisarius himself narrowly escaped death by sacrificing one of his bodyguards.

In the end Caesena was the first to fall, the last Gothic city in the Aemilia, and then Faesulae, which had been besieged by Cyprianus and Justinus. "My Faesulae!" the king had cried when he heard it. He had been commander of that city, and nearby was the house in which he and Rauthgundis had lived. "Now the Huns are probably camping in the ruins of what was my hearth!"

But when the captured garrison from Faesulae was led in chains before the defenders of Auximum, and when those prisoners described any prospect of relief from Ravenna as hopeless, the brave *bandalarius* and his starving army finally surrendered.

He himself had made free conduct to Ravenna a condition. But his men were led out of Italy as prisoners. Indeed, so much had their national spirit declined that some of them, under Count Sisifrid of Sarsina, served under the flag of Belisarius against their own countrymen.

The victor had placed a strong garrison at Auximum, and then he led the troops which had been involved with the siege back to Ravenna, where he also took back the supreme command from Cethegus, to whom it had been temporarily entrusted.

It seemed as if there was some evil curse on the head of the hapless king, on which the crown was resting so heavily. As he could not ascribe his failures to any fault or oversight on his own part, nor doubt the justness of the Gothic cause, his simple godfearing mind could see the outcome as nothing other than the will of heaven. Again and again therefore, as he went over the situation in his mind, he came back to the idea that God must be punishing the Goths for some past sin, as yet unforgiven. That kind of outlook was consistent not only with the Old Testament, which ruled the thinking in much of the world at that time, but also with much Germanic mythology.

Such thoughts were constantly on the mind of this worthy man, and night and day they gnawed at the remaining strength in his soul. Long ago he would have cheerfully passed the crown to another, were it not for the fact that such a move would now be seen as nothing but cowardice. Hence even this way out, which to him was the most attractive, was closed to him. And so the normally so strong and confident man spent much of his time sitting silently, his head bowed, only occasionally uttering a sound or shaking his head.

The daily sight of this quiet, proud and silent suffering did not pass without making an impression on Matesuentha, as we have already seen. She also thought that for some time she had noticed his eye looking at her more kindly than usual, with a melancholy expression and even fondness. And thus her great hope, which she still bore although she was only partly aware of it herself, drove her more and more to the king. Perhaps it was remorse, perhaps pity, and perhaps both, mingled with what was left of her former love.

Also they were now often united in joint works of mercy. During the last weeks the population of Ravenna had started to suffer hunger, while the besieging army outside was able to procure plentiful supplies from Calabria and Sicily. Only the very rich were still able to pay the very high price of grain. The king's kind heart did not therefore hesitate to give grain daily to the poor and needy, from his ample storehouses which promised to last twice as long as it would take for the Franconian army to arrive. He was also hoping for the arrival of some grain ships, which the Goths had assembled in the upper Padus region, and which they were now trying to bring into the city by using the river.

In order to ensure that there would be no abuse of this privilege, and to avoid extravagance, the king himself supervised the distribution of grain, which took place daily after the Gothic troops received their own rations. One day Matesuentha had found him among the begging and grateful crowds, and she had sat down beside him on the marble steps of the Basilica St Apollinaris and helped him distribute the bread. It was a beautiful sight to see the royal couple there, he on the right and she on the left, distributing bread to the crowd from large baskets.

While they were standing thus Matesuentha noticed among the seething masses – there were many people from country areas there as well, having fled from the war and sought refuge in the city – that on the bottom step of the basilica, off to one side, there sat a woman in a simple brown cloak, which she wore half pulled over her face. The woman did not force her way up the steps to ask for bread for herself like the others.

Instead she leaned forward, her head resting on her hands, behind a column of the basilica. She looked at the queen the whole time.

Matesuentha thought that the woman refrained from joining with the beggars out of shame, or fear or pride, and so she gave Aspa a special basket of bread, to go down and give it to the woman. Carefully she heaped the bread into the basket with her own hands.

When she looked up her eyes met those of the king, which had been watching her with a kindness and gentleness as never before. The blood shot hotly to her cheeks, and she trembled slightly as she lowered her eyes. When she looked up again the woman in the brown cloak had disappeared, and the spot by the column was empty.

While she was filling the basket Matesuentha had not noticed how a man wearing a buffalo hide and helmet, who had been standing behind the woman, had grasped her arm and pulled her away gently. "Come," he had said, "this is not a good place for you."

And she had replied, as if in a dream: "By God, she is beautiful."

"Thank you, Matesuentha!" the king said in a friendly tone, when the bread destined for that day had been distributed. His look, his tone, his words cut deeply into her heart. He had never called her by her name before, but had always seen only the queen in her and addressed her accordingly. Oh how that word, coming from his mouth, delighted her! And yet, at the same time, his kindness weighed heavily on her guilt-ridden soul. Evidently she had earned this warmer relationship with him out of her work with the poor. "Oh, he is so good," she said to herself, almost weeping with emotion, "I will be good too."

With these thoughts in her mind she returned to the courtyard of her wing of the palace – Witigis occupied the other, right wing. As she entered Aspa hurried toward her busily. "An envoy from the camp," she whispered to her mistress. "he brings a secret message from the Prefect – a letter in our language in Syphax's hand – he is waiting for a reply."

"Leave it be," Matesuentha replied with a frown, "I don't want to hear or read anything. But who are these people?"

And she pointed to a staircase, which led from the atrium to her rooms. There, on the red stone floor, cowered a large bunch of women, children, old and sick people, Goths and Italians clad in rags – a gathering of abject misery.

"Beggars, poor people, they have been here the whole morning. There is no getting rid of them."

"They are not to be got rid of!" said Matesuentha, coming closer.

"Bread, queen! Bread, Amalung daughter!" several voices cried out to her.

"Give the gold, Aspa, all you have with you, and fetch…"

"Bread! Bread, queen, not gold! There is no bread to be had for gold in the city any more."

"It is distributed every day free outside the king's storehouses. I have just come from there. Why didn't you go there?"

"Oh queen, we could not get through," an emaciated woman wailed. "I am old, and my daughter here is ill, and that old man there is blind. The young and healthy people push us back. We have tried in vain now for three days, but we cannot get through."

"No, we are starving," the old man grumbled. "Oh Theodoric, my king and master, where are you? Under your sceptre we had plenty. In your day the poor and the sick did not have to go without. But this disaster of a king…"

"Be silent!" Matesuentha replied, "the king, my husband," and as she said this an appealing colour came into her face, "does much more than you deserve. Wait here, I will get you bread. Come with me, Aspa!"

Quickly she walked away. "Where are you going?" Aspa asked, puzzled.

Matesuentha drew her veil about her face as she replied: "To the king."

When she reached the outer chambers of the wing occupied by Witigis the doorman, who recognised her with surprise, asked her to wait. "An envoy from Belisarius is having a secret audience. He has been in there for quite a long time, and will be leaving soon."

At that moment the door opened, and Procopius was standing on the threshold, hesitant. "King of the Goths," he said, turning around once more, "is that your last word?"

"My last, as it was my first," the king replied with dignity.

"I will give you more time. I will be in Ravenna until the morning."

"From now you will be welcome as my guest, but not as an envoy."

"I repeat: if the city is taken by storm, then every Goth who is taller than Belisarius's sword will die – he has sworn it! Women and children will be sold as slaves, you understand? Belisarius has no use for Barbarians in his Italy! You might be attracted by the idea of a hero's death, but think of the helpless ones. Their blood, before the throne of God…"

"Envoy from Belisarius, you are in God's hands just as we are. Farewell!" These words were spoken so firmly that the Byzantine had to go, much as he wanted to do otherwise. He was greatly affected by this man's simple dignity, but it affected the listener too.

As Procopius closed the door he saw Matesuentha standing before him, and took a step backwards in admiration, blinded by such beauty. He greeted her with deference: "You are the Queen of the Goths!" he said, regaining his composure, "you must be."

"I am," she replied, "I should never have forgotten that."

As she brushed proudly past him Procopius said to himself: "These Gothic men and women have eyes such as I have never seen before."

Chapter 20

Meanwhile Matesuentha had entered her husband's chambers unannounced. Witigis had left all the rooms formerly used by the Amalungs Theodoric, Amalasuntha and Theodahad, which were located in the centre of the vast palace, untouched. Instead he had moved into a few rooms in the right wing, which he had used previously when he was performing guard duty at court. He had never donned the golden insignia and purple robes of the Amalungs, and his rooms were devoid of all traces of royal pomp. A camp bed with low iron legs had his helmet, sword and a number of documents on it, and apart from the bed, a long oak table and a few pieces of wooden furniture, the room was bare.

After the envoy had departed Witigis sat down exhausted on a chair, his back to the door, resting his head on both hands, his elbows on the table. Thus he had not noticed the queen's light footfall.

Matesuentha halted on the threshold as if spellbound. Never before had she gone to him like this. Her heart was beating wildly. She could neither speak, nor approach him more closely.

At last Witigis rose with a sigh, and saw the motionless figure standing by the door. "You here, queen?" he said, astonished, and took a step toward her. "What brings you to me?"

"Duty – compassion," Matesuentha said quickly. "Otherwise I would not – I have a favour to ask."

"It is the first favour you have asked for," Witigis replied.

"It does not concern me," she interrupted quickly. "I only want to ask you for bread for the poor and the sick, who…"

The king held out his right hand to her. It was the first time he had done that; she did not dare to take it, and yet she longed to do so! In the end he himself took her hand and gently pressed it.

"Thank you, Matesuentha, and accept my apology. You do have a feeling for your people and their suffering. I would never have believed that. I thought of you as being hard."

"If only you had always thought otherwise of me, perhaps many things might have turned out better."

"I doubt it! Misfortune seems to follow on my heels. Just now – you have a right to know – my last hope has been shattered. The Franks, on whose aid I was counting, have betrayed us. Relief is now impossible, and due to desertions by the Italian population the numerical superiority of the enemy is now just too great. There is only one thing left to do, and that is to die as free Goths."

"Let me share death with you!" Matesuentha cried, and her eyes glowed.

"You? No, Theodoric's granddaughter will be received at court in Byzantium with honour. Everyone there knows that you became my wife against your will – you can appeal to them on that basis."

"Never!" Matesuentha said passionately.

Witigis continued, virtually thinking aloud, taking no notice of her: "But the others! The thousands! The hundreds of thousands of women, of children! Belisarius will do as he has sworn! There is only one hope left for them, because all the forces of nature have combined against me. The Padus is suddenly so shallow that the two hundred grain ships I was expecting could not be brought down the river quickly enough, and the Byzantines have intercepted them! I have now written to the king of the Visigoths and asked him to send us his fleet – as you know our own fleet is in enemy hands. If it can get into the harbour, then let those flee who cannot fight and must not die. You too, if you wish, can escape to Spain on one of their ships."

"I want to die with you, with my people!"

"In a few weeks the sails of the Visigoths could appear outside our city. My stores of grain will last until then, our last hope. But that reminds me of your request: here is the key to the main gate of the storehouses. I carry it with me day and night. Look after it well, as it guards my last hope. It holds the lives of many thousands, and that was the only one of all my efforts which has not failed. I am amazed," he added sadly, "that the earth did not open or that fire did not come down from heaven to swallow up my stores as well."

With that he took the heavy key from his jacket. "Guard it well, Matesuentha, it is my last treasure."

"I thank you Witigis – King Witigis," she said, correcting herself, and reached for the key, but her hand trembled and it fell.

"What is the matter with you?" the king asked, pressing the key into her right hand. She placed it into the belt of her white undergarment. "You are trembling. Are you ill?" he asked, concerned.

"No, it is nothing. But please don't look at me like that, like you did just then and this morning…"

"Forgive me, queen," Witigis said, turning away. "I don't want to offend you with my eyes. I have had much, much sadness these last days. And when I thought about it, trying to think with what guilt I earned all this ill fortune…" his voice became soft.

"Then? Oh speak!" Matesuentha begged. She no longer had any doubt as to what he was thinking.

"Then often I wondered, among all my nagging doubts, whether it might not be my punishment for a harsh deed I committed against a magnificent creature. Against a woman I sacrificed for my people," and quite unintentionally he looked at his listener whilst in the emotional turmoil of his own words.

Matesuentha's cheeks were aglow, and she reached for the backrest of a chair for support. "At last, at last his heart is softening, and I – oh what have I done to him!" she thought, "and he is sorry…"

"A woman," he went on, "who suffered unspeakably on my account, more than words can describe."

"Stop!" she whispered, so softly that he did not hear her.

"And then, when I saw you moving about me these last few days, softer, kinder, more feminine than ever before, it moved me mightily and tears came to my eyes."

"Oh Witigis!" Matesuentha sighed.

"Every sound of your voice cut deep into my soul. Because you remind me so much of…"

"Of whom?" Matesuentha asked, and grew deathly pale.

"Of her whom I sacrificed! Of her who suffered on my account, of my wife Rauthgundis, the soul of my soul." How long had it been since he last spoke her beloved name! Now, at the sound of it, he was overcome by grief and longing, and he sank back into his chair, covering his face with his hands.

It was as well he did so, because it meant that he did not notice how the queen trembled as if she had been struck by lightning, and how her lovely face had become distorted like a Medusa. But he did hear a dull thud and turned around. Matesuentha had sunk to the floor. Her left hand still clutched the broken back of the chair beside which she had fallen, while her right hand rested firmly on the mosaic floor. Her pale face was bent forward, her magnificent red hair flowed over her shoulders, and her delicate nostrils trembled.

"Queen!" he cried out, rushing over to help her rise. "What has come over you?"

But before he could touch her she jumped to her feet with the speed of a snake, and stood up straight: "It was only a weakness," she said, "it has passed now. Farewell!" Unsteadily she reached the door, and as soon as she got outside she collapsed unconscious in Aspa's arms.

Meanwhile the threatening face of nature outside had become even more ominous. The little round cloud which Cethegus had noticed the day before had become the forerunner of an enormous wall of black cloud, which had risen in the east overnight. Yet it had remained there motionless since early morning, above the ocean, full of foreboding and covering half the horizon.

But in the south the sun was burning with an almost unbearable heat from the cloudless sky. The Gothic guards had removed their helmets and armour, preferring to risk enemy arrows rather than endure the insufferable heat. Not a breath of air stirred. The easterly wind, which had brought the cloud, had suddenly fallen away. The sea lay there, flat, calm, heavy and grey as lead. The poplars in the palace gardens stood silently, and not a leaf was moving.

But the animal world, which on the previous day had been as silent as the landscape around it, now seemed possessed by fear. Swallows, seagulls and swamp birds flew along the hot sands of the coast uncertainly, aimlessly, very close to the ground and from time to time letting out shrill shrieks. In the city dogs were running from the houses whimpering, and in the stables horses tore themselves loose and struck out with their hooves, snorting impatiently. Cats, donkeys and mules were uttering mournful wails, and three of Belisarius's dromedaries died struggling and foaming, trying vainly to escape.

It was almost evening, and the sun was about to set. In the Forum of Hercules a citizen of Ravenna was sitting on the marble threshold in front of his house. He was a wine grower and, as the dried vine above his door indicated, he served some of what he grew in his house. He was looking at the threatening clouds. "I do wish it would rain," he sighed. "If we don't get rain, then there will be hail instead, and that would completely ruin what enemy horses have left of my vines."

"Are you calling our emperor's troops enemies?" whispered his son, a Roman patriot, because a Gothic patrol was just rounding the corner.

"I wish Orcus would swallow them all, Greeks as well as Barbarians! At least the Goths are always thirsty. Look, that's tall Hildebadus coming along there, he is one of the thirstiest. I would be amazed if he does not want a drink today, when even the stones want to burst with dryness."

Hildebad had just relieved the nearby guard and was now approaching slowly, his helmet under his arm and his spear carelessly slung over his shoulder. He walked past the wine shop, much to its owner's astonishment, turned into the next side street, and very soon he was standing in front of a massive, tall round tower, known as the tower of Aetius. Up on the wall, in the shade of the tower, a young Goth was pacing up and down. His long, light blond hair was flowing over his shoulders, and the delicate pink and white of his face, together with his pale blue eyes, gave him almost girlish good looks.

"Hey, Fridugern," Hildebad called out to him, "Are you still alive on that grilling rack up there? And with shield and armour too?"

"I have the watch, Hildebad!" the youth replied gently.

"Nonsense, watch! Do you think Belisarius is going to storm in this heat? I tell you, he is glad if he can just breathe, and he wants no blood today. Come with me – I came here to fetch you. The fat Ravennite on the Forum of Hercules has old wines and young daughters. Let's go and sample both."

The young Goth shook his long locks and frowned. "I am on duty, and I am not interested in girls. I will admit I am thirsty though; will you have a goblet of wine sent up to me?"

"Of course, in the name of Freya, Venus and Mary! I forgot that you have a bride up there in the mountains near the Danube! And you think that you would already be unfaithful to her if you so much as look into the black eyes of a Roman girl here. Oh dear friend, you are still very young! Still, that's your affair, and you are not such a bad fellow otherwise. You will get older in time. I will have a goblet of red wine sent up to you, then you can drink to Allgunthis's love."

He turned and had soon disappeared into the inn. Soon afterwards a slave brought the young Goth a goblet of wine. He whispered: "Your health, Allgunthis!" and drained it in a single draught. Then he placed the spear back on his shoulder, and slowly walked up and down the wall. "I can at least think about her, and dream of her," he said, "duty does not forbid that. I wonder when I will see her again?" He walked on, and then he stopped thoughtfully in the shadow of the tower, which looked down on him, black and threatening.

Soon after Hildebad had gone, another group of Goths passed. They were leading a blindfolded man in their midst, whom they let out by the Porta Honoria. It was Procopius, who had waited the agreed three hours in vain. No message had come from the king, and the envoy left in low spirits. It seemed as if the Prefect's clever plan had foundered on the simple dignity of the Gothic king.

Another hour passed. It had become darker, but not cooler. Suddenly a strong gust of wind rose from the sea in the south, pushing the black clouds northwards before it with great speed. Now they lay over the city, thick and heavy.

But the sea, in the southeast, was still not free. Another wall of black cloud had appeared there, and had now become one with the first. The entire firmament over land and sea was now a single, black dome.

Tired from the wine Hildebad now walked back to his night position on the Porta Honoria: "Still on watch, Fridugern?" he called out to the young Goth. "And still no rain! The poor earth! How it must be thirsting, I feel sorry for it! Have a good watch!"

Inside the houses it was unbearably hot: the wind blew from the hot, sandy deserts of Africa. The people were hurrying out into the open, frightened by the threatening appearance of the sky. They moved through the streets in thick throngs, or else they camped in groups among the columns of the basilicas. Many people were crowded together on the steps of the St Apollinaris basilica. It seemed to be darkest night, even though the sun had only just gone down.

★

Matesuentha, the queen, was lying on a her bed in her bedchamber, deadly pale; she was almost unconscious, but not asleep. Her open eyes were staring into the darkness.

She had not uttered a syllable in reply to Aspa's anxious questions, and in the end she had dismissed the weeping girl with a wave of her hand. Again and again the same words recurred in her monotonous thoughts: Witigis – Rauthgundis – Matesuentha! Matesuentha – Rauthgundis – Witigis! For a long time she lay thus, and it seemed as if nothing could break the vicious circle of her thoughts.

Then, suddenly, a ray of red light flashed through her room, and in the same instant a tremendous clap of thunder erupted over the trembling city, thunder such as she had never heard before, growling, crashing.

Cries of fear from her womenfolk struck her ears. She shot up and then sat on her bed, upright, listening. Aspa had removed her outer garment, so that she was wearing only the silken undergarment. She threw her thick red hair back and listened. It was a frightening silence. Then another flash of lightning, and another clap of thunder!

A gust of wind howled through the courtyard and tore open one of the windows. Matesuentha stared into the darkness outside, which was now broken by lightning every few seconds. The thunder rolled on ceaselessly, drowning out even the dreadful noise of the storm. This battle of the elements did her good, and she listened greedily, resting on her left hand, and slowly stroking her forehead with her right.

Then Aspa hurried in with a light. "Mistress, you... but, by all the gods, what do you look like? You are like a Lemura, a goddess of revenge!"

"I wish I was!" Matesuentha replied. It was the first word she had spoken for many hours, but she did not take her eyes off the window. Flashes of lightning and claps of thunder followed one another without a break.

Aspa closed the window. "Oh queen, the pious ones among your maids are saying that this is the end of the world coming, and that the son of God will soon be coming down on clouds of fire to judge the living and the dead. What a flash of lightning! And still not a drop of rain. Never have I seen such a storm! The gods must be very angry."

"And woe be to him against whom their anger is directed. Oh how I envy the gods! They can love or hate as it pleases them, and crush anyone who does not return their love."

"Oh mistress, I have just come in from the street. The people are streaming into the churches, praying and singing, in order to assuage heaven. I am praying to Kairu and Astarte – mistress, are you not praying too?"

"I am cursing! That is also a kind of prayer!"

"Oh, what a thunderclap!" the slave girl screamed, and fell to her knees trembling. Her dark blue cloak slipped from her shoulders. The thunderclap and lightning had been so strong that Matesuentha jumped from her bed and hurried to the window.

"Mercy, mercy, ye great gods! Have mercy on us humans!" the black girl prayed intensely.

"No, no mercy! Curse and damnation over the wretched human race!" Matesuentha retorted. "Ha, look at that, how beautiful it was! Can you hear them crying with fear in the street below? Another clap of thunder, and another bolt of lightning! Ha, gods, if there is a god or gods in heaven – I envy you only one thing! I envy you the sheer might of your hatred, and the deadly lightning at your command. You can unleash it with all the anger in your hearts, and your enemies perish while you stand by and laugh. Thunder is your laughter! Ha, what was that?"

A bolt of lightning and thunder even stronger than any before! Aspa rose from the floor, terrified.

"What is that big building there, Aspa? That great dark mass opposite us? I think the lightning has struck. Is it burning?"

"No, thanks to the gods! It is not burning! The lightning only illuminated them, the king's grain stores."

"Ha, you aimed badly, gods, didn't you?" the queen screamed. "But mortals too can use the lightning of revenge." She leapt away from the window, and suddenly the room was in darkness.

"Queen, mistress, where are you? Where did you go?" Aspa cried. She felt her way along the walls, but the room was empty, and Aspa called out for her mistress in vain.

In the street a pious procession was moving toward the basilica of Saint Apollinaris. They were citizens of Ravenna and Goths, children and old men, and a great many women. Boys with torches led the way, followed by priests with crosses and flags. And through the thunder a moving old hymn was heard: "*Dulce mihi cruciari, parva vis doloris est: malo mori quam foedari: major vis amoris est.*"

And then the other half of the chorus replied thus:

"*Parce, judex, contristatis parce pecatoribus, qui descendis perflammatis ultor jam in nubibus.*"

And then the procession disappeared inside the church. The nearest supervisors from the grain stores also joined the procession.

The woman in the brown cloak was sitting on the steps of the basilica, right opposite the door to the grain stores. Despite the tumult of the elements she sat in silence and without fear, her hands folded in her lap. The man in the helmet was standing next to her.

A Gothic woman, on her way to the church, recognised her during a flash of lightning: "You here again, countrywoman? Without shelter? I have offered you my house often enough. You seem to be a stranger."

"I am a stranger to Ravenna, but I do have shelter."

"Come into the church and pray with us."

"I will pray here."

"You are praying? But you neither speak nor sing?"

"God will hear me just the same."

"Please pray for the city too. They fear the end of the world is coming."

"I do not fear it when it does come."

"And pray for our good king, who gives us bread every day."

"I pray for him."

Now the sound of men in arms could be heard approaching. Two Gothic patrols were passing in front of the basilica. "All right then, thunder as much as you like," the leader of one patrol muttered angrily, "but don't interfere with my commands. Halt, Wisand, is that you? Where is the king, in church too?"

"No, Hildebad, he is on the walls."

"Well done, that's where he belongs! Forward march, hail the king!" And their footsteps disappeared.

Shortly afterwards a Roman teacher passed with a group of his pupils. "But *Magister*," the youngest of them asked, "I thought we were going to church? Why else are you taking us out into this awful weather?"

"I only said that to get you out of the house. Who needs a church? I tell you, the fewer walls and roofs I have around me, the happier I am. I am taking you out into the big, open meadow outside the main city. I wish it would rain. If Vesuvius was closer I would think that today Ravenna is about to become another Herculaneum. I know the air we are smelling today, and I don't trust it." And so the group went past.

"Won't you come with me, mistress?" the man in the helmet said to the Gothic woman. "I must go to see Dromon, our host, and I must go now; otherwise we will be without shelter again tonight. I can't leave you alone here in the dark. You have no light with you."

"Can't you see how the lightning shines for me? You go on ahead, and I will follow. I still have some thinking and some praying to do." And the woman remained alone. She pressed both hands firmly to her breast and looked up into the black sky, her lips moving very slightly.

Suddenly it seemed to her as if, in the vast halls and corridors of the stores building opposite her, she could see a light moving about, up and down. It had to be an illusion caused by the lightning, because any open flame would immediately have been blown out by the wind in the open building. But no, it was a light after all. It had to be, because it appeared and disappeared again in regular intervals, as if someone was carrying it hurriedly along the corridors, past the pillars and partitions. The woman looked sharply into the darkness, searching for the light.

But suddenly, oh terror, she shot up with a start. It seemed to her as if the marble step on which she had been sitting had become a sleeping animal. Now it seemed to be waking, and was moving to and fro, first slowly and then more strongly.

Suddenly lightning and thunder ceased abruptly. And then there was a shrill cry from the stores. The light burned brightly for a moment, and then it went out.

But the woman in the street also let out a small cry of fear. Because there could no longer be any doubt: the ground was trembling beneath her! A slight tremor, then suddenly two or three strong shocks, as if the ground was rolling from left to right in waves.

Loud screams of fear could be heard coming from the city. The crowd of worshippers was rushing out of the basilica in mortal terror, screaming loudly. – Another shock! – The woman was able only with difficulty to remain on her feet.

And from the distance, from outside the city, there came a mighty, dull crashing sound, as if huge and heavy masses were falling and crashing to the ground.

A terrible earthquake had struck the hapless city of Ravenna.

Chapter 21

Whilst she was turning in the direction of that dull, crashing sound, the woman had turned her back on the stores for a moment. But almost immediately she turned to face them again, for she thought she had heard a heavy door closing. Searchingly she looked at the huge building, but in the pitch darkness she could see nothing. Only her ears picked up a slight sound, as if someone was rushing silently along the outer wall of the building. And she thought she could hear somebody sighing deeply.

"Halt!" The woman cried, "Who goes there?"

"Quiet, quiet," a strange voice whispered, "the earth is shuddering over it, quaking with disgust and horror. The earth is trembling – the dead are rising. The day of judgment is coming, and then everything will be uncovered. Soon he will know. Oh!" There was a long wail, a rustling of clothing, and then silence.

"Where are you? Are you hurt?" the woman asked, searching in the darkness. Suddenly there was a bright flash of lightning, the first since the earthquake, and it showed the shape of a female figure right in front of her, in white and dark blue clothing. The woman reached out for the figure's arm.

But the latter sprang to her feet at the woman's touch, and an instant later she had disappeared into the darkness with a cry. The whole thing had happened so quickly and so strangely that it seemed unreal, like a dream. Only a broad golden bracelet with the image of a green snake, made of emeralds, remained in the woman's hands, as a reminder that the whole thing had indeed been real.

★

Once more the heavy footsteps of Gothic patrols could be heard.

"Hildebad, Hildebad, come and help!" Wisand cried.

"I am here – what is the problem? Where do you want me?" the latter asked, hurrying to Wisand's aid with his own patrol.

"To the gate of Honorius! The wall has collapsed there, and the great tower of Aetius lies in ruins. Help! Into the gap!"

"I am coming – poor Fridugern!"

★

In that same instant, outside in the Byzantine camp, the Prefect Cethegus was storming into Belisarius's tent. He was fully armed, with the purple plume fluttering about his helmet. His body stood proud and erect, and there was fire in his eyes. "Come! What are you waiting for, commander of Justinian's army? The walls of your enemies are collapsing of their own accord. The Gothic king's last refuge lies open before you. And you? What are you doing in your tent?"

"I am paying homage to the greatness of the Almighty!" Belisarius replied with a dignified calm. Antonina was standing next to him, her arms around his neck. A tall cross and a prayer stool were evidence of the activity in which Cethegus had disturbed the couple.

"Do that tomorrow, after your victory. But now storm!"

"Storm now?" Antonina said, "What sacrilege! The earth is trembling in its foundations, shaken and frightened. The Lord our God is speaking to us through this storm."

"Then let Him speak, and let us act! Belisarius, the tower of Aetius and a large part of the wall there have collapsed. I ask you again: will you storm now or not?"

"The man is no fool," Belisarius replied, as the lust for a good scrap awakened in him. "But it is still pitch dark!"

"I will find the way to victory and into the heart of Ravenna in the dark. In any case there is lightning to aid us."

"You suddenly seem very eager to fight!" Belisarius hesitated.

"Because now it makes sense to fight. The Barbarians are in confusion. They have been so busy fearing God that they have forgotten their enemies."

At that moment Procopius and Marcus Licinius rushed into the tent. "Belisarius," the former reported, "the earthquake has overthrown your tents at the northern moat, and half a cohort of your Illyrians are buried under the rubble!"

"Help! Help! My men!" Belisarius cried, and hurried from the tent.

"Cethegus," Marcus reported, "a cohort of your Isaurians also lies buried under the tents."

But the Prefect, impatiently shaking his helmeted head, asked: "What about the water in the Gothic moat outside the Aetius tower? Has the earthquake diminished it at all?"

"Yes. The water has disappeared, and the moat is quite dry. But listen to those cries! They are your Isaurians; they are groaning and crying out for help under the rubble."

"Let them cry!" Cethegus replied. "So the moat is really dry? Let the tubas sound for a general storm, and follow me with every mercenary or legionary who is still alive!"

Amid thunder and lightning, which were once more raging without pause, the Prefect hurried to his entrenchments, where his Roman legionaries and the remaining Isaurians were standing fully armed. Quickly he cast his eye over them: there were not nearly enough of them to capture the city alone. But he knew that a quick success would bring Belisarius into the fight straight away. "Lights, bring torches!" he commanded, and with a torch in his hand he stood before the line of his Roman legionaries. "Forward!" he commanded, "draw swords!"

But not a single arm moved.

All of them, even the leaders, were speechless with horror and astonishment as they looked at the demonic man who, among this terrible turmoil of the elements, could think only of his goal, and who saw this terrifying display of God's might as nothing but a means to further his own ends.

"Well? Do you obey me or the thunder?" he cried.

"General," said a centurion, stepping forward, "they are praying. The earth is trembling."

"Do you think Italia will swallow her own children? No! Romans, the very soil of holy Italia has risen against the Barbarians. The ground is rearing up to break their yoke, and their walls are crumbling. *Roma! Roma eterna!*"

That worked. It was one of those Caesarean words which carry men and their arms with them.

"Rome! *Roma eterna*!" The Licinius brothers were the first to echo the cry, and thousands of Roman youths followed their example. And they followed their Prefect through the night and the storm, through lightning and thunder they followed the man whose demoniacal drive carried them with him. Their enthusiasm gave them wings. In a very short time they had crossed the wide moat, which normally they hardly dared approach. Cethegus was the first man to reach the opposite side. The storm had blown out the torches, and he was feeling his way in the dark. "Here, Licinius," he called out, "follow me, this must be a gap."

With that he leapt forward, but ran up against something solid and stumbled back. "What's that?" Lucius Licinius asked behind him, "a second wall?"

"No," a calm voice replied from the other side, "but Gothic shields."

"That is the king, Witigis," the Prefect muttered fiercely, and mustered the dark figures of his opponents with hatred. He had counted on the element of surprise, and now his hope was dashed. "If only I had him," he said angrily to himself, "then he could do no more damage."

Suddenly many torches appeared from behind, and the trumpets sounded. Belisarius was leading his army to storm the breach in the wall. Procopius reached the Prefect's side: "Well? What are you waiting for? Are new walls holding you back?"

"Yes, living walls! There they are!" And the Prefect pointed with his sword. "Those Goths, among the ruins as they are falling around them, yet still they stand there and defy us!"

"Indeed!" Procopius cried. "*Si fractus illabatur orbis, impavidos fereint ruinse!* They are truly brave men!"

But now Belisarius had arrived with his powerful forces, massed to attack. One moment more – the leaders were rushing about issuing a few final commands – one moment more and a terrible carnage must commence. And then, suddenly, the entire horizon above the city glowed red. A column of flames shot skywards, and countless sparks flew everywhere. It seemed as if fire was raining from the sky. The whole of Ravenna glowed in a red light. It was a sight of awesome beauty.

Both armies, about to become engaged, stopped in their tracks.

"Fire! Fire! Witigis! King Witigis!" a Goth on horseback cried as he came racing from the city, "it is on fire!"

"We can see that. Let it burn, Markja! First we must fight, then we will put out the fire."

"No, no Sir! All your stores are on fire! Your grain is flying through the air in a million sparks."

"The stores are on fire!" Goths and Byzantines cried as one.

Witigis was unable to speak; his voice failed him. "The lightning must have struck in the interior of the storehouse some time ago. It has burnt everything from the inside out. There, look!"

Another powerful gust of wind tore into the blaze and fanned it to a gigantic height. Flames flew onto the roofs of the nearest houses. At the same time it seemed as if the wooden ridge of the roof on the tall building was collapsing. A dull crash, and the thousands of sparks rose skywards once more. It was a sea of flames.

Witigis was about to raise his sword in command, but his arm dropped wearily.

Cethegus saw this: "Now!" he cried, "storm now!"

"No, halt!" Belisarius bellowed in his leonine voice. "He who draws his sword now is an enemy of the Empire and a dead man. Back to the camp – that means everyone. Now Ravenna is mine, and tomorrow it will fall by itself."

And his thousands followed him and withdrew. Cethegus ground his teeth in anger. By himself he was too weak, and he had to give in. His plan had failed. He had wanted to take the city by storm, so that he could entrench himself in the key positions, just as he had done in Rome.

He could see that the whole of the city would now be delivered into the hands of Belisarius, and angrily he led the withdrawal of his troops.

But it was to turn out quite differently to the way Belisarius and Cethegus envisaged.

Chapter 22

The king had entrusted the defence of the breach in the wall to Hildebad, and rushed straight to the scene of the fire. When he arrived there he saw that the fire had started to die down, but only because there was nothing left to burn. The entire contents, the store buildings themselves, the wooden frame and roof, everything combustible had been destroyed down to the last splinter and the last grain of wheat. Only the stone walls of the original circus of Theodosius, blackened by soot, were still standing.

There was no trace of the bolt of lightning which had struck the building. Obviously the fire had been burning unnoticed from the inside for a long time, from the spot where lightning might have initially ignited it, and spread from there, destroying everything. By the time flames and smoke became visible it was too late to do anything about it. Shortly afterwards the building collapsed, and the occupants of nearby houses had their hands full trying to save their homes, some of which had already been ignited. In this they were aided by the rain, which had come at last, and which finally put an end to thunder and lightning.

When the sun rose it no longer shone on the stores which had been there the day before, but on a cheerless heap of ashes and rubble within the confines of the original circular marble building.

Silently, with his head lowered, the king leaned for a long time against a marble column of the basilica, opposite the ruins. He stood there motionless, only occasionally pulling his cloak more tightly about him. His chest was heaving, and in the sight of these ruins he had come to a difficult decision. Now he was silent, silent to the innermost core of his being, silent as the grave.

But in the square around him Ravenna's miserable poor were milling about, praying, swearing, crying.

"Oh, what is to become of us now?"

"Oh how lovely the white bread was, which I was given here only yesterday."

"What are we going to eat now?"

"Pah, the king will have to help us. The king will have to do something!"

"The king? Poor man, where is he to take it from?"

"That's his concern. He alone brought us all this misery."

"It's all his fault! Why didn't he surrender the city to the emperor long ago?"

"Yes, to its rightful master!"

"A curse on the Barbarians! They are to blame for everything."

"No, not all of them, only the king. Don't you see? It's God's punishment!"

"Punishment? For what? What crime did he commit? He gave the people of Ravenna bread."

"Don't you know? How can an adulterer hope for God's mercy? The sinful man has two wives at once! He lusted after beautiful Matesuentha, and would not rest until she was his. He sent his rightful wife away."

Witigis heard this, and walked on in disgust. The masses now revolted him, but they recognised his step.

"There is the king! See how fierce he looks," they shouted, and stepped aside.

"Oh, I don't fear him! I fear hunger more than his anger. Get us bread, King Witigis! Do you hear us? We are hungry!" a ragged old man said, and grasped for his cloak.

"Bread, King! Good king, give us bread!"

"We are desperate, help us!" and the crowd milled around him.

Witigis tore himself loose, calmly but firmly. "Be patient," he said earnestly, "by the time the sun sets you will have help," and he hurried away to his chambers.

When he arrived there, several of Matesuentha's servants and a Greek physician were waiting for him.

"Sir," the latter said with deep concern, "the queen, your wife, is very ill. The horrors of last night have confused her mind. She is hallucinating, and talking in her fever. Don't you want to see her?"

"Not now, you look after her."

The physician continued: "She handed me this key, with great concern, this key here, to give to you. In her feverish dreams it seemed to be the only thing that concerned her. She pulled it out from under her pillow, and made me swear that I would give it only to you personally, as if it was of utmost importance."

With a bitter smile the king took the key and cast it to one side. "It is not important any more! Go, leave me, and send my scribe to me."

★

An hour later Procopius allowed the Prefect to enter the tent of Belisarius. As he entered Belisarius, who was pacing up and down in some agitation, called out to him: "That's what comes from your schemes, Prefect! Of your cunning, and your lies! I have always said that lies lead to disaster, and I have always been true to that principle. Oh why did I follow your advice this time? Now I am in desperate trouble!"

"What is the meaning of all this virtuous talk?" Cethegus asked his friend.

The latter handed him a letter: "Read this! The Barbarians are unfathomable in their great naiveté. They defeat the devil with the mental processes of a child. There, read it!"

With astonishment Cethegus read: "Yesterday you disclosed three things to me. Firstly that the Franks have betrayed us. Secondly that you want to tear the western Empire away from the grip of your ungrateful emperor, and thirdly that you offer the Goths free passage over the Alps, without arms.

"Yesterday I answered you that the Goths would never lay down their arms or surrender Italy, the conquest and inheritance of their great king, and that I would rather die with my entire army. I still speak thus today, even though fire, water, storm and earth have joined together and rebelled against me.

"But tonight, as I watched the fire consume my supplies, I saw clearly what I had always darkly suspected: There is a curse on me, and the Goths are perishing on my account. I alone am the misfortune of my people, and it must no longer be so. Only my crown has prevented me from taking an honourable way out, but now it will do so no more.

"You rebel rightly and justly against Justinian, the disloyal and ungrateful tyrant. He is our enemy as he is yours. Very well then, instead of relying on an army from the treacherous Franks, you can rely on the entire Gothic nation, whose strength and loyalty are known to you. With the former you were to divide Italy between you, but with us you can have it all. Let me be the first to greet you as emperor of the Occident as well as the King of the Goths! My people will retain all their rights, and you will merely take my place. I myself will place the crown on your head, and I assure you that no Justinian will take it away from you. If you refuse this offer, then prepare for a fight such as you have never fought before. I would then break into your camp with fifty thousand Goths. We will fall, every one of us, but so will your entire army. It is either one or the other. I have sworn it. Choose! Witigis."

For one moment, and only one moment, the Prefect was gripped by mortal terror. He took one quick, searching look at Belisarius, but that one glance calmed him completely. "He is Belisarius, not Cethegus," he said to himself once more. "But still, it's always dangerous to play with the devil. What a temptation!"

He handed the letter back and said with a smile: "What a crazy idea! It is incredible what desperation drives men to do."

"The idea would not be all that bad," Procopius remarked, "If..."

"If Belisarius was not Belisarius." Cethegus concluded the sentence, smiling.

"Save your laughter," Belisarius scolded, "I admire the man, and I can no longer regard it as an insult that he thinks me capable of rebellion. After all I myself told him those lies." And he stamped his foot. "Now advise and help me! Because you two have brought me to the point where I have to make this dismal choice. I cannot agree, and yet if I refuse I will have to regard the emperor's army as annihilated. And on top of all that I have to admit that I lied about rebellion."

Cethegus stood there thoughtfully, stroking his chin with his hand. Suddenly a thought flashed through his mind, and a look of joy came over his face. "This way I can destroy them both," he thought, very pleased with himself. But first he wanted to make quite certain of Belisarius: "Sensibly there are only two things you can do," he said aloud, hesitantly.

"Speak, but I can see neither one nor the other."

"Either you really accept..."

"Prefect!" Belisarius roared furiously and went for his sword. Procopius held him back, startled. "No more jokes like that, Cethegus, if you value your life."

"Or," the latter went on calmly, "you appear to accept. Next you march into Ravenna without striking a blow. And then – you send the Gothic crown together with the Gothic king to Byzantium."

"That is brilliant!" Procopius cried.

"That is treachery!" cried Belisarius.

"Actually it is both." Cethegus added imperturbably.

"I could never again look the Gothic people in the eye!"

"That won't be necessary. You have the captured king taken to Byzantium in chains, and the disarmed people will cease to be a nation."

"No, no! I could never do that."

"Very well, then you had better arrange for your whole army to make their last will and testament. Farewell, Belisarius! I am going to Rome. I have no desire whatever to watch as fifty thousand Goths fight with the courage of desperation. And how Justinian will praise the man who destroyed his best army!"

"It is an awful choice!" Belisarius fumed.

And then Cethegus slowly walked up to Belisarius. "Belisarius," he said in a deep, moving voice, "you have often thought of me as your enemy, which indeed in some ways I am. But who can stand next to Belisarius in battle and not admire the hero?"

These words were spoken so solemnly and convincingly, such as the sarcastic Prefect had never done before, that Belisarius was moved, and even Procopius was surprised.

"I am your friend where I can be. And in this moment I want to prove that friendship through my advice to you. Do you believe me, Belisarius?" With that he offered the giant his right hand and laid his left on his shoulder, looking him straight in the eye.

"Yes," said Belisarius, "who could mistrust a look like that?"

"You see, Belisarius, no man ever had a more suspicious master than you. Justinian's last letter was a most severe insult to your loyalty."

"Heaven knows you are right!"

"And no man—" now he grasped both of Belisarius's hands "—has ever had a more magnificent opportunity to put the most vile distrust to shame, to avenge himself most gloriously, and to demonstrate his loyalty clearly beyond all possible doubt. You have been accused of lusting after the crown of the Occident. Very well, now you hold it in your hands. Move into Ravenna, let Goths and Italians pay homage to you, and let them place two crowns on your head. Yours is Ravenna, yours is your own blindly loyal army, the Goths and the Italians. Truly, you will be untouchable. Justinian will tremble in Byzantium, and his proud Narses will be like a straw against your might. But you, who hold all this in your hand, you lay all that power and glory and magnificence at your emperor's feet and you say: 'Truly, Justinian, Belisarius would rather be your servant than master of the Occident.' Never in history, Belisarius, has loyalty been proved so nobly on this earth."

Cethegus had struck at the very core of Belisarius's heart. His eyes were aglow. "You are right, Cethegus, and I thank you. That is indeed worthy of greatness. Oh Justinian, you shall die of shame!" And with that he embraced the Prefect. Cethegus withdrew from the embrace and made for the door.

"Poor Witigis," Procopius whispered to him, "will be sacrificed to this show of loyalty. Now he is lost!"

"Yes," Cethegus replied, "lost he most certainly is." And when he reached the outside of the tent he threw his cloak over his shoulder and said to himself: "But you, Belisarius, are even more certainly lost."

★

As he reached his quarters Lucius Licinius came to greet him, in full armour. "Well general?" he asked, "the city has not yet surrendered. When does the fight begin?"

"The fight is over, Lucius. Lay down your arms and prepare for a journey. You will leave today with secret letters from me."

"To whom?"

"To the emperor and empress."

"To Byzantium?"

"No. Fortunately they are quite close, in the baths of Epidaurus. Hurry. You must be back in fifteen days, not even half a day later. The fate of Italy depends on your speedy return."

★

As soon as Procopius had transmitted the message from Belisarius verbally to the Gothic king, the latter called the leaders of his army together in his palace, also including a few of the most important Gothic noblemen and a few representatives of the common people. He simply communicated to them what had taken place and asked for their agreement.

Certainly they were greatly taken by surprise at first, and an astonished silence followed his words. At last Duke Guntharis spoke, deeply moved, and looking straight at the king: "The last of your royal deeds, Witigis, is even more noble than any that went before it. I will always regret having fought against you, and I have long sworn to make up for it by following you blindly. And indeed, in this matter you alone can decide, because it is you making the ultimate sacrifice, your crown. But if some man other than you is to be king, then the Woelsungs would find it easier to take second place to a foreigner than to another Goth. And so I agree with what you have done, and I say this: you have acted well, and with greatness."

"And I say no! A thousand times no!" cried Hildebad, "think what you are doing! A foreigner our king?"

"How is that different from what other Germanic tribes have done before us, Quadi, Heruli, Markomanni, even the Franks under that Roman Aegidius?" Witigis asked calmly. "Indeed, how is it different to what our most glorious kings, even Theodoric, have done? They served the emperor under arms, and in return they received grants of land. That is how the contract is worded under which Theodoric accepted Italy from the emperor Zeno. I regard Belisarius as no less a man than Zeno, and I certainly do not think myself superior to Theodoric."

"Yes, if it was Justinian," Guntharis added, "I would never subject myself to that cowardly and treacherous tyrant. But Belisarius is a hero. Can you deny that, Hildebad? Do you remember how he threw you from your horse?"

"May thunder strike me if I ever forget it. It is about the only thing I like about him."

"And luck is with him, just as ill fortune was with me. And we will remain in this rich country here, free as we have always been, and will only help fight his battles against Byzantium, our common enemy."

Almost all the assembled men agreed. "Well, I cannot argue against you in words," Hildebad cried, "I have always been better with the axe than the tongue. But I feel it clearly; you are wrong. If the Black Count was here, he would be able to put into words what I feel. May you never regret it! But at least allow me to depart from this ghastly mixed Empire; I have no wish to live under Belisarius. I will go off and seek adventure in the great wide world. One can go a long way with shield and sword and a strong arm."

Witigis still hoped that he could divert the loyal fellow from what he planned by persuasion. He therefore continued with the matter, which was so close to his heart. "Above all Belisarius has asked for absolute secrecy until he has occupied Ravenna. He has cause to fear that some of his commanders will want no part of any revolt against the emperor Justinian. Those men must be firmly under the control of reliable followers of Belisarius, and suspect parts of Ravenna must be firmly under the control of Goths, before the decision is announced."

"Beware," Hildebad warned, "that you do not fall into the trap yourselves! We Goths should no more take up fine needlework than a wild bear should try tightrope-walking – sooner or later he will fall. Farewell, and I hope it all turns out better than I fear. I will go now to say farewell to my brother. He, as I know him, will probably find a way to come to terms with this Roman/Gothic state. But Black Teias, I think, will come away with me."

★

That evening the rumour of an impending capitulation swept the city. The conditions were uncertain. What was certain was that Belisarius, at the king's request, had sent large quantities of bread, meat and wine into the city, which were now being distributed to the poor. "He kept his word," they said, and they blessed the king.

The latter now inquired after the well-being of his queen, and learned that she was slowly calming down and recovering. "Patience," Witigis sighed with relief, "she too will soon be free, and rid of me."

It was already becoming dark when a strong detachment of mounted Gothic soldiers approached the Aetius tower from within the city. Their leader was an unusually tall man; then followed a group which was carrying a covered load in heavy chests on crossed lances. The remaining men, all heavily armed, concluded the group.

"Open the emergency gate!" the leader cried, "we want to leave the city!"

"Oh, it is you, Hildebad!" Count Wisand called out. He had the watch and gave the order to open the gate. "Did you know that the city will be handed over tomorrow? Where are you going?"

"To freedom!" cried Hildebad, and spurred his horse.

Chapter 23

Several days had passed before Queen Matesuentha was able to leave her sickbed for the first time, after the wild fantasies of her fever and the sleep and troubled dreams which had followed.

She had remained totally disinterested and apathetic to the world around her, and to the momentous decisions and events which were then happening. She seemed to have no feeling left save for one of terrible remorse for her many treacherous and evil deeds.

The wild rejoicing of her hatred, when she had stormed through the night, torch in hand, had soon turned into remorse, dread and self-disgust. The very moment she had done the awful deed, the earthquake had thrown her to her knees, and her conscience, which at the time was stirred by all her pent-up passion, led her to believe that the earth itself was shaking with disgust at what she had just done. She could see only heaven's revenge breaking over her guilty head.

And when she had regained her own rooms, and saw the blaze which she had started rise to the sky in one gigantic flame, when she heard the thousands of Gothic and Italian voices cry out in pain and sorrow, suddenly every single flame seemed to be eating at her own heart, and every wailing voice accusing her personally. She lost consciousness, and collapsed under the load of the consequences of her deed.

When she finally came to again, and slowly managed to remember what had happened, the strength of her hatred against the king had broken completely. Her very soul was almost broken. Deepest remorse over what she had done, and fear of ever having to face him again, those were her only thoughts. She knew, and was told from all sides, that the loss of his stores had forced the king to surrender, and this fact only intensified her feelings of remorse and disgust with herself.

She did not see the king himself. Even on the one occasion when he did find time to inquire after her health, she had prevailed upon the astonished Aspa not to admit the king under any circumstances, so that she would not have to face him. Yet she had been leaving her sickbed for several days, and had often received poor people from the city; indeed she had gone out of her way to invite the needy to dine with her. She would then distribute food intended for the court with her own hands, and she also gave away jewellery, gold and other precious items.

She was waiting for the visit of such a beggar one day, when a man in a brown cloak and helmet begged her to grant the favour of an audience, not to him but to a poor woman of his people, alone and without witnesses. It concerned the welfare of the king, he said. It was about the need to warn him of active treason, which was threatening his crown and perhaps his life. Eagerly Matesuentha granted the audience. Even if it was a mistake, or an invented excuse, she could not dare to refuse anything which might conceivably help to save him. She gave instructions that she would receive the woman at sunset.

The sun had gone down. There is almost no twilight in the south, and it was almost dark when a slave girl finally waved to the woman, who had been waiting in the anteroom for a long time. The slave told the woman that the queen, ill and without sleep at night, had only just now been able to get some rest. Just awake, she was still very weak, but nevertheless she was willing to see the woman if it concerned the welfare of the king.

"Are you certain that is the truth?" the slave girl inquired. "I do not want to trouble my mistress in vain." It was Aspa. "If you are only using this as a trick to get money, then just tell me. You can have all the money you want, but please spare my mistress. Is it really something to do with the king?"

"It is something to do with the king!" With a sigh Aspa led the woman into Matesuentha's bedchamber.

In the background of the large room Matesuentha rose from her bed. She wore a veil wound around her head and hair, and was dressed in a long white gown such as was customary for the sick. A round mosaic table stood in front of the bed, and the golden lamp above it had already been lit. She remained seated on the edge of the bed and said wearily: "Come closer. It concerns the king? Why do you hesitate? Speak!"

The woman pointed to Aspa. "She is discreet and faithful."

"She is a woman." On Matesuentha's signal the girl removed herself uneasily.

"Amalung daughter, I know! Only the needs of the Empire, not love, led you to him (how bewitchingly beautiful she is, even though she is so pale). Yet, Queen of the Goths, you are his queen, even if you do not love him. His Empire, his victory must mean everything to you."

Matesuentha reached to the table for support: "That is how every beggar woman in the nation thinks!" she sighed.

"To him I cannot speak, for reasons of my own. Therefore I am now speaking to you, as you are more concerned than anyone for his welfare, and therefore it is fitting that you should be the one to warn him against treason. Listen to me." And she came even closer, looking sharply at the queen. "How strange," she said to herself, "what a strange resemblance in build."

"Treason? Still more treason?"

"So you also suspect treason?"

"What does it matter? From where this time? From Byzantium? From outside? From the Prefect?"

"No," said the woman, shaking her head, "Not from outside, from within. And not from a man but from a woman."

"What are you saying?" Matesuentha asked, becoming even more pale. "How can a woman…"

"Harm a hero? By hellish evil in her heart! Not by force, but through cunning and treachery. Perhaps soon with a secret poison or, as has already happened, with fire."

"Stop!" Matesuentha, who had already stood up, tumbled back again to the mosaic table on which she was leaning.

But the woman followed her, whispering softly: "Let me tell it to you, unbelievable and disgraceful as it is! The king and the people think that lightning from heaven burnt his grain. But I know better, and he too shall know it, through you. Once you have warned him he can investigate and then render the threat to him harmless. That night I saw a torch hurrying through the corridors of the grain stores, and it was a woman who threw it into the grain. You shudder? Yes, a woman. Do you want to go? No, just listen to one more thing, and then I will let you go. Her name? I do not know it, but she collapsed in front of me and left this behind. It should make it easier to recognise and identify her. Here, look at this snake made of emeralds."

And the woman stepped close to the table, close to the light from the lamp, raising the bracelet.

At that the tormented Matesuentha rose up in terror, and held up her bare arms to hide her face. But as she moved, rapidly, the veil dropped and revealed her red hair, flowing down to her shoulders. And through her hair, on her arm, a golden bracelet with a snake of green emeralds glistened clearly in the lamplight.

"Ah!" the woman screamed aloud. "By God! It was you! You yourself! His queen! His own wife is the one who betrayed him! A curse over you! He shall most certainly know about this!"

With a shrill scream Matesuentha fell back on her face on the bed. The scream brought Aspa from the next room, but as she entered the queen was already alone once more. The curtains at the main entrance were still moving, but the beggar woman had gone.

Chapter 24

On the following morning the astonished citizens of Ravenna watched as Procopius, John, Demetrius, Bessas, Acacius, Vitalius, together with a number of lesser commanders from the army of Belisarius, moved into the royal palace, where they discussed with him details and conditions of the formal handover.

For the moment all the Goths knew was that a peace had been concluded. The main aims for which their nation had borne the whole of the long war would be achieved. They would remain free and in possession of the rich country of Italy, which had become so dear to them. After the serious state of the Gothic cause, compounded by the retreat from Rome and the now inevitable surrender of Ravenna, that alone was more than they had come to expect. The heads of the leading families and the influential leaders of the army, who were now informed of the next step Belisarius would take, fully concurred with the decision which had been taken, and with the main conditions.

Those few who did not agree were granted freedom to leave Ravenna and Italy unhindered. But quite apart from that the Gothic army was now dispersed in all directions. Witigis could see the impossibility of trying to feed not only the people of Ravenna and Belisarius's army, but his own army as well, from the severely depleted surrounding countryside. For that reason he had agreed to one of the main conditions imposed by Belisarius, namely that the Goths, in groups of hundreds or up to a thousand or so, should be led out of the city by all the gates and dispersed in all directions to their homes.

Belisarius feared an outbreak of Gothic desperation once the treachery he planned became common knowledge, and that was why he wanted the army disbanded and scattered. Once securely in possession of Ravenna he could be confident of crushing any possible uprisings in the flat countryside around it. Moreover, Tarvisium, Verona and Ticinum, the last fortified cities still held by the Goths, would not be able to hold out for long against the entire might of Belisarius, now directed against them.

It took several days to carry out all these various arrangements.

Belisarius delayed his own entry into the city until the Gothic garrison in Ravenna had been reduced to a mere handful of men. Even this handful was divided into two halves, of which one was transferred into the Byzantine camp. The other half was divided into small groups and quartered in various parts of the city, under the pretext that they were being held in readiness against possible uprisings by diehard loyalist supporters of Justinian.

But the one thing which most surprised the native population of Ravenna, and those Goths not in the know, was the fact that the blue Gothic flag flew as before from the pinnacles of the palace. To be sure, one of Belisarius's lancers now stood guard by it, and the palace was full of Byzantines.

Belisarius had taken great care to foil any plan on the part of the Prefect to grab control of the most important strategic points in the city, as he had done in Rome. Cethegus saw through these precautions easily, and smiled. On the morning of

Belisarius's planned entry into the city Cethegus entered Belisarius's tent in full armour. As he entered he found only Procopius there.

"Are you ready?" Cethegus asked.

"Completely!"

"When will the decisive moment come?"

"When the king mounts his horse in the palace grounds in order to ride out and meet us. We have thought of everything."

"Everything? Again?" the Prefect smiled. "There is one thing which you have so far omitted. There can be no doubt that, once our plan has succeeded and become known, wild fury will break out all over the country. Pity for their betrayed king and thirst for revenge could lead the Goths to do desperate things.

"Now this whole enthusiastic support for Witigis, and the fury against us, would be nullified from the start, if only the Goths would think they had been betrayed by their king, and not by us. Suppose the king was to verify in writing that he handed the city over, not to Belisarius as the new Gothic king and rebel against Justinian, but simply to Justinian's general? That way the supposed rebellion by Belisarius against the emperor, which will of course never take place, would appear to the Goths as a mere lie, dreamed up by their king to try and hide the shame of surrender."

"That would be brilliant, but Witigis would never fall for it."

"Certainly not knowingly, but perhaps unknowingly. You had him sign only the original of the contract, is that so?"

"Yes, he signed only once."

"And that document is in his possession? Good! I will now have him sign this duplicate here, drawn up by me, so that Belisarius too," he smiled, "will have a copy of the valuable document."

Procopius saw through the plan: "If he signs that, then certainly no Gothic sword will be drawn on his behalf, but..."

"Let me worry about the 'if' and 'but'. Either he signs it now, willingly, without reading it and under the pressure of the moment..."

"Or?"

"Or," Cethegus concluded with a threatening look on his face, "he will sign it later, unwillingly. I will hurry on ahead. Please forgive me if I do not accompany your triumphant entry today. And please convey my regards to Belisarius."

But at that moment Belisarius himself entered the tent, followed by Antonina. He was unarmed, and staring ahead gloomily.

"Hurry, general," Procopius exhorted him, "Ravenna is waiting for her conqueror. Your entry..."

"Entry nothing!," Belisarius replied fiercely. "Call off the soldiers. I am now regretting the whole deal."

Cethegus halted at the entrance to the tent.

"Belisarius!" Procopius cried, horrified, "which demon has put that into your head?"

"I have," Antonina replied proudly, "what do you say now?"

"I say that great statesmen should not have wives!" Procopius cried angrily.

"Belisarius only disclosed your plans to me last night. And I, in tears..."

"Understandable," Procopius grumbled, "they always come at just the right time."

"In tears I begged him to desist. I cannot bear to see my hero thus stained with horrible, black treachery."

"And I no longer want any part of it. I would rather ride into Orcus vanquished than ride into Ravenna as a conqueror this way. My letters to the emperor have not yet left, so there is still time."

"No," said Cethegus from the door in a dominant tone, striding back into the tent. "Luckily for you there is no longer time, it is too late. Let me tell you this: I wrote to the emperor eight days ago, told him everything and congratulated him on the fact that his general was able to capture Ravenna with only minimal losses, and thus conclude the war."

"Oh Prefect!" Belisarius cried, "you seem very eager to serve the emperor? Why this sudden burst of enthusiasm?"

"Because I know Belisarius, and his hesitancy and his changes of heart. Because one has to force you to achieve your own success. And because I want an end to this war, which is tearing my Italy apart." In a threatening manner he moved closer to the woman, who was now also unable to escape the commanding spell in his eyes: "Dare if you like! Try and withdraw now, disappoint Witigis and sacrifice Ravenna, Italy and your army to your wife's whim, and then see if Justinian will ever forgive you for it. Let the responsibility for all this rest on Antonina's soul! Listen, the trumpets are calling; arm yourself! You have no other choice!" And with that he hurried outside.

A shocked Antonina watched him go. "Procopius," she asked, "does the emperor really know about everything already?"

"Even if he did not, there are already too many who know of the whole arrangement. He would certainly hear about it afterwards, that Ravenna and Italy were his, and – and that Belisarius had sought the Gothic crown and the Imperial crown of the Occident. The only thing which can now excuse him before Justinian is the fact that he hands it all over."

"Yes," Belisarius added with a sigh, "he is right. I have no choice."

"Go then," said Antonina, now somewhat frightened. "But please forgive me if I do not accompany you on this entry into Ravenna. It is more like setting a trap than a triumph."

★

The people of Ravenna, even though they were in the dark as to the detailed conditions of the surrender, knew at least that a peace had been concluded, and that there would now be an end to the long and heavy suffering of the terrible war. Full of joy and relief at the imminent end to their troubles, the citizens of Ravenna had cleared their streets of rubble from the earthquake and festively decorated their city. The streets were decorated with ivy, flowers, flags and gaily coloured rugs, and the people were crowding into the great Fora, the canals and baths and basilicas, in joyful agitation. They were eager to see Belisarius and the army which had threatened their walls for so long, and had finally defeated the Barbarians.

Already strong detachments of Byzantines were entering, proud and triumphant, while the few remaining Goths watched from their scattered posts as the hated enemy moved into the palace which had once served as residence to Theodoric.

In the royal palace itself, also gaily decorated, the most noble of the Goths had assembled near the king's apartments. The latter, as the hour of Belisarius's entry into the city drew near, donned his royal robes. He had the satisfaction of knowing that this would be the last time he would have to wear the insignia of an office which had brought him only pain and failure.

"Go, Duke Guntharis," he said to the Woelsung, "Hildebad, my chamberlain, has left me. Will you take his place this time? The servants will show you the golden chest among the royal treasure which contains Theodoric's crown, purple robe and helmet, sword and shield. I will put them on today, for the first and last time, to hand them over to the hero who will wear them, I trust, with honour. What is all that noise there?"

"Sir, a woman," Count Wisand replied, "a Gothic beggar woman. She has already forced her way in here three times. She wants to tell her name only to you. Have her thrown out!"

"No, I will hear her – tell her to ask for me in the palace this evening."

After Guntharis had left, Cethegus entered with Bessas. The Prefect had given Bessas a copy of the contract, without telling him the contents in detail, which he was now to get the Gothic king to sign. He thought that Witigis might be less suspicious accepting the document from such an innocent bearer.

Witigis greeted the two men as they entered. As he caught sight of the Prefect a shadow came over his face, which had been looking more cheerful than it had for months. But he kept his self-control and said: "You here, Prefect? This war did end differently from what we expected! And yet, you too have reason to be pleased with the final outcome. At least no Greek emperor, no Justinianus, will rule over your Rome."

"Nor shall he, not as long as I live."

At this point Bessas interrupted: "I have come, King of the Goths, to place the contract with Belisarius before you for your signature."

"But I have already signed it."

"It is the copy which is intended for my master."

"Give it to me then," said Witigis, and was about to take the document from the Byzantine.

At that moment Guntharis and the servants rushed into the room: "Witigis," he cried, "the royal treasure has vanished."

"What was that?" Witigis asked. "Hildebad alone had the keys to the treasure chamber."

"The whole golden chest with its contents, as well as other chests, has gone. In the empty niche where they used to be we found this strip of parchment. The writing is that of Hildebad's scribe."

The king took the parchment and read: "Crown, helmet, sword, purple and shield of our great king Theodoric are in my keeping. If Belisarius wants them he will have to get them from me. Hildebad."

"He will have to be pursued until he surrenders the treasure," Cethegus said bitterly.

Then John and Demetrius hurried into the room. "Hurry, King Witigis," they urged. "Can you hear the tubas? Belisarius has already reached the Porta del Stilicho."

"Let us go then," said Witigis, and had his servants place a substitute purple cloak around his shoulders, and a golden coronet on his head, and handed him a sceptre in place of his sword. He turned for the door.

"You have not signed, Sir!" Bessas urged him.

"Give it to me then," and he took the document and started to read. "It is very long," he said.

"Hurry, King!" John urged again.

"There is no time now to read it all," Cethegus said indifferently and handed him a reed pen.

"Then there is no time to sign it either," the king replied. "You know that, as the people say, I am a peasant king. Peasants will not sign a single line until they have read it carefully. Let us go." With a smile he handed the document back to the Prefect and left the room. The Byzantines and all those present followed.

Cethegus clutched the parchment fiercely: "Just wait," he whispered, "you will sign it yet." Slowly he went to follow the others.

The hall outside the king's chambers was already empty.

The Prefect stepped out into the arched balcony which surrounded the entire first floor of the palace in a huge square. From here he had a clear view of the courtyard below, which was full of armed men. All four exits were guarded by Belisarius's lancers. Cethegus leaned against one of the pillars, out of sight, following the events below. He said to himself: "Well, there are enough Byzantines to capture a small army! Friend Procopius is very careful – there! Witigis has appeared in the portal. His Goths are still a long way behind him on the staircase. The king's horse is being led forward... Bessas is holding the stirrup for the king... Witigis approaches, and raises his foot... There, the trumpet... The heavy door into the palace falls shut, and traps the Goths inside. On the roof Procopius is tearing down the Gothic banner... John has grasped the king's right arm, well done John! The king calls out: "Treachery! We have been betrayed!' He is defending himself mightily, but his long cloak is hindering him... There, there, he stumbles... He has fallen to the ground... There lies the Gothic Empire..."

★

"There lies the Gothic Empire!" Procopius used the same words to start his entry into his diary that evening: "Today I helped make an important piece of world history by day, and I will now record it all here tonight.

"When I saw our Roman army march into the gates of the royal castle of Ravenna today I could not help thinking once more: it is not virtue or righteousness that decides the course of history.

"There is another, higher power, that of inescapable necessity.

"In terms of numbers and courage the Goths were superior to us, and they certainly did not spare every possible effort to defeat us. The Gothic women in Ravenna openly ridiculed their menfolk to their faces as they watched the small men of our not so very numerous army march into their city. Conclusion: despite having the most just of causes, and the utmost heroism and effort, a man or even a whole people can yet be defeated if faced by all-powerful forces which by no means always have right on their side.

"Today my heart beat in protest, knowing the wrong I was doing as I pulled down the Gothic banner and replaced it with Justinian's golden dragon, the flag of injustice and wrong in place of the flag of justice and right.

"Not justice, but some great necessity beyond our understanding rules the fate of men and nations.

But that does not deter a just man. Because it is not what we experience, suffer and endure, but the way in which we do it that makes a man into a hero. The Goths are more honourable in defeat than we are in victory. And this hand, which tore down the banner of the Gothic nation, will record their glory for the generations of the future. However, be that as it may, there lies the Gothic Empire."

Chapter 25

And indeed so it seemed! Thanks to careful preparation by Procopius the coup had succeeded perfectly. As they saw their flag fall on the palace tower and their king taken prisoner, the Goths everywhere knew they were surrounded and outnumbered, outnumbered everywhere, in the streets and squares of the city and even in their own quarters – wherever they looked a forest of lances stared back at them. And so, almost without exception, the stunned Goths laid down their arms without offering any resistance. Those few who did try to resist, such as the men in the king's immediate vicinity, were mown down without mercy. Witigis himself, Duke Guntharis, Count Wisand, Count Markja and the other leaders who had been captured with them were placed in separate custody, and the king himself was incarcerated in Theodoric's Tower, a strong tower within the palace itself.

The procession of Belisarius from the Porta del Stilicho to the Forum of Honorius took place without incident. Once he arrived at the palace he had called the Senate of the city together, and had them swear an oath of allegiance to the emperor Justinianus. Procopius was sent to Byzantium with the golden keys of Naples, Rome and Ravenna. His mission was to report in detail, and to request an extension of Belisarius's appointment until Italy was again fully at peace, which was to be expected shortly. After that he requested for himself the honour of a triumphal procession in the Hippodrome, as had been granted to him after his successful campaign against the Vandals. The procession was to include the captive King of the Goths.

Belisarius saw the war as being over. Cethegus almost shared that belief, but he feared an outbreak of Gothic anger in the provinces over the treachery which had been committed. He therefore took great care to ensure that no news passed beyond the city gates as to the manner in which the city had fallen. At the same time his mind was busy trying to find a way in which he could use the captive king himself as a tool, to dampen any possible re-awakening of Gothic nationalism. He also persuaded Belisarius to have Persian cavalry under Acacius pursue Hildebad, who had escaped in the direction of Tarvisium.

The Prefect also vainly tried to speak to the queen. She had still not fully recovered from that night of terror, and would see nobody. She had even received the news that the city had fallen with dull silence. In order to be sure of her the Prefect ordered a guard of honour, because he still had great plans involving her. He then sent her the sword of the captive king and with it he sent a note: "I have kept my word. King Witigis has been destroyed. You are avenged and you are free. Now it is your turn to grant my wishes."

A few days later Belisarius, now without his faithful adviser Procopius, sent for the Prefect to come to him in his quarters, in the right wing of the palace.

"Unbelievable mutiny!" Belisarius called out to Cethegus as he entered.

"What has happened?"

"You know that I had Bessas and his mercenaries occupy the entrenchments by the Honorius gate, one of the most important strategic points in the city. I heard that the mood of those troops was insubordinate. So I ordered them relieved, and Bessas..."

"Well?"

"Bessas will not obey."

"What? Without a reason? That's impossible!"

"He does give a reason, ridiculous as it is. He says that my appointment to command expired yesterday, and so he says that since midnight I am no longer in a position to give him orders."

"That's disgraceful! But strictly speaking he is right."

"Right? In a few days the emperor's reply to my request will arrive, and of course he will re-appoint me as commander-in-chief, following my conquest of Ravenna, until the war is ended. The news could be here the day after tomorrow."

"It may even be earlier, Belisarius. The lighthouse keeper at Classis reported a ship approaching at sunrise, coming from the direction of Ariminum. Apparently it is an Imperial trireme. It could be here at any time, and then the knot will unravel of its own accord."

"But I want to hack through it first! I want to have my bodyguard storm the entrenchments, and that mutinous Bessas shall pay..."

And then John came rushing into the tent, breathless: "General," he panted, "the emperor Justinianus himself is anchoring in the port of Classis."

Quite involuntarily Cethegus quivered slightly. Was such a sudden bolt of lightning out of the clear blue sky a mere whim on the part of the unpredictable despot? Was the final and almost complete culmination of all his plans to be foiled at the last moment, just before fulfilment, in spite of all his efforts?

But Belisarius asked, with eyes aglow: "My emperor? How do you know that?"

"He has come himself to thank you in person for your victories. Such an honour has never yet been bestowed on a mortal. The ship from Ariminum bears the Imperial purple banner. Purple and silver. And you know that means the emperor himself is on board."

"Or a member of his immediate family!" Cethegus corrected him, with a sigh of relief.

"Let us hurry to the port to greet our master!" Belisarius urged.

★

His pride and his joy were somewhat dashed when, on their way to Classis, they met the first Imperial courtiers. They were seeking quarters not for the emperor himself, but for his nephew, Prince Germanus.

"At least he did send the first man in the Empire after himself," Belisarius said, consoling himself as he continued on his way with Cethegus. "Germanus is the most noble man at court. He is incorruptible, just and pure beyond temptation. They call him the 'lily in the swamp'. But you are not listening to me."

"Forgive me. I noticed among the crowd over there a young friend of mine, Lucius Licinius."

"Salve Cethegus!" the latter cried, making his way over to the Prefect.

"Welcome to liberated Italy! What do you bring me from the empress?" he asked in a whisper.

"The word '*nika*' (victory) as a parting message, and this letter," the young messenger whispered just as quietly. "But," and he frowned as he went on, "never send me to that woman again."

"No, no my young Hippolytos, I don't think that will be necessary."

With that they had reached the harbour itself, where the prince was just mounting the steps from his ship to the shore. His noble person, surrounded by a splendidly attired following, was greeted by the troops and the rapidly growing crowd with full Imperial honours.

Cethegus mustered him with his keen eyes. "His pale face looks even more pale than it did before," he said to Lucius Licinius.

"They say the empress is poisoning him, because she can't seduce him."

The prince had by now made his way through the crowd, thanking the people as he went, and as he reached Belisarius the latter greeted him with the utmost respect. "My greetings to you also, Belisarius," he replied in a serious tone, "please follow me to the palace immediately. Where is the Prefect Cethegus? And Bessas? Ah, Cethegus," he said, shaking the latter's hand. "I am delighted to see Italy's greatest man again. You will accompany me at once to Theodoric's granddaughter. My first mission is for her. I bring her gifts from Justinianus and my personal respects. She was a prisoner in her own Empire. At the Imperial court in Byzantium she shall be a queen."

"That she shall," thought Cethegus. He made a deep bow and said: "I am aware that you already know the princess from some years ago. Her hand was intended to be yours."

Colour came to the pale face of the prince: "Unfortunately not her heart. I did see her here, many years ago, at her mother's court, and since then her picture has been constantly before me."

"Yes, she is the most beautiful woman on earth," the Prefect replied calmly, studying the ground at his feet.

"Please accept this gem as a token of thanks for those words," Germanus replied, and placed a ring on the Prefect's finger.

Meanwhile they had arrived at the palace gates.

"Now, Matesuentha," Cethegus said to himself, "now your second life will begin. I know of no Roman woman, except perhaps one girl I once knew, who could resist a temptation like that. Could it be that this coarse Gothic woman is able to do so?"

As soon as the prince had somewhat recovered from the rigors of his sea voyage and changed his travelling clothes for more suitable garments, he appeared at the Prefect's side in the great throne room of Theodoric in the middle of the palace.

Trophies from former Gothic victories still hung proudly from the walls in the vast hall, which was surrounded by rows of pillars on three sides. In the centre of the fourth wall stood Theodoric's majestic throne.

The prince scaled the steps to the throne with regal bearing. Cethegus, with Belisarius, Bessas, Demetrius, John and a number of other commanders remained in the centre of the hall.

"In the name of my Imperial master and uncle I now take possession of this city of Ravenna and of the Occidental Roman Empire. This letter from our master the emperor is for you, *Magister Militum*. Open it and read it to the assembly yourself. That is what Justinian commanded."

Belisarius stepped forward, received the Imperial letter on his knees, kissed the seal, rose again, opened the letter and read aloud:

"Justinianus, Imperator of the Romans, master of the Orient and the Occident, conqueror of the Persians and the Saracens, the Vandals and the Lazi and Sabiri, the Alani, the Huns, the Avars and the Slavs and latterly also the Goths, to Belisarius the consul, formerly the *Magister Militum*.

"We have been informed of the events which led to the fall of Ravenna by Cethegus the Prefect. At his own request his report will be communicated to you in full. However we are unable to share the favourable opinion which he expresses in his report of you, your successes and the means whereby you achieved them. We therefore now relieve you of your position as commander-in-chief of the army. And we command you, as soon as you have read this letter, to return immediately to Byzantium, where you will answer for your actions before our throne. We are unable to grant you a triumph such as was the case after your victory over the Vandals, because neither Rome nor Ravenna fell as a result of your bravery. Rome fell by peaceful capitulation, and Ravenna through earthquake, God's anger at the heretics, and finally as a result of some highly suspicious dealings which you, accused of high treason, will justify before our throne. In the light of your former services to the Empire we do not wish to judge you without having heard your defence, and therefore we will not arrest you as your accuser demands. Orient and Occident shall always remember us as the emperor of justice, and you will therefore face our Imperial presence with no bonds other than those of your own guilty conscience."

As he reached this point Belisarius trembled – he staggered. He could not continue, covering his face with both hands instead. The letter fell to the floor.

Bessas picked it up, kissed it and went on reading: "As your successor in command of the army we appoint the strategist Bessas. Ravenna will be under the command of the Archonius John. The administration of taxes, despite the very unjust accusations made against him by the Italians, will remain in the hands of our eager and loyal servant Alexandros. And as Governor of Italy we appoint the worthy Prefect of Rome, Cornelius Cethegus Caesarius, who is very much in our debt. Our nephew Germanus, who acts in our name and with full Imperial powers, will see to it that you proceed without delay to our fleet in Ariminum, and from there Prince Areobindos will take you to Byzantium."

Germanus rose and ordered everyone except Belisarius and Cethegus to leave the room. He then descended the steps from the throne and walked over to Belisarius, who was no longer aware of what was happening around him. He stood motionless, his head and left arm resting against a pillar, staring at the ground.

The prince took his right hand: "It pains me, Belisarius, that I have to be the bearer of such news. I accepted the mission because a friend can execute it more kindly that any of the countless enemies who vied for the honour. But I must be frank with you. To my mind this last victory of yours nullifies the glory and the honour of all those which went before it. Never would I have expected such a web of lies from the hero Belisarius. Cethegus has asked that you be permitted to read his report to the emperor. It is full of praise for you; here it is. I think it was the empress who kindled Justinian's anger against you. But you no longer hear me..." and he placed a hand on Belisarius's shoulder.

Belisarius shook off his touch. "Leave me alone, boy – what you bring me is – the true thanks of a crown."

Germanus rose to his full height with dignity: "Belisarius, you are forgetting who I am, and who you are."

"Oh no, not at all. I am a prisoner and you are my warden. I will go to your ship immediately – only spare me chains and bonds."

★

It was not until much later that the Prefect finally managed to get away from the prince, who had been discussing affairs of state and his personal wishes with him in the fullest confidence.

As soon as he was alone in the room which he occupied in the palace, he eagerly started to read the letter from the empress, which Lucius Licinius had brought him.

It read: "You have won, Cethegus.

"When I received your letter I was reminded of old times, when your letters to Theodora were written in the same secret code, but dealt not with wars and affairs of state, but with kisses and roses…"

"They always have to remind one of that," the Prefect interrupted himself.

"But even in your last letter, dry and matter of fact as it was, I could still recognise the irresistibility of that mind, which once captivated the women of Byzantium even more than your youthful good looks did. And so I once again acceded to the wishes of an old friend, as I once acceded to those of a young one. Oh, how I like to think back to our youth, and how sweet it was. And I recognised clearly that Antonina's husband would be in altogether too secure a position in the future, if he did not fall this time. And so I whispered in the emperor's ear, as you suggested: 'A subject who is able to play such games with crowns and rebellion is altogether too dangerous. No general can be exposed to such temptation for long. What he did this time, for show only, he may well do next time in earnest.' Those words carried more weight than all the victories Belisarius had won, and all my requests, which are your requests, were granted.

"You see, suspicion and distrust are the very soul of Justinian. He believes in the loyalty and faithfulness of only one person on earth, that of Theodora. Your messenger Licinius is handsome, but he is also dull and unfriendly; he has nothing but Rome and fighting on his mind. Oh Cethegus, my friend, the youth of today are not those we knew – those days have gone. 'You have won, Cethegus,' do you remember the night when I whispered those words into your ear? But never forget to whom you owe your victory. And remember this: Theodora will allow herself to be used as a tool only for as long as she herself wishes it so. Never forget that."

"Certainly not," said Cethegus, carefully destroying the letter. "You are far too dangerous an ally, Theodora – no, Demonodora! Let us see if you are irreplaceable. Patience: in a few weeks Matesuentha will be in Byzantium… What have you got there?" he asked Syphax, who was just entering the room carrying magnificent armour.

"Sir, a farewell gift from Belisarius. After he read your report to the emperor he said to Procopius: 'Your friend deserves my gratitude. There, take my golden armour, the helmet with the white plume and the round shield and send them to him, as a last greeting from Belisarius.'"

Chapter 26

The round tower in which Witigis had been imprisoned was situated in the far right corner of the palace, in the same wing he had previously occupied as king.

The tower with its iron door formed the end of a long corridor leading to a small courtyard, from which it was also closed off by an iron gate. Immediately opposite this latter heavy iron gate lay the small apartment of Dromon, the *carcerarius* or jail warden of the palace. The apartment consisted of only two small rooms. The first of these, separated from the second by a curtain, was only an anteroom. The second room had a small window, through which one could see the courtyard and the tower. Both rooms were furnished with the utmost simplicity; there was a straw bed in one room and a table and two chairs in the other. Some keys on the wall completed the sparse furnishings of the small apartment.

There was also a wooden bench under that window, and on it sat a woman, day and night, silently and in thought. Her eyes were constantly on the narrow niche in the wall, which was the only source of light and air to the king's lonely dungeon. She was Rauthgundis.

Not for even a moment would she allow her gaze to wander from that niche in the wall. "There," she would say, "his eyes are fixed on it also, and all he yearns for is the world outside it." Even as she talked to Wachis, her companion, or to the old warden who had given her shelter, her eyes never deviated from that niche. It seemed as if she was determined that her stare should ward off all evil or ill fortune from the inhabitant of the tower.

Today she had again sat thus for a long time. It had become quite dark.

The tower, mighty, threatening and dark, was silhouetted against the night sky. It cast a huge shadow on the courtyard and the left wing of the palace.

"Thank you, kind God in heaven," she said, "even your heavier blows lead to salvation. If I had gone away into the high mountains in the north to be with my father, then I might never have known about the misery down here, or at least much too late. But instead of going back to the mountain, as I had planned, yearning for the place where my child died drew me back to my old hearth. I could not live there, of course, for how was I to know if his new wife, the queen, might not stop there too? And so we lived in a forest hut near Faesulae.

"And when all the terrible events took place, when news of one disaster followed that of another, when Saracens set fire to my house and I could see the flames even from my hiding place, by then it was too late to escape to my father in the north. The Italians had blocked all the roads, and if they caught anyone with yellow hair they were immediately delivered to Belisarius's Huns. There was no place left to go, and no road open except the road leading here, to Ravenna the raven city, where I had never wanted to come as his wife. I arrived here as a fugitive beggar woman, and only his horse Wallada and his farmhand Wachis were left to me.

"But it was for his benefit. Even though I did not want to come I was forced here by God, and I am here in time to save him, and to free him from the dreadful treachery of his own wife. And from the malice of his enemies. Thank you, dear God! I could no longer live with him, but I – I, Rauthgundis, may yet be able to save him."

Something rattled opposite her. It was the iron gate. A man with a light came out, walked across the courtyard, and a moment later he was in the anteroom. It was the old warden.

"Well? Speak!" Rauthgundis cried, leaving her seat and hurrying to meet him.

"Patience, patience – just let me put my lamp down first. There! He did drink, and it did him good."

Rauthgundis placed her hand on her feverishly beating heart. "What is he doing?" she asked.

"He sits there silently the whole time, in the same position on his wooden stool, his back to the door and both hands resting on his knees. He will not answer me, no matter how often I try to speak to him. Usually he does not move at all; I think that sorrow and pain have done that to him. But today, when I held out the wine to him in a wooden cup and said: 'Drink, dear Sir, it comes from loyal friends.' He looked up. His face was sad, so very sad. And he drank deeply and then he let out such a deep sigh that it cut clean through to my soul."

Rauthgundis covered her eyes with her hands.

"God only knows what dreadful plans he has for him!" the old man mumbled quietly to himself.

"What did you say?"

"I say it's time you had something to eat and drink too. Otherwise your strength will leave you too, and you are going to need it, you poor woman."

"I will have strength."

"At least have a cup of wine."

"This wine? No, that is for him alone." And she went back into the inner room, where she took up her former position by the window.

"There is plenty left in the jar as yet," old Dromon went on, to himself. "And I am afraid we will have to save him soon, if he is to be saved. There comes Wachis. If only he has some good news, otherwise…"

Wachis entered. Since his visit to the queen he had exchanged his helmet for Dromon's clothes. "I bring good news," he said on entering. "But where were you an hour ago? I knocked in vain."

"We had both gone out to buy wine."

"Oh yes, that's why the whole room smells so good – what's that I see? That's old Falernian, and expensive too! How did you manage to pay for that?"

"With what?" the old man repeated, "with the most precious gold in the world!" His voice was trembling with emotion. "I told her that the Prefect was deliberately making him go hungry, so as to destroy his spirit. For many days now they have given me no food for him at all. Against my conscience I was able to feed him only by making the other prisoners go short. But she did not want that. So she thought for a while, and then she said: 'Is it true, Dromon, that Roman ladies will still pay a very high price for the yellow hair of a Germanic woman?' And I, unsuspectingly, said 'Yes'. And she goes and cuts off her hair, her lovely golden brown tresses, and brings them to me. And that's how the wine was paid for."

At that Wachis rushed into the next room, threw himself to the ground at her feet and covered the hem of her gown with kisses. "Oh mistress," he cried, "you woman of pure gold!"

"What have you been doing, Wachis? Stand up and tell me."

"Yes, tell us," Dromon added, joining them. "What did my son advise?"

"What do we need his advice for?" the woman said, "I, and I alone want to finish it."

"We need him very badly. The Prefect has made legionaries out of the young men of Ravenna, just as he did in Rome, and he has set up nine cohorts of them. My son Paulus too was conscripted. Luckily he has entrusted these legionaries with guarding the city gates. The Byzantines are camped outside in the port, and his Isaurians here in the palace."

Wachis went on: "The gates are watched very carefully, and they are secured at night. But the breach in the wall near the Aetius tower has not yet been repaired, and is secured only by the guard on duty."

"When will your son have the watch?"

"In two days. He will have the night watch."

"Thanks be to all the saints in heaven! It must not go on much longer: I am afraid…" he hesitated.

"What? Speak!" Rauthgundis said resolutely. "You can tell me everything."

"It might be best in the end if you do know everything. You are more clever and resourceful than either of us. And I am afraid they have evil things in store for him.

"As long as Belisarius was in command, he was still well taken care of. But as you know he has been taken away and the Prefect, that cold and silent demon, is master here in the palace. That makes things look much more dangerous. Every day he visits him personally in his dungeon.

"And then he speaks to him, intensely and threateningly, for hours. I have often listened in the corridor outside. But I don't think he is achieving much, because the master does not seem to be giving him any answer at all. And when the Prefect comes out again he looks as black as – as the king of shadows. For six days now I have been given neither food nor wine for him, other than a small piece of bread. And the air down there is damp and mouldy, like a tomb."

Rauthgundis sighed deeply.

"And yesterday, when the Prefect came out, he looked even blacker than ever – and then he asked me…"

"Well? Say it, whatever it might be!"

"He asked me if the torture implements were in order."

Rauthgundis paled, but said nothing.

"The vile wretch!" cried Wachis, "and what did you—"

"You need not worry. All is well, at least for the time being.

"'*Clarissime*,' I replied – and it is the absolute truth – 'the screws and pincers and the weights and the hooks and needles and all the other torture implements are all neatly together in the one place.'

"'Where?' he asked.

"'At the bottom of the sea. I personally, on orders from King Theodoric, threw them into the ocean'. You see, mistress Rauthgundis, a long time ago, when your husband was still only a simple count, he saved me once when those instruments were going to be used on me. At his pleading torture was abolished entirely, and so I owe him not only my life, but my limbs as well. And that is why I will risk my neck for him, with pleasure. If there is no other way I will leave this city with you as well. But we must not delay much longer, because the Prefect does not need pincers and screws if he wants to torment the marrow from someone's bones. I fear him as I fear the devil himself."

"I hate him as I hate a lie!" Rauthgundis added fiercely.

"That is why we must hurry, before he is able to put his evil plans into effect. Because I am quite sure he is planning something dreadful against the king. So hear my plan, and mark it well. On the night when my Paulus has the watch, when I go to bring him his evening drink I will unlock his chains, throw my cloak over him, and then lead him out of the dungeon and the corridor into the courtyard. From there we can reach the palace gate unhindered. There the guard will ask him for the password, which I will give him.

"Once he is out in the street, we must hurry to the breach in the wall, where my Paulus will let him through. Outside in the pine forest, in the grove of Diana, Wachis will be waiting for him, and will help him mount Wallada. But nobody must accompany him, not even you, Rauthgundis. He is safest alone."

"What do I matter? He must be free, that's what matters, without being tied down even by me. Don't even mention my name to him. I have brought him nothing but bad luck. I just want to see him one more time, from this window, as he walks outside to freedom."

★

The Prefect, during this period, was enjoying himself at the full pinnacle of his power. He was the Governor of Italy. On his orders the fortifications in all the cities were being repaired and reinforced, and the citizens were being trained in the use of arms. The representatives from Byzantium were unable to compete with him in any way. Their commanders were having no successes, and the sieges of Tarvisium, Verona and Ticinum were making no progress.

And Cethegus heard with glee that Hildebad, whose little group had grown to about six hundred men along the way, had fiercely and bloodily repulsed Acacius and his one thousand Persians, who had pursued and attacked him. But then a powerful Byzantine force, moving against him from Mantua, blocked every escape route he might have taken – he was trying to get through to Totila in Tarvisium. Finally he was forced to take refuge in the fortress Castra Nova, occupied by Goths under Count Thorismuth. Here the Byzantines now held him surrounded, but they had not been able to take the powerful fortress. Already the Prefect could see the day coming when Acacius would call on him for help, and then he would at last destroy the hated Hildebad, who by then would have nowhere left to escape to.

It pleased him to see that the military might of Byzantium, following the departure of Belisarius, was unable to break up the last remnants of Gothic resistance. And then there was the severity of Byzantium's taxes and financial administration; there was nothing he could do to prevent the country from being sucked dry as ordered by the emperor. These taxes served to arouse or intensify the dislike of the people for their new masters, both in the cities and in the country. Cethegus took care not to prevent the worst excesses of the tax collectors, as Belisarius had done, and he saw with joy that in Naples, and then also in Rome, the people started to rise up in open rebellion.

Once the Goths had finally been wiped out, if the power of the Byzantines in Italy was small enough and the hatred against them strong enough, then at last he would be able to rouse the Italians to call themselves free, and the liberator and the new ruler of a free Italy would be – Cethegus.

In all of this there was only one thing which caused him concern, and that was the fear that the Gothic war could break out anew. The last Gothic resistance had by no means been wiped out, and he was concerned that renewed hostilities could be sparked by just indignation at the treachery which had been committed against the Gothic people and their king.

It also concerned the Prefect that the most effective of the enemy leaders, Totila and Teias, had not been caught in the net in Ravenna. In order to forestall a nationalistic uprising the Prefect tried all the more to extract from the king some form of declaration to the effect that he had surrendered the city and his people unconditionally, and that the king now called on the last of his followers to abandon all further forms of futile resistance.

He also wanted his prisoner to tell him where Theodoric's treasure was hidden, as this treasure was of the utmost importance to him to pay mercenaries and attract foreign rulers. Once the Goths lost that treasure they also lost any hope they might have had of bolstering their weakened forces with foreign mercenaries. Furthermore it was most important to the Prefect that this treasure, which was said to be immense, should not fall into the hands of Byzantium. The emperor's constant need for money, and the resulting tyranny, were an important component in the Prefect's plans. He wanted the treasure for himself, as his private fortune was not inexhaustible.

But all of his efforts seemed to be foundering on the unshakable determination of his prisoner.

Chapter 27

The arrangements to free the king had been completed.

Rauthgundis had gone with Wachis outside the city, in order to have details of the little pine forest clearly in her mind, where the faithful farmhand would be waiting for them with Theodoric's horse Wallada.

The Gothic woman had returned to the jailer's little home, calm in the knowledge that plans for the release of her husband were well in place. But she grew pale when old Dromon hurried to meet her, evidently in despair, and drew her into the little room. There he threw himself on the ground at her feet, beat his chest with his fists and tore at his long white hair. For a long time he could not speak.

"Tell me what is the trouble," Rauthgundis commanded, and pressed her hand to her wildly beating heart. "Is he dead?"

"No, but escape is now impossible! Everything is lost! An hour ago the Prefect came and climbed down into the king's dungeon. As usual I unlocked both gates for him, and then..."

"Well?"

"He took both keys from me, and said that he would henceforth look after them himself."

"And you gave them to him?" Rauthgundis snarled.

"How could I refuse? I did not dare to do more than withhold the keys from him and say: 'Sir, don't you trust me any more?' And then he gave me one of those looks that cut through heart and soul and replied: 'From now on, not any more!' and he tore the keys from my hand."

"And you allowed it to happen! Still, what is Witigis to you?"

"Oh mistress, you are hurtful and unjust! What could you have done in my place? Nothing more!"

"I would have strangled him with these hands! And now? What now?"

"What now? Nothing! Nothing more can be done."

"He must be freed! Do you hear me? He must!"

"But mistress, I do not know how!"

Rauthgundis picked up an axe, which was leaning against the stove. "Let us smash down the doors!"

Dromon tried to wrest the axe from her: "Impossible! They are made of thick iron plates!"

"Then call the demon. Tell him Witigis wants to talk to him. Then I will slay him outside the door with this axe."

"And then? You are raving! Let me out. I want to call off Wachis from his fruitless watch."

"No, I cannot imagine that he will not be free tonight. Perhaps that demon will come back of his own accord. Perhaps," she said, thinking, "Ah!" she cried suddenly, "sure, that's it! He wants to murder him! He wants to sneak down to the defenceless man on his own. But woe be to him if he dares to come again! I will guard the threshold of that door there like the holy of holies, better even than I guarded my child's life. And woe be to him if he dares step over it." She leaned against the inside of the door to Dromon's apartment, weighing the heavy axe in her hand.

But Rauthgundis was mistaken.

Cethegus had not taken the keys in order to murder the king. He had gone to the southern or left wing of the place with them. Late that afternoon Cethegus, on his way back from the king's dungeon, went to Matesuentha's quarters. The calmness of death and feverish emotion alternated so quickly in the seriously ill woman that Aspa was able to look upon her mistress only with tears in her eyes.

"Oh, most beautiful daughter of the Occident," said Cethegus, "let go of those white clouds over your temples and listen to me."

"How is it with the king? You have given me no news. You promised to set him free once the decision had fallen, and to have him led across the Alps. You are not keeping your word."

"I did promise that, under two conditions. You know them both, but you have not yet fulfilled yours. Tomorrow the emperor's nephew Germanus will return from Ariminum, to take you with him to Byzantium. You will give him hope that you will become his bride. Your marriage to Witigis was forced on you, and it is null and void."

"I have already told you: no, never!"

"Then I am indeed sorry, for my prisoner. Because he will not see the light of day again until you are on your way to Byzantium, with Germanus."

"Never!"

"Do not provoke me, Matesuentha! I would have thought that the girlish foolishness which once led you to pay a high price for an Ares bust is now a thing of the past. After all, the very same girl is the one who betrayed the Gothic Ares to his enemies. But if you do still live for that girlish dream you once had, then at least save the man whom you once loved."

Matesuentha shook her head.

"I have until now treated you as a free woman, indeed as a queen. Do not remind me that for all practical purposes you are completely in my power. You will become the wife of that noble prince – and soon his widow. And then Justinian, Byzantium, the whole world will lie at your feet. Daughter of Amalasuntha, is it possible that you do not also love to rule?"

"I love only... Never!"

"Must I force you then?"

She laughed: "You? Force me?"

"Yes. I will force you. And my second condition is that the prisoner puts a name into this empty space here – it is the name of the fortress where the Gothic royal treasure is hidden – and that he then signs this document. Thus far he has refused to do either, with a stubbornness which is beginning to make me angry. Several times now I have gone to see him – I, the victor – and he has not yet spoken a single word to me. Only the first time he gave me a look, and for that look alone he deserves to lose his head."

"He will never give in to you."

"That is debatable. In the end constant dripping water will wear away the hardest granite. But I cannot wait that long. This morning I received news that the madman Hildebad defeated Bessas in a sortie, and beat him so badly that the latter is only just able to continue the siege. Gothic rebellion is becoming evident everywhere. I now have no choice but to stamp out these sparks of rebellion, and I want to do that with the water of disillusionment rather than with blood. To do that I must have the captive king's signature and I must know the whereabouts of that treasure. Therefore I now tell you this: unless you are on your way to Byzantium as the prince's companion by noon tomorrow, and unless you have by then obtained the prisoner's signature, authenticated by yourself, then, I swear it by Styx, I will…"

Matesuentha, terrified by the threatening look on the Prefect's face, sprang to her feet and grasped the Prefect's arm: "Surely you are not going to kill him?"

"Yes I am. First I will have him tortured, then blinded, and then I will have him killed."

"No! No!" Matesuentha screamed.

"Yes, I have made my decision. The executioners are ready. And you will tell him of it; coming from you, in your despair, he will believe that I am serious. You may be able to move him, whereas the sight of me merely serves to intensify his stubbornness. He may still be under the illusion that the soft-hearted Belisarius is in command here. You will therefore tell him just who it is that now has the ultimate power over him. Here are the two documents, and here are the keys. You can choose your time to suit yourself, and these keys will unlock the dungeon."

A flash of joyful hope shone from Matesuentha's soul through her eyes. Cethegus saw it, but smiled calmly and went out of the room.

Chapter 28

Soon after the Prefect had left the queen it became dark in Ravenna. Strong winds were driving ragged clouds over the city from the direction of the new moon, and short intervals of weak, uncertain light alternated with periods of darkness, which looked even darker because of it.

Dromon had completed his evening rounds, and he returned to his little anteroom, tired and sad. There was no light in the room, and it was only with difficulty that he could make out the form of Rauthgundis, who was still leaning against the door post, motionless. She was still holding the axe in her hand, and her eyes were fixed on the door to the dungeon.

"Let me make light, mistress, and share my evening meal with me. Come, you are standing there and waiting in vain."

"No, no light, and don't light a fire. That way I can see better what is happening out there in the moonlight."

"Very well, but at least come inside and sit down. Here, some bread and meat for you."

"Am I to eat while he has to go hungry?"

"Unless you eat you will die! Anyway, what are you thinking about all this time?"

"What do I think about?" Rauthgundis repeated, always with her eyes fixed on the courtyard outside. "Him. How we used to sit on the porch outside our lovely house, with the spring bubbling merrily in the garden, and the cicadas chirping in the olive trees. And the cool night air would caress his dear face, and I would snuggle up to his shoulder. We would say nothing as the stars slowly passed on their way above us. And we would listen to the breathing of the little child who had gone to sleep on my lap, his little hands around his father's wrists like bonds. Now he has to wear different bonds, bonds of iron, which hurt him." And she pressed her face against the iron grating of the window, more and more strongly, until she herself felt pain.

"Mistress, why do you torture yourself so? There is nothing you can do to change it!"

"But I want to change it! I must save him and – Dromon, come here quickly! What is that?" she whispered, and pointed outside.

Silently the old man rushed to her side. Outside in the courtyard a tall figure was gliding silently along the wall, dressed in white. The moonlight illuminated her briefly, but clearly.

"It is a *lemura*! A ghost of the many people who have been executed here," the old man whispered, trembling. "May God and the saints preserve me!" He crossed himself and hid his face.

"No," said Rauthgundis, "the dead do not return from the next world. Now it has disappeared – dark everywhere – look, there, the moonlight has broken through – there it is again! It was moving toward the dungeon entrance. What is that there, something red in the light? Ah, it is the queen – her red hair! She has stopped at the door. She is unlocking it! She is going to murder him in his sleep!"

"You are right! It is the queen! But murder him? How could she?"

"She could! But she will not, not while Rauthgundis lives! After her! A miracle is opening his dungeon for us! But softly! Quietly!"

With that she moved from the little room out into the courtyard, the axe in her right hand, carefully seeking the shadows along the wall and walking softly and silently on her toes. Dromon followed immediately behind her.

Meanwhile Matesuentha had unlocked the door to the corridor and made her way down the many steps along the narrow passage, feeling her way with her hands in the dark. Now she had reached the door to the actual dungeon, and carefully she unlocked it also.

A narrow beam of moonlight, coming from the hole left by a missing tile in the roof far above, illuminated the prisoner just enough for her to see him. He was sitting on a block of stone, his back to the door and his head resting on his hands, motionless.

Trembling, Matesuentha leaned against the frame of the door. A draught of icy cold air met her, and she felt cold. She was speechless with horror.

And then the slight draught made Witigis aware that the door was open. He lifted his head, but did not look around.

"Witigis – King Witigis," Matesuentha stammered at last, "It is I. Can you hear me?"

But the prisoner did not move.

"I have come to save you – flee! Freedom!"

But the prisoner merely lowered his head again.

"Oh speak! At least look at me!" And she entered. She would have liked to touch his arm, his hand, but she did not dare. "He wants to kill you – torture you. He will do it – unless you flee."

And now she stepped closer, with the courage of despair. "But you must flee! You must not die! You are going to be saved – through me! I beg of you – flee! You do not hear me. Hurry! One day you shall know everything. But now run, flee, flee to life and to freedom. I have the keys, and the way is open. Flee!" Now she grasped his arm, and tried to pull him to his feet. But as she did so she caused the chains on his hands and feet to rattle – he had been locked to the stone block.

"Oh, what was that?" she cried, and fell to her knees.

"Stone and iron," he replied tonelessly. "Let me be. I will die in any case. Even if these bonds were not holding me here, I still would not follow you. Back into the world? It is a great lie! Everything is a lie!"

"You are right! It is better to die. Let me die with you. And forgive me, because I too have lied to you."

"It could well be. It does not surprise me."

"But you must forgive me before we die. I hated you – I rejoiced at your downfall – I have – oh, it is so difficult to say it! I don't have the strength to confess it. And yet I must have your forgiveness, even if I have to steal it! Forgive me – give me your hand as a sign that you forgive me."

But Witigis had returned to his brooding.

"Oh I beg of you – forgive me, for whatever I have done to you."

"Go away – why shouldn't I forgive you? You are like the rest, no better and no worse!"

"No, I am worse than anyone. And yet I am better, or at least more repentant. Yes, I hated you, but only because you rejected me and pushed me away from you! You would not let me share your life – forgive me! God, all I ask is that I be allowed to die with you. Give me your hand, just once, to say you forgive me." On her knees, imploring him, she reached up to him with her hands.

The king raised his head. His basic kindness had been roused, and drowned out his own agony.

"Matesuentha," he said, "go, I am sorry for you. Let me die alone. Whatever you have done to me – just go! I have forgiven you."

"Oh Witigis!" Matesuentha sighed, and tried to grasp his hand.

Chapter 29

But as soon as she had said these words she could feel herself being violently pulled away. "Night arsonist! He shall never forgive you! Come Witigis, my Witigis. Follow me! You are free!"

The king jumped to his feet, as if the sound of that voice had woken him from a deep sleep. "Rauthgundis! My wife! No, you have never lied! You are true and loyal. Oh, can it be true that I have you back?" And then, taking a deep breath and letting out a cry of rejoicing, he spread out his arms as much as the chains would allow. His wife threw herself at his breast, and they both cried sweet tears of love and of joy.

But Matesuentha, who had also regained her feet, stumbled against the wall. Slowly she stroked her long red hair out of her face and looked at the couple, who were now brightly illuminated by the moonlight coming through the hole in the roof.

"How he loves her! Yes, her he would follow into freedom and into life anew. But he has to stay and die – die with me."

"Don't dally any longer!" Dromon's voice urged from the door.

"Yes, hurry, my life and my joy!" Rauthgundis cried. She drew a little key from her bosom and searched for the small keyhole among the chains.

"Will I really be free once more, and get out of here?" the prisoner asked, partially reverting to his former state of semi-conscious apathy.

"Yes, out into the fresh air and to freedom," cried Rauthgundis and threw the now unlocked chains to the ground. "Here, Witigis, a weapon! An axe! Take it!"

Eagerly the Goth took the weapon thus offered him, and took a lusty swing with it: "Ah, a weapon! How good it feels! It is giving me back my strength!"

"I knew that, my brave Witigis!" Rauthgundis cried, and then she knelt down and unlocked the chain which shackled his left foot to the stone block. "Now, stride out! You are free!"

Witigis rose, stretched to his full height and then, holding the axe in his right hand, made for the door.

"And she was able to unlock his chains!" Matesuentha whispered.

"Yes, free!" said Witigis, taking a deep breath of relief. "I do want to be free and go with you."

"He wants to go with her!" Matesuentha cried and threw herself at her husband's feet, barring his way. "Witigis – God be with you – go! Only tell me once more that you forgive me."

"Forgive you?" cried Rauthgundis. "No! Never! She is the one who destroyed our Empire. She betrayed you. It was not lightning from heaven but her hand which burned down your stores!"

"Oh, be cursed then!" cried Witigis. "And away from this snake straight out of hell!" Flinging her away from the door he crossed the threshold, followed by Rauthgundis.

"Witigis!" Matesuentha screamed, getting to her feet again. "Stop! Wait a moment! Listen to me once more, Witigis!"

"Be quiet!" Dromon said, gripping her arm, "You will attract attention and destroy him!"

But Matesuentha, no longer in control of herself, tore herself free and followed them up the steps into the corridor.

"Stop!" she screamed, "Witigis! You must not go like this! First you have to forgive me!" And then she collapsed unconscious.

Dromon hurried past her, after the fugitives.

But Matesuentha's piercing cries had already woken the man with the lightest sleep in Italy. Cethegus, only partly dressed and with his sword in his hand, stepped out onto the arcade outside his bedchamber, from where he could see out into the palace courtyard.

"Guards!" he cried, "To arms!" But some of the soldiers had also heard the commotion, and been alerted by it. Witigis, Rauthgundis and Dromon had barely made it out of the corridor and the second iron gate into Dromon's apartment opposite, when six Isaurian mercenaries came storming into the corridor.

Quickly Rauthgundis raced out of the apartment, ran toward the heavy iron door, threw it shut and turned the key in the lock. "They are locked in and harmless!" she whispered.

Quickly the reunited couple now hurried from Dromon's rooms to the main exit leading from the courtyard into the street. The last man of the guard, his spear felled, came to meet them. "Give the password!" he cried, "Rome and?"

"Revenge!" said Witigis, and cut him down with the axe.

With a loud cry the mercenary fell, but managed to hurl his spear after the fugitives before he collapsed. It pierced the last of the three fugitives, Dromon.

Running down the marble steps and out into the street the couple could hear the trapped mercenaries beating loudly against the strong iron door. They also heard a command: "Syphax, my horse!"

And then night and mist swallowed them up.

A few moments later the palace and the courtyard were a sea of torches, and mounted soldiers flew to every gate of the city.

"Six thousand *solidi* to him who brings him in alive, or three thousand dead!" Cethegus cried, leaping into the saddle of his black stallion. "Now go to it, you sons of the desert wind, Ellak and Mundzuch, Huns and Massageti. Now ride as you have never ridden before!"

"But to where?" Syphax asked, racing out of the palace gate at the side of his master.

"That's difficult to say. But all the gates are locked and guarded. They can only be heading for one of the breaches in the wall."

"There are two major breaches; which one?"

"Do you see Jupiter there, just coming out of the clouds? There, in the east? He is waving to me. Isn't the breach near the Aetius tower there?"

"Yes, it is."

"Good! We will go there! I will follow my star!"

★

Meanwhile husband and wife had made their way through the breach in the wall, allowed to pass by Dromon's son Paulus, and had found the faithful Wachis waiting with two horses in the nearby pine forest of Diana. The couple both mounted the broad back of Wallada.

Quickly Wachis led the way in the direction of the river, which at this point was very wide. Witigis held Rauthgundis in front of him, behind the neck of the horse. "Oh my wife! When I lost you I lost everything that mattered! I lost the will to fight and the will to live. But now, for the sake of the Empire, I am willing to try once more. Oh soul of my soul, how could I ever let you go?"

"Your arm is sore from the pressure of the chains! Here, put it on my neck, oh you, my life and my all!"

"Go, Wallada, go quickly, it's life or death!"

With that they turned out of the thicket and into the open. They had reached the river's edge. Wachis tried to drive his reluctant horse into the dark waters. The animal shied and struggled, and Wachis dismounted. "It is very deep, and flowing fast. There has been high water for three days. The ford is useless. The horses will have to swim, and the current will carry us a long way to the right. There are rocks in the river too, and the moonlight is so deceptive and changeable." At a loss he walked up and down the riverbank.

"Listen! What was that?" Rauthgundis asked. "That was not the wind in the stone oaks."

"That's horses," said Witigis, "and they are closing fast. We are being followed – I can hear the sound of arms. There – torches! Now into the river, life or death, but quietly!"

And he led the horse to the water's edge by the reins.

"It is too deep now, the horses will have to swim. Hold onto the mane, Rauthgundis. Go, Wallada!"

The animal stared into the black flood, trembling and snorting, its mane flying wildly in the wind. It had dug in its forelegs, not wanting to go into the water.

"Go, Wallada!" and then Witigis whispered softly into the great horse's ear: "Dietrich von Bern!" At the sound of those words the fine animal leapt proudly into the flood.

Already the pursuers were racing out of the wood, Cethegus in the lead, Syphax with a torch at his side. Now he raised the torch and said: "Here, Sir, the trail disappears at the water's edge."

"They are in the water! Forward, you Huns!"

But the Huns held their reins tight and would not budge.

"Well, Ellak? What are you waiting for? Into the water! Now!"

"Sir, we cannot do that. Before we go into the water at night we must first pray to Phug, the water god, for forgiveness. We must pray to Him first."

"Pray as long as you like later, when you are on the other side, but now…"

At that moment a stronger gust of wind blew across the water, blowing out all the torches. Water sprayed over them.

"You can see, Sir, Phug is angry."

"Quiet! Did you see something? There, on the left?"

The moon had broken through the patchy cloud cover, and it showed the light coloured undergarment of Rauthgundis. She had lost her brown cloak.

"Aim there, quickly!"

"No Sir, first we must finish praying."

And then it was dark again. Cursing, Cethegus tore the Hunnish chieftain's bow and quiver from his shoulder.

"Now hurry, quickly," Wachis whispered softly – he had almost reached the opposite bank, "before the moon comes out again behind that small cloud there."

"Stop, Wallada!" said Witigis, jumping off to lighten the horse's load and holding onto the mane. "There is a rock there! Don't hurt yourself, Rauthgundis."

Horse, husband and wife stopped for a moment at the towering rock, where the water raged past it. And then the moon came out once more, brightly illuminating the river and the little group on the rock.

"There they are!" Cethegus cried, who had the bow ready; he aimed and dispatched the arrow. The long arrow with its black feathers flew from the bowstring.

"Rauthgundis!" Witigis cried, shocked, because she suddenly gave a jerk and sank forward onto the horse's mane. But she did not complain.

"Have you been hit?"

"I think so. Leave me here. Save yourself."

"Never! Let me help you."

"My God, master, down! They are taking aim now!"

The Huns had now finished praying. They rode right down to the riverbank, readied their bows and took aim.

"Leave me, Witigis! Flee! I will die here."

"No, I will never leave you again!" He tried to lift her out of the saddle and onto the rock. The little group was clearly visible in the moonlight.

"Give yourself prisoner, Witigis!" Cethegus cried, spurring his horse right into the water.

"A curse on you, you liar and traitor!"

And then twelve arrows flew at once. Theodoric's horse reared high up in the air once more, and then disappeared for ever in the depths of the river.

But Witigis too had been mortally wounded. "With you!" was the last thing Rauthgundis was able to utter.

Witigis embraced her firmly with both arms: "With you!" And they both vanished into the river, locked together in a final embrace.

On the other side of the river Wachis called out their names three more times, with despair in his voice. But he received no reply, and so at last he spurred his horse and raced away into the night.

"Get their bodies ashore!" Cethegus commanded ominously, turning his mount. And now the Huns did ride and swim right up to the rock in the river, searching.

But they searched in vain. The rapidly flowing river had carried them with it, and soon the reunited couple were swept out into the deep, free and open ocean, for ever.

On the same day Prince Germanus had returned from Ariminum to Ravenna, ready to take Matesuentha to Byzantium with him.

Matesuentha was only aroused by the workmen, who were breaking down a wall in order to free the trapped mercenaries. The princess was found collapsed on the steps leading to the dungeon. She was carried to her rooms with a high fever, and there she was laid on purple cushions, where she lay without moving or making a sound, but with her eyes wide open.

Around midday Cethegus let himself be announced. The look on his face was dark and threatening, and his manner icy cold. He walked right up to her bed. Matesuentha looked him in the eye.

"He is dead!" she said calmly.

"He wanted it that way, he and – and you. There is no point in reproaching you. But you can see what happens when you go against my will. No doubt the furore which will follow his demise will drive the Barbarians to renewed fury. You have thus made a lot of work for me, because it was you alone who led him to flight and death. The least you can do for me now is to grant my second wish. Prince Germanus has landed in order to fetch you. You will go with him."

"Where is the body?"

"We did not find it. The river carried it away, him – and the woman."

Matesuentha's lips trembled. "Even in death? She died with him?"

"Never mind the dead! In two hours I will return with Prince Germanus. Will you be ready to receive him by then?"

"I will be ready."

"Good! We want to be punctual."

"So do I. Aspa, call all my slaves. They shall adorn me. Diadem, purple, silk!"

"She has lost her mind," said Cethegus as he left. "But she will get it back! Women are tough. They can live without a heart." With that he left in order to console the impatient prince.

Even before the two hours had elapsed a slave came in order to bid the two men proceed to the queen's rooms. Germanus hurried to her chambers as quickly as he could. But at the door he stopped, stunned. Never had he seen the Gothic princess look so magnificent.

She had placed the high golden diadem on her shining hair, which flowed freely over her shoulders. Her white silken undergarment, of heavy silk and embroidered with golden flowers, was visible only below her knees. The remainder of her person was covered by a splendid purple cloak. Her face was marble white, but her eyes burned with an eerie fervour.

"Prince Germanus!" she called out as he entered, "You have spoken to me of love. But do you know what you were saying? To love is to die."

Germanus looked questioningly at Cethegus. The latter stepped forward, about to speak.

But Matesuentha began once more, in a clear voice: "Prince Germanus, they call you the most educated man at a court where the solving of difficult riddles is much practised. I too will set you a riddle; see if you can solve it. By all means let the clever Prefect help you – he is such an authority on human nature. What is it that is a woman and yet still a girl? Widow yet never a wife? You cannot solve it? You are right! Death alone solves all riddles."

Quickly she threw the purple cloak aside. A broad sword flashed, and with both hands she plunged it deep into her breast.

With a loud cry Germanus leapt to her aid from in front, as Aspa did the same from behind. Cethegus caught the falling princess without a word. She died as soon as the sword was withdrawn from her wound. He knew the sword. He himself had once sent it to her.

It was the sword of King Witigis.

BOOK SEVEN

Totila – Part One

"Glory be to us that this sunny youth lives!"

Margrave Ruediger von Bechelaren

Chapter 1

A few days after the death of Matesuentha and the departure of the deeply shaken Prince Germanus, a deputation arrived from Castra Nova, which necessitated the sending of Byzantine troops from Ravenna.

A few Gothic fugitives were still managing to steal their way through the enemy lines, and one of them had informed Hildebad of the treacherous way in which the king had been arrested. When he heard this Hildebad released a few prisoners and sent them to Ravenna in order to challenge Belisarius and Cethegus to a duel, either separately or together "if they have so much as a single drop of courage in their veins."

"He seems to think Belisarius is still in the country, and he does not appear to be exactly afraid of him," said Bessas.

"This might present us with an opportunity," Cethegus replied thoughtfully, "to destroy that irrepressible ruffian once and for all. Of course it would require courage, the kind Belisarius had."

"You know that I am his equal in that respect, as I am in all other ways."

"Good!" said Cethegus, "come with me to my room. I will show you how to destroy that giant. You shall succeed where Belisarius failed." But to himself he added: "True, Bessas is an admirably bad general, but Demetrius is no better, and he is more easily manipulated. Also I still owe Bessas a debt from the Porta Tiburtina, in Rome."

The Prefect's fear that news of the treacherous end met by their king might renew the by now almost non-existent Gothic resistance was not without foundation. This was why he had tried, using every means he knew, to extract that declaration from Witigis, because that would have served to choke any nationalistic anger and thirst for revenge. So far, no definite news had reached old Hildebrand in Verona, Totila in Tarvisium or Teias in Ticinum. They had heard only that Ravenna had fallen, and that the king was a prisoner. There were dark rumours of treachery, but nothing definite. And in spite of their anger and sadness the three friends could not help feeling that the impregnable fortress and their able king had not been defeated by military action alone. Rather than discourage them, the bad news had actually stiffened their resistance. By means of repeated sorties, all successful, they managed to weaken their besiegers to such a degree that they were already close to having to give up the respective sieges.

From all directions important signs reached them, indicating that conditions in Italy were about to undergo significant change.

One such change was a change of heart on the part of the Italian population, particularly the middle class, the merchants and tradesmen in the cities and the peasants in the country. Everywhere the Italians had cheered the Byzantines as their liberators, but it was not long before this cheering subsided. Behind Belisarius came a whole army of officials and tax collectors from Byzantium, sent immediately by Justinian to gather the fruits of victory, and above all to fill the always empty coffers of the eastern Empire from Italy's riches. These eager servants of the emperor commenced their work even as the war was still raging. As soon as Belisarius had captured and occupied a city, the *logothetus* (principal tax collector) with him would call a meeting of all free citizens in the *curia* or the Forum, and there he would ask the citizens to voluntarily divide themselves into six classes, according to their wealth. Then he called on each class to assess the wealth of the next highest class. On the basis of these estimates the Imperial officials imposed a tax on each of the six classes, calculated as high as possible. And since they, because of repeated shortages and delays in their own pay, were forced to fill their own pockets as well as the emperor's coffers, the financial pressures on the population soon became unbearable. The *logotheti* were not content with the high taxes, which the emperor demanded be paid three years in advance, nor with the "special levy for freedom, gratitude and joy", which had been imposed on every "liberated" city in Italy. And then there were substantial secondary taxes, which Belisarius had to collect for the food and pay of his army, as Byzantium sent neither money nor supplies. And even apart from all these taxes, these financial masterminds were able to think of yet more ways to extract still more taxes.

And so they instigated checks of tax lists everywhere, found discrepancies or overdue payments from the Gothic reign, or even from the era of Odoacer, and so they gave the citizen concerned the choice between huge settlement payments or prosecution by the fiscal officials of the Empire, who had never been known to lose a case. And if, as was often the case in those unsettled times, the lists were incomplete or missing entirely, then the officials "reconstructed" them at their whim.

In short, all the financial trickery which had led to the ruination of all the Empire's eastern provinces was now being practised in Italy, wherever the Imperial occupation extended.

Without compunction and with no thought whatever for the needs of the war or of individuals, the officials would unharness the peasant's ox from his plough, take a tradesman's tools from his shop or a merchant's goods from his warehouse, to pay for so-called taxes. In many cities the population rose in open revolt against the oppressors, who of course returned soon afterwards in greater numbers, and went on about their business with even greater severity. The emperor's Moorish cavalry, aided by savage bloodhounds, would chase desperate peasants from their hiding places, where they had fled to escape the tax collectors.

But Cethegus, who alone might have had the power to help, stood by and watched with calculated calm. It suited him well that Italy would get to know the tyranny of Byzantium even before the war was over. It would make it all the easier for him to stage a revolt later, with all of Italy rising in support of him, so that he could then shake off the Byzantine yoke just as he had shaken off the Goths. With a shrug of his shoulders he would dismiss the complaints from envoys representing the various cities, who came to him for help. He would simply give them the laconic reply: "That is Byzantine government – you will just have to become used to it."

"No!" the envoys from Rome had cried, "one cannot become used to the unbearable. And if this goes on, then the emperor may well experience a reaction he did not imagine even in his worst nightmares."

Cethegus took this threat as meaning only one thing, a revolt throughout Italy, a war of independence. He did not know what else it could mean. But he was wrong. As much as he despised his own countrymen, he thought he had been able to inspire them by his own example. But the idea of "Freedom and renewal of the Roman Empire," so familiar to his own mind and as necessary to him as air is to others, was one which his generation was no longer able to grasp. The decadent population could only choose between masters. And since the yoke of Byzantium was proving unbearable, many began to think back once more to the mild and benevolent rule of the Goths. That was a possibility which had never even entered the Prefect's head, and yet it was to be so.

What had started in a small way in Tarvisium, Ticinum and Verona was also brewing on a much larger scale in Naples and in Rome. The Italian population was rising against Byzantine officials and soldiers, just as the native population of the first three smaller cities was supporting their Gothic garrisons.

Thus it eventually came about that the beleaguerers of Tarvisium not only had to abandon the siege, but were forced to concentrate on defending their camp, after a sortie by Totila, supported by local peasants, had destroyed most of the camp's defences. Totila was now able to obtain provisions for his men from the surrounding countryside.

One evening, as he completed his evening rounds on the walls of Tarvisium, he felt more joy in his heart than he had felt for a long time. The sun, setting behind the Venetian Mountains, imparted a golden glow to the countryside before him, and little red clouds were gathering overhead. It touched his heart as he watched peasants from the region around Tarvisium pouring into the city through the open gates, bringing his half starved Goths supplies of bread, meat, cheese and wine, as the latter ran out into the fields just outside the city. There Goths and Italians were soon celebrating their joint success, their arms around one another, united in hatred of their common enemy.

"Could it really be that it is impossible," the victor said to himself, "to maintain this harmony, and to have it spread throughout the land? Must two peoples always remain in conflict? How well this friendship suits both sides! Did we not also do wrong to treat them as enemies, as a conquered people? We treated them with suspicion instead of trust, and we demanded their obedience but never sought their love. And that may well have been worth seeking. Had we won it, then Byzantium would never have set foot here. The fulfilment of my promise, Valeria, may not be that unattainable. If only it were granted me that I could fight for that goal in my own way!"

And then his thoughts were interrupted by a messenger coming from the outer guards with a report that the enemy had hastily abandoned their camp and were in full retreat southwards to Ravenna. There was also a cloud of dust approaching from the west, where a strong detachment of cavalry appeared to be coming. They were thought to be Goths.

Totila received the news with joy but cautiously, and took every precaution against a possible trap. But during the night his doubts were resolved. He was woken with news of a Gothic victory, and the arrival of the victors. He hurried out into the antechamber and saw Hildebrand, Teias, Thorismuth and Wachis.

His friends greeted him with the cry: "Victory! Victory!" and Teias and Hildebrand reported that the population had risen against the Byzantines in Ticinum and Verona also, helping them and their Goths to attack and defeat their beleaguerers, forcing them to withdraw after destroying their camps.

But there was an even greater than usual melancholy in the eyes and voice of Teias. "What sadness do you have to report with all this joyful news?" Totila asked.

"The wretched end of the finest man of us all!" he replied, and motioned to Wachis, who now related the suffering and death of the king and his wife.

"I escaped the arrows from the Huns," he concluded, "in the reeds by the side of the river, and that is why I am still alive. But I now live for one reason only, and that is to avenge my master and mistress against their murderer and betrayer, the Prefect."

"No, the Prefect's head is mine!" Teias stated, in a manner which bore no argument.

"The next claim," said Hildebrand, "is yours, Totila. Because you have a brother to be avenged."

"My brother Hildebad?" cried Totila. "What happened to him?"

"Shamefully murdered, Sir," said Thorismuth, "by the Prefect! In front of my eyes! And there was nothing I could do about it."

"My strong Hildebad dead!" Totila lamented. "Tell me what happened!"

"The great warrior was with us in the fortress Castra Nova near Mantua. The rumour of the king's disgraceful end had reached us. Hildebad therefore challenged both of them, Belisarius and Cethegus, to a duel. Soon after that a herald arrived and announced that Belisarius had accepted the challenge, and would expect your brother to meet him in the plain between our walls and their camp. Joyfully your brother rushed out, and we followed on horseback. And indeed, out of his tent strode a figure familiar to all of us, Belisarius, in his golden armour, with a closed helmet with white plume and a round shield.

"Only twelve mounted men were following him, and at the head of them all rode the Prefect Cethegus, on his black stallion. The other Byzantines halted in front of their camp, and Hildebad ordered me to follow him with eleven mounted men at the same distance.

"The two warriors greeted one another with their spears, the tuba sounded, and Hildebad spurred his horse and charged at his opponent. A moment later the latter fell from his horse, pierced by Hildebad's spear.

"Your brother, quite unharmed, dismounted and cried: 'That was not one of Belisarius's thrusts!' and he opened the dying man's visor. 'Bessas!' he cried and, angry at the deception, looked toward the enemy.

"And then the Prefect gave a signal. The twelve Moorish mounted soldiers hurled their spears, and your brother fell, mortally wounded."

Totila covered his head, and Teias approached him sympathetically.

"Hear me out," said Thorismuth. "We who saw the murder committed were gripped by a mixture of grief and furious anger. And so we charged ferociously at the enemy, who had followed from the camp, hoping that we might be demoralised by Hildebad's fall. After a fierce engagement we drove them to flight, and the Prefect, who had been wounded in the shoulder, was saved only by the speed of his hellish black stallion. Your brother lived to see our victory, and his eyes shone with pride. He had us bring down the chest which we had brought with us from Ravanna, then he made us open it and said to me: 'Here are Theodoric's crown helmet, shield and sword. Take them to my brother!' And then, with his last breath, he said: 'He shall avenge me and renew the Empire. Tell him that I loved him very much!' and with that he fell back on his shield and his wonderful soul was gone."

"My brother, oh my dear, dear brother!" Totila cried. He leaned against a pillar, and the tears flowed freely down his face.

"Lucky is he who can still weep!" Teias said softly.

There was a pause, a pause of grief and sorrow.

"Remember your oath and your duty!" Hildebrand cried at last. "He was doubly your brother! You must avenge him!"

"Yes!" cried Totila, and instinctively he tore the sword from the scabbard which Teias was holding out to him. "I shall avenge him!"

It was King Theodoric's sword.

"And you shall renew the Empire!" said old Hildebrand solemnly, standing up straight, and then he firmly pressed the Gothic crown on Totila's head. "Hail, hail King of the Goths!"

Suddenly Totila was frightened. Quickly he reached for the golden crown with his left hand and said: "What are you doing?"

"That which is right! Your dying brother spoke a prophesy. You shall indeed renew the Empire. Three victories call on you to take up the fight once more. Remember your oath! We are not yet defeated, and we are not defenceless. Are we to lay down our arms? To strike our colours to lies and treachery?"

"No!" Totila cried, "that we will not do! And we do well to choose a king, as a sign of new hope! But there is Teias here, more worthy, older and more proven than I am. Choose Teias!"

"Me as an advocate of hope? No!" said the latter, shaking his head. "First it is your turn! It is to you that your dying brother sent sword and crown. Wear them, and may fortune be with you! If the Empire can indeed be saved, you are the one to save it. And if it cannot be saved, then there must still be an avenger left!"

"But right now," Hildebrand interrupted, "the first and most important thing we have to do is to instil confidence and belief in ultimate victory into the hearts of all of us. That is your task, Totila! Look, a new day is rising, shining and bright. The first rays of the sun are coming into this hall and kissing your face. That is a sign from the gods! Hail King Totila! You shall renew the Gothic Empire."

And the young man pressed the crown firmly onto his golden head and held out Theodoric's sword toward the rising sun.

"Yes!" he cried vehemently, "if it is within human power to do it, then I shall renew the Empire."

Chapter 2

And King Totila kept his word.

Once more he restored the might of the Gothic nation, whose hold on Italian soil at the time he was crowned had shrunk to three small towns and a few thousand men in arms. Once more he established the Gothic Empire, mightier and more glorious than it had ever been, even in the days of the great Theodoric.

With one fateful exception he drove the Byzantines from every city and every fortress on the peninsula. He regained the islands of Sardinia, Sicily and Corsica. But even more than that, with victory upon victory he expanded the Gothic Empire beyond its previous borders, and as the emperor stubbornly refused to recognise Gothic sovereignty in Italy, Gothic fleets were almost compelled to spread terror and destruction deep into the provinces of the eastern Roman Empire itself.

And in spite of the war, which had never entirely ended, Italy under his mild and benevolent rule bloomed once again, as it had done during the reign of King Theodoric.

It is significant also that legend, both Gothic and Italian, soon started to celebrate the lucky young king, either as a grandson of Numila Pompilius, or Titus, or Theodoric, or as a reincarnation of Theodoric's genius, returned to earth in youthful form to restore his Empire.

Totila's rise seemed like the rising of the morning sun after a dark and cloudy night, bringing endless light and blessing. At his coming the dark shadows retreated, step by step; luck and victory accompanied him everywhere, and the gates of cities and the hearts of men opened to him virtually without exception and without resistance.

The genius of a general, ruler and man, which had lain dormant in this youth, had been suspected only by a few, such as Theodoric and Teias. But nobody had fully recognised that genius which, given the scope to do so, was now able to unfold fully and magnificently. The cheerful youthfulness which had been his essence had not died in all those long years of pain and trial, in Naples and before Rome, and yearning for his distant beloved. It had matured into a serious manliness. But that shining basic feature of his character had remained, and everything he did bore its mark, especially his almost boundless benevolence and amicability.

Inspired by his own idealism Totila turned trustingly to the idealistic streak in everyone with whom he came into contact. And most men, indeed all men who were not already possessed by some hostile demon, found that his confidence and his trust in everything noble and beautiful was quite irresistible. As light illuminates everything it touches, so the noble mindedness of this enlightened king seemed to transmit itself to everyone at his court or in his vicinity, and it even had a conciliating effect on his opponents.

"He is as irresistible as the sun god!" the Italians cried.

Upon closer examination one finds that the secret of his success lay largely in his very special skills, with which he was able to turn bitterness on the part of the Italians against their Byzantine oppressors into gratefulness for his own Gothic benevolence.

He was able to do this more by following his natural instincts than by following any preconceived plan, and in time this pro-Gothic feeling became stronger and stronger.

We have already seen how this changed mood had begun to affect the peasant population, the wealthy merchants, the tradesmen in the cites and the middle class in general, which made up by far the largest part of the population as a whole. The personality of the young king now served to turn them away completely from the Byzantine tyrants, whose luck seemed to have deserted them in any case, and their allegiance and sympathies switched strongly to the Goths. From the moment the Goths started to charge into battle with the joyful cry of "Totila!" there seemed to be nothing that could stop them.

Certainly there was a small minority which remained inflexible. It included the orthodox church, which considered any form of truce with the Gothic heretics to be treason, together with stubborn republicans and the core of the catacombs conspiracy, the proud Roman aristocratic families, and last but not least the followers of the Prefect. But by comparison with the full-scale defection by the masses the numbers of these diehards were so small that they were relatively insignificant.

The new king's first act was to issue a proclamation to all Goths and Italians. To the former, it explained exactly how the fall of Ravenna and the downfall of King Witigis had been the result of treachery, rather than a military defeat, and it also exhorted them to revenge, which had already started with the three victories achieved to date. As for the Italians, who were starting to realise by now what a poor bargain they had made by exchanging Gothic rule for Byzantine tyranny, they were urged to return to their old friends.

In return the king promised not only a complete pardon, but also equality with the Goths. This included the abolition of all existing Gothic privileges, and in particular it permitted the formation of an Italian army. Furthermore, in marked contrast to the example set by the Byzantines, it abolished all taxes on Italian property and wealth until the end of the war. Another very clever move was based on the fact that the nobility was mainly pro-Byzantine, but the peasants predominantly pro-Gothic. Hence a law was introduced to the effect that any Roman nobleman who did not surrender to the Goths and accept Gothic jurisdiction within three weeks would forfeit all his property, in favour of the peasants who had until then been his *coloni* and serfs.

Finally the king offered a substantial premium, paid from the Gothic royal treasure, for all mixed marriages between Goths and Italians, and he promised gifts of land to such young couples, taken from the confiscated estates of Roman senators.

The proclamation concluded: "Italia, bleeding still from the wounds caused her by Byzantium's tyranny, shall rise again under my shield. Help us, sons of Italia, our brothers, to drive our common enemies, Justinian's Huns and mercenaries, from our holy soil. Then, in our new Empire, a new nation of Italians and Goths shall emerge, sired out of Italian beauty and civilisation by Gothic strength and loyalty, a new people the like of which the world has never seen, unsurpassed in terms of glory and splendour."

★

When the Prefect Cethegus rose from his camp bed in Ravenna one morning, where his wound had kept him convalescing, news of Totila's uprising reached him. With a curse he jumped up from his bed.

"Sir," the Greek physician warned him, "you must take care! Your wound…"

"Didn't you hear? Totila wears the Gothic crown! Now is not the time for taking care of myself. Syphax, my helmet!"

And then he tore the proclamation from the hands of Lucius Licinius, who had been the bearer of the news, and read it eagerly.

"Isn't that ridiculous? Utter madness?" Lucius remarked.

"It would be madness if the Romans were still Romans. But are they? And if they are not? Then it would be us, and not the Barbarians, who are mad in trying to do what we have been aiming at. That test must not be allowed to take place, and this new danger must be crushed right now, in its infancy! That new law against the nobility and in favour of the peasants is a masterpiece. It must not be given time to work! Where is Demetrius?"

"He left yesterday, to march against Totila. You were asleep, and the physician would not let us wake you."

"Totila king, and you let me sleep? Don't you know that flaxen head is the genius of the Gothic nation? Demetrius is trying to gather the laurels for himself. How strong is he?"

"More than double the Gothic strength, twelve thousand against their five thousand."

"Demetrius is doomed! Go and get your horses! Arm everyone who can carry a spear, and leave only the wounded on the walls. That flame Totila has to be extinguished in its first flicker, or no ocean of blood will put it out later. My arms! My horse!"

"I have never seen the Prefect like this before," Lucius Licinius said to the Greek physician. "Is it the fever? He grew pale."

"He has no fever."

"Then I do not understand it. It certainly cannot be fear. Syphax, let us follow him."

Relentlessly Cethegus drove his men onwards, so much so that only a small part of the cavalry was able to keep pace with his headlong progress on Pluto, his tireless black stallion. A considerable distance behind him came Marcus Licinius and Massurius with the Isaurian mercenaries, and Balbus with the hastily armed citizens of Ravenna. Cethegus had indeed left only old men and children with the wounded in Ravenna.

At last the Prefect made contact with the rearguard of the Byzantine army. Totila was moving south from Tarvisium in the direction of Ravenna. Hordes of armed Italians from the provinces of Liguria, Venetia and Aemilia joined him, encouraged by his promise of new hope and a better future. They asked to be permitted to fight the first battle against the Byzantines with him.

"No," Totila had replied, "make your final decision after the battle. We Goths will fight alone. If we win, then you may join us. But if we lose, then at least you will not suffer Byzantium's revenge. Wait!"

When news of such a high-minded attitude spread, it served to attract further masses of Italians to the Gothic flag.

But Totila's army grew stronger by the hour as it marched, due to Gothic soldiers who joined it. Alone or in small groups they had either escaped their captors or were emerging from their hiding places, now that they heard about the treachery which had been committed against King Witigis, and that the war had been re-kindled under a new king.

Both Totila and Demetrius were urging their armies to utmost speed, the former because he wanted to exploit the fresh enthusiasm of his men before it could cool, and the latter driven by the ambition to defeat the Goths alone. It was not long before the two armies clashed. It was at Pons Padi, and the battle is known as the battle of the Padus Bridge.

The Byzantines stood in the plain; the river, which they had so far crossed only with half their infantry, lay behind them. Suddenly the Goths appeared on the heights in the northwest.

The Byzantines were blinded by the setting sun.

Totila looked over the enemy position from the top of the hill, close to the enemy. "Victory is mine!" he cried, drew his sword and charged down on the enemy with his cavalry as a falcon swoops on his prey.

Soon after sunset Cethegus reached the last deserted camp of the Byzantines with his cavalry. Already the first fugitives were running toward him: "Turn your horse, Prefect," the first rider called out, recognising him, "and save yourself! Totila is upon us! He cut through helmet and head of Artabazes with his own sword, and he was the bravest of the Armenian commanders."

And the fugitives raced on without stopping.

"A god from heaven is leading those Barbarians!" cried a second one. "All is lost! The general has been taken prisoner! Everyone is in full flight!"

"This King Totila is irresistible!" a third fugitive cried, and tried to get past the Prefect who was barring his way.

"Pass it on in hell!" Cethegus replied, and cut him down. "Forward, men, attack!"

But he took back the order almost as soon as he had uttered it.

Already the Byzantines were flooding toward him in mass, beaten and in full flight. The Prefect saw that it was impossible to halt the flight of thousands with only his handful of men, and for a time he stood and watched, undecided.

Already the first Gothic pursuers became visible in the distance. And then Vitalius reached him, one of Demetrius's commanders, himself also wounded: "Oh friend," he called out to the Prefect. "There is no holding this! This pursuit will go on right to Ravenna!"

"I believe you," Cethegus replied, "they are more likely to sweep away my own men with them too than stand and fight."

"And yet only half the victors are pursuing us, under Teias and Hildebrand. The king himself turned away even as he was still on the battlefield. I saw him turn away, to the southwest."

"Where to?" Cethegus asked attentively, "say that again! In which direction?"

"To the southwest!"

"He is heading for Rome!" Cethegus cried, and pulled his horse around with such ferocity that the stallion reared high in the air. "Follow me, to the coast!"

"And the defeated army? Without a leader?" cried Lucius Licinius. "Look at them, how they are fleeing!"

"Let them flee! Ravenna is secure! It will hold out. Didn't you hear? The Goths want Rome! We must get there before him, we must! Follow me! To the coast, the way by sea is open! To Rome!"

Chapter 3

The valley through which the Passara runs from the north into the Athesis, which in turn flows from the west to the southeast, is famed far and wide for its loveliness. Far away in the distance the Meridola, leaning forward in the distance on the right bank of the Athesis, is like a figure yearning for the lovely southern land. Here, upstream from the point where the Passara enters, lay the Roman settlement of Mansio Majae. The castle Teriolis lay a little further upstream, on a commanding rock. Today the town is called Meran, and the castle gave its name to the county of Tirol. The name Mansio Majae lives on in the village of Mais.

But in those days the castle of Teriolis was occupied by a Gothic garrison, as was the case with all the mountain strongholds on the Athesis, the Isarcus and the Oenus. They were a line of defence against thieving hordes of Suevi, Allemanni and Markomanni or Bajuvari, who lived in Raetia, on the Licus and the lower Oenus. Quite apart from the garrisons a number of Ostrogothic families had settled here in the fertile valley, which was not too hostile and which had ample feed for their flocks and soil to till.

Even today the peasants of this region are a handsome lot, with a grave beauty about them which sets them apart from their neighbours. They are much more refined than the descendants of the Bajuvari on the Inn, the Lech and the Isar, and even today they tend to say little. Their speech and legend also suggest that perhaps a few displaced Goths lived on here, and that these people are their descendants. The legend of the Amalungs and Dietrich von Bern and the Rosengarten still live on here in place names and in folklore.

On the left bank of the Athesis, on one of the highest mountains, the Goth Iffa had once settled, and his descendants still lived there. The mountain is known to this day as the Iffinger Mountain.

Halfway up the southern slope of the mountain a simple village had been built. Gothic immigrants had already found other cultures in existence here, and the traditional alpine house, which had already been found by Drusus, had undergone no change during Roman times, being ideally suited to the climate. The Romans had built their villas in the valleys, and their watchtowers on the hilltops.

The almost entirely Romanised people of the Etsch Valley had calmly remained on their properties after the Gothic invasion from the east. In fact the Goths had not invaded here, but further to the east from the direction of the Save, across the Isonzo River. This was where the Goths had forced their way into the peninsula, and it was only after Ravenna and Odoacer had fallen that Theodoric had despatched his hordes, into northern Italy and the Etsch Valley as well, with the aim of peaceful occupation.

And in this way Iffa, too, had managed to share the mountain, which still bore its ancient name, with the Roman settlers he had found there already established. As had been the case everywhere else the Goths had taken over one third of the fields, forests, houses, stock and slaves from their Roman hosts. Over the years however the Roman *hospes* found this enforced closeness to the Barbarians somewhat uncomfortable. He therefore sold the remainder of his property to Iffa the Goth for thirty pairs of cattle, which the Goths had brought with them from Pannonia, and which they knew how to breed expertly. The Roman then moved further south, where the population was predominantly Roman.

And so the Iffinger Mountain became entirely Germanic. The new master sold the few remaining Roman slaves, and replaced them with field hands and maids of Germanic descent, mainly captured Gepidae. The present owner was called Iffa, like his ancestor. He lived alone, a silver-haired old man, his wife, brother and a daughter-in-law having been killed by an avalanche some years before. A son, a younger brother and his son had followed the call to arms of King Witigis, and had not returned from the siege of Rome. And so only his two grandchildren remained, the son and daughter of the son who had fallen before Rome.

The sun had set gloriously behind the mountain, which formed the border of the Etsch Valley in the west. A warm, golden glow lay over the mountain, like a dark red wine.

Walking up the gentle slope, her hand before her eyes to shield them against the setting sun, was a child – or was she already a young girl? She was driving a herd of sheep before her, up the slope, on top of which the stables were situated near the house.

She gave her charges plenty of time to dally along the way, so that they could pick and choose among the alpine grasses which grew there, and using the hazel rod she was carrying in place of a shepherd's staff she beat the time to a simple little song she was softly singing to herself.

She was silent now, and with her little head leaning forward she peered into the deep and narrow chasm to her left, which the fast flowing stream had cut into the hillside. Now, in summer, the stream was only half full, and on its other side the cliffs rose steeply skywards.

"Where could he be?" she asked. "Usually his goats are already climbing down the slope by the time the sun has turned to gold. If he does not come soon my flowers will have wilted."

She sat down on a stone block by the wayside, letting the sheep go on grazing, and placed the hazel rod beside her. Then she let down her apron of sheepskin, which she had been holding hitched up, and masses of the loveliest alpine flowers rained down on the meadow at her feet. She started to make a garland.

"The blue ones suit his brown hair the best," she said to herself, working away busily. "I get tired much more easily when I have to herd my sheep alone than I do when he is with me, even though we climb much higher when we are together. I'd like to know why that is. Oh how my bare feet burn! I suppose I could climb down to the little creek to cool them off. And then I would see him straight away as he comes down the slope on the other side. The sun is not burning any more."

With that she removed her hat, and as she did so her white blonde hair was revealed, tied at the back of her head with a red ribbon. Now it flooded like a sea of sunlight over her neck and back. She was wearing only a simple woollen shift reaching just below her knees, held together by a leather belt.

She tested the size of the garland she was making on her own head. "Of course," she said, "his head is larger! I'd better add these alpine roses!" And now she joined the two ends of the garland together, jumped to her feet and shook the remaining flowers from her apron. Then, the garland in her hand, she started climbing down the steep slope, at the foot of which the little stream raced past the rocks.

"No, you stay here and wait! You too, Snowdrop! I will be back in no time." And she drove back the lambs which tried to follow her, and who stood bleating after their mistress.

The agile girl climbed quickly down the slope with practised ease, holding on to a shrub one moment, and jumping from stone to stone the next.

At one point the rock crumbled under her foot, and as she was about to follow the fragments down the slope she suddenly heard a sharp, threatening hissing sound. And before she could turn away a large copper coloured snake, probably disturbed in its sleep, was rearing up at her. The child took fright, her knees failed her, and she cried out at the top of her voice: "Adalgoth, help! Help!"

Her cry for help was immediately answered by the bright shout of "Alaric! Alaric!," like a battle cry.

The shrubbery to her left crackled, stones hurtled down the hill, and a moment later a slender lad stood between the frightened girl and the viper. He was wearing a shaggy wolf skin, and he hurled his sturdy staff like a spear. He did this so skilfully that an instant later the staff's iron tip had pierced the viper's head and pinned it to the ground. Its long body wound itself around the shaft in death throes.

"Gotho, are you all right?"

"Thanks to you, my ever-reliable hero!"

"Then let me say the snake charm while the viper still twitches; that will banish its relatives from this vicinity for three hours."

He raised the first three fingers of his right hand, as if swearing an oath, and recited the ancient rhyme:

"Wait, you wolf worm! Twitch and writhe, viper!
Bite the dust with your poison venom;
Men and maidens you shall not harm:
Down, worthless worm, poisonous vermin,
into the night with you. High above the heads
of scaly snakes walk the shining Gothic people."

Chapter 4

When he had finished reciting and bent down to inspect the dead snake, the girl whom he had saved quickly pressed her garland on his short, curly brown hair.

"Hail, hero and helper! Look, your victory garland had already been made for you. How the crown suits you!" And she clapped her hands in joyful admiration.

"Your foot is bleeding!" he said, concerned, "let me suck out the wound – if that poison worm has bitten you…"

"It was only a sharp stone. Would you rather die yourself?"

"For you, Gotho, willingly! But the poison would be harmless in my mouth. Let me wash the wound anyway; I still have vinegar and water in my leather flask here. And then I will dress it for you with sage."

Gently he pressed her down onto the stone once more, knelt before her and took her bare foot in his hand. He washed it with the mixture from his flask, and then jumped to his feet and went looking for the necessary herbs. In a moment he was back, and dressed the wound with the herbs he had found, tying them securely with a strip of leather which he had removed from his own foot.

"How good you are!" she said, stroking his hair.

"Now let me carry you – only to the top of the slope!" he begged, "I like holding you in my arms so much."

"You will do nothing of the sort!" she laughed, jumping up. "I am not a wounded lamb! Look how I can run. But where are your goats?"

"There they come, out of the juniper bushes. I'll call them!" He placed the horn to his lips and blew, and he waved his staff above his head in a circle. In a moment the sturdy goats were with him – they did not want to be punished! And now, leaving a thin trail of salt from his pocket behind him for the animals to lick as they followed him, he walked up the slope with his arm gently around the girl's neck.

"Tell me, dear one," she said when they had reached the top and started gathering the sheep together, "why did you attack the dragon today with that cry 'Alaric!' again? It was the same the other day when you drove off that eagle, which already had Snowdrop in its claws."

"It is my battle cry!"

"Who taught it to you?"

"Our grandfather, the first time he took me wolf hunting; the time I killed the wolf whose skin I am wearing now. When I cried: 'Iffa! Iffa!' when we had the wolf cornered and I was about to attack him with my sword, just as I heard him do it, grandfather said to me: 'You must not shout 'Iffa!' like I do, Adalgoth. When you go to attack another warrior or a wild animal you must shout: 'Alaric!' and that will bring you victory."

"But none of our ancestors or relatives are called that, brother, and we know them all."

By now they had reached the stables, driven the animals inside, and sat down on a wooden bench outside the front door of the house.

"There is," the girl recited in thought, "our father Iffamer, our uncle Warga, whom the mountain killed, grandfather Iffa, our other uncle Iffamuth, his son and our cousin Iffaswinth, great grandfather Iffaric, and then Iffa again, but no Alaric."

"And yet, you know, it is almost like a dream, of the time when I first started running around the mountain here as a small boy, before the great avalanche that killed uncle Warga. Somehow it seems to me as if I used to hear that name a lot more. And anyway, I like it. Grandfather told me about a great heroic king of that name, who was the first among all the heroes to conquer the fortress Roma, you know, the city from which our father and uncle Iffamuth did not come back. And King Alaric died when he was young, like Siegfried the dragon slayer and Baldur, the heathen god. His grave is in a deep river. There he lies, under a golden shield among his treasures, and tall reeds surround him. And now there is another king, by the name of Totila, so the troops which have just relieved the garrison at Teriolis tell me. They say he is like Alaric and Siegfried and the bright sun god all in one. And grandfather said that I am also to become a warrior. One day I am to go down to join King Totila and charge among the enemy with the cry: 'Alaric! Alaric!' Anyway, for some time now I have been growing tired of climbing around this mountain and herding goats, where there is no enemy to be fought except an occasional wolf, or perhaps a bear who steals the grapes and the honeycombs. And you all praise the way I play the harp and my singing. But I feel that I will never amount to very much up here, and that there is nothing more our old grandfather can teach me. And I want to sing songs much more proud than those I sing now, songs of King Totila's victories. The other day I gave old Hunibad, whom the king sent up here to recuperate from his wounds, the finest deer I have ever bagged, just so that he would tell me the story of the Padus Bridge battle for the third time. I love hearing him talk about the way in which King Totila is even defeating the dark king of hell, the dreadful Cethegus. I have already composed a song about it, to be accompanied by the harp, which starts like this:

"'Tremble and flinch, stony Cethegus:
Your cunning won't help you. Teias the courageous
will shatter your pride: And as bright as sunlight,
as the morning sun emerges out of night and darkness,
the shining one of the heavenly master above:
the shining knight, our brave new king.'

"But that is as far as it goes. And I cannot go on composing songs and poems by myself. I need a knowledgeable teacher, both of words and the harp. I also want to finish an incomplete song about the spear-wielding Teias, whom they call the Black Count, and who is said to be a wonderful harpist. And I tell you this: I would have left long ago, even without asking grandfather's permission – he keeps saying I am still too young – if there was not the one thing holding me here." And he jumped hastily to his feet.

"And what is that, brother?" Gotho asked innocently, remaining seated.

"If you don't know that then I cannot tell you," he replied, almost angrily. "I must go now and make some new arrowheads over in the workshop. Just give me one more kiss, dear little sister, there! And let me give you one on each eye! And one for your fair hair! Farewell now, until suppertime." And he hurried away to a nearby building; a grinding stone and various tools and implements could be seen outside the door.

Gotho rested her cheek on her hand, looking thoughtfully at the ground before her, and then she said aloud: "I cannot guess what he is trying to say. He would take me with him of course. We could not live without one another." With a little sigh she stood up and walked toward the meadow beside the house, to see to the linen which she had bleaching there.

But inside the house, behind an open window, old Iffa had been sitting and listening, and he had heard every word that had been said. "That will no longer do!" he said to himself, vigorously rubbing his head. "I have never had the heart to separate the two children. After all, they were only children! I have always waited just a little bit longer. And now I have waited almost a little too long. You will have to go, young Adalgoth!" And he walked out of the house and over to the workshop.

There he found the lad busily at work. He had a good fire going, blowing into it vigorously to keep it hot, and he was holding arrowheads in the fire to make them hot enough and soft enough to be worked. Then he would pick out one arrowhead with the tongs, place it on the anvil and hammer out the point and the barb at the same time.

As his grandfather entered he merely nodded to him, without pausing in his work. He was beating away at the anvil with such vigour that the sparks were flying. "Well," the old man thought to himself, "right now his mind is only on iron."

But suddenly the young blacksmith concluded his work with one last blow from the hammer, threw it into a corner, wiped his hot forehead and, turning to Iffa, he said: "Grandfather, where do people come from?"

"Jesus, Wotan and holy Mary!" the old man cried, taking a step backwards in shocked surprise, "what makes you ask that, my lad?"

"The thought just occurred to me. What I mean is, where did the first men come from, the very first? Tall Hermegisel over in Teriolis came from Verona, where he ran away from the Arian church. He can read and write, and he says that the Christian God made man out of clay in a garden, and as he slept he took one of his ribs and from that he made a woman. Surely that's laughable, because no matter how long the rib was, nobody could make a whole girl out of it, even a very tiny girl."

"Well, I don't believe it either!" the old man confessed thoughtfully. "It's difficult to imagine. And I remember, my father told me one evening by the fire that the first men grew on trees. And old Hildebrand, who was his friend although he was a good deal older, and who had visited us during a foray against the wild Bajuvari, was sitting next to him. It was still early in the year and very cold. And Hildebrand said that it was true about the trees, but that men did not grow on them. He said that two heathen gods – Hermegisel calls them 'demons' – once found two trees lying by the seashore, an ash and an alder, and from them he made a man and a woman. There used to be an old song about it too. Hildebrand still knew a few words from it, but my father had no longer been taught the song."

"That I might be more willing to believe! But in any case, were there only a very few people in the beginning?"

"Certainly!"

"And there was only one family at the beginning?"

"Yes, that's right."

"Then I'll tell you something, grandfather. If that was so, then either mankind had to die out, or, since they have not died out – you see what I am getting at – in the beginning brothers and sisters must have often married until there were several families."

"Adalgoth, you are talking nonsense."

"Not at all. What I am trying to say is this: if it could happen then it can still happen now. And I want my sister Gotho for my wife!"

The old man jumped to his feet and tried to hold his hand in front of his grandson's mouth.

But the youth avoided him: "I already know what you are going to say. Up here I suppose the priests of Tridentum would soon find out about it, and then the King's Count. But I could take her with me to a far away country, where nobody knew us. And she would come with me, that I know."

"So you have already established that, have you?"

"Yes, I know she would, I know for certain."

"But here is something you don't know yet," the old man said now, seriously and very firmly: "This night will be the last night you will spend up here on the Iffinger Mountain. Go Adalgoth, I now command you as your grandfather and your guardian. You have a duty of honour to fulfil, the duty of revenge, at King Totila's court and in his army. It is a holy mission from your uncle Warga, who lies buried under the mountain. It is something you must do for – for your ancestor. You are now old enough and strong enough to do it.

"At first light tomorrow you will leave for the south, to Italy, where King Totila punishes injustice, helps the just to victory, and fights the evildoer Cethegus. Come with me to my room. I have something there to give you from your uncle Warga, and I have many words of advice to give you to help you along your way, words of advice and words of revenge. Say nothing to Gotho, because if you do you will only make it difficult for her too. If you follow my advice and that of your uncle, then you will become a strong and worthy warrior at the court of King Totila. Then, and only then, you and Gotho will see one another again."

Very serious now, and suddenly pale, the young Goth followed his grandfather into the house, where they talked softly for a long time. At suppertime Adalgoth was missing. He let his sister know through his grandfather that he was more tired than usual, and had gone to bed early.

But that night, while she slept, he tiptoed into her room. The moon was shining on her angelic face, and he stopped on the threshold, merely holding out his right arm to her.

"I will see you again," he said very quietly, "my Gotho!"

Shortly after that he walked outside the simple alpine house. The stars had just begun to fade, and the night was fresh and clear. He looked up at the sky, and as he did so he saw a falling star in the south. At that the youth raised his staff in his right hand and said: "The stars call me to the south. Now watch out, evildoer Cethegus!"

Chapter 5

After the battle of the Padus Bridge the Prefect had sent messengers to the troops following him, first to his mercenaries and then to the slower Ravenna citizens, ordering them to return to that city. The fleeing troops of Demetrius were left to their fate. Totila had captured every flag and standard of the twelve thousand men, "something which has never before happened to Romans" as Procopius was to write angrily.

Cethegus himself, with only a few men, hurried diagonally across Aemilia to Italy's west coast, which he reached near Populonium. There he boarded a fast warship and, aided by a strong northwesterly wind, he sailed for Rome's harbour of Portus. The wind, he said, had been sent by all the gods of Latium.

He would no longer have been able to force his way through by travelling overland, because after the Padus Bridge victory the whole of Tuscany went over to the Goths; the open country went over completely, as did all those cities which were not restrained from doing so by strong Byzantine garrisons.

At Nucella, a day's march from Florence, the king defeated another strong Byzantine army under eleven leaders, who were all at cross purposes one with the other. They had gathered together the Imperial garrisons from the various towns and cities in Tuscany in order to halt the king's progress. Justinus, the commander-in-chief, managed to escape to Florence only with great difficulty. The king treated his numerous prisoners with such kindness that many of them, both Italians and Imperial mercenaries, soon took up service under the Gothic flag. And by this time all the roads of central Italy were crowded with Goths newly rushing to arms, and by countless peasants who, under Gothic leadership, now followed Totila's march to Rome.

Cethegus made preparations for the defence of Rome as soon as he had arrived in that city. After his second victory at Nucella Totila was now approaching with lightning speed, with virtually the only thing slowing his progress being the enthusiastic reception he received from cities and fortresses along the way. Almost all of them opened their gates to him, and competed with one another in welcoming him. Those few fortresses which did resist, being held by strong Imperial garrisons, were simply surrounded by small forces which Totila formed out of Italian volunteers, with a core of a few Gothic troops.

Totila was able to do this as his might was growing rapidly during his march on Rome, due to a steady influx into his ranks of both Goths and Italians, in large and small numbers.

Italian peasants, whom he had declared free, rushed to his flag in their thousands. In small towns the citizens rose against their Byzantine garrisons, disarming them or forcing them to leave. Even some of Belisarius's mercenaries, who had received no pay from Byzantium for months since the departure of Belisarius, were now offering their services to the Goths.

And so it was a very considerable army of Goths and Italians which Totila led before the gates of Rome, a few days after the Prefect's arrival there.

Soon afterwards the brave Woelsung Duke Guntharis, Wisand the *bandalarius*, Count Markja and old Count Grippa were received into the Gothic camp with loud cheering. Totila had managed to arrange their release from Ravenna by exchanging them for the Imperial commander-in-chief and several of his generals. All had been taken prisoner at the Padus Bridge, and the exchange had been negotiated with Constantinus and John, who were now commanding Ravenna.

Cethegus now faced the almost insurmountable problem of trying adequately to man his magnificent fortifications. Not only did he lack the army of Belisarius, but also the major portion of his own mercenaries, who were arriving only gradually and in small numbers by ship from Ravenna. In order to man the entire circumference of Rome even sparsely, Cethegus found it necessary to not only impose extraordinarily arduous duty and very long watches on his legionaries, but also to increase their number by forcible means. From sixteen-year-old boys to sixty-year-old men he called "all the sons of Romulus, Camillus and Caesar" to arms, "to defend the heritage of our forefathers against the Barbarians."

But his proclamation was barely read, and brought him only a trickle of volunteers. At the same time he had to stand idly by and observe how the Gothic king's manifest, which was thrown over the wall in many places every night, was circulated everywhere and eagerly read by large groups of people in Rome. He therefore issued an order that anyone caught picking up, posting, reading or circulating the manifest would be punished by confiscation of his property or enslavement. But it continued to be read just the same, and his list of volunteers, sent to every part of the city, remained almost empty.

He therefore had his Isaurians enter every house, and he had them drag young boys and old men forcibly onto the walls. Before long he was more feared, and indeed hated, than he was loved. Only his iron will and discipline, coupled with the gradual arrival of his Isaurians, were able to hold the dissatisfaction of the Romans in check.

But in the Gothic camp one piece of good news followed the next.

Teias and Hildebrand had pursued the fleeing Byzantines right to the gates of Ravenna, which were defended by Demetrius and Bloody John following their release by the Goths. The port of Classis was defended by Constantinus against Hildebrand, who had captured Ariminum in passing. Its population had disarmed the Armenian mercenaries of Artasires and opened the gates to the Goths. On the other hand Teias defeated the brave Byzantininan commander Verus, who had tried to prevent his crossing of the Santernus with handpicked Pisidian and Silesian mercenaries, and killed him in a duel. Teias then marched right through northern Italy, Totila's proclamation in one hand and his sword in the other. In a few weeks every city and fortress with the sole exception of Mediolanum had either been captured or had voluntarily gone over to the Goths.

Totila, with the experience of the first siege of Rome, did not want to subject his army to the task of storming the Prefect's terrible walls, and moreover he did not want to expose his future capital to the inevitable destruction which that would bring. One day he called out to Duke Guntharis: "I will enter Rome on wooden bridges, and with wings of linen!" He then left Guntharis in charge of the siege and, with his entire cavalry, he hurried to Naples. There, in the port, lay a weakly manned Imperial fleet.

Totila's march along the Via Appia through southern Italy was more like a triumphal procession than an act of war. Those areas which had suffered the worst under the yoke of Byzantium's rule were now the most eager to greet the Goths as liberators.

The young girls of Terracina received the handsome Gothic king, decked out with flowers.

The people of Minturnae received him by driving a gilded carriage to meet him, then lifting him from his horse and into the carriage and driving it into their city amid cheering and rejoicing.

"Look at him!" was the cry in the streets of Casilinum, an old cult city dedicated to the goddess Diana, "Phoebus Apollo has come down from Mount Olympus and he now enters his sister's city in peace."

And the citizens of Capua begged him to strike the first coins of his reign in their currency with the inscription: "*Capua revindicata.*"

And so it went on to Naples, along the same road he had once covered in nocturnal haste as a wounded fugitive. The Armenian mercenaries in the city, a brave but small force, were commanded by the Arsacidian Phaza. The latter did not dare trust the population in the event of a siege, and he therefore opted to lead his lancers and the armed citizens of Naples to meet the king in open battle.

And there, before the battle began, a man on a white horse rode out from the Gothic lines, removed his helmet from his head and cried: "Have you forgotten me, men of Naples? I am Totila! You loved me once, when I was naval commander of your city, and now you will bless me as your king. Do you remember how I helped your women and children to flee from Belisarius's Huns in my ships? Let me tell you, those same wives and daughters of yours are once again in my hands, as my prisoners. You took them to the fortress Cumae to protect them from the Byzantines, and perhaps also from me. Now hear this: Cumae has surrendered to me, and all those who fled there are in my power!

"I have been advised to use them as hostages, and by so doing to force you and other cities to surrender. But that goes against my nature. I let them all go free – I had the wives of Roman senators conducted to Rome. Men of Naples, your wives and children are now in my camp, not as my hostages or my prisoners, but as my guests. Look over there: there they are, streaming out of my tents. Open your arms to receive them – they are free!

"Do you now want to fight against me? I cannot believe it! Which of you will be the first to aim at this breast?" And he opened his white cloak wide.

"Hail King Totila, the benevolent!" was the resounding reply. And the hot-blooded people of Naples threw down their arms, poured towards the Goths, joyously greeted their wives and children and kissed the hem of the young king's gown, and even his feet.

The leader of the mercenaries rode over to the king: "My lancers are surrounded and too few to fight against you alone. Here, oh king, take my sword. I am your prisoner."

"Not so, brave Phaza! You are unconquered, and therefore you are not a prisoner. You are free to go where you like, with your men."

"I am conquered and taken prisoner by the nobility in your heart and the glow in your eyes. Please permit that we henceforth fight under your banner." And thus Totila had gained a unit of excellent soldiers, who were to hold out loyally by his side from then on.

He entered Naples through the Porta Nolana under a rain of flowers. Aratius, who commanded the fleet in the port, tried to raise anchor with his warships. But even before he could do so the crews of countless merchant ships in the port, together with old admirers and grateful protégés of Totila, had overpowered the crews of the warships and captured the leaders.

And so the Gothic king had captured a fleet along with the third city in the Empire without bloodshed.

But that evening he stole away quietly from the celebration feast which the joyful city had prepared for him. Gothic guards looked on in astonishment as their king, in the still of the night and without followers, disappeared beside an old olive tree growing by a collapsed tower near the Porta Capuana.

On the following morning a proclamation was made by King Totila to the effect that henceforth all Jewish women and girls in Naples would be exempt from the poll tax which had been imposed on them until that time. Furthermore, as they were not permitted for other reasons to wear jewellery in public, they would henceforth be permitted to wear a golden heart on their bosom as a sign of honour.

And in the little garden, where the stone cross and a gravestone had become completely covered by weeds, a memorial stone of black marble was soon erected with the inscription; "Miriam Valeria."

And there was not one person in Naples who could understand what those words meant.

Chapter 6

And now envoys started to stream into Naples from all sides, in order to invite the Gothic king to enter their own walls as liberator. They came from Campania and Samnium, Bruttia and Lucania, Apulia and Calabria. Even the important and powerful Beneventum surrendered voluntarily, as did the neighbouring fortresses of Asculum, Canusia and Acheruntia. And there were thousands of instances in these areas where the local serfs were instructed to take over the estates of their former masters, who had fled to Rome or to Byzantium. Apart from Rome and Ravenna, of the major cities only Florence under Justinus, Spoletum under Bonus and Herodianus, and Perusia under the Hun Uldugant, were still held by the Byzantines.

Within a few days the king, who was an expert in naval matters, had managed to man his fleet with the help of thousands of Italians, who had come to join him from all parts of southern Italy. And so he now led his fleet out of the harbour, under full sail and richly decorated with flags, while his cavalry proceeded northwards overland on the Via Appia.

The goal of both ships and horses was, of course, Rome. In the meantime Teias had captured the entire area between Ravenna and the Tiber, the fortresses of Petra and Caesena having surrendered without a blow being struck. Teias had also accepted the surrender of Aemilia, the whole of Tuscany and furthermore he had won control of the Via Flaminia. He was now marching on Rome along that road with a third Gothic army.

The Prefect recognised that the situation he now faced was deadly serious, and he resolved to defend himself fiercely, with the determination of a dragon trapped in his own lair. He looked with pride at his great walls and battlements, his colossal achievement, and to his companions, who were troubled by the approaching Goths, he said with apparent confidence:

"Rest easy! They shall shatter against these walls a second time."

But in his own mind he was not nearly as confident as his oratory and his outward demeanour suggested. It was not as though he had any regrets about his past deeds, or that he thought his ambition unattainable. But the fact was that his great work, which after repeated disappointments and setbacks he had brought so close to a successful conclusion, seemed as far from fulfilment as ever following the rise of Totila. And that was something which had its effect even on the iron strength of a Cethegus. "Water will in the end wear through stone!" he replied when Lucius Licinius asked on one occasion why he looked so gloomy. "And also, I cannot sleep like I used to."

"Since when is that?"

"Since – since Totila! That blond boy has robbed me of my slumber!"

No matter how secure and superior the Prefect had always felt in the past, no matter who had been his enemy, the shining and open character of this youth, together with his easy successes, had aroused in him a fierce and almost passionate hatred. There were now times when even his icy calm would melt for a moment of heated passion, while Totila opposed him, confident of victory, almost as if for him there could be no such thing as failure.

"He is lucky, that milksop!" Cethegus snarled when he heard of the effortless way in which Naples had been captured. "He is as lucky as Achilles and Alexander. But fortunately they never grow old, these eternal youths. The soft gold of their souls grows brittle, while we lumps of solid bronze are more durable. I have seen this dreamer's laurels and roses, and it seems to me that I am soon to see his cypresses also. It cannot be that I am to be defeated by that boy, who is almost like a girl. Luck has carried him this high in a very short time, and he will fall just as quickly and just as far. But will his luck last long enough to carry him over the walls of my Rome? Fly away, young Icarus, fly effortlessly in the warm sunshine! But I will be waiting when the sun's treacherous kiss melts the wax in your daring wings, and you will perish at my feet like a falling star."

But it did not look as if this was about to happen soon.

Eagerly Cethegus awaited the arrival of a powerful fleet from Ravenna, which was to bring him the remainder of his mercenaries together with every man who could be spared from his legionaries and from the army of Demetrius, as well as ample provisions. Once these reinforcements arrived he would be able to grant the grumbling Romans some relief from their endless tours of duty on the walls. The citizens of Rome were becoming ever more bitter and threatening, and for weeks he had been able to console them with the promise of that fleet. At long last a fast scout ship sailing in advance of the main fleet reported that the main body was now passing Ostia. Cethegus had the news spread by heralds through the streets to the sound of tubas, and he announced that on the next Ides of October eight thousand citizens would be released from their duty on the walls to return to their homes. In addition he had double wine rations distributed on the walls.

On the *ides* of October a heavy fog covered both Ostia and the sea. On the following day a small sailing boat flew into Portus, the harbour of Rome, from Ostia. Its trembling crew, legionaries from Ravenna, reported that King Totila had attacked the triremes with the fleet from Naples under cover of thick fog. Of the eighty ships he had burnt or sunk twenty, and the other sixty had been captured together with their crews and their cargoes.

At first Cethegus refused to believe it. He rushed aboard his own fast galley, *Sagitta*, and raced down the Tiber. But he only managed with great difficulty to escape the king's ships, which were already blocking the harbour of Portus, and were now sending small warships upstream along the Tiber.

The Prefect now had a double barrier constructed across the river with great urgency. The first barrier was made of logs and the second, an arrow-shot further upstream, out of iron chains, as Belisarius had done before. The space between the two barriers was filled with a large number of small boats.

The loss of the fleet had dealt Cethegus a fearful blow, and he felt it intensely. For one thing his eagerly awaited reinforcements had fallen into enemy hands, so that instead of being able to offer the Romans relief he now had to place even greater burdens on them, because the river now also had to be defended against never-ending attempts by Gothic ships to break through. Worst of all Cethegus could now feel that most dreadful of all enemies creep ever closer. That enemy was hunger.

The sea road by which he, like Belisarius before him, had brought provisions aplenty into the blockaded city was now closed to him. Italy did not possess a third fleet, and the two fleets from Ravenna and from Naples were now blockading Rome under the Gothic flag.

Worse was to come. The last mounted scout whom Marcus Licinius had sent reconnoitring and foraging along the Via Flaminia came racing back utterly terrified, and reported that a powerful Gothic army was approaching in forced marches. Its leader was the terrible Teias, and his vanguard was already at Reata. The next day Rome was surrounded to the north as well, the last side which had still been open, and had only her own citizens to defend her. And those citizens were weak, no matter how strong the Prefect's walls might be. For weeks and even months their courage and their spirits crumbled, and yet the iron will of Cethegus held them together.

Already it was becoming apparent that the city must ultimately fall, not by storm but from hunger. And then a totally unexpected event occurred, which revived the hopes of the beleaguered Romans afresh, and which was to put the genius and the luck of the young Gothic king to his hardest test thus far.

In the theatre of war there appeared once more – Belisarius.

Chapter 7

Soon news of disaster after disaster started to arrive in the golden palace of the Caesars in Byzantium, the defeats at the Padus Bridge and at Mucella, the renewed siege of Rome and the loss of Naples along with most of Italy. Suddenly the emperor was woken from his dreams with a terrible start.

These events made it easy for friends of Belisarius to put forward the argument that all these failures had been caused by the recall of that hero. It was clear to all that, as long as Belisarius was in Italy, victory followed on victory, and as soon as he turned his back defeat followed defeat. Even the Byzantine generals in Italy now openly admitted that they could not take Belisarius's place. Demetrius wrote from Ravenna: "I cannot hold Totila in a pitched battle, and in fact I can only barely hold this powerful fortress in the swamps. Naples has fallen, and Rome could fall any day. Send us back the lion of a man whom we were vain enough to think we could replace; send us the conqueror of the Vandals and the Goths."

And Belisarius, although he had sworn never again to serve his ungrateful emperor, immediately forgot all his hurt and disappointment the moment Justinian smiled upon him once more. And then, after the fall of Naples, the emperor had embraced him and called him "my faithful sword". He claimed that he had never believed Belisarius capable of treason, but was merely unwilling to accept his almost royal status. At that neither Antonina nor Procopius could restrain Belisarius any longer.

But the emperor was reluctant to incur the cost of a second war in Italy whilst Narses was waging the war in Persia, successfully but at great cost. Ambition and greed competed within him, and this inner conflict might have lasted longer than the resistance of Rome or Ravenna if Germanus and Belisarius had not given him a convenient way out.

The noble-minded prince was driven by a longing to visit Ravenna and Matesuentha's grave, and to avenge her against the coarse Barbarians; Cethegus had told him that the enforced marriage to Witigis had destroyed her mind and caused her death. Belisarius, on the other hand, could not bear the thought that all his gains and victories in Italy were now being questioned. His detractors at court were asking if a nation had truly been defeated if it was able to rise again so magnificently within a year. He had given his word that he would destroy the Goths, and he intended to keep it. And thus Germanus and Belisarius suggested to the emperor that they would conquer Italy for him at their own expense. The prince offered his entire fortune to equip a fleet, and Belisarius was willing to contribute his newly reinforced bodyguards and lancers.

"That suggestion is exactly what Justinian's heart desires!" Procopius cried when Belisarius told him about it. "Not one solidus out of his own pocket, possibly a province with laurels for him and the Empire, destruction of the infidels to please Theodora as well as God and heaven, and all without any expense! You may rest assured that he will accept your offer and give you his paternal blessing. But apart from that he will give you nothing. I know that you are just as difficult to restrain as your horse Balan when the trumpet sounds, but I will not be a witness as you are shamefully defeated."

"Defeated? Why, you prophet of doom?"

"This time you will have the Goths as well as the Italians against you. But you were not able to defeat the former while you had the whole of Italy on your side."

But Belisarius scolded him for his cowardice, and put to sea with Germanus soon afterwards. The emperor did indeed give them nothing except his blessing and the big toe of St Mazaspes to aid their cause.

The Byzantines in Italy breathed a sigh of relief when they heard that an Imperial fleet had landed near Salona in Dalmatia. Even Cethegus, as he heard the news, sighed: "Better Belisarius in Rome than Totila!"

The Gothic king was also deeply concerned. Above all he had to establish the exact strength of Belisarius's army, and then make his decisions accordingly. He might even have to abandon the siege of Rome so that he could march against the mighty relief army.

Belisarius sailed from Salona to Pola, where he mustered his ships and his troops. There two men came to him who identified themselves as Heruli mercenaries, and who thus spoke Gothic as well as good Latin. They claimed to be envoys from Bonus, the commander in Spoletum. Luck had helped them through the Gothic lines, and now they pressed the general for speedy relief. They asked for precise information about his strength, the number of ships he had, cavalry and infantry, so that they could raise the morale in their beleaguered city with the good news. "My friends," said Belisarius, "you will have to exaggerate what you see in your report. The truth is that the emperor has left me entirely to my own resources." Belisarius then spent a day showing them his fleet, his camp and his army. Next morning they had vanished in the night.

They had been Thorismuth and Aligern, whom King Totila had sent out to gather the desired information, which they now brought him. That was a bad start, and the campaign which followed did nothing to enhance the reputation of the brave Byzantine general. He did, however, manage to reach the port of Ravenna with his fleet, and to bring that city fresh supplies.

But on the very day of their arrival Germanus suffered a recurrence of an old illness, and collapsed at the sarcophagus of Matesuentha, who had been laid to rest next to her young brother Athalaric. Germanus died, and in accordance with his last wishes he was laid to rest beside the beloved he had never won.

But in a small and insignificant niche in the vault there rested another heart, which had beaten loyally for Queen "Schoenhaar". Aspa, the Numidian, had not survived her mistress. "In my country," she had said, "servants of the fading sun goddess often willingly follow her into the flames. Aspa's sun goddess, the beautiful and shining one, has faded away too. Aspa will not live on alone in the cold, but she too will follow her sun." She had heaped flowers high in her mistress's death chamber, even higher than she had done in decorating the same room as a bridal chamber. She had then lit some unknown incense made from African rosin, and the aroma soon caused the other servants to leave. She alone remained all night. Next morning Syphax, who had been attracted by the old familiar smell, secretly made his way into the room. There he found complete silence, and at Matesuentha's feet her "antelope" also lay dead. "She died," he told Cethegus, "to follow her goddess. Now I have only you left on earth."

After Germanus had been buried Belisarius left Ravenna with his entire fleet. But his very first operation, an attempt to attack Pisaurium, was a failure with heavy losses.

In fact King Totila, who was now precisely informed of the small size of Belisarius's army, mounted some daring raiding parties, supported by ships and commanded by Wisand, and captured Firmum on the same strip of coast. The Byzantines Herodian and Bonus surrendered the important Spoletum to Count Grippa, after the thirty days in which they hoped Belisarius might relieve the city had expired. Assisium was commanded by a Gothic deserter named Sisifrid, who had joined Belisarius at the time of Witigis's misfortunes. The man knew what awaited him if he should fall into the hands of old Hildebrand, who was conducting the siege in person. Bitter hatred had influenced the old man to undertake this task rather than take part in the siege of Ravenna. The Goth defended his city stubbornly, but when the old armourer's stone axe smashed his helmet and his head during a sortie the citizens forced their Thracen garrison to surrender. The prisoners taken included many distinguished Italians and some members of the catacomb conspiracy, together with three hundred Illyrian cavalry and bodyguards from Belisarius's first army.

Placentia fell soon afterwards, the last city in the Aemilia, which its garrison of Saracens had still been holding for the emperor. It surrendered to Count Markja and his small siege army. In Bruttia the fortified town of Ruscia opened its gates, and the important port of Thurii surrendered to the brave Aligern.

Belisarius now despaired of reaching Rome by land and, hearing of the city's growing need, he tried without further delay to relieve Rome from the sea and to break the Gothic blockade of the harbour Portus. But at Hydrunt, as he was rounding the southern tip of Calabria, a violent storm scattered his ships, and he himself with a few triremes was blown south as far as Sicily. The major part of his fleet, which had sought refuge in a bay near Croton, was attacked by a Gothic fleet which the king had sent from Rome, and which had been waiting in ambush near Squillacium. The Byzantine ships were overpowered and captured, and that in turn meant a significant increase to Gothic naval strength. As we will soon see, this in turn placed the Gothic fleet in a position where it could seek out the Byzantines in their own islands and coastal towns.

Since that defeat the army of Belisarius, which had been inadequate from the start, was powerless. All the generalship and courage in the world could not make up for the lack of ships and men. The hope that Italy would join with the Imperial forces, as it had done in the first campaign, never materialised. And thus the campaign was a complete failure, as Procopius had predicted, and which he has recorded for posterity in most unflattering terms. The emperor did not even reply to pleas for reinforcements. And when Antonina repeatedly begged the empress to allow Belisarius to return, she replied sarcastically that one did not dare recall the hero a second time, thus interrupting his string of victories. And so it was that Belisarius came to spend a period of impotent inactivity and indecision near Sicily.

Chapter 8

Meanwhile in beleaguered Rome the situation had become critical, with the population suffering from exhaustion and need.

Hunger was decimating the guards on the walls, already insufficient in number. The Prefect tried his utmost, but in vain. Without success he tried all his old skills and tricks and every other means at his disposal, sometimes persuasion and at other times brutal force. He wasted his gold in vain, trying to obtain fresh provisions for the city, because the supply of grain which he had originally imported from Sicily and stored in the Capitol had been consumed almost to the last mouthful.

He promised incredible rewards to any ship which managed to break the king's blockade with fresh supplies, and to any mercenary who dared to sneak out through the enemy camp and back again with food. Gothic vigilance under Totila was just too good. In the beginning greed had tempted a few to try their luck at night. But when Count Teias had their heads thrown over the wall near the Porta Flaminia the following morning, even the greediest lost their desire for the Prefect's gold.

The cadavers of mules killed in the fighting were sold for high prices, and hungry women fought over the weeds and thistles growing on heaps of rubble. Hunger had long taught them to eat even that which was inedible. And the number of deserters who ran over to the Goths from the houses and over or through the walls could no longer be counted. Teias had wanted to drive them back into the city by a phalanx of spears, so as to force a surrender all the sooner. But Totila ordered that they should all be received and fed, the only condition being that they were to be carefully watched, to stop them dying of overeating whilst still suffering the extremes of hunger. Initially this had happened a number of times.

Cethegus now spent every night on the walls. At all hours he would personally inspect the guards, carrying a shield and spear, and here and there he would personally relieve a guard whose spear was threatening to fall from his grip out of tiredness or hunger. Certainly this personal example did have an effect for a while, reviving the more courageous defenders. The Licinius brothers, Piso and Salvius Julianus stood by the Prefect still, with unbowed admiration and enthusiasm, as did the blindly loyal Isaurians.

But this did not apply to every Roman, such as gastronomes the like of Balbus.

"No Piso," Balbus said seriously, "I can stand it no longer. It is just not human, or at least not for me. Holy Lucillus! Who would ever have believed it of me? Why, the other day I gave my last and biggest diamond for half a stone marten."

"I can remember the time," Piso replied, "when you had a cook put in irons for letting a crab boil a minute too long."

"Oh, crabs! By the Saviour's mercy! How can you say that word? How can you place such a vision before my eyes? I would give you the whole of my immortal soul for one claw, or even for the tail. And one can never sleep enough! If hunger does not wake me, then the horn does."

"Look at the Prefect there! For fourteen days he has not slept fourteen hours. He lies on his hard shield and drinks rainwater from his helmet."

"The Prefect! He has no need to eat. He lives on his pride as a bear lives on his fat, and he sucks on his gall. After all, there is nothing of him except sinews and muscles, pride and hatred! But I, oh I had accumulated such a lot of lovely white fat that the mice were starting to nibble at me in my sleep; they thought I was a Spanish ham! Did you hear the latest? Today they drove a whole herd of fat cattle from Apulia into the Gothic camp, favourites of gods and men alike!"

Early the following morning Piso and Salvius Julianus called on the Prefect early, waking him where he slept on the wall by the Porta Portuensis. It was close to the river barrier, the weakest spot in the defences. "Forgive me, I am disturbing you in a rare moment of sleep."

"I was not sleeping. I was awake. What have you to report, Tribune?"

"Last night Balbus fled from his post with twenty other citizens. They lowered themselves down the wall on ropes by the Porta Latina. The Apulian cattle were bellowing all night, and apparently they found that call irresistible."

But the smile disappeared from the young tribune's face when the Prefect fixed him with his stare: "A cross, thirty feet high, will be erected in front of Balbus's house on the Via Sacra. Any deserter who falls into our hands again will be nailed on it."

"But General, the emperor Constantinus abolished crucifixion in honour of the Saviour!" Salvius Julianus warned.

"And I am re-introducing it again, to honour Rome. I doubt that the emperor would have thought it possible that a Roman knight and tribune would betray the city of Rome for a piece of roast beef."

"But there is more to report. I am no longer able to man the tower on the Porta Pinciana. Of my sixteen legionaries nine are either dead or ill from hunger."

"Marcus Licinius reports almost the same thing from the Porta Tiburtina," Julianus added. "Who is going to defend us against the dangers threatening from everywhere?"

"I will, and Roman courage! Go now, and let the heralds call everyone still left in the houses to the Forum Romanum."

"Sir, there are only women and children, and the sick..."

"Obey, Tribune!"

And then the Prefect, a fierce dark look on his face and in his eyes, climbed down from the wall and mounted Pluto, his magnificent black Spanish thoroughbred stallion. Then, followed by a detachment of his loyal mounted Isaurians, he went on a slow round of a large part of the city, by a roundabout route, checking on the guards and their preparedness everywhere he went. At the same time, by doing this, he was giving the heralds and the citizens time to follow his call.

And so he rode upstream along the right bank of the Tiber. People were coming from the houses only in ones and twos, dressed in rags, and staring at the mounted men in utter despair. Only as they reached the bridge of Cestius did the crowd become a little more dense. Cethegus pulled up his mount in order to inspect the guards posted there.

Suddenly a woman came rushing out of one of the houses, her hair flying wildly in the wind, a child on her arm. Another child was pulling at her clothes. "Bread, bread!" she cried. "Will tears turn stones into bread? Oh no, they remain hard! As hard as – hard as that man there! Look at him, children, that is the Prefect of Rome. That one there, on the black horse with the purple plume on his helmet, with the terrible look in his eyes! But I do not fear him any more. You see, children, he forced your father into his army and onto the walls. And there he served, day and night, until he collapsed dead. A curse on you, Prefect of Rome!" And she clenched her fists at the mounted Cethegus, who had stopped.

"Bread, mother! Give us something to eat!" the children wailed.

"I can give you nothing to eat, but plenty to drink! Here!" the woman cried, clutched one child in each arm, and with both children she jumped from the bridge into the river. A cry of dread and of horror, along with curses, went through the crowd.

"She was mad!" the Prefect said aloud, and rode on.

"No, she was the most sensible one among us all!" a voice from the crowd replied.

"Be silent! Legionaries, let the tubas sound! Forward! To the Forum!" Cethegus commanded, and the mounted group galloped away.

Via the Fabrician Bridge, through the Porta Carmentalia and past the foot of the Capitoline Hill the Prefect reached the Forum Romanum. The vast space looked empty, not even nearly filled by the few thousand people who were hovering in rags on the steps of the halls and temples, or who were standing upright with an effort, leaning on spears or sticks.

"What does the Prefect want?"

"What more could he possibly want?"

"We have nothing left but our lives!"

"Maybe that's just what he does want."

"Have you heard? Yesterday Centumcellae on the coast also surrendered to the Goths."

"Yes, the citizens overpowered the Prefect's Isaurians and opened the gates."

"Oh if only we could do that!"

"We will have to do it soon, or it will be too late."

"My brother dropped dead yesterday, the boiled thistles still in his mouth. He could no longer swallow them."

"On the Forum Romanum yesterday a mouse was weighed in gold."

"For a week I secretly obtained roast meat from a butcher; he would not deliver it raw…"

"Count yourself lucky! They will storm any house where they smell meat cooking."

"But the day before yesterday he was torn to pieces in the street. He had been luring beggar children into his house, and it was their flesh he was selling to us."

"But do you know how the Gothic king treats his prisoners of war?"

"Like a father treats his helpless children."

"Most of them immediately sign up under his flag."

"Yes, but even those who don't want to do that are given money for their journey."

"Yes, and food and clothes and shoes."

"The wounded and the ill are nursed and looked after until they are well again."

"And then he has guides escort them to the coast."

"In some cases he has even paid for their passage on merchant ships to the eastern Empire."

"Look, there is the Prefect getting down from his black horse."

"He looks like Pluto!"

"Not Princeps Senatus any more, but Princeps Inferorum."

"Can you see the look in his eyes? Look at it!"

"Cold, and yet it's as if his eyes were shooting arrows!"

"Yes, my aunt is right. Only a man who no longer has a heart can look like that!"

"That's nothing new. Evil spirits have eaten out his heart at night."

"Nonsense! There are no evil spirits! But there is a devil, because it says so in the Bible. And he has made a pact with the devil. That Numidian there, holding his horse, is a messenger from hell, who accompanies him everywhere. No weapon can so much as scratch the Prefect's skin. He feels neither night watches nor hunger, but he can never smile again because he has sold his soul to the devil."

"How do you know that?"

"The deacon from St Paul's told me all about it the other day. And he said it's a sin to go on serving such a man. After all, did he not betray our bishop Silverius to the emperor and have him sent to Byzantium in chains?"

"And just the other day he had sixty priests, both Arian and of the true faith, expelled from the city for suspected treason."

"That is quite true!"

"But he must have also promised the devil that he would bring every possible suffering to Rome and the Romans."

"But we will not endure it any longer!"

"We are free, as he himself has told us often enough. I will ask him what right he has..."

But the courageous speaker stopped in mid-sentence. A glance from the Prefect had struck him as he mounted the small podium, looking over the crowd as he did so.

"Romans," he began, "I now call on you all to become legionaries. Hunger and, a shameful thing to say about Roman men, hunger and treason have thinned the ranks of our fighting men. Can you hear the hammer blows? A cross is being erected for deserters! Rome must now ask for even greater sacrifices from you Romans, and you have no choice. Citizens of other cities may choose between surrender and defeat, but we who have grown up in the shadow of the Capitol do not have that choice. In our streets there walk the memories of a thousand years of heroism! No cowardly thought may be heard here. You cannot permit the Barbarians to tether their horses to Trajan's columns again, and so a last great effort is called for. In the sons of Romulus and Remus the marrow of heroes matures early, and men who drink the water of the Tiber retain their strength into very old age. I now call on all boys from the age of twelve, and all men up to the age of eighty for duty on the walls. Quiet! Do not complain! I will go with my tribunes and my lancers from house to house, but only to ensure that no boy who is too delicate, and no man who is too feeble, is called upon to bear arms. What are you grumbling about over there? Does anyone have a better idea how we can defend ourselves? Let him say so! Let him tell us all aloud from this place here, which I will gladly vacate in his favour."

At that silence reigned wherever the Prefect's eyes had flashed.

But behind him, among those whom his eyes did not restrain, there now arose angry and desperate murmuring, becoming louder and louder. "Bread!" ... "Surrender!" ... "Peace!" ... "Bread!"

Cethegus turned around to look at them: "Are you not ashamed of yourselves? You have borne so much, worthy of your name. And now that all you have to do is to hold out for a few more days you want to give in? A few more days, and Belisarius will have brought us relief."

"You have told us that seven times already."

"And after the seventh time Belisarius lost nearly all his ships!"

"And now those same ships are helping to blockade our harbour."

"Give us a time when you will put an end to our misery, rather than let it go on for ever. I feel desperately sorry for these people."

"Who are you?" Cethegus asked the invisible last speaker. "You cannot be a Roman!"

"I am Pelagius the Deacon, a Christian and a priest of the Lord. And I do not fear men, but only God himself. The king of the Goths, although he is an infidel, is said to have promised that in all the cities he has conquered he will give back to the true faith all the churches which his fellow infidels, the Arians, have taken from us. It is also reported that he has already sent heralds to the citizens of Rome three times, offering the most favourable terms for surrender, but they were not permitted to speak to us."

"Be silent, priest! You have no fatherland other than your heaven, no country apart from the kingdom of God, no people except the communion of saints, and no army but for the angels. Leave the Empire of Romans to men, and restrict yourself to putting your heavenly Empire in order."

"But the man of God is right!"

"Give us a time limit!"

"Not too far away!"

"We will hold out until then."

"But if there is no relief by then…"

"We will surrender!"

"We will open the gates!"

But this thinking was unacceptable to Cethegus. Having had no news from the outside world for weeks he had no idea just when Belisarius might be expected to appear at the mouth of the Tiber.

"What?" he exclaimed, "am I to dictate to you how long you may still be Romans, and when you must become women and slaves? Honour does not know time limits."

"You are saying that because you no longer believe in relief!"

"I am saying it because I believe in you."

"But we want it this way, all of us! Do you hear us? You have spoken to us often enough of Roman freedom and liberty. Very well then, are we free or are we already slaves, slaves to your will like your mercenaries? Do you hear us? We demand a time limit. We want it, and we want it now!"

"We want it!" the chorus of the crowd repeated.

But before Cethegus could reply the sound of tubas could be heard coming from the southeastern corner of the Forum. People and armed men were streaming in from the Via Sacra, a great crowd of them, and in their midst there rode two men in very strange armour.

Chapter 9

Lucius Licinius was galloping ahead of them all, and flew up the steps to the speaker's podium: "A herald from the Goths! I was too late to turn him away again the way I did before. The starving troops at the Porta Tiburtina let him in."

"Down with him! He must not be allowed to speak!" said Cethegus as he leapt down from his position and drew his sword.

But the crowd was quick to guess at what he was about to do, and amid loud cheering they formed a protective cordon around the herald.

"Peace! Salvation! Bread!"

"Peace! Listen to what the herald has to say!"

"No, do not listen to him!" Cethegus thundered. "Who is Prefect of Rome? Who is it that defends this city? I do, Cornelius Cethegus Caesarius, and I say: Do not listen to him!"

And with that he charged among the crowd with his drawn sword.

But the women and old men clustered together like a swarm of bees to block his way, whilst the armed men maintained their protective barrier around the herald.

"Speak, man! What message do you bring us?" they asked.

"Peace and relief from your suffering," cried Thorismuth, and waved his white staff. "Totila, the king of the Goths and the Italians, sends you his greetings and asks for free passage into your city, so that he can convey important news to you and offer you peace."

"Hail to him!"

"Let us hear him!"

"Let him come!"

Cethegus had hurriedly mounted his horse, and now he had his men sound the battle signal on the tubas. At that it became quiet on the Forum.

"Listen to me, herald! I, the commander of this city, refuse the free passage you seek. I will treat any Goth who enters this city as an enemy."

But his words were greeted by a thousand angry voices.

One citizen climbed onto the podium: "Cornelius Cethegus, are you our governor or our tyrant? We are free! And as you have often told us yourself: the greatest thing in Rome is the majesty of the Roman people. Very well, the Roman people command you that the Gothic king shall be heard. People of Rome, is that not so?"

"We want to hear him!"

"It is the law!" cried the crowd. "Did you hear us? Are you going to obey the people of Rome or defy them?"

Cethegus returned his sword to its scabbard as Thorismuth turned his horse to fetch his king.

The Prefect gathered his young tribunes around him.

"Lucius Licinius," he commanded, "to the Capitol! Salvius Julianus, you will defend the lower river barrier, the wooden one. Quintus Piso, you will defend the upper chain barrier. Marcus Licinius, you will hold the entrenchment which protects the approach from the Forum to the Capitoline Hill and my house. The remainder of the mercenaries will gather in close formation behind me."

"What are you trying to do, general?" Lucius Licinius asked before he hurried on his way.

"To attack and destroy the Barbarians."

Some fifty mounted mercenaries together with about a hundred lancers now grouped themselves around the Prefect, once the tribunes had gone on their way. After a short pause the sound of Gothic army horns could be heard approaching along the Via Sacra.

And now the Gothic delegation could be seen approaching from that direction. In the lead were Thorismuth, Count Wisand the *bandalarius* with the blue Gothic banner and six horn blowers. The king rode between Duke Guntharis and Count Teias, and another ten or so other Gothic leaders followed. They were almost all unarmed. Only Teias openly displayed his much feared broad battleaxe.

Earlier, as this procession was just leaving the Gothic camp in order to ride into the city by the Porta Metrona, Duke Guntharis could feel someone tugging at his cloak. He looked down, and beside his horse he saw a boy or youth, with short brown hair and blue eyes, carrying a shepherd's staff in his hand.

"Are you the king? No, you are not. And he over there? He must be the brave Teias, the black Count as he is called in song."

"What do you want from the king, boy?"

"I want to fight under him, in his army."

"You are still too young and too tender. Go and come back in two years' time, and meanwhile look after your goats."

"I may be still young, but I am no longer tender. And I have tended goats long enough. There, now I see him! That must be the king."

And he stepped before Totila, bowed in a very becoming way and said: "With your permission, Sir King." He then reached for the reins of the king's horse in order to lead it, as though it was all ordained to be so. And the king looked down on him with a pleased look on his face, and gave him a smile, as the boy led his horse by the halter.

But Guntharis said to himself: "I have seen that boy's face before. No, he only looks like him – but I have never seen such an incredible resemblance. And what an aristocratic bearing he has for a young shepherd!"

And now, as the Gothic king approached the Roman people, loud cheers of: "Hail King Totila! Peace and deliverance!" were heard.

But the young boy who was leading the king's horse looked up at Totila's shining face, and he sang softly but with a voice of silver:

"Tremble and flinch, tough Cethegus! Your cunning won't help you.
Teias, the courageous, will shatter your pride.
And bright as daylight, as the morning sun emerges out of night and darkness,
comes the shining darling of the heavenly master above;
the shining knight, our brave new king!
Every tower and every gate opens to him, as do halls and hearts,
as anger, winter and pain retreat before him, conquered."

At a signal from the king there was silence.

But this was the moment for which Cethegus had been waiting. He now spurred his black stallion forward among the crowd, and cried: "What do you want in my city, Goth?"

After giving him a withering look Totila turned away from him: "To him I will henceforth speak only with my sword, for he is a liar six times over as well as a murderer! I have come to talk to you, unhappy, betrayed people of Rome. Concern over you and pity for you are tearing my heart asunder. I have come to end your misery. I come unarmed, because I believe that Roman men are men of honour, and that honour will guard me better than any sword and shield could do."

He paused. Cethegus did not interrupt him again.

"Romans, you have known it yourselves for a long time now: I could have stormed your walls with my army of thousands weeks ago! Because you now have only stones, and no men to defend them. But if Rome was to fall by storm, then Rome would also go up in flames. And I will tell you this quite frankly: I would rather never enter Rome if it meant I had to destroy Rome first. I am not here to reproach you about the manner in which you have repaid the benevolence of Theodoric and the Goths. Have you forgotten the days when, in gratitude, you struck coins with the inscription '*Roma Felix*'? Indeed, you have been punished enough. You have suffered more punishment from hunger and plague and Byzantium and that demon there than our severest justice could have inflicted. More than eight thousand of your men, not counting women and children, have perished. Your deserted houses are collapsing. You are eagerly devouring the grass which now grows in your temples, and you drag yourselves hollow-eyed through streets of despair.

"Starving mothers, Roman mothers, have eaten human flesh, the flesh of their own children. Until today one could understand the fight you have put up, and even admire it, even though one felt sorry for you. But from today any further resistance is madness. Your last hope was Belisarius! Let me tell you then: Belisarius has returned home to Byzantium from Sicily. He has abandoned you."

Cethegus ordered the tubas sounded to drown out the roar of the people. For a long time it was in vain, but ultimately the metallic sound had its desired effect. When the noise had died down a little the Prefect cried: "Lies! Don't fall for such clumsy lies!"

"Have the Goths ever lied to you? Have I ever lied to you, Romans? But you shall believe only your own eyes and ears. Step forward, man, and speak. Do you know this man?"

A Byzantine in splendid armour was led forward by Gothic soldiers.

"Konon! Belisarius's skipper!"… "We know him!" cried the crowd. But Cethegus grew pale.

"Men of Rome," the Byzantine began, "Belisarius, the *Magister Militum*, sent me to King Totila. I arrived today. Belisarius had to return to Byzantium from Sicily. In parting he commended Rome and Italy to the well known benevolence of King Totila. That is my message for him and for all of you here."

"Very well," Cethegus interrupted with thunder in his voice. "If that is so then the day has come for you to show whether you are Romans or bastards. Listen to me and mark my words well! Your Prefect, Cethegus, will never surrender Rome! Never will he yield his Rome to the Barbarians! Think back to the days once more when I was everything to you, when you called my name in the same breath as that of Christ, and ahead of the saints. Who was it that gave you work, and bread, and – most importantly

– arms all these years? Who was it that defended you, Belisarius or Cethegus? Who defended Rome when there were a hundred and fifty thousand of these Barbarians outside our walls? Who saved Rome from King Witigis with his blood? Now, for the last time, I am calling on you to fight!

"Hear me, descendants of Camillus. Just as he swept away the Gallic hordes, who had already won our city, from the Capitol by the sheer force of Roman swords, so I too will sweep away these Barbarians. Gather around me for a sortie! And prove to all the world what Roman strength can do when it is led by a Cethegus and driven by despair! Choose!"

"Yes, choose!" Totila cried, rising high in his stirrups. "Choose between certain doom and equally certain freedom! If you decide to follow that madman one more time, then I can no longer help you. Listen to Count Teias of Tarentum on my right here. I think you know him. I can protect you no longer."

"No!" cried Teias, raising his mighty battleaxe, "there will be no more mercy, by the god of hatred! If you refuse this very last boon, then not one life will be spared within these walls. I have sworn it, as have thousands with me!"

"I offer you a complete pardon for all wrongs committed in the past, and I will be a kind and benevolent king to you. Ask the people of Naples if I know how to do that! Choose between me and the Prefect!"

"Hail King Totila! Death to the Prefect!" was the unanimous response from the crowd.

And then, as if by some prearranged signal, the women and children threw themselves on their knees before the king, as if in prayer. At the same time the thousands of armed men around them raised their swords and spears against the Prefect, cursing and threatening, and a few javelins were actually hurled in the Prefect's direction. They were the very weapons which he himself had once given them.

"They are dogs, not Romans!" Cethegus snarled furiously, and turned his horse. "To the Capitol!"

And his great thoroughbred took a mighty leap over the rows of kneeling, screeching women, and through the hail of missiles which the Romans were now throwing at him. The few courageous ones who tried to bar his way were simply trampled down by the determined Prefect.

Soon his red plume had disappeared, and his men followed him with a will, the mounted mercenaries in the lead. The lancers retreated slowly and in good order. In this way they reached the high battlement occupied by Lucius Licinius, which guarded the approach to the Capitol and to the Prefect's house.

"What now? Shall we follow him?" the Romans asked the king.

"No, halt! Open all the gates. There are wagons with bread and meat and wine ready in our camp. Let them be taken to every part of the city. Give the people of Rome food and drink for three days of feasting. My Goths will watch over you and make certain that nobody comes to any harm from overindulgence."

"And the Prefect?" Duke Guntharis asked.

"Cethegus Caesarius, the former Prefect of Rome, will not escape the gods of revenge!" Totila replied, turning around.

"Nor me!" cried the shepherd boy.

"Nor me!" said Teias, and galloped away.

Chapter 10

As a result of the events in the Forum Romanum, most parts of Rome were now in Gothic hands. The only parts still held by Cethegus were that part of the city on the right bank of the Tiber, between the Porta Portuensis in the south and Hadrian's tomb in the north. That area also included the two barriers across the river.

On the left bank the Prefect now held only a small but dominant section west of the Forum Romanum, with the Capitol in its centre. This section was surrounded by walls and high battlements stretching from the riverbank at the foot of the Capitoline Hill east to the Forum of Trajan and west between the Circus Flaminius and the theatre of Marcellus, including the latter but not the former, as far as the bridge of Fabricianus and the island in the Tiber.

The liberated Romans in the city spent the remainder of that first day feasting and drinking. The king had arranged for eighty wagons of food and wine to be driven to the main squares of the city, and the starving people were now settled around these wagons. They were sitting on stones or hastily made wooden benches, thanking God, the saints and the "best of all kings".

The Prefect had immediately arranged for all gates leading from the Gothic part of the city into the regions still held by him to be securely locked and barred, particularly the approaches to the Capitol and the gates Flumentana, Carmentalis and Ratumena. He had then, with great strategic insight, divided the few men remaining to him among the most important points. Indeed, it was approximately the same section of Rome he had held before, under and against Belisarius.

"Salvius Julianus will receive another hundred Isaurians for the lower river barrier! The Abasgan archers will join Piso on the river to defend the upper barrier. Marcus Licinius will remain on the battlements at the Forum."

But then Lucius Licinius, who had been guarding that part of the city barricaded off while the decision in the Forum Romanum was made, and had therefore not taken part in the events which occurred there, reported that the remaining legionaries under his command were becoming very difficult.

"Ah!" cried Cethegus, "the aroma of the roast beef which their cousins down there have exchanged for the honour of Rome is tickling their nostrils. I am coming."

And he rode up to the Capitol, where about five hundred legionaries stood in orderly rows, with fierce and threatening attitudes. Slowly, with appraising eyes, Cethegus rode along their front.

At last he spoke: "I had intended to let you earn immortality for yourselves by defending the Capitol against the Barbarians. I did hear that you prefer the roast beef down there, but I cannot believe it of you. Surely you will not desert the man who taught you to fight and win again, after centuries! Let him who will remain with Cethegus and the Capitol raise his sword!"

Not one man moved.

"Evidently hunger is a more powerful god than the Jupiter of the Capitol," he said disdainfully.

A centurion stepped forward. "It is not that, Prefect of Rome. But we do not want to fight against our cousins and brothers, who are now on the side of the Goths."

"I ought to hold you as hostages for your fathers and brothers, and throw your heads at them when they storm. But I am concerned that would not be enough to halt their valour, coming from their full stomachs. Go! You are not worthy of saving Rome! Open the gate, Licinius! Let them turn their backs on the Capitol, and on Roman honour!"

And the legionaries moved off, except for about a hundred men, who remained behind undecided, leaning on their spears.

"Well? What are you waiting for?" cried Cethegus, moving right up close to them on his horse.

"To die with you, Prefect of Rome!" one of them cried.

And the others repeated: "To die with you!"

"I thank you! Licinius, there you see one hundred Romans! Are they not enough to establish the Roman Empire anew? To you I will allocate the place of honour: you will defend the battlement which I have adorned with the name of Julius Caesar."

He jumped down from his horse, threw the reins to Syphax, called his tribunes closer and said: "Now listen to my plan!"

"You already have a plan?"

"Yes, we will attack! If I know these Barbarians we are safe from any attack today. They have won three quarters of the city, and that victory must first be celebrated by a hundred thousand Barbarians drinking themselves senseless before they will think about the last quarter. By midnight the entire army of golden haired drunkards and heroes will be immersed in wine and blissful sleep. And the hungry populace down there will not be far behind them today, when it comes to indulging themselves. Look at them, and the way they are stuffing themselves and dancing about, adorned with garlands. And so far only a small portion of the Barbarian army has moved into the city. That is our hope of victory! At midnight we will charge at them out of every gate at once. They will not be expecting an attack from a force which they outnumber so greatly, and we will slaughter them in their sleep."

"Your plan is extremely daring!" said Lucius Licinius. "But should we fail, then the Capitol will become our tombstone."

"You are learning from me," Cethegus smiled, "words as well as deeds. My plan is one of desperation. But it is the only hope we have. Now – are the guards at their posts? I will go to my house and sleep for two hours. Nobody is to wake me earlier. Wake me in two hours."

"You can sleep, general, even now?"

"Yes, I must. And I hope that I will sleep well. Awake or asleep, I must gather my own thoughts – after ceding the Forum Romanum to the Barbarian king. That was too much! It calls for refreshment. Syphax, I asked you yesterday: is there no more wine to be found on the right bank of the Tiber?"

"I enquired, Sir. The only wine left is in the temples of your god. But the priests say it is already dedicated for the altar."

"That will not have spoilt it. Take it away from the priests, and distribute it among the hundred Romans on Caesar's battlement. It is the only thanks I have left to give."

Followed by Syphax he slowly rode towards his own house and stopped outside the main entrance. Cethegus dismounted and patted his great horse's chest: "Our next ride will be a hard one, my Pluto, whether into victory or flight. Give him the white bread you saved for me." The horse was led away into the stable next to the main house. The marble stalls were empty, and Pluto now shared the huge stable only with Syphax's bay stallion. All the Prefect's other horses had been slaughtered and eaten by the soldiers.

The master of the house walked through the magnificent vestibule and atrium into the library. The old *ostiarius* and scribe Fidus, who was too old to carry a spear, was now the only servant or slave in the house. All the other slaves and freedmen were on the walls, alive or dead.

"Give me the scroll with Plutarch's Caesar! And the big goblet with the amethysts with water from the well." The Prefect was still in the library. The old man had lit the candelabra with precious aromatic oils, just as he had done in times of peace. Cethegus tool a long look at the line of busts, statues and sculptures, whose shadows fell on the mosaic floor.

There they were, almost all of them, the heroes of Rome in times of war and peace, small marble busts on pedestals bearing brief inscriptions with their names. They dated from the days of the mythical kings through the long rows of consuls and Caesars to Trajan, Hadrian and Constantine.

His own ancestors, the "Cethegi", formed a separate, crowded little group. The empty socket had already been fixed to the wall which would one day hold his own bust. His would be the last bust on this side of the room, for he was the last male member of his family. But on the left side there was another complete arcade of pillars with empty niches, intended for future continuation. Cethegus hoped to perpetuate his name into future generations, not by marriage but by adoption, for many glorious centuries.

To his astonishment, as he walked along the row of busts deep in thought, he saw one such bust standing on the empty socket which was one day intended for his own bust.

"What is the meaning of this?" he asked. "Bring the lamp over here, old man. What bust is that in my place?"

"Forgive me, Sir! The socket up there, one of the very old ones, had to be repaired. I had to take the bust down. And so I put the bust on this socket so that it would not be damaged."

"Shine the lamp on it! Higher! Who could it be?" And Cethegus read the brief inscription on the bust:

"Tarquinius Superbus, tyrant of Rome, died, driven out by the populace because of unbearable oppression, into exile far from the city. As a warning for future generations."

Cethegus himself, in his youth, had composed the inscription and had it placed under the bust. Quickly he now removed the marble head and placed it to one side. "Away with the omen!" he said.

Steeped in serious thought he went into his bedroom, where he leaned his helmet, shield and sword against the bed. The slave lit the lamp on the tortoiseshell table, brought the goblet and the book, and left.

Cethegus picked up the scroll, but soon put it down again.

This time even he could not force himself to be calm. It was just too unnatural. In the nearby Forum Romanum, Roman citizens were drinking with the Barbarians to the health of the Gothic king, and to the downfall of the Prefect of Rome, the *Princeps Senatus*! In two hours he was going to make a daring attempt to wrest Rome from the

Barbarians. He could not bring himself to spend the brief pause reading a biography which he knew almost by heart.

Thirstily he drank from the goblet, and then he threw himself on the bed. "Was it an omen?" he asked himself. "But there is no such thing as an omen for one who does not believe in omens. Homer tells us that 'there is but one token, and that is to fight for one's country.' Certainly Cethegus fights not only for the soil of his country. He also fights for himself, and perhaps that is even more important. But has this day not shown it up most shamefully? Rome is Cethegus, and Cethegus is Rome, and not these so-called Romans who cannot remember great names. Today Rome is Cethegus even more than – even more than Rome was once Caesar. Was he not also a tyrant in the minds of fools?"

Impatiently he got up and walked over to the huge statue of his great ancestor. "Divine Julius, if I could pray then I would pray today, pray to you. Help your descendant complete his great work! How hard, how ruthlessly have I fought ever since that day when the great idea of renewing Rome came to me out of your marble head. There it was, ready and fully armed, as Pallas Athena sprang from the head of Zeus!

"Oh how I fought, with both sword and mind, night and day!

"And if I was forced to the ground seven times by the superior might of two nations, then I picked myself up again seven times out of the dust, unconquered and unbowed! A year ago my goal seemed to be so close. And now, this night, I must wrestle with that fair-haired boy for the last few houses in Rome, for my own house and for my life. Is it conceivable? Am I to be defeated after all? After all my efforts? After such deeds? By the lucky star of a mere boy? Is it really impossible, even for a descendant of the great Caesar, that one man can take the place of his people until he is able to rebuild them so that they rise anew? Can a man from the world of the Barbarians or the Greeks win through in the end? Cannot Cethegus first halt the wheel of fate, and then start rolling it in the opposite direction? Must I be conquered because I stand alone, a general without an army, and a man without a nation at his shoulder? Can it be that I must cede this, my own Rome? I cannot, and I will not think of it! Did not your star also darken for a while just before Parsalus? And did you not swim across the Nile to save your life, bleeding and with a hundred arrows after you? And yet you made it through, and you returned to your Rome in triumph. I, your descendant, will fare no worse! No, I shall not lose my Rome, nor my house, nor this your godlike image, which has so often given me strength and hope as the cross of the Christians does for them. And as a token of my trust in you, let that remain with you which is safest when concealed under your shield! Where on earth could there be safety and security if not with you?

"It was in an hour of weakness when I tried to entrust these secrets and many a treasure to Syphax, to be buried in the earth. If Rome, this house and this sanctum should be lost to me, then let these records be lost also. In any case, who is to decipher these secrets? No, you shall guard my treasures as you shall guard my letters and my diaries."

And with that he withdrew a sizeable leather sack from his tunic. He had been wearing it under his armour. In it he had hidden his most precious pearls and his most valuable gemstones. Then he touched a spring on a lower left rib of the statue, just under the edge of the shield. A small opening appeared, and from it he took a small oblong ivory case, delicately carved and with a golden lock, which contained a number of documents on small papyrus scrolls. He placed the little leather sack into the box.

"There, great ancestor, preserve my secrets and my treasures for me. Where could they be safe, if they are not safe with you?" He closed the opening again, and not the slightest crack betrayed the fact that there was an opening there.

"Under your shield, next to your heart! As a token that I trust you and my caesarian luck, that I cannot be swayed away from you, or from my Rome. At least not for long! If I do have to go, I will return. And who would think to look for my treasures and my secrets with a dead Caesar? Look after them for me."

Had the water in the amethyst goblet been the strongest wine, the drink could not have had a more intoxicating effect on the Prefect than this inner struggle and debate with himself; he was half talking to himself and half to the statue, which he almost worshipped.

The superhuman efforts of mind and body these last few weeks, the failure on the Forum today, the new and desperate plan he had conceived immediately after his defeat, and the tension of yearning for the hour of decision to arrive, all these factors had increased both emotion and exhaustion to the limit, even in this man of steel. He was thinking, speaking and acting as if in a delirium.

Exhausted he threw himself on the bed at the foot of the statue, and almost instantly he was asleep. But it was not the untroubled sleep which, until now, he had found after every guilty deed, and before every danger he had faced, the result of his mighty and resolute mind, aloof over any emotion. This sleep was an uneasy sleep. Changing dreams troubled him, confused like those of a man in the delirium of fever. At last the dreams became a little clearer and less confused.

He could see the Caesar statue at the foot of the bed grow and grow, and the majestic head kept rising higher and higher. It had forced its way through the roof.

The head with the garland of laurels was disappearing beyond the night clouds among the stars.

"Take me with you!" Cethegus begged.

But the demigod replied: "From my height I can barely see you. You are too small! You cannot follow me!" And with loud crashing the timbers of the roof collapsed over him, seeming to bury him under the rubble of the room. Even the statue seemed to be collapsing.

The blows were still sounding. Cethegus woke with a start, sprang to his feet and looked about him.

Chapter 11

The thunderous blows were still sounding, and they were real, not a dream!

They were smashing against the door of his house. Cethegus reached for helmet and sword as Lucius Licinius and Syphax rushed into the room: "On your feet, general!"

"It can't be two hours yet. I wanted to attack in two hours, not before."

"Yes, but the Goths! They beat us to it! They are storming!"

"A curse on them! Where are they storming?" And already Cethegus was at the front door.

"Down at the port. At the river barrier. The king sent fire ships up the river, with burning towers on deck, full of pitch and sulphur and resin. The first barrier, the wooden one, is already in flames, and so are all the ships behind it! Salvius Julianus has been wounded and taken prisoner. There, you can see the flames yourself in the southeast."

"What about the chain barrier, is it holding?"

"So far yes, but what if it breaks?"

"Then I will be the barrier of Rome, as I was once before. Forward!"

Syphax led the Prefect's snorting black stallion forward, and Cethegus swung himself into the saddle. "To the right, over there! Where is your brother Marcus?"

"On the battlements at the Forum."

A moment later they met up with the mercenaries, Abasgans and Isaurians, who were fleeing from the port. "Flee!" they cried, "Save the Prefect!"

"Where is Cethegus?"

"Here – to save you! Turn around! To the river!"

He galloped before them, the light from the burning logs and ships clearly showing the way. As he reached the riverbank he dismounted. Syphax carefully led the horse to safety in an empty warehouse.

"Torches! Into the boats! There are a dozen small boats there, ready for just such an eventuality as this. All archers into them! Follow me! Licinius, you take the second boat! Row to the chain barrier, and then place yourselves right next to it, but above it. As soon as you see anyone coming up river and close to the chain, let them have a hail of arrows. The high walls reach right down to the river on both sides, so they have to pass here, where the chain is!"

Already a few isolated Gothic boats had tried to approach. But some of them had caught fire from the burning ships between the two barriers, and others had capsized in the tumult. One boat, which had come to within half an arrow shot of the heavily manned chain barrier, was drifting downstream again soon afterwards without a helmsman; its entire crew had fallen victim to the arrows of the mercenaries.

"Did you see that? There goes a ship of the dead! Nothing is lost! Hold out! But find some torches, and some firebrands. Set the shipyards there on fire too. Fire against fire!"

"Look over there, master!" Syphax warned. He had not moved from his master's side.

"Yes, there comes the decision floating up river."

It was a superb spectacle. The Goths had quickly recognised that the chain barrier could not be passed or broken by small boats. They had therefore set about removing enough of the burning first wooden barrier to make room for a larger ship to pass through the burning logs, a warship.

But moving slowly through the flames like this, driven only by oars, could turn out to be even more disastrous for a large ship than it had been for the much smaller "ship of the dead", especially with the hail of arrows which could be expected from the defenders.

Hesitantly the Goths paused below the burning logs. And then, suddenly, a strong southerly wind arose, causing the surface of the water to ripple.

"Can you fell that breath? That is the breath of the god of victory. Hoist the sails! Now follow me, my Goths!" a joyous voice cried.

The sails went up and spread like wings from the mighty Gothic warship, a ship called *Wild Swan*.

A magnificent spectacle now presented itself as the mighty ship, in full sail and pushed forward also by a hundred oarsmen, accelerated upstream, illuminated on both sides by the burning logs and Roman boats.

The ship was moving upstream with a wild, destructive urgency. On both sides of the upper deck, high above the enclosed lower decks of the oarsmen, a number of Gothic warriors were kneeling in a tight cluster, their shields held close together, a wall of bronze against the arrows. At the bow a huge swan spread its wings high in the air. And between those wings, sword in hand, stood King Totila.

"Forward!" he commanded. "Pull, oarsmen! With all your might! Get ready, Goths!"

Cethegus recognised the tall, youthful figure, and he could also clearly hear the familiar voice. "Just let the ship approach, very close, to twenty paces, and then shoot. No, not yet. Now! Shoot your arrows!"

"Take cover, my Goths!"

A hail of arrows rained down on the ship, but they bounced off the wall of shields without effect.

"Curse them!" Piso cried behind the Prefect. "They are trying to snap the chain by the ship's momentum. And they certainly will, even if we could kill every man on deck. We cannot reach the oarsmen, and we cannot wound this southerly wind."

"Fire into the sails! Fire into the ship! Quickly, fire!" Cethegus commanded.

The threatening swan came ever closer, and also ever closer came the deadly clash with the chain. Already some of the torches being thrown were reaching the ship. One flew into the sail of the mizzen mast, but it flared momentarily and went out.

A second one, which Cethegus himself had thrown, touched the king's long hair as it fluttered in the wind. The firebrand fell down beside the king, who had not noticed it. But then a boy leapt to his side who, instead of any weapons of either offence or defence, was carrying only a rough shepherd's stick. He stamped out the firebrand with his feet, and the other firebrands bounced off the shields into the water, where they went out.

The bow of the galley was now only eight paces from the chain, and the Roman defenders were trembling in anticipation of the coming impact.

And then Cethegus stepped right forward, into the bow of his boat, where he took careful aim with a heavy javelin.

"Watch carefully," he said. "As soon as the Barbarian king falls, quickly throw more fire!"

Never had the experienced warrior taken more careful aim. He drew back the spear, and then he hurled it with all the might of his hatred and all the strength of his arm.

Those around him waited with breathless anticipation. But the king did not fall. He had recognised the man taking aim, but he put down his small and narrow shield just the same. He watched the spear coming, facing it with his shieldless left side. The spear came hissing through the air at precisely the right height, where the king's bare neck was showing above his armour. Only when it was about to strike did the king react, catching it deftly with his left hand and then, with his right, immediately throwing it back at him who had thrown it. It struck the Prefect in the left arm, above his shield, and Cethegus fell to his knees.

In the same instant the bow of the ship struck the taut chain. It burst, and most of the Roman boats which had been situated above it capsized, including the Prefect's boat. A few boats shot downstream out of control.

"Victory!" Totila rejoiced. "Surrender, you mercenaries!"

Cethegus managed to reach the left bank of the Tiber, swimming and bleeding profusely. The Gothic ship lowered two small boats, and the king jumped into one of them.

An entire flotilla of smaller Gothic boats and vessels, which had sailed upstream under the cover of the royal galley, now also broke the lines of his archers and landed troops on both banks.

Cathegus could see his archers, who were neither equipped nor in the mood for hand-to-hand fighting, surrender to the Gothic troops either singly or in small groups. He could also see a hail of arrows now being directed from the royal galley at the defenders on the left bank.

Worse still, he could see the king's boat fast approaching the bank at the very spot where he was struck, dripping wet.

He had lost his helmet in the water, and dropped his shield in order to reach dry land more quickly. He was about to throw himself at the Gothic king with his sword alone when an arrow strafed his neck.

"Well done, Haduswinth!" a young archer cried happily, "better than the last time at the marble tomb!"

"Good shot, Gunthamund!"

Cethegus swayed. Syphax caught him, and at the same time he felt a hand on his shoulder. He recognised Marcus Licinius.

"You here? Where are your men?"

"Dead!" Marcus replied. "The hundred Romans fell on the battlements. Teias, that awesome Teias, stormed it. Half your Isaurians fell on their way to the Capitol. The rest of them are still holding the gate of the Capitol and the entrenchment in front of your house. But it cannot go on. Teias's axe went through my shield and into my ribs. Farewell, oh great Cethegus! Save the Capitol, but hurry! Teias is quick." And with those words Marcus sank to the ground.

Flames were leaping high into the air from the Capitoline Hill.

"There is nothing, nothing left to save down here at the river," the Prefect said with an effort, as his loss of blood was considerable and was weakening him rapidly. "I will save the Capitol! To you, Piso, I will leave the king of the Barbarians.

"You have already struck one Barbarian king on the threshold of Rome. Now strike a second one, but make sure you strike him mortally! You, Lucius, avenge your brother. Don't follow me."

Cethegus threw one last angry look at the king, around whose feet the Abasgans were now gathering, begging for mercy. The Prefect sighed deeply.

"You are swaying, master?" Syphax asked with concern.

"Rome is tottering!" Cethegus replied. "To the Capitol!"

Lucius Licinius took his dying brother's hand for the last time. "I will follow him," he said then, "the general is wounded."

As Cethegus, Syphax and Lucius Licinius disappeared into the night Piso took cover behind a column of a basilica, which lay immediately on the path up river.

Meanwhile the king had left the Abasgans, who had surrendered to his followers. He took a few steps upstream and pointed his sword at the flames rising from the Capitol. Then he turned around and faced the river, and the Goths landing behind him.

"Forward," he urged. "Hurry! There is some fire fighting to be done up there. The fight is over. Now, my Goths, preserve Rome, for Rome is precious!"

Piso spotted his opportunity. "Great Apollo," he thought, "if ever my verses found their mark, now let my sword do likewise." He leapt forward from behind the pillar with drawn sword at the king, whose back was turned. But a few inches short of the king's body he dropped the blade with a scream. A sharp blow from a stick had stunned his hand.

Immediately a young shepherd flew at him, pulled him down and knelt on his chest.

"Surrender, you Roman wolf!" he cried, with the bright voice of a boy.

"Hey, it's Piso the poet! He is your prisoner, boy!" said the king, who had now come closer. "And it will cost him plenty of gold to buy himself free. But who are you, young shepherd, my friend?"

"He saved your life, King!" old Haduswinth interjected. "We were too far back to help you when we saw the Roman charging at you, and we could not even warn you. We owe your life to that boy!"

"What is your name, young hero?"

"Adalgoth."

"And what is it you seek here?"

"The evil Cethegus, Prefect of Rome. Where is he, Sir King? Just tell me that. I was told to come here, on the ship. Here, I was told, is where he would be trying to repel your attack."

"He was here. But he has fled, probably to his house."

"Are you trying to defeat the king of hell with that stick?" Haduswinth asked.

"No!" cried Adalgoth, "because now I have a sword!"

And he picked up his prisoner's sword from the ground, swung it high in the air above his head, and vanished into the night.

Totila handed Piso over to the Goths, who had now landed in large numbers on both sides of the river.

"Hurry!" he repeated. "Save the Capitol, which the Romans are trying to burn."

Chapter 12

Meanwhile the Prefect had left the river and taken the road to the Capitol.

He managed to reach the Forum Boarium through the Porta Trigemina. At the Janus temple he met up with a crowd of people, who held him up for a while. Despite his wound he moved so quickly that Licinius and Syphax had difficulty in keeping up with him. Repeatedly they lost sight of him, and it was only now that they finally caught up with him. His aim now was to hurry through the Porta Carmentalis and thus reach the rear of the Capitol.

But he found the gate already occupied by Goths, among them Wachis, who recognised him from afar.

"Revenge for Rauthgundis!" he cried, and a heavy stone struck the Prefect's bare head, now without a helmet. He turned and fled.

Now he remembered a low part of the wall to the northeast of the gate, and resolved to try and scale the wall at that point. But as he approached the spot flames from the burning Capitol met him once more.

Opposite him three men jumped over the low part of the wall. They were Isaurians, and they recognised him. "Flee, master! The whole of the Capitol is lost. That black Gothic demon!"

"Did he – did Teias start the fire?"

"No! We ourselves set fire to the wooden barricade when the Goths took a foothold in it. The Goths are fighting the fire."

"Barbarians saving my Capitol." Full of bitter agony, Cethegus leaned on a spear, which one of the Isaurians had given him. "Now I must somehow get into my house."

And he turned right in order to reach the main entrance to his house by the shortest route.

"Sir, that is dangerous!" one of the mercenaries warned. "Soon the Goths will be there too. I heard how the black Gothic Count kept calling you and looking for you. He was looking for you everywhere on the Capitol. Soon he will go looking for you in your house."

"I must get to my house one more time!"

But he had only advanced a few steps when he was met by a strong force of Goths, Romans among them, who were coming toward him from the city, heading straight for him.

The men in the lead, who were Romans, recognised him.

"The Prefect!"

"Rome's destroyer!"

"He had the Capitol set on fire!"

"Down with him!"

Arrows, spears and stones were flying in his direction. One mercenary fell, and the other two escaped. Cethegus was hit by an arrow, which struck him lightly in the left shoulder. He pulled it out. "A Roman arrow, with my stamp on it," he laughed out loud.

With great difficulty he managed to escape into the darkness of the nearest alleyway. In front of his house a huge mob was trying vainly to smash down the massive front door, but their spears and swords were not up to the task. Cethegus heard their cries of frustration over their wasted efforts.

"The door is strong!" he said to himself. "By the time they get in I will be far away." He reached his house by way of a narrow back lane. There he pressed a secret spring, hurried into the courtyard and from there, leaving the door open, into the house.

Suddenly an entirely different sound was coming from the front door, much louder. "A battleaxe!" said Cethegus, "That's Teias!" He hurried to the small niche in the wall, through which he could see the main street from a corner room. It was indeed Teias.

His long black hair was fluttering about his bare head. In his left hand he held a piece of burning timber, from the Capitol. The much feared battleaxe was in his right, and he was spattered with blood all over.

"Cethegus!" he cried out aloud with every blow against the door. "Cornelius Cethegus Caesarius! Where are you? I sought you in the Capitol, Prefect of Rome! Where are you? Must Teias go looking for you at your own hearth?"

And then Cethegus heard rapid steps behind him. Syphax had reached the house, and had followed him through the back door. He saw his master. "Flee, master! I will cover your flight with my body!" And he hurried past his master, through a number of rooms, to the front door.

Cethegus turned quickly to the right. He was barely able to stand. He still managed to reach the Zeus room, but there he collapsed. A moment later he was back on his feet.

A loud crashing and splintering sound was coming from the front door. The solid door had been smashed at last, and with a loud thud it fell inside the house. Teias entered the house of his mortal enemy.

On the threshold the Moor sprang at him from a cowering position, like a panther. His left hand was on Teias's throat, and a knife flashed in his right. But the Goth let go of the axe, and with a jerk of his right hand the attacker was flung to one side, where he flew out through the door and rolled down the steps into the street.

"Where are you, Cethegus?" the voice of Teias was coming closer, in the atrium, and now in the vestibule. A few doors which the faithful Fidus had bolted were soon smashed, and there were now only a few paces between the two men.

With a desperate effort Cethegus had managed to reach the centre of the Zeus room. He was still hoping to get into his study, and to retrieve the treasures and documents from the Caesar statue.

And then another door burst with a loud crash, and Cethegus could hear Teias calling from the study: "Where are you, Cethegus?"

Cethegus listened breathlessly. He could hear how the mob, which had followed Teias, was now smashing the busts and sculptures of his ancestors.

"Where is your master, old man?" Teias's voice cried.

The slave had fled into the study: "I don't know, by my immortal soul!"

"Not here either? Cethegus, you coward! Where are you hiding?"

By now the mob had apparently reached the study also. Cethegus could no longer stand, and he leaned against the marble Jupiter.

"What will happen to the house?"

"It will be burnt!" Teias replied.

"The king has forbidden burning!" Thorismuth warned.

"Yes, I know! But I asked for this house as a special favour from the king. It will be burnt and made level with the earth. Down with the devil's temple! Down with his holy of holies, the idol here!"

There was a terrible smashing blow, and the Caesar statue fell to the mosaic floor in many fragments and pieces. Pieces of gold, boxes, jewels, capsules rolled about everywhere.

"Oh, the Barbarian!" Cethegus cried, beside himself. Forgetting all else, he was about to storm into the study with his sword, and then he collapsed unconscious once more at the foot of the Jupiter statue.

"Listen, what was that?" a boy's voice cried.

"The Prefect's voice!" cried Teias, and tore open the door which separated the study from the Zeus room. Holding his torch before him, and swinging his battleaxe, he leapt into the room. But the room was empty. There was a pool of blood at the foot of the Jupiter, and a trail of blood led from there to the window overlooking the courtyard. The courtyard also was empty. Pursuing Goths found the little wooden gate shut, and locked from the outside. The key was in the keyhole, on the side facing the street.

Eventually this gate was also smashed, after much effort. Other Goths had reached the small side lane almost at the same time, by rushing through the front door and around the corner. But there was no sign of the Prefect. Only his sword was found lying in a corner. The slave Fidus recognised it.

With a look of foreboding on his face Teias took the sword and returned into the study. "Pick up carefully everything which the idol statue contained. Did you hear me? Everything! Especially any documents, and take them to the king. Where is the king?"

"He went from the Capitol to the chapel of St Peter with Goths and Romans, to offer prayers of thanks with all the people."

"Good! Find him in the church and take everything to him, also the sword. Tell him Teias sent it."

"It shall be done. But you – are you not also going to church with the king?"

"No!"

"Where will you spend the night of victory then, and say your prayers of thanks?"

"On the ruins of this house!" said Teias, and plunged his torch into the purple cushions on the bed.

BOOK EIGHT
Totila – Part Two

Chapter 1

And from that day onward King Totila held court in Rome, splendidly and happily. It seemed that the most difficult part of the war's aims had been achieved. After the fall of Rome, most of the smaller fortresses on the coast or in the Appenine Mountains opened their gates, and only a few had to be besieged and conquered. For these tasks the king sent his generals, Teias, Guntharis, Grippa, Markja and Aligern, while he himself remained in Rome to undertake the statesman's task of restoring the Empire, devastated as it had been by the long war. The Empire had to be calmed and reorganised, and indeed established anew.

Totila sent his dukes and counts into every city and every county, to convey the king's thoughts in every area of government. They also had to protect the native Italian population against acts of revenge by the victorious Goths, because he had announced a general and all-embracing pardon from the Capitol, with one single exception. That exception was the former Prefect of Rome, Cornelius Cethegus Caesarius.

Everywhere he had the destroyed churches rebuilt, those of Catholics and Arians alike. He also had property ownership reviewed everywhere, and he restructured and reduced the taxation system.

The fruits of his efforts were not long in coming. From the moment Totila had assumed the crown and issued his first decree, the Italians in all parts of the country had resumed their long-neglected work in the fields. Gothic warriors were under the strictest instructions not to interfere with this, and to prevent any interference by the remaining Byzantine troops as best they could. It so happened that the fields proved to be exceptionally fertile that year, resulting in a bountiful harvest of grain, wine and oil such as had not been seen for more than a generation. And this seemed to provide ample proof that even heaven had sided with the young king.

In Byzantium news of the capture of Naples and Rome was received with amazement, because the Gothic Empire in Italy was already regarded as extinct.

Merchants were attracted in large numbers by the strong protection offered them by the newly re-established law and order, the thoroughly patrolled roads and seas in and around Italy, and the economic boom which was taking place under the young king. In grateful admiration they spread word everywhere of the king's benevolence and justice, of the glory of his reign, and of the splendour of his court in Rome. In his capital Rome the king gathered the senators about him as they returned from flight or rebellion, and he also gave to the people plentiful grants of food and superb circus games.

The Frankish kings could see the altered situation in Italy, and sent gifts, but Totila refused them. They sent envoys, but Totila would not see them. The king of the Visigoths offered him an open alliance against Byzantium and the hand of his daughter. Avar and Slavic brigands on the eastern border were disciplined. Peace and order reigned in the entire Gothic Empire, as it had done in the most golden days of Theodoric, with the exception of Ravenna and Perusium, which were still under siege, and a few small castles.

But with all of this the king did not lose sight of the wisdom of moderation. Despite his victories he recognised the threat from the still militarily superior eastern Roman Empire, and he earnestly sought peace with the emperor. He decided to send a deputation to Byzantium, who were to offer peace on the basis that the emperor recognised the Gothic regime in Italy. On the other hand he was willing to cede Sicily, where no Goths remained at all and where Gothic settlement had never been extensive. He was also willing to give up those parts of Dalmatia which were still occupied by Byzantines. In return the emperor was to vacate Ravenna first and foremost, which no effort or generalship by the Goths had been able to capture.

As the man best suited to undertaking this mission of peace the king chose the one man whose rank and reputation were admired in Byzantium as well as in Italy, and who was also known for his great love of both Italy and the Goths. Totila chose the wise and honourable Cassiodorus.

Although the pious old man had withdrawn from affairs of state for many years, the king had managed to persuade him to undertake the rigours and dangers of a journey to Byzantium for the great aim of securing lasting peace in his beloved Italy, and Cassiodorus agreed to leave the seclusion of his monastery. But Totila could not possibly expect the old man to undertake the strain of such a journey alone, and so he sought after another, younger man imbued with the same Christian kindness and love for Italy and the Goths, to travel with Cassiodorus as his companion.

A few weeks after the fall of Rome a royal messenger took the following message across the Alps:

"To Julius Montanus Totila, whom they call King of the Goths and Italians.

"Come back, my dear friend, come back to me!

"Years have passed. Much blood and many tears have flowed. Everything around me has changed more than once, with both pain and joy, since the last time I shook your hand. Around me everything is different, but nothing has changed inside me, or between you and me. I still worship those gods whose altars we once visited together, and where we offered sacrifice with the first tears of youth, even if those gods have matured in my mind as I have myself matured.

"You departed from Italian soil when evil, violence, treachery and all the powers of hell ruled here. But you see, they have gone, swept away and bleached out by the new sun. The conquered demons have retreated far away, and a rainbow now rises above this Empire.

"As for myself, after better men yielded with little or no luck, the mercy of heaven has allowed me to see the end of the terrible thunderstorm, and to sow the seeds of a new era. Come now, my Julius, and help me fulfil those dreams at which you once smiled as being nothing but dreams. Help me to make a new, integrated nation of both Goths and Italians, combining the strengths of both sides but without the faults of either. Help me to build a kingdom of justice and peace, of freedom and beauty, ennobled by Italian charm and protected by Germanic strength.

"You, my Julius, have built a monastery to the church. Now help me build a temple for humanity.

"I am lonely, my friend, at the pinnacle of my success.

"My bride waits in loneliness for that oath to be fulfilled, and the war has taken my dear brother. Won't you come, my friend? In two months Valeria and I will await you in the monastery at Taginae."

And Julius read it, and then, deeply moved, he said to himself: "My friend, I am coming."

★

Before leaving Rome for Taginae King Totila decided to pay a debt of the greatest gratitude, and to give dignity and beauty to a relationship with which, until then, his bright and harmonious nature had not been entirely compatible. That relationship was with his nation's greatest hero, Teias.

They had been friends since early boyhood. Although Teias was several years older, he had always recognised and respected the depth and strength in the younger man, beneath the exterior joyfulness and youthfulness. They had also been drawn together by a shared leaning to idealistic and artistic thinking, and even by a common pride.

Later on of course the two men, who had been very different from the start, had been drawn very far apart by vastly different fortunes. The sunny nature of one was in stark contrast with the other's gloomy despair.

With the impatience of youth Totila had rejected the darkness and pessimism of his friend, which he could neither share nor understand. After several failed attempts to change his friend Totila had chosen to keep the latter's views away from his own, as if they were somehow diseased. First his friendship with Julius, also serious but more gentle, and then his love for Valeria had pushed the friend of his younger days into the background.

But these last years since that nightly meeting, where he and the others had sworn the oath as blood brothers, the suffering and dangers he had faced since the deaths of Valerius and Miriam, the burning of Naples, the siege of Rome, the treachery at Ravenna and now the duties and concerns of the crown had not been without effect. These events had so matured the once impatiently joyful youth that now, at last, he was able to better understand his dark and gloomy friend.

And what had that friend not achieved since that night! When others tired and stopped; Hildebad's vigour, Totila's drive, the steady Witigis and even old Hildebrand's icy calm, Teias had never complained and had always done his duty, never hoping yet always daring. At Regata, before Rome, after the fall of Ravenna and again before Rome – what incredible feats he had achieved! And what a debt the Empire owed him!

And he would accept no thanks. When Witigis had offered him the honour of a dukedom, land and gold, he had refused them as if they were an insult. Lonely and in silence he walked the streets of Rome, the last shadow in the sunshine around Totila. His black eyes always lowered, he was the one who stood nearest to Totila's throne. Without a word he would steal away from the king's feasts. His body was never without armour, and he never without arms. Only very occasionally, in the heat of battle, did he laugh, as when charging among Byzantine spears with a courage that defied death, or perhaps sought it. Then alone all seemed to be well with him. Then, and only then, everything about him was life and fire.

It was well known among the Gothic people, and Totila in particular knew it from his younger days, that the melancholy hero possessed the gift of song to an unusually marked degree, both in melody and poetry. But ever since he had returned from a period of imprisonment in Greece, nobody had been able to persuade him to sing one of his deep and fiery songs in front of others. Yet it was known that his small triangular harp was his constant companion in war and peace, as inseparable from him as his sword. During a battle, or while storming a fortress, he was occasionally heard to sing a few fragmented lines in time to the Gothic horns. And if anyone secretly followed him at night, which he liked to spend alone in the open among the white marble of Roman ruins and remote bushes, then he might well hear a lonely tune from his little harp, to which he sang a few dreamy words. But if one asked him – something few had dared to do – what was the matter with him, he would simply turn away silently. Once, after the fall of Rome, he had replied to just such a question from Duke Guntharis: "The Prefect's head!"

The only person with whom he had more frequent contact in recent times was Adalgoth, whom he had taken under his wing. The young shepherd had already been promoted by the king as his herald and cup bearer, as thanks for his brave deeds on the bank of the Tiber, and he had saved the king's life more than once. He had brought with him a strong talent for singing and story telling, although he had enjoyed very little training. Teias had found pleasure in his gift, and it was said that he was secretly teaching the eager youth his own superior art, although they were as different as night and day. "That's precisely why," Teias had replied when his brave cousin Aligern had pointed this out to him one day. "There has to be something left when the night fades away."

The king felt instinctively that he alone could give this man the one thing anyone could give him, and that one thing was neither gold nor honours.

One evening – the stars were already appearing in the sky – the king left the evening banquet in his palace. He had chosen as his palace the former house of the Pincians, where Belisarius had also resided. From there, unaccompanied, he went to seek out the shy hero in the wilderness of stones and laurel trees which filled the gardens of Sallustus, where Teias normally lived when he was in Rome.

Adalgoth the cup bearer had asked for leave from the king's table that evening, and the latter had guessed that he would spend the hours of darkness with his gloomy harp teacher, as he had so often done before. The king knew therefore that Teias would also be in the garden.

And indeed teacher and pupil were sitting under ancient Roman pines that evening, practicing the art of playing the Gothic harp.

"Now listen one more time please, Count Teias," the youth began, "to what I have made out of the few lines you composed the other night. With you it is all so sad again! And that leap into the river at the end, without hope! I have made it all much more cheerful."

"If only it were true."

"Oh, as long as it is beautiful! And true! Is the truth always sad?"

"Unfortunately, yes."

"Is there no joy in the world?"

"Oh yes, but it never lasts long. The end is always – that one perishes."

"Perhaps, but often not until very late. And that which comes between sunrise and sunset – has that no value? Is it not worth something?"

"Yes, it is something that must be. It is what a hero lives for!"

"Well, anyway, listen. I kept your beginning, and the sad part in the middle, but I conclude my song with a victory. I have left out your ending where they jump into the Isis River without hope. The way I have written it our old armourer Hildebrand..."

"If only he had Ravenna at last!"

"And I have brought our great king Theodoric into it, as the child Dietrich von Bern who was saved to inherit the Empire. And I want to perform the whole piece for our dear master soon, at the great royal feast. But make no mistake about it: I composed the whole thing in the new style of verse which you taught me, and which is much more appealing to the ear and soul than the old alliteration we used in our heroic songs and ancient proverbs. But where did you get the idea of rhyming the lines at the end?"

"The monks sing their Latin songs like that, and so do the priests in church. I heard it one evening in the basilica of St Peter. The curtains of the church were open, the twilight was flooding the interior, and the candles on the altar added their own glow. There were clouds of aromatic incense, and invisible choirboys were singing from the crypt with bright, clear voices. That is where I first heard the sound which is the same, and yet not quite the same. Hearing it was like magic to my ears, and I tried to do the same thing in our language. And as you see, it works beautifully."

"Yes, the closing sounds fit together like – like head and helmet, or like sword and sheath. Like lip on lip in a kiss."

"Oh, so you already know about that too? You are very young for that!"

"I have only ever kissed my beautiful sister Gotho," the youth replied with a blush.

"Well, let's get back to the verses! For many things the rhyming type of verse is certainly lovely. But you must not entirely neglect the alliteration of our fathers either."

"Yes, for some songs it is as if made to order, and it is much stronger than the meltingly soft rhymes. You know, when they sing our old verses, our powerful heroic songs, then it seems to me like a mighty wind blowing through the forest, bending saplings and trees alike in its path."

"Dear boy, the god of song has certainly touched your lips. You may not realise it, but beautiful sounds come from your mouth without your even trying, just as your tongue demands and the senses yearn for. Now tell me, how does your version of my song about Gothic loyalty go?"

"I start the same as you do: 'Slain, with half his army, there lay the Gothic king, Theodermer.' And so on. But then, where they all despair and jump into the river without hope, then in my song there is a ray of hope after all, a hint at a better and safer future, like this:

"'Slain, with half his army, there
lay the Gothic king, Theodemer.
The Huns rejoiced in the bloody plain,
and vultures bore down on the many slain.
The moon shone bright, the wind blew cold.
In the forests howled the wolves so bold.
Three men rode through the heather field,
with battered helmet and splintered shield.
The first one on his saddle did bear
his king's blood spattered, broken spear.
The king's crown helmet the second bore,
with a gaping hole a battleaxe tore.
The third man's loyal arms concealed
a precious bundle behind his shield.
And so they came to the Danube's tide:

the first man stopped his horse and cried:
"A broken spear and a helmet cleft,
nothing more of the Goths is left!"
And the second man said: "Into the deep
we give our treasure, for the river to keep.
We'll follow from the river's sand.
Why do you hesitate, Master Hildebrand?"
"You good men have the king's helmet and spear,
but I have more, something very dear!"
His cloak opened wide, so they could see:
"I have the Goths' great future with me!
You saved spear and helmet, nobly done.
I have saved our king's small son!
Awake my boy: we greet in you
young Dietrich, the Gothic king, we do!"

"Not bad at all. But the truth is…"

"I suppose the only truth is the sad future you see in your dreams? Tell me, how did that other poem go, the one you dreamt?"

"It was not altogether a dream, nor a poem. But I fear it will become altogether true. Before falling asleep I had thought for a long time about Gelimer, the last Vandal king, the brave man who had nothing left of his splendid Empire in the end but his harp, with which he later sang of his sadness in the hills of Africa. Finally I went into a sleep, or rather a dream. There I saw before me a landscape in Campania, as lovely as any in this splendid country. In the foreground I saw the Bay of Naples, with the sun shining on its waters. In the background was the mighty mountain with the fiery breath and cloud of smoke."

"What is it called again?" the young shepherd asked eagerly.

"Mons Vesuvius. And coming down its slopes I could see a group of warriors in our Gothic arms, sad yet proud. They were covered in blood, their helmets were battered and their shields broken. And on their spears they carried a dead man, their king."

"Totila?" the youth asked, terrified.

"No, calm yourself," Teias replied, with a melancholy smile. "The pale dead man had black hair. And they marched right through the midst of their enemies, who stood and watched in admiration, in a solemn procession to the edge of the sea. There lay a proud and mighty fleet, neither Greek nor Gothic, with huge dragon heads at the bows of each ship. The dead man was to be put on board one of the ships. And then I heard the words of a song of mourning in honour of their dead king. They were:

"'Give way, ye peoples, to our step! We are the last of the Goths:
We carry with us no crown; we carry only a dead man.
Shield to shield, and spear to spear we go to the north land's winds
until, in the distant grey sea we find the island of Thule.
They say it is the island of truth, where honour and oath have meaning still!'

"That is as much as I heard of the song of mourning, and then the horn of a Gothic patrol woke me, which our king thoughtfully has patrolling the streets at night. Make a point of remembering that beginning. Perhaps a day will come when you will finish it.

You have learned so much in such a short time that soon you will know more about harp playing and singing than I do."

"If only you could teach me to fight like you do as well!"

"That will come with the years, nay, with the weeks! You have done enough for your seventeen years. If a helper had jumped to the aid of our worthy King Witigis when the poet hurled a stone at him, as you did when our king was mortally threatened, then we might have won Rome that day and chased the Prefect out of Italy years ago; what a pity he has escaped us again!"

"Yes, unfortunately! You know, the events in the Prefect's house that night have been on my mind for some time now. They would make a wonderful song, but unfortunately there is no end to it yet."

"Just wait. Perhaps you will see the end to it, and then you won't have to invent it. By the way, I left the Prefect's house the very next morning after our victory, to pursue the legionaries who fled. And so I don't know what happened later. Tell me about it!"

Chapter 2

"Very well then, let me tell you. After I could not find the Prefect anywhere, neither by the Tiber nor in the Capitol, I decided to seek him out at his own hearth. All I found was a trail of his blood and his sword. But after you smashed his idol and burned his house, and after the whole structure collapsed right down into the cellar, I searched about once more near the foot of the statue. And there I found another hollow space, full of gold, jewels and documents.

"I carried everything I had found to the king on a broad shield. And he had his readers carefully search through the documents, as well as browsing through them himself. And then, suddenly, he cried: "So, Alaric of the Balti was innocent!" The next day, after I had been appointed a royal herald, my very first task was to ride about the streets of Rome on a white horse, with a golden herald's staff, and to announce to all the Romans and the Goths: 'Adalgoth, the king's herald, calls! In the house of the former Prefect there was found, by the hand of Adalgoth the shepherd, written proof that Alaric of the Balti was innocent of the charges which caused him to be sentenced to death for high treason twenty years ago!"

"How was that discovered?"

"Cethegus himself had recorded in his diary, using a secret code which Totila succeeded in breaking, that he had caused the hated Balti nobleman to be suspected of high treason. He did this by using forged letters, which he caused to fall into the hands of the deceived king. The noble and proud Alaric then managed to anger the Amalung further by his stubbornness, and one day he suddenly vanished from his dungeon. Nobody knew how he did it or where he went to. And I had to go on announcing in the streets: 'Alaric of the Balti is innocent. His property, which was confiscated, is hereby restored to him or his rightful heirs. The dukedom of Apulia, which he held, is given back to him or his rightful heir. Let Duke Alaric or his rightful heir make himself known openly to the king! Gold and gifts, land, property, cattle and carriages, weapons and ornaments, honours and the rich dukedom of Apulia shall be his, or his heir's. Where is Alaric? Where is the heir of the Balti?'

And the king's other heralds walked the roads and streets of Italy as I was doing, announcing the news and seeking information as to the whereabouts of Alaric of the Balti, and his rightful heirs. Wouldn't it be wonderful if they managed to find the exiled old man somewhere, and if we could restore his dukedom to him once more with all honour and glory?"

"And as he would owe his honour and his dukedom to the shepherd Adalgoth, I suppose he might give that lad a nice castle, on the seashore perhaps, near the Garganus Mountain among laurels and myrtles, eh?"

"No, that had not occurred to me."

"But I very much doubt that the old duke could still be alive."

"Well, perhaps we will find the young one. Duke Guntharis told me that he knew the distinguished hero well, and that he had gone to his exile with a little boy. And although his own house, the Woelsungs, had a long-standing feud with the Balti, yet he said that he himself had never believed in the proud man's guilt, because he had been an arch-enemy of the Italians, and a thorn in their sides. And he said that he had never seen a finer looking boy than Alaric's little four-year-old son.

"I keep thinking: where could he have got to? Won't he be surprised when he hears the heralds announce his reappointment as Duke of Apulia? He is probably living under a false name somewhere in a little town or village, because the whole of Alaric's family was affected by the sentence of death and banishment. That would make a nice ending to a 'Saga of the Balti' or 'Song of a fugitive'. What do you think? 'The song of the fugitive duke's son'. It has a nice sound to it!"

"With you all songs turn out quite well!"

"But now tell me the beginning of the other song, which you made up yourself after you awoke from that dream."

"Very well! Now, the song of mourning which I heard in my dream I only heard, I did not compose it. But after I woke up I placed myself in my mind's eye into that familiar landscape near Vesuvius, just opposite the Mons Lactarius or milk mountain. There is a superb stony chasm there, made of lava from the fire mountain. It is very steep, with only a small gap where one can enter it. It is so narrow that a single man with a shield could defend it for hours against any force, no matter how large or strong…"

"With every mountain or valley you immediately think how it could be stormed or defended."

"And then the words came to me of themselves:

'Where the lava cliffs rise at the foot of Vesuvius,
One can hear through the night sounds of deepest woe.
Neither shepherd, thief nor peasant dares enter the stony chasm:
And a fearful shadow lies brooding over the black stones.
Did a battle of nations rage here in the past?
Or is the battle still to be fought which will immortalise this place?'"

And he played a few notes softly on his harp, to which Adalgoth replied like an echo, just as softly.

Those were the sounds which led King Totila to the two men.

Along densely wooded paths the king followed the sounds he could hear coming from a clump of cypresses. They came softly and at intervals, words half spoken and half sung, accompanied by two distinctly different stringed instruments and carried to his ears by the night wind. Without being noticed Totila, whom not even the moonlight had betrayed, made his way through the ruined walls surrounding the vast gardens, and into the partly overgrown cypress and laurel pathways leading to their inner part.

Teias could hear the steps of a man approaching and he laid down his harp. "It is the king," he said, "I know his walk. What do you seek here, my king?"

"I am looking for you, Teias!" the latter replied.

Teias jumped up from the piece of broken column on which he had been sitting. "Are we going into battle?"

"No," Totila replied, "but I deserve that reproach." He took the hand of Teias and pulled him down onto the marble seat once more, sitting down beside him. "I am not looking for your sword, I am looking for you. I need you, but not your sword arm; I need your heart. No Adalgoth, you may stay. You shall hear how one must admire and love the proud man whom they call 'The Black Count'!"

"I have known that since I first saw him. He is like a dark forest through which a gentle breeze blows, deep and yet appealing."

Teias looked at his king through his sad eyes.

"You see, my friend, I have been so immensely fortunate, and our dear God in heaven has bestowed so many rich gifts on me! I won back an Empire which was half lost – should I not also be able to win back the lost half of a friend's heart? Certainly that friend did more than anyone as the Empire was being won back, and here again he will have to play a major part. What is it that estranges us? Forgive me if I, preoccupied by my own luck and happiness, have somehow neglected or offended you. I know well to whom I owe this crown, but I cannot wear it with joy unless I have your heart as well as your sword. We were friends once, Teias, a long time ago. Oh let us be friends once more, for I cannot do without you!"

And he tried to put an arm around his friend. But Teias took both the king's hands in his own, and pressed them sincerely.

"This nocturnal walk does you more honour than your victorious march through Italy. The tear which I just saw in your eye is worth more than the most precious pearl in your crown. Will you forgive me? I have done you injustice. Your luck and fortune and your cheerful nature have not harmed your heart at all. I was never angry with you! I have loved you always, and it was with pain that I saw our ways drawing ever more apart. Because deep down you and I do belong together, and you have more in common with me than you did with the worthy Witigis, or even your dear brother."

"Yes," said Adalgoth. "You two do belong together, like light and shade."

"We feel the same way, just as spontaneously and just as intensely," the king added.

"Where Witigis or Hildebad," Teias went on, "would walk straight down the road through life and war, it is as if some impatient wind always wants to carry us through the air before it. And it is because we do belong together like this that you, in your happiness, seemed to think that anyone who could not laugh as you do was a sick fool. Oh, my king and my friend, there are hammer blows of fate and pain which change the way a man thinks! He who has once endured such blows and thought those thoughts has lost the art of being able to smile for ever!"

Totila replied with earnest admiration and respect: "If a man performs his every duty with the same heroic strength as you do, then one may feel sympathetic towards him, but nobody has the right to scorn him because he rejects life's pleasures."

"And you believed that I felt anger at your luck or your cheerful nature? Oh Totila, it is not anger but rather nostalgia with which I look upon you and the way you are. Just as a child can move us to nostalgia as it imagines that summer, sun and life will go on for ever, not yet knowing that winter, cold and death also exist, you believe in the ultimate victory of goodness and joy in the world. But I hear only the wing beat of fate which is as pitiless and deaf to prayers as it is to curses and thanks." And with that he stared in front of him into the night, as if he was trying to peer into the shadows of an unknown future.

"Yes," the young cup bearer added, "it reminds me of an old verse, which Iffa used to sing up on the mountain. He learned it from Uncle Warga:

"'The world is not ruled by luck and ill fortune.
That is something which only we foolish humans thought of.

There is an eternal will, which has its way regardless:
To it we must be obedient, but we must resist it too.'

"But," the youth asked thoughtfully, "if we cannot avert that which is pre-ordained, even with all our might, why then struggle and wring our hands at all? Why then don't we simply await in gloomy brooding that which will come about anyway? Where is the difference between hero and coward?"

"That is something which is not determined by whether or not one is victorious, my dear Adalgoth! It is determined solely by the way in which a man fights and bears his fate, and by that alone! The fate of men and of nations is not decided by justice, but by necessity. Often in the course of history the better man, the greater nation and the nobler cause has perished before a lesser or meaner one. Certainly goodness and greatness are forces also. But they are not always strong enough to triumph over the greater might of other, lesser or more sinister forces. Heroism, justice and uprightness can always sanctify defeat, and glorify it, but they cannot always avert it. And that is our final consolation. The greatest honour on earth is not what we do or bear, but the manner in which we do it. Often the finest laurels belong not to the victor, but to the vanquished hero."

The king leaned on his sword deep in thought, and stared at the ground. "How much you must have suffered, friend," he then said with feeling, "before you arrived at such a black and wrong outlook! You have indeed lost your God in heaven! To me that would be worse than losing the sun up in the sky, or going blind. I could no longer breathe if I could not believe in a just God, who looks down upon us from heaven to observe what we do, leading to victory all that is good and pure and just!"

"And King Witigis? What crime had he committed, that fine man without fault and without wrong? Or I myself, and…" He did not finish his sentence, and was silent.

"I know nothing of your life since our ways parted when we were very young men."

"Enough of that for today," said Teias. "I have revealed more of my innermost self tonight than I normally do in years. I suppose that a time will come for me to reveal what I have experienced and thought." He stroked Adalgoth's golden hair. "I don't want to put gloom too early into the song of our nation's best and youngest singer."

"Very well," said the king, rising to his feet, "your sorrow is holy to me. But I do ask this of you: let us now put into practice our renewed friendship. Tomorrow I am going to Taginae to my bride. Come with me, if it does not offend you to see me happy with a Roman girl."

"Oh no, not at all! It touches me! It reminds me of… I will go with you!"

Chapter 3

A few days later the king arrived in Taginae with Count Teias, Adalgoth and a considerable following. On a steep and densely wooded hill above Taginae stood the convent of the Valerians, where Valeria still lived.

The place had lost its terrors for her, not only because in a physical sense she had become accustomed to it, but also because the serious religious forces which resided here had influenced her soul more and more. At first she had resisted this, but gradually she was being won over by the church. As she met the king on his arrival in the garden it seemed to him that she was even paler than usual, and that she walked more slowly than before.

"What is the matter with you?" he scolded her gently. "When it seemed that our oath could almost certainly never be fulfilled you managed to keep up hope and courage. And now that your beloved wears the crown of Italy, and virtually only one city in the country is still in enemy hands, you want to lose heart and give up hope?"

"I have not lost heart or hope for our happiness," Valeria replied seriously, "but I want to renounce it. No friend, hear me out. Why have you kept from me what the whole of Italy knows? What everybody else knows and expects of their king? The king of the Visigoths in Toledum has offered you an armed alliance against Byzantium and the hand of his daughter. The Empire wishes and expects that you will accept both. I do not want to be any more selfish than that noble-minded daughter of your people, Rauthgundis the mountain peasant's child, of whom your poets already sing and tell in the streets. And I know that you too can make a sacrifice like that humble man who was your king."

"I certainly hope that I could do it, if it were necessary. But fortunately that is not the case. I do not need foreign help. Look about you, or rather take a look outside the walls of this convent church some time. Never before has the Empire bloomed the way it is blooming now. I intend to offer the emperor my hand in peace one more time. If he refuses it again, then a fight will erupt such as has never before been seen. Ravenna must fall soon, and indeed, my strength and my courage are stronger than ever, as are my people. I am in no mood to renounce anything. The air within these walls has finally sapped your strength. You must get away from here! Pick the loveliest city in Italy as your home! Let us rebuild your father's house in Naples!"

"No, leave me here. I love this place and the peace within its walls."

"It is the peace of the grave! And you know very well, don't you, that renouncing you would also mean renouncing my life's dream? You are the living symbol of all my plans; to me you are Italia herself. That is why you shall become the Gothic king's own, totally and irrevocably. And both Goths and Italians shall take their king and queen as an example; they shall become one and happy as we will be. Now, no more objections and no more doubts! I will smother them all, like this!" And he embraced and kissed her.

★

A few days later Julius Montanus arrived from Genoa and Urbinum. The king went to meet him with his followers outside the convent garden. For a long time the two friends embraced without speaking.

Teias stood to one side and watched them, a serious look on his face.

"Sir," Adalgoth whispered, "who is that man with the deep set eyes? Is he a monk?"

"Inside he is, but not on the outside!"

"He is such a young man, and yet he looks so old. Do you know whom he looks like? That picture there, on the golden background."

"Yes, he does look like the sad, gentle apostle John."

"Your letter," Julius said at last, "found me already resolved to come here."

"You were going to look for me? For Valeria?"

"No, Totila! I came to be tried and, if I am worthy, initiated into holy orders by Cassiodorus. The pious and holy man Benedict of Nursia, who fills our century with miracles, has built a monastery which draws me mightily to it."

"Julius, you must not do that! Why has this spirit of wanting to escape from the world gripped all those who are nearest and dearest to me? Valeria, you, and even Teias!"

"I flee from nothing," the latter replied, "not even from the world!"

"How did you come to what, to me, is virtually suicide," the king went on as he led his friend by the arm to the inside of the convent, "in the best years of your life? Look, there comes Valeria! She must help you change your mind. Oh, if ever you had known love you would certainly not turn your back on the world!"

Julius smiled, but said nothing. Calmly he took the hand which Valeria cheerfully offered him, and went with her to the door of the convent, where they were met by Cassiodorus.

It was only with great difficulty that the king was able to persuade Julius to accompany the aging Cassiodorus to Byzantium after an interval of a few days. Julius was reluctant to face the splendour, the noise and the sins of the Imperial court, until in the end the example set by Cassiodorus changed his mind.

"I think," the king concluded, "that there are deeds in this world which please God more than those performed in monasteries. Surely a mission which is aimed at preventing another war between the two Empires is such a pious work!"

"Certainly!" Julius agreed. "A king or a warrior can serve God just as well as any monk. I do not fault your way of serving God, but leave me to my own way. And it seems to me that we are living in a time where an old world is disappearing, and a new one emerging among many a storm. All the evils of decaying paganism are blended with the wildness of countless Barbarians, while the whole world is filled with abundance, lust and bloody violence. Perhaps now is a good time to establish places far removed from the outside world, where poverty, humility and love may dwell in peace."

"But to me splendour, love and joyous pride do not seem like a sin before God. What do you say of our difference of opinion, friend Teias?"

"It has no meaning for me," the latter replied calmly. "For your God is not my God."

★

On the evening before the two envoys were to leave for Firmum, from where they were to embark for Byzantium by ship, Cassiodorus took Totila, Julius and their group of friends to a little chapel he had built, close to the monastery and located on a high cliff of the same mountain. "You will like it there, my Totila!" Valeria had said.

The friends reached the peak of the lovely rounded rocky outcrop just before sunset. From there, high above the surrounding countryside, they had a superb view of the landscape of Picenum around them. In the north and the east the view extended to the magnificent terraces of the Appenine Mountains, with those classical and lovely shapes which only an Italian landscape can possess. The glow of the setting sun shone in the west, like a precious golden belt, and its light was reflected in the waters of the River Classis, which joins here with two smaller rivers, Sibola and Rasina. And to the south the River Tinia glistened among the mountains of Nuceria and a fertile plain.

Under this laughing sky a bountiful harvest – it was the year of Totila's miraculous reign – had removed all traces of earlier devastation and desolation. Many hundreds of white marble houses, villas and castles could be seen among the green of the laurel trees or the silver grey of the olive groves, and the endless expanse of grapevines. On the southern slope of the hill stood an ancient watchtower, possibly from pre-Roman times. Its walls, as well as the entire crest of the hill, were covered by a delightful confusion of ivy, fig trees, vines and chestnut trees.

The setting sun threw a cloak of purple over the vast plain, a warm red glow, while the distant hills were covered by a layer of violet beauty. Surprised, and blinded by so much beauty, they all stopped in their tracks, and for a long time none of them could find words.

"I imagined Italia to be something like this," Adalgoth whispered to Count Teias, "when I looked southwest from the Iffinger, or even from the Mentula. But it is even lovelier than I dreamed."

But the king cried: "Now Teias, am I not right in loving this land like a bride? And in wanting to preserve it for our people at any price? Truly, this place is the best justification imaginable for what I am trying to achieve! Heavenly air and golden light surround this place!"

And he continued, with liveliness and emotion in his voice: "Yes, friends, Cassiodorus, this is where I want to be buried!" He laid his right hand on a mighty ancient sarcophagus of weathered dark marble. Its broken lid lay on the ground beside it, and its interior was filled entirely with wild ivy.

"What a happy coincidence!" Cassiodorus said seriously. "Do you know what this place has been called since ancient times? Spes Bonorum, the place of good hope. And do you know who, according to legend, once lay in this casket here? Another wise and kindly ruler who loved peace, originally probably an ancient Tuscan king. Local legend later had it that the tomb was that of Numa Pompilius, the benevolent one. Even the heathens worshipped here as an ancient place of peace, of blessing and of refuge. When I built my new chapel at the outbreak of the war, I dedicated it to Emmanuel, the god of peace. It would do my chapel the greatest honour if you, the king of peace, were to choose it as your final resting place."

"No!" cried Totila, "Forgive me, dear father! I do not want to rest in the dark crypt of your building. No, here under the blue Ausonian sky is where I want to rest when I die!" And he patted the side of the sarcophagus with his hand. "Here on this golden hill, surrounded by sunlight, by nodding laurel bushes and the singing of birds, is the place for me. I will get along very well with the spirits of the king of peace. Do you hear me, my friends? That is my wish. You listen most of all, Adalgoth, as you are young enough to survive us all, Adalgoth my favourite!"

"How can you think of the night in the noonday sun?" Adalgoth cried. "Who can do such a thing?"

"Those with a sense of foreboding," said Teias. "Look how quickly the sun has disappeared with her warm and cheerful light. Already a blanket of red, like a blood-soaked shroud, lies over the Valley of Taginae. And the violet shadows have already turned a deep black! So quickly and so suddenly! In all lands fate and death come even more rapidly than the night falls here in Italy."

Chapter 4

On the same evening Adalgoth was watching the sun go down at Taginae, Gotho, the shepherdess, was also watching the sunset. She was leaning on her staff, on the southern slope of the Iffinger Mountain.

Around her the sheep were frolicking about and grazing, eventually tiring and gathering around their guardian, eager to return to their stable for the night. But they waited and bleated in vain.

The lovely child was busying herself, sitting on a mossy stone by the bank of a clear mountain stream. In her apron she held a pile of sweet-smelling flowers, which she had gathered on the mountain slope. There was thyme, wild roses, mint and deep blue gentian. And as she sat there she was busy thinking and talking to herself, her flowers and the gurgling mountain stream. And she kept throwing flowers into the water, first singly, and then in small bundles or half finished garlands.

"How many?" the child said to herself and the waves, throwing her long golden plaits back over her shoulders, "how many of you have I already sent out to greet him? He went south, and these waters flow south too. But I don't know that you are delivering my messages, because he still has not come home. But look at the way you are dancing up and down with the waves, as if beckoning me to follow you. Oh if only I could! Or if I could follow the little fishes as they flit downstream like little dark arrows! Or even the swallows as they fly through the air, free as thought itself. Or the red-winged evening clouds, when the mountain wind carries them swiftly to the south. I am certain that my heart would find him, wherever he is, if only I could follow him south from this mountain into the distant, sunny land of Italy.

"But then, what would I do down there? Me, a shepherdess, among warriors and the clever women of the court? And yet I know that I will see him again, just as surely as I will see the sun again, which has just disappeared behind the mountain there. I just know I will! And yet every moment from the time the sun sets to when it rises again is filled with longing for the blessed sun to return."

Her thoughts were interrupted by the sound of her grandfather's horn blowing from the farmhouse.

Gotho looked up. It had become darker, and already she could see the fire burning red in the hearth through the open door. The sheep answered the familiar signal with loud bleating, and turned their heads toward the house and their stable. The shaggy brown dog jumped up against her, beckoning.

"All right, I am going," she smiled, calming all her animals. "Oh, sheep will tire of grazing long before the shepherdess tires of thinking! Come on now, Snowhite, you are quite big now!"

And she walked down the hillside towards the valley where the house and stables lay, for protection against the wind. The sun had disappeared completely, and the first stars were coming out. She looked up at them fondly: "They are so beautiful because he looks at them often."

A falling star flew overhead and fell to the south. "It is calling me, to go there," Gotho said to herself with a start. "Oh how I would love to follow it!" And so she drove her sheep more quickly, settled them in the stable, and then walked into the single large room on the ground floor of the house.

There she found her grandfather Iffa stretched out on a stone ledge by the fire, his feet covered with two large bearskins. He looked older and more pale than usual.

"Sit down here, next to me, Gotho," he said, "and have a drink – here is some milk mixed with honey – and listen to me. The time has now come of which I told you long ago. We have to part, because I am going home. My tired old eyes can barely make out your lovely face, dear child, and when I went down to the stream yesterday to fetch some water my knees gave way. And that's when I felt it; it is getting close.

"And so I sent the boy from the next farm to Teriolis with a message. But you are not to be here when old Iffa's soul leaves his mouth. Human death is not a pretty thing, at least not when an old man dies in his bed. And you have never seen anything sad, so I don't want this shadow to fall into your young life.

"Tomorrow, before the cock crows, the brave Hunibad will come from Teriolis to fetch you, he promised me that. Although his wounds have not yet fully healed, and he is still weak, he says he can no longer bear to remain idle when the fight is about to break out again at any moment. He wants to join King Totila in Rome, and you are to go with him with a most important errand. He will be your guide and protector.

"Bind strong soles of beech bark under your feet, for you have a long journey ahead of you. Brun, the dog, may go with you both. And take the goat leather pouch over there too. There are six gold pieces in it, from Adalgoth's – from your father. They belong to Adalgoth, but you may use some of the gold if you need it. You will have enough money to get you to Rome. And take a bundle of fragrant hay with you from the Iffinger meadow. You will sleep better at night if you rest your head on it.

"Once you have found Rome and the king's golden house in it, walk into the great hall and look to see which of the men has a band of gold on his head. If that man also has eyes which shine on you like the morning sun in the mountains, then you may be sure that man is King Totila.

"Then bow your head a little before him, but only a little. And do not bend your knee, for you are the free child of a free Goth. And then you must give the king this scroll here, which I have kept faithfully for many years. It is from your uncle Warga, whom the mountain buried."

And then the old man removed a brick from the base under the hearth, and from the dark space behind it he produced a papyrus scroll, carefully tied and sealed, and wrapped in a parchment, also written on and sealed.

"Here," he said, "take good care of these writings. The outer one, which is written on the donkey skin, contains what I told tall Hermegisel over in Majae to write for me. He swore to me that he would keep it to himself, and he has kept his word. Now he cannot speak at all, from under the church where they buried him. But you and Hunibad, you cannot read, and that is good. That's because it could be dangerous for you and – another person – if people should find out what that scroll contains before the kind and just King Totila knows of it. Particularly hide the scroll from the Italians.

"And whenever you enter a town or city, ask someone whether Cornelius Cethegus Caesarius is in it, the Prefect of Rome. And if the gatekeeper says he is, then turn on your heels. And then, no matter how late it is or how tired you are or how hot the midday sun, go away from that place and do not stop until you have put three stretches of water between you and that man Cethegus.

"And there is something else which you must guard just as carefully as these writings. You can see that I sealed them with tree resin that comes from the pines, and I scratched on it our house mark, which identifies our cattle and implements. The other thing which you must guard carefully is this old and precious gold!"

He reached back into the hollow space under the hearth, and produced one half of a broad bracelet made of gold, such as the Gothic warriors wore on their bare arms. With almost devout respect he kissed the gold and the runic characters on it. "This goes back all the way to our great King Theodoric, and it comes from him, from my dear – my son Warga. Remember, it belongs to Adalgoth, and it is his most precious inheritance. When the boy went away I gave him the other half of the bracelet, and the other half of the inscription on it. Once the king has read the inscription, and if Adalgoth is nearby, as he has to be if he followed my instructions, then call Adalgoth over to you and join the two halves of the bracelet together.

"And then listen to what the king says. They say that the king is intelligent, clear headed and kind, and that he is able to see through everything like a ray of sunshine. He will find the right thing to say, and if he does not then nobody ever will. Now give me one more kiss on each of my tired eyes, and go to bed early. May God in heaven watch over you and guide your steps, God and all his bright eyes, the sun, moon and stars.

"And once you have found Adalgoth, you will probably live with him in the little rooms of the stuffy houses in the city and in the narrow city streets. If ever it becomes just too small and tight and stuffy for you down there, then think back to the days of your childhood up here on the Iffinger Mountain. It will be like a breath of fresh mountain air to you."

Silently, without raising any objection, without fear and without asking any questions the child obeyed. "Farewell, grandfather!" she said, and kissed him on his eyes. "Thank you for all your love and caring."

But she did not weep, for she did not know what it is to die.

And she walked away from him to the threshold of the farmhouse, where she stopped and looked out into the mountain landscape, which had by now become quite dark. The sky was clear, and all about her the mountain peaks were glistening in the moonlight. "Farewell," she said, "you Iffinger, and you Wolfhead, and you, old Giant's Head! And you down there, shining Passara River! Do you know already? Tomorrow I will leave you all. But I go gladly, because I am going to him!"

Chapter 5

After many weeks Cassiodorus and Julius returned from Byzantium, without having secured peace. Cassiodorus went to his monastery in Apulia immediately after his ship landed, leaving Julius to travel alone from Brundusium and to report to the king in Rome. Totila received him in the Capitol, in the presence of the leading Gothic commanders and nobles.

"At first," Julius related, "our chances seemed favourable enough. The emperor, who had refused to even receive earlier envoys from King Witigis, could not refuse an audience to an envoy of the standing, wisdom and piety of Cassiodorus. And so we were received honourably and pleasantly in the palace. Important advisers, including Tribonianus and Procopius, advised the emperor to negotiate for peace, and he seemed to be favourably inclined to their advice.

"His two great generals, Belisarius and Narses, were both busy on the constantly threatened eastern borders of the empire, fighting Persians and Saracens in different places. And the campaign in Italy and Dalmatia had been so costly and so prolonged that the emperor had grown tired of the whole idea of the Gothic war.

"It is true that he was reluctant to entirely abandon the idea of regaining Italy, but he could see the impossibility of carrying out that aim, at least in the foreseeable future. He therefore gladly entered into peace negotiations with us, and received our proposals for consideration. For a while, he told us, he still had in his mind a temporary division of Italy, at the Padus River. By far the larger part of Italy in the south was to go to the emperor, with only the part north of the river to remain Gothic.

"One day at noon we left the Imperial palace with excellent prospects. The audience had been more favourable than earlier ones. But on the evening of that same day we were surprised by the *Curopatala* Marcellus, who had the usual parting gifts sent to us by palace slaves, which was an unmistakable sign that negotiations were terminated.

"Taken aback by this sudden turn of events," Julius continued his report, "Cassiodorus resolved nonetheless to risk incurring the Imperial wrath in the interests of peace, by requesting a further audience with the emperor even after the parting gifts had been received. The highly respected Tribonianus allowed himself to be persuaded to act as our go-between, and to seek this unheard of favour from the emperor. As an old friend of Cassiodorus, Tribonianus had always opposed the war.

"The emperor's reply was a most unfriendly threat of banishment if Tribonianus should ever again dare to request anything against the clearly indicated Imperial will. Never, not under any circumstances, would the emperor sign a peace treaty with the Barbarians until they had left the last sod of earth in the empire. Never would he regard the Goths in Italy as anything other than enemies.

"We tried in vain," Julius concluded his report, "to uncover a reason for this sudden change in attitude. We were only able to find out that, immediately after our last noon audience, the empress had invited her husband to dine in her rooms. It is said that the empress is ailing much of the time these days, but it is also well known that, although the empress was one of the most eager supporters of the war in the past, she had been in favour of peace rather than renewed war for some time."

"And what," the king asked, who had been listening earnestly to the report, but with a threatening rather than concerned demeanour, "brings me the honour of such a change in mood on the part of the circus wench?"

"It is whispered in Byzantium that she is more and more concerned about the welfare of her soul, and so she really does not want to see the limited Imperial funds spent on a war, the outcome of which she does not expect to see. Instead she wants every effort made to build churches, especially the St Sophia cathedral. She wants to be buried under the foundations of that church."

"She probably wants to use it as a shield against the anger of the Lord on the day of judgment! The whore wants to disarm God with a hundred churches and bribe Him with their cost. What madness this religion breeds!" Teias muttered darkly to himself.

"And so we found not a single clue. The only thing I did see, a mere shadow and possibly an error that slipped past me in the night, can hardly be described as a clue."

"And what was that?" Teias asked attentively.

"As I was leaving the palace late at night, considering the unfavourable report from Tribonianus, a gilded sedan chair belonging to the empress was carried quickly past me by her slaves. It was coming from the direction of Theodora's wing of the palace. The shutters had been raised a little by the occupant of the sedan chair. I saw him, and it seemed to me as if I recognised…"

"Well? Who was it?" Teias asked.

"My unfortunate fatherly friend, the long lost Cethegus," Julius sadly replied.

"Hardly!" said the king. "He fell. It was probably a deception when Teias thought he could still hear his voice in the house."

"Me? Fail to recognise that voice? And the sword which Adalgoth found in the street?"

"Could have been lost by him earlier, when he was hurrying from his house to the Tiber. I saw him there, clearly commanding the defence from his ship. That spear was aimed at my throat with all the skill and force that only hatred can engender. Also Gunthamund, who is an outstanding shot, told me he was sure he had hit him in the neck. His cloak was found on the riverbank, with holes from many arrows and completely covered in blood."

"I suppose he must have died there," Julius said in a grave voice.

"Could it be that you are all such good Christians, and yet you do not know that the devil is immortal?" Teias asked.

"That may be," the king replied, "but light is immortal too!" And he knitted his brows threateningly as he went on. "Now, on your feet, my valiant Teias, there will be work for your brave sword. Hear me well, Duke Guntharis, Wisand, Grippa, Markja, Aligern, Thorismuth, Adalgoth: soon I will have plenty of work for all of you. The emperor Justinian refuses us peace or the peaceful possession of Italy. Evidently that is because he considers us to be just too peaceful. He thinks that it can do no possible harm to have us as his enemies. At worst we would sit quietly in Italy, waiting for him to attack. And Byzantium can choose to attack us at any time they want to, again and again, until at last they succeed. Very well, we will show him that we can be very dangerous as enemies, and that he may be well advised to leave us in peace here in Italy rather than provoke us into attack.

"He does not want us to live in Italy? Well then, he shall see the Goths in his own country once more, as was the case in the days of Alaric and Theodoric. But for the time being I will say only this, for secrecy is the womb that will bring us victory. We will enter the eastern empire with wings of linen, and on bridges of wood. Just as we entered Rome in this manner, so shall we penetrate to the very heart of the eastern Roman empire. Now, Justinianus, prepare to defend your own hearth!"

Chapter 6

Some considerable time after news of the failed peace mission had reached Rome, two men were engaged in a confidential discussion in the dining room of a house on the Forum Strategii in Byzantium. The house was built simply but in exquisite taste, and it commanded a view over the incomparable strip of coast known as the Golden Horn, and the magnificently laid out new city of Justiniana.

. The master of the house was our old friend Procopius, who now lived in Byzantium, having acquired the high rank of a senator. He was eagerly pouring more wine for his guest, but was using his left hand in doing so. His right arm ended in a concealed stump.

"Yes," he said, "at every move my missing right forearm reminds me of an act of foolishness. It is true that I don't regret it; I would do the same again, even if it was to cost me the eyes in my head. It was a foolishness of the heart, and to have such a foolishness is the greatest happiness a man can possess. I was never quite the kind of man who falls in love with women. My one love was and is: Belisarius. I am perfectly well aware – there is no need to look quite so disdainful, my friend – I see and recognise the faults and shortcomings of my hero very well. But that is just what makes a foolishness of the heart so agreeable. The heart loves the faults of a loved one too, more than the virtues of other people.

"Well then, I will make it short. During the last Persian war I warned the man with the lion's courage and the child's heart once again not to ride through an unknown and unsafe forest with only a small force to protect him. It was near Dara. Of course that only made him more determined than ever to do it, the silly, dear fool. And of course Procopius, the intelligent fool, rode with him. And it all happened just as I had foreseen and foretold. Suddenly the entire forest was alive with Persians. It was as if the wind was shaking dry leaves and twigs from the trees, but they were all spears or arrows.

"It was just as it had been at the Porta Tiburtina in Rome, only this time Balan, his faithful stallion, drew his last breath as well. Riddled with spears the noble animal fell dead, and I lifted my hero onto my own horse. And then a Persian nobleman who is almost as tall as his name is long – the man is called Adrastaransalanes – took a swing at the *Magister Militum* with his sword. It happened so quickly that I could use only my arm to deflect it, because my shield was already occupied defending my commander against a Saracen. The blow was a good one, and had it struck Belisarius's head it would have split it in two like a seashell. As it was the blow merely sliced off my right forearm as cleanly as if it had never been there."

"Belisarius, of course, escaped, and Procopius, of course, was taken prisoner," said the guest, shaking his head.

"Correct on both counts, oh thou possessor of great intellect, as my friend Adrastaransalanes would call you. But that same man with the long body, sword and name, which I hope you won't insist on my repeating again, was so impressed by my 'elephantine bigheartedness', as he put it, that he released me soon afterwards without demanding any ransom money. He merely requested a ring, which had been on a finger of my former right hand, as a souvenir, or so he said. Since then there has been an end to my campaigning," Procopius continued in a more serious vein. "But I interpreted the loss of my writing hand as a kind of punishment also. With it I have written many an unnecessary or not entirely truthful word. True, if the same punishment were meted out to every writer in Byzantium, then there would soon be no man left with two arms to write anything. My writing is now somewhat slower and more laborious. And that is good, because I now think a little longer about every word, whether it is worth the effort and whether writing it down can be justified."

"I have read with great enjoyment," said the guest, "your *Vandal War, Persian War* and, as far as you have completed it, your *Gothic War*. During my prolonged convalescence it was my favourite book. But I am amazed that you were not sent to join our friend Petros in the mines of Cherson with the Ultzigarian Huns. If Justinian punishes falsification of documents that severely, how savagely must he punish truthfulness in a historical account? You dared to criticise the fickleness of his mind, his greed and his errors in the choice of his generals and officials mercilessly! I am amazed that you are unpunished!"

"Oh, I am not unpunished," the historian replied grimly. "He left me my head, but he did try to take away my honour. And that goes even more for her, the beautiful devil in female form, because I had suggested that he, Justinian, is totally dependent on her apron strings. And she wants to continue – and keep secret – this dominance she has over him, both with equal intensity. And so she sent for me after my books had appeared.

"When I entered and saw those books on her lap I thought: 'Adrastaransalanes took the hand that wrote it, and this woman will take the head which thought it!' But she contented herself with extending her small golden shoe for me to kiss, and then she smiled most beautifully and said: 'You write Greek like no other man of our time, Procopius. So beautiful and so true! I have been advised to despatch you to the company of the silent fishes at the bottom of the Bosporus. But the man who best knew how to tell us the truth when it was bitter medicine to us will also write the truth when it is music to our ears.

"'The best critic Justinian has had will also become his greatest eulogist. Your penalty for your book about Justinian's works of war will be – a book about Justinian's works of peace.

"'You are hereby commissioned by the Imperial court to write a book about the emperor's buildings. You cannot deny that he has tremendous achievements to his credit in that regard. If you were a better lawyer than your life in Belisarius's camp has allowed you to become, then you would be required to describe his greatest mosaic creation, his legal code. But your legal training is not sufficient for that, oh brave shield bearer of Belisarius (and she was quite right, the beautiful demon). You will therefore write a book *The Buildings of Justinianus*, and you yourself will become a living memorial to his magnanimity. For you will agree that under earlier emperors many a writer has lost his eyes, nose and other parts which are not pleasant to do without. No emperor has yet permitted such things to be written about him, let alone reward such liberties with a commission. Should *The Buildings of Justinianus* not be to your liking, then I fear that you would not long survive such lack of taste, for the saints would soon punish your ingratitude with death. And you see, I have worked out a reward for you, the reward I have just described, because Justinian was only going to make you a senator. And so you will have been right after all, when you wrote of Theodora's all-powerful influence.'

"And then another kiss for her shoe, and this time she used the occasion to strike me on the mouth with it in good natured jest. I had made out my last will and testament before the audience. Now you see how this demon in female form has taken her revenge against me! It is true, one really cannot be critical of Justinian's buildings. One can only praise them – or remain silent.

"If I choose to remain silent it would cost me my life. If I choose not to remain silent and not to write praise, then it would still cost me my life, and my love of the truth as well. And so I have to praise or die, and I am so weak," sighed the host, "that I would rather praise and live."

"To have enjoyed so much of Thucydides and Tacitus, both in dry and liquid form," said the guest as he refilled both goblets, "and yet never to have been a Thucydides or a Tacitus!"

"I would rather have my friend with the long name hack off my left hand too than write that book with it about Justinian's buildings!"

"Keep your hand! And with that same hand, after you have written publicly in praise of the buildings, write secretly another book – about the evil works of Theodora and Justinian."

Procopius jumped to his feet. "That is fiendish! But it also great! That advice is worthy of you, friend. For that I will give you one of the nine Muses of Herodotus from my cellar – my oldest, noblest, purest wine. Oh, posterity shall be amazed at that secret book! The only pity is that I cannot tell of the worst of murder and filth, for I would perish from sheer disgust. And even what I do write will be regarded as wild exaggeration by later generations. But what will posterity think of Procopius if he writes a criticism, a eulogy and an accusation against Justinian?"

"They will say: 'he was Byzantium's greatest historian, but he was also a victim of Imperial tyranny'. Avenge yourself! She has left you your very clever head and your left hand; now your left hand will not know what your right hand has written in the past. Paint a picture of this emperor and his woman for all the generations of the future! Then they will not have triumphed with their buildings, but you yourself will have done so with your secret history. She meant to punish what she considers your boundless impertinence; now you punish her by a boundless revelation of the truth. Every man avenges himself with a weapon of his own choosing, a soldier with his sword, and a writer with his pen."

"Even if, or perhaps especially if," said Procopius, "only one hand is left to him. I thank you, and I will follow your advice, Cethegus. I will write the *Secret History* as revenge for the *Buildings*. But now it is your turn to relate what has happened to you. I know what happened until that hour when you were last seen in your house, from letters and from verbal reports by legionaries, who were released by Totila. Some say that you were last heard in your house. Tell me now, oh Prefect without a prefecture."

"In a moment," said Cethegus, "but first tell me: what happened to Belisarius in the Persian campaign?"

"Oh, the usual. You had no need to ask that, nor should you have done so! Belisarius had indeed defeated the enemy, and was about to force the defeated Persian king Chosroes, the son of Kabades, to conclude a permanent peace on terms favourable to us. And then that Prince of Snails, Areobindos, appeared in the camp with news that Byzantium had agreed to an armistice for six months behind the back of Belisarius. Justinian had long ago commenced negotiations with Chosroes – he just happened to be short of money again. Once again he pretended that he did not entirely trust Belisarius, and for five hundred hundredweight of gold he allowed the Persian king to slip the noose just as we were about to draw it tight around his neck.

"Narses was much smarter. When the Prince of Snails came to him, on the Saracen section of the theatre of war, he declared that the messenger had to be either a forger or mad. So he took him prisoner and continued the war until he had defeated the Saracens completely. Then he sent an Imperial envoy to Byzantium with an apology. But the best apology was the keys and treasures from seventy castles and cities, which he had wrested from the enemy during the armistice implemented by Belisarius."

"That Narses is…"

"The greatest man of our time," Procopius interrupted. "And that even includes the Prefect of Rome, because unlike the latter, Narses is not trying to do the impossible. But we, that is Belisarius and the cripple Procopius, we returned to Byzantiumn, ever angry, ever critical, but also ever as loyal as poodles and, as usual, none the wiser from our experience. We maintained the armistice with constant grinding of our teeth, and now we are back here awaiting new orders, new laurels and new kicks from Imperial feet. Luckily Antonina has given up her former fondness for the verses and flowers of other men, and so the happy couple, the lion and the dove, are now quite happily living here in Byzantium. Belisarius of course spends his days and nights pondering just how he can best demonstrate his loyalty and his courage to his Imperial master once more. Justinian is his weakness, just as Belisarius is mine. But now it is your turn to talk."

Chapter 7

Cethegus took a deep draught from the goblet in front of him, which was fashioned from solid gold in the shape of a tower.

He was a changed man since that night in Rome. The lines around his eyes were etched even deeper now, and his mouth narrower than before, with its lips tightly closed. His lower lip was raised, giving his face a severe look, and that ironic smile, which had once made him look younger and more handsome, appeared much more rarely now. His eyes were now almost habitually half closed.

Only once in a while did those eyes open fully, to reveal the much feared piercing look in them, and that look was now more devastating than ever.

It seemed not so much that he had grown older, but that he was now even more a man of iron than before, more determined and more relentless.

"You know," he began, "what happened up until the time when Rome fell. That night I saw the city fall, and the Capitol, my house and my Caesar with it. The crashing end of that statue hurt me more than Gothic arrows, or even Roman ones.

"I lost my senses out of pain and anger, as I tried to punish the man who murdered my Caesar. I collapsed in the library before the Zeus statue.

"I was awakened again by the feel of fresh night air and by the Tiber, which revived a mortally wounded Cethegus once before – twenty years ago."

A dark cloud moved over his majestic forehead.

"Of that, perhaps, I will speak another time – or perhaps never," he said, cutting off any possible questions on the part of his host.

"This time I was saved by Lucius Licinius, whose brother fell for Rome and for me, and by my faithful Moorish slave, who had managed to escape that black maniac Teias as if by a miracle. The Barbarian threw the slave out through the door, not taking the trouble to murder him in his hurry to get to the master. Syphax hurried to the back door, where he caught up with Lucius Licinius, who had just reached my house through the masses of people outside by a side street.

"Both of them now followed the trail of my blood through the open doors until they found me in the Zeus room. There they found me unconscious, and they barely had time to wrap me in my cloak and lower me into the courtyard like some piece of lifeless merchandise. Syphax jumped down first, and he caught me after the tribune let me down. The latter followed, and together they carried me out of my burning house in my cloak, through the back door and down to the river.

"When they got down there it was almost deserted. All the Goths and all the pro-Gothic Romans had followed the king to the Capitol in order to put out the blaze there. He had expressly ordered – to his doom, I hope – that all non combatants were to be left alone. And so my two bearers with their load were allowed through everywhere. Everyone thought they were carrying a corpse, and for a while so did they.

"Down by the river they found an empty fishing boat full of nets. They put me in it, and Syphax threw my blood-soaked cloak with the purple insignia of the *Princeps Senatus* onto the riverbank in order to lead the enemy astray. Then they covered me with pieces of canvas and nets, and rowed downstream through the boats and barriers, which were still burning. Once we were past them I came to, as Syphax washed my forehead with water from the Tiber. The first thing I saw was the burning Capitol.

"They say that my first cry was: 'Go back! The Capitol!' And they had to forcefully restrain me, in my feverish eagerness, from going back. Of course my first clear thought was: 'Revenge! Recapture of Rome!'

"In the harbour of Portus we came upon an Italian grain ship with a crew of seven oarsmen. My rescuers drew alongside the ship in order to try and obtain a little bread and wine, as they were also both wounded. And then the oarsmen recognised me. One of them wanted to deliver me as a prisoner to the Goths, certain that I would bring a high reward. But the other six had been workmen who had once worked for me on the walls at Hadrian's tomb; I had fed them and their families for years. They slew the seventh, who was calling for the Goths in a loud voice, and they promised Lucius that they would save me if there was any possible way they could do so.

"They hid me from Gothic patrol boats in a big heap of grain as they left the harbour, and Lucius and Syphax sat themselves at the oars in the garb of fishermen. And that is how we made good our escape. But while we were on that ship I came close to death as a result of my wounds. Only my faithful Moor and the fresh sea air saved me. For days, they say, my only words were: 'Rome, Capitol, Caesar.'

"Once we had landed at Panormus, under Byzantine protection, I recovered quickly. My old friend Cyprianus, who had once let me into Theodoric's palace when I was to become Prefect of Rome, happened to be harbour master there, and he received me most hospitably. Barely recovered, I travelled from Sicily to Asia Minor, or Asiana as you call it, to my estates. As you know I had glorious estates at Sardes Philadelphia and at Tralles…"

"Don't you have them any more? They were superb villas!"

"I sold them all. After all, I had to hire new mercenaries at once, so that I can free Rome and Italy."

"*Tenax propositi!*" Procopius cried in surprise. "You have still not abandoned that hope?"

"Can I abandon myself? What they fetched was not insignificant; Furius Ahalla bought the villas on the coast at Ephesos and Jassos. And so, with the gold from the sales, I went to my old friends in the lands of the Isaurians, Abasgans and Armenians. I had to kill one Isaurian leader, because he attacked my tent one night, hoping to get hold of my gold without giving anything in return other than a dagger thrust. After that I managed to hire a good many mercenaries.

"But of course Narses has made them expensive; he spoils them and he has ruined the trade. They are no longer willing to die as cheaply as they used to. He has won many a brave chieftain over to his colours.

"And so I had to look around for other peoples as well. Now, down in Pannonia, there happens to be a Germanic tribe, not very numerous but strong and courageous. I only discovered them from your writings, my friend – they are known for their bloody wars against the Gepidae."

"Ah," cried Procopius, "the savage Lombards! May God have mercy on your Italy if ever they set foot in it. The Lombard is like a wolf compared to the Gothic sheepdog, or the golden fleeced sheep, Italy."

"But Rome herself is to become the she-wolf of old once more. I will find a way to get them out again, Alboin and his Barbarians! I have sent Lucius Licinius to these long beards – that is what I believe the name means – to do a deal with them. It would give me the greatest pleasure," he concluded bitterly, "to destroy one Germanic tribe through another. With every wound that Lombard and Goth inflict on one another Rome will be the winner."

"You have learned the wisdom of Tiberius from your Tacitus. But let's leave the Tacitus be, it is too dry. Here is an excellent drink: Ammianus Marcellinus! Truly a fine fellow!"

"I wonder how posterity will judge 'Procopius' as a drink?"

"Buildings," the latter replied, "stuffy!"

"Persian and Vandal Wars – golden clear," said Cethegus.

"Gothic War – too sour!" the author of the latter contributed, pulling a face.

"But Secret History," Cethegus smiled, "fiery stuff – to be sipped drop by drop only at the end of a meal."

"Bah, an emetic!" Procopius replied, shaking himself.

"But I," Cethegus went on, "hurried over here into the den of the – shall we say 'lion'?"

"That would be an exaggeration," Procopius commented, "even the 'Buildings' will not contain a lie like that."

"Very well then, your fox or your hamster. Because I am not as naïve as the great Belisarius, and so I do not deceive myself that the Goths can be defeated with mercenaries alone. Those Barbarians have the undeserved luck of being a nation, and their king is the living symbol of that nationhood. It is extremely difficult to defeat a nation, even a clumsy, stupid, dull nation like those Barbarians."

"What you mean is," Procopius nodded in agreement, "that it is difficult to defeat a nation without being a nation."

"But Byzantium, even though it may not be a nation, is at least a state. And that state without a nation can defeat a nation without a state, because what the Goths choose to call their 'Empire' cannot be called a state. It is merely a horde which has settled somewhere. Didn't they have three Gothic armies fighting against one another under that Witigis? Even the Byzantium of your *Secret History* is superior to that kind of foolishness, immaturity and barbarism. And the emperor Justinian did give his word that he would liberate Italy. Be assured that he will be reminded that he should keep that word. I will keep on reminding him until at last he does it."

"You may have to go on reminding him for a very long time!"

"So it seems. Religion, fame, gold, nothing seems to motivate him any more. Let us see if perhaps fear will serve to do it."

"Fear? Of whom?"

"Of Cethegus – and the – unknown. Nameless horrors are always the most gruesome. Naturally I had pinned much hope on the empress. We were friends once, in our youth, and we valued our common strengths even then. She was the most beautiful woman I had ever seen – at that time. And I?"

"You were Cethegus," said Procopius.

"But in spite of the old attraction, which she did not deny when I appeared before her again now, the empress is not in favour of my war. I cannot quite understand her. Suddenly she deems it more Christian to build churches than it is to burn cities! Why this sudden change? After all, she is too young for that journey common to the likes of her, shall we say from Cypros to Golgatha."

"So you don't know," Procopius interrupted, "what everyone in the Eastern Empire knows, except Justinian and you? The beautiful empress is ill, being consumed from within by a terrible disease. You are surprised? Yes, she not only endures it, but with incredible willpower she even manages to hide it from Justinian. Because he, the greatest and the smallest of all selfish men, hates sickness! He cannot bear to have anything near him which reminds him of suffering or death.

"The empress's hold over him is incredibly strong. But even so I am sure that, if he were to discover her suffering, he would send her to the furthest corner of the Empire to recover, ensuring of course that she had every care. After all, he did the same with Germanus, whom he genuinely loved.

"That is why the empress bears up to the tortures of hell with a smile on her lips. They say that her nights are terrible. But by day, when she is near the emperor, at the table, in church or at the circus, she hides her pain with superhuman strength. Even her beauty has barely suffered, because her arsenal of cosmetic tricks is inexhaustible. She has become still more delicate in her body, but her mind has grown even more in its all-powerful dominance."

"A wonderful woman!"

"Yes, and much as she practises her cunning and intrigue in small things, in the bigger things such as affairs of state, she never deviates from her convictions."

"Never! Or at least only with great reluctance. The emperor was already about to accept the Gothic peace proposals; Cassiodorus and – another man were about to triumph over me. Theodora was not in favour of war, and it seemed to me that everything was lost. And then, at the last moment, it occurred to me to appeal to her piousness.

"I was able to discover from her directly that Justinian had summoned the two envoys to the palace for a favourable decision. Just before noon on the same day I hurried to her and said: 'You are building churches for the saints with all your gold. At best you can build a hundred more. But if you cede Italy to the Goths you will take more than a thousand churches away from Christus, the son of God, and hand them over to His hated enemies, the Arian heretics. Do you think that a hundred new churches will make up for that?'

"That worked. She leapt from her bed and cried: 'No, that is not a sin I want to commit! And if indeed we are too weak to wrest those churches away from the heretics, we will certainly not openly hand them over. The emperor must never let them have Italy without a struggle! I thank you, Cethegus! The saints will forgive us many a joint sin from our younger days, because you have kept me from committing this, the greatest sin of all.'

"And then she invited her husband to dine with her, and under her flowers, prayers and kisses Justinian became inflamed with the cause of Christ once more, refused the peace offers, and so the wise Cassiodorus had to leave without having achieved his aims. Peace has been prevented. I do not yet have the means to force an immediate war, but I will find them. Because Rome must again become free of those Barbarians."

Calmly Cethegus halted, raised his goblet and drank. But within him there still burned a deep, if controlled, passion.

Chapter 8

Procopius laid his hand on the shoulder of his friend Cethegus and said: "Cethegus, I am truly amazed. I am amazed that, in this time of decay, there is still such power and force in a man's breast.

"I am even more amazed that the same fire burns for a high and unselfish goal, like the freedom of Rome. Let us assume that this goal is merely an impossible dream, as I think it is. Even if that is so your goal is not a selfish one, and for that reason I am willing to forgive the many dark and crooked paths you have taken to achieve it, and which you have caused others such as Belisarius and myself to take, through treachery, cunning and sin. But should I ever find that your goal is a selfish one after all, then much as I admire your mind and your drive, from that day I would have to call an end to our friendship."

But Cethegus merely laughed: "Could it be that I still hear from your lips the same old ethic from our schooldays in Athens, half Christianity and half Plato? You are an incorrigible disciple of the Imperial court and the army camp! Are you still clinging to that girlish morality? Selfish or unselfish – what, who is there that is unselfish? Who can be so? Every one of us wants what he must want.

"Whether I am to become Rome's liberator or perhaps her tyrant, either goal is selfish. For love is the greatest passion only because it is the sweetest form of selfishness."

"And Christ? Are you suggesting that he died selfishly too?"

"Certainly. He died for a noble-minded daydream! His egotism was aimed at humanity, which rewarded him by crucifying him for his love. Just as Justinianus rewards Belisarius, and as Rome will reward Cethegus. The selfishness of weaklings is despicable, but the selfishness of the strong is greatness! That is the only difference among men."

"No, friend! That is the logic of a powerful passion. The highest goal is to aim for something good by good means alone. And for that ultimate goal Procopius is too small, and our time too weak.

"But let us at least serve only good causes by evil means, not baser aims, nor selfishness! Woe betide me if ever I should find that I misjudged you. I believe in the hero of the sword, Belisarius, and the hero of the mind, Cethegus. Woe be me if ever my hero Cethegus should become a demon. I can understand that men avoid you and fear you like Lucifer, the fallen angel of the morning star. 'All his enemies perish before him,' Antonina once told me, who fears you with an almost superstitious intensity. And she is right! Think of Gothelindis, Petros our cunning fellow student, who is now sawing marble and cutting stone with the Huns, Pope Silverius whom the emperor still holds imprisoned on the island of Sicily, like Scaevola and Albinus. From the latter he took his soul as well, which means his money."

"I could quote even more examples," said Cethegus, knitting his brows, "but I do not want to provoke angry shadows out of their graves. I will mention only fat Balbus," he laughed. "I had intended for him the honour of dying like the son of God. But he willingly sacrificed himself to his own god, namely his stomach. I heard of his end from Quintus Piso, whom the Barbarian king released without ransom money, like Marcus Massurius and Salvius Julianus.

"With his last gold pieces Balbus bribed the Gothic guards, who were there to prevent excessive overeating by the ravenously hungry, to let him eat as long as he wanted to. He ate for three hours, and in the fourth hour he dropped dead! He died on duty! But of what use is the undoing of all my minor enemies to me? As long as there is an enemy in Rome who is indeed great," and he paused for a moment before continuing intensely, "but only in terms of sheer luck!"

"Are you not being unjust against King Totila? Don't you think that one day his historians will write a different…"

"I am not his historian, but his enemy to the death. Ha, I must live to see the day when that boy's heart's blood is dripping from the end of my spear!

"I can fully understand Achilles, and why he dragged the body of the slain Hector around the walls three times. Ever since I began fighting for my Rome, again and again that flaxen head with the girlish face has opposed me, and has almost always been victorious.

"He took away from me my adopted son and my Rome, and in the end he even took my Pluto. Piso says that, when they were pursuing me, they found only my stallion where Syphax had hidden him by the Tiber. And of all the booty in Rome the Barbarian wanted for himself only the 'Prefect's horse'. Throw him off, my Pluto, and then smash his skull with your hooves!"

"You hate with real heat!"

"Yes, I hate him not only out of common sense, but from a fundamental animosity between his being and mine. When I had to vacate the Forum Romanum in his favour I swore it: he will die by my hand!

"But," he concluded, calming himself, "When? When?

"When will I find the means to hurl this lazy colossus whom they call Justinianus, the emperor of the Romaeans, against the Gothic Empire? When will fate call me back once more to the great battlefield called Italy? Oh, when will the tuba sound?"

At that moment Syphax came rushing into the room. "Master," he said as he bowed, "I request a messenger's reward. There has been a storm somewhere, and I think it is coming quickly to this city. Something is brewing in the air. There is much busy activity in the golden palace. Guards have been posted at every entrance, so that any envoys or messengers are immediately taken to the emperor in closed litters. The messengers are to speak to nobody. And a moment ago a messenger in a golden outfit delivered this letter to your house – from the empress."

Hastily Cethegus tore open the purple strings from the seal – it was a dove – and read: "To the Jupiter of the Capitol. Do not leave your house tomorrow until I send for you. Tomorrow you will be called by your fate and – Kypris."

Chapter 9

The following morning found the emperor Justinian standing before the tall, golden cross in his room. He was deep in thought, and the expression on his face was grave, but it showed neither dismay nor doubt. There was a look of calm determination on these features, which could not normally be described as handsome or noble, but at this moment they did betray a high degree of intellectual and mental ability. Almost threateningly he raised his eyes up to the golden cross and said: "You have subjected your loyal servant to great trials, oh God of the cross! I would have thought I had deserved better, Christ Jesus! You know all the things I have done in order to honour your name. Why then don't you strike at your enemies, the heretics, instead of me? Why me? But since you seem to want it this way, you will see that Justinian can do more than build churches and consecrate pictures."

He paced through the room, and as he did so his gaze fell on the row of busts of earlier emperors, which were standing there on small pedestals along the wall.

"Great Constantinus, founder of this eastern Empire and protector of the true faith! Do you fear for your creation? Do not be afraid, but take heart! You built it, and Justinian will preserve it. The others there among you had it easy, being great and creating greatness: Augustus, Trajanus, Hadrianus – all of you were there at the beginning or at the height of the Empire, but it is left to me to arrest the progress of the wheel as it rolls down from the peak into the valley below. And stop it I will! I have already halted it. And with great effort I have even managed to push it back a little way up the hill. I look you in the eye with my conscience clear, for I have no reason to feel ashamed. Where is the Empire of the savage and heretic Vandals? The grandson of Gaiseric, the feared king of the seas, knelt before me in the Hippodrome. Let us see if Justinian cannot recapture Rome as he did Carthage. Those Barbarians in Italy have sought to gain peace by sheer persistence, and they shall find it, the peace of the grave!"

The *valerius* entered and announced: "Sire, the Senate is assembled in the great hall of Jerusalem. The empress is just mounting the lion steps."

"Good," Justinian replied, "you may go. The hour of trial has come for Theodora, and also for all those who call themselves my advisers. They are never at a loss where small means are to be used to achieve small goals. Oh how inventive they are, and how clearly they can think when they are sitting comfortably on silken cushions, busily justifying banishment or confiscation as a punishment for one of their colleagues! The majesty of emperor and Empire are the alpha and omega of these slavish lips. We will see if they manage to remember that today also. Oh may it be granted me that today, of all days, the ultimate art of a great ruler will not fail me! What I need today is to be able to deceive, to pretend, utterly and totally convincingly. Today, oh statesmen of Byzantium, I will truly test your strength. I have a good idea how you will all rate, and it delights me! Your pitiful weakness is the strongest support my throne could have, and the finest justification for my way of ruling! I will make it very clear to you, you frightened, cowardly, stupid and honourless slaves, that what you need is not a ruler, not an emperor, but an utter tyrant!"

The chamberlain now appeared in order to dress him. Justinian exchanged his morning gown for the Imperial gown of state, and the *vestiarii* assisted him, kneeling.

He put on the white *tunica*, reaching to his knees, embroidered in gold on both sides and held together by a purple belt; even the very tightly fitting trousers were made of purple silk. The cloak slave now cast the magnificent Imperial cloak over his shoulder, bright purple with a broad "*clavus*" (or border) of pure gold, embroidered with red circles and various animal shapes in green silk, especially birds. But the masses of pearls and precious stones which were liberally scattered over the whole garment made the embroidery scarcely discernible. In addition they made the entirety of his regalia so heavy that the assistance of train bearers would not be entirely unwelcome.

Each of his forearms was covered with three broad bracelets of gold. The diadem, which was broader than his head on both sides, was made of solid gold crowned by two arches of pearls. The cloak was held over the right shoulder by a clasp inlaid with the most precious jewels. Finally the guardian of the sceptre placed the golden ruler's staff in the emperor's right hand. It was taller than a man, made of solid gold. On top of it was a globe of the world, made from a single emerald, topped with a golden cross.

The emperor grasped the sceptre firmly in his hand, and sprang to his feet.

"What about the sandals, Sire. The, er, *coternus* (built up) sandals?" a kneeling attendant asked.

"No, today I need no *coternus*," Justinian replied firmly and strode from the room. The emperor walked down to a chamber located one floor down, a large conference hall in the palace known as the Hall of Jerusalem via the lion steps, so called after the twenty-four marble lions which Belisarius had brought back from Carthage.

The Hall of Jerusalem derived its name from the porphyry columns, onyx bowls, golden tables and countless golden implements which adorned the walls and columns on all sides, and which according to legend had originated from the temple in Jerusalem. The emperor Titus had taken the treasures with him to Rome after capturing Jerusalem. Later the Vandal king Gaiseric had taken them, together with the empress Eudoxia, on his dragon ships to his capital of Carthage. And now Belisarius had brought them back to the emperor of the eastern Empire.

The dome of the great hall was fashioned after the greater dome of heaven, made of a mosaic of semiprecious blue stones. Apart from the sun, the moon, the eye of God, the lamb, the fish, the birds, the palm, the vine, the unicorn and other Christian symbols the entire zodiac and countless stars of solid gold had been incorporated in the huge mosaic. The cost of this dome alone was estimated in Byzantium to have cost as much as all the taxes of the Empire for forty-five years.

Opposite the triple entrance arches, which were the only means of entering the hall, and which were closed off by curtains and guarded on the outside by the Imperial bodyguard of the "golden shields," stood the throne of the emperor at the focal point of the semicircular hall. To its left, a little lower, stood the throne of the empress.

As Justinian entered the hall with his huge following of palace servants, the entire assembly, including the highest nobles of the Empire, prostrated themselves face down on the floor in a humiliating gesture of subordination. Even the empress rose, bowed deeply and crossed her arms over her bosom; her attire was very similar to that of her husband. Her white *stola* was also covered by a purple cloak, but the Imperial *clavus* was missing. She also carried a sceptre, but a shorter one made of ivory.

The empress cast a tired but disdainful glance over the patriarchs, archbishops, bishops, patricians and senators who, more than thirty in number, occupied the golden chairs with the silk cushions, which had been arranged in a semicircle.

Justinian now strode along the aisle which divided the hall into two halves, and then he mounted his throne with a swift, assured step, swinging his sceptre as he did so.

Twelve of the foremost palace officials stood on the steps of both thrones, with white staffs in their hands. Now the sound of trumpets gave the signal for the prostrate assembly to rise.

"We have called you together," the emperor began, "holy bishops and distinguished senators, to hear your advice in a matter of great importance and gravity. But why is our *Magister Militum per Orientem*, Narses, not here?"

"He only arrived back from Persia yesterday, and he is confined to his bed gravely ill," the Proto-Keryx reported.

"And our *Quaestor Sacri Palatii Tribonianus*?"

"Has not yet returned from your mission to Berytus about the *Codices*."

"Why is Belisarius, our *Magister Militum per Orientem extra Ordinem*, not here?"

"He does not live in Byzantium, but over in Asia, in Sycae, in the Red House."

"He is keeping very much to himself in his Red House. That displeases us. Why does he keep himself out of our sight?"

"He could not be found there."

"Not even in the house of his former slave Photius, in the House of Shells?"

"He has gone hunting, Sire, to try out the Persian hunting leopards," Leo, the *Comes Spathariorum*, replied.

"He is never there when he is needed, and always when he is not wanted. We are not pleased with Belisarius. Now, hear what has been happening, and what we have learned these last few days from numerous letters. Finally you shall also hear the verbal reports of the messengers.

"As you are aware we allowed the war in Italy to lie dormant because we had – other tasks for our generals. You know also that the king of the Barbarians proposed peace, and requested that we cede Italy to him. We refused that at the time, waiting for a more suitable occasion.

"The Goth has now given us his answer, not in words but in very daring deeds. You do not know of it as yet, because we kept the news to ourselves, thinking it to be impossible, or at the least greatly exaggerated. But we know now that everything we have been told is true. Listen therefore, and advise me.

"With utmost secrecy and great urgency the Barbarian king sent a fleet and an army to Dalmatia. The fleet entered the port of Muicurum near Salona, and the army landed and took the fortified city by storm. The fleet also caught the naval city Laureata by surprise.

"Claudianus, our commander in Salona, sent numerous and well manned *dromonas* to recapture the city from the Goths. But in a major naval battle a Gothic Duke, Guntharis, defeated our fleet so decisively that he captured every single one of our ships without exception, and he then sailed victoriously into the harbour of Laureata.

"The king next equipped a second fleet of four hundred large ships at Centumcellae. That fleet was largely made up of galleys of ours, which had been sent to Sicily from the Orient for Belisarius, not knowing that the Italian ports were once more in Gothic hands. The entire fleet with crews and cargoes was captured by another Duke, Grippa. The goal of this second fleet was also unknown.

"Suddenly the Barbarian king in person appeared with that fleet off Regium, the fortified harbour city at the southernmost tip of Bruttia, which he had captured right at the beginning of the first campaign and held ever since. After a courageous defence the Heruli and Massageti of our garrison surrendered.

"The tyrant Totila then turned quickly toward Sicily, in order to wrest from us this island, which had been Belisarius's first major gain. He defeated the Roman *Comes* Domnentiolus, who faced him in a pitched battle, and from there he quickly captured the entire island. The last we heard only Messana, Panormus and Syracusae were still safe behind their strong walls. A fleet we sent to reinforce our forces and recapture Sicily was scattered by a storm; a second fleet was blown back to Greece by the northwesterly wind.

"At the same time a third fleet of triremes was despatched by that tireless king, under a Count Haduswinth, against Corsica and Sardinia. The former island soon fell to the Goths after the Imperial garrison of its capital Aleria was defeated in open battle. Although the wealthy Corsican Furius Ahalla, who owns most of the island, was far away in India, his *institori* and *coloni* were under instructions not to hinder the Goths in any way, but to assist them as best they could.

"From Corsica the Barbarians turned to the island of Sardinia, where they defeated the troops which our *Magister Militum* of Africa had sent to defend the island at Caralis. And then the Goths captured and occupied that city, likewise Sulci, Castra, Trajani and Turres.

"Now the Barbarians have made themselves at home on both islands, Corsica and Sardinia, treating them like permanent additions to their Empire. They installed Gothic counts in all the cities. And they imposed taxes according to their Gothic constitution. They are, amazingly, much lower than ours! And the populace there has declared shamelessly that they would rather pay the Goths fifty than pay us ninety. But that is not all!

"Sailing northwest from Sicily the tyrant Totila combined his fleet with a fourth fleet under Count Teias near Hydrus. A part of this combined fleet, under Count Thorismuth, landed on Corcyra, occupied the island, and from there captured all the surrounding islands, particularly the Sybotian islands. And that is still not all!

"The tyrant Totila and his Count Teias have already attacked the mainland of our Empire."

At this point the Imperial speaker was interrupted by a general cry of horror all round.

The emperor continued in a grim and sinister tone: "They landed at the port of Epirus Vetus, captured the towns of Nikopolis and Anchisus south-west of ancient Dodona, and they also captured a number of our ships in the coastal waters of that area. What we have told you so far may have aroused your indignation at the sheer daring of these Barbarians. But now let us tell you something which will have an altogether different effect on you. Very briefly and simply, after the messengers who arrived here yesterday there can no longer be any doubt. The Goths are now marching directly on Byzantium with their whole army!"

At that a few of the senators jumped from their seats.

"They are attacking us on two fronts. Their combined fleet, under Duke Guntharis, Count Markja, Count Grippa and Count Thorismuth, has defeated our fleet in the island province in a naval battle, which lasted two days. The remnants of our fleet have been driven into the straits of Sestos and Abydos.

"Their land army, under Totila and Teias, is moving diagonally across Thessalia via Dodona against Macedonia; Thessalonica is already under threat. The 'new walls' which we built there have been stormed and levelled by that Count Teias.

"The road to Byzantium is now open to them. And there is no army left between us and the Barbarians. All our troops are on the Persian border.

"And now we will tell you what the Barbarian king has offered us. By some miracle a god has blinded him and concealed our weakness from him. He is offering us peace on the same terms as those that applied several months ago, except that he now wants Sicily as well. But he is willing to vacate and hand over to us all his other conquests without striking a blow in anger, provided that we recognise him and his regime in Italy.

"As we have no means of halting his progress if he should choose to advance further, we have requested a temporary truce. This he has accepted on the condition that peace will be concluded on the terms he had already named. To that we have agreed…"

At this point he looked about him searchingly, taking a sidelong glance at his empress also.

Everyone in the room breathed a deep sigh of relief.

The empress closed her eyes in order to hide the expression in them. Only her tiny hand gripped the golden armrest of her throne as if in a cramp.

"We have made only the one reservation that we wished to first consult with our empress, who has always favoured peace, and also that we wished to hear the opinion of our Senate. We added that we ourselves were in favour of peace."

At that the worried expressions on the faces around him relaxed a little.

"And we believed that we could judge in advance what the opinion of our learned advisers would be. Upon receiving our reply the advancing cavalry of Count Teias halted reluctantly before Thessalonica on orders from King Totila. Unfortunately they took the city's bishop prisoner first. But then they sent him here, together with other prisoners, messengers and letters. Hear their own stories now, and then make your decisions. But before you do remember this: if we refuse peace, then the Barbarians will be at our own gates within a few days.

"We are being asked only to give up something which the Empire had already given up as lost many decades ago, and which two campaigns by Belisarius failed to win back, Italy! Admit the messengers!"

A number of men were now led in through the entrance arches by bodyguards. They were dressed in clerical garb, military armour or the dress of civilian officials. With much trembling and sighing they prostrated themselves before Justinian's throne, and there were a few tears also. Upon a signal from the emperor they rose, and stood in a line before the throne.

"We have already read your letters and reports yesterday," the emperor said. "*Protonarius*, read out only the one letter, the combined one from the bishop of Nikopolis and the wounded *Comes of Illyricum*, who has since died of his wounds."

"To Justinianus, the invincible emperor of the Romaeans Dorotheos, bishop of Nikopolis, and Nazares, *Comes per Illyricum.*

"The place where we write this is perhaps the best proof of the seriousness of this report. We are writing this on board the ship of the Gothic king, *Italia* by name. As you read these words you are probably already familiar with the defeat of our fleet, the loss of the islands, the storming of the 'new walls' and the scattering of the land army of Illyricum.

"The Gothic pursuers reached us faster than the fugitives or even the news from these battles. Nikopolis was captured and spared by the Gothic king. Anchisus was taken and burnt to the ground by Count Teias.

"I, Nazares, have served in arms for thirty years, but never have I seen an attack like the one in which Count Teias cut me down in the gate of Anchisus. He is invincible! His cavalry is racing through the whole country from Thessalonica to Philippi.

"The Goths in the heart of Illyricum! Nothing like this has been known for sixty years! And the king has sworn to return every year until he has either a peace treaty, or – Byzantium. Ever since his capture of Corcyra and the Sybotian islands, he is standing on the bridge into your Empire. And as God has stirred the heart of this king, so that he is offering you peace at a cheap price – in fact only for something which he already has – we now beg of you, in the name of the trembling subjects of your smoking cities: conclude peace! Save us, and save Byzantium! For your generals Belisarius and Narses will halt the north wind and the morning sun in their paths before they can hope to stop King Totila and that awesome Teias."

"Both the authors of these letters were prisoners," the emperor interrupted. "Perhaps they were writing under the influence of fear, or under the threat of death by the Barbarians. Therefore we now ask that you speak to us directly, Bishop Theophilos of Thessalonica, you, *Logothetes* of Dodona, Anatolius, you, Permenio, valiant commander of our Macedonian lancers: all of you are now safe here in our palace, but you have seen the Barbarian leaders. What is your advice?"

At that the old bishop of Thessalonica prostrated himself once more and said: "Oh emperor of the Romaeans! The Barbarian king is a heretic, and he is therefore eternally damned. That knowledge could lead me to doubt the basic teaching of the true church, because I have never seen a man so richly endowed with all the Christian virtues. Do not wrestle with him! In the next world he is lost for ever. But – I cannot fathom it – here on earth God seems to bless his every step. He is irresistible."

"I understand it quite well," Anatolius the *Logothetus* interjected. "His supposed cleverness wins all hearts over to him, but it is in fact teamed with the crassest hypocrisy and deception, which greatly exceeds our much lauded and criticized Greek wisdom. The Barbarian is acting out the role of a merciful and benevolent friend of mankind, and he is doing it so convincingly that he almost had me deceived as well, until I told myself that there cannot possibly be anyone as perfect and good in this world as the character which that Goth is acting out. He acts as if he really does feel sympathy for his beaten enemy! He feeds the hungry, and he allows the money from our Imperial coffers to be distributed among the peasants whose fields have suffered as a result of the war. He gives the men back their wives, unharmed and unsullied, from the forests where their husbands have hidden them, and where his omnipresent horsemen manage to find them. He rides into the villages to the accompaniment of a harp, played by a handsome boy who also leads his horse. And do you know what the result is? Your own subjects, oh emperor of the Romaeans, are flocking to him! They help him, give him news, and deliver to him in chains the officials who obeyed your commands in respect of taxes. The peasants of Dodona delivered me in this very manner. That Barbarian is the greatest actor of our century, for what he does certainly cannot be real.

"The clever impostor has the ability to do other things besides fighting. He has commenced negotiations with the distant Persians and your arch-enemy Chosroes, with the aim of forming an alliance against you. We ourselves have seen the Persian envoys as they rode east out of his camp."

Then the Macedonian captain spoke: "Ruler of the Romaeans, ever since Count Teias won the military road from Thessalonica to here nothing stands between your throne and his terrible battleaxe except the walls of this city. A man who stormed the 'new walls' eight times in a row, and then succeeded at the ninth attempt, that same man will scale the walls of Byzantium too, at the tenth attempt. The only way you can stop the Goths is with an army seven times stronger than theirs. If you have no such army then make peace."

"Peace! Peace! We beg of you in the name of your trembling provinces Epirus, Thessalia, Macedonia!"

"Get the Goths out of the country for us!"

"Do not allow the days of Theodoric and Alaric to return, more terrible than ever before!"

"Peace with the Goths! Peace! Peace!"

And all the envoys, bishops, officials, senators and soldiers sank to their knees with the imploring cry of "Peace!"

The effect of the news just announced on the assembly had been terrifying indeed. Certainly it was not an uncommon occurrence for Persians or Saracens in the east, Moors in the south or Bulgarians and Slavs in the northwest to cross the farthest borders of the Empire, perhaps defeating the nearest Imperial garrison, and then escaping unpunished with their haul.

But that Greek islands should be under enemy occupation for long periods, that Greek coastal cities were under Barbarian control, or that the roads leading to Byzantium were in Germanic hands – such things had been unheard of for many decades.

With terror the senators thought back to the days when Gothic ships and Gothic armies had overrun all the Greek islands, and when they had repeatedly stormed the very walls of Byzantium, letting up only when all their demands had been met in full. They could already hear the battleaxe of black Teias smashing against their city gates. And so every face in the room bore an expression of helpless fear.

Calmly Justinian looked at the rows of men to his right and left. "You have heard," he began once more, "what the church, the state and the army want. We now seek your counsel. We already have an armistice. Is it to become peace, or renewed war? One word will secure peace, and that is the secession of Italy, which is lost in any case. If there is any one among you who still wants war, let him raise his arm."

Not a single arm was raised. The senators feared for Byzantium, and they had no reason to doubt their emperor.

"So our Senate chooses peace unanimously. We had predicted that it would," Justinian said with a strange smile. "We are accustomed to always following the advice of our wise counsellors. And our empress?"

And at that Theodora sprang from her throne like a coiled up serpent, and she flung her ivory sceptre away from her with such violence that it flew far into the hall.

Terror was reflected on every single face in the room.

"There goes," she cried with utmost intensity and with a tremendous effort, "there goes what has been my pride in all these years, my belief in Justinian's greatness as an emperor! With that sceptre there goes any part I may ever have had in the cares and honours of this Empire. Woe be to you, Justinianus, and woe be to me too, that I ever had to hear such words coming from your mouth!"

And she concealed her face in her purple cloak, thus managing to conceal the physical pain which this emotional outburst had caused her.

The emperor turned to her: "What is this? Does the Augusta, our consort, who has always with few exceptions urged for peace ever since the second homecoming of Belisarius, does she now, in such a time of danger, advise…?"

"War!" cried Theodora, letting the purple fall. And in this grave moment her face assumed a beauty such as she had never possessed in times of playful jesting.

"Must I, your wife, remind you of where your honour lies?

"Are you prepared to accept that these Barbarians settle in your Empire, and that they then force you to accede to their demands by threats? You, who once dreamed of recreating the Empire of Constantine? You, Justinianus, having assumed the names Persicus, Vandalicus, Alanicus and Gothicus, are you now willing to let that Gothic boy pull you by the beard whenever he wants? If all that is so, then you are no longer the Justinianus whom Byzantium, the world and Theodora have admired all these years. Our worship of you was a monumental error!"

And then the Patriarch of Byzantium plucked up courage. He was still under the impression that the emperor had already irrevocably decided on peace, and so he dared to oppose the empress, who did not always meet the ideals of Christian virtue as preached by him.

"Do I hear correctly that the noble lady advises in favour of war? It is true that the holy church has no reason to speak in favour of the heretics. However, it is said that the new king is extremely kind towards Catholics in Italy, and so perhaps we should wait for a more opportune moment, until…"

"No, priest!" Theodora interrupted. "The sullied honour of this Empire cannot wait. Oh Justinianus…" The latter still remained silent, and he had closed his eyes so that his thoughts would not be betrayed by the expression in them. "Oh Justinianus, do not allow me, or the world, to lose faith in you! You must not allow yourself to be bluffed into yielding something which you have refused to give before! Must I remind you how, once before, your wife's advice and strength saved you, and your honour and your throne as well? Have you forgotten the dreadful Nika rebellion?

"Have you forgotten how the combined parties in the circus, the blues and the greens, together with the rampaging mob of Byzantium was bearing down on this very house with what seemed irresistible might?

"The flames and the cries of 'Down with the tyrants!' drowned out everything else. All your advisers, all those holy bishops and distinguished senators, and even the leaders of your army, advised you to either flee or make concessions. Narses was far away in Asia, and Belisarius was already trapped by the rebels in the Ocean Palace, which they had surrounded. They all gave up hope, all these men.

"And your wife, Theodora, was the only one to stand by your side. If you fled or surrendered, then your life, your throne and most certainly your honour were gone for ever. You were in two minds, and you favoured flight.

"'Stay, Justinian, and die if you must,' I said to you at the time, 'but die wearing the Imperial purple!'

"And you stayed, and your courage saved you. You remained where you were, with me, on your throne, waiting to die there. But God sent Belisarius, and with him He sent victory.

"And that is the way I speak to you today also. Do not yield, emperor of the Romaeans, do not yield to the Barbarians! Stay firm! Let the ruins of the Golden Gate bury you, if that Goth's axe should shatter it. Die there if need be! But die as the emperor!

"The purple you wear is stained by the boundless insolence of those Germanic Barbarians. Here, I now throw it from me, and I swear this, by the infinite wisdom of almighty God: I will not wear it again until not a single Goth remains on the soil of this Empire!"

With that she tore the purple cloak from her shoulders and flung it onto the steps of the throne. And then, completely exhausted, she was about to sink back into her seat.

But Justinianus caught her in his arms and embraced her enthusiastically. "Theodora!" he cried with a sparkle in his eyes, "My splendid wife! You need no purple around your shoulders; your mind is already clad in purple. You alone understand Justinianus. War and destruction to the Barbarians!"

A mixture of astonishment and shock went the rounds, as the senators watched this rare performance.

"Yes," said the emperor, turning this time to the senators, "this time, wise fathers, you were just too clever to be wise, or even to be men. Certainly it is an honour to be called the successor of Constantine, but I am afraid it is no honour to be your master. I fear that our enemies are right! Constantine only transplanted the name and the ashes of Rome here; Roma's soul had already fled!

"Woe, what is to become of this Empire? Had it been free, or a republic, today it would have sunk in shame! It has to have a master, just as a lazy horse has to have a master, so that he can save it from the morass into which it is about to sink. Only a firm hand on the reins, a cut with the whip and plentiful use of the spurs will save that horse – or this Empire!"

At that moment a small, crippled man made his way into the room through one of the entrance arches, leaning on a crutch. He limped right through the room as far as the throne.

"Emperor of the Romaeans," he began, rising from his gesture of prostration, "the dark news of what the Barbarians have dared to do reached me on my sickbed, as did news of the decisions which are to be made here at this hour. So I forced myself to my feet and dragged myself here. I must know, from your own mouth, whether I have been a fool to have regarded you thus far as a great ruler despite many petty traits in you, and whether I must throw my commander's staff into the deepest well I can find, or whether I may go on carrying that same staff with honour and with pride? Say just one word: War or Peace?"

"War, *Magister Militum*!" Justinian replied, and his face beamed.

"Victory, Justinianus!" the general replied, and threw away his crutch. "Oh permit me to kiss your hand, Imperator." And he limped up the steps to the throne.

"But *Patricius*," Theodora said scornfully, "could it be that you are suddenly a man? You have always been opposed to the war against the Goths. Have you, all of a sudden, found a sense of honour?"

"Honour rubbish!" Narses cried. "Let the great child Belisarius run after that pretty soap bubble! Not honour, but the Empire itself is now at stake.

"As long as serious danger threatened from the east, I advised you to wage war against the Persians. There was no threat from the Goths. But now your piety, oh empress, and the heroic sword of Belisarius have been poking around in this hornet's nest for so long that the swarm of hornets is angry, and they are not only annoying but also quite dangerous. Now there is indeed danger from the Goths, and the threat is real and urgent, and that is why Narses now advises you in favour of war against the Goths. The Goths are now closer to Byzantum than Chosroes is to our eastern border. This man Totila has been able to pull one Empire out of the abyss, and the same man can just as easily throw another Empire into that very same abyss. That young king is a worker of miracles, and those miracles must be checked, quickly and completely."

"Today," Justinian said, "I have experienced the rare pleasure that my empress and Narses are of the same mind." And he was about to dismiss the assembly.

But the empress grasped his arm. "Stop," she said, "my consort. Today I have earned for the second time the honour of being your best adviser, is that not so? Very well then, hear me out once more, and follow my second piece of advice also.

"Keep this entire assembly, except Narses, prisoners in the palace until tomorrow. Do not tremble, you *Illustrissimi*! This time your lives are not at stake. But you are unable to keep silent, unless your tongues are cut out. This time incarceration will suffice in place of that drastic measure. Justinianus, there is a conspiracy against your life, or at least against your power to make free and independent decisions.

"There are some who were determined to force you into war against the Goths. True, that war has now been decided upon. But the conspiracy is to break out tonight or tomorrow, and it will therefore be necessary to let the conspirators go about their task undisturbed until then. They must not be distracted from what they are doing by the news that their goal has been achieved in any case.

"There are some dangerous men among them, oh Justinianus, and – some wealthy ones too! It would be a pity if they were to escape the net which I have already set for them."

Justinian had shown no sign of being startled by the word "conspiracy".

"I knew of it also," he said. "But is it already as far advanced as that? Tomorrow morning already? Theodora," he cried, "you are worth more to the Empire than Belisarius and Narses. *Archonius* of the Golden Shields, you will hold everyone here as a prisoner until Narses comes to fetch them. In the meantime, wise and pious fathers, think about this hour, and the lessons which can be learnt from it. Narses, come with us and the empress."

And with that he descended the steps from the throne.

The entrances were soon filled with a sea of spears.

Chapter 10

The emperor beckoned to his empress and Narses to follow him to his rooms.

Once he had arrived there he embraced his wife once more, with great fondness and sincerity, undisturbed by the presence of a witness. "Oh how your enthusiasm rejoices me, and how it raises my spirits! Truly, I am proud to call such a woman my wife! Oh Theodora, how well your righteous anger suited you. How can I reward you? Choose any favour, any symbol at all of my gratitude. You are my best adviser of all, nay, you are my fellow ruler in Byzantium!"

"Am I, a mere weak woman, really to believe that I may play a part in your thoughts and plans? Then pray take me into your confidence, and tell me how you plan to conduct this war."

"Well, one thing is for certain, I will send two generals to Italy. Never again will I rely on only one, ever since Belisarius played with a crown in that country. But I will most certainly send Belisarius again, on that I am firmly resolved."

"In that case permit me the honour of suggesting the other one," said Theodora. "Narses," she went on, "will you be the other one?" She was out to remove him from consideration as quickly as possible.

"Thank you," Narses replied with bitterness. "You know that I am a stubborn and quarrelsome horse; I am of no use pulling the same cart with any other animal. Justinianus, one must have a commander's baton or a woman in one way only."

"And how might that be?"

"Alone – or not at all."

"Then for you it will be not at all," Justinian replied gruffly, "you must not deem yourself indispensable, *Magister Militum*!"

"Nobody on earth is indispensable, Justinianus. By all means send the great Belisarius again! Let him try his luck for the third time in that country where the laurels grow so thick. My hour will come! I daresay that I am superfluous here as a witness to your marital bliss. And in my house, opposite my sickbed, there is a map of Italy. Permit me to continue my study of it, as I now find it much more interesting than the map of our Persian border.

"But before I go, permit me to offer you one more piece of advice. In the end you will have to send Narses to Italy anyway. The sooner you send him, the more you will save in defeats, in frustration and – in money! And if gout or the treacherous epilepsy should take Narses before that King Totila lies on his shield, who then will defeat him for you? I hear that you believe in prophesies, and so let me tell you that in Italy this saying has been going the rounds for some time: 'T defeats B, N defeats T.'"

"Is that supposed to mean: Theodora defeated Belisarius, and Narses will defeat Theodora?" the empress asked scornfully?

"That was not my interpretation of the riddle. It was yours. But all the same, I will accept your solution also. Do you know which was the wisest of your laws, Justinianus?"

"Which law was that?"

"The law which fixed the death sentence on anyone who dared to accuse the empress. It was the only way to preserve her for you." And with that he took his leave.

"The insolent dwarf!" Theodora hissed, following with a look like a dagger. "He dares to threaten us! As soon as Belisarius is out of the way, Narses must follow quickly."

"For the time being we still need them both," Justinian commented. "And I suppose that you will now suggest, seriously this time, the same second general you had in mind before we sent Cassiodorus away?"

"Yes, the same one."

"But my reasons for distrusting that ambitious man are now stronger than ever before."

"Have you forgotten who it was that revealed the true nature of Silverius to you, and who rendered him harmless? Or who it was that first warned you when Belisarius was toying with the crown, secretly and before anybody else?"

"But here he keeps company with the very men who are involved in the conspiracy against me."

"True, Justinianus, but he is doing it at my behest, so that he is in fact helping us to destroy them."

"If only that were true! But what if he has deceived you too?"

"Will you believe him and me if he brings the conspirators to you in chains tomorrow, including their secret leader, who is so far not known to you?"

"I know who he is. He is Photius, Belisarius's freedman."

"No, oh Justinianus, you are wrong! The leader is the very man whom you were about to send to Italy again, if I did not warn you. He is Belisarius himself."

At that the emperor grew visibly pale, swayed, and grabbed at a chair for support.

"Will that make you believe in the dedication of that magnificent Roman, and persuade you to send him to Italy in place of the treacherous Belisarius?"

"Of course, of course," Justinian replied, "whatever you say! So Belisarius is a traitor after all? Then we must act quickly. Let us act now!"

"I have already acted, Justinianus. My net has already been set, and there is no possible escape. Just give me the authority to pull it tight!"

The emperor signalled agreement.

And Theodora, as she was leaving the room, commanded the *valerius*: "Fetch Cethegus Caesarius, the Prefect of Rome, from his house to me at once!"

Chapter 11

Shortly afterwards Cethegus was standing before the still seductively beautiful friend of his youth, who was lying stretched out on the divan in the bedroom with which we are familiar.

From time to time Galatea administered drops to her from an onyx bowl. They had been prescribed by a Persian physician – Greek physicians were no longer adequate.

"I thank you, Theodora," Cethegus said. "If it has to be that I must thank someone other than myself, and a woman at that, then I gladly owe my gratitude to the friend of my youth."

"Listen to me, Prefect!" said Theodora, looking at him very seriously. "You are precisely the man – and I am unsure whether to call you Barbarian or Roman – to first kiss a Cleopatra to whom Caesar and Mark Anthony once paid homage, and then still lead her to the Capitol in triumph. That is the kind of thing Octavian might have had in mind, if that queen of snakes had not beaten him to it. A Caesar I have never yet been able to find, but who knows, I may yet find a snake."

"You do not owe me any thanks, because I spoke and acted entirely out of my own conviction. This danger, and the insults from those Goths, must be choked in blood.

"At times I may not have been the faithful wife Justinian thought me to be, but I have always been his best and his most loyal Senator.

"Belisarius and Narses cannot be sent to Italy together, much less either of them alone. Therefore you shall go! You are a hero, a general and a statesman, and yet you are too weak to harm Justinian."

"I thank you for the compliment," Cethegus replied.

"Friend, you are a general without an army, an emperor without an Empire, and a helmsman without a ship. But let us not talk of that. You evidently don't believe me.

"I am sending you to Italy out of deep conviction. I know you hate the Barbarians. The second commander, whom Imperial distrust will no doubt send after you, shall be Areobindos, the prince of snails; he will not hinder you very much. But it pleases me to think that I can help my friend and the Empire at the same time.

"Oh Cethegus, what would I give for youth? For you men it is a shining hope or a golden memory; for a woman – it is life itself! Oh what would I give to re-live just one day from the time when I used to give you roses, and you gave me verses."

"Your roses were beautiful, Theodora, but my verses were not."

"They seemed beautiful to me at the time, because they were meant for me! But quite apart from an old love my decision, which the welfare of the Empire demanded in any case, is made even sweeter by hate, both old and new. Belisarius must not aspire to any further honour and glory. No, he shall fall, this time completely and for good, as truly as I rule here in Byzantium."

"And Narses? It would suit me better if you were to topple that head without an arm than the arm without a head."

"Patience! One after the other."

"What has the good-hearted hero done to offend you?"

"He? Nothing! But his wife! That plump Antonina, whose entire triumph lies in her healthy blood." Angrily the empress clenched her little white hand into a fist, even more transparent than it used to be. "Ha, how I hate her! Indeed, how I envy her! Stupid people are always healthy, but she shall not rejoice while I must suffer!"

"And it is by such women's hatreds that the fate of the Capitol depends," Cethegus said to himself, "down with Cleopatra! The foolish woman has delusions about her husband's fame and greatness, and that is where I can deal her the most telling blow! Just wait, Theodora!"

A twitching over her delicate face betrayed an acute attack of pain; she slumped back in her pillows.

"But my little dove," Galatea warned, "do not upset yourself! You know what the Persian said. Any emotion, be it love or hate…"

"Ha, to hate and to love is to live. And as one grows older hate becomes even sweeter than love. Love is faithless, but hate is always true."

"In both of them," said Cethegus, "I am a clumsy beginner compared to you. I have always called you the 'Siren of Cyprus'. One can never be certain whether you will not suddenly tear your sacrificial lamb to pieces in the middle of a kiss, be it out of love or hate. And what suddenly turned your love for Antonina to hate?"

"She has suddenly become virtuous, the hypocrite! Or could she really be that naïve? She has the blood of a fish, which never did stir with real passion, and she was always too cowardly for a real love affair or for a determined crime. She is too vain to do without flattery or flirtation, and too small of mind to return love when she finds it. Ever since she has been accompanying her husband on his wars she has again become quite virtuous. Ha, she is virtuous out of sheer necessity, just as the devil fasts when he has nothing to eat! You see, I have been keeping her admirer a prisoner here!"

"Anicius, the son of Boethius? Yes, I heard about it."

"Oh yes, in Italy she decided to become entirely her husband's dutiful wife again, sharing both his triumphs and his failures. Ever since then she has been another Penelope, the perfect wife. And after she arrived back here, do you know what the stupid goose did? She accused me of trying to tempt her away from the path of true virtue! And she swears that she will get Anicius released from my bonds. What is more, she will do it too, the little snake! She has aroused the fool's conscience, and every day she drives him further away from me, faithless chamberlain that he is. Of course, she is only doing it so that she can keep him for herself!"

"So you cannot imagine," Cethegus asked, "that a woman should try and reclaim a soul for heaven without – what?"

"Without claiming salvage rights? No! But she is deceiving both him and herself with her pious talk. And oh, how that young man loves being saved by his healthy, blooming saviouress, away from my arms, sick, wilting, consumed before my time by this wretched malady. Oh," she cried passionately and jumped up from the divan, "oh that the body must lie down, tired, before the soul has had time to indulge in even a one thousandth part of its thirst for life. But to live is to rule, to love and to hate!"

"You seem to be insatiable in these arts and pleasures."

"Yes, and I am proud of it! And yet I am destined to soon step down and leave the richly set table of life, down from this throne, with all my fervent hunger for joy and for power! Only a few more drops will I have time to sip! Oh, nature is an incompetent, miserable muddler!

"Once in an eon she sires, alongside myriads of cripples who are ugly in body and incompetent of mind, a single body and soul like those of Theodora, beautiful and strong and demanding to live for ever and enjoy immortality to the full. And after three decades, after I have only just tasted the cup of life, now nature refuses to allow my parching thirst to go on living! A curse on the envy of the gods! But men too can be envious, and envy can make demons of them. Others shall not laugh as I writhe in pain, night after night! And that proud, healthy peasant wench shall not find joy with any faithless man who was once Theodora's, and who could still manage to think of another woman, or of virtue, or of heaven.

"Only today he told me that he could no longer endure this idle life in my women's quarters, without fame or honour; he said that heaven and earth were calling him away. He shall live to regret it – with her! Come, Cethegus," she said venomously, gripping his arm, "we will destroy them both."

"You are forgetting," Cethegus said coldly, "that I have no reason for hating either her or him. What I do, therefore, I do for your sake alone."

"Not quite, you icy Roman, clever as you are. Do you imagine I can't see through you?"

"I hope not," Cethegus thought to himself.

"You want to keep Belisarius away from Italy, because you want to fight and win there on your own. At most you want a shadow with you, such as Bessas was or Areobindos will be. Do you really imagine that I did not see through you when you engineered Belisarius's recall from Ravenna in such a masterful fashion? Care for Justinian indeed! What do you care for Justinian?"

The heart of Cethegus was beating furiously.

"The freedom of Rome! How laughable! You know that only strong and simple men can endure freedom. You know your present day Romans. No, your goal is something much higher."

"Could it be that this woman sees through what neither my friends nor my enemies have even suspected?" Cethegus thought, with growing concern.

"Your aim is to liberate Italy on your own, and then to rule as Justinian's governor alone, nearest to his throne, and much higher than either Narses or Belisarius. You want to be next in rank after Theodora, and if there was a still higher aim, then you would be the man to strive after that too."

Cethegus breathed a sigh of relief. "That would scarcely be worth the effort," he thought.

"Oh, it is a proud feeling indeed to be first among Justinian's servants!"

Cethegus thought: "Of course, she cannot think beyond her husband, even if she does betray him almost every day."

Theodora added: "And then to rule him, the emperor, as Theodora's accomplice."

"The flattery and artifice of this court will dull and confuse even the greatest mind eventually," Cethegus thought. "That is the madness of the purple! She can think only of herself as the ultimate, all-powerful ruler."

"Yes, Cethegus, if any other man was to even think these thoughts I would never tolerate it. But with you I will even help you to attain your impossible goals, and then share control of the world with you. Perhaps it is only for the sake of a foolish memory from our youth. Do you remember, years ago, when we divided two cushions between us in my little villa? We called them Orient and Occident. That was an omen. Let us allocate Orient and Occident again now. I will rule the Orient through my Justinian. And I will also rule the Occident through my Cethegus!"

"You arrogant, insatiable woman!" Cethegus thought. "If only the maidenly Matesuentha had not died on me! If she was at this court – you would be finished!"

"But first," Theodora went on, "Belisarius must be got out of the way once and for all. Justinian was determined to send him again, as your commander-in-chief."

Cethegus frowned.

"Again and again he puts his trust in the faithfulness of Belisarius. Somehow he must be convinced that he is utterly disloyal, and for that I need some tangible and demonstrable proof."

"That will be difficult," Cethegus commented aloud, "Theodora is more likely to learn loyalty than Belisarius the opposite."

A blow on the mouth from Theodora's small hand was his punishment. "Foolishly I have remained loyal to you, or at least I still have your interests at heart. Do you want Belisarius back in Italy a third time?"

"Not at any price!"

"Then help me ruin him, together with Boethius's son."

"So be it," the Prefect replied. "I have no reason to spare the brother of Severinus. But how? How do you propose to obtain proof that Belisarius is disloyal? That is something I am really eager to find out. If you can find a way to do that, then I will be the first to admit that I am a clumsy beginner compared to Theodora, in scheming as I am in loving and hating."

"That you certainly are, you clumsy son of Latium. Now listen – but this is so dangerous that I must ask even you, Galatea, to stand guard so that no one can come in and listen. No my little golden one, not in here! I must ask you very nicely: outside the door please. Just leave me alone with the Prefect. This concerns – unfortunately – only a secret of hatred!"

A considerable time later, as the Prefect was leaving the room, he said to himself: "If this woman was a man, then that man would have to die. He would be more dangerous than the Barbarians and Byzantium put together. But then, of course, if she was a man then her cunning and her scheming would not be so utterly and impossibly demoniacal!"

Chapter 12

Soon after the Prefect arrived back at his own house, Syphax announced the son of Boethius, saying that the empress had sent him.

"Let him in, and then admit no one until after he has left. Meanwhile, send urgently for Piso, the tribune."

Young Anicius entered. He had matured into a man. He was dressed simply and his hair, which was normally carefully curled and oiled, today hung straight down to his shoulders. His gentle features, which were reminiscent of Camilla, wore a determined expression today.

"You remind me greatly of your lovely sister, Anicius," were the words with which the Prefect greeted him.

"It is on her account that I have come, Cethegus," the youth replied seriously. "You were my father's oldest friend, and my family's also. You kept Severinus and me hidden in your house, and then you helped us to flee when the Barbarians were looking for us. That involved you in considerable danger on our account. You are the only man in Byzantium to whom I can come for fatherly advice in a matter of duty. A few days ago I received this mysterious letter.

'To Anicius, the son of my Patronus, Corbulo the freedman...'"

"Corbulo? I remember the name."

"He was my father's freedman, with whom my mother and sister found refuge, and who..."

"Fell outside Rome with your brother."

"Yes, but he did not die immediately. He died in the Gothic camp, where he was taken with my dying brother from the village of Aras Bacchi. He had been seriously wounded also. That is what Sutas told me, one of Belisarius's Armenian mercenaries. He is the one who brought me this letter, which Corbulo was unable to complete. Here, read it for yourself."

Cethegus took the little wax tablet with its barely legible writing and read: "The last words of your dying brother were: Anicius must now avenge mother, sister and me. All of us were destroyed by that same demon of our house..."

"Unfortunately the letter ends there," said Cethegus, handing back the tablet.

"Yes. The mercenary said that Corbulo lost consciousness."

"There is not much you can do with that," Cethegus remarked, shrugging his shoulders.

"True, but the mercenary heard one more thing, which my dying brother said to Corbulo – they were lying in the same tent – and that could be the key to it."

"And what was that?" Cethegus asked, now very alert.

"Severinus said: 'I sense it. He knew of this ambush, and he deliberately sent us to our deaths.'"

"Who?" Cethegus asked calmly.

"That is the question."

"You have no idea?"

"No, but it can't be impossible to find out whom my brother meant."

"How do you intend to go about doing that?"

"He said: 'Sent to our deaths.' That could only have been one of the commanders, who commanded or persuaded my brother to take part in that early morning mission with Belisarius out of the Porta Tiburtina. Now, at that time Severinus was not a member of Belisarius's army, but he was a tribune of your legionaries. If you, or Belisarius, together with Procopius were to thoroughly investigate the whole incident, then it must be possible to discover who it was that caused my brother to go with that mission. You see, he was not commanding any other legionaries; apart from him there was not one other of your men in that party."

"That is correct," Cethegus said, "as far as I can remember."

"No, not one. Procopius, who is unfortunately abroad just now inspecting some of Justinian's buildings, was personally there. He often listed the names of all the other participants for me. When he returns I will enquire and delve very carefully to find out with whom my brother had contact before that foray, or in whose house or tent he had been beforehand. I will neither rest nor pause. I will ask the surviving comrades of Severinus where they saw him last, before they rode out of Rome."

"You have a very sharp mind for one so young," the Prefect said with a strange smile. "Just think what will happen when such a mind matures! But of course, you are living in a place which is a good school for sharpness of mind and wit. Does the empress know of your mysterious letter?"

"No, and she must never know about it. Do not even mention her name to me! This duty of revenge is a last message from God, telling me to tear myself away from her."

"But I thought that it was she who sent you to me?"

"Yes, on a different errand, but that errand is going to end very differently from the way she intended. Earlier today she sent for me; once more she asked me if it was really so difficult to live for a little longer in the golden cage. But the woman revolts me! And I thoroughly regret the many months I have wasted with her, while my brother fought and fell for his fatherland. I gave her such a rude reply that I quite expected an outburst of rage in response. But to my surprise she remained quite calm and said, smiling:

'So be it, then, no loyalty lasts for ever. Leave me, and go to Antonina or to virtue or to both of those goddesses. But as a final sign of my favour I will save you from certain death.

"There is a conspiracy in Byzantium of Roman and Greek young men, against either the life or the freedom of the emperor. They want to force him to take up war against the Goths once more, and to appoint Belisarius commander-in-chief. Quiet, I know all about it. I also know that you have already been half won over to their cause, that you have not yet visited any of their meetings, but that you are the custodian of the conspiracy's documents. I have let them be until now, because there are a few of my old enemies among them, whom I hope to destroy for good this time. I plan to spring the trap in a few days, but I want to warn and save you. Go to the Prefect; he can get you out of Byzantium as one of his men or mercenaries. Just tell him that you are in some danger, and that Theodora sends you. But say nothing to him, or any of his tribunes, about the conspiracy. Several of them are among the conspirators, whom he would no doubt like to save, but I am going to destroy them!'

"And so I have come to you, but not in order to flee. I came to warn you and my Roman brothers in arms. I also intend to visit the assembly today – the empress assured me that it would be quite safe today – so that I can warn them all, and tell them that the conspiracy has been discovered. You must not go, Prefect! You cannot afford to expose yourself any more, as Justinian already does not quite trust you. The fools want to wait until they have won Belisarius over to their cause! And they may all be behind bars as early as tomorrow if they are not warned. So I will now hurry to warn my friends. But after that I will not rest until I know who it was that murdered my brother."

"Both very praiseworthy," said Cethegus. "By the way, where have you hidden the conspiracy's letters?"

"In the same place," the youth replied, colour rising in his face, "where I have also hidden other secrets, even holier ones – letters which are very dear to me – and where I also intend to put this tablet. I will tell you about it, for you are the oldest friend of my family, and I hope that you will help me complete my work of revenge. I have also hidden there what the mercenary Sutas has told me of barely understandable things which the two dying men said: they talked of 'murder by poison', of a 'murderous command', of an 'accusation before the Senate' – so the perpetrator must have been a Roman senator – of a 'purple plumed helmet', and of a 'black horse from hell' among other things."

"And so on," Cethegus interrupted. "Where is the hiding place located? It may be that you really do have to flee in a hurry one day – I advise you not to trust the empress – and you may not have time to get to your house one day before you must flee."

"And in that case it would be necessary that you take up my task for me. I was going to tell you anyway: in the cistern in the courtyard of my house – the third brick to the left of the waterwheel is hollow.

"There is also another reason," he went on in a sinister tone, "and you may as well know of it. I think you are right with your warning. For some time now I know that I am being followed, but I don't know if they are the emperor's men or those of the empress. Should it come to pass that my friends, the conspirators, cannot be saved, then I intend to make a quick and bloody end of it! What would my life matter then? If I cannot fulfil the last dying wish of my brother Severinus anyway, then – I have to report to the emperor every morning how the empress slept – then I will strike the tyrant down right in the midst of his slaves!"

"You madman!" Cethegus cried, with genuine shock, for it now suited his plans to keep Justinian alive and on the throne. "Just what is remorse and a life of useless idleness driving you to? No, the son of Boethius must not end his life as a murderer. If you want to make up for your past life in blood, very well then, fight among my legionaries. Purify yourself in Barbarian blood, but with a hero's sword, not an assassin's dagger."

"What you say is great, and true. And you are willing to place me, untried, among your knights? How can I thank you?"

"Forget the thanks until the task is completed – until we meet again. In the meantime warn the conspirators tonight. That in itself will be a trial of courage, because I don't think it out of the question that you are being followed. If you are afraid – just say so openly."

"Me? Fear the first test of my courage? I will go to warn them even if certain death awaits me!" With that he took the Prefect's hand, and hurried on his way.

As soon as he had gone – the Prefect followed him with only a single glance – Syphax brought the tribune Piso into the room by another entrance.

"My poet tribune," Cethegus said as he entered, "you will now need to be as fleet of foot as your verses. Enough of intrigue and conspiracy here in Byzantium! You will go immediately and seek out all the young Romans who have been to the house of Photius. There must not be a single one of them left within these walls by nightfall! Your lives are at stake. None of you must go to the 'evening meal' at the house of Photius. Go, in small groups or alone. Go hunting, go sailing on the Bosporus, do what you like; but hurry and get away immediately!

"The conspiracy is quite unnecessary. Very soon the tuba will sound once more for the fight against the Barbarians in Latium. Go, all of you, and wait for me in Epidamnus. I will come with my Isaurians and fetch you there – and lead you in the third struggle for Rome. On your way! Syphax," he now asked, alone in the room with the slave. "Have you enquired in the house of the great general? When is he expected back?"

"Before sunset."

"And his faithful wife is waiting for him in his house? Now, I need a litter, but not mine. Hire the nearest one from the Hippodrome, one with shutters that can be closed completely. Then lead it to the harbour area, to the street where the dealers in second-hand goods live."

"Master, the worst rabble and the worst criminals in this city of rabble live there. What do you want among those beggars?"

"I want to get into the litter there. And from there I want to go to the Red House."

Chapter 13

In the Red House, Belisarius's palace in the new city called Justiniana (Sycae), Antonina was sitting in the women's chamber, busily embroidering golden laurels on a cloak for the hero Belisarius.

On the little citrus table beside her lay a luxury edition of *The Vandal Wars* by Procopius, a recently published book about her husband's most splendid campaign. It was written in purple ink, and bound in an ornate cover set with precious stones.

At her feet lay a magnificent animal, one of a pair of tame hunting leopards which the Persian king had given to Belisarius after his most recent victory. It was a precious gift, as it was unusual for the taming process to be completely successful. Many hundreds of such animals, captured when they were very young or even born in captivity, had to be killed after many years of training as not being trainable and therefore unsafe. The beautiful animal, big and very strong, had not been taken on the hunt for fear that the taste of warm blood might bring out the wild beast in it. Like a domestic cat it now lay contentedly on the hem of Antonina's dress, playing with a ball of golden thread, waving its tail and rubbing its head and chest against the feet of its mistress.

And then a slave girl announced a strange man. She said he had arrived in a plain litter and was wearing a plain cloak. The door slave had tried to turn him away, as the mistress did not receive visitors when the master was away. "But it is impossible to resist him! He ordered us to say: 'Tell Antonina that the conqueror of Pope Silverius is here to see her'. What shall we do?"

"Cethegus!" Antonina cried, growing pale and trembling. "Have him admitted at once!"

In her mind she now remembered how the mighty mind of this man had remained calm and steadfast when her husband, Procopius and all the other generals had been helpless against the priest. That event, when she had first met Cethegus, convinced her of the latter's superiority. Entirely on his own Cethegus had conquered the conqueror and humiliated him. Later, during the march into Rome, the battle of the Anio Bridge, the defence of Rome against Witigis, in the camp outside Ravenna, during the conquest of that same city, always and everywhere this man had shown his superiority of mind again and again, yet he had never used it against her husband. She remembered how misfortune and failure invariably followed whenever his advice was ignored, and how his every suggestion had always led to victory. All of these memories were now flooding through her mind.

The Prefect's footsteps approached, and she rose quickly. The leopard, thus roughly pushed away and disturbed in its play on account of the intruder, leapt to its feet with a low snarl. Baring its powerful teeth it looked toward the entrance as Cethegus entered, throwing back the curtain with an impatient gesture. His head was half concealed by his cloak.

That either frightened or annoyed the leopard, because during the initial stage of taming Persian lion and tiger tamers used long woollen rugs, and covered head and shoulders with a protective covering made of similar material. Perhaps the memory of an old adversary arose in the animal, which had never been entirely tamed. With a dreadful cry of anger it now crouched for the deadly leap, beating the floor with its long tail and spitting saliva, both signs of extreme anger.

Antonina saw this and was terrified. "Flee, flee Cethegus!" she cried in desperation.

If he did that, if he turned his back, then he was certainly doomed, as the animal would have him by the neck in the very next instant. There were no solid doors to protect his exit, only curtains.

Quickly he took a step forward, threw back the hood of his cloak and looked straight into the leopard's eyes. The index finger of his left hand was raised commandingly, and in his right hand he was holding a shining broad dagger straight out in front of him. "Down! Down! Or hot iron threatens!" he called out to the snarling animal in the Persian language, taking another step forward.

At that the leopard let out a long, wailing cry of fear. Its muscles, tensed for attack, grew slack, and with a whimper it crawled along the floor toward Cethegus, trembling with fear. And then it licked his left sandal while he placed his right foot firmly on the animal's neck.

Antonina, petrified with fear, had sunk to her knees, watching the awesome spectacle spellbound. "The animal would never prostrate itself for Belisarius! Dareios always became angry whenever he demanded it. Where did you learn to do that, Cethegus?"

"In Persia, of course," the latter replied. And he gave the now completely subdued animal such a powerful kick in the ribs that it raced away with a loud cry of pain, seeking refuge in the furthest corner of the room, where it lay trembling.

"Belisarius conquered only the cities, but never the language of the Persians," said Cethegus. "But these beasts do not understand Greek. I must say, you are well protected when Belisarius is away," he went on, returning the dagger to his cloak.

"What brings you to his house?" Antonina asked, still trembling.

"Old friendship, albeit often misunderstood. I have come to save your husband, who has a lion's courage, but lacks the nimbleness of even a mouse! Unfortunately Procopius is abroad, or I would have sent him to you, a more trusted adviser. I know that severe danger threatens Belisarius from the emperor. It must be averted. The emperor's favour…"

"Is changeable, I know that. But Belisarius's achievements…"

"Are the very thing that threatens to destroy him. Justinian would never fear an insignificant man, but he fears Belisarius!"

"We have found that out often enough," Antonina sighed.

"Then let me tell you this. You shall be the first to know something which nobody outside the palace even suspects. The emperor has made up his mind, in favour of war with the Goths."

"At long last!" Antonina cried, and her face brightened.

"Yes, but – think of the shame of it! Belisarius was not named as commander-in-chief."

"Who then?" Antonina asked angrily.

"I am one commander." She looked at him suspiciously. "Yes, that has been my ambition for a long time, I admit it. But the second commander is to be Areobindos. I cannot do anything with that shadow of a man. I cannot conquer the Goths alongside him, with him, hindered by him and by his stupidity. Nobody except Belisarius will defeat the Goths, and that is why I must have him with me again, above me if necessary as commander-in-chief. You see, Antonina, I consider myself the greater statesman."

"My Belisarius is a warrior, not a statesman!" the proud wife said.

"But it would be ridiculous if I tried to compare myself to the conqueror of the Vandals, the Persians and the Goths as a general. So you see, I admit it freely, I am motivated not only by a concern for Belisarius, but by selfishness as well. I must have Belisarius as my companion in arms."

"I can see that," she said agreeably.

"But Justinian cannot be persuaded to name Belisarius. Worse, he distrusts him anew, more than ever."

"But by all the saints in heaven, why?"

"It is true that Belisarius is innocent, but he is also very careless. For months now he has been receiving secret letters, notes and other messages, slipped into his clothing at the baths or thrown over the wall into his garden, all urging him to become part of a conspiracy."

"Great heaven, you know about that?" Antonina stammered.

"Unfortunately I am not alone in that. Others know too, including the emperor himself!"

"But the emperor's life or throne are not under threat," Antonina said soothingly.

"No, only his freedom to act independently. 'War against the Goths', 'Belisarius as commander-in-chief', 'it is shameful to serve the ungrateful tyrant' and 'force the emperor for his own good' – that is how the messages sound, am I right? Now it is true that Belisarius has taken no notice of them. But at the same time the careless man failed to report the first suggestion that there is such a conspiracy to the emperor, and that could cost Belisarius his head!"

"Oh Saints have mercy!" cried Antonina, wringing her hands. "It was at my urging that he did not report it. Procopius advised him, just as you are now doing, to report everything to the emperor at once. But I was frightened of the emperor's mistrust, which might interpret even the fact that Belisarius was invited to join the conspiracy as proof of his guilt."

"I doubt if it was that alone," Cethegus said carefully, first checking that nobody was listening, "which influenced your advice, which of course Belisarius then followed as he always does."

"What else? What are you getting at?" Antonina asked softly. She was blushing all over.

"You knew that good friends of your house were part of it. You wanted to warn them first, and separate them from the clearly guilty before they were accused."

"Yes," she stammered, "Photius, his freedman..."

"And another man also," Cethegus whispered, "one who had just been released from Theodora's golden prison, and whom you did not want to go straight into the dungeons of the Bosporus."

Antonina hid her face in her hands.

"I know everything, Antonina. I know all about your guilty conscience from former times, and your more recent good intentions. But here the old affection has influenced you. Instead of thinking of Belisarius you thought only of this young man's welfare. If Belisarius was now to perish because of it who is at fault?"

"Oh stop it, have pity!" Antonina begged.

"Don't despair," Cethegus continued. "After all you have one powerful ally left, one who can plead with Justinian on your behalf. Even if there was a threat of banishment – surely your friend will avert the worst."

"The empress! Oh God help us!" Antonina cried, terrified. "How will she describe all this to him? She has sworn to destroy us."

"That is bad," said Cethegus, "very bad. Because the empress also knows about the conspiracy and about the invitation to Belisarius to join it. And as you know, much lesser guilt that that has been known to…"

"The empress knows? Then we are lost! Oh please, you know of ways out of a trap where nobody else can see one. Please help, save us." And the proud woman sank to her knees before the Prefect, pleading.

From the corner of the room there came a pitiful wailing sound. The Prefect cast a quick glance at the cowering leopard, and then he gently helped Antonina back on her feet.

"Get up, there is no need for the wife of Belisarius to despair. Yes, there is one way to save Belisarius."

"Should he report everything now, as soon as he comes home?"

"No, that would be too late. And it would not be enough – they would not believe that he means what he says. No, he must prove his loyalty with deeds. He must take all the conspirators prisoner and deliver them to Justinian, all at once."

"How can he take them prisoner all at once?"

"They have invited him themselves. Tonight they will meet in the house of Photius, his freedman. He must tell them that he is willing to become their leader, and then appear at the meeting and take them all prisoner. Anicius," he added quickly, "has been warned about tonight by the empress herself. He has been to see me and told me so."

"Oh, and even if he has to die! What matters now is to save Belisarius. He will have to do it! I can see that. And it is daring, dangerous. He will see it as a challenge."

"Will he sacrifice his freedman?"

"We have warned the fool in vain seven times. What does Photius matter where Belisarius is in danger? If ever I have had any power over him, tonight I will convince him. There was one other time, long ago, when Procopius advised him to prove his loyalty by such brutal means, as he called them. Then too he did not report it when he was first invited to join an earlier conspiracy. I will remind him of the advice Procopius gave him then. You may rest assured, he will follow our joint advice."

"Good. He must be there before midnight. When the guard on the walls announces the twelfth hour I will break into the hall. To make quite sure, tell him to enter only if he sees my slave Syphax in the niche behind the statue of St Peter in the house. He could station a few of his bodyguards outside the house too; they can cover him in the event of an emergency, and testify in his favour. He will not be called upon to pretend. He is not to enter until just before midnight, so that he will only have to listen, not talk, Our guards will wait in the wood of Constantine outside the back door to Photius's house. We will break in at the sound of midnight, as the tubas sound the changing of the guard. That can easily be heard, as you know, so he will not even have to give a sign."

"And you – you will be there for certain?"

"I will be there. Farewell Antonina."

Quickly he had reached the exit, walking backwards, his eyes on the subdued animal and the dagger in his hand. The leopard had been waiting for this moment; he was now stirring in his corner, getting to his feet.

But then Cethegus, who was already passing through the curtains, raised the dagger once more and threatened: "Down Dareios, or hot iron threatens." And with that he was outside.

The leopard lowered his head onto the mosaic floor and let out a howl of impotent fury.

Chapter 14

Meanwhile King Totila had returned to Rome with his fleet and his army, leaving only small garrisons behind in the captured cities, since the emperor at his request had opened peace negotiations and sought an armistice of six months. Peace was to be concluded by Byzantine envoys before the six months expired, and the emperor had promised to send those envoys to Rome soon.

Totila's luck and the glory of his regime were now at their peak. The successful attacks on the Byzantine Empire had added even more lustre to his name, and even Italy felt the glow of his fame and his successes. The last two cities in Italy still in enemy hands were Perusia in Tuscany and the unconquerable Ravenna. Perusia now finally surrendered to Count Grippa after a long and fiercely fought siege, and even in Ravenna the oldest and most important part, the harbour city of Classis, finally capitulated to old Hildebrand, who had been holding the fortress surrounded for eighteen months. Supplies to Ravenna could now be cut off, and Totila ordered that all the separate Gothic naval units should regroup into a single powerful fleet near Ancona, and then blockade the port of Classis. Thus an early fall of the city through starvation could now be expected with some confidence.

Only one small obstacle therefore now remained before Totila could regard the promise he had made to Valeria's dying father as being fulfilled. Only on the land side of Ravenna were there still Byzantines on Italian soil. A few more weeks, and that city too would have to open its gates, and then nothing would stand in the way of a marriage between the Gothic king and the loveliest girl in Italy.

Totila decided to prepare for that event by a formal and public engagement and betrothal, which was to be combined with a magnificent festival to celebrate and glorify his victories. He also planned to use this occasion to draw his beloved away from the influence of the cloister, which no longer pleased him, and to show off his future queen to his court and the country. Until now only Teias and a few close friends had known of Totila's love or his bride. Cassiodorus and Julius had accepted the task of bringing the king's betrothed from Taginae to Rome.

Southwest of the present day Monte Testaccio, where the Tiber runs along the Aurelian wall before leaving the city, there stood on a slight hill an old Imperial villa from the days of the Caesars. Totila loved this place, which commanded a beautiful view along the river and into the Campania. The river was once more full of small merchant ships, which plied their trade from the harbour of Portus, bringing the freight and cargoes of the larger ships from there into the city. The Campania had now recovered from most of the destruction caused by the war, and houses and villas once again dotted the countryside.

Totila had managed to restore the old palace, and it was once more pleasantly habitable. The festival was to take place on the broad terrace in front of the villa, at the top of the marble steps which reached right down to the river. Totila had summoned the old sculptor Xenarchos from Naples, the same man who had sculpted the *dioscuri* years before, and had given him the task of selecting the best of the many statues to be found in Rome and nearby cities. These statues were then to be placed on the vacant bases either side of the marble steps. The old man had fulfilled his task with loving enthusiasm, and thus it was not long before those marble steps were lined with a double row of gods, goddesses and heroes on both sides.

A large purple tent had been placed over the terrace, such as those used over amphitheatres, as protection from the sun but open to the breezes from the river. The rear of the terrace adjoined the vestibule of the villa, borne by many pillars. The royal tent, the steps, the vestibule and the whole villa were covered everywhere by evergreen ivy, which adorns Italian gardens in summer and winter alike.

From the top of the tent Totila's splendid new royal banner fluttered proudly against the Roman sky. Valeria and her companions at Taginae had sewn it with gold and silver thread on light blue silk, depicting a golden swan flying with spread wings into a star-studded sky. On the right, even higher, there rose the famous old Amalung banner of Theodoric, with the rising golden lion. Somewhat lower, on the left, there was a trophy; it was the banner of Belisarius, which Totila had captured outside the Porta Tiburtina. It had been hoisted with its point lowered, to indicate that it represented a victory.

Chapter 15

The victory celebration had been set for the day coinciding with the *calends* of June.

From earliest morning the population of Rome was out and about, moving through the gaily decorated streets and squares toward the Aventine hill and the river, which was covered with numerous gondolas. All around the villa there were tents, shelters and tables, where the people of Rome were being feasted by their Gothic king.

After Cassiodorus had betrothed the daughter of his old friend to the king in St Peter's cathedral and rings had been exchanged, the young couple moved to the river in a festive procession, across the gaily decorated bridge of Theodosius and Valentian, and from there to the villa below the emporium. The ceremony of betrothal had taken place with prayers by both an Arian and a Catholic priest – the latter was Julius – so as to satisfy both the Gothic and the Italian people.

After arriving at the villa, they stood before the assembled Gothic people's army under the king's golden shield, which was supported on a spear. There the Roman girl placed her foot into the left shoe of the Gothic king, and he laid his armoured right hand on her dark hair, which was covered by a transparent veil. And so the betrothal had been concluded according to the customs of the church, Romans and Goths.

Now the bridal couple took their places at the central table on the terrace. Valeria was surrounded by noble Roman and Gothic women, and the dukes and counts of his army stood assembled around Totila. Gothic and Roman singers and flautists sang and played in turn, and Roman dancing and the sword dancing of Gothic youths entertained the crowd. Meanwhile on the river, on both banks and on all sides around the villa, the Roman and Gothic guests of the king ate and drank together, toasting their benevolent master and his lovely bride in turn.

Valeria was looking into the distance with a serious look on her face, her lips moving gently.

"What was the name you spoke just then?" the king asked, holding out his goblet for her to drink.

She replied: "Miriam," drank and returned the cup.

"Our thanks and eternal honour to Miriam!" the king replied as he solemnly raised the goblet to his lips.

But then there arose the golden clear sound of harp strings; clad in a festive gown of pure white, a garland of laurel and oak leaves on his head, Adalgoth stepped before the royal pair. Questioningly he glanced once more at his harp teacher and weapons master, Count Teias, and then he sang in a bright voice, to the accompaniment of his harp:

"Hear this, ye peoples near and far,
Byzantium, listen well!
The king of the Goths, Totila,
reigns high up on the Capitol!
How very far from the Tiber stream
ran the hero Belisarius:

Only Orcus now, not Rome it seems
is ruled by ex-Prefect Cethegus.
How well the laurel garland suits
our good King Totila.
And at his breast the beauty
of his bride Valeria.
Of peace and justice the defender
with sword and shield is he:
Oh olive, for the peace protector
your pious leaves lend me!
Who carried the sword of vengeful fury
mightily to Byzantium?
Come laurel, green of victory,
be part of a garland meant for him!
But not from Roma's ancient dust
did his strength for victory grow:
Nay, only true Germanic oak leaves must
reward him, the great hero.
Hear this, ye peoples near and far,
Byzantium, listen well!
The king of the Goths, Totila
reigns high up on the Capitol!"

The roar of applause followed his song as a Roman youth and a Gothic girl knelt before the royal couple, handing each of them a garland of roses, olives, laurels and oak leaves.

"Even our singers, Valeria," Totila smiled, "are not entirely displeasing. Nor are they lacking in strength or loyalty. I owe my life to that young musician there." And he laid his hand on Adalgoth's head. "He was not at all gentle when he struck the clumsy fingers of your countryman Piso, as punishment that those same fingers wrote many a scandalous verse against me or to my Valeria, and also as punishment that those same fingers were poised to swing the deadly iron against me."

"There is only one sound, my Adalgoth," Teias said softly to the youth, "which I would have rather heard than your song of rejoicing."

"And what sound is that, my Count of harp and sword?"

"The death rattle of the Prefect, whom unfortunately you only sent to hell in your song."

But Adalgoth was called down the long staircase by a group of Gothic warriors, and for a long time they would not let him go again. To the ears of his Gothic audience his song had been much more pleasing than it might have been to you, dear reader.

Duke Guntharis embraced him and then led him aside, where he said: "My young hero! The resemblance is incredible! Every time I see you my first thought is: Alaric!"

"Hey, that's my battle cry!" Adalgoth replied, and they disappeared into the crowd deep in conversation.

Chapter 16

While all this was taking place, the king looked over in the direction of the villa itself, because the flutes there had suddenly stopped. He could clearly see the reason for this, and with a cry of astonishment he jumped to his feet himself.

For there, between the two garlanded centre columns of the entrance, stood an apparition which did not seem to be of this earth. An indescribably lovely young girl in a pure white gown stood there, a shepherd's staff in her hand and a garland of white flowers around her light blonde hair.

"Oh what is that? Could that lovely vision be a living soul?" the king asked in amazement.

All the assembled guests, all the men and women around him, followed his eyes and to where his hand was pointing, as astonished as he was himself. The space between the flowers in the entrance was indeed filled by an utterly lovely apparition, the like of which none of them had ever seen.

The child, or young girl, had fastened her gown over her left shoulder with a sapphire clasp. Her broad golden belt was adorned with sapphires too, and the sleeves of her white gown fell from her shoulders like a pair of white wings. Her entire figure was surrounded by ivy; her right hand was holding a bunch of wildflowers to her breast, and her left the shepherd's staff, also adorned with flowers. Beside her stood a huge, shaggy brown dog, again with flowers around his neck. There she stood, quite without fear, thoughtfully looking at the splendid assembly before her. For a while the guests remained silent in utter astonishment, while the girl herself stood motionless.

At last the king rose from his throne, went over to her and said: "Welcome to the Gothic royal hall, if you are an earthly being," he smiled. "But if, as I would almost rather believe, you are the queen of the elves or the queen of light, you are welcome just the same. In the latter case we will have to arrange a throne for you high above where the king sits." And thus, greeting her with great charm, he beckoned her with both arms to come closer.

And she did come closer, gliding over the steps onto the terrace, and then she blushed and said: "What lovely foolishness you speak, Sir King! I am not a queen. I am only Gotho the shepherdess. But you, I can tell from the brightness on your face more than by the circle of gold on your head, you are Totila, the king of the Goths, whom they call the King of Joy.

"Here are some flowers for you, and for your lovely bride. I heard that this feast was taking place to celebrate your betrothal, and as Gotho has nothing else to give I picked these and made them into a garland as I was walking through the forest on my way here. And now, King, defender of orphans and champion of justice, hear me and give me your protection."

The king resumed his seat next to Valeria. The girl stood between them, and there the bride took her hand as the king placed his hand on her head and said: "I swear it on your lovely head, you will receive justice and protection here. Who are you? And what is it you seek?"

"Sir, I am the child and grandchild of mountain peasants. I grew up on the Iffa Mountain among flowers and isolation, and there was nobody I loved except a brother. He went away to go and look for you. And when the time came for my grandfather to die, he sent me to you. He said that with you I would find my brother, justice and my future fate.

"He gave me old Hunibad from Teriolis to accompany me, but his wounds had not fully healed. They soon broke open again, and he could go no further than Verona. For a long time I had to nurse him before he died too. And after that I walked through this big hot country quite alone, with only my dog Brun here for company, until I finally found the fortress Roma and you.

"And I must say, Sir King, you keep good law and order here in your country; I have to praise you for that. Your roads are guarded day and night by your soldiers and lancers, and they were all very kind and friendly to this lonely child. And every night they showed me to the house of some good, kind Gothic people, where the lady of the house looked after me and my wants. And they said that you keep such strict law and order in this country that one could safely leave gold bangles lying in the streets, and many nights later one could go back and be sure of still finding them there.

"And in one city, I think it was called Mantua, there was a great commotion just as I was walking through the marketplace, and a lot of people had gathered there. And your *sajoni* were leading a Roman to his death in their midst, calling out: 'Marcus Massurius is to die by order of the king, who had set him free after taking him as a prisoner of war. And then the insolent devil robbed and violated a Jewish girl by force. King Totila has renewed the law of our great King Theodoric.' And then they cut off his head in the open marketplace, and all the people knew fear at the knowledge of King Totila's justice. Well, faithful Brun, here you can rest; nobody will harm you or me here. Today, in your honour, I even adorned him with flowers."

Gently she patted the huge dog's shaggy head, and then the latter went before the king's throne with an intelligent look on his face, and placed his front paw trustingly on the king's knee. The king gave him spring water to drink from a shallow golden bowl. "For such faithfulness," he said, "Brun deserves a golden bowl. But who is your brother?"

"Well," she said thoughtfully, "after much of what Hunibad told me on our way and on his sickbed, I am not sure that his name is the right one. But he is easy to recognise," she added with a blush. "His hair is golden brown and wavy, and his eyes are bright and blue like this gemstone here. His voice is like that of a lark, and when he plays his harp he looks up at the sky as if he was looking at the heavens, wide open to him..."

"Adalgoth!" cried the king.

"Adalgoth!" the Goths around him repeated.

"Yes, his name is Adalgoth," she said.

When he heard his name called, Adalgoth came flying up the steps. "My Gotho!" he cried, overcome with joy. And they were in one another's arms.

"They belong together," said Duke Guntharis, who had been following the youth.

"Like dawn and morning sun," Teias added.

"But now," said the girl, freeing herself from her brother's embrace, "let me fulfil my mission, as my dying grandfather commanded me to do. Here, King, take these scrolls and read them. Grandfather said that they contain the past, the future and also the destiny of both Adalgoth and Gotho."

Chapter 17

And then the king broke the outer seal and read: "'This was written by Hildegisel whom they call the tall one, the son of Hildemut, formerly a priest but at the time of writing this a soldier in the garrison at Teriolis. It is written as it was told to me by old Iffa, and has all been truly written down.

"Now: here it comes. The Latin may not always be as it is sung in church, but you will be able to understand it Sir King, because where the Latin is bad the Gothic is good.

"Now here it comes, really this time. Thus spoke Iffa, the old one: 'Sir King Totila. That which is written in this wrapped scroll here was written by the man Warga, but he was not my son, nor was his name Warga. His name was Alaric, and he was of the Balti clan, the banished Duke of ...'"

A cry of astonishment went the rounds of the assembled Goths. The king paused, and Duke Guntharis spoke: "Then Adalgoth, who has been calling himself the son of Warga, is really Alaric's son, whom he has been seeking everywhere in his role as the king's herald, riding his white horse through the land. Never have I seen a greater resemblance between father and son that that between Alaric and his son Adalgoth."

"Hail to you, Duke of Apulia!" Totila cried with a smile, and took the lad in his arms.

Speechless with surprise Gotho sank to her knees. Her eyes filled with tears and then, looking up to Adalgoth, she sighed: "So you are not my brother? Oh God! Hail, Duke of Apulia. Farewell, for ever!" and with that she rose and turned to leave.

"Not my sister?" Adalgoth cried overjoyed. "That's the best part of the whole dukedom of Apulia! Wait right there," and he caught her and pressed her little head to his breast. Then he kissed her heartily on the mouth and said to the king: "King Totila, will you betrothe us? Here is my bride, my little duchess."

Totila, who had by now quickly scanned through both documents, smiled: "Indeed, there is no need for the fabled royal wisdom of King Solomon to find the right thing to do here. Young Duke of Apulia, as of this moment you and your pretty bride are betrothed."

With that he took the child in his arm, who was crying and laughing at the same time. And then he said to the Goths around him: "Permit me to sum up for you the miracles which are written here in Hildegisel's clumsy Latin – I knew him, and he was better with a sword than a pen – and also in the Duke's testament. Duke Alaric states here that he was innocent."

"His innocence is already proved, through his son!" cried Guntharis. "I never did believe him guilty!"

"He did not discover until late in his life who his secret accuser was. Our Adalgoth has brought his name out into the light from the ruins of the shattered Caesar statue. The Prefect Cethegus had been keeping a kind of diary, in a secret code, but Cassiodorus has been able to decipher it, and he has been shocked and disgusted at the crimes of the man whom he had so long admired. In the diary I found this entry, written some twelve years ago: 'Duke of Apulia sentenced. Only he himself and his accuser now believe that he is innocent. A man who strikes at the heart of Cethegus shall not live. When I awoke from that deathlike state of unconsciousness by the Tiber, my first thought was this revenge. I swore to carry it out, and now I have kept my word.' The reasons for this vengeance are still not known to us, but they must somehow be connected with our friend Julius Montanus. Where is he?"

"He has already returned to the church of St Peter with Cassiodorus," Count Teias replied. "They asked to be excused by you. They are praying night and day for peace with Byzantium. And Julius is also praying for the Prefect's soul," he added with a bitter smile. "King Theodoric found it difficult to believe in the guilt of the courageous Duke, who had been his close friend."

"In fact," Duke Guntharis interrupted, "he once gave him a golden bracelet with a runic inscription."

The king continued, reading from the scroll: "'I took this bracelet here with me into banishment as I fled with my little son. May this bracelet, broken in half through the inscription, serve one day to prove my son's noble birth.'"

"He carries that proof in his face," Guntharis commented.

"But I have the golden proof too," said Adalgoth: "Old Iffa gave me one piece of it anyway. Here it is," and he produced one half of the bracelet, which he had been wearing on a piece of string around his neck. "I never could fathom the meaning of the inscription:

"'To the Balti –
to the falcon –
in need –
to a friend—'"

"You are missing the other half, Adalgoth," the shepherdess said, and produced the other piece from the bosom of her gown. "You see, here the inscription says:

"'—the Amalungs,
– the eagle,
– and in death,
– a friend.'"

And then Teias, holding the two halves together, read:

"To the Balti the Amalungs,
to the falcon the eagle,
in need and in death,
to a friend a friend."

Totila continued: "'But in the end the king could no longer protect me, after forged incriminating letters were placed before him. They were so skilfully forged in imitation of my own hand that I myself, when they showed me a single sentence cut out of the parchment, said without hesitation: 'Yes, I wrote that'. The sentence was harmless enough, but when they fitted the piece back into the whole parchment and read out the entire document I found that I was supposed to have written to the court in Byzantium; the document said that I was planning to murder the king and give up southern Italy, in return for Byzantium recognising me as the king of northern Italy. And then the judges found me guilty.

"'As I was led from the hall I met Cethegus in the corridor, who had been my enemy for many years. I had once succeeded in wresting a young girl whom he was courting from his evil grasp, and I married her off to a worthy friend in Gaul. Cethegus forced his way through the guards, slapped me on the shoulder and said: "He whom love eludes, hate consoles." And I could see from the look on his face that he, and none other, was my secret accuser.

"'As a last favour the king granted me the means enabling me to flee from my dungeon. But I was banished, and along with my entire family I was hunted mercilessly, with all my property being confiscated. For a long time I drifted about in the northern mountains, until I remembered that there were some old and faithful followers of my house living on the Iffinger Mountain near Teriolis. So I went there with my little boy and the few pieces of treasure which I had been able to save and take with me.

"'And the good people there took me and my son into their house, and they gave me shelter under the name of Warga, "the banished one". They said that I was old Iffa's son, and got rid of all unreliable hands who might have betrayed me. And so I lived in hiding for many years. But I and the Iffings after me will bring up my son to exact revenge against the traitor Cethegus.

"'I hope that there will come a day when my innocence is proved. But if that should take too long, then my son shall go down the valley into Italy as soon as he is old enough to carry a sword. He shall go from the Iffinger Mountain to avenge his father against Cethegus Caesarius. That is my last word to my son."

"'But soon after he had written this,'" the king read on from the other scroll, "he was buried in a landslide on the mountain with several of my relatives. I, old Iffa, have brought up the boy as my grandson and as Gotho's brother, because the family of the Duke was still being hunted, and I did not want the hatred of that man from hell to be directed against Adalgoth also. And in order to make quite sure that the boy could tell nobody of his dangerous origins, I took care to tell him nothing in the first place.

"'But when he was old enough to carry a sword, and I heard that a kind and just king was ruling in Rome, who was fighting the hellish Prefect as the sun fights the night, I decided to send young Adalgoth down to seek revenge. I told him that he was to avenge a protector of our family, a great nobleman, against the evil traitor Cethegus on his father's instructions.

"'But I did not tell him that he was the son of Alaric, the Duke of Apulia, because I was afraid of the sentence of banishment which still lay on him. As long as there was still guilt associated with his father's name, that name could do him only harm, not good.

"'And I sent him away quickly when I discovered that he was developing a most unbrotherly fondness for my granddaughter Gotho, even though he thought her to be his sister. I could have at least told him that Gotho was not his sister. But far be it from me to try and marry my granddaughter, the child of a simple shepherd, to the heir of my noble duke's house by such deception. No, if there is any justice in this world, then he will one day be Duke of Apulia, as his father was before him. And as I feel that I am soon to die, and Adalgoth has as yet sent no news of the Prefect's death, I have asked the tall Hildegisel to write all this down.

"'(And I, Hildegisel, received twenty pounds of the best cheese for writing this and twelve jars of honey, which I acknowledge gratefully, and both were very good indeed.)

"'And so I sent the child Gotho to the just King Totila with all this, with the blue gemstones and the fine clothes from the Balti inheritance and with a few pieces of gold. King Totila will pardon the innocent man, and lift the sentence from his innocent son. Once Adalgoth knows that he is a descendant of the noble Balti family, and that Gotho is not his sister, then he may choose to do as he pleases; he can either choose the shepherdess or avoid her of his own free will. But you should know that the Iffing family has always been free and never enslaved, even though they were under the protection of the Balti. King Totila, you shall decide what is to be done with her.'"

Chapter 18

"Well now," the king smiled, "you have already saved me the trouble of having to make that decision, Sir Duke of Apulia."

"And the young duchess," Valeria interjected, "is already dressed as if she had somehow sensed that this was going to be her wedding day."

"That was for your betrothal," the young shepherdess replied. "When I heard about this feast outside the gates of the fortress Roma I opened the bundle, as my grandfather told me to, and dressed myself in your honour."

"The day of our betrothal," Adalgoth said to his bride, "fell on the same day as that of the royal couple. Shall we make our wedding day the same as theirs too?"

"No, no!" Valeria interrupted quickly, almost fearfully. "Not another oath, coupled to an earlier one which as yet has not been fulfilled! You are children of happiness and good fortune. Be wise; today is the day you found one another, so hold on to the golden present, for who knows what the morrow holds in store."

"You are right," Adalgoth rejoiced, "this very day will be our wedding day!" and he raised Gotho high in the air on his left arm, showing her to all the people. "Look, good Goths, look at my little duchess here."

"With your permission, Sir King," a modest voice spoke from the crowd. "On a day where there is so much joy and happiness among the highest in our nation, there are more lowly members of that same nation who would like to partake of that same happiness too." A plain-looking man stepped before the king, a pretty girl on his arm.

"It is you, worthy Wachis," Count Teias cried, walking up to him, "and no longer a serf, but a free man with long hair?"

"Yes Sir! King Witigis, my unfortunate master, freed me as he dismissed me with the mistress Rauthgundis and Wallada. Since then I have been growing my hair long, as a free man. And I am sure that the mistress Rauthgundis intended to free her maid Liuta here too, so that we could wed as free Goths. But she never managed to get back to the house near Faesulae. I did get there however, from my hideout in the forest, and just in time! I just managed to take my Liuta from the villa and to safety, and the next day Belisarius's Saracens came and burnt the town and murdered the people. After the mistress died without an heir – her father Athalwin had already been killed by an avalanche before she died – Liuta is now the property of the king. I now seek a favour. Please, Sir King, make me a serf again too, so that we will not be punished if we wed, and..."

Totila did not let him finish: "Wachis, you are a true and faithful man," he cried, deeply moved. "No, you shall wed as free citizens according to ancient Gothic custom. Does anybody have a gold piece?"

"Here, Sir King!" Gotho cried eagerly, taking a golden coin from her pouch. "It is the last one left out of the six my grandfather gave me for Adalgoth."

The king took it with a smile, laid it on Liuta's outstretched right palm, and then struck her hand from below so that the piece of gold flew high in the air before falling to the mosaic floor with a clatter. Then the king said:

"Free and without restraint I leave you, Liuta, single and unburdened! Go and wed happily with our royal blessing."

And then Count Teias stepped forward and said: "Wachis, you have already carried one luckless master's shield. Will you be my shield bearer from now on?"

The faithful man grasped the Count's hands, with tears in his eyes. Teias raised his golden goblet and said solemnly:

"Here you are, lucky and happy! The glow of the glorious sun shines on you both with favour: yet, sadly, spare a thought for the faithful dead as well! Without luck or glamour, but true, brave and worthy the warrior fought with honour. Witigis, Waltari's son, should be toasted by you today. Joyful favourites of benevolent gods and golden feasts: may the Gothic people honour now and always the luckless couple in sacred memory. I urge you now to drink sadly to great true love, that of the bravest man and his worthy wife. I drink to the love of Witigis and Rauthgundis."

And they all joined him, silently and respectfully.

And then King Totila raised his own cup once more and said aloud to all the people: "He earned and deserved a kingdom, but fate left me to attain it. Eternal and never to be forgotten honour to him!"

After they had resumed their seats, the other two couples having been placed at the royal table also, Count Thorismuth of Thurii mounted the steps to the throne. Thorismuth's bravery had been rewarded by making him a Count, but on his own wish he had retained his office of herald and royal shield bearer. Now he bowed before the king with his herald's staff and said: "King of the Goths, I come to announce strangers, guests from afar. That great fleet of more than a hundred sails, which has been reported for several days now near your coast, has entered the harbour of Portus. They are North People, courageous men of the sea, from the distant island of Thule. Their dragon ships rise high out of the sea, and their enormous figureheads spread terror from the bows of their ships. But they come to you in peace. Their royal ship launched some boats yesterday, and important guests are sailing upstream in them. I have hailed them, and in reply they said: 'King Harald from Gotaland and Haralda (apparently his wife) come to greet King Totila!'"

"Bring them here. Duke Guntharis, Duke Adalgoth, Count Teias, Count Wisand, Count Grippa, go to meet them and accompany them."

Shortly afterwards, to the warlike sounds coming from their strange horns made from seashells, and surrounded by twenty warriors in heavy steel armour, two tall figures appeared on the terrace, towering even over the tall Totila and his table companions.

King Harald wore the foot-long wings of the black sea eagle on his helmet, and the helmet itself was covered with the feathers of the same bird. From his back hung the hide of an enormous black bear, its head and paws hanging over heavy bronze chest armour. More armour woven from iron wire reached down to his knees, and was held around his waist by a belt of seal leather, set with seashells. His arms and legs were bare except for some heavy golden bracelets, which served to adorn and protect them at the same time. A short sword hung from a steel chain at his side, and in his right hand he carried a long spear with a sharp barb. His thick light blond hair flowed freely over his shoulders like a mane.

On his left, shorter by only the breadth of a finger, stood the Valkyrie-like figure of his companion. Her bright red hair had an almost metallic sheen, and reached down to her waist from her open golden helmet topped with the wings of a seagull. The white

skin of a polar bear covered her back, more as a cloak than an adornment. Closely
fitting armour made from tiny platelets of gold served to accentuate this warrior
maiden's magnificent build, following her every movement. Her undergarment
reached down to her calves, and was made from the white fur of the snow hare. Her
arms were covered with rings of amber beads, which glowed golden in the light of the
setting Roman sun. And on her left shoulder there sat the delicate white falcon of
Iceland. There was a short hand axe stuck in her belt, and over her shoulder she
carried a tall harp, made of silver in the shape of a swan.

The Roman masses followed them, staring, agog at the sight of such strange people.
Even the Goths had to admire them, looking at how much whiter their arms were, and
how their eyes had the fire of a strange vitality.

"After the black warrior who received me," the Viking began, "told me that he was
not the king, then only you can be he," and he held out his hand to Totila, first
removing his sharkskin fighting glove.

"Welcome to the Tiber River, cousins from Thuleland," Totila cried, drinking to
them both.

Chairs were quickly fetched, and the royal pair joined King Totila's table, with
their companions sitting at tables nearby. Adalgoth poured them wine from tall jars.

King Harald drank, and looked about him admiringly.

"By Asathor," he cried, "it is beautiful here!"

"This is how I imagine Valhalla!" his companion added.

The Goths and these northerners were barely able to understand one another.

"If you like it here with me, brother," Totila said slowly, "then stay here awhile
with your wife, as my guest."

"Hoho, King of Rome!" the giantess laughed, and threw back her head so that her
red hair flowed freely about her, as her falcon flew around her three times, screeching,
before returning to her shoulder. "As yet no man has come who can tame Haralda's
heart and hand. Only Harald, my brother, can bend my arm, jump farther than I or
throw a spear further."

"Patience, little sister. I feel sure that a virile man will come along soon enough,
who will master your stubborn spinsterhood. This king here might look as gentle as
Baldur, and yet he looks like Sigurd, who defeated Fafnir. You two should compete in
the spear throw."

Haralda took a long look at the Gothic king, coloured a little and pressed a kiss on
her falcon's head.

But Totila replied: "Only evil, so the singers tell us, came from the battle between
Sigurd and the shield maiden. Instead let woman greet woman in peace. Haralda, take
my bride's hand."

And he signalled to Valeria, to whom Duke Guntharis had translated the essence of
what had been taking place into Latin.

Valeria now rose with noble dignity from her chair. Beauty surrounded her like
music as she stood there in her long, flowing Greco-Roman gown, white with a
golden belt and golden shoulder clasp, and a laurel branch from Adalgoth's garland in
her hair. She held out her hand to her northern sister.

The latter had cast a quick, and not exactly admiring, glance at her Roman rival.
But in an instant admiration took the place of angry surprise in her face, and she said:
"By Freya's necklace, you are the most beautiful woman I have ever seen! I doubt if
there is a girl in Valhalla to match you. Do you know, Harald, whom this princess

resembles? Ten nights ago we devastated an island in the blue Greek seas, and we plundered a temple with pillars. In it there was a woman of marble. She held a head with snakes instead of hair against her breast and had the night bird at her feet, and she wore a flowing gown. Unfortunately Sven smashed her to pieces because of the jewels in her eyes. That marble goddess is who this royal bride looks like."

"That I must translate for you," Totila smiled at his beloved. "Not even your poetical admirer Piso could have flattered you more charmingly than this Bellona from the northern land. They landed on Melos, from what they tell us, and there they smashed the Athena of Pheidias. She says that you look like her! You must have waged a terrible campaign," Totila went on, "I have heard it from all the islands between Cos, Chios and Melos. You must have really left havoc in your wake. What is it then that brings you to us so peacefully?"

"That I will tell you, brother, but not until I have had another drink." He held out his deep goblet to Adalgoth. "No, don't spoil this godly liquid with water! Water has to be salty, so that one cannot drink it at all unless one is a shark or a walrus! Water is good for carrying us on its back, but not in our stomachs. And this grape beer of yours really is some drink! I get tired of our mead every now and again – it is like some watery, sweet food. But this grape mead, the more one drinks of it the thirstier one becomes. And if one should drink too much, which is difficult to imagine, it is different to having drunk too much mead or beer, where one is tempted to ask Asathor to forge a ring around one's skull with his hammer. No, this intoxication from grape mead is like the sweet madness of our legends, and it makes one feel like the gods themselves. But that is enough of drinking and wine.

"We have come here for a reason, and I will now tell you what it is."

Chapter 19

"Now, we live in what the singers call Thuleland, but we call it Gotaland, because Thuleland is a country where nobody lives. It is the land beyond the icebergs.

"Our Empire extends from the sea and our island of Gotland where the sun rises, to Hallin and the bay of Skioldungen where the sun sets. In the north is the Svealand, and in the south, where the sun is at midday, we border on Smaland, Skone and the land of the Sea Danes.

"The king is my father Frode, whom Odin loves. He is much wiser than I. He has now crowned me as his fellow king, because he is almost a hundred years old and blind.

"But in our halls the singers still tell of how you Goths with the Amalung rulers and the Balti nobles were once our brothers, and how you became lost during your wanderings and so drifted ever further to the south. You followed the flight of the cranes from the Caucasian Mountains, while we followed the wolf."

"If that is so," Totila smiled, "then I prefer the cranes as my guides."

"It may well seem that way to you now, in your proud mead hall here," King Harald said seriously. "But my wise father Frode thinks otherwise. But be that as it may. I can barely believe that we are brothers, because if we are brothers we should be able to understand one another more easily, but we do honour the old blood relationship highly, and if we are not brothers then we must be at least cousins.

"And for a long time only good and joyful news came from your warm southern land here into our cold country. Once my father and your King Thidekr, whom our singers and harpists praise, exchanged gifts and envoys, arranged through the Estonians who live where amber abounds on the Austr River. They conducted our envoys to the Wendi on the Wyzala, who in turn brought them to the Lombards on the Tisia. The Lombards conducted them to the Heruli on the Dravus, and from there they travelled through Savia to Salona and Ravenna."

"You are a man who knows his way about lands and journeys," Totila remarked.

"A Viking has to be, for otherwise he gets nowhere. And often he never gets back from where he has been. And so, for a long time, we heard only news of fortune and fame from you.

"But then merchants started to come, only one at first, and then more and more. They buy furs, eider duck feathers and amber from us, which they take to the Friesians, Saxons and Franks, and they bring back artefacts of gold and silver for us. The news became more and more sad. We heard that King Thidekr had died, and that after his death much misfortune had befallen your Empire. We heard of defeat, treason, regicide, war of Goth against Goth, and the superior might of the false rulers in Grekaland.

"And we heard that thousands upon thousands of you smashed your skulls against the walls of your own Roma castle, which however you did not have. A man like Asathor had it, with a second man who was even worse, like Loki the fire demon.

"And then we asked if there was nobody who was helping you, out of the many kings and dukes who had once begged favours of King Thidekr. At that the Franconian merchant laughed and said, in my father's hall where he was offering fine cloth for sale: 'When luck breaks, loyalty breaks too. They have all deserted the Gothic heroes, on whom fortune no longer smiles, and left them to their own devices, Visigoths and Burgundians, Heruli and Thuringi and most of all we Franks, because we are more clever than most other peoples.'

"But when we heard that my father Frode smashed his staff down on the ground angrily and cried: 'Where is Harald, my strong son?'

"'Here, father,' I said, and took his hand.

"'Did you hear,' my father went on, 'about the disloyalty of the southern kings? No one shall sing or speak the same about the men of Gotaland. Even if all the others have deserted the Goths of Garderike and raven, we will keep faith with them and help them in their need.

"Go, my strong Harald, and my brave Haralda! Equip a hundred ships and fill them with men and arms. Dig deep into my royal treasure in Kingsala and don't spare the rings of gold which are heaped there. Then sail, with Odin's breath in your sails.

"From Konghalla you must first sail past the Island Danes and the Jueti heading to where the sun sets, then towards the coast of the Friesians and the Franks through the part where the sea narrows. Then sail around the country of the Suevi and also around the land of the Visigoths. Then turn south and make your way through the narrows of the great ocean, where Asathor and Odin have placed two columns. You will then be in the sea of Midilgardh, where there are countless islands with trees and bushes which are always green, and among them great white halls of marble, made from huge round logs of stone.

"These islands you must devastate, because they belong to the false rulers of Grekaland.

"And after that sail to Roma or Ravenna and help the people of Thidekr against their enemies, and fight with them on land and sea, and stay loyally by their side until they have defeated all their enemies.

"But after that is done go and say to them: This is what King Frode advises, who has seen almost a hundred winters, and who has seen the fortunes of many peoples and their rulers rise and then fall again. He has also seen the southern land himself when he was a young man, as a Viking.

"And King Frode says to you: Give up your southern Gotaland, wonderful as it is. You will not last there.

"You will not last, any more than an ice floe lasts as it drifts into the southern ocean. Sun, air and the waves gnaw at it ceaselessly, and no matter how great and strong it might be in the end it must melt, and not a trace of it will be left.

"It is better to live in the poor North Land than it is to die in the rich South Land. Go aboard our dragon ships, and build some more of your own. Then load all your men, women, children, field hands and maids, cattle and horses and weapons and treasures onto the ships. Go away from the hot earth which will otherwise surely swallow you, and then come to us. We will move closer together if we have to, or else you may take as much land as you need away from the Finns, the Wendi and the Estonians.

"Here you will survive and prosper, fresh and blooming. But down there the southern sun will burn you and dry you up.

"That is the advice to you from King Frode, whom men have called the wise one for fifty years!

"Certainly we heard, as soon as we entered the sea of Midilgardh, how your fortunes have been reversed by a new king, whom they liken to the god Baldur, and that you had won back the Roma fortress and all the land from Garderike, and how you have even devastated Grekaland itself.

"And now we can see with our own eyes that you have no need for armed aid from us. You are living splendidly and happily in this fine mead hall here, and everywhere we look we see red gold and white stone. And yet I must repeat my father's advice: follow it! He is wise, and everyone yet who has spurned the advice of King Frode has had cause to regret it."

But Totila took his hand with a smile and said: "Tell King Frode that we are most grateful to him and to you for your noble and rare loyalty. Such brotherly faithfulness shall not be forgotten in our Gothic songs, and we will sing of our loyal North Land heroes always. But, King Harald, follow my example and look about you."

With that he rose, took his guest by the hand and led him to the door of the tent, where he drew back the curtains. There lay the river and the countryside and the city in the golden glow of the setting sun: "Look at this land, incomparably beautiful, and immeasurably rich in sun and soil and art! Look at the lovely Tiber River there, with happy, joyous and beautiful people on its waters. Look at these bushes of laurel and myrtle! Look there at the palaces of marble columns, over there in Rome, in the light of the evening sun, and look at the tall marble statues here on these steps! And now tell me yourself, would you vacate this land if it was yours? Would you exchange this splendour for the pines and firs of the north, for long icy winters, and for smoke-blackened huts on a misty heath?"

"Yes, by Thor's hammer, I would indeed! This country here is a great place in which to pillage, to indulge oneself and win victories, but once that is done, then home with the spoils as quickly as can be! But you Goths have been thrown in here like drops of water on hot iron. And if ever we sons of Odin should come to rule in the South Land, it will only be by those sons of Odin who have the support of many other sons of Odin in their rear, to the north.

"But as for you, you are already quite different to us. You, your fathers and grandfathers have married southern women. If that goes on for a few more generations, then you will become one with these southerners. You are already smaller than us, darker of skin and eyes and hair, or at least many of you are.

"I long to get away from these warm shores and out of this mild air, back to where the north wind roars over our forests and the waves. Yes, and I even long to be back in the smoke-blackened hall, where the names of the gods are carved in runic letters into the wooden pillars, and where the holy fire in the hearth flickers with everlasting hospitality. I yearn for our North Land, for it is my home."

"Then allow us to love our homeland too, this land Italia!"

"It will never be your home, but it may become your tomb. You are foreign here, and foreign you always will be. Or you will go under, and become southerners like them. But you will not remain here in this land as the sons of Odin."

"My dear brother Harald, let us at least try," Totila smiled. "Yes, we are different after living here for two generations among the laurels. But are we any the worse for that? Is it necessary to wear a bear skin in order to be a hero? Does one have to steal golden images and smash marble statues in order to enjoy them? Can one only be either a Barbarian or a southerner? Is it not possible to retain the virtues of Germanic peoples, but rid ourselves of their faults, and to acquire the virtues of the Italians without taking on their faults as well?"

But Harald shook his head. "I would be truly delighted if you should succeed in doing that. But believe it I do not. A plant cannot assume the nature of the sky or the earth. And I would not want to do so, even if I and those near and dear to me could. I prefer our faults to the Italians virtues – if they have any."

Totila was reminded of the words which he himself had once said to Julius, "all strength goes out from the northern peoples; the world belongs to them alone."

"Why don't you tell them," Haralda interrupted, "in the words of your favourite song?" and she handed him the harp.

Harald took the harp and started to play and sing an ancient song in alliteration verse. Aalgoth translated it into rhyming verse for Valeria, and it sounded thus:

"Thor stood at the midnight end of the world: his heavy battleaxe he threw:
'As far as the soaring hammer flies, mine is all the land and the seas!'
And from his hand the hammer flew, it flew across all the world,
Down it fell at the earth's most southern tip, so that the whole earth was Thor's.
And ever since it has been Germanic right to conquer land by the hammer:
We are of the hammer god's people, and we are going to inherit this world!"

Loud applause from the Gothic listeners rewarded the royal singer, who looked as though he was fully intent on putting his song into reality, and was quite able to do so.

Harald drained his deep golden goblet once more, and then he cried: "Come little sister Haralda, and my sailing brothers too! We will be on our way now, for we must be back on board the *Midilgardhserpent* before the moon shines on her. How does the Viking saying go?
'A ship sleeps badly when the helmsman lies ashore.'
"Long friendship, short farewells, that is the northern custom."

Totila placed his hand on his guest's arm: "Are you really in such a hurry? Are you afraid to become southernised along with us? Stay awhile, it will not happen that quickly, and you seem to be enjoying yourselves here in this softness and luxury."

"You are right there, King of Rome," the giant laughed, "and by Thor's hammer, I am proud of it. But we must go. We had three things to do, according to the orders from King Frode. One was to help you in your war, but you don't need us. Or do you? Shall we stay until the war flares up again?"

"No," Totila smiled. "Peace, not renewed war lies ahead. And suppose there was to be more war. Am I to admit to you, brother Harald, that we Goths are not strong enough to defend our Italia alone? Did we not defeat the enemy before without your help? Can we Goths, alone, not do the same again?"

"I don't doubt it," the Viking replied. "Our second task was to bring you all back to our northern land, but you don't want to come with us. And the third task was to wreak havoc on the islands which belong to the king of Grekaland. Now that is a delightful business, and one of which we have not nearly had our fill. Come with us! Help us! Avenge yourselves at the same time!"

"No, the word of a king must be honoured. We have an armistice, which still has months to run. And listen, friend Harald, don't confuse our islands with those belonging to the emperor. I would not be at all pleased if..."

"No, no!" Harald smiled. "You need not concern yourself about that. We have already seen how well your ports and coasts are guarded. And here and there you have had tall gallows erected with inscriptions on them in Roman runic signs. Your naval commander in Panormus translated them for us:

"'Bandits on land hanged and pirates drowned; that is the fate of thieves under Totila's justice.'

"They saw that my sailing brothers quickly developed a strong aversion to your gallows and inscriptions. Farewell now, King of Roma and the Goths; may your luck last! Farewell also, you beautiful black-haired queen. Farewell, all you heroes; we will meet again in Valhalla if not before."

And the Vikings took their leave quickly, and strode away. Haralda threw her falcon into the air: "Fly ahead, Snotr, to the ship!" and the intelligent bird flew away like an arrow, straight over the river.

The king and Valeria conducted their guests to the second last step, and there they exchanged a final handshake.

The Viking maiden took one last look at Totila. Harald noticed it, and as they descended the last step he whispered to her: "Little sister, it was for your sake that I took our leave so quickly. Don't mourn over the handsome king. You know that I have inherited from our father the gift of recognising men who are doomed to die. I tell you, I saw death by a spear on the sunny brows of that king. He will not see the moon change again." And the warrior maiden wiped a tear from her proud eyes.

Count Teias, Duke Guntharis and Duke Adalgoth went with their guests to their boats, and remained there until they had pushed off.

Teias followed them with a serious look in his eyes. "Yes," he said, "King Frode is wise. But sometimes foolishness is sweeter than wisdom, and more splendid too! Go on back to the tent, Duke Guntharis, I see the king's messenger boat coming up the river. I will stay to see what news it brings."

"I will stay with you, my master," Adalgoth said with concern. "You look so terribly solemn. What is it that troubles you?"

"A premonition, my Adalgoth," said Teias, placing his arm about the youth. "Do you see how quickly the sun sinks? Let us meet the boat. It will land down there, by the old marble ruins."

Meanwhile Totila and Valeria had returned to the tent. Valeria said to him: "My beloved, were you moved by what that stranger said? Teias and Guntharis explained it to me – it was very serious."

But Totila quickly raised his head, which had been lowered in thought. "No, Valeria, it did not move me. I have taken the work of the great Theodoric upon my shoulders, together with the dream of my youth, and the ideals of my reign. For that I shall live, and die if must be. Come! Where is Adalgoth, my cup bearer? Let us drink once more to the future and fortune of this Empire."

He raised the goblet to his lips, but was not able to drain it, because Adalgoth came flying up the steps, followed by Teias.

"King Totila!" Adalgoth cried breathlessly, "prepare to receive dreadful news! Take hold of yourself!"

Totila paled, set down his goblet and asked: "What has happened?"

"Your messenger ship brought the news from Ancona. The emperor has broken the armistice! He has..."

And then Teias reached the scene, his long black hair fluttering in the wind. His face was deathly pale, but his eyes spewed fire: "On your feet, King Totila!" he cried, "get that garland out of your hair and put on your helmet! An Imperial fleet, in the region of Senogallia near Ancona, has attacked our own fleet without warning. Our ships were lying peacefully at anchor. The armistice has been broken, and our fleet mercilessly attacked.

"Our fleet no longer exists. Of four hundred and seventy sails only eleven have been saved! A powerful Imperial army has landed. And its commander is Cethegus the Prefect!"

Chapter 20

In the camp of the Prefect Cethegus at Setinum, at the foot of the Appenine Mountains a few miles north of Taginae, Lucius Licinius was pacing up and down outside the commander's tent, talking animatedly to Syphax. Licinius had just arrived by ship from Epidamnus.

"My master has been eagerly awaiting your arrival for several days, oh tribune," the Numidian said. "He will be delighted to find you in the camp. He should be back from a reconnaissance ride soon."

"Where did he ride to?"

"Towards Taginae, with Piso and the other tribunes."

"Yes, that is the nearest fortified Gothic city south of here. But now, you clever Moor, tell me the latest news from Byzantium. As you know, your master sent me on a mission to hire Lombard mercenaries, long before a decision had been reached in Byzantium. When I returned from my journey to the Lombards and the Gepidae, and entered the Empire of Justinian once more by way of crossing the Ister River at Novae, I called on my host at Nikopolis for further orders from the Prefect. But the only order that reached me was a curt command to meet him in Senogallia.

"I was amazed, because I did not dare hope that he would ever again set foot in Italy as a victor, at the head of not only an Imperial army but also an Imperial fleet. From Senogallia I followed your march here as quickly as I could. The commanders whom I have met in the camp thus far did tell me in general terms what had taken place just before Belisarius was arrested. But as to exactly what happened then or since, they do not seem to have any precise knowledge. But you, I should think..."

"Yes, I know these things, almost as well as my master, for I was there when it happened."

"Was it true? Was Belisarius really a conspirator against Justinian? I would never have believed it."

Syphax smiled knowingly. "Syphax has no right to pass judgment on such things. I can only tell you what happened. Now let me tell you, but come into the tent first for some refreshment. My master would scold me if I was to leave you out here without something to eat and drink. Also it is safer inside," he went on, closing the curtain of the tent behind Lucius.

As he bade his master's guest sit down, and served him food and wine, he commenced his tale: "At nightfall on that fateful day I was hiding in a niche in the house of Photius, a freedman of Belisarius, behind a statue of some Christian saint. I don't know his name, but he had a good broad back, and from behind his shoulders I could see out through a hole in the wall, which is there to let fresh air in.

"There was not much light, but I could make out Photius and a number of nobles, whom I had often seen entering or leaving the palace, or the houses of either Belisarius or Procopius. My master had made me learn the language of the Greeks, and the first thing I understood was the host saying to another man as he entered: 'Rejoice! Belisarius is coming. After he barely acknowledged me yesterday when I approached him hopefully at Zenon's riding school, today he himself addressed me as I walked slowly past the open door of his house. I knew that he would return home from hunting with his Persian leopards toward evening. Carefully he placed this wax tablet in my hand, looking about him carefully to make sure nobody was watching. And on it is written: I will no longer resist your efforts to win me over. My hand is being forced by new considerations. I will come tonight.'

"'But where is Piso, or Salvius Julianus and the other young Romans?' Photius asked.

"'I don't think they will come tonight,' the other man replied. 'I saw almost all of them on boats on the Bosporus. I suppose they were going to dine at the Prefect's house, by Constantine's gate.'

"'Let them be, we don't need either the brutal Latins, nor do we need the proud and treacherous Prefect. Belisarius surely is worth more than they.'

"And then Belisarius entered. He was wearing a large cloak. The host rushed over to greet him, and they all crowded around respectfully. 'Great Belisarius', said Photius, 'we gratefully acknowledge what you have done. You have come, and you should be our leader.'

"And then he made him accept a small ivory staff, such as the leader of an assembly carries, and led him to the highest seat in the hall, which he himself had just vacated. 'Speak! Command! Act! We are prepared.'

"'I will act when the time is ripe,' Belisarius replied sternly, and sat down on the seat of honour.

"And then young Anicius rushed into the room, his hair flying in the wind, his clothing in disarray and a sword in his hand.

"'Flee!' he cried, 'we have been discovered and betrayed!'

"Belisarius rose expectantly.

"'They forced their way into my house. My slaves have been arrested. Your weapons, which I had hidden, were found, and your letters and documents were taken from the safest of all hiding places, known only to me. And alas, my own letters and documents have disappeared too. But there is more! When I came through the wood of Constantine to this house I thought that I could hear men and arms in the shrubbery. I have been followed. Save yourselves!'

"The conspirators raced for the doors. Only Belisarius remained calm, remaining seated.

"'Be calm!' Photius the host urged. 'Follow the leader's example!'

"But then I heard the sound of the tuba from the main entrance. That was a sign for me to leave my listening post and join my master, who was storming into the house at the head of the Imperial Lancers and the Palace Guard. The Prefect of Byzantium and Leo, commander of the Imperial Guard, were with him. All doors and windows were surrounded. My master did look magnificent!" Syphax cried with enthusiasm. "As he stormed into the room his purple plume was flying, and he held a torch in one hand and his sword in the other. That must be how the fire demon looks in Africa when he comes out of the fire mountain.

"I drew my sword and sprang to his left, to take the place of the missing shield on that side. He had ordered me to render young Anicius harmless straight away. 'Down with all who resist!' Cethegus commanded. 'In the name of Justinian!' His sword was red with blood all over, and he had personally helped in cutting down the bodyguards which Belisarius had placed at the exit.

"'Surrender, all of you!' he called out. 'You, commander of the Palace Guard, arrest all the conspirators! Did you hear? All of them!'

"'Can it be? Shameful traitor!' young Anicius cried and flew at my master with his sword. 'Yes, that's the purple plume on his helmet! Die, my brother's murderer!'

"But the next moment he lay dead at my feet. I withdrew my sword from his chest and disarmed Photius, who was the only one to offer resistance. The others let themselves be taken like sheep.

"'Well done, Syphax! Search his clothes for any written material! Are you finished, Leo?' my master asked.

"The latter had halted hesitantly before Belisarius, who was still calmly seated in his place of honour. 'What,' he said, 'the *Magister Militum* is to be arrested too?'

"'All of them,' my master replied. 'Can't you understand Greek? You can see for yourself – you can all see! He is clearly the head of the conspiracy; he has the staff and the seat of honour.'

"'Ha,' Belisarius cried now, 'is that how it is? Guards! Help me, my bodyguards, Marcellus, Barbatio, Ardaburius!'

"'The dead have no ears, *Magister Militum*. Give yourself up! In the name of the emperor! Do you see his large seal here? He has appointed me as his representative for tonight, and there are a thousand lancers around this house.'

"'Loyalty is madness!' Belisarius cried, and held out his strong arms to Leo to be bound.

"'Into the dungeon with all prisoners. Photius and Belisarius are to be separated from the others and placed in the Tower of Anastasius, in the palace itself. I will now hurry to the emperor and bring him this ring and this iron,' my master said as he picked up Belisarius's sword from the floor, 'and I will tell him that he can sleep in peace. The Empire has been saved!'

"The very next morning the trials for high treason began. Many witnesses were heard, including me. I swore that I had seen Belisarius being greeted as head of the conspiracy, and then act as such. And I showed them the incriminating wax tablet, which I had personally taken from Photius.

"Belisarius was going to rely on the testimony of his bodyguards, but they were all dead. Photius and the other prisoners admitted under torture that Belisarius had at last agreed to be their leader. Antonina was placed under tight guard in the Red House, and the empress refused to grant her the audience which she furiously demanded.

"Antonina herself was under grave suspicion when spies from the empress reported how they had seen young Anicius stealing his way into the house of Belisarius by night for weeks. The fact that both Belisarius and Antonina stubbornly denied this, even though it was proven beyond doubt, annoyed the judges immensely.

"Immediately after Belisarius was arrested I had to convey a message from my master to Antonina that he was very surprised to find that Belisarius really was the head of the conspiracy. I also had to tell her that Cethegus had found not only letters of hatred in Anicius's cistern. I still don't know what that means, but when she heard those words the lovely woman collapsed unconscious.

"We left Byzantium before the sentence on Belisarius had been pronounced, but Photius and most of the other conspirators had already been sentenced to death when we sailed with the Imperial fleet to Epidamnus, where my master's tribunes and strong Imperial forces were waiting for us.

615

"My master had been granted the new title of *Magister Militum per Italiam*, and with it command of the First Army. The Second Army was to follow under Prince Areobindos, after he managed to conquer the Gothic garrisons in Epirus and a few islands with an army five times larger than the Gothic forces in that area. They are doomed."

"What is known of the punishment which awaits Belisarius? I would never have believed that this man would betray his emperor."

"The judges must surely sentence him to death, because he really was caught red-handed. There is some speculation that the emperor may exercise clemency, and commute the death sentence to blinding and banishment for life. My master says it is very foolish of Belisarius to continue denying everything. And he misses his friend and lawyer Procopius, who is abroad in Asia looking at buildings.

"My master managed to embark his army at Epidamnus so secretly that the stupid Goths barely heard about it; and anyway, they were relying on the armistice and expecting an early peace. The pretext for preparing the fleet was some devastation on the emperor's islands by foreign ships from Thuleland. And so our fleet caught the Gothic fleet by surprise at night, while their crews were asleep on the shore. More than four hundred of their ships were captured, sunk or burnt, almost without bloodshed.

"But listen, that's my master now! I know his walk; only the lion in my homeland walks like that."

Chapter 21

"Welcome, Licinius, to Italy and to victory!" Cethegus called out on entering. "Where are the Lombards?"

"*Salve*, destroyer of fleets," the tribune replied. "The Lombards are coming, twenty thousand of them."

"That is very many indeed!" Cethegus said, suddenly very serious. "I had wanted only seven thousand. I don't even know how I am going to raise enough gold for almost three times that number. You see, it is important that they are paid by me, and not by the emperor."

But the young knight replied, with a proud and happy look in his eyes: "I trust that you will be satisfied, *Magister Militum*. The Lombards are coming without pay."

"Really? And that many?"

"Yes. The son of their king Audoin is one Alboin. Germanic legend already sings his praise from the Bajuvari on the Oenus to the Saxons on the Wisurgis. He is a very courageous and, for a Barbarian, a very intelligent young man…"

"I know of him. He served for some time under Narses," Cethegus commented, becoming suspicious.

"This intelligent and brave Barbarian made his way into Italy last year, disguised as a horse trader, and so he managed to explore the whole country from Rome to Naples without being recognised. He knows the roads and fortifications and defences of the Goths. He would have stayed even longer, had not the same Goth who killed my poor brother…"

"The black Teias?"

"Yes, Teias. He became suspicious, followed Alboin, and in the end threatened to arrest him as a spy, so that Alboin fled back to Pannonia. But he took back with him wine and delicious fruits from our country to his father and his people, and ever since then all the Lombards are inflamed with a desire to come and see this land of wonders. Alboin asks only for the booty which his Lombards acquire, and does not demand pay. They are splendid Barbarians, these long beards, much more savage and rougher than the Goths. 'Yes,' Alboin laughed when I told him this, 'we have a saying that the Goth is a deer, and the Lombard a wolf.' He drinks from the skull of the Gepidae king, whom he slew in battle. You will be pleased with him and his mounted warriors – they are worth more than Isaurians or Abasgae."

"Thank you for your eagerness," Cethegus said hesitantly. "It is almost too much eagerness. There are so many of them!"

"Alboin would not agree to a lesser number. 'Wolves hunt in packs!' he laughed."

"Well," Cethegus concluded, "I trust that, with two Imperial armies and Italy behind me, I will be able to ensure the obedience of even that number of wild animals. You are sure they will not go over to the Goths?"

"No, my general. There is some ancient hatred in the history of these two peoples, originating from one of those unfathomable causes as only Germanic tribes can find for hating one another. At some time in the distant past some Lombard queen had a

617

Gothic ruler slain, or the other way round – who can remember these things? From then on it has been a sacred duty for Goths and Lombards to hate and murder one another. 'We are the gravediggers and the inheritors of these Goths,' Alboin told me."

"They are free to inherit the misfortunes of these Goths," Cethegus said threateningly, "otherwise there is nothing the Goths have to pass on. They will die as foreigners on Italian soil. And when will they come, these wolves from Pannonia? I will need them soon."

"That is something Alboin was not able to tell me as yet. They have an alliance with the savage Avars, who are not Germanic, against the poor Gepidae. They plan to completely annihilate that Germanic tribe and murder every last man among them. Then they plan to divide their country between them."

"A fierce and dangerous people," said Cethegus, shaking his head.

"I daresay they are. Alboin told me laughingly: 'Wolf and vulture hunt together, and then they share the deer. Once this deed is done, we will move via Dravus, Savus and Sontius to Venetia next. I know the way.' That is what he said."

"He knows the way so well," Cethegus said, more to himself than to Licinius, "that he must not be allowed to return home along it again later. Licinius, I need new reinforcements, strong ones. The beginning was good, but now we are not making much headway. The Italians, disgraceful as it is having to say it, are not rebelling but siding with the Barbarians," he smiled angrily, "for the same reasons as my late friend Balbus, who ate himself to death. I feel certain that the Gothic king is already on his way, from Rome, with a strong army to avenge his fleet. I know him well; he will attack! And so I have sent messenger after messenger to Areobindos, who really is a prince of snails, asking him to bring the Second Army up to join me quickly. I want him to leave the scattered Goths in Epirus be – they will be annihilated in any case by the sheer audacity of their position. But no Areobindos comes. And with the Byzantines I have I cannot defeat this Totila in open battle, especially as he will have numerical superiority."

"And Ravenna? Will it be able to hold out if you do not relieve it quickly?"

"Ravenna has been relieved. After the destruction of the Gothic fleet I sent thirty of my triremes under Justinus to Classis. They forced their way into the harbour there and brought fresh supplies to the city. And a few days ago I heard that old Hildebrand had abandoned the siege on the landward side as well, and that he has moved around us to the west. He is now reported to be near Florence or Perusia with his few thousand men. The supposed reason for this, which is an impossibility, is that an enormous Imperial army is moving up by land from Dalmatia through Venetia, and that it is closing on Ravenna in forced marches.

"If only that was true! But unfortunately I know better. The Second Army, which by the way is smaller than mine, is neither in Dalmatia nor in Salona, which are both held by the Goths. Instead of that they are gathering in Epidamnus, unbelievably slowly. Prince Areobindos, who they wrongly think is capable of forced marches, would rather go on picking easy laurels in Epirus.

"Your beautiful friend the empress, my Licinius, is still favourably disposed towards me, that is true. But neither she nor the emperor of the Romaeans want to see me win too quickly. And so I will just have to wait and wait, until the prince of snails finally gets here. But the place for us is not up there at Senogallia. I am drawn towards Rome!

"In any event the positions up there are too weak to be held against a superior enemy. This splendid position here at Setinum, Caprae and Taginae is one I had picked out long ago.

"And so I hurried here, quickly! But not quickly enough. I had time to reach Setinum, but not Caprae or Taginae, which I needed to give me cover in my rear.

"And yet, Taginae is the key to this whole position. Without Caprae and Taginae my position is like a fortress with a wall but no moat. The three small rivers at Caprae and Taginae serve as natural moats. I raced over to Taginae with my Saracen cavalry from Setinum as quickly as I could, but too late.

"Count Teias must have been riding on the wings of the storm wind from Rome! Teias got to Taginae just before me with a fast mounted detachment, moving ahead of the main army. Although my Saracens outnumbered them seven to three, Teias and his Gothic mounted troops with their battleaxes repulsed us with bloody losses. Once he had split the younger Saracen king Abocharabus in half with his battleaxe, through his turban and right down to his belt, there was no holding my men. Screaming, the Saracens turned their horses and raced back via Caprae, tearing me away with them.

"Today I tried to ascertain just how strong the garrison in Taginae is, because I want to crush that accursed Teias before the main Gothic army gets here. But the position at Caprae was already impenetrable today. The Barbarian king is supposedly already approaching himself. They say that Duke Guntharis is leading the vanguard.

"Oh where is my Second Army? When, oh when, will it finally get here?"

Chapter 22

On the following day King Totila did indeed arrive in Taginae with a part of his army. Valeria, who was now safest in the king's camp, accompanied him as did Julius, who was trying to return to his monastery in Gaul, and Cassiodorus.

The main body of the army, under Duke Guntharis and Wisand the *bandalarius*, was to march up from the south along the Via Flaminia, whilst Hildebrand was approaching from the west, via Florence. An attack against the Prefect's very strong position could not be contemplated until all these troops had arrived.

Cethegus too was busily trying to restrain his impetuous young knights, who were spoiling for the fight. "I have not come to win battles, but to win Italy. Soon we will have superiority in numbers, and that is the time when we will attack."

One morning Julius stepped into the king's tent, and silently handed him a letter. Totila, who recognised the handwriting, frowned as he read:

"To Julius Montanus Cethegus, Prefect of Rome and *Magister Militum per Italiam*. I have heard that you are staying in the Barbarian camp. Licinius saw you riding alongside the tyrant. Could it be that the impossible happens, and that Julius takes up arms against Cethegus, son against father?

"Grant me a meeting with you tonight so that we can talk, at sunset, at the ruins of the old Silvanus temple between the Barbarian lines and ours. The tyrant has robbed me of Italy, Rome and your soul, and I will take all three away from him again, beginning with you. Come: I command you as your father and your teacher."

"I must obey him. I owe him so much."

"Yes, you must," Totila replied, handing back the letter. "But the Prefect's meetings can be dangerous.

"You have asked me never to speak with you about your 'fatherly benefactor' again. I gave my word and I have kept it. But I can warn you, and indeed I must."

"He will not threaten my life."

"No, but he may threaten your freedom! Take fifty cavalry with you. I will not let you out of the camp without such a guard."

At sunset Julius and his guard reached the ruins of the temple. Only a few columns of the old structure had remained standing, and the roof of the building had partly collapsed also. Ivy was growing around the stumps of broken columns, and thick weeds covered the marble steps leading up to the temple.

This time Totila had mistrusted the Prefect without cause. When Julius arrived at the foot of the small hill with fifty men, with a further fifty following him from the camp at a distance, on the king's orders, he could see Cethegus alone, pacing up and down inside the temple.

Julius had dismounted and was climbing the steps. Cethegus received him with an accusing look on his face. "You let me wait for you, the father for the son? At our first meeting after such a long time? Is that the morality the monks teach? And you come well guarded too! Are the Barbarians following us here as well?"

With that he pointed to the leader of the Gothic soldiers, a man in a brown cloak with a hood, who had just dismounted with twelve of his men and taken up position on the steps.

Julius tried to get them to move away, but another of their leaders, Count Thorismuth, replied curtly: "King's orders!" and with that he sat down on the second highest step.

"Speak Greek," Julius said, "they don't understand that."

Cethegus held out both hands to him. "And so Odysseus, the much travelled one, sees his Telemachos once more."

But Julius withdrew from the outstretched hand. "There are dark rumours circulating about you, Cethegus. Has that hand of yours shed blood only in battle?"

Cethegus clenched the rejected hand into a fist in anger: "Have the lies of your bosom friends poisoned your heart against me completely?"

"King Totila does not lie. For months now he has not even mentioned your name. I asked him not to, because I could not defend you against his terrible accusations. Is it true that you murdered his brother Hildebad by…?"

"I have not come to offer apologies, but to demand them. For years now the struggle for Rome has raged with priests, Greeks and Barbarians. And I stand alone. Tired, wounded, half despairing, carried high by the tide of fortune one moment, and flung deep into an abyss the next, but always alone. And where is Julius, the son of my soul, to encourage me with his love? In Gaul among monks, in Byzantium or in Rome as the guest or the tool of the Barbarian king, but always far from me and my paths."

"I warned you against the path you were taking! There are red and black blemishes on it, and I cannot walk along it with you."

"Well then, if you were so wise and so eager to follow the teachings of your faith, where were you to save me and illuminate my ways?" Cethegus now despatched his most telling missile of persuasion, which he had been saving to the last. "If indeed my soul was becoming more and more hardened and stony against love and warmth, where was Julius to warm me again? You find fault with me, but have you fulfilled your duty toward me either as a son, a Christian or a priest?"

These words had a shattering effect on the sensitive and pious young monk. "Forgive me," he said, "I can see now that I have failed you."

Cethegus saw his advantage and decided to exploit it quickly. "Very well, then make it good again. I do not ask that you take sides in this war. Wait for the final outcome. But wait for it in my camp, by my side, and not with the Barbarians or in Gaul. If I am Saul who has forfeited God's mercy, then you can be David and cast light into my soul, which is often darkened by shadows. The sacred duty of your own conscience forces you to my side. Otherwise the responsibility rests on your head! Yes, you are the good influence in my life. I need you and your love if I am not to fall victim completely to those forces which you hate. If there is a voice which can convert me to the belief which, as you teach, brings salvation, then that voice is yours, Julius. Now decide, according to your own conscience."

The eager and dutiful Christian could not resist his own emotions: "You have won! I will follow you, my father!" and he was about to embrace Cethegus.

"Accursed liar and hypocrite!" a strong, clear voice called out. That cavalry leader, who had been lying on the topmost step, leapt into the interior of the temple and threw back the hood of his cloak. He was King Totila, his naked sword in his hand.

"Ha, the Barbarian here!" Cethegus cried with the intensity of extreme hatred. His sword flashed too, and the two mortal enemies clashed in deadly hate; their blades crossed. Just in time Julius threw himself between the combatants, and managed to separate them for a moment. But the two of them still stood opposite one another threateningly, swords at the ready.

"Have you been eavesdropping, king of the Barbarians?" the Prefect snarled. "I must say that is most regal of you, the actions of a true king."

But Totila did not answer him. Instead he turned to Julius and said: "It was not your physical freedom and safety which concerned me. I knew, or rather suspected, that he would make an attempt to ensnare your soul. I have promised never to accuse him again in his absence. But now he stands before us both. He shall hear me through and defend himself if he can. I will show you that his mind, his soul and every thought within him are black and dirty and evil, as false as Satan. Even the words he has just spoken, which appeared to have been inspired by the warmth and the emotion of the moment and which almost won you over, even those words were false, carefully thought out years ago. Look here, Julius, do you know this handwriting?"

And he showed the astonished Julius a papyrus scroll with handwriting on it.

"Usually the Barbarians steal only gold," Cethegus said angrily. "To steal letters is infamous, without honour." And he tried to snatch the scroll from Totila's hand.

But Totila continued: "Count Teias captured it in his house, in a secret hiding place. Oh what an abyss it was that his diaries opened to my eyes! I will say nothing about his crimes against others, but here is what he wrote about you: 'Julius I have not yet given up as lost. Let us see if the duty of saving souls will not win over the foolish idealist. He will imagine that he has to grasp my hand in order to "draw me up to the cross". But my arm is stronger than his, and I will pull him down with me into my world. The only thing I will find difficult is to mimic a convincing tone of despair. For that I will have to study Cassiodorus."

"Cethegus, did you write that?" Julius lamented.

"I would have thought that you would recognise the style. But he will deny it of course! He will deny everything I either know or suspect about him. He will deny that he falsely accused the Balti Duke Alaric, that he brewed poison for Athalaric and Camilla, that he had the other three Balti dukes murdered, that he sent assassins after me, that he betrayed Amalasuntha to Petros, Petros to the empress, Witigis to Belisarius, and Belisarius to Justinian. He will deny that he sent the son of Boethius to his death, that he murdered my brother, that he broke the armistice and treacherously attacked our ships – he will deny all these things, for his very breath is nothing but one great lie."

"Cethegus," Julius begged, "say 'no', and I will believe you."

But the Prefect, who had at first listened to Totila's words with his eyes closed as if they were blows from some invisible club, now returned his sword to its scabbard, stood up erect, crossed his arms over his chest and said: "Yes, I have done those things. And others too. I have removed whatever obstacle barred my way, with strength and with cunning, because my path led to the ultimate goal, the glory of the Roman Empire. And to the throne of the world at the same time! But my successor to this throne – was to be you, Julius. What I have done I did for Rome and for you, not for myself. Why for you? Because I love you, you alone in the world. Not with your Christian love of thy neighbour, which is supposed to embrace the whole world equally. No, that is a lukewarm weakness which I have always despised. No, I love you with a passion, with heat and with pain. Instead of loving humanity I love – you. Yes, my heart did indeed turn to stone from despising the smallness of men. There is only one feeling left in this block of granite – my love for you. You never deserved that love.

"But there was a creature whose features you bear, and whom you bring back to me every time I look at you, from the grave back to my past. There is a magical bond between you and her. Hear then the secret, in the presence of your enemy, which you were only to learn the moment when you became fully my son.

"There was a time when the heart of young Cethegus Caesarius was soft and tender, just like yours. And within it there lived a love, pure and holy as the stars, for a creature who was – beyond comparison. And she loved me as I loved her. But there was an ancient hatred which had separated the families of the Cethegi and the Manilii for centuries."

When he heard this Julius grew pale. Totila returned his sword to its scabbard and, leaning with both hands on its hilt, listened to Cethegus most attentively.

"They were on the side of the Senate, we with the Gracchi. They were with Sulla, we with Marius. They with Cicero, we with Catilina. They with Pompey, we with Caesar. And yet I had finally succeeded in gradually wearing down her father's stony opposition to our love, and it seemed at last that he was willing to give us his reluctant blessing. He could see that we loved each other. She followed me as iron follows a magnet, and I could feel that she was made for me. And then a Gothic duke came along, whose soul may be for ever damned to the furies of hell, who had known me and hated me for years. He came to warn Manilius, who looked upon him with trust because he had protected him and his house against oppression when the Barbarians had first conquered Italy. He warned her father against the man Cethegus with the evil eyes, as he put it, and he managed to revive the old hatred. He would not rest until the father had agreed to betrothe his child, reluctant as she was, to a Senator from Gaul who was a friend of the duke.

"Manilia begged for mercy, but in vain. In the end we decided to flee, to elope. They lived in a villa on the Tiber, outside the Porta Aurelia. But the father rushed the marriage, driven on by suspicion. When I scaled the wall on the prearranged night and made my way into her bedchamber I found it empty. But I could hear hymns and the sound of flutes coming from the Atrium. Breathlessly I made my way to the curtains and looked in. There I could see my Manilia resting by her father's side, dressed as a bride with her groom beside her, and countless guests. I saw Manilia's pale face, and her eyes which had been weeping. I saw Montanus place his arm around her neck, and then a senseless despair took hold of me! I stormed into the room, took her in my arms and drew her away with me, with my sword drawn.

"But there were ninety of them, brave men that they were. For a long time I was able to fend them off, and then the accursed Duke Alaric's sword struck me! They tore the screaming Manilia from my arms and threw me over the garden wall by the bank of the Tiber. They thought I was dead as I was bleeding severely. But that day, almost six lustra ago, the breath of the river god revived me from my deathlike state, just as it did more recently after the Barbarians took Rome. Fishermen found me, cared for me, and I recovered. But my heart had been torn from my breast that night.

"And many, many years passed. I hated the world and its god, if one existed.

"But the Manilii family and that Duke Alaric came to know that I was not dead. They fled from the country, in disgrace, all of them, struck severely by my revenge. Only one picture remained in my soul, incomparably and touchingly beautiful.

"And then, many years later, on my travels I came to the River Rhodanus in Gaul. There had been a war between the Barbarians. Franks and Burgundians had invaded Gothic Gaul and burned a villa on the Rhodanus. And as I was looking at the ruined *atrium* and the devastated garden a little boy came running out of the house, crying, and he called out to me: 'Help, Sir! My mother is dying!'"

"Oh Cethegus!" Julius cried, his voice shaking with emotion.

"And I forced my way into the house, which was still smoking from the fire which had just burned itself out. There, in the women's chamber, lay a pale woman, with an arrow in her breast. Otherwise the house was empty; all the slaves had gone, having either fled or been dragged away. And I recognised the dying woman, and her child's name was Julius. Her husband had died soon after you were born. And she opened her eyes when she heard my voice, for she loved me still.

"And I gave her wine and water to drink out of my helmet. She drank and thanked me, and then she kissed me on my forehead and said: 'Thank you, my beloved! Will you be my boy's father? Promise me that you will.' And I promised her I would as I held her hand, which was becoming colder and colder. Then I kissed her and closed her eyes. Whether I have kept my word as far as that little boy goes, that is something you must decide."

As he finished speaking the man of iron had great difficulty keeping his emotions in check, and his chest was heaving.

Julius broke into tears: "Oh my mother!" he cried.

Totila said nothing. Deeply moved he paced up and down in the rotunda.

Cethegus continued: "And now choose! Choose between me and your 'unsullied' friend. But let me tell you this: all of those deeds of mine, which you abhor so much, I did mainly on your account. Go from me then if you wish, and leave me a lonely man. I will do nothing more to hold you back. Go to him if you like.

"But if Manilia's shadow should ever come to ask me about you, then I will have to reply truthfully: 'I was a father to him, but he was no son to me!' Now choose!"

Julius concealed his head in his cloak.

But Totila halted before the Prefect and said: "You are tearing at his heartstrings in a most unfatherly fashion. You can see how he is being torn to and fro by conflicting emotions. Come, I know a way whereby we can spare him the need to make that choice. Let us end the war which threatens both our peoples on our own, Cethegus. A second Gothic king now challenges you to a duel. Here, in the presence of your favourite, I call you to your face: liar, counterfeiter, traitor, murderer, villain without honour. I demand revenge from you for my brother's blood.

"If you are a man then draw your sword. Let us duel for life, for Rome and for Julius, and put a speedy end to this long hatred. Defend yourself!"

And spurred by the most bitter hatred they both drew their swords, and their blades clashed a second time.

"Stop it, you cruel men of hate and the world. Every blow strikes at my bleeding heart. Listen to me, both of you. I have made my decision. I can feel it, my mother's spirit is calling out to me."

Angrily both men lowered their swords, but did not sheath them.

"Cethegus, you have indeed been a father to me for more than two decades. What you have done and where you have sinned, that is not something for a son to judge. I take your hand with love; even if it was still more deeply stained with blood and murder, my prayers and my tears will purify it again."

Totila angrily took a step backwards, and there was a gleam of victory in the eyes of the Prefect.

"But," the monk went on, "what I cannot bear is your terrible statement that you did it all for me, that you sinned on my account. So you must understand this: never and under no circumstances, even if I was otherwise tempted, which I am not, never could I accept your inheritance on which such crimes and curses hang. Only the crown of thorns from Golgatha attracts me, not the bloodstained crown of Rome. I am yours, but you too must be a son, a son to my God. Belong to Him and to me, not to the world and hell. If you really love me, then forego your criminal plans and worldly ambitions. But more than that, more! You must repent and seek and beg for God's forgiveness. Without repentance and prayer there can be no salvation. And I too will wrestle with God in prayer, until he forgives you. Repent, and in your own mind take back the evil deeds you have done."

"Stop there," Cethegus said, and stood up to his full height. "What are you talking about? How can you, the son, speak to your father of repentance? Don't worry about my deeds, and leave them to rest on my head. I am the one who must bear them, and not you."

"No, Cethegus, never! If you persist like that, then I cannot follow you. Repent, humble yourself before God the Father, your supreme ruler and mine."

"Ha!" Cethegus laughed. "Do you think you are talking to a child? Even if everything I have done had never happened, I would do it all again."

"Cethegus!" Julius cried, horrified, "what a terrible thing to say! Can it be that you really do not believe in any God?"

But Cethegus, annoyed, went on: "You say repent. Does fire repent the fact that it burns? You can only choke it, but never restrict it from burning as long as it lives. Praise it or berate it, but fire will always be fire! In the same way Cethegus must follow the idea that runs in his mind as surely as blood flows through his veins. It is not that I want to do it; I am compelled to want it! A mountain stream races down from the heights, through flowering meadows here and through wilderness there, spreading growth and fertility in one place and deadly destruction in another. It does not ask whether it is right or wrong, it accuses no one and seeks no thanks for what it does, but races always toward its goal. In the same way fate carries me with it, and that fate is dictated by the world around me, by the moment and by events which occur. Am I to regret what I destroyed along the way, what I had to do? I would do it all again!"

"What ghastly words! What you have just uttered carries Satan's breath! How can you hope to be saved unless you see that you have sinned? Man's will is free."

"Yes, it is as free as a stone which has been thrown, and which therefore imagines it can fly."

"Oh fear, Cethegus, fear the living God!"

But Cethegus laughed, more fiercely than before. "Ha, where is He, this living God of yours?

"I have searched heaven and earth, the stars and the cruelty of nature. I have researched the ever more cruel history of mankind, but nowhere have I been able to find a god! If there is a god at all then it is necessity and the right of the strong over the weak, a dreadful goddess with a glance that turns man to stone like the Medusa. You, childish boy, are trying to hide in the cloak folds of your imagined god, hiding your head in His lap, even if fate is staring at you as a Gorgon might. Do that if you wish, but do not be critical of a man who returns the terrible glance of fate and says: 'There is no God!' even if he turns to stone for saying it.

"To smile and to weep are two sweet pleasures. But Prometheus did not smile when Pandora offered him the beguiling box, nor did he weep when strength and brute force forged him to the rock. As for the vulture that gnaws away at his liver – well, he grew used to it. And fate will tire of plaguing the Titan before ever the Titan bends to fate."

"Cethegus," Julius implored him, "don't talk like that! I tell you, there is a God!"

"There is? Then where was He when Manilia was forced into a marriage she did not want, and when the heart of Cethegus was poisoned for ever? Where was He when blind accident buried a Frank's arrow in her heart? Ha, I too believed in Him once, and just as long as I did I was the toy of others.

"Later on I started acting under the assumption which my own fate had taught me: 'There is no God!' And ever since that day all my conclusions have been the right ones!

"Where was he, this almighty, just, wise, benevolent God, when Camilla drank from the cup which was not mixed for her? Where were His angels and His miracles then? When Calpurnius threw the young son of Witigis from the cliff, why didn't God's angels catch the child and tear the murderer apart? After all, not even a sparrow falls from a roof unless God wills it so, or so you tell me! Where was your God when I despatched the arrow at that fine woman Rauthgundis? Ha, if there was a God in heaven, then that arrow would have bounced back, turned around and pierced my own breast! But the arrow was well aimed, and it was sharp, and that is why Rauthgundis died, just as if she had been a gull on the Padus. So don't talk to me about a living God, you foolish boy."

"Cethegus," Julius replied, "I shudder. That is the most terrible blasphemy I have ever heard."

Totila turned away in disgust and threw his sword into its scabbard. "Anyone who thinks like that," he cried, "has been punished enough. But, Prefect of Rome, you do not know as yet the final outcome of your deeds. Wait for that, and perhaps then you will believe in an avenging God."

"The end of my deeds," Cethegus laughed, "will be my death. That I have known for a long time. Whether I will find death on the throne of the Occident, or that of the whole world, whether in a lost battle or a victorious one, that matters little in our question as to whether or not there is a God. And if there is a hell, very well, even after he was forged to that rock in the Caucasian Mountains Prometheus remained true to himself. But enough of words, more than enough. Come here, Julius, come to me, for you are mine."

"I am God's, our Lord's, not yours!" Julius replied, crossed himself and backed away.

"You are my son – obey me!"

"But you are God's son, just as I am. You deny our common father, whereas I acknowledge Him. I now sever myself from you for ever!

"If, as our belief teaches, there is a Lucifer, the first among the demons and once the morning star and the first among God's spirits, who sank to hell through pride and blasphemy, then that Lucifer has to be you, you horrible, evil, repulsive man."

"Ha, but Lucifer rose from being a mere servant of heaven to being an emperor, even if he was the emperor of hell. It is better, much better, to be the first in hell than second in heaven. Follow me!" Carried away by the passion of the moment he drew the monk over to him by his arm.

And then Totila's sword and that of the Prefect clashed for the third time. And this time it was in deadly earnest. This time Julius was not able to separate the two mortal enemies.

Totila aimed at the Prefect's forehead. The thrust was too powerful to be deflected completely, and the Roman's helmet flew from his head backwards as blood flowed from his cheek.

The Prefect's counter-thrust cut through Totila's cloak, and whilst his armour prevented him from being injured, the force of the thrust flung Totila backwards half a pace.

The next clash threatened to be a deadly one, as neither man carried a shield.

Again they clashed. There was a cry of pain from the monk, who had thrown himself between them and in so doing had received a cut on his left hand from the Prefect's sword. That cry would not have been enough to separate the two combatants, but now they were being pulled apart by the strong arms of other men who, while Cethegus and Totila were locked in a deadly duel, had hurried up the temple steps without being noticed by either of them.

Totila was restrained by Thorismuth and Wisand, and Cethegus by Syphax and Licinius.

"The reinforcements have arrived, together with important news from the south," Count Thorismuth cried. "Count Wisand is here as the representative of Duke Guntharis. Come quickly, the battle lies ahead."

"Come back to the camp quickly!" Lucius Licinius called out to Cethegus, "the Second Army has arrived."

"With Areobindos?"

"No, master," Syphax cried: "The empress Theodora has died suddenly. Narses is the general they have sent, and he comes with one hundred thousand men."

"Narses?" Cethegus asked, growing pale. "I am coming! Farewell, Julius my son!"

"I am God's son!"

"He is mine!" said Totila, placing his arm around him.

"Very well, the struggle for Rome will decide that struggle too. I will fetch him directly from the Barbarian camp."

And with that he hurried down the steps. Moments later Cethegus with his men was galloping to the north, while Totila and his following, including Julius, flew to their camp in the south.

Chapter 23

When the Prefect arrived back at his tent he did not find Narses himself as yet, nor any messengers from that general, which somewhat surprised him. Piso and Salvius Julianus, whom he had sent to Areobindos with urgent despatches in the direction of Ancona, had already met up with the vanguard of Narses at Cale. They were Germanic cavalry, they said, and from them and from a Byzantine *Archonius* by the name of Basiliskos they had received information which had caused them to hurry back in order to warn Cethegus.

"Yes, he evidently tried to catch me by surprise," Cethegus said, deep in thought, "but just you wait, Narses," he concluded fiercely. "Belisarius also stood at Capua with a greatly superior force, and in the end I mastered him just the same as long as he remained in Italy. And in the end I pushed him out, out of my Italy. Let us see if the cripple is stronger than the lion-hearted hero was."

"Be careful, my general," Piso warned. "There are evil tidings in the air; clouds are gathering above your head. This Basiliskos is a confidant of Narses. I know him from Byzantium, and he made me feel very ill at ease."

"Yes," Salvius Julianus added, "he was just so secretive! There was nothing to be learned from him except what he himself wanted us to know."

"Our slaves found out more from their slaves than we were able to learn from him."

"But when the leader of the Germanic cavalry happened to pass by as they were chatting, he slew one of Basiliskos's slaves, on the spot there and then."

"And after that the surviving slaves became almost as silent as their dead comrade."

"And so even what we did manage to find out is disjointed, conflicting, confused and incomplete."

"Only one thing is certain: there must have been a very sudden change in the political climate in Byzantium."

"In fact it must have happened on the very evening of your departure from that city."

"They say that the empress took her own life – choked on coal fumes, they say."

"The trial of Belisarius," the lawyer interrupted, "seems to have taken an unexpected turn. They say it was because of intervention by Tribonianus, and perhaps Procopius as well. In any event rumour has it that the emperor has reversed the sentence which had been imposed by the Senate."

"The names Narses, Antonina, Anicius and Procopius are being talked about in some connection, but just what that connection is we could not find out."

"Prince Areobindos has supposedly fallen ill, and has therefore been replaced by Narses."

"But I fear that it is a disease from which others are more likely to die than the Governor of Snails."

"And my fourteen messengers to the Second Army?" Cethegus asked, with a frown.

"I think," Licinius replied suspiciously, "that Narses had them arrested as soon as they arrived."

"The Germanic horsemen laughed most sarcastically when I asked after them," Julianus confirmed.

"Narses really has marched from the gates of Byzantium with an army such as that meanest of all emperors has never before given to any general."

"And everything which you dismiss as being impossible is true, oh general!"

"Narses did not go to Epidamnus. The troops stationed there, together with the remaining units of Areobindos's Second Army, are quite insignificant compared to his own enormous force. He has therefore ordered Areobindos's Second Army to Pola in Istria by sea, and he himself moved into Gothic Dalmatia overland, and in forced marches. He rolled irresistibly through Dalmatia, and the few thousand Gothic troops stationed there were swept before him like dry leaves blown by a storm wind. He took Salona, Scardona and Jardera."

"Yes, and in doing so he follows a terrible system. Wherever he goes he leaves not a single Goth. He has them all taken prisoner, every last man, woman and child, and then he has them shipped to Byzantium as slaves immediately. And so he rolls over the Gothic nation like a massive iron roller, crushing everything in its path. Wherever Narses has passed not a single Goth remains, either in a city or countryside."

"That is good!" said Cethegus. "It is a sign of greatness!"

"They say that he has sworn by Justinian's sceptre that he will not rest until not one free Goth remains in the Orbis Romanum. And in battle he takes no prisoners."

"That's good," Cethegus agreed.

"Once he joined up with the Second Army in Pola he marched into the Gothic Venetia, and moved through the country there on a very broad front, turning with his right wing while his left wing acted as a kind of fulcrum. From the sea in the south to the mountains in the north his army moved like a walking wall of iron, mowing down everything before it, or forcing the few defenders into the cities, which soon fell one after the other.

"'The art of the siege is something which my Narses understands like no other man,' Basiliskos told us, who also told us about these other events of war without reserve. 'Soon that will be no secret to the Prefect either,' he smiled maliciously. 'The Prefect will soon even understand the greatest strategic idea Narses has yet expressed. Narses says that; "Italy is a boot, and therefore one must get into it from the top down. My impetuous colleague Belisarius was foolish enough to try and slip in from the bottom, near the big toe. If one tries to drive the Gothic fleas from below, from the water upwards into the mountains, then they will not die. Instead one must drive them down from the mountains toward the sea, gradually further and further, until in the end they are all crowded together on the last bit of land, right at the big toe of the boot. All that is then left to do is push them all into the water so that they drown. For the splendid *Magister Militum* has already taken their fleet, although in fact he really stole it rather than took it,' that is how Basiliskos concluded."

"We heard rumours that your title *Magister Militum per Italiam* has long since been revoked again." Julianus added.

"If that were so then surely I, the bearer of that title, should know about it too."

"Who knows? Rumour has it that you have been replaced. Narses has brought with him secret sealed orders from the emperor, which he is to open and carry out once Totila has been destroyed."

"Who said that?" Cethegus asked quickly, "Basiliskos himself?"

"Oh no, he only talks about the war. No, that slave told us, and it was the moment after he said it that the Germanic leader slew him with his club."

"That was a pity," Cethegus said thoughtfully. "I mean, he struck too soon."

"This is what Basiliskos told us: 'It was a magnificent spectacle, that march, crushing everyone and everything before it. It was like a man trapping birds with a net, closing over the frightened, flapping little creatures, yet there is no escaping the net. Only a few thousand managed to escape via Tridentum and Bolzanum to the north, in the direction of the Athesis and Passara Valleys, taking their women and children with them. They obtained reinforcements from the garrison of the Castrum Teriolis near Mansio Majae, and they defeated the pursuing *Archonius* Zeuxippos so severely that he was forced to rejoin the main army with utmost haste.

"But with the exception of that one group which escaped into the hills, not a single Goth is left living in Narses's rear, other than the garrison of Verona, and that is surrounded and will fall shortly. Aquileja, Concordia, Forum Julii, Ceneta, Tridentum, Tarvisium and Comaclum all fell to Narses.

"From there he hurried to Ravenna. The Gothic siege army quickly escaped the huge army of Narses by moving in a circle to the west. In Ravenna he settled his differences with Bloody John, Basiliskos told us, and…"

"I don't believe it," Cethegus interrupted. "John is the most loyal follower Belisarius has, and he hates Narses even more than Belisarius himself does."

"That's what we thought too, and yet Basiliskos said that he had won him over. He also told us to 'expect many other things from Narses, which you Roman knights and tribunes don't even suspect as yet.'

"And it is a fact that Bloody John now serves under Narses just as he formerly served under Belisarius. He commands the bodyguards and the Huns."

Cethegus shook his head in disbelief.

Piso continued: "Basiliskos then went on to tell us that, unfortunately, Martinus the weapons master had a fatal accident soon after the departure from Ravenna."

"What did you say?" Cethegus asked in amazement, "Is Martinus the mathematician and long-time Belisarius supporter now also serving under Narses? You are right, there is definitely something very strange taking place."

"Apparently, according to Basiliskos, Narses struck the first serious obstacle to his progress not long after he left Ravenna, not by soldiers but by some fortifications which the Barbarian king had built. Totila had a particularly effective system of defences constructed by his general Teias, which was to protect Italy against any attack from the north. The defences are already complete in Aemilia, but fortunately for us they are not yet completed in Venetia, as otherwise even the huge army of Narses would not have been able to advance so rapidly. Apparently Totila and Teias managed to defend every strategic point on the heights and the roads so skilfully with ditches and barricades that even a small force of defenders could delay the largest of armies for days behind every one of these obstacles.

"Narses saw these defences with admiration. 'This Totila is a much better general than Antonina's husband!' he cried. He had planned to move through Aemilia on a very broad front also, crushing all Gothic life in his path.

"He had to abandon his plan to march westward through the countryside after Martinus had his fatal accident. It happened when he was trying to destroy such a battlement in a very secret way near Imola. As Narses was standing before the fortress, at a loss what to do and saying that his entire plan was in danger because of obstacles such as these, he became so troubled that he even suffered an attack of the terrible sickness *Epilepsis*. And then Martinus said to John, who had suffered a nasty chest wound during an unsuccessful attempt to storm the fortress: 'The avenger of Belisarius shall not be delayed by these stones if Martinus has calculated correctly. Admittedly,' he went on, 'the last little experiment nearly cost me my head, which was almost torn off. But then Belisarius must be avenged, and to do that I would gladly risk my head.' And that night Martinus, with only a few stonemasons, secretly made his way to the stone wall, and they drilled a small hole into it in one place.

"Suddenly we were all awakened in our tents by a terrible crashing sound, the like of which we had never heard before. We all hurried to the stone wall.

"When we got there it was blown to pieces as if it had been struck by lightning, but from bottom to top instead of top to bottom. The Gothic defenders on the walls had been torn to pieces, but our Martinus and his men also lay there, all blackened and mutilated, with Martinus himself several paces from his clever little head. They were all dead."

"Mysterious," said Cethegus. "Do they know what did it?"

"No, Martinus took the secret into the grave with him. He had said apparently that he was not yet quite finished with the invention. In his tent they found a small pile of little grains, like black salt. Narses commanded that it be brought to his tent straight away, in the middle of the night, but a spark from one of the torches fell into the open dish, and the poison flashed and flickered until it was all gone in just a moment, but this time there was no bang and no damage."

"I wish I had that black salt," Cethegus sighed, "then both Narses and Byzantium had better beware."

"Yes, I think Narses may have thought the same," Piso smiled. "Basiliskos said that he personally searched through all the dishes and all the writings which the dead Martinus had left behind, but evidently without success."

Salvius Julianus then went on: "Basiliskos said that after the accident they had Imola, true, but not long afterwards they encountered another such barricade, near Castrum Brintum. And there was now no Martinus to blast it out of the way. Narses stopped, puzzled as to what to do next.

"'John,' he asked at last, 'you know the coast road from Ravenna to Ancona to the south intimately, is that correct?' – 'Yes,' John replied, 'it was the road along which I won some of my most splendid victories under Belisarius.' – 'I don't think there will be obstacles there,' Narses said happily, 'because the Barbarian king thought he could control the natural barriers, the rivers which run through there to the sea, by means of his fleet. Now that fleet has conveniently been removed by our friend the Prefect of Rome. Turn about! Break camp, we are marching southeast by closely following the coastline.' – 'But how do you plan to cross the rivers without bridges?' Basiliskos asked in surprise. 'My friend,' Narses replied, 'we are carrying the bridges with us on our shoulders.'"

"I want to hear this," Cethegus interrupted.

"And so they moved southeast toward the coast at first, and from there along the coast due south, led by John. Meanwhile the fleet sailed close to the coastline, keeping pace with the army, and wherever a river hemmed the army's progress over land the fleet would launch numerous small boats and send them upstream, so that the troops could cross on them. And where two rivers were separated by only a narrow stretch of land, horses and men would carry their light vehicles across on their backs and shoulders. That is how they crossed over the Sepis to the old city of Ficocle, across three arms of the Caesarian Rubicon, across another river and then across the Ariminus to Ariminum. That is where Usdrila, the valiant Gothic leader, fell during a sortie.

"It was impossible to advance along the Via Flaminia, as it was blocked by the fortress Petra Pertusa. So they turned to the southwest and marched across the Metaurus to the Appenine Mountains, 'so as to make sure that the great *Magister Militum per Italiam* would not be crushed like a grain of corn in a mill by King Totila and Count Teias,' so they said."

"But the fact that your messengers were detained in Epidamnus," Piso went on, "means…"

"I am certain that the clever Byzantine tried to detain us as well," Julianus interrupted. "He tried very hard to have us taken further away from you, 'to Narses', and they had a 'guard of honour' placed outside our tents, Germanic horsemen. And when we saw what he was up to and left our tents at night, our 'guard of honour' sent a few arrows after us, killing two of our slaves and a horse."

"So the great epileptic was determined to catch me by surprise, and has kept me away from him until the last possible moment. Good! Syphax, my horse; we will ride to meet Narses this very night."

"Oh master," the Moor whispered softly, having overheard the entire conversation, "if only you had sent me to Epidamnus, as I asked you to do!"

"Then they would have imprisoned you too, like the other messengers."

"Master, in Africa we have a proverb: if the fire from the mountain is not coming toward you, then be content, and do not walk toward the lava."

"That could be translated into Christian terms," Piso laughed: "If you don't want the devil to get you, don't go and look for him. Who would ride to hell of his own free will?"

"I would! In fact I have felt that way for some time now," Cethegus smiled, "farewell, you Roman tribunes. Licinius will represent me here in the camp until I return. I imagine that by now the Barbarian king also knows how close and how strong the army of Narses is. He will not attack tonight, as he did that time in Rome."

After the Roman knights had left the tent, Cethegus said to Syphax: "Unbuckle my armour."

"But master, tonight you are riding into the camp of Narses, not Belisarius."

"That is precisely why! Get the outer chest armour off, and give me the protective vest instead, the one worn under my tunic."

Syphax sighed deeply: "Now things are getting serious. Now, son of Hiempsal, be on your guard!"

Chapter 24

Later that night Cethegus, deep in thought, rode out with a handful of men to meet Narses. When the tribunes urged him to increase the number of men in his party he had replied: "What difference does it make? I cannot take one hundred thousand with me, whatever I do!"

At first light he met the vanguard of the approaching army. They were wild-looking men on horseback, whom he encountered near Fossa Nova. Their pointed helmets were decorated with black horse tails, and they wore wolf hides on their backs, heavy armour, and they carried broad swords and long lances. Their arms and legs were bare, and they wore only a single spur on their left foot, attached by means of a strap. Although they used no saddles they sat very firmly on their sturdy mounts.

The leader of these men wore armour heavily plated with gold, and on his helmet the wings of a vulture took the place of the horse tails his companions wore. This man flew towards Cethegus at top speed on his huge red horse, and stopped only a pace or so short of the Prefect, who was riding at the head of his own little detachment. Long red hair, parted in the middle, flowed down to his shoulders, and he also wore a long and thin red moustache. His pale grey eyes suggested bravery and cunning.

For a long while the two men mustered each other with searching looks. At last the man with the vulture wings exclaimed: "You must be Cethegus! The protector of Italy."

"I am he."

And the other man turned his horse around and galloped away even faster than he had come, past his own men and into a small wood, from which infantry could now be seen approaching in thick columns.

"And who are you? Who is your leader?" Cethegus asked one of the horsemen in Gothic.

"We are Lombards, Cethegus, in the service of Narses," the one whom he had asked replied in Latin, "and he over there is Alboin, the son of our king."

"So that is why your efforts were wasted, Licinius!"

Already Cethegus could see the open litter which carried Narses approaching from afar. It was made of plain timber, without decoration of any kind, and in place of the usual purple cushions it contained only a woollen rug. The cripple was carried not by slaves, but by specially selected soldiers, who took turns at the honour of carrying him as a special reward for particularly valuable services.

Alboin was riding at his side with drawn sword, and was whispering to him: "So you really don't want to do it, Narses? That man looks dangerous to me, very dangerous. You do not need to say anything; just a blink of your eyelids and it is done."

"Don't push me, oh future hope of the Lombards! Otherwise I might be led to believe that you want that man out of your own way rather than mine."

"We sons of the Gambara have a proverb: A slain enemy is seldom regretted."

"We Romaeans also have a proverb," Narses replied. "Don't throw the ladder over until after you have climbed the wall. First, my eager young friend, let us use Cethegus to destroy Totila. Cethegus knows Rome, the Italians and the Goths even better than

Alboin the horse trader. As for this former *Magister Militum per Italiam* himself, his fate is already sealed!"

Alboin looked at him questioningly.

"Yes, sealed with the Imperial seal. When the time is right I will – unseal it for him, and then I will carry out the emperor's wishes."

Shortly after that Cethegus halted by the litter. "Welcome, Narses," he said: "Italy greets the greatest general of the century as her liberator."

"Forget the compliments. Did my coming surprise you?"

"When one expects an Areobindos as helper, and finds a Narses instead, one can only be delighted. But of course," he added searchingly, "as Belisarius has been pardoned he too could have been sent to Italy again, in accordance with his own wishes."

"Belisarius has not been pardoned," Narses replied curtly.

"And my benefactress, the empress? How did she die so soon?"

"Only she herself knows that. And by now the devil probably knows too."

"Here lies a secret," said Cethegus.

"Yes, but let it lie. However it is no longer a secret that Narses now stands in Italy. You are probably aware from past experience that Narses never shares a command. The emperor has placed you and the First Army under my supreme command. If you choose to serve under me in my camp I would be pleased, for you understand warfare, Italy and the Goths. If you do not wish to serve under me then you may as well dismiss your mercenaries, as I do not need them. I command one hundred thousand men."

"You have come with great means."

"True, for I am going to achieve great ends, and my enemies are not small ones."

"You are numerically very much stronger than the Goths, unless they move their southern army here also, from Regium."

"They cannot, because I have two fleets with twenty thousand men cruising off the port of Rome and around Regium, which are keeping the Gothic southern army fully occupied."

Cethegus was genuinely surprised. Here was another unexpected turn.

"But now you must choose," Narses said. "Will you be my guest or will you serve under me as one of my commanders? In my camp there is no third alternative."

Cethegus could see the situation clearly. He was either a subordinate of Narses, or his prisoner. "I am honoured to serve under the conqueror of the Persians, who has never been defeated!" And to himself he added: "Just wait; Belisarius also appeared here as my superior, but in Rome I became his master instead."

"Very well," Narses commanded. During the discussion his litter had been placed on the ground, resting on high legs like stilts. "Let us then march against the Barbarians together. You may carry your father again, my dear children."

And the warriors returned to the litter and lifted it once more. Cethegus tried to guide his horse to the right side of the commander's litter, but Alboin called out to him in excellent Latin: "Nothing doing, Roman! I am known as the right hand of Narses, and the place of honour on his right is mine. The left side, the side of ill fortune, is still free. We have saved it for you especially."

Silently Cethegus rode over to the left side. "I don't know," he said to himself, "whether this right hand should fall before its head or after it! Ideally both must fall at the same time."

Chapter 25

On the evening of that day Narses and his army arrived at positions between the mountains of Helvillium and Taginae.

And mighty indeed was this army which Narses had brought to Italy. This time the mean, spendthrift Justinian had not tried to cut costs; instead of that he had spent freely with both hands. For this undertaking his character, normally a strange mixture of the grandiose and the petty, seemed to have shed its petty side completely. The great upheavals in the capital and at his court seemed to have shaken him awake. His able mind, which was much better suited to external politics than to domestic and administrative matters, had clearly recognised the extent and significance of the Gothic threat. The accusation that he himself had been the one to provoke this danger by needless attacks made it a self-imposed duty to suppress and avert it.

"He hated the very name of the Goths, and he swore to wipe them off the face of the Empire," Procopius wrote at the time.

Narses had pointed out this duty to his emperor in tough, uncompromising terms, and at the same time he added a most intelligent piece of advice as to how this aim might be accomplished. "These Germanic peoples will only be defeated by other Germanic peoples," he had exclaimed. "If I am to break these Goths, then I will need raw Germanic strength in addition to the usual mercenaries from Asia. I need that raw strength right from the primitive forests where they live! For a long time I have been warning you not to disturb these peaceful men, who were no threat to us, and instead to fight off the Persians, who were a very real threat indeed. You would not listen. Now that these Goths have gone over to the attack they are very dangerous, more dangerous even than the Persians with whom, by the way, they have already formed an alliance. Now they must be destroyed at any price, for they have already uncovered your Empire's weakness. Therefore I now say to you: we must have Germanic strength in order to break Germanic strength. I have a courageous people ready, together with the son of their king, who are filled with a thirst for conquest."

"Who are they?"

"That is my secret. I will hire savage, courageous hordes from among them as my bodyguard. But they alone will not be enough. I will need Franks, Heruli and Gepidae to help as well. You will concede to the Franks that which you cannot refuse them anyway, namely their new conquests in Gaul, Massilia and Arelate."

"In addition I will give them the right to strike coins with the images of their own kings; that will appeal to and flatter their childish conceit, both of the people and of their leaders. King Theudebert in Mettis, who had been won over by this King Totila like Childebert in Paris, has died. His young heir Theudebald needs our support."

"As for the Heruli, those ever hungry eternal mercenaries, give them a piece of Dacia near Singidunum. In return they will send their villainous lads to you in droves. Then make peace with the Gepidae, those the Lombards have left, and give them back Sirmium. They will fight for you, if only out of their old hatred for the people of Theodoric and Witigis."

"Those are a lot of concessions!"

"We will soon take them back from the dogs with whom we will hunt the Gothic lion, but first the lion must be defeated with their help."

And so Narses had completely persuaded and won over the ruler of the Romaeans.

The gold in the coffers of the Imperial treasury, which until now Justinian had always claimed was empty, was spent freely to equip a magnificent army for Narses. The latter, by no means modest in his demands, was amazed at the richness of this treasure, which until now had always been kept carefully concealed. The great war with Persia as well as the various smaller wars with neighbouring peoples were speedily concluded, with some sacrifices having to be made. Thus the tried and proven veterans, who had served for decades under Belisarius and Narses both in Asia and in Europe, all became available to be used against the Goths.

And the very enemies whom until now Justinian had fought, Persians, Saracens, Moors, Huns, Slavs, Gepidae, Heruli, Franks, Bulgars and Avars, now suddenly supplied mercenaries for substantial payments in gold.

All able-bodied men were conscripted from various parts of the Empire itself. The army Narses put together also included three thousand Heruli cavalry under Vulkaris and Wilmuth, seven thousand Persians and a company of selected Gepidae. One hundred and fifty wild adventurers under Asbad were hired, also ten thousand men of infantry from every part of the Franks' Empire. The Meroving rulers from Paris, Mettis and Aurelianum supplied Burgundians and Alemanni.

Furthermore on this occasion Narses, in addition to his own well trained commanders, had the use of the best commanders who formerly served under Belisarius as well, who had never previously been willing to serve under Narses. The mysterious reconciliation of the two great rivals, together with the fact that the borders were secure in all directions, made it possible to combine the best troops with the best commanders for the campaign in Italy.

Thus the two excellent *Archonti*, Orestes and Liberius, served under Narses. They were very close friends, and were often referred to as Orestes and Pylades. Their eager cooperation in all things made their friendship one of military importance as well. Later, during the battle of Taginae, their mutual affection would prove to have grave consequences.

Then there was Cabades, the nephew of the previous Persian king by that name, who with his Persians had long subjugated himself to the emperor. Also there were John, Basiliskos, Valerianus, Vitalianus, Justinus, Paulus, Dagisthaeos and Anzalas the Armenian, all of them tried and able commanders. The fleet which was cruising off Rome was commanded by Armatus, and that between Sicily and Naples by Dorotheos.

Thus it was that an army of one hundred thousand men stood facing the Goths at Caprae under Narses and Cethegus, while Rome and Naples were under threat from a further twenty thousand.

Chapter 26

King Totila no longer commanded anything like the army which Witigis had been able to muster, at that time one hundred and sixty thousand men, and he knew that he was numerically inferior.

Huge gaps had been left by the war. The losses before Rome alone numbered seventy thousand men, and were compounded by pestilence and hunger, as well as the prisoners who had been taken in Ravenna and at Senogallia. All these gaps had been only partly filled by Italian peasants, who enlisted only as the volunteers demanded it. The entire army at the king's command numbered about seventy thousand men, of whom ten thousand under Duke Guntharis and Count Grippa had to be left behind in Rome to defend that city against the threatened landings. A further ten thousand had been sent to the Greek islands, and to various cities and fortresses in Italy and Dalmatia. Many of these troops had already been slain or taken prisoner by Narses.

Thus King Totila now had barely fifty thousand men to put into the field at Taginae, against an enemy almost double his own strength.

When Cethegus pointed out this numerical comparison of the two opposing armies to Narses, the latter replied: "My great friend Belisarius has often been victorious with an inferior force, but even more often he has been defeated by a larger one. I, Narses, have sought to establish my own fame solely by winning every battle I fight, even if not with an inferior army. That rather more modest but also more useful fame has not eluded me. It will not elude me this time either."

The Gothic camp, of course, recognised the superior strength of the Byzantine army too. Among the king's council of war there were those who advised against meeting Narses in open battle, and instead to retreat into cities still held by the Goths and to drag out the war by a strategy of tough and uncompromising defence. But the king, for good reasons, rejected this advice and resolved to offer battle at Taginae.

Valeria had gradually guessed, with growing fear and apprehension, that the decisive battle would take place here, in the very valley of all her sorrows.

The king had recommended the cloister and chapel on the two hills behind the army as a safe refuge for the other women who accompanied the army, including the newlyweds Gotho and Liuta. He thought that Spes Bonorum was the best and safest place for them. Even if the enemy should prove victorious, these Catholic places of worship were most likely to be respected as a refuge by their Catholic conquerors.

The king's camp and surrounding areas, however, became more and more crowded every day by members of the Gothic nation, of both sexes and all ages, who had fled from areas which had either fallen to or were threatened by Narses. His terrible systematic approach to the eradication of all traces of Gothic life had soon become known, and so the terrified Goths fled in their thousands before the awesome juggernaut crushed them too in its relentless path.

They saw now that this was not merely a political war, but a war of genocide against their entire nation. Not only the Gothic warriors, but everyone with a drop of Gothic blood was under threat by Narses.

In addition the Italians also now recognised that both the nature and the purpose of the renewed fighting had drastically changed. And now the old hatred against the Barbarians, and their differences in blood, culture and religion, broke out anew. The reconciliation that had followed the hardships of the previous war, inspired by the benevolent regime of the peace-loving king, had been artificial and to some extent enforced, and ran contrary to their innermost convictions. Now that the tables had turned once more their true beliefs, and the old hatreds, came to the fore once again. Wherever they thought themselves safe and protected by the Romaeans, the Italians would show them the homes or hiding places of Gothic families, or indeed take them prisoner themselves to be sold into slavery.

And so, unlike the previous war against Belisarius, this time the Gothic settlements could not duck and wait for the tide of war to pass them by, to rise up again like blades of grass after a thunderstorm once the war had passed on. This time, wherever Narses had been, the end of Gothic life went with him, and once he moved on there was not a trace of such Gothic life left behind him.

And so all those who could flee had run before the slowly moving wall of annihilation, and from both north and south they had found their way into the king's camp. Because of this the war was shaping up like one of the ancient wars of migratory nations, whose fates were intimately tied to battle and the camp. For such people the barricade of wagons joined together, with tents on them, often represented the only homes they knew. Such a war was no longer merely a matter of defending a country and its inhabitants against an invading army. Indeed, other than in the king's camp and the surrounding areas protected by it, there were almost no Goths left in Italy. Totila had already started making arrangements, if only to avert the threat of famine which such a huge concentration of people brought with it, to move many of the non-combatants further to the south, and to spread them out over a larger area.

One evening the king was riding in the vicinity of the Spes Bonorum, on the heights, on a reconnaissance mission. When they spotted the cloister, young Adalgoth reminded him of the time when they had first visited the chapel there. The king smiled: "Yes, I remember. That was when I chose the site for my own grave at Numa Pompilius. Well, if I should fall in the coming battle, at least you will not have to carry me far."

But deep in his heart the king was much concerned about the outcome of the battle which lay ahead.

His greatest concern was his lack of cavalry, as most of his mounted troops were stationed with Guntharis and Grippa near Rome. Somehow the king had to find a mounted force of roughly equal strength to put into the field against the courageous Lombards on their strong horses, whom Narses was sure to use as one of his main weapons in the coming battle.

But then it seemed as if the king's old luck had returned once more, to help him out of this very difficulty.

Chapter 27

In the Gothic tents dark rumours had been going the rounds for days. It was reported by Gothic fugitives that new auxiliary forces were approaching from the east.

The king knew of no aid to be expected from that direction and therefore, in order to forestall any possible flank attack by the Byzantines, he sent out Count Thorismuth, Wisand the *bandalarius* and young Adalgoth with a handful of mounted troops to investigate the reports.

They returned the very next day, and as Count Thorismuth entered the king's tent with Adalgoth he exclaimed joyfully: "I bring you an old friend at just the right time, oh king!

"He looks just like the Bengal tiger which you showed to the people during the last circus games in Rome. Never have I seen such a resemblance between man and beast.

"You will be most pleased to see him. There he is already!"

And there, before the king, stood the Corsican Furius Ahalla. He bowed his proud head, his face even more brown than before, and placed his left hand on his chest: "Greetings, King of the Goths."

"Welcome in Italy, you world traveller. Where do you come from?"

"From Tyre."

"And what brings you back?"

"That, oh king, I can tell only to you."

Upon a signal from Totila the others left the tent. As soon as they had gone the Corsican grasped both of Totila's hands in feverish emotion: "Say yes, say yes! My life – no, more than my life depends on it!"

"What are you talking about?" the king asked as he took a step backwards, somewhat unpleasantly surprised. The hot, savage, hasty manner of this man was very different to his own, and it repelled him.

"Say yes: you are engaged to the daughter of Agila, the king of the Visigoths, and Valeria is free?"

The king frowned and angrily shook his head, but before he could speak the Corsican went on, wild with emotion: "Don't be surprised – and don't ask questions! Yes, I love Valeria with all the fire in me. I love her so much that I almost hate her. I courted her years ago. Then I discovered she was yours, and I withdrew in your favour. Had it been any other man I would have strangled him with these hands here! I hurried away, and in India and in Egypt I threw myself into new adventures and new dangers – and new delights too. But it was in vain. Her image remained indelibly impressed on my mind and soul. I suffered the agonies of hell out of longing for her. I thirsted for her as a panther thirsts after blood. And I cursed her, and you, and me. And I imagined that she had become yours long ago.

"And then, in the port of Alexandria, I came across some ships from Spain, Visigothic ships. Their commanders, old trading friends of Valerius and myself, told me that you had been made king, and when I asked after your queen Valeria they told me that you were unmarried. They also told me that their king Agila had offered you his daughter's hand and an alliance against Byzantium, and that you had accepted both. But above all they repeated – in fact they swore – that you were not married, and that your former bride Valeria, who was well known to them, was living a lonely life near Taginae.

"'Valeria is free!' everything within me rejoiced. That very same night I weighed anchor with my ships and hurried to Italy. Near Crete I came across a substantial fleet. They were Persian cavalry, whom Justinian had hired, and whom he was sending to Italy under their chieftain Isdigerdes, an old acquaintance of mine. They were to fight against you. I also learned from them what a huge army Narses had put into the field against you.

"And then, King Totila, I decided to repay my old debt to you. I was able, by offering double pay, to win Isdigerdes and his men over into my own service. They really are exceptional, hand-picked troops. I now bring them to you to provide you with reinforcements which, according to your counts, are most welcome indeed. They number more than two thousand horses."

"They are very welcome indeed," Totila replied, pleased, "Thank you!"

"I was able to confirm that you are still unmarried," the Corsican continued, "but – they say – they say that Valeria is not free – that she is still – I wouldn't, couldn't believe it – still can't give up the hope that – no, no, don't shake your head! I implore you, say yes, she is free." And again he reached for Totila's hands.

But Totila tore himself free, not without signs of anger. "Still the same old, destructive, boundless fire! When oh when will that lava ever cool? Still, yes that young singer is right – you still have that frightening manner of a tiger. At any moment I can feel your claws in my neck!"

"Do not preach to me, Goth!" the Corsican fumed. "Say yes or no, is Valeria…"

"Valeria is mine," the king cried violently, "mine now and for ever."

At that the Corsican let out a cry of pain and anger, and beat his forehead furiously with both his fists. He then threw himself onto the camp bed in the tent, shook his head to and fro among the cushions, and let out a muffled groaning.

For a while Totila stood and watched this display in silent astonishment. A last he went over to him and took his right hand, which had been beating away at his chest. "Control yourself! Are you a man or a wounded boar? Is that worthy of a man, of a human being? I would have thought you had learned your painful lesson as to where such senseless fury can lead."

With a loud cry Furius sprang to his feet, his hand on his dagger.

"Ah, it is you who speaks like that? Who dares to admonish me? You alone may do that – you alone can! But I warn you just the same; don't do it again! It is something I cannot bear, even from you! Oh, you should not admonish me, you should pity me.

"What do your northern hearts know of the fire in my veins? That which you call love is a mild twinkling of the stars. My love is a burning fire, just like my hatred – yes, lava, you are right! If only you knew how I have suffered on her account, how I glowed with renewed hope, how I blessed and loved you, and now – now it is all gone." And he began to rage once more.

"I don't understand you," Totila said severely, walking up and down in the tent and leaving the raging man to his own devices. "You have a low, repulsive attitude to women."

"Totila!" the Corsican threatened.

"Yes, a lowly, brutal attitude. You seem to regard a woman like some chattel, like a horse perhaps, which a second man can have if the first will let it go. Does a woman not have a soul, a will of her own, a right to choose?"

"Do you really imagine, if I had really died or married another, that Valeria would then simply have become yours? We are, after all, very different people, Corsican! And a woman who has loved Totila would hardly take Furius Ahalla in his place."

The Corsican sprang to his feet again as if struck by lightning.

"Goth, you are suddenly very proud! Such arrogance was once foreign to you. Has that golden crown given you such superior airs? You dare to look down on me? That I will not tolerate from any man, not even from you. Take back what you just said!"

But Totila shrugged his shoulders. "Your jealousy, your blind rage are confusing you. I said that a woman who has loved me would not love you after me. And that is so true that even you must see it. Imagine Valeria, withdrawn, strictly brought up, marble-like. And then imagine your own wild, undisciplined character. Valeria is not a soft Syrian girl like that Zoe."

"Don't mention her name!" the Corsican groaned.

"Valeria is repelled by your savagery; she told me that herself once. She said that you terrify her."

Furius flew at the king and grasped both his shoulders with his hands. "You told her that? Have you revealed that story of disaster to her? You have? Then you shall not..."

But Totila now pushed him away rather roughly. "Enough of this unworthy raging. No, I have not told her – until now. But you would certainly have deserved it. Still, even after such an experience..."

"Do not speak of it!" the Corsican threatened.

"Still you cannot control yourself in love, hate or anger! You grab hold of your friend as if he was a beast of prey, like a madman. Truly, if it was not for the fact that I know the noble core within you, this savagery of yours would have turned me against you long ago. Control yourself or leave me!" And the king fixed his eyes on the Corsican, not without a suggestion of superior dignity.

This look was something which the passionate man could not bear. He covered his eyes with his hands and then, after a pause, he said in a broken tone: "Forgive me, Totila. It is over. But never repeat that tone, or that look. During that night of terror it held me back even more than your arm did. I fear it and I hate it at the same time. If I have hurt you I will apologise by personally helping you fight your battle tomorrow, by your side with my men."

"There, Furius," the king said, "that is your noble core coming to the fore, the fact that you are still willing to give your gift despite your – disappointment. I thank you again. Your help and your cavalry make it possible for me to execute a splendid plan of battle, which I had been forced to abandon regretfully, because I lacked sufficient mounted troops."

"Your generals, whom you summoned for a council of war, are waiting outside your tent!" a *sajone* reported.

"Show them in! No, Furius, you may stay and hear everything. Your task in tomorrow's battle will be the most important of all my commanders."

"I am proud of it, and I will perform in such a way that you will be satisfied with the 'wild animal'!"

Chapter 28

And now the king's generals assembled around him. There were old Hildebrand, Count Teias, Count Wisand, Count Thorismuth, Count Markja, Aligern and the young Duke of Apulia.

Totila pointed to the wall of the tent, where they saw a map of Taginae and its surroundings, drawn by the king himself with a skilful and knowledgeable hand. It was based on an old Roman road map of the area, particularly the Via Flaminia, and on it Totila had drawn the most important places and features.

"My valiant warriors," he began, "I would like nothing better than to simply storm at the enemy in the ancient Gothic wedge formation, and try to thrust through his heart. But by using the ancient wisdom handed down to us by Odin," he smiled, "we will not defeat the greatest general of our century, at the head of an army twice as strong as ours and in a position which he himself has chosen."

"Don't anger the god of victory by jesting about him on the eve of battle!" old Hildebrand warned.

But Totila went on: "Very well then, we will see whether the great strategist, who wants to destroy one Germanic people through another, can't be defeated by his own methods. The decision tomorrow will fall here, in the centre between the two positions, near Taginae. The two wings will only need to hold their own.

"Hildebrand, you will command our left wing across from Eugubium; I will give you ten thousand men. The forest there, and the little River Sibola, which runs into the larger River Classis here, will give you good cover. The same with you, Teias—" Teias was standing close by Totila's shoulder "—on the right wing, with fifteen thousand. You will be positioned here on the mountain behind Caprae to the right, which reaches almost to the hill with the cloister of the Valerii and the tomb of Numa."

"Oh king, let me fight near you tomorrow, on your shield side. I had an evil dream," he added in a whisper.

"No, my Teias," Totila replied, "we are not going to arrange our plan of battle based on a dream. You will both have more than enough fighting to do once the decision has fallen here because, and I say it again, right here is where the battle will be decided, in the centre." He pointed at the space between Caprae and Taginae.

"That is why I have placed half of our army, twenty-five thousand men, here in the centre of our position.

"The centre of Narses's own position will be the Heruli and – his best troops, the Lombards. He will not alter that arrangement now because he, great master of battles that he is, has probably seen long before I did that tomorrow will be decided by the clash of the two centres. Now pay close attention.

"I know the Lombards, their eagerness to fight, and the impetuosity of their cavalry. That is what I am building my plan on. If Narses wants to defeat us through Germanic strength, then he shall fall due to Germanic weakness.

"With the few Gothic mounted troops we have I will charge from Caprae against the Lombards, who are deployed at Helvillium, in Narses's powerful centre. They will not hesitate to charge at me with their numerical superiority. Then I, apparently thrown back by the ferocity of their charge, will race back to Caprae's northern gate in what will look like disorderly flight. I will have that northern gate closed behind us, so that they don't become suspicious, but I will not defend it.

"Knowing the Lombards I would be very much surprised if they, full of eagerness for the chase, don't continue the pursuit with their fast cavalry alone, far ahead of the much slower infantry. I am certain of it; they will tear open the gate and chase us through Caprae, out of the southern gate, and out into the open field between Caprae and Taginae – here!

"But immediately before Taginae the Via Flaminia is flanked on both sides by wooded hills, the Collis Nucerius on the right, and the Collis Clasius on the left. Can you see? Here! Now on these wooded heights, hidden by the forest, our great Corsican's cavalry will wait in ambush; as soon as the Lombards are here, between the two hills, I will turn from feigned flight to attack on the Via Flaminia itself. The horn will sound a cavalry charge. Upon that signal your men, Furius, charge down on the Lombards from both sides at once, and…"

"They are doomed!" Wisand the *bandalarius*, rejoiced.

"But that is only the first half of my plan," Totila continued. "Narses will either have to abandon the flower of his army to their fate…"

"He will not do that," Teias said calmly.

"Or he will have to follow with his infantry. But I will have our archers hidden in the houses of Caprae, and our spear bearers in the houses of Taginae. When Narses's Armenians try to become involved in the cavalry duel between the two cities they will be attacked simultaneously from the front and the rear by our infantry, charging out of the gates of the two cities. Wisand, you will be in command in Caprae, and you, Thorismuth, in Taginae."

"I would not want to be a Lombard tomorrow," Furius commented.

"Their beards will be long, but their pleasure short," Adalgoth laughed.

"Not one of the Armenians will escape," said Markja.

"True, if the plan succeeds," Teias added.

"You two, Hildebrand and Teias, as soon as you see the Byzantine infantry start to move against Caprae, will also move toward Caprae with those of your forces nearest to the centre. Leave only just enough men there to defend your wings, and in that way you will help us crush the centre. When that is done we will turn towards both wings; it will not be difficult to split their position in two to the left and right, because without Helvillium they have no base. Their huge numbers will become an embarrassment among the narrows and chasms there once we attack their flank from Helvillium."

Old Hildebrand shook the king's right hand. "You are Odin's favourite!" he whispered in Totila's ear.

"That's bad!" the king replied, also in a whisper but smiling. "You know, in the end the spear given one by Odin must fail, and the god of victory takes his favourite with him to Valhalla. Now, farewell and good luck, my valiant generals!"

After the generals had left the Corsican hesitated at the door for a moment. "I have one favour to ask of you, king. Tomorrow, after your battle has been fought and won, I will put to sea, never to return. Before I go let me say farewell – to her. Let me impress her image into my soul for one last time."

An angry look came over the king's face. "What for? It can only cause pain and agony, both for you and for her."

"No, it will please me. And you – are you jealous? Or are you afraid to even show what you possess? Are you jealous, King of the Goths?"

"Furius!" the king cried, hurt and embittered within at the way in which the Corsican was behaving. "Go and find her, and then satisfy yourself just how different she is from you, in every way!"

Chapter 29

Almost at the same time as the Gothic council of war was making its fateful decisions Narses, who had suffered badly from repeated attacks of epilepsy in the last few days, had himself carried from his tent to a hill at the rear of his centre. He was surrounded by his commanders, and from this vantage point the entire area known today as Gualdo Tadino could be seen.

"Here," he said, pointing with his crutch from his litter. "here, between Caprae and Taginae, is where the battle will be decided. If only you had managed to occupy Taginae, or even Caprae, Cethegus!"

"That black Teias beat me to it by three hours," the latter retorted angrily.

"There is no other position like this one on the whole Via Flaminia between here and Rome which is more ideally suited to being defended against a superior foe," Narses went on. "Truly, these Barbarians have chosen this position with masterly insight. If they had not managed to gain control of those hills there, then our army could roll on unhindered as far as Rome. Now listen carefully to every word I say. I am not finding it easy to talk, and Narses says nothing twice. Now, Lombard, what are you thinking about?" He touched Alboin's shoulder with his crutch. Alboin was standing there, admiring the landscape as if in a trance.

"Me?" Alboin replied, startled out of his daydreaming. "I am thinking how wonderfully rich and beautiful this country is, and what fertility abounds everywhere! It is the land of wine we sing about in our songs."

"Thou shalt not covet thy emperor's Italy, nor all that is his," said Narses, threatening with his crutch. "The grape Italy, fox Alboin, hangs very high indeed."

"Yes, as long as you are alive, Narses, it is sour too!" the Lombard replied.

"For the time being the Gothic king, whose Empire you want to inherit, is still alive," said Narses. "Now, here is my plan: Orestes, you and Zeuxippos will take our left wing to the *Busta Gallorum* (Tombs of the Gauls), opposite the high wooded hill with the white cloister buildings on it."

"What was the origin of the name?" Alboin asked.

"It is the site," Cethegus answered him, "where the Roman consul Decius, dedicating his life to the fatherland, defeated a vastly superior army from Gaul. The soil here is sacred, and it is a good omen for Rome. Also," he concluded bitterly, "it is an evil omen for Barbarians."

"When was that?" Alboin inquired further.

"In the four hundred and fifty-eighth year of the city."

"That was a long time ago," the Lombard commented.

Narses continued his briefing: "John, with Valerianus and Dagisthaeos, will command our right wing by the rivers Classis and Sibola. You will remain positioned here and do nothing until the decision has fallen in the centre – here! As soon as that has occurred – for he who has superior strength and does not use it to outflank his enemy does not deserve to have it – you will both move toward the centre, from both wings. You will reach far beyond the narrow Barbarian front line, and then you will close the net and cut off their retreat to Rome. You will meet up on the Via Flaminia east of Taginae, near Nuceria Camillaria. If the plan succeeds then the war will be over with a single blow."

"Pity!" was Alboin's comment.

"Yes, my little wolf, your heart will not bleed if you can butcher the emperor's Italy by hacking away at it in a nice long war, but my heart will! It is not my manner to win many battles – that is the special joy of my friend Belisarius – my aim is always to conclude a campaign successfully at one blow. That is my style. But first, before you can move on the flanks, the bloody groundwork has to be done down here, in the plain. I will have to storm Caprae and Taginae. If those Barbarians have any sense they will not show themselves in the open field outside Caprae. My wolves would run them down there, right, my wolf king?"

"What a magnificent plain for a cavalry battle!" Alboin exclaimed. "I can already see them fleeing back to the gates of Caprae."

"They will not oblige you by venturing out this far, my little wolf. But under no circumstances are you to try and attack Caprae with your mounted troops alone."

"Oh," Alboin replied, "we are used to having to dismount and fight on foot where necessary. The horses just stand still like obedient little lambs, and when we whistle they come after us in a trot."

Narses was shaken by a severe convulsion; his features became distorted. "Long beard," he said after regaining control over himself, "don't annoy me! Annoyance and fright bring on this horrible shaking. If you dare to attack Caprae before my infantry gets there, I will send you straight home after the battle."

"That would indeed be the worst punishment you could mete out."

"You, Anzalas, will command the Armenian infantry, and you, Cethegus, the Illyrians, together with your own splendid Isaurian mercenaries. Together you will storm Caprae and Taginae. I myself will follow behind you with the main force of the Macedonians and Epiroti." Another convulsion shook the commander-in-chief.

"I fear that these attacks will return tomorrow, and that they will become worse. If that happens you, Liberius, will stand in for me and command until I am again able to speak and give orders."

Cethegus looked annoyed.

"I would have given you the task of taking my place, Prefect," Narses said, noticing it. "But you will not want to be watching idly from Helvillium. I will need you and your much-feared sword as our troops storm the two fortified cities."

"And if I should fall in the process the Imperial General will no doubt survive the loss."

"We are all mortal, oh Prefect!" Narses replied. "Only a very few of us become immortal, and then only after our death."

Chapter 30

On the evening of that same day Valeria went for a walk within the walled garden of the cloister, among the cypress trees there. She knew, or rather sensed, that the long awaited battle lay ahead on the morrow, and in her heart she was afraid.

She climbed the little tower at the corner of the garden wall. A small circular staircase led up to the tower, and from here one had a splendid overview of the entire valley where tomorrow her own fate as well as that of Italy would be decided.

In the west behind the Classis River, directly in front of her, the sun was setting into blood-red clouds.

To the north she could see the great expanse of the Byzantine camp, with its countless tents of dark skins and hides as well as coarse blackened canvas. The camp seemed to stretch on and on for ever, beyond the horizon from *Busta Gallorum* in the east to Eugubium (the ancient Iguvium) in the west. The cold, dark shadows of the night were already moving over the camp, silent and threatening.

Immediately below her feet she could see the Gothic tents, close to the small town of Taginae. At first she was shocked to see how few they were, even though Totila had told her that the majority of his troops were billeted in the houses of Caprae and Taginae.

The Gothic camp, too, was already in the shadows.

She alone, a white figure standing high on the cloister wall and sharply contrasted against the stones of the battlement, was still standing in the full glow of the setting sun. The little chapel at the tomb of Numa Pompilius, to the east of her and a little higher still, was also still bathed in sunlight.

For a long time Valeria, filled with dark foreboding, stood there and looked out at the peaceful landscape. What kind of spectacle would she witness from here tomorrow? How many hearts, still beating today full of warmth and confidence, would by then be cold and still for ever? Thus she stood and daydreamed, alone with the heavens above and the fields below.

Meanwhile the sun had long gone down, and it was rapidly becoming dark, but she was barely aware of it. Already a few fires could be seen burning in the camps below her.

As she stood there the young woman allowed her thoughts to drift over events of the recent past, and she said to herself: "It is strange, the way I have lived happily for years, having almost forgotten about the promise that binds me to this place. Suddenly a hand reaching out from the clouds takes me back here to the place of my destiny, and not my choice, as if by some secret force. And then after a long, sad wait I escaped these walls once more out into the world, following my friend's call, to happiness and joy and love. I exchanged the tomb-like silence here for the tumultuous bridal feast in the king's castle.

"And once again, almost on the eve of my wedding, the hand of fate takes hold of me once more, and tears us all away from happiness and rejoicing. And fate takes me and my beloved to meet our destiny here, of all places, to the site of my fate.

"Is that some form of warning by fate? A premonition? Is that same dark spell which binds me here going to take hold of my friend also? Is his fate to be tied to mine? Can I save him from it if I give him up and fulfil the promise my mother made?

"Will he be the one who has to pay for the fact that we, my father and I, failed to keep that promise? Alas, heaven remains deaf to the anguished questions of a frightened human heart. It only opens its gates to punish. Its terrible language is thunder, and its fateful light is as the lightning that accompanies it and destroys all. Are you satisfied, you severe god of the cross? Or do you still demand the soul, unrelenting, which was once promised to you?"

It had by now become quite dark, with the moon as yet doing little to illuminate the high-walled garden. She was aroused from her thoughts by the footsteps of a man, who was approaching quickly from the garden. She could hear the sand of the garden paths being crushed under his feet.

That was not Totila's light, gliding walk.

The maiden climbed down the marble steps and was about to walk back to the house along the narrow path between the cypresses and the wall, when suddenly the man barred her way. He had recognised her coming, but he himself was almost unrecognisable in his dark cloak. It was the Corsican.

His sudden appearance frightened her. She had long been aware of the man's passion for her, but that knowledge filled her with a strange dread, almost fear. "You here, Furius Ahalla! What brings you to these sacred walls?"

For a moment the stranger remained silent. He was breathing heavily, and seemed to be searching for words. Gradually the moonlight started to creep over the wall, and soon afterwards it clearly showed the face and figure of the lovely Roman girl. At last Furius spoke, with effort and in fragmented sentences: "My desire brings me here… to say farewell, Valeria. Farewell for ever. Tomorrow we fight a bloody battle. Your… king has allowed me to see one more time the… that which I would begrudge to any other man but him alone. Or," he added passionately, staring at her intensely and slightly raising one arm, "that which I should not begrudge him, and yet… cannot help begrudging him."

"Furius Ahalla," Valeria replied, retreating a step backwards with dignity, for she had not failed to notice the movement of his arm, "I am the bride of your friend!"

"Oh I know that, only too well!" And then, following her, he took a step forward. "That knowledge is written in my heart with the burning letters of pain. Oh I could hate him fiercely! Why did he, he of all men, have to step between you, you magnificent woman, and my raging passion? If it was any other man I would tear him apart! It is very difficult not to hate him."

"You are mistaken," Valeria replied calmly, "and the only reason I stood here and listened to such talk is to tell you this: Even if I had never set eyes on Totila, yet I would never have been yours."

"Why not?" Furius asked, irritated.

"Because you and I are not suited to one another. Because the very things which attract me to Totila repel me from you."

"Oh, you are wrong! To be loved as fiercely and as passionately as I love you must surely be enough to win any woman!"

"Your love would have… filled me with fear. Now let me into the house."

But the Corsican blocked her path. "Fear? That does not matter. Sweet fear is the mother of love. There are many different ways to love, or to pay court. The mating habits of the lion have always had the most appeal for me. He leaves his bride no choice but love or death."

"Enough of these words, which are as unseemly for me to hear as they are wrong for you to utter. Let me pass!"

"Ha, are you afraid of me, Vestal Virgin?" And he took another step closer.

But Valeria stood her ground, and looked him up and down with cold contempt. Calmly and with dignity she said: "Afraid of you? No."

"Then you are altogether too brave, Valeria, because you have every reason to be afraid. If you knew of the passion that has been burning within me all these years, if you knew how tortured my nights are with longing for you, then you would tremble! Oh, and even if you cannot love me, even to see you tremble as you are trembling now! To make you tremble would be a joy in itself."

"Be silent!" Valeria cried, and tried to force her way past him through the trees. But again he barred her way and, by now barely in possession of his senses, reached for her cloak. "No, I don't want to be silent," he whispered heatedly. "You will at least feel it, and know that it burns within you as long as there is breath in your body. I can already see the shudder of dread running through your proud limbs. I will not cut short the joy of watching you tremble. Oh how you would tremble in my arms! How your proud figure would melt under the hot breath of my mouth... how you would..." and with that he gripped the struggling girl by both her shoulders.

"Help! Light! Help!" Valeria screamed.

Already people were rushing to her aid from the house, with lamps and torches.

But the Corsican, his back to the door, would not let her go.

"Let go of my arm!"

"No, for once you will..."

But in the next instant he was pulled back with the strength of furious anger, so that he was forced to let Valeria go and stumbled against a wall. Totila shone his torch into the Corsican's heated face. Terrible but righteous anger burned in the king's eyes. "Tiger!" he cried, "are you trying to murder my bride, like you did your own?"

With a piercing cry of fury the Corsican flew at him, both hands clenched into fists. But Totila stood motionless, merely fixing him with his stare. Furius managed to regain control over himself.

And then Valeria threw herself at Totila's breast. "Oh take me away from here, quickly! He is mad! He killed his bride, did you say?"

That question, coming from Valeria, was more than the Corsican could bear. He cast one more look at Totila, saw him nodding to Valeria in agreement, and in a moment he had vanished in the shadows behind the cypresses.

"Yes," said Totila, "it's true. Did the madman frighten you much?"

"It is over. You are with me now."

"I am sorry I permitted him to see you. I became concerned, and so I hurried here, driven by love, regret and concern."

"I am glad it was you who came, and not the people from the house. How that would have shamed him! I only cried out when I really thought he was mad. But what an awful deed! His bride?"

"Yes," Totila repeated, placing his arm about her and handing his torch to a slave woman, who had come out of the house. "But let us walk a little in the moonlight first."

And so the two lovers walked deeper into the garden once more, walking up and down. "I am sorry that righteous anger forced those words from my lips. It was a secret by means of which I had won a strange power over the black panther. Many years ago, as I returned from hunting Libyan pirates with my ship, I met him in the harbour of Beronike on the coast of the Pentapolis. He was about to wed Zoe, the daughter of a Syrian merchant who had settled there in Africa to ply the ivory trade.

"The Corsican had always been favourably inclined towards me, I suppose because I had often helped him with his shipping trade, and so he invited me to be a guest at his wedding on board his richly decorated ship. I accepted the invitation, and the feast was a very happy one, but the bridegroom was in a mood which was one of cruelty rather than tenderness.

"Finally the bride's parents were about to leave the ship with me, in a small boat. The ship was to take the newlyweds to Corsica, and it had been only with great reluctance that the parents finally agreed to give their gentle, tender child to a stranger whose violent temper and wild savagery had already been in evidence during the courtship.

"Zoe was understandably moved by the emotions of saying farewell to her parents. Again and again she threw herself tearfully into the arms of her mother and father. I noticed that the groom, seeing this, gradually worked himself up into a tremendous rage. Finally he called out to Zoe aloud whether she preferred her father to him. Did she not love him any more? What she was doing looked as if she was having regrets about having married him, and so forth. The more he threatened and scolded, the more the poor child wept and cried. In the end he cried out to her furiously that she was to stop her crying at once and come over to his side of the ship so that, according to ancient sailor's custom, he could sever the anchor rope with the axe he was holding in his hand.

"Zoe obeyed. She tore herself away from her father, and then her eyes met her mother's frightened face and eyes filled with tears. Instead of walking over to Furius she turned and, bursting into tears again, threw herself into her mother's arms to embrace her once more. Furius, now in an uncontrollable rage, flew forward, his axe flashed and then glanced over the top of the girl's head, wounding her slightly; he would have slain her on the spot if…"

How awful!" Valeria cried.

"If I had not caught his arm and torn the axe from his grasp with a look which suddenly tamed him. Lysikrates carried his bleeding child from the ship and to his house, and he refused to allow his daughter to marry such a dangerous suitor."

"And what happened to her after that?"

"She died soon afterwards, not so much from her wound as from the shock of it. And you were to take Zoe's place in the heart of lonely Furius Ahalla."

Valeria shuddered. "He frightens me. He is like a wild beast, only half tamed, unreliable and unpredictable. His deadly savagery could awaken at any moment."

"Let him be. Under his crude exterior he has a noble heart. He will give full vent to his rage now and exhaust himself – did you hear his horse galloping down the hill? Tomorrow, during the battle, he will make up for it all. I will gladly forgive him – he was not in control of himself. But now let us return to ourselves, to our love and our happiness."

"Have you been able to find happiness in our love?" Valeria asked thoughtfully. "Think how much stronger you would be in the battle tomorrow if you had wed the daughter of the Visigothic king, or that Haralda, who seemed much smitten with you…"

But Totila drew her to him. "Who can replace Valeria?"

"Your happiness? Your lucky star?" Valeria repeated anxiously. "Will we ever become one? They say that the enemy outnumbers you by two to one. Are you not concerned over the battle tomorrow?"

"Never in my life have I looked forward to a battle more confidently. Tomorrow is the day I will earn an honoured place in history! My plan is sound, and I am looking forward to defeating Narses, the great master of battles, by his own methods. I am going to ride into this battle as if I was riding to a feast. You must therefore decorate me, and my horse and my weapons, with flowers and garlands and ribbons."

"With flowers and ribbons? That is how sacrifices are decorated."

"And victors too, Valeria."

"Tomorrow, at sunrise, I will send your weapons down to the camp for you, adorned with flowers still damp from the morning dew."

"Yes, I want to ride into what will be my finest victory looking like a victor. Tomorrow I will win my bride and Italy with the same single stroke. In my heart you are one, because in you I have always loved Italy as well."

Chapter 31

When at last the king arrived in the small house in Taginae where he had set up his headquarters, he saw a man sitting there, on the edge of the cistern. He was wearing a dark cloak, and on his knees a small harp glistened in the moonlight. His fingers were playing a soft tune on it.

"It is you, Teias? Don't you have work to do on your wing?"

"I have everything in order there. Here is where I have business – with you."

"Come into the house with me. Is Julius outside?"

"No, he has gone to the basilica of St Paul to pray for your victory, but I expect he will be back soon. I have brought you a suit of armour, and I ask a favour of you. Wear it in the battle tomorrow. It is strong and will protect you well."

Totila stopped in his tracks, touched: "What a thoughtful gesture from a true friend!"

Together they now walked into the middle chamber of the house. There, on a marble table, lay a complete suit of armour, from the helmet to the steel-clad shoes. It was made from the finest Spanish steel, light and yet impenetrable, a masterpiece of workmanship. But it was plain and lacked any trace of adornment. There was not even a plume on the helmet, but it did have a tightly closed visor. The entire outfit was made of dark blue steel.

"What master blacksmith could have made this superb masterpiece?" Totila asked admiringly.

"I did," Teias replied. "As you know I have always been interested in the making of weapons and armour. And so, as I do not sleep much at night, I made this up for you. You must accept my gift."

"Yes," Totila smiled, "for my funeral; in this suit of armour I would like to accompany my own funeral procession. But tomorrow, my friend Teias, I will ride into battle in my full royal robes and insignia. Italy shall not say that her king and bridegroom went into hiding on his day of glory. No, whoever tries to find the Gothic king tomorrow shall have no trouble doing so."

"I was afraid you would say something like that," Teias sighed. "Let me at least fight by your side then; relieve me of my command on the right wing."

"No, it is most important. I can take care of myself, but you must cover the mountains for me, and the road to Rome. In the event of a mishap your wing is our only hope of retreat."

At that moment Julius entered with Count Thorismuth and Duke Adalgoth, together with their servants. The latter also included Wachis, who had accompanied Teias as his shield bearer. They brought with them the evening meal of meat, fruit, bread and wine.

"Just think, Julius," Totila said, smiling to the latter as he entered, "the bravest hero in the Gothic nation has become afraid."

"Not for myself," Teias replied. "But my dreams usually come true. And they are always black."

"What about your dreams," Totila smiled and looked at the young Adalgoth and Wachis, who was filling a goblet for the king. "I guess your dreams, you newlyweds, are not black!"

"I can't complain about them, Sir King," Wachis grinned, "But I do wish that…"

"What can you have left to wish for, now that you have Liuta?" Totila asked.

"I wish the tall one was here."

"Which tall one?"

"You know, the tall one who would have towered even over your brave brother Hildebad by a head, the one with the bear skin and the woman falconer. What was his name again?"

"Harald!" Teias replied seriously.

"Yes, he is the one I mean. He and his giants would be useful tomorrow."

"We will not need him."

"But it is always better to be on the safe side, Sir King. And if I had been the king, well – I would have had him sent for, as soon as war broke out again."

"We do not need him!" the king said again, slightly annoyed.

"I thought as my shield bearer does, oh king," Teias interjected. "On my own initiative, as I was doubtful you would agree, I sent for him. I doubt that you would have sent him away again if I had been able to bring him back. I too was impressed by that trusty northern giant; his men would have been good against those Lombards. Unfortunately my small ship was unable to catch up with his fleet."

"Thank you, Teias, that was just like you once more. But I am glad you could not catch him. We will fight and win alone. My plan cannot fail – if only…" and here a cloud passed over the king's face.

"If the Corsican does his part," said Teias.

"Tell me, Thorismuth, I sent you from the cloister to Furius because I had a slight disagreement with him. You were to ask if everything was still the same between us. What was his reply?"

"He gave me this open letter, addressed to you."

"Where did you find him?" Totila asked, taking the wax tablet from him.

"Outside Taginae. He was already showing his men their positions in the ambush. He has complied exactly with everything you asked of him."

The king read: "Tomorrow I will do what you expect of me. After the battle you will have nothing to accuse me of."

"He added," Thorismuth explained, "that a few hundred of his horses, somewhat affected by their journey on the ship, were marching a little more slowly, but would surely be here by tomorrow. They have already been reported coming from Septempeda. He suggested that you delay the decision, if you can, until they have arrived."

"Why does he not come here himself?" Teias asked angrily.

"He is trying his hardest," Thorismuth replied. "I saw it with my own eyes. He is showing his men the exact location where the decision will fall tomorrow. He has been conducting practice charges from the hills down to the road, in the moonlight."

Totila concluded: "I know why he did not come to join me for the evening meal. It has no significance."

And now they all took their places on the various camp stools and boxes around the table, and commenced their simple meal.

"The king," Teias began, "will not allow me to fight by his side tomorrow. I therefore command you, brave Thorismuth, to guard his life."

"He will not always be able to do that," Totila smiled as he drank. "Thorismuth has to command my spear bearers in Taginae for me."

"As long as I am by the king's side, nothing will happen to him," Thorismuth replied calmly. "I will go and have one more look at the front lines outside Caprae." And with that he left the room.

"Yes," Totila exclaimed, "he was the one who saved me in Naples, at the Porta Capuana."

"And in Rome, on the Tiber, it was the young duke with the harp here," said Teias. "Where will he be tomorrow? He shall guard you again!"

"No!" Adalgoth replied. "I asked to be permitted to lead the cavalry charge, and to carry Domna Valeria's new banner."

"Well then, my pious Julius," said Teias, "you will not be expected to fight. Will you guard the king's life? I know that you love him, in your own way, and surely it would be no sin to try and protect him?"

"I will stay by his side. But even more than my weak arm, or even your strong one, Count of Tarentum, my prayers to God will protect him."

"Prayers!" Teias sighed. "No prayer has yet got through the clouds. And if one did it would find heaven empty."

Chapter 32

"No!" the monk exclaimed. "You cannot also deny God, as Cethegus did! You cannot deny the God of love his own world, can you? Are you denying the one God, the wise, almighty and loving father, who directs the ways of all men on earth from heaven?"

"Yes!" Teias cried, and his hand flew to the hilt of his sword. "Him I deny! If there really was some being up there who controls what happens down here, then one would have to pile mountain on mountain and stone on stone so as to storm his heaven, and never rest until the bloody spirit up there has been toppled from His blood-spattered throne, or fallen victim to his own bolt of lightning."

Julius, horrified, sprang to his feet: "Has the evil of blasphemy, of denying God, gripped hold of all the world's mightiest men? I cannot bear to listen to such words!"

"Then do not ask me!" Even the king looked in surprise at his normally quiet friend, as his breast suddenly allowed some fierce and long hidden agony to burst from it.

"Are you surprised," Teias went on, "that quiet Teias can still feel so intensely? Sometimes it surprises me too. But tomorrow is the day of the summer solstice. That is the day when the sun turned away from me for ever, long ago, and every year that day returns and my old wounds ache all over again."

"Now I understand why you are so depressed, you unfortunate man," Julius said after a pause. "Yes, I cannot even understand how you are able to live. I could not so much as breathe without God."

"Who told you, monk, that Teias has no god? Because I do not see Him as you do, according to your faith, humanised through love, hate, anger or envy? Because I cannot believe that He, the omniscient one, can create beings only to torture themselves and others, and to be damned in the end anyway? Because I do not see how those beings can then be saved through the blood of an innocent, blameless man? Because I cannot imagine Him like an unskilled carpenter, who built His house badly and so has to patch it again and again with miraculous hands? Let me tell you this: the majesty of my god is so terrifying that in his presence your angel king vanishes, before His terrible, relentless and merciless might, as the dome of a church is a mere nothing when compared to the dome of the universe.

"No, if there really was a father up there in the clouds, and if He was unable to steer the cruel paths of fate down here, then He Himself would be overcome with grief. Terribly He would suffer from the cries of his suffering children, just as your gentle Jesus suffered. That story has always moved me deeply, the way in which He bore the suffering of all mankind up there on the cross at Golgatha.

"Now, my Totila, I promised that I would sing and play the harp for you once more. Listen to the song, then, which I have put in the mouth of Father Odin." His hands touched the strings of the little harp, which had lain next to his weapons, and he sang in a deep and solemn voice Father Odin's song:

"My soul sighs in unbearable suffering over the sad, painful fate of humanity.
Everything in this world that breaks , burning in every breast, again and again,
I must suffer too, feel it, fight it, lament it all!
All and everything, for they call me 'father of the world'.
Sometimes it is for a conquered, good man, defeated by one who is evil,
his soul on fire as he writhes in death's agony and curses the cruelty of fate.
Sometimes it is for a lover's mortal anguish, as his arms reach out into empty air,
life slowly ebbing from him with his longing never satisfied.
And the widow's woe, the orphan's tears and the last despairing cry of a sinking soul.
All this misery, senseless and empty, I must share it all as the father of all.
How few, by comparison, are the small joys which life brings; they are like lost rose petals
scattered on a stormy sea in the endless ocean of woe and suffering.
There is but one consolation, and one only: there is a goal, set to put an end to all the
      misery;
there will be an end to it. I bless the day when the burning Sutur crushes the last of mankind
together with the tired earth; finally it will still the fountain of pain and the last human heart.

"Welcome to that day! And if men were wise, they too would yearn for it to come sooner. That is how I once imagined the soul of some kind god. But since then I have thought about it a great deal, and I have found another god, my own, terrible god. But of course, to understand that god one must have experienced Him in the death agonies of one's own twitching heart."

Chapter 33

Julius remained silent, shaking his head. But the king asked: "And how did you experience Him, this terrible god?"

"The hour has come, Totila my king and my friend, for you to know that which I have kept from you all these years: the story of my past, and the shadow which fell into my life and threw it into darkness for ever. No, Christian, stay! You too may hear what I have to say, and then try to justify it or explain it in terms of God's mysterious ways, how He punishes those He loves, or by such other pieces of wisdom such as you monks teach. Think like that if you wish, but don't say it! I cannot bear to hear it, at least not today. Totila, you know about the dreadful fate which befell my parents, because the two of us were educated together in old Hildebrand's school of arms in Regium."

"Yes, and we loved one another like brothers," said the king.

"In the beginning I was shy, withdrawn and depressed by what had happened to my parents. But being near you and your sunny personality I began to cheer up again. And then, suddenly and in peacetime, ships of the emperor attacked Regium. There had been some quarrel between the emperor and our king over a border dispute in Sirmium, apparently. In any event, together with other prisoners they took us forty youths with them also, sharing us out among the various triremes. You alone escaped them, because the king had summoned you to his palace in Ravenna the day before, as his cup bearer.

"As soon as they heard about what had happened old Hildebrand and Count Uliaris set out after the Greeks with the Sicilian fleet, and caught up with them near Catana, where they captured their ships and released all the prisoners. Only one ship escaped the liberators, the fast trireme *Naus Petrou*, in which I lay in bonds together with two companions.

"The ship's commander was a man by the name of Lykos, and rather than take us to Byzantium he chose instead to sell us as slaves and pocket the sale price. He entered the harbour of the island of Paros, where he sold us to the merchant Dresos, who was not only his friend and host but also the wealthiest man on the island.

"And so Teias, the son of Count Tagila and a free Goth, became the slave of a Greek. I resolved to kill myself as soon as I had shed my chains and regained the use of my limbs. But then, as we were brought ashore in small boats, my eyes saw – oh my friend – I saw – I saw…" and he paused, placing his hand in front of his eyes.

"My Teias," said the king, placing his hand on his friend's shoulder.

"I saw the richly ornamented golden litter which stopped beside Dresos – and I saw a girl – unbelievably beautiful! Soon afterwards we were taken to the villa of Dresos, not far from the city. Dresos was a man who maltreated all his slaves with beatings, overwork and not enough food. Indeed he even mistreated his ward Myrtia, the lovely girl I had seen.

"I met with a somewhat better fate than the others. When Dresos learned from me that I was skilled in the art of forging weapons and also making jewellery – I had been practising these skills since boyhood – he started to treat me better. He built a workshop for me near the villa, and placed me in charge of the other slaves who worked there. He even had my chains removed by day, but at night I was chained to the anvil in the workshop together with two Gothic fellow slaves.

"I could have attempted to flee by day, but alas, I did not flee. Myrtia had cast some kind of spell over me! To see her, to speak to her was all I wanted in life, for she often came to the workshop to order some item of adornment or jewellery, to watch me work or just to hear me play the harp.

"And oh, ye eternal stars, what a time of bliss those days were! What had in the beginning been only pity with her gradually became love, love in the fullest, noblest sense. I could doubt it no longer, for she herself admitted it when I kissed her.

"I cannot describe her; her hair was golden, her eyes were golden and her heart was golden – and Teias too was happy for a time, and he believed in luck and happiness and in a god above the stars.

"And then, one evening, my loved one came to me, desperate and in tears, to talk to me in the workshop. Her guardian had given her in betrothal; he had virtually sold her to the same Lykos who had sold us into slavery. Pleas, tears, begging on her knees were all to no avail. Her marriage had been arranged for the day of her sixteenth birthday. That was only a few weeks away.

"For a long time I had dreamed of our fleeing together, and that plan now quickly matured in my mind. I had already made for myself a file to cut through our chains, and now I made a key to fit the workshop door as well. I took my fellow prisoners into my confidence, and they knew of my plan. We knew that we could not remain hidden on the small island, and that we would therefore have to flee across the sea.

"Close to the garden and the workshop there was a little bay to one side of the villa, and in it a small sailing ship belonging to Dresos lay at anchor. It was always there, and always ready for pleasure trips of various kinds. This was the ship we decided to use for our flight to Italy. We had managed to save some provisions from our daily food ration, and of course there was no shortage of weapons.

"The birthday fell on the *calends* of July, and the wedding had been arranged for that day. The plan was that I, the night before, would file through my chains and open the door. Once I freed my companions they would then hurry around the villa to the bay and the ship, whilst I would go silently to the other side of the villa, where the women's quarters were, and where Myrtia would be asleep. A small rope ladder would suffice to bring her down from her room into my arms; and I was then to hurry to the waiting ship with her. It had all been planned and prepared meticulously and with utmost care."

Chapter 34

Teias paused for a moment, and then went on: "But Lykos, the man I hated so intensely, arrived a full two weeks before the wedding day. The same man who had sold me as a slave now wanted to steal my beloved away from me.

"I hated him immensely, so much so that I could barely restrain myself from killing him on the spot, when he came up to my anvil with Dresos and some of the other wedding guests. Dresos had brought them to the workshop to show them my skill. But I controlled myself – for Myrtia's sake.

"But she complained to me that her hated bridegroom was becoming impatient, and that he was pressing with increasing fervour for the wedding to go ahead. In fact her guardian was only dissuaded with difficulty from giving her away there and then. Her freedom and her coming and going were being watched ever more closely.

"So we decided to flee earlier than we had originally planned. We chose the night of the summer solstice, because we knew that the men in the villa would be celebrating the festival that night, and a lot of wine would flow. We hoped that it would be easy for us to make our getaway once the revellers were overcome by drink and by sleep. As soon as the stars indicated that it was midnight I was to help Myrtia elope from the women's quarters.

"On the day of the solstice Lykos came to my workshop with Dresos and bought a precious golden necklace I had made. 'And do you know who it is for, slave?' he laughed. 'For my wife Myrtia. And let me tell you this, you Gothic dog: if you dare to look at her once more in the impertinent manner of a slave, the way you did yesterday when she came in here – you did not see me in the *taxus* bushes, but I saw you – then I will ask Dresos to give you to me. And then watch out!' And with that he struck me in the face with the shaft of his spear.

"I screamed and reached for my blacksmith's hammer, but my cousin Aligern, who was one of my fellow prisoners, caught my arm. Lykos left with a curse. Oh how I hated that proud helmet with the silver wolf on it, and the yellow cloak he always wore.

"At last the night came, and with it darkness. We could hear the wild carousing and noise of the feast coming from the villa, and we could see the lights shining from the house above us. Dresos, Lykos and the other guests would by now be quite drunk.

"It was not yet quite midnight. I had already freed my companions, and they had successfully reached the ship, and the cry of the wild swan sounded three times. That was the sign I had arranged with Aligern. I was just making my way out of the door to hurry to the women's quarters when I clearly heard the sound of the iron gate opening, which led from the villa into the garden. Now suspicious, I stopped in my tracks, and looked in the direction the sound had come from.

"Indeed there a man in armour was slowly feeling his way towards me through the *taxus* bushes, walking on his toes. It was Lykos! I could see the silver wolf quite clearly in the moonlight, above the closed visor of the helmet, and the yellow cloak as well. In his right hand he carried a spear.

"Carefully, looking right and left, he came closer, looked around to check if anyone was following him, and then made directly for the workshop, past where I was hiding in the shadows. There could be no doubt; he had become suspicious and decided to keep an eye on me overnight. Our plan to flee had evidently been uncovered. I leapt at him fiercely, and plunged my sword deep into his chest.

"I heard a cry – it was my name. It was not Lykos! With horror I opened the visor, and before me lay Myrtia, dying."

He was silent for a moment, and hid his head in his cloak.

"My poor, unhappy friend," said Totila, reaching for his friend's right hand.

But Julius said, so softly that neither of the others could hear: "Mine is the revenge, and I will punish! Thus sayeth the Lord."

Teias raised his head and continued: "I fell down beside her, unconscious, totally numbed. When I came around I could feel the fresh breath of sea air blowing about me. My friends, particularly Aligern, had become concerned about the length of time I was taking, and had returned to the workshop to look for me. There they had found us both.

"Before she died Myrtia told me briefly how Dresos and Lykos, both drunk, had suddenly decided right there in the middle of the feast that the wedding should take place that very night. Shortly before midnight the struggling girl had been fetched from the women's quarters and dragged to the villa and the wild drinking feast. The marriage was to be performed there and then; Dresos placed her trembling hand into that of Lykos. Only just enough time was to be allowed so that Lykos could change his clothes for the ceremony, which was to take place aboard his ship, and also so that he could send out orders for the bridal chamber to be prepared aboard.

"And so the newly married girl was left alone – for a moment. She decided to make use of that brief moment and hurried into the hall, where she had seen Lykos's cloak and helmet lying on a chair. Quickly she threw herself into this disguise, closed the visor and hid her women's clothes in the folds of the long cloak. Then she hurried past some of the drunken guests, without being recognised by them, and directly to me in my workshop. By now everyone in the women's chambers was fully awake, so she could not return there, and her idea was that we could flee from the workshop together. And her last breath had been a word of blessing for me.

"My friends had to restrain me, for I wanted to throw myself into the sea. I fell victim to a severe fever, and many days later I woke on board a Gothic warship. The ship was commanded by Duke Thulun, and it had picked us up near Crete.

"And then Aligern suddenly saw that we were being followed by Lykos's trireme. It had set out in pursuit of the fleeing slaves, and was just rounding the point off Kydonia. As soon as he saw the Gothic flag the Greek hoisted every sail he could to try and escape. But Duke Thulun and Aligern gave chase, caught the Greek, and then they boarded the trireme and slew Lykos, Dresos and the entire crew of thirty.

"And I, when I awoke, was the Teias I still am now. And I no longer believed in a god full of love and mercy, and now every word I hear about such nonsense sounds to me like a poor jest, as if the speaker was holding Myrtia up to ridicule. What crime had she committed? What had I done wrong? Why did God, if there is a God, allow such a dreadful thing to happen?"

Chapter 35

"And so, because this one rose perished, you now deny God, summer and sunshine?" Totila asked, "and instead you think that the world is ruled by blind chance?"

"No, I do not believe that. But I do see an eternal and inescapable inevitability in the movement of the stars above; and that same eternal law rules over the earth and the fates of men as well."

"But you say that this law makes no sense?" Julius asked.

"It does make sense, but it is not aimed at making us happy. It has only one single purpose, and that is to fulfil itself. And woe be to any fools who imagine that there is someone above the stars who counts their tears. Or perhaps they are lucky; their self-delusions make them think they are happy!"

"But your way of thinking," Julius replied, "does not make you happy either. I cannot see what your purpose is in living, with such an outlook."

"I will tell you what it is, Christian! It is to do what is right, to do my duty and what honour demands, without looking for rich rewards in some other world for every noble deed. It is to love my people and my fatherland and my friends, with a true and manly love, and to seal that love with blood. It is to tramp everything evil into the dust, wherever I find it, for a thing that is evil is no less ugly because it cannot be otherwise. One kills serpents and thistles too, even though it is no fault of theirs that they are not nightingale and rose. Finally my purpose in life is to do without all forms of happiness, but to seek only that deep peace which is as eternally serene and earnest as the sky, and on the way to that peace to allow my thoughts to travel up and down my path like bright stars. And then I listen to the pulse beat of the world's fate, which I can hear as clearly in my own breast as I see it in the stars. That too, Christian, is a very special kind of life, and one worth living for."

"But it is difficult," Totila sighed, "immeasurably difficult, and almost too difficult for mere human strength. No Teias, even if I cannot share with my pious friend here every facet of the faith which rules our world at this moment, yet there is one truth to which I must cling and which I cannot do without: there is a kind and loving God, who protects what is good and punishes what is evil. And it is into the hands of just this God that I place my own fate and the fate of my people too, for our cause is a just one. And it is in this belief that I confidently look forward to victory tomorrow. Right and justice are on my side; they cannot lose."

"Justice is often defeated by injustice. Witigis was defeated by Cethegus!"

"Yes, on earth," Julius interjected. "But our home is not here. There is a next life, where all wrongs are wiped out, and where only the good and just will triumph."

"That belief is a pleasant compensation," Teias said as he rose, a look of bitterness on his face. "Only one cannot imagine such a next world, only dream about it. As for me I have enough. I have no wish to wake up in some other world when one day a spear does finally pierce my heart."

At that moment Count Thorismuth entered, just back from a reconnaissance ride: "Put your mind at ease, Sir King, I have just checked again myself. The Corsican's cavalry stands ready in the right place, and the first of his reinforcements, which were lagging behind, have also already arrived. But he still expects three hundred more of the bravest, and he asks that you delay the attack of the Lombards tomorrow until he has had their arrival reported to you. 'They are the fiercest of them all, and I don't want to be without them!' is what Furius said."

"Very well then," Totila called out cheerfully, raising his golden goblet. "I think we can manage to do that with a little horsemanship. And now, let's have a last drink and then go to our beds. Teias, let the battle of Taginae tomorrow resolve our debate. Let it be a true judgment of God! Let God himself tell us if he lives or not! I say that there is a God, and that is why our good and just cause must be victorious tomorrow."

"Stop!" Julius exclaimed. "You must not put God on trial!"

"You see," Teias said as he stood up and threw his shield on his back, "he is afraid for his God."

Chapter 36

On the following morning the sun rose majestically into the sky, and its very first rays already found the Gothic camp a hive of activity.

As the king stepped from his house into the marketplace of Taginae he was met by Duke Adalgoth, Count Thorismuth and Phaza the Armenian, the faithful former prisoner from Naples.

"Hail King, and victory! Here, your bride sends you your milk white warhorse and your weapons, richly decorated for victory."

And the king placed his shining helmet, which had no visor, on his golden hair. On the helmet there was a tall silver swan, around which Valeria had wound red roses. And then Totila patted the chest of his horse Hveit-fulas; it too had mane and tail decorated with flowers and ribbons.

He swung himself into the saddle, and as he did so his weapons rang. An attendant was leading two spare horses for the king as well, one of them being Pluto, the Prefect's black stallion.

Totila's cloak flowed from his shoulders, held under his throat by a heavy golden clasp. His armour was made of shining silver, richly inlaid with gold, depicting a flying swan. The edges of his armour were lined with purple silk around his arms, his neck and his belt. His arms and legs were covered by a white silk battledress, which also covered his hips. His arms were protected by broad rings and battle gloves, and his legs by leg armour. His narrow, delicately shaped shield was decorated in silver, gold and purple, again depicting a flying swan, and the horse's harness was also richly adorned. In his right hand Totila swung his spear; Valeria had affixed four long pennants to its point, and they now fluttered in the morning breeze.

Thus adorned, shining and glittering, the king rode through the streets of Taginae at the head of his cavalry. Count Thorismuth, Phaza the Armenian, Duke Adalgoth and Julius were also among his followers. Julius carried no offensive weapons, but he was using the shield Teias had presented to the king in order to protect himself.

Never had Totila looked so magnificent. And during his ride all the people everywhere he went greeted him with loud cheering and great enthusiasm. At the northern gate Aligern came riding towards him.

"You were to fight on the right wing. What brings you to me?" the king asked.

"My cousin Teias has commanded me to stay near you and to guard your life."

"How typical! He never ceases to concern himself with my safety. What a wonderful, loyal friend!" the king cried as Aligern joined the rest of the king's followers.

Count Thorismuth now assumed command of the archers and spear bearers hidden in the houses.

From the northern gate of Taginae King Totila rode along the line of his small force of mounted Goths, and he now revealed his plan to the leaders of the cavalry. "Today I will demand the utmost from you, brothers in arms. I will ask you to flee.

But your flight will only be a deception. In truth it will serve to show your courage, and it will help to destroy our enemy."

And now the small detachment rode along the Via Flaminia and past the site of the ambush between the two hills. The king convinced himself that the Corsican's Persian cavalry were ready and waiting in the trees on either side of the road. On the right side they were led by Furius himself, and on the left by their chieftain Isdigerd.

The king then rode on and entered Caprae by the southern gate. Here Totila again instructed the archers positioned in the town, who were commanded by Wisand the *bandalarius*, that they were to wait until the Persian cavalry charged down on the Lombards. Then, and not before, they were to come out of the houses where they had been hiding, to break out of the southern gate and attack Alboin from the rear. At the same time the spear-bearing infantry would charge at the Lombards from the northern gate of Taginae.

"In this way the Lombards, together with any of Narses's infantry that follows them, will be trapped on all four sides at once. And then they will be crushed, by Thorismuth and myself from the front, by Furius and Isdigerd from the flanks, and by Wisand in the rear. They are doomed!"

"Doesn't he look just like the sun god?" Adalgoth asked the monk, delighted.

"Quiet! You must not worship graven images, nor people, and not the sun either! And today is the day of the solstice!" Julius replied.

By now the king had reached the northern gate of Caprae. He had the gate opened, and then he charged with his small force across the wide, open field outside Caprae towards Helvillium.

Here was where Narses was positioned with his main force, directly opposite. Alboin and his cavalry stood in the front line. Behind them, some distance away, were Narses in his litter, surrounded by Cethegus, Liberius, Anzalas and other leaders.

Narses had suffered a bad night with an attack of mild convulsions. He was weak and unable to stand for long in his open litter, which had been set on the ground. He had again expressly warned Alboin not to attack unless he was clearly and specifically ordered to do so.

King Totila now gave his men the signal, and the thin line of Gothic cavalry advanced at a trot against the vastly superior Lombards. "Surely they will not insult us by attacking with that handful of lances!" Alboin exclaimed.

But attack did not seem to be the king's immediate aim at all.

He had advanced well beyond the line of his own men, who had suddenly stopped, and he now drew all eyes to himself with a superb display of horsemanship and fencing skill. The spectacle which he thus provided was so strange that the amazed eyewitnesses reported every detail to Procopius. The latter, astounded in his turn, tells us about it. "On this day," he wrote, "King Totila wanted to show his enemies the kind of man he was. His horse, his arms and his person glittered with gold. There were so many purple pennants flying from the tip of his spear that they alone announced the king's coming from afar. And so he put on a splendid display on his magnificent white horse, right there between the two opposing lines. He would ride around in circles or delicate semicircles, throw the richly decorated spear high over his head in full gallop and then catch it again by the middle of the shaft, before it could fall to the ground, performing this feat with equal skill with either hand. Thus he demonstrated his amazing skill to both armies." After the battle the Byzantines were also to learn the purpose of it all, which was to gain time until the last detachments of the Corsican's cavalry arrived at their positions.

For a time Alboin watched as all this went on. Then he called out aloud to one of his Lombard leaders, who was astride his horse by his side: "He rides into battle as if he was going to his wedding. What magnificent armour! We don't see armour like that back at home, cousin Gisulf! And still we have not been given the signal to attack! Is Narses asleep again?"

Chapter 37

At long last a mounted Persian galloped through the Gothic lines to the king. He was carrying a message, and once he had delivered it he raced straight back to where he had come from.

"At long last!" Totila cried, "now that's enough of play! Brave Alboin, son of Audoin," he called out to the enemy. "So you really want to fight against us, on the side of the Greeks? Very well then, son of a king; a king challenges you to a fight!"

When he heard that Alboin could restrain himself no longer; "He just has to be mine, he and his armour and his horse," he cried, and with his lance couched he charged furiously at the king.

With just the lightest pressure from his thighs Totila brought his dancing mount to a standstill; it seemed that he intended to stand still and await the clash. Already Alboin was upon him, but another slight pressure from Totila's thigh and the horse leapt slightly to one side; and the Lombard flew past the king without touching him. But in the next instant Totila was hard on his heels, and he could have run his spear through Alboin without any difficulty.

The Lombards, seeing this, cried out aloud and hurried to the aid of their leader.

But Totila swung the lance in his hand, and contented himself with striking his opponent so hard with the blunt end of the shaft, into Alboin's left side, that the latter flew out of the saddle and fell to the ground. After that Totila calmly rode back to his own lines, swinging his lance above his head.

Meanwhile Alboin had remounted his horse, and he now led his men in a charge against the much weaker Gothic line.

But even before the clash occurred Totila called out to his men: "Flee! Flee into the city!" and with that he turned his mount and raced away in the direction of Caprae. Speedily his men followed him.

For a moment Alboin hesitated, dumbfounded. But the next moment he cried: "There cannot be any mistake! That's a case of full flight if ever I saw one! Look, they are already racing through the gate. Yes, display of horsemanship is one thing, and real fighting another. After them, my wolves, into the city!"

And so they raced after the Goths towards Caprae, tore open the gate which the fleeing Goths had only shut but not locked, and raced along the main street to the southern gate, through which the last of the Goths were just vanishing from view.

Narses had until now managed to stand in his litter, and he had watched everything that had occurred. "Stop!" he now cried out aloud, "Stop! Sound the tubas to retreat! Call them back! That's the clumsiest trap in the world! And yet that Alboin thinks that every time somebody runs away from him they are serious."

But the trumpeters blew in vain. The sound of the tubas was drowned out by the victory cries of the Lombards, or else those Lombards who did hear ignored the signal.

With a groan Narses watched as the last of his Lombards disappeared into the gates of Caprae. "Alas," he sighed, "so I am forced to commit a foolishness with my eyes wide open. I cannot let them perish because of their own stupidity, as they deserve! I still need them. In the name of madness then, advance! By the time we catch up with them they could be half torn to pieces. Forward Cethegus, Anzalas and Liberius, with your Isaurians, Illyrians and Armenians! Into Caprae! But remember, the city cannot be empty! It is a trap, into which we are following these Lombard oxen with our eyes wide open. My litter will follow you. But I cannot stand any longer." Tiredly he leaned back, and a slight trembling, such as sometimes overcame him when he was gripped by tension, shook him somewhat.

The infantry, under Cethegus and Liberius, now advanced against Caprae at a running pace, with both leaders riding ahead.

Meanwhile fleeing Goths and their pursuers had passed through the little city. The last of the Lombards had made their way through Caprae, and their vanguard with Alboin among them had reached the spot on the Via Flaminia, halfway towards Taginae, where the road was flanked by two wooded hills on either side.

For one more horse's length the king fled, then he halted, turned and waved. Adalgoth by his side blew into the horn, and in the next instant Count Thorismuth was breaking out of the northern gate of Taginae with his lancers; at the same time the Corsican's Persian cavalry charged down from both sides of the road, in double ambush, to the loud sound of cornets and trumpets.

"Now turn, my Goths! Forward to the attack! Now woe to our deceived enemies!"

Perplexed, Alboin looked about him in all directions. "Never before have we ridden into an evil hole like this, my wolves!" he cried. He wanted to turn back but there, out of Caprae's southern gate, Gothic infantry was now also moving into the attack.

"Now all that is left for us is to die cheerfully, Gisulf. Greet Rosamunda for me if you happen to get out of this alive." And with that he turned against one of the Persian cavalry leaders, wearing a richly decorated open golden helmet, who had by now reached the road and was charging down on him.

Already they were very close and their clash was imminent. Suddenly the one with the golden helmet cried: "Turn, Lombard! Those are our common enemies, over there! Down with the Goths!" And in the next instant he ran a Gothic rider, who was threatening Alboin, through with his spear.

Almost immediately after this the Persian cavalry, racing past the Lombards on both sides, started to strike at the shocked Goths.

For a moment the Goths stood their ground, taken completely by surprise. But when they saw that it was no misunderstanding, and that the ambush was aimed at them rather than the Lombards, they cried aloud: "Treason! We have been betrayed! All is lost!" and they raced back toward Taginae in full flight, real this time, tearing down everything that barred their way and even mowing down their own infantry as they swept past.

The king's face lost its colour too as he saw the Corsican slashing away at the Goths by Alboin's side.

"Yes, this is treachery!" he cried. "Ah, the tiger! Down with him!" And he spurred his horse to charge at Furius. But before he could get to him Isdigerd, the Persian chieftain, had come down from the left side and stormed out onto the road between the Corsican and the king.

"Get the king!" he called out to his men. "Aim every spear at the king! That's him over there, the white one, with the swan on his helmet! Everybody after him!"

A thick hail of spears flew through the air, and the next moment the king's shield had more than a dozen missiles sticking in it. And then the Corsican also recognised the tall, shining figure of the king from afar. "It is he! His heart's blood is mine! I want him!" And he cleared a path for himself through Isdigerd and his Persians. Soon only a few horse lengths separated the two bitter foes, but before they could clash Totila met with Isdigerd. An instant later the Persian fell dead from his horse, his throat and neck pierced by the king.

Another instant, and Furius and Totila had to clash. Already the Corsican raised his spear to take aim; he was aiming at the open face of the king, unprotected by a visor.

But suddenly the white cloak and the swan helmet disappeared from view. Two spears had struck down the king's white horse, and at the same time a third spear had penetrated his shield and severely injured his shield arm. Both horse and rider fell.

The Persians rejoiced wildly and closed in; Furius and Alboin spurred their horses.

"Spare the king's life! Take him prisoner! He spared my life too!" Alboin cried. It had touched him deeply when Gisulf told him how he had clearly seen Totila exchange the point of his spear for the shaft end.

"Down! Down with the king!" Furius cried.

And already the Corsican was upon the wounded king and hurled a spear at him, just as Aligern was trying to lift him onto the Prefect's horse to lead him out of the fray. That first spear thrown by Furius was parried by Julius, who was using the fine shield Teias had made. Furius called for a second spear, and aimed at the turmoil around the king. Phaza, the Armenian, tried to parry it with his shield, but it was hurled with such force that it penetrated Phaza's shield and armour and pierced his heart.

By now Furius had managed to work his horse very close to the king, and he swung his long, curved sword at him. But before he could strike the blow the Corsican flew backwards out of the saddle. The young Duke of Apulia had struck him in the chest with his flagstaff so hard that the shaft broke.

But now Totila's banner, the skilfully made and precious work of love which Valeria and her helpers had made, was in utmost danger in young Adalgoth's hand. All the Persians now closed in on the courageous young flag bearer; the Lombard Gisulf struck at the shaft with his axe, so that it broke again. With quick determination Adalgoth tore the cloth from the broken flagstaff and tied it firmly around his waist.

And now Alboin was on the scene and called out to the king: "Give yourself prisoner, King of the Goths! Surrender to me, also the son of a king!"

By this time Aligern had completed the task of lifting the king onto the Prefect's horse, and turned to face the Lombard. The latter wanted to prevent the king's flight, but without killing the king. He therefore bent far forward and aimed his spear at the black horse, wounding it in the hindquarter. But at the same time Aligern cut through his helmet with his sword, and a stunned Alboin swayed in the saddle.

Having thus held up the leaders of the pursuit for the moment Adalgoth, Aligern and Julius had gained sufficient time to safely lead the king out of the fight to the northern gate of Taginae.

Here Count Thorismuth had been able to restore order among his lancers. The king tried to lead the fighting himself once he reached the gate, but he was barely able to sit in the saddle.

"Thorismuth," the king commanded, "you will hold Taginae; Caprae will be lost for the time being. A speedy messenger will bring Hildebrand and his entire wing here, because the road to Rome must be held at all costs. Teias and his wing, I hear, are already engaged in the battle. Cover our retreat to the south, that is our last hope!" And with that he lost consciousness.

Count Thorismuth replied: "I will hold Taginae with my lancers to the last man. No cavalry will get in there, be they Lombard or Persian. As long as I can still raise one hand I will cover the king's life and the rear. Take him further back, to the hills there, to the monastery, but quickly! I can already see the decision coming from the gates of Caprae over there! The infantry of Narses, and look there: Cethegus the Prefect with the Isaurians. Caprae and our archers are doomed." And so it was.

Wisand, following orders, had not defended Caprae, and instead of that he had allowed Cethegus and Liberius to enter. The street fighting did not start until they were in the city, and at the same time he threatened the Lombard cavalry by sending a thousand men against them out of the southern gate.

But as the Persian attack from the ambush had been aimed at the Goths instead of the Lombards, the latter together with Furius and the Persians now annihilated the handful of mounted Goths. In addition the attack by the lancers from Taginae did not now take place. The Gothic archers were therefore quickly crushed by the vastly superior foe, on the Via Flaminia between Caprae and Taginae as well as in Caprae itself.

Wisand himself, although wounded, somehow escaped to Taginae as if by a miracle, and there he reported the destruction of his men. Narses was carried into Caprae in his litter, and the storm on Taginae by the Illyrians commenced. Count Thorismuth offered heroic resistance, fighting to cover the Goths' last avenue of retreat.

Shortly afterwards he was reinforced by Hildebrand's forces, hurriedly drawn from the wing, while the major part of his own force was led by the old armourer around Taginae to the south, and from there onto the road to Rome.

Just as the storm on Taginae was to commence, Cethegus met up with Furius and Alboin, who had just recovered from their respective blows. Cethegus had heard about the Corsican's decisive intervention, and shook his hand: "There, friend Furius, on the right side at last, against the Barbarians!"

"Their king must not escape alive!" the Corsican hissed.

"What? He is alive? I heard that he had fallen?" Cethegus asked.

"No, he was wounded, but they managed to get him out."

"He must not live!" Cethegus cried. "You are right! That's more important than taking Taginae; Narses can perform that heroic feat from his litter. They are ten against one. Come, Furius, what are your Persians doing here idle?"

"Horses cannot climb walls."

"No, but they can swim. Come, you take three hundred and I will take three hundred. There are two ways around the city, on either side. No, they have destroyed the bridges. We will pursue them across the Classis and the Sibola. Surely the wounded king – can he still fight?"

"I doubt it."

"Then he has fled via Taginae, to Rome or…"

"No, to his bride!" Furius cried. "Of course, he has been taken to Valeria in the cloister. Ha, I will kill him in her arms! Come Persians, follow me. Thank you, Prefect! Take as many men as you want. You ride to the right, and I'll go around the left side, as there are two ways to get to the cloister." And with that he vanished from sight, turning to the left.

Cethegus spoke to the remaining Persians in their own language and ordered them to follow him. He then rode over to Liberius and said: "I will catch the Gothic king!"

"What? He is still alive? Then hurry!"

"Meanwhile you take Taginae," Cethegus went on: "I will leave you my Isaurians." And he rode away, with Syphax and three hundred Persians.

Meanwhile the king had been brought through Taginae into a small thicket, where he drank from a spring and recovered somewhat. "Julius," he said, "ride up to Valeria and tell her that the battle is lost, but not the Empire and not I, and therefore not hope. As soon as I feel stronger I will ride up to the Spes Bonorum, where I have ordered Teias and Hildebrand after they have done their part. Go, I beg of you. Console Valeria for me, and take her there also from the cloister. You don't want to go? Then I will go myself, up the steep slope to the cloister. Won't you do that for me?"

Julius did not like parting from his wounded friend.

"Oh, take off my helmet and my cloak, they are so heavy," Totila asked, and Julius removed both for him.

Chapter 38

And then an idea flashed through the monk's mind; had they not switched clothes before, the two *dioscuri*? And had he not once before, by doing this, deflected the deadly steel from Totila to himself? Now it all came to him with lightning speed: what if they were pursued? He thought he could hear horses approaching. Aligern – Adalgoth was holding the king's head in his lap – had gone to the edge of the little wood to investigate. "Yes, they are coming," he called out as he returned. "Persian cavalry is closing in on this spot from two sides."

"Then hurry, Julius," Totila begged, "save Valeria for me. Take her to the strong tomb, to safety, to Teias."

"I am on my way, my friend! Until we meet again!" With that he shook his friend's hand once more and mounted the black stallion Pluto, leaving his own and as yet uninjured horse for Totila. Without being noticed by Totila he quickly placed the swan helmet on his head, draped the white, blood-spattered cloak around his shoulders and galloped from the wood toward the hill with the cloister on it. "This way," he said to himself, "is quite open and without any cover whatever, whereas the path the king will take to the tomb leads through many trees and vineyards. I may just succeed in diverting the pursuers from Totila and draw them to myself."

And indeed, no sooner had he ridden out into the open and started his climb uphill, than he saw the mounted Persians start to follow him eagerly as they came around Taginae. In order to divert attention from the king for as long as possible, and to delay their recognising the deception, he spurred his mount to utmost speed. But the black stallion was wounded, and the slope was rocky and very steep. The pursuers drew closer and closer.

"Is that the king?"

"Yes, that's him!"

"No, it is not the king, he is too short," said the leader, riding in the first line. "And would he flee alone?"

"That would be his wisest move if he wants to get away," another man replied.

"Of course it's him, the swan helmet!"

"And the white cloak!"

"But he was riding a white horse, wasn't he?" the leader asked.

"Yes, at first," one of the others replied. "But it fell by my spear. I saw them lift him onto that black stallion – I was very close at the time."

"Good," the leader cried, "in that case you are certainly right. And I know that black stallion."

"What a great animal! How it is holding out, uphill, even though it is bleeding."

"Yes, it is a noble animal! And he will stop, that black stallion; watch this: Halt, Pluto! On your knees!" And the intelligent, faithful animal stopped, snorting and trembling, and in spite of spur and blow on its hindquarter. Slowly it lowered its front legs into the sand.

"It is not healthy for Barbarians, Totila, to ride the Prefect's horse! There! Take that for the Forum, and that for the Capitol, and that for Julius!"

And with great strength the leader threw three spears, one after the other, his own and two more which he took from Syphax behind him. They were aimed at the fleeing man's back with such force that they pierced him entirely, their points emerging through his chest. Then Cethegus leapt from his horse, drew his sword and tore the fallen man's head up toward him by the helmet.

"Julius!" he cried in horror.

"You, Cethegus?"

"Julius! You must not die." Passionately he tried to stem the flow of blood from the three wounds.

"If you love me," said the dying man, "then save him! Save Totila!" And his gentle eyes closed for ever.

Cethegus felt for his heart; he laid his ear on the man's bare chest.

"It is over," he said in a toneless voice. "Oh Manilia! Julius, oh Julius, you I did love! And he died, with the Barbarian's name on his lips! It is over," he added fiercely. "The last bond between me and human love, and of all people it had to be me that severed it by a ridiculous coincidence. It is almost a mockery, but also the end of my last weakness. Now, humanity, as far as I am concerned you are dead. Lift him up onto my noble horse; Pluto, that can be your last service in life. Take him – there is a chapel up there. Take him there and have him buried properly by priests. Tell them only that he died as a monk, that he died for his friend, and that he deserves a Christian burial. But I," he concluded with a terrible threat in his voice, "I will go and look for his friend once more! I want to unite them quickly, and for ever." And with that he mounted his horse again.

"Where to?" Syphax asked. "Back to Taginae?"

"No, down into that little forest there. That's where he will be hidden, because that's where Julius came from."

★

While these events were taking place the king had recovered somewhat, and he was now riding with Adalgoth, Aligern and a few mounted Goths straight through the forest, along the eastern edge of which the path led to the chapel. Already they could clearly see the walls through the trees.

But then there was a sudden shouting from the south, from their right, and in a moment a strong detachment of cavalry was charging across the open field from the Classis River, straight at them.

The king recognised their leader. And before his companions could restrain him he had spurred his horse, felled his spear, and was charging at his enemy in full gallop. The two riders clashed like bolts of lightning from two opposing thunderstorms.

"Arrogant Barbarian!"

"Miserable traitor!"

And both fell from their horses. They had clashed with such force that neither of them had thought about protecting himself, seeking only to strike at the other.

Furius Ahalla had fallen dead from his horse. The king had thrust his spear at him with such force that it pierced his golden shield and armour, and then broke in half as it went through his heart.

But the king also collapsed dying into the arms of Adalgoth. The Corsican's lance had torn into his throat and chest just below his chin.

Adalgoth tore Valeria's blue banner from his belt and tried to stem the flow of blood, but it was in vain. In moments the bright blue was soaked with blood.

"Gotia! Italia! Valeria!" were his last words.

At this moment, before the uneven struggle could begin, Alboin reached this spot with his Lombards. He had followed the Corsican, reluctant to remain idle while the battle raged around Taginae.

Silently and reverently, the deeply moved Lombard leader looked down on the body of the king. "He spared my life – but I came too late to save his," he said earnestly.

One of his men pointed to the dead king's valuable armour.

"No," said Alboin. "This royal hero must be buried with full royal honours, and in his full armour."

"Up there, on the rocky hill there, Alboin," Adalgoth said sadly, "his bride and his grave, which he himself chose, have been waiting for him."

"Take him up there. I will grant free passage to the noble body and its worthy bearers. You, Lombards, will follow me back into the battle."

Chapter 39

But the battle was over, as both Alboin and the Prefect were to find out to their surprise and disappointment when they arrived back at Taginae.

As the Prefect was just entering the pine forest from the north in order to follow the king's tracks, a messenger from Liberius approached him in utmost haste, conveying to him an order to return at once. Narses was unconscious, and there was extreme danger demanding an immediate decision.

Narses unconscious, Liberius at a loss, the victory which had already seemed certain now in doubt – in the end these considerations weighed more heavily on Cethegus than the prospect of dealing the king a final blow, which in any case was doubtful. Cethegus therefore raced back along the way he had come at top speed.

As he arrived Liberius called out to him: "Too late; I have already decided and made all the necessary arrangements. A truce has been concluded. The remaining Goths will withdraw."

"What?" Cethegus thundered. He would have liked to shed every last drop of Gothic blood on his favourite's grave as a sacrifice. "Withdraw? Truce? Where is Narses?"

"Unconscious in his litter, suffering severe seizures. The shock, the surprise, they overcame him, which is hardly surprising."

"What surprise? Speak, man!"

Briefly Liberius explained how they had finally entered Taginae under terrible bloodshed, "for those Goths stood with their spears like walls of stone." Every house and every room had to be wrested from the defenders one by one in bitter street fighting. "There was one leader, who jumped into a breach in the wall after running his spear through Anzalas, whom we had to literally hack to pieces inch by inch before we were finally able to enter the city over his body."

"What was his name?" Cethegus asked eagerly. "Count Teias, I hope?"

"No, Count Thorismuth. When we were half finished with the bloody work and Narses was about to have himself carried into the city, a messenger from our left wing reached us – our left wing no longer exists by the way – it was the wounded Zeuxippos, accompanied by Gothic heralds."

"Who did…?"

"Oh, the one you mentioned before, Count Teias. He saw, or was told, that his own centre was severely threatened and that the king was wounded. He evidently realised that he would be too late to affect the outcome in the centre, and so he made a courageous and desperate decision. Suddenly he threw himself from his waiting position in the mountains onto our left wing, which was slowly moving uphill opposite him. He defeated our left wing at his first onslaught, pursued the fleeing troops into the camp, and there took ten thousand of our men prisoner, among them my Orestes, Zeuxippos and all their leaders. He sent Zeuxippos with Gothic heralds to report what happened, and demanded an immediate truce for twenty-four hours."

"Impossible!" Cethegus exclaimed.

"Otherwise he had sworn that he would kill all ten thousand prisoners, including their commanders!"

"So what?" was the Prefect's comment.

"It may not matter to you, Roman. What does a myriad of the emperor's troops matter to you? But Narses thinks otherwise. The awful surprise, and the terrible decision he had to make, shook him to the core. A severe attack of his illness overcame him, and as he fell he handed me his baton. I accepted the truce."

"Of course! Pylades had to save his Orestes," Cethegus retorted angrily.

"And ten thousand men of the Imperial army."

"Your agreement is not binding on me," Cethegus cried, "I am going to attack again."

"You must not do that! Teias took most of the prisoners and all the commanders with him as hostages. He will slaughter them if another arrow is fired."

"Let him slaughter them. I will attack."

"Try it and see if the Byzantines will follow you. I immediately conveyed the command from Narses to your troops. As far as you are concerned I am Narses for now."

"You are a dead man as soon as Narses regains his senses."

But Cethegus saw that he alone, with his handful of mercenaries, could do little harm to the Goths. The latter had by now managed to regroup in strong positions, after both Teias with his hostages and Hildebrand had gained the Via Flaminia near the hill with the cloister and the chapel, with considerable sacrifices. Pursuit by John had been hindered both by the two rivers and the truce. Cethegus now eagerly waited for Narses to regain his senses, hoping that he might not recognise the truce agreed to in his name.

Chapter 40

Meanwhile Teias and Hildebrand had both been able to gain the hill of Numa, with the chapel on it, where they had been advised the wounded king had been taken. News of subsequent events had not yet reached them.

Just before reaching the walls of the chapel the two leaders had agreed on a plan, which they proposed to put to the king. In their opinion there was no other alternative but a speedy withdrawal to the south, under the protection of the truce.

But what a sight confronted them as they entered the little walled courtyard. Sobbing loudly, Adalgoth rushed towards Teias, and led him by the hand to the ivy-covered sarcophagus of Numa.

Inside the sarcophagus King Totila lay on his shield. The solemn majesty of death lent his features a dignity which was even more beautiful than any which happiness and joy had ever lent to this splendid face while he lived.

To his left, resting on the separate long lid of the sarcophagus, lay Julius. The resemblance between the two *dioscuri* had become even more startling in death.

And in the middle, between the king and his friend, a third figure had been laid out by Liuta and Gotho on the king's blood-spattered cloak. There, on a small mound, with her noble head resting on the edge of the cistern, lay Valeria.

After being summoned from the nearby cloister to receive her wounded betrothed, she had thrown herself across the broad shield without a cry or complaint, as Adalgoth and Aligern carried it through the gate at a slow and solemn pace.

Before either of them had spoken she cried: "I know it, he is dead." And then she had helped to lay out the handsome corpse to rest in the sarcophagus. Whilst doing so she had said to herself in a soft voice, without shedding a tear:

"Do you not see how handsome, how shining is Achilles?
And yet death and dark fate await him.
When his life escapes from him in the turmoil of battle,
whether it be by an arrow or by a spear,
may it be granted that I enter the shadow of death with him."

And then, slowly and without haste, she had drawn his golden dagger from his belt, and with the words: "Here, relentless Christian God, take my soul! Thus I fulfil the promise made!" the Roman girl plunged the sharp steel deep into her heart.

Cassiodorus, deeply shaken and with a little cedar cross in his hand, was walking about deep in prayer; tears were running down his dignified old face and into his white beard. He kept walking to and fro, from one body to the other.

And gently the nuns from the cloister, who had accompanied Valeria, now started to sing:

"*Vis ac splendor seculorum, belli laus et flos amorum labefacta mox marcescunt.*
Dei laus et gratia sine aevi termino vel fine, in eternum perflorescunt."
(Soon into ashes must vanish that which we now see, strong and lovely,

all the pride and beauty of a time. Without fail God's mercy,
and without bounds God's love, will go on into eternity.)

Gradually the courtyard had filled with warriors, as had the little forest around it.
Their leaders, including Counts Wisand and Markja, had been able to follow their men
unhindered because of the truce.

Silently Teias had received the weeping Adalgoth's report. Now he stepped close to
the dead king.

Without a word or a tear, he laid his armoured right hand on the king's wound,
bent over him and whispered in his ear: "I shall complete what has to be done."

Then he stepped back under a tall tree, which rose above some long forgotten
grave, and he addressed the small group of men around him. They stood there in
silence and respect, gripped by what fate had dealt out to them.

"Gothic men: the battle is lost, and the Empire is also lost. If any among you want
to go to Narses and surrender to the emperor, I will not stop you. I will hold no one.
But I am willing to fight on to the end, not for victory but for the free death of a hero.
Any of you who wish to share that fate with me may remain. You all want to stay?
Good."

Then Hildebrand spoke: "The king has fallen. The Goths cannot fight without a
king, not even if it is only to die with honour. Athalaric – Witigis – Totila – there is
only one man fit to be the fourth after that great trio, and that is you, Teias, our last
and our greatest hero."

"Yes," Teias replied solemnly, "I will be your king. You will not live happily under
me, but you will die magnificently under my reign. Silence! I want no rejoicing, and
no clashing of arms to greet me. Let him who wants me for his king follow my
example."

With that he broke a small branch from the tree under which he was standing, and
wound it around his helmet. Silently they all followed his example.

Adalgoth, who was standing next to him, whispered: "Oh King Teias! They are
cypress branches – that is how beasts of sacrifice are adorned, after they are dedicated!"

"Yes my Adalgoth, it is a prophesy you speak!" and he swung his sword in a circle
over his head, "they, like us, are dedicated to die."

BOOK NINE

Teias

*"I must now describe the most memorable of battles,
and the great heroism of the man who is second to none
of the great heroes of history – that of Teias."*

Procopius, *Gothic Wars IV*, 35

Chapter 1

And now the fate of the Gothic Empire moved rapidly to its conclusion. The rolling stone was approaching the abyss.

When Narses had regained consciousness and learned of the events which had occurred, he immediately gave orders that Liberius be arrested and sent to Byzantium to give an account of his actions.

"I am not saying," he said to a confidant, Basiliskos, "that he made the wrong decision. I myself would have done exactly as he did, but there are other reasons. His first concern was to save his friend, and then the ten thousand men. That was a mistake! Given the decision that faced Liberius, as Liberius, those ten thousand had to be sacrificed because he did not see the total situation of this war. Liberius did not know, as Narses knows, that after this battle the Gothic Empire is doomed. Whether it is finally annihilated here at Taginae or later near Naples is not important. That is the only reason why one could, and in fact had to, save those ten thousand men."

"Near Naples? But why not near Rome? Don't you remember those terrible walls and defences which the Prefect created? Why would the Goths not retreat into Rome, where they could offer long months of resistance?"

"Why? Because... because there is something special about Rome. That is something of which the Goths know no more than Liberius does. But it is also something which must not become known, least of all to Cethegus. So keep it to yourself. Where is the City Prefect of Rome?"

"He hurried ahead, so as to lead the pursuit as soon as the truce expires."

"But you saw to it that..."

"Have no fear! He wanted to leave with his Isaurians only, but I, or rather Liberius on my advice, also gave him Alboin and his Lombards. As you know..."

"Yes," Narses smiled, "my wolves will not let him out of their sight."

"But how much longer is he to...?"

"For as long as I need him, and not an hour longer. So the young royal miracle worker lies on his shield? Now Justinian may call himself 'Gothicus' with good reason, and sleep peacefully once more at night. But of course I doubt that Theodora's disappointed widower will ever sleep peacefully again."

So it seemed that the two leaders, Teias and Narses, had formed the same opinion regarding the fate of the Gothic Empire. It was indeed doomed.

At Caprae and Taginae the flower of the Gothic infantry had fallen. Totila had put twenty-five thousand men into the field there, and less than one thousand of them were saved. The two wings had also suffered losses, so that there were now barely twenty thousand men left for King Teias to lead hastily to the south, along the Via Flaminia.

He was also driven to haste by the appeals for help from the small army of Duke Guntharis and Count Grippa, which was under heavy pressure from the Byzantines. A force outnumbering the Goths by more than two to one, led by Armatus and

Dorotheos, had landed between Rome and Naples, and now posed a real and urgent threat.

Finally he was driven to utmost speed by the pursuit which Narses had put into effect the moment the truce had expired. That pursuit was being conducted true to his system of the "moving wall". While Cethegus and the Lombards set out in relentless pursuit, slowly followed by Narses, the latter spread two terrible wings to the left and right, reaching from the sea in the southwest beyond Tuscany to the Ionic Sea in the northeast past Picenum. As these two wings moved through Italy, from north to south and west to east, they crushed and wiped out all traces of Gothic life in their path.

This process was made very much easier by the fact that the Italians were now deserting the lost Gothic cause in their thousands and tens of thousands. The benevolent king who had once won them over had now been replaced by a dark warrior whose very name was feared. Those who hesitated were soon won over, not out of a desire to be ruled by Byzantium, but from fear of Narses and later reprisals. Every Italian who still sided with the Goths at this stage of the war was faced with the threat of death, and those few still left in King Teias's army now left and joined Narses instead.

Instances where Goths were betrayed by their Italian neighbours now became more frequent than had been the case even before the battle of Taginae. This was especially true in areas where the Goths were greatly outnumbered by the local Italian population, or where the *hospes*, who had been forced to cede one third of their estates to the Goths, now seized on this opportunity to get even. In some cases, where the Italians outnumbered the Goths by a large margin, they would take them prisoner by themselves and then deliver them to Narses, whose two fleets were slowly moving along both the western and eastern coasts. They were following the progress of the land armies and taking all captured Goths with them, men, women and children.

The cities and fortresses, weakly manned because King Totila had strengthened his small army by drawing heavily on their small garrisons, mostly fell to their native populations. In city after city the native Italians overpowered the few Gothic troops, just as they had done to Imperial forces when Totila had first risen a few years earlier. In this way cities such as Narnia, Spoletum and Perusium were lost. The few which resisted were surrounded and besieged.

And so Narses was like a giant moving through a narrow passage with his arms outstretched, pushing before him everything that tried to hide. Others likened him to a fisherman, wading upstream behind his spread net, leaving no trace of life where he had passed.

Those Goths who were able to save themselves fled in fear, with their wives and children, from the "iron roller" as it rolled towards them. From all directions they fled to the king's army, and it was not long before the king had many more women, children and old men in his camp than warriors.

Once again the Ostrogoths were engaged in a massive migration as a hundred years before, but this time the unrelenting net of Narses followed behind them. Before them was the peninsula, becoming narrower and narrower as they moved on, and then the sea. And there were no waiting ships to take them to safety.

The Gothic nation was truly trapped.

Chapter 2

In addition to all of the above problems there was one further unavoidable necessity, which further reduced the number of men able to bear arms in the army of King Teias, and which caused his small force to continue shrinking in the most terrible way.

From the moment the pursuit started Cethegus with his Isaurians and Saracen and Heruli cavalry, together with Alboin and his Lombards, had firmly attached themselves to the heels of the retreating Goths. If that retreat, which was in any case slowed down by the large numbers of women and children, was to make any progress at all, then drastic measures were called for. Thus a small group of brave warriors had to be sacrificed almost every night; they would halt at some favourable and easily defended spot, and there they would delay the pursuers by stubborn last ditch defence, literally to the last man. This dreadful measure did, however, ensure that the main body of the army could keep ahead of its pursuers.

This cruel but necessary tactic meant that Gothic troops had to be sacrificed on every such occasion, some five hundred in some cases, and even more in others where the defence had to cover a broader front.

King Teias had announced this aloud to the entire army before the departure from Spes Bonorum. The men had received the terrible announcement in silence, but accepted it as inevitable.

And every night the men eagerly competed for the honour of dying for their fellow Goths, so much so that King Teias, often with a tear in his eye, had to decide by drawing lots so as not to offend one man by preferring another. The Gothic warriors could now see the certain demise of their nation and their Empire before their eyes, and in many cases they knew that their wives and children were already in enemy hands. And so they virtually raced one another to their deaths. And in this way the Gothic retreat also became a monument to Gothic heroism; almost every resting place became a milestone of death-defying, courageous sacrifice.

The leaders of these "rearguards of death" included old Haduswinth at Nuceria Camillaria, the young archer Gunthamund at Ad Fontes, and the fast horseman Gudila at Ad Martis.

But these sacrifices, and the king's generalship, were not to be without benefit to the fate of their people.

Near Fossatum, between Tudera and Narnia, a night engagement occurred between the pursuers and the rearguard under the brave Count Markja. It started at midday, when Cethegus and his cavalry first engaged them, until the following dawn. As the rising sun shone once more on the hastily constructed Gothic defences there was total silence everywhere. The pursuers approached with utmost caution. At last Cethegus jumped from his horse onto the first line of barricades, with Syphax immediately behind him.

And Cethegus waved to his men: "Come on, there is no danger! You will only have to walk over your enemies, for they are all dead, all one thousand of them including Count Markja down there. I know him."

But when the horsemen had removed the barricades and started the pursuit afresh, they soon learned from peasants on their way that the main Gothic army had not passed through along the Via Flaminia here at all.

Thus, by the noble sacrifice of Count Markja and his one thousand men, King Teias had not only gained a considerable headstart, but had also managed to completely deceive Cethegus as to the direction he had taken. The pursuers had lost all contact with the retreating Gothic army. Cethegus advised John to take a portion of his force to the right, in a southeasterly direction, whilst Alboin and his Lombards followed the Via Flaminia to the northeast, in order to pick up the trail once more.

But Cethegus himself was drawn strongly to Rome. He hoped to get to Rome before Narses, and without Narses, so that he would be able to call check to him from the Capitol, just as he had done with Belisarius before. After he discovered that King Teias had given him the slip he called his trusted tribunes together, and told them that he intended to rid himself of the constant supervision by Alboin and John, using force if necessary. Having weakened both of them by sending strong detachments from their respective forces after the Goths, he now proposed to hurry with his Isaurians directly along the Via Flaminia to Rome, as that road was now no longer blocked by the Goths.

But even as he spoke Syphax brought in a Roman citizen, whom he had wrested from the hands of the Lombards with great difficulty. The latter had asked for the Prefect, but the Lombards had laughed and said that they would "treat him in the usual manner."

"But," Syphax added, "there is a large contingent coming from the rear. I will investigate for you and report back."

"I know you, Tullius Faber," the Prefect said, "you were always loyal to Rome and to me. What news do you bring?"

"Oh Prefect!" the man lamented. "To see you still alive! We all thought you were dead, as you gave no reply to eight messages which we sent to you."

"I did not receive a single one of them."

"So you do not know what has been happening in Rome? Pope Silverius has died in exile in Sicily. The new Pope is your enemy Pelagius."

"I know nothing. Tell me all you know!"

"Oh then you will not be able to help or offer advice. Rome has…"

At that moment Syphax entered, but even before he could speak Narses followed him into the Prefect's tent, leaning on the arm of Basiliskos. "You allowed yourself to be delayed so long by a thousand Gothic spears," he said angrily, "that the healthy Goths managed to get away, and the sick Narses caught up with you. That King Teias can do more than break shields; he can also weave veils over the eyes of the Prefect. But I see through all veils, including this one.

"John, recall your men. He cannot have escaped to the south, but must have moved north instead. By now he will know what concerns the Prefect of Rome more than anyone. Rome has been wrested from the Goths."

Cethegus's eyes sparkled.

"I had a few clever men smuggled into the city. They encouraged the citizens to rise against the Goths, quickly and at night. Almost every Goth in Rome was slain. Only five hundred escaped into Hadrian's tomb, and they are holding it."

"We sent eight messengers to you, Prefect!" Faber added.

"Get that man outside!" Narses motioned. "Yes, the citizens of Rome are remembering their Prefect with affection, to whom they owe so much: two sieges, hunger, pestilence and the burning of the Capitol! But the messengers they sent to you somehow always ran into the teeth of my wolves, and I suppose they have torn them to pieces. But there was also a deputation from the holy father Pelagius, and that did get through to me. And so I made an agreement with him which I am sure that you, Prefect of Rome, will find acceptable."

"I will not be able to do much about it."

"The good citizens of Rome fear nothing more than a third siege. They begged us to do nothing which could lead to a new struggle over the possession of their city. They think that the five hundred Goths in Hadrian's tomb will soon fall victim to hunger, and they have sworn to defend their walls themselves. They also say that, once the Goths have finally been conquered, they will surrender their city only to its rightful master, the Prefect of Rome. Are you satisfied with that, Cethegus? Read the agreement – give it to him, Basiliskos."

And Cethegus read, in deep and joyful emotion. So they had not forgotten him after all, his Romans! And now that the final decision was drawing close they were calling him, and not the hated Byzantines. They wanted him back on their Capitol, him, their rightful master and protector. Already Cethegus could visualise himself back at the pinnacle of power.

"I am satisfied," he said, handing back the document.

"I have agreed," said Narses, "that I will make no attempt to take Rome by force. First that King Teias must follow his predecessor Totila into Hades.

"After that Rome – and many other things. Follow me into the council of war, Prefect."

When Cethegus left the discussion in Narses's tent later, and inquired after Tullius Faber, there was not a trace of him to be found anywhere.

Chapter 3

Being the great general that he was Narses had clearly recognised the direction in which King Teias had evaded Cethegus from the Via Flaminia.

He had initially swerved to the north, to the coast of the Ionic Sea, and from there he had led his people with rare skill and local knowledge via Hadria, Aternum and Ortona to Samnium, without being troubled by his pursuers. The news that Rome was lost to him reached him by way of scattered Gothic fugitives shortly after Nuceria Camillaria.

And now the king was faced with the urgent need to do something about the rapidly growing number of his prisoners, whose number was by now almost half as great as that of his army. Feeding and controlling them was becoming a problem, and King Teias had to threaten death to anyone who tried to escape. In spite of this the prisoners made an attempt to escape en masse soon after the Goths turned north after Fossatum.

A large number of prisoners were killed by Gothic forces in the mass escape attempt. On the king's orders, while the Goths were crossing the river, all those who were left, including Orestes and all the other commanders, were bound and thrown into the river Aternus, where they drowned.

When Adalgoth pleaded with the king on behalf of the prisoners, the latter had replied sternly: "They have slaughtered defenceless Gothic women and children in their thousands by their home fires. This is no longer a war of warriors, but it has become a war of mass murder against whole nations. Let us therefore play our part in this game also, as far as we can."

From Samnium the king hurried with his best remaining troops to Campania, leaving the mass of unarmed women and children to follow slowly with only minimal protection, as there was no threat of pursuit here. He arrived there so suddenly that he caught the small force of Duke Guntharis and Count Grippa almost as much by surprise as the enemy, who were already confident of victory. The small Gothic force under Guntharis and Grippa had shrunk considerably from numerous engagements with the vastly superior enemy.

Teias learned from Guntharis, who was in a secure position between Naples and Beneventum, that the "Romaeans" were now threatening Cumae from Capua. "No," cried Teias, "that is one fortress which they must not reach before I do. I still have some important business to conclude there."

Strengthened by the garrison of his own city of Tarentum, under the courageous Ragnaris, the king decided to attack the Byzantine army which was trying to overrun Cumae, by secretly marching on that city himself from Capua. The Byzantine army greatly outnumbered the force which Teias was able to hurl against them, but he caught them completely by surprise, and he defeated them decisively with bloody losses. With his feared battleaxe he personally split the head of their leader in two, the *Archonius* Armatus. At his side the young Duke of Apulia ran his spear through

Dorotheos as well, and the terrified Byzantines ran north without stopping, as far as Terracina.

It was to be the last kiss of sunshine with which the god of victory would favour the Gothic flag. On the following day King Teias entered Cumae.

Totila, contrary to his usual manner, had decided to take hostages so as to guarantee that the city of Rome would keep faith with him when the Gothic army marched from that city. Nobody knew where those hostages had been taken.

On the evening after he entered Cumae King Teias had the walled up courtyard of the *castellum* of Cumae broken open; here the Roman hostages had been kept prisoner. They were mostly patricians and senators, among them Maximus, Cyprianus, Opilio, Rusticus and Fidelius, three hundred all told, and the most respected men in the Senate. They were all members of the old catacombs conspiracy against the Goths.

Teias had them informed by the few Goths who had managed to escape from Rome, how the Romans had suddenly risen against the Goths one night, spurred on by emissaries from Narses. They were also told how the Romans had murdered every Goth who had fallen into their hands, including women and children, and then forced the remainder to retreat into the Moles Hadriani.

The eyes of the king, which glowered at the hostages while these events were being recounted, held such a terrifying expression that two of the hostages could not endure listening to the end of the tale. Instead of that they smashed their own skulls by running against the hard rock walls. After the escapees had finished their tale at last, and demonstrated the truth of what they had said, the king turned around silently and walked from the courtyard without saying another word. An hour later the heads of the three hundred hostages stared down from the walls of the *castellum*.

"But it was not only this dreadful work of judgment that drew me to Cumae," Teias said to Adalgoth. "There is a great secret to be lifted here as well."

And he invited Adalgoth, together with the other leaders, to join him for his cheerless, plain evening meal. At the conclusion of the sad supper the king motioned to old Hildebrand. The latter nodded, took a pitch torch from an iron ring on the central column of the hall, and said: "Follow me, you children of younger days, and bring your shields with you."

It was the third hour of the July night. The stars were showing the hour of midnight.

Out of the hall, following the king and the ancient armourer, walked Guntharis and Adalgoth, Aligern, Grippa, Ragnaris and Wisand the *bandalarius*. Wachis, as shield bearer to the king, concluded the little procession with a second torch.

Opposite the little walled garden there stood a huge round tower, known as Theodoric's Tower because the great king had caused it to be restored and reinforced. And now old Hildebrand was leading the little procession into the old tower.

But instead of climbing the staircase from the empty ground floor, the old man stopped. He knelt down and carefully measured fifteen breadths of his huge hand along the floor, from the door to the middle of the room. The entire floor seemed to be made from three great slabs of granite. Hildebrand shut the door leading to the outside, and where the thumb of his hand indicated after his measuring the fifteenth width, he struck the floor with his stone axe. It sounded hollow, and a small hole appeared in the stone. Bidding the others to stand to one side, the old man dug the point of his axe into the hole, and then he levered the entire stone slab to the right.

And now a space appeared below them, as far down as the tower rose above them, yawning a gaping black.

There was just enough room in the opening to allow one man to pass. From here a narrow staircase, hewn into the rock, led downwards for more than two hundred steps.

Silently the men descended. When they arrived at the bottom they found that the circular room had been divided into two halves by a stone wall. That half in which they were standing was empty.

And now King Teias measured ten hand widths upwards from the ground along the wall. At the precise spot he pressed against the stone, and another narrow opening appeared, revealing a small door opening to the inside. Hildebrand stepped inside, followed by the king, who lit two further torches on the wall.

And then the other men drew back blinded, placing their hands over their eyes. When they looked up again they saw, and immediately recognised, the secret they were looking at. It was the entire rich Amalung treasure of Dietrich von Bern.

There before them, here carefully arranged and there in disorderly array, lay weapons, jewellery and implements of all kinds. There was a helmet from ancient Etruscan times, made of bronze, which had been taken by traders in ancient times to the Goths on the Baltic Sea or the Pruth or the Dniestr, and then brought back by the southerly migration of the same people a century or more later, possibly to the very same spot where it had once been fashioned. Beside it lay a sealskin fur and the head of a polar bear, spread over a wooden frame. There were pointed Celtic helmets, proud Roman and Byzantine helmet plumes, armour and neckbands of bronze and iron, silver and gold. There were shields, from the rough wooden shield as tall as a man, designed to protect an archer like a wall, down to the beautiful little cavalry shield of some long-dead Parthian, covered all over in pearls and precious stones. Beside ancient chain mail of almost crushing weight there were lightweight suits of armour made of purple linen, together with swords, and daggers of stone, bronze and iron. There were axes and clubs, some still made from the bones of the mammoth, roughly fashioned and with a deer antler for a handle, down to the Frankish *Francisca* and a delicately worked little Roman throwing axe, with which Roman circus riders would split an apple in two at full gallop. There were spears, lances and javelins of every kind, from the crudely worked tooth of a whale to an ebony shafted and gold inlaid spear dating back to a Vandal king of Carthage. There were the massive golden javelins of the same rulers, with flamingo feathers and a steel point a foot long, and cloaks made from every kind of material, from the fur of the blue fox to the hide of the Numidian lion and the most precious purple from Sidon. Shoes ranged from the long snow shoes of the Skritofins to golden sandals from Byzantium. Coats of Friesian wool and tunics of Chinese silk lay among countless implements and tableware: tall jars, flat bowls, round goblets and urns of amber, gold and silver, tortoiseshell and ceramic ware. There were bracelets and clasps of various materials, strings of crystal, amber and pearls, and many more items for eating and drinking, clothing and ornamentation, weapons and household items.

"Yes," said King Teias, "this hollow here was known only to us blood brothers. Hildebrand had it hewn into the rock here forty years ago when he was Duke of Cumae. It has been the treasure house which held the Gothic royal treasure.

"That is why Belisarius found so little when he captured the treasure in Ravenna. The rarest and most precious items were missing, all the presents and gifts, the collection of Amalung honours in peace and war going back far beyond Theodoric to

Winithar, Ermanaric, Athal, Ostrogotho and Isarna to Amala. We hid them all here. We kept in Ravenna only coined gold and such implements whose value lay more in gold than in honour. For months now the enemy has been walking over the top of these treasures, but the faithful deep remained silent.

"But now we are going to carry these treasures with us. We will heap them on our shields and hand them up the stairs, one to the other. Then we will take them with us to the last battlefield which will ever see a Gothic army fight. No, don't be afraid, young Adalgoth, even after I have fallen and everything is lost, these treasures will never fall into enemy hands, and our honour will be safe.

"You see, I have chosen for us the most splendid final battlefield. It will swallow up the very last of the Goths, with their fame and their honour and their treasure, and hide them for all time."

"Yes, and that will include not only treasure, but our highest fame and honour too," said old Hildebrand. "Look here, my fellow Goths!"

With that he withdrew the curtain which closed off the innermost part of the semicircle, and shone his torch into the space behind it.

Respectfully they all fell to their knees. They immediately recognised the great man, dead, sitting upright on the golden throne, clad in a royal robe of purple and his spear still in his right hand.

It was the great Theodoric. The art of embalming, which had found its way from ancient Egypt to Rome, had preserved the great king in almost gruesome, lifelike majesty. Deeply moved, the men were speechless.

"For a long time now," Hildebrand began at last, "Teias and I have had our doubts about the star of the Goths. And so, when I had the guard of honour in the round marble mausoleum in Ravenna, where Amalasuntha had laid her dead father to rest just before the war broke out, I did some thinking. I felt little affection for that building, and less still for the priests, forever stinking of incense, who were there praying for the great man's soul. And then I thought that, if ever all traces of us Goths should vanish from this southern land, then Italians and Greeks must not be allowed to mock or desecrate the remains of our great hero.

"No, my great king had to find a last resting place where no one would ever find his body, so that nobody would ever desecrate his memory. Just as the Visigothic king Alaric found his grave in a riverbed, safe from all, my great king had to be safe also. And so, with the help of Teias, one dark night I removed the noble body from the mausoleum and the company of the wailing priests, and then we brought it here as part of the Amalung treasure, in a sealed trunk. Here he would be safe, and if in some future century blind chance should find him, who would then recognise him, the king with the eagle eye? And so the sarcophagus in Ravenna is empty, and the monks are singing and praying there in vain.

"Here is where he had to rest, with all his treasures and honours, sitting upright in all the splendour due to him; and as his soul looks down from Valhalla it would much sooner see this than see him lie under a stone slab, surrounded by the stink of incense."

"But now," Teias concluded, "the hour has come for him and the Amalung treasure to rise once more from the deep. After you have raised the treasure to the surface we will raise the body of our precious hero also. Tomorrow we leave this city. The vanguard of Narses and the Prefect has already been reported approaching, and we will march to the last battlefield of the Goths with king and treasure. I have already sent the women and children to that battlefield, which I have been seeing for many years in my troubled dreams. It is that battlefield which will see us and our nation go down gloriously and which, even after the last spear has broken, can take all those who are willing to die into its burning womb. That is the final battlefield which Teias has chosen for himself and for all of you."

"I sense it now," Adalgoth interrupted, "the name of that last battlefield is…"

"Mount Vesuvius!" Teias replied. "To work!"

Chapter 4

After that council of war at Fossatum Narses had moved south as rapidly as his terrible system of annihilation would allow, moving through the country on the broadest possible front in order to either crush all remnants of Gothic life, or hurl them into the sea.

He despatched only a small force to Tuscany and another to Luca, under his commanders Vitalianus and Wilmuth the Heruli chieftain. Their task was to break any last pockets of resistance in the few remaining fortresses in those regions. He also sent Valerianus still further against the still unconquered Verona, which had made it a great deal easier for the remaining Goths to escape through the Athesis Valley to the Passara. Meanwhile Valerianus had succeeded in capturing Petra Pertusa, which blocked the Via Flaminia above Helvillium.

At the same time Narses had hurried south with all his remaining troops. He himself moved along the Via Flaminia past Rome, whilst John moved along the Tyrrhenian coast, and the Heruli under Vulkaris along the Ionian coast, forcing the Goths ahead of them on all three fronts.

However none of the three armies now encountered much resistance, and there was little for them to do but move on. In the north the few remaining Gothic families had already been absorbed into the king's army, which Vulkaris was not able to overhaul. In the south the Goths had also long been roused from their settlements, and were moving via Rome to Naples, where they had been ordered to proceed by fast messengers from the king.

"Mons Vesuvius!" was the word which had been given out to all Gothic fugitives; here was where they were to assemble.

Narses had specified Anagnia as the place where his two wings were to reunite with the main army.

Cethegus had gladly accepted the invitation from Narses to remain with him and the main army; there were, after all, no great events to be expected on the two wings.

Furthermore Narses would be moving via Rome!

In the event that Narses, in spite of his promise, should make an attempt to take Rome by force after all, Cethegus would be on the spot. But, almost to the Prefect's astonishment, Narses kept his word, and with his huge army he moved peacefully around and past Rome.

In addition he invited Cethegus to be a witness to his discussion with the new Pope Pelagius and the other ruling figures in Rome. This meeting was held outside the walls, between the Porta Flaminia and the Porta Salaria, at the Porta Belisaria (formerly Porta Pinciana).

Once again the Pope and the Romans swore faithfully on the remains of the saints Cosmo and Damian (who according to legend were twin brothers and Arab physicians, who allegedly died as martyrs under Diocletian) that they would open their gates only to the Prefect of Rome once the remaining Goths on the Moles Hadriani had been overcome. However any attempt to take their city by force would be resisted with force, as they had no wish to become involved in any future fighting which might yet erupt around Rome.

Narses proposed that he loan the Romans a few thousand of his troops, so that the Goths in Hadrian's tomb could be overcome more speedily. However, much to the Prefect's delight, this offer was politely but firmly refused.

"They have learned two things these last years," Cethegus said to Lucius Licinius as they departed, "to keep the 'Romaeans' at a safe distance, and to associate Cethegus with the welfare of Rome. That is already a great deal."

"Commander," Licinius warned, "I cannot share your joy, nor your confidence."

"Nor I," Salvius Julianus concurred. "I fear Narses, and I distrust him."

"Oh, you are all too clever," Piso said scornfully. "One must exaggerate nothing, not even doubt or caution. Have events not changed beyond our wildest dreams since that night when a coarse shepherd lad struck the immortal hand of Rome's greatest poet? That night when the mighty Prefect of Rome was floating downstream in a pile of grain? When Massurius Sabinus was recognised by Count Markja in a woman's clothing in which he was trying to escape, and when the great lawyer Salvius Julianus was fished from the river, bleeding, by that less than gentle Duke Guntharis? Who would have thought then that a time would come again when we would count on our fingers the number of days left to the time when not a single Goth would remain standing on Italian soil on his own two feet?"

"You are right, poet," Cethegus smiled. "Those two are suffering from Narses fever, just as their hero suffers from epilepsy. To overestimate one's enemies is also a fault. Those remains which the priests brought to the wall in their ivory and silver caskets are really holy to them; I am certain that they will not break an oath they swore on them."

"If only," Licinius replied with concern, "I had seen just one of our old friends up there on that wall, with the priests! But they were all tradesmen, butchers and the like. Where is Rome's aristocracy, and where are the men from the catacombs?"

"They were taken away as hostages," Cethegus replied, "and it serves them right. After all they did return to Rome, and they did pay homage to the Gothic king. If the new black Gothic king now lops off their heads, then they have asked for it. Do not fear; you see things too black, all of you! You have been intimidated by Narses and his enormous army. He may be a great general, but the fact that he agreed with Rome to admit no one but me shows that he is not dangerous as a statesman. Let us first breathe the air of the Capitol again; epileptics cannot breathe that air and remain healthy."

And when, on the following morning, the young tribunes came to fetch their leader from his tent to break camp and move against Teias, their leader received them with a gleam in his eyes.

"Well," he beamed, "now tell me who it is that knows the Romans, you or the Prefect of Rome? Listen – but keep this to yourselves. Last night a centurion of the newly established city cohorts, Publius Macer, sneaked into my tent. He is in command of the Porta Latina, and his brother has been placed in command of the Capitol by the Pope. He showed me the documents confirming both appointments. I know the handwriting of Pelagius; the documents are genuine.

"The Romans have long tired of being ruled by the clergy. They want to see me and you and my Isaurians walking up and down along the walls of Rome once again, the walls of Aurelianus and the Prefect. He left me his nephew Aulus, as proof and as a hostage at the same time. Aulus will tell us the exact night and the time and place where they will open the Capitol to us. The Romans will communicate with him by seemingly harmless letters, which will be in code and contain the necessary information. Narses can hardly complain if the Romans let us in of their own free will, can he? After all, I will not be using force. Now, Licinius and Julianus, speak! Who is it that knows Rome and the Romans?"

Chapter 5

Narses now moved on Anagnia, and two days after his arrival there the two wings also arrived, according to plan.

After a few days of resting, mustering and reorganising his enormous army the commander-in-chief moved to Terracina, where the remainder of Armatus's and Dorotheos's troops also joined him. Soon after that the huge juggernaut rolled on once more against the Goths, who were holding an excellent defensive position south of Naples. The Gothic position was based on Mount Vesuvius and Mons Lactarius opposite Nuceria, and it was also protected by the River Draco, which flows into the sea north of Stabiae.

The Gothic army, after its departure from Cumae, had moved past Naples to the final battlefield chosen by Teias long ago. The citizens of Naples had locked their gates, recently so well repaired by King Totila, and declared that they would follow the example of Rome and lock their city to all combatants until the eventual outcome of the struggle became clear. The Gothic garrison of a mere three hundred men had easily been overpowered.

After arriving at his chosen position King Teias proceeded to further strengthen his already strong position by every available means. In addition to that he had as much foodstuff as was possible brought to the mountain from the rich countryside all about him, so that he would have enough food to feed his people until the last day of the Gothic nation was to dawn.

For many years historians have tried in vain to find a location on either Mount Vesuvius or Mons Lactarius which corresponds exactly with the description that Procopius has handed down to us. None of the many chasms and passes on either mountain seems to match his description exactly. Nevertheless there is no reason to doubt the validity of what has been handed down to us by eyewitnesses, i.e. by the commanders and soldiers in the army of Narses, all of which corroborate the account of the Byzantine historian Procopius. A likely explanation for this apparent absence of a site matching the descriptions of that last battlefield is the changes which have occurred over the centuries, due to the activities of the volcano. Vesuvius has been continually active for the last thirteen centuries, and flows of lava, landslides and erosion have all taken their toll. Credible reports by various Italian authors about other and unrelated events which occurred on the mountain also, cannot be substantiated today. It is therefore likely that the ground which once soaked up the heart blood of King Teias has long since been covered by layers of lava.

Even Narses had to admire the foresight with which his Barbarian opponent had chosen this position for a last ditch defence.

"He wants to fall like a bear in his own lair!" he said as he approached in his litter from Nuceria in the north, and saw the entire Gothic defences for the first time. "And many of your wolves," he said to Alboin, "will reel from the blow of his paw as they try to sneak into that narrow pass over there."

"In that case so many wolves must run into that hole at the same time that the bear has both paws full, and has no time to strike a second blow."

"Well, be patient. I know a pass on Mons Vesuvius from my younger days, when there was still hope that I might be cured of my malady. Once I spent several weeks convalescing on Mons Lactarius over there. That's when I found the pass, and I remember it well. Once they are in there, then only hunger will drive them out."

"Winning the battle that way will become drawn out and dull."

"True, but also necessary. I have no wish to sacrifice another myriad of imperial troops, just to stamp out the last few sparks."

And so it was to be. After Narses arrived the two armies were to stand facing one another for a further sixty days. Very slowly, fighting for every step forward with bloody losses, Narses drew his net tighter and tighter until it was almost choking the hapless Goths.

In a huge semicircle Narses covered every possible point of escape to the west, north and east of the Gothic position. Only the southern side, bordering on the sea, was left open, as the Goths had no ships on which they could flee. Narses himself was camped on this southern side, on a beach. The Tyrrhenian fleet was already occupied shipping Gothic prisoners to Byzantium, there being no need to patrol the coast as the Goths had no ships to either escape or bring in supplies. The other Ionian fleet was expected soon. A few ships from it had already been detached to cruise in the bay of Bajae as far as Surrentum. After the last few remaining ships had been surrendered by their commanders there were no more Gothic sails.

And so Narses, despite his huge numerical superiority, had no choice but to proceed slowly and tenaciously, overlooking nothing. In this way he gradually occupied Piscinula, Cimiterium, Nola, Summa, Melane, Nuceria, Stabiae, Cumae, Bajae, Misenum, Puteoli and Nesis.

Soon afterwards Naples also knew fear at the might of Narses, and voluntarily opened its gates to him.

And from all sides the Byzantines were closing in on the encircled Goths.

After some heavy fighting Narses succeeded in forcing the remaining Goths away from Mons Lactarius to the right bank of the Draco River, where the remnants of the Gothic nation were now camped on a plateau behind the incomparable narrow pass, which Narses had previously praised. The pass was close to one of the many secondary craters which existed at that time, but the occupants of the camp had to suffer the fumes and smoke from the mountain only rarely, when the wind came from the southeast.

Here, in the numerous chasms, caves and hollows in the side of the mountain, the masses of Gothic civilians had made camp, either in the open air, in the warm August weather, or under the wagons and tents they had brought with them.

The only access to this encampment was by way of a narrow pass, so narrow at its southern end that one man with a shield could fill it comfortably. This pass was guarded day and night by rotation, an hour at a time. That watch was shared by Teias himself, Duke Guntharis, Duke Adalgoth, Count Grippa, Count Wisand, Aligern, Ragnaris and Wachis. Behind them stood a Gothic company of one hundred men, which also changed regularly.

And so the whole terrible war, the struggle for Rome and for Italy, had now led, inevitably and true to the system of Narses, to a struggle for the possession of a single cleft in the rock. That cleft was just wide enough to be defended by a single man, at the southern tip of the much loved and fiercely defended peninsula.

Even the factual historic accounts of the last days of the Goths read like the final act of a great tragedy of history.

Narses had pitched his camp on a beach just below this pass. The Lombards were with him. To his right was John, and to his left Cethegus.

The Prefect put it to his tribunes that Narses, by leaving Cethegus to defend this position which he himself had chosen, had thereby shown that he was either very careless or very naïve. "Because you see," he explained, "by doing this he has left the road to Rome open to me. Had I been placed either in the centre or on the right wing then that road would have been closed to me. So be ready, as soon as the signal arrives from Rome, to hurry there secretly with all the Isaurians."

"And you?" Licinius asked, concerned.

"I will remain here, close to the feared Narses! If he had wanted me murdered, then he could have done so long ago. So evidently that is not his wish. He does not want to act against me without some plausible, legal pretext. And if I follow the call of the Romans, then I will be honouring our agreement, not breaking it."

Chapter 6

Above the narrow pass on Vesuvius, which we will call the Goths' chasm, there was a narrow but deep hole in the black volcanic rock; here is where King Teias had hidden the Gothic royal treasure, together with the embalmed body of Dietrich von Bern. Theodoric's banner had been hoisted outside the entrance to the chasm. A royal robe of purple, spread out over four spears, formed the antechamber and curtain to the rocky cave, where the last king of the Goths had set up his royal hall. A block of lava, covered with the hide of a black panther, served as his last throne.

Here is where King Teias spent his time when the jealously guarded turn to stand guard at the entrance to the chasm fell to another. The chasm was under constant attack from arrows, javelins and rocks hurled from a distance. From time to time there would also be an attack by the vanguard of Narses, resulting in close hand to hand combat. Not once did one of these heroic guards return from his turn of duty outside the chasm without either bearing the signs of such combat on shield and armour, or leaving the signs outside the chasm in the form of slain enemies.

This was happening with such frequency that the decay of the fallen – for no one dared to try and remove the bodies – threatened to make it impossible for anyone to remain near the entrance of the pass.

It seemed as if Narses had been counting on this. Once, when Basiliskos was lamenting at the useless sacrifice, he had replied: "Leave them there! Perhaps they will serve the emperor better dead than they ever did alive."

But King Teias replied by having the corpses hurled down the rugged mountainside during the night, so that they would arrive at the bottom terribly mutilated and torn to pieces, as if to deter anybody else from attempting to attack the pass. After that Narses quickly requested permission to have all the fallen removed each evening by unarmed men, to which the king agreed.

Since their withdrawal into this pass the Goths had not lost a single man in combat, as only the very first man in the pass at any one time was accessible to the enemy. This guardian of the pass, supported by his comrades standing behind him, had never yet been conquered.

One evening, after sunset, King Teias was walking back to his lava cave, his spear over his shoulder, having been relieved at the front of the chasm by Wisand the *bandalarius*. It was September by now. The traces of the battle of Taginae had almost disappeared, and the flowers which Cassiodorus and the inmates of the cloister had planted by the graves of Totila, Valeria and Julius were already showing fresh shoots.

When King Teias arrived outside his cave he was greeted there by Adalgoth, who handed him his golden goblet in a respectful kneeling position. "Allow me to attend to my duties as your cup bearer anyway; who knows how much longer I will be able to do so."

"Not long now," Teias replied seriously, sitting down. "Let us stay outside, in front of the cave here. Look how beautifully the whole bay of Naples is glowing in the light of the setting sun, from Bajae to Surrentum; even the sea itself is blood red. Truly, this southern land has no finer frame in which to set the scene of the Goths' last battle. Let us make sure that the painting is worthy of the frame. The end is drawing near. It is strange how everything has come to pass, just as I sensed – dreamed – and described in my poems." And the king rested his head on both his hands.

He looked up again only when the silver note of a harp roused him from his reflections. Unnoticed by the king, Adalgoth had fetched his small harp from the cave.

"Listen to this, Sir King," he said, "hear how I finished your song about the lava chasm – or rather how it finished itself. Can you remember the night near Rome, out in that wilderness of ivy, marble and laurel trees? It was not some past battle you described then, but our own coming heroic last stand, right here on this spot. You must have somehow seen it in your mind, like a foreboding."

And he played the harp and sang:

"Where the lava cliffs rise at the foot of Mount Vesuvius,
through the night air one hears cries of deepest mourning, here and there,
for the curse of many brave dead men clings here to the rocky slopes:
It was the great Gothic nation which perished here in glory."

"Yes, glory, my young friend. That is something which neither fate nor Narses shall take from us. The terrible sentence and judgment of the all-powerful god, which took Totila from us, has indeed been cruel to all of us, to Totila, his people and his Christian God. No just God in heaven weighed our fate in the balance, as poor Totila believed. There is no justice in heaven, if there is a heaven. We will fall by the betrayals of Romans and Byzantines, betrayed a thousandfold, or by sheer superiority of numbers. But the way in which we fall, unconquered, proud even in death, that is something no fate can decide. Only our own worth will determine that!

"And after us? Who will rule after us in this magnificent land? Those Greeks with their treachery won't last long, and the Italians will not rule in their own right again for centuries. There are still many Germanic peoples living in the north, beyond the mountains – they are the ones who will become our heirs, and who will avenge us."

Slowly he now picked up the harp, which Adalgoth had put down, and then he sang softly whilst looking down upon the sea, which had quickly become quite dark. Already stars were shining overhead.

And he sang, touching the strings of his harp only once in a while:

"Extinct now is the bright star of the high and noble Amalungs.
Oh Dietrich, worthy hero of Bern, your army's shield is burst.
Cowardice has won, and virtue is conquered. Truth and courage perish:
Scoundrels are rulers of the world. Come, fellow Goths, let us die!
Oh lovely south land, oh evil Rome, oh sweet blue skies of Italia,
oh bloody Tiber River, oh false southern loyalty!
As yet the north brings forth many brave sons as heirs to our hate and courage:
The thunder of revenge already rolls. Oh Goths, it's time for us to die!"

"I like the song," Adalgoth cried, "but is it already finished? What about the ending?"

"The ending can only be sung to the tune of sword blows," Teias replied. "I think that you will soon hear the ending too."

And then he got to his feet. "Go, my Adalgoth," he said, "leave me here by myself. I have already kept you too long from—" and in spite of his sadness he smiled "—from the loveliest of all duchesses. You will not have many more evening hours together, you poor children. You – if only I could save you, you young ones, budding new life of the future…" and he brushed his hand across his forehead.

"Foolishness," he said then. "You too are but a part of a nation that is doomed to die, even though you are the best part."

Adalgoth's eyes had suddenly filled with tears as the king remembered his young wife. Now he stepped closer to Teias and placed one hand on his shoulder, questioningly.

"Is there no hope at all? She is so young!"

"None," Teias replied, "for there are no angels in heaven to come to our aid. I am not the all-powerful God of the Christians. But not a single woman or girl of our nation needs to become a slave to Byzantines, unless she herself chooses disgrace rather than death as a free Gothic woman. Look over there, my Adalgoth: already the night shows us the glow of the mountain – look over there, a hundred paces to our right – how the flames are rising out of the crater! Once the last defender of the pass is dead – one leap, and no Roman's cheeky hand will ever soil any of our pure women. Think of them, even before you think about us, because we Gothic men can fall and die anywhere. It was for the sake of our Gothic women that I chose this place for our last stand: Vesuvius!"

And now Adalgoth, no longer despondent but filled with the fire of inspiration, grasped the hands of his king.

Chapter 7

A few days after Cethegus had taken up his chosen position to the left of Narses, news reached the Byzantines that the last remaining Goths in Hadrian's tomb had been annihilated. Thus Rome once more belonged entirely to the Romans; not a single Goth, nor to the joy of Cethegus a single Byzantine, remained within the walls of Rome.

If he could now find a way to occupy the city with his Isaurians under the leadership of his tribunes, then Cethegus would be able to face Narses on even more favourable terms than those with which he had faced Belisarius, with whom he had had to share possession of the city.

One of the messengers who had conveyed the news from Rome also gave a letter from the two centurions in Rome, the Macer brothers, to Aulus, who was still being held as a hostage. The letter read: "The bride has recovered from her long illness; as soon as the bridegroom comes, there will be nothing to prevent a marriage before the next *ides*; so come, Aulus."

Those were the prearranged words. Cethegus conveyed them to his Roman tribunes.

"That's good!" Licinius said, determined. "So I will be able to erect a memorial stone after all, on the spot where my brother fell for Rome and for Cethegus."

"Nobody can deny the right of Romans to Rome," Salvius Julianus added.

"Only take care, Prefect, that our departure does not become known to the greatest cripple of all time until he can no longer catch us. We will need to leave in secret."

"No," Cethegus replied, "there will be no need for that. I have already checked, and I know that the most cautious of all heroes has placed sentries far beyond our left wing; his Lombard wolves are distributed everywhere. What we thought were our own outposts are in fact surrounded by his outposts. We cannot depart against his will or without his knowledge, either by force or through cunning. It would also be much wiser to act openly. He can stop us if he chooses to, and he will find out in any case. But he will have nothing against it – you will see! I will tell him what I have decided to do, and he will agree to it."

"General, that is very daring; it is greatness."

"It is the only possible way."

"Yes, you are right Cethegus, as always," Salvius Julianus agreed after some thought. "Force or deception are impossible. And if he does agree, then I will gladly concede that my own reservations…"

"Were based on your overestimation of Narses as a statesman. You have all been intimidated by numbers, and by the cripple's great ability as a general, and that is admittedly difficult to overestimate. I will admit it to you, things looked grim for me before Taginae, but as I am still alive those assumptions must have been – in error. I will send you both to Narses with my request immediately. Now you are both suspicious, and so you will watch his reaction closely. Go and tell him that the Romans want me, their City Prefect, in their city now, even before the Goth Teias has been finally defeated. I wish to ask if he will permit me to depart for Rome with my Isaurians immediately, and whether he would see that as a violation of our agreement. Tell him that my Isaurians and I would not leave without his consent."

The two tribunes left, and Piso laughed as he walked from the tent: "Your minds have been rendered useless by the crutches of Narses for even longer than my fingers were stunned by that shepherd's stick."

When they had gone, Syphax hurried to his master: "Oh master," he said earnestly, "don't trust that sick man with the calm, piercing eyes. Last night I questioned the snake oracle again. I divided the discarded skin of my god into two halves and placed them both on the hot coals. The piece 'Narses' lasted much longer than the piece 'Cethegus' did. Won't you let me try once more? You know, one little scratch from this dagger, and he is doomed. What does it matter if they impale Syphax, Hiempsal's son? It cannot be done through cunning; the leader of the long beards sleeps in his tent, his camp bed across the threshold, and seven of his 'wolves' sleep outside the entrance. The Heruli stand guard outside. As you instructed me to do I have checked out his quarters every night since Helvillium, but I doubt that even a blowfly would escape detection by either the Heruli or the Lombards if it should fly into the tent. But openly, by day, a leap into his litter – a flesh wound – and he is a dead man in a quarter of an hour."

"But before that not only Syphax, but Cethegus too would be just as dead. No. But listen: I have found out where the commander holds his secret discussions with Basiliskos, and with Alboin too.

"Not in his tent, because the camp has a thousand ears, but in his bath! The physicians have ordered him to take a morning bath in the saltwater mud in the gulf of Bajae. They have built a bath hut for him, out over the sea, which can only be reached by boat. Before their commander's bath Basiliskos and Alboin are as well informed as – well, as Basiliskos and Alboin. But after they return from there they are always as full of knowledge as Narses himself. They know exactly what letters have come from Byzantium, and other things. Right around the hut there are reeds. Syphax, how long can you dive, and how far can you swim under water?"

"Long enough," the Moor replied not without pride, "for the clumsy and suspicious crocodile in our rivers to take a look at the gazelle put out as bait, and start to swim slowly towards it – and then a knife into its belly from below. That Narses is a little like a crocodile. Let me see if I can't outstay him too, in a long and patient dive."

"Splendid, my panther on land, and my duck on the water!"

"I would jump into fire for you too, as your scorpion."

"Yes, go and listen to what the sick man says in the bath."

"And that will coincide nicely with another little game. For several days now I have been watching a fisherman, who always looks at me so stupidly. He always throws his nets night and morning, and yet he never catches anything. I think he is trying to catch me, instead of the fishes. But those long-bearded wolves and their Alboin are always on my heels; perhaps, as I emerge from beneath the water, I will find out what that fisherman is trying to tell me."

Chapter 8

In a solemn mood, but no longer in a state of tearful depression, Adalgoth had told his young wife of the decision the king had made, and about the final escape from slavery and disgrace. He had expected to hear an outburst of painful emotion, such as he himself had just conquered.

But to his surprise Gotho remained unshaken. "I have seen that coming for a long time, my Adalgoth, and I do not see it as a great misfortune. It is only a misfortune to lose that which one loves in life. I have experienced the highest joys earth has to offer. I became your wife. Whether that lasts for ten years, or twenty, or barely half a year, that matters little. So we are to die together, on the same day, and probably in the same hour. I am sure that King Teias would not mind, after you have done your part in that last battle and come back here, probably wounded and no longer able to fight, if you then take me in your arms. It will be just as you have done so many times back on the Iffinger Mountain, and then we will jump down into the crater together. Oh my Adalgoth," she cried, embracing him passionately, "how happy we have been together! Let us now earn that happiness by dying bravely, without complaint. The Balti dynasty shall not say," she smiled, "that a shepherd girl was not equal to its aristocratic spirit.

"I can feel the grandeur of our mountains mightily. Uncle Iffa told me to always think back to the fresh mountain air, whenever life in these small, stuffy golden rooms down here weighed too heavily on my soul, and that thinking of our aloof, proud heights would do me good. We were never troubled by small, golden rooms. But now that we will have to face the thought of death I had to lift my spirits out of their sad, melancholy mood. Like you I was depressed too. But then I thought of home, and thinking about our wonderful mountains gave me the strength to face death with courage. I said to myself: 'You should be ashamed of yourself, daughter of the mountains! What would the Iffinger and the Wolf's Head and all the other stone heroes say if they saw the shepherd girl despairing? Be worthy of those mountains, girl, and of your Adalgoth!'" And Adalgoth drew his young wife to himself, proud and happy.

Behind the duke's tent there was a small shelter made of leaves, in which Wachis and Liuta lived. Liuta, after having been told by Gotho what lay ahead, had to talk long and hard to her good husband before he finally agreed with her, and came to the same decision as she had done. He was sitting there, shaking his head as he worked on repairing his shield, which had suffered considerable punishment from Lombard spears during his last watch.

"I can't believe," the simple man said, "that our good God in heaven can stand idly by and watch all this happening. I am one of those who never likes to say: 'Now all is lost!' Sure, the proud ones like King Teias and Duke Adalgoth, with their heads held high, they always run into the barriers of fate. But we little people are used to ducking and crawling; perhaps we will find a little crack or mouse hole yet, by which we can get away. It is just too mean! Miserable! Low! Cruel!" and every word was accompanied by a lusty blow of his hammer. "I just cannot believe it of our dear God! All these thousands of brave women and pretty girls and little children and old men, all into that hellish fire there! Why must they all jump into the fire of this accursed magic mountain, as if it was a merry solstice feast and they were all going to come out again on the other side, hale and hearty? I could have let you burn in the house at Faesulae. And now, not only are you going to burn, but our unborn child too, whom I have already called Witigis in advance."

"Or Rauthgundis!" Liuta whispered, leaning on her husband's shoulder, who stopped his hammering. "Think of that name, Wachis. Think of the mistress Rauthgundis! Was she not a thousand times better than the maid Liuta? And yet she would not hesitate for a moment to die with her people, would she?"

"You are right, woman!" Wachis cried, with one final lusty blow of the hammer, so that the sparks flew. "You know, I am only a peasant, and we peasants don't like to die at all! But if heaven should fall in, it will crush all of us peasants also. And before that – hassa! I will strike many a good blow yet before that happens! That would meet with the approval of Master Witigis and Mistress Rauthgundis too! In their honour and in their memory – yes, you are right, Liuta – we will live bravely for as long as we can. And if a day should come when there really is no other choice left to us, well then, we will die bravely too."

Chapter 9

Not long afterwards the two tribunes returned from Narses's tent to that of the Prefect, most pleasantly surprised. "You have won again, oh Cethegus!" Licinius exclaimed.

"You were right, Prefect of Rome," Salvius Julianus added, "I don't understand it, but Narses is really letting you have Rome."

"Ah," Piso added happily, who had just entered the tent. "Cethegus, that is your old luck of the Caesars once more. Your star, which seemed to wane as soon as this cripple appeared on the scene, is on the ascent again. I think that his mind must be suffering from the occasional epileptic seizure as well as his body; surely if his mind had been healthy he would not have given you Rome without a struggle. No, *quem deus vult perdere dementat!* Now Quintus Piso will walk on the Forum once more and look in the bookshops to see whether the Goths are buying his *Epistolas ad Amabilissimum, Carissimum Pastorem Adalgothum et Ejus Pedum* (Letters to the Most Noble and Much Adored Shepherd Boy Adalgoth and his Stick)."

"So you have been writing poems while you were living in exile, like Ovidius?" Cethegus smiled.

"Yes," Piso replied, "the hexameters come more easily since they have no longer had to duck from the Goths, who are so tall that no verse can match them in length. Anyway, even in peacetime it was never easy to write poetry with the noise of Gothic drinking bouts going on."

"He has written some funny verses about that, with Gothic words among them," Salvius Julianus interjected. "How did they start again? '*Inter Hails Gothicum skapja*' – and then?"

"Do not commit grave sin by misquoting my words. The immortal must never be rendered inaccurately."

"Well then, how did the verses go?" Cethegus asked.

"Like this," Piso replied.

"De conviviis barbarorum.
Inter: 'Hails Gothicum! Skapja matjan jah drinkan!'
Non audet quisquam dignos educere versus:
Calliope madido trepidat se jungere Baccho!
Ne pedibus non stret ebria Musa suis."

(About Gothic drinking bouts. Among Gothic shouts of: 'Hail! Bring food and drink for the Goths!' no sensible person can think up a tolerable little verse: the intimidated muse trembles long under the influence of Bacchus and intoxication, and as for the befuddled verse! Alas, its feet simply fail.)

"Terrible poetry," was Salvius Julianus's comment.

"Who knows," Piso laughed, "whether Gothic thirst might not be immortalised by these verses."

"Perhaps. Now tell me exactly what Narses said in reply to my request, will you?"

"At first he listened to us in apparent disbelief," Licinius replied. "He said: 'Are the Romans, who are normally so careful, really asking for another occupation by Isaurians, of their own free will? And they want the Prefect back, to whom they owe so much hunger and involuntary bravery?'

"But I replied by telling him that he probably underestimated the patriotic spirit of the Romans, and whether you had been deceived or not was, after all, your concern. If the Romans would not let us in, then seven thousand men were certainly not enough to take the city by force. He seemed to see the logic of that. He only asked us to promise that, if the Romans did not let us in, we would not try force but return here straight away."

"And we thought that was something we could promise in your name," Salvius Julianus added.

"Yes, you could," Cethegus smiled.

Licinius went on: "Narses said: 'Good. I have no objection as long as the Romans accept you.' And he is so completely naïve that he does not even want to keep you here as a hostage, because he asked: 'When does the Prefect wish to leave?' So he must have assumed that you would be leading your Isaurians to Rome in person! And he does not even object to that! He was clearly surprised when I told him you preferred to remain here to watch the final downfall of the Goths."

"Well then, where is he, the terrible Narses, the superior statesman? Even my friend Procopius overestimated him greatly when he referred to him once as 'the greatest man of the century'."

"The greatest man of our time – has another name!" Licinius exclaimed.

"Procopius of course has to recognise the man who conquered his friend Belisarius as being the first among all the sons of the earth. But that clumsy mistake by the 'greatest man' to let me go to Rome myself is one which we are almost obliged to exploit." Cethegus went on, thinking: "The gods may be angered if we fail to exploit such miracles of blind stupidity, which they have worked in our favour. I will alter my resolve. I am drawn to the Capitol, and I will go to Rome with you. Syphax, we leave immediately. Saddle my horse."

But Syphax gave his master a warning look.

"Leave me, tribunes, for a moment," Cethegus said. "I will call you back shortly."

"Ah master," Syphax said eagerly as soon as they were alone, "do not go yet, not today. Send them ahead. Tomorrow morning I will fish two great secrets from the sea. Today I already managed to speak to that fisherman, by diving under his boat. He is not a fisherman. He is a slave, a scribe owned by Procopius."

"What was that?" Cethegus cried, softly but eagerly.

"We were able to whisper only a few words. The long beards were standing on the shore, watching me. Seven letters from Procopius, sent both openly and secretly, have not reached you. That is why he chose that clever slave as his messenger. Tonight he will fish for tuna by torchlight, and then he will give me the letter from Procopius. And tomorrow morning Narses will bathe in the mud again – today he was too sick. I have found a hiding place among the reeds, very close, and if they should happen to see bubbles rising from the water I know how to whistle like an otter. I saw the Imperial mail arrive today, thick packages of it, all sealed and protected. Basiliskos took it all into his possession. Just wait until tomorrow morning. I am sure that Narses will discuss the latest secrets from Byzantium then with Basiliskos and Alboin. Or leave me behind if you like…"

"No, for that would immediately mark you as a spy. You are worth more than ten times your weight in gold, Syphax. I will stay behind until tomorrow," he called out to the tribunes as they returned to the tent.

"Oh general, come with us," Licinius begged, "away from the oppressive proximity of this Narses."

But Cethegus became angry: "Does he still tower over me in your eyes? The same fool who lets Cethegus out of his carefully watched camp and out of the sight of his Lombards to Rome, throwing the pike back into the sea from his net? He has intimidated you far too much! I will follow you tomorrow evening. There is still some business I have to do here, which I must handle personally. To occupy Rome without resistance is something you can do without me. I will catch up with you along the way, probably before you reach Terracina, but if not don't worry about me. Just move straight on to Rome. You, Licinius, will guard the Capitol for me."

With gleaming eyes Licinius replied: "You do me great honour, my general! I will defend it with my heart blood if need be. May I ask a favour?"

"What is it?"

"Don't expose yourself so recklessly again to the spears of the Gothic king! The day before yesterday he threw two spears at you at once, one with each hand. If I had not caught the one from his left with my shield…"

"Then, my Licinius, the Jupiter from the Capitol would have blown it away from me. He still needs me! But you mean well."

"Do not allow Roma to become a widow!" Licinius warned.

Cethegus looked at him with an overwhelming expression of respectful affection. And then he went on:

"Salvius Julianus, you will occupy Hadrian's tomb; you, Piso, the rest of the city on the left bank of the Tiber, especially the Porta Latina. That is the gate through which I will follow you. You will not open the gates to Narses alone any more than you would have done to Belisarius alone last time. Farewell, and greet Rome for me. Tell Rome for me that the last struggle for her possession, between Narses and Cethegus, has ended in victory for Cethegus. Farewell until we meet again in Rome! *Roma eterna!*"

"*Roma eterna!*" the tribunes repeated with enthusiasm, and hurried on their way.

"Oh why couldn't that Licinius have been Manilia's son?" Cethegus said to himself, following the young man with his eyes. "Oh foolishness of the heart! Why are you so persistent? Licinius, you shall be my heir in place of Julius! Oh if only you could have been Julius!"

Chapter 10

Cethegus's departure for Rome was delayed for several days. Narses, it is true, did nothing to detain him. In fact he expressed surprise that the 'Ruler of the Capitol' was not drawn more strongly to the Tiber River.

"Admittedly," he said, "I can understand that you have watched the Barbarians rule in Italy for so long that now you are keen to see them fall in your Italy. But I cannot say how much longer that will take. That chasm cannot be stormed, certainly not while it is being defended by men like that king. More than a thousand of my Lombards, Alemanni, Burgundians, Heruli, Franks and Gepidae have already fallen in front of that accursed pass."

"Why don't you send your brave 'Romaeans' against the Goths sometime?" Alboin interjected angrily. "The Heruli Vulkaris and Wilmuth fell from King Teias's axe almost as soon as they arrived here. Asbad of the Gepidae fell from the spear of that boy Adalgoth, my cousin Gisulf lies severely wounded by Duke Guntharis, the Franconian Count Butilin was stabbed by Wisand the *bandalarius* with the point of his banner, the Burgundian Gernot had his brain smashed in by old Hildebrand's stone axe, Liuthari of the Alemanni was slain by Count Grippa, and my own shield bearer Klaffo by some common Gothic soldier. And around every one of our dead heroes a dozen or more of their men lie dead too. Last night at midnight the block of lava on which I was standing slipped most conveniently and intelligently just as King Teias, who can see in the dark, was about to throw his accursed lance. Had that rock not slipped when it did then Rosamunda would no longer be the most beautiful wife in the Lombard Empire, but the most beautiful widow. As it was I escaped with only nasty abrasions, which will never be praised in any song, but which I much prefer to King Teias's best spear in my stomach. But it seems to me that it must by now be the turn of some other hero. It's time your Macedonians and Illyrians tried their luck too. We have shown them often enough how one dies in front of that wretched mouse hole."

"No, my wolf, diamond alone will cut diamond!" Narses replied with a smile. "Always Germanic peoples against Germanic peoples. There are too many of you in this world."

"It seems, *Magister Militum*," said Cethegus, "that you hold the same fatherly opinion of the Isaurians, at least of mine. Just before they left for Rome you ordered them to attempt a general storm of the pass, the first such storm you have ordered. Seven hundred of my seven thousand now lie dead on those rocks, and my tried and proven Sandil, who has fought so many battles by my side, found King Teias's axe too sharp for his helmet too. A pity! He was worth a great deal to me."

"Well, at least the remainder of them are now safe in Rome. But as for those Goths, nothing will drive them out of that hole except fire. If only the earth would tremble just once to help me, as it did for Belisarius at Ravenna."

"Is there still no news about the outcome of the case against Belisarius?" Cethegus probed. "I hear that some letters arrived from Byzantium a few days ago, is that so?"

"I have not yet read them all. If not with fire, then perhaps we can drive them out with hunger. And when they do charge out of that pass in their last battle, then many a man in my army will wish he was hearing the Ganges roar, and not the Draco. Not you, Prefect, I know you can look death in the eye!"

"I want to wait and see how things develop here for a few days before I leave for Rome. The weather is bad for travelling; it has been raining and storming incessantly. I will leave on the first sunny day."

That was indeed the problem. The night after the Isaurians had left the weather had suddenly changed. The fisherman, who lived in a house near Stabiae, could not risk going out in this weather, not so much on account of the weather as the Lombards, who had been watching him suspiciously and almost took him prisoner on one occasion. It was only when his old father hurried along and swore before witnesses that Agnellus was really his son, and nothing but a harmless fisherman, that they reluctantly let him go. But he did not dare to appear to be fishing when no other fisherman was casting his nets. It was only far out on the water that Syphax could speak to him unobserved, but the fisherman could not venture out that far, and therefore no meeting between them could take place.

The exits of all the camps, including the now half empty camp of Cethegus, where Narses had placed only some three thousand Persians and Thracens into the empty tents left by the Isaurians, were being watched day and night by the Lombards.

Narses also had to postpone his mud bath until the rain gave way to sunnier days. But those secrets, i.e. the letters from Procopius and what Narses would discuss in the bath, were what Cethegus was waiting for.

Chapter 11

It looked as if the Prefect's old luck was even about to change the weather. On the morning after his discussion with Narses the sun shone brightly on the blue bay of Bajae, and hundreds of fishing boats hurried out to make the best of the weather.

Syphax had disappeared at first light, after leaving the entrance to his master's tent in the care of the last four remaining Isaurians.

After Cethegus had completed his morning bath in the next tent, and was returning to his own tent for his breakfast, he suddenly heard Syphax shouting loudly as he ran through the camp.

"No," he was crying, "this fish belongs to the Prefect. I have paid good money for it. Surely the great Narses does not want to eat another man's fish?" And with these words Syphax tore himself loose from Alboin and several of the Lombards, as well as a number of slaves belonging to Narses.

Cethegus stopped in his tracks. He recognised the slave who was chief cook to the cripple, who was always ill and of the most moderate habits. This slave had to work almost exclusively for Narses and his personal guests.

"Sir," the well educated Greek slave said, with an apology, addressing the Prefect in his own language: "Please don't blame me for this unseemly behaviour. I care nothing for one fish! But those long-bearded Barbarians want to claim the basket of fish which Syphax has brought back for Narses, no matter what the cost."

A quick exchange of glances between Cethegus and Syphax was sufficient. The Lombards had not been able to understand the conversation in Greek between Cethegus and the slave.

Cethegus struck Syphax on the cheek and cried in Latin: "You worthless, insolent slave! Will you never learn manners? Why shouldn't the sick general have the best?" With that he tore the basket roughly from the slave's grasp, and gave it to the Greek cook. "Here is the basket. I hope that Narses will enjoy the fish." The slave, who thought he had refused the gift quite clearly, went on his way shaking his head.

"What did that mean?" he asked on parting, in Latin.

"That means," Alboin who was following him replied, "that the best fish is not in the basket but somewhere else." Back in the tent Syphax eagerly reached into his belt of crocodile skin, which held a bundle of papyrus scrolls protected from the water. He handed them to his master.

"You are bleeding, Syphax?"

"Only a little. When the Lombards saw me swimming in the water they pretended I was a dolphin, and shot at me with their arrows."

"Take care of yourself – one *solidus* for every drop of your blood! This letter is worth gold and blood, it seems. Look after yourself! The Isaurians are to admit nobody."

Now alone in the tent the Prefect started to read. As he did so his features became darker, the great crease in the centre of his forehead grew deeper and deeper, and his lips were tightly closed.

"To Cornelius Cethegus Caesarius, the former Prefect of Rome and former friend of Procopius of Caesarea, Procopius for the last time.

"This is the saddest piece of writing I have ever had to do, with either my former or my present writing hand. And I would gladly give my left hand here, as I gave my right hand for Belisarius, if I did not have to write it. This letter will put an end to our friendship, which is now almost thirty years old.

"I believed in two heroes in this time where heroes are so few. I believed in the hero of the sword, Belisarius, and the hero of the mind, Cethegus. The latter I must in future hate, indeed almost despise…"

The reader threw the letter down on the *lectus*; then he picked it up again and went on reading:

"Only one thing could have been worse, and that is if Belisarius had been the traitor you made him out to be. But the innocence of Belisarius has been proved, just as gloriously as your black treachery and deceitfulness has been uncovered. For a long time now I have felt uncomfortable on your dark, devious and crooked paths, along which I too accompanied you for a good part of the way. But that was because I believed in what I thought was your high and unselfish ideal, the liberation of Italy. But now, at long last, I can see through you, and I see now that the one and only great driving force in you is your boundless passion for power, and your insatiable thirst to rule. Any goal and any passion which requires means such as those you have chosen must be evil. You tried to destroy that great man with the loyal and childlike soul through his own wife, while she herself had only just started striving to correct her ways. And you did all this as a sacrifice to your shameful friend Theodora and your own thirst for power. That is demoniacal, and I now turn away from you once and for all."

Cethegus closed his eyes for a moment.

"It should not surprise me," he said to himself. "He too had his idol, Belisarius! To the clever Procopius it is as unbearable to have Belisarius harmed as it is to a Christian to see the cross as nothing more than a piece of wood. Therefore it should not surprise me, but it does hurt!

"That is the power of thirty years of habit. How habit does weaken one! The Goth took Julius from me, and Belisarius took Procopius. I wonder who will take away Cethegus, my last and oldest friend? Nobody shall do that, not even Narses or fate. Away with you, Procopius, out of my life. You are dead! The eulogy which I have just held in your honour was almost too long, and certainly too emotional. What else does the dead man have to say?" And he read on.

"But I am writing all this to you because I want to conclude our long friendship, which you terminated with your attack on Belisarius, by doing you a favour. I want to warn you and save you, if you can be warned and saved.

"Seven of my earlier letters have apparently not reached you, for if they had you would no longer be in the camp of Narses; yet his reports about the war lead me to believe that is where you are.

"I have therefore entrusted this letter to my trusted slave Agnellus, the son of a fisherman from Stabiae, where you are now camped. I am giving him his freedom, and this letter is to be his last task in my employ. Although I should hate you, Cethegus, I find that I love you still, my long-time friend. I do not know why that should be so, but somehow I cannot let go of you, and I want to save you if I can.

"When I arrived back in Byzantium soon after your departure – the news that Belisarius had been arrested reached me along the way, like a clap of thunder – I thought at first that you must have been deceived as the emperor had been. I could not believe Belisarius guilty of treason against Justinian.

"In vain I sought an audience with the emperor; his anger was directed against all those who had been friends of Belisarius. In vain I tried to get to Antonina, with every means and trick at my disposal. Thanks to your instructions she was being expertly watched in the Red House. In vain I demonstrated the impossibility of his guilt to Tribonianus; he merely shrugged his shoulders and said: 'I don't understand it either! But the proof is conclusive. Why does he persist in denying those visits to his house by Anicius? He is doomed!'

"And doomed indeed he was. Sentence had been passed; Belisarius received the death sentence, and Antonina banishment. The emperor's mercy commuted the sentence to blinding, banishment to a place far away from Antonina, and confiscation of his estates.

"The news lay heavily on Byzantium. Nobody believed in his guilt, except the emperor and his judges. But nobody could prove him innocent, or turn his fate for the better. I made up my mind that I would go with him, the one armed man with his blind idol. And then a man came along who saved him, and may he be blessed for it in all eternity! It was his great enemy Narses, whom I have already described to you as the greatest man of our century."

"Of course," Cethegus grumbled, "and now the noblest as well."

"As soon as the news reached him, the sick man rushed directly to Byzantium from the baths at Nikomedia, where he had been convalescing. He called for me and said: 'You know that it would be my greatest joy to defeat Belisarius in open battle. But I will not have him miserably destroyed like this, by lies. The man who was the greatest enemy of Narses deserves a better fate. Come with me; you his greatest friend, and I his greatest enemy, together we will save him, the great fool!'"

Chapter 12

"And then he demanded an audience with the emperor, which was immediately granted to a known enemy of Belisarius. And Narses said to Justinian: 'It is not possible that Belisarius could be a traitor. His only fault has always been his blind loyalty to you in spite of your ingratitude.'

"Justinian remained deaf, but Narses would not give in. Instead of doing so he laid his commander's baton at Justinian's feet and said to him: 'Well then, either you overturn the verdict and permit a re-trial, or you lose both your commanders on the same day, because Narses will go into exile on the same day as Belisarius. Then see who will defend your borders against Goths, Persians and Saracens.'

"At that the emperor swayed, and asked for three days in which to consider the matter. In the meantime Narses and I were permitted to examine all documents connected with the case, and also to speak with Antonina and the other accused.

"I soon saw from the documents that the most damaging evidence against Belisarius was the secret nightly visits by Anicius to his house, which Antonina, Belisarius and Anicius himself had persistently denied. The only other really incriminating evidence was his agreement to be part of the conspiracy, written on a wax tablet, and I thought that I would be able to explain that away.

"When I spoke to Antonina alone I told her: 'Those visits from Anicius, and your lies about them, will destroy him.' To that she replied, with a gleam in her eye: 'Very well then, in that case only I am lost, and Belisarius is saved. Belisarius really knew nothing of those visits, because Anicius was not visiting him but me. The whole world shall know, and Belisarius too. He will kill me, but he will be saved.' And she gave me a bundle of letters from Anicius which, if presented to the emperor, would indeed explain everything. But they would also indict the empress terribly.

"And you know how highly Justinian valued his Theodora, and the extraordinary position of valued trust she held in his eyes. I took the letters and hurried to Narses with them. The latter read them and said: 'Good. Now we are no longer concerned merely with the downfall of Belisarius; now we are all doomed, or else Theodora herself, that lovely devil in human form, is doomed. Now it is a matter of life and death! First, before we do anything else, come with me to Antonina once more.' And from Antonina, accompanied by armed guards, we hurried to Anicius, who was slowly convalescing in his dungeon."

Cethegus stamped his foot.

"And after that the four of us went to Justinian. The noble-minded sinner Antonina confessed her nightly meetings with Anicius on her knees before Justinian, but she also added that their only purpose had been to extract the youth from the web the empress had woven around him. She gave him all of Anicius's letters, which described the temptress and her secret tricks, as well as details about the secret passage into her chambers and the revolving Justinian statue.

"It was terrible to see how the poor, deceived husband rose in defence of Theodora. He wanted to have us all arrested on the spot for insulting the throne and for boundless lies. But Narses said: 'You can do that tomorrow! But today, while the empress sleeps, let Anicius and myself lead you into your wife's chambers through the secret passage and the revolving Justinian, take possession of her letters and make her face Anicius and Antonina. Have the old witch Galatea tortured as well, and then see if you don't find out much more than you will enjoy hearing. And if we are wrong, then you can punish us tomorrow in any way you choose.'

"The revolving Justinianus, and the insistence by Anicius that he had often gone through the secret passage, were both so clearly demonstrable, and so challenging, that they could hardly have been mere inventions on our part. Justinian therefore accepted our proposal.

"That night Anicius led the three of us and the emperor into the garden of the empress. A hollow tree concealed the entrance to the secret passage there, and the passage itself ended under the mosaic floor of the antechamber to Theodora's rooms.

"Until that moment Justinian had remained steadfast in his belief that the empress was innocent. But then Anicius really did push a marble plate aside, and opened a secret lock with a key that had been fetched from his house, revealing the statue on the other side. At that the emperor sank into my arms, half conscious. At last he regained his composure and entered the chamber alone, past the statue.

"The room was filled with a half light. Theodora's bed was visible in the pale light of a lamp. Softly, with trembling step, the betrayed husband walked to the bed. There Theodora lay, fully dressed in her imperial robes. A shrill scream on the part of Justinian drew us all to his side; it also drew Galatea, coming out of a side chamber, whom I took into custody immediately.

"Justinian, rigid with shock, pointed to the empress. We all stepped closer – she was dead. Galatea, no less surprised than we were, started to sob convulsively.

"In the meantime we searched the room, and on a golden tripod brazier we found the ashes of countless papyrus scrolls. Antonina called for slaves and light. And then Galatea regained her composure and told how the empress had left her garden toward evening, which was the time of our audience, without any following. She planned to seek out the emperor alone in his study, as she often did at this hour.

"She had come back very quickly, calm but noticeably pale. She had asked for the brazier to be filled with glowing coals, and then locked herself in her rooms. Later, when Galatea knocked, she had replied that she had retired early and did not require anything further.

"The emperor threw himself across the much loved body of his wife once more and then, in the light, he saw that the little poison capsule in her ring was open. The ring had once been Cleopatra's; it was clear that the empress had taken her own life. And on the citrus table there was a strip of parchment with her old motto: 'To live is to rule through beauty.'

"Still we had our doubts. Perhaps the pain of her illness or depression, and not the discovery of her imminent downfall, had driven her to the desperate deed. When news of her death reached the palace the emperor's chamberlain, Theophilos, hurried into the death chamber almost in despair. He prostrated himself at the emperor's feet, and confessed that he thought he knew what had happened.

"He, Theophilos, had been secretly in the pay of the empress for years, and he always let her know whenever the emperor granted audiences of this type, where he normally refused in advance to allow the empress to attend. Theodora had then usually witnessed the proceedings unobserved from a side chamber, no matter how secret the discussions may have been.

"This was what he had done yesterday also, when he learned that we had been granted an audience, and specific instructions had been issued that the empress was not to be admitted. Soon after the audience commenced the empress had appeared in the side chamber, but she had no sooner heard a few words uttered by Anicius and Antonina than she uttered a muffled cry and collapsed among the curtains. She had then quickly regained her composure, risen and left, bidding him to say nothing.

"After hearing this Narses tried to persuade the emperor that he should have Galatea tortured in order to extract further secrets, but Justinian replied: 'I do not wish to inquire any further.' For a whole day and night he remained alone with the dead woman whom he still loved, locked in her rooms. On the next day he arranged to have her buried with full imperial honours in the church of St Sophia. It was officially announced that the empress had died from coal fumes, and the tripod brazier with the coals was publicly exhibited.

"That night Justinian had become an old man.

"And now it became apparent from the statements by Antonina, Anicius, Belisarius, Photius, Antonina's slaves, the litter bearers who had carried you to the Red House just before his arrest and others that you, in collusion with the empress, had persuaded Belisarius to give the appearance of heading the conspiracy. To this end you had used Antonina as a tool to your advantage. All the various statements agreed, and I swore that Belisarius had expressed to me his abhorrence at what Photius had in mind some time before.

"Justinian hurried to Belisarius's dungeon, embraced him in a tearful scene, and begged Belisarius for forgiveness, not only for himself but also for Antonina. The latter now freely and dutifully confessed all her innocent love trysts, and in return received complete forgiveness from Belisarius.

"The emperor then begged Belisarius to accept the top command in Italy in order to make good the wrong he had done to him. But Belisarius replied: 'No, Justinianus, my work on earth is done! I will go with Antonina to my furthermost villa in Mesopotamia, and there I will bury myself in my past. I am cured of the sickness of trying to serve you. If you wish to grant me one last favour, then give Narses the command in Italy, Narses my great friend and my saviour. Narses shall avenge me against the Goths and against the Satan called Cethegus.' And the two great former enemies embraced before our eyes, moving us all deeply.

"All of this had been cloaked in the greatest secrecy in order to protect the memory of the empress. Justinian loves her still. It was announced that the innocence of Belisarius had now been established by Narses, Tribonianus and myself, and by some newly discovered letters by the conspirators. And Justinian pardoned all of the convicted men, even Scaevola and Albinus, whom you had once toppled.

"But I am writing this to you in order to warn you and to save you if I can. Although I do not know how he plans to do it, I feel certain that Justinian has sworn your demise, and that Narses is to carry out your destruction.

"Flee! Save yourself! Your goal of a free, rejuvenated Rome, ruled by you alone, was a dream which could never be realised. To it you have sacrificed everything, even our beautiful friendship.

"I am going to accompany Belisarius and Antonina, and then I will try, near them and as a witness to their happiness now that they are completely reconciled, to forget all the horror, disgust and doubt about everything that is human."

Chapter 13

Cethegus jumped from his camp bed to his feet, threw the letter to the ground and started to pace rapidly up and down in the tent.

"You weakling, Procopius! And weakling Cethegus too! How could you let yourself be upset over one more lost soul, Cethegus? Had you not lost Julius long before you killed him? And yet you live and fight on! And as for this Narses, whom they all fear as if he was God the father and the devil in one; could he really be all that dangerous? Impossible! After all, he blindly entrusted Rome to me and my men! It is due to no master stroke on his part that I am not in Rome at this moment, out of his reach, ruling Rome from the Capitol and defying him. Pah, I am too old to learn fear now. I will place my trust in my lucky star once more! Is that extreme daring? Or is it the calmest of wisdom? I don't know, but it seems to me that the same kind of confidence led Caesar from victory to victory. Indeed, there is scarcely anything more to be discovered from what Narses says in his bath, certainly nothing more than I already know from this long and explicit letter."

And he tore the papyrus scroll into small pieces.

"I will leave this very day, even if Syphax hears nothing more during Narses's bath hour, which should be now."

A few moments later the *Archonius* John was announced by the Isaurians, and upon a signal from Cethegus he was admitted.

"Prefect of Rome," John addressed the latter, "I have come to make good an old injustice against you. My grief at the death of my brother Perseus made me suspicious at the time."

"Forget it!" Cethegus replied. "It is past."

"But I have not forgotten," John continued, "your tremendous bravery. It is to honour it, and at the same time make good use of it, that I now come to you with a proposal. My comrades and I are used to Belisarius and his hearty way of attack, and we find the cautious habits of the great Narses very dull. For two months now we have been lying here before this pass; we are losing men every day, and we are certainly not gathering any laurels in the process. The commander-in-chief wants to starve the Barbarians out! Who knows how much longer that might take? And when they do eventually break out of that pass there will be a nice piece of butchery, as they will sell every drop of blood dearly. It is quite clear to me that, if only we had the entrance to that accused pass..."

"Yes, if!" Cethegus replied. "It happens to be rather well defended by that Teias."

"That is exactly why he must fall. He, the king, apparently is the only thing now which holds the whole bundle of loose spears together. That is why I have made a pact with the best blades in the camp, about a dozen or more of them. What we are trying to do is this. As you know the pass is so narrow that only one man at a time can approach it for hand to hand combat. We propose to take it in turns to challenge that Teias whenever he has the watch; we will draw lots as to who goes first. The others will stop behind the fighter in front as close as possible, save him if he is wounded, take his place if he is slain, or force our way over the king's body if we are successful. Apart from myself the pact includes the Lombards Alboin, Gisulf and Autharis, the Heruli Rodulf and Suartua, Ardaric the Gepidae prince, Gundebad the Burgundian, the Franks Clothachar and Bertchramm, the Alemanni Vadomar and Epurulf, Garizo the tall Bajuvar, Kabades the Persian, Althias the Armenian and the Illyrian Taulantius.

"We would like to have you and your feared sword among our number also. We know that you hate that black haired hero. Will you be one of us, Cethegus?"

"Gladly," the latter replied, "while I am still here. But I will soon exchange the camp here for the Capitol."

A strange, scornful smile appeared on John's face, and this did not escape Cethegus. But he did not interpret it correctly. "You can hardly doubt my courage, after what you said before," he said. "But for me there are more important things than stamping out the last glimmering coals of the war against the Goths. The orphaned city wants its Prefect. The Capitol is calling for me."

"The Capitol!" John repeated. "I would have thought, Cethegus, that the death of a free hero was worth something too."

"It is, but only after one has achieved one's aims in life."

"None of us knows, Cethegus, how close he has come to his goal. But there is one more thing. It seems to me that there is something brewing among the Barbarians up there on that accursed fire mountain. From the hill on my side of the camp it is possible to look over the top of the lava outcrops, through a crack. I would like you and your trained eyes to take a look. If they do decide to break out, then at least we don't want to be caught by surprise. Come over there with me. But say nothing to Narses about our pact; he does not like such things. I chose his bath hour to come and call on you."

"I will come with you," Cethegus replied. He then donned the rest of his armour and left, after vainly asking the Isaurian guards outside the tent for news of Syphax. He followed John through his own camp, then through the main camp of Narses, and finally they arrived together at the outermost camp on the right side, which was John's.

A number of leaders were already standing on the crown of the hill to which John had referred earlier, peering through a small dip in the lava to a part of the Gothic camp clearly visible from here.

After Cethegus had looked in the direction of the Gothic camp for a while he exclaimed: "There is no doubt! They are clearing the eastern part of their camp, the part in front of us. They are moving the wagons and pulling them to the right, to the west. That would indicate they are moving closer together, and it could mean that they plan to break out."

"What do you think?" a young commander asked John. He had apparently just arrived from Byzantium, and Cethegus did not recognise him. "What do you think? Could we not reach the Barbarians from that rocky outcrop over there with the new ballistas, which my brother had to take to Rome? You know, the last machine Martinus invented before he was killed?"

"To Rome?" Cethegus cried, and threw a searching glance at both the young man and at John.

Suddenly he was overcome by hot and cold shivers, which went right through him. It was more frightening, more devastating, than the news of Belisarius's landing had been, or the news of Totila's uprising, or Totila's diversion to Rome at Pons Padi, or Totila entering Rome from the Tiber, or even the news that Narses had invaded Italy.

He felt as if some great hand was gripping both his brain and his heart at once, like a claw. He saw also that John was signalling the young questioner to be silent, by fiercely knitting his brows.

"To Rome?" Cethegus repeated, piercing John and the stranger in turn with his eyes.

"Well, yes, of course to Rome!" John said at last. "Zenon, this man is Cethegus, the Prefect of Rome." The young Byzantine bowed with an expression such as one might use when meeting some famous or notorious monster for the first time. "Cethegus, the *archonius* Zenon here has been fighting on the Euphrates until now. He only arrived from Byzantium last night with his Persian archers."

"And his brother?" Cethegus asked, "has gone to Rome?"

"My brother Megas," the Byzantine replied, now back in control, "has orders to make the new ballistas available to the Prefect of Rome." And here he bowed his head once more. "He embarked long before me, and so I thought he had arrived long before me too, and left for Rome with you. But his ballistas are very heavy.

"And I am delighted to meet the mightiest man of the Occident, the glorious defender of Hadrian's tomb, face to face."

But Cethegus cast one more sharp look at John and turned to go, with a brief word of farewell to those present. After taking a few steps he stopped suddenly and looked back; he saw how John was clenching his fists and speaking in a threatening manner to the young *archonius* from the Euphrates.

A cold sweat overcame the Prefect. He resolved to go back to his tent via the shortest possible route, and then mount his horse and leave for Rome immediately, without waiting for Syphax to report what he had found out. In order to take the shortest path he tried to leave John's camp, and to get to his own camp by walking in a straight line across the huge semicircle of tents.

A few Persian archers from the camp were riding in front of him. A few peasants, who had been selling wine in the camp, were also allowed to pass freely by the guards. They were Lombards, to whom Narses had entrusted guard duty here as he had in every other part of the camp. They stopped him with couched spears as he tried to follow the peasants. Angrily he reached for the spears, quickly parting them.

At that one of the Lombards blew into his horn, and the others closed in a tight formation around Cethegus once more. "Orders from Narses!" Autharis, their leader, said.

"What about them?" Cethegus asked, pointing to the peasants and the Persian archers.

"They are not you!" the Lombard replied.

A group of other guards had arrived at the scene by now, attracted by the sound of the horn, and now they stood facing Cethegus, their bows at the ready. Silently Cethegus turned his back on them and went back to his tent along the same way as he had come.

Perhaps it was only because his suspicion had suddenly been aroused, but it seemed to him as if all the Byzantines and Lombards whom he passed were evading him with looks which seemed to be a mixture of jeering and pity.

On arriving back at his tent he asked the Isaurian guard: "Is Syphax back yet?"

"Yes master, long ago. He is waiting for you in your tent. He is wounded." Quickly Cethegus threw back the curtain and entered.

As soon as he did so Syphax, pale under his bronze skin, rushed towards him and put his arms around the Prefect's knees. Then he whispered to him, desperately, urgently: "Oh my master, my great lion! You are trapped – doomed – nothing can save you now!"

"Control yourself, slave!" Cethegus ordered. "You are bleeding…"

"It is nothing! They did not want to let me back into the camp. They started to quarrel with me as if in jest, but the thrusts from their knives were in bitter earnest…"

"Who? Whose knives?"

"The Lombards, master, who have been holding every entrance to your camp occupied for the last half hour."

"I will ask Narses why!" Cethegus said threateningly.

"The reason, or rather the excuse, is the threat of a Gothic breakout. He sent the Persian Kabades to tell you that. But oh my lion – my palm tree – my spring – my morning star – you are doomed!" And once again the Numidian threw himself face down on the ground, and covered his master's feet with hot tears and kisses.

"Tell me everything, one thing after the other, in order!" Cethegus commanded, leaning with his arms crossed behind his back and his head held high against the central pole of the tent. He seemed to be looking into the far distance, and not into the tear-stained, despairing face of Syphax.

"Oh master – I will not be able to do it in clear order. Well, I arrived at the hiding place among the reeds – I barely needed to dive because the reeds were so thick that they hid me well. The bathhouse is made of wood and canvas, newly rebuilt after the storm the other day. Narses came in his small boat, accompanied by Alboin, Basiliskos and three other men. They were disguised as Lombards, but I recognised them; they were Scaevola, Albinus and…"

"Not dangerous," Cethegus interrupted.

"And Anicius!"

"Are you sure you are not mistaken?" Cethegus cried.

"Master, I know his eyes and his voice! From the conversation – I could not understand all the words – but the meaning was clear to me…"

"I wish you had been able to tell me the exact words!"

"They were speaking Greek, master, which I do not understand as well as your language; and the wind and the waves were making a noise too."

"Well, what did they say?"

"The three of them arrived from Byzantium last night. They demanded your head immediately. But Narses said: 'No, not murder. He shall be properly tried, and then lawfully punished.'

'But when? When?' Anicius urged, and Narses replied: 'As soon as it is time.'

'And what about Rome?' Basiliskos asked. And Narses said: 'he will never see Rome again.'"

"Stop!" Cethegus cried. "Stop for a moment! I have to be quite clear about this." He wrote a few lines onto a wax tablet. "Is Narses back from his bath?"

"Long ago."

"Good." He gave the tablet to one of the Isaurians in front of the tent. "You will bring me a reply immediately. Go on, Syphax!" Cethegus could no longer stand still, and started pacing up and down.

"Oh master, something terrible must have happened in Rome – I was not able to understand exactly what it is. Anicius asked a question, which was somehow related to your Isaurians. 'I got rid of that leader Sandil,' Narses said. 'And the rest are in good hands in Rome, those of Aulus and the Macer brothers, my decoys,' he added with a laugh."

"Did he use the word decoy?"

"Yes master. Then Alboin spoke: 'It is a good thing that the young tribunes are gone; that would have meant a sharp fight otherwise.' And then Narses concluded: 'All the Isaurians had to be moved away from here some way. Otherwise we might have been forced to fight a bloody battle right here in our own camp. What if King Teias had charged suddenly into the middle of it?' Oh master, I am afraid they have taken your most loyal supporters away from you."

"I think so too," Cethegus said gloomily. "But what did they say about Rome?"

"Alboin asked about a commander, whose name I had never heard."

"Megas?" Cethegus asked.

"Yes, Megas, that was his name. But how did you know?"

"It does not matter. Go on, what about this Megas?"

"Alboin asked how long Megas had been in Rome? Narses replied: 'Long enough and soon enough for the Roman tribunes and the Isaurians.'"

At this Cethegus groaned with deeply felt agony.

"Then Scaevola asked: 'But the citizens of Rome, they regard this tyrant and his tribunes almost as gods!' And Narses replied: 'Yes, they did once. But now they hate nothing more than the man who tried to make Romans and heroes out of them by force. They hate him now!' And then Albinus asked fearfully: 'What if they decided to admit him to Rome again just the same? His name is almost all-powerful?' And Narses replied: 'Twenty-five thousand Armenians in the Capitol and in Hadrian's tomb will have an even stronger influence on the Romans!' "

Cethegus struck his forehead with his hand.

"Narses went on: 'They are even more firmly committed than Pope Pelagius to their agreement and oath.' Scaevola asked: 'What agreement and oath?' and Narses replied: 'As you know they swore that they would open the gates of their city only to the Prefect of Rome. But you see, they have known for three months now that the name of the Prefect of Rome is – Narses! They have sworn allegiance to me, not him!'"

When he heard that Cethegus threw himself silently on his bed and hid his head in his cloak. But no sound or complaint came from that powerful chest.

"Oh my precious master – it will kill you! But I have not yet finished. You must know everything, so that desperation will give you untold and ultimate strength, as a lion is most powerful when he is cornered."

Cethegus rose to his feet again: "Go on and finish what you have to say! Anything further I have yet to hear is unimportant, as it concerns only me and not Rome."

"But it does concern you – terribly! Narses went on to say: 'Yesterday, at the same time as I received the long awaited news from Rome…'"

"What news?" Cethegus asked.

"He did not say. What he did say was: 'At the same time Zenon brought me the order to open the sealed letter from the emperor. The latter is assuming, with every justification from my last report, that the final destruction of the Goths could now occur any day. I opened it and' – oh master, it is dreadful!"

"Speak!"

"Narses said: 'The whole pettiness of the great Justinian is evident in this. I think that he could perhaps forgive Cethegus for almost leading the emperor of justice to blind the ever-faithful Belisarius, but he cannot forgive that he conspired with Theodora, as "a seduced victim of Theodora!" What a terrible anachron… something'. That was all I could understand."

"Anachronism!" Cethegus calmly corrected him.

"'Of having deceived the emperor. The lot which he almost contrived for Belisarius, blinding, shall now strike him instead…'"

"Really?" Cethegus smiled, but he reached for his dagger.

" 'And also that punishment which he re-introduced in his Rome, blasphemously insulting the memory of Jesus Christ, and breaking the law handed down by the great emperor Constantine…' What could he mean by that?" Syphax asked anxiously.

"Crucifixion!" Cethegus replied, replacing the dagger.

"Oh master!"

"Don't despair, I am not hanging in the air yet! So far I still have my feet firmly on the ground. Go on!"

"And then Narses said: 'But I am Justinian's general, not his torturer; he will have to be satisfied if I bring the brave man's head back with me to Byzantium.' Oh master, not that! If we must die – not that!"

"We?" Cethegus smiled, quite composed once more. "You had no part in betraying the great emperor of the Romaeans with Theodora. You are not in any danger."

But Syphax went on: "Don't you know? Oh please do not doubt me – the whole of Africa knows this. If a body has no head, then the soul must crawl like a lowly worm through mud and excrement for centuries. Oh no, they must not be allowed to sever your head from your body!"

"For the moment it is as firmly attached to my neck as the world rests on Atlas. Quiet! Someone is coming."

The Isaurian whom he had sent to Narses brought back the sealed reply: "To Cethegus Caesarius Narses, *Magister Militum*. There is no objection to your wish to return to Rome, today any more than yesterday."

"Now I understand!" Cethegus said.

"The camp guards are under orders to let you leave the camp if you wish to do so. However, in case you do insist on leaving, I will give you a bodyguard of a thousand Lombards under Alboin, because the roads are being made unsafe by scattered Gothic troops.

"As there is every indication that an attempted breakout by the Goths will take place today or tomorrow, and since we have sustained severe losses of both troops and commanders when they have left the camp alone, courageously but foolishly, no one is now permitted to leave the camp perimeter without my permission. Accordingly all guard duty, including that on individual tents, has been entrusted to my dependable Lombards. That includes guards outside the tents of commanders too."

Quickly Cethegus jumped to his feet and tore open the door of his tent. He was just in time to see his four Isaurians being taken away and replaced by twenty Lombards under Autharis. "I was thinking about trying to escape tonight," he said to Syphax. "That is now impossible. And perhaps it is better this way, and more honourable. I would rather die from a Gothic spear in my chest than a Greek arrow in the back of my neck. But Narses has not finished yet." And he read the remainder of the letter.

"In my tent you will be informed about the measures which I have taken to counter the bloodbath which threatens if the Barbarians do break out. It could become a very great bloodbath. But I have yet to give you a piece of unpleasant news. A report which reached me from Rome by ship last night indicates that the majority of your Isaurians in Rome, as well as your tribunes…"

"Oh my Licinius, Piso, Julianus!" Cethegus cried, roused from his usual icy calm by the pain of it all.

"…have been killed. After being peacefully admitted into the city"—"Ha, tricked into entering is more likely"—"they refused to take the oath of allegiance to the emperor. Contrary to the agreement they then tried to use force. Licinius tried to take the Capitol by storm, Salvius Julianus attempted the same with Hadrian's tomb, and Piso with the Porta Latina. They all fell, each before his target. The remaining mercenaries have been taken prisoner."

"My second Julius has followed the first!" Cethegus lamented. "Well, now I no longer have any need for heirs, because Rome will never be mine to leave to anyone. It is over! The great struggle for Rome is lost! Sheer brutal superiority in numbers, coupled with petty cunning, have won out! They have triumphed over Gothic swords just as they have over the mind of Cethegus. Oh Romans – Romans – 'you too, my sons!' Yes, you are my Bruti! Syphax, you are free. I will go on and seek death. You are free to go back to your desert."

"Oh master!" Syphax cried, sobbing aloud and throwing himself at his master's feet, "Don't push me away from you! I am no less loyal to you than Aspa was to her mistress. Let me die with you."

"So be it!" Cethegus said calmly, placing his hand on the head of the faithful Moor. "I have been very fond of you, my panther. Die with me if that is your wish. Give me my shield, helmet, sword and spear."

"Where are we going?"

"To Narses first."

"And then?"

"Then to Vesuvius!"

Chapter 14

The intention of King Teias had been to hurl himself at the Byzantine camp that night, with every able bodied soldier at his disposal except for a few guards to defend the pass. His plan was to create one last dreadful bloodbath in the camp of Narses, aided by the darkness and the element of surprise. Once the last man of his Goths had been killed, and when a general attack on the pass threatened at daybreak, it was intended that all the women and children who had chosen death rather than slavery would seek a free tomb in the nearby crater of Vesuvius. After that the few defenders left at the pass would make a quick end of it by charging at the enemy from the pass.

It had filled the king with joyous pride to see that not one among the thousands of women and girls – all boys from the age of ten had been armed – had chosen the disgrace of slavery rather than a free death in the crater. Teias had put the choice to them all in the camp, and all had chosen the same fate.

His heroic nature found solace in the thought that his entire nation was to end dying freely as one man, a deed without precedent in history. This desperate plan of the grim last king of the Goths was not to become reality; instead his breaking eyes were to see a different, brighter, more humane spectacle of hope.

Narses, always watchful and cautious, had noticed the threatening enemy preparations even before John and Cethegus, and he had called his council of war into his tent to discuss the threat and to take countermeasures. This meeting was to take place at the fifth hour.

It was a wonderful, golden September, full of light and warmth; the rich aroma of flowers and the sea filled the air. It was a kind of beauty which only the Bajae gulf region of Italy knows. The little white cloud of Vesuvius rose vertically into a clear blue sky, and the waves of the ocean lapped the shores of this lovely land.

And there, walking along the shore so that the waves lapped at his armoured feet from time to time, a man paced along slowly, coming from the left wing of the camp. He was a powerful figure; the sun was reflected by his round shield and his magnificent armour, and the sea breeze rustled the purple plume on his helmet.

It was Cethegus, and he was on his way to die. Only the Moor was following him, at a respectful distance.

When he had reached a small strip of sand, which reached out into the sea, he walked along it to its furthest point, and from there he looked to the northwest. That was where Rome lay, his Rome.

"Farewell!" he said to himself, deeply moved. "Farewell you seven hills of immortality. Farewell, Tiber River, as you roll along, carrying the debris of the centuries with you. Twice you have drunk my blood, and twice you have saved me. This time you cannot save me, friendly river god! I have wrestled and struggled and fought for you, my Rome, as no man has done before me, not even Caesar. The battle is over, and the general without an army is defeated. Yes, I see it now. A single great mind can do anything, except to take the place of a nation which no longer exists.

"A mind can keep itself young, but it cannot rejuvenate other minds. I have tried to do the impossible. But achieving that which is possible is – ordinary! And if the great thought of this struggle for Rome should come to me again from the marble head of my shattered Caesar, armed to the teeth as Athena sprang from the head of Zeus, I would fight the whole fight again! For it is better to yield while wrestling with the impossible than to surrender meekly to mundane everyday events.

"And you shall be blessed." He knelt down and splashed his hot forehead with cool seawater under his bronze helmet. "You shall be blessed, holy seawater of Ausonia; blessed also shall be Italy's holy soil!" And he picked up a handful of sand from the beach, letting it run through his fingers. "Your most faithful son takes his leave from you gratefully; I am shaken, not by fear of my approaching death, but by your magnificence. I see many centuries of crushing foreign rule ahead for you. I was not able to divert that from you, but I am offering you my heart's blood as a sacrifice toward a better future. Even if the laurels of world rule have dried up for ever for you, at least I believe that the olive of freedom and the free spirit and individuality of Italy's people will live on, for under the dust they are still green. And one day there will be a dawn, my Rome, when no foreigner rules on Italy's sacred soil. And then, once more, you will belong only to yourself, from the holy Alps to the holy sea."

He now rose calmly and started to walk toward the central camp and the tent of Narses, his step now faster and more sure.

As he entered he found all the commanders already assembled, and Narses called out to him in a friendly tone: "You have come at a good time, Cethegus. Twelve of my commanders, who made a pact and whom I caught planning a foolish deed of the kind which Barbarians might commit, but never commanders whom I have trained, have mentioned your name as their excuse. They say that anything in which the great and mighty Cethegus has a part cannot be foolishness. Speak, did you really join that armed pact against Teias?"

"I did, and after I leave here – let me go first, John, without drawing lots – I am going directly to Vesuvius. The king's hour on guard is approaching."

"That was a noble action on your part, Cethegus."

"Thank you, it will probably save you a great deal of trouble, *Prefect of Rome*," Cethegus replied.

A gasp of complete surprise went the rounds; even those in the know were amazed at Cethegus's detailed knowledge of the situation. Narses alone remained calm. Softly he said to Basiliskos: "He knows everything, and that is good."

"It is not my fault, Cethegus, that I did not inform you earlier of your replacement; the emperor strictly forbade me from doing so. Your decision is praiseworthy, Cethegus, for it fits in with my best intentions. The Barbarians shall not have the pleasure of slaughtering another myriad of our men tonight. We are moving against that pass immediately with all our troops, including the wings, until we are just out of range of the Gothic spears in front of the pass. They must not be given room to move, and the very first step they take out of that pass shall lead them straight into our lances. I have no objection, Cethegus, if volunteers want to duel with that king of terror. His death, I hope, will mean the end of Barbarian resistance.

"Only one thing concerns me. I ordered the Ionian Fleet here some time ago, as I had expected the final decision to fall a few days earlier. But it has still not arrived. I need it in order to ship the captured Barbarians directly to Byzantium. Has the fast messenger ship returned yet, Nauarchius Konon, which I sent on a reconnaissance mission through the straits of Regium?"

"No, general! A second ship which I sent has not returned yet either."

"Could the last storm have damaged the fleet?"

"Impossible, commander, for it was not strong enough. And according to the last news we received the fleet was safely at anchor in the port of Brundusium."

"Well, we cannot wait for the ships. Forward, my generals! We will all leave for the pass immediately, myself included. Farewell, Cethegus! Don't let the shock of what you have learned worry you too much. I suspect that many a tedious and unpleasant legal procedure and trial would await you at the war's conclusion. You have many enemies, some rightly and some not. Evil omens are threatening you everywhere. But I know that you believe in one omen only: 'There is but one valid purpose in life!'"

"To die fighting for one's country. I ask one more favour. As my Isaurians and my tribunes are either dead or imprisoned in Rome, allow me to gather about me the Italians and the Romans who are serving in your army, so that I can lead them against the Barbarians."

Narses thought for a moment: "Very well, gather them and lead them!" And in a whisper he added to Basiliskos: "To their deaths. There can be no more than fifteen hundred of them at the most. I do not begrudge him the joy of dying at the head of his countrymen, nor them the joy of dying behind him! Farewell, Cethegus."

Silently, saluting Narses with his raised spear, Cethegus left the tent.

"Hmm" Narses said to Alboin. "Take a good last look at him, Lombard. There goes a strange piece of history. Do you know who that is, going away from here just now?"

"A great enemy to his enemies," Alboin replied seriously.

"Yes, my little wolf, take a good last look at him. There goes, on his way to die, the last Roman!"

After all the commanders other than Alboin and Basiliskos had left the tent Anicius, Albinus and Scaevola rushed into it from a side entrance, still in Lombard clothing, with shock and dismay mirrored on their faces.

"What?" Scaevola cried, "You are going to save this man from his proper judges and punishment?"

"And you are robbing the executioner of his body, and his accusers of his fortune?" Albinus added. Only Anicius was silent, clenching his fist.

"General!" Alboin cried. "Make these two old women take off the clothes of my people. Their yapping disgusts me!"

"You are wrong, my wolf! You no longer need that disguise," Narses said. "I no longer need you as accusers. Cethegus has been tried and judged. The sentence will be carried out by – King Teias! But you vultures shall not pick away at the body of the dead hero."

"And the emperor's orders?" Scaevola asked stubbornly.

"Even Justinian cannot blind or crucify a man once he is dead. Once Cornelius Cethegus has fallen, I cannot bring him back to life, to meet with the emperor's cruelty. As for his gold, Albinus, you will not receive a single *solidus* of it; nor will you, Scaevola, taste a single drop of his blood. His gold belongs to the emperor, his blood to the Goths, and his name to immortality."

"You are going to allow this villain to die as a hero?" Anicius now grumbled.

"Yes, son of Boethius, for he has earned it.

"But you have a valid right of revenge against him. You shall hack off his head after he has fallen, and take it to the emperor in Byzantium! Sound the tubas! Can you hear them? The battle has started!"

Chapter 15

When King Teias saw the army of Narses starting to move toward the mouth of the pass, he said to his warriors: "Very well then, it looks as though the last battle of the Goths will be witnessed by the midday sun rather than the stars. That is the only change in our resolve." He positioned a number of soldiers outside the lava cave, showed them the body of Theodoric sitting up on a purple stretcher, and also the royal treasure. He instructed them, whilst the battle raged around the pass, to hurl both body and treasure into the crater on a signal from Adalgoth; he had entrusted the last defence of the pass to Adalgoth and Wachis.

Those who could not bear arms, the women and children, were now crowding around the cave. There was not a tear to be seen, nor a sob to be heard. The warriors themselves were arranged into companies of one hundred men, and within the companies into families, so that fathers and sons, brothers and cousins could fight shoulder to shoulder. This was an ancient form of battle order which the Romans had found to be extraordinarily tough and coherent as far back as the days of the Teutons and the Cherusci of Ariovistos and Arminius. The natural topography of this final Gothic battlefield almost dictated that the Goths should assume the ancient Germanic battle formation of the wedge, with the king at its point as taught by Odin himself, for their charge from the pass.

The deep, thick columns of Byzantines were arranged in echelon formation reaching from the coast to within a spear-throw of the pass itself; it was a magnificently beautiful, but also a terrifying spectacle. The sun was reflected a thousand fold from their weapons, whilst the Goths were standing in the shadow of the mountain. The Goths could see far beyond the standards and lances of their enemies to the blue ocean smiling in the distance. Seldom had the Italian landscape been more majestic.

King Teias was standing next to Adalgoth, who was carrying Theodoric's banner, at the entrance to the pass. For the last time the poet stirred within this king of heroes.

"Look there," he said to his favourite, "could there be a more beautiful setting for us to die in? Nowhere could be lovelier than this, not even the Christian heaven or the Asgardh or Breidablick of Master Hildebrand. Come, Adalgoth, let us die here, worthy of our nation and of this glorious setting."

And with that he threw back the purple robe he was wearing over his black armour, took the little harp in his left hand and sang, in a soft and restrained voice:

"From farthest north to Byzantium and Rome – what a string of victories!
In glory did the Gothic star ascend, and in glory shall it set.
Raise high your swords, and with your last strength strive for lasting fame!
Farewell, proud Gothic heroism; to battle, Goths, let us die!"

And then, with a powerful blow, he smashed the little harp against a rock to his left. The instrument gave one last ringing note as it died.

"Now, Adalgoth, farewell! If only I could have saved the last remnants of my people! Not here, but by free retreat to the north. But it was not to be. Narses would hardly grant it now, and in any case the last of the Goths do not beg. To death!"

And then, raising his feared battleaxe on its long shaft in his hand, he placed himself at the head of the wedge. Behind him stood his cousin Aligern and old Hildebrand. Behind them were Duke Guntharis of Tuscany, the Woelsung, Count Grippa of Ravenna and Count Wisand of Volsinii, the *bandalarius.* Behind them were Wisand's brother Ragnaris of Tarentum and four counts, all relations of Wisand and Ragnaris. And behind them, in successive rows, there stood six, eight, ten Goths, more and more as the wedge widened further back.

Behind the main wedge stood the masses of the people's army, ordered in tens and hundreds.

Wachis, who stood next to Adalgoth defending the pass, gave the signal with the Gothic army horn upon a sign from his king. And immediately the Gothic army burst forth from the chasm, in their last and desperate charge.

Not far from the pass, on a small rocky platform, John was standing with the warriors who had formed the pact with him. Only Alboin, Gisulf and Cethegus were still missing. Behind these ten commanders stood Lombards and Heruli in the front lines, and they immediately started to hurl a rain of spears and arrows at the charging Goths.

The first man to challenge the king, who was conspicuous by the crown helmet above his closed visor, was Althias the Armenian. He fell instantly, his head cleft in two.

The second man was Rodulf the Heruli chieftain, who charged at Teias with his spear. The latter caught the blow with his small shield, quite undisturbed, and as the attacker stumbled backwards Teias thrust the point of his battleaxe into his groin.

Even before Teias could extract his weapon from Rodulf's chainmail the latter's cousin Suartua, the Persian Kabades and Garizo the Bajuvar all charged at the king at once. Teias struck the last of the three, nearest to him and most dangerous, in the chest with the point of his shield, and he tumbled over the cliff on his right and slid down the steep mountainside. "Now help me, oh holy wood nymph of Naples!" the tall Garizo prayed on his way down, "you, who have protected me through all the years of this war, help me now!" And, lucky once more, Miriam's admirer arrived at the bottom little the worse for his experience, apart from being rather stunned by the fall.

Suartua was the next to charge, and as he swung his sword over the head of Teias Aligern leapt to the aid of his king and severed the attacker's arm from his body, sword and all. He screamed and fell. The Persian Kabades, trying to lunge at the king with his curved sword from below, had his visor, face and brain smashed by the old armourer's stone axe.

Teias, once more in possession of his beloved battleaxe and rid of his nearest attackers, now charged into the attack himself. He hurled his axe at a warrior who wore a helmet with the head and tusks of a wild boar. It was Epurulf of the Alemanni, and he fell backwards. His cousin Vadomar bent over him, trying to grasp the Gothic king's dreaded axe; but in a flash Teias was on the spot, his short sword in his right hand. It flashed high in the air, and the next moment Vadomar fell dead on top of his dead friend.

Next the Franks Chothachar and Bertchramm charged together, each swinging a *francisca*, a battleaxe not unlike Teias's weapon. Both axes flew at once; Teias caught one with his shield, and parried the other with his own axe. The next instant he was standing between the two enemies, and swung his axe in a terrible circle above his head. At a single blow both Franks fell to his left and his right, their helmets and heads split in two.

And then a spear struck the king's shield from very close quarters, piercing the edge of the shield and slightly grazing Teias's shield arm. As Teias turned to meet this new enemy – it was the Burgundian Gunobad – Ardaric of the Gepidae charged at him from behind with his sword and struck Teias a heavy blow on his helmet; in the same instant Ardaric lay dead, pierced by the spear of Duke Guntharis. The king forced the Burgundian Gunobad to his knees with his shield, even though the latter was defending himself fiercely. He lost his helmet, and Teias thrust the point of his shield into his throat.

But already Taulantius the Illyrian and the Lombard Autharis were facing the king. The Illyrian smashed at the king's shield with a heavy club made from the root of a stone oak, and smashed a portion of the bottom steel edge from it. Simultaneously the Lombard threw his spear and struck the shield also, tearing away another section of rim and sticking fast in the shield, pulling the latter down by its weight. And already Taulantius was raising his club against the king's visor.

Quickly Teias decided to abandon the half-ruined shield; he smashed the Illyrian's face with its point as he let it go, and at the same time he thrust the point of his axe through the armour of the charging Autharis and into his chest.

But now the king stood without a shield, and the enemy troops doubled their missiles from a distance. With sword and axe alone Teias parried the hail of spears, which came flying at him from all directions. And at the same time the sound of a horn from the pass forced him to look around.

As he turned he saw how the major part of the troops he had led from the pass had fallen; the countless missiles from afar had mown them down; and already a strong force of Lombards, Persians and Armenians had attacked them from the flank, and was now engaging them in hand to hand fighting. And from the right the king could see a strong column of Thracens, Macedonians and Franks starting to attack the guardians of the pass with couched spears. Meanwhile a third force, Gepidae, Alemanni, Isaurians and Illyrians, was now threatening to cut off the retreat for him and the small remaining force behind him.

Teias took a sharp look back to the pass; there the blue banner of Theodoric vanished for a moment, and it looked as if it had fallen. That made up the king's mind. "Back, back to the pass! Save Theodoric's banner!" Teias called out to those fighting behind him and he charged backwards, trying to break through the encircling enemy forces.

But this time the situation was deadly serious, for John was in command of the Isaurians. "Attack the king!" he cried. "Don't let him through! Don't let him retreat either! Spears! Throw spears at him!"

By now Aligern was on the spot. "Take my shield, quickly!" Teias accepted the buffalo shield thus offered; in the same instant John's javelin flew through the air, and would have pierced the king's visor if he had not parried it with the newly won shield.

"Back to the pass!" Teias cried once more, and charged at the attacking John with such force that he fell flat on his back; two of the nearest Isaurians were slain by the king. And now Teias, Aligern, Guntharis, Hildebrand, Grippa, Wisand and Ragnaris were hurrying back to the pass as quickly as they could.

When they arrived there the fight was already raging. Alboin and Gisulf had stormed here, and a heavy, jagged block thrown with both hands by Alboin had struck Adalgoth on the thigh, momentarily forcing him to his knees. But in the next instant Wachis had picked up Theodoric's banner, and Adalgoth himself was back on his feet and pushed the Lombard out of the pass with the point of his shield. The sudden return of the king and his warriors relieved the pressure on the defenders of the pass. The Lombards were now falling by the score through being attacked from behind, and at the same time the defenders of the pass now charged at the Lombards as well. A few moments later the Lombards were in full flight down the slope, tearing their commanders with them. But they had not got far before they were absorbed by the strong force of Isaurians, Illyrians, Gepidae and Allemanni under John. The latter had regained his feet, adjusted his helmet while gnashing his teeth in anger at his earlier humiliation, and he then ordered his troops to turn and advance against the pass, which Teias by now had reached.

"Advance!" he commanded. "Come over here to me, Alboin, Gisulf, Vitalianus, Zenon! Attack! Let us see if that king is really as immortal as he seems to be."

By now Teias had regained his old position at the entrance to the pass, where he now stood cooling off, leaning on the shaft of his battleaxe.

"Now, Barbarian king, the end is near! You have crawled back into your snail shell, have you? Come out, or I will punch a hole in your house! Come on out, if you are a man!" Thus John taunted the king, weighing his spear.

"Give me three spears!" Teias said, and handed his shield and axe to the wounded Adalgoth standing beside him. "Now! As soon as he falls, follow me." And now, without his shield, he took a step out into the open, spears in each hand.

"Welcome to the outside, and welcome to Hades!" John cried and hurled his spear. It was expertly aimed, directly at the king's visor. But Teias bowed his head to the right, and the lance, which had been thrown with a great deal of force, shattered against a rock wall.

As soon as Teias despatched his first spear with his right hand John threw himself face down on the ground; the spear struck and killed Zenon behind him. In a flash John was back on his feet and hurled a second spear at the king, as fast as lightning, at the same time catching the king's second spear with his shield. But this time Teias, the instant he had hurled one spear with his right hand, despatched a second spear with his equally skilled left. This second spear, which the attacking John had not noticed, pierced armour and chest of the courageous man, protruding again through his back. He fell.

When they saw this his Isaurians and Illyrians were gripped by terror, for John was regarded in Byzantium as the finest warrior after Belisarius himself. They cried out aloud, turned and fled in long bounds, downhill in utter disorder, pursued by Teias and his men.

For a short while the re-assembled Lombards held out. "Come, Gisulf, grit your teeth and let us stand up to this king of death!" Alboin cried. But already Teias was standing between them, and his dreaded battleaxe flashed. Alboin fell, cut deep into the right shoulder through his armour, and in the next instant Gisulf had fallen too, his helmet shattered. And now there was no holding them any more. Lombards, Gepidae, Alemanni, Heruli, Isaurians and Illyrians all fled as one, downhill in blind, disorderly flight.

Cheering loudly Teias's men pursued them. Teias himself remained at the pass, and contented himself by having Wachis hand him spears, which he then threw in a high trajectory over the heads of the Gothic pursuers, killing an enemy with every spear. These were the emperor's best troops, and they carried the advancing Macedonians, Thracens, Persians, Armenians and Franks with them as they fled, and the flood of fleeing troops raged on right up to Narses's litter. The latter, worried, rose from his cushions.

"John has fallen!"

"Alboin is severely wounded!" they cried, fleeing past their commander.

"Flee! Back to the camp!"

"A new attacking column must be…" Narses said. "Ha, look, there comes Cethegus, just at the right time!"

And it was he. He had now completed his long ride through the camp to round up all the Italian forces which Narses had allocated to him, and he had arranged them in five detachments of three hundred men each. Now he moved at their head, his troops in attacking formation, calmly marching ahead. Anicius followed from a distance and Syphax, carrying two spears, was walking immediately behind his master.

Slowly the Italians advanced, allowing the fleeing Imperial troops to pass through gaps in their ranks. Most of the Italians were former legionaries from Rome and Ravenna, loyal to Cethegus. The Gothic pursuers hesitated as they came upon this fresh, strong and well ordered attacking force, and slowly they started to withdraw back to the pass.

But Cethegus followed them.

Across the bloody, corpse-strewn spot where Teias had first destroyed the pact of twelve, over the spot where John had fallen a little higher up, on and on he marched at a steady, even pace, shield and spear in his left hand, and his sword in his right. Behind him his legionaries followed, spears couched.

Silently, without the sound of tubas, they advanced up the slope.

The Gothic warriors did not want to retreat into the pass behind their king. They halted outside the entrance. Guntharis was the first man Cethegus reached.

The duke's javelin shattered against the shield of the Roman, and in the next instant Cethegus thrust his spear into the Woelsung's side, the deadly shaft breaking in the wound. Count Grippa of Ravenna tried to avenge the duke; he swung his long sword above his head, but before he was able to strike Cethegus had run under the sword and thrust his own short Roman sword into the right breast of Theodoric's old follower, who fell and died. Angrily Wisand, the *bandalarius*, now advanced against Cethegus; their blades crossed, sparks flew from their swords and helmets, and then Cethegus skilfully parried an over-enthusiastic thrust. Before the Goth had time to protect himself again the Roman's short sword had found his thigh, so that his blood spurted high into the air. Wisand swayed, and two of his cousins carried him out of the fight. His brother, Ragnaris of Tarentum, charged at Cethegus from one side, but Syphax came to his master's aid and deflected the well-aimed thrust upwards. Before Ragnaris could let go of the spear and draw his hand axe, Cethegus had thrust his sword between his eyes. He fell dead.

The shocked Goths now began to avoid the terrible Roman and forged past their king into the safety of the pass. Only Aligern, Teias's cousin, would not budge. He threw his spear with such force at Cethegus's shield that it pierced the latter, but Cethegus let the shield go and caught the furiously charging Aligern on the point of his sword. Struck in the chest, Aligern fell backwards into the arms of old Hildebrand who, letting his heavy stone axe fall, now tried to carry the severely wounded Aligern past the king into the pass.

But although Aligern had also aimed well – the shield arm of Cethegus was bleeding profusely – the Roman took no notice of it. Pursuing Aligern and Hildebrand he tried to kill them both. At that moment Adalgoth saw his father's hated destroyer. "Alaric! Alaric!" he cried out in his clear voice, and as he leapt forward he picked up the old armourer's stone axe from the ground. "Alaric!" he cried once more.

Cethegus listened attentively as he heard this name called. In the same instant the stone axe, well aimed, flew through the air and struck Cethegus on his proud helmet with a loud, smashing sound. Cethegus fell, stunned. Syphax came to his master's aid and carried him out of the fray with both arms.

But the legionaries would not retreat. They could not have retreated even had they wanted to, as two thousand Thracens and Illyrians whom Narses had sent were moving up the slope behind them.

"Spears! Javelins!" their commander Aniabades ordered. "Don't get close to him! Narses has ordered it! Keep throwing spears at the king until he falls!" Gladly the troops obeyed this command, which promised to spare their own blood. Almost as soon as their commander had spoken a hail of missiles started to fly at the narrow entrance to the pass, a hail so thick and so terrible that not a single Goth was now able to step out of the pass and in front of his king.

And now King Teias defended the pass with his body, covering the gap with his shield and himself alone, and for a long time, a very long time, he defended his Gothic nation entirely alone.

Procopius has described this last stand by King Teias for us with obvious admiration, based on eyewitness reports. "And now it is for me to describe the most memorable of all struggles, and the heroism of one man, which yields not an inch to the bravery of any whom history calls heroes, that of Teias. There he stood, visible to all, behind his shield, his spear at the ready and at the head of his own battle formation. All the bravest among the Romans, of whom there were a great many, now charged at him. They thought that, with his fall, the fight would be over.

"All of them thrust and hurled spears and lances at him, but he caught every one with his shield, and in sudden lunges forward he killed many of his enemies, countless numbers of them. And when the missiles sticking in his shield made it so heavy that he could no longer hold it, he would call to his shield bearer for a fresh shield. Thus he stood, not once turning around or putting the shield on his back, but instead standing firm as if cemented to the earth. He stood like a wall, hour after hour, hurling death and destruction at his enemies with his right hand, and fending off their missiles with his left, constantly calling to his shield bearer to hand him fresh shields and spears."

Wachis and Adalgoth were the ones who constantly kept him supplied with fresh weapons. Shields and spears had been brought in their hundreds from the royal treasure.

At last their courage started to fail the Romans, Thracens and Persians, as they saw all their efforts bounce off this living shield of the Goths. They saw the best and the bravest among them fall, one after the other, to spears thrown by the king. They swayed; the Italians fearfully called for Cethegus, and before long they started to flee.

And then Cethegus regained consciousness.

"Syphax, a fresh spear! Halt!" he cried, "stand fast, you Romans! *Roma, Roma eterna!*" And with that, rising to his full height, he moved against Teias.

The Romans recognised his voice. "*Roma, Roma eterna!*" they replied, and they stood their ground.

But Teias too had recognised that voice. His shield was bristling with twelve lances; he could not hold it any longer. But when he saw the approaching Cethegus he no longer thought about changing shields.

"No shield! My battleaxe! Quickly!" he cried. And Wachis handed him his favourite weapon.

And then King Teias let his shield fall and, swinging his battleaxe high above his head, he stormed out of the pass at Cethegus. "Die, Roman!" he cried.

For a second the two great enemies stared each other in the eyes for one last time. And then axe and spear hurtled through the air together; neither of them thought about defending himself, seeking only to destroy the hated enemy.

And both fell. Teias's axe had pierced shield and armour of Cethegus, and its point buried itself deep into the Roman's left breast. "*Roma! Roma eterna!*" he cried once more, and fell to the ground dead.

But his spear had struck Teias in the right side of his chest also; he was not dead but mortally wounded as Adalgoth and Wachis carried him back into the pass. And they had to hurry as they did so, because when the enemy saw the Gothic king fall at last – he had been fighting continuously for nearly eight hours, and it was now almost evening – they found new heart. And so all the remaining Italians, Thracens, Persians and Isaurians charged at the pass once more from below, in large numbers and with renewed determination. Adalgoth was now covering the pass with his shield, with Wachis and Hildebrand standing behind him.

Syphax had picked up the body of his master with both arms and carried him out of the melee to one side.

Sobbing loudly, Syphax held the noble head in his lap. In death the features of Cethegus had acquired a majesty which bordered almost on the superhuman. In front of him, around the pass, the battle raged on.

And then the Moor suddenly noticed that Anicius, followed by a group of Byzantine soldiers including Scaevola and Albinus, was coming closer to him with an authoritative look on his face.

"Stop!" Syphax cried, jumping to his feet. "What do you want here?"

"To bring the Prefect's head to the emperor!" Anicius replied. "Obey, slave!"

But Syphax let out a piercing cry. His javelin flew through the air, and Anicius fell. And then, with lightning speed, before the others could get to him because they were busy with the dying Anicius, Syphax had taken the precious load on his broad back. Now, with the speed of the storm wind, he raced straight up the mountainside along impassable paths, at times climbing almost vertically straight up the steep lava cliffs near the pass, walls which both Goths and Byzantines had thought could not be scaled. Syphax made his way up, faster and faster. His destination was the little cloud of smoke on the other side of the lava cliffs; there, just beyond the topmost rocks, was one of the small secondary craters of Vesuvius.

For a final moment Syphax stopped on the crest of the black rocks. Then, with both of his strong arms, he raised the body of Cethegus high into the air once more, horizontally, showing the proud figure to the setting sun.

And suddenly both master and slave had disappeared.

The fire mountain had buried the dead Cethegus together with the ever-faithful Syphax. The dead Roman's greatness and guilt alike were buried for ever in its molten interior. He had escaped the petty hatred of his enemies.

Scaevola and Albinus, who had watched the entire process, hurried to Narses and demanded that the crater should be searched for the body.

But Narses replied: "Leave the great Roman to rest in the tomb that is worthy of him. He has earned it! I fight with the living, not the dead."

But in almost the same instant the noise of fighting around the pass suddenly stopped, where Adalgoth had been resisting the charging masses of the enemy with skill and with courage, worthy in every way of his tutor in both fighting and harp play, Teias.

Suddenly Hildebrand and Wachis, standing behind Adalgoth, called out: "Look toward the sea! The sea! The dragon ships! The northern land heroes! Harald! Harald!" At the same time, from below the pass, the sound of tubas called for the fighting to cease, for a ceasefire. The Byzantines gladly lowered their swords, tired from fighting all day."

King Teias was lying on his shield. Hildebrand had ordered that Cethegus's spear was not to be removed from the wound – "for with his blood his life will escape too."

Now the dying Teias asked in a low voice, almost a whisper: "What's this I hear? The heroes from the northern land? Their ships? Harald is here?"

"Yes, Harald, and safety for the remnants of our nation, for us and – for the women and children," Adalgoth rejoiced, kneeling by his side. "So it was not in vain, you wonderful, ever-dependable hero, your incomparable courage and your endurance out there for hour after hour, far beyond human strength! Basiliskos just came as an envoy from Narses: Harald has destroyed the emperor's Ionian Fleet in the port of Brundusium. He now threatens to land and launch a fresh attack on the tired Byzantines. He demands to take with him those of us who are still alive, with their weapons, property and possessions, to freedom in Thuleland. Narses has agreed; he says that he honours and respects the heroism of King Teias, and he wants to demonstrate that respect to the remnants of his nation. May we? Oh may we, my king?"

"Yes!" Teias replied, as his eyes were breaking. "You may, and you should. Free, the remnants of our nation are free! The women and the children – now I will not have to lead them into Vesuvius after all! Yes, take all the living to Thuleland with you, and take the two dead as well, King Theodoric and…"

"And King Teias!" Adalgoth completed the sentence, and lightly touched the forehead of the dead Teias with his lips.

Chapter 16

And so it came to pass.

As soon as Narses left his tent, a fisherman was brought to him, who had just rounded the spit of Surrentum in a small, fast ship. The fisherman assured Narses that a huge fleet of Gothic warships was approaching, but Narses laughed. He knew quite well that not a single Gothic sail remained anywhere on the oceans. On closer questioning the fisherman did admit that he had not actually seen the fleet himself. Merchantmen had told him about it, and they had also told him about a great naval battle, in which the Goths had destroyed the emperor's Ionian Fleet in the port of Brundusium. Now Narses knew very well than this was impossible. And after the fisherman had described the appearance of these supposed Gothic ships, according to the reports of his merchant friends, the commander exclaimed: "Now, at last, they are coming! Triremes and galleys; those are our ships that have been sighted, not Gothic ships at all."

As for the Viking fleet, which had disappeared four months ago, and which was thought to have returned to the north, nobody gave it a thought.

A few hours later, whilst the battle was raging about the pass and claiming the commander's full attention, Narses was informed by coast guard ships that a huge fleet was indeed approaching, a huge Imperial fleet. The flagship of the Ionian Fleet, the *Sophia*, had been clearly identified, however the number of sails was much larger than expected, and it also included the ships Narses had sent to Brundusium to urge the fleet to hurry. In fact those ships were sailing in the front line, and the fresh southeasterly wind meant that the fleet would soon reach the region of the camp. Soon afterwards Narses himself was able to watch from his litter, on top of a small hill, the splendid spectacle of the vast fleet approaching at full speed, both under sail and propelled by oars.

Thus reassured, he turned his attention back to the fighting on the mountain. Then suddenly messengers reached him from the camp, who not only fully confirmed those terrible rumours, but in fact had worse still to report. They had been sent ahead of a larger delegation, which reached Narses in his litter just as Cethegus was going out to face Teias in his last fight. The delegation consisted of commanders from the Ionian fleet, with their hands tied, together with four representatives from the Viking fleet who had brought their captives to act as interpreters.

They reported briefly that they had been attacked in the port of Brundusium one night by the Viking fleet, which they thought had long since disappeared. Almost all their ships had been captured; not one had been able to escape in order to warn Narses, as the Vikings had blocked the harbour.

After he heard about the annihilation which threatened the last Goths, crowded together on Mount Vesuvius, Jarl Harald had sworn that he would either avert their fate or share it. And now, wisely sending the captured Greek ships ahead and hiding their own dragon ships behind them, they had come flying to the scene on the wings of the east wind.

"And so," the interpreter concluded, "this is the message from Harald the Viking: 'Narses, you have a choice. Either you agree that all remaining Goths, with their arms and possessions, withdraw from the southern land to our ships in order to return home with us. In that event we will release the thousands of prisoners we have taken together with all spare ships of yours which we do not need to accommodate the Goths. Alternatively, if you do not agree to this, we will immediately kill all our prisoners, land and attack your army and your camp from the rear. Then see how many of you, attacked by us and the Goths from the front and the rear at once, survive, because we northlanders will fight to the last man if it comes to that. I have sworn it, by Odin.'"

Narses immediately granted the Viking's demands and agreed to let the Goths withdraw. "I have sworn only that I will eliminate the Goths from the Empire, not that I will wipe them out of the world. It would bring neither me nor the emperor much glory if I was now to throttle to death the last remnants of such a great nation, by sheer superiority of numbers. Furthermore I honour the heroism of this man Teias; in forty years of war I have seen nothing like it. And I have no desire at all to find out how my tired and badly shaken army, which has a day of the most terrible fighting behind it, and which has lost almost all its leaders and its bravest men, would now stand up to these Nordic giants, fresh and full of wild daring."

And so Narses had sent messengers to Harald's ships at once, and to the pass as well. The fighting stopped, and the Gothic withdrawal began.

The army of Narses formed a long double line of honour, from the mountain to the sea itself. The Vikings had landed four hundred men, who now received the Goths as they reached their ships on the coast.

But even before the procession commenced, Narses waved to Basiliskos and said: "The Gothic war is over, and the great deer has been shot. We must now get rid of the wolves who chased the deer for us. How is it with the leaders of the Lombards? How are their wounds?"

"Before I reply," Basiliskos said respectfully, "will you accept the laurel wreath here, which your army has wound for you? The laurels are from Vesuvius, from the pass up there. There is blood on the leaves."

At first Narses refused the wreath with a motion of his hand, but then he said: "Thank you, give it to me." But instead of placing it on his head he put it beside him in his litter.

"Autharis, Warnfrid, Grimoald, Aripert, Agilulf and Rotharis are dead. They have lost more than seven thousand men. Alboin and Gisulf are lying motionless in their tents, badly wounded."

"Good! Very good! As soon as the Goths have embarked, you will see that the Lombards are led away. They are dismissed from my army. And to Alboin, as a farewell, you will say only this: 'After Narses is dead, perhaps, but certainly not before!' I am going to stay here in my litter; support me with some cushions, for I cannot stand any longer. But this unique spectacle is one which I must see."

And indeed it was a splendid, a movingly grandiose spectacle which now unfolded before his eyes: the last of the Goths were turning their backs on Vesuvius and on Italy and embarking on the long ships, which were to take them safely to their new home in the north.

The procession began with the solemn, earnest sound of Gothic horns coming from the unconquered Teias chasm, which no enemy had been able to enter. The sounds of the horns were interspersed by long pauses, and in between those sounds the ancient death songs of the Goths could be heard, monotonous, solemn and moving, but certainly not soft or wailing. Men, women and children sang them together.

Hildebrand and Adalgoth, the last two Gothic leaders, had organised the procession, the silver-white past and the golden future of their nation.

At the head of the procession marched five hundred Gothic soldiers, proud and stubborn, led by Wisand the *bandalarius*. The latter, in spite of his wounds, had insisted on leading the march and was now doing so, using his spear as a crutch.

Behind them followed, laid out on his last shield, without his helmet and with the spear of Cethegus still in his chest, Teias. He was carried by four warriors. His pale face was framed by his black hair, and a purple robe covered his body.

Behind him walked Adalgoth and Gotho.

And Adalgoth sang softly, to the accompaniment of a small harp in his left hand:

"Give way, ye peoples, to our step!
We are the last of the Goths; we carry with us no crown, we carry only a dead man.
Shield to shield, and spear to spear we go to the north land's winds until,
in the distant grey sea, we find the island of Thule.
They say it is the island of truth, where honour and oath have meaning still!
There we will bury our king in a coffin of oaken spears.
Here we come – give way to our step – out of Rome's false gates:
we carry only our king with us – the crown he wore is lost."

When the pallbearers reached Narses, the latter ordered them to halt, and in a strong, loud voice he called out in Latin:

"Victory was mine, but the laurel belongs to him. There, take it! Whether future generations will ever see a greater display of personal courage nobody knows; but for today, King Teias, I salute you as the greatest hero of all time!" And he placed the laurel wreath, which his army had wound for him, down on his dead foe's pale temples.

The pallbearers picked up their load again and slowly and solemnly, to the sound of the horns, the songs and Adalgoth's harp, they walked slowly to the sea, which by now was glowing splendidly in the light of the setting sun.

Not far behind Teias a tall, purple throne was being carried; on it sat the tall, silent figure of Dietrich von Bern, his crown helmet on his head, his shield leaning by his left arm, and his spear against his right. To his left walked old Hildebrand, his eyes firmly fixed on the body of his great king, which shone majestically in its purple robe in the rays of the setting sun. Hildebrand was holding the blue Amalung banner with the rising golden lion high above Theodoric's head; the giant flag fluttered mightily in the evening sea breeze, almost as if it was saying farewell to the air of Italy in its own way.

As the body was carried past Narses the latter said: "I can tell from the strange thrill running through me: that is the wise king of Ravenna! First a stronger man, now a wiser one is being carried past us. Let us act accordingly." With an effort he rose in his litter and bowed his head respectfully before the corpse.

Next came the wounded, either being carried on stretchers or leaning on others for support. The first of them was Aligern, who was being carried on a broad shield by Wachis, Liuta and two warriors.

After them came countless chests and trunks, boxes and baskets, in which Theodoric's royal treasure and the possessions of individual families were being carried away in accordance with the agreement.

They in turn were followed by the masses of unarmed women, children and old men; boys from their tenth year onwards had not wanted to give back the weapons which had been given to them, and they formed a special group. Narses smiled as he saw the little blond heroes look up at him so stubbornly and angrily. "Well," he said, "it seems that care has been taken to ensure that the emperor's successors and their generals will also find work to do."

The procession was concluded by the remainder of the Gothic people's army, arranged in companies of one hundred men each.

The people and their possessions were ferried out to the high-sided dragon ships.

The bodies of Theodoric and Teias, the royal banner and the royal treasure were taken on board the flagship of Harald and Haralda. The great Dietrich von Bern on his throne was placed leaning against the main mast, and his lion banner was hoisted to the top of the mast. Old Hildebrand settled himself by the feet of his dead king.

But the body of King Teias was laid in front of the rudder by Adalgoth and Wisand. Sadly Harald and his lovely sister came closer to the dead hero.

The Viking laid his armoured hand on the dead man's chest and said: "I was not able to save you, you brave black king, neither you nor your nation. So let me take you with me, together with what is left of your people, back to the land of loyalty and strength which you should never have left. Thus I will bring back the Gothic people to King Frode after all, as he instructed me to do."

And Haralda added: "And I will preserve the body of the noble dead king by secret arts, so that it will keep until we reach our homeland. There we will build a great tomb for him and King Thidekr near the sea, where they will be able to hear the waves and talk to each other. These two are worthy of one another.

"Look over here, my brother: the enemy army stands gathered on the beach. They are lowering their spears respectfully, and the sun is sinking into the sea behind the islands of Micenum and the other islands over there. Purple is covering the ocean like a royal robe. Purple is also colouring all our sails, and our weapons glow golden in the evening light. Look how the south wind is moving King Thidekr's banner! The wind is pointing us to the north, and the wind knows the will of the gods. Come, brother Harald, let the anchors be raised! Turn the helm and point the dragon's bow northward! Go, Freya's clever bird, fly, my falcon!" And she cast the falcon high into the air. "Show us the way, to the north, to Thuleland! We are bringing home the last of the Goths!"

Translator's Postscript

As stated in the Preface most of if not all the major events portrayed in this book actually occurred, and all the major characters in it did live, the one notable exception being Cethegus.

As also stated in the Preface the author drew heavily on the *Gothic Wars* by Procopius, but to my regret I have not so far been able to lay my hands on an English or German translation. The following comments are therefore based on information I have been able to find in other sources, notably Gibbon's *Decline and Fall of the Roman Empire* and my 1966 edition of *Encyclopaedia Britannica*.

Theodoric (also known as "The Great," and as "Dietrich von Bern" in Germanic mythology) did live; he did conquer Italy, and he was not only a great warrior and conqueror, but he also became a wise and benevolent ruler afterwards, something which few men in history have been able to do. Under his rule Italy experienced a golden era of peace and prosperity. However along the way he did have Odoacer murdered. He also had Boethius and Symmachus executed, and there is doubt whether that sentence was just. I am uncertain as to whether Rusticiana or any of her three children are historical. Theodoric also had Alaric of the Balti banished on charges which later proved false, but whether Alaric had a surviving son Adalgoth I have been unable to confirm.

Hildebrand appears with his king in the legend of "Dietrich von Bern," and while the real Hildebrand probably did live, the real and the mythological Hildebrand have become one. Given that Hildebrand was "almost a hundred" in 535 when Theodahad ascended the throne (Book 4, Chapter 1) he must have been well over a hundred by the end of this story, and yet he was still a formidable warrior. This is not as unlikely as it may seem, and extreme longevity seems to have been a Germanic characteristic. For example, according to no less an authority than Gibbon, the great Ostrogothic king Ermanaric (or Hermanric) fought most of his many and successful campaigns at the head of his army aged between eighty and a hundred and ten.

Amalasuntha, Cassiodorus and Athalaric were all historical figures. Amalasuntha did act as regent for her son Athalaric, who did die young but whether he was poisoned, and if so by whom, I cannot say with certainty. Amalasuntha later ruled in her own right, and she did have the three Balti Dukes murdered. Her most trusted adviser was indeed Cassiodorus, and she did have a daughter Matesuentha. Although I have not been able to confirm that the latter actually married Witigis, it seems probable.

Silverius lived and became Pope. Whether any of the other catacomb conspirators lived I have not been able to confirm, but Albinus probably was a historical figure, and the family of Scaevola certainly existed. Whether any of Cethegus's Roman tribunes as named in the book actually lived is uncertain, but men like them certainly did.

Theodahad is historical and was a weak ruler much as described; Gothelindis was probably also real, but I have not been able to confirm this. Petros was real, he did travel to Italy as an envoy for Theodora, and he did contrive to have Amalasuntha murdered, although on his return to Byzantium he was rewarded and honoured, not sent to the metal mines.

Witigis lived, he did have an enviable war record against the Gepidae, he was a simple but honest and able soldier, and he did become king. Whether there was a Rauthgundis, and whether the couple died as portrayed in the book, is uncertain, but the major Gothic victory over Belisarius and the subsequent siege of Rome are historical. In fact Rome changed hands several times during these wars, and according to some sources it was virtually uninhabitable for some years. Ravenna was also besieged, and there was widespread dissension among the Goths as to who was their rightful ruler.

Descriptions of crippling taxation under Byzantine rule and devastation in the countryside are also historical. There is no doubt that Italy suffered terribly during the wars described in this book.

Justinian and Theodora certainly lived, as did Belisarius, Narses, Tribonianus and Procopius.

Theodora did start life as the daughter of a lion tamer in a circus, and at a very young age she and her sister Comito became prostitutes. According to one source Belisarius was one of Theodora's early clients. Theodora was notorious early in her life for her shamelessness and wantonness, and repeatedly danced naked before paying customers. She travelled widely as a prostitute and had an illegitimate son, who was later put to death on Justinian's orders. It is beyond question that Theodora was a noted beauty, as well as extremely clever. These qualities enabled her to ensnare Justinian, and eventually to become empress. Descriptions of the luxury in the Imperial palace and the extreme lengths Theodora went to in order to preserve her beauty are also based on known facts. Equally, Theodora's intrigues are legendary.

Belisarius was a heroic general much as described. His role in the "Nika rebellion" is historical, and he did lead two armies into Italy. He later fell out of favour with Justinian, but accounts of his being blinded and banished are generally considered untrue.

Narses was a eunuch, and very much the successful general portrayed in this book. Nothing I have read elsewhere suggests that he was either a cripple or an epileptic; he may have been, but given that he died at ninety-five his health cannot have been too precarious. The animosity and rivalry between Narses and Belisarius are historical.

Totila became king after Witigis, and the battle of the Padus Bridge is historical. His brother Hildebad (or Hildebad) also lived.

According to the *Encyclopaedia Britannica,* Witigis ruled from 536 to 540, Ildibad and Eraric 540 to 541, Totila 541 to 552 and Teias 552 to 554. Ildibad and Hildebad are almost certainly the same, and brief rule by him is not inconsistent with this book, noting that Britannica does not say he ever actually became king. Whoever Eraric was he does not feature in this book, probably because his rule, as king or otherwise, was brief.

Totila was certainly a benevolent king, and Italy experienced a second golden era under his eleven year reign. Julius is probably fictional. Valeria and her father may have lived, but I cannot be certain.

The battle of Taginae is historical, and Totila was killed at it. Whether Furius Ahalla lived is something I have been unable to confirm, but I suspect that both he and his role in the battle are fictitious. But Alboin and his Lombards were real. True to the warning given to Alboin by Narses, some twenty years after the battle of Taginae the

Lombards did invade Italy, and Alboin reigned briefly as their king. Lombard rule in Italy was to last some two hundred years, even though the Lombards never controlled all of the peninsula.

The battle at Mount Lactarius did occur, and it is historical fact that the last Gothic king Teias defended the remnants of his nation for several hours entirely alone. Many attempts have been made to find the "Teias chasm" as described by Procopius, all without success, but this is not surprising as volcanic landscapes do change with time. His death occurred when he was changing shields, largely as described.

Viking fleets certainly did wreak havoc in the Mediterranean from time to time. I have been unable to confirm whether Harald and Haralda, and the last-minute rescue of the surviving Goths, are historical. Dahn himself in his novel *Die Kreuzfahrer* (the crusaders) refers to a successful deal struck between the surviving Goths and Narses for a free retreat north over the Alps, which seems more probable. But it seems unlikely that the annihilation of the Ionian fleet is merely an invention by the author, and the fact that the remnants of the Gothic nation were all embarked in one evening suggests that their number by that time was quite small. Therefore it seems possible that the Viking rescue may be loosely based on fact.

I apologise to my readers for not being able to state with more certainty what is historical and what is not, but I am not by profession a historian, and have had to rely on such information as I have been able to gain from those sources which are available to me.

But as I said in the Preface this book is first and foremost a novel. As such I believe it is a masterpiece, and such history as one learns while reading it is simply a bonus.

To my mind this book is somewhat like the literary equivalent of one of Gustav Mahler's colossal symphonies, which are conceived on a similarly vast scale. Mahler once said: "A symphony should contain everything!" and that also applies to this novel. He also said: "My time will come!" which it most certainly has. I hope that, through this translation, I may have contributed to the same holding true one day for Dahn's mighty epic.

Above all I hope that you, the reader, have enjoyed this book as much as I have.

Herb Parker
Redcliffe, Queensland, Australia
October 2004

Printed in the United States
103500LV00003B/1/A

Made in the USA
San Bernardino, CA
15 November 2018